Cover design by Opulent Designs
Edits by Lilly

www.ellemaebooks.com

NOTE

This is a work of fiction. Names, characters, business, events and incidents are the products of the author's imagination. Any resemblance to actual persons, living or dead, or actual events is purely coincidental.
Before moving forward, please note that the themes in this book can be dark and trigger some people. The themes can include but are not limited to; sexual assault, death, gore, domestic abuse, character deaths, trafficking, dubious consent, mention of CSA, flash backs of CSA, double penetration, blood play, self harm, cannibalism, explicit sex, and violence.
If you need help, please reach out to the resources below.

National Suicide Prevention Lifeline
1-800-273-8255
https://suicidepreventionlifeline.org/

National Domestic Violence Hotline
1-800-799-7233
https://www.thehotline.org/

Before you continue

This book is a boxset of all five Winterfell Academy books, plus bonus content, and a special villain novel in the back.

Please make sure to read the content warnings as I make sure to try and be as accurate as possible when making them so that I can protect my readers. If needed at any point please reach out to your support system.

In this book will encounter bi characters, lesbian characters, non-binary, and trans characters. If that doesn't interest you please close this book now.

As always, I hope you enjoy the ride!

Also by Elle Mae

Stand Alone:

Contract Bound: A Lesbian Vampire Romance

Other World Series:

An Imposter in Warriors Clothing

A Coward In A Kings Crown

Winterfell Academy Series:

The Price of Silence: Winterfell Academy Book 1

The Price of Silence: Winterfell Academy Book 2

The Price of Silence: Winterfell Academy Book 3

The Price of Silence: Winterfell Academy Book 4

The Price Of Silence: Winterfell Academy Book 5

Short and Smutty:

The Sweetest Sacrifice: An Erotic Demon Romance

Eden Emory (Contemporary):

The Ties That Bind Us

Don't Stop me

Don't leave Me

Two of a Kind

For all my readers out there.
Thank you for believing in me even when I didn't believe in myself. Because of you I have been able to go on this wonderful journey with Rosie and the gang.
Enjoy and I hope to see you again soon.

THE PRICE OF SILENCE

BOOK 1

ELLE MAE

Prologue
Rosie

Nine years ago

It takes only about seventeen minutes for a house to burn down.

If that house coincidentally has a volatile low-level demon in it that controls fire, it only takes about ten.

The house was filled with smoke darker than my ten-year-old eyes could see through, but luckily I was small enough to crawl under the tables and chairs and push my way out of the burning kitchen and into the living room.

"Mom!" My scream was followed by a cough. The smoke filled my lungs, making it hard for me to breathe. My body was working overtime just to keep me conscious.

My father's form was the first thing I saw.

The second was the hideous burned flesh that marred the left side of his face. It stood out against his pale skin.

Did I do that?

"Rosie," he choked out.

My mother's scream was followed by a bright light that hit me square in my chest, causing my body to soar across the room and smack against the melting walls.

The last thing I saw before I lost consciousness was a pair of laced-up heels and a perfectly manicured hand reaching for me.

This birthday sucks.

Chapter One
Rosie

Rosie Miller,
Welcome to Winterfell Academy.
The words stuck out to me like they were burned into the page.

This had to be a mistake. My heart raced as I turned the letter over in my hands. It was a thin piece of paper but in my hands, it weighed a thousand pounds and threatened to pull me down with it into the ground. Scanning the page, I was sure that this had to be some elaborate scam that was played on unsuspecting low-levels. They not only extended an offer to me but accepted it for me in the same letter. I mean why would someone of my birth even dare to reject them, right?

"Mom," I called out to her. The tingling came before the pain. I winced, feeling a slash across my back. Just as it came, the wound quickly began to heal leaving only a ghost of pain. I winced again at the pain of the healing but after being subject to it for more than nine years, I'd gotten used to it. A day without pain was unheard of.

My mother raced into the kitchen not a moment later looking frazzled. Her black hair was a mess around her head and her green eyes were wide. "Rosie don't hurt yourself like that," she chided and reached for the letter in my hand.

She had been like that since I was cursed. It was on my tenth birthday that a witch barged into our house and made both my parents and me regret the day I was born. I had never seen a witch before that, only heard of how terrible and power-hungry they could be. I was, as expected, fearful when she came into our house and demanded that my parents pay her back. So I did the only thing I could think of. I burned the house down and in return, she cursed me.

Witches had a funny way of cursing people nowadays. There was no prick of your finger. There was no awakening by true love's first kiss. No, instead the witch thought that the ten-year-old would need a much darker curse to pay for her parents' misdeeds.

She turned my words into weapons.

After that birthday party, the same sides that used to ache with laughter were now aching and burning because cuts covered them. It happened with any noise I made. A sigh, a laugh, a groan—even a sneeze now subjected me to pain. It was a testy curse and even after nine years it still managed to surprise me. Sometimes the curse thought I deserved pain that was even worse than a cut. Those were the dangerous ones.

That happened when I was fifteen.

I had the curse down pat; I never spoke, relying solely on this stupid little whiteboard that I carried around to communicate with teachers and classmates. Well, when someone takes that whiteboard and shoves you to the ground so hard your skull feels like it will break...you are bound to make a noise. And then I realized that if I made a small noise the pain would be in vain. Why waste pain if no one could hear you besides the snarling bullies that stood over you? So, I screamed.

And that's when we found out the stronger the emotions, the more words I spoke, the longer they were drawn out...the more it would hurt. I was left with three broken ribs after that.

My mother had a funny way of fussing over me. Sometimes I thought it was real, but other times it seemed like just a show she put on. There were times where she thought I wasn't looking and I would catch her narrowed eyes and scowl. The hate was mutual though, so I didn't feel too bad about it, nor did I try to cover it up as hard as she did. There was a wall that I put up after the incident—I had to, given that my only way to form a connection had been taken from me. I was thankful every day that my parents were on the other side of it.

"What did you need?" my dad asked walking in. He was barely above a human on the scale. He had aged considerably in the last few years while my mother had retained some of her youth. Dad's previously black hair was almost white, but his blue eyes had kept their luster. With the lack of demon powers came the absence of immortality. Only the powerful demons could obtain that. Meaning he was also stuck with a permanent reminder of my birthday in the form of a nasty scar that covered half his face. I thanked god that even though my parents were weak, I was able to inherit fast healing from whatever high-level ancestor we had, if not the curse would be much more obvious.

My mom's hand was clasped tightly over her mouth as her eyes devoured every single line.

"Oh my god Rosie." My mom gasped and showed Dad the letter. "She has been picked because they want to begin expanding their enrollment to lower-level demons!" She was practically vibrating.

"The tuition is covered?" Dad asked. Dad may regret my existence, but this was no doubt a chance to show everyone that they still mattered. Hope bubbled in my chest, threatening to push its way out onto my face.

"What's the catch?" I asked and held in my groan as each word was carved into me. The wound on my arm bled through my shirt.

"Don't do that!" Mom snapped and lifted the back of my baggy black sweater. I had hoped the blood wouldn't soak through. At least it was black and if I washed it, I could probably keep it for longer. It had been a while since they gave me money to buy new clothes and I didn't want to show up to school in rags. "This is a once-in-a-lifetime chance. That you *will* take."

"Use your phone," Dad grumbled as my mouth opened to speak. I swallowed and typed on my phone for them.

No tuition? Low-level demon entry? What else, a stipend? It doesn't feel right. Mom and Dad looked over the letter carefully. I could almost see the way that their minds turned with possibilities.

"Actually, they will give you a stipend for food and such. Two hundred dollars a week," Mom said looking at me. She couldn't keep the smile off her face.

"We could use that money too," Dad said eyeing me, waiting for my reaction. I gave him none. "They say you can move in before the term starts to meet the new arrivals like yourself."

"I have to go tell Cynthia!" my mom squealed and left to go call her friend. I rolled my eyes at her retreating form. Then stiffened when I realized I was now alone with Dad. My eyes flitted to his fists; they were relaxed.

"If you can get a degree from this school Rosie..." He rubbed his hands through his untamed facial hair. "You could work in the demon sector. Help this family out."

All low-levels were forced to either work with other low-levels or humans. But if I could get a degree at such a sought-after school, there very well may be a possibility for me to get a better job. But that wasn't what was pushing me to take the chance on this school.

Elle Mae

When is the start of the term? I typed to my dad. He had to squint to read it.

"Two weeks from tomorrow but they are allowing you to have time to settle next week," he replied reading off the letter.

Sounds like a snap decision.

"Don't look a gift horse in the mouth, Rosie," he said as his hand came to tug a strand of my black hair lightly. It was a gesture he had taken up long ago as a warning. "Get your education. Get a good job. Help your parents rebuild the *shit life* they were left with."

I stayed tense even as his hand left my hair without pulling it.

Afterward, Dad went to go take his regular seat on the beat-up recliner that was permanently stationed in front of the television. This was what he was like when it had been a busy day for him, a rough day. But every day was a rough day for him. Because of his status, he was put in with the human work and cleaned the various schools around the area. He no doubt would have to face the torment of any demon who thought himself higher than him, as was the way it was. If he wasn't such a horrid being I may have felt bad for him.

For thousands of years, society had been separated into three different categories. You had your humans; they were weak and had practically no value left in society. There were many still in the government and they liked to pretend that they were superior, but it was obvious that they were the ones in danger.

The other group, and my most hated, was the witches. Many demons were not privy to the knowledge of how witch covens worked, but they did tend to tie themselves to the higher-level demons when they were not grouped amongst themselves. They were known to have outbursts and some even went on killing rampages throwing curses around to see what would stick.

The last group was the demons, and we were still severely divided to this day. There were demons that were classified as "high-level" and they were rumored to have not an ounce of human blood in them, or at least very little. Low-levels on the other hand, were polluted with it. And that in turn made us unworthy of being mixed in with those higher-level demons.

Growing up, I didn't understand what had made us so different from the higher-level demons. We had separate schools. Separate places of work. The only time I ran into them was on the occasional shopping trip, but even then it was only at a distance since my parents rarely allowed me to leave the house.

And now I was going to a school filled with them.

Winterfell Academy

Opening the school homepage on my phone, I almost scoffed at how cringy the page was. It was so stereotypical it was laughable. Like every other high-level demon school, it looked like it was forged from old money. High-levels, usually the older families, liked for everything to have a colonial feel. Lots of brickwork and statues dedicated to the founding demons. Their slogan was what stole the cake. I had to cover my mouth with my hand so my parents wouldn't hear the giggle even as it tore up my sides.

It read, "Live with passion. Die with no regrets."

Their heads were way too far up their asses.

It was better than nothing though. I had no choice but to either go to a cheap community college in the area or Winterfell. At least at Winterfell I had money and a clean place to live, not to mention I would be away from my parents, which was by far more valuable than anything that could come out of the degree.

I chose to leave my parents to their own devices and go up to my room on the second floor. This was the only house we could afford after the other one burned down. It was much farther than our other one, we were forced to move from Hartford to Holyoke. A new state and new city. Perfect for a new start after a suspicious fire. I was forced to change schools, but at least it was spacious enough to house us. I didn't mind the mold in the bathrooms so much anymore.

When I reached my door I ran my fingers over the metal door sign that I took from our other house. You could see on the edges where it was blackened by the flames. I had been so surprised when I found this in the rubble. Before we found this house we were living in a hotel not too far away from the previous house, I used to sneak away from school in hopes to find anything of what our life was like there. It was so different then—happy. I was ecstatic to find something that reminded me of a better time, but it also made me realize how horrible my power was. When I was younger, the other low-level children would beg me to show them and scream with joy when a small flame showed up in the center of my palm.

They didn't realize how permanent fire was though. The scene from the house wasn't cleared for months but when it was...I was hit with the guilt and fear of what I did. It wasn't just the house that burned. My fire was so hot it destroyed the foundation underneath the house and during the renovations they had to tear the whole thing out, leaving a gaping hole in the dirt.

I didn't return after that.

I sighed, ignoring the bruise on my leg, and pushed myself into my room. I would need to prepare if I wanted to hide this curse from the high-levels. I doubted anyone would even talk to me, but it was better to be overprepared than underprepared.

The student's uniforms were light—white button-ups and brown bottoms. If I were forced to speak I would definitely bleed through them.

That would be a great introduction to the curse, I thought wryly.

I would have to pack an extra layer; black would be best, and probably long sleeves and leggings. As I was tearing through all of the worn and torn clothing, I paused.

What was I even thinking?

How would someone like me even hope to live among all those higher-levels? I couldn't even speak. I would need to show them that I belonged there. Force them to see me as an equal rather than as a punching bag with no brain cells...but how could I do that if every time I spoke it was like a kitchen knife was slashed across my body?

Die with no regrets.

"You're going," I whispered to myself, wincing at the scratch on my side. At least it wasn't a cut this time. By the time I had packed my main staples the ache was gone. Looking down at the overflowing suitcase I was satisfied with what I packed. Sleep clothes were free range so I packed shorts and long shirts that I had had for years. I had also packed enough underclothes so that even if I was forced to speak and bled through my shirts, I would be covered for a while.

I ruffled through my underwear drawer and paused when my hand reached a particularly see-through black lace one.

A gift.

I snorted. Courtesy of the only romantic connection I was able to build while being a cursed mute. Demons tended to have the irrational fear that curses could travel from one person to another, which made even the most compassionate ones stay far away from me in hopes of saving their own hide. I understood though; it just didn't help me overcome the barrier that forced its way between me and literally everyone I ever met. Sometimes when I got a smile, or someone sat next to me, the barrier would seem less like a brick wall and more like a see-through fence, but it never got any clearer than that. Even the romantic connection seemed put off by the wall after a while.

Maybe a high-level demon would feel as though a low-level like myself would be worth degrading himself to be with.

I packed the underwear without a second thought.

Chapter Two
Rosie

From our town Holyoke, it had taken an hour for us to get to the Winterfell campus which was classified as its own small town on the map even though it was just a few short miles from Hartford. The campus had a few small shops on the way but the rest of it was surrounded by thick forest.

"We are not allowed in, apparently." Mother sneered.

I couldn't help but thank the Originals for the gift. My mother most likely just wanted to enter and take pictures of the campus to show her friends. It would only cause more trouble for me and I didn't want to add to the bad image I probably already had as a low-level. If they saw how human my parents looked, I would never live it down.

"It's okay," I whispered. The bruises were on my back this time. "I love you." Those words tore but not deep.

Because you don't mean it, a voice whispered but I pushed the thought away and reached over to awkwardly give them hugs.

"Don't show them your curse," Dad reminded me. "Tell the faculty but let them know you will tell the students you are mute."

"Don't let them find out," Mom fussed. "We don't want high school all over again."

Ah yes. The broken ribs.

I nodded at them, choosing not to inflict any more pain on myself. I quickly grabbed my overfilled suitcase and scrambled awkwardly out of the car.

Elle Mae

Here we go.

I straightened my shoulders and walked toward the gated entrance that held the guard who had refused my parents' entrance. He gave me a sidelong glance, his dull blue eyes looking over my stature suspiciously. He may have been a low-level as well, but that would just mean that he knew better than anyone that I didn't belong here. He took my admissions paper and let me through.

The buildings were as ridiculous as they had looked in the pictures online. They towered over me as I walked past, their old brick adding a colonial feel that seemed to reek high-level demon stature. They just loved to hang on to whatever old demon traditions, unable to move on from when they ruled everything with an iron fist.

I mean, they still did sometimes. They just liked to give off the idea that we were somewhat equal. It seemed that low-levels were sometimes treated worse than humans.

The buildings seemed to hum as I walked past, as if they were living and breathing. I almost expected one to get up and move if I looked away for long enough. Everything appeared to have been there for hundreds of years, but the walls of the buildings and the stone paths were so clean. Even the grass was trimmed perfectly short. Not a blade out of place.

A clock tower chimed in the distance and when I looked over toward the sound I was taken aback by how huge it was. It was behind a few buildings, but even from where I was I could see how it towered over the whole school.

I stuck out in loose torn jeans and a turtleneck. I was lucky that it was still chilly outside, or else my turtleneck would have looked even worse. It would be harder to keep this up when it got into the warmer months. At least, that was if I lasted until then. There was an air about this place, like it had its own personality. A playful one. It made my fingertips tingle, similar to how the curse felt before it attacked.

"Are you lost?" a soft feminine voice asked from behind. Turning, I was met with a petite girl with a warm smile. She was in uniform, a pressed button-down shirt with a plaid skirt. I had read over the school handbook before coming and could see that her skirt length was far away from the required knee length, baring her milky thighs. Her curly red hair was pulled back in a tight bun which only let a few strands fall loose onto her face. Her eyes were what caused me to suck in a sharp breath. They were the brightest green I had ever seen, and it almost looked like there were swirls of other various greens in them if you looked close enough.

This was what a *real demon* looked like up close.

I nodded to her. I had a general idea of where to go after studying the map for hours on end but I would take her assistance over the stumbling of my two feet any day. She paused for just a moment when her eyes met mine.

"This way for new students." Her voice was still pleasant; maybe me being a lower-level demon didn't faze her. "What's your name by the way?" she asked after we had entered the main building. "I'm Emma."

I took out my phone to respond.

I'm Rosie. Apologies, I am mute. I made the font bigger so she wouldn't have to come too close. Her mouth dropped open when she read my message.

"I didn't know that could happen," she mused and cocked her head to the side. She opened the double doors to what looked like an office space where a soft-faced secretary smiled at us. "Magic can't fix it?"

I winced at her question but just shook my head at her. I handed the secretary my admission letter. Looking at her eyes I could tell she was also on the lower side, but her eyes had a similar glow to what my mother's had.

"Nice to meet you deary... Ms. Miller, is it?" She waited for me to respond. I only nodded my head at her.

"She's mute, Tammy." Emma spoke for me. I didn't miss the way "Tammy" rolled off her tongue. Maybe she was not as nice as I pegged her to be.

"Oh my," Tammy responded and dialed a number on the phone. There was a muffled "What?" on the other side. I internally groaned; entitled high-level demons were what I was dreading. "Rosie Miller is here for you." I didn't hear him respond, but a door to my left opened and out walked a suited man with long braided purple hair and matching purple eyes. His tanned skin seemed to glow as bright as his eyes did. It was Mr. Winterfell himself.

"Ms. Miller, welcome. Come into my office." He gestured for me. "Thank you Emma."

"Any time, Principal Winterfell." She giggled. *Gross.*

"Please sit, you must be tired from the ride over." He pulled out the seat across from his desk. It was a modest office for a principal but was definitely more than he needed. This room alone was three times the size of my bedroom. It was hard not to be sour when high-level demons were just so extravagant. "You came from somewhere near Holyoke, right?"

He paused like he was waiting for me to answer. Then he gave me a smile before continuing. "As you are more than aware, Winterfell has never accepted low-level demons."

Ouch.

"But I decided we change that this year. One of my goals for this year has been to create a more diverse environment for our learners and push them together with people who have not had the chance to be in a place like this." He leaned back in his chair and folded his hands together. "That's where you—and a few other students—come in. We have opened our doors to three outstanding low-level demons this year across all three years. You are in the freshman class and I am sure you will have time to meet the others at another point."

That's it, three? I prepared myself for the pain before I spoke.

"I am not outstanding." It was in my stomach this time. I felt the blood soak into my tank top but I trusted it wouldn't bleed though.

The importance of layers.

"But your curse is." He was leaning forward now. The twinkle in his eye intensified. "That must have hurt."

"Yes." Cue the dull ache in my shoulder.

"I heard Emma say you told her you were a mute? Smart move." I opened my mouth but he waved his hand. "Type if you need to speak." A rush of relief swept through me.

The story is I am a mute until I cannot hide my curse. If you knew about my curse then why am I here? I showed him my question.

"Because this is by far the most outstanding curse I have seen. I do not know what you did to deserve it but it is powerful and for it to last so long... Nine years right?" I nodded. He hummed. "We also have a pool of talented witches here; maybe they will find this interesting as well."

So a test subject? I typed with shaking fingers. Anger flared in me.

"A chance. Don't mistake it as anything else. This is a chance for you to show the world what you are made of." He paused. "And who knows, maybe you will find some answers here."

I sighed.

"Is it a different place every time?" he asked. "What did that sigh just get you?" My lip twitched. I couldn't tell if I was annoyed or amused by his morbid curiosity. I pulled up my sleeve to show him the slowly disappearing bruise. It was too loud a sigh, apparently. "Fascinating."

Is there anything else? I typed to him.

"Nope. I would just like biweekly check-ins for your first few months, then after that you are free," he said and got up to hold the door open for me. "Let me know if you run into any issues, Ms. Miller." I nodded but did not turn around on my way out. I did flash the secretary a smile, which she wholeheartedly returned.

* * *

It was easy enough to find my dorm even as I lugged the heavy suitcase around. It was a long walk across the campus, and by the time I got there I was out of breath. I was not sure if it was supposed to be a single room but when I opened the door to see that I would be the only one bunking there, my shoulders sagged with relief. It would be impossible to hide my curse if I had to dorm with other people.

The single room came with a decent-sized queen bed, a small kitchenette, and a single desk. There was also an attached full-size bathroom. The colors in the bathroom and room were all muted browns that seemed to match the rest of the aging school. There were two small windows across from the entrance that were surrounded by exposed brick. My insides fluttered with excitement as I took in how nice the room was.

Way better than staying at home, I summarized. Even our first home didn't have such a feel as this.

I quickly unpacked my suitcase and headed to shower off the caked-on blood that had formed between my clothes and my skin. The hot water washed away the chill in my body and warmed my freezing toes. I was never more grateful than as I was right now to be in a rich school. Showers were my sanctuary and the only place where I could be myself. I sighed again and watched as a bruise formed on my stomach.

This was the routine. Now that I was forced to keep up the image of a mute I would have to find some time to let my voice out. I found it easier this way, in the shower. I was alone and the water would wash off any blood spilled.

I thought of this as a type of twisted therapy. I would push myself and experience this pain now so that I had something to anchor myself onto later when I had the itch to speak. When I went on for too long without speaking I felt it bubble up inside me; maybe it was the curse or just wanting to be heard, but I couldn't keep silent for long without feeling like my insides would explode. My skin would become itchy, I'd get irritable, and my body would always feel too small for the emotions inside me.

"This was a bad idea."

Slash down my leg.

"Very bad."

Small cut on my neck.

"It will only get worse from here."

Slash all the way from my right shoulder to my left hip. I had to steady myself against the cool tiled wall of the shower as the cut took the breath out of my lungs and made me lightheaded.

I sighed. "Okay." Small cut on my wrist.

I waited for them all to heal and for my breathing to normalize before showering off. At least no one would chastise me for talking here.

My parents found out early on what I was doing in the shower and began shortening the time I was allowed to shower. One time when I was younger, right after the curse hit, I stood in the shower crying and muttering to myself for an hour. It was more than I had ever let myself say in months, all bottled up inside me fighting for the surface. I healed just as quickly as I do now but the phantom pains ached all over my body for days. After that I was more careful, limiting it to make sure I would be able to bounce back.

There was a small, timid knock at my door as I slipped a fresh turtleneck over my head. I opened to find another low-level demon in front of me, and he was so tall I had to step back to peer up to his face. He was handsome for sure. He had a straight nose, high cheekbones, dull grey eyes and reddish-brown hair that complemented his tawny skin.

Damn.

"I am Matt. Your fellow low-level." He gave me a smile a model would kill for. *If his attractiveness was normal for this school, I would be so screwed.* "Principal Winterfell asked me to give these to you, and he thought it would be good for us to get acquainted as there are only three of us this year. I am in year three; the person from year two hasn't arrived yet so it's just us." He paused to take in a breath of air. "Also he told me that you were mute so don't worry, I won't ask you to talk. Rosie right?"

I had to blink a few times to catch up to the stream of words that flew out of his mouth at breakneck speed. I slowly nodded when I realized he had asked me a question. He pushed the uniform toward me with a smile.

"Great, get changed and we can grab dinner. He said that you would prefer pants but gave you both pants and a skirt." I nodded and started to close the door before he rambled on again. After the door was closed I let out another sigh.

What a team.

A mute and a person who wouldn't shut up. I had never encountered someone who was willing to speak so much to me so my skin pricked with annoyance, but I tried not to let it bother me.

I put my button-up over my turtleneck and slid the light brown pants up over my leggings. I did not want to ask how the principal knew my size.

I opened the door to find Matt pacing. This kid had way too much energy.

"Uhm..." he trailed and tried to sign the phrase "Do you know ASL?" to me. A smile made its way to my face and the irritation I had felt earlier disappeared. Only a few people learned sign language to communicate with me and that was usually before they found out about my curse. They viewed can't talk and won't talk as two very different things.

A little, I signed back at him and watched a smile spread across his face. I wasn't going to lie, it was contagious.

"Mine is very bad. I took it last year. If I knew I would actually have had to use it I would have tried harder." He rubbed his already messy hair in embarrassment.

I sign. You talk, I signed to him. I was happy to stop typing on my phone for once. My inner cynic told me it wouldn't last long but I pushed the thought away. My parents tried for a while too but they never got the hang of it. I tried to push the anger down and keep my fake smile for Matt.

"Right, well let's go to the mess hall to grab dinner. I have been here since this morning so I had time to explore." He began leading me down the dorm stairs and out the building. "The mess hall is not too far. There also are a few other students that came back early. Mostly freshman. Most people have been staying away from me given our demon status but I don't mind too much; I am just here to finish my degree."

I could understand why he had so much to talk about and how the words just fell from his mouth. I had felt like that once too, when I was still excited about the world around me, before the hope was beaten out of me.

I let him talk without interrupting. It was nice to be around so much energy. He told me all about his family. The younger siblings he had back home. His single mom who was happy to the point of tears for him. He only paused when we entered the mess hall; it was rows upon rows of long tables and at the very end was the buffet table. He halfway dragged me to the front.

The lack of people made me anxious. There were only a few small groups of people and they very obviously stopped their conversations as we passed by. Matt didn't let it bother him though.

"Rhonda, I found my other friend!" he said loudly to the lady at the counter. She gave him a smile. I was surprised to see that she was even a higher level than my mom, the indicator being the vibrant blues of her eyes.

"Oh my what a surprise and what is your name, pumpkin?" Her voice had a sweet southern twist that made me want to spill my guts to her.

"Her name is Rosie and she is mute!" I almost wanted to hide my face in embarrassment at his volume.

"Well don't go yelling to the whole world now," she shot at him. He gave her a pout in return. "It's nice to meet you, Rosie. As you see here this is the buffet table, but if you want to order something you can do it here. When you get your card you will scan it here." She pointed to the screen near the edge of the counter. "And it will take it out of your account. But don't worry, all new students get free meals for a month so you don't have to worry too much about that."

What kind of dream school was this? Single dorms with showers? Free food? Stipends? Instead of the happiness or excitement that someone would normally feel in this situation, it left me extremely uncomfortable.

I didn't trust this.

"Look, the menu is there," Matt said. "It's numbered so you can just show them the number if you want. No talking needed." I followed his pointed finger and my mouth started to water at the food pictured. I had only seen food like this in movies and it all came with a huge price tag. Looking at the menus I was not surprised to see the cheapest thing, a garden salad, priced at thirty dollars. That two-hundred-dollar stipend made sense now.

"The buffet is only twenty dollars and you can pick as much as you want if the food that day doesn't tickle your fancy," Rhonda said noticing my panicked look. The buffet didn't look bad but looking at the menus above, it paled in comparison.

I held up the number four to her.

"Ohh, the truffle pasta with scallops looks good." He paused. "Is there anything else you want to try? We can share if you want. At least while the food is still free." He gave me another big smile. The big brother vibe he gave off was almost suffocating and caused emotions to stir inside me that I couldn't put a name to. I nodded at him and showed him the other steak pasta dish on the menu. "More carbs? I can get behind that."

"Gotcha. Go help yourself to the drinks and sides at the end, they are included in every meal." Rhonda sent us away with a smile. Matt grabbed himself a coke and raised his eyebrow asking me what I wanted. I took his coke instead.

He followed me to an empty table. People stopped staring but I personally wanted to stay as far away from the others as possible.

"Wow, this place is great. Free everything and a dorm all to myself." He sighed happily. "I wish I could have started as early as you."

You don't find it suspicious? I signed to him while taking a sip of my coke.

"Uhm...what's that sign?" he asked sheepishly. I spelled it out for him. "Suspicious?" He paused as if this was the first time he thought about it. Our food appeared in front of us before he could speak. I sent Rhonda a smile. "Nah, this is the heaven that rich people feel."

I heard a laugh from a nearby table. It was Emma. "They don't understand that they are alone because Principal Winterfell knows that their kind is not welcome here." She spoke loud enough for everyone in the quiet mess hall to hear, but Matt simply devoured his food. My body began to heat at her words. I knocked my hand on the table to get Matt's attention. His eyes met mine hesitantly.

Do you have a power? I asked after feeling my hands get unbearably hot. I would have to expel this anger at some point.

"Sorta." He held out his hand. I watched as a small flower grew out of his palm. He smiled and handed it to me. "My sister loved it growing up."

I smiled feeling a warmth spread in my chest at his gesture. *I love it. Watch mine*, I signed and in an instant the flower in my hand burnt to a crisp. I don't know if it was that people were obviously watching or that I wanted to talk about something other than the situation at hand, but I didn't feel scared to use my power. The witch had left a fear inside me that never left, but the guilt at what I did to my father's face and the house was stronger than any fear, making me want to never use my power again.

"Holy shit." Before he could let out the excitement that was building in his chest, a squeal from Emma's table caught our attention. I looked over to see her and her friends looking to the entrance and not a moment later, the same tingling sensation that I usually felt before my curse took effect spread through me. But this time was different. This one had a source and it was *warm*.

Looking over Matt's shoulder I was met with three of the most beautiful demons that I had ever seen in my life. I understood Emma's reaction now because inside I was doing the same, much to my dismay and slight disgust.

The first two had to be from very powerful families because their eyes were brighter than any I had seen before. Even from so far away I could see them glowing, and even if I couldn't the air had shifted and I felt something on the back of my tongue. You could *literally* taste their power.

The girl leading the group had a cocky smile that made my heart skip a beat. Paired with her long, slicked-back blonde hair, blue eyes, and pale skin, there was no doubt she commanded everyone's attention. And from the confident way she walked to the smile that seemed permanently engraved on her face, she had to have known that too. She was not in uniform, instead she wore a fitted black button-up that was fully buttoned, with a single white tie and matching black slacks.

The next girl by her had gleaming topaz eyes underneath her rectangular glasses. Her black hair was cut short on the sides but on top there was a definitive curl. Her expression was the exact opposite of the first. Instead of a smile, she had a small, deep scowl. She had a confident walk, but her narrowed eyes sent a chill through me and made the air run cold. Her olive skin tone stood in stark contrast to her pure white sweater and burgundy pants.

And last but not least there was a man trailing behind the two with a sour look on his face. This one looked like he was ready to fight anyone that even dared to cross his path. He was the most casually dressed in an over-sized Metallica shirt and loose ripped jeans. His bare arms showed two full black and grey sleeves of tattoos. My mouth watered at the sight. The tattoos wrapped around his strong arms so beautifully that it looked like they were made to fit every dip and curve. His messy brown hair was almost the same color as his eyes.

Wait.

His eyes weren't glowing like the other two's. They were brown. Very similar to my own, but I had yet to meet anyone with the same colored eyes as me before.

As they got nearer I became aware of two things.

One: they were fucking huge. If I stood up I would probably not even come to their shoulders and all of them, even the girls, were so fit that their biceps had to be the size of my head.

Two: the tingling I felt came from one man, the brown-eyed one. As they passed our table it licked at my skin. And as if in response, my curse magic moved under my skin but didn't even try to reach the surface; it just shifted like it was awoken from a type of slumber. Before I got lost in the way the tingling warmed my body, I got one more surprise.

A black long-haired cat trailed behind the group. It paused when it got to our table and its yellow-sliced eyes met mine. I smiled at it and patted the seat I was on hoping that it would reward me with its attention. It hesitated to look at the trailing group but then decided to join me on the bench.

"Oh my god, what a cute cat!" Matt cooed. It sat in front of me like it was waiting for something. I eagerly began petting it behind the ears and scratching its chin. If we were alone I would coo sweet nothings in its ear, but I was playing a part now. My parents never were fond of animals. Especially cats. They were convinced cats were the witches' spies and any cat that came near was trying to harm us. The cat began purring and nudged its head against my hand.

Nothing this cute could do any harm.

As soon as the thought passed through my head I felt the same tingling sensation as before shoot up my arm. I paused. The cat's eyes opened to check why I was stalling.

"Amr," a deep husky voice called from the end of the mess hall. I felt my heart stumble at the sound. Looking over I saw the brown-eyed one staring at us with an unreadable expression.

"He's degraded himself to flirting with a low-level for attention." The blonde girl with the cocky smile spoke her words loudly. Her arm was currently wrapped around the brown-eyed one and she was smiling at us. The smile seemed malicious now though, curling at the edges of her lips, and her eyes narrowed at us. Embarrassment rose up in me faster than I could stop it.

Of course, the hot ones had to be bitches.

The cat looked at them and then back to me. I smiled at the movement and patted his head.

Go, I signed to the cat.

"He probably can't understand the sign. She says go," Matt supplied helpfully. I rolled my eyes.

It's an obvious sign, I signed to him and turned away from the cat to finish my dinner.

The cat must have taken the order because it left my side.

"I can't believe Daxton's cat went to *her*," Emma's friend tried to whisper to her friend group. "I have been trying to grab that little shit since middle school."

My eyes trailed to the man that now sat a few rows away from us. My heart skipped a beat when brown eyes met mine. *Daxton*, apparently.

Do you know them? I asked Matt and he shook his head. He switched our pastas and began digging into mine.

"Maybe we can ask our friends over there." So, he was capable of whispering. His tone was so snarky I almost wanted to let out a laugh.

That's a battle for another time. He gave me a confused look. *Battle, really? B-a-t-t-l-e.*

"Yaaa... I have been here awhile and I am getting tired so it may best be left for another time. After dinner we can just rest before tomorrow."

What's tomorrow? I asked. I thought we had a free day.

"You get a personal tour from this guy." He pointed his thumbs back at himself in an exaggerated gesture. I let myself mime a laugh, careful to not make any noise.

Can't wait.

Chapter Three
Rosie

As it turned out, the third person would never be joining us.

We only found that out after we were asked to go visit Principal Winterfell in the middle of my personal tour. I had to admit, Matt was a breath of fresh air to be around after I had gotten used to his ramblings. No one had quite been this energetic around me before and it felt like I had something akin to the start of a friendship with him. I tried not to let myself get too excited though; it was only our second day.

"Please, Ms. Miller alone first if you don't mind Mr. Thompson." Matt gave him an okay and sat back down in the lobby chair. I followed Principal Winterfell into his office and sat down in the same seat as yesterday without him prompting. I imagined that I might as well get comfortable as I would be meeting with him regularly. He shut the door softly. "I have news to tell both of you but I wanted to give you a suggestion before we continued." He paused, the twinkle in his eyes back in full force. "You need to tell Mr. Thompson of your curse."

"Why?" I asked and a sharp pain blossomed on my calf. I guess that had too much panic infused in it.

"You are alone here and it would be good to have someone on your side that can help you hide the curse if needed." His words made sense. If just one person could help keep this a secret it would be a shared burden...but a burden nonetheless. I didn't want to do that to him.

"I'll think about it," I rushed out and bit my lip to stop the groan that was forcing its way up my throat. They all landed on my back on top of one another.

"How far has it gone before?" the principal asked rubbing his chin, obviously more fascinated in my pain than he should be.

"Three ribs." As if the curse were self-aware, its next spot spanned across my ribs. A warning. He nodded and got up to call Matt back in. Matt's smiling face made its way through the office.

"So, some bad news," Principal Winterfell said with a sigh and took his chair in front of me with Matt to my side. "The second year who was supposed to join us declined the offer, meaning that you will be the only two to join us this year. Since you are already well acquainted I don't have to tell you to stick together but...here is a word of advice. People will not be happy. When—and I do mean *when*—they decide to take that up with you, talk to me about it. Get their names and come to me. I will not stand for the harassment of fellow students." His words surprised me and made me uncomfortable at the same time. This was the same person who brought me here just to observe my curse and now he was acting like he cared about our wellbeing.

Maybe I was just being too untrusting, but I didn't like how the people around here made a full one-eighty and decided that I was actually worth their time now.

"Aw, that's nice Principal Winterfell. Rosie and I are fast friends. I was concerned about our classes being in different buildings but I am not sure if you can change that?" Matt replied sending me a smile when he said "fast friends." Damn him. Now I felt bad about keeping my curse from him.

As if the principal could read my thoughts he shot me a look before responding. "Yes, unfortunately we cannot have the different years in the same buildings for classes. Far too many students, you see." He shuffled around in his desk and pulled out two packets for each of us. "But now that everyone is here. I wanted to give you a chance to look over the different majors that you can choose from while you're here. Mr. Thompson, I recommend taking one as close to the one you already have been taking in order to keep up with your classes. For Ms. Miller, you are a clean slate and can choose from whichever major you want."

"Yes, I would like to stick with mathematics..." His voice trailed off as he was shuffling through the packet. Looking at my own I realized there were only a few categories one could pick when coming into this school.

Demon History and Culture
Government Relations and Politics
Science
Mathematics

"While high-level demons can have any job, we want this school to focus on obtaining government positions and the advancement of science." He paused. "Barely any students are in the other majors and it would be a waste to spend money on resources to expand the list."

So I was an experiment.

I pointed to Demon History and Culture.

"Good choice. There are not many people in that major so hopefully your classes will go by smoothly." He leaned back in his chair looking pleased with himself. "Expect your schedules within the next few days. Until then, enjoy your time away from classes!"

We both were dismissed and as soon as we were out of his office Matt jumped back into the flurry of words that he had been holding back since we had entered.

* * *

After much deliberation—to be honest it wasn't much, it only took one puppy dog look from Matt—I decided that Principal Winterfell was right about one thing: it may be safer to have someone on my side. This would be a first for me and it made me uncomfortable to divulge such a secret.

Would Matt be afraid? Would he look at me differently? There were so many ways this could go and I worried that the closest thing I had to a friend would disappear right before my eyes. I had come here to just get away from my parents, but finding Matt already was like finding a diamond in the rough.

We were lying in the courtyard now, enjoying the nice breeze. It was his idea. He was so much like a golden retriever that I couldn't help but give in to his demands. There was no one around, thankfully, so this would be the perfect time to bring it up. I also didn't want to wait around to see what the stuck-up high-levels would think of us *sullying* ourselves in the dirty grass. I tapped Matt on the shoulder lightly.

Can I tell you a secret? I signed. He furrowed his brows together like he was confused.

"Of course you can," he said and rolled his body toward me so I had his full attention. I took a deep breath to prepare myself.

Now or never, Rosie.

"I am cursed." And I was slashed right across the chest and once on my wrist. I hurried to lift up my shirt sleeve before the cut healed. Matt's eyes widened when he finally heard my voice but they snapped to my now bleeding wrist. He scrambled up on his knees and gripped my wrist, watching as it healed. "Can't speak," I explained and in front of Matt a line slashed down my arm once more.

"Holy shit," he said breathlessly. He thought for a moment and dropped my wrist as if it were contagious. I tried not to feel hurt when he did that.

I thought it would be best you knew, I signed to him. His eyes met mine slowly. This was the longest I had seen him go in silence.

"When?"

My tenth birthday.

"Why."

I had to finger spell debt.

I have to say, this was not the reaction I was expecting but it was the normal one. People got scared when they saw the curse in action and tended to run for the hills. Or on the off chance they liked to wreak havoc, they would take advantage of it. There was never any in-between.

Matt surprised me even further by pulling me into a hug. I stiffened but he held me tighter, engulfing me into his warmth. His fresh scent filled my senses and my breath caught. It had been too long since I had been held like this. His hand cupped the back of my head and pulled me tighter into his chest.

"It must be so hard for you," he said after a moment and pulled me back at arm's length. "You need a witch."

A witch did this, I signed to him.

"Then they can fix it!" he insisted.

How do you find a witch? I asked him, already giving in. I had never seen one before out in the open. Even the one that showed up at my birthday had been clouded by the smoke that overtook the burning house, leaving her features unidentifiable.

"We are literally in the best place to!" he exclaimed and scrambled us to a standing position but didn't remove his hands from my shoulders. "I heard that they have hundreds here! And if they can get in here they must be powerful!"

Or rich. He ignored my sign.

"Ew, the low-levels have bonded." Emma's snide voice broke through the moment we were having. I prayed to god they didn't hear anything.

"Perfect!" he exclaimed looking at the group of high-levels that were making their way down the path. "Do you guys know the name of a witch?"

Emma and her posse stopped. Her green eyes widened slightly and then narrowed once more. "Why would you need a witch?" My heart skipped a beat and I gripped his shirt tightly.

"For research of course," he explained like it was the only possible answer.

"Is the mute not a witch?" asked a girl with a black bob. Her eyes were a bright hazel and stood out against her pale skin.

Me? A witch?

"Shut it, Marie," the girl with long blonde hair next to Emma said. She had the same eye color as her. Maybe a similar family?

"If she was I wouldn't need to ask." He pouted at them.

"Most witches have brown eyes. Just seek them out," Emma provided looking to the ground quickly. The handsome brown-eyed boy I saw in the mess hall flashed through my mind. I had a bad feeling that if what Emma said was true, that he would be a witch too.

"I see!" Matt sent her a smile. "Thanks!" He leaned over to pick up the bags on the ground and pulled me with him across the campus.

I tried to sign to him, but he was intent on searching the grounds. After we had crossed almost the entire campus, searched in all the common areas, and even walked the halls of some of the dorms, we finally found people that we could ask. My heart dropped when I saw who it was.

It was the blonde girl that we saw yesterday. She was leaning against the wall of the building, this time actually in the required school uniform and it fit her even better than those all-black clothes had. It fit her *too well.* Heat rose to my face when I saw how tight the shirt was over her chest. She had opted for pants like myself, but I couldn't tell if I was envious of the way she looked in them or turned on at the sight. As we came closer to her it was clear that she was smoking. She tipped her head back showing her long, toned neck and jaw, then ever so slowly exhaled the smoke. Her eyes lazily made contact with mine.

Fuck.

I panicked and averted my gaze, and that was when I realized she wasn't alone. The man with brown eyes was sitting on the ground next to him, also smoking.

Daxton. The rumored witch.

His form was hidden from our view previously but seeing him now, I knew we were fucked if we went up to them. His eyes were narrowed in our direction and his mouth formed a scowl. His brown orbs burned into my skull even from the distance we were in now. He would be in no mood to talk.

I pulled harshly on Matt's hand. He stopped in his tracks and looked back to me with a questioning gaze.

Don't talk to them, I signed to him. I wasn't sure what I felt coming from them but it was not just their looks that made me pause. Even from here the tingling sensation radiating off Daxton, and even the blonde girl, had some type of dangerous aura. It caused the hair on the back of my neck to raise and my blood to pump wildly.

"Why? I told you I would find a witch for you." He gave me the same pout that he gave Emma earlier.

You heard them yesterday, I signed. *They don't like us.*

"No one here does, Rosie," he said giving me a small smile.

I was about to sign but I saw the blonde girl's form suddenly tower over us, shadowing us from the previous sunshine. Even Matt couldn't compare to her height. The cigarette was still in her hand but she met us with the same cocky smile that she had before.

"So the low-level really can't talk," she jabbed. "I was curious to see it myself. How do you expect to survive here when you can't even speak?"

"She can sign and has a phone. It works," Matt answered for me, obviously not understanding the difference in status here. The blonde girl did not even look at him.

"I'm Eli," she said to me and stretched her hand out to me. I stared at her large, scarred hand not knowing what to do.

Would it be rude not to accept?

High-levels were known to get temperamental against our kind, beating whoever crossed them.

"I won't bite," she joked but the smile never left her face, "outside of the bedroom."

I took my chances and slipped my hand into hers. It was rougher than I expected and practically swallowed mine. My mind automatically thought of what it would be like to have hands as big as hers trail themselves along my body, around my throat, gripping my hips. Before I could actually get farther in those fantasies her fingers tightened around mine painfully. At first I thought she was just messing around but it got more and more painful every second that passed. I had to bite my lip to stop any noise from escaping my lips.

"What are you doing?" Matt hissed at Eli. She only tightened her hand more and my knees buckled at the pain causing me to kneel in front of her. A whimper tried to make its way up my throat but I refused to let it out. A pained breath left me.

"This is a good position for you, low-level. I have never met a mute before, and wanted to see what happened when they were in pain." I swear if she squeezed any harder she was going to break my hand.

Do all high-level possess such strength? I was so weak in comparison it was laughable.

"No, just me. Don't think to compare me to the other mediocre demons that go here," she replied like she was responding to my thoughts.

"Cause I am," she said with a smile.

I panicked with this information. If she could read my mind how much could she see? Surface thoughts? My whole life story. Embarrassment flooded. She definitely heard what I thought about her hands.

I met her eyes; that damn smile was still there but her head was leaned back now and her eyes were hooded. She seemed to be enjoying this immensely. She brought the cigarette in her free hand to her lips and inhaled slowly. She then looked at it quizzically.

"Let her go, now," Matt demanded.

"Don't talk to me, low-level." Her eyes met mine again. "Can mutes scream?" She twirled the cigarette between her fingers.

Please don't, I begged her. Suddenly the tingling sensation heightened, and a sense of relief filled me. Daxton appeared next to her. He was only slightly shorter and his brown eyes met our conjoined hands. My hand was now starting to turn purple under the pressure.

"This is a waste of time, Eli." His eyes met mine slowly. "Even if you cut off her arm she wouldn't be able to scream." A cold chill washed over me at his words. Was this really a save or was he just giving her more ideas?

"No one is going to save you, low-level," Eli responded, but let go of my hand nonetheless. "Find me if you want an encore. You have some *interesting* thoughts there."

With that she turned on her heel and left. Daxton paused and followed her a moment after. He seemed to be searching for something but whatever it was he didn't find it. Matt's worried face entered my view and he gripped my hand softly.

"What an ass," he muttered looking at my healing hand. The bruise would be gone in another minute and thankfully there were no broken bones.

I sighed and looked over his shoulder. Their forms were rounding a corner of one of the various school buildings, just about to disappear from view.

"Fuck him," I let myself whisper, not caring about the pain in my back.

As if Daxton heard it he stopped in his tracks and his eyes snapped toward mine. The waning tingling sensation suddenly intensified and his eyes felt like they were burning holes in my head. It was Eli that grabbed his arm and dragged him away. If they had super hearing *and* strength, we were even more fucked than I thought.

* * *

The rest of the week went by without incident from the duo. Matt and I settled into a routine that was broken for the first time on the weekend when he went to go visit his family.

Mom had asked if I wanted to visit them on the weekend but I told them that I wanted to stay to prepare for the start of the term. They took the excuse at face value and for that I was glad. I contemplated telling the principal what happened but Eli's hooded expression flashed through my mind once more. She would probably enjoy any excuse to knock me around.

Psychopaths.

After dinner I decided to take the path back to the dorm that Matt had shown me on one of our free days. It looked to be less commonly used and there was even a full secret garden on the way. I had been itching to speak all day since Matt was gone. He didn't chastise me for speaking when I chose to but he did worry when I started to push into full-blown sentences. Honestly, I shouldn't have been pushing my curse like this, but he was one of the only people outside my family that knew and I didn't realize how lonely it had been to not have anyone know about the curse.

Still, I decided to push it just a little more. I could sense when it was too much and I wouldn't subject myself to anything crazy in public, but the curse, my words, became so bottled up that I wanted to scream.

I turned into the small garden and was happy to see that it was still empty. There was an elaborate dry fountain that was in the middle, surrounded by overgrown rose bushes. The orange sky was visible when you looked up, along with the large Winterfell tower that read six o'clock. I walked around it and sat down on the fountain's edge in a way that would hide me from view even if people came.

"This was a stupid idea." I let myself groan as the pain radiated through my legs and was rewarded with a slash on my arm. "A bit too loud huh?" I whispered and was rewarded with another, yet less severe slash. I waited while I healed. "I hate this curse." The curse must have known that I was talking about it because I was rewarded with a strong one on my back.

I didn't have another chance to say anything because I heard someone coming through the path I had taken.

"I felt it." Daxton's voice rang through the garden. There was something off about it; it was frenzied and I heard the way his feet rubbed against the pavement. He was searching for something and I knew that Eli would probably be close by.

Find me if you want an encore. Her voice twirled around in my head, teasing me as if she stood right over my shoulder.

"Fuck," I whispered, suddenly regretting that I let it slip out. There was a pause. My heart was pounding in my ears. Did he leave?

A strong hand lifted me up and slammed me against the edge of the fountain painfully. His arm circled around my waist and a large hand gripped my chin roughly and forced me to look up, right into Daxton's frenzied brown eyes. His normally cool expression was gone and in its place was something akin to a feral animal. I let out a small gasp in surprise, my back burned once more.

Daxton inhaled deeply. My heart skipped a beat and I couldn't stop myself from watching his full lips as they parted. The action made my stomach warm and my mouth dry. He then leaned his face closer to mine but instead of kissing me like I had thought—and foolishly hoped—he stuck his face in the crook of my neck and inhaled again.

"This is the most potent magic I have ever come across." He groaned and pushed his hips roughly into mine. He was already hard. I tried to push him away but his grip was strong, making sure that there was no space in between us.

I debated whether or not I should speak. Even though I had only seen him once or twice, anyone could have guessed that this was not his normal character. And as hot as he was, this was not how I imagined my next sexual encounter to take place.

He bit hard into my neck through my clothes and I had to stifle a yelp. He bit harder, breaking the skin. Tears pricked my eyes. These demons seem to like pain. He pushed down my turtleneck and his tongue reached out to lick the sore area, then he trailed up to my ear, biting it.

"Daxton," a voice called out. His arms tightened around me in response as if he was afraid to let them take me. "Let the low-level go. If you want magic go find a witch."

"No," he growled and yanked at my hair. "Her magic is so potent."

Chapter Four
Daxton

Principal Winterfell had warned me that the school's magic may overwhelm me, but his explanation had been less than a third of what I was actually hit with when coming onto the campus for the first time.

As soon as I stepped on campus my own magic reacted to it violently. In less than ten minutes my magic became so angry that my body swelled with it painfully. It started to fight underneath my skin begging for me to expel it. I would have to find a witch to exchange some magic with me as soon as possible. I was not partial to bloodletting so that only left two choices. Amr not being an option knocked that list down to one, but I had yet to come across a witch since I got here.

There was something else in the campus though. It played with my senses and aggravated my magic even further. It had a musky aura, aged even. So it had to be old, even older than the campus itself, and it was strong.

So strong that I could taste it. Like a waft of whiskey just barely enough for the tip of my tongue. I knew that as soon as I found it, if I was in the right mind I would need to keep the source as far away from me as possible. I didn't need a repeat of *that night*.

"I'm sure a little witch would be honored to help you *expel* some magic," Eli teased as she took a drag of her cigarette. I inhaled my own, enjoying the way it burned my throat. I needed something to calm me down before I sought anyone out. The semester had yet to start and there was no sign of any witches yet. Maybe Jess would be here soon. She had hinted that she would be coming to Winterfell Academy. She was a proficient enough witch to help with my magic and she also had a tight little ass so you could guess the way she liked to take my magic. I wasn't complaining; anything was better than bloodletting, but sex magic was definitely a sweeter deal.

Eli knew all about it. Hell, she has been there for most of it. If we had not built up the relationship we had, I would have been in real trouble when I lost control on the witch of choice that evening. I had felt so guilty, still did honestly, but she was from an old witch family so she understood the struggle when the magic overtook your senses.

I still blamed myself though. I should have kept up with my growing magic. I should have kept a pulse check on it but I let it slip and almost paid for it with a person's life. I would never forget the way her life force flickered when the magic was almost drained out of her body.

"They are not here yet," I said with a sigh and took another drag, trying to chase the stray thoughts away.

"Oh?" I recognized that tone from Eli. I looked over to see what gained her attention. It was the two low-levels, the first to ever come to this academy. They either had balls of steel or a death wish. "I heard that girl's a mute."

"We saw her yesterday," I reminded. Principal Winterfell must hate low-levels more than the average demon if he thought to extend the first spot to a mute. There was no way she would survive here, especially if she caught the attention of Eli so quickly. She may not kill in cold blood but she would make you wish she had if you were subject to her torments.

She best leave if she knows what's good for her, I thought watching Eli's face. She was already too interested in her for her to get out of this unscathed.

"Yeah, but it's not like I was paying attention to her." Her eyes narrowed at the two. It looked like they were coming over here until the mute low-level yanked the ginger boy back.

A death wish.

They had a death wish if they wanted to approach Eli when she was already so interested. "I wonder..."

She pushed off the wall and walked over to the two low-levels. Amr had also shown an unusual level of interest when it came to the girl. He never approached someone before; he wasn't supposed to. That's why it made all of this far odder.

I watched as Eli went to go talk to them. The girl obviously had more common sense than the boy. She cowered as she approached but the boy stood straight as if Eli's presence didn't even scare him.

Eli introduced herself with her hand extended out to the girl. I snorted at her actions. Of course she would use her powers on them—it was a perfect chance to get into her head, literally.

I stomped out my cigarette and walked over to her. It wouldn't do any good to cause so much trouble before the term started. Afterward, I didn't care so as long as she didn't get kicked out. If she left there was no way I would stick around with just Honor Student here to keep me company. Going back to my parents' house was out of the question; I vowed that as soon as I was able to I would leave that damned place. This school was the easiest way to get out of their grasp.

A shiver ran through me when I got close enough to look at her face. She was attractive for a low-level, too attractive. Her black hair was a mess around her head and brought out the stark contrast of her pale skin. Her freckles sprinkled delicately over her nose and cheeks and she had small but plump lips that were now almost bleeding due to her teeth biting into them so hard.

The image went straight to my cock.

It didn't help that my magic was itching under my skin. I wanted nothing more than to expel this magic, but sex with a low-level wouldn't suffice. I needed a witch to take some magic at least or this would be all for naught. Not that Eli would ever let me live it down.

"This is a waste of time, Eli," I told her. More for my own sake than the girl's. "Even if you cut off her arm she wouldn't be able to scream."

"No one is going to save you, low-level," Eli told her but she let go of her now bruised hand anyways. "Find me if you want an encore." Eli pushed past me but I lingered, watching as the low-level boy huddled over her. I wondered what Amr saw in her.

I followed behind Eli closely as we left. Her back was tensed but her face showed no hint of anything but her arrogant smile. She wore it like it was her job, never letting anybody see anything different. I was about to ask what she saw in her mind but a sudden flash of that old powerful magic filled my senses. My magic roared to life and I snapped my head back over to the low-levels. Inhaling deeply I could tell it was coming from their vicinity. My mind didn't want to make any connections. The only thing I wanted was to get closer to the magic, devour it and everything in its path.

Eli grabbed my arm roughly and pulled me along with her when she realized I was not following. "I know that look," she grumbled. I wanted to laugh at her antics but also felt like tearing my hand away from her and hunting down that magic. "Don't forget last time."

"Yes, ma'am," I told her, my voice coming out in a growl. I didn't want to lose myself again. It was a deep hole that was hard to get out of and that's why witches gained such a bad rep.

We are pure. Without hate. Without desire. Without violence. My mother's words washed through my mind. They were fucking ridiculous if they thought meditation and light spells would get rid of the desires that came with magic of this caliber. It was angry. It was violent. And there was nothing pure about it.

"That low-level will be interesting," Eli said snapping me out of my magic-filled haze. "I look forward to playing with her."

The panic-filled look she gave me filled my mind again.

"She's good looking for a low-level," I responded.

"Interested in hearing her scream in a different way but I'll let you have her when I'm done." She sent me a wink.

"Mutes can't scream," I reminded her once more.

"We will see," she said, a dangerous light flashing through her eyes.

Rae met up with us not much later. She was already looking worn out.

"Honor Student," I greeted as she walked over to the bench we were currently sitting at. Eli handed me another cigarette.

"Dax, seems like you are having trouble with your magic *again*." Her topaz eyes narrowed in my direction. We had a more strained relationship than her and Eli. I didn't like her whole good girl act she put on in front of everyone. I knew it was because of her parents mostly, but it annoyed the living hell out of me that she thought she was above everyone else. I do owe her for her help in covering up the incident with the witch though.

"He just needs to find a witch to bend over." Eli chuckled.

"There are none yet, I checked the roster. None of them have checked in," Rae said. I didn't let my surprise show on my face but she must have felt it. "Just covering our bases," she said in response to my emotions.

"Can't Amr take some?" Eli lit her cigarette and then passed the lighter to me.

"He's sleeping," I muttered. Amr had taken a lot over the break and it had worn him out more than usual. Guilt gnawed at me. He was supposed to be a strong familiar and he had been able to keep up for years, but my magic grew the summer before senior year and he had been struggling to adjust.

"Maybe you can trade him for a new version," Eli joked. "A girl, since you seem so against him in his shifted form."

Disgust rolled my stomach.

"Witches who take advantage of their familiars are trash," I growled at her. "You know not to joke like that."

"Testy," she teased and exhaled some smoke. A dirty smirk graced her plump lips. "I could always extend my services if you want to take an edge off."

I thought over it while taking a drag. I wouldn't mind it to be honest, but I wasn't sure if it would wind my magic up even more. It was too volatile right now to tell. Eli and I had formed a sexual relationship almost as soon as we had met years ago. She came onto me almost right away and I didn't know what to expect when my experience back then was so little and corrupted by my parents' *teachings* and *rituals*, but she definitely showed me a side of sex that I'd never thought I'd allow myself to feel. I was grateful for her.

"You know you can't help him," Rae answered for me, saving me from having to reject Eli. She may have been annoying but her ability to read emotions paid off more than once.

"Just come knocking when you want me," Eli said with a wink.

* * *

The week had been one of the hardest I had experienced since my magic first began growing. Every day the magic underneath my skin grew bigger and bigger, leaving my skin aching.

I did end up taking Eli on her offer, coming into her dorm in the middle of the night and practically jumping her bones. She was more than happy to please and didn't let me leave until she had thoroughly left me shaking and delirious. Eli's skill with a strap was unparalleled and a very needed distraction.

It was only but a small distraction though.

The next day I was back with them in the area that we had deemed ours. I was lying in the grass, Eli sitting next to me. She had stolen a demon's jacket and used it to sit on the grass so it wouldn't dirty her pants. The demon didn't dare fight when they saw who was stealing their jacket.

Rae was standing near the tree not daring to get her clothes dirty. It was times like these, when we were all together, where I could actually rest and let a sort of peaceful calm fill me. The magic may have been terrorizing my insides but at least the other two were here to keep an eye on me.

Eli turned to me. Her eyes had a playful glint. Her hand brushed the hand that was resting on my stomach, sending me a message before moving south.

Can you stay quiet? she asked in my head.

I swallowed thickly as her hand brushed my cock. It responded to her immediately, springing to life and getting painfully hard. The magic fighting inside me plus her touches were driving me insane.

Her fingers expertly traced the outline in my pants but before I could close my eyes and enjoy what Eli was about to do, the old magic flared once again. I stiffened.

"Dax?" Eli asked confused at my change.

I felt the magic flare once more. It was so close. I gritted my teeth together painfully. It was strong. So strong.

Every time since it had started, it had only been one or two bursts, but now it was consistent and with my magic already on edge, I couldn't control the thoughts racing through my mind.

Destroy. Devour. Dominate. The magic commanded me, pushed me forward taking control of my body. I had to give it what it wanted; I had to find the source. Annihilate it.

I leaped up and began moving toward the source of the magic.

I heard the others call for me as my feet moved faster but there was no way I could stop now. They were trying to keep up but they couldn't, and the more the magic infiltrated my senses the more I felt certain that I would die before I let them stop me. I followed it in between the buildings and down a forgotten path. I stopped when I found myself in the middle of an empty garden and inhaled deeply. It was here.

"I felt it," I growled to my magic.

Find it. Find it. Find it, my magic seemed to demand.

My eyes narrowed in onto the side of the fountain. *There.*

The magic was *so pleased.* I didn't recognize the magical signature of the witch it came from. The only thing I could focus on once I found the witch was ripping the magic from her. I forced the witch's face up to mine and wrapped my arms around her. She was strong, I could smell it, but the magic swirled through her oddly.

"This is the most potent magic I have ever come across," I told her and ground my already formed erection into her. I would take her and her magic. With magic this potent I could destroy worlds once it tangled with mine.

I had to have it.

I inhaled her scent deeply by burying my face in her neck.

Yes. The magic egged me on. Hers was so sweet I had to taste it. I bit into her clothed neck and the magic sprang to life. I bit harder, enjoying the way it felt against mine. I moved her turtleneck down and licked the area. The magic from the small bit of blood began to enter my body easily. My own magic was sucking it up like a vacuum. It didn't help that she was turned on; the magic latched onto the intoxicating feeling adding fuel to the fire.

"Daxton." Rae had found us. I tightened my arms around her refusing to let her take her. I didn't want anyone else to take this magic from me. I wouldn't let them separate her from me. "Let the low-level go. If you want magic go find a witch."

Was she blind? She was obviously a witch. How could she not be with *this* type of magic spilling out of her?

"No," I growled at her and pulled the witch's hair back to expose her neck more. "Her magic is so potent."

Hands grasped at my shirt and pulled me roughly away from her. I let my arms loosen just enough that she wouldn't be injured when I was pulled away. I didn't want the good to be hurt before I could get any magic, so it was either let her go or have her crushed by whoever chose to fight me.

"I told you that you could have the low-level after I was done with her," Eli teased and pulled my arms back painfully. Rae stood near the woman. Her scared brown eyes met mine. Her magic was still calling out to me.

Rae grabbed a small knife that she conveniently kept in her school jacket and walked toward me.

"Don't you dare, Rae," I growled at her. It was infused with magic and sounded more animal than human at this point. I hoped the witch took that as a sign of my power. She would come crawling once she understood the power I could offer her.

"She's not a witch. Look," Eli whispered by my side. "She can't help you expel magic." I met her wide eyes once more. Only then did I realize that it was the low-level mute that we met earlier. Even at the realization my magic didn't recoil; it kept pushing forward begging me to take her, becoming feral when it realized what Rae wanted to do.

In my distraction Rae lunged forward and slashed her knife across my chest deep enough for blood to start pouring out. I groaned but did not quit my fighting against Eli.

"I don't want to *expel* magic. I want to take hers," I growled. The magic in my blood began expelling quicker than I wanted it to. I became frustrated. My power was draining from me, spilling all over me then to the floor. A waste. Such a fucking *waste*. "Let me take hers. I won't hurt her. I want it so bad."

"Look at you begging," Eli teased again. "It's been a while since I had the honor to see this." Her lips lowered to my ear once more. "Kinda turns me on."

I wasn't pushing hard enough for you to beg last night, huh? Maybe a bigger strap next time, if you can take it, her voice whispered in my head.

My magic flared at her words. Anything she offered paled in comparison to this girl's magic and it was angry that I even considered it.

Rae slashed me again down my arm and I fell to my knees. I let out a loud exhale, feeling the magic seep out through my blood. Rae left me on the ground and wiped the blade off with a cloth she pulled out of his pocket.

"Apologies, Ms. Miller," she told her in a polite tone. There she goes again. "He has trouble with magic. Curious though as to why he thought you were exuding any type of magic?" The way she spoke was low and direct. "Last I checked, you are the new low-level."

She shifted slightly. Her chest was moving up and down erratically trying to catch her breath. She patted her pockets searching for her phone and began typing furiously. She showed her the screen not a moment later, her face lit by the artificial light.

"Don't play dumb, low-level," she snapped.

I was calm enough to shake Eli off. I shuddered as I stood. Bloodletting was always horrible, it left me weak and like I had lost a part of myself. Most of our magic hides in our blood so if it's let out by blood without transfer it just dissipates. I would much rather take her blood than let mine.

I hated wasted magic.

"I know you know more than you are letting on," she pushed her. "Come on dirty little low-level." Eli's voice was smooth as if she did not just insult her. "Tell us."

Her eyes met mine then. Did she think I would stop them? I was also curious and I desperately needed to know if she could help. I was on the verge of begging her, giving her anything she wanted if she could supply me just an ounce of whatever magic she had.

She must have realized I wouldn't help because she picked up her discarded school bag and began to walk away. Rae grabbed her shirt, stopping her from leaving.

"What if I told you I already knew?" she asked her. She acted like the air was punched out of her. A loud exhale came from her and I felt the magic again. The whiskey taste filled my mouth. I gritted my teeth and stayed planted against the ground. It was small but it was there.

Chapter Five
Rosie

*F*uck.

How did I already fuck this up? School hadn't even started yet and my secret had spilled.

"It's easy to find out information when you know the right people. I also took the liberty of looking into your past and found something...interesting." Her voice was low and threatening. I hated the situation she put me in but her voice was so demanding and it made shivers run down my spine. "Do you want to tell them? Or should I? I suggest you do or else I will let it slip to the entire school."

I swallowed thickly. I guess I didn't have a choice.

"I'm cursed," I said barely above a whisper and was rewarded with a pain in my back. Daxton let out a groan.

Was it my curse that was causing him to go crazy? What was his problem?

Eli let out a disappointed sigh. "That's not any fun. I enjoyed the thought of the mute better." Anger flared through me.

"Good, you crazy bitch," I hissed at her but regretted it as the curse slashed my chest, causing me to bleed through my shirt.

Rae gave me a smile that showed me that she was not at all surprised with the outcome. But Daxton slowly got up and began walking toward us. I tried to pull out of Rae's grip but she didn't let me.

"Do you think a cursed individual will work as well as a witch?" he asked Rae but his eyes were crazed and poised on me as he spoke. There was something far too disconcerting about the look he was giving me now.

"Not sure. We should probably test it," Rae offered. I had no idea what that meant but from the look in her eyes I knew I should probably be scared. But at the same time, my core clenched. Rae gave me an odd look. "I would expect a low-level to have better self-preservation strategies."

"This is so boring guys," Eli whined and started kicking at the rose bush. "Who cares about a stupid curse?"

"Eli," Rae started and her pink-tinted lips twitched as Eli hit another rose bush. "Watch what happens when she speaks." Rae's other hand pulled at the edge of my shirt and tried to force it up, effectively giving them a full view of my light pink bra. "Speak," she commanded.

I didn't speak at first. Instead, I just glared at her. I didn't want to let her push me around like this.

"Fuck you," I responded. The curse must have liked her because two slices ran themselves down my sides near my ribs, giving them a perfect view of how it worked. The fabric must have been stained by the sheer number of cuts I received today but even so, a look of absolute excitement graced Eli's girlishly handsome face. I shuddered at the way she told me she wanted to hurt me before. Now that she knew this, I was sure she was going to push me just like the other school bullies.

"Oh my god." Eli began laughing. She had to hold her stomach in order to contain herself. Daxton's warm hand came out to brush across my bare stomach. "This is fucking perfect. Too good." She came to stand by Daxton and watched as he trailed his fingers where the cuts just were. I tried to ignore the way it sent shivers down my spine and I hoped to god they couldn't see my nipples through my bra. "I think you have the right idea," she whispered to Daxton. "Let's share, hmm?"

I flushed, thinking of those two together in bed. Their stature? At both of their mercies? At the same time? They would fucking destroy me. Eli sent me a smile. Daxton grabbed her harshly by the wrist. They locked gazes and the tension was almost palpable. I stepped back and pulled my shirt down, practically ripping it from Rae's grasp.

I typed on my phone quickly and pushed it in Rae's face. *Get your stupid friends off my back and don't let them touch me again.* Her shoulders sagged and she put a hand on her hip, almost like an act of defiance.

"It's not like I'm in charge of them, and from the way arousal is rolling off of you I guess you don't mind it." I flushed with anger at her words and tried to type my response but Eli's scarred hand covered mine.

You can use me if you want to speak. Her voice came into my head. I met her eyes but her expression remained unchanged.

I don't need your help. Don't touch me, I thought hoping it would land.

You may want to rethink that, pathetic low-level. You should feel honored to even receive our attention like this.

Fuck off you entitled asshole. I tried to yank my hand out of hers but she began crushing my fingers much like she had before.

She leaned her face down close to me and for once the smile was wiped clean off her face. "You won't live long enough to regret those words," she vowed.

Those words were sharp and pierced me like knives. I was angry, furious at their actions. High-level demons didn't give two shits about my kind but their blatant disrespect only angered me further. I grimaced at the pain and let out a throaty laugh, almost enjoying the way the small scratches littered my legs. I made a split-second decision and gripped onto her shirt. Her eyes widened.

The school shirt went up in a blaze. She let out a yelp and tried to pat down the flames. The other two jumped but seemed too shocked to move. Rae narrowed her eyes in my direction.

I gave her a small smile and used this as a chance to escape, only stopping to look at my work once I was near the end of the walkway. All of the dried rose bushes were now up in flames leaving the garden in a sea of red. The three demons stood in the middle unmoving. It was scarier seeing them standing in the middle of all that fire than when they were close enough to actually maim me.

The fire surrounded them and licked at their clothing, but as if it knew that those demons meant trouble, it never got close enough to harm them. Even Eli's shirt was charred but no longer actively burning. The similarity to Dante's *Inferno* and the Rain of Fire was uncanny, but it just made me realize how big the gap between myself and them was.

It's terrifying, I concluded.

Eli's eyes met mine and on her face was no longer the cocky smile but a twisted one that belonged in a horror movie. She threw her head back and let out a booming laugh.

I ran at top speed to my dorm and didn't look back until I was safely unlocking my door. Slamming the door to my room shut I finally paused to catch my breath.

What the fuck just happened?

I checked the lock on my door multiple times before I collapsed into a heap on my bed. I was expecting some type of bullying when I entered this school but coming face to face with those demons was more than I could handle. If they were the norm here I would be out before even finishing the first quarter of the year.

The witch was the one that presented the most problems. Daxton. There was something about my curse that affected him enough that he would lose himself and become exactly like those witches my parents warned me about. The image of Rae slashing his chest caused me to flinch and made my stomach clench painfully. It was deep, deeper than I had seen on another person. I had seen it on myself before but I was rarely in a situation where another person had to be hurt. And when his blood soaked his shirt, suddenly the animal was gone. It lingered but at least his eyes seemed to clear.

And he had mistaken me for a witch. The irony of it all was too painful.

I just hoped that our search for a witch did not end with him.

I stared at my shaking hand as another thought gripped me.

That was the first time I had used my power to such an extent since the fire. I hated that the fire was such a permanent and destructive part of my life. When I thought about it before I felt like I would burst into tears, or fear would claw at my throat because I'd remember the witch that cursed me. But now...

I couldn't tell if this change was a good or bad sign.

* * *

"I can't believe I missed it!" Matt exclaimed as we sat down with our breakfast. "I'm glad you are okay though. That must have been scary...facing them head-on I mean." Matt had gotten back to the dorm late the night before and we hadn't had time to catch up, so he had to get all the details over breakfast.

Eat. Talk later, I signed to him. There were many more students here now that classes were finally starting. I felt like I had lived a whole life here at Winterfell while others were just starting. I was disappointed to see that our once quiet and peaceful sanctuary had turned into a hectic and overly loud mess hall.

One thing was certain though: most students already knew that they now had to share classes with two low-levels, and the overall sentiment seemed to be that they were very dissatisfied with the principal's decision. We received more than enough hateful glares and people refused to get close to us. Even with the mess hall almost bursting at its seams with people, we had ample space on either side of our seats.

We still had a few days until the start of class, but anxiety has been at an all-time high between Matt and me. His because of school, mine because I was looking over my shoulder constantly for the psycho whose shirt I lit on fire.

I sighed softly and took a sip of the bottled coffee I took from the buffet earlier.

"Uh...Rosie?" Matt's voice quivered as he spoke. I didn't need him to tell me that the trio was fast approaching. The power that radiated off the witch was already tickling at my senses.

A rough hand pushed down my head and tore the bottle out of my hands.

"I knew low-levels had shit taste but really? Bottled coffee?" Eli's snide voice said from behind me. I gripped her wrist ready to burn it off.

I wouldn't if I were you, her voice warned in my head and her fingers tangled through my hair as a warning.

Amr jumped up onto the table and meowed loudly. Eli's hand loosened enough for me to yank it off. I sent the feline a smile and scratched his chin lightly. He purred in response and closed his eyes. Daxton's tattooed hands snatched Amr off the table. Neither Daxton nor Rae met my eyes as they passed. Rae sent a pointed look to Eli and she rolled her eyes in return.

"See you around low-level," Eli commented, but before she left she took the chance to pour the bottled coffee all over our table. Matt and I both scrambled away from the liquid that threatened to spill over the edge and stain the only uniform set we both had.

"I'll make you clean that up next time!" yelled a familiar southern twang. Rhonda stomped up to our table with towels and a replacement bottled coffee. Her concerned expression made my heart flutter and ache at the same time. "Don't let those *children* get to you dear."

I took the bottle from her outstretched hand with a smile. Even the teachers back in the low-level schools wouldn't bat an eye when I was bullied, yet here this woman was defending me over something as small as spilled coffee.

"Thanks from both of us, Rhonda," Matt said giving her a dazzling smile.

"Don't you worry your pretty little head," she huffed as she cleaned the table. I grabbed my book bag from the seat before the coffee could. "I'll always be on the lookout for y'all." Her words caused my eyes to sting.

Stupid response.

"Let's go, Rosie," Matt said looping an arm around my shoulders. "Maybe you can show me the extent of that power of yours later. I heard it was *hot*."

I cringed at his joke but he laughed it off and led me out of the mess hall.

* * *

"How big can it get?" he asked as we watched the flowers he had just conjured burn up in a flame.

We decided to go back to the courtyard I had burnt to a crisp and do a little makeover, but before we did he was dead serious about showing him how my curse worked.

"However big I want it," I whispered and winced at the pain radiating down my back.

"I can only manage a measly garden," he pouted, not saying anything about my curse. It was a refreshing change. "That power is dangerous if used right."

"Deadly," I told him. "Except against those three." I had to steady myself against the fountain as the next wave of pain made its way through me.

He waved his hand over the dead rose bushes. Small green sparkles left his hand and the once dead rose bushes sprang to life and grew almost as tall as him.

"What's your favorite color?" he asked. His grey eyes met mine and I had to look down at my feet because of the intensity.

"Purple," I replied, peeking up just in time to watch him conjure another bush. This one was full of purple roses. He picked one off the stem and stalked toward me silently with it in his hand. Instead of a smile his lips were relaxed and his eyes were locked on mine, missing their usual twinkle.

"For you," he said. His free hand covered mine and he dropped the purple rose into my open hand. My heart started beating wildly in my chest. Matt was handsome, of course, but I had seen him as more of an older brother until this very moment. "Be careful." He brought his hand to his mouth and I realized that it was bleeding. His tongue shot out to lick up the blood.

"You're hurt," I said. My voice was huskier than I wanted it and from the heat in my face I knew I must have been blushing.

"They symbolize love at first sight," he said. "Maybe I should start bringing you purple roses everyday then, hm?" He stepped closer. My mind was trying to keep up with the sudden change in demeanor and I couldn't think of what to do.

I was saved by a loud meow and Amr weaving around my legs. Matt stepped back and let out a sigh. The smile found its way back to his face when he caught sight of the long-haired cat.

"That cat likes you," he commented looking down at the long-haired feline.

"And I like him," I said and placed the purple rose on the fountain's edge before bending down to pick him up. I brought the cat up to my face and kissed its face softly. "Now that we are alone I can tell you what a good boy you are." Even whispering didn't stop the curse but it was worth it once the cat purred against me and licked my fingers softly.

While I was distracted Matt used that as a chance to build the garden back to its once beautiful state in a matter of minutes. I was in awe at his power, jealous even. He could create such beautiful things while I could only destroy and harm.

"Let's visit the library today, ya?" he said and pushed me and the cat along with him out of the courtyard. "Let's see what we can find out about witches."

The walk to the library was short. Apparently, a campus this big had to have multiple and we just so happened to be by the biggest one. I was expecting the librarians to refuse the cat but there was no one when waiting for us when we walked in. Instead we just came into contact with a large study area filled with long tables surrounded by hundreds of rows of books. The air was warm against the chill of the outside and it smelt faintly of old and worn antiques, much like my first house did before it burnt down.

How comforting.

"I came here my first day before I came to get you," Matt said pulling me up to the second floor and into a row of books that looked just about as old as the school. None of the spines had titles and each seemed to be bound in a thick material close to leather.

Matt walked down the aisle slowly looking over the place cards. I petted Amr absentmindedly. Matt grabbed a few books and we snagged ourselves a table on the first floor.

"This is about the witches' history. You can have this one first," he said pushing a book toward me. It was as big as my torso and about as thick as one of the trio's biceps. "I will take a look at the curse book."

I frowned at him.

I want that one, I signed. Amr shifted in my lap but remained seated.

"Let's share notes afterward," he said with a smile and cracked the book open. I pushed down my irritation and opened my own book.

Most of the book seemed to be in a language I didn't understand but luckily for me there were some sections that were transcribed. I started in the section labeled "The New Era" and began reading.

The section outlined a witch's conception to death. For a witch to be born both parents had to be witches. There was no such thing recorded as half witches; the book only showed that if witches conceived with weaker witches, as the bloodline went on they would find themselves getting so weak that at some point they may be at risk of losing their powers and it would effectively end their blood line. So having children with a human would just create more humans.

They said it was also almost impossible to conceive with a demon as well. From the examples they had cited it sounded like the magic in the witch's DNA and the powers infused with the demon's DNA become volatile during the gestation period, and any infant conceived with those two sets would end up in miscarriage regardless of which race was holding it.

The section also mentioned some of the rumors that came with the creation of witches in this world. Some stated that the witches showed up at the same time as demons, others stated that they were a product of the demons' powers, and the last one which I thought was the most interesting was stating that witches came from humans trying to take a demon's power by drinking their blood and consuming their flesh—and as a punishment the Original demon families had put the first curse ever to exist on the witch race. They could have their powers but only at the cost of it being so violent and bloodthirsty that they would fall to the point of insanity.

I cringed at the thought and closed the book.

Matt was still face down in his book and I wasn't ready to talk just yet. I sighed and leaned back, giving some attention to the cat in my lap.

This book was useless. I didn't care about how they came to be. I really just wanted to know how to break this damn curse. Daxton was an option that I didn't really want to take. I wasn't even sure if he or any witch at this school would know how to break it. From the way the people here were dressed it was easy to tell that many people probably came here for the name and not the education. We had uniforms but that didn't stop the students from flaunting their expensive handbags and designer shoes, ties, and watches.

There was also no guarantee that the witch would even want to help us. A shiver raced down my spine when I remembered the clacking heels of the witch in my burning home. The last thing I wanted to do was end up like my parents—almost dying because they owed a witch for more than they could pay. I tried to probe my parents about what the debt was, but they always got defensive when I asked and insisted that it no longer mattered.

"Done already?" Matt asked. I nodded. "I am not sure that this book is the one we are looking for. So far I have found out that you can curse someone so that their feet would dance nonstop until the magic wore out or they died. The other was so that whenever they say a certain trigger they would blurt something embarrassing."

That's stupid, I signed to him.

"Tell me about it." His eyes locked onto Amr. "Do you know anything about that, Amr? Don't you live with a witch? If you can talk tell us now." I mimed a laugh when Amr's eyes met mine. "Just blink twice if you would spill all the secrets you know."

Amr continued to stare at me.

That's a no, I signed to Matt. He let out a loud sigh.

"A witch's cat that can't talk?" he whined.

This isn't Sabrina, I signed to him.

"I've never watched that show. We never had a TV." He paused. "Come on little kitty, anything. The low-level you've taken a liking to needs your help."

"Of course he is here with you," a sultry voice said from behind me. I leaned my head back and came eye to eye with Rae's belt. I scrambled to sit up straight, jostling the cat in my lap. Amr let out a loud whine.

"The cat seems to like Rosie," Matt supplied. I gulped and stood up to hand Amr to Rae. She looked me up and down with a slight sneer and gripped the skin behind Amr's neck and held him away from her body.

I covered my mouth with my hand and let out a small gasp.

"Don't hurt him!" I whispered to her looking around to make sure we had no witnesses.

"It doesn't hurt him," she said. "Is there a reason you are researching witches, Ms. Miller?" She raised an eyebrow at me but her eyes did not waver from mine even as the cat growled in her grip.

"You know why," Matt said and stacked the books on top of each other. "You could always help spill what you know as well." His smile was gone when he looked up to meet Rae's eyes. "Isn't your *best friend* a witch?"

"Something like that, Mr. Thompson." Rae's amber eyes drilled into me once more before she turned to leave. "Do be more careful, Ms. Miller. Don't want your *condition* to get out."

I let out a sigh as she left.

"She's kind of an ass."

Chapter Six
Rosie

Each day leading up to the first day of classes became more unbearable than the last.

It seemed that Eli would purposefully go out of her way to cause some type of hell in my life. After the coffee, it was knocking my lunch over.

Then it was a shove against a table that bruised my hip.

Then it was my bag being torn off my body and thrown across the hall leaving all my books scattered on the floor.

I was one more incident away from staying in my dorm the rest of the free days. Matt would be upset that we couldn't explore the campus while we had a chance, or continue to add to the garden, but if it would get Eli to stop bothering me, I would do anything. I chose to try and ignore her when she acted out like a child bully. I would look at her with a blank expression, then leave. The last few times I could tell that it started to get on her nerves because I was no longer met with a smile. Her eyes became narrowed, and her hands clenched into fists.

After the last incident we ended up making it to the first day without anything too exciting. I got up and got ready as usual but checked my bag to make sure I had all my school supplies in the right places so if my bag was thrown, I wouldn't have to degrade myself by getting on my knees and picking up all my various colored pens. I checked my hair in the mirror for the tenth time. Making sure it wasn't too frizzy and that there were no tangles. Tangles made it more painful if the bully decided to yank it.

I made my way to the mess hall to meet Matt alone.

All of the students were here now and it was hard to walk through the halls without bumping into anyone. I made sure to keep my head down so they wouldn't see my eyes. The only good thing was that if they did, maybe they would think I was a witch. I was jarred and a bit offended when they first made that assumption, but I chose to use it to my advantage instead.

"I'm so nervous about the first day of classes," Matt said through bites of his food as I joined him at the table with my own food. "I have no idea if I will even be able to keep up with the people here." He let out a loud sigh.

I didn't tell him, but I was nervous too. Nervous about having to talk in class. Most teachers, once my curse came to light, refused to call on me. These were high-level demons though, and I wouldn't put it past them to dock my points if I didn't respond. Nervous about the possible bullies that lay in wait. Nervous about the trio.

I nibbled on my bagel lightly, feeling a bit nauseous as my anxiety skyrocketed. Matt was almost done with his food; seemed as though the nerves only made him even more hungry while it had the opposite effect on me.

All first-years had orientation before they started their classes. It was held by Principal Winterfell himself. I'm sure it was supposed to be an honor to many of the demons here but there was something suspicious about that man.

How did he even find out about my curse?

"Are you okay, Rosie?" Matt asked as he cleaned up his trash. "You barely ate."

I'm okay. Not hungry. He eyed me disbelievingly.

"Sacred the trio will get you back for burning the shirt off their backs?" he whispered wide-eyed. "Or maybe they'll make you pay for a new one."

I rolled my eyes at his lame joke. I couldn't even afford my own clothes.

A deep bell rang throughout the campus. We both stood up and followed the crowd of first-years out and into the orientation hallway. As I looked at Matt's smiling face I felt a pang of guilt. I hoped the demons treated him well. I was used to being lonely given my curse, but I doubted someone like him ever had been alone in school. Personalities like his were just far too easy to get along with and would pull in anyone within a mile radius. I hoped that the demons would at least go easy on him.

My foot caught and I was slammed into a brick wall. A hiss escaped my lips. I clutched my head and glared at the culprit. Bright blue eyes with flecks of gold met mine. Eli paused only for a moment. Her lips were pushed together in a thin line and her eyes were narrowed. She didn't even wait for a reaction before she walked down the hall. Rae and Daxton were waiting for her at the end. Amr rested comfortably on Daxton's shoulders, the only one looking like nothing was wrong. The other two gave Eli a look as she passed them.

I couldn't get over the fact that demons that looked *like that* were first-years.

Matt helped brush off my clothes and pulled me down the hall. I contemplated shrugging off his hands but the warmth was nice. I leaned into him slightly. He sent me a smile and removed his hands without me having to ask.

When we entered the auditorium we quickly found a seat toward the back, not wanting to attract any attention. Matt's demeanor changed slightly when more and more people started to pile in. He began fidgeting and his eyes watched each person that came in.

The seats filled all too quickly and the seats next to us were taken without a second's notice. I turned to gauge Matt's reaction but he was engaged in a conversation with a young girl next to him. She gave him a kind hesitant smile. I sucked in a breath when her eyes met mine. Chocolate brown.

"I know, it was so horrible! My sister is still experiencing side effects. You wouldn't happen to know how to get rid of those would you?" He paused and smiled sheepishly. "I don't know much about witches' powers so I apologize for my ignorance."

"Not at all," her voice squeaked. A blush rose in her cheeks. "Um, for small curses even low-levels can break it. Just a soak in natural untainted water should do the trick. But if the witch was powerful you would need another witch to remove the curse."

Damn, Matt was good at this. Even though he was a low-level he had no problem getting this girl to talk to him. Even caused her to blush. She gripped her bag tighter to her and fluttered her eyelashes.

I didn't need to be worried about him it would seem.

"Ah, we tried the water." He sighed and rubbed his chin. "Are their witches who specialize in curse breaking? Maybe I can find one of those?"

I stayed still in my seat waiting for her answer. Since I had been cursed my parents had tried what they could, but they outright refused to go to another witch. They said it was too risky to entrust another witch and they would have to find another way. It had been years since they stopped searching. Sometimes I think they gave up because they thought it was a good enough punishment for scarring my Dad's face so bad.

"Ahh you have to be pretty powerful to break curses but anyone should be able to do it if they have enough power." She paused. "I am not sure many people here have enough power. Maybe you can ask around or wait till the rankings come out and search then. I wouldn't recommend going outside for help. Those witches get power highs and are unlikely to work *fairly* with low-levels."

I could not agree more with her words. If an outside witch did this to my low-level parents, there was no saying what the risk was to go searching for one.

"The rankings?" he asked but she shushed him as Principal Winterfell came into view. He was as eccentric as he was when I first saw him but seeing him just reminded me of what Rae said the other night. He meddled too much and his wanting me here was suspicious.

"New students! Winterfell Academy welcomes you!" There was a small round of applause. "All of you should have gotten your schedules so if there are any questions please reach out to me or the other attendants here. This morning we wanted to go through the rules here and then you are free for the rest of the day. Classes start tomorrow!" A slideshow appeared on the wall behind him. It showed the history of the campus as well as some famous alumni. "Winterfell Academy has been in my family for over a thousand years. This was the first place that we demons took as our own after we came out of the shadows and became members of earthly society." The slideshow went on showing various pictures of the first few years between demons and humans. This was common knowledge. Learned it since young. "We have been adamant about keeping this a demons-only place for fear of human attacks but after a few years we started to take witches as well and now..." He paused. "Low-levels as well."

The crowd broke out into murmurs and a few eyes shifted to us. "Damn," Matt swore under his breath. If people didn't know before there was no hiding it now. We were absolutely fucked. I started to doubt if this education and time away from my parents was worth it.

"We need to move on with the times. Demons have been territorial and prejudiced since the beginning and it is our turn to become a more diverse and accepting community. Not one person here will grow without the other so please don't make this difficult." He met everyone with a smile. "Now the rules!"

The rules showed on the screen and dread filled my stomach.

1. No hate crimes of any kind including against demons, witches, and humans.

2. No abusing your powers against other students or faculty.

3. No plagiarism and/or cheating.

4. Any other type of harm including but not limited to murder.

"Wow only four, right?" He laughed and shook his head. "No, these are just the ones that will get you expelled." The screen changed to show font so tiny that I could barely make it out. "We have many other rules that will result in detention and or down ranking. Learn them; you are no longer children and you will be held to the standards of adults." He clapped. "Any questions?"

The rest of the two hours were miserable. My head hurt by the end and I only came out knowing two things that I didn't before.

First, we were all ranked on a combination of our powers and class work. Meaning low-levels were at a severe disadvantage. Even if we did well in our classes there was no way we would ever beat the high-levels when it came to the rankings.

Second, everyone here had been in school together since they were in diapers. It was easy to pick out the new people—they were the only ones alone. Apparently this school sourced from the same two schools that they have for the past hundred years and even those schools have a reputation for being filthy rich and only reserved for the powerful.

It was a disaster.

"Let's get some fresh air before lunch. My head hurts," Matt groaned. I followed him in silence. This was the first time I had seen him act like this. He seemed more dejected than when everyone came into the auditorium. We walked to a secluded area and sat under the tree. There was a small breeze and instantly a weight lifted off of my chest as we sat in silence. "I regret what I said," he whispered. I raised my eyebrow at him. "I don't envy you for being stuck here for three years."

My heart skipped a beat when I realized that I would be the sole low-level here in just a year's time. *You just realized?* I teased.

"At least we got good information about the witches," he mused and looked up to the sky. It was a clear day despite the slight chill. "I hope you can wait until next month to get some answers."

I gave him a smile and patted his shoulder. I'd been waiting over nine years for answers. A month would not kill me.

"We could always ask around before then," he offered but I shrugged at him. I was in no rush.

* * *

We spent most of the day inside and went our separate ways to our dorms. I felt uneasy being away from Matt after what happened but tried to pull my big girl panties on and walked in the dark by myself. He offered to walk me but it would have been just as dangerous for him as it was for me. There were still some people left out but no one paid any mind to me as I weaved through the hallways. I made sure to avoid the hallway from the other day and pick a different route back to the dorm.

As I rounded a corner, I was slammed into a brick wall for the second time that day. I couldn't help the whine that came out of me. A dull ache formed in my stomach from the curse. A hand was wrapped around my neck and the other was on the wall next to my face. Familiar blue eyes pierced into mine.

"I thought it was time to get you back for that little fire trick you played the other day since *apparently* you have ignored my other methods." She leaned in toward me and whispered in my ear. "This could have gone such a different way," she cooed. The hand on the wall slid down the leg of my pants. "No one has been brash as you to attack me." She chuckled darkly and slid her hand up to my belt. "I wanted so badly to tear you limb from limb yesterday. Hang your body in the front hall for the rest to see. Then you started to ignore me. And I thought, what's the fun in hurting someone that doesn't even care about anything other than her fellow low-level?"

When her hand hit the bare skin of my stomach I shivered. What did Matt have to do with this? Her eyes widened slightly and there was a small twinkle in them.

Forget about him, her voice snapped in my head. *You're not scared?*

Never, I spit. *You are just like a high school bully. I've dealt with much worse.* Against my will images of my bullies shot through my mind. They would hit me, degrade me. Literally do anything so they could get my curse to work. Just like her. *Like a child.*

Oh, I'm not like them, she chuckled. Her words were like a whisper in my ear. And that's when my eyes started to get blurry. An image took over. It was me tied and gagged. I was fully naked and spread eagle on a large bed, then there was Eli. She was also naked but that wasn't what surprised me. Up until now she had carefully hidden all of her skin with her uniform and now with her skin bare I saw that she was covered with tattoos, but all very particular tattoos that I swore I could have seen before.

"So this is what you like? Maybe this is a better way to get a reaction from you," naked her said teasingly as her hand ran across her breast and pinched her own nipple. "You'll like this more." She smirked and her hand trailed from her chest, over her scarred abs and to a surprisingly big strap-on.

Oh fuck. I panicked. I had never done something like this with a girl before nor had I ever tried toys. And now I was faced with both in some type of weird alternate reality.

I tried to look away but vision me had other plans. Her legs spread wider and only now could I feel how wet she was.

She's not me, I cried in my head. Eli leaned over my body and slowly ran her fingers down my wetness. I could feel every moment of it. It wasn't like a daydream; I could actually feel it. Feel the heat spread throughout my body. Feel her rough fingers teasing my core.

And I *liked it.*

"Make a noise," she commanded. "And I'll reward you." The vision me groaned and a wound opened up on my stomach. Her fingers plunged into me. They stretched me and began pounding into me furiously. The pain from the cut mixed in with the feeling of her fingers moving inside me and the illusion of me arched against the bindings. She let out another moan and Eli added another finger intensifying the pleasure. Each time her hand snapped into me it hit my clit just right and sent shocks through me.

I lost myself quickly in it and didn't know if it was vision me or real me that began thrusting to meet her hand.

"Look at how much you're enjoying this," Eli purred as she gripped my thigh. "Such a filthy low-level."

The words sent another jolt through me and I knew that soon Eli would bring me to my limit.

As soon as I felt vision me about to climax I was back in the dark court-yard with Eli.

"You could have that," she whispered, her voice husky. I was panting now. It had felt so real, all of it. Her hands, the cut, I couldn't help but want more. "It was in a way...another perk you could say." She leaned closer, her lips close to mine. I wanted so badly to close the space and continue what she started. After feeling her fingers inside me I couldn't think of anything I wanted more. "If you say yes, I'll make you come right now. I want to see your little low-level curse in action so badly that it hasn't left my mind for days. I can't wait to make you beg."

My stomach tightened at her words. They turned me on but they also made me look at the situation with clarity. The haze cleared just enough for me to rethink what I was doing.

Fuck off or I'll light your ass up.

Instead of getting angry like I thought she would, she backed off and let out a laugh. Just like the time she was surrounded by flames. I rubbed the area of my throat that her hand was once clenched around.

What was so funny about this?

"You'll come. Voluntarily," she vowed, wiping the fake tears from her eyes.

"In your dreams," I shot at her. She laughed again and waved me off. I watched her walk away with a glare.

How dare she do that to me?

I was even angrier to see Rae there waiting for her. She seemed to have gotten an eyeful of the sick show Eli put on. I stomped away from them and hightailed it back to my dorm once again, humiliated.

Chapter Seven
Rae

I didn't understand the fascination with that low-level.

Curses were not uncommon. This one was unorthodox but there was no use getting *this* excited over it. Watching them lose control over a single woman irritated me beyond belief. Eli and Daxton were similar and tended to feed off of each other's more volatile emotions, but Daxton usually had his own reasoning. Eli had no need to involve herself. She even decided to stake a claim on the low-level, jealousy spiking in her whenever she saw her and Mr. Thompson together. Both of them had so much riding on this education and were more than capable of resisting a low-level.

Now...all I saw was two starving dogs fighting over a piece of meat and it was so irritating that even just looking at her sent me whirling.

"Don't look so pissy, Rae," Eli said brushing the imaginary dirt off my shoulder. "I know you like a little rebellion sometimes."

"Not this. Not with a low-level," I snapped at her.

"But you knew," she whined. "You knew exactly what you were doing when you told me about her curse. I bet you knew even before we saw her but you chose to tell me when you knew I couldn't resist."

I had found out before she even came here but that was beside the point. She was right. I wanted to see what would happen. I hoped something would. "I didn't think you would try to get in her pants like a dog in heat." I crossed my arms across my chest. She raised an eyebrow at me. "Just keep it together. The principal is secretive about her and my education is more important than *that* low-level."

She made a noncommittal noise and waved me off.

I took a deep breath as they both left the area, letting out all the tension those idiots had brought up. The emotions that were pouring out of both of them were hard to separate from my own and the last thing I needed to do was get involved with a low-level. I had many things weighing on my education here—government offices, demon association, fuck, I could take on the White House if I wanted to—and I would not let anything deter that.

Noticing the time, I steeled myself and walked my way toward the principal's office for the umpteenth time since my arrival. I gave a smile to the office lady and she returned mine with a small blush. She was such a gossip when you gave her a little attention; no doubt she was tired of her life as a low-level and enjoyed the attention of a higher-level demon.

I was unsure if she would be interested in girls. Meeting her the first time I was met with conflicting emotions. Most of all confusion and hesitation with a small amount of arousal. I tried to play on the arousal, hoping that because I presented more masculine that she would overlook what was in my pants and give me what I needed.

"Mr. Winterfell is already waiting for you, dear. Let me know if you need anything," she told me. A flurry of excitement and nervousness fluttered through my chest. It was easy to separate her feelings from my own; I have never felt such useless emotions.

"Of course, Tammy. Thank you," I told her with a smile. I ignored her reply as I walked into Principal Winterfell's office. His discomfort seeped out from under the door and expanded into the office. I gave him a smile as soon as I stepped in and his anxiety skyrocketed.

"Here to probe for more information, Ms. Ashwell?" His voice was polite, but he couldn't fool me. He resented my entire existence.

"Just a chat, *James*." I sat down in front of him. He may have thought he had the whole school fooled but not me. "I think it's time you tell me the truth about the cursed low-level."

"I told you all that I know," he dismissed. His lips were curling into a smile but his emotions contradicted his playful expression.

"My family doesn't take well to lies," I told him. "You know I don't give a damn about low-levels. But a cursed one is something different. You have a motive and I want to know what it is."

He shifted in his seat and leaned toward me.

"There are things in this world that are more powerful than you or your family, Rae. You know that I am more than happy to divulge any information I can to you but there is nothing more about the low-level that I can tell you.

Anything else you will need to figure out through her." His eyes dared me to continue.

This wasn't the first time that someone had been so unwilling to share information, but James had been very forthcoming in the last few years. He usually forked over any information I asked for but this was the first wall he had given me. Given his words, there was someone stronger pulling the strings, but who was stronger than father? He had the senate eating out of his goddamn hand. The low-level couldn't possibly be better than that, could she?

But you are different, my mind reminded me. *Father doesn't think a girl like you can hold that type of power.*

I would prove him wrong.

"First you ask me to watch over her and now you are practically forcing my hand," I commented crossing my legs and checking my nails, showing him that his actions didn't bother me in the slightest even if they enraged me inside.

"It's not me who has to know everything about everyone. I'm just suggesting that if you want to know something, get the information yourself." He shrugged and lowered himself back down to his seat. His emotions were still a wreck. He was scared.

Information is power and my family just so happened to be the world's most powerful information broker out there.

"I thought I could count on you more." I tutted and stood up from my seat. "I hope we don't run into this issue again. Remember, I hold your career in my hand."

"My hands are tied. They have my life; my career is nothing in comparison."

I cursed internally. I needed to figure out who needed this low-level here. It was not normal for something to be so far out of my grasp. Nor would father approve of such a weak roadblock, and it would only prove him right in the thoughts he had about me.

I left without another word but not before stopping in front of Tammy.

"Do you by chance have Principal Winterfell's calendar handy? I would like to schedule a regular meeting but I want to make sure it doesn't clash with my extra-curriculars." I leaned toward her giving her a smile that sent a blush running up her cheeks.

"Sure, let me pull it up." Her long nails clacked on her keyboard. "He has three, five, and seven. Available on Tuesdays and Thursdays," she replied.

"Do you mind if I see?" I asked sweetly. "I am a *visual* person." I let my eyes rake down her form. She loved it and had no idea how I wouldn't dare lay a finger on her. I sent a little bit of arousal to her in hopes of goading her into giving me what I wanted.

"S-sure," she stuttered and surprised me by printing out his schedule for me instead of just showing me on the screen. "For you, dear." Her hand brushed mine as she handed the paper to me.

"I knew I could always count on you," I purred and walked out with a small goodbye.

When I was far away enough I looked at the schedule. Not only did she print out the whole month but it had names on it and everything. It was mostly packed with faculty meetings. I saw that the low-levels had biweekly meetings with him but besides that no other names stood out.

Which meant that whoever was keeping him from talking was not meeting him here, or at least, not on the schedule.

It was a shot in the dark anyways, I thought and folded up the paper to put it in my pocket for when I would need it.

The low-level had already messed up the group dynamic by being here for just a week. Daxton was barely controlling himself and probably off fucking the nearest witch he could lay his hands on. Bloodletting would be so much easier but he was so stubborn. It was literally the answer to all of our issues at the moment.

Well...not all. The frenzy she threw Eli into was something else. She would normally never corner someone like that if it wasn't for her work. Any demon or witch she wanted came to her and yet the low-level refused no matter how much it seemed that she wanted her.

I didn't even want to think of how Daxton had tried to stop Eli from touching her when he wasn't in control of himself. There has never been a time where they had fought over a woman and I didn't need it to start now. This education was important to all of us even if Eli refused to admit it.

I sighed loudly as I entered my dorm. It wasn't hard to get us all into separate dorms and I would never degrade myself to sleeping in the same room as other students. Even just being *in the dorms* was embarrassing enough as it was.

There was a knock at my door and without opening it I felt Daxton's emotional pattern. I cursed internally. If there was anyone more anxious than that low-level, it would have to be Daxton.

Could I get a moment of peace?

"Yes Daxton?" I asked as I opened the door. I loosened my tie feeling like it was too tight all of a sudden. He was calmer but his magic continued to restlessly move inside him. It was such an odd feeling, his magic. It was like it was something else living inside of him but their emotions were so in sync it was barely distinguishable.

"Have you seen Amr?" he asked, his eyes searching behind me as if I was harboring him.

"Is he wandering off again?" I asked remembering when I saw him cuddled up to the low-level in the library. I didn't have to guess where he might be and it only angered me more. Not that I would show it though. Openly showing anger was a foolish move.

"It's hard to keep track of him recently," he admitted with a frown.

"Can your magic call out to him?" I asked.

"He's not answering. And I felt his presence around here but I can't pinpoint it." His facial expression barely showed his thoughts but unease and anxiety rolled off him in waves.

"I guess the witch wasn't enough huh?" I asked and shut my door behind me joining him in the hallway. "Let's see if we can feel him while we can walk?" He nodded and started down the hallway. I felt the prick of irritation at my words and it made me smile. He hated coming to me even if he wouldn't show it and that had to be my favorite part about what my family did. Not the knowing, but the feeling of when people knew they had to come to you but actually hated themselves for it.

I let him lead me but I had no doubt in my mind that this journey tonight would probably lead us right into the low-level's territory.

I didn't need him to tell me when he felt him the closest. His own magic became antsy and I could feel the curse magic radiating through the door in front of us. His magic and anxiety was soaring as each second passed. I sighed again and removed my glasses to rub my eyes.

This was a tiring fucking night.

I didn't wait for him to make a move. I stepped forward and knocked on the door. There was a small shuffling and low and behold the low-level's wide brown eyes came into view. Looking down I was surprised to see that she was wearing a tank top and shorts, much more skin than I had seen her show before. It was all milky white and the droplets from her wet hair rolled down her perky chest. My throat dried at the sight. What didn't surprise me though was the cat in her arms that was cuddled close to her form. Amr lowly growled at us, obviously not wanting to be interrupted.

I wondered what the low-level would think if Amr shifted in her arms. The absolute giddiness I felt when I thought about spilling this information should have been illegal.

"Amr, what the fuck?" Daxton growled back at the cat. Daxton's arousal raised as he saw her.

"So glad you found our cat *again*, Ms. Miller. We were worried," I told her and grabbed the offending feline ignoring his hissing. My hands brushed across her skin sending heat waves up my arm.

There is no time for that, I chided myself.

I threw the cat in Dax's arms and pushed them both down the hall without so much as a goodbye. I heard her door shut only after we were almost at my dorm.

"I don't care what you see in that low-level, don't fucking do that," Daxton hissed at the cat. The cat growled and jumped out of his arms, preferring to walk by himself.

"You have to get your magic under control," I reminded him as I opened my door. "We can't have another incident like last time. There is too much unknown about her."

"What do you mean unknown—I thought you researched her?" he hissed.

"I *did*," I hissed back, frustration filling me. Such a *kid*. "I can only learn so much and we still don't know about her curse."

"You were the one that had the idea to use her like a witch," he accused, his anger rising. He was mad because he couldn't bed her? Really?

"I offered it before she almost burned the school down," I hissed. "If you want to chance it, go ahead but I won't clean up your mess if you lose control *again*."

It was a low blow, but I couldn't stop the words from coming out of my mouth. Shame filled him immediately. I swallowed my guilt. It was a lie—of course I would help whenever he would need me to, but I couldn't help but get angry at his actions.

"Whatever," he spat at me and turned on his heels to his dorm.

I closed my door once again and let out yet another sigh.

This low life was going to be a fucking pain.

Chapter Eight
Rosie

"For you," Matt said handing me a purple rose. This time there were no thorns. I smiled at him and accepted it.

Thank you, I signed to him.

"Are you ready for your classes?" he asked throwing his arm around my shoulder. "I am nervous about mine but I have never been more ready to get them done with and graduate. I know you have to be here for another few years but I have no idea how you are going to do it." He leaned close to whisper in my ear. "Do you see what some of the girls wear? They are definitely not here for an education."

Let a girl wear what she wants, I signed to him with a frown. I agreed that the designer fashion was a bit overboard for school and most were here for the name of the school on their diploma, but putting this just on how women chose to wear their clothes rubbed me the wrong way.

"You know girls only dress like that for a reason," he said with a pout. I gritted my teeth at his comment and for show I held out the flower he gave me and set it ablaze.

That's an ignorant comment, I signed to him after brushing off the soot that lingered on my hand from the rose.

"I guess I deserve that," he said with a sigh and removed his arm from around my shoulders. "This should be your class," Matt said as we arrived at the first-year door. "Demon History and Culture, Class A. Going to be weird getting used to the classes thing."

We had both assumed that this college would be like any other but after we got our schedules it was clear that high-level colleges worked a bit differently. Apparently we were each assigned a classroom and we would be taking the same classes as the others in our major. Every day, every hour, same classes for three years together.

Thank you. See you later, I signed to him and walked into my class. I was immediately discouraged to see that there were not single desks and instead lab-like tables that sat two people at a time. I didn't see any assigned seats and students started filling in so I quickly grabbed one near the window and hoped that it would make me as unnoticeable as possible. I put my book bag on the table adjacent to the window and began laying out my supplies and schedule.

Just a few minutes before the bell was supposed to ring I heard the chair next to me move and a warm body filled it.

Did someone want to sit with me? A small flutter of excitement filled my heart.

I looked over to meet the newcomer and my heart dropped immediately and all positive emotions left me.

It was Eli.

"Well hello there, little low-level." She chuckled, that stupid grin still on her face. "What a coincidence." I frowned at her.

Fuck off, I told her in my head but she seemed to ignore it.

"Ms. Miller," the person who I assumed was the teacher said coming up to my desk. His light brown hair was slicked back and his glasses perched low on his nose. His eyes shined a similar blue as Eli's. "I hope you have been settling in. I am Mr. Falkner. The principal told us about your *condition* so we thought it would be best for Ms. Groten here to assist you if needed in the class. I will try not to call on you to answer but having someone with a mind-reading skill would stop you from having to write everything."

I felt a twinge of annoyance at Mr. Winterfell's *consideration.* What was he playing at?

Eli's rough hand covered mine.

A perfect excuse to touch you.

Are you stupid? I tried to move my hand away but she gripped it tightly. Mr. Falkner forced a smile, his eyes narrowing at Eli.

I have to touch you to read your mind, unfortunately. It didn't sound like she thought that was such an unfortunate thing. Her voice almost purred when she spoke.

"She said she appreciates the consideration," she replied smoothly to Mr. Falkner and he nodded then headed back to the front of the class. Before I could yell at Eli in my mind a familiar black cat jumped up on our table and rubbed itself on my chin.

Amr! I took my free hand and gave him scratches behind the ear. The cat began purring and nudged his head into my hand.

Such a sweet baby. Maybe if the cat can stay with me the class may be more bearable.

Eli let out a deep chuckle and I flushed realizing that she could still hear my thoughts.

"I could make it more enjoyable if you wanted," she purred. Her hand removed itself from my own hand and placed itself on my thigh. "I realized that you are a bit *new* to this but there is no need to worry, you'll enjoy it."

I was at a loss on how to respond and was saved by the volatile witch once more.

"Of course, he's with the low-level *again*," Daxton's voice grumbled as he took the empty table in front of us. It seemed like he was the only one without a seat mate. He sat so his back was against the window and his front facing toward the opposite wall of the classroom. His head was against the wall and tilted upward showcasing his long tattooed neck. He looked better than the last time I saw him. His hair was still a mess but he overall seemed calmer and more collected. My eyes trailed to the other tattoos peeking out of his unbuttoned shirt collar. I couldn't make out the shapes but the grey and blacks were so pretty against his skin.

"I didn't know you liked tattoos so much," Eli commented reading my thoughts once more. I wanted to push her away but at the same time I kind of enjoyed not having to hurt in order to get my point across. Thinking about it now it probably wouldn't be safe if Daxton was so close. "Don't worry. He is satiated for now."

Daxton's eyes lazily made their way over to us, just barely showing underneath his messy black hair. "Talking shit?"

"Only a bit," she teased.

If you must do this, can you rest your hand somewhere else? I hissed at her. Surprisingly, and without a fight, she removed her hand completely.

"You touch me if you want to talk," she told me and got out a notebook and pen from her book bag. I raised my eyebrow at the act.

Amr meowed, trying to get my attention. I gave him a smile and kissed his wet nose lightly not caring that I could feel the others' stares. He laid down in front of me and I began absentmindedly petting him. I looked around to see that the class was pretty much filled and most of the people were looking toward us.

It's not like I wanted the attention of these people. If anything it would make my time here worse. My eyes shifted to Daxton. Was there an actual possibility that he could break the curse? The magic that radiated off of him was strong but with the little knowledge about witches that I had, I couldn't be sure what it took to break a curse like mine.

Maybe I could ask him when Eli was not around. God knows what she would do when I asked for their help. Another trip into a brick wall? Those stupid daydreams of hers?

I shuddered lightly remembering what she had shown me. Daxton met my eyes once more.

I quickly shifted my gaze and instead of focusing on him I looked toward the front of the classroom and saw some notes already on the board.

Mr. Falkner started class with a short introduction before jumping into the questioning.

The teacher paced the room, looking everyone in the eye, probably checking to see if we were actually paying attention in the classes that cost more than I would make in my entire life.

"I will be your main teacher and will be teaching you a majority of what you need for your degree. We will have a few specialized teachers that will come in and teach you more of what I cannot, but for the most part you will be stuck with me," he said and sent the class a smile. "Also, once a month you will be given a day off from class to compete for the rankings."

His eyes met mine for a second then looked toward another student. I swallowed thickly. I was sure to utterly fail whatever test they had for the rankings system and I would hate to see what people would do once they realized how weak I was.

"As far as curriculum for this year...we are going to push the beliefs that we grew up with in this class." His voice boomed off the walls, jarring some students that were dozing off. "First question, why are we called demons?"

He tapped his pen on the desk of a blonde girl that looked more interested in her nails. She looked to him with a raised eyebrow.

"Because the humans thought we crawled up from hell," she answered in a bored tone.

"Because we scared them," he pushed back. "Because we were something unknown to them. All of a sudden they were no longer just among their fellow humans but instead came face to face with things that had the ability and the want to utterly destroy them. It is no secret that when our ancestors started to congregate they decided very quickly that their goal would be to rule over the humans."

"We already know this," the boy next to her grumbled.

The teacher only smiled down at him.

"Does anyone know when the first *recorded* interaction with humans was?" he asked the class.

"The Salem witch trials," Daxton answered with a bored tone. "It wasn't just witches that were burned at the stake."

"Good." Mr. Falkner hummed. "There were of course many other interactions and many of the folk tales during that time revolved around the demons that attacked their towns, their livestock, and even kidnapped their children. But the first time they actually wrote us down in history as *demons* was during the Salem witch trials."

"Originals were powerful though. Why did they allow themselves to get burned at the stake?" a boy asked toward the back.

"Does anyone know the answer?" Mr. Falkner asked. He pushed his glasses up and with a huff answered once no one else did. "Rumor has it they took something the demons loved."

"Stupid," Eli muttered next to me. For once, I agreed with her.

Originals were the first recorded demons and witches to ever walk this earth and they were supposed to be the most powerful beings that have ever lived. They were pure power that no one could stand in the way of though it still begged the question: why did they get defeated during that time? And why would they throw away thousands of years of their lives for something as flimsy as love.

An image of my parents during a school science fair popped through my mind. It was a month before the accident and it was one of the happiest I remember seeing them. They gushed to my teachers about how proud they were of me. Mom's arm was even comfortably tucked into Dad's and a smile was on his perfectly smooth face that would turn ugly and scarred after my birthday.

The accident made me realize that love was flimsy. A parent's love could vanish overnight and be replaced by silence and sharp glares. And a love between husband and wife...well let's just say it'd been a while since I'd seen my dad look at my mom with anything but contempt.

"If anyone has any better arguments I would love to see them in your future papers." He gave everyone a smile and there were a few groans around the class.

"Another one, since you all seem so tantalized by this debate," he said leaning against his desk meeting the annoyed glares of some of his students. "What if I told you we descended from angels and not demons?" he argued. There were a few chuckles.

"Humans would shit themselves if they learned they killed angels," one boy murmured.

"Wishful thinking," Eli commented while crossing her arms over her chest.

"Why?" the teacher pressed her. There was a small frown on his face. "Some Originals had wings."

"We all have our things," Eli responded with a shrug.

"It is my job this semester to make you rethink everything that you know about demons...and witches." He looked pointedly at Daxton. "And your final paper will include a section where you try to convince me that I am either right or wrong depending on which you believe more. Every few classes we will go over some of the rumors of our creation. You choose your favorite and fight me in your final paper."

After a series of lectures and debates the ringing of a bell jolted me and the cat. If I could talk I would have loved to question some of the points brought up, especially about low-levels, but I would never get that chance to. I looked up to see a pair of brown eyes staring intently at me.

"You really don't give a shit about school do you?" he asked.

I looked toward Eli and she was already looking at me. Her hand was out. An invitation to speak. I put my hand in hers lightly, my fingers barely brushing her palm.

School hasn't always been my favorite but today's lesson was interesting. Easy but interesting.

Eli relayed my message. "Demon History and Culture is the easy major," she commented. "Why do you think we are in here? Could you see people like us in a science or government major?"

Remembering both of their tattooed bodies I would have assumed they would want to do something more creative, but Demon History and Culture hadn't crossed my mind. The arts maybe? Anything but actual school if I was being honest.

"This is the stupid people class," Daxton responded dryly. His eyes shifted toward the cat that was still cuddled into my arms. "I can't believe he degraded himself to such levels."

He's one to talk, I scoffed in my head.

I was curious as to why Eli and Daxton were even conversing with me in the first place. Eli obviously had a bone to pick after the shirt incident, but Daxton had no motive.

Maybe it was his magic? As if on cue my fingertips began tingling, sending shock waves up my arm.

"You can feel magic? You keep getting more and more interesting," Eli whispered. I forgot my hand was still connected to hers and pulled it away quickly. Daxton's eyes snapped up to mine. There was darkness there that made my toes curl. "And don't get us wrong. You definitely repulse us as a low-level but there are some *attributes* that hold our interest."

Her voice caused shivers to go down my spine. The images she sent to my mind yesterday pushed to the front and my face flushed.

* * *

"Come on, eat with us," Eli whined pushing her bottom lip out in a fake pout and tried to push me through the hallway.

I have to meet my friend, I hissed in my mind. I tried to keep hold of my book bag while trying not to jostle the sleeping cat in my arms. Thank god the cat slept like the dead or else I was sure it would have attacked me by now.

"Ah the other low-level," she mused slipping her arm around my shoulder. I shoved her arm off and there was an audible gasp in the hallway. I looked around and saw more people staring at us.

Were these demons really such a big deal?

"This isn't a charity case, Eli," Daxton growled coming up beside me. His magic was tingling my arms and making my hair stand on edge.

"Oh come on it will be fun," she promised, her eyes flashing slightly.

You don't want to be seen with low-levels. Even being so close to me has no doubt tarnished your reputation, I said once Eli's hand came to rest on my neck as she guided me to the mess hall. I tried to look for Matt's tall form but it was hard when Eli kept pushing me around and forced us to get in line for food.

"Nonsense. We don't much care about reputation. Right, Dax?" And as if to prove my point she took two cigarettes out of her book bag and handed one to Daxton. I watched as Eli lit up her own and leaned close to Daxton to light his. Apparently, Daxton's move wasn't good enough for her. Eli gripped his chin roughly and forced his face closer. Daxton's neck was stretched and his face angled up toward Eli. Eli helped him light up.

Oh my god. It slipped in my mind and I couldn't deny how dominating the move looked and how it sent butterflies through my stomach. The two most beautiful demons I had ever seen getting so close was almost too much for me to handle. I tore my eyes away from the scene and searched the mess hall finally finding Matt's messy mop of red hair. He gave me a panicked look when I saw him. I tried to leave my spot but Eli's rough hand wrapped itself around my hair and pulled me back in line.

I bit my lip hard to stop the groan that threatened to come out. I wouldn't dare think of the other emotions her actions stirred in me. I must have been going crazy if I found the *bullies* attractive.

"Not so fast," she said blowing a puff of smoke in my face. She waved Matt over to us. Matt paused but began to march over, his eyes narrowed at the way Eli gripped my hair.

"What is going on, Rosie?" Matt said coming up to our spot in line. He eyed the two next to me wearily.

They are in my class. I'm sorry I tried to leave—I signed to him but Eli cut me off.

"No, none of that. You will talk through me," Eli said gripping my hair harder before letting go and looping her arm around my shoulder. "The principal has asked for my assistance due to her *condition* so I am just helping out a fellow student." Her body was hard against mine and I got a strong whiff of her cologne mixed with smoke. It was musky and smelt like burning wood and the damp forest late at night.

Matt's eyes met mine.

Let me go with him. If you don't we may have another fire accident, I demanded to Eli but her hold only tightened. She sent an image of a beat-up and bloody Matt into my mind and my heart stopped. *You wouldn't.*

I wouldn't? she teased and sent another image of the scene in front of me but instead of Eli being draped around me as she launched himself at Matt and easily overpowered him with a punch to the face. *Let's bet.*

I must have lost control of my grip because the cat meowed softly. I gritted my teeth looking down at the cat. He met me with curious eyes.

"Isn't smoking against school rules? Especially inside?" Matt asked eyeing the two.

"Like anyone would ever stop us," Eli said with a chuckle taking another drag.

I couldn't help the sigh that escaped my lips.

"Perfect, you both just don't listen to literally anything I say," grumbled Rae's familiar voice.

"It was Eli," Daxton said in almost a whine. It was akin to a kid getting caught with their hand in the cookie jar and then blaming it on the cat. "And Amr won't leave her side."

"Put those out," Rae commanded. Eli paused for a moment but then did just that by throwing it to the stone ground and stomping it out. Daxton did the same.

"No fun," Eli whispered in my ear.

"Now that that's done with, we might as well use this as a way to get to know the first low-levels that are to join this academy. You never know where the connections will lead us one day." I looked up to meet Rae's calculating eyes. She had a cold but polite smile. "What do you say, Mr. Thompson?"

Matt shifted slightly and watched my reaction. I nodded at him.

Good choice, Eli cooed.

"Sure, I would love that. It's usually only Rosie and me so company is greatly appreciated," he said slipping into his normal excitable tone. He joined my side on the opposite side of Eli. "Look at the cute kitty," he cooed and petted his head lightly. I smiled at his actions. The cat sniffed his hand and looked toward me.

I gave the cat a small smile and he nudged his head against Matt's hand. Matt's arm brushed mine and Eli quickly pulled me closer to her side and away from Matt's.

We made it to the front of the line and were met with our friend, Rhonda. Eli let go of me and let me step forward with Matt.

"So lovely to see you two! I hope those troublemakers are treating you well." She eyed the trio behind us, no doubt remembering the coffee incident. "What will it be today?"

"I was thinking number three. Rosie what do you want?" he asked me. Number three was a lamb dish. My eyes flitted toward the only pasta on the list today. I showed them a number five. "Good choice, I knew I could count on you to try the carbs." Matt elbowed me playfully.

I smiled at him and made my way down the line grabbing a fruit and an iced tea. We were about to go to an empty table when Eli's hand gipped the top of my hair and forced me to a table that already had people in it. I swallowed when they all looked at us with surprise and some glares were sent toward me and Matt.

"Move," she ordered and in less than a minute the tabled was cleared for us. "Sit," she ordered this time to us and pushed me down on the seat. "Dax on the other side of her."

I was suddenly pushed in between two warm bodies that barely gave me any room to breathe. It didn't help that Daxton's magic kept reaching out to me leaving my body tingling. I shifted uncomfortably as Matt eyed me from the other side of the table. I let out a shaky breath in an attempt to calm myself, but it only made the pounding of my heart worse because now I was sure they knew how anxious I was between them.

"So Mr. Thompson, it would seem that you are the oldest here and the only math major," Rae started sitting next to him. "Tell us how the third-year classes are."

"Oh—um," he stuttered, trying to find his words. "I would say it's not much different than what I experienced before. The teachers do seem a bit more relaxed, though I am not sure if that's because of the school we are in or the year. The class has been friendly so far as well."

"That's good to hear. And the curriculum, is it what you expected?" Rae asked meeting him with a smile. Her eyes never wavered from my fellow low-level.

"Well, it hasn't been that long but I can already tell that low-level schools have subpar education," Matt said with a sigh.

"A gap Winterfell will surely need to fill now that we are more inclusive."

Matt seemed to relax slightly under Rae's attention. As anxious as I may have been around these three, I was relieved to see that Matt had somewhat of a chance here. I wondered if it continued like this, maybe Matt would be safe from Eli.

Are you worried about your fellow low-level? Eli's voice asked in my head. *You like that boy too much.*

He's my friend, I told her. The tone she used irritated me as much as it worried me.

Sure he is. Just don't make me angry and he will be fine. He's not as entertaining as you are anyways. Eli let out a laugh in my head that made my ears hot.

Can you tell the kitty to move? I am afraid I cannot eat like this, I asked her trying desperately to change the conversation away from any violence surrounding the red head that was currently gushing to Rae.

"Amr. Move," she told the cat. He peered up at her with what looked like annoyance but simply moved over to Daxton's lap. I felt the magic that was reaching out to me calm suddenly and reel back toward Daxton. "He's Daxton's familiar," Eli explained. "Helps contain the magic inside him."

"Oh ya!" Matt interjected but paused as our food made its way to our table. "Rosie we should ask about that *thing.*"

I swear to fucking god. I shook my head at him. I didn't want to breach that subject here or with these people. They had already tried to make me their little experiment. There was no way I would want to get involved with them any further.

Eli gripped my hand under the table and began squeezing.

"Don't hide stuff from us, low-level. Go ahead. *Say it.*" She leaned closer to me daring me to speak. Her actions caused me to lean back but I was trapped against Daxton's side. I gulped at the intensity of her stare. The gold flecks in her eyes twinkled.

You can't be serious?

"Eli," Rae warned.

"Please don't talk. I'm already on edge," Daxton piped up digging into his food. He shifted against my weight but didn't try to move.

"It's okay! I can talk instead," Matt said, laughing to try and get rid of the tension that was forming.

"No I want to hear her *say it*," Eli pushed and she twisted my hand painfully under the table. I let out a small whimper and Daxton stiffened against me as a blooming ache showed up in my arm. Daxton's magic reached out to me again, the same way I had felt it that night when he pushed me against the fountain.

We need a witch to help to get rid of the curse, I shouted at her through my head.

"That's not what I asked," she growled at me and forced another whimper out of me.

"*Fuck* Eli," groaned Daxton. He shifted and right when I thought he was going to leave his arm circled around my waist and pulled me closer to him, forcing space between me and Eli. "Stop it with that. I just visited a witch yesterday."

I blushed when his head dipped closer to mine. His eyes seemed darker than before, and the magic beast that was hiding behind them was coming to the front.

"I will have the principal put her in a different class if you two do not behave," Rae threatened. Eli let go of my hand and Daxton reluctantly let go of my waist, both giving me enough space on the bench. "Now, Mr. Thompson. Explain."

"Uhm...Matt is fine." I noticed there was also a light blush on his cheeks. I felt a twinge of shame fill me. Even though I was just playing along because I wanted to protect Matt there was some little part inside me that enjoyed the attention. "We wanted to find a witch who could break a curse and were going to wait until the rankings came out to show us who was the most powerful. But since we have you here it may have been better to just ask if you can do it."

"Why would we want the curse broken?" Eli asked, the cocky grin still grazing her perfect lips. I leaned forward and begun eating my pasta, not liking how this conversation was going.

Matt spluttered trying to come up with a response but never found one.

"It would be good publicity if a couple of college students were able to break a curse as strong as hers," Rae mused. "The governor would love to hear all about it."

"I want the magic though; I don't want to break it." Daxton's voice was almost a growl.

"Then find a way for you to take it from her and consume that magic for yourself," Rae offered. I met her gaze. Her smile was one that scared me the most. It was cold and her eyes watched over us like a hawk. I wouldn't be surprised if we were playing right into her hand.

"I don't even know where to begin," Daxton grumbled.

"A low-level without the curse would be boring." Eli pouted.

The bell rang before anyone else could say anything. I hurried and got out of my seat to walk toward my class but Eli stopped me once more by grabbing my wrist. She pulled me down to sit next to her once more.

"Free period for Class A, didn't you read the schedule?" Eli teased.

Matt sent me a look that was full of sympathy.

I'm okay, go, I signed with a small smile, trying but definitely failing to reassure him by the look on his face.

"Mr. Thompson and I have class. Let's go," Rae said and without so much of a glance backward she left the mess hall with Matt.

The students in the mess hall all started to leave except the few who also had a free period.

"We will stay here and eat. Why don't you go find your witch, Daxton," Eli said and pushed my food back in front of me.

Daxton began to grumble but did exactly as Eli said and brought the cat with him. I refused to look Eli in the eyes and continued to eat my food. She sent another vision to me that almost made me choke on my food.

We were still in the mess hall. Everything looked the same from the time of day to the people that were sitting at the tables eating their food. The only difference was instead of the sitting position I was in I was bent over the table with zero clothes on. I couldn't see Eli but I knew that she was behind me. Her rough hands gripped my hips and roughly pulled them to her, and what I assumed was a strap-on pushed into me. I was wet and ready to take it without any fight.

As soon as it showed up it was gone. I sent her a glare. My stomach twisted painfully and I had to clamp my thighs together when her eyes met mine again.

Stop that, I snapped at her in my head ignoring the heat that traveled across my body.

"Just say the word and we can do much more," she purred. Her hand was removed from mine and she dropped some of her food on my plate. It was the same thing that Matt had ordered.

This time it was me who reached out. I lightly touched her arm.

What do you want?

"Many things," she mused. "But like I said I want you to come willingly, and it seems you respond better to nice guys like that low-level."

Don't play games. First you corner and bully me and now you are saying you want to be nice to me? Just admit you want to see the curse and leave it at that.

"No one has rejected me before, Rosie." Her voice was low as she spoke. "The curse is a nice touch but never in all my years has someone had the balls to not only light my shirt on fire but then ignore me so easily." She paused again, a light smile forming on her face. "Think of it as a conquest. The easier you give in the easier I'll get bored of you and leave."

You're not afraid of catching the curse? I asked hesitantly.

"You and I both know it doesn't work like that. And I would be more than happy to see that curse in action." She sent me a smirk. "I guess you could say I have an interest in pain." I dropped my hand from her arm and focused on the food in front of me.

I was glad that she wasn't touching me because an odd sense of relief filled me. I didn't mind the thought of having sex with her, far from it really. Bullying and arrogance aside, she was attractive.

It also didn't help that I hadn't been with another in over a year long. And she was open to my curse; she wasn't scared of catching it nor did it seem like she would back down if it showed during sex.

I sighed and tried to finish my food and ignore her for the rest of the free period.

Chapter Nine
Rosie

"I'll do it," Daxton said the next day before class started. "But...you cannot push me, Eli. I mean it. If I lose control you have to pull me out."

"What's the fun in that?" Eli pouted. She obviously would not be happy if she didn't get anything out of a low-level without a curse but I didn't let her ruin the flutter of hope that ran through me. I reached over to her hand and threaded my fingers through her rough ones.

Please, Eli, I whispered in her mind. Her smile dropped and her eyes snapped to our hands.

Tricky little low-level. Her eyes met mine. *I will only say yes if you promise me something,* she shot back. She faced her body toward mine and leaned in close. My breath hitched. *Promise me that I'll be the first to have you.*

What are you talking about? Heat fanned across my face and I tried to scoot away from her but she grabbed my shirt and forced me closer.

I have seen how you feel about Daxton and Rae. God, even the other low-level has a chance with you if he tried. I'm a competitive person. Promise that you won't let them touch you until I do. Her eyes narrowed at me.

What are you insinuating? I snapped.

I'm insinuating that you are a woman with needs and can get them satisfied with the bat of an eyelash. I don't know how you did it but you have got all of us waiting in line for you to make a decision, she replied. There was no smile in her tone; she was being completely serious no matter how ridiculous her words may have seemed.

Don't exaggerate.

I'm not and you know it. Her eyes were almost too intense for me to handle.

I licked my dry lips feeling a heat rise up in me. A different type of emotion soared through my chest.

And if I do allow them to touch me first? I dared to ask. A burst of confidence fluttered in my chest.

Then I'll let him do whatever his magic wants him to do and I can promise you last time that happened it wasn't pretty. I expected her to show me but she didn't. Instead, she just stared into my eyes with a serious expression.

I never knew someone of your status would resort to begging for someone to sleep with you. I paused when she growled in my mind. *And you think I want you?*

I know you do and there is no need to beg. You'll thank me after and then you will be the one begging for more.

I have never been with a girl before, I admitted embarrassed. I never denied my attraction to girls but getting close to anyone was almost impossible.

I'll take care of you, she promised me, her face slightly softer now.

My stomach dropped and I looked over to Daxton. He was watching our interaction with a dark gaze. Was it really that bad when he lost control? I really didn't have much to say no to; I knew what I wanted...and *needed.*

I promise, I told her and pushed her away as the teacher came into the room. I didn't have to look at her face to know that she was still watching me intently.

"It's a deal," Eli told Daxton.

The teacher stood with his hands on his hips and gave us a large smile. "Welcome to your first ranking. Everyone get your bags and follow me out to stadium three. After you are done you may have the rest of the day off."

I swallowed my fear and stood with the rest of the class.

* * *

From the murmurs it seemed like today would be only for a few first-year classes and the other years would be taking their rankings on other days. I was sandwiched once again between Daxton and Eli as we waited to be called.

"Alright listen up!" yelled a teacher dressed in athletic leggings and a tight jacket. Her short hair stopped at her chin and her bright green eyes were surrounded by charcoal liner. "You will walk to the middle of the field where you will demonstrate your power. We will ask you a series of questions and then you will get your scoring around your next testing period. Any questions?"

All of the first-year teachers stood behind her. None really stood out except Mr. Falkner and the only reason he stood out was because his eyes were drilling into mine. I looked at the ground to avoid his gaze.

Slowly each student was called into the middle of the field while the rest of us stood on the first track that surrounded it. I shivered after the fifteenth student was called up. The chill was starting to make its way through my layers.

"Maybe you can use that fire to heat yourself up," Eli said and wrapped her arm around my shoulder. I was enveloped in her warmth and immediately stopped shivering.

Remove your arm. People are already staring, I hissed and removed her arm. Her hand lingered in mine.

Don't care so much what other people think. Insecurity is not a good look for you.

I wanted to retort but I was cut off by a booming voice.

"Is that all you got?" yelled the teacher in charge of the rankings.

The high-level man that was in the middle of the field was surrounded by tiny rocks that levitated around him stuck in midair.

"I can only levitate small things!" he yelled back and the rocks dropped by his feet.

"What other limitations?" she asked writing notes on her clipboard.

"I can only hold it for less than ten minutes. Right now it's about eight minutes." Even from far away I could tell that the high-level was embarrassed by his power.

I was a bit confused that a high-level could have such a weak power. I assumed all high-levels were as powerful as Daxton and Eli but maybe even high-levels could be weak.

"Fine," huffed the teacher. "Next! Rosie Miller."

I froze at hearing my name. Murmurs surrounded me and I was roughly pushed forward by Eli. I sent her a glare but she returned my glare with a smile.

I walked to my place in the middle of the field and turned to face the teacher and students. Standing in front of them now made me feel like I was a freak show and they had all paid to watch me really fuck up. Many eyes that had been turned now looked at me straight on. Even the teachers all turned to watch.

"I understand your *condition* so just follow the prompts," she yelled from across the field.

I flushed with embarrassment but nodded at her anyways to show I understood.

"Show us your power," she commanded.

I started a small fire in my palm and held it out for her to see. There were a few snickers in the crowd. My eyes met Mr. Falkner and he sent me a small encouraging smile.

"Make it bigger," she commanded. I made the flame in my hand bigger but she shook her head as if annoyed. "Are you immune to your own flame?"

I nodded to her understanding where she was going. I pushed my hands out palms faced down and commanded the fire to grow around me. The warmth shot through my body and in seconds the fire was roaring around me.

"Alright," the teacher said and started writing down on her clipboard. I was about to extinguish the flames when Mr. Falkner moved next to her.

"I think you can do more than that," Mr. Falkner called out. The athletic teacher raised her brow and whispered something to him, but he just nodded.

"Alright, make it as big as you can, Ms. Miller," she commanded.

I shifted uncomfortably and looked around taking note of the length of the field. I could probably try to stretch it to the end of the field, but it would get too close to the students and that would be pushing farther than I had ever gone before. Mr. Falkner nodded when I met his gaze. I sighed and pushed the fire out around me.

There were audible gasps but the larger the fire got the less I was able to hear the murmurs of the group. I may have been immune to the flame but the heat, the smoke, and the noise was an entirely different story. People may not realize but being inside the middle of a roaring fire is very loud. It was like the sound of waves but amplified. It caused your blood to rush and pound in your ears. *That's* what made it so *terrifying.*

I pushed and pushed the fire as far as it could go. When the smoke surrounded me I knew it was time to pull back before I was on the ground heaving for air. With a snap of my fingers the raging fire that had painted the entire field red was gone. The black smoke stayed in the air and I was met with an interesting sight.

I had in fact burned the entirety of the field all the way up to the bleachers. I was surprised that I was even capable of all that, and even a little proud of myself. I never thought after the accident that I would even be capable of being proud of such a destructive thing.

The most interesting thing though, was all of the teachers and students were crowded in a circle behind Daxton. Daxton stood facing me; his hands were up in the air and around them was a small protective veil that shone blue in the light. The dirt and grass around them was left unharmed.

The athletic teacher and Mr. Falkner were the first to peer over Daxton and the only ones to leave the veil. As soon as they did Daxton lowered it and it evaporated into nothing but left a few sparkles in the air. His eyes burned into mine with an intensity that I have never seen before. It almost frightened me more than the two high-level teachers that were stomping their way over to me.

"That was more than we expected from you, Ms. Miller," Mr. Falkner said. He clapped his hand on my shoulder as if to congratulate me.

"That was amazing!" the athletic teacher gushed. My jaw nearly dropped when she held my hands in hers. "We have so much to test you on! Next time we need to try more of a tactical practice. How hot can you make the fires? Is it always red? Ever try to make them blue?"

"You know she can't answer, Linda," Mr. Falkner chided with a laugh.

"I know but that was the biggest fire I have seen in centuries!" she said still giddy as we walked back toward the students. "And did you see Mr. Reid's shield? Beautiful!"

"Okay, okay," Mr. Falkner said with a groan. "Let's get on to the others now."

The students were back in their lines and were absolutely silent as I walked back to my place between Eli and Daxton. I shifted uncomfortably when no one spoke.

"So, I guess that was cool," Daxton commented.

"Cool?" a high-level boy with cropped brown hair and yellow eyes said from behind us. His hands came to rest on my shoulders and pulled me back into him. "That was insane! I had never thought a low-level would be capable of that power!"

Eli let out a small growl but it was Daxton who pulled me out of his grasp.

"Be careful or she'll light you up," Eli commented.

After that a normal level of chatter resumed amongst the students and I was surprised that some even had praised me for my show. I received a few more dirty looks but I ignored them and tried to watch the rest of the rankings.

"Daxton Reid, I will take your actions from earlier as part of the test so we will move on to Eliza Groten?" the athletic teacher said.

"It's Eli," Eli corrected. "And no need to." Eli walked straight up to her and placed a large hand on her shoulder. It was so big in comparison that it almost covered her entire shoulder.

"Oh I see," she mumbled and started writing furiously down on her clipboard.

Eli turned back to us with a smile. The next name was called. She put her arm across my shoulder and I couldn't help myself.

Eliza, such a pretty name, I cooed in my mind.

Can it, she hissed back at me.

"Maybe the little low-level has some power after all," Eli teased changing the subject.

Don't let it get to your head, she said in my mind.

That's not very nice for someone trying to be a nice guy, Eliza. My lips twitched slightly.

Oh she jokes now? Maybe my charms won her over? I could hear the smile in her voice even in my head.

Don't let it get to your head.

* * *

"Wait so you'll really help us?" Matt asked excitedly as he sat down at our lunch table.

Eli, Daxton, and I had left as soon as the teachers allowed. There was a surprising amount of high-levels that had either useless powers or just weak ones. The worst one that I saw had to have been the person who could summon bugs and only then managed to summon a fly. It made me look at the people around us in a new light.

"I will help *her*," Dax corrected. "In return I get her magic."

"Then what are you in for?" Matt questioned Eli. "It would be stupid to think that you are only going along with this because you are Daxton's friend."

My heart pounded when Eli leaned forward as if to tell Matt a secret. "That's between me and *Rosie*, low-level." The way my name rolled off her tongue had to be a crime.

"Did you coerce her into something? How low are you to take advantage of someone's curse." Matt sneered at her. His face was twisted, and his hands gripped at the edge of the table. I was taken aback by his attitude.

I shot a look around at the students that filled the mess hall. There were still many people that were at the rankings, so it was safe for the moment.

"It's not like that," I whispered gritting my teeth against the pain on my side. Matt's face suddenly relaxed at my intervention. *It's a different promise,* I signed to him not wanting to provoke the curse.

"Okay, Rosie," he murmured and suddenly his food was more interesting than Eli's provoking.

"If I tried to coerce her, she would burn me to a crisp, wouldn't you?" Eli teased and stabbed a piece of chicken off my plate to pop it into her mouth.

"She almost did," Daxton huffed. Amr snored lightly in his lap but did not stir at his response.

Poor cat must be exhausted.

Even sitting next to him now, I could feel the magic building up. Whatever Amr was used for it would not hold him off for long. Guilt shot through me and I suddenly regretted speaking aloud.

There was an awkward pause and a small shuffling. Suddenly Matt's head shot up and sent a glare to Eli. They were both locked onto each other and both refused to look away. So far communication had been smooth between all of us; this was the first time I had ever seen them act like this.

"Let's take a walk, Rosie," Matt said getting up. I scrambled up as well, thankful that I was able to get away from the awkwardness.

I followed him out of the mess hall without another word to the others. He didn't speak again until we were out in the courtyard and far away from any high-levels.

"You don't have to feel indebted to them, Rosie." Matt turned around and gripped my arms tightly. "Him getting whatever magic the curse has is enough. You don't have to go through this *deal* you made with Eli."

I'm not going through anything, I tried to sign to him, but I was unsure if he understood given how his hands were stopping my movement.

"She showed me," Matt whispered, his grey eyes searching mine. "What you agreed to. Her leg brushed mine under the table and she showed me what you said in class."

"That's none of your concern," I said and yanked my arms out of his grasp as they were filled with cuts. "You are not in charge of what I do...with my body." I sucked in a deep breath as a particularly nasty cut made its way down my side.

"Don't speak, I'm sorry," Matt rushed out and tried to reach out to me but his hands failed as he tried to find a place to put them. "I just wanted to make sure you aren't getting hurt. Stupid older brother complex, right?" He let out a panicked laugh. "I won't interfere, I promise. Just tell me if you need me to step in."

I wanted to point out that I was more than capable of protecting myself and it was actually the fact that Eli threatened to beat him up that got us into this whole mess anyways.

That's a lie.

It was me lighting up her shirt.

It's fine, just trust me okay? I signed to him and stood up straight as the last cut healed itself. *Don't provoke her. Them. They are all dangerous. We will get the curse fixed, then leave.*

"Okay I get it." He sighed and ran his hand through his curls. "I know I was the one that asked them to help but...are you sure about this? There will be no turning back."

I paused to think about it but there was nothing that was going to change my mind.

I'm sure, I signed to him.

Matt gave me a hesitant smile and was about to speak but we were both soaked by ice-cold water that seemed to have magically fallen from the sky.

I gasped and wiped the water out of my face. I was already soaked down to my underwear and in this chill there was no telling how fast it would take for low-levels like us to get sick. Looking up I came face to face with Emma and her posse of high-levels.

"Sorry, didn't want a repeat of what happened earlier." Emma sneered. The other girls laughed behind her. "Let's try not to show off too much, right low-level?"

The group of cackling bullies left faster than they came. I wanted so badly to send some fire after them, but her throwing water on me had the same effect as throwing it on an actual fire and I would be left like that until I was able to dry off.

I met Matt's eyes and almost laughed at his bewildered expression.

First time? I signed.

"Did I miss something, Rosie?" he asked and flung his soggy curls out of his face.

It's a long story. You can dry off in my room if you want?

"Yes please, mine is way too far and I still have class later," he said with a sigh.

I mimed a chuckle and walked toward my dorm in soggy clothing.

It was too long and too soggy of a walk to be comfortable. By the time we reached my hallway my teeth were chattering.

A door in front of us opened and I crashed into a hard chest. The person sighed and stepped away from me without touching me any more than was necessary. Looking up I realized it was Rae.

"You just can't help but show up wherever I go, hm?" she said giving me a cold look. I looked down at my feet suddenly feeling like I was intruding. "Why are you both wet?"

"Some girls dumped water on us. Something about Rosie showing off," Matt grumbled.

"Ah yes the field of fire," Rae mused, her expression still cold. Her eyes trailed down my form and I felt like I was being scrutinized.

Looking at Rae now Eli's words about having them waiting in line seemed to be about as true as fiction.

"A whole field?" Matt exclaimed and I tried to hide my face under the tangled, wet mess of my hair.

"Yes, *apparently* the only thing that saved the students was Daxton's shield. She was praised by teachers and students alike." Rae opened her door back up and gestured for Matt to come in. "You can change in here."

"Ah...sure...okay." Matt paused before entering but I just sent him a wave. He looked mildly disappointed.

Rae spared one last glance at me then shut her door behind her leaving me soaking wet and alone in the hallway.

I snorted. Maybe Matt was more her type.

Chapter Ten
Rosie

The next time I saw Rae it was with the rest of the trio and she still had a distasteful look on her face when her eyes met mine. I tried to ignore it but her gaze was so intense that it made me anxious. It didn't help that Matt was suspiciously late.

"I assumed as much," Rae hummed after Daxton explained that he wanted to take the magic for himself. "I have already prepared a schedule. If we want to make this work before the semester ends we will need to meet—"

"The end of the semester is too fast," Daxton interrupted.

"You are not suggesting we waste an entire year on this, are you?" Rae asked, her tone becoming sharp.

"Let's see what we can do in a semester," Eli said, her arm snaking its way around my waist. "If we can do that maybe we can just quit school completely."

Don't act so familiar, I hissed at her.

Don't act like you don't like it, she shot back. *Or are you afraid I'll out you?*

*That's not it...*I trailed in my mind.

"Unlikely," Rae said with a huff. Her gaze went to Eli's grip on me, then to me. I gulped.

If we do this, can we leave Matt out of it? I asked Eli. She leaned forward on the table, loosening her hand on my waist and rested her head on her hand. From my view I could see a bit of her colorful tattoos peeking out.

"Why do you not want the other low-level to join?" she asked. All attention was on me in that moment, and I felt my face flush.

He doesn't like you; it will be hard to get anything done with you two at each other's throats. Her eyebrow raised at my explanation. My face must have been red as a tomato. *And Daxton reacted weirdly to my curse last time. I don't...want him to see that.*

"So, without him then," Eli summarized.

"We will do it twice a week," Rae said interrupting the staring contest between me and Eli. "Mondays I can join but I have prior engagements most other nights of the week so you can pick another day that suits you."

"Friday then," Daxton said. "So I can rest in case it gets to be too much."

I swallowed my guilt and nodded.

"We will wait until the Monday after next," Rae said. "Daxton needs time to get his magic under control and there is no way I will leave you three alone the first time."

"Yes, mom," Eli said, distaste evident in her tone.

The week and a half moved in the blink of an eye, far too quickly for my liking if I was being honest. Each day made me more and more anxious and had me fidgeting in my seat whenever Daxton got near. The first test would have to be the worst because it required Daxton to consume the curse's magic. Eli constantly teased Daxton, asking if he had fun with his witch. It was all fun and games for her but it only made me more on edge. I should have been happy to finally get rid of this curse, but after last time I didn't know what to expect.

When the time finally came, Daxton moved to an empty space in the garden and Eli stood behind him, hands placed firmly on his shoulders so she would be able to keep him steady in case.

Rae decided to stay close to my side, for which I was grateful. She was close enough that if I shifted my weight my arm might brush across hers. I looked up to see her writing furiously in her notebook. Her eyes scanned the page before meeting mine. My heart leapt in my throat but I couldn't tear my gaze from her, those hazel eyes were so intense they pinned me in place.

"You will be fine," Rae whispered behind her notebook. I gulped and prayed to the Originals that her words would be true.

"Go," Daxton ordered.

"Okay," I said slowly feeling the pain radiate through my legs. "I'm not sure what I am supposed to say." I had to say the words slowly and paused.

"Tell us about how you got the curse," Rae offered, jotting down more notes. Daxton's eyes were firmly shut and he was trying to center his breathing but I could already tell it was becoming erratic. His clenched fists began to turn white. Eli's eyes were firmly on mine.

"It was my tenth birthday," I said raising my voice. "A witch came and demanded payment from my parents." I took a deep breath when a sharp pain spread across my ribs. I stumbled slightly. "They fought," I pushed out. The cuts were getting deeper even though I tried to force the words out of me as fast as possible. The blood began to soak through the front of my turtleneck. "And I burnt the house down."

The figures of Daxton and Eli began to blur and the world spun around me. I felt myself tipping to the side but before I fell onto the dirt, Rae's arms circled around me. I wanted so badly to relax into them but Eli's words rang through my head.

Promise me that I'll be the first to have you.

I stood up straight and pushed Rae away softly. Looking over at Eli and Daxton, I was not even sure if either even caught what just happened. Eli was now holding Daxton in a chokehold while he was clawing at her arms.

"Am I to assume that position means that we do not know more than we started with?" Rae called out to them. Both shot glares at us. I swallowed thickly at the look in Daxton's eyes. The beast was back.

"He knows. I heard him. He recognizes it. Fucking stop it," Eli hissed at Daxton and tightened her chokehold. Daxton's jerks started to lose their strength. "He just got lost in it *again*. Whatever it is I heard enough to know it's extremely old magic. Maybe Original."

I didn't dare speak but I was certain we all had the same question. How the fuck did my parents get in touch with an Original?

"They never told you anything about the witch?" Rae asked. I shook my head at her; my parents never dared to even mention it. One question was all it took for my Dad to explode and I never wanted to risk his temper more than I already had.

Daxton became slack in Eli's arms and his body was pushed to the ground with disgust. She stood up and brushed the dirt off her clothes, but it was useless—after the tumble she had with Daxton her whole uniform was covered in soot and dirt. Her white shirt that was rolled up to the elbows giving me a rare look at her intricate tattoos that were also covered in dirt. She huffed and angrily marched up to me. Her blue eyes had a shine that first captivated me but now looked like blue fiery pools that were ready to burn whatever was in their path.

Her hand gripped me, fingers digging into the soft flesh of my shoulder. She stepped closer, so close our noses almost touched. I would have been nervous at the closeness if not for her murderous look.

"Remember your *fucking promise* to me. I don't roll around in the dirt for some bullshit like this. Especially involving a disgusting low-level." So maybe she did see it.

Her breathing came in pants and her tone was dangerous. Small beads of sweat rolled down her face and her blonde hair hung messily in her face.

What did it say about me if I admitted I was turned on by this?

I reached out letting my fingers brush softly against her exposed skin.

I thought you would wait for me, hm? Giving up the nice guy act so easily? My eyes trailed down to her semi-exposed chest, a bead of sweat falling in between the channel of her breasts.

Fuck that. Circumstances changed. Having me roll around in the dirt, degrade myself all while you run into her a—

Rae's hand brushed dirt softly off of Eli's shoulder, stopping all of Eli's angry ranting in my head. "Seems like Daxton is not the only one on edge." Eli let go of her harsh grip on my shoulder and pushed me away from her in disgust, severing our connection. "This is not just for her, remember. Who knows what we could gain from solving this? Maybe the principal would even let us graduate early."

"That is wishful thinking." Eli spat on the ground.

Anything you wanted was in the realm of possibilities when you were rich. Students here were rewarded differently than at other low-level schools. You do good, get a little publicity, and that would be far more valuable to the school than if you actually sat in class. It wasn't like they needed any more money anyways.

"It's happened for people who make great scientific breakthroughs or contributions to the school. Don't forget, for some reason the principal likes her." Rae's molten eyes met mine. "Likes her so much he hides things from even me."

Daxton chose that moment to wake up with a loud groan. "Jesus Christ, Eli."

"Tell us what you felt," Rae demanded going back to taking notes without wasting another precious second.

"I think it's something akin to an Original's magic. I didn't think the Original witches still existed, but the magic is too old not to be." He rubbed his head but remained sitting on the floor. "If I could separate the magic from her and take it for myself there is no telling how powerful I'd become." He let out a breathless laugh.

"Would you be able to control it though?" Rae asked.

"The fuck you would know about that?" Daxton growled at her.

Rae gave out a sigh. She seemed to be the only rational one tonight. "We are done for today. Next time bring us a solution and we will test to see if it works." She paused and looked to me. "It would be best to remain silent and only speak for the purposes of these tests. We won't be around to hold Daxton back all the time."

I nodded at her and grabbed my book bag to leave. No one moved so I decided to go by myself. Even as I left the garden not a single person moved.

* * *

"I hope the school has been treating you well, Ms. Miller," Principal Winterfell commented as I sat down in the chair across from him. "I heard you even made some new friends?"

"Sure, friends," I murmured.

"Where was it that time?" he inquired, his purple eyes twinkling in the light.

"Leg," I answered. "How did you find out?" I got out my phone after that, not wanting to go through any more pain.

"About your friends? It's unusual, for people as high of a status as they are to take interest in a low-level," he explained and leaned back in his chair. His previously braided hair was down today, and he twirled one of the loose purple waves through his fingers.

I meant the curse but you've piqued my curiosity. What makes them so high status? I typed out and showed to him.

"Rae's family is in deep with the government, and I wouldn't be surprised if that girl takes over for the governor at some point," he said with a smile. "A dangerous one, always *prying* for information. Eli's story is hers to tell. Daxton is a part of the most prominent witch family, one of the only ones that have positive ties to the government."

I mulled over this new information. There was no way I would ask Eli about her ties but the way the principal skipped over it made me curious.

Didn't know you would give so much information about your students to a random person, I typed.

"You are also a student, Ms. Miller." He smiled and leaned forward. "And I just thought that you should know of their ties. It's all public knowledge anyways."

"The curse?" I asked not liking the way he dodged my question.

"I have many ties to other schools. How do you think I get the best of the best here? Of course, we have to share information." He leaned back with a smile.

"Which teacher?" I asked then winced at the pain in my side.

"All that matters is you are here now, right?" he responded. "You have the chance at an education with people who once deemed you as unworthy."

"A great opportunity," I murmured but didn't back down and kept my gaze firmly on him. It was weird. This situation, him dodging my questions. All of it.

"Who was it?" he asked and hummed lightly. He looked up and to the side like he was trying to remember. "Eleventh-grade math teacher I believe?"

"Oh, Mrs. Davids?" I asked knowing full well I never had a teacher by that name.

"No need to speak if it pains you Ms. Miller," he said. His narrowed eyes pierced through me. "There is no Mrs. Davids, Rosie. Don't think I am incapable of doing research myself."

I gulped when he said my name. He stood up and leaned against the side of his desk so he towered over my sitting form.

"That would have been smart if it was anyone else," he said. "Don't ask stupid questions that will get you in trouble. Or worse...hurt." His fake smile was plastered back on his face. "This was a nice meeting, Ms. Miller. I am glad you are getting along with your classmates."

I took the cue to stand up and tried to hurry out but his voice stopped me.

"Do be careful around those others, hm? Focus on your education," he called out.

I slammed the door shut, sending Tammy a sheepish smile, and then hurried out of the office with my heart pounding in my chest.

* * *

"I'm going to try and consume it," Daxton said as we entered the garden for the second time that week. I was still anxious from my chat with the principal earlier and his words added a whole new panic to my life that I so did not need right now.

"Like hell you are," Eli growled, a scowl gracing her lips. "I am not tumbling in the dirt with you again."

"I haven't found any solid research to make a potion yet," he shot back. "And this is another test to see—if I do consume her power—if I can handle it."

I looked between the two not understanding what was going on.

"How do you plan on doing it?" Eli asked taking her place at my side. Her hand made its home on my shoulder.

"There are two ways. Like I normally do with my witches." He paused and grimaced. "Or bloodletting. But that one is gross."

Eli's hand squeezed my shoulder. I looked up at her but her eyes were narrowed at Daxton.

Did I miss something? How does he plan to consume it? I asked her. She met my eyes after a long pause.

"He's offering to fuck you," she hissed. "You will blood let. I expect you to keep my promise."

I looked at Daxton. His brown eyes were clear. No sign of the beast underneath. Which meant he was offering this clear-headed and fully aware of his choices. Heat pooled in my stomach.

Don't you dare consider it, she hissed in my mind. *I told you I am competitive.*

"You aren't in charge of her," Daxton fought back.

Is bloodletting like the time when Rae cut him? I asked.

"Yes," came Eli's clipped response. She sat down on the fountain edge and pulled me in between her open legs and flush against her chest. "Blood-letting."

Speak now if you want this to stop, she said in my mind.

Daxton grumbled on his way over to us and pushed up my shirt to expose my arm.

We should at least try something. Even as I told her this, uncertainty left me feeling anxious and scared to see what would happen if Daxton did lose control. *You'll stop it if it gets too dangerous anyways, like last time.*

Eli let out a small chuckle.

"Let's get started, Dax. The low-level is ready." Her voice was right by my ear and low enough to cause shivers to go down my spine. I took a calming breath.

Daxton's eyes flitted between the two of us and then he scowled while looking toward my arm.

"Disgusting," he hissed and pulled a small knife out of his pocket. "This will hurt." Without any other warning the knife dug its way down my fore-arm. I bit my lip to stop the noise from my mouth and dug my fingernails into Eli's arm. Eli in return only held me tighter against her, breathing heavily in my ear.

Good girl, she cooed in my mind.

Daxton brought the wound to his mouth and began licking at the blood. An odd tingling sensation filled me once more. Just like before the cuts came but this time it was intensified, and I leaned my head back into Eli in hopes to center myself. I guessed it was his magic that started to coarse through me. It started in my arm and washed slowly over my entire body.

No wonder he went crazy over this. Just him taking the small amount of blood had my whole body on edge yet gooey at the same time. It didn't help that Eli's arms were clasped around me and I could hear every breath she took.

Daxton moved to stand in between our legs. His grip tightened on my arm as he began sucking on the wound trying to get the blood out faster. His eyes met mine and my breath caught.

Does that feel good? Eli asked as her hand slipped into my shirt and rested against my bare stomach. It sent jolts down my body.

Daxton moaned against the blood. He cut deep enough that it would take a few moments to heal but those moments were like a lifetime and with each stroke of his tongue an uncontrollable fire began raging inside me. It was so inappropriate to be stuck in between the two like this but I absolutely loved it.

Not so against it now huh? Eli's smug voice said in my head.

In one motion her hand slipped under my bra and she rolled my nipple between her rough fingers. I gritted my teeth refusing to make a noise. Instead, I leaned my head back against her chest and took a deep breath. She slipped the hand under the other side and pinched the other nipple. A small gasp escaped my lips. There was a small pain that radiated in my arm but Daxton was far too involved in his letting to give us a second thought.

What are you doing? We are not alone, I snapped at her through our connection.

I told you that I would be the first to touch you but I never said we would be alone.

Her hand unbuttoned my pants and slipped through to cup me over my underwear. I wanted so badly to whimper but I didn't dare. Her fingers began to rub against the length of my wet core expertly teasing me, knowing exactly where I wanted her fingers but not quite giving in to my desires.

Not now. I pushed back but her fingers brushed over my clit and I let out a small whimper. Daxton froze and removed his mouth from my wound. When his eyes met mine now they held a different kind of fire.

"Go on Dax," Eli mused near my ear with a chuckle. "Continue to blood let while I make this little low-level beg." Her pressure increased and she began rubbing fast circles against the nerve endings. Against my better judgment my legs opened wider for her, her actions far too mouthwatering to further deny this.

"That's not fair," Daxton whined. Eli hooked her legs through mine and pulled them apart giving her hand easier access.

"Do as I say," she growled. Daxton pouted and made another cut in the same place as the healed one without another word. When his lips met my arm once more, my head swam.

"Are you going to speak for us, low-level?" she purred and dipped her hand teasingly to my wet entrance. She was purposefully not going inside my underwear and it was driving me crazy. I no longer cared that we were out in public and with each stroke of her fingers against my folds I lost myself.

Fuck you, I told her in my head and her hand stopped. The one that had been rolling my nipple came up and gripped my throat tightly.

"Say the words," she groaned in my ear. Her hand pushed aside my panties finally and played achingly with my entrance. "Who would have thought you'd get so wet by having Dax's lips on you. Maybe I should have tried that tactic sooner." The hand attached to my throat tilted my head and exposed my neck enough for her tongue to flick out and drag across it.

I let out a groan this time and she rewarded me by rubbing up the length of my slit.

Fuck, Eli. Please, I begged and bucked against her hand unable to stop myself.

"If you are not going to fuck her I will," Dax hissed and left his position at my arm. His hands cupped my face bringing his lips to mine. Eli chose that time to slip two fingers into me stretching me further than I expected.

I let out a gasp and Daxton's tongue entered my mouth. There was a burning cut on my back but I couldn't even pay attention to it as Eli's fingers pounded into me.

Such a low-level slut. She pushed toward me. *Look at how easy it was to get you to open your legs for us.*

Daxton grabbed my hand and brought it to his erection, moaning once contact was made. He ground against my hand and began to undo his pants.

A moment of panic entered my mind when it caught up with my actions.

Do you regret making your promise? she teased and pushed a third finger into me. I decided in that moment that none of the hesitation or fear inside me mattered. I tried to help unbutton Daxton's pants but we were interrupted by a sigh.

"I leave you three alone for less than an hour and this is what I come back to?" Rae's voice caused Daxton to freeze and step away slightly. His brown eyes were too calm to be normal.

There probably wasn't a lot of magic in your blood, Eli told me but she didn't remove her fingers from inside me. Instead, she picked up the pace.

"Glad you could see this, Rae," Eli told her. "I'm going to be the first to make her come and now both of you can see me reap my prize."

"Wait I—" I tried to speak but a combination of the pain and Daxton's lips returning to mine once more stopped me. Embarrassment filled me at the thought of Rae watching this happen.

She likes it. You think someone that looks like that likes dick? Eli asked.

I kissed Daxton back stronger as I felt my release build. His hands wound themselves in my hair, pulling harshly. A different kind of tingle made its way through me and into Daxton but I couldn't follow the feeling as Eli's fingers sent me over the edge.

Neither Daxton nor Eli pulled away until I had come down from my orgasm. When Daxton did I saw that there was a light to his eyes. Eli removed her hand that was clamped on my throat and I took a deep breath of air.

"It does work the same as the other witches," she commented toward Rae. "It's not a lot but it's potent."

"Your magic is calmer than I expected," Rae noted. Eli removed her fingers and looped her arm around my neck and popped them into her mouth. I hurried to try and button my pants, but she turned my head to a painful angle and kissed me. Her lips were much softer than I expected, and I could taste myself on her. She bit my lip hard before removing her mouth from mine and giving me a grin.

"It calmed when I took some of her magic. It's like it knew I couldn't take much so it didn't try to push it. For once it stopped asking for more," Daxton continued.

"That may not be a good thing," Eli commented.

"No. It may mean the curse is more powerful than I expected. If it could scare my magic…I would hate to see what else it could do."

Eli stood us both up and reached down over me to button my pants.

"Don't think this stops here," she warned, sending another wave of shivers down my spine.

* * *

I couldn't look Matt in the face the next morning when we met for breakfast. It was a mix of shame and embarrassment. I could never tell him what happened, nor did I want to when I thought of his reaction to Eli before.

"I swear whatever they have been feeding us in those low-level schools is straight bullshit." He moaned into his eggs as he ate. "I have been doing homework and studying every night until 3 a.m. because they said they would drop my ranking even lower if I failed the test. And the free food deal is over now. I thought I'd be able to save more. Life is so hard now."

Our money should be deposited. We will be fine until that runs low, I signed to him and ate my bagel slowly.

"You'll be stuck here for two more years, Rosie," he reminded. "Anyways how's classes? Lots of homework?"

Almost none. We will have a big paper at the end of the term. It was true, we had not received a lick of homework since we started...not that I'd even be able to complete it with how demanding those high-levels were. Mr. Falkner just asked that we made sure to write careful notes and to pay attention in class so we'd be prepared when the paper came.

"Lucky," he whined.

A hand found its way to my shoulder and Amr jumped onto my lap with a loud meow. I looked up to see Eli smiling down at me. Her knowing smile caused a blush to immediately burn at my face.

"Let's get to class," she said pulling me up lightly. I had to drop the rest of my bagel back onto my plate and grip Amr tightly so he wouldn't fall.

Matt cursed and scrambled for his things.

"Let's go together, Mr. Thompson," Rae said appearing from behind us.

"Ah, sure, of course," he said and rubbed his hand through his messy curls. He didn't look at her while he packed up. He gave me a small wave and walked out of the mess hall. Rae gave me a sidelong glance before following him.

I gulped at her reaction. Rae probably hated me.

She doesn't, Eli's voice rang through my mind. I stiffened and grabbed my bag, tearing her hand from my shoulder.

"Don't act so shy, low-level," she teased and grabbed my bag from me, slinging it over her shoulder. I flushed again and followed her out of the mess hall. Daxton was still nowhere to be seen. I hugged Amr close while I watched Eli's back. Her moods were like a roller coaster and I was nervous to see what would push her spiraling back to that hot-headed bully she was not too long ago.

We entered the room and seated ourselves at our normal seats by the window. She handed me my bag and I rummaged through it to find my notebook and pens. Students started to pile in but I paid them no mind as I reviewed the previous class's notes.

"How do your parents feel about their kid getting into this school?" Eli asked and placed her hand on top of mine. Her scarred one covered mine completely and left a pleasant warmth.

I replayed their reactions in my head. My mother's excited face and my father's words.

Get an education. Get a good job. Help your parents rebuild the shit life they were left with.

"A charmer," Eli teased. "Wasn't that their own fault for the deal?" I peeked out from behind her, my eyes darting around to see if other students heard. Only a few glowered in my direction but no one else gave any notice that they heard anything.

Be careful about what you say, I snapped.

"Don't worry so much," she said giving me a smile that showed her teeth. "Have you contacted them since?"

What's with the interest in my parents all of a sudden? I asked, not wanting to answer a question that so obviously had nothing to do with her.

"Just curious," she said as her eyes trailed down to my lips. I couldn't help myself from wetting them, suddenly feeling self-conscious under her gaze.

Daxton finally took his seat in front of us interrupting our stare down. Amr meowed but made no effort to be removed from my lap. Daxton pushed a large iced coffee across our table.

Is that for me? I asked Eli.

"Treating her to coffee now, hm?" Her smile dropped as she spoke.

"A thank you," Daxton responded. His still shimmering brown eyes met mine. "For making my magic calmer than it has been in the last two years. It's the real version of the bottled one you like so much."

I hoped my face didn't show how shocked I was because if it did my jaw would have hit the floor by now. Gifts? Bag carrying? Remembering what I liked? I barely did anything with them and now this was how they treated me?

A warm feeling bloomed in my chest. The same one that I felt when Matt gave me a hug after I told him about my curse... It was a nice feeling.

"Don't look so surprised," Eli said with a chuckle. "Dax is good with aftercare, aren't you?"

Daxton responded with a snort. I freed my hand from Eli's to grab the coffee. I took a careful sip, fully feeling every second their eyes were on me. A mix of chocolatey sweetness and the bitterness of espresso filled my mouth. My eyes widened and I shot Daxton a smile.

I smacked my hand down onto Eli's arm and shouted through our connection.

Tell him this is delicious! Tell him it's the best thing I have ever tasted! Tell him thank you and that I will—

Before I could finish Eli tore her arm from my grasp. I shot her a look but she met me with a look of her own.

"You've never had real coffee before?" she asked. I shook my head and reconnected my hand to her arm once more.

Just the cheap stuff and nothing ever tasted this good.

"She said it was delicious. She thanked you," Eli finished with a grunt and a small scowl.

I sent a smile to Daxton and gave him a thumbs up. His eyes widened and a light blush played at his cheeks. I removed my hand from Eli and focused fully on the delicious coffee in front of me.

"Happy to see all of your *smiling* faces once more," Mr. Falkner said with a sarcastic drawl as he walked in. He eyed my coffee but said nothing about it. "We have a specialist here today. Sarah Collins—she is known for finding the first Original demon bones."

A murmur passed around the class.

"Winged ones, to be precise," Mr. Falkner said and sent Eli a knowing look.

The clack of high heels was heard before we saw a tall blonde woman enter the room. She was dressed in a tight-fitting dark brown suit with a skirt and dull yellow heels. Her bright blue eyes searched the room, pausing only when they reached our table.

"Thank you, Mr. Falkner. I am so honored to be here to share my story today." Her light voice was something akin to ringing bells and the smile she gave Mr. Falkner was even sweeter. "If you would please pull up the presentation I will begin as soon as you are ready."

Mr. Falkner smiled at her then sat at his desk. The light shut off and the projector flashed images across the whiteboard. The first, and most shocking, was the picture of what looked to be a half-mummified demon.

"When I was fresh out of college I visited an excavation site where I dug up this mummified demon," she said and traced the outline of the figure with her fingertips. "This was the closest I had been to such an old demon and I was beyond amazed at what I found." The next slide showed the demon face down on a metal table with bones sticking out of its back. "As you can see these bones are not just an accident; skin was enclosed around them but whatever was previously attached to them remained no longer.

"If you look closely you can see a jagged edge to the bones with the other connecting bones angled in an unnatural way, meaning they were violently pulled off and probably when the demon was still alive given how uneven the right is compared to the left. With the help of digital reconstruction we were able to remake what we thought its wings looked like." The next slide showed a digital image of wings that were twice the size of the man's body. "But the bones sticking out of the back were so odd. We wanted to find out where the bones had gone and how they were taken off."

"This is stupid," Eli muttered. Her hand rubbed from my knee up into my mid-thigh but she was blocked by Amr's purring form lounging across my lap. "Move, cat." Amr jumped up to sit on the table.

"We found the wings after several weeks of digging up various mass graves. They were mummified as well and after that it was easy to confirm that its wings were torn off." She raised her voice loud enough to draw Eli's attention and to stop her hand from moving up my thigh and rubbing circles in the sensitive flesh. "It is not an unknown fact that the humans had hated our kind for centuries. We believed that this was just one painful example of the attacks that our kind had to endure."

She went to the next slide and instead of just the single body in the grave we were hit with a gruesome image of ten to twenty bodies of all sizes stacked on top of each other in a shallow dirt grave.

There was an eerie silence that surrounded the classroom that no one dared to break. Eli removed her hand fully from my thigh and shifted in her seat. My stomach twisted painfully looking at the picture and my breakfast threatened to show itself once more.

It was a baby.

"I am not here to remind you of the tragedies of our kind." She spoke after letting us stew in the silence for a minute longer than necessary. "I am here to show you that we were once very different from the people you see around you. We were hated for a different reason. Back then we were hated because humans rejected the idea of us. Beings as powerful as us in their minds was a direct threat to their lives. We as demons decided after years of torture and abuse that we were not going to take it any longer. We knew we were superior and finally, we started acting like it."

"Sarah," Mr. Falkner warned from his place at his desk.

"I am not trying to reignite the hatred of the human race," she said, eyes narrowing in the direction of Mr. Falkner. "There is a high possibility though that we will go extinct after some time. Many of us call ourselves *high-level* demons, but what does that mean? How are we better than the low-levels when our blood is *just* as tainted as theirs?

"Remember that within a class the size of this one there may only be one person that has blood closer to the Originals than anyone else." Her eyes shifted around the class until they landed, once again on our table. "And even then, their line will not last unless they breed with other demons a similar strength to them."

A shiver ran up my spine. I didn't like the way her eyes honed on Eli. If the monster behind Daxton's eyes looked dangerous, the one behind Sarah Collins' looked pure evil.

After another two hours of looking at the bone structure of some of the earliest demons, we were all released to lunch.

"Don't forget, ranking results come out tomorrow and we will head to the area for our monthly testing," Mr. Falkner yelled out after the class but Eli paid no mind. She practically stormed out of the classroom.

Eli was beyond pissed but the only way you could tell was the fact that the smile that always seemed to be etched on her face was now replaced with a deep frown.

"I'm skipping the rest of the day," Eli said as we walked toward the mess hall. Her eyes were trained on her phone. We had taken the long way this time hoping to avoid the crowd and were now walking on a stone path surrounded by trees and bushes, barely another student in sight. "I'll be back tonight so make sure Rae doesn't go ape shit and send a search party out."

Daxton huffed. "She only did that once." His eyes shifted to mine before he responded, "Work stuff?"

"Something like that," she responded and left us, walking back the way we came at a quickened pace. Her normal relaxed stance was now hunched, her school shirt stretched across her back tightly.

What's got her in such a mood?

"Let's get to lunch," Daxton murmured and pushed me down the walkway. I felt the heat rise to my face when his hand lingered near the back of my neck.

For some reason, I was bothered by Eli's quick disappearance and a dark foreboding feeling hung over me for the rest of the day.

Chapter Eleven

Eli

The heel of my boot smacked against the demon's face with a satisfying crunch. His face was already a bloodied mess. My gang and I had been here awhile and I didn't feel the need to hold up all the pent-up anger and frustration that filled me. The demon had resigned to keeping his position on the floor and just let the blood flow after the fifth kick had been delivered.

I needed this after the way that stupid teacher looked at me today. *Sarah Collins*. Something about her didn't sit right with me. For all intents and purposes she looked like a weak woman but when her eyes met mine...the classroom's air had thickened and there was a small connection that formed between us. If I'd thought it was possible I would say that the connection had to have been her reading my mind, but it seemed impossible to believe.

Not impossible, but I refused that anyone other than that *fucker* Malik could ever hold one over me. I was pissed at Rae once too, for having the audacity to be born with a better power then me, but I got over that once I realized how much I'd grown to like her.

Now a stupid teacher; I would not even entertain the thought that she could possibly have a more powerful gift than me *and* use it so blatantly on me. I wouldn't allow it.

This dumbass worker picked a hell of a day to get me angry. I kicked him again enjoying the way blood splattered out of his mouth. It sent a shiver up my spine.

No one invades my privacy like that. Not again. Never again.

I stared down at the scum of a worker that laid on the ground. Normally I wouldn't draw it out like this. Normally, I would have just had my men kill him and be done with it but I was pissed, and this attack was personal. Women? Car? Property? Take it, I couldn't give a damn, but when you take my money? We have a problem.

"Ple—ase…" he choked out, trying to shield his face from my next kick. Like that would even work. I kicked straight through his hand and his skull bounced off of the carpeted floor. He didn't try to get up this time.

I narrowed my eyes at my blood-coated boots. They were leather so they would be easy to clean but the laces would need to be replaced. *Just another thing to make me angry today.*

"Boss." An underling next to me spoke. I think his name was Chris or something mundane like that. He shifted as he came up to my side, obviously hoping that he would escape my wrath. "We found the money in his bedroom safe."

"How much?" I asked and gestured for the others to grab the low-level off the ground. I didn't even bother to remember their names—they wouldn't last long here anyways nor would they ever be anything important. Even if they somehow managed to make it under me without pissing me off, I didn't know how long I would stay here. If I could ever take a sector I sure as hell wouldn't want to take anyone with me that didn't even have enough power for me to remember their name. That's what it all boiled down to after all: power and making sure the people who were important knew that you had it.

"A few thousand."

"You wasted your life for a *few thousand*," I hissed as the others brought him up to me. His body was hanging limp from their arms and blood from his multiple head wounds dripped to the ground. The carpet was a light cream but with the beating it had turned dark and made wet noises as the others walked over it. "At least take a million if you knew you were going to get caught."

I grabbed a cigarette from my jacket coat. The one next to Chris shakily came to light my cigarette. I met his eyes.

Cute.

He reminded me of Dax in a way. The only difference were his green eyes; they were so dull. A pity. I was hoping to find someone to satiate this anger since beating the low-level to within an inch of his life did nothing for me.

The low-level from school flashed through my head and I hardened when I remembered the way her tight pussy felt wrapped around my fingers that night. I had prepared my strap and wore it to school in preparation. I was going to take her today, teach her just how enjoyable being with a woman could be, then I'd finally be done trying to be a *nice guy*. I would fuck her and leave her, then she would never look at me with a face that made my knees weak again. Instead she would hate me just like the others.

A groan from the traitor brought me back from the delightful thought.

I walked toward the now unconscious low-level and began searching his pockets. There was nothing save for his phone. It wasn't password protected and I easily was able to scroll through his recent messages.

"Stupid *and* careless," I mused.

Inhaling the lit cigarette I paused and blew the smoke directly into his dripping face. No movement. I threaded my hand through his hair and yanked it back to show me his throat. I pushed the butt of my cigarette into the soft skin on his neck and was rewarded with a scream so blood-curdling that it made my belly warm.

I wished the low-level would make that for me. Being nice to her was so exhausting. I couldn't count how many times I wanted to bend her over the table in the classroom today and make her regret the day she rejected me.

"I'm sorry. They made me. Please I swear." His voice went on and on even after I had removed my cigarette off his neck. I sighed. Way to ruin the moment.

I looked away from him feeling disgusted. Something in the place stood out to me once my head had cleared slightly. My group had checked this place out earlier but it seemed too perfect. And there were no pictures of family or anything that could identify him as a person. The furniture barely looked lived in and when we got here he was sitting on the couch...but the TV wasn't even on nor was there anything else to occupy his mind.

"Damon," I concluded and was awarded with hoarse laugher that radiated through the room.

"Ah... That was too fast Eli, have a little fun, hm?" Damon's grainy voice filled the room around us. Why was I not surprised that the lunatic had cameras and speakers installed in this house. "I'll be waiting in the basement."

I huffed and waved off the men around me. As much as I didn't care about them I didn't want to subject them to whatever I was about to see with that motherfucker. Damon loved games and I should have known that with my attention occupied by school he would get antsy at some point and try to pull something. I walked down the only hallway in the single house and a door slowly opened at the end of the hallway to show a puff of white hair and gleaming blue eyes.

"What is this Damon?" I huffed and followed him down the stairs of the basement. The stairs creaked under my weight. In the room I was met with hundreds of computer screens and his normal army of men dressed in suits. Damon was the current head of our gang. He renamed it *The Fallen* after he had taken over and if that wasn't indication of his character enough I didn't know what was. There was a warrant out for his head, so he insisted that he had dozens of men always surrounding him. I think it was just so he could have his pick of anyone of them, if I was being honest.

He sat down on the red sofa that was so dark that when he sat down his all-black attire blended in with the couch. It was a staple in this organization —even if you didn't see the tattoos, if you knew anything about demon gang activity you could recognize us by our matching attire.

A slim but muscular man wearing only a thong wrapped himself around Damon's form, kissing along the bare skin of his neck. The man's tattoos still shone against the light, leading me to believe that this was what Damon had given him as his first job in order to secure a spot in the gang. All of the pleasant thoughts and feelings the low-level had blossomed in me promptly died at the sight before me and the anger that I felt earlier began burning hotter than before.

"Why don't you smile for me anymore, Eli?" he cooed and let his hand trail down the naked male's chest. "I saw the pictures of you and your friends at school and you look so happy." His hand left the man's chest and he began to unbutton his own pants. "I'm jealous, even when you beat that man you barely smiled."

The man didn't need to be told what to do. He unleashed Damon's limp dick and began sucking on it. I almost felt bad to see him like this; I knew better than anyone what a manipulative bastard Damon could be even if he didn't have any powers.

"Get to the point," I growled.

"I was going to say that I am surprised that you came to a job on a school night. I thought I told you to focus." The sounds coming from the naked man were starting to fill the room. The guards were used to this by now and they showed no signs of discomfort at the sight.

It was expected; Damon ran a tight ship here and no one wanted to be the guy that was forced to suck him off next time. I forced my hands into my pockets so he wouldn't notice the way they clenched.

The more affected you show him you are, the more he will capitalize on it.

"So this was a test to see if I would come?" Damon never once looked at the man currently sucking him off. Instead, his narrowed blue eyes were fixated on me. His tongue wet his lips and by the look on his face, he was imagining the man in his lap to be me. He had told me once, long after I put a stop to it, that no one could ever compare to what I had offered him. He was obsessed with the child I once was and it made me so sick that I almost had to look away.

"A test to see if you could delegate work." He let out a small groan and gripped the man's hair. "You failed horribly." He started bucking up into the man's mouth—his saliva was pooling in Damon's lap and his gagging filled the quiet room. "Yes, just like that. I'll reward you after this."

"I am ahead in my classes. They are easy," I told him. Why did he act like he cared about this shit?

"If you cannot delegate work I cannot give you your own sector. You know that." He broke eye contact only to lean his head back.

"You were always adamant about not giving me my own sector," I spat at him. My blood was boiling. I would love to kill this bastard right now. How dare he hold that over my head? The man pulled away from Damon swallowing his seed with a smile.

I bet he just wanted me here so he could show me that I was still under his control. He hated being at a disadvantage as much as I did. This had to be his punishment for not thinking of him while away at school.

"I changed my mind," he said and tucked himself back into his pants. He pulled a cocaine-filled baggie out of his pocket and handed it to the man. "If you do well in school and learn how to lead I would have no problem giving you a position amongst leadership."

Damon's leaders were the only ones that really held the power here. Malik was a perfect example of that. I had once thought they were brothers because of their similarity but I didn't ever get close enough to Malik to ask about it. I envied him from afar. His power, his men, he had so much more power than I and it burned my soul to think of how unfair it was. Even though I had my own team of men they were still under Damon's order. Their allegiance was to him. But if I could lead like Malik...

"I can lead without an education." The anger was evident in my voice. The careful relaxed facade was broken and his eyes twinkled in response.

"I made a deal with your father when he decided to sell his baby girl. He practically begged for you to get an education." Damon hummed and walked over to me. He placed his hands on my shoulder. I blocked out his thoughts. "I am a man of my word, and of course you know I see you as my own even if it's not through blood."

I wanted to shiver in disgust at his words but instead I focused on the blinding rage it brought me. I imagined tearing his limbs from him and stuffing his own dick down his throat.

"There is the smile I have been missing," he cooed. His eyes flitted down to my mouth then back up to my eyes. It was a mistake to let him live. A mistake to let him control me.

"So, I graduate and then you give me a sector?" I paused. "Which one?"

"Any one you want," he purred. He knew that he had a tight leash on me now. The carrot he was dangling in front of me was too good.

"If you are lying I'll kill you for real this time," I vowed. I could feel the tension coming off his men in waves. I didn't care, even though my power was at a disadvantage I trained like hell in order to close the gap.

"Good thing I am not lying." He gave me a smile and waved me off as he made his way back to the man on the couch.

I took the dismissal and left before he began fucking the drugged-out man.

* * *

I roamed the dark streets hoping that there would be someone stupid enough to be out this late. I was about an hour away from the campus and in the heart of the city yet there was not a soul around.

My hands were itching. Beating that idiot's face did nothing for me. I needed to crush my fist into someone. Needed to hear the scream as I broke their bones. I stopped in a dark alleyway and slammed my fist against the jagged concrete.

Fuck that woman.

I punched again.

Fuck Damon.

And again.

Fuck Malik.

And again.

Fuck this stupid life.

And again.

"How dare he?" I spat and punched the wall again. "All of a sudden he puts restrictions on me?"

I punched the wall again.

"Fuck that school."

It was a stupid school filled with brain-dead high-levels that wanted to be a legal version of Damon. They thought that they were better than all those dirty humans and low-levels but those high-levels were just as bad if not worse. It was a part of my job to know all of those children's parents. Not only were they in some deep illegal shit but we knew their kids would follow in their footsteps sooner or later. Damon had me worm my way into their families and get close to them since I was eleven, and offer them things illegally that would either boost their image or hurt others. In return they would make sure to overlook all of our other illegal dealings.

Rae's family was one of my first assignments and while it failed spectacularly, I didn't regret the relationship that came from it. She was so young back then but already so bright that she caught onto my act right away. Her father acted all high and mighty but there was no way he could compare to Rae's level of genius.

After the pounding in my hands ceased, I let out a long sigh.

Thinking about Rae calmed my anger enough so that I could think straight. She was the rock of this group. Between myself, Daxton, and Amr, the only rational one would always be Rae. I wanted to look out for them; that was my plan when I realized how much shit all of them had been through...but Rae was always the one to keep us grounded. She was the one to dreamed for all of us when Daxton and my path filled with fog and we couldn't see straight.

Rae wouldn't be disappointed when she figured I had a job with Damon tonight, but there still was one thing that I couldn't get my mind off of and there was no way Rae would be happy with it. I didn't much care about that right now though; I'd cross that bridge when I came to it.

After hearing the low-level's sweet gasps in the garden and the way she tightened around my fingers, there was no way I could stop myself. I was already too deep to pull out.

And there was no way any other girl would suffice. I have seen their looks, I have been cornered a few times this year when I was away from that low-level, it was cute that they thought they had a chance with me. I was even considering just taking one on a right, but none of them could hold my attention. None of them had the gall to deny me like she did.

Her mind was so different from the others. She wasn't scared or disgusted, and she absolutely loved the way I took control of her in the garden. She would be disgusted though, after I was done with her.

My dark chuckle filled the silent alleyway.

* * *

When I finally made my way back to the dorm, courtesy of Chris I think, I didn't pause on my way to the low-level. I headed straight to the first-year dorms. I passed my own. Then Dax's. Then Rae's. I shouldn't have been surprised when Rae's door swung open after I was only a few feet past it.

"Your anger can be felt from a mile away, Eli," she hissed. "Calm yourself."

"Why does it matter to you?" I asked turning to face her. Her glasses were off and she was in a loose cotton shirt and light pajama pants. "Were you waiting for me?"

"No, I literally felt your anger when you pulled up. You woke me up." She huffed and ran her hand through her hair. "I know where you are going."

"Good." I didn't move from my spot even though I knew that regardless of what she said it wouldn't stop me from going to that low-level.

"Just..." She sighed again and this time when she met my eyes I felt myself calm slightly. "Don't hurt her too badly okay? She's important."

"To the school?" I asked. "Or to you?"

"Don't be stupid." From the resigned look on her face she realized she wasn't going to get any further with me tonight. "Be gentle."

I didn't wait for her door to close fully before I headed down the hall. I stopped at a door that I had never been to before but I knew the number by heart.

503.

Rae's warning rang through my head as I stood outside the low-level's door. Stupid girl. For as smart as she was, I never imagined that a low-level would warrant a reaction like that.

She makes you act stupid too, a voice in the back of my head told me. *Bag carrying. Waiting for her to give in to you. Ignoring perfectly good women for even just a chance to wet your fingers.*

It was a lie when I told her that I would move on. I didn't even fully know it was a lie when I had told her, but standing here outside her door it became painfully obvious that I wouldn't be going anywhere even if I was successful in what I planned for tonight.

I didn't bother knocking and tried the handle. It was locked, of course. She was not as stupid as that dumb face of hers gave off sometimes. I twisted the door handle the opposite way and cracked it clean off. The metal clanged to the floor and if it wasn't two o'clock in the morning, I would be worried about someone coming to investigate. It was easy from there to get the door open.

I shut the door softly behind me when I found out that the noise hadn't woken her already. A thrill ran through me. I had been anticipating this since the night in the garden. The way her heat surrounded my fingers. She took all three fingers with ease making me fantasize about what else she could take. She refused to be alone with me and Dax since then besides our classes. But even in them that bastard cat Amr would swat me when I tried to touch her. I would have loved to chuck him in front of a moving car if he didn't help Dax as much as he did.

Walking toward her sleeping frame in the bed I repositioned the harness around my waist, tightening the straps. I noticed that she had on a large shirt that was currently riding up her slightly toned stomach and giving me a full view of what I assumed were light pink panties. The darkness made the color hard to decipher but I could tell that they were a lighter material. Her tight cheeks were in full view and her leg wrapped around the pillow like she was cuddling with a person.

She was too attractive for a low-level.

I wondered briefly how I should wake her up. My mouth on those pink panties? Better yet fingers inside her? She would hate me for it, and I would easily accomplish what I set out to. It would make it easier for me. The realization was almost painful when I looked at her.

I don't want her to hate me. Not really.

I didn't have time to decide as she took this moment to roll over and her eyes slowly fluttered open. When she saw me her eyes widened, and a smile began to form on my face as a response. She scrambled to a sitting position.

"Aw, you could have had such a pleasant awakening if you just stayed asleep," I joked and stalked toward her bed. She didn't move as I did. Instead, her wide eyes watched me intently. I used my hands to spread her legs open and climbed over her. She stayed up on her elbows and without a second thought I brought my lips down to hers.

First gentle, I told myself. I wasn't sure anymore if it was because of Rae's warning or my own fucked up emotions.

She seemed to pause at the contact, but she ever so slowly parted her soft lips giving me entrance to her mouth. I greedily took the invitation, exploring her mouth with my tongue. I pushed her lightly back down onto the bed and ground the strap-on into her. Her hands wrapped around my shirt and pulled me closer to her while gasping in my mouth.

Her mind was a flurry of thoughts and emotions but as I ground against her more, her thoughts became clearer and clearer. She was so eager for this. She wanted this, badly.

Finally coming to terms with this? I teased.

There was nothing to come to terms with. You know how I felt.

Why don't you show me?

She showed me how much she thought of it after our encounter in the garden. Showed me the way my fingers felt inside her.

Will this...affect the group? Her question made me pull away. Her eyes shone lightly in the darkness, and I could see my own shine in their reflection.

"Why would it? You know how they feel. If anything they'd want a turn," I told her. She bit her lip.

Is that okay?

I dove forward and captured her lips once more.

Don't think of fucking other people when I am trying to make good on our promise, I sent to her mind. *You are nothing but a release to us. Don't over-complicate this.*

Even her mind stilled at my response. Could she sense the lie?

Regretting it now? I asked and bit her lip hard. She gasped. I wondered if that was a bruise or a cut. I brought her top up over her head, breaking our kiss but not for long. I swooped down and took her nipple lightly in my mouth. She arched into it and tangled her hands in my hair. I growled and bit down, enjoying the gasp that rang out in the silence of the room. I ran my hands up the sides of her ribs feeling her silky, unmarred skin.

Her thoughts became slightly panicked. *Good,* I thought. *Hate it, hate me.*

"Don't touch the hair," I hissed at her, moving myself from her nipple, and began undoing my belt. The look on her face sent another thrill throughout my body. I could feel my own wetness between my legs. I regretted not bringing the double strap-on. I grabbed both her wrists and tied them tightly to the metal headboard.

She didn't fight me. *Do it, fight me,* I chanted in my head but didn't push it toward her.

Why do I like this? her mind asked itself. She scolded herself because she was so turned on by it. There were various scenarios running through her mind, each dirtier than the last.

"We can get to that at some point but tonight will be relatively vanilla." Even though I hated myself for the words on the inside, on the outside I smirked at her. There shouldn't be a next time. I let my hand rub her already soaked panties.

Please, she begged in my mind. I slowly removed her panties and ran my fingers down her glistening slit. She bucked her hips against my fingers. *Please, Eli.*

"Please what?" I asked her out loud. "I can't hear you." I let my fingers run over her clit and her whole body arched. She had been waiting. She had been aching. Her mind told me. I slowly undid my pants and pulled the flesh-colored strap-on out.

Her eyes widened when she took in the toy I had chosen for tonight.

"Don't tell me you've never used one of these before?" I teased even though I already knew the answer. This poor low-level was practically a virgin. I rubbed the tip against her wetness and dragged it across the length of it.

She shook her head. I smiled and plunged my fingers into her. Her eyes rolled into the back of her head but I didn't give her the satisfaction. I used the rest of her wetness to coat the base. She would need it.

"Don't get shy now," I said with a laugh and teasingly ran the tip against her swollen folds. Her hands gripped against the belt on her wrists.

Fuck. Fuck. Fuck, her mind chanted. Her hips bucked against me, almost pulled the toy into her. I tsked.

"I will leave you like this, *Rosie*," I threatened.

"Fuck me," she ordered quickly, surprising me. The thought to speak didn't even register in her mind. Her voice was not more than a whisper but I saw a cut run across her chest. It was so beautiful. So feral. So uncontrolled.

I didn't bother waiting any longer. Instead, I lifted her hips and brought myself closer to her. I slowly eased into her tight pussy. She sucked it in without pause until it was fully buried in her.

It was blissful, her face. The way she arched into me. The way her legs clenched around me. Even without the curse in action, a warm emotion filled me deep in my stomach. I hated it...it was almost like being able to be so close to her was worth more than the curse was. It didn't even matter if I was getting off, this was more than worth the weight, having her at my mercy.

Please. Eli please.

She didn't have to tell me twice. I almost fully pulled out of her and then slammed my hips into her. I was rewarded with a gasp and saw the bruise float across her stomach. I did it again and was rewarded with another. I gripped her hips hard and began slamming into her at a faster pace. The sight of her orgasmic face and the bruises were too delicious a sight. But on top of that her mind chanted to her.

Hold it in.

Hold it in.

"Don't hold it in," I growled and dug my nails into her hips pounding harder into her. I wanted her to hate it so bad, but her mind screamed at me to go harder. "Don't hold it in and I'll go harder," I told her and slowed my thrusts. I brought my thumb to her clit and gave her a harder thrust. I was rewarded with a gasp. "No, more," I growled and slammed back into her. She finally moaned and I was rewarded with a nasty bruise across her thigh.

Darker than I'd seen before on her skin. She was still holding back. I brought her leg up over my shoulders and leaned forward continuing to snap my hips harder into her.

Her moans were hesitant at first but in this position, she couldn't hold them back. Each moan, the louder it got, brought a cut to her skin.

Except one.

Just as she orgasmed, she let out the loudest moan but no cut appeared on her naked skin. I turned her over; the restraints twisted against the headboard. Her back was free of wounds. I didn't stop my thrusts. And her moans didn't stop.

Did she realize?

I watched slowly as another cut began to show. The sight and her noises were almost enough to send me over. Almost. I gripped her hips, nails digging into her soft supple skin and pulled her back to meet my frenzied thrusts. I pulled out as soon as her mind told me she was about to come.

I could hear her annoyance that I did so. *Good.*

I filled her with three fingers. She let out a surprised gasp.

"Remember me," I told her and my fingers stretched her. Even after taking a pounding, she was still so tight. "Remember my skin. Remember the feeling of my fingers inside you. Remember that while we do this *I own you.*"

She arched her hips. "Yes, Eli. God," she moaned, each time a cut marring her skin.

Gentle first, I reminded myself and the urge to make her bleed descended over me like a tidal wave. The cuts were healing too fast for my liking.

Why did I care?

I snapped my hips into her and against my hand forcing the fingers in deeper, harder.

Why was I being gentle?

She bucked her hips against my hand and cried out.

Why do I feel like this?

She began trembling.

It's not fair that a stupid low-level can make me want something so badly.

It was not long until she came on my hand again. After I pulled my fingers out she collapsed on the bed. I pushed the strap-on back into my pants and buttoned them back up. I helped her undo her hands but before I left, I gripped tightly at her throat and pulled her lips to mine. Biting them hard enough to bleed.

"Keep the belt for next time," I told her putting more pressure on her neck. "Consider this your luck that I had already let out my anger. I will be back to see what your curse actually can do."

I'll be waiting, came her cheeky-ass response. I wondered if she would still be saying that when I rode her face.

I pushed her back and without another look I left her in the bed.

The warm feeling in my chest felt like it would explode. I allowed myself to smile as I walked through the hallways. I would let myself have this, then after this I would try to cut myself off.

It was the biggest lie I could tell myself.

Chapter Twelve
Rosie

I*'ll be waiting?*

Seriously, she was going to fucking kill me.

I met them in the morning for breakfast like I had done regularly. Eli and Daxton were already waiting for me. I swallowed thickly and took a deep breath, preparing myself for the shitstorm ahead of me. There was no way this woman would stay quiet.

"Let's try not to burn down the whole field this time, low-level," Eli said and wrapped her arm around me as if it were any other day. She sent me a shit-eating grin.

You broke my fucking door, I snapped at her in my mind.

I didn't hear you complaining last night, she snapped back. *How does that pussy feel? Ready for round two?*

I felt my face flame up at her vulgar language.

I thought you were a hit it and quit it type of person, I commented. My food was placed in front of me by one of the workers. An everything bagel with cream cheese.

I changed my mind, she said as I was taking a bite of my bagel. I would have choked on it if Daxton had not handed me my favorite bottle of coffee. I took a swig and sent him a small smile.

"Not the real kind but all I had time for," he said. There was a slight blush on the top of his cheeks again. "But yes I'd like to save some magic today so please don't blow up the field."

Tell him there is no need to keep buying—

"Morning!" Matt's cheerful voice interrupted my complaining to Eli. "I see Eli has already begun monopolizing your time."

"I have done more than that, low-level," Eli shot back.

Speak again and last night will never happen again, I shot toward her as quick as I could. She sent me a glare but listened and turned her attention away from Matt.

This was going to be a long day.

* * *

When it was time for the rankings, we as a class made our way to the field once more. It was only when the field came into view that we were stopped by a group of chattering people. They were in front of a bulletin board that held three large pieces of paper, with names scribbled on them.

The rankings.

"You nervous?" Eli asked and slipped her arm over my shoulder.

Why would I be? Like they would even put a low-level on the list.

Daxton pushed his way through the crowd with Amr in his arms. People started moving once they realized who was trying to get through. Many eyes met mine, but none were filled with hate. Instead, I saw some hesitation in their eyes.

Daxton stopped in front of the boards and let out a low whistle. My heart stopped when I found my name. It jumped out immediately.

1. Malik Hendrix
2. Rae Ashwell
3. Daxton Reid
4. Rosie Miller

"You aren't even in the top ten, Eli," Daxton teased with a small smile pulling at his lips.

I looked and saw her name placed at number twenty-two.

"The nature of the power," Eli responded but the smile had already dropped from her face and her eyes narrowed in on the name that held the first spot.

Who is number one? I asked her but was given no response. Daxton noticed her change in demeanor and looked at the number one spot.

"Eli, isn't that...?"

"Unfortunately," she said with a sigh.

What am I missing? I asked again. Her eyes drifted toward mine but then shot behind me. Her jaw twitched.

"Eli. Still lagging, I see," said a smug voice from behind me.

I turned and caught an eyeful of pure white hair before Eli's rough hands forced my face into her chest obstructing any view of the newcomer.

"Malik," came Eli's gruff response. "I didn't know you were playing the college student now."

"I decided to go back to school. Sue me." There was a shuffling. "Hello Daxton, you look better than last time."

There was no response from Daxton.

"You won't even look at me?" Malik asked. "Who's that you're hiding?"

Don't look him in the eyes Rosie. Once you do, he can control you. Blood rushed through me, pounding in my ears.

Does he know about the curse Eli?

I have no clue, she responded.

"No one," Eli responded. "We have to test soon. We will leave first."

Eli positioned me under her arm once more with her hand pushing my head down and began moving toward the field.

"Let's meet later, Eli," Malik said stepping in front of us. His shiny leather shoes and slacks entered my view. I could just barely see his hands from my view but I could tell they were as rough as Eli's. "To talk about your sector."

"I don't have one," Eli responded. I raised my head just slightly and caught Malik's rolled-up sleeves. He had almost the same exact tattoos Eli had.

"Because I'm giving you mine." Eli stood straight as a rod at Malik's words. "Let go of her head." There was a swirl of something in the air at his words. It was so similar to Daxton's magic and left a tingle as it swirled past. "Don't let this brute control you. A peek couldn't hurt, trust me."

Eli's hand dropped from my head like it had been burned. Malik's voice was sweet like honey and his power washed over me with a warming sensation.

I wanted to look. I really wanted to.

"We will be late," Daxton interjected and pushed me roughly away from Malik. His hand was firm against the back of my neck stopping me from raising my head.

"I will meet you later," Eli said as we walked away.

"Stay away from him, Rosie. If you think we are dangerous you have no idea what he can do."

Eli was absent the rest of the day.

* * *

"Why the fuck didn't you tell me he was here?!" Eli snapped at Rae.

We met inside the garden once more. It was supposed to be for curse testing but as soon as I saw Eli pacing in the courtyard, I knew it would not be a fun time.

I was surprised she even showed.

"I didn't see his name on the roster, Eli. If I knew I would have told you," Rae said. Her arms were crossed and she was leaning back against the fountain. A relatively casual stance but if the twitch of her eyebrow said anything, I would bet she was pissed.

"You are supposed to know this stuff! He almost made eye contact with the low-level!" Eli grabbed my shoulder roughly and pushed me toward Rae. "The curse is supposed to be a secret is it not? What if he made her talk? You should know well that he is far crueler than I am and in a second this *stupid science project* will go up in flames."

"Did you not think that you shielding her from him would cause him to be more suspicious? Did you even think that through? Or were you just worried he would take your toy?" Rae stood straight as she spoke. Even as she stood in front of me her narrowed eyes never left Eli's. Eli's hand tightened painfully on my shoulder.

Stop it, I sent her.

"This was your idea. An idea that you promised would have us graduating early. He is a complication that *you* overlooked."

"He's here for you Eli. It's your ties to the gang that forced him here." Rae's hand clamped down on Eli's and tore it off my shoulder. "This is your responsibility to take care of. I won't clean up your messes *again.*"

"That's enough," Daxton said. His tone had an edge to it. "We came here for a reason."

With one last glance at Eli, Rae turned me around to face Daxton.

"I'm not a doll," I said and winced at the pain in my back. I was already irritated from their stupid arguments and now they were throwing me around like a stupid toy.

Don't let this brute control you. Maybe Malik had a point.

Eli let out a huff and stalked toward the edge of the garden, kicking at the plants as she passed. I should have lit her shirt on fire again. I'd gotten too comfortable with them.

"No, you are not," Rae murmured, her grip on me lessening. "Let's get this started."

Daxton let out a sigh and stepped forward.

"This is something I made with the magic I took from you last time," Daxton said handing me a bottle of dark blue liquid. The shiny liquid had waves of glitter floating in it.

Was this what magic looked like in physical form?

It was too beautiful to be anything that that disgusting curse gave me. I tilted my head back to meet Rae's eyes and she nodded for me to take it. Her anger seemed to have faded. It's not like I could actually trust any of them but at least she was the most rational. Without a second thought I uncorked the bottle and drank its entirety. A heat shot through my body.

It was pleasant at first but then it quickly turned into a scorching fire. My knees buckled and I found myself falling to the ground. I clamped my hands tight over my throat and tried to breathe in but it felt like with every breath, shards of glass embedded themselves in my esophagus.

Rae's hands were back on me. She was calling out to me but I couldn't make out the words due to the pain clouding my mind. I still tried to take deep, gulping breaths of air. The oxygen disappeared from my lungs, like the flames that the potion had ignited were swallowing up all the air inside of me leaving nothing for me to live off.

Then it was gone.

In an instant the fires that were coursing through my blood were gone and in its place was a tingling sensation. An all too familiar tingling sensation. I waited for more pain, but it never came. Instead, the tingling spread across my body like a thin sheet, covering every part of my skin.

As I came to, I realized that Rae's arms were around me. Her hands were pulling at mine. Daxton was crouched in front of me, his hands out in front of him. They were glowing bright blue. Eli was still at the opposite side of the garden. She watched us with a scowl.

"What did you put in that stupid potion?" Rae growled. She helped me to my feet slowly. Daxton followed with a blank look on his face.

"It's the curse's own magic. I tried to use it against itself." His voice trailed off as he reached out to grab my arm. I could feel how the sheet of magic rippled when his skin met it. "Try to speak. I feel something here. It may have worked."

I tried to swallow my nerves. "It feels..." I paused as the cuts ran down my leg. I sent a glare toward Eli and held out my palm toward her. A small smile graced her lips and she stalked over to us. Rae's hands left me.

I feel it on my skin, but it didn't protect against the cuts.

Eli relayed my message to them. Daxton gave a small pout.

"The potion I gave you should protect you from outside spells," he murmured. And then paused. His hand was still on my arm and in a sudden flare his hand was engulfed in flames. I yelped and pulled away. Surveying my arm, the fire did no damage to me. "Well...that's not good."

Panic clawed at my throat. Gripping Eli's hand once more I demanded an explanation.

If he couldn't protect me from it then who could? Would I be stuck like this forever?

I wanted to scream.

"I know about magic as much as you do," she said with a shrug.

"I'm guessing," Rae started, "that it means her spell resonates from inside her instead of lying across her skin like you assumed." Daxton nodded.

"Most spells should act as a barrier on the skin. Cloak the person." He shifted uncomfortably. "I have never encountered one within the person. Never heard of a witch strong enough to do that. "

There was a heavy silence that descended onto the group. If Daxton was the strongest witch that we knew and even he had not seen anything like this before...what did that mean for my future? How would I live the rest of my life with this curse? Already with only having it for nine years I wanted to give up.

Eli must have been listening to my inner monologue because she linked her arm around my neck and pulled me close to her chest.

"I can show you how much fun a curse like that could be," Eli purred against me.

Let go of some more built-up anger, she added in my mind.

Didn't you already? I shot back, still not quite over being thrown around.

Feisty. Her fingers threaded through my hair.

"Oh that was nothing, little low-level. I was being *gentle*." She chuckled.

"No wonder you acted like that around Malik," Rae muttered.

"Shut up would you already, Eli?" Daxton growled from behind us.

Why did you have to open your mouth? I snapped at her.

"They knew I would just didn't know when. It was a matter of time," she said with a chuckle and wrapped her arms tighter around me. "We can share next time."

Daxton huffed in response. *Next time.* I shivered at the thought.

"What are the next steps, Daxton?" Rae asked.

"I need to do more research. Maybe reach out to some of my old teachers," Daxton supplied.

Can I talk to you alone? I have some questions.

"You can ask whatever you want. I have no secrets from them," Eli said out loud. I cursed internally and pushed myself off her but kept a hand on her arm. I took a deep breath trying to work up the nerve to ask her, suddenly feeling like I was prying.

So a gang? And Malik?

"Ah. Now what will I get in return for this information?" she asked with a smile playing at her lips.

Have I not already been honest?

"It's not about honesty, low-level. I have been giving and giving and giving to you with barely any repayment." I rolled my eyes at her but there was something deep down that told me she wasn't wrong. All of them have gone out of their way to help me even if nothing was guaranteed.

What do you want?

Stay away from Malik.

That's it? I asked raising a brow at her.

"I could keep adding on more if you'd like."

Fine, I shot back angry that I caused this.

"I grew up in the biggest gang in the state. My boss and *adoptive father* promised that if I could graduate from school that I could leave his sector and run one all on my own. That's where Malik comes in. He's dangerous. The only reason someone of his age is here has to be to keep an eye on me, which I should have figured would happen since I was called on a job last night. Malik says he wanted to give me his sector, but I doubt that it will come for free. The timing is *too* perfect."

"Isn't he like as old as the principal?" Daxton asked.

"I tried to find out but even my sources in the Demon Regulation Society have no clue," Rae chimed in. It seemed now the angry air between the others had dissipated.

"And they have been tracking every demon for the last thousand or so years. So he has to be older right?" Daxton asked. It was refreshing to see him interact so much.

"Or he just slipped through the system like the slimy rat he is," Eli said aloud.

Chapter Thirteen
Daxton

Malik may not have been my problem to deal with but his presence here worried me. Not only was he pretending, though not very well, to be a college student but he had let us all rest for a few months before showing his face.

What was his plan?

"What did he say to you?" I asked Eli as soon as she showed up for our weekend meetings. The space was cool with a small breeze but as Eli strode over to us it was like a dark cloud came over us.

"Who?" Eli asked as she sat down in the grass beside me. She pulled out her cigarette almost immediately and lit it. She didn't look at me and a lock of her blonde hair fell into her face. Her eyes stayed firmly on the grass.

"Malik, of course," Rae said for me from her place against the tree. Honor Student wouldn't degrade herself and sit on the dirty grass. Eli was picky with what she allowed to stain her clothes but god forbid Honor Student get even a grass stain on the cuff of her pants.

"Same thing I told you earlier. He wants to give me his sector," she responded.

Neither I nor Rae spoke. Eli's eyes were still on the ground, averting our questioning looks. I looked over to Rae. Her eyes met mine for a second and then drifted back to Eli.

"Is it about Rosie?" I asked. Eli's fingers snapped her cigarette. She cursed when the lit embers fell on her and threw the wasted cigarette into the dirt. I waved my hand, dousing it with water so that it wouldn't burn down the only quiet place we had.

"He wants to know why I shielded her from him," she said with a sigh. Finally, her eyes drifted up toward the blue sky that was partially covered by the tree leaves. "I'm not sure why he came but if he wasn't interested in her before, he will be now."

"Besides the mind control...is that really such a bad thing?" I asked. Her eyes met mine, expression unreadable.

"I'm not sure anymore." Eli paused, her eyes shifting away from mine.

It was in moments like this that I would remember how human Eli was. The moments that she didn't have words for. From an outsider's perspective Eli always had a smile and the rare time she didn't it would be because she was angry. But those emotions had names and were easy to read. Her averted gaze and clenched fist was not one I understood.

"He hasn't done anything yet and we do not know his motives," Rae said acting as the voice of reason once more. "Let's not think too much about it. It's probably because he has never seen Eli act like that before, right? Take his offer as a blessing and take advantage of it. The faster you are rid of Damon the better."

"You are right." Eli's shoulders slumped. "It was stupid. When I figured it was him I knew I was already screwed but I thought in that moment...what if he made her talk? What if he made her scream? Would he know it would kill her?"

There, I saw the anger flood into her expression once more. Jaw tight and eyes narrowed.

She likes her. Something tugged at my chest when the realization hit me. I had thought she was just playing with her but this...was something different. Looking at Rae once more, she didn't meet my gaze either. Her expression was also nothing I could decipher.

"You like her a lot," I noted looking back at Eli. She didn't even shy away from the question, instead she met me head-on with a sad smile.

"You know what the first thought people usually have when they find out what I do? Who I *really* am?" she asked but didn't wait for a response. "Disgust. Always. But her...she never felt that way when it came to me. And she has already seen so much but her thoughts never change."

There was a pause between us, and I had no idea how to respond.

"Can I have a light?" I asked trying to unclog the knot in my throat. Eli snapped out of her angered state and patted herself down for a cigarette, handing me one and her lighter.

"What about your magic?" Rae asked me. I took a heavy drag of the cigarette and let it be an excuse to gather my thoughts.

"It acts like a puppy," I explained. Rae raised her perfect brow at me and I saw amusement twitch at her lips. "After I got a taste, my magic has not lashed out. You felt it. It's waning but...nothing like before."

"The curse is strong," Eli commented. I nodded.

"It was the best thing I ever felt but when I was taking it, my magic didn't dare try to consume more than necessary... I'm not sure it wants to consume it to be honest." I took another drag. The thought haunted me in my dreams.

What if I couldn't consume it? Would the magic disappear when the curse was lifted? Such a waste.

"You will find a way," Rae said with conviction.

"Never heard you believe in me so much," I teased dryly. Rae responded with a blank look.

I wasn't so sure I knew where to go from here. Potions and consuming it were all I knew. It wasn't like a curse had ever lasted this long before.

"It stopped working," Eli said after taking a long drag of her cigarette.

"What stopped?" Rae asked.

"Her curse," she said. I took a drag of my own cigarette. "When I was fucking her."

I let out a heavy sigh. I guess today would revolve around her even if she wasn't here. I'm not sure I minded but I was just so tired of not knowing what to do.

"Explain," Rae said with a huff and brought out her notebook. She of course had to document whatever Eli was going to spout.

Amr, who was previously lying near the tree base, came to lay by my side like he wanted to hear more.

"That's just it. The curse was working like normal but just once there was a time when the curse didn't hurt her." A grin finally played at her lips.

"Curses have loopholes," I told her. "Maybe you found hers."

"An orgasm?" she asked incredulously. There was a glint in her eyes once more. I rolled my eyes.

"Did anything else happen during that time when you noticed the curse wasn't working?" Rae asked. I heard her pen pick up its pace on the paper.

Eli hummed. "I don't think she was thinking of the curse." She paused. "At least she was aware of it when the cuts showed but she didn't even notice that time that it didn't show."

I hummed. Was this it? But could a curse read your mind?

"I'll talk to my teacher about it," I said. "He will be at the banquet tonight with Honor Roll's parents. It would probably be the only other chance I have to ask another witch."

"And yours," Rae replied.

"Aw, do I get an invite?" Eli teased.

"You know they wouldn't turn you away," Rae said. "Just make sure your tattoos are shown or else they may think you are ordinary."

"With this face? Ordinary?" Eli said with a chuckle.

I absentmindedly petted Amr's soft fur. I couldn't stand the thought of seeing my parents again. I had to force down the bile that rose in my throat when memories of our magic sharing flashed through my mind like a tidal wave. This was important though, and if I didn't show I had no doubt that they would send someone to force me home. I would bear it for now and find out as much information as I could.

My eyes flashed toward Eli once more. At least she would be there just in case.

* * *

I fiddled with my suit buttons and slacks, already feeling out of place. I hated having to dress up for these stupid events ever since I was a kid. My parents loved to flaunt their wealth in front of people they thought would care. Meaning I would have to always dress up in brand named suits that were itchy at the seams.

After some careful thought I unbuttoned the top few buttons of my shirt to show more of my tattoo-clad chest. I smiled when the intricate face of the devil showed itself from underneath my clothing. My parents would *fucking* hate it.

It was a painful reminder for them that I would never be as *pure* as they wanted me to be. Nor would it help their image in front of the governor. They liked to lie to the demons about the type of magic they consumed. They thought as long as it came from within the family, it would count as pure, and they could pass themselves off as different from the other crazed witches that tried to rebel. My looks would barely dent that reputation that they have carefully crafted for themselves, but it was fun to see them freak.

I met Amr's eyes in the mirror. He was waiting near my door as if he was ready to leave with me.

He's more obsessed than Eli. I wonder how Rosie would react when she realizes that Amr is not a normal cat.

If she stayed around, she would find out eventually that Amr was a full-grown man but I hoped that it would not come to that. I didn't want to say goodbye to Rosie but there was no way I could break this secret for a third time. Having Eli and Rae know was nonnegotiable, but Rosie...

"Don't think I don't know that you are off to Rosie's dorm," I chided.

He stuck his nose up in the air and pawed lightly at the door. Amr had gone missing more than once and I didn't have to guess that he had been sneaking off to her room. He had never shown much interest in anyone outside our circle; he wasn't supposed to. Usually, he would just wander around, soak up magic, sleep, and sometimes when I wasn't looking cuddle up to Rae.

I pulled out my phone with a jolt when I realized Rae was probably waiting for me. I was a minute later than she had asked for us to show up. I cursed and let Amr out. He walked toward Rosie's dorm just like I had thought he would. I almost collided with Rae in my haste to leave my room.

"It's been a while since I have seen you without glasses, Honor Roll," I joked and brushed off her suit jacket. Her hair looked to be newly trimmed, and she was decked out in a fancy-looking suede suit, with noticeably absent glasses. She gave me a polite smile that was worthy of an Oscar.

"Yes. Well, you know how important the night is," she explained as we both turned to walk down the hall.

"Yes," I grumbled. "You and your fancy politics."

Eli was waiting for us outside, smoking as usual. She gave us her signature smile before pushing off the wall. She normally kept her tattoos hidden at school, but she had done just as Rae asked and displayed as much of her tattooed skin as she could. Much like myself her button-up was rolled at the sleeves. The only difference was that she had unbuttoned more than just the three top buttons of her shirt. I honestly think she should have just foregone the shirt all together. Not only were the sides of her breasts showing but the shirt was also so tight that it left nothing to the imagination. Her black slacks hugged her figure perfectly.

Rosie is lucky.

Eli and I were by no means strangers to each other. She had stopped me from fucking many girls to death when my magic took over my senses and made me the beast my parents so loved to lock behind closed doors. She was more caring than she let on, making sure we would send the girl off pleasantly and then take care of me. She didn't care how much the monster consumed me and she always brought me back from the edge.

Her eyes met mine and her grin turned into something sultrier.

"Rae is serious tonight," she commented and stomped her still-lit cigarette on the ground.

"Our car is waiting for us," Rae said dismissing us and walking toward the parking lot.

"I hate when she gets in moods like this," Eli murmured watching her retreating form. Rae wasn't a nervous person, but she carried tension in her shoulders so obviously that I wouldn't be surprised if that suit ripped from the force.

I hummed in agreement but followed her anyway.

The car ride was almost silent the entire way there. I preferred to be in silence so I enjoyed the only time I would get it before I would be forced into a room too small to house both my parents and me. Dread weighed on the entire car but I couldn't be sure if that was from me or if Rae was projecting.

The role my parents wanted me to play would be so much more suited for Rae. Even though I knew she was on edge she had loosened the tension in her shoulders and the mask she held was cool. She would be controlling the party as soon as she stepped in and I couldn't help but envy how put-together she was.

Rae had about as good a relationship with her family as I did mine but instead of letting it control her every waking moment, she was using their position to her advantage. Proving that she was already a politician in her own right.

A dangerous one who has a thing for blackmail, a snide voice in my mind commented chasing away any positive thoughts about the demon I had.

"Daxton. Eli," Rae said just a block before we arrived at the famed Connecticut governor's manor. "You should be milking these events for all that you can." She paused and put away the notebook she was reading in the inner pocket of her suit. "I know you *loathe* them, but you are both powerful demons and you cannot live off of your...*families* forever." She paused when she said families, her eyes shifting over toward Eli. "Think of after graduation."

I bristled at her comment, but I knew deep down she was right. I got into school because of my parents' money. I lived comfortably only because my parents allowed it and their comfortable positions afforded it. But I didn't even know what I wanted to do after school. I enjoyed the life we built for ourselves, between the four of us.

"I have a reason to go. For the curse knowledge," I murmured knowing that was not what she was looking for.

"I don't want to get involved with the scum that deals in Damon's trafficking rings," Eli hissed.

"You'd be surprised how many of the lonely housewives have bad drug addictions," Rae commented. "Senator Bennett's wife in particular loves to host cocaine-filled parties with the other housewives. Quite an income source."

Eli shifted at her words. "I could work with that," she muttered sounding as if she wasn't pleased, but I saw the glint in her eyes.

"These are opportunities to build ourselves. Don't forget it. Just look a little harder and you'll be surprised at the opportunities that present themselves," she said and quietly prepared herself to exit the car as we stopped in front of the grand mansion.

I exited after her, followed by Eli. The bulky white eyesore of a mansion looked the same as always, grand staircase, high columns, and even a touch of green gardens surrounding the property, the whole deal. Staff—decked in penguin suits—were waiting outside to welcome guests. Paparazzi and news stations were being pushed back by the gates and guards. The grass even seemed just as green as it did last summer.

My family had some notorious good relationships with the Bennetts so I was often forced to come here while they ratted out witch clans left and right in exchange for money and status. If it wasn't for the lone witch in their service, I would have gone crazy sitting in this mansion. Luckily, she was a great distraction while she was bent over the kitchen sink.

We went inside and it wasn't long before the three of us were surrounded by various groups of rowdy people. I didn't try to put on a mask like Rae; I didn't care much for the fanfare. She gave everyone a cool smile and greeted them each by name and asked them about their various families.

"Mr. Walker, nice to see you! How is Emily? Did she ever get on the soccer team?"

"Caroline, so great to see you, how are those negotiations with the Demon Regulation Society?"

"James what a pleasant..."

Rae's voice became muffled as the crowd grew and it wasn't long until my parents descended on me like hawks. I stopped my hand from reaching itself out to Eli.

I fucking hated this already.

"Daxton, you could have dressed nicer," my mother whispered as she pulled me away from the crowd and effectively away from the person she deemed as *the worst mistake I could make.* "You will be meeting with Governor Bennett and his wife. You must thank them for inviting you. They want to hear about how school is going. As you know their daughter is attending Winterfell next year."

My mother rattled on while my father stayed by her side in a stoic silence. No doubt he could already sense the change in my magic and was getting pissy. Their magic felt as disgusting as it had always been and reached out to my own as if it wanted to slide through any of the cracks. I had to fight to keep the scowl off my face when it oozed around me.

They steered me toward the Bennetts and I was met with a familiar aging face and his far-too-young-for-him wife that was clinging to his arm. This governor was a demon but from the looks of it he had to either be super weak or super old because he was currently aging like spoiled cheese.

No wonder the trophy wife turned toward drugs; I couldn't imagine what the old fart was like in bed. Just looking at his clothed beer belly and his oily face made me nauseous.

"Governor Bennett, Daxton has finally made an appearance. He had schoolwork to attend to but I am sure you have *many* questions about Winterfell." Father spoke for Mother, not trusting her to keep it short.

"Yes!" he said clapping his hands together. "Martha and I were just discussing if Winterfell is right for Hayley. Curious how your experience has been so far?"

A familiar arm wrapped around my shoulders and I had never been so relieved to be in Eli's arms as I was right now.

Thank you, I shot toward her. *I owe you one.*

She sent me a picture of me on my knees that made heat coil in my stomach.

"It's been fantastic, hasn't it Dax?" Eli spoke to the Governor as if they had been lifelong friends. He and his wife both zeroed in on her tattoos right away. The Governor narrowed his eyes at Eli and looked her up and down like she was a street rat. His wife on the other hand had a distinctive look in her eyes.

"Yes. Many learning opportunities," I added on. My parents backed away from us slightly. They loathed Eli. She had no purity left, they told me. Said their magic *felt* how tainted she was. I almost scoffed at their lies when they told me. They were just afraid she would get me to think for myself and finally leave their house of horrors.

"Yes, especially magical ones. Speaking of that, isn't that your old teacher?" Eli pushed me away from the group and pointed to a figure across the room. I was surprised that she even recognized Professor Wilton but there was no way in hell I would ask. Steeling myself I walked toward him.

"Professor," I called out to the lanky professor. His warm brown eyes met mine and he sent me a light smile. He had not changed in the years since I had seen him last. I hadn't taken classes from him after I was able to control my magic but I always greeted him at functions like this. And it was not just to be polite—other than my family he was the best-known witch in the area. If there was anyone who could give me information, it was him.

"Daxton, I almost didn't recognize you. I heard you got into Winterfell?" he asked but I knew his comment about not recognizing me was not just about the growth spurt I went through. His magic reached out to my own. It was warm and pleasant but tiny in comparison to mine. I let his magic float around me, checking the weak spots I knew were not there. If he was frightened his face did not show it in the moment.

"Yes. It's the topic of the night apparently," I told him. A server handed me a glass of alcohol. I took it without facing her.

"Well it's a good school. What are you majoring in? Your parents told me government but I highly doubt that," Professor Wilton said, his tone light and playful.

"Demon History and Culture," I responded and took a swig of champagne trying to find the right way to ask the questions that were forming on my tongue. I looked around, my eyes catching Rae speaking to a man of similar height as her in a grey suit. It was her father.

As if on cue Rae met my eyes. Her lips showed a barely visible scowl. If I hadn't known her for the last few years I wouldn't have noticed, but Rae got *that* particular look when her family were being assholes. She paused for only a moment and then left her father to disappear into the crowd, no doubt finding another politician to schmooze.

"Professor, I actually came today because I wanted to ask you what you knew about curses," I rushed out bringing my attention back to the professor. I wouldn't have much time before my parents tore me away from him.

"More than your average witch, I guess. What specifically were you looking to learn about?" He replaced his empty champagne glass with another as the server passed. His finger tapped at the glass and a nervous smile played at the left side of his mouth.

Interesting.

I kept it short. Told him that I met a girl who had a curse that seemed to latch onto something inside her. A curse that had no rhyme or reason and seemed to ooze Original magic. His eyes widened as I spoke and his normally white skin became green. He nodded his head like he was listening, but his eyes darted around us like we were gossiping.

"Well curses cannot be more than skin deep. If you found that there has to be another reason for it. Even the most powerful witches cannot accomplish that." He paused and cleared his throat. "A curse only works on the skin because it can pull magic from the person who cast it. It will last a certain predestined time unless other conditions are met. Also magic cannot penetrate the skin of a...non-magician. It would die faster than the person could keep it up."

His eyes shifted slightly. "It's happened. I am telling you. I felt it and consumed some of it," I told him.

"You consumed some?" My old professor looked like he was about to faint. "Has your magic reacted at all?" Just like how his magic had checked for weak spots it came back once more with more force. He had done it many times before I was used to it but one of his jabs caught me off guard and made me spill some of my drink.

"I'm fine. Tell me what else you know," I growled at him while wiping the alcohol off my shirt. My patience was wearing thin. I clearly described in detail the situation and now he's acting like it's not even possible?

My father's familiar clammy hand clamped down on my shoulder and I would have pushed it off if it was not for the way his magic poked at my back, warning me to do no such thing. A cold sweat covered my skin.

"Glad to see you still keep in contact with each other," My father said, his hand tightening on my shoulder in warning. Obviously, he was mad I had ditched the governor. "I am terribly sorry, but I must be taking Daxton now. Nice to see you, Wilton."

Professor Wilton looked relieved. I glared at my father as he pushed us away from the professor and back to where my mom awaited with a non-alcoholic punch.

"That was rude, Father," I hissed. He paid no mind to me and proceeded to hand me off to my mother. She then decided that I needed to do rounds of all the most influential people in power. Many had asked about my education but after hearing my one-worded response they quickly redirected the questions to Mother and Father to comment on the biggest witch uprising. My mother and father gave perfect rehearsed responses that left me rolling my eyes.

"So sad we couldn't come to an understanding."

"It's because their magic was stained."

"Yes, a pity. Tainted magic does terrible things."

I wanted so badly to spill that the only difference between my parents and them was the matter of a closed door and government ties. But I kept my mouth shut.

I tried to get Rae's attention when I saw her next but she paid no mind to me. Instead, she continued to work the floor, floating from guest to guest. Her expression never wavered from the cool smile she had put in place after meeting with her father. Eli had also disappeared not too long ago and I had a nagging suspicion that Mrs. Bennett was occupying her in another room.

It wasn't until eleven o'clock rolled around that my parents had finally decided it was enough and that they needed to leave. The party size had been cut in half by then and even the governor had retired more than an hour ago.

"Morning magic ritual," they told the people. "Must be consumed as the first waves wash over us to keep the purity." If there were any other witches in hearing range, they would snicker at their obvious lie.

My mom turned toward me as I walked them outside. "I can feel your tainted magic, Daxton. It's disgusting and diseased," she whispered. "Come home for a cleanse."

"Don't you dare ever mention a cleanse to me again," I snapped at her. I didn't dare let my mind conjure up the images of the cleanse; I couldn't handle it nor did I want to know what it would do to my magic. Trauma and panic tended to aggravate it.

"You know you need it, my boy," Father added on. His face was filled with mock sympathy. "We could feel the filth in your magic as soon as you walked in the door."

"Yes Daxton, sweetie," my mother said clinging to my shirt exposing my naked chest even further. I wanted to barf. "Like old times. Like a family. We can unite and cleanse together."

I growled deep in my chest trying to disguise my panic as anger. My magic seemed to flare at her words just like I feared. "If you say another word, I will spill to everyone what those *cleanses* entail, *Mother*."

She blanched at my words and my father pulled her away from me.

"You know those are holy rituals. They are pure. Purer than whatever witch you have been fucking," he hissed. My mother curled into his chest acting like a kicked puppy. Her act was disgusting.

"Just leave me alone and be assured that your *disgusting ways* will never come to light and you can stay in your comfy positions. If you continue to goad me I cannot promise you that you will still have your jobs in the morning."

My father fumed at the accusations. His temper was always short but now it seemed nonexistent. "Why you—"

"Oh yes," Rae purred from beside me holding her notebook. Eli's arm found its home across my shoulders. "Witch rituals are not commonly known to many of the demons in government. Quite frankly, they hate any thought of witches. So they are willing to accept any of the crap you spew about purifying magic." My heart soared at her words.

You okay? Eli asked in my mind.

Fine, just want to get out of here.

"But we are not just any other demons, right Dax?" Eli noted and even though I couldn't see her face I knew that she gave them a smile that made their faces lose all color.

"You don't know anything," Father stuttered out but backed away slowly. "You are just as soiled as the rest of them."

"Correct me if I am wrong, Dax. But there are only three ways to release magic. Sex, bloodletting, and a familiar, right?" Rae asked. Her voice was light but her words were heavy.

"You are right," I answered, my eyes squarely on my father's. I wished for the day I could show him what I really thought about him.

"It is easy to guess which one you partake in," Rae told them. "Don't make this hard."

We didn't have to say another word. They knew they were fucked and they practically ran to their car.

"Thank you," I whispered after my parents left. Instead of relief though, I felt a tightening in my chest and my magic was lashing out wildly as if it too refused to go back to that dark place in my memories. Gone was the puppy that Rosie's curse created and in its place was the monster I had come to know so well.

It would be in my best interest to find a witch and expel all this magic but what I wanted to do was carve into my skin and watch as the magic spilled onto the floor. Force the memory of *their* magic out. The memory of it crept along my spine.

Maybe Amr would suffice.

"Let's go get that bastard cat of yours," Eli whispered.

We all left the party in silence and headed back to the dorm.

* * *

"You broke her fucking handle," Rae said with a sigh. Her mask slipped just enough for us to see how annoyed she was. There was a small scowl that graced her lips and her forehead was wrinkled, no doubt a leftover from the conversation with her father.

"Your face will stick like that if you're not careful," Eli responded and then proceeded to show us how she had entered last time.

"Both of you are going to send me into an early grave," Rae grumbled in response.

As soon as the door was wide enough a flash of white streaked by us and crashed into Eli's face, then fell to the floor with a thud. Despite the current cloud of dark emotions that hung around me, laughter bubbled up inside me.

Eli's mouth was hanging open and she seemed to be momentarily stunned as she processed what just happened. Rae was also noticeably pleased at the turn of events. A smile played at the corner of her lips.

I heard Amr hiss from inside.

"I just want the cat," Eli called and then peeked her head in through the open doorway. "Dax's cat but I would like a taste of the other one while I am here as well." Her voice sounded like she was smiling.

My magic purred at the thought that raced through my mind. Watching Eli go down on her while I sucked the magic out of her would be far too decadent. I couldn't see her but I hoped that her cheeks were painted with that beautiful red I had seen the last time in the garden.

I heard the small shuffling of her feet and her pajama-clad body came into view with Amr in her arms. She locked eyes with me and held the cat out to me. He meowed unhappily but I couldn't even bother to look at him, I was too entranced by the light blush that spread across her face, only interrupted by her freckles. I swallowed thickly and tried to ignore the coiling in my stomach.

When I took Amr from her arms and accidentally brushed my skin against her, my magic jumped up to the surface and reached out to her. Then in a matter of seconds, the monster disappeared in a poof and instead it was like a dog tugging at its leash, whining to get a taste of the curse.

There has to be another reason.

My teacher's voice rang through my head, and I was suddenly brought back to the feeling of Amr struggling in my arms. Rae grabbed the fallen pillow and handed it to Rosie before she and Eli pushed my dazed form down the hallway and to Rae's dorm. As we walked, I pushed my magic out to Amr and he sucked it up like a black hole, purring as he did.

"What did your teacher say?" Rae asked as she pushed me into her room. It was just like any other dorm, but I didn't miss the expensive coffee machine on the counter of her kitchenette.

"He doesn't think a curse can last that long inside a person without a witch being near," I told them and made myself comfortable on the floor with my back against the wall. Having the hard surface against my back calmed my pounding heart and a sense of security flushed over me. If I could see everything my magic would calm.

"But there is no other witch around," Eli mused. "So if it's not a really strong curse what is it?"

"There is no doubt a curse," I told her. "It's just odd how long it has lived on without intervention." There was a thought that I didn't want to breach.

It was there, just below the surface and was glaring obviously at us yet so out of this world that it had to be impossible.

"So there is another power source feeding it," Rae concluded.

My stomach sank even further, and her eyes met mine. I wondered briefly if it was her that had the mind-reading power and not Eli.

"I think she has magic in her," I told them. "My magic couldn't tell the difference and when she blood let it acted like normal magic."

"That's impossible. You saw her conjure fire. That's a demon trait. And the healing," Eli pushed.

"I have done both of those things as well," I reminded her.

"With magic," Eli countered. "Her body healed itself just like any other demon."

"Regardless of whatever it is, it is feeding off something in her." I paused and looked at Eli. "And you found a way around it that night."

"So she either separated the curse from the magic source, which is unlikely," Rae supplied. "Or..."

"The conditions the original witch placed on it weren't met," I finished.

There was a small silence as we each stewed over this information.

"What was she thinking about when it didn't work last time?" Rae asked.

"I told you, dude. The only thing on her mind was my—"

"Okay, let me rephrase," Rae cut Eli off. "What was different about every other time?"

There was another silence. I had a feeling I knew the answer. It was right on the tip of my tongue. And it felt so simple.

If I was that witch, how would I make this the most effective? What was the surefire way to make the victim suffer from this curse? Something they couldn't break. Every curse has some type of loophole, how would I make that smaller?

It had to be something the person couldn't control, or at least would be very hard to control. Thoughts are easy to control if you work at it hard enough but...

"Holy shit," I gasped, the dots finally connecting. "That witch is evil but also a pure genius. It can't be that she just wasn't *thinking* about it. If that's true, she would never not have cuts."

"But she wasn't thinking about it," Eli said.

"It has to be instinctual," I told them. "Something like a gut reaction."

"It's based on emotions," Rae concluded. There was a small light in her eyes.

"When her curse is triggered what does she feel?" I asked Rae. She rubbed her chin searching for the answer.

"Fear. Pain. Anxiety and anticipation," she answered. "But that's a common feeling for her."

"Maybe it's a specific fear? Fear of pain? Can magic do that?" Eli asked her voice was hesitant and there was a small frown on her face.

"Magic does not have many bounds. Particularly curses. If you have the reserves anything is possible," I explained remembering the time I witnessed a witch place a squeaking curse on a mortal. Anything was possible if you were powerful enough.

And this witch was an Original based on the taste of the magic.

I looked down at Amr. His eyes were closing sleepily, the magic taking a toll on him.

"So, what. We just tell her not to fear her curse? The one that's been tearing apart her skin for years?" Eli scoffed.

"And breaking her bones," Rae added.

"No, we stop it," I said.

"Her emotions?" Eli was getting more irritated by the second. It seeped into her voice like poison. "Another orgasm?"

"Is sex the only thing you think about?" Rae snapped.

"We can test it," I piped in before Eli blew up and gestured to Rae. "We have the perfect tool. We don't even have to tell her until we are sure."

"That would take a lot of power," Rae said with a sigh.

"You have enough power to be ranked second most powerful in the school," I reminded.

"And I would have to be close to her in order to control it."

"Then we do it on a weekend," I said with a smile. "We can make a sleepover out of it. Say it's so we can monitor her after last time."

Rae paused as she thought over my plan. I knew it was the best we could do with the circumstance. And she needed to be watched because if she went and tried to talk by herself while still fearing the curse, our cover would be blown.

"What's our excuse? Anyone could monitor her. Why Rae?" Eli was mad again, barely concealing her glares toward Rae.

"I'll say because I'm the only one that doesn't want to get in her pants," Rae answered with a sigh. She ran her hands through her hair.

Was that true though?

Chapter Fourteen
Rosie

"It's like you've been avoiding me," Matt whined as he sat down at the only available table in the small café we found ourselves in. It was only five minutes away from the campus and perfect walking distance. It was a rare sunny day and I had originally planned to stay holed up in the dorm but Matt changed those plans unexpectedly. This was a rare occasion when Matt decided to not visit his family. Almost every other weekend he was busy but this weekend I guess was the only time he could get to himself. I felt for him; if not studying or in school he was traveling to his family's house.

You know I'm not, I signed to him. His eyebrows pulled together and he gave me a pout.

I was, but he didn't need to know that. It was hard to get free time away from the trio and even if I did, I wasn't sure what I wanted Matt to know just yet.

"How's the thing with, *y'know*," he asked gesturing toward me with his hand.

Before I could respond there was a loud clang from across the café, making us both jump in our seats.

"Stupid low-level couldn't even get my order right," grumbled a high-level in a suit. The staff member who had been serving him now had a huge stain on her black apron and there was coffee spilled all over the floor. She looked to almost be in tears.

I felt a pang in my chest at the look on her face. This was normal for us. I shouldn't feel like this after seeing it so many times. She just looked so helpless, and she was so young, at least half the age of the angry demon.

"Rosie," Matt whispered. "Not our problem." His eyes were wide like he thought I might do something.

I am not stupid, I signed to him. *It's fine. No progress yet.*

"I'm sure it just takes time," he said with a sad smile. His eyes shifted to the space behind me. "Hey! You're in my class! Nice to see you here, Malik right?"

I have never felt coldness like the one that washed over me when I realized that Malik was so close to Matt this entire time. I kept my eyes firmly on Matt's face.

Don't look at him. The ghost of Daxton's hand was on my neck guiding my head to stare at the ground.

"Yes. I was interrupted by the rude demon and I couldn't help but notice a familiar head of hair and wanted to say hello." Malik's deep voice vibrated around us and sent a chill down my spine.

"Have you met Rosie?" Matt asked. "She can't speak but she can sign or type to us if needed."

"I have seen her but have yet to meet." Malik moved around us so that his torso was standing in my line of sight. He thrust his hand out toward me. I couldn't help but notice that it was as scarred as Eli's but far more delicate-looking. He was wearing a short sleeve that gave me a full view of the tattoos that covered his skin.

I shook his hand but refused to look him in the eye.

"Sorry for the wait, here are your lattes," the staff member said and placed them gently on our table, breaking the tension around us. "Sir yours is coming up, would you like me to bring it here?"

Please no, I chanted in my head.

"That would be lovely," Malik said and brought a nearby chair to sit down with us. I had to avert my gaze to the latte in front of me so I would not make accidental eye contact.

"Did you hear that Malik got number one in the rankings?" Matt asked. "Crazy right? He won't tell me his power though and when I asked others about it they said they didn't know what they saw."

I gulped down the bitter coffee. I wanted to enjoy the rare real cup of coffee I could get but I couldn't with the tension around us.

"Rosie knows," Malik said with a chuckle. It was light but I read it as threatening. "But I would like to keep it a secret. Keeps things *more interesting*."

"What? Rosie how did you find out?" Matt asked, his voice rising slightly.

I peeked up at Matt. I could make out Malik's white hair near the corner of my vision.

Let's go, I signed to him and stood up, carefully averting my eyes from Malik. A cold hand clasped on my wrist, and something shot out in front of my foot and in an instant, I was falling toward the floor.

Malik caught my fall. He did so by standing and pulling me to his chest. He was wearing a dark shirt that had a type of print that scratched my cheek.

"What's the rush *Rosie*?" he asked, his lips centimeters away from my ear. "No need to fear me."

He pushed me back down in my seat and then sat back into his.

"Here you go, sir," the staff person said and placed a cup down in front of him.

"Thank you kindly," he said and I caught sight of him forcing something into the girl's hand. "A tip for dealing with the bastard."

That was it. The shock of the action is what tore my eyes to the waitress. Her eyes were still red but she had on a new apron now and was looking at Malik in shock.

"Oh, my that's too much sir. Please," she said and turned a bright crimson.

"Nonsense," he said. "You deserve it." She left and it only took two more seconds to make the worst mistake of my life.

Brown met gold.

Fuck.

A small smile graced his lips. He had a puff of curly white hair that surrounded his head and eyes as golden as the sun. The pale skin on his face was marred by a white scar that ran from his left eye to the right side of his mouth. His features were delicate and boyish-looking and if it wasn't for the tattoos that marred his bare arms I wouldn't have guessed that someone like him would be in a gang. Model work would fit him better regardless of the face deformities—if anything they worked in his favor.

"There we are. Not so bad right?" he asked and leaned forward. "I apologize for starting off on the wrong foot. Eli is a bit brash at times."

"Eli? How is she involved here?" Matt asked but Malik's eyes stayed on mine.

"Why is she so interested in you, hm?" Malik asked. I waited for his power to kick in but there was no shift in the air. "No pressure to answer. I'm just not as she portrayed and wanted to make that clear."

I eyed him warily. It would seem that way but putting on a front was easy and I had only known him for a short while.

But is Eli someone you can trust? asked a voice in the back of my head. *Is Daxton? Rae? They have only proven that they want to use you,* the voice continued.

I use them too, I reminded myself.

"Does Eli not like you or something?" Matt asked. Malik tore his eyes away from mine.

"You could say we fell out of sorts. She's always looked up to me," Malik said with a small smile. "She grew up in a shitty way so I didn't blame her when she stopped putting me on a pedestal, I just wished I could see that starry-eyed kid once more."

Ask him what he did to make Eli not trust him, I signed to Matt. Matt hesitated slightly. I sent him a small glare.

"She asks—" Matt was cut off by Malik.

"I know. I studied sign language at one point too," Malik said. My heart skipped a beat. "It's been around for centuries."

So have you, I signed to him not caring that Matt was watching. Malik let out a chuckle.

"Eli has loose lips it seems." Malik licked his lips as if to emphasize his point. "I didn't *do* anything other than show her my power. She asked to see it, begged even. How could a kid her age resist?"

"How could that make her not trust you?" Matt asked. "Especially if you were so close?"

"I didn't say we were close," Malik responded. His eyes narrowed and there was a sly smile on his lips. "And I wouldn't say she doesn't trust me..."

She fears him, I concluded without his help.

He was dangerous. I could see it now even without feeling his power. The way his eyes narrowed. The way he zoned in on you when you spoke. He no doubt followed us here. He sensed right away something was different with Eli and he went out of his way to find out.

Like a cat watching its prey.

I slept with her, I signed. *That's it.*

"Rosie are you serious?" Matt spluttered.

Malik's smile widened. "So she didn't want me to encroach on her plaything." He clicked his tongue. "How childish." He took a sip of his coffee and sighed. "I thought it had to be more interesting than that. Daxton too? Don't tell me you also slept with the glasses bitch?"

The way he talked about Rae irked me but I let it go. I was just relieved that he took the bait.

Just Eli, I signed.

"I would have assumed she would want Daxton in on it too. You know they are *very close*."

"Eli and Daxton? Like as in *sleeping together* close?" Matt asked with a small gasp. Was he blind? I was silently fuming at his reaction.

So what? I asked.

"You don't mind your woman with another man?" Malik asked.

I wanted so badly to yell at him. Scream at him. Why did he care?

No, I signed. *She's not mine.*

"Hmm how progressive of you," Malik commented with a smirk. Malik stood and smoothed down his pants. "It was nice talking Rosie, but I best get going. I'll be open to talk if you have any more questions about your lover, just find me. See you in class, Matt."

I clenched my cup hard in my hand as he walked away. It was only when I heard Matt's chair squeak that I met his face.

"You can tell me more about it on the way back," he said with a strained smile.

* * *

The air had chilled on our walk to the garden. I am not sure if it was imagined, the leftover fear I had, or if the winter air was finally catching up to us. The tall rose bushes covered us, which made it a great place to talk, but it also made me uneasy when Matt was so angry.

"I don't see how *magic* makes people jump one another, Rosie," Matt said, his voice sharp. His hands were balled into fists at his side.

"I don't have to explain anything to you." I kept my voice low enough so the curse wouldn't cause significant damage, but I couldn't let Matt keep rambling about how wrong it was that I slept with Eli. From the walk back to Winterfell until now he had been grumbling about my sexual proclivities.

"I have been trying to look out for you this whole time Rosie and you literally just jump straight into danger!" He threw his hands up in the air and stalked around the small garden.

"It was literally your idea," I reminded him. I took a deep breath to steady myself against the pain that racked through my body. Matt's pacing paused and his eyes met mine.

"That was before I knew how dangerous they were," he said. His voice was lower now and his eyes were pleading. "After the talk with Malik I don't think it's okay to trust them. I think we need some distance. We can figure out something else for the curse."

"How are they dangerous?" I asked. The blood seeped its way into my pants.

"Eli's in a gang, Rosie! And not to mention Daxton can't even control his own magic! Did you know what he did in high school? Hm?" With each word he took a step toward me. "He almost fucked a witch to her death. Her magic was completely depleted when he was done, and Eli has been helping him cover it up. They cannot *live* without magic, and all of them are in on it."

My blood ran cold at his words. The news about Daxton's behavior was almost as surprising as Matt knowing about Eli's gang ties.

But...you cannot push me, Eli. I mean it. If I lose control you have to pull me out.

What's the fun in that?

Was that what losing control looked like? I balled my shaking hands and hid them behind my back and outside of Matt's sight.

That time in the garden when Daxton first became drunk on my magic, he was ready to take anything he wanted. It was Eli who stopped him. But didn't he tell Eli not to push him?

Information was hitting me at all angles. It made my head spin.

"Who told you that?" my voice rasped.

"I asked around," he said with a huff and cast his eyes down to the grass below our feet. "Don't hurt yourself by talking."

"Don't tell me what to do," I hissed at him. "Your class is third-year. They are first. What could you know?" I grit my teeth against the pain of the cuts, getting angrier with each word out of his mouth.

"Everyone knows the truth," he whispered. When his grey eyes met mine, they seemed sad. "Except you."

I had enough.

I regretted letting Matt in at all. I should have pushed him away from the beginning. Why did I listen to the principal when I knew talking about the curse was a bad thing?

"I'm done with this. Done with you," I said and pushed past him.

His wrist shot out to grab mine. Flames engulfed my arm. Matt let out a yelp and scrambled away from me. I thought I saw tears when his eyes met mine, but I couldn't be sure because I turned away.

"Rosie..." His voice was low.

* * *

I made the decision to skip breakfast the next morning in exchange for a few extra minutes of sleep.

It's not like I wanted to see Matt any time soon.

Or Daxton.

Or Eli.

I curled in my bed and sighed into my pillow.

Times like these were when the wall between me and the rest of the world was just too high to comprehend. I had hope, when they told me that they could help get rid of my curse. The wall became a fence during that time. I felt seen. There was still something dividing us but at least for the first time in my life the wall seemed like something I could conquer.

But now...

I realized it was only my imagination. What I thought was the journey to belonging was just a very vivid daydream. It was all a product of my overactive imagination, just like when I told my parents when I was younger that I saw an angel fly across the sky. Who could understand and accept someone who could barely speak?

A knocking snapped me out of my wallowing. I got out of the bed but froze when my hand hit the cold metal knob.

A small bit of hope rose in me. Did they notice I was gone? Maybe they came to get me so their group would be complete. A small smile graced my lips and I opened the door.

My hope crumbled and burned when I was met with the person on the other side. The wall that had seemed to crack was now higher and stronger than ever.

"You look like you could use a day off," Malik said with a smile. The scars on his face shone under the fluorescents in the hallway. He was out of uniform in an oversized black shirt that was tucked into fitting black cargo pants and Doc Martens.

What do you want? I signed to him.

"I noticed you were not having breakfast with the others," he said his eyes shifting behind me, checking my room. "And I already was going to skip classes and was wondering if you would like to ditch with me."

Why me? I signed, suspicions rising.

"Given the state of Matt's burned hand I thought that you may also need a day off," he said with a shrug. "Not a big deal if you don't want to come. Just thought you could use someone on your side."

I met his shining gold eyes.

Someone on my side.

"It's okay," he said. "Next time." He turned quickly and left down the hall.

Something in me jolted. I was not sure if it was because of everything that had happened the last few days or just how honest he was, or maybe it was that I finally had something that I could choose for myself.

I just...couldn't let him just walk away from me.

I hurled myself out into the hallway and banged on the wall to get his attention. His head cocked toward the sound and a small smile played at his lips.

Wait, I signed to him. He shoved his hands in his pocket and leaned against the wall.

I rushed back into my room and pulled on the ratty band t-shirt I got from the thrift store with a pair of dark jeans that had more than a few accidental holes in them. I would normally wear a turtleneck with a short sleeve shirt but I didn't want to chance him waiting any longer. I was almost afraid that when I checked the hallway he would be gone.

I dove into the bathroom and harshly brushed my teeth then pulled my long black hair into a ponytail. There were bags under my eyes from the incessant thoughts that had plagued my mind during the night. I sighed and splashed my face with water and ran back out to grab my phone and wallet.

When I was done, I paused by the doorway once more. I spotted a bottle of cheap perfume on the desk. I hadn't even thought to use it since I unpacked it on the first day. Without a second thought I dabbed the scent on my wrists and neck and ran out the door.

I was happier than I would like to admit when I saw Malik leaning against the same spot I left him in.

"I saw that band in concert when they first became popular," he commented with his eyes narrowing in on the shirt I was wearing. "Let's go, little rocker."

I blushed as I followed him through the dorm.

"Where do you want to go?" he asked as he held the dorm doors open to me. "I don't really have a plan, so I am hoping you do." I paused, looking for an answer. I bit my lip trying to think, feeling under way more pressure than normal.

Beach? I signed to him.

"The beach? Good idea," he said and ruffled his hand on my head. "I have a car. Follow me."

He led me into the parking lot and to a black BMW. It shone like it had just been washed. He opened the passenger side door for me. I paused and met his eyes once more.

"Trust me." His voice was smooth, and it was topped off with a smile. "Just a quick trip and we will be back before you know it."

Why wouldn't I trust him? my mind asked, but it was simple. He had yet to show me I couldn't. Even the others had their cracks and paired with the added information Matt gave me...

I sat down on the cool leather seats. The musky warm scent of men's cologne filled my senses.

My stomach flipped when I realized just how odd the situation I was in was. Skipping class with a high-level demon that had to be a minimum of a thousand years old and liked to hold doors open and take you to the beach.

Was this even okay? Eli would surely be angry with me.

Stay away from Malik. I promised her that but here I was in his car.

"Whatcha thinking about so hard, hm?" Malik said as he turned on his car. I snapped out of my musings and looked at him in the driver's seat. His white hair stood out against the all-black interior but his clothing seemed to blend right in.

Eli will be mad, I signed to him with a small pout.

"Not if we don't tell her," Malik said with a smile and put the car in drive and pulled us away from the parking lot. "It will be about an hour to the sea from here. Connect your phone and play some music if you'd like. I won't be able to watch you sign so just tap me if you need something."

I nodded and searched my phone for some music. I settled on some light instrumental music that seemed to be trending on the music app. He didn't comment and I let myself relax against the cool seat and watch as the scenery zoomed past us.

The cool morning air would be chased away with something a bit warmer soon, but this was the first time that I had been out in public in a short sleeve in over nine years. It was weird for my arms to be so bare, vulnerable. I rubbed my hands against my skin, feeling uneasy.

"You cold?" Malik asked and turned the heater up a notch. I turned my attention to him and watched as he drove.

Was he really in the same gang as Eli? Was he really so dangerous?

His scarred hands gripped the steering wheel loosely and there was still a small smile on his face. He had to be as tall as Eli but he was leaner and seemed to take up less space. If Eli was the muscle, he would most likely be the brains in whatever organization they were in.

"We will be there in another few minutes," he told me.

I looked around and noticed that the trees around us were thinning and beyond them was a dark greyish-looking sea. My breath caught in my throat.

My parents never took me to the sea. After the accident they refused to go out in public if it was anything other than work or school.

Malik pulled into an almost empty parking lot. There were only a few cars and I had no idea what beach we came to, but I was absolutely in love. The sun shone off of the grey-blue waves and the sand here seemed dark and rocky; it was perfectly moody. The waves were so loud I could hear them from in the car. Malik sent me a small smile.

"Let's go get our feet wet, if you can handle it," he said.

You know it, I signed at him. I let the smile that was pushing against my mask grace my lips and pushed myself out of the car.

"Take your shoes off. You can leave them here," Malik said jabbing his thumb behind him, toward the trunk of the car. I nodded and did as he told. Malik was by me taking his own Doc Martens off and shutting the trunk. I am not sure what made the movement so intimate but something warm blossomed in my chest.

He sent me another smile when he sensed my gaze and motioned for me to go toward the waves. Without another look back I jogged lightly to the sand. The cool air was refreshing in my lungs and the sand was slightly warm even if the air around it was cold.

I made a hard stop near the waves. The sand was dark and wet here, sending a chill through me. I buried my toes in it and let out a small sigh. Looking up I saw some boats near the horizon. Their little white sails were carrying them farther than my eyes could see.

Icy water splashed around my feet and I jumped. A small sound escaped my lips and I felt a bruise form on my ribs. I froze and searched for Malik. He took a step forward and stood silently behind me.

"Beaches on the west coast are warmer," he told me. "Maybe next time we want to ditch school we can take a plane there."

The tension left my shoulders when I realized he wasn't going to mention my noise.

Maybe he didn't hear?

The waves pulled away from our feet and I watched as small bubbles pushed up to the surface of the wet sound. Curious, I squatted down to get a closer look. A wave bigger than last washed up and soaked my jeans. Strong hands pulled me up quickly before I could fall.

Malik's deep laugh radiated through his body and his chest moved against my back.

"Have you never been to the beach before?" he asked.

I leaned my head back against his chest and looked up to meet his gaze. His gold eyes were already staring at me. I shook my head.

In a moment of courage—or stupidity—I reached up and tapped on his scar. His eyes widened and then he smiled down at me like he understood my question.

"Witches can cause demons to scar," he explained. "I have had more than my fair share of fights with them throughout the years. The witch that caused that one just so happened to be easy to anger."

My heart skipped a beat. *Would he know about curses? He's been around for years—how could he not know?*

Do you know about curses? I signed to him. His smile dropped slightly, and his hand tightened around my arm. His movement was enough to remind me of my position against him and I stepped away and turned to face him.

"Not really. Unfortunately, I am not as *friendly* with witches as Eli is," he said and then cocked his head. "What does a little thing like you want to know about curses?"

The wave lapped at my feet once more.

Nothing really, just curious.

"Curiosity killed the cat," he said. "Best stay away from witches. They can lose control easily."

I couldn't control the grimace that showed on my face. He was obviously talking about Daxton.

They told me to stay away from you too, I signed to him.

"I know," he said. "Yet here you are. More than an hour away from the campus with me." He gestured to the phone in my pocket. "And they didn't even call to check on you. Great friends."

His words stung but they were true.

They don't have my number, I signed to him. A small chuckle passed his lips. He held his hand out. I slowly grabbed my phone, unlocked it, and placed it in his hand. He typed on it quickly and handed it back to me. A smile made its way to my face when I saw what he did.

He put his number in and his contact's name was *A Real Friend.*

Who said we were friends? I signed to him. I was anything but serious and I couldn't keep the smile off my face.

"I did," he answered with a smile. "I don't know about you but I am starved. Let's get some food and then we can head back."

I didn't mean to pout but he saw it right away. His hand landed on the top of my head and he rustled my hair.

"If you can successfully keep this from Eli, we can come back," he said.

I nodded and followed him back to his car.

$* * *$

Another two hours later with a belly full of the most delicious clam chowder, we arrived back at the campus. It was still early but students would be getting out of class soon and I wanted to beat the rush and hide out in my dorm for as long as I could.

The thoughts of the trio and Matt had escaped me while I was enjoying my time with Malik. I felt so normal with him today. It was the first time that I could relax.

This was being seen, I concluded.

"Text me when you are in," Malik said. "I have some stuff to do so I must leave but please let me know when you get in." He paused for longer this time. "And if you need anything don't hesitate to text me. For anything. On your side, remember that." His eyes were almost smoldering.

I nodded, not really looking at him, and gave him a smile as I left his car. He gave me a small wave and pulled away once my feet had hit the curb. I kicked my shoes against the concrete, feeling the sand sit uncomfortably at the bottom of my sole. I sighed but continued, my smile never wavering as I did.

The walk to my dorm was short but it wasn't like I was paying attention anyways. My head was too busy being so far up in the clouds. My cheeks hurt from smiling so hard. The beach was perfect, everything I needed.

The trip made it so much easier to separate myself from everything that was going on. Think critically. I would have to be wary about the others from now on. They had been trying to help me so far but who knew what their real motives were? Was it just graduating? Sex? I really didn't know anymore but one thing was for certain, *they had to be wrong about Malik.*

I rounded the corner into my hall and walked quickly toward my room. The trio plus a nervous-looking Matt stood in my hallway in front of my door.

Amr meowed loudly as I came up, drawing everyone's attention away from their heated conversation and toward me.

"Rosie, where the fuck have you been?" Eli asked. There was a growl in her voice as he spoke. She stalked toward me and clamped her hands down on my shoulders. Her bright blue eyes held flames behind them.

Don't you dare lie, she warned in my head.

I had a fight with Matt and I didn't feel like going to school today, I responded and pushed her hands off my shoulders.

"I didn't ask why I asked where, and with who?" she yelled at my retreating form. I stood in front of the other three and glanced at Matt's hand. I forgot he couldn't heal like me and his hand was currently bandaged. Guilt punched me in the gut.

"We wanted to let you know that the experiments will be paused this week. We will begin again on Friday night," Rae said. I looked over toward her.

Matt's words rang through my head once more. *What's her reason? How much did I not know?*

I knew Rae would have all the answers and the more I looked at her the angrier and more suspicious I got.

Why would they not tell me something like that?

Why would they? a voice in my head asked.

Eli's hand clamped on the back of my neck.

"Matt says Malik was missing as well," Eli growled in my ear.

I sent a glare to Matt.

Didn't he just tell me how bad the trio was?

Were you with him, low-level? Eli asked.

No, I answered back and walked toward my door to open it with shaky legs, but I was pushed harshly against it.

You have a thing for pushing people against the wall, I snapped in my head.

"Eli, stop," Rae said from behind us. Eli pushed herself against me, her hot breath tickling my neck.

You are lying, she said.

Why does it matter to you? I shot back. *So what if he controls me? Afraid he'll kill me? Then what? You'll get to go back to your normal life.*

"What are you talking about?" she asked. "Don't act like you don't know why we are helping you in the first place. I am getting out of here early with my degree. I hate this school as much as I fucking hate entitled low-levels like you. Why else would I agree to this?"

My stomach dropped at her words.

"Eli," Rae warned and Eli was pulled off me. "We will leave you to rest. Apologies about this."

Without looking back, I opened my door and slammed it shut behind me.

Chapter Fifteen
Rosie

I sat on the brickwork around one of the various communal areas that scattered the campus. It was still early so the air had a slight chill to it. I took a deep breath and watched as the high-levels mingled with each other. A group passed me and they laughed loudly at some joke one of the students made. Carefree. Unburdened.

I wished to be them.

I had thought it may be best to skip again today. If it wasn't for a shitty home life, I would have left the school as soon as I thought possible. I didn't have many options waiting for me out there. They didn't employ low-levels in positions that paid them enough to live. The sullen face of the wait staff at the café filled my mind.

That's what I would be left with. Serving people who didn't give a damn about me. Except...

Trust me.

I'm on your side.

I shook the thought away from my head. This was all much more trouble than it was worth.

"Rosie!" Matt's screeching voice rang through the busy communal area.

I let out a sigh and turned to face the voice. Matt's hair seemed messier than usual and his tie hung loose around his neck. The bandage from yesterday was still wrapped around his hand.

"I was looking for you everywhere!" he said through pants. He wiped the back of his hand against his forehead. "You weren't at breakfast."

I looked around. There were so many people here, so many possible witnesses. I turned back to Matt and stalked close to his form. So close my nose almost touched his chest. I watched his expression changed to a confused one, and it only angered me.

"Rosie?" His arms stretched out like he was going to embrace me, but they stayed frozen in the air.

"What the fuck, Matt?" I asked with as much venom as I could muster. The cuts seemed to feed off the hate and they stung worse than normal. "You told me you didn't trust them."

"Rosie don't talk please." Matt looked around us frantically.

"Yet you snitch on me to them," I said and took a breath to steady my aching body.

"I didn't snitch, I was worried!" he said with a hushed voice.

They are mad now. If they are so dangerous why chance their anger? I signed to him. His eyes widened. *I thought you were on my side. What were you thinking?*

If I was honest, deep down the only real reason I was angry was because Malik asked me not to tell Eli. If I told Eli, the moment on the beach, the freedom, they would fall out of my reach and never be accessible to me ever again. It also meant that all the attention they had shown me as of late would wane. It was completely and utterly selfish but regardless, Matt acted without a thought.

Matt's choices were erratic; they didn't make sense. First, he pushed me straight into them. Then, he pulled me away. Then back again.

"I just wanted you safe..." He stepped back, his eyes shifting to the ground for just a second before they met mine again. "I am sorry Rosie, I didn't think."

You never think, I signed with a scowl. *I thought we were friends.*

I turned away from him before I could see his reaction and stormed to my class. People seemed to notice the anger radiating off me because despite my low-level status, no one dared to get near me and as soon as I would pass their eyes would be glued to the ground.

Good.

As I entered the classroom door a ball of fur launched itself into my arms. Amr meowed loudly and nudged his head against my cheek. I smiled softly and gave him a small kiss on the head. The classroom was starting to fill and the people who I dreaded seeing were already sitting in their seats.

Daxton's eyes met mine and he patted the seat next to him. I raised my eyebrow at his action and my eyes drifted toward Eli.

She was put together as well as she normally was. Slicked back hair.

Tight button-up. But her eyes were cast down toward the table and her face was graced with a small scowl.

I hate this school as much as I fucking hate entitled low-levels like you.

My feet shuffled on the way to Daxton's table. I didn't know if I should be sitting next to him right now. He had his button-up rolled at the sleeves showing off his tattoos, and some of his hair was tucked messily behind his ear showing off some metal earrings. There was a small quirk of his lips that made me realize he was smiling. I'd kissed the lips of this man without a care; I'd enjoyed it. Thinking about what he did...

A shiver ran down my spine.

I swallowed thickly and sat down next to him and placed Amr in my lap.

A blank notebook was passed toward me with a small note on it.

Glad to see you joined.

A wrapped pastry and a bottled coffee were pushed next to the notebook. I looked up at Daxton in surprise.

He grabbed the notebook back and wrote on it once more. I heard Eli scoff behind me.

If we write like this Eli can't eavesdrop. Finally, a taste of her own medicine. Use this if you need it.

He slides the notebook and the pen back in front of me. I look at the food in front of me with suspicion. Hunger gnawed at my stomach.

It's packaged. He couldn't really do anything to it right?

I hesitantly ate the breakfast. Daxton relaxed against the wall in his usual position but only now did I realize how uncomfortable it would be to sit here. His whole body was turned toward me.

I peeked to the side and saw his head tilted back against the wall, showing his long-tattooed neck. His eyes were covered slightly by his hair but they were not looking at me like I assumed.

They were closed.

He looked so peaceful. I almost wondered how on earth could a man rumored to be so out of control and violent toward a woman look so peaceful. Did the magic inside him rage so uncontrollably that he was driven to such measures? What was the magic doing now?

"So you just move on to the next one in line, huh?" Eli's angry voice came from behind me. "How mad would that low-level be if he knew you were already planning to bed the next one?"

I crushed the bottled coffee in my hand. Were all the demons surrounding me such crybabies?

"Eli, now is not the time. You are still in the shit hole for yesterday," Daxton warned.

I turned to look at Eli. Her eyes were narrowed at us. A light bulb went off in my head. It was almost blinding. I slapped my hand down on hers.

I don't talk to murderers like you, I snapped before my courage went down the drain with whatever was left of my brain.

Eli pulled her hand away harshly. She looked out the window and crossed her arms over her chest.

Sitting back in my seat, my eyes met Daxton's. He was watching me with a calculating gaze.

"Alright class. Welcome to another beautiful morning," Mr. Falkner said drawing my attention away from Daxton. Daxton on the other hand seemed to be perfectly content with watching me for the rest of the period.

* * *

"Please Rosie," Matt said rushing after me as I tried to escape the after-class rush.

It had been an awkward class. Daxton didn't question me as to what I had said that caused Eli to do an entire one-eighty but I felt his eyes lingering the entire day. It didn't take a genius to know he was asking without saying the words. Daxton may be quiet, but he was sharp and caught even the slightest flinch. I wouldn't be surprised if he already started to question Eli.

I turned on the balls of my feet and faced Matt. He faltered mid-step at the sudden change and took a step back, inhaling a sharp breath.

Leave me alone, I signed to him angrily.

"I don't want to fight, Rosie." He picked at the bandage on his wrist as I glared at him.

Let me cool down, I signed to him. *I can't think straight when everyone is crowding me.*

He shifted and thought about my request for a few seconds before running his hand through his messy curls. There were bags under his eyes now and his frown seemed so deep that it'd become permanent.

"...Okay." His voice was small when he spoke. The next sigh he let out seemed to deflate his entire being. With hunched shoulders he turned and walked away from me.

I turned in the opposite way and headed to my dorm. With each step the weight of the day became heavier and heavier. By the time I got to my door I was hunched over much like Matt had been and I was so not ready to come face to face with yet another demon.

At least this one is more tolerable.

"You look like you've had another shit day," Malik commented. He was dressed in the school button-up but put his own black jeans on. His white puff of hair hung in his eyes slightly and he had a soft smile on his face.

What are you doing here? I signed to him.

"You didn't text me," he said. I frowned.

Sorry, I was busy, I signed and opened my door. After a moment of consideration, I opened the door wider for him.

He gave me a bigger smile and pushed past me into the room. His scent wafted over me as he did so. He smelt just like the ocean we visited yesterday. In that moment all of the stress and anxiety left me.

Malik made himself comfortable and sat down on the chair by the desk. He looked at the various school supplies I had there. He picked up a particularly bright blue pen with a soft smile.

I dumped my bag on the floor near the desk he sat at.

You came here just because I didn't text? I signed to him after poking at his shoulder to get his attention.

"And I wanted to see how mad Eli got," he said with a smile.

She was angry. She put two and two together even if I didn't tell her.

"She's smarter than she lets on," he said. His eyes narrowed in on my neck. "Why do you wear so much?"

My hand subconsciously tugged on the fabric of my turtleneck and my previously calm heart began pounding in my chest. The tension of the day came back tenfold, and I swallowed hard. I didn't want to lie to him, I *really* didn't. He had been so kind, the only person that didn't want anything from me. Everyone had their ulterior motives, but he *saw* me.

Malik stood up. His frame towered over me. His hands moved to my arms and rubbed them soothingly. "Are you okay, Rosie? Did I say something?"

I shook my head and met his golden eyes. His eyebrows were pulled together, and his eyes were wide.

Concern.

I opened my mouth to speak. I didn't want to hide this from him. Emotion swirled within me, almost choking me.

There was a knock at the door.

"Can we talk?" Eli said from the other side.

Fuck. I met Malik's eyes; he had a small smile as if to ask...*so what now?*

I looked around the room and made a quick decision. I pushed Malik into the bathroom. He gave me a look but I shut the door in his face.

Eli knocked again.

"I heard the door," she said. I let out a sigh and tried to calm my heart as I made my way to the door.

These others are going to kill me.

With a silent prayer that Malik would stay undiscovered, I opened the door and came face to face with Eli. One arm was stretched out against the threshold of the door and the other was up as if she was going to knock again. I looked around her and noticed for the first time in a while, she was alone.

"Can I come in?" she asked lowering her arm. I was taken aback by her tone. I had only seen her a few ways and this...calm yet sullen demeanor wasn't one of them.

I grabbed her hand.

What do you want? I snapped in her mind.

"Why did you say that earlier?" she asked. There was no anger—her words sounded strangely hallow.

Because it's not hard to put two and two together, I said trying to find an excuse, but I couldn't stop the memory of Matt and me in the garden from popping up.

Eli pushed her way in and shut the door behind her. Her grip on my hand tightened.

"I knew that low-level deserved the burn you gave him." Eli spat the words out. "Why would you lie like that? Just because Daxton can't control himself doesn't mean I am the same."

I raised my eyebrow at her words.

"I've done bad things but I am not vindictive. I am in control," she insisted. I tried to step back but she pulled my hand to her chest. "I didn't choose this life you know that, right?"

I swallowed thickly. The last time we were this close and in my room...

It bothers you when I think of you as the gang member you are, I noted.

"Because I'm more than that!" she snapped. Her words almost threw me off; they were pained and vulnerable. I understood this reaction too well. I knew where she was coming from. Just like her gang status, I was not just my curse.

What about Daxton? I pried.

"I can't speak for before I met him but he never lost control that bad when I was with him," she answered.

Almost did, I pushed.

"I stopped him before it got that far," she admitted. Her other hand clamped down on my shoulder.

Why are you here, Eli? I asked getting tired of the back and forth. *So you are not a dangerous gangbanger murderer? Great. Doesn't excuse your behavior.*

Eli let out a loud sigh.

"Look, yes I came because I couldn't have you thinking I was this murder crazed... When you said that, I could hear the disgust in your mind... I just didn't... I couldn't...not from you." She let out another sigh. "...*I'm sorry.*" Her voice was so small I almost didn't hear it.

I was so stunned I could only blink at her words. Eli pouted slightly, pulled me forward harshly and crushed her lips to mine. It was a short kiss, a peck, and over before my mind caught up. Her hand was already on the door when she spoke next.

"I won't mention the Malik thing again... I was just worried." She gave me a small smile that looked out of place on her face.

I was so grateful she wasn't able to hear my mind right now because the only image I had was how Malik was locked away in the bathroom not ten feet away from us.

I stood there stunned even after she left and shut the door behind her. I heard Malik open the door and come to stand by my side.

"Ooohhh little Eliza has a crush," he said with a laugh.

Chapter Sixteen
Rosie

By the time Friday came the feeling of guilt had almost become unbearable.

Eli was back to her normal self and never mentioned the apology after the fact, but I couldn't get it out of my head. I couldn't bring myself to care about what they were hiding anymore. I was too consumed with my own guilt.

I wanted to tell Eli she was right, I did see Malik, but he wasn't as bad as they said. I wanted to tell her that Malik could *see* me. But...

Looking at her now over breakfast I couldn't bring myself to do it. She was smiling as if she was on top of the world and I didn't want to fight with her anymore. That apology... That was *seeing* me too wasn't it? That counted, right?

"Eat," Daxton said from my other side and pushed my plate in front of me. "You need energy for tonight."

Matt choked on his food. I didn't pay him any mind. Daxton's eyes were asking questions again. My guilt intensified. The need to apologize to him even though I never uttered my disgust to him, overwhelmed me. Could he see through me? I should have known Daxton wasn't the way Matt portrayed him.

Eli's hand found its way to mine. *I didn't tell him what Matt said. He's sensitive about it.*

I feel bad, I confessed and looked away from Daxton's questioning gaze.

He did lose control. You were on the right track, but he won't hurt you. I won't let it get to that, Eli told me and then removed her hand once more.

"Can I come this time?" Matt asked with a pout. He rested his now fully healed hand under his chin. Daxton offered the other morning to heal his hand and my guilt grew as large as Winterfell tower. With one look at Matt I knew that he must feel it too.

"No." Eli, Daxton, and Rae spoke at the same time.

Matt lowered his head with a loud sigh.

* * *

Please tell me this one doesn't hurt, I begged Eli as I threaded my hand into hers.

"This one doesn't hurt, right Daxton?" Eli asked.

Apparently, due to the type of experiment this was, they preferred to stay away from our usual spot in the garden and go to a more *private* area that just so happened to also be Rae's room. I tried not to let my mind race at the thought of being stuck in such tight quarters with three of the hottest demons in school. It didn't help that I had already kissed two of them. At least once this was over, I could leave to my own dorm quickly.

We did more than kiss, Eli shot back at me.

"It won't hurt. I tested it on Amr," Daxton told me. I glared at him.

Animal cruelty.

"He's magical—it doesn't count," Eli responded to my thoughts. I took the vial but again hesitated and looked toward Rae hoping that she would change her mind, or at least warn me if it would be painful. Instead of answering my prayers she just gave me a nod.

I sighed and downed it.

This one was much more pleasant than whatever poison they had given me before. At first, it was a strong cooling sensation and then it felt like the weight was taken off my shoulders. For a moment, my body felt suspended in air, but as soon as it started it stopped. I was left feeling nothing. It was like a dream; no happiness or giddiness came with it, just something akin to an out-of-body experience.

I met Daxton's intense gaze and cocked my head. "Is that it?" My words came out without a second thought. I waited and waited. I expected the cuts to come but they didn't. I looked at my hands and pushed up my sleeves searching for something. Was time just slowing? But no, the cuts never showed.

I looked at the demons around me. They were all staring at me, even

157

Amr. They were waiting for an answer. I could tell they were holding their breath.

"It worked," he said. "Say more."

"I don't know where to begin," I told them. Again, no cuts. "I've never been able to do this before. So, I don't even know how to do this."

"Amazing," Rae whispered. I looked over at her and watched as she furiously wrote on her notepad.

"Well now that you can speak. Tell us what you have been dying to. Or ask us anything," Eli teased but her smile didn't reach her eyes.

"You are upset that my curse is gone," I summarized and pulled my fingers away from her.

"I did want to play around with it more," she admitted. "But we will have time for that later." She gave me a wink.

"Later?" I asked looking at Daxton.

"We suspect that the potion will last for a month. But at least during this time, it is gone," she said, her eyes shifting from mine slightly. Did she normally not look at me when she talked?

"Gone?" I mused and looked at my hands. They all of a sudden didn't look like they belonged on my body.

"What's something you always wanted to do?" Eli asked. "Choose anything."

Instead of answering I brought out my phone. I thought to call my parents, but instead a perfectly useless idea popped into my mind. I dialed a number that had been saved in my phone for years.

I was met with a polite voice on the other end.

"Hi, I would like a pizza delivered to Winterfell Academy." I paused when they asked me a question. "Uhh large I guess? Cheese please. And cinnamon rolls please." They confirmed my order and said it would be delivered in thirty minutes. I met the surprised stares of the demons in front of me.

"You can talk and the first thing you do is order a pizza?" Daxton asked.

"I wanted to talk on the phone," I explained. "And I think I'm hungry."

"That's all?" Rae asked this time.

I shook my head. I never thought this moment would come but I took a deep breath in and let out a scream. It was so loud and raw that I had to cover my own ears. My voice had not been able to do this since I was ten and it wore my vocal cords out before Eli could slam her hand over my mouth. She tackled me and pushed my head into the carpet so even if I wanted to continue screaming I could not.

"Jesus, low-level what the fuck?" she yelled at me. There was a pause, probably waiting to see if anyone came running. I replied but my voice was muffled. Her hand that was gripping my hair pulled back roughly, exposing my neck and making me arch painfully against her chest.

"My name is Rosie," I groaned out. "Not low-level."

"Yes, *Rosie*." My name coming out of her mouth sounded so dirty. "Do you realize you could have just outed your secret to everyone here?"

"No, I just needed to scream," I said truthfully. "You are starting to hurt my hair," I added and she pushed me off her.

"I am not sure this potion was worth this," Eli grumbled.

"Time will tell," Rae told her.

* * *

The others made sure that I stayed near them all day. Luckily, I had my pizza to tide me over. After being able to talk for a few hours, I realized that I did enjoy being silent—if I had a choice when I could speak that is.

I didn't know how to talk to them or what to say now that I had endless words. For the last nine years I had been nothing but an observer and only hoped that someone would care enough to *see* me for who I really was because I didn't have a chance to connect with them like a normal human. This was how normal people did it, I realized. They would force themselves to talk and connect. I had been waiting for this moment for the majority of my life and now that it was here...I had no idea what to say. All the words that were on the tip of my tongue died as soon as I had the ability to speak.

I can't do this, I summarized. I wanted to be normal and talk with them but I could not contribute to anything of value.

Amr stretched lightly from across the room and walked over to where I was sitting on the ground with my pizza in hand. Rae was the only one who opted to sit on a chair. It took some convincing, but she also accepted a slice of pizza. Eli and Daxton were comfortable sitting on the floor with me. Eli was laying on her side and Daxton was sitting cross-legged. They were hovering like they thought I would have a meltdown or something. They would look over at me but didn't bother to really try to start a conversation. I put my pizza down on the plate, wiped my hands on my pants, then scooped up the sleepy cat, burying my face in his fur.

"You were the one that I really wanted to talk to, but you have been such a sleepy head," I cooed at him and held him at arm's length. These words almost felt like a lie coming out of my mouth. I didn't really want to talk at all. Was that what I was boiling down to now, a bunch of lies? The cat even cocked his head like he was confused. "You should visit me more often. My bed is cold without you."

There was a choked laugh that came from Eli. She was already on her fifth pizza, but she put it down to shoot me a smirk. "I could change that."

"No," I replied simply and gave the cat a small kiss on the nose. Another pause filled the air.

"You will have to be watched tonight anyways though," Rae said from her spot at the table. "During the time you are under the potion you will be staying here."

"Why you?" I asked. Her topaz eyes met mine. There was something behind there I couldn't read.

"Because I can read your emotions," she replied like it was a stupid question. "And someone has to make sure there are no adverse side effects. I am the only one that can keep an eye on you *without touching you*." My eyes shot toward Eli.

"Why do you need to watch me at all?" I brought the cat back to my chest. "Amr is sufficient enough, no? I thought you said he was magical." His soft paw batted at a strand of hair as I spoke to him.

"If you want to chance having your airways cut off again, be my guest." She huffed lightly. I paused and as if on cue, a small sliver of panic played at my senses. It was so small that I almost didn't feel it but compared to the cool numbing of the potion it felt like a tidal wave.

"I'll stay," I whispered wanting the panic to go away. The coldness was a much better feeling. When the residual panic subsided, I stuffed a cinnamon roll in my mouth and let Amr lick the icing off my fingers. "Sugar is bad for you," I scolded but didn't push him away.

"I want to stay too." Eli fake pouted.

"I thought you were bored without my curse?" I shot at her.

Eli opened her mouth to answer but Rae cleared her throat. "There is only one bed and I would rather gouge my eyes out than see Eli naked again."

Trust me she likes it, Eli's twinkling eyes whispered to me.

* * *

"I will study for the next few hours," Rae told me after the others had left. I looked toward the clock; it was already past eleven. "Feel free to...wash and sleep."

I nodded at her and rummaged in the overnight bag that I had brought with me. Eli had gone with me to pack extra clothes earlier to make sure that

I would be prepared. She'd tried to start something in the room by pushing me against the wall and groping me but the action that would normally cause my knees to go weak didn't really seem like much in the moment. Besides that, neither Eli nor Daxton had much of anything to say about my *sleepover* with Rae, but you could tell in the way that they lingered that they were none too happy with the idea.

After I found my nightclothes and toiletries I went to wash in the connected bathroom While her dorm may have been the mirror image of mine it didn't stop the feeling of being out of place. It wasn't really a feeling, but more of a fact. Looking at her tidy bathroom sink it was painfully obvious who lived here. There was a case for her glasses, organic skin care, a fancy electric toothbrush, and even teeth whitening stuff.

I placed my clothes on the counter and opened up one of the many creams that spanned across the entire marble surface. It smelt light and fresh and had a hint of...rainforest? I shrugged and placed it back on the counter. I turned on the shower and as I waited for the water to heat up, I found the same brand of hair care and body care products tucked away in the shower.

She sure is on brand, I thought to myself. *I wonder how much she spends on all this?*

Undressing, I caught myself in the mirror. It wasn't enough to jar me— not that I could really process much of anything now—but it was obvious enough to make me pause. I had gained weight since being at this school. Turning in front of the mirror I caught sight of my newly filled out body; it was a nice improvement.

I wouldn't say my parents *abused me...* More like they wanted to forget I existed but it wasn't like they withheld food from me at any point. I ran my hand across my lightly protruding stomach. It was because I tried to stay away from them as long as I possibly could, leading to missed dinners and late-night snacks when they were asleep.

"Ms. Miller? Everything alright?" Rae asked behind the closed door. I cocked my head at her voice, watching in the mirrors as my long black hair fell around me.

I would need to get that cut soon too.

"Yes, fine," I responded and entered the piping hot shower.

Even after spending so long in the bathroom, I found myself lingering under the spray. Lathering up my body with soap longer than necessary, and washing my hair not once, but twice. Uneasiness was creeping up on me, but I couldn't tell from where.

"Is this it?" I asked myself staring at my pruned hands. "Is this what my life will be now?"

"Ms. Miller, are you alright?" Rae's voice was muffled by the sounds around me.

"I'm not dead yet," I responded and washed the excess soap off my body. It was maple, I realized after washing it off.

After drying and dressing in an oversized shirt and shorts I went back out to the room. Rae was at the table bent over various papers and a book that seemed to weigh at least five pounds. Her eyebrows were pushed together and she was scribbling on one of the notebooks near her. I walked over and peered over her shoulder to get a closer look at the culprit that could cause someone like her to make a face like that.

It was a third-year U.S. Government book. I tried to decipher some of the words on the paper but I didn't get very far as my wet hair began dripping onto the white paper leaving semitransparent dots all along the sheet. Rae looked up at me with a sigh. With her out of the way I could see what she was reading.

Demon uprisings.

My vision was blocked by a blinding white.

A fluffy towel had been draped over my head. I lifted my hand to remove it but I paused when two strong hands start ruffling the towel over my head. Rae was gentle as she toweled off my hair, never too rough and she didn't pull at my hair as she squeezed it dry. I felt her warmth behind me but she didn't try to breach the space between us.

"That textbook probably costs more than anything you've ever paid for in your life," she commented. Her voice was still even, with no hint of anger. I leaned back into her ministrations. A feeling of warmth, though small, sparked throughout my cold body. She paused and removed the towel. "There is a dryer if you need it." She pushed the towel in my hands and sat back down at the table focusing back on the still wet textbook.

I watched her for only a moment before returning the towel to the bathroom. I decided to forgo the blow dryer and head straight to bed, exhaustion prickling at my senses. The first thing I noticed about her bed was that she changed the standard school sheets and comforter to something expensive. The fabric was smooth as I ran my hand down it and the comforter was at least five inches thick. Peeling back the cover I wrapped myself in it and let out a sigh as I sunk into the bed. It also smelt like her maple body wash but there was another unknown scent.

My consciousness began to slip easily and before I knew it I was falling asleep to the soft scratching of Rae's pen against her many notebooks.

It was soothing to no longer be left in silence.

* * *

My chest became unbearably tight. I couldn't breathe. My lungs were on fire. There was something on me. Hot and heavy. I clawed at the figure but it did not budge.

I was thrown violently by the demon that held me in my dream and sat up and pushed the covers off of my shaking form. I took gulps of air trying to calm the pounding in my chest. My mess of hair clung to my sweaty face and I pushed it off in a hurry to catch whatever I had felt in my dream.

There was nothing moving in the dark. The only thing that broke the stillness of the night was the pounding of my heart and my deep breaths of air. Rae. But she must have been deep asleep because she didn't even stir when I awoke.

My eyes flitted to the mass under the covers beside me. The moonlight coming through the dorm window provided just enough light so that I could see the outline of Rae's features.

They were more relaxed than I'd ever seen on her and with her glasses absent it was like I was looking at a different person. The face that was always so guarded, the same one that watched the entire group like a hawk, was slack. The crease between her brows was gone, her jaw was loose, and her lips were parted slightly.

One of her arms was caressing the pillow underneath her head and the other was stretched out like she was trying to reach for something. My heart had calmed when I realized it was Rae that was beside me but seeing, and feeling, her so close made it speed up again.

I laid back down but this time I faced her. I had to push myself further away from her as her hand reached forward once more. Searching. I gulped, suddenly nervous.

Her lower lip quivered lightly and her brow creased. My heart melted in that instant and I knew that I had no choice.

It's not like anyone would know, I thought to myself.

With that thought swirling around my head I hesitantly intertwined my fingers with hers. The same gut-wrenching feeling that I now could name as terror battered my body. I snapped my hand from hers. This time she did move but only slightly and it was to clench her hand around the empty air.

I watched her for a second more. There was barely a twitch. My mind whirled with possibilities.

I can sense emotions, she had told me, but could she also project them?

Her stillness was so unnerving that I almost thought that I had dreamt it all up. This time I lightly brushed the tip of my finger on her hand. Terror shot through me like a jolt of electricity, leaving my finger tingling as I pulled away.

I swallowed thickly. *Well... Better to ask for forgiveness than permission.*

I kicked her shin with my foot hoping that it would wake her from her deep slumber. It may have been a bit too hard because a groan filled the silent room. I ignored the shivers it sent down my spine.

"What the fuck, *Rosie?*" Her voice held obvious annoyance. Not a second later all the emotions that were making my chest heavy washed away. I could make out the soft glowing of her hazel eyes in the moonlight.

"I think you were projecting," I told her, gripping the blanket tight against me as I backed away from her.

"You felt it?" she asked, surprise filling her voice. I could see just barely how her eyes widened.

I cleared my throat. "Yes." I was unsure what I should mention. Would she be angry? Get defensive? She was normally so stoic and to catch her so... vulnerable was something I didn't know how to handle.

"Sorry... Was it bad?" Her voice was barely above a whisper.

"I should be asking you that. You were feeling some pretty heavy stuff."

I could only slightly make out the way her hands ran themselves across her face. "Just stress."

"Does that..." I paused as she shifted. I didn't know if she was aware how much closer that made our bodies. The heat was radiating off of her. "... Happen often?"

"More than I'd like to admit," she replied. I wondered briefly if she was more comfortable talking in the dark like this. She let out a long sigh and I heard the blanket rustle, like she was holding it closer. "It's hard to sleep well with someone in a bed. The dreams make it almost impossible."

"I can sleep on the floor," I told her and sat up ready to launch myself onto the floor. The emotions came then, the self-consciousness. It was small but enough for me to realize that I was overstepping. Not only did I ask her such personal questions but I took over her bed. She never wanted me here, obviously, but she did it to aid me. To aid her friends in graduating earlier.

"No." Her hand shot out and wrapped around my wrist. I held my breath. Her hand was strong and warm against the chill of my skin. "*Please just stay.*"

I didn't have time to even think about how vulnerable the words sounded. Even as dismissive as she had been the entire time I had known her, the words that she spoke were filled with something that made my stomach clench. A wave of exhaustion hit me like a truck and all thoughts of moving left me as I flopped back to the bed.

"If you want something just ask," I said in a weak voice. I curled into a ball leaving space between us but I did not dare try to pry her fingers off my wrist. There was something there, a connection. I wanted to put it down to the tiredness, but I knew that where her long fingers circled around my wrist, was a connection.

Darkness consumed me before I could think about it. I could have sworn I heard a curse coming from Rae but that, I knew, had to be a dream.

* * *

I was awoken by a violent pounding.

Bolting up from my sleeping position I looked through blurry eyes to see what was happening.

"Eli, calm down," Rae groaned from the end of the room. She had a coffee cup in hand and was already dressed in somewhat casual clothing. This was only the second time that I had seen her in anything but a uniform. She had on a loose cream cable-knit sweater and black jeans.

God those jeans. My still sleep-heavy brain could not see anything other than the way those dark jeans hugged her lower half as she walked past the bed. Opening the door, we were met with a casually dressed Eli as well. The first time I had seen her she was in a button-up, but now she was wearing a large band t-shirt and tight black jeans. Her hair was still slicked back but paired with her outfit, she looked like a whole mess of trouble. It didn't help that her tattoos were out in the open.

"Does the low-level want to get out of here?" Eli asked with a devilish grin completely ignoring the glare Rae was giving her.

"Um..." I floundered for words and pushed myself out of the bed.

"Where is Daxton?" Rae asked and shut the door behind Eli. It took me this long to realize that Rae was not wearing her glasses. Her hazel eyes met mine and I played with the edge of my shirt to rid myself of her gaze.

Get yourself together, Rosie, I chided myself.

"Sleeping as usual," Eli answered. It only took three strides for her to reach me and yank me into a standing position. "Let's leave the others and go get some breakfast, hm?"

Eli pulled me to her chest. Her blue eyes were almost twinkling, and her head was dipping closer to me.

"I'm coming too," Rae said and yanked the back of Eli's shirt effectively detangling her from me. "It would be a good experiment."

Eli glared at Rae. Rae just stared back and sipped her coffee, never breaking eye contact.

I sucked in a deep breath and made my way to the bathroom.

* * *

"You're ordering," Rae told me from across the booth and closed her menu. Eli let out a snicker from beside me and also put down her menu.

They brought me to a small diner that wasn't too far away from the campus. I was surprised that they would dare choose something so cheap-looking but when I looked at Rae for an answer she just shrugged and walked in.

It was a normal American diner that was already filled with people. Many were low-levels and they paused when we walked in, obviously feeling the aura that the high-levels that were on either side of me gave off. Apart from their stares, I noticed the delightful smell of a sweet blueberry syrup that I knew I would have to try.

"I don't know what you want," I said in a harsh whisper as the waitress walked over. I had watched her take the orders of the other patrons but her smile and laugh were real at that time. Now her smile was tight as she walked to our booth.

"Take a guess, *Rosie*," Eli said from my side. Her hand reached out to graze mine. *It's not food.*

I met Rae's eyes. Nervousness was flooding into me, then was extinguished like a flame. I let out a small sigh.

"Welcome, what can I get for you," the waitress said as she came to a stop at the end of our table. Her brown hair was up in a bun and she donned solid black clothing. She had smile lines but besides that, her face was youthful. She didn't have a paper or pen to take orders, I noted.

"Um... I would like the pancakes with blueberry syrup, please," I told her and searched the menu for the others. "A coffee for both of them, and uhhh..."

"Eggs benedict for me," Rae said saving me from having to decide for her. "French toast for her." She gestured toward Eli. "And sunny side up eggs with hash browns for our friend who will join us shortly. Oh and two iced teas."

The waitress shifted and with a nod she headed back toward the rear of the building where the kitchen staff was. They were all glaring daggers at us.

"At least you got a coffee for us," Eli said with a smug voice.

The waitress came with a tray and set down the drinks in front of us. "Creamer?" she asked with a dull tone.

"If you would be so kind," Rae responded politely. She put down a bowl of creamer so roughly I thought the ceramic would crack. I jumped at the noise.

"I can't believe you guys left me." Daxton's voice came from behind me. The waitress was the one to jump at his interruption. Daxton's tall form moved around the waitress with grace and plopped down into the booth next to Rae. Amr was resting comfortably in his hands.

"Animals are not allowed in here," the waitress said with a huff.

"That's weird," Eli said with a chuckle. "Then why are you here?"

The waitress looked horrified with her comment. I wanted to hate the comment, I really did, but the way she stomped away ignited a small trickle of amusement in me.

Rae shook her head and pushed an iced tea toward Daxton and then one toward me. I raised my eyebrow at her; she merely sipped her coffee.

"How was the sleepover?" Eli asked from beside me.

I couldn't help but look at Rae, remembering the way her voice sounded last night. Her glasses fogged up slightly when she lifted her cup.

"She has expensive taste in bedding," I commented then sipped on my tea. The sweetness washed over my tongue and I let a smile grace my lips. It was pretty good.

Daxton let out a snort. "You should see her room at home, it looks like it was built for a queen."

"I didn't take you as Rae's type." The words left my mouth before I could stop them. Rae choked on her coffee. Eli looped her arm around my neck and began laughing. Daxton just looked at me with an expression mixed with shock and slight amusement.

"As opposite as they seem..." Eli said, noting just how odd they looked sitting together. Rae was sitting up straight in her booth looking put together while Daxton's hair was a mess on his head, and he wore a ratted oversized shirt with a cat in his arms. "They do get along well enough."

"She can be annoying sometimes," Daxton commented and took a sip of his iced tea. The comment held no weight and there was a slight smile playing at Rae's lips.

"At least I'm not brain dead," Rae replied. Eli let out a snicker.

"I'm not the one who let the lab rats loose *right before* the class was going to dissect them," Daxton shot back, a smile playing at his lips as well.

"It just wasn't their time," Rae said not denying the claim at all.

"Rae loves animals," Eli mentioned leaning close to me as if she was telling a secret. I drank it up. Everything I was witnessing seemed like something that no one else would see. "The first time I met her she was telling her dog all the reasons why she should not be allowed to jump on furniture *yet* she couldn't help but let her sleep in the bed at night."

"Eli, stop telling lies," Rae said not looking at her. The tips of her ears were flushed.

"There is no lie," Daxton said and lifted up Amr as if he was a baby. "Isn't that right Amr? I swear Rae started cussing Amr out for clawing at the dog."

"He made her bleed."

"See?" Eli said gesturing to Rae's blushing face. "There is no lie here."

A giggle bubbled in my chest and made its way through my lips. All three heads snapped toward me.

My laughter ceased immediately.

"What?" I asked not liking the way they stared at me. Daxton looked toward Rae but her eyes were firmly on mine.

I don't think we've ever heard your laugh, Eli said through the mental bond. *It's nice.*

The waitress brought us our food with a scowl and the rest of the meal went with small conversations in between each bite.

The softness of the moment did not get past me. It was nice to be a part of something so intimate. From the outside it looked like just a bunch of college kids having breakfast but from the inside...I don't remember a time where I felt so content.

I don't remember a time where I could share something like this moment with anyone else. I was finally a part of something that no one else would see. They wouldn't have the chance to. I was overjoyed at the thought of being able to call this moment in time *mine.*

Rae called for the cheque after we had all eaten our fill.

The blueberry pancakes were divine. Way more syrup and sugar than I needed in the morning but even as I downed the rest of my tea, I couldn't come to regret it.

"This has already been paid for by table three," the waitress said and muttered just loud enough for us to hear as she walked away. "Not like you need it."

I looked over my shoulder to the table she had motioned to, and two feelings hit me simultaneously. First, bone-chilling panic comparable to being flung off the clock tower at Winterfell.

The second, was a happiness that I did not know I possessed. It was unabridged, uncontrolled; it ran free through my veins as I met golden eyes.

There at the lone booth sat a mess of fluffy white curls that I would recognize anywhere. A grin broke out on his face. He sent a wave to our table.

A rough hand cupped itself over my eyes and I was thrust into darkness while Eli cradled me to her chest.

"Don't look," she said with a growl.

"She already did," Rae said. Her voice had an edge to it. "I felt his satisfaction."

There was a shuffling but no one moved.

"Come on Eli, she already saw me, nothing you could do now." Malik's voice came from in front of me. "Don't fight me." I could feel the magic that his power held when he spoke. It swirled around the table and similarly to Daxton's it licked at my limbs.

Malik's cold fingers pried Eli's hand away from my face without a fight, just like he knew they would. I knew I shouldn't be happy. I knew I shouldn't give any sign to the others but a smile played at my lips before I could stop it.

"Interesting," he murmured. His eyes searched my face. "Hello little low-level."

My mouth opened and then Eli's hand cupped over my mouth.

What the fuck do you think you are doing? she asked angrily in my mind.

I still in her arms.

What *was* I doing?

"Malik, we don't need your money," Rae said and pushed Daxton out of the booth. "Let's go."

Malik moved so we could leave our spot as well. Eli kept a hand on my neck as she pushed us out of the booth. Malik didn't stop us as we left.

All three others were silent as we made the walk back to the campus.

"Is it too late to get coffee?" I asked after I spotted the coffee spot that I had met Malik in originally.

"Are you kidding?" Eli growled at me, her hand finding its way to the back of my neck once more. I looked toward Daxton and tried to conjure a small pout. To my surprise it was Rae that spoke.

"If he wanted to do something he already would have, Eli," Rae said with a sigh. "No harm in a cup of coffee."

With a smile I moved out of Eli's grip and followed Rae into the coffee shop.

Chapter Seventeen
Rae

Coffee or not, it was not the pout that had me saying yes to this coffee. It was her reaction to Malik.

For this experiment, I had started with taking away all of her emotions and just letting a few of the most potent ones out. I acted like a leech, sucking out all of her emotions and quickly building a wall to keep them behind.

It was arduous work and after more than a few hours I felt myself struggle to keep it up. Contrary to the others' belief, just because I was holding her emotions from her doesn't mean they didn't exist. They still fully rage inside me so everything that she would feel I am now subject to. I suspect that the projecting last night was because of the strain it caused on my powers.

I decided to create cracks in the wall, letting the emotions slowly flow through, but I paid careful attention to those involving fear, anxiety or apprehension of any kind. A few wisps could make their way out, but any more than that put this experiment in danger. Happiness, insecurity, embarrassment, would be fine at the beginning.

Imagine my surprise when I felt a rush of emotions flood through her when she saw Malik. It was like the flood gates had opened. I had worked tirelessly with a village of teachers my father had hired over the years to help me with my power. I knew my shit and I knew how to use it in a way that suited me...but I was not prepared for her emotions.

He caught us all off guard *except* Rosie. When she met his eyes, she was expectant, and when he met hers... He knew he had won.

I eyed her as she waited for her coffee at the end of the counter. Her happiness was almost palpable, but I didn't let that fool me.

What are you hiding?

She gripped the iced latte that the barista handed to her and turned to leave and join Daxton and Eli outside but before she did, I stopped her by placing my hand on her shoulder.

"Is there anything you need to tell me?" I leaned down to whisper in her ear.

The panic was cold and spread across my own body in a cool wave. I let it trickle to her.

"No," she said and took a sip of her latte. I eyed her watching as her brown eyes flitted to mine.

"He's dangerous," I warned her. "His power can ruin you. Don't get carried away no matter how...pleasing he may look."

The confusion that ran through her caught me off guard. It was followed by slight...amusement?

My own anger rose. Was this a game to her?

"I am not thinking of..." She let out a small breathy laugh and met my eyes once more but this time she was prepared. A sly smile spread across her face and for the second time today, her words surprised me. "If you are jealous just say so, *Rae*."

My name on her lips felt like a sin.

She brushed off my hand and left the coffee shop to join the others outside. Eli put an arm over her shoulder, her anger momentarily forgotten as she swooped down to take a sip of her latte. Daxton watched them with an amused smile.

* * *

Eli and Daxton left almost as late as they did the other night but after a slight push and a threat of being late to school in the morning, they left with a grumble.

"Is this the last night?" Rosie said as she climbed back into the bed.

"Let's see how you do tonight then we can rethink our arrangements," I told her and turned off the lights. I knew this wouldn't be the last night though. My words were just to soothe the panic she couldn't even feel.

The act of climbing into a bed with a woman should have put me on edge, but I didn't feel even the slightest bit anxious. Instead, I was looking forward to her next to me as I slept. Last night was the first time that I had slept deeply enough to have a dream. It was a horrible nightmare, but it was something.

After almost being crushed to death in my dream, I was glad to see Rosie's concerned face over me. Even if I was awoken by a kick that bruised my shin. I almost laughed at the absurdity of it but when I felt the emotions rolling off her, I couldn't bring myself to. She was actually worried about me.

When I was a kid, I would pray that I would experience those emotions directed toward me one day by a person that cared about me. I had felt it between other people. Mothers and their children, lovers, friends even, but never my mother or father for that matter. So when a person felt that way toward me, there was no way they could sleep on the floor.

No, after I put her to sleep...I allowed myself to pull her closer. Allowed myself to revel in the feeling of her sleeping body next to me.

The best part?

When I held her she was happy; she felt safe. My heart soared.

So that's why as I got into bed with her now, I cast everything that happened today away. I cast away the thoughts of Malik. I cast away the feeling of her happiness when she saw him. I cast away the thoughts of defending a group that barely felt that kind of worry for me.

Instead, I focused on all the emotions she felt now.

Nervousness, excitement, and a small bit of relief. I let her feel them for now as well.

"Can I ask you something?" she asked. Her small body was facing away from me but as she spoke she turned around. I had taken my glasses off, but she was close enough that I could make out the way her long eyelashes fluttered against her cheek.

"What is it?" I asked.

She brought the cover closer to her. Nervousness was gnawing at her. I took away a little hoping her courage would overpower it.

What could she possibly want to know?

"How did you meet Eli?" she asked and after some deliberation, added, "Actually both. How did you meet them?"

Ah, the power this information could hold, I thought.

"Why not ask them?" I prompted not fully wanting to give her information that could harm them.

I saw her pout again. "I feel like you'd be more truthful," she said. There was something sour playing at her emotions. *A lie.*

"Try again," I told her. The panic was small but enough to up her anxiety.

"I feel...more comfortable asking you," she confided. "Maybe it's the dark but I just...feel okay to talk like this. Ask about things that have been bothering me."

"Why has our relationship been bothering you?" I asked. "I mean mine and the others," I clarified when there was a flash of embarrassment.

"Well Eli is in a gang...and I am not sure about Daxton...but Principal Winterfell said that you had something to do with the government?"

I scoffed at the information she provided. "So, the principal mentioned us? What's the context?"

"To warn me about interacting with you," she said.

Bastard. He deserves what's coming to him.

"My family is powerful," I told her. "People like Eli feed on powerful people like they have never seen a piece of meat in their lives. And well... Daxton's family is also powerful. It would be weird if two powerful families didn't know each other, right?"

She ate up every word I told her with wide eyes. I almost wanted to spill everything to her. The attention she gave me was addicting. It wasn't all that interesting, and I left out enough for it to lack power...but she hung onto every word.

"So that's it. Eli saw an advantage but...people like me are not easy to fool. And with Eli came unfortunately, Daxton," I told her.

"You pretend too much," she said with a small smile. "I saw how you acted today with him."

Her words stirred something in me.

"We get along in our own way," I responded.

"You protect them," she said while lifting her head up and resting it on her arm.

"They are not children," I reminded her. "They do not need protection."

"But you do so anyways," she said, her smile getting bigger. "I've seen it. You are never far from them and you are always guiding them no matter how much they say it annoys them. They listen because they know you know what's best."

My chest swelled painfully. Her words were too much for me to handle. I wouldn't say I was protecting them...it was a group thing. Anything to keep our group...a kind of fucked up makeshift family alive and thriving.

I didn't know if Daxton or Eli ever saw it, but here this random cursed low-level saw right through everything that I had hidden away. I was angered and excited at the same time.

"Let me ask you a question," I said changing the subject before I got too lost in the emotions that were engulfing me. "Were the pancakes that good?"

Confusion rose in her and even if I weren't able to feel emotions the sudden change in her face gave it away. "You were just...really happy while eating them. But if we are being honest...the food was subpar at best."

She let out a small giggle. It was as perfect as the one earlier today, the first one I ever heard from her. And this one was all mine to hear.

"I was just happy to be included in something," she said. "With someone so skilled in reading emotions I would have assumed you knew that."

"I can read emotions," I said with a sigh. "Not their reason for being."

She nodded in the darkness.

"My curse has made it hard for me to be accepted," she said. "From family to friends, I always found myself lacking. And today it really felt like I had found a place that I felt comfortable enough to just...be."

Her words scared me as much as they pained me. There was a part of me that pitied her. Growing up I knew how it felt to be outcasted, to feel like there was nothing I was actually a part of. But the other part did not want a person to ruin our group, even if it was her. We had forged this group together and it was the only thing to this day that I could say that I really belonged.

We were too vulnerable, I realized now after replaying all of our interactions with her in my head. No one had ever gotten as far as her. We didn't *let* anyone because there was just no one that we found worthy enough. And on top of that we all knew the risks of someone getting close enough to know our secrets. We were screwed if this went on any longer.

And I was the one that let this happen.

"That's a lot to spill," she said with a nervous laugh. "Sorry it's just, I think I am getting used to talking."

"It's okay," I told her. "But we should sleep. School tomorrow, remember?"

"Right," she said and plopped down into the bed and turned to face the wall. "Night."

I pumped exhaustion into her and waited until I heard her deep breaths before releasing the wall.

I did not dare try to breach the space between us that night.

* * *

I once thought that the low-level was ruining the group dynamic, but that was an understatement. She absolutely annihilated it and then proceeded to rebuild it in a way that I hadn't thought possible.

It scared me if I was being honest.

Watching her now, sitting next to Eli and Daxton, the pull she had on them was way too obvious. Every twitch, every sigh, every sip of her bottled coffee would cause their eyes to shift toward her.

Eli was more obvious, but that was in her nature. I was not surprised with how she acted around her. I was surprised though by how quickly Daxton came around. He was quiet, always had been. But with the silence came his disinterest in almost all things. Yet his silence was different now; even in his silence he paid attention to her.

Daxton had worried more for this girl than he had for himself through the entire time that I had known him. He had a sense of longing that surrounded him but when he watched Eli interact with her...there was only warmth and content that radiated off of him.

Eli was a different story though. There was normally a prick of lust, a dust of pain, but recently there was an emotion so small and soft starting to sprout that it almost made me stop in my tracks when I first felt it. And watching her now, with her arm around Rosie and her eyes glued on her as she slowly nibbled on her bagel, I felt it once more. If anyone looked at her from the outside they would see the cocky facade that she put on. It looked like she was terrorizing her. But inside...

This was my fault, I summarized.

I told her to stay away because Principal Winterfell had some powerful people looking out for her and I did not want to risk our group's safety. It only catapulted them together. I should have seen it coming: she was not one to listen to rules and the idea of her excited her far too much.

I thought she would be done with her as soon as she had gotten what she wanted—at least that was the lie she spouted to me.

I took a sip of my third coffee today trying to ignore the way the emotions around me made me feel. Eli's hand caressed the back of Rosie's neck and I felt a spike of arousal emanate from her. I knew Eli had to be showing something to her in her mind by the way she blushed and I couldn't help the anger that flared in me.

"We have class, Mr. Thompson," I said getting up from my seat.

I hadn't planned on going through with my plan to abuse Principal Winterfell on one of his free hours so soon but I was not sure how much more I could handle. It was bad enough that she made me go through such stupid emotions, but to have to watch Eli and Daxton react to her in such a way just hammered in how much of a failure I was at protecting our group.

I needed to find out why Principal Winterfell thought she was so important.

Mr. Thompson and I separated with a small wave at the hallways that divided our years, and I watched him walk out of sight before I turned on my heel and headed the opposite way to the office. I was greeted with a cool rush of air as I walked into the office and a very surprised Tammy. She flushed slightly as I walked up to her desk.

"Oh dear, what a surprise." She giggled.

"I suppose so." I sent her a smile. "I have some urgent matters to discuss with Principal Winterfell that cannot wait. I saw that he has a free time now, you wouldn't mind if I squeezed myself in would you?"

Tammy stuttered but before she could fully get out another word the answer showed itself. A man and woman, both with russet hair and brown eyes, left Principal Winterfell's office. It didn't take long to guess that they were witches. Their brown eyes along with the restlessness that resided within them gave that away. But the most surprising thing was that on the outside they looked completely guarded. They looked me over with feigned indifference, but I knew better.

Surprise.

Anger.

Disgust.

Resentment.

And then the emotions coming from Principal Winterfell sealed the deal. *Panic.*

I had to fight to keep the smile off my face. I knew the principal was hiding something and thanks to the anger I felt this morning, I may have just stumbled upon the one thing I needed to seal this deal. I watched as the witches nodded to the principal and left the office without ever looking back at me.

A sort of giddiness rose in me as the principal's eyes met mine from the slightly ajar door to his office. I walked in slowly, enjoying how his panic rose with each step I took.

"To what do I owe the honor?" he asked trying to feign the same indifference that the witches had.

"You know..." I trailed running my hand across the chair. "Witches tend to be wary of high-levels. Especially people in government like me. But..." I met his eyes enjoying the way he flinched. "They seemed to know me. Sadly, I cannot say the same."

"Your family is prominent, who doesn't know you?" he asked.

"Oh come on," I said in mock playfulness. "This couldn't possibly hurt, right? Not like they are important right?"

"I have no information to give you," he said with a tight smile.

"Not even if I tell you I have solved our little curse issue?" He stilled at that.

Curiosity.

Mistrust.

Anxiety.

"Did you now?" he asked trying to not act like he knew of the carrot I was dangling in front of him. It was too irresistible though and he knew that.

I hummed. "Yes. And I would be more inclined to keep you updated about our *project* if you tell me who those witches were."

He sucked in a breath. I was so close to getting what I had been prepping for. I could at least do this for us.

"You have to tell me how you do it," he demanded.

"Only if we succeed," I said. "Tell me, have you been giving them reports on me?"

"Of course. Ever since your gang laid eyes on Ms. Miller." He crossed his arms.

I almost snorted at the way he labeled us. Like *a gang* could hold a candle to what we could do.

"When we succeed, I want us all recognized." He was about to protest but I held up my hand. "And for us to graduate early."

"Impossible." More panic.

"Then I will tell you nothing."

"You get more out of this deal," he fought standing up from his chair and slamming his palms down on the table.

"Then what do you want?" I raised a brow at him.

"Keep her away from Mr. Reid."

I grit my teeth at his words. Why Dax of all people? Was it his parents?

"We are a group package," I insisted. There was no way I would break the group up for her.

"Something *they* aren't too happy about," he said with a huff. He was no doubt referencing the two witches that left earlier.

"Are you afraid he would hurt her?" I pried. My hand clenched the chair so hard that I heard the fabric tear.

"Among other things," he admitted, his eyes suddenly transfixed on the floor.

"Then I can promise you I will not let him hurt her."

"Keep their alone time to a minimum," he ordered.

"Fine," I spit out. "Names."

"Claudine and Maximus," he gave.

"Last names."

"Believe it or not they don't have them. Or at least that is what they told me." I could not sense his lie so I nodded and turned to leave.

"I will update you once we succeed."

"I expect more information in our next meeting," he called. "And remember, I have eyes."

I rolled my eyes at his threat not caring if Tammy saw. She had outlived her usefulness.

I stalked down the hallway with anger swirling deep in my chest. I was the one that got us into this mess and while I didn't feel too bad about having to pull Daxton away from Rosie...I did feel bad about hiding my motives.

It was my fault anyways.

* * *

"I need more magic," Dax said that night as we settled in my room once more.

"Out of the question," I answered. Daxton and Eli's spikes of arousal were enough to send me reeling. I had to grind my teeth and take a deep breath before I responded. I couldn't let such a useless emotion cloud my judgment like it had been.

"It's the only thing that calms it," Dax hissed at me.

The principal's words weighed on my mind.

What if it wasn't alone?

I could oversee it, make sure that nothing happened. My mouth went dry when I remembered the way they handled her in the garden.

"Eli has to leave," I told them.

"Not fair!" She pouted.

I hadn't been as strict on Rosie's emotions and I watched a small smile curl at her lips while amusement rolled off her in waves. It made my heart tighten painfully.

I didn't mean to talk so much. My own actions in regard to her opening up weighed on my conscience.

"What happened last time is not happening again. Especially because we don't know how the *potion* will react to it," I told her and glared at them daring them to ruin that plan we put together. I glanced toward Rosie. "Are you willing to help him?"

She thought over it for a second biting her lip softly. I wanted to tell her to stop that after feeling the others' emotions, but she came to her conclusion too fast. "Will a kiss work?" she asked. Eli let out a laugh.

"Not unless other things are happening with it," Daxton explained. Her eyes sought mine. She was looking for an answer that I could not give her.

"I can give you some blood. But Eli can stay as long as she won't touch me," she said after some consideration. I was surprised to hear that she listened to me. I didn't like the way it made my heart pound and my chest swell.

"You didn't say that last time." Her smile fell. "Don't tell me you didn't like it?"

"I liked it." She paused and I knew that if I let her emotions go just slightly, her cheeks would be bright red. "Just not really in the mood." Cue the daggers from both Eli and Daxton.

The satisfaction that I felt at their annoyance was too sweet.

Rosie held out her arm for Daxton as an invitation, her eyebrow raised slightly as if she was taunting him. He dug around in his pocket for a knife and wasted no time in slicing a thin line down her forearm.

When his mouth was on her wound I had to grab onto the table next to me. Daxton's rituals were hell normally but now that I was in charge of keeping her emotions under lock and key I could think of no worse punishment.

His lust was suffocating the room as the magic from the curse entered him. I found myself losing control slightly as heat pooled in my stomach. Eli gave me a knowing smirk but her attention was drawn to Rosie when she let out a whimper. I tried to patch the holes in my defenses but the emotions were overpowering and I could not keep a hold on them.

I was relieved when Dax detached his mouth from her arm without me asking. Any longer and I would have been on my hands and knees begging for him to let up.

"It's the same as last time."

"Obviously," I hissed at him letting out a deep painful breath. I had to shift slightly in my chair. I shouldn't have gotten that wet from those feelings. "That's enough. You two leave for the night." They didn't argue this time, but Eli did stop to give Rosie a passionate open-mouthed kiss. She sent me a look before leaving.

Bastard.

* * *

Rosie was curled under the blankets just as she had been the night before. There was nothing different from last night. Or there really shouldn't have been.

Just a low-level...in my bed. Just a low-level that had caused all sorts of emotions to course through me that I hadn't been prepared to handle. Just a low-level that just so happened to have more mystery surrounding her than demon heritage itself.

I keep women out of my bed for a reason, but our current situation literally forced us together and it was hard not to regret doing this even if the pros outweighed the cons by tenfold. It was my fault anyway.

I had let go of her emotions as soon as she fell asleep and it was like a weight had been lifted off of my shoulders. Even hours after the others had left, the effects of the magic transfer were still evident in the room. I clenched my fist against my pajama pants and with a huff I entered the bed with her.

I was relieved when she stayed still. Her emotions were stable and dulled in her dream state. I let out a sigh and tried to force myself to sleep. Only after a minute Rosie's warm body pressed against mine.

My eyes snapped open and I was met with a cloud of black hair. Rosie had pushed her back all the way to my chest and now lay flushed against me. I stiffened against her unsure what to do or where to put my hands. The other nights she had maintained space, and even when I had held her the other night it was all me.

I should push her away.

It took all that I had last night to not wrap my arm around her. I inhaled her scent deeply. She smelt just like my shampoo. I couldn't help myself this time, my resolve from the day had already been destroyed. I wrapped my arm around her body and pulled her closer without a second thought.

No one would know. The principal asked me to keep her away from Daxton...which I did. He didn't say anything about me. And it wasn't like I would be able to push her away from us, that was obvious. If it was my fault she was here with us...then I might as well take advantage of this.

Man, the possibilities, Eli had said this morning as we watched Rosie bolt out of the room. She then gave me that stupid fucking smile. I prided myself in being able to know everything about everyone around me but Eli was the only one that could *truly see me.* Even without reading my mind she knew exactly what I wanted.

I inhaled against her hair deeply once more. I liked that my scent surrounded her. I liked it a bit *too much.*

She sighed deeply as she slept and wiggled against me, trying to get closer to the heat I assumed. My throat dried when I felt her ass wiggle against me. I gritted my teeth and buried my head in her hair. I closed my eyes and tried to think of anything other than her soft body. But with the pungent magic that was left in the room and the far too powerful emotions, it only exacerbated the problems and my grip around her tightened.

She wiggled again.

This time I felt her surprise as she woke. Maybe I could pretend I was asleep?

"Rae?" she whispered. I wasn't holding her emotions back so I expected to feel her curse, but it never came. Instead, there was a dull arousal that weighed low in her.

"I'm sorry," I told her hoarsely and loosened my grip slightly. She gripped my wrist and wrapped my arm around her higher. Did she not understand what she was doing to me? My hand twitched wanting so badly to feel her.

"Don't be," she said her voice equally as hoarse. Still no panic but arousal sharply rose in her followed by a dust of confidence.

Oh no.

Her slim hand slowly trailed along my arm and then down to my hand where she linked her hand with mine. In one swift movement she brought my hand and placed it under her shirt on the smooth skin of her stomach. Her hand lingered for a moment and then trailed back up my arm and out of her shirt.

She was giving me a choice. A stupid choice. Horrible choice.

Her breath hitched when I slowly inched my hand upward lightly trailing along the underside of her breast. My heart was going to burst out of my chest but I couldn't stop the images of what I wanted to do to her from flooding me.

"Are you sure this is what you want?" I asked her rubbing the pad of my finger ever so lightly over her nipple. She gasped and arched.

"Please," she rasped.

"Is this just because of the bloodletting?" I asked grinding against her backside. I knew the arousal from earlier was affecting her even as I asked. I could dream though couldn't I?

"No," she said with a gasp when I lightly trailed circles around her nipple feeling the peak harden under my touch.

"Are you sure?" I asked one more time. "When I want to bed a woman I want it to be because they *want me.*"

"*I want you.*" In turn her hand came back in between us then pushed itself between my legs. I groaned against her and widened my legs for her. She quickly slipped her hand into my pajama pants, past my panties, and made direct skin-to-skin contact. I hissed and began pinching her nipples lightly. When her delicate fingers began to tease my clit I lost myself. Yanking her hand out I climbed over her and connected her lips with mine.

They were softer than they looked.

Her mouth opened and I brushed my tongue across her, enjoying the way it ignited sparks in me. She moaned against my mouth and her hands yanked at my sleep shirt pulling me closer to her. Her tongue played against mine, trying to dominate me but I wouldn't allow it.

I pulled off her shirt between our frantic kisses. She tried to pull off mine but instead I pushed her hands to her shorts and I rose to take off my shirt myself. I paused to look at her naked body. She had taken off her underwear and shorts already. I desperately wished I had my glasses so I could get a good look but even now seeing her bared to me and waiting to be fucked caused my core to clench. She tried to pull my pajama pants down but I grabbed her wrist.

"Later," I told her and leaned down to give her a chaste kiss. She wrapped her hands in my hair gently. I trailed my hand slowly down the length of her body. Past her hips. And pushed her legs farther open. I teasingly ran my finger up her already wet slit. I was praised with a small moan from her. She was still not panicked at the noises she was making.

Good.

I slowly massaged her folds enjoying the way she bucked against me. She tried to pull me down so our lips connected but I refused to give her the satisfaction. The look on her face was just far too sweet to miss. Her parted, swollen lips. Her pants. The way her eyes widened when I circled her clit.

I could feel the pleasure inside her build and I had never been more thankful for my gift than right now. I entered two fingers into her slowly, watching as she threw her head back and arched into me. I rubbed her clit with my thumb and pulled out my fingers only to enter her again. She was so wet and clamped so tightly around my fingers. I couldn't wait to see what she looked like when she came around me. But I would wait, and I would relish every sweet moment she gave me during this time.

If I would throw everything away like this for her it better as hell be worth it.

"Faster," she groaned.

"No rushing," I scolded her but captured her lips once more and just to satiate her I began to push my fingers into her harder. She met each thrust with one of her own. It was a slow build up that I felt rise in her but it was persistent and doubled when I gave her clit the attention it deserved. She gripped tightly at my hair and not a moment later did I hear her cries of release.

I removed my fingers only to bring them up to her own lips. She licked the wetness off eagerly. Her eyes never left mine.

Chapter Eighteen
Rosie

Being with Rae was painfully slow, but I loved every moment of it. She took her time. There was not an inch of my body that she left untouched. It was like she had been starving and couldn't bear to let a single thing slip past her.

She left a line of wet kisses down my body and only stopped so she could hook my leg around her shoulder. She kissed down my thigh slowly, her eyes watching every breath I took, every moan that spilled out of my lips. When her lips finally met my swollen wetness I couldn't help but cry out. Her tongue flicked my clit. I gripped her hair trying to push her closer but I quickly learned, she never gave in. She was calm, collected, and knew exactly what she was after.

"I didn't understand their fascination," she said against me, her voice vibrating through my core. She plunged two fingers into me once more. I gasped for air. "You changed them." I let out a cry when her pounding became more erratic. With each thrust of her fingers I met her hand. With each thrust I felt myself get tighten around her. *Almost there.* Then she stopped.

Her lips were on mine again. I loved the taste of myself on them. "Please," I begged and pushed her pants down with my feet. She let me while never removing her mouth from mine, her slick wet tongue exploring me.

She turned me over harshly so that I was on my stomach. She lifted my hips closer to her and entered three fingers inside me this time. I gripped the sheets and pushed myself against her, allowing her fingers to go deeper.

"Fuck," she groaned from behind me. "Spread them wider."

I did as she commanded and was rewarded with her hand pinching my clit. My mind clouded and I could barely think anything other than how good she felt inside me.

"Rae, I'm so close," I moaned to her. My legs began shaking and I felt as though I would collapse any moment.

It was sensual, the way she moved. She was taking her time, but it wasn't like she was inexperienced and that was why she was slow. Instead, she knew all *too well* what she was doing. No touch was wasted.

Something rose in me faster than lightning and I shuddered as the most powerful orgasm I had ever experience wracked my body.

I collapsed in a heap on the bed as Rae carefully turned me over. Her eyes met mine again briefly and then she swooped back in for a kiss. This one was soft. Her hand was placed on my neck and her fingers pushed my chin up to meet her lips.

"Stay there," she said, her voice in a whisper. She pulled out and went to the bathroom. I admired her stark-naked form as she walked. She was beautiful in the daytime but seeing her at night like this is magical. The moon shone off her skin in an iridescent hue and I was sure that if she had been born just a few centuries earlier, it would be her body that we would see in the stone sculptures that littered the Louvre. I heard the faucet running and not a moment later she came back with a damp towel. She sat on her heels and began cleaning in between my legs. My face flamed at her actions and I didn't know how to react to this. "Don't be embarrassed," she told me.

"You are gentler than I imagined," I whispered as she finished cleaning me. She slowly helped me put my panties back on, pushing my hands away when I tried to do it myself. Next was the shorts but before she pulled them up she left a light kiss on my mound.

"I'm pleased to hear you imagined this," she teased in a light playful tone. She dressed me fully before attempting to put on her own clothes. My hand shot out to stop her.

"Can I try something?" I asked her. Her brow raised in the darkness, and she paused for a moment before putting down her clothes and nodding.

I pushed her back on the bed hungrily taking in her nakedness. She watched me intently as I moved over her. I spread her legs and gulped when I saw how turned on she was by this. I leaned closer but instead of kissing her lips I lightly kissed her cheek, then her jaw, then I trailed my kisses down her neck. She inhaled sharply when my tongue came out to lick her neck.

Her hand threaded through my hair as I trailed down. I looked up at her, meeting her eyes before taking her nipple into my mouth and sucking on it. Her legs spread and she let out a small moan.

I ran my hands up and down her inner thigh loving the way her breath hitched as I got closer to her folds.

"Rosie," she groaned as I bit down and trailed kisses down her stomach. "You don't have to."

"I want to," I said once I came face to face with her swollen pussy. I hesitantly gave it an experimental lick, watching as Rae's head fell back and her hand wrapped tightly around my hair. I dove in and tried to emulate what she had done previously to me. Her soft moans filled the room pushing me forward.

I let my free hand roll her clit and was rewarded with a flurry of curses.

"Fuck, yes. Rosie just like that." She bucked against my mouth.

"Is this good?" I asked and rubbed her clit harder.

"Yes, Rosie. Good. Like that." She pushed me closer to her and I could tell she was going to come soon. "So good."

She came with a loud moan. I leaned up to kiss her and she pulled me closer to her to deepen the kiss.

I tried to clean her up like she did to me but she ended up just taking both of us to the bathroom for a shower. Seeing her in the light of the backroom made me swoon even more for her.

We found ourselves tangled in the sheets not long after our shower. I cuddled to her chest and she played with my hair lightly.

"You don't...act like this around the others," I commented.

"No," she said. "And they will never get to see me like this."

"Why?" I pushed.

"It's not just them," she explained. "This is how it will be for the entire world." She paused. "I don't think that I need to tell you that you probably won't see me act like this again."

No. She did not. I had a sinking feeling that this may be the only time that I would see her like this. "I guessed."

"It hurts your feelings," she commented. Damn empath.

"Yes," I said. "But I'm okay keeping this to myself." I hooked my outstretched pinky on hers. "It's our secret."

She chuckled and hooked her pinky around mine. "Our secret."

* * *

I woke up earlier than I had expected to the smell of coffee and some rustling in her room. I didn't notice the coffee machine before but peering over the covers now it was hard to miss it. And it was most definitely expensive.

"Do you drink hot coffee?" she asked. My heart skipped a beat when she looked at me. She had glasses on now but I didn't forget the heat in those same eyes last night and the way her voice egged me on as she came on my tongue.

"I take it sweet if you have it," I told her with a scratchy voice.

"It may take a while for you to get used to using your voice. I hope you don't lose it," she murmured. "You may want to get ready. In less than an hour Mr. Thompson will be at your door."

I nodded and slowly got out of bed enjoying the small ache that bloomed between my legs. A cup of sweetened coffee was waiting for me when I finished my morning routine. I met Rae's eyes and my heart skipped a beat. I stood up on my toes and before I could back out, I brushed my lips across hers.

"Thanks," I said and took a deep sip of my coffee. Rae was still frozen when a knock came at the door. I didn't wait for her and instead went to open the door for the others, not even surprised when Eli and Daxton walked in.

"How do you feel?" Daxton asked closing the door behind him. Eli's grin looked a little dirtier than usual.

"So far so good," I replied inhaling my coffee. "Maybe we can stop the potions since it is going so well," I offered. Eli wrapped her arm around my shoulder.

"And lose my time with you?" she teased.

My curse doesn't work anymore. You should move on like you said you would, I reminded her. I don't know why I suddenly had the balls to say it but I almost regretted it.

You don't want that, her voice echoed in my head.

And you do?

"We can start experiments tonight," Daxton commented going for a coffee of his own. "Just to see how the potion is holding up."

Did you fuck her? Her voice startled me, but I took a quick sip of my coffee and pushed forward the image of when she came into my room. Glowing eyes. Rough kisses. Her belt that still hung in my room.

Nice deflection. She snorted aloud but did not remove her arm.

"Your low-level will be waiting for you," Eli reminded and pushed me toward the door "Let the high-levels talk, now."

I flipped her off but did as she said.

* * *

I couldn't help replaying my night with Rae in my head. It was great, probably the best I ever had. I couldn't compare it to Eli because there was just no way those two could even be compared to each other. They were so widely different that comparing them would be like comparing a demon with water affinity to one with fire. Neither would win against each other and to be honest, I didn't want either to. I was...content with how things were.

I wondered how long we would keep this from the others though. I narrowly got away from Eli's probing and I doubted it would stop there. She was willing to "share" with Daxton...but would it be the same for Rae?

My face heated when I realized just how much of a mess I had gotten into with this group. A smile followed when I thought of the diner. I think I was okay with it. I think I was content just being able to be a part of a group like this.

I didn't lie to Rae when I told her that I had been lacking in friends and family connections up until now; I just didn't expect to be able to tell anyone that, especially someone like her.

A knock at my door pulled my head out of the clouds.

I walked across my room to open the door.

"Morning, Matt," I said in a low voice still acting as if the curse affected me.

But it was not Matt that met me at my door.

Instead, it was the second secret I had been keeping. Malik.

"Such a lovely voice, Rosie," Malik commented. "Let's go for a drive, ya?"

He didn't give me a chance to speak, instead he grabbed my wrist and pulled me out of my dorm. My heart beat in my chest as he pulled me down the hallway to the opposite end of the others' dorms.

The dorms were oddly empty, but even if I were to catch sight of an onlooker the only thing that would have given away my predicament would be my face. Malik strode as if there was nothing wrong. He stood up tall with a smile so big that it rivaled Eli's when she was in a good mood.

I tried to pull my hand out of his grip but all it succeeded in doing was cause me to stumble over my own two feet.

"Malik stop," I said in a half yell.

He ignored me.

Once we had reached the exit his eyes finally met mine and I felt the presence of his power before it hit me.

"Stay quiet." It was like a million bricks had fallen on my shoulders. His power overtook my senses and filled my body with a heat that rivaled a volcano. I didn't try to speak this time. I knew it would be no use.

An icy coldness chased away the fire of Malik's power and I was instead left with pure panic. The Malik that I had trusted was still in front of me but there was no way to explain his actions. Why would he use his powers like that?

I looked behind me hoping that there was someone finally roaming the hallways but to my dismay there was no one. I slid my foot back ready to bolt.

Don't look at him Rosie. He's dangerous. His powers can ruin you.

I was so stupid. I can't believe I doubted Eli.

"Whoa Rosie! It's not that serious," Malik said. I turned back to give him a glare and he rubbed the back of his head as if he was caught doing something embarrassing. "I just don't want you to hurt yourself on the way to our destination. And if the others heard, you know for sure they would not let you come with me."

I looked him up and down. His stance was casual with a hand in the pocket of his black jeans. He didn't look like he was going to tackle me and throw me in the back of his car like a kidnapper.

Remove it, I signed to him and folded my arms across my chest. The fight-or-flight response was still screaming at me to flee.

He sighed before meeting my eyes and a coolness washed down my spine.

"I told you to trust me and that I am on your side, okay? Believe me." He had a frown on his face that made him look like a pouty two-year-old.

"Where are we going?" I demanded.

"The beach, it's the perfect weather." The side of his lip twitched. "Don't try to talk, you can just sign to me."

"How do you know?" I asked trying not to show just how bothered I was about letting yet another person know about my curse. He had a full-blown smile now. He took a step forward; our bodies almost touched.

"I'll tell you if you come with me," he said with his voice low. "I have been dying for some clam chowder."

I weighed my options carefully. Eli would be pissed again, and she would no doubt figure out by now that I was with Malik. I wouldn't know what would make her angrier, that I was with Malik or that I had been lying to her about it.

"Rosie?" Matt's voice called from the hallway. I stiffened and watched

Malik with wide eyes. Malik's golden eyes shimmered and he lifted up a hand to wave at Matt.

"Hey carrot top, want to join us for some clam chowder?" Malik asked.

I gripped the front of his shirt.

"You promised—"

"Nothing," he finished for me in a whisper.

I stepped away from him and my stomach churned.

"I would love to!" Matt exclaimed from down the hall and I felt the vibrations of his sprint toward us. "I've never skipped class before, this is so exciting!"

Matt stood close to me and even patted my head like all was forgiven but I had never hated him more than at this moment. I sent daggers at Malik, but it only seemed to widen his smile.

"Then we have to go all out!" Malik said and opened the door. The chill of the wind filtered through the open door.

Matt pushed me forward with him and out into the courtyard.

"What do you even do when you skip besides getting clam chowder?" he asked slipping an arm around my shoulder. I pushed him off and sent him a glare. "Rosie are you still mad at me?"

"That would be my fault," Malik said as we reached the edge of the parking lot. "I may have forced her to ditch with me. But in my defense, we had so much fun last time that I couldn't help myself."

"Wait the last time you were really with him?" Matt asked.

Malik's car unlocked with a small beep and I glanced one more time at the school before opening the door and getting in the car. The car was slightly warm and smelled too much like Malik's cologne.

He had to have been in here before he came to get me.

"Unfortunately," I grumbled in my seat. Matt gasped when he heard the words come out of my mouth.

"Oh, don't act so surprised carrot top it's not like it's a well-kept secret," Malik said while looking in the rear-view mirror at him.

"Explain," I demanded. Malik shot me a wild grin, started the car, and peeled out of the parking lot.

"Where is the fun in that?" he replied. "A little suspense is needed in life to make it interesting."

I huffed and crossed my arms across my chest.

"Eli is going to be pissed," Matt said from the back. His voice had a small quiver in it.

"Who fault is that?" I growled at him from my seat.

"Don't bleed on my seat," Malik warned. "I put a lot of money into this car and I don't want to put any more to get blood out of the seat."

"She's right," Matt said from the back. "I'm sorry Rosie I wasn't thinking when I told them Malik wasn't in class."

"Oh so that's what *that* apology was about. Poor Eli, so tongue-tied," Malik said with a chuckle.

"Who apologized? Eli? Really?" Matt asked, his voice holding obvious surprise. "I never would have guessed she was capable."

"You wouldn't believe it, it was almost like she was a kid again." Malik was laughing now.

Anger flared inside me.

"Don't talk about her like that," I hissed.

"Touchy," Malik jabbed.

The ride was silent except for the occasional comment from Matt. I ignored them both as best as I could. With each minute my anxiety got worse and worse.

I really shouldn't have lied to them. If I hadn't I wouldn't be in this position, skipping when I didn't want to. Eli was going to be bad enough but Rae... I wasn't sure I could face her.

What would she think? I literally ditched right after our first night together. *Only* night together, my mind corrected.

"We will be there in a few minutes," Malik announced.

I looked at the freeway exit coming up and realized we were still at least twenty minutes away from the last place we went to.

"This is a different place," I commented. I looked in the side mirror trying to catch a glimpse of Matt.

"There is more than one clam chowder place," Matt answered. His nose was still buried in his phone. I frowned at his actions.

"This one is better, trust me," Malik said and sent me a small wink.

"Don't be so anxious Rosie," Matt commented. "If you are so worried about their reaction, just don't go back."

My eyes snapped back to Matt in the side mirror. His arms were crossed and there was a rare deadpan look on his face. It unsettled me greatly and it had the exact opposite effect of what he said.

We pulled off a freeway exit I had never heard of before and I was presented with what looked like a town that was older than Winterfell itself. There was only one other car in the street besides ours and the buildings were all made out of brick. Even the street signs were browned with age.

"Welcome to Montnesse," Malik said with an excited tone. "The last hidden witch settlement."

Chapter Nineteen
Amr

I watched as Eli paced angrily inside Rosie's empty dorm.

"She was alone for less than fifteen minutes!" She growled and grabbed hold of the chair attached to Rosie's desk throwing it cleanly across the room. It smashed against the brick wall and I had to duck under the bed to hide from the raining wood splinters.

Stupid demon.

Eli was always the angriest and I hated her for it. She was rash and never thought anything through. I blame her for this happening. When Daxton brought me into Rae's room and I heard that Eli had dismissed her I went to go find her immediately.

When she did not answer I ran back to the dorm. I looked over toward the others. I didn't need any power to understand that the others were just as worried as Eli. Daxton's jaw was clenched and Rae's face was pale. But all they did was *stand* there.

With a yowl I commanded my body to shift.

Shifting back into a human was the worst pain. It had happened for the first time when I was six and I thought that I had to be dying. Back then, when my grandpa explained to me that my shift would mean I would be tied to another witch for the rest of my life, I thought that dying would surely have been better. My kind, shifters—or as witches like to call us, familiars—were indebted to forever serve the witches. It was the only way we could live safely. If I created a bond with a witch, no other witch would dare touch me.

Rumor had it that witches liked to eat us and absorb our powers and I wasn't brave enough to chance it.

I was lucky that Daxton chose me though, he was a fair witch that didn't look down on my kind. Nor did he ever try to take advantage of our bond... like his parents did to him.

"You are getting on my nerves," I growled at Eli and stood up slowly as my bones cracked into place. I rolled my head from side to side trying to get the kink out of my neck.

"I swear to god Amr I am not against skinning a cat," Eli hissed at me.

"Like you could," I growled at her. Shifters had a different way of holding magic than witches. It was like a bank for us instead of something that had its own mind. While I may get overwhelmed by having to take Daxton's power, it also meant that I had an almost never-ending supply of magic at my disposal and there was no way a *demon* could stand a chance at that power.

"Amr you should shift back," Daxton said in a weak voice. I gritted my teeth at his words.

"Ya, no one wants to see that shit," Eli spat at my naked form.

"Is that an order?" I asked Daxton. He let out a sigh and shook his head. "Eli all of this is your fault, since we have met Rosie you have been so *careless* with her."

"Like a *cat* would know better," she said and stalked over to me. Our chests touched and I could not tear my eyes away from her blue ones. I gripped her shirt and pulled her closer.

"I shifted to tell you that *Malik's* scent is in here." As the growled words sunk in, her eyes widened, and she stepped back. "That why this is your fault. Your fucking gang ties followed you here and have been hanging around *my Rosie.*"

"Your Rosie?" she said with a laugh. "She thinks you're still a cat! And you think you have got some claim on her? Don't be stupid!" Magic swirled in my palms at her words.

"Even as a cat I treated her better than any of you!" I yelled. "I was constantly watching her. Even this morning, I was the first one to find her. Why do you act as if she is just a plaything?"

"Amr that's enough," Daxton said in a commanding voice. "Shift back."

The weight of our bond on my shoulders began pulling me down but I stood firm even as it felt like my bones were bending under the weight of it.

"I refuse," I hissed at him. "Rae, surely you see reason."

"Let's hear him out, there is not use in fighting," Rae said after a moment of silence.

"You can't be seriously trying to listen to a *cat?*" Eli growled.

"Do it, Daxton," Rae ordered.

"You are released," Daxton muttered. I let a sigh once the weight was lifted off me.

"As I was *saying*." I gave a pointed stare to Eli. "Malik's scent is here, in the room. But it's old."

"He took her from here?" Eli asked and I rolled my eyes.

"There is no sign of struggle," Daxton remarked.

"He controls people, why would she need to struggle?" Rae said. "The only thing we have going for us right now is that she thinks the curse is gone."

"Did it show up at all during the last few days?" Eli asked.

"I didn't feel it," I said.

"She was fine during the night. I stopped controlling her emotions so heavily yesterday and nothing happened. As long as she continues to believe it works, it will. That's how placebos work," Rae added. "We also shouldn't jump to the conclusion that Malik kidnapped her."

"What else would it be, Rae?" Eli kicked a pile of clothing that was on the floor. I remembered her words about that very pile only a few days prior.

"Don't judge me Amr. I will do laundry at some point," Rosie said with a playful tone. I rubbed across her legs and purred as she picked me up and rubbed her nose against mine. "You are the only one I really look forward to being with, you know."

"Don't ruin her stuff," I growled at her. "Take your anger out on something useful."

"That's it I am going—"

"Both of you two stop," Rae said harshly. I froze when she spoke. I had never heard her so angry. Exasperated, tired, annoyed, but never so angry. "Amr change back, we are going to the principal. The others will stay here and wait in case she comes back."

I nodded and shifted back, feeling my body shrink and fur sprout out of my skin. As much as I enjoyed my time being human, I was so much more used to being in this form. Rae's hands scooped me up and without another word she left the room.

"They are such children," she commented.

I couldn't help but agree.

The office was empty as usual when we entered. I hated the smell in here. That front desk lady always sprayed way too much of that liquid that girls like to put on. Rosie had put it on rarely and when she did it was never much.

My gut churned. Even if I wasn't as rash as Eli, my stomach still twisted in knots at the thought of Rosie being taken. Eli was right though... I was just a cat in her eyes and if I obeyed the contract, I would never be anything more.

It hurt when I realized what they had all been able to do to her while I was stuck in this form and forced to watch from afar. They were so callous with her. I had only seen Daxton treat her with kindness and even that was in the form of small gifts like a coffee. She deserved so much more and in my cat form I tried to give her some comfort but there would never be a chance for anything more than that.

The thoughts hurt me. I had wished that in another life she could have been a witch and I could be her familiar...but that was only a dream.

"Oh, deary now is not a good time," the office lady said in a voice that felt like it would rot your teeth out.

"Not now, Tammy," Rae said in a clipped voice.

She stalked over to a closed door that I assumed was the principal's office and opened the door without even knocking. We were met with a naked rear end.

The purple-haired man looked over his shoulder at us in surprise and from my position in Rae's arms I saw what looked like a student turn her head back to face us. Her skirt was pulled up around her hips and her face was flushed.

Rae let out a chuckle that vibrated in her chest. "Oh Emma, you did so well."

I didn't know it was possible for her to flush even deeper. The purple-haired man pulled out of the woman and zipped up his pants hastily. Emma did the same with her skirt.

"Is this her doing?" the man asked with a pointed glare at the girl. She smiled sheepishly and moved past us and left us alone in the room. "What did you promise her?"

The man was flushed with anger and was shaking so violently I thought he'd explode.

"Just a date to the governor's New Year ball," Rae responded and stretched to close the door behind her. "Now, I don't even have to try that hard anymore."

"You're evil," the man said.

"At least I don't fuck my students," Rae responded. "Listen, I need you to tell me what you know about Malik and why he is here."

"I don't know anything about a Malik," he huffed.

"Now is not the time to play stupid." Rae leaned back on the closed door. I was thankful she didn't step closer; the room already smelt putrid.

"I am being truthful! Shouldn't your stupid ability get that?" The man tugged on his braids harshly.

"White hair? Like a few centuries old? Works with Eli's gang? He's in the third year." Rae's voice was getting impatient.

"Why would I allow someone that old into the academy?" he hissed back at us. "I know every problematic student that comes in *those*"—he gestured to the space behind us—"goddamn doors. I would know if someone like that had a place here."

Rae stilled.

"Keep it in your pants or you may just owe me more than the cost of this school," Rae threatened and left the door in a hurry.

The Emma girl was waiting outside.

"You have my word," Rae said as she passed.

It didn't get past me that the girl went back into the room and shut the door softly behind her.

"Amr," Rae spoke, and she hurried back to the room. "We really fucked up."

Chapter Twenty
Rosie

"You are fucking insane," I hissed at Malik as he pulled us into an almost empty parking lot. "The witches hate us. I literally have a curse on me!"

Ice-cold fear was rising in me faster than I could keep up with. This was a bad idea, horrible. Not every witch here would be like the ones in school and with my luck we would run into one that had to hate low-levels with a burning passion. The clack of the witch's heels on my tenth birthday played repeatedly in my mind.

There was an elephant sitting on my chest.

The car shrank by half.

I reached for the handle of the passenger door and pulled. And pulled. And pulled again praying that it would open. Nothing. I was stuck.

"Rosie stop, it's okay," Malik said from besides me but I didn't listen. I tried the door again.

I would die if we stepped foot in that place. They would find me, just like Daxton had. They would find me. There would be nothing Matt nor Malik could do to help me.

"Get me out of here." I tried to pry the lock open but my hands were shaking so violently that I couldn't even wrap my fingers around the hard surface.

Malik's hand gripped the back of my shirt and pulled me away from the door.

"Rosie I wouldn't put you in danger, trust me," he said. I tried to slap his hand away. "Rosie, calm." This time I barely felt his power before it hit me. The only thing that tore me from my panic was the ice that had formed in my veins shattering into thin air.

The car resumed its normal size. The world became clearer. I took a deep inhale of breath and noted it tasted sweeter now, like my lungs were savoring the air around us. My body stopped shaking and I slouched against the chair.

"That turtleneck is saving your life right now," Malik said and let go of the back of my shirt. "Get out. I promise no one will hurt you here."

Malik left the car. I turned my head to catch a glimpse of Matt, but he had already exited the car as well. I didn't have it in me to be mad at Malik for calming me but if he thought I'd forget about him taking us here, he was wrong. I took one more steadying breath and exited the car.

"Time is different here," he said as he walked toward one of the shops that lined the parking lot. "Eli and her *friends* will feel as though we have only been gone as long as the drive." Malik gave me a smile as he pushed open an old-looking shop door. "But we can stay here for days. Months. Years, even and no one would notice."

"How is that even possible?" I asked and wrapped my arms around myself feeling cold even under the warm rays of the sun.

Malik only cocked his head in response. He was daring me to trust him once more.

I held my breath and stepped into the shop. There was a flash of light and then a sharp pull in my stomach. I shut my eyes against the feeling and gripped the closest thing next to me in hopes that I could catch myself before I made a fool of myself and fell to the floor.

The feeling disappeared, and my senses slowly came back to me. I didn't feel like we had moved, my feet were still planted on the hard ground, but the air had turned mustier than it had before.

"I always hate that feeling," Malik said from beside me. He cleared his throat.

I was about to open my eyes, but a sour taste exploded in my mouth. There was retching behind me. I opened my eyes in a start and leaped forward in hopes to get out of the line of fire.

Malik was still at the door, but Matt was on his knees wiping his mouth. I pinched my nose when the smell threatened to invade.

"That was horrible," Matt moaned and slowly tried to stand on his shaky legs. "...Sorry."

"It usually is," Malik commented and stepped over the puddle. "How about you? You okay Rosie?"

I opened my mouth to speak but my stomach immediately flipped, and I had to clamp my hand over my mouth. I just gave him a meek nod and focused on my breathing.

"Every time I see you, I feel as though you have a new scar on that ugly mug of yours," a playful voice came from behind us. "Also, don't bring people with weak stomachs anymore."

I looked behind us and realized that we were in a small bar. There were patrons in the bar stools, but it was the bartender that caught my attention. He was a man with kind brown eyes, a soft face, and a mustache that was perfectly combed.

"How would I know he'd do that?" Malik joked back.

The bartender waved his hand and there was a tingle of magic by my side. Looking down, the once puke-covered floor was now clean. My eyes widened and I looked to Malik but he just pushed our group forward.

The other patrons barely looked up as we passed them, as if people appearing out of thin air was a normal occurrence for them.

"Visit me before you leave!" the bartender called out as we crossed the bar and moved toward the exit on the other side.

"I thought you said you didn't get along with witches," I hissed at him.

He shot me a smile and pushed open the back door.

"I partially lied. Some hate me, others love me." With a wink he pushed me outside.

My jaw dropped comically when I took in the sight in front of me.

It was like a mirrored image of the town we had entered but instead of being run down, everything was shining. From the street to the lamp posts, to the cars, everything gleamed as if freshly painted. The best part was even though buildings remained the same, the colors had changed, giving the space a whole new mood. Streetlamps were purple, and there seemed to be beautiful murals covering every building corner.

And the people...god some of the people looked like they stepped out of an old Hollywood movie. There were women dressed in floor-length gowns, men in suits, even the most casually dressed seemed to hold a certain style that didn't seem to exist anymore in modern society.

It was more than just a small town; it was a bustling city. Cars were lined up at the streetlights, the previously emptied parking lot was now filled with all different makes and years of cars, and the sidewalk was filled with people.

I turned to look at Malik. Was I dreaming?

"What is this place?" Matt asked in a whisper.

"I told you," Malik said and clapped a hand on his shoulder. "Montnesse. The witches, and a handful of worthy demons, migrated here and created a barrier so that their world would never be bothered again. If you want, I can take you to the museum in this town. They love to share their history with newcomers."

"How did you get invited into such a place?" I asked him, breathless. With each breath I took, magic entered my lungs; it was addicting.

"I migrated here with the rest when demons were under siege. They trust whoever I bring in, so they won't question either of you but trust me when I tell you..." He put a hand on my shoulder as well and gave a threatening squeeze. "If you ever so much as breathe a word about this, I promise to kill you and anyone you tell."

His golden eyes were in slits and even without his hand firmly on my shoulder I would have felt the spike of his power. He didn't use it but it was like he was powering it up, getting it ready.

"These people have been here since the uprising?" I asked in shock not fully able to comprehend the amount of time it would mean that these people had been here. "Wait, you have been here since then?"

"I am an old man, Rosie," he said. "And I care about these people."

"Why did you show us this?" I asked, a different sort of feeling snuggling its way in my chest. Something that I had never felt before. Something I could not even name.

"I'm on your side Rosie. You belong here as much as I do," he explained.

I belonged. The feeling exploded in my chest. What was this feeling?

"Well geez, I guess I really am just here for the chowder, huh?" Matt said jokingly, breaking the connection between me and Malik.

"Ah yes, let's eat first. They do have an amazing clam chowder," he said with a small smile.

* * *

"Oh my god," Matt moaned into his chowder.

"Good, right?" Malik asked with a small chuckle.

It *was* good but I had other things on my mind.

"So when you are here do you not age?" I asked him unable to keep the question to myself.

"Nope," he answered. "There are some lucky mortals here, but most left when they realized it was time."

"What happens when they leave?" Matt asked between bites.

"They age and die in an instant," Malik answered as easy as talking about the weather. "Demons and witches are lucky like that. They can come and go, that's why this place is such a mix of things. Whenever they find something they like, they just bring it back through the barrier."

"How do they get the cars in?" Matt asked. He already finished his bowl and I pushed mine toward him still feeling nauseous from entering the barrier.

"What?" Malik asked with a raised eyebrow. Matt grabbed my bowl and started eating the remnants.

"It's a good question, we entered through a door to a bar. How do people get cars in?" I asked.

"There is a gate on the other end of town, I believe. I don't deal in that so I wouldn't know," he answered with a shrug and took a sip of his beer.

"What do you deal in?" I placed my chin on my hand and leaned forward to meet his eyes. He gave me a sidelong glance.

"You are very talkative today," he commented. "Aren't you afraid of bleeding through your clothes?"

"Yeah Rosie, don't talk so much," Matt said with a sigh and leaned back in the booth to rub his still full belly.

I shot Matt an irritated glare.

"It hasn't hurt since I entered the barrier," I lied to them.

Matt leaned forward then, and Malik stilled next to me.

"Really?" Matt asked, his eyes now full of light.

"Really," I told him. "Maybe it's a time thing and when I leave the cuts will appear all at once."

"Or it's a magic thing," Malik commented. "Maybe the barrier is affecting it because it's pure magic."

"I am not complaining," I told them and sat back to take a sip of my own iced tea.

"Rosie, tell me. Is there something you've always wanted to say? I mean you have a perfect chance now," Matt said with excitement.

I remembered the way it felt to finally scream when the others had fixed my curse. The guilt of it all made me nauseous when I realized how fucked I was being to them right now. If they found out they would be so pissed.

...I was just so worried. Eli's words made my heart clench even tighter.

"I want to say that I think next time you should think of an alibi for me rather than telling the trio that Malik was missing and so was I," I said to him. I let the edge show in my voice.

"But I never go to class anyways," Malik commented. A new fury rose in me.

"You didn't think to mention that Matt? When Eli was having a heart attack?" I growled at him. He looked down with a sigh.

"I'm sorry Rosie. I know I messed up," he whispered. "Just please forgive me, I'll be better."

Damn. Matt's pout turned into a full puppy dog face and I shifted uncomfortably.

"She was just mad that she was caught in a lie," Malik said. "You shouldn't take it out on him when *you* feel bad that you lied to your lover. No wait, is it lovers now?"

My heart stopped. I was ready to scream at him. Burn him to a crisp. Fight him. But it only took one moment for me to reassess my guilt and realize that it truly was my fault all along.

"No I really did—" Matt tried to say but I lifted my hand to stop him.

"He's right Matt, I am sorry," I said and reached out my hand to cover his. "I will be the one that will be better. I was caught in a lie and was selfish about it. I am sorry."

Matt gave me a smile and flipped our hands so he could bring it to his mouth and give it a small kiss. He then opened my hand and I saw a small purple flower bloom in my palm.

"Forgiven."

"Alright, as sweet as that was, I am sure you guys are dying to see the rest of the town," Malik said and slammed money down on the table and got up to leave.

Matt blushed lightly and followed suit.

They both paused when I didn't follow right away. Malik with a small smile and Matt with an outstretched hand.

The feeling was back again, pulling at my chest.

"Let's go, Rosie."

* * *

The town was beautiful. Malik explained that the witches had to keep themselves busy somehow and many had turned toward more artistic ways to express themselves. To prove his point further we were taken to a park that was full of sculptures that even towered over some of the tallest trees in the area.

I ran my fingers across a particularly colorful one that called to me as soon as I entered. It was an array of colorful metal poles that were bent and knotted around each other forming complex paths that were hard to follow with the eye. It was called *Fear* and I couldn't help but believe that if fear could take on its own shape, this would be an accurate representation.

"No wonder Daxton looks the way he does," I murmured admiring the art. I didn't know how old he was or if he had ever seen this town but something told me that he would love it. I tried to imagine what he would look like if he saw this: widened brown eyes probably and maybe a light blush, he wouldn't say much but I would really want to hear what his mind went through when looking at this.

"Your mind is never far from them, huh?" Malik said from behind me. I jumped, startled at the proximity of him. I turned to meet his intense gold eyes.

"They accepted me when no one did," I told him and turned my attention back to the art.

"You mean they bedded you," he said. "And used you as an experiment."

My face flamed.

"I don't know what you mean," I told him. My gaze flitted toward Matt. He was admiring another art piece across the park leaving me and Malik in almost full privacy.

"You think I wouldn't make the principal tell me all the juicy gossip?" he asked. His hand trailed along the length of my spine. "Don't worry, I made him forget that I ever asked him. Wouldn't be good if Rae found out I had been snooping. That girl has a way of finding out things."

"Is that how you found out?" I asked finally getting the courage to turn to him. His hand reached for me and I couldn't help but flinch. He paused and then proceeded to rub between my eyebrows removing the tension and wrinkles from there. My breath caught.

"Of course," he said. "I originally came to keep an eye on Eli but I thought the curse was interesting."

Why did I feel so disappointed at those words?

"That's usually how that works," I said with a sad smile.

"And then," he said and moved his hand to the bottom of my chin, lifting it. "I found the person to be much more interesting than the curse."

Blush painted my face and my mind slowed.

"You knew they were trying to break it," I said. He nodded, and his eyes trailed from my eyes to my lips. My mouth went dry.

"But I don't know the outcome," he said, voice breathless. "Did they succeed?"

I swallowed thickly.

"No." My voice cracked at the lie. He gave me a smile and then pulled away from me.

"Then we may have to take you here more often, so you can finally be *free*," he concluded.

I nodded but didn't move until his back was turned to me and he was walking toward Matt. I turned so they wouldn't have a chance to look at my face and slapped my cheeks.

"Don't act like such a whore, Rosie. Get your shit together," I whispered.

Next was the museum he promised to take us to. We were met with a short-haired witch. They greeted with hugs and the girl took us in with open arms.

"Listen, you will get my extra special tour today," she gushed as we walked. "But Malik has been on it like hundreds of times, so he doesn't get to come."

"A hundred and thirty-two times to be exact," he said and gave use a small wave. "I will meet you guys afterward. I need to say hello to some people anyways."

I gave him a small wave back and turned my attention back to the girl.

"Alright," she said in a mock whisper. "The real reason I want him gone is because there would be no history without Malik."

I held my breath as she walked us through the various exhibits. The paintings and sculptures were mostly around the town being built. There were photos of a grand opening in the center of town that we had passed on our way here, pictures of demons covered in sweat and work clothes, then a picture of a speaker decked out in a suit and standing on a podium looking excited. I assumed the person was a mayor of this town given his looks. Next to him I saw a familiar white tuft of hair.

"Malik was one of the few founders here that helped create a safe haven," she said looking over my shoulder at the grainy photo. "As you probably know, demons and witches were being exiled and killed for just being us."

Malik was behind the mayor, also dressed in a suit. The chairs on either side of him were taken. One by a tall man with light hair and a large smile, the other by a woman with long black hair and dark eyes. She was more serious.

The tour guide took us to the next picture and my chest caught when I recognized it. It was a mass grave filled with bones and even some mummified bodies. I sucked in a breath of air when I realized that this was the exact same picture that the speaker showed in class that one day.

What was her name again?

"Malik acted as an informant from the outside and helped get information in and out of the town. Really if he weren't here, I am not sure we'd be safe. There were many times where people stumbled upon our town when our protection was weak and if he wasn't there to catch them... Well, you could guess."

"Was he the only one to venture outside all those years?" I asked looking over some of the pictures of people gathered in the square. I caught Malik's puffy white hair immediately, I could see the smile on his face and this time his face was far smoother than it was now.

"No there were a few others, but no one wanted his job because during that time the humans still tried to kill us any chance they got," she told me.

It was hard to comprehend just how old Malik was even when the proof was staring me right in the face. It almost didn't make sense in my head and it felt like this was all some weird, fantastic dream. The more she talked about the town and the more pictures I saw with Malik in them, the more I realized that I had no clue who he was. Nor did I know anything about the supernatural world around me. How could something like this even exist and be kept secret for so long?

The whole tour took an hour and after she was done, I already felt the weight of the day on my shoulders. Matt and I sat in silence on a bench outside of the museum after saying our goodbyes to the hyper tour guide. My mind was whirling, and I didn't know how to put my thoughts into words.

"This has to be a dream," Matt said breaking the silence for me.

"I feel like I've gone crazy," I told him.

"I knew witches were secretive but...damn," he said and rubbed a hand across his face.

Silence fell over us as we watched the people live their lives right before our very eyes. A mother pushing a stroller. Kids chasing each other laughing. A couple holding hands and walking down the street.

"How many of the world's witches do you think are in this town?" I asked him.

"Believe it or not every witch in the history of the United States has had to have made their way through here at some point. If they live outside of this town, they or someone in their bloodline was exiled," Malik said with an exceptionally large iced coffee that entered my view.

I gave him a smile and started sipping from it happily. I hoped that this would keep me through the rest of the day.

"I thought witches were violent," Matt said. His eyes were trained on the kids chasing after each other. "But it's peaceful here."

"Magic is violent when not harnessed properly," he said, his eyes meeting mine and I knew he was talking about Daxton. "We exile power-hungry people that like to bend the rules of nature for their own selfish gain."

"What are you even doing?" I asked him, looking over his scarred face. "Why work for that gang?"

"Maybe if you come again, I'll tell you," he said. "Trust needs to be earned."

"Then why ask that I trust you so easily?" I raised a brow at him while I took another sip of the mocha.

"It's not like you actually do," he said and his expression dared me to fight him but he was right. "Alright children, let's head back."

Chapter Twenty-One
Rosie

I tapped my foot against the leg of the table as I waited for the teacher to arrive. True to Malik's words, we had arrived just past the time that breakfast had ended, and I had enough time to make it to my class without being suspicious. The others were not in their usual spots, and I assumed they had gotten breakfast without me. Meaning they would be here any minute now.

I didn't have my books with me today since Malik practically dragged me out of my dorm, but it wasn't like the teacher even cared. I took another sip of my coffee and stared at the slowly moving hands of the clock. I started to get more anxious when the others didn't show up.

Did they figure it out already?

They couldn't have. They must have just assumed I missed breakfast—nothing weird about that. The only reason they worried last time was because Matt had spilled that Malik was missing...but if both Matt and I were missing there should be nothing to give us away.

Having already stayed awake for almost a half day, I found myself drinking my coffee faster than I usually would. I had a feeling it would be hell trying to get through the classes with nothing but this coffee to keep me going. I should have skipped for real and just slept the rest of the day.

A loud meow tore me from my sleepy haze, and I jumped when Amr slid across the table. I moved my coffee out of the way and gave him a small smile. It didn't seem to calm him though because he continued to meow.

I put a finger to my lips hoping he would be quiet and then scratched the bottom of his chin. Looking around, some of my other classmates were already staring. I smiled sheepishly and gave a half-serious glare to Amr.

Both Eli and Daxton chose that moment to rush into class, both panting as if they had run here. As soon as their eyes landed on me there was a pause and I watched as Eli's eyes narrowed.

I swallowed the knot in my throat.

"Rosie where the fuck have you been?" she said once she stalked close enough to our table.

I showed her the coffee cup in my hand. She glared at it and reached out to grab my wrist so tightly that I had to bite my lip from crying out.

Why did Amr smell Malik in your room? her voice said in my head.

I gave a questioning glance to Amr.

The cat? I asked her. Does that cat talk now?

I saw Eli's lip twitch like I had just told her a joke. The bell rang.

"We were worried," Daxton said for her. "You owe us an explanation."

I pried my wrist away from Eli before any thoughts of guilt could spill out. I showed Daxton my cup again and raised my brows at him.

"About Malik," he finished. Instead of taking his normal position in his seat—back against the wall—he sat sideways and plopped his chin on his open palm and continued to stare at me.

I took a sip from my coffee and averted my eyes from his gaze.

Amr nudged his head against my arm. I gave him a strained smile and scratched behind his ear. And what did the cat have to do with Malik's scent? Maybe because he was magical, he had some type of power?

I couldn't help the sigh that came out of my lips.

"Alright, to the field!" Mr. Falkner yelled as he entered class.

I cursed internally. Was it already time to do more testing? There was a collective groan that came from the class.

"I think your mood will change when you get there!" Mr. Falkner responded to everyone's groan with a wink.

I doubted that.

I grabbed my coffee and Amr, then got out of my seat to follow the crowd out but Eli grabbed my waist before I could leave.

"Not so fast," she said, her lips centimeters from my ear. I could feel her hair tickle my neck. "You will not leave my sight after this morning."

I shivered at the feeling of her voice in my ear but just nodded to her. She stood up as well and put an arm around my shoulder.

As we walked Daxton scooped Amr out of my arms and I felt his magic spike. I looked up to him for an explanation.

"I heard they are pairing people off to battle," he responded.

"How considerate of you," Eli commented.

But still useless, she said in my head.

Why? I asked back.

Because even if he gives Amr all the magic he can take, Dax will still absolutely murder whoever he is paired with, Eli responded. I didn't need to look at her to know that she was smiling. Her emotions practically vibrated off her in waves.

You are so bloodthirsty.

You haven't seen anything yet, she said. *Just wait till you see Daxton fight.*

I didn't know if I should be excited or worried about what I was about to see. I already knew of the *situation* with the girl but...how far would he go when he actually wanted to hurt someone?

I snuck a peek at Daxton from the corner of my eye. There was a frown on his face and his eyes were intently on Amr.

We made it to the field without any issues but it was obvious that it was more than just first-years here. When I saw Matt's bright hair my heart sped up. If he was here, it meant Malik was too.

The students slowly placed themselves on the bleachers with their classmates and a loud chatter settled in the field. Many seemed to be excited with wide grins stretched across their faces. The others, who were probably going to fight, seemed to be giving everyone that passed them a nervous glance.

The realization came at me like a ton of bricks. I would have to fight as well. I would have to engulf someone in flames. They wanted me to burn *students* alive and watch them scream in front of the entire school. My father's gnarled and nasty scar flitted through my mind.

Oh I cannot wait to see you burn someone alive, Eli purred in my mind. *I may just take you right then in front of the whole school.*

I smacked her arm off my shoulders severing the connection between us. She let out a small chuckle but I didn't find anything about the situation funny.

"Ms. Miller," Rae called as she pushed through the students and came to stand in front of us. I wouldn't really say she had to actually push them; the students parted as soon as they saw her form towering over them. Her eyes were intense as she looked over me and I couldn't help but flush.

It has only been less than a few hours since we...

"You should think carefully about the situation you are in," she told me. Her voice lost whatever warmth it had last night and her eyes held an emotion that made my chest ache. "After this stupid show of power is over, you have some questions to answer."

I tried to push down the panic; she would be able to feel it. Instead, I just shook the half-finished coffee in my hand.

"No one believes that Rosie," Daxton replied. "And even if we did there is still one thing you have to account for."

"I'm surprised you aren't raging right now," Rae commented toward Eli. She shrugged in response.

"She's here now. If I don't let her out of my sight, we will never have this problem again." She paused and an almost sinister smile graced her face. "And I have a few ideas for punishment."

Should I feel relief or more guilt? I really couldn't make up my mind and my emotions just seemed to be a mess because paired with my exhaustion there was no deciphering what my mind wanted.

We decided to stay standing with a few other classes of students. There just wasn't enough room for the entire student body on those bleachers. Our teacher, as well as all the others, stood in the middle with a surprise guest: Principal Winterfell.

"Welcome!" The principal spoke into a microphone with a cheery voice. His voice echoed across the field and there were small cheers. "You should know why you are all here by now but today we have something very special for you!" He walked forward and waved his arms around. I almost snorted at the theatrics. "This year is a very special one and I had a thought: why not up the stakes of the rankings? This year we will officially start the Battle of Winterfell!"

There were even louder cheers that echoed across the field now and my heart seemed to want to beat out of my chest. I looked around at the students here. My name was remarkably high so if I tried, I could beat them...but I couldn't even think of what I would have to do to them. Burning a field of dying grass was one thing, but purposefully setting someone on fire...

"We will start from the bottom at number one hundred and number ninety-nine. They will battle and the winner of that battle will then face number ninety-eight, and so on so forth. We have medical witches standing by but there is one thing they cannot reverse: death." Silence fell over us at his words. "Do not fight to kill. Fight to maim or surrender. If there is a death we are not responsible for the damages and whoever is responsible *will be apprehended.*"

"That's no fun," Eli groaned from next to me.

I eyed her warily...was this all a front for her? Or another lie?

The principal gestured to one of the teachers and in an instant, there was a white rectangle hanging in the sky. Slowly the names seemed to be burned onto the material. There were murmurs across the students at this show of magic. I was too distracted by the names on the board to even pay attention to it though.

How could I forget about the order of the names?

1. Malik Hendrix
2. Rae Ashwell
3. Daxton Reid
4. Rosie Miller

Pure horror laced my senses. I slowly turned to Daxton. His jaw was tight and as soon as I looked over his eyes met mine.

He wouldn't hurt me would he?

"I'll forfeit," he assured me.

"Then I'd have to fight her," Rae said from in front of us. Her hazel eyes met mine; they gave no indication to what she was feeling. I shrunk under her gaze.

"Just put her to sleep or something," Eli offered. "Whatever it is don't let her get to Malik."

I reached out to Eli and laced my fingers in her rough ones.

I'll forfeit instead, I told her. She sent me a look as if she didn't believe my words.

"She wants to forfeit," Eli told them.

Daxton let out a breath and I saw his shoulders sag. It was a cowardly thing for me to do, but there was no way I was going to go up against these people.

"Let's start!" Principal Winterfell yelled. At his command two names popped up on the board and that signaled the start to the Battle of Winterfell.

* * *

My fingernails were almost gnawed to the nubs when it came time for number five. I had watched each battle trying to size up the competition but all in all, they seemed pretty weak. I noticed that Matt didn't even make it into the top one hundred. I spotted him in the bleachers and I wasn't surprised to see the bane of my existence sitting next to him. When he noticed my gaze he gave me a wave and I had to avert my gaze so the others around me wouldn't see the interaction.

We had found a seat near the field as we were waiting for our turns. Eli had come and gone. She forfeited saying that she didn't want to risk the stamina. Her power worked differently so it wouldn't have given her an advantage; she would have had to do hand to hand.

"I didn't want to get my clothes dirty," she said when her turn was up. "You know how much I hate rolling around in the dirt."

There was a pause for a break once we reached number five.

"Numbers one through five please make your way to the field," Principal Winterfell called from his place on the field. I looked to Rae and saw her eyes narrow at the principal. I gulped, that didn't feel like a good sign.

"What does he need from us?" Daxton asked Rae.

"I don't like this," Rae responded.

I gave Amr to Eli, and she sent us off with a tense nod. Her previously relaxed posture became rigid after the announcement and her eyes firmly watched Malik.

We all walked to the center field, Daxton to my right, Rae to my left. Malik and number five walked together. Daxton's hand cupped the back of my neck as Malik came close.

"Okay so as the last five, I expect you to put on a show," the principal said once we lined up in front of him. "But please no killing, especially you Mr. Hendricks."

"I thought you didn't know of Mr. Hendricks?" Rae cut the principal off. He gave her a confused look in response. I was just as confused and looked toward Daxton for an answer, but he just shook his head at me.

"Not now," he whispered.

"You of all people should know that I know every single student that walks through these doors Ms. Ashwell," he replied.

Rae looked over at Malik with clenched fists and a tight jaw. Malik had a small smile on his face when he looked over to us.

"If that's all I'll just sit back and enjoy the show," Malik said and dismissed himself.

"Yes well, Ms. Miller and Mr. Evans. Please get into your places," Principal Winterfell said and gestured for us to take our places at the opposite ends of the small clearing they left for us in the middle of the field.

I sized up the small demon in front of me. I had watched his last battle intently. Even if I planned to forfeit, I couldn't help but try and see where his weaknesses were in the off chance that we fought. He was plain-looking with cropped brown hair and green eyes. He had the power of air vibrations from what I could tell—he made the last opponent's eardrums pop. I hoped I could raise my hand fast enough or else the whole field would know me being mute was a sham. The last contestant did not stop screaming until the medical witches fixed his ears.

The witch teacher conjured the number five in between the open space that we left. It slowly counted down.

4.

I clenched my fist ready to raise it.

3.

My opponent straightened and his eyes widened. His face went slack and it almost looked like he couldn't see me any longer.

2.

There was a film on his eyes and I watched as his Adam's apple bobbed in his throat.

1.

Something was wrong, he was twitching.

The number disappeared and faster than I could raise my hand number five's mouth opened.

"I forfeit!" he yelled across the field.

Pure dead silence followed. No one moved and I swear even as vast as the field was you could hear a pin drop.

Then there were cheers.

My head snapped open to where the others were waiting on the bench. They were tense except Malik; he had a smile.

"Uhh alright, up next!" Principal Winterfell said and I stood still as Daxton got up and jerkily walked toward the middle of the field.

My eyes were still on Malik as Daxton walked over. Was this his doing? There was no way the demon would forfeit against a low-level.

He sent me a wink and then his mouth moved but he was so far away I couldn't hear it. Even if I had, it would have been useless because in less than a second the same fiery heat that I had felt this morning was washing over my body.

I gave Daxton a panicked look and I couldn't help the words that came out of my mouth.

"Fuck."

Chapter Twenty-Two
Rosie

The numbers appeared once more without even a break. I tried to look around them and get in Daxton's sight, but he was flexing his fists. I didn't know exactly what Malik had done to me, but it couldn't have been anything good.

4.

3.

2.

1.

I was met with Daxton's face. He gave me a smile and an encouraging nod. I slowly willed my hand up. Slowly I inched it up the length of my side. Once I turned my hand to raise it, it stopped listening completely and snapped back down against my side.

Daxton raised an eyebrow at me.

I tried with the other arm.

As soon as I turned it once more it snapped back to my side. I looked across the field once more to Malik. I tried to read the words that came out of his mouth.

...Trust me?

I didn't care what other secret magical towns he could take me to, I was going to kill him when I had the chance.

I jogged over to Daxton; he tensed as I did so. His hands raised. He was preparing to fight me.

I stopped just a few feet away.

"What are you doing? I thought you'd forfeit?" he asked. I jerked my head hoping that he would get the idea and look over at Malik. He looked over to Malik's direction. I felt the power swirl around us before I saw it take effect. Whatever invisible power that was surrounding us made Daxton stiffen.

His eyes glazed over just like number five's had, but instead of yelling his forfeit his eyes snapped over to mine.

I took a step back.

Daxton raised his arm toward me.

I ran as fast as I could in the opposite direction. My fight-or-flight instincts took over. The noise of the crowd made the blood that was heating up and pumping through my veins run hotter than I ever thought possible.

Faster, I chanted as I pushed my weak legs further from Daxton. I didn't know where I was going but I just knew that I needed to get away from him before I ended up like that women.

"What's wrong low-level?"

A voice loudly asked from the crowd.

"Where are you going?" Another just as loud.

They loved seeing this. A struggling low-level get what they deserved. The tears burned as I ran. I was sent out like a lamb to slaughter, and Malik made this happen.

I slammed face-first into an invisible barrier that knocked me back so hard the wind rushed out of my chest. I tried to scramble back up through pained gulps of air. My hands searched the air around me. They came into contact with a cool surface but there was nothing physically in front of me. I got up and tried to run in the opposite direction but was met with the same cold invisible wall that I ran into before.

I was trapped.

I saw Daxton slowly stalking toward me.

"Rosie..." Daxton's solemn voice was muffled by whatever box held me. "I can't stop." I flattened myself against the invisible wall behind me staring at Daxton as I did. There was a frown on his face as he lifted his arm up once more. "I don't know how to make this less painful. I'm sorry."

"Daxton don't you dare!" I heard Eli growl from the sidelines.

I lifted my own arm. It was shaking so violently that I had to use my other arm to hold it still. Through the fear I tried to focus as much as I could on the ground beneath Daxton's feet.

I'm sorry, I whispered in my mind.

The grass below him burst into flames so high that they engulfed his body before he could even register what was happening. The barrier around me dropped and I scrambled to catch myself before I fell to the ground.

Turning back to look at Daxton I saw that he had already extinguished the flames. His pants and shirt were charred at the ends and his face had a layer of soot on it, but other than that he seemed to be in one piece. He coughed lightly into his elbow.

I used this chance to send a ball of flames toward his form. He ducked left and stepped right into another pit of flames I had set up beside him. This time I heard a curse before he had extinguished the flame. I made sure these ones were higher, hotter. I pumped as much as I could into it and with each push of power, something in my chest tightened. When Daxton had finally stumbled out of the flames the skin on his arms was starting to char. The shirt of his chest was open, and his skin was bright red. His face was what caused me to regret my entire existence.

There was a small smile on his burned face, and the ugly twisted skin was worse than my dad's after the night of the fire. He let himself fall to the ground with a thud.

I pushed myself toward his twitching body. The run had already winded me but I could not see anything other than his charred body struggling to inhale.

"Number four is the winner!" Principal Winterfell announced. The crowd cheered but I felt no excitement at this announcement. They were bloodthirsty demons and this game would only egg them on more.

I kneeled by Daxton's body. My hands were flailed out beside him. I didn't know where to put them as there was not any part of his body that wasn't burned. Even his hair was almost burned to a crisp.

"I'm so sorry Daxton. I'm so sorry, it's okay the medical witches will be here, you won't hurt for long," I blubbered over him. My tears were coming out steadily and fell over his burned body. His magic spiked and I watched as he was slowly engulfed in a soft blue light.

The burned flesh started to knit back together and repair itself presenting a new layer of soft unblemished skin. I had never been more thankful that magic existed until this very moment. I hated the fire. I hated the pain it caused but at least Daxton was strong enough to repair himself. His clothes were still ripped and charred but the magic worked its way slowly up his body. Finally, his face which still had the smile on it, began to clear until it looked the same as it once was.

Relief crashed through me violently. I didn't care about the crowd. I threw myself over him and sobbed into his bare chest.

"You surprised me," he said with a warm chuckle that radiated through his chest. "I wasn't expecting *that*."

"I'm so sorry Daxton I didn't want to hurt you," I said into his chest.

"It hurt like a bitch but at least I didn't have to hurt you," he said and let out a sigh. "Save your voice, people are coming."

I nodded but continued to sob against him.

"It's okay, stop crying," he cooed in a voice gentler than I could imagine from him. "I let you burn me. It was the only way to stop it, I could have protected myself."

I inhaled deeply and pushed myself off of him. His brown eyes were warm and he still had a smile on his face.

"That's my girl," he whispered and pinched my cheek. "Don't feel sorry ever for defending yourself."

I sniffled as the medical witches gathered around us.

"Oh my god."

"He's healed?"

"Did you guys see how gnarly his body looked?"

Daxton sat up with a groan, the light finally faded.

"What happened to forfeiting?" Rae's angry growl came from somewhere above us.

"Isn't it obvious?" Daxton replied looking up at Rae. I noticed now his hair was still singed and I had an unobstructed view of his face that would have normally been covered by thick black hair. For the first time, I noticed fancy script that lined the side of his temple. I ran my finger down it. "Ya, healing doesn't include the hair so I will need a cut."

He gave me a boyish smile and reached his hand out to me. I tried my best to lift him up but he ended up slouching over me.

"Rae's power is limited by distance," he whispered in my ear taking advantage of our position. "I don't know what Malik has planned but I would love to see you kick Honor Roll's ass."

"Alright. I got it from here," Eli said coming up from my side and lifting Daxton from my shoulders. "Don't act like such a princess."

Daxton shot her a smirk and stood up on his own. "It's only so you can be my prince."

"Please leave the field so we can continue!" yelled the principal from his place across the field.

The medics, Eli, and Daxton left leaving only me and Rae alone in the field.

We took our places across from each other. The numbers showed between us. I could feel the irritation rolling off Rae in waves and I was already nervous. The last fight, as much as it had pained me...it had also left a strange sensation in my veins.

I was *excited* to see what I could do against someone like Rae, the girl who had slept with me then wanted to act as if nothing happened. To *save* her precious reputation. At least if I landed a hit it would be great payback for the blow to my ego it caused.

"I will not forfeit," she told me as the numbers counted down.

4.

I positioned myself in a wide stance. Rae's eyes widened.

3.

"Ms. Miller," she warned. I took a deep breath and exhaled. I let the giddiness make its way up my body and shot her a smile.

2.

"Rosie," she warned her voice getting angrier.

1.

"Don't you da—"

I took off running in the opposite direction as fast as my short legs would take me. I didn't look behind me I just kept on pushing forward.

The crowd cheered. This time I relished in it. Allowed it to make my heart pump faster. Held onto it as the fear and excitement coursed through me, powering me faster and faster.

Rae's power began to work on me. Exhaustion started to make my limbs heavy, but I tried to push through it. I used the panic to help fuel me, used it to anchor me. I pushed and pushed my almost dead legs. My chest was burning.

"Rosie stop running," Rae's voice boomed from the other side of the field. It was far.

A small bit of hope flared inside me. She was *far*. Of course Rae wouldn't degrade herself by running after a *low-level*.

The exhaustion did not lift from my limbs just yet; I felt myself slowing. I was nothing more than a light jog now.

Then a walk.

When I had to rest on the ground was when I finally looked back.

I was right. There Rae stood in the same spot as I left her in.

Stupid prideful girl, my mind purred.

With the last ounce of power I had I focused on not just lighting the fire under her feet, but something much bigger. If I wanted to stand a chance at winning I would have to force her to move back since I was in no state to drag myself across the field. I made a line of fire appear before her and she instinctively jumped away from it.

More, I chanted at it.

She was pushed back once more.

More, I chanted as my eyes began to close.

She was pushed further. She was trying to yell something, but I couldn't hear it. She was too far and the flames were louder than her voice.

Awareness pricked at my senses. I finally felt it, her power was slowly leaving me. I pushed myself on the ground further away from her, crawling. My fingers dug into the ground and pulled myself further. I didn't care about my clothes that were now stained with dirt, I forced my knees to push against the ground and away from her power.

I gulped in deep breaths of air as my heart started to beat erratically once more, trying to catch up with the wave of emotions that hit me. The exhaustion was almost gone and I could feel the energy pouring back into me.

Looking back Rae's head peeked just over the line of fire. She was pissed.

"I'm sorry," I whispered and with a flick of my arm the area around her burst into flames.

There was no scream and that haunted me more.

I pulled back the flames almost as soon as they engulfed her. Her body fell to the ground and medical witches were on her in seconds.

"Number four is the winner yet again!"

The crowd cheered.

Daxton ran to Rae and pushed the medics away. He engulfed Rae in the same blue light and I watched as Rae sat up almost immediately.

"You shouldn't have done that," Eli said pulling me up from the dirt. Eli lifted me up by the back of my shirt like a mother would to a kitten and walked me across the field. As soon as Rae spotted us she pushed everyone off her and stalked toward us.

"What was that out there, huh?" Rae asked as she stood in front of us. Her hands gripped the front of my shirt and she pulled me out of Eli's grasp. "You realize next is Malik, right? Did you think that through?"

Rae's glasses were broken, her cropped hair lightly singed and there was a layer of soot that covered her. Her eyes were fierce and caused my heart to pound in my chest. She pulled me closer to her, her face inches from mine,

"He could out your curse, did you think of that? He could make you scream. He could force you to degrade yourself in front of the entire school. He could literally make you say or do anything. Every *secret* that you hold is in his power and could be shouted to the school in seconds. You wouldn't even realize what happened. Do you understand?" Rae's voice was harsh as she spoke, it made my stomach twist and my throat constrict.

Every secret. She was never afraid of me getting hurt. She was afraid of her reputation. I should have known. Why would I think any different?

"Rae, it's okay," Daxton said appearing behind Rae. I paid no mind to him and instead kept my gaze locked on Rae.

"No, Dax," Eli told him from behind me. "You know he's bad news."

"It was me that told her about her range," Daxton admitted. "If you have anyone to be mad at, it's me."

Rae let go of my shirt and I fell against Eli's front. Her arms wrapped around me.

"There will be a break and then we will get to see the last battle!" Principal Winterfell's voice came through the speakers.

Rae turned to Daxton.

"You realize she knows too much right? And that you literally handed her to the worst person possible?" Rae's voice was a growl, but she didn't dare approach Daxton. She wouldn't fight him, that much I knew.

Unlike me, he belonged. Bitterness filled me.

"What will she give him that he doesn't already know Rae?" Daxton asked. "You already saw what he did to the principal, he probably planned this before the games started. And there still is the question of why he was in her room, which she still hasn't answered. Who knows, maybe they have been in contact long before we knew?"

Daxton somehow saved me and doomed me in one breath.

Do you have an answer? Eli asked in my mind. Her voice carried no anger, no accusation, it was more soothing than anything.

No, I said back. *Not one that I am ready to share.*

Her chest rumbled against my back and she pushed me forward, severing our connection.

"Good luck then, Rosie," Eli said and she left my side. Rae and Daxton both gave me one last look and then left as well.

I saw Malik's white hair in the distance before I registered him. His lanky figure walked toward me at a lazy pace, long legs stretched out in front of him, and his hands were in his pockets. He was even wearing his school uniform.

I met him halfway.

They are mad, I signed to him. A smile broke out across his scarred face.

"That's to be expected, isn't it?" he mused. He began stretching the tendons in his neck. "I mean who wants to be defeated so badly by a low-level."

I don't know what to tell them about us, I signed.

"Oh so there is an us now?" he said with a chuckle.

You know what I mean, I signed.

"Tell them the truth," he said, his eyes wandering over to where they now sat at the bench. "That I cornered you in a café. Skipped class with you to go on a date to the beach. And even bought you coffee."

It wasn't a date, I told him with a small pout.

"Wasn't it?" he said his eyes returning to mine. "Or you think they'd be mad that you've taken an interest in someone outside their group?" He closed the space in between us and leaned down to whisper in my ear. "I say let them be mad. Because that's what this is right, an interest?"

My mind came to a screeching halt. Was that what this was about? No, it couldn't be. He had to have just been trying to throw me off so he would have an advantage in this battle.

"Take your places!" Principal Winterfell made me jump away from Malik.

He walked back over to his space and the numbers appeared before us once more. I jogged back to my place and sent him a glare when I turned back to face him. I was met with a smile.

5.

4.

I tensed and readied my stance. I didn't know what Malik was going to pull but if I wanted to stand a chance, I'd have to be fast.

3.

2.

1.

The numbers disappeared and I came face to face with Malik once more. I readied my power. It burned in my veins before it materialized. I made it hotter, forced it into something akin to lava, ready to explode the moment I was ready.

Malik's hand raised.

"I forfeit!" he yelled.

There was a pause.

What the fuck?

Pure chaos erupted. Cheers broke out from some. Others cursed the day I was born. Chairs were thrown into the field. I started at him gobsmacked that he would forfeit to someone like me. He was old and didn't care for school, but didn't losing to a low-level bother him? He could destroy every last student in this place, and this would insult anyone.

Once my brain wrapped around what just happened, I jogged toward him. With one simple word echoing through my brain.

Why? I signed to him.

"Don't look a gift horse in the mouth, Rosie," he said with a smile. The same words my dad echoed to me before I left. My stomach filled with lead. "You are now the first-ever champion of the Winterfell Games on the year that they just started to allow low-levels into the academy. A mute and a low-level all wrapped in one, what a thing for the history books."

I shook my head unable to think straight.

"I truly am on your side, Rosie," he said.

Before I could respond the trio crowded around us.

"Malik, you have some nerve," Rae said in a growl.

"What? What's so wrong with giving up? Or are you just mad that the low-level beat you?" he said and gave Rae a smirk that no doubt pissed her off.

"What was the point?" Eli asked, her arm already looping around my shoulder.

"Ask Rosie, I am sure she has some answers for you now," he said and then added after a pause, "though I can't promise not to skip class with her again. That was far *too enjoyable.*"

Eli stiffened next to me and her nails bit into my shoulder.

You lied to me, she said in my head. *I apologized to you, and you lied to my face.*

With a wave Malik left us. None of the others moved nor even dared to look in my direction.

Chapter Twenty-Three
Rosie

I twiddled my thumbs as the gaze of all of the trio and Amr weighed on me. The silence was almost unbearable but none of them decided to talk. The worst had to be Eli's gaze; I couldn't decipher the thoughts behind her eyes. Rae looked more than unhappy, and Daxton was the only one who looked uncomfortable about the silence no doubt regretting the tip he gave me about Rae's power.

The games had ended over an hour ago and after the fanfare and rounds of congratulations they had ushered me back to my own dorm. I had a feeling this was their own way of punishing me for what I had done. I had been racking my brain for what to tell them since the games ended but I really had no excuse.

"I lied," I admitted casting my gaze downward into my lap to avoid having to look at them while I came clean.

"Obviously," Rae noted.

"I have a good reason," I started but was cut off by Eli.

"What reason could you have?" Eli asked. "Didn't you promise you would stay away from him? I told you he was dangerous and yet you still went to him?"

I would have so much rather Eli yell and scream at me. Break the stuff around me, but she did none of that. Instead, her voice was a cool calm that didn't falter as she spoke. It set me on edge. What was she planning?

"I did and I broke it," I told her. "It just happened. He met me and Matt in a coffee shop and I looked at him. There was no undoing it."

"What is your relationship with him?" Daxton asked. "Skipping class? Coffee shops?"

"There is nothing *like that* between us," I said. "He took me to the beach once, the day I skipped class. And then this morning, we got coffee with Matt."

"He was in your room," Daxton said. "That doesn't sound like nothing."

I swallowed thickly and finally had the courage to look up. I wish I didn't because I met Eli's eyes immediately and I did recognize the look finally, one that I had seen more often than not.

Disappointment.

Tell them the truth, Malik had said. But what would happen if Eli knew that Malik was in the bathroom while she was apologizing to me for something that wasn't even her fault?

"He came in once. Asked me why I did not text him to tell him I got home safely. He knew you would be mad and worried I would be...*unsafe,*" I said.

Eli snorted. "Let me guess, after that he wooed you with his words?" Eli crossed the room and put her hands on either side of me on the bed. I had to lean back but it only made our position worse. Her blonde hair hung loosely in front of her and tickled my face. Her eyes were narrowed, and her chest was heaving as if she ran a marathon. "Did you let him fuck you in this bed?"

My heart hammered against my ribcage.

"No, it's not like that," I said quickly and cast my eyes downward to her balled fists.

"Then what is it like, hm?"

"Nothing really, a friendship maybe. I don't trust him still." I hope she could hear the truth in my words.

"You will stop meeting with him. You will not be his friend. You will not even talk to him." Eli grabbed my chin harshly and forced me to look at her. "You are ours. Not the low-level's and certainly not *Malik's.* Remember that the next time he comes knocking."

You are ours. The same unnamed feeling fluttered in my chest again.

"Does he know about your curse?" Rae asked breaking the trance between me and Eli.

"Yes," I answered but still kept my eyes on Eli. I couldn't help but have my eyes wander to her slightly open mouth. Hot breath wafted across my face. "The principal told him."

"That's funny," Rae said. "Because the principal told me that Malik doesn't even go here."

"You saw how he talked to him at the tournament, he must have messed with his memory," Daxton said from beyond Eli's form.

"He did say something about messing with his memory," I murmured. Eli's tongue reached out to moisten her lips.

"What else did he say, low-level?" Eli asked, her voice a low whisper. She leaned forward slightly.

Eli was being very careful to not touch me. Her hands stayed by my thighs and her face was far enough that there was no chance of her reading my mind, but I still got nervous when I thought of the town.

"We didn't talk much about you guys. He knew sign language; it was easy to talk... He said he was on my side." I couldn't help but finish the sentence with a blush.

"Do you think I'm not on your side, *Rosie?*" Eli asked. I hated and loved the way she said my name.

"You guys...have each other," I told her truthfully. "Sometimes I feel like I belong but...most times I feel like you don't *see me.*"

I don't think she expected that truthful of an answer because she paused and leaned back to look at me.

"And Malik does?" Rae asked after a moment.

I paused at her words. Did I really need to tell them this?

"You belong to us Rosie," Eli said. "Don't make us worry again or you will pay the price, not Malik."

"We don't even know what he wants with you," Daxton said. "If you go with him again, we can't stop him if he wants to hurt you."

"He doesn't want—" I started but was cut off by Eli's hand on my mouth.

"She won't have a chance because she will be guarded by one of us at all times," she said. "Don't you dare try to fight me. I have heard enough of your *Malik* talk. I promise you," she continued as her other hand squeezed roughly at my thigh, "I'll make you forget his name and your own before the morning comes."

I swallowed thickly.

"Are we done with the questions?" I asked them. "Thanks to you two I am covered in dirt and would like a shower."

* * *

True to Eli's words, there was someone with me at all times. Even as I got out of the shower Amr was waiting for me on the bed and Eli had promised to return later that night after "some business" she and the others needed to take care of.

I dressed in my night clothes and joined Amr in the bed. I lay on my back and lift him above me. His head cocked at my actions. I giggled lightly.

"There they are off again," I said to him. "Doing group things and just proving my point from earlier."

Amr meowed at me. I brought him down to lay on my chest and hugged him close. His long fur tickled my chin.

"But you and me man, we still got each other." I ran my hand down the length of his spine and buried my fingers in his soft fur. "Malik really isn't that bad, Amr. I wish the others could see that. He doesn't do this type of stuff; he even tells me things I don't ask him—oh!"

I lifted Amr up to look at him once more, a light bulb going off in my head.

"You know Malik told me not to tell anyone. Well threatened to kill me actually and everyone I told...but you don't count!" Amr meowed unhappily. "Listen Amr, he took me someplace wonderful. A place that seemed to be straight out of a movie. I don't even know how it's possible but there is a place—a town. That is stuck in—"

I was cut off by a knock. I frowned at Amr.

"I'll tell you later," I finished and got up to open the door. Eli was standing there with a bag in hand. She pushed past me without a notice. I sighed and closed the door while juggling Amr in my hands. "At least you knocked this time."

"I thought you'd be happier to see me," Eli said as she threw her bag down on the floor. When she did, I finally realized how many piles of clothes I had still left on the floor. I felt a bit of shame when I realized that they all saw how much of a mess this was earlier.

Eli came to stand in front of me tearing my eyes from the mess. Her rough hand gripped my chin and forced it up. Her lips crashed into mine. Her teeth sank into my lower lip and I groaned and opened my mouth for her. Her hot tongue entered immediately, and my knees weakened.

God, how long has it been since we kissed like this?

Too long, she answered back.

She pulled away, a line of spit following her. She took Amr and threw him across the room. I gasped in horror.

"Eli no!" I looked around her and saw that Amr landed on his feet across the room. He gave out a small, disgruntled hiss.

"He will not want to see this anyways. I said I would make you forget your name but I am not *that* forgiving just yet. You will have to earn it," she answered. "Strip."

I gulped at the command.

"Eli I—"

"Did you not hear me?" she asked and pulled me back into her chest and leaned down for another kiss. This time she allowed me to bury my fingers in her hair without pulling them away. She brought her hand down to my lower back and pushed me into her.

She sent a vision into to me. It showed her on my bed sitting on the edge with her feet firmly on the ground. Her legs were spread and between them was me but I was stark naked on my knees in front of her.

She pulled away from me and the image went with her.

"Strip."

She undressed completely and sat down on the bed just like she had shown me. I paused under her stare and let my eyes roll down her body. The tattoos bled into her chest around her perky breasts and when she spread her legs I caught sight of her pussy. It was mouthwatering.

I took my clothes off. First the shirt, her eyes watching hungrily as I did so. She did a sharp intake when she realized I wasn't wearing a bra. Next I slowly pulled down my shorts and my underwear in one motion. She spread her legs further and her hand trailed her body teasingly. I was about to kneel before her but she stopped me.

"Actually, I was going to save this for later but, hand me my bag," she said. I gave her a look but managed to get her bag to her on shaky legs. She unzipped it and when she found what she was looking for she threw the bag back across the room.

I saw a flash of pink and her lips were on mine again. Her fingers brushed across my slit and I writhed against them. Her thumb pushed against my clit and two fingers slowly and painfully teased my slit. I met her passion, pulled her closer by the neck deepening our kiss. Her other hand came over to pinch my nipple. I let out a moan.

She moved even faster and inserted two fingers into me.

"Damn you don't even need much to get you ready," she said against my lips and pumped her fingers in me twice before removing them completely. I whined against her actions. She gave me a chaste kiss and then held something in front of my face.

It was pink and egg-shaped with a leather string-like handle attached to it.

"You aren't serious," I said.

"I am," she replied. "I told you I'd make you forget your name. Let's see if we can make a game out of this. Use this and let's see if you can get me off first. If I come first I will remove it, if you come first this bad boy gets to stay in as long as I want."

The words sent shivers down my spine and my belly pooled with heat. "I've never..."

"It's not hard. Spread your legs further," she ordered. When I did she brought the pink vibrator down and teased my wet slit with it. Before entering she showed me the remote with her other hand and turned it on to level four. I let out a yelp when it turned on and began vibrating against my clit. The sensation was odd at first but my apprehension was quickly replaced with shocks of pleasure. I began grinding against it needing more friction.

She dragged it across my opening then inserted it inside me and I buried my head in her lap and moaned loudly against the feeling of it filling me. It was vibrating against a spot that made me see stars. I would definitely lose this challenge.

"Eli this isn't...fair," I said with a moan. I gripped onto her thigh. My weak legs were barely holding me up anymore.

"I would get started if I were you," she said and pushed my hair away from my face. "It doesn't seem like you'll last long."

I swallowed and quickly began working on her. I let my tongue run the length of her folds and sucked on her clit lightly.

Eli's hand gripped at my hair rougher and I could have sworn I heard something akin to a sigh from above me. I got to work moving my tongue where I thought it would feel best and brought a hand over to rub her clit. Eli let me take my time, giving me encouraging moans when I did something she liked.

The vibrations caused my thighs to shake violently and my movements became frenzied. I moaned into her and that seemed to stir something in her because until now I had free rein but after the sound vibrated around her she pushed me harder into her.

"Yes, like that Rosie," Eli cooed from above me. "If you want to level the playing field go pick a toy," she said loosening her hand. I drove for the bag and quickly found a bright pink dildo. I looked to her for an explanation. Her eyes were hooded and her free hand was pinching her nipple lazily. "It's as easy as it seems Rosie."

I crawled my way back in between her legs. She pulled me closer and put her leg over my shoulder, positioning herself for me. I closed my eyes against the feeling of the toy inside me trying to ground myself.

"Go on," she cooed and guided my hand to rub the dildo across her entrance, rubbing the sticky wetness all over it. Her hand pushed into mine and I watched as she stretched around the dildo.

Her hand knotted itself in my hair. I managed to look up at her and was caught with a sight that sent a jolt through me. Her head was back and her mouth was open just slightly to allow her pants through. She was beautiful like this, her neck long and lean, sweat glistening on her skin lightly, and the noises she made were only plunging me harder into oblivion.

I thrust the dildo into her and tried to build a rhythm with the help of her hand.

"Now harder," she moaned letting me fully take control and moving her hand to her clit. I did as she said and was rewarded with beautiful moans that made my pussy throb.

She must have felt it or heard it in my mind because her eyes snapped to mine. I grabbed my hand tightly in the sheets beside her as I continued to thrust the dildo into her. I paused only to cry as the orgasm rocked my entire body.

"If only you could listen this well in real life," she said with a groan.

There was no break and Eli did not stop the toy, instead she gripped my hand and forced the tempo up. Her hips met the thrusts and she froze as the orgasm wracked her body.

"You lose," she said and chuckled darkly. She pulled the toy out of her and threw it somewhere in the room. She pulled my face closer to hers, lips brushing across mine. "You look so sinful like this, so beautiful."

I shook against her lips. The vibrator inside me was still going without stop and I was already so desperately ready for another orgasm.

"Eli, please..." I begged her.

"You know the deal." She let go of my hair and patted her lap, giving me a sinful smile.

I climbed on top of her and without wasting another second tangled my hands in her soft blonde locks and crushed my lips to hers. She grabbed my hips tightly. One of her hands reached between my legs and dipped a finger inside me pushing the vibrator deeper within me.

I let out a cry against her lips. She chuckled in response and moved her now wet fingers to the middle of my back. She broke our kiss and with another smile she leaned down and took a nipple into her mouth. I couldn't help but arch into her.

"Eli...Eli, please," I said between the moans that were freely coming out of my mouth now. I tried to grind against her lap but the hand on my hip stopped me and forced me to still. I yanked at her hair harder and she bit down on my nipple.

"Please, what?" she asked and moved on to the next nipple.

"I can't...it's too much." I couldn't find my thoughts, I couldn't think of the words, I couldn't think of anything other than how good her tongue felt circling my nipple. "Fuck."

Eli grabbed harder and bit down on the other nipple. "Such a bad mouth," she said. "But this doesn't really seem like a punishment if I give you what you want."

"Eli, I—"

"I think this is a pretty sweet deal. Maybe…" She leaned away from my nipple and gave me a hooded look. "I should just not touch you at all." Her hand started to move from my hip.

"No, Eli." I gripped at her shirt and forced her back to me. "Please." I tried to kiss her again as I felt myself tightening once more. God I could barely think. She leaned out of my grasp.

"Let me see this," she commanded. "I want to see your face when you come."

Her free hand rested between my legs and she began to circle my clit.

I came, crying her name and shuddering above her. I was pushed to the bed and she was on top of me pulling out the vibrator only seconds after my orgasm. With the amount of wetness that was already gathered she easily slipped it out.

"Eli please," I begged still feeling the aftershocks of my orgasm. I reached down between her legs but she caught my wrist.

"Jesus, Rosie," she growled and flipped me over. She pulled me to the end of the bed. "Lift."

I complied and lifted my hips and spread my knees. Her fingers entered me from behind and I rocked into them.

"You are soaking," she said with another thrust. "Tell me how much you wanted this." She relentlessly finger fucked me so hard that I had to brace myself against the bed. I did not mind though—she was reaching far deeper than that toy did and spread me wider when she entered another finger.

"Fuck," I moaned. "So bad, Eli."

"You will be good from now on won't you?" she asked rubbing my clit.

"Yes," I moaned and continued to arch further against her.

"Say it," she commanded and removed her finger from my clit. I shuddered at the feeling of her leaving me.

"I'll be good Eli," I cried. "Just for you. I'll be good for you."

My toes curled when she began rubbing circles on my clit once more.

"Good girl," she praised.

I came with another cry. I collapsed into the bed in a sweaty wet mess; Eli was next to me panting heavily.

"I'm the only one sleeping here from now on."

Chapter Twenty-Four

Eli

"I fucking hate it here Dax," I grumbled as we pulled up to his parents' house. The farmhouse had been in sight for over twenty minutes now as we rounded the long driveway, but I couldn't bring myself to speak. I was too busy trying to calm myself. I may be all for bashing those witches' heads in but Dax would be less than happy. I had one of my workers drive us over in hopes of a quick getaway if anything went wrong.

I couldn't get over how disgusting these freaks were. They acted all perfect and pure in public parading around like they didn't have their own fucked up *rituals* at home. The demons who had seen the destructive powers of the witches over the years believed their bullshit without a second thought but everyone who even had the slightest clue about magic knew that they spewed nothing but lies.

When Daxton first revealed to me the years of abuse he had suffered through, I went on a rampage. I was ready to destroy everything in sight. I almost did. But a tearful Daxton told me that if I did that, I would be no better than them. Daxton had his share of rebellion years but when push came to shove, he really didn't want any violence without reason.

I watched him fidget in the back seat and take a deep breath. He had tried so hard these past years as his powers grew to control himself, but slips happened and every time they did I saw a little piece of him break off and die. It seemed at times that the wounds Rae and I so carefully sewed back together were ready to break at the seams. This was one of those times. He didn't like to admit that Rae had any part in his healing, but we all understood better just how thorough Rae was with clean-up.

"Let's just get this over with," he said and let himself out of the car.

I cursed under my breath and followed him. I gave instructions to the driver to wait for us in case we needed to make a hasty getaway. These witches were crazy and last time we barely left in one piece. That was over a few years ago but still...I didn't trust them to change.

The black iron gate to the property was slightly ajar as if waiting for us to arrive. Daxton slipped in and I followed after him making sure to keep as close to him as possible. The front yard was filled with colorful flowers and trimmed hedges in the shape of various animals. My eyes roamed across the property; besides the light wind everything was still. I kept my hands firmly in my pockets careful not to brush anything. The last time they had caught us was because I had set off a magic alarm that was attached to one of the doorknobs. The less I touched the quicker this would be.

Daxton paused and waved his hand out in front of him. A wave of translucent magic blanketed itself across the property and clung to our skin. A shiver went through me at the cooling effect it left.

"I don't feel them," he said in a whisper and continued onward.

Daxton stayed silent as he walked up the white-painted porch and opened the unlocked door. We made quick work of the trip and moved from the overly decorated front room, up the stairs and to the back of the second story where Dax's childhood bedroom stayed unchanged. Unlike the rest of the house that was painted in a light mint color, his bedroom was as dark as you could get it, from black walls to dark red sheets.

"Stay by the door," he ordered not looking back at me as he crossed the room and began to dig through his dresser drawer. I did as I was told and perched myself near the door of his room watching the hallway. I listened intently for footsteps; I heard none.

I was out there for less than a minute before I saw someone enter the hallway. Her shoes did not even make a whisper of a sound as she walked. I cursed internally and slipped back into his room and shut his door softly, making sure to lock it. I listened to the steps of what I assumed was their wait staff. She slowly made her way down toward Dax's room. I held my breath and she passed the room. Her footsteps stopped near us as she paused.

I promised myself that if she did not move on in five seconds, I would go out there and deal with her myself. Anyone that saw us here could snitch and his parents would descend on us like hawks. I looked over at Dax and noted that he was still rummaging through the drawer, his back turned to me.

One.

There was no movement, I couldn't even hear her breath.

Two.

A shift? Maybe an inhale?

Three.

Nothing.

Four.

I braced myself ready to barge out of this door.

Five.

I heard her footsteps as she quickly walked away from where we were at the end of the hallway. I let out a sigh and stepped away from the door. Dax paused in his rummaging. I looked over and met his wide eyes. There was a second of utter silence before he went back to his rummaging. He pulled out three jars of a blue swirling liquid and wrapped it into a black hoodie that he didn't come here with.

"Is that for Rosie?" I asked him, noting that the bottles looked exactly like those ones he gave her for her curse. For relaxation, he had said. I didn't need to ask why he had so many stocked up in his room, but it pained me nonetheless to think of the nights he spent here before I met him and dragged him away from this hellhole.

"We told her a month," he said and stood. "If we want to keep up this experiment, we will need to convince her that the potions work."

"Why not just tell her?" I asked. "Coming here is more than it's worth."

"The curse itself is a form of trauma, Eli. You of all people should know trauma doesn't disappear overnight."

If he was talking about himself, I would understand but the way he used me as an example made something itch under my skin.

"Whatever," I dismissed. "Let's get out of here."

"I don't think my parents are home," he said and moved to exit out his door. "They would have known by now."

"Still, I hate it here," I told him.

"Me too," he answered. He paused with his free hand on the door. His brown eyes met mine. His short hair gave me such a better view of his face and it would be a lie if I said I didn't enjoy every minute of it. I took the moment I had and leaned in close brushing my lips against his. He let out a sigh.

"I like this new look," I told him. I let my finger trail the tattoo on the side of his face.

His eyes stayed trained on mine through the interaction. "I thought you would have given me up for Rosie," he said. I chuckled at his response.

"Would you give me up for her?" I asked. Blush ran across his face in the cutest way.

"No...well...it's difficult to say." He paused and let out a breath. "Do you think she'd be okay with this?"

"Since when were you so worried about her reaction, hm?" I asked him with a smile even though I knew exactly why he was worried and there was some part inside me that was just as worried.

"We have lied to her enough, Eli," he deadpanned. I ruffled his hair.

"We had no choice," I said and planted a chaste kiss on his lips once more.

"Do you really think she will forgive us for these lies?" he asked in almost a whisper.

"You are not talking about us," I concluded. I let out a sigh. "I told you I am for telling her about the curse. It would be easier for us than continuing to do this. But if you and Rae are right, if we told her, it is possible that the curse would snap back in place."

"You didn't answer the question," he said with a small frown.

"I think when she finds out she will be mad but if she doesn't understand that this was for her own good then she is not as smart as I thought," I told him earnestly.

"Is it really for her own good though? Do we really care about the curse or is this still just a tool for graduation?" he asked.

I paused and thought over my words carefully.

"I can't tell you what you should feel or what motivates you to help her. That's for you to decide."

He nodded and without another word he opened the door. As soon as his sneaker-clad foot crossed the threshold, alarms sounded.

"Shit *they are* here," Dax cursed and began running down the hallway at full speed. Normally, I wouldn't degrade myself to such a chase but I under-stood from past experience that if I lingered the witches would be on me in seconds.

Instead of going out the front door, Dax led us further into the house and up to the third floor. This had been the way we both snuck out years ago so I knew the path like the back of my hand. That's not what bothered me. What bothered me was the multiple pairs of feet that I heard running down the hallways after us. I chanced a look back and when I did I almost let out a crazed laugh.

"We really pissed them off last time huh?" I yelled at Dax as I saw the very large snouts of two wolf-like dogs that scrambled after us. They were at least three times the size of a normal dog and their jaws seemed like they could break my leg in half.

"They are familiars, like Amr," he said through pants and flung the door to the third-floor balcony open.

We didn't stop as we ran full speed to the balcony's end. As serious as the situation was I couldn't help but smile at the sight in front of me.

This was my favorite part.

We dove headfirst off of the balcony. The garden floor came quick, my stomach flipped, and mild panic clouded my senses when I didn't feel the pull at first. But then, something with the feeling akin to a cloud enveloped me and the ground stopped only a few feet short of my face.

I let out a laugh as Dax dropped whatever power he was using to hold us and we both fell to the ground. I wiped the dirt off my pants and then helped him up from his position. He was looking over the bottles in almost a frantic manner.

"Go," I told him and pushed him toward the front.

A heavy warm force that felt like a tank covered in a wiry type of blanket hit me from above and I went crashing to the ground. Before I could even let out a sound I had to bring up my arm to protect my face from the beast's jaws. He was positioned over me stopping any move of escape.

Looking over to Dax I was relieved to see that it was only the one hound that had jumped after us, but the other would probably be soon to follow. I sent a kick to the hound, but his jaws stayed tight.

I sent another.

Then another.

Then another.

"Argh!" I yelled and used all the strength I could muster to maneuver the hound to one of my sides so I could at least free my legs. There was a red light that filled my eyes and the hound stiffened. I was able to easily push him off then and watched as his stiff body fell to the ground.

I sent a look over to Dax.

"Thanks," I said and half jogged over to him. He just nodded and turned to lead us back to the front of the yard. It was a maze of hedges that we had to work through, each feeling like their thorns were purposefully reaching out to scratch us. As we made our way through the last batch of hedges the black sedan we had used to get here came into view. I sped up my steps along with Dax.

The other hound loudly crashed through the front door and out into the garden.

"They have gone overboard," Dax said with a sharp tone. He lifted his free hand balancing the wrapped hoodie in his other hand. The same red light that I saw on the other hound exploded from his hand and began racing toward the creature.

This time it dodged then began running toward us.

Dax sent another beam that the hound just narrowly ducked and rolled out of the way of. With a shake, the hound began circling us. Dax's magic shifted, and instead of the red light the air cleared. There were small wisps of magic that seemed to circle around his hand.

The hound ran into an invisible wall much like the one Rosie been confined to during the games. The hound rammed its body into the invisible wall.

"Can that break?" I asked Dax, watching as the hound continued to ram its body up against the wall.

"Yes," he answered simply and his hand grew red once more. Vein-like red bands wrapped around the hound's body and it stiffened and fell to the ground just like the other had. "Let's go."

I nodded and we both jogged to the car that was waiting for us. Neither of us wanted to stick around to see just when his parents wanted to show. Dax was a hell of a witch but if it actually came down to a fight we were severely disadvantaged due to the annoying fact that I was *just a demon with a mind-reading power* as they had once said when they had met the girl who was sneaking into their son's room at night.

The car pulled away from the house and we held our breaths in the back seat as the farmhouse disappeared from view. I looked over to see Dax's eyes closed, a small droplet of sweat formed on his forehead.

It was another twenty minutes before he let out a sigh and his eyes opened. When they did, I felt my heart skip a beat. My favorite monster was back.

"I didn't know you used so much magic," I jabbed playfully. His eyes snapped toward mine.

"I didn't until we left. I had to keep the magic going so they wouldn't follow. The further away the harder it is to control, the more magic it needs," he explained. "And now it wants more."

I let my hand rest on his inner thigh.

"I think we have a solution to that."

Chapter Twenty-Five

Rosie

I used to think I hated the solitary life. The lonely nights with no one to talk to, silent meals, cold beds, but now after being followed by the trio every minute...maybe the solitary life wasn't as bad as I thought.

No matter where I went, even the bathroom, there was someone waiting for me. There was not a moment where I could just have a moment to think to myself. I told them that Amr would cut it but they begged to differ.

And today may have been the worst because I was stuck with Rae.

She had been moody since the day of the games and refused to talk to me really about anything. She would ask simple questions but when we were alone she stayed silent more often than not. Today, we were in her room once more. She was at the table doing her work and I sat on the floor against the bed reading one of the books she had stashed near her bed. It was boring and I couldn't even get through one paragraph. If I wasn't so mad at her, I would have felt flustered when I thought about what we did when we were alone in her room the last time but now every time I looked at her glasses-covered face and stupid curly hair I became irritated.

"What are they even doing?" I asked her with a huff.

"Daxton has to pick up some elixirs from his house," she answered. Her homework seemed more important than this conversation.

"And Eli has to do that with him?" I asked, my tone sounding way too bratty even in my ears. Rae peered over her shoulder.

"Yes," she answered and then looked back at her work.

I let a minute pass.

"Are you still mad at me or something?"

She let out a sigh and turned around to face me fully now.

"Why must everything be about you, Rosie?" she asked, her tone cold.

"You are obviously mad *at me!* I would say that has a lot to do with me." I crossed my arms over my chest.

"Tell me something and I will tell you why I am angry with you," she said.

"What is it?"

"In your room, the day of the game. You were hiding something," she accused. The blood rushed to my head.

"You mean other than fucking you?" I deflected.

Rae's eyes narrowed.

"About Malik," she clarified.

"You wouldn't know the difference," I commented and tried to look back at the book I was reading. I really hoped my words were true—based on what she said before she could only read the emotions not what they stemmed from.

"Tell me, did you tell Malik we were together?" she asked.

Were together. I wanted to scoff.

"Not everything is *about you*, Rae," I echoed her words back at her. I peeked over the book and saw her jaw twitch.

"Answer the question." She slammed her pen down on the desk.

"He does seem to think I have slept with all of you."

It wasn't a total lie, he did call them my *lovers*...it just wasn't what I was worried about.

"And you told him?" she pried.

"I didn't," I said. "I let him think what he wants."

"I am mad you won," she confessed. "I am mad you lied about Malik. I am mad that you were so careless to get yourself in that situation. You could have spilled so many of our secrets and even after we warned you, you still went to him."

I swallowed thickly at her words.

"I don't have secrets to share," I forced out.

"You do, Rosie," she pushed. "You see us every day, eat with us, take classes with us, hear us talk about our business dealings, sleep with us. No one has the secrets you do."

"Why do you think you are all so important, hm?" I said my irritation getting the better of me.

"Even as a low-level you should know the attention that is on all of us. You do not know how many people have tried to weasel their way into our beds so they can take advantage of our positions." She spat her words like a curse.

"Not like you would give them the time of the day," I said with a huff.

"Because of *my hard work*," she replied. "You yourself said you saw how I protected them. Imagine what else you could accidentally spill now that your curse is gone? We play with powerful people Rosie and they like to gamble with *lives*."

I couldn't respond. I didn't know how to. God why did these others have to make me feel so guilty?

She turned back to her work with a sigh.

"And another thing," she said. This time she didn't look toward me as she spoke.

"Yes?"

"If he asks again...when he asks again, tell him that we were never together. I don't care about what you say about Daxton and Eli but leave me out of it." I heard her pen against the paper as if her words did not mean anything. As if, she couldn't feel the hurt radiating off of me. She could feel it right? The hurt?

I was saved by the opening of the door and the entrance of the two in question. They both had dirt stains on their white school uniforms. Daxton had a rip in his school pants and Eli's sleeve was almost completely torn off. Daxton set down what looked like a black bundle of clothing near the entrance.

"I thought you were just going to your house," I commented.

Daxton's eyes shifted to mine and I felt a jolt run through me. The magic was back behind his eyes, watching. The last time I saw him like this was when we were in the garden and he was having trouble keeping a handle on himself.

"We did but now," Eli spoke for him, "he needs magic."

"Did they send guards this time?" Rae asked from the table, her eyes running over their torn clothing.

"Hounds," Daxton spoke, his voice low and almost growl-like. "They were mad."

Rae let out an uncharacteristic snort.

"Do it somewhere else." Rae raised her hand in dismissal.

Eli's eyes met mine and a sly smile passed her face. I knew what the smile usually meant and as much as I didn't want *that* I still felt my insides clench.

"Rosie," Eli said in a purr as she crossed the room and knelt down in front of me. "You want to help Daxton, don't you?" Her rough hands gripped my ankles, and she pulled my legs and placed them on the sides of her hips. I had to catch myself on my elbows in order to stop my head from hitting the edge of the bed.

"Eli maybe we shouldn't..." I trailed off when Daxton stalked over to us. He leaned down and threw the book across the room; it landed with a loud thud.

"I told you to go somewhere else," Rae growled.

Daxton pushed me up into a sitting position and sat directly behind me with his legs on either side of me. I could feel that he was already hard against my back. One warm hand made its way under the hem of my shirt and the other made its way to my neck. He pushed my chin up forcing me to lean my head back into his chest and look into his eyes. His hair had been cut since the games and it now gave me a full view of his face. What was once hidden under a mess of black hair was now shown to the world. His strong jaw, high cheek bones, the script tattoo, and most importantly his eyes were left unobstructed giving me a rare chance to gaze into those brown depths.

"You want to help me don't you, *Rosie?*" he asked me, his breath fanning across my face.

I swallowed and felt his hand tighten ever so slightly on my neck. I couldn't speak and the argument with Rae was close to forgotten. Eli's hands began massaging my legs starting from my ankle to my thigh. I had taken advantage of my curse the last few days and forgone the undergarments, and I almost regretted it when I felt the warmth of Eli's rough hands on my inner thighs.

With the hand that was in my shirt Daxton reached behind me and unclasped my bra with one hand. I couldn't help my sharp intake of breath.

"You wouldn't make me blood let, would you?" Daxton asked. "You remember how good the time in the garden felt, right?

"Daxton," Rae warned. I paid no mind to her especially when Eli's hand came to undo the button on my pants. Since when did I feel so unashamed about this?

Tick tock, low-level, Eli said in my head. *Daxton is showing tremendous strength but I on the other hand am not willing to wait to see how long it takes for Rae to kick us out.*

"Yes," I forced out and watched as Daxton let out a small smile.

Eli used a free hand to pull my chin down causing Daxton to loosen his grip on my neck, and forced two fingers inside my mouth.

"Wet them for me," Eli commanded.

I did as she asked and took the two fingers in my mouth. I bit them lightly before running my tongue along the digits. Eli watched me with hooded eyes. She removed her fingers with a plop. They were gleaming with spit.

Daxton forced my chin up once more so we could make eye contact. His free hand pinched one of my nipples and I bit my lip to stop the moan.

"Don't hide your sounds," Daxton said. I felt Eli begin to pull my pants down. Even just being between the two caused my pulse to skyrocket, but now that I was at their mercy the wetness gathered between my legs even faster than before.

I had been at the mercy of Eli before but god...*both of them?*

Eli threw my jeans behind her and spread my legs even further, then let out a chuckle. Daxton rolled my nipple between his fingertips. His eyes were on me the entire time, never wavering. The intensity made me blush and it only caused the situation between my legs to worsen. I averted my eyes but he let out a low animalistic growl.

It startled me as much as it excited me.

"Don't look away from me," he commanded and squeezed at my throat. It made me lightheaded. Eli's fingers played with the wetness that was on my thigh and began trailing it down my leg.

Fuck. I wanted Eli's teasing to stop. I widened my legs and let out a whine.

"I wish you could hear her thoughts right now. She wants it so bad," Eli said playfully.

"You have to ask nicely, Rosie," Daxton said, his voice almost condescending.

Eli's finger lazily played with the wetness coming out of my slit. I gasped at the feeling and Daxton leaned down and licked at my open lips.

"You heard him, Rosie," Eli added on, flicking my clit. "Use that pretty little voice to beg us."

I tried to move against her hand but Eli's other hand wrapped around my hip and stopped me from moving. The other was still lazily rubbing along my aching core.

"Get on with it," Rae growled from the other side of the room. I had forgotten she was here until now.

"Don't be jealous Rae," Eli teased back, her finger dipping just slightly into my opening. I moaned against Daxton's lips and tried to kiss him but he pulled just far away enough that I couldn't reach him. "I'm sure you will have your turn. Maybe Rosie will want you when we are done."

I couldn't help the images that popped into my mind. The night I stayed here, the way her lips traveled my body. I wouldn't put it past me to want her even if she was acting like an asshole. I panicked and tried to send a warning to Eli in my mind but she beat me to it.

"Beg, Rosie," Eli demanded. *And I won't tell Rae you just spilled her secret.*

"Please," I said with a groan. Even as I held Daxton's stare, I could feel the smile when Eli let out a chuckle. She inserted one finger into me achingly slow. Daxton leaned down once more to cover my mouth with his while his free hand continued to tug at my nipple.

She slowly removed the single digit and then entered it with slightly more force. I tried to meet her hand with my thrust but the hand on my hip pinned me in place.

Daxton's tongue entered my mouth, wrestling with my own. I couldn't bring myself to pull away from him to demand that Eli move faster. The way he kissed me, paired with the way his hand wrapped firmly around my throat, was far too addicting. Daxton's magic was already reaching out to me. I felt it under my skin and it rippled like waves. It traveled all the way from my head to my toes and I couldn't help but moan at the feeling.

Eli inserted another finger, giving up whatever game she was playing and began pumping into me hard and fast. I widened my legs so her knuckles could hit my clit as she thrust her hand into me. Daxton pulled away from our kiss when I was unable to kiss him back. His hand removed itself from my throat and lifted my shirt and unhooked bra up to my neck leaving me exposed. I cried out as Eli hit a spot that made me see stars.

"Look Rosie," Daxton's voice rumbled in his chest. I opened my eyes. Eli, still pounding into me, began to lean forward and she took the free nipple and brought it into her mouth. Eli began to bite and suck on it. Daxton's ministrations lightened to a feather-light touch. "Do you like this Rosie? Being between us?"

I more than liked it, I wanted to tell him, but my orgasm was fast approaching. Eli pulled away from my nipple leaving it pink and sore. She gave me a smirk, like what she was doing was all fun and games and barely fazed her.

"Look at the low-level. She fucking loves being used by us, don't you?" Eli said and inserted a third finger. I let out a loud moan only for my mouth to be covered once more by Daxton. "I bet she dreams about being fucked by us, one after another."

Daxton moved a hand in between my legs and Eli shifted slightly so that Daxton could begin rubbing my clit. I shuddered violently as I came. If Daxton wasn't covering my mouth I would have no doubt been heard through these walls. Eli nor Daxton stopped as I came and instead picked up the pace.

I whimpered against Daxton. He pulled away.

"One more," he cooed softly. "You don't want us to stop now right?" His voice was so soft and sweeter than any candy I could remember tasting. I felt the magic build up inside me as the second orgasm came following the first with no hesitation. The feeling that made my toes curl was back and I felt it spill over to Daxton. He groaned and his head fell back onto the bed.

There was a pause where it felt like we were wrapped in a cocoon of warmth. The magic that had been flowing in between us seemed to stretch outward and expand across the space. After what felt like we were being suffocated from the thick magic, it snapped into us.

Both Daxton and I out a loud gasp.

"What the fuck?" Eli asked as she pulled her fingers out of me. I saw Rae's form tower over the three of us and through blurry eyes I saw her hand a damp towel to Eli.

Eli wiped between my legs, then her fingers. I couldn't focus on her actions as the magic slowly settled inside me. It seemed to rock inside me as if trying to get out, but after a moment it settled into a stillness. But unlike how the curse felt before, this was different. It was like even though it was still, it was living inside me, just waiting for its moment.

"That's not right," Daxton said from behind me.

I heard a shuffle, then something hit Eli. She grumbled and then I felt her pull my pants up and my shirt down. My eyes were still trying to clear as I took deep breaths. Rae's features slowly came back into focus.

"It's inside me," I choked out. "I feel it."

"Feel what?" Rae asked.

"My magic," Daxton answered for me, his arms snaking around me and holding me tight. "Witches mutually exchange magic. The exchange and expulsion of magic is what calms it. Before, I just took magic. Usually it would make me unstable, but the magic was so powerful..." Daxton's voice trailed as if he was also mesmerized by the feeling.

"It was satiated," Rae finished for him. "Are you saying *the curse* took it back this time?" Rae gave him a hard look.

"But how could it if I took that potion?" I asked. "Doesn't it get rid of it?"

"It's dormant, that's how I was able to take magic before," Daxton explained.

I thought to the last time I blood let in this very room.

"Wait..." I paused trying to find the words. "So we still don't know how to fully get rid of it. Rae didn't you just say it was gone?"

Eli stood up and cast a look toward Rae. Rae met her eyes and then mine. She had a small frown.

"It's not...fully gone," she answered.

"Then why is it not working?" I asked. There was something prickling at my senses, a familiar tingling.

"We found a loophole," Daxton answered from behind me.

"Which is?" I asked, my voice hard. What was so hard about the truth? I tried to pry Daxton's hands off me but they stayed firm. "What are you guys hiding from me?"

"You can't know the loophole," Rae told me. "We are still not sure; we have to keep watching."

"How much longer?" I asked my voice rising slightly. "What were you doing this entire time if not watching it?"

No one spoke. Daxton finally loosened his arm and I pushed away from him, scrambling to stand up and put some space between myself and the others. I backed away from them, my back toward the door. Amr came out of his hiding place and ran toward my legs.

"Why can't I know the things you do?" I asked, my voice cracking against my wishes. This was stupid, I would not cry over something so stupid. "How is it that you *still* won't let me into this little group you have?"

"Ms. Miller," Rae started to speak but I cut her off with a glare.

"Don't you Ms. Miller me, Rae," I hissed at her. "How many more secrets do you have that I don't know about? You said that I already knew *too much* but I feel like I know nothing at all!"

"This is the reason we didn't tell you," Rae explained. Both Eli and Daxton averted their gaze but Rae was staying strong. "We didn't know how you would react and the curse is—"

"It's my curse!" I yelled at her, tears filling my eyes. "I should know!"

The wall that seemed so transparent with them firmly rebuilt itself and I couldn't help but feel like the people in front of me were those that I didn't even recognize anymore. Every touch, every kiss, the gifts, the gestures...how much was a lie?

"I feel what's happening, don't do that," Rae said and took a step toward me. I raised my hand to stop her and the lights in the room went out, startling everyone but myself. I was too over it. Over all the lies.

"This whole thing was a lie wasn't it?" I asked. "You brought me in here, made me feel welcomed, but what was it, the sex? The early graduation?"

"You knew what we wanted out of this deal," Rae said. Daxton stood up.

"Rae," Daxton warned.

"There was never a promise of anything more," she continued. "You willingly let Daxton and Eli do whatever they wanted but we told you what we were like. You knew we wanted something that benefited us."

Was it my heart that broke into pieces or the windows? I couldn't tell anymore. Why was I so surprised anyways? She was right, they told me from the beginning. It just turned out that I wasn't anything that benefited them so I couldn't be involved in these talks.

I thought through every time they dismissed me. Every weekend where they would be nowhere to be seen, leaving me on my own and all by myself until Matt came back. They never wanted anything more than a fuck buddy. Why was I surprised?

I let out a pitiful laugh and opened the door.

"Next time find a different bitch to fuck, Rae," I said in a dull tone and left the dorm.

I should have known there was no tearing down this wall.

Chapter Twenty-Six
Rosie

Matt gave me a sheepish look as he opened the door to his dorm. The third-year dorms were slightly roomier than the first-year's but they all had the same exposed brick, wooden desk that seemed as old as the school, and a rickety bed. There were clothes strewn across his floor. I wouldn't judge though, my room had its fair share of messes. It's not like I gave him a lot of time to prepare anyways; I came here right after I exploded on the others.

"I'll clean up and you can take the bed," he said and reached down to pick up the clothes.

"Thanks for this," I said and sat myself at his desk.

"It's not a problem at all." Matt threw his clothes into the hamper that was hidden behind the bathroom door. "Some company would be great anyways, you know? I also feel like it has been a long time since we were able to talk."

I felt a pang of guilt. It was because I had pushed him away to work on the curse with the others and just ended up staying with them and ignoring Matt. *Stupid mistake.* I wished they didn't even pretend like I was a part of their group. That would have been easier than this.

"Ya..."

"Do you wanna talk about what happened with the trio?" he asked, his eyebrows pushing together. I felt my throat close at the thought of them. I just wanted an explanation. Why was that so hard to ask for?

"Not really," I replied.

"Ahh that's okay." He began to reorganize the nightstand. Then he came to the desk and began straightening his papers and putting them in a spare notebook. When he looked down at me, he gave me a sad smile.

"What did you think about the town?" he asked and moved away from me to throw away whatever papers he had crumpled in his hands. "Insane right? I couldn't wrap my head around something like that. I have so many questions, like when they leave the magic bubble, do they return to their time? Are there people from before World War Two there? Crazy."

His normal droning would have been welcome if I wasn't so wound up and the questions were just slighter easier to think of. Just trying to wrap my head around how that magic worked made pain blossom behind my eyes.

"Maybe it moves on a different plane? Can people choose when they want to come out? Like maybe you wanted to take a trip to see the moon landing?"

"Matt," I said tearing him from whatever cleaning he was doing. "Let's ask Malik when we see him next."

"That's a lot of words Rosie, be careful," he warned, his eyebrows knotting together. "And...Malik hasn't been at school for a month."

I raised my eyebrow at this.

No sign at all? I signed just to satiate him.

"Nope," he said and sat down on his bed. "Maybe he's in the town."

That's a long time, I signed to him.

"Maybe it would be like thousands of years there," he said with a smile. "Maybe time just moves slowly, not stops all together."

I sent him a shrug.

Why do you think he showed us? I asked him. It had been nagging at me since we came back. Since he had pushed me in front of the whole student body and had me declared as winner of the games.

"I dunno," Matt said then sent me a sad grin. "Maybe he needs friends." I rolled my eyes in response.

Him being in that gang with Eli is weird, I signed to him.

"Ohh, I have an idea," Matt said his face lighting up. "Maybe the gang has been a front for that town. I mean a town stuck in time, how do they make money? How do they import stuff? Can animals even live there? Think about it—they had cars, but where was the gas coming from? Oh my gosh what about the electri—"

"Please, Matt," I said and placed a hand on my aching temple.

"You know what Rosie, if you *really* wanted to get away from here you could just go to the town with Malik. Think things over and come back refreshed." He let out a chuckle. "A vacation if you will."

My phone felt like it would burn a hole in my pocket. I had his number; I could text him.

I am on your side.

Trust me.

Before I chickened out, I picked up my phone and chose to call him instead of text. Matt gave me a questioning look.

I brought the phone to my ear with a shaky breath.

"What's wrong?" answered a familiar voice on the other end of the line. The background was quiet and I could hear him shuffling something like papers.

"You left school," I replied lamely. There was a small laugh.

"Did you miss me?" he asked. The smile in his voice was evident.

"Not even one bit," I replied and even though the events from the day still weighed heavily on my chest, the corner of my mouth twitched.

"Aw, and here I thought we had made some progress," he teased. Matt was watching me closely as I spoke. He seemed to be holding his breath. "Then if this isn't you worried about my wellbeing, how can I help you?"

"Take us back," I said. He paused on the other side of the phone and then I heard a sigh.

"I told you it's about trust." There was another ruffling. This one sounded like fabric.

"How do I get you to trust me?" I asked.

"I'll text you an address, meet me there in three hours," he said.

"Is it safe?" I asked, an uneasy feeling settling deep in my stomach.

"Trust me and I'll trust you, Rosie." He hung up without another word.

* * *

Matt and I called for an Uber because neither of us was rich enough to afford our own car. It would be better this way. Matt had said something about the town not *totally* being stuck in time, or at least that was his idea, and it made more sense to me but that would mean at some point the others may figure out that we had left. If there was no car, I hoped they'd assume that I wouldn't leave the campus. I was positive Malik didn't tell them about the town, but the less they could track, the safer that town would stay.

The address Malik had sent us was nowhere near the town. Instead, it was in the opposite way and closer to the city. I tried not to let the obvious switch up bother me. It was a test of trust; it was supposed to make me uncomfortable. I would imagine that Malik divulging a carefully guarded secret to people he barely even knew made him more uncomfortable than I could be right now, sitting in the back of an old Toyota on my way to meet a gang member with a golden retriever as a sidekick who didn't even rank in the top four hundred in the school rankings.

Not worried at all.

As if he read my thoughts Matt reached across the seat between us and gave my hand a gentle squeeze. I lifted my face to catch his eyes and he gave me a small smile.

"It's okay Rosie," he said. I nodded at him.

The driver stopped in front of a well-lit building that was at least fifteen floors tall. We were in the middle of the city and the setting sun made the building reflect the orange rays off its glass front. Cars honked at our stopped car.

"This is it," the driver grumbled. "Get out before there is an accident."

I gulped and hurried my way out of the car and into the sidewalk in front of the building. I had rarely had a chance to go to the city since I was cursed. I remember when I was younger that my parents would frequent the city and take me with them as well sometimes. The buildings seemed just as large now as they did back then to my five-year-old self. A light wind passed through the area and left a chill on my bare arms. I'd decided to dress in a t-shirt and jeans because I assumed that when we left for the town, I would be able to speak freely.

"That's a fancy place," Matt said with a whistle as he stood beside me. "Well, we better get in before it gets dark, huh?"

I nodded and walked toward the double door. There was a doorman waiting for us. I expected him to demand us for some identification, but he simply looked toward me then to Matt behind me and opened the door with a nod. Matt slipped his arm around my neck, a gesture much like Eli had done in the past.

"Don't be so stiff," he whispered in my ear and guided me into the build-ing. It was sleek inside with grey walls, light marble floors, and jet-black furniture. The only other people were two large men, one bald and the other with slick back hair that guarded an elevator.

The bald man pushed the button for the top floor, and I felt his eyes on me but I was too nervous to make eye contact. Instead, I just wrung my hands together and waited for the elevator.

"So, you guys just stand here and press buttons all day, huh?" Matt asked in a joking tone. "Your boss must hate you." I froze but relaxed as soon as I heard one of them laugh.

"He's not too bad," the one who laughed joked back. I peeked up to see both of their eyes on Matt. They had small grins.

"His sense of humor could use some work though," the other one added on.

The elevator dinged and opened in front of us. I saw myself and Matt reflected back at me. Matt had a grin on his face and after only a moment, he pushed us in.

"Keep up the excellent work boys," he said just as the elevator doors began to close.

"Sure...*boss*," the bald one said sarcastically. The doors closed on us and I was met with our reflections once more. Matt's grin drops and he let out a sigh.

"So tense, right?" he commented.

"I'm surprised they played along," I muttered. Matt grabbed my arm, startling me.

"Where were they?" he asked. It took me a moment to realize he was talking about the curse.

Back, I signed to him automatically kicking myself internally for making such a rookie mistake. He nodded and let go of my arm.

The elevator was silent as we rode our way up. I watched the numbers at the top of the door with waning confidence. Each time we got closer to the top floor I felt my heart drop lower and lower into my stomach until it was left on the first floor with those guards.

We reached the sixteenth floor and the doors opened to reveal a penthouse apartment. The sun had set on our way up and we were greeted with a twinkling view of the city. Much like the bottom floor the walls and floors were greyish, and the furniture was all black though all that I could see beyond the mouth of the elevator was a small bench against the floor-to-ceiling windows.

Matt pushed me out of the elevator and I scrambled to catch myself before falling on the floor.

"Nice to see you made it," Malik's familiar voice called from my right. I looked over to see the familiar scarred face and white hair. He was dressed in a button-up black shirt with the top three buttons unbuttoned and black slacks, though instead of dress shoes, he had fuzzy grey house slippers on. They brought a smile to my face.

"She acted like she was going to keel over at any moment on the way here," Matt said coming out of the elevator. I sent him a glare for the earlier push, but he just gave me a smile.

"Glad to know you trusted me, Rosie," Malik said.

I used this chance to look around. The penthouse was an open floor plan beside two doors on the other side of the room which I assumed was a bedroom. The furniture was indeed all black, from the sectional couch to the bar stools that surrounded the kitchen island. His appliances were black too, but it didn't make the space depressing. Instead, paired with the small glow of the LED lights sprinkled around the rooms, it gave the feeling of a cool and safe environment.

"Let's go discuss things in the office before your drool makes a puddle," Malik joked and showed us toward one of the closed doors. "You can come back anytime you'd like; the guards will know your face from now on so if you want to drool over this place again, feel free to."

I shot him a look; he just shrugged it off.

When he opened the door, we were met with a sleek black desk and the view of the other side of the city, but that wasn't what made me step back in surprise. It was the two red-headed people that stood near the window. Their conversation stopped when they spotted us. Their features looked so familiar, but I couldn't place my finger on exactly what it was. Their eyes did not have a glow, so even though I could not see the color exactly there was no doubt they were witches or at least very weak low-levels.

"Claudine, Maximus," Malik said and placed a hand on my back pushing me forward into the room. "This is Rosie, the cursed one."

I shot him a panicked look but he only gave me a small encouraging smile.

Trust me, his face seemed to say.

"Obviously. I could feel her magic from when she entered the building," Maximus spoke. He stepped forward; his long hair was pulled into a low ponytail the rested on his shoulder. His counterpart stayed behind but I realized that they were twins given their looks. The woman, Claudine, had longer hair than Maximus and it was pulled up into a tight ponytail at the top of her head. She watched me with a guarded stance.

"Nice to meet you," he said and reached a hand out. I gave him mine hesitantly. He grabbed mine softly and shook it, then it was over and he was stepping back over to Claudine. "This is my sister Claudine, she's not good with new people so excuse her."

"Your magic is potent," she observed.

"The curse is potent," I corrected. There was no use in hiding my voice and if they asked, I was resigned to say the cuts were under my clothes.

"So ignorant," Maximus commented. I raised my eyebrow at his harsh words. I looked over to Matt and Malik but they both had no reaction to his words. "Am I to assume that you have a healing trait? There is no blood streaming from wherever those cuts that must have stemmed."

"Yes," I whispered.

"Sit Rosie," Malik said and pushed me toward the chairs in front of his desk. He leaned against the front instead of taking a seat behind the desk. Matt stood behind me and put a supportive hand on my shoulder. I looked up at him. The worry should have been obvious in my face.

Who are these people? I wanted to ask. Why did he have witches flanked at his side now? And why did they look so—*oh.*

Looking over Matt's face I realized why the two in the corner looked so familiar. They looked like Matt, or should I say Matt looked like them? I couldn't tell their age from the dim room. It was weird to see how similar they looked but there was no way they could be related...they were full-blooded witches, and witches and demons couldn't cross breed.

"This is my home, Rosie," Malik explained. "Or at least one of them. This is also where this sector's headquarters are. Maximus and Claudine help oversee anything related to witches here."

"Sector..." I repeated slowly. Eli had said it once before. "A part of the gang you are a part of?" It was a shot in the dark and I didn't want to look any more stupid than I already was in front of the newcomers. I could already feel their gazes.

"Yes, that's correct Rosie," he said with a smile. His arms crossed snugly on his chest. "We dubbed it *The Fallen.*"

"Then you oversee the demons," I guessed again feeling slightly better that the first one was right.

"Don't bleed over my couches," he warned.

"Guess again, cursed one," Claudine said from her corner of the room. I gave Malik a confused look.

"Are we really trying to teach a child here?" Maximus asked obviously annoyed.

"Patience, *Maxi,*" Matt said in a pleasant tone from above me. His hand squeezed my shoulder. "This is all new for her, right Rosie?"

My gaze snapped over to Maximus. Matt was pushing his luck. The guards were one thing but now high-level gang members? To my surprise Maximus just gave him a glare and backed down.

"Right. But Claudine is right, it's not me Rosie," he said.

Matt's hand became tight on my shoulder and I felt him lean down. His lips were by my ear.

"*It's me,*" Matt's voice said near my ear with a chuckle.

I let out a sigh and swatted his face away.

"Can you not joke right now, Matt?" I hissed at him and turned around to stare at him. He had a smile on his face.

There was a pause that lingered between the group. Finally, Maximus began laughing.

"His sense of humor is pretty bad, but if anyone else tried to make that joke they'd be put in their place faster than you could blink," Maximus said after clearing the laughter from his throat.

Matt shrugged. I looked back to Malik; the headache was back again.

"Why would I believe that a low-level is in a high position in a gang?" I asked him. Anger was steadily boiling under my skin. They made my anxiety skyrocket and now they wanted to joke.

"He's not a low-level," Claudine said as Malik began to speak. Malik pushed his lips together into a thin line.

"Okay you must think I'm stupid but, please. I am not *that stupid*," I growled at them.

Now they were all teaming up to play this stupid joke? How many people wanted to hide the truth from me? The emotions in me felt like they were colliding. First the trio, now Malik wanted to bring me here and make me a laughing stock?

"You are stupid if you refuse to believe what's in front of you," Maximus said. "Didn't you notice the resemblance?"

"Now you are going to tell me you are related," I hissed and moved to stand up but Matt put both hands on my shoulders, halting my movements and forcing me back down into the chair.

"We are siblings actually," Matt confessed. "I'm sorry, Rosie. I have been lying to you."

I took my chance to look up at him. The seriousness in his tone extinguished the fire in my veins, leaving a cool numbness.

They all lie, I wanted to say. *But Matt?*

"He's the product of an experiment," Malik explained. "Neither he nor his siblings got perfectly fused genes. Claudine and Maximus got witches' genes only. While Matt here, got a mix of both but as you have seen, it doesn't mix well enough for him to do any real damage."

"The hurts, Malik," Matt said giving him a pout, but his eyes returned to mine shortly after. "We thought it was time to give you the truth Rosie. It's about trust, yes...but also we can't put this off any longer."

"Put what off?" I whispered straining my neck to hold his stare. There was no panic rising in me. No fear. Barely any confusion. Just numbness.

"It's time to tell you why you really came to Winterfell," Matt continued and gave me a sad smile. "There is no scholarship Rosie, not really. They never had plans to let low-levels in and it is not because of your curse that they did. It was a front Malik fed to the principal with his power.

"We brought you there to keep you safe as you come into your powers. It was a task given to us but after seeing how powerful you are and how deep you have fallen with those who are...less informed, we needed to step in. We would rather give you the full truth than have you blindly follow the trio."

"That was your fault, Matt," I hissed.

"Yes well, that wasn't his most thought-out plan," Malik commented.

"Once they found out how deep you had gotten in I worked to separate you from them," Matt explained.

"And when he failed, I made my appearance," Malik said with a smile. Was this supposed to be funny? If their words were true that would mean that nothing in my life up until now had been my choice. Only a very carefully constructed lie by the only people I thought I could trust.

The headache was back. I couldn't believe I let myself feel bad about cutting Matt off.

"Who gave you this task?" I said in a whisper. Anything more would have my head splitting.

"Your mother," Malik responded. "Your *real mother*."

"You're telling me I'm adopted," I asked incredulously, my eyes trailing over to Malik.

"You are like us, cursed one," Claudine said. "But you were the only perfect specimen."

"A witch and a demon came together to birth you," Malik said.

"Not true," I cut him off. "My mother would never cheat on my father. Witches and demons can't even procreate anyways."

"Aren't you curious about the debt they owed?" Maximus asked. "That's how they get them. They wrangle couples that have issues with conceiving, promising that they can fix their issue, as long as they give the witch their first-born child."

"All the while the parents never knew the witch had placed a magic embryo inside the woman before they even got home. Many embryos do die in the womb but you four...you made it," Malik finished for her. "That's how you were made Rosie, but your parents never gave you back, they moved instead."

"But she found you," Mat said.

"She found me..." I echoed. The heels that haunted my nightmares played through my mind at such a volume that I was sure my eardrums would explode. I began shaking violently. "You lied, she cursed me."

"Yes but it was for your own good," Matt cooed from above me.

"The curse tears my skin apart," I responded to his ridiculous notion. How dare he insinuate it was to protect me?

"She had to keep your magic in check. She sent us to help you acclimate to this life. Prepare you for what is to come." Matt's hand brushed my hair. An act meant to be soothing, but it made me even angrier.

"She sent you," I echoed. There was something underneath my skin, bubbling. Not anger—it was something different, something living. "You are going to take me to her."

"She wants to meet you. She has been waiting," Malik said. "We can take you to her."

"No," I choked out.

"No?" I don't know who asked it but I didn't care.

"You lied to me. Befriended me," I said, my breath coming in pants. I pulled at my shirt collar. My skin was too hot and the shirt felt too itchy against my skin.

"It's not like that," Malik tried to say. "We were sim—"

"Silence," I commanded. Both the room and the people in it paused as if listening to me. "You were never on my side. You never wanted to help me."

"Calm down," Maximus said breaking the silence. "You are getting too worked up."

"Your magic, cursed one," Claudine added on.

"You are sending me to my death." I stood up abruptly, Matt's hands falling away. "Right into the person who harmed me the most. She ruined my life and for what? Because my parents didn't give up a child they *birthed?*"

Was I yelling or was the room just so quiet that my voice sounded like screaming? Ever since the moment in the room, everything seemed to be running together.

There was a rumbling far in the distance.

"I have been in pain every single day for *nine years*. She took away my voice." I grabbed Malik roughly by the shirt and brought his face closer to mine. His eyes were wide as I spoke. "My freedom. She made me a target. And now you want to hand me to her."

The bubbling, I felt like I would explode with it. I wanted to scream. I wanted to destroy. It clouded my mind; I let it. I wanted to feel this anger. I was owed this anger. My life up until now had been resentment and fear but no more, I would ride this.

I readied my voice.

"Rosie, no!"

I screamed and with it came a burst of light. Glass shattered into a million pieces, and I felt like I was flung across the room.

Then, I was falling.

Then, came darkness.

THE PRICE OF SILENCE

BOOK 2

ELLE MAE

Prologue

I never understood why mother and father would yell at each other. I hated when they did it. I heard other kids at school talk about how they would wake up to fights in the middle of the night, but I never had that luxury.

I jumped as blue glass hit the wall and rained down on my hidden form behind the couch. It was my favorite place to hide when they got angry like this, I was out of sight and hopefully out of mind, but it didn't stop the glass from cutting open my skin. Tears pricked my eyes at the first few cuts but they closed up quick enough thanks to the healing ability I had.

"I am not going to another witch!" my father scream at my mother. I could hear his bated breaths and knew that this fight would be coming to an end soon. Father was getting older, the human in him showing more and more as the years went on.

"The people are whispering!" My mother yelled back. "Michelle came to me last week and acted like she had some *disease!* Can't you see how bad this is for our reputation?"

My father let out a mocking laugh that made my skin heat.

Of course it was about the curse. Everything had been about the curse. Barely anyone at school talked to me anymore but when they did it came in the form of taunts and things being thrown at me. They started this new game recently, trying to see who could make the ugly curse rear its fangs.

Sometimes I indulged them just to get them off my back but sometimes... it just made those monsters hungrier.

"Our reputation? Really?" he asks. There was silence and I heard his fist swing before my mothers cry. "We are the lowest low-levels there are. We *have no* reputation." He spit on her. "This is your fault anyways. I knew that whatever came out of that shriveled up body of yours would just bring us bad luck. If I had any sense I would have gotten rid of her and you long ago."

When he left the room neither I nor my mother moved from our spots but I could hear her soft sobs. I moved to crawl out side of my dark hiding space but froze when I heard her spoke again.

"I should have never had a child," she said with more distain and anger than I had ever heard her utter in my short life.

I slept behind the couch that night and didn't leave my space until I knew that they had both left for work. I didn't bother going to school and when my parents did finally come back for the day, they didn't even blink in my direction.

After this I would be stuck with years of the same glares while they barely succeed in trying to act like a loving family.

Chapter One
Rosie

The air whipped past me leaving cold burns across my skin as I flew through it. I had never once felt as free as I did in this very moment. Nothing was holding me down; the ground that seemed to want to swallow me up was missing and my body felt as light as a feather. The only thing that called me back to myself was the searing pain in my left eye, and that was when I realized that I was not flying. In fact, I was falling.

I opened my eyes to see the concrete ground coming at me fast. I shielded my face and prepared for the impact that was sure to come. I had lived a miserable life up until Winterfell and I couldn't help but feel a sharp pang of disappointment when I realized this was it for me.

I was yanked up by two strong arms that circled around my waist.

"You are going to pay for that," Malik hissed in my ear.

His hands were around my waist holding me suspended in midair. There was a small flapping in the wind and out of the corner of my eye I could see a brilliant white. I cocked my head to the side and came face to face with a pair of wings. Wings that were attached to the person holding me. They were steady yet looked as worn as the person who they sprouted out of. The tops of the soft feathered wings were thick but scarred, with missing feathers in places where scars showed through.

Malik. The very old demon turned gang leader. He had that small understanding smile on his face that was only broken by a scar that ran through his lips. His golden eyes burned into mine with an unnamed emotion and his white mess of hair fluttered around his face with the ebb and flow of the wind. If his scarred yet handsome face told you anything it would be that he wasn't one to back down from a fight. A fight for his people. A fight for the people he cared about. Or at least that was what I had thought before this. Malik was there when I thought no one was on my side, convincing me that I could trust him...but now I was not sure I could. And now he even had wings.

My awe was interrupted by a screeching sound. While we were suspended in air I saw the top of Malik's apartment engulf in flames and start bending. My heart dropped a few thousand feet to the concrete below. The building and all the people in it would be crushed in mere moments.

"Matt!" I yelled and reached out to the now burning building.

"We are here!" came Matt's voice. Coming from below us I saw Matt being held up by wings, the same as Malik's. An auburn-haired golden retriever of a boy who had been the first at Winterfell to show me what a friend could really be...but he too had a horde of secrets he was keeping from me. His grey eyes were wide as they watched the building burn. He held his sister in one hand; she hung limply but sent me a strained smile when her eyes met mine. Matt's brother was in a normal standing position and was being pushed up by an invisible force. They both looked so much like Matt save for their slightly darker hair and brown eyes giving away their witch status.

"You could have killed us!" yelled Maximus. He had looked murderous since we met but now I could feel his anger rolling off him in waves even across the wide space. This was the person Matt thought of so fondly when he spoke to me back in Winterfell. In my eyes both he and his sister had been young children that relied on Matt, but apparently they helped Malik run his gang... It was all absurd.

I tried not to look at the commotion below. Cars were honking and there were the tell-tale sounds of screeching tires and crushing metal that told me the building collapsing was causing havoc on the ground level. I could hear the ghost of screams below.

"The people," I choked out as the building continued its slow destruction.

"A pity," Malik replied. His voice called me back to him. When I turned to face him his long fingers trailed the left side of my face. They were light, ticklish almost, more intimate than I expected. It reminded me of the him I knew before all of this. When they brushed over a tender spot I couldn't help but flinch.

"Why do you guys have wings?" I asked Malik, and he gave me a smile when I turned to get a better look at the wings behind him. That teacher's images flooded through my mind once more. "Are you angels?"

Malik let out a throaty laugh.

"Let's get out of here. We can talk more in the town." When he pulled his hand back from my face his fingers were stained with bright red blood. "We match now."

The town... *Montnesse*. The town that had been kept a secret for hundreds of years after the uprising against demons and witches. A safe haven that was stuck in time, never changing even as the world around it went into total chaos.

It would do for now...at least until I get some answers.

* * *

The women of my nightmares like to dress in Gucci.

From the pumps, to her skirt, to her blazer, hell even her nails had Gucci emblems on them. She had been waiting for us in the town just like Malik had promised.

On the very east side of the hidden town there was a house that overlooked the entire area. It was a three-story Victorian mansion and from Malik's explanation, housed my mother and a few choice Originals who had claimed the town as their permanent residence. I had overlooked it since the last time I was in this town but when we reentered, it was the first thing I saw. It towered over the town and the invisible aura around it commanded the attention of all who entered. . It's white trim and soft purple paint was supposed to look harmless but with knowing who resided inside made it all the more sinister. The dark windows seemed to have shadows in them and the creaks became frightening.

It would have to, if it really housed the Originals. They were the first of our kind, the people who paved their way in society and demanded our rights. They were akin to gods. To ignore them as such would be an insult.

Malik had silently brought me into a foyer that was twice the size of my living room back home. There was a light carpet that sprawled across the marled floors, painting were strewn across the light green walls but none were familiar to me, and last but not least there was a huge mammoth skull on top of the fire place. It was extravagant, unnecessary... but if I guess this was how the oldest, richest, most powerful; beings in our world acted.

By far the thing that command the most attention was my *mother* and another gentleman that I had come to recognize as one of the founders of this town. He had blonde long hair that was slicked back, he dressed in a fancy suit that had a yellow brooch on the right pocket. His chair was facing the fire place and he had a relaxed smile on his face. If he was a founder, he had to have been as old as Malik... if not older.

My *mother's* chair however did not face the fireplace, instead she sat on the other side of the table from him and faced the door so that the first thing I would come into contact with was her brown eyes and black hair. Besides that, the similarities ended. She was much taller than me and I couldn't see myself in any of her facial features.

I felt a pang of hurt, maybe guilt when I saw her and couldn't help but think of my own parents. I had been unhappy with them, but they were still the ones who had raised me, had fed me, had clothed me and this women in front of me had the audacity to uproot everything I had known up until this point. How dare she look at a struggling low-level couple and do this to them?

I know my low-level mother must love me, even just a little bit, and now she would be forced to watch as I was taken away from her. All she had wanted was to start a family. Low-levels did not have the luxury to travel or have big dreams... but perhaps a small one? A family that would sleep in with you on Sundays and watch a beat-up television, go to a park, eat dinner with every night, but she could never have that.

I could never have that.

"I cannot tell you how ecstatic I am to finally meet you Rosie," she told me her voice as sweet as honey suckle.

"We met once," I told her, not trying to hide the growl that made its way up my throat.

"Ahh yes, well... let's not count that." She said and stood on her long legs. She came to me with an outstretched hand. Her nails were painted dark red and were as perfectly manicured as I remembered them "My name is Xena, your biological mother."

I did not shake her hand. Let's not count that? That *single* moment has literally ruined my life. Been the bane of my existence and has almost proven that I am not fit to even be on this earth. Malik squeezed my shoulder harshly.

I was not having any of it. She had left me, cursed me, I wanted nothing to do with her. I should have been scared but the betrayal of it all, and the unstable magic that resided in me only fueled my anger.

"Take the curse off," I demanded. Her smile dropped slightly and she took a step back.

"From the feel of it..." She paused and I felt my sides tingle. *Her magic,* I realized. It was strong, so strong that after a brush of it, my body began vibrating. "You have found a way around it...have you not?"

Malik tightened his grip once more.

"Rosie, why did you lie to me?" Malik asked. "Tell us the truth, did you break your curse?"

His power washed over me. Eli had told me that Malik was dangerous because of his power to control people, but I never believed it...until now. With the combination of my own magic I felt my skin heat up almost unbearably.

"No," I told them on command. "It's not broken...just paused."

"Don't be so forceful Malik." The man spoke from his chair. He also stood to introduce himself. His blue eyes shone in the light of the fireplace and I felt myself shiver under his gaze. I was used to feeling witch magic but the aura that was radiating off of this man...it was terrifying. It licked at my ankles, sent a chill through my body, all without him lifting a finger. When he did raise his hand I flinched. "Ezekiel. Nice to meet the woman who has had my daughter wrapped around her finger."

"Daughter?" I asked looking towards Malik. He gave me a smile that pissed me off.

"Eliza," Malik answered for him.

I was going to faint. My head felt dizzy and my body couldn't handle everything I had put it through. Not to mention the whole left side of my face burned like crazy. I had yet to look in the mirror but from the feel of it I would guess there was a large cut that made its way down my face.

What the fuck was going on here? First I figure out I am the product of an experiment and now Eli herself has ties to this? Does she even know?

"That was my bad," Matt spoke from the entrance. "I wanted to get her used to the idea of witches like we spoke about but they got...more tangled than I anticipated."

I didn't turn to look at him. I didn't want to. After the adrenaline of a near-death experience left me, my anger came back like a tidal wave. The man who had been the first person that I could really call a friend had been lying to me since day one. He knew everything about me, he even had a task to complete but he sat there and acted like an idiot while I stressed over the curse. He had all the answers yet refused to give them.

"That's actually what I wanted to talk to you about," Xena said and crossed her arms. "I think this is a great opportunity to shift gears."

"Xena, let's not push the dear too much yet, hm? She looks ill." Ezekiel said and put an arm on her shoulder. "What do you need from us, Rosie was it?"

"I need to you tell me what this is all about. Why did you curse me? Why did you leave me with my parents? Why did you bring me to Winterfell? What the hell is up with this town? And why will no one tell me the truth?!" My voice rose with each word along with the bubbling inside me inside me and my eyes stung with unshed tears. I knew now based on what Malik and Matt had told me that this was my magic. It was just as angry as I was, and it wanted to be let out. The house began shaking violently. Cups began falling over and the picture frames on the wall shook violently.

Xena put a slender hand on my shoulder and I felt my magic reel itself in and calm immediately.

"That is why, my child," Xena said. "You have magic that is far too powerful for your body. If you cannot harness it, you will go mad."

"Sit," Ezekiel said and left to bring Xena's chair over to me. I did as I was told, my legs almost collapsing from under me as I sat. "Just like my own daughter." He knelt in front of me like he was speaking to a child. "I had to leave her because dangerous people were after me. The only place I am safe is here in this town, but this is no life for a child. Both you and Eliza are far too important to be sheltered in this life for what you are destined to do. You needed real-life experience to help you survive."

"*Eli*," I corrected. "You put Eli in a fucking gang."

"Rosie," Matt chastised me from behind. I ignored him.

"And you," I said towards Xena. "You fucking put a curse on me that tore me up every single day of my life. And for what?"

I tried to keep my voice steady but the anger and confidence that I had was wearing fast. I was tired and hurt and I wanted nothing more than to bundle myself in my blankets back at Winterfell and cry my heart out, preferably while cuddling with Amr.

"The curse helps you expel magic," she said. "Without me around you could not learn how to properly harness it so I put measures in place to ensure that the magic would not take control of you."

"We will not hide anything from you any longer, Rosie," Ezekiel said.

"Who are you even?" I hissed at both of them. Ezekiel gave me a small smile.

"I was in the group of the first witches ever created," Xena answered first.

"And I am one of the first demons to get banished from the heavens," Ezekiel finished. "Malik is the second generation."

"My father and mother, were eaten by Xena and her gang of witches when they were still human," Malik explained. My brain stalled and I looked at Xena with new eyes.

The rumors were true. Witches were crafted out of violence and destruction just like the books claimed. Everything had seemed so far-fetched, there was no way I could believe it yet here were the people who started our race standing in front of me, not looking a day over thirty-seven.

The air was knocked out of my chest.

"How are you standing next to the person who killed your parents?" I hissed at him.

"That was over a millennia ago," he answered.

"And it's wasn't me who killed them," she said. "My group and I were what was known as demon sympathizers back in the day. When they killed demons they would force us to eat their flesh as punishment."

I wanted to vomit. I felt it shift in my stomach and I had to cover my mouth with the back of my hand to steady myself. Eating the flesh as punishment? What kind of sick people would make someone do that? I had not care for the shell of a mother that stood before me but I would not wish that on anyone.

"I told you about Winterfell," Malik said. "We wanted you to be accustomed to other demons and witches. We had hoped once Matt led you to the discovery about your powers that you would come to understand more about witches. We had planned at that time to step in and teach you but...things got out of hand."

"I really just wanted to prove to you that we are not bad, Rosie," Matt pleaded. "Please believe me when I say that's all I wanted."

"Why would I ever trust witches after what *she* did?" I hissed.

"That's the point," Malik said. "You met Daxton, you have been friends with Matt, you yourself are a witch. Don't you get it? Witches are not what this world has been feeding you."

"When will you tell Eli about this?" I asked changing the subject. "She is just as affected by me. I have no idea what she had to do in a gang growing up but this is a whole world she has yet to see."

"Eliza went through a test when she was younger. She proved to be easily swayed, so we have put the plan to tell her on hold until we can be sure she will not ruin our plans."

"What plans?" I asked. "About this stupid town?"

Xena let out a laugh. "You must get your attitude from your father."

"Let me guess, he's also dead," I hissed at her. I realized it was a low blow when her face contorted.

"Right before your tenth birthday," she said. "It was what put the plan into action."

"What plan?" I asked again.

"We will only tell you if you agree to help us," Xena said.

I gritted my teeth. I didn't want to help them.

"Remove my curse," I argued.

"I will after you agree to help us *and* prove it." She watched me like a hawk. She may have said she had good intentions but there was no way she was doing this for anything other than her own gain.

"Isn't the curse not an issue?" Matt asked.

"It is," I growled back still locking eyes with Xena. "How will I prove it?"

"We will give you a task. Once it is completed you will have earned our trust," Xena said.

"I am not agreeing, but what is the task?"

She sent me a smile. "I will not tell you until you promise to help us."

"Just say yes, Rosie," Malik said from above me. "Trust us, okay? I haven't let you down yet."

"You lied to me this entire time, Malik." My voice cracked as I spoke, the tears threatening to spill.

"Until I was able to tell you the truth," he said, his voice softening.

I thought over their offer. I could promise but if the task seemed too daunting maybe I could just back out, even if that meant I would forever be stuck with a curse. At least the trio found a way to break it.

My chest ached at the thought of them. This was so much bigger than any of them thought. Bigger than I ever imagined. A few months ago I was a low-level with no prospects and now I was talking to the literal gods of our race.

"I promise," I told them, with no intention of keeping it. I would have to run back to the trio for their help or see if I could find other allies in the school.

Xena nodded towards Malik.

Malik lifted my chin and made contact with my eyes.

"If you betray us you will turn yourself over to me right away. Once the first thought of betrayal enters your mind you will pick up your phone and tell me your location. After that you will not talk until I get you again." This time his power was cool as it ran down my back.

My body felt like it would explode with anger and I felt my magic lash out wildly as if wanting to fight him as hard as I did. It took all that I had to stay seated while my insides told me to pounce.

"Fuck you," I hissed at him through barred teeth.

"Such dirty language in front of your own mother," he teased.

I looked at said mother with a scowl. My skin felt hot and I could feel my hands beginning to shake.

"Fuck you," I hissed at him.

"Such dirty language in front of your own mother," he teased.

I looked at said mother with a scowl.

"There are people in the government that threaten our existence. We need you to get close to them and find a way to exploit them. When you report back to us we will use this information to weaken them, then kill them. The first one should be easy for you." Mother cleaned the dirt under her fingernails as she spoke to me.

I had a bad feeling about this. "Who is it?"

"The first target is Daxton's parents," Malik said from above me.

I froze in my chair. *Are you fucking kidding me?*

Chapter Two
Rosie

They were in fact, not kidding. I gave them a few moments hoping that someone, anyone, would burst out into laughter. My gaze snapped over to Matt but his normally smiling face was solemn and his gaze downcast. His sister, Claudine, who was standing at his side playing with the hem of her sleeve met my gaze head-on. Her long red hair that had been tied on top of her head was now messily strewn across her face from the fall off the building. Her gaze felt like she could see into my soul and caused me to panic even further. Maximus gave me a disgruntled look and a glare as if he couldn't believe what he was seeing. He was much more put together than his sister, his long hair still in a loose ponytail. The only indication he had taken the fall was the rumpled look of his shirt.

"You really want me to kill Daxton's parents?" I asked, my magic freezing around me feeling as cold as the words that left my mouth.

"We will kill them," Malik said from behind me, his hand giving my shoulder a squeeze. "You just need to give us an in."

Xena nodded at his words and raised her eyebrow as if asking me to speak the words that were raging through my head.

I couldn't. *I can't.* I cannot be responsible for someone's death like this. Especially Daxton's... We were not close enough to even be friends but I couldn't deny that I had been drawn to him, all of them. I was mad at them for keeping secrets but that paled in comparison to the mountain of information the group in front of me had kept from me. If I really thought about it, the ones who *really* wanted to help me were Daxton, Eli, and Rae. And this is how I repay them? By killing their parents?

"You will not be responsible for killing someone Rosie," Ezekiel said and came to kneel in front of me. His warm hands grabbed mine, a comforting gesture but it made me squirm nonetheless. "These are bad people, child. The entire reason we must hide in this town is because people like them are still alive to exploit their position. They are evil and only want what will give them the most power. Sirene and Lars are the worst of them. They go about spouting rumors of dirty magic and unholy practices while they themselves are the ones tarnishing the witches' image."

"I don't know how to do this," I confessed. "I don't know what information to give you. I do not know how to create an in. I don't even know these people. How do I even know they are as bad as you say they are?" My voice cracked and I had to clear my throat in order to continue. Ezekiel's blue eyes watched me carefully. "I am not this type of person."

"You are this type of person," Xena said. "You were *made* to be this person. Why else would we send you to Winterfell? The games? You think that was a coincidence? All of this is to prepare you to step into the light."

She's insane, I thought and Ezekiel let out a small chuckle.

"Let's not get ahead of ourselves," Ezekiel said without looking back at Xena. She huffed in response.

"I see where Eli gets her powers," I mused giving Ezekiel a smile even as I felt my magic trying to lash out wildly. The feeling of his hands anchored me, much like Eli's had when I felt them on the back of my neck, guiding me.

"Yes, well, we could never tell if it was from me or her mother but if I had to guess she got a bit of both," Ezekiel answered and let out a sigh before continuing. "They have done unspeakable things Rosie. They have murdered, even if not by their own hands, they have ordered the murder of thousands of witches that live outside these walls. They infiltrated the government alongside others and whispered in the ears of leaders, sealing our fates." Malik cleared his throat behind me. "When you meet with Daxton again you can ask him about his relationship with them."

"I don't see how—" I started but Malik's hand over my mouth cut me off.

"Rosie, you are bleeding and have expended a lot of magic. Let's rest for the night. I promise you that you can ask all your questions later." I sent him a glare and he returned it with a soft smile. "We don't have to rush here. You can digest this information and start anew tomorrow morning."

Having enough of his lying attitude I opened my mouth and bit into his palm. Malik's eyes widened and he jumped back with a surprised yelp.

"I didn't bite you that hard," I grumbled.

I didn't want to stay here, but I knew that Malik's suggestion wasn't one at all and they expected me to stay here until they could guarantee I wouldn't leave without proving to them I was on their side. My eyes washed over Ezekiel's amused face once more.

What is the extent of your power? I asked through our still connected hands. *I assume you are much more powerful than Eli.*

"Wise assumption," he noted and disconnected our hands. He did not give me another indication that he was going to answer my question.

Exactly like I thought, I mused in my mind. Malik wasn't kidding about the gaining trust thing. I would have to navigate this whole thing carefully if I ever wanted a chance to go back to Winterfell.

"Alright," I said with a sigh. "Where am I staying?"

"I'll take you to the guest room closest to mine," Malik said snaking an arm around my shoulders. Probably so I wouldn't run, not like I'd get very far anyways.

"We will continue this talk tomorrow," Xena said. "I hope you can move on from the past and work together with us for the sake of our people."

I didn't look back at her as Malik led me out of the room. Matt and his siblings stayed behind. I didn't miss the way Matt's eyes washed over me; I didn't need or want his pity.

Malik led me up the staircase to the third floor. We passed over twelve rooms before we stopped at one at the very end of the hallway. Even though this house had to be ancient, it stayed in impeccable condition no doubt thanks to the barrier that protected this town, but also the maids that could be seen scurrying about. Even on our way up we had passed three, all wearing the same black uniform that I had only seen in cliche movies. They all smiled at Malik as they passed and paused when they took in my appearance. I imagined myself to be a bloody mess and when Malik opened the door to the room and I caught my reflection in a mirror that was propped up against the wall, that was an understatement.

My hair was a mess around me, telling me that I would need a lot of conditioner to brush out those tangles. There was a nasty open wound that started above my left brow and went over my eye extending onto my cheek. The blood was dried over my entire face and neck. I cupped my mouth and leaned into Malik with my eyes closed.

"You didn't tell me my eyelid was cut in half." My voice was muffled by my hand and it took all I had not to vomit all over Malik. The pain that had been a dull ache seemed to intensify now that I could properly see the damage.

"Almost," Malik said cheekily. "Once they are done down there one of them will come up to fix it."

"Just another thing you are hiding from me," I replied and straightened myself enough to put space between us. I gave him a momentary glare before turning my gaze to the rest of the room, carefully avoiding the mirror that stood on the dresser.

The room was strongly modern. There was a bed with an upholstered black bed frame, dark purple sheets, and a mountain of pillows. There were two black beside tables next to it that had a freshly pluck purple rose. The windows had heavy drapes on them but they were pulled open giving me a twinkling view of the town below us. If I was more at ease I would have loved to pull up a chair right to the to open window and stare at the bustling city below, enjoying the way the cold air would brush my skin... but this was more of a nightmare than anything else. A well hidden one that was made to look like a dream world. It scared me, made me want to hide, but a small part of me, probably the magic, pushed me to fight. It was hungrier now that it had awoken, and more vicious than I could stand to be.

The rest of the room was furnished with a few lounge floral loveseats and a dark oak dresser that was probably just for show. There was an open doorway that led to a bathroom and a closed door which I assumed was the closet. Just like I had felt at Winterfell... this was great, better than I could have imagined but I felt out of place here.

"Not bad right?" Malik commented avoiding my snarky comment about their lies. "We heard purple is your favorite." I turned to him ready to launch into a lecture but a throat clearing from the open doorway stopped me in my tracks.

Maximus stood there with a scowl on his face and his auburn brows pulled together. If he had any less dignity I was sure that scowl would turn into a pout. An anxious looking Matt stood by him fidgeting as I stared. I could not wrap my head around the fact that this *golden retriever* of a person was a gang leader. Someone who gave orders to bloodthirsty demons involved in things like drug deals and hell probably even human trafficking.

"Sit down on the bed so I can get this over with," Maximus commanded and crossed the room in large strides. A sneer showed itself on my own face in response to his attitude. "Or don't, just remember I will not catch you if you fall."

Losing my courage, I sat down on the edge of the bed. He positioned himself in front of me carefully avoiding any physical contact.

"If I disgust you so much why are you even here?" I asked him in a whisper.

With a huff I sat down on the edge of the bed. He positioned himself in front of me carefully avoiding any physical contact.

"If I disgust you so much why are you even here?" I asked him.

I swear I could see a vein pop on his forehead as he glared down at me.

"It is me or your mother," he said. "You choose."

I remembered the way Daxton's magic made me feel and shuddered. He was the better bet by far.

"It won't make me...feel things will it?" I asked hesitantly. There was a quirk of a smile on his lips.

"That only happens in the act of *sharing* magic," he explained and brought his hand over my left eye partially blocking him from view. "And you do not disgust me. I just wish someone as important as you had a head that wasn't so empty."

There was a warm tingling on my eye that stopped me from spitting fire at him. I could feel the wound over my eye close, slowly sewing itself together. The pain vanished when he pulled his hand away. He carefully looked over my eye and nodded before stepping back and giving Malik a signal.

"Looks pretty cool," Malik commented as he also looked over my face. I finally took the chance to see what I looked like in the mirror. The blood was still on my face but the open wound was shut and I could see a bit of discoloration of what I assumed to be a scar but couldn't fully tell because of my distance.

"So magic can scar demons," I mused to myself remembering Malik's words. I looked over at the group. All three of them had their eyes on me. "What?" Maximus looked towards Malik but his eyes were trained on me. "Is this about me destroying a building?"

Malik's lips twitched.

"About that—" he started but I held up my hand to cut him off.

"I will not be paying you back."

There was a sigh from Matt that drew my attention. His facial expression was much more relaxed now. And he even shot me a small smile. I didn't want it though. I was pissed at him. At all of them.

"We are waiting for you to lash out," Matt said softly from the doorway. "Your magic should be raging, you used so much from the explosion that a normal witch would be drained."

I licked my lips and looked down at the floor. I had a feeling it was because I took Daxton's magic while we were still on campus. Pushing my embarrassment aside I took a deep breath and met Matt's eyes.

"I'll tell you why I think that is if you promise to no longer lie to me," I said. "Think of it as a trade and we can keep it going as long as you hold up your end."

"Look at you kitten, trying to hold your own," Malik teased. "We are on your side remember? You should trust us."

"You have not proven trustworthy," I hissed at him. "While you may have brought me here and explained a bit about what you know, I have a feeling that there is *way more* than what you have told me and given Ezekiel's and Xena's reactions downstairs I am assuming you will keep everything on lock until I—" I took a studying breath. "Until I find a way for you to *murder* Daxton's parents. This pact is the least you can do."

Malik's shoulders sagged, and he ran a hand through his fluffy white hair before speaking. It was not as vibrant a white as before, probably from the dust of the explosion.

"Fine," he vowed. "I promise to no longer lie to you. Understand though there are things that you are yet to know until you complete your task. After that everything will become clear but from here on, I promise to not create any new lies."

I gestured to Maximus and Matt. Maximus grumbled his response while Matt almost chirped it from the doorway.

"I took some of Daxton's magic," I told them. "Right before I saw Matt. I thought it was the curse taking it...until you told me I was a witch."

Silence descended on the room like a title wave. No one moved, no one spoke. I could feel the collective thought between them, but no one dared to utter it. Malik was the first to shift.

"Go tell Xena," Malik commanded Maximus. "Tell her we have some damage control to do."

Maximus hurried out of the room and Matt rushed in to stand next to Malik while they looked over me as if I had a disease.

"They know," Matt said anxiously.

"Of course they know, stupid," Malik replied.

"I thought we told the principal to limit their alone time," Matt said. "I rarely saw them alone, at least not enough to swap magic."

The anger that flooded me as they talked about me like an object did not rise over the panic that spilling this had caused. I didn't realize that sharing the magic was such a big deal. It shouldn't have been—Daxton seemed to do it all the time.

"Who are you to limit my time with someone?" I hissed at the two as they continued to talk like gossiping old ladies in the corner.

"Magic making you testy, huh?" Malik asked in a teasing tone, his once understanding and soft exterior was long gone. This was a Malik I didn't know and couldn't tell if I liked even if my magic had already made it's mind up.

"Answer," I grumbled.

"We had a plan," Malik said. "I'm not sure how we will come back from this." He directed the last part at Matt who nodded.

"They were not supposed to know," Matt explained as he rubbed his hand over his face. He had changed from anxious to downright stressed. He began to pace the length of the room. "We told the principal to somehow keep you two apart because if he got a taste—" He paused to look at me before diving to the ground near my feet. He took both of my hands in his much like Ezekiel had done. "He would know you are a witch and this whole plan would be ruined. So, tell me how it happened."

Even through the panic and anger a blush managed to make its way onto my face heating my skin.

"We were testing the curse," I said. "And he realized he could take magic from it." It wasn't a total lie, but at least it would save some dignity.

"How did he realize?" Malik asked. I looked up at him slowly. His face was blank. "I don't have to think too hard to realize how it could have happened, but I need to get an idea of how many times from you."

I swallowed and met Matt's eyes. He let out a sigh and stood back up.

"More than once," I said. "If what you say is true then he probably knows."

I gripped the fabric of my shirt. Was this what they were trying to keep from me? Why wouldn't he just tell me?

"I am going to have a talk with that principal," Malik grumbled.

"Maybe your power was faulty," Matt supplied. "How would he even keep them apart anyways? Not like he can watch them all the time."

"Still deserves some sort of punishment," Malik said with a sigh.

"In his defense," I said looking up at them sheepishly. "We were never alone."

It was Malik's turn to rub his hands over his face. "So they all know."

"Like they would hide anything from each other anyways," I said and avoided Matt's eyes.

"Wait but how did he even find out? Was it when he found you in the garden before school? Didn't Eli stop him?" The more Matt questioned me the hotter my face felt. "Maybe he got a taste of your blood? Or oh—"

"Oh, is right," Malik commented with a grin. "I applaud you. I knew you were with all of them, but at the same time. Can't believe Eli really shared you."

"Don't comment on my sex life," I growled. "Can you both leave? I would like to shower and sleep. I am tired."

Matt sent me a look before shrugging and walking out. Malik stayed behind to shoot me a grin before walking towards the door.

"I bet you are tired after all that magic sharing," he teased and shut the door just as I sent a pillow flying towards him causing it to smack against the wood and plop to the floor.

I was starting to think that I should have listened to Eli when she told me not to trust Malik. If I had listened to her, maybe I wouldn't be stuck here.

Chapter Three
Daxton

I didn't think I cared much about Rosie. I tried to stay away from others, not form any connections. Even with the witches I had regular magic sharing sessions with I had made it very clear that I wanted nothing to do with them, that they were nothing but a means to an end. When the more sensitive ones cried it wouldn't even bother me, but with Rosie...

It started after the games. Seeing her cry so easily over just a few burns warmed my heart. Before then I had been focusing on her and Eli's relationship. I was too caught up in the change of Eli to notice how my own feelings had changed in response.

I liked that she cared; I am sure that's what drew Eli to her in the first place. She had said as much. Even though Eli had grown up in a gang without any real parents, she and I were more alike than I would like to admit. My parents were horrible to say the least. They said they did everything in love, but I knew even at a young age that no one would ever do the things they did to me out of love.

I think because of them it became hard for me to decipher others' emotions. I could to a point with the emotions I could feel myself...and that's why I was so sure of Rosie's.

Rosie cared in a different way. Even if she never said it, I saw it. She wanted to be around us, around me. No matter what we had done in the past, and not because she had anything to gain but instead because she herself needed a place to belong. We all did.

And Rae just ruined it all.

It's hard to admit when someone is wrong. Especially someone as close to us as Rae is. She had a hidden temper that rivaled Eli's and Rosie knew just enough to slam her outside her comfort zone. Rae was just reacting to that unknown feeling... I know that, but I cannot help but be angry at her saying those things to Rosie.

"Would it be so bad to just tell her?" I asked Rae as she settled at her table. She rolled up the sleeves of her button-up and smoothed down her slacks. She gave me a glare that told me she was tired of my questioning.

We had just returned to the dorm after trying to check on Rosie. We had waited thirty minutes until after she left. I say waited but it was mostly Rae and I forcing Eli to give her a chance to breathe. Eli was ready to run after her on a moment's notice and refute Rae's claims. I explained she needed time to calm down. The magic would calm once her emotions did and we definitely did not want to be at the end of that attack right now.

Rosie was not there when we arrived. I wasn't surprised; we really pissed her off. She was probably with the other low-level right now.

"I told you that would ruin the plan," Rae said as she pulled off her glasses to pinch the bridge of her nose. For the first time in a while I got to see how much of a mess she looked. Her shirt was untucked, her short curly hair slightly askew. It was small but enough to know that she was just as affected as Eli and I were.

"What plan, Rae?" Eli asked. She was still wearing her school uniform but she had also rolled up her sleeves showing her colorful tattoos. No doubt she would hear from Rae later about wearing "outside clothes" on her clean bed. She propped herself up on Rae's bed so she could throw a pillow in her direction. Rae smacked it away with ease. "We have no idea what we are doing or how to get rid of the curse. All we know is that if she doesn't fear her words, the curse doesn't work. Tell me how you planned to get rid of it."

Rae bared her teeth at Eli. I felt the tensions rise sharply in the room. Eli let out a low growl in her chest, her blue eyes alight with anger and her normally slicked back blonde hair fell messily in her face.

"Guys, stop," I said and stood in between them as Eli readied another pillow. "Rae said what she said to protect Rosie, even if it doesn't seem like it."

Eli lowered the pillow and sent Rae a glare. "Why didn't you tell us you slept with her?"

I looked to Rae; I wanted to know too. I didn't even get that far with her, and she had been adamant about not wanting to touch her. How did it go from that to all the sudden sleeping with her?

"I want to know too," I said. "I thought you didn't like her."

Rae placed her glasses on her head and met my gaze head-on. Rae was many things...but never a liar. So why now?

"I didn't think it would happen," she said after a pause. "It happened the night she stayed over."

"Obviously," Eli spat at her from behind me.

"The bloodletting affected both of us and we agreed not to mention it," Rae said and cast her eyes downwards. "It was a mistake."

"You have been open about your...encounters," I noted. "I don't understand why Rosie is different."

I was caught off guard when Rae's eyes narrowed in my direction.

"Don't you see that she is already too intertwined in our lives?" she asked, her voice as sharp as a knife. "She can't be getting comfortable with us, and I don't want her thinking that whatever happened between us will happen again."

Eli stood abruptly from the bed, her face dead serious. She had an expression I couldn't read again. I hated when she did that.

"Then more for me and Dax," Eli declared. "If what you say is how you really feel then I better *never* see your hands on her ever again."

Eli had never said something of that nature to Rae. They fought, hell Rae and I fought often, but never like this. This was serious. But... I understood Eli's words. Something in my stomach turned sour when I heard Rae's words to Rosie earlier. I didn't like to see Rosie cry, nor did I want her to be mad at us.

It would take more than a coffee to make this up to her.

"See?" Rae said and threw her hands up into the air. "We would have never fought like this before. And we are acting like this over some low-level."

"She's a witch." The words came out before I could stop them. "I am almost certain. But that doesn't change the issue at hand. When Rosie comes back from the low-levels we should really consider telling her."

There was a scratching at the door that drew out attention. Eli went to open it and in ran Amr. Eli caught him by the back of the neck before he could make it very far.

"He said they were not in his dorm, but the scent was still fresh, probably left shortly after she left here." Eli spoke his thoughts for him and then threw him to the ground.

Amr gave her a hiss before running to my side. Amr was a godsend in times like these.

"Thank you," I whispered as I picked him up and scratched behind his ears.

He was another person to worry about, one that cared too much for Rosie. We were supposed to be secretive, yet he had been itching to reveal himself to her and followed her around like he was her familiar instead of mine. But if she was a witch...

A shrill ringing cut through the silence in the room. Eli patted her pockets before answering her phone. Eli didn't have anyone that normally called her so I assumed this would have to be work. It was getting late, but I guess that was the perfect time to start gang activity. Just like Eli, they thrived while hiding in the shadows and stalking their prey. The hunt would be starting soon.

"What the fuck?" Eli's voice sounded alarmed. I met Rae's gaze before looking towards Eli as she stood frozen by the door. "Let me be clean up."

She argued with the person on the other line for a few short moments before hanging up with a growl.

"That sounds troubling," Rae commented. Eli shot her a look.

"Malik's home base was blown up," she replied. "By witches."

"Where is he?" Rae asked.

Eli typed furiously into her phone before looking up to meet Rae's gaze. There was a crease starting to show itself between her eyebrows. We all disliked Malik but she... I knew she grew up around him, looked up to him. But she never would tell us exactly what their relationship was like before she began hating him. My guess was she wanted to forget it. Hearing the news of his home base seemed to worry her. Worry her in a way that told me she didn't really hate Malik as much as she let on.

"I don't know," she replied. "There is no sign of him, and Damon asked me to send some men to go clean up the mess."

"But not you," I commented. She nodded and ran her hand through her short golden hair.

"He said he doesn't want me there in case the authorities are snooping around. It wouldn't look great if they catch wind of a college student being involved."

"But they know you are in *the fallen*," Rae noted. "So why now does he want you to stay away?"

It was odd, now that Rae mentioned it. Damon wanted Eli to clean up everything, do all the dirty work. I had never seen Damon call Eli without asking for her to do something. Even though Damon had multiple people in his organization he always fell back on Eli.

"I don't know," she answered.

"Are you worried about Malik?" I ask her. Her gaze is sharp when it reaches mine.

"Never," she said but the crease between her eyebrows never smoothed out.

Chapter Four
Rosie

My body was more exhausted than I had realized because after I had showered, I fell straight into the comfy bed and didn't move until morning. It had taken me forty minutes to wash all the blood off and detangle my hair and I couldn't even be bothered to dry it before I went to sleep. As I forced my eyes open, I could still feel the wet strands sticking to my skin.

My body felt heavy, and it took a tremendous amount of effort to even look around at the room. I hadn't forgotten where I was. I knew exactly the things that waited for me when I awoke but I didn't trust for one damn minute that I would be left alone. I stifled a groan as I pushed myself into a sitting position. My arms felt like lead and my eyes burned. Whatever magic I had done last night had taken a toll on my body.

I slowly peeled myself out of bed and forced myself to stand on unsteady feet. I straightened my back trying to stretch out the knots hat had formed but I could barely roll my shoulders.

There was a knock at my door.

"Come in," I called. My voice was hoarse and I had to clear my throat against the itchiness.

Both Matt and Malik showed themselves into my room looking much better than they had the night before. Matt's curly red hair was no longer matted on his head and his skin had been wiped clean of soot. He had a nervous smile on his face.

Malik's white hair which was once grey was now back to a brilliant white. His normally scarred face did not seem to have accumulated any new scars so it was really only I who had gotten injured by my own magic. My newly healed scar itched at the thought. I had stared at it for a long time last night, twisting my head around in the mirror. I had never had a scar; my body always healed my cuts too fast. I wasn't sure how I felt about my skin being marred.

"It's already two in the afternoon," Malik commented and shifted his weight to one foot. "Come out with us, into the town."

I forced my limbs to move, rolling my shoulders then swinging my arms as I walked towards the dresser. There were clothes in here that were two sizes too big but they were comfy enough. Ignoring their looks I picked an oversized t-shirt and shorts that tied at the waist. I decided that if I was being honest about the curse I might as well wear whatever I wanted. It had been ages since I had worn shorts. Maybe once the curse was gone I could finally put on the school's uniform skirt. It was cute and I was beginning to get envious when I saw the other girls style it in ways that I never could.

I quickly brushed my teeth and combed through my wet hair before pulling it into a messy ponytail. I stripped out of my night clothes and donned the oversized clothes I had picked from the dresser. The shirt ended at mid-thigh, hiding the shorts underneath. I quickly tucked the shirt into the shorts and tied it at the waist tightly so there would be no chance of them slipping. I felt unbearably naked in such little clothing. I steeled myself and walked out of the bathroom grabbing my cracked phone off the dresser before I joined them.

"I am assuming this will not work here," I noted and stretched my arms once more. The ache was still there but the more I moved the easier it became.

"Correct," Malik answered.

Matt paused before coming to my side. He gripped my wrist and lifted my arm to shoulder height. I winced at his motion and sent him a glare.

"Maxi and Claudine had this happen before too," he said and moved my arm in slow wide circles. He positioned himself behind me and his other hand cupped my shoulder. I couldn't help the yelp that came out of my mouth. "When their magic went haywire, they were sometimes stuck in bed for days." He moved onto the other arm once I began to relax into his motions. "I would do this for hours." His thumb dug into a sore spot between my neck and my shoulder blade and tears sprang in my eyes. "Our bodies are not made for this type of magic. Even if you are the perfect hybrid there are bound to be some issues with you adjusting."

Just before he began to massage the rest of my back I stepped away from him. A frown pushed itself onto his face and his eyebrows pushed together. *Like a puppy dog face.* I hated how guilty it made me feel. I should be furious with him. I should yell at him until my throat is sore...but he was trying to be nice and now the pain in my shoulders and arms was much more bearable.

"Thank you," I said softly before turning to Malik. "No clam chowder please."

Malik gave me a small smile and gestured towards the open door. "I will take you wherever you want to go."

"And pay," I added feeling a dust of confidence wash through me. His eyes twinkled.

"And I will pay."

* * *

I made him drop by the coffee shop where he had previously gotten me coffee at. This time I tried a cinnamon vanilla latte and on the first sip my knees almost buckled. It was delicious. I had missed a lot after being kept in the house my entire life, hidden by a pair of low-levels that angered a witch who was literally the most powerful one on the planet. By far the thing I had come to love the most was this coffee. I had snuck out after school to go try things my parents could never afford...but this was different. It was heaven.

"Blueberry pancakes? Really?" Malik asked as he walked us through the bustling sidewalk. Cars were still driving on the streets but it looked like a majority of the people in this hidden away sanctuary loved to walk. They would stop people in the streets, talk to them, laugh and then continue on with their day. Many people have waved hello to Malik. He would politely wave but didn't stop as he marched through the town. He weaved expertly between the narrow alleyways between shops. It was hard to keep up with him but Matt pushed me in the right direction when I lost him in the maze of shops.

"Have you ever tried them?" I asked him picking up my pace so that I could follow him through the narrow street he was taking us down. People passed on all sides of us and jostled us as we moved. "Delicious."

"Rosie, you need to get out more," Matt said from behind me. He grunted as a passerby crashed into him. His tall frame made it hard for him to slip between people and he had reached out to grab my shoulder more than one time to keep up. "You are in a town that has been untouched by the decades, and you want pancakes?"

"Are you saying I cannot get pancakes?" I hissed at him, shielding my coffee as people kept jostling my sides.

Finally, Malik turned a corner and we were met with a large square where the people were more dispersed. I let out a sigh and smacked Matt's hand off of my shoulder.

"I'm just saying there are other things—" I cut Matt off with a glare.

"So, you lie to me this entire time, and take me into the den of a gang leader, force me to help you mur—" Malik dove forward to cover my mouth. People that had been sitting at the tables that surrounded the square turned to look at the commotion. Malik's golden eyes were hard as he glared at me.

"We are in public," he hissed. "If you act like a *brat* I will not indulge you as much as I have been. I like you Rosie but do not forget that there are many sides to me and I *choose* to show you that one you have seen up until now. Push me and I can take that away."

"She has a right to be angry," Matt said from behind me and slowly lifted Malik's hand from my mouth. Good thing too because I was just about to bite him again. "We will give you information in time, Rosie. We just want you to enjoy your time here in the town. See that we are not as bad as you believe. Think of it as a rest, a vacation. One you *deserve*."

I continued my stare down with Malik. He had been caring up until now. This was the first time I had seen him so annoyed. Albeit this was also the first time I really mouthed off to him. I didn't want to see the other sides that he talked about. Eli had told me they existed, but I was content living in a world where I could still see Malik as someone who *saw* me, as someone who finally gave me a choice even if it was as simple as ditching class to go to the beach.

"I may be less angry when I have pancakes in my stomach," I told him. Malik's face deflated and I swore I saw a bit of a smile there. It was a compromise from both of us.

"Can you settle for maple walnut pancakes?" Malik asked and gestured to a small diner that stood on the corner of the square. It was a cute white building with a green trim and the entire front was made of glass showing piles of sweets. My mouth watered at the sight.

"It'll do."

* * *

Maple walnut pancakes were better than blueberry. Malik had been right to choose what he had. But what was even better was he had asked for the owners to set us up in a private room on the second floor so that we could talk privately.

"Ezekiel comes here sometimes," Malik said as he sipped the coffee the waitress had just poured for him. He had eaten a small bowl of oatmeal with a side of bacon and eggs while Matt and I dug into the most heavenly pancakes I had ever tasted. "It's the most private we can get so ask away."

I swallowed my food and quickly downed some water. This was what I had been waiting for.

"So Ezekiel really comes from heaven?" I asked. Matt slowed his eating as if to listen as well.

"That's what he tells us, but he said his memories are hazy after the fall. He woke up here when humans could barely fend for themselves but he had been alive much longer than that. He said he had watched them." Malik paused, looking over us before speaking again. "After that he started to find others like himself who had been cast out. Not many live anymore. Some are in this town, others hiding around the world."

"And you were here to hide from humans? Or the people in the government that you want me to...help you with," I asked being careful about mentioning murder. Malik seemed to get testy when I brought it up.

"Both," he answered. "Those like us saw a way to manipulate the humans in a way that benefited them. Our people have suffered because of them."

"Daxton's parents," I supplied and Malik nodded. "This is why you got me close to them?" I asked Matt. His eyes widened and he shook his head furiously.

"I didn't know this was the plan, I swear," Matt said. "I feel bad now that I know."

"Matt was not aware of everything until just recently," Malik said his eyes shifting to Matt. "He had undergone his test; everyone does and when they pass they get to know the plans. It is to protect us."

I looked over Matt carefully. His expression was pleading. I still couldn't understand how someone as sweet and kind as him could really deceive me like this the entire time. I wanted to see him being the bad person I thought he would be but even now his personality stayed the same. Still like a stupid older brother, still like a puppy.

"I don't even know these people," I told Malik. "I don't even know how I would begin at finding an in for you."

"Google them," Matt supplied. "They are pretty famous."

"And you want me to get close to Daxton so...what? He can bring me home and introduce me to his parents?" I let out a scoff at the idea. Like any of them would take this as a serious relationship. While I may not be as mad at them as before, what Rae said had still stung... But she was right. They didn't want me for anything other than what they had outlined at the start.

"That is unlikely," Malik said as if he had the same thought as me. "Getting close to Daxton is so you can learn about his parents' habits. A schedule, an event, what they like to do in their free time, when they see him, when they don't see him, an affair, a love child. Information."

Rae's words hit me like a truck. She was right. This entire time. Everything I had thought was unimportant was now being thrown in my face. She was right to be worried. I was literally about to hand over all this information to them. I wondered if they knew how messed up Daxton's parents were. I wouldn't put it past her to know but that would only make all this more complicated.

"Daxton doesn't share, and even if he did Rae is careful about what she allows to be let out," I told him.

"Then get close to her too," he supplied.

"I don't want to betray them like that," I hissed at him and stabbed my fork in my remaining pancakes. I felt my magic shift under my skin. It startled me. It had been laying low all morning until now. It felt weird now, like it had a mind of its own. I could feel its restlessness; it wanted out.

"They will come to realize which side is the one in the right," Malik promised. "It's not betrayal, you are protecting them. Their parents are evil people, they probably already know this. If anything, you are doing them a favor."

With a shaky hand I took a sip of my almost empty coffee trying to focus on anything other than killing Daxton's parents and the new magic within me. It was a lot to take in and way too much to process in such a short amount of time. Everything I knew had been ripped away from me and torn to shreds, leaving in its place something that hardly resembled the world I once knew.

"I want to see them," I demanded Malik. I sat up straight and held his gaze, showing him I would not back down. "If I am going to do this I do not want to be an information mule. I want to see the people you want me to destroy. To understand. It's the least you can give me in return for such a big ask."

Malik's face hardened under my gaze and I caught sight of the other side he had shown me earlier. It scared me, caused my heart to pound and my palms to sweat. This was the powerful demon to be feared.

"The internet is a powerful tool," Malik said through clenched teeth.

"Or," Matt said slowly and turned to look towards Malik. Malik gave him a hard look. "They should be at any government gathering. If you can get Daxton to bring you to one you could meet them."

Maybe forgiving Matt wouldn't be all that hard.

"Forget about it," Malik hissed. "It is dangerous to be around them alone."

"I wouldn't be alone," I said quickly, a small bit of hope sparked in my chest. I didn't know why seeing them was so important but it was my first step into truly understanding what I got into. "Daxton, Eli, and Rae would be there."

"I mean us," Malik corrected. "If they find out you are a hybrid no one can protect you. It's not you that can't see them, it's them who cannot see you. Not yet."

"From what you told me they already know," I pushed. "If they wanted to tell their parents wouldn't they have done it by now?"

There was a pause.

"They shouldn't even know to begin with," Malik growled. I could feel something around us thicken the air, maybe his power? I couldn't name it but it caused the hair to stand on the back of my neck. "End of discussion. No gala, no gathering, if I hear you even step foot in the vanity of them I will personally hunt you down and show you why you should fear me."

Malik stood and threw money down on the table before leaving the private room. Matt looked at me with a worried gaze and I tried to clamp down on the mischievous feeling that was forcing a smile to my face. I liked to see Malik lose himself like that. My fear easily mixed with my excitement and before I could stop it a plan bloomed in my mind.

I was going to get to that gala whether they came with me or not. I deserved answers and I would not wait until they decided to give them to me.

Chapter Five

Rosie

"So you're telling me," I said with a sigh as I rubbed my pounding head, "that the gang *really* does only exist to fund this town."

I thought Matt's ramblings were utter nonsense but it turns out there was some truth to what he had been trying to tell me before. I sat in a room much like the one I had first met Xena in while they answered may questions about their *employment*. This time there was no skull, but their was a fire place. This room also seemed to have a very specific theme, lilacs. They were on every corner, plastered n the wall paper, hell even the couch was a purple color. The fireplace was nice at first but the heat it provided started to make me sweat as I was hit with a truck load of information.

Malik sat quietly across from me as he watched me take in everything. His eyes were heated and I couldn't help but remember the way they bored into me earlier; it made my palms sweat on top of the anxiety of all this new information. He had changed into an oversized t-shirt and sweats, making him look almost uncomfortably at home. His intricate and colorful tattoos were on full show to the world. Matt sat on the ground in front of the couch in jeans and a t-shirt. Claudine was currently lying her head in his lap as he absentmindedly braided her hair. She had worn a dress that was so big on her that it made her look like a child who had gone shopping in her mother's closet. Maximus had yet to make a presence but if anything I was thankful that he wasn't here to glare at me as I tried to digest this information.

"It's the only thing that we can do so that no one would notice the movement of money or goods," Malik said. "You've seen how many people are here. They live full lives here and we have to get income in here at some point, or else everything you've seen would be wasteland."

"I wondered what the townspeople would think when they realize their lives are being funded by blood money," I muttered and took a sip of the tea Claudine had made for me. It was bitter but she had said that it would help control my magic, or at least calm it down to a point where it would no longer feel like I was going to jump out of my skin.

"It's how all governments work, cursed one," Claudine said dreamily from Matt's lap. "We do what we can to keep them safe."

I nodded at her.

"And the tattoos?" I asked noting that Matt and his siblings were missing the ink that both Malik and Eli shared.

"You are all in testing phase," Malik said as he propped his chin on his hand. He lifted the other arm up so we could see the designs that were hidden from us due to his position. "When you are trusted and full members of our organization you will have the opportunity to get your own."

"Wouldn't that ruin the point of my role?" I asked him. There had been a thought bothering me for a while and I guessed now was a time more than any other to breach the subject. "You guys said there were multiple people in the government you needed to go after. I am assuming Daxton is not the end of this?"

Malik gave me a small smile. He had gotten over my battiness from earlier and was now unfazed when I challenged him. I didn't know if I liked it, a part of me wanted him to get angry like he once had so I could let my own festering anger out but the other part, the bigger part, wanted to go back to a time where I knew nothing. To when I could just enjoy the attention that was being thrown at me. I was asking all these questions, but I didn't really want the answers. I was in over my head, I knew that...but it seemed there was no going back.

"We will cross that bridge when we get to it," he said and looked towards Matt. "You can get yours whenever, as long as you hide them at school."

"Was that his whole task? Bringing me to this point?" I asked, anger slipping into my tone. Malik gave me a harsh look while Matt gave me one full of pity.

"His job is none of your concern," Malik said. His voice was even as he spoke but it had dropped to a dangerous tone that made my stomach flip.

My magic shifted inside me as if waking from a deep sleep. It tugged at my stomach and I felt it come close to the surface of my skin.

"You will need to do something about that," Claudine said from her position on the floor. She twisted so she was able to hug Matt's waist. "Maximus and I can help if you so choose or we can find you a witch...more suitable to your taste. Bloodletting without a partner is messy and not ideal. In order to get stronger, you need to keep your magic, not let it go." Her voice was muffled but it rang loudly through the room. I felt my face heat.

"I didn't know you could feel my magic from over there," I noted trying to talk about anything other than magic sharing.

"When it spikes I can feel it. You will start to feel others' too if you practice more," she said, her voice still muffled by her face against Matt. She sat up, her eyes met mine, and I had the distinct feeling they were seeing into my soul. "Either way the next few days will be uncomfortable for you if you leave it."

I shifted uncomfortably in my seat. Maybe I could leave the town and go find Daxton instead? Surely the magic couldn't be that bad, right? Either way doing *that* was not something I really wanted to do with anyone other than him.

"I'll think about it," I told her earnestly. "If worst comes to worst... I will leave the town and go back to Winterfell." I paused, watching Malik's response. "Back to Daxton for assistance."

The similar feeling I had felt back in the restaurant came back full force. I didn't know what other type of power Malik had but the one that he was exuding right now caused even my magic to shrink back in fear. His expression did not change as he spoke.

"You have already given him enough magic to out our entire plan. We do not need you to jeopardize us any more than you have," he growled and stood preparing to leave, probably to storm off just like he had done earlier.

"You know our relationship. How else do you think I will get information from him?" I asked. It wasn't in my plan to use this as a manipulation tactic. I really wasn't sure how to go about the task they had set forth for me. I was still debating if I could even go through with it. I tried to remind myself that it was just information but even just talking about this caused my insides to shrivel with disgust.

"I already told you that them knowing is a thorn in our side and now you want to give them more to grab onto?" he spat at me, his eyes watching me dangerously as I stood from my own chair. Everything told me to run away from him, to back down, but I was done doing that.

"What do you suggest then, hm?" I asked him, coming close enough that our chests almost touched. "I go back to school and just have the magic overtake me until I am literally bursting at the seams? You really think they are going to trust me if I go behind their backs and share magic with others? Do you know how Eli reacted to me even getting close to you? What I do with them shouldn't even be your concern."

Malik's jaw twitched as I spoke, and his breathing became erratic. For someone who had been able to control himself so well up until now, it really took so little to push him over the edge. I found myself wanting to push him, just to see how far he would fall. Wanting to see what the man who had concocted this plan looked like when he realized that I refused to be as swayed as he wanted me to be.

"Be real with me, Malik," I said in a low voice and ran my hand across his chest teasingly. His stunned expression only egged me on. "Maybe you are just a bit jealous?" I paused and leaned even closer so I could whisper to him, "Or is it because Eli finally one-upped you?"

The widening of his eyes then the quick narrowing caused my heart to race inside my chest. I didn't know where these actions or wants stemmed from. I didn't know when I had started to change or who I was becoming... but I think I liked it. I liked seeing how worked up I could make Malik. Even though I had no power here I liked how I could cause the dynamic to change in an instant. Power like this could quickly become intoxicating. My magic pushed me further, wanted me to continue pushing him. It was just as excited as I was. It too had been locked in a cage and now...it was finally ready to come out and play.

Malik tilted his head slowly to the others behind him and without a word they both silently left the room. Matt gave me a pitiful look as he closed the door behind him. The fact that I was alone with Malik in this room caused my palms to sweat and a different type of nervousness overcame me. As soon as the door clicked shut Malik spurred into action. His long fingers tangled themselves in the hair on the back of my head and he pulled harshly so that my head would be forced back and my throat was stretched in front of him.

"I never lied to you when I said I was on your side Rosie," he said in a low growl. His hands tightened in my hair and I let out a low groan at the pain. "I wanted to be the person that you could come to. That you could trust. Because god knows those *children* will put you through hell and back. But it seems that I may have been too lenient with you since coming here." I swallowed thickly at his words. What was he getting at here? "I am in charge here, Rosie. I am for all intents and purposes your boss. I do not care who your mother is, if you continue to act like you have any sort of power here I will show you just how wrong you are."

I shouldn't like this. I should hate the way he was speaking to me. Hate the way his hand gripped into my hair. I should be angry at him for treating me like this, yell at him for the audacity...but even my magic seemed to purr at the action and the way his commanding voice sounded. I was seriously messed up to like this. Not to mention Eli may quite literally kill me for having these thoughts.

"How would you show me?" I asked before I could stop myself. A sick smile tugged at the left side of his lips. I watched it and licked my own lips before meeting his eyes again.

Yes. My magic seemed to purr when he watched my mouth. *This is what we need.*

"I understand now," he said in a low tone. "You did this on purpose."

I wanted to fight him, say that I didn't but even I couldn't be sure anymore. I had been all over the place since coming here and didn't even understand much about myself anymore. I was once scared to be handled in such a way by Malik, scared he would force me to do something...but for some reason I had a feeling it was all talk.

"And if I did?" I asked, my voice also lowering. Malik leaned in slightly before his lips spread into a full-blown smile.

"Then you will be disappointed," he said. "Kneel." His power swirled around us and my knees gave out from under me at his command. I lifted my gaze to glare at him. He stood back and looked down at me with a smug smile on his face. Anger licked at my soul. I was stupid to play so easily into his hand.

"That was rude," I spat at him and tried to stand but my knees stayed planted on the ground. "Let me up."

"Apologize," he commanded and his power snapped into place easily. I tried to cover my mouth with my hands but my skin became unbearably hot and I was forced to let the stream of apologies out of my mouth. "Say, I was wrong, Malik. I'm so sorry I didn't listen to you."

"I was wrong, *Malik*," I spit his name like a curse. "I am so sorry I didn't listen to you."

"Next time I will make Matt watch as you grovel," he threatened. Humiliation crashed through me like a tidal wave. He leaned down to look me in the eyes. "You trust me," he noted. I tried to speak but he gave me a glare that said it would be better if I stayed quiet. "You wouldn't push me as such if you didn't. It's a good thing, trust. But don't get comfortable, understood?"

"I understand," I said through gritted teeth.

"Now tell me, with your big girl words instead of throwing a tantrum like a child, what you require from me," he said, his voice losing its edge. His words twisted my stomach in a way I liked too much and my magic fanned out around me causing my body to shake. Was this what Daxton was feeling all of the time? It was horrible and humiliating to be at the mercy of something so disruptive. It clouded my senses and at times I felt like I wasn't myself any more.

"I am angry at you all, still," I said. He nodded slowly as if asking me to continue. "But what I *need* is to expel some magic. It's..." I trailed, unable to think of a way to describe the way my magic was pushing me.

"Overwhelming. Making you anxious. Something new," he finished for me. I nodded at his words. "So you are taking control in the way you know how. Seeking comfort...or something from someone you trust."

I swallowed thickly, not able to look at him. My knees were already sore and I wanted desperately to go hide in the room and never come out again. I averted my eyes from his and focused on a carpeted spot on the floor.

"Something like that," I grumbled.

"I cannot fix the problem with your magic, you know that right?" he asked in a soft voice like he was speaking to a child.

"That's why I said I want to go to Daxton," I said trying to sound angry but it came off as a whine. "But you got angry."

"I apologize," he said startling me enough to cause me to look back at him. "For losing my temper. I have been working on this *project* for many years and when I learned that all my work may have been for nothing... I got angry." He sighed and took my hands in his. "I release you. Let's go ask your mother for help." He tried to pull me out of the room but I pulled him back. I didn't want to see her, not again. Even if she said she did this to me for my own good that didn't take away from the horror of what she did. "I'll be with you the whole time."

I nodded and followed him out of the room.

* * *

We found her in a different sitting room than before and this time Ezekiel was still with her. It was a small room with large windows that overlooked the town below. One of them was open, allowing a light breeze in. There was no fire this time but there were a few candles spread about giving off a light floral scent. The room was decorated with some portraits of people I didn't recognize and there were floral patterns on all the furniture.

Ezekiel was enjoying a cup of tea while my mother held a glass of whiskey delicately between her fingers, which now had a black shimmery coat on them. He had on a button-up shirt with some dark jeans that seemed all too normal for him while Xena had on a deep emerald green dress. They were not sitting closely together, on opposite ends of the room oddly enough, but finding them together once more made me question their relationship. Friends? Partners in crime? Coworkers? Did neither of them have loved ones?

"Her magic needs help," Malik explained for me. "And she refused to exchange with anyone but Lars' son."

Xena's lips puckered as if she tasted something sour. "That is not an option at this point."

My anger renewed itself. Who were these people to tell me what I can and cannot do? Surely they wouldn't force me to do something so...intimate with someone I didn't trust? I was tempted to demand that they let me leave right now if that was the case. I'd rather be stuck with this curse forever.

"How about something to take the edge off, hm?" Ezekiel suggested looking at Xena. "Maybe a trick that would help expel some magic? That wouldn't harm anything would it?"

In the light of the room he looked so much like Eli that it almost pained me. I didn't miss her, *them*, but they were all I had up until now and I would feel much better if it was her hand that squeezed my shoulder instead of Malik's. I trusted Malik in a different way than Eli. She may have been hot headed and a bully, but in her own right I knew I would be safe with her.

"Come here, child," Xena commanded, her long finger beckoning me. Malik pushed me forward lightly. I left his side with a small scowl and stood in front of my *mother*.

Getting closer to her only intensified that hate that had festered deep inside me. Here she was in this comfy mansion of a home while I had been left to suffer my curse alone in a house where my parents were less than loving.

She held out her palm face up and a purple light shimmered in her hand. A small semi-transparent purple butterfly appeared and flew up to land itself on my nose before it disappeared in a flash of shimmering magic.

"This is how children get rid of their magic while they are still growing," she said. "Until they are of age to share magic. You would do well to learn this; there will come a time where you teach this to your own children."

"I refuse to have children," I growled at her. There was nothing in the world I would want them to experience and to doom an innocent life to a world like I had grown up in was unspeakable.

She grabbed my hand and forced it palm up.

"Your magic is a part of you, your wants and desires. When you are more in tune with it you can call upon it without even thinking about it. But for now, command it to do what you want it to," she explained and took another sip of her whiskey as she stared at me.

I shifted in my place. I could feel my magic but how could I command it to do such a thing?

Uhh...please help? I asked inside my mind. It shifted inside me restlessly but nothing appeared in my hand. *Make butterflies appear in my hand?* I asked again. This time there was a tug in my chest but nothing happened. *Please?*

Visualize it, a voice in my mind commanded me. I jumped at the voice and shot a glare towards Ezekiel. He sent me a smirk that rivaled his daughters. *Witches visualize their magic when they call it forth even if they don't realize it.*

I sighed and closed my eyes. Feeling everyone watching me in this moment only caused my heart to pound harder in my chest. I imagined the purple magic that swirled around Xena's hand now coming out of my own. The magic worked its way to my hand leaving a trail of fire as it moved. I held onto the image and felt my magic flare to life and burst through my skin.

I snapped my eyes open when I felt the weight of it on my hands. Instead of the purple magic though, there was a reddish magic that poured out of my hand much like my fire had shown before, but this was more transparent and wafted through the air like smoke.

I could feel the magic leave me as it poured out of my hand. I focused on molding it, this time into a bird rather than a butterfly. I was happy that she was teaching me magic but that didn't mean I would take her teachings and replicate it. I didn't want to be her. A sparrow formed in my hand. I could feel the weight and the feathers of it brushing against my hand. Its beady eyes looked at mine and then it ran out of my hands before flying away. It made it only a foot away before it disappeared.

Thanks, I told Ezekiel in my head assuming that he could hear.

"That will suffice," I said to Xena. I wouldn't thank her; she had done the bare minimum. "How long are you planning on keeping me here?"

Xena let out a snort as she downed the rest of her glass.

"You are free to leave at any time. You are here for your own benefit. I recommend you leave here when you are ready and not a moment sooner."

I stepped back looking her up and down critically. She gave no indication of lying. I nodded and turned to leave the room. Malik was following behind me a second later.

I am glad someone cares enough about Eliza to miss her. Ezekiel's voice rang through my head.

I faltered in my step.

At least someone should be thinking of her, I shot back and left the room.

Chapter Six
Rosie

After they admitted that I could leave at any time...the fight in me had decreased drastically. I allowed myself to live the days in this town with little to no worry about the task that was set in front of me. I used this time to understand the people around me. The only people who were anything close to what I was.

Matt, Maximus, and Claudine might not be exactly like me but they knew the struggle of having two different entities raging inside of me. My demon side felt normal and I never noticed any changes, but my magic that seemed to linger just below my skin became volatile and tried to push itself out any time it got.

That's how I got to be in the situation I was in now.

Myself, Claudine, and Malik were in the garden that stood right outside the property and we were testing the extent of my magic. The garden was filled with flowers I did not know the names of and multiple iron tables and chairs, perfect for teatime. During my time here I felt as though I was the daughter of an extremely rich aristocrat, everything I asked for was at my hands in minutes. A girl could get used to this type of life... if she wasn't sharing it with the person who cursed her.

I had thought a lot about Xena and my low-level parents recently. I didn't know what to do with them... do I go back home and pretend like nothing happened? Never go home again? Go home and spill everything I knew?

The latter was obviously not an option with Malik's power hanging over my head.

I hated Xena, feared her at times... but there was a part of me that wished I could have been here growing up. It was a clean and calm environment. No one was hungry and every time we walked the town, people were smiling and waving at us. For the first time in my life I wasn't ashamed of what I was or hiding my face in public. I had more freedom and control than ever before... even if I still had the chain tied to my ankle.

Claudine's whine brought me out of my thoughts. I had strayed too long and the birds I were making almost disappeared.

I had learned that I could keep the birds form as long as I concentrated on the magic. Once my mind wandered even slightly it would disappear. It took a lot of concentration, and it was perfect because I needed to connately funnel magic into them.

"Again. Make a hummingbird," Claudine commanded and giggled as a sparrow tugged at her hair. They had a mind of their own which made this all the harder. I had to watch out for them carefully as they flew through the air going every which direction. I had gotten up to four birds now and all of them seemed to enjoy Claudine's company. She let out another giggle as a raven landed on her head.

The raven was hard; it took a lot of magic and wasn't even the right size. I conjured the hummingbird with ease because of its small size. It sprang to life out of my hand and instead of flying to Claudine it flew to my cheek and gave me a light, loving nudge.

It was enough to break my concentration on all the other ones.

Claudine let out a noise of disappointment. The hummingbird nudged me once more before disappearing as well.

"Make some yourself. Aren't you also a witch?" I teased her when she gave me a small pout.

I came to learn that Claudine was a sweet girl that had a very childlike mind. It was refreshing to be around someone so simple. Not to mean she was dumb or anything of the sort; the way her eyes honed onto you at times made it clear she knew far more than she let off. She was just very open about what she did and did not like or want.

"How does the magic feel now?" Malik asked giving me a pointed stare that made my stomach flip. I didn't forget the way I was ready to jump him the other night and in turn he made me humiliate myself in front of him... and I *liked* it. I couldn't wait to finally leave this town so I could go back to the trio.

That posed another problem... I would have to *beg* Daxton to share magic with me while trying to skirt around me actually being a witch.

"Better," I said a bit too quickly. I cleared my throat. "I will need to meet with Daxton soon after I leave this town though."

"Remember for them it will be like almost no time has passed," he said. "So you may need to wait a few days...unless they are into that type of thing."

I blushed furiously and ran my hand through my hair.

"It doesn't help that we fought before we left," I admitted.

"Make up sex," Claudine said from her sitting position in the grass. She wore a bright yellow dress that made her look younger than she was and it made her words all the more startling.

Malik let out a loud laugh. "No need to be embarrassed, Rosie. This is normal for witches and you should get used to this talk."

"It's just..." I trailed off trying to find the words. "This wasn't how my life was before."

In truth I had lived a very sheltered life up until now under the careful watch of my parents. Most of what I learned about adult relationships had come from them or from the gossips of other low-levels during my time in school. No one prepared me for this, no one taught me how relationships were supposed to be like.... And now with those three controlling every aspect of my life....

"It's overwhelming," Claudine summarized for me with a sweet smile. "Magic and the things it makes you do."

I swallowed thickly and stared at my unchanging hand. I looked the same, save for the scar on my face. But nothing about me was the same anymore. To start I wasn't even the race I thought I was. There was no hiding in the crowds of low-levels anymore. Before I had been furious at seeing the way low-levels were treated but now that I knew what blood really resided in me, I couldn't help but wish to be an ignorant low-level once again.

"I don't understand it," I said in a weak voice. "Anything."

I looked over at Malik and he met my gaze with a soft smile. That was the Malik I liked, not this gang leader, or angry demon that forced me to beg. All of that was hot, sure, but what I needed was this person right now.

Seeing his smile almost made tears spring to my eyes.

"In time you will," he promised. "It's not as bad as you are making it out in that pretty little head of yours, I swear."

I let out a weak laugh.

"Please don't tell me we have another mind reader among us?" I asked teasingly.

The clearing of a throat caused us to pause and look toward the intruder. Ezekiel stood there in a light white shirt and light brown pants, the most casual outfit I had seen him in to date. His hair hung limply around his face.

"Can I have a moment with Rosie?" he asked. I looked towards Malik and Claudine but they were looking at me, waiting for me to make the decision.

"Sure," I said to him and the other two vacated their seats immediately.

"Find me when you are done and we can go get the best ice cream you've ever tasted," Malik said and sent me a wink before walking with Claudine back into the house.

Ezekiel sat in Malik's previous spot and gave me a soft yet hesitant smile.

"I should be honored to receive such a visit from an Original," I teased. In the last few days I had relaxed significantly around him. He was quiet and much calmer than I had expected which meant Eli was probably more similar to her mother than him. The joking started when I bumped into him on accident one night. I thought it was Malik and began cursing at him only to find him staring down at me. He smirked and told me someone with a mouth like mine would stand up against Eli well.

"You are leaving soon," he noted. "I wanted to meet with you alone before you did."

I shouldn't be surprised by his words. We had all felt it. We had overstayed our welcome and it was a nice break from reality but there were things to do back in the real world.

"A warning?" I asked. "Worried I'll ruin the plans?"

"Actually," he said then cleared his throat. "I was wondering if you could tell me about Eli."

I sat there in a stunned silence. His eyes were sincere and he still had that hesitant smile on his face.

"What do you want to know?" I asked.

"Everything," he said and seemed to deflate a little. Was he thinking I would have refused? "Yes. I thought you would see me as unfit and think that I had no business in her life but...this is the closest I can get to her."

I nodded slowly, mulling over this.

"It's not pretty," I told him. "She's mean and brash. She can be unkind."

He sat back against the chair and closed his eyes as if focusing on something. I startled when I realized it was my thoughts. I played the image of Eli walking into the mess hall inside my mind and a smile tugged at his lips.

"It's to be expected. It's okay, tell me what you can."

So I did. I told him about the bullying but also made sure to mention the sweet times. To mention the way she looked out for me. Mentioned the way she worried about Malik hurting me even if it came off as jealousy and anger.

He laughed at her actions thoroughly enjoying the stories I told him as they left my lips.

"She's so much like her mother," he said with a sigh. "Her mother is so hot headed and has a glare that could kill a person."

"She is alive?" I asked slowly. I hadn't heard much about her until now and I was curious about who she was.

"Yes," he said with a nod. "But she too must stay away since they have identified her. She can move freely from this town because she is not an Original and they could care less about her powers, but she still must stay vigilant."

"Eli would freak if she heard her mother was anything less than an Original," I said with a smirk.

"Oh she is powerful don't get me wrong, just a few generations younger than me so the power is different," he explained and stood up brushing off his pants. "Thank you Rosie. I know we are sending you on a task that you disagree with but I would appreciate you continuing to look out for Eli."

"It's her that looks out for me," I corrected but he just shook his head.

"Come back in one piece and I can share more stories about what we do here with you. I think you will grow very powerful Rosie and I can't wait to see what you do with it." He paused before turning to leave, looking at me with a hard to read expression.

"Is there something wrong?" I asked.

He cleared his throat. It looked like he didn't want to breach this subject. My mind immediately went to the gutter.

"No," he choked out with a laugh. "I actually wanted to talk to you about your parents."

I cocked my head to the side.

"Xena?" I asked not understanding where this was going.

"The other ones," he said with a forced smile. "I heard... in the main room when you first got here. You feel bad for them."

I stiffened at his words. Sure, I felt like it was unfair for my parents... and we didn't have a great relationship but...

"They are losing a child," I said and shifted in my seat. "They have no idea what's happening right now and think I am just living my life at Winterfell."

"Have they... contacted you?" he asks hesitantly.

I looked at my intertwined fingers.

"No," I whispered.

He paused for a long moment.

"She's not as bad as it may seem," he said. "She's not replacing them and didn't want to cause them harm."

It was much easier to believe him then Xena. It was the way he carried himself, the calm, sure manner in which he spoke. He felt trustworthy.

"Her curse cuts open my skin," I noted calmly. When I met his gaze there was no smile on his face.

"I hope you can find your place among us, Rosie," he said and with a last, sad smile, he left.

* * *

As the day passed by, the anxiety that had been at bay for the days started to catch up to me. I had been living here as peacefully as I possibly could and forgetting all about the real world. Forgetting about the task that they had asked me to complete. Forgetting about *them*.

We were fighting when I left and now all of that seemed meaningless. Rae's words had hurt me, sometimes still did, but I really couldn't bring myself to be mad at them anymore especially when the secrets they kept were like child's play compared to what I had found out during my time here.

And none of them even knew what they were facing out there in the world. None of them knew what was hiding behind the veil that the people around us had crafted so carefully.

Or maybe they did know? This would be another thing I would have to pry from Rae's stone-cold grip. She obviously knew more than the other two but how far did that information extend?

I had come up to my room over an hour ago trying to calm myself and think through what I would do when I got back to Winterfell. I had something to achieve now, a plan I needed to put in place. One with so little direction and assistance that it made me stressed every time I thought about it. I told myself that once I calmed myself and thought through a plan for the trio, I would tell Malik I was ready to leave... But nothing came to mind. I had no idea how I was going to pull this off especially with a mind reader and an empath in the group.

I gathered the belongings that lived through the explosion. My t-shirt and jeans were washed and looked as good as new. Even the blood stains had been removed. My cracked phone which was still frozen lay on top of the folded clothes. Besides that, I had the shoes on my feet and nothing else to bring back.

A knock at my door startled me out of my thoughts. Thinking it was Malik I told him he could enter. I was thoroughly disappointed when brown eyes and black hair peeked over my door.

"Xena," I greeted. She gave me a nod and forced an awkward smile to her face. "If you are here for some mother-daughter bonding I do not want it."

She shut the door softly behind her effectively trapping me in here with her. This room was far too small to house the both of us and I felt the familiar ice-cold fear wash down my back. It was instinctual even though she had yet to harm me the entire time I was here. I still could not bring myself to stop fearing her.

"I came to give you a choice." She paused, her eyes looking over the room and flashing to my pile of belongings.

"I didn't know I had a choice in anything I do here," I said not hiding the venom in my voice.

She closed the space between us stopping at the end of my bed. Close enough that her floral scent invaded my senses but not enough to touch. It was still enough to lock my knees and cause my heart to beat rapidly.

"You can stay here," she said. "You can learn to harness your magic. You can." She paused to take a shaky breath. The act caught me off guard and made her seem more human than I was ready to believe. "We can be together. Close the gap between us."

I averted my gaze from hers and stared at the clothes that lay out on my bed in front of me. How many times had I wished for a better relationship with the parents who weren't even my real ones? And now she was acting like I actually had that chance?

"Do I have siblings?" I asked grabbing the clothes and bringing them to my chest, a movement that made me feel safer.

"No," she answered. "I know this task seems—"

"Murder," I interrupted her. "You want me to help you murder someone. My—" I paused, unable to find the word and looked up at her before continuing. "Someone's parents. Someone I care about."

"It is important Rosie," she insisted, her manicured hand reaching out to touch my arm. I flinched away from her touch. "For us to live a safe life outside these walls."

"When this is over. This task, I mean." I paused taking a steadying breath. "On top of removing the curse I want you to take me away from my parents. I do not want to go back there."

"Anything else?" she asked. Her expression didn't change as if the request was nothing to her.

"An apartment would be nice," I admitted. "The semester will be concluded in a few short months... I do not know if I will complete the task before then but I do not want to go back to my parents' house during the break."

She nodded and replied without hesitation, "Consider it done. Do you..." She paused again. The awkwardness between us was almost palpable. "Do you have plans for the short break in a few weeks?"

The shock must have shown on my face because her eyes shifted to the floor. I should appreciate how hard she was trying here but I really couldn't get over how much she had ruined my life. The road to forgiveness would be a long and bumpy one that I was sure she would not be able to stand.

"I was thinking of staying at the school," I told her.

She nodded and trailed her finger across the bedspread.

"It would be a good time to get close to Daxton," she said slowly. "From what I have heard he doesn't go back home. He tends to stay with Eli or Rae."

There it is, I thought. *Did she really stage this conversation just to get to this point?*

The hope that fluttered in my chest was squashed to pieces by that simple sentence. I am not sure why I though our relationship could change. Ezekiel had said he hoped for me to find a place here, but how can I when every nice thing comes with a price tag too big for me to handle?

A real, caring parent wouldn't ask this of her child. I wish there was a world in which my real mom could care for me in a way that didn't require me to murder people. It made my heart ache for my low-level mom.

"The break is soon. If I can mend the relationship between me and them I will see about how I can join them on their break."

Her shoulders sagged at my response. "Good. Good."

She turned to leave without another word.

"I will have to share magic with Daxton once I get back. You cannot stop this, I hope you know that," I warned her. Both Malik and her had shown how against it they were in multiple conversations but I made it clear I would not go to anyone else... At least not now.

"I know," she said and sent me a small smile as she opened the door. "Ezekiel is very adamant to let you do what you please. He made us swear we would at least give you this amount of freedom."

My throat tightened so much I had to clear my throat in order to continue.

"He did?"

She nodded. "He thinks you're important to his daughter and apparently thinks your happiness is directly correlated to Eliza's."

"Oh," I said not knowing how else to react.

"We are not monsters Rosie. Even if we have done cruel things in the past...we care for our children."

When I didn't reply she took it as the cue to leave. When she did I was able to let out the breath that was caught in my throat.

It was time.

* * *

Malik brought the group to the same bar that we had entered from. Matt, Claudine, and Maximus came with us this time. It was almost odd seeing the whole group together. This entire time, except now, we hadn't been hanging out as a whole and I couldn't say that I had missed Maximus' bad attitude. Before leaving Malik ordered us all shots of vodka stating that we needed to loosen up a bit. I was grateful for anything that could give me at least some bit of courage.

The soft-faced bartender gave us five shot glasses and I smacked Malik's hand away when he tried to grab his own and instead downed both mine and his. The liquid burned on the way down but in comparison to the way the magic was heating up my skin it almost seemed cool. He had a smirk on his face as he watched me.

"I need it more than you," I told him and walked over to the door we had entered from, waiting for the others to finish their shots before they joined me. Malik watched me the entire time, only moving to follow me to the door.

"It won't be that bad," he said and wrapped an arm around my shoulders. My body automatically leaned into his. It felt safe and warm but I would never admit that to him.

"You don't have to make up with them and then manipulate Daxton into giving up information about his parents," I grumbled.

Matt was the first to bounce over to us. He gave me a large smile that showed his pearly white teeth. My eyes trailed down to his now tattooed arms. As soon as Malik had said he could get them he ran out the next day to do it. Apparently they were infused with magic and not only healed faster than normal tattoos but only took one six-hour session to complete. I hadn't decided yet if I wanted them but seeing them on Matt made me just a bit envious.

Claudine glided over with a soft smile as well with Maximus on her heels. They had both refused, given that they would need to be undercover for whatever their task was.

"Alright children, let's go," Malik said and without removing his arm from my shoulder he reached behind him to push the door open.

The same gut-wrenching feeling struck me as the magic swirled around us. This time I was prepared and held on to Malik for dear life. I swear I heard him let out a chuckle as I did so. Even with the violet onslaught of magic it still caused my skin to tingle in inappropriate ways.

When the magic had left us and we were hit with the cool air of the outside, Matt pushed past us to lose the contents of his stomach onto the sidewalk. My own stomach was in knots but I had gotten used to it on the second trip and prepared myself on what to expect, so my reactions were never as bad as his. I let out a sigh and walked over to him to pat his back.

"You need to tougher stomach," I muttered as I patted his back. He shot me a sheepish look that was only exacerbated by the sickly green look on his face. "I can't believe you are a gang leader."

"He's a damn good one too," Malik said from behind me.

The dead and rundown town hadn't changed a bit since we left it. Every time I left the barrier I had expected something else to meet us on the other side, but there was nothing. The blacktop was still cracked, the store fronts still dusty and barren, and Malik's care was still the only new thing left in the lot. After letting out a noise of disgust, Malik pushed us both to his car which hadn't moved from where we parked it. Malik pushed me into the passenger seat while the three siblings took upon the back seat.

Malik turned on the car and without a second to waste started driving the way back to Winterfell. I took out my cracked phone and saw that the time had already changed

"So," I said breaking the silence that had descended on the group. "It's been what, forty minutes? What's the plan when we get back?"

Malik's eyes shifted towards mine, his face lit by only the street lamps that littered the highway. It made his expression look all the more grim.

"If my workers do a good job, Eli would have heard of the explosion right after it happened." Malik's eyes shifted to the clock on the dashboard. "It took us almost an hour to get from the city to the town so they have had an hour and a half to freak out. There is no reason they should think of you being connected to it and given what you told me, you were already fighting so you should be safe until the morning."

"Hand that to me," Matt said from the back. When I gave him a questioning look he pointed to my phone.

I hesitantly handed it over and watched as he gave it to Maximus.

Maximus sent him a glare but his hands began glowing a light blue. When he was finished Matt grabbed it from his hands and gave it back to me with a big smile. It was good as new.

"We have to go to the principal," Maximus said from the back. "Get information and change the order."

"The order?" I asked. Malik sent me a small smile.

"Well, it's not like I can ask him to keep you and Daxton apart anymore can I?"

I nodded and tried to relax in my chair. So far it sounded easy. The hardest part would just have to be acting as if I didn't just open the door to an entirely new world. The drive felt shorter than it had before, and before I knew it we were stopping in the parking lot of Winterfell. Students were still walking in the darkness either laughing in groups or hurrying to their dorms. Curfew here wasn't strict and they practically let the high-levels do whatever they wanted, so we wouldn't stand out if we were wandering at this time.

"You guys go to the principal, he will listen to you," Malik ordered looking at the group through the rearview mirror. "I will walk Rosie to her dorm."

I almost wanted to refuse his help but one look at him told me better not to fight it. His words from the other night flashed through my head.

I am in charge here, Rosie. Ya, I didn't doubt that anymore but if I did not get to Daxton soon my magic would not take this as an answer. Without another word I climbed out of the car not being able to stay in such a tiny space with them any longer. The cool air almost hurt when it hit my over-heated skin.

We parted and Matt gave me a small wave as he ushered his siblings along. Malik slipped his arm over my shoulder and pushed us towards the dorms.

"We should enter from the back or the others may hear us as we walk past," I whispered to him careful to not speak too loud. My cover as a mute had to be firmly back in place in order to keep up with appearances. Not to mention we had no idea when the curse would be lifted so I would need to be careful in case it ever came back full force.

"We probably should, huh?" he said. His voice was slightly teasing. He led us to the main entrance against my protests. The air in the dorm room was warmer than the outside and I felt a nostalgic feeling crash over me even though I had only been gone a few days. My heart pounded as we walked down the hallways. We would have to pass Rae's door and if they heard me with Malik...

"*Malik*," I hissed at him and tried to dig my heels into the ground but he only held me tighter against him. His hand brushed at the exposed skin on my neck and the featherlight touch pulled a hiss from my mouth. "If you are going to do this can you please just not touch me like that?"

Rae's dorm was getting closer and the panic that was clawing at my insides turned into surprise when Malik's fingers tangled themselves in my hair instead and pulled just hard enough for me to feel a prick of pain.

"Trust me," he whispered. "If I know anything about young demons this should work surprisingly well for you."

"What are you talking about?" I hissed back but instead of responding he just pushed me past Rae's door quickly. My heart pounded with each step fully expecting the door to swing open but instead it stayed shut. My door was only a few more paces away but before we reached my door Malik turned me towards him, his molten gold eyes meeting mine.

"Will you trust me on this?" he asked quickly. "Hurry we don't have time."

My heart caught in my throat. I didn't know what he was planning but if there was anything the last few days had proven, we had the same goal even if I was reluctant to be a part of it.

"Yes," I whispered to him, my own heartbeat louder than my words.

A small twinkle made its way to his eyes and in a flash he backed me up to the wall beside my dorm. I sucked in a sharp breath of air as he pressed his chest to mine and lifted my chin.

What the fuck was he doing? This would piss them off, not help me.

His hand snaked around my waist pushing us closer together, his lips were mere centimeters from mine.

"How real do you want to make this?" he whispered to me, his breath wafting across my face. His eyes trailed down my face. "I can give you what you were asking for."

Fuck, was he serious?

"You are messing with me," I whispered.

"Not at all," he said in a serious tone. His fingers trailed down my arm and I almost let out a moan right there. *Stupid magic.*

I heard it then, the footsteps. Even if they hadn't opened the door I had no doubt that it was the trio that was coming up on us.

""Demon, gang leader, whatever.... I am still a man with needs," he said. He leaned even closer, stopping just a breath away. "When Eli tries to enter your mind... distract her with something pleasant."

My brain stalled and I waited too long while trying to decipher his meaning. The footsteps stopped all together.

"Malik, get off her," Eli growled from somewhere to our left. Malik let a smirk grace his lips and lifted his head to peer at Eli.

"You have no say here," Malik said and let out a small chuckle. "This poor little low-level was such a mess when I caught sight of her. If you are going to keep her as a pet the least you could do is take care of her better." His eyes met mine once more. "Isn't that right Rosie?"

I tried to look at the group but Malik grabbed my face harshly and kept it straight towards him. He leaned down close to my ear.

"Say yes," he growled. "And don't show them your eye, not yet."

"Yes," I choked out. His lips brushed my ear as if rewarding me.

"Rosie come here," Daxton growled. Hearing his voice sent a pang of guilt through me. He had no idea what was to come. No idea that the person I was now was entirely different from the person he had seen a few hours ago.

"What was it that Rae said?" Malik asked me and licked the length of my throat. I could feel my core clench and my magic lash out wildly trying to grab onto anything.

"She said—" I was cut off by Eli pushing Malik off of me. She stood in front of me her back almost pressed to me as she glared at Malik.

I used this chance to look over at Rae and Daxton. They were both in the same clothes I had seen them in a week ago. Their school uniforms were wrinkled as if they had rolled around in them. Rae's hair was slightly messy, which was odd for her. Her hazel eyes narrowed on me, and I could almost hear her brain whirring to life behind those sharp eyes. Daxton's short brown hair was also a mess above his head sticking every which way, but it only made him more endearing. As endearing as a huge, tattooed person with a mean glare could be.

For them, nothing had changed but from me I couldn't help the feelings of guilt that crashed through me. Another warm emotion played at my senses, but it was overshadowed when Daxton's brown eyes met mine. I could see the predator behind his eyes one more and wondered if my eyes reflected the same thing. Amr, his cat familiar, was near his calf and stared at me curiously.

"What the fuck happened to your eye?" Daxton demanded in a voice that sounded near animalistic. My hand came up to cover the scar over my left eye, but Eli was too fast and her rough fingers yanked my hand away from my face. Her blue eyes had a fire behind them, and her teeth bared as if ready to attack.

It was frighteningly beautiful.

Chapter Seven

Eli

"Did he do this to you?" I demanded Rosie. Her once perfectly smooth and freckled skin was now marred with a scar that started from above her left eyebrow and stopped in the middle of her cheek. There was no blood on her so that bastard probably had her healed before we found them here. Did that bastard really think we wouldn't notice?

She looked at me with wide brown eyes and her pink lips slightly parted. Even like this, regardless of my anger, her beauty stirred my senses to life.

I fully blamed Rae for this. If she would have just kept he mouth shut we wouldn't have to pull her from Malik *again*. I would have words with Rosie about running to Malik every time we had a fight but that was not the problem now.

"No," she said all too quickly for my liking and tried to avert her gaze but I held her face in my hands, listening to the stream of her thoughts. They were everywhere and nowhere at once. She could barely focus on any one thing. There was something there though, tugging at her mind that I hadn't heard until just a few hours ago. It was like Daxton's magic when he was about to lose himself.

I didn't want to believe their theories about Rosie being a witch but listening to her thoughts now there was no denying it. It was magic reaching out and I could feel its intention. It needed to consume.

"She did this to herself," Malik said from behind me. His voice ignited the anger inside of me once more and I sent him a glare.

"You really expect me to believe that?" I growled at him. "Why are you with her anyways, didn't your place get blown to pieces?"

He shrugged and stuffed his hands in his pockets. The smile that played at his lips pissed me off.

"A stray witch on a rampage. Luckily, I ran into Rosie when I did or I would have been torn to pieces in that place." His eyes shifted towards Daxton. "And let's not beat around the bush; you have most likely figured it out faster than me. I was lucky enough to see her explode in a burst of lights before I realized there was more to her *curse* than meets the eye."

I could hear Rosie's shocked thoughts before I could register my own.

What the fuck is he saying?

Ya Rosie, what the fuck is he saying? I asked her keeping my eyes on Malik.

"We learned earlier," Rae admitted. "Why don't you tell us what's really going on here Malik?"

Malik didn't even look at her as he walked closer to me and put a hand on my shoulder.

Come on, Eliza, his voice said in my mind. *Jealousy is unbecoming of you.*

"I was just helping out a friend in need. You know how crazy magic can make a person," he said so low I could barely hear.

"Let me go," Rosie said from behind me. "I want to go to bed, it's been a long day."

I whipped my head around to glare at her. Her brown eyes were wide, scared almost.

"You really think I will let you go like that? We have been apart for a few hours and I see you with him? Didn't we have this talk already or do you need a refresher?" I growled at her. What did she not understand about this? Her mind told me she would like nothing more than to relive that experience with me.

I was pulled away from her by Malik. I smacked his hand away.

"Amr," Rosie called. She gave the feline that sprinted towards her a small smile before opening her arms for him to jump into. He rubbed his head against the underside of her chin and she let out a soft sigh. "As for you three—" She paused before meeting my eyes. "Don't bother me any longer. Give me some time before you jump back into your routine."

"Rosie," I warned in a growl. "I know Rae hurt you but we have things we need to—"

"Stop talking." Rosie cut me off. Her voice was so hard and full of anger that it caused my back to straighten. I could almost feel her words weigh down on me like an anchor. I didn't like the feeling it left in my chest. "Rae was right." She sent Rae a small smile that caused the dark-haired girl to blink owlishly. "I have gotten comfortable and forgotten what we wanted to do here. So thank you, for helping with my curse up until now. Once we feel as though we are ready, we can start up again."

There was a pause between us until Malik let out a chuckle from behind me.

"I think you guys just got dumped," he teased. "Let me know if you want me to visit you tonight Rosie. Or I could always take you to mine."

I swung my elbow back connecting with his stomach. I enjoyed the way the air rushed out of him and how he had to steady himself against the wall in order to regain his composure.

"The *curse* is unstable. Let me stay with you," Daxton spoke up finally. I didn't like the look in his eyes. Even though he had just gotten rid of some of his magic it looked like he was barely holding on.

"Not alone you're not."

"Forget it."

Rae and I spoke at the same time. Normally I would have liked that we were on the same page but I still couldn't look over the reason why we were all here.

"Amr will be with me," Rosie said and scratched the long-haired cat's chin. "He will come to you if I need help."

"We will talk about this later," Rae told Rosie. It was more of a threat than anything but instead of Rosie looking away like she normally would she met Rae straight on with an unwavering gaze.

"No, we won't," she said and opened her dorm room with one last look at us. "Thank you, Malik. I don't know what would have happened if you hadn't found me when you did."

The fire in my veins roared to life and I was ready to beat Malik into a pulp. How come he got a better thank you? I vowed that I would make her beg in ways Malik couldn't even dream of.

"Anytime Kitten. You have my number," he replied and sent her a wink. That time she did look away and there was a slight blush on her face.

The door shut with a click before I lunged myself at Malik.

"What are you doing with her?" I hissed at him. He raised his hands palms out.

"Apparently more than you guys are. What do you take her for? You really didn't think she would get tired of being your doll? What does she even get out of this deal?" he asked. Each word tested my patience. "Let go." His power washed over me and against my will my hands left him like they were burned.

"We are getting rid of her curse," Rae spoke from behind us. "But it's an awful coincidence that you just *happen* to be there when she exploded? Also, what was that thing with the principal? What is your goal here Malik?"

Malik rolled his eyes and brushed invisible dirt off his shirt.

"I'm here for Eli of course," he responded. "I need to see how my successor is faring. We can't have someone ill-informed running the biggest part of our gang."

A burst of excitement filled me when he called me his successor. When I was younger I would have died to hear those words out of his mouth. All I wanted before was him to look at me like I was worth something. I couldn't care less about Damon but Malik...even Damon was scared of him.

"And the principal?" Rae reminded.

"Why does he need to be in my business?" Malik said and brushed past me. His voice only took a second to enter my mind.

After the break let's meet at our spot. He continued walking as if nothing happened and pushed past both Rae and Daxton with a shit-eating grin.

Our spot. A place in the city he took me to when I was younger. When I was ready to end it all. A place where for the first time I felt like I mattered to someone. It was a lie; I didn't know it back then but it became clear when I figured out the type of person Malik really was.

And now he had his claws in Rosie.

I looked at her closed door debating whether or not to barge in there and put an end to this but it was Daxton that snapped me out of my daydream.

"Let's give her time," he said. "Amr is with her, that should be enough for now."

"So she really is...?" I let my sentence trail off purposely. I almost didn't want to say it out loud, afraid it would jinx what we had going for us.

"I'm not positive," Daxton replied. "But it's looking like it."

"How do we tell?" Rae asked.

"The only for sure way is to see her do magic but if you ask me what we have seen is enough," Daxton replied. "I've never seen a curse act like it had a mind of its own."

"We shouldn't push her too hard just yet," Rae said after a pause. "You saw what happened in the room. We need to navigate this carefully."

I nodded and even though my entire being was telling me to go get her I listened to my friends and left with them down the hall.

* * *

Elle Mae

When I saw her the next day my heart almost jumped out of my chest. I was by no means someone who would actually degrade myself into kneeling for a mere low-level but when Rosie showed up in a *skirt* of all things to class, I thought for sure right there I would give her anything she wanted. Her legs were smooth, and her hips swayed as she walked into the classroom with Amr in her arms. The scar that now marred her beautiful face did nothing to take away from her beauty, if anything it created an aura around her that told anyone who looked not to mess with her.

It made my mouth water and I wondered if she would let me put my hand up that skirt of hers. I had to remind myself that she may not even be a low-level anymore, but something else entirely. A witch? A low-level with a curse that acted independently of her?

Why did the thought of her being a witch displease me?

She sent me a small smile from the doorway and I swear my stomach did a flip. I looked towards Dax to see if he was as affected as I was and noticed his grip on the desk caused his knuckles to turn bone white.

That was no reaction to the skirt. I had known him long enough to know that his magic was unstable. I reached out and brushed my hand against his arm. His eyes flashed dangerously in my direction as if on high alert.

Do you need to leave? I sent him in his mind.

I am not leaving until she leaves with me, he growled back. I rolled my eyes and withdrew my hand just in time to watch Rosie slide into the seat next to Daxton instead of the one next to me.

"Not a good idea, low-level," I warned. She sent me a look that told me she didn't care much for my comment. *Why was she mad at me?* Rae was the one who fucked this up.

Daxton took this time to slide the cup of iced coffee he had already got for her over to her side of the table. She flashed him a pretty smile and shifted in her seat so she could cross her legs. Her already too short skirt rose under the table gaining the attention of both Dax and me. Amr jumped out of her arms and sat down in Dax's lap. His eyes cleared slightly but he still could not take them off Rosie.

"The scar is a nice touch," Dax commented. "Did a witch heal it for you or did you do that yourself?"

She took a sip of coffee before reaching her hand out to me. The immediate reaction of mine to grab her hand disgusted me.

A random witch helped, she said. *Can you thank him for the coffee? It is delicious.*

What are you doing? I asked her and held onto her hand tightly before she could remove it from mine. *The skirt? Ignoring us? It was Rae that pissed you off, not me.*

I wanted to wear a skirt; it's been a while, she responded back. *And about that... You didn't really fight her right? And you also kept secrets, still do. I knew what you wanted, you told me as such. It was my fault for thinking I could actually belong somewhere.*

And Malik? The question came before I could stop myself and the jealously that sparked when she showed me what it looked like from her perspective when Malik looked over her, the way she wanted him to touch her.

Her audacity only flamed my anger. Not only did she partner with Malik and run to him at every chance she got, but now she wanted him to touch her? She needed a lesson.

I threw her hand back at her and gripped Dax's shoulder.

After class, I told him. *Let's show her who she belongs to.*

His eyes flashed dangerously when he peered back at me.

You're on, he said and placed his hand on her thigh. Rosie's reaction gave away her cool exterior. She jumped slightly and her skin flushed a perfect-looking red. I gripped his shoulder tighter.

Switch places with her. Have her sit near the wall. I don't want anyone else to see this... Yet. I sent him an image of what I wanted him to do and he let out a chuckle that caused Rosie to jump.

"Switch with me, Rosie," Dax said smoothly. He stood while pulling Rosie into his previous spot. Amr meowed angrily in response and jumped onto the table to get out of the way. Rosie scowled as she was pushed closer to the wall and it deepened as Dax pulled his own stool closer to hers. There were a few stares and odd looks but they hastily looked away when I sent them a glare.

Rosie tried to reach out to me but this time I didn't give her my hand and watched with sweet satisfaction as Dax brought the leg closest to him over his lap. I couldn't see inside her skirt from my position but I could see as Dax trailed his hand up her thigh teasingly.

We were in the perfect position for this. We were at a table near the corner of the room closer to the back. If she didn't make a noise no one would be the wiser as to what we were just about to do to her. But she would have to sit there and squirm as Dax bent her to our will.

We were the best partners and I couldn't wait to see what else we could make Rosie do. Dax was more rational than me and didn't jump headfirst into things, but with the right coaxing...he could be a beast. That magic, that stamina, paired with a bit of direction? The perfect combination.

Rosie's face was flaming as Dax leaned close to whisper to her. "Don't freak, Rosie. You wore that skirt and thought I could resist such a perfect opportunity?"

She covered her mouth with her hand and shot me a look. I shrugged and leaned forward to whisper as well even though I didn't really give a damn about the other students hearing.

"Let us help you *Rosie*." I put emphasis on her name and she looked down at the table. "Since apparently we didn't do enough last night."

"I won't do anything you can't handle," Dax whispered leaning almost close enough to kiss her. Her face lifted as if she expected him to. "I won't even go *inside* even though I can already feel how wet you are for us."

She shuddered as his hand reached lower and lower until I was sure he was touching her. Just then, Mr. Falkner walked in and greeted everyone. His eyes washed over us just for a second but then they were on the whiteboard. I heard Rosie's sigh and watched as she shifted so Daxton would have better access to what was under her skirt.

The movement set my body on fire. Watching her like this was far too sweet. The little low-level didn't even know how good she looked when she was embarrassed. I loved watching her squirm. She came in here acting like she was in control but as Dax began working in between her legs she began to lose control quickly. She leaned forward on the table, hand still covering her mouth and tried to look like she was interested in the lecture, but her legs were shaking underneath the table.

Mr. Falkner rambled on about the acceptance of demons in the early seventeenth century without even noticing what Dax was doing. Dax even nodded to him when he spoke about witches, ever the perfect little student but in reality he was getting his fingers wet by the low-level.

I saw the moment when Daxton went against his word. In one movement I could see him fiddle with her underwear and her hand on his arm told me he had entered her. There were tears in her eyes and I could hear her breathing pick up. He pumped once, twice, then Rosie's hand came to grip his wrist and instead of pulling him away she pushed him harder into her. The action made my own clit throb. Dax's eyes met mine and I nodded to him.

"You like this, Rosie?" he whispered to her barely audible. "You feel the way your cunt clenches around my fingers. Don't you have any shame? Acting like this in front of all these people?" He pumped once more. "It only turns you on even more, doesn't it?"

She was about to come and just like I had showed Dax he pulled his fingers out of her and pushed her leg off of his. He wiped her wetness on her own thigh. A degrading, angry act.

The glare she gave me was worth everything. She would be begging for this soon. She wanted to act out, run after Malik, this is what she got.

Chapter Eight

Rosie

This was the worst class ever. I had worn the skirt for a reason, but I never thought he would be so bold as to finger me during class. I tried desperately to listen to Mr. Falkner but my clouded brain couldn't hold on to a word he said. I had started the day thinking that this would be my chance to share magic with Daxton but instead he left me hanging the entire time. Now that class was finally over they ushered me through the mass of chattering students and into a secluded hallway that I had never been to before.

It only took two seconds before Daxton turned on me and began attacking my mouth with his own. I had suffered through the class but here it was *finally*. I kissed him back furiously and allowed him to wrap my legs around his waist. He claimed me with his mouth, leaving no space untouched and pushed us so close together. I could barely move. Even pinned like this I could manage to grind against him trying to release the pressure building up inside me.

"Eager are we Rosie?" Eli asked as she watched us. Daxton trailed kisses down my neck and I hastily unbuttoned my shirt for him not caring if anyone walked in on us. I needed this and every magic fiber of my being felt like it was pushing me towards this moment.

Daxton pulled my bra down just enough so he could latch onto one of my nipples. I was so strung tight that I almost screamed when his tongue circled around it.

"Fuck," I moaned and reached in between us to unbutton his pants.

"This is not how I wanted our first time to go, Rosie," Daxton said with a growl and slapped away my hands. Instead, he pushed my underwear aside and plunged two fingers into me without warning. They stretched me almost painfully as I clamped around them. I pushed my chest into him and was rewarded with a hard bite on my nipple.

"Please Dax," I moaned as his thumb came to circle my clit. I was already so wound up that I felt myself quickly falling towards the edge until—

"Stop," Eli commanded. And Daxton immediately pulled his fingers out. I whined and sent Eli a heated look.

"What game are you playing?" I hissed and she gave me a sticky sweet smile.

"There is no game, Rosie," she said. "Why don't you show us how much you want it? Maybe then I will finally let you come."

I wanted to fight her so bad but the aching need between my legs would make that impossible. These were the people I needed to deal with and the first step into making this work was to not only get my magic taken care of, but to get them to trust me.

"Let me down," I growled at Daxton. He did and I immediately dropped to my knees and finished unbuckling his belt. Eli let out a laugh but I paid her no mind as I pulled out Daxton's already hard cock. My mouth watered when I saw the piercing that sat on the underside of the tip. I had never seen something like this before and I was dying to know what it would feel like inside of me.

I was nervous since I had never done this before but I didn't let that stop me from diving forward and taking as much of him in me as possible. He let out a hiss and his hand tangled in my hair.

"Look at how good she's being," Eli teased as she moved to stand behind Daxton and stare down at me. When I looked up at both of them, I felt myself swell unbearably. The heat from their stares was doing things to me I never thought possible. Eli was whispering in his ear and left kisses on his neck that made him sigh.

I gave an experimental suck and ran my tongue along the underside of him. He let out a groan and his grip on my hair tightened. I paid close attention to his reactions making sure that if his hand tightened at all, that I would do what I did over again. I thought I was getting the hang of it until Eli's hand pushed my head forward and caused me to gag on his length. She continued to push until I couldn't breathe and finally let me up only to force me back down again. I felt Daxton swell inside my mouth and tried to hold on even as tears spilled down my face. Eli pulled my hair hard enough that Daxton fell out of me and his hot seed spilled all over my face and chest.

I felt the magic play at my senses but it left faster than I could grasp onto it. We were not touching as he came and I had a feeling that it had stopped us from sharing our magic. Looking up at Daxton his eyes showed that he was more rabid than ever, meaning he also did not get to expend any magic.

"You look so good like this Rosie," Eli cooed as she came behind my kneeling form. Her arm circled around me so that she could lift up my skirt and play at the dampness between my legs. "I should call everyone over here so they can get a good look at how much of a whore you are."

Her words stung but it was not enough to dampen the feeling she elicited between my legs as her fingers found my clit.

"You're horrible," I said but let out a gasp when she pulled me against her and bit my neck enough to burn. Daxton watched us with hungry eyes but didn't dare move, waiting for instructions.

"At least anyone who sees this would know that you are ours, but it seems like it is you who has trouble realizing that," she said and pulled my underwear aside. Her fingers finally pushed themselves through my folds and I let out a loud moan.

"Make him hard again, we aren't done here," Eli commanded. I gripped Daxton's pants pulling him closer and taking him in my mouth. "I thought I told you to stay away from Malik."

Daxton's length twitched in my mouth and I ran my tongue over his piercing earning me a loud groan. Eli began pumping two fingers into me slowly. I tried to grind down on her hand but when I did she pulled my hair. The groan that spilled out of my mouth seemed to spur Daxton into action. He swelled painfully large and began fucking my mouth, trusting into me like he had lost control.

I shouldn't like to be used like this but with each thrust I felt myself tighten around Eli's fingers.

"We could be so good to you Rosie," Daxton groaned between thrusts.

"From the feeling of it maybe she would prefer we weren't," Eli said. "Is that what you want Rosie? Do you like it when we use you like this?"

I couldn't answer because with one final thrust Daxton and I were both coming. The expansion of magic that I had felt in the dorm was back and this time even more intense than before, knocking the air out of me. If I wasn't so winded, I would have screamed through the most powerful orgasm I had ever experienced.

The magic snapped back in place and for the first time since I exploded on them I felt my magic settle into me. Daxton pulled out of me and I collapsed against Eli. This time I swallowed the seed in my mouth. She caught me with ease and her chuckle filled my ears.

"Now walk back to the dorm and don't you dare clean yourself until you get there," Eli commanded. I opened my mouth to protest but Rae's voice did it before me.

"And you say I'm the one that hurt her," Rae muttered and I looked up at her in shame. I only now realized how horrible this looked. I loved it in the moment and probably would have listened to Eli but now that Rae looked at me with such pity in her eyes it made me want to cry. I didn't want her pity.

"You always have to ruin everything," Eli grumbled and lifted me into a standing position fixing my shirt as she did so.

"Was this really necessary?" she growled at Eli. She grabbed a handker-chief out of her jacket pocket and walked towards me. She paused looking over me. "Can I help you clean up?"

I couldn't bring myself to speak so I only nodded to her. She began slowly wiping what she could, her eyes tracing over my features in a way so soft it made me feel self-conscious.

"She needed to know who she belonged to after whatever the hell went down with Malik yesterday," Eli said and swept the hair off my shoulder as Rae wiped the area.

"Wet this," she commanded Daxton as she held out the fabric for him. He complied and the next time the fabric touched my face it was pleasantly warm. I could no longer bring myself to be mad at her, not when she was looking over me so carefully.

"Rae is getting major brownie points right now," Eli commented. I pushed her away not wanting her to listen any longer. I wasn't mad at her, I just really didn't want her to hear the thoughts in my head because the only thing I could think of was how fucked up it was that I would be betraying them soon. They could degrade me, use me for sex, I didn't care. I was willing and she was right. I *loved* it. And that was the problem; this would be much easier if I just didn't care at all.

Rae's bright hazel eyes washed over my face. They had unsaid words in them that I couldn't decipher. It felt like they were looking into my soul and I was afraid that maybe it was her that had a mind-reading power rather than Eli. I averted my eyes to the right looking over her shoulder to the hall behind her. My heart skipped a beat when I realized we were not alone in this hallway.

Claudine and Maximus were at the end of the hallway staring at us with differing expressions. Maximus was unsurprisingly disgust, I didn't expect anything to change from him regardless of what I did with my life. He had hated me from the beginning. His long hair was pulled into a low ponytail and he was wearing the school uniform but it looked out of place on his form. A person that serious rivaled Rae and both of them fit better in a stuffy government position than as a college student.

Claudine's expression was one of pity. Her eyes were clouded but there were lines on her face that showed her dislike of the situation. She was also dressed in the uniform but she had been the only girl in this school that I had seen wear her skirt longer than her knees. She paired them with thick wedges and on her it looked more like a style than forced school clothing.

Why were they here? And dressed in uniform?

My face quickly flamed and I tried my best to right my clothing. How much had they seen? Malik had joked about my relationship with the trio before but I didn't want them to see this...something so intimate and also so... embarrassing. Who in their right mind would let themselves be used like this? So violently without a care and actually like it?

Rae caught my expression and looked over her shoulder at the siblings. She stood up straight and froze almost as if she hadn't been expecting them. Her expression darkened like a cloud had magically appeared on top of us and I could hear her teeth grind together.

"Can we help you?" she asked in a tone that was less than friendly.

Claudine looked up at Maximus. His eyes stayed planted on us in his usual glower.

"Are you okay, miss?" he asked. "Do you need help?"

I jumped at his question. What the hell did he think he was doing? They should have walked away as soon as they saw us here. Even being this close was putting us all at risk.

"She's obviously fine," Eli spoke for me. Her hand brushed my shoulder, but I stepped away from her afraid I couldn't control my thoughts.

"I didn't ask you," Maximus shot back. He took a step forward and it spurred those around me into action. Eli pushed me behind her and stood at the front with Rae. Daxton pulled me close to him enveloping me in his warmth.

"She's a mute," Rae answered. "She will not be able to answer you anyways."

"Nod if you are okay, shake your head if you want me to pull you out," Maximus said.

Pull me out. Of this mission? What was his motive?

I quickly nodded my head, overexaggerating my movements so he would clearly see them. He looked over the two in front of me with disbelief written on his face.

"She said yes," Daxton spoke from my side. "Move on."

Maximus turned with another glance towards me. Just as he was about to leave Rae spoke up.

"Do we know each other?" she asked their retreating forms.

"No," Claudine answered, her soft voice barely audible. "Unless you've lived in California before."

"Visited once," Rae said offhandedly. "You have pretty strong feelings there for someone you've never met."

Fuck. Rae was too perceptive for this.

"I don't like those who take advantage of those weaker than them," Maximus responded with a sneer.

"You had the same feelings when I saw you in the office," Rae said. "But now you seem to be parading around as students. When you are obviously not."

"You must have us mistaken," Maximus said and grabbed his sister's arm.

"What are you doing with the reports you requested on us?" Rae called as they walked away but they left without a look back.

"Reports?" Daxton asked from behind me.

We were fucked. How did we get such a group of incompetent people together?

"The principal told me they asked for reports. On me." She turned to meet my gaze. "On us."

She turned fully and stepped closer to me. "You know them."

I tried to swallow my panic.

"I don't," I whispered.

"Recognition," she said. "You felt it."

"That they are witches," I said. My heart pounded against my ribcage painfully. She continued to stare me down, waiting for me to budge.

"Let's not fight, Rae," Eli said in a teasing voice. She looped an arm around Rae's shoulders. Rae shot her a look and took a step back. "We just made up."

I jumped when I felt Daxton's lips on the top of my head. It was a sweet gesture. Something so foreign and completely opposite to what just happened that it jarred me.

"You should skip the rest of the day," Daxton's deep voice came from above me. His hand squeezed my shoulder and I looked up into his brown eyes. His short hair gave me an unobstructed view of his perfect face and I could see a small smile playing at his lips. He ran a hand through his hair as if embarrassed. "I will come by later."

"Insatiable," Eli said with a chuckle.

"For a gift," Daxton replied, a small blush lining his cheeks and the tops of his ears.

"I don't need it," I said a bit too quickly. Rae gave me a look. "I just mean you have done enough to help me." I let out a shuddering breath. "I'll head to my dorm."

I ran out of that hallway as fast as my legs would take me without looking like a bat out of hell. Only when I got close to my dorm did I exhale the breath that had been lodged in my throat since Rae gave me that penetrating gaze.

We were so out of our league. I had no idea how I got myself into such a shit show. I just wanted to be seen. To be desired. To feel good. And now I had landed myself in a sticky situation.

It got worse when I finally got to the dorm. From the outside everything looked fine but when I opened it I was met with a six-foot-something white-haired scarred man that almost gave me a heart attack.

"Get out," I hissed at Malik. He did not give me a small smile like normal, instead he just looked at me seriously.

"Maximus seems to think they are forcing you." He paused. "Hurting you."

That literally just happened, and he called Malik over already? I wanted to groan aloud, stomp my feet like a frustrated child.

"I am doing what you told me to do," I said with a huff. "How I do it is none of your business. Yell at him for almost fucking up this entire thing."

"I'm not yelling," he said and his stance relaxed just slightly. "What did he do?"

"Rae recognizes them. She feels their emotions and mine. They hate her, know her, and I know them. Keep them away and get the hell out of my way."

Malik's lips twitched. He nodded once and moved past me to leave.

"As you wish," he murmured. I turned to close the door but stopped short.

"The magic is...taken care of," I whispered. "And don't come anymore... The cat knows your scent."

Malik cocked his head as if asking for more but I didn't oblige and instead slammed the door in his face. I quickly turned to open the windows. There would be no use if they kept being this careless.

It's like they wanted me to fail, I thought wryly.

* * *

Even though I had insisted that he leave me alone, Daxton knocked at my door no more than an hour later. I had changed into a short-sleeve shirt and shorts not expecting him to come after I already told him no. I opened the door ready to feel irritated but my heart melted when I saw him. He had a nervous sort of smile on his face and Amr was lounging lazily over his shoulders. His short brown hair was sticking up in every which way giving him a boyish look even though the tattoos that covered his face and most of his body gave the opposite look. His uniform shirt was still partially unbuttoned showing tattoos of what I thought was a...devil? He had his book bag over his shoulder and a something in his hand that made my heart skip a beat.

It was a white plastic bag with the name of the diner we had visited before, and his other hand had an iced coffee. The scent of sticky blueberry pancake wafted from inside the bag. My mouth watered just from the smell.

"You didn't eat earlier," he said and pushed himself behind me. He set the food on the desk and mentioned for me to come over. With a small smile of my own I closed the door and joined him near the desk. Amr jumped off his shoulders and wound himself around my legs meowing loudly.

"Yes, I missed you too Amr," I cooed and picked him up. He licked my chin with his bumpy tongue.

"Here," Daxton said. He already had the containers open and was cutting the pancakes with a fork. He stabbed a few pieces before offering them to me, carefully keeping the container underneath them so the syrup wouldn't drop onto the ground. I hated the act and loved it at the same time.

Hated it because I didn't deserve it.

Loved it because this was all the attention I had been craving. He even remembered my favorite food. It was little but it was enough to make my chest warm.

"You outdid yourself," I commented and leaned forward to eat the delicious gooey mess of pancakes that awaited me. He watched me intently as I chewed and swallowed. There was a light in his eyes and a smile on his face as he did so.

"More," he insisted, and we repeated the process over and over again until I had finished the pancakes. I wanted to tell him it was enough but the intimacy of it all made the words die in my throat. Instead, the same heart-warming feeling spread throughout my body and I found myself smiling wider with each bite. I even let out a giggle at one point.

"You didn't eat," I commented as he began throwing away the trash.

"I did earlier," he said and picked the coffee up bringing it to my lips.

I took a long sip.

"Breakfast for lunch is the best idea you've ever had," I said.

He smiled and leaned forward. I thought it was to kiss me and froze, but instead he placed a kiss on my forehead.

"I was...rough earlier," he said his voice dropping an octave. "I apologize. I will control myself better next time."

It was my turn for my cheeks to flush.

"I liked it actually," I said not looking at him. He let out a small chuckle. "Maybe more aftercare would be better."

"Pancakes?" he asked teasingly.

"Intimacy. Hugs? Kisses maybe? I liked the ones on top of my head." The words out of my mouth surprised me. I didn't know I was that affected by it until they began cleaning my face. That was when I realized that I could take the hardness as long as there was...some softness as well.

Eli was an exception to this. She barely was intimate afterwards but Daxton...

I liked the way he touched me. It made me feel warm. Needed.

He placed the coffee back on the desk and led me to the bed without a word. My heart raced and my palms began to sweat. Was he already ready to go again?

He pushed me onto the bed. Amr jostled in my arms and jumped to the floor. Daxton pushed me over and turned me to my side. He then laid behind me and wrapped one arm around my waist and the other rested under my head. His chest was flush with my back and his heat enveloped me pleasantly as we lay in bed.

He's spooning me, I realized with a jolt of surprise. I tried to turn to look at him but he just buried his head in my hair and inhaled deeply. It sent shivers down my spine.

"Something like this?" he asked, his voice low and almost sleepy. I nodded.

"This is nice," I said. My voice was high. I was taken aback if I was being honest; I had never done this with anyone other than Rae. And here we were in the middle of the day spooning on my bed after he brutally fucked my mouth then fed me pancakes.

Amr meowed and padded across the bed only to stop and lay by my chest, almost as if he wanted to be the small spoon. I chuckled and ran my fingers through his fur. I felt oddly comfortable between the two. So much so that I felt my eyelids droop. Daxton reached over to pet Amr as well.

Before I knew it, I fell into the darkness with the purring of Amr near my front and the heat and soft snoring of Daxton at my back.

Chapter Nine
Rosie

I was awoken when the heat began to feel like it was choking me. I didn't know if Daxton being a witch had anything to do with his body temperature, but his hold quickly became sweltering. He was still snoring when I removed his arms from my waist. I sat up slowly, careful not to jostle him too much. Amr opened his eyes and stretched.

"Let him rest." I whispered to the cat as he let out a small mewl. He blinked sleepily at me and I couldn't help but smile at him. "It was a good nap, wasn't it?"

I sat on the bed with my back against the wall so that my body was facing Daxton as he slept. Amr climbed into my lap and quickly fell back asleep. The two were so much alike, both falling asleep so easily and snoring lightly when they did. I looked over at Daxton, trying to savor the rare time where I could look at him uninterrupted, my thoughts free of being spied on.

His face was slack and showed the boyish charm I had seen when he opened my door. His hair stuck up every which way and my fingers itched to trace the script tattoo that lined his temple. His body was still curled as if holding onto me and his tattooed arm stretched out. He was deep asleep and his mouth twitched slightly like he was dreaming about something funny. He looked innocent here and not at all like a person who would drain people's magic in a moment of lost passion.

His magic had to be worse than mine to lose such control but even back in the town I had felt like I was jumping out of my skin. I was lucky to have provoked them in such a way that I could expend some magic because if not... I would have gone crazy.

I wore the skirt for that reason... Well, also because I didn't have to worry about the curse, but I hadn't hoped to achieve what I did in the hallway. I would have rathered it be in the dorm and not out in the open where everyone could see us... I let out a sigh.

Who was I kidding?

I may have liked it more because I was at their mercy.

My eyes snapped towards Daxton as he turned onto his back. He groaned lightly before relaxing again, his snoring getting a bit louder. He was so defenseless here...it only reminded me of how much of a monster I was. His life would never be the same when I was done with it. And if he ever found out, if the others found out... I should expect a worse punishment than sex.

"I'm surprised Eli hasn't barged in here yet." Daxton's voice was husky and full of sleep as he spoke. His eyes fluttered open and he turned his head to look at me. His fingers grabbed at my ankle and traced mindless patterns up my calf. The action sent shivers up my spine. "I told them to give us time."

"Why would you do that?" I asked and placed a sleeping Amr at the end of the bed then crawled back over to Daxton. He accepted me with open arms and pulled me tightly to his chest and rested his chin on the top of my head.

"Well Rae would be the most considerate, don't tell her I said that, but she wouldn't likely come at the cost of whatever pride she has," he said as his fingers combed through my hair. I let out a sigh and wrapped my arms around him to pull him closer. "Eli just doesn't care for this type of intimacy."

"No, she doesn't," I echoed. "So...you felt bad."

Daxton gave me a kiss on the top of my head before speaking.

"I'm being selfish," he said and continued again after a pause. "Rae and Eli seemed to have both been very selfish with you but I never got my turn." He pulled away to look at me. His brown eyes were unreadable. "Is it wrong I want you to like me more than them?"

His question stunned me. Daxton may have shown a sexual attraction to me but this topic was never breached...between any of us. It was I who expected more from them, yearning to be a part of this club that they built for themselves. After everything that happened with Malik...maybe it was best they never let me in. Maybe I could longingly hope from the outside. But now...

He laughed and shook his head.

"Your silence hurts," he teased. I panicked for a response, but he shushed me. "It would be unfair if you liked any of us more than the other... We are a jealous group after all."

I swallowed thickly and nodded. He stood abruptly and walked over to the bag he brought with him and rummaged around until he brought out a bottle with blue swirling liquid inside. The same one they treated my curse with.

"Is that...?" I trailed off unable to voice it. He sent me a smile and nodded. He walked back over to the bed and I scurried to sit on the edge of it. He dropped to his knees in front of me, his head still almost reaching my chest. I instinctively spread my legs and he chuckled at my action but moved between them nonetheless.

"Yes, but I can't take the credit... It was Rae's idea," he said and his big hand landed on my bare thigh while the other handed the bottle to me. "She said you have been feeling anxious since the fight. Scared even."

My chest constricted. If only she knew it wasn't because of her. If only she knew that it was what I was being forced to do.

But you didn't have to, a voice whispered in the back of my head. *You could live with this curse forever and just live your life with them.*

That voice was delusional. I could never remain with these three forever. I knew that now. And I couldn't go back... After stepping into that town there was only one fate that awaited me.

"But that's for the curse," I said in a whisper.

"It's actually a calming potion," he corrected. I grabbed the bottle and uncorked it hesitantly. "I brewed them a while ago and stocked up recently so you could have them."

"You brewed them for me?" I asked in shock. How far ahead had he been thinking? He rubbed the back of his head messing up his hair even further and averted his gaze from my eyes.

"I brewed them for myself," he admitted. "I used them when I was still at home." He paused again this time looking me in the eyes. "Family troubles."

This is it, I thought. *I will have to be careful how I proceed.*

I nodded before saying, "I have family troubles too... If I had this I am sure I would have had a much better time growing up." I paused, shifted before downing the potion. It was the same cooling effect I felt when I took it last time. In mere seconds it felt like the tension I had been holding disappeared.

I didn't realize how tense I was this entire time until I felt all of my muscles relax at once. Even my head became clear. I locked onto Daxton's gaze and sent him a sincere smile.

"It's great, isn't it?" he asked as he took the bottle back but didn't move to get rid of it. Instead, he kept a hand firmly on my thigh and watched me.

"It is," I said and leaned back slightly, looking at him through my eyelashes. "I may need to take this home with me during the break, I hope you have extra to spare. They may be happy I am at Winterfell but..." I averted my eyes purposefully. "Let's just say, I'll miss this place."

He squeezed my thigh forcing me to make eye contact with him.

"Maybe you could—"

He was cut off by Eli strolling into my room. She had a shit-eating grin and was followed by a stoic Rae who paused when she saw our position.

I cursed them in my head. That was a perfect chance I may not get again and they just had to ruin it.

"You must have broken my door again," I hissed at her. She stood behind Daxton with her hands in her pockets and stared down at me with bright blue eyes that told me everything she was thinking. And it was *filthy*. It made my body heat and my magic pulsed inside me.

"I never fixed it," she responded and her eyes drifted to Daxton who still didn't get up from his spot between my legs. "Sorry I interrupted."

"I wasn't there yet but since you brought it up..." Daxton trailed off and leaned forward. I panicked and pushed his head away. Rae was halfway to closing the door when she stopped.

"What do you need?" I asked Eli. Her eyebrow raised silently asking what my problem was.

"We have to leave for the night," Rae spoke from behind her. "Work stuff and you need a babysitter since every time you are alone Malik finds you."

Even through the potion I felt my skin light with anger. How dare they?

"I am a grown woman," I hissed. Daxton's once sweet touches turned rough and he gripped my chin forcing me to look at him.

"For your protection," he said. "You'll trust me, right?"

Fuck him. I hated and loved the way his pleading voice sounded.

"Where will you take me?" I asked giving in to their demands.

"My house," Rae spoke up. I turned to glare at her. "We have stuff to do there. You will stay in one of the rooms."

My heart pounded with excitement. This was exactly what Malik warned me *not to do.*

"What are you doing there?" I asked drilling holes into her hazel eyes.

"None of your business," she said with a cold voice full of spite.

Two could play at that game. I smiled sweetly down at Daxton and did something I never thought I'd have the balls to do.

"Maybe you are my favorite," I teased Daxton and hooked my leg over his shoulder. A smirk spread across his face and he handed the empty bottle to Eli's awaiting hand before his fingers wedged between my waistband and underwear and ripped them off me. Rae smiled and the door shut with a bit too much force.

He wasted no time bringing his lips home and I enjoyed the way Rae's eyes narrowed in my direction. I held nothing back and even went as far as moaning Daxton's name while holding her gaze.

The more I watched her the more I realized that some small part of me did hang on to the grudge. I was still hurt even though I had bigger things to worry about now. I was satisfied with this small act of rebellion though. She brought this on herself and if she thought she could treat me like this...then she had other things coming. I would make her watch as they ravished me and deny her the one thing she was so adamant about hiding that she wanted.

* * *

The drive to Rae's house was almost as satisfying as watching her heated gaze burn me as Daxton fucked me with his tongue. Rae was silent the entire way and I swear I could hear her plotting my death throughout.

Eli and Daxton on the other hand were content in the silence and each took a side of me to themselves. Eli seemed happy to let her rough hands roam my bare legs while Daxton had my head on his lap as he played with my hair. The limo was spacious enough that I could be spread across a whole seat without touching anyone but that wouldn't be fun and I had already gone so far... What was wrong with enjoying this moment?

Eli's hands tugged at my short school skirt and she sent me a dirty smile. The sleeves of her black button-up were rolled up showing the colorful tattoos she normally kept hidden.

"You have to know this skirt does things to me," she commented, her fingers trailing down my inner thigh. I had changed back into my school uniform after seeing Eli's and Rae's clothing. They both had button-ups on and slacks; seemed like they were dressing for something important. Daxton and I were the only ones in the school uniform still.

You could fuck me in it, I sent to her and conjured an image of me over a desk wearing no panties.

She let out a whistle and chuckled.

"What happened to make you so dirty? Was it me? Did I finally corrupt you?" she asked teasingly. Her words made my stomach clench and I knew that if her hands trailed any further they would come into contact with my wet panties. She did just that and found my clit through my panties easily. I let out a gasp.

"Stop it both of you," Rae hissed. "We are closing in on the house and the last thing my father needs to see is you fucking a low-level in the family car."

Eli pulled away with a scowl but kept a hand on my calf. I felt my own annoyance rise.

Why would she care what Rae says?

"Rae's family firmly believe in a straight partnership between high-levels." Her eyes looked up and down my body. "And no one else."

"She doesn't need to know that," Rae hissed at Eli.

This is how it will be for the entire world. The words she whispered to me in the darkness suddenly made too much sense. When I looked at her angry face I felt my own anger dissipate and instead I felt a pain in my chest.

"I don't need your pity, low-level," Rae hissed at me. The way she called me a low-level hurt more than any curse anyone had sent my way. There was no name or degradation tactic that worked better than finally hearing her curse low-level to me with so much hatred. The pity and sadness I held for her in my heart was easily swatted away by her and instead I was left with hurt and anger.

The car stopped softly and without any other word Rae pushed out of the limo faster than the driver could open the door for her. The driver ran over to our side and opened the door with a nervous smile.

"Don't mind her," Eli said with a scowl still marring her beautiful face. "She can get testy."

She helped me out of the car and held onto me reminding me that I was still supposed to act as a mute. It was better this way. I didn't know what else my anger would make me say or do.

My jaw almost dropped when I saw the elegant house in front of me. It was a beautiful light periwinkle with white trim and maybe...three stories? Either way it looked magnificent. We had pulled into the rounded cobblestone driveway and I hadn't noticed how gated the area was. Even those black iron gates were decorated with vines that had colorful flowers sprouting out of them. The grass around the house was perfectly trimmed and greener than I had seen before.

It was perfect, all of it. *Too perfect.* It felt like no one lived here, like this was all some type of display.

I gripped Eli's arm tightly. She cast me a look.

What is her father's power? Will he know about my curse? I asked her.

Her blue eyes looking over my face before answering.

I don't know, she admitted. *I never found out, or cared to. He is in his position for a reason, that alone should scare you enough from trying to pry.*

I wanted to reply but Rae stopped in her tracks and sent us a glare.

"Hold on to Daxton," she hissed. I understood immediately and moved to Daxton's arm with a smile.

"Hey beautiful," he said, his voice low enough to give me butterflies. The potion did wonders for my thoughts; I could actually focus on my mission now without feeling like the guilt was eating me alive but that voice...it did things to me the potion couldn't help.

"Not fair," Eli muttered from next to us.

No one spoke as Rae opened the all-white door that stood before us. I didn't know what to expect but I hoped that her father was not behind those doors. When the room came into view my mouth dropped open again. The foyer had a set of twin white staircases that led up to the second story. The floor was a glossy marble and spanned on in front of us for what seemed like forever.

There were two maids in there both busy with tasks. One was arranging flowers on a table to the right of us and the other was wiping down the banister. Both looked as we walked through and smiled pleasantly at Rae.

"Welcome, young mistress," they said in sync then went back to their tasks as if Rae wasn't even there. Their eyes were variants of colors indicating their low-level status.

She silently walked us up the stairs where the maids weren't present. I stared at them when we reached the top but they never turned to watch us. Daxton pushed me down the hallway to follow Rae.

The inside of the house reminded me of the Victorian house I had seen in the town. The molding, old portraits, and frill all held the same type of feel. The only difference was it felt much colder here and I could not hear the running of maids or guests. Rae opened a room at the end of the second hallway as we walked down and ushered us inside. It was a lavish seating room with windows that let in the daylight. The entire room was decorated in floral patterns that made the room seem light. I wouldn't be surprised if this was a tearoom back in the day for the mistresses. Daxton brought me over to a spare couch and forced me to sit while they stared at me.

"What?" I whispered feeling awkward with all of their eyes on me at once.

"You cannot leave this room," Rae commanded with a firm voice. "If a maid or anyone else comes in here type on your phone and tell them you are waiting for Daxton."

"Fine," I said and reclined on the couch with my arms crossed.

"I mean it," she said with an angry tone.

"I know," I grumbled sending her a glare. "Go do whatever you came here to do and keep it from me like you always do. I'll just be here like a good little girl."

My words stunned them. Eli was the one to let out a bark of a laugh.

"Damn Rae, you really brought out something in her," Eli said.

Rae rolled her eyes and left the room, motioning for the group to follow her. Eli sent me a wink before she left the room, Daxton a small smile, and Rae a heavy glare. Then there was silence. I let out a sigh a relaxed into the couch.

It only took ten minutes for my peaceful silence to be interrupted by whispers outside the door.

"I think they left something in here," came the male whisper from the other side of the door. I sighed and pulled my phone out of the pocket in my skirt but refused to move from my comfortable position.

There was a shuffling, then the door was pushed open and two male faces poked in. They had to be Rae's brothers because besides the missing glasses, slightly longer hair, and lanky form they looked exactly like her. They even had the same hazel eyes.

Twins? I thought looking at them.

"A girl?" one whispered looking me up and down.

"A witch?" the other asked and his expression showed something akin to slight fear.

I typed on my phone quickly and waved it at them.

They looked at each other then slowly walked into the room. The one with the fear in his eyes stayed behind the other. I noticed he was also slightly taller.

"I'm waiting for Daxton. Sorry can't talk, I'm mute?" the one with the leering gaze read aloud and lifted a perfectly trimmed brow. "What witch can't fix their own voice?"

I decided not to correct them and typed an introduction on my phone.

I am Rosie, am I to assume you are Rae's brothers? I showed them my phone.

"My name is Nathaniel and this is Benjamin," the one in front, Nathaniel, said and jabbed his thumb back to gesture towards the fearful one. I looked Benjamin up and down; his Adam's apple bobbed as I critiqued him. "We are her *older brothers*." He looked me up and down again with a smile on his face. "Let me know if you want a real heir. I would gladly oblige."

I rolled my eyes and stood up typing on my phone before shoving it in his face.

"Daxton's girlfriend?" he asked with genuine surprise in his voice. He looked back at Benjamin and he shook his head to his twin brother as if to say he didn't know.

Telepathy gift maybe?

"I didn't think Daxton ever kept his girlfriends." When Benjamin finally spoke his weak voice matched his stance. Rae really was the shining one compared to these two.

My eyes drifted towards Nathaniel. He said he was the *heir*. Maybe if what Eli said was right Rae would never get the family money if she wasn't a man. That would only make too much sense.

"That must mean there is something special about her," Nathaniel answered and walked closer making it a show as he licked his lips. "Good in bed?"

I smiled through my anger.

Ask him when he gets back, I typed to him. *I wonder what he will say when the two older brothers of his friend forced themselves into a room where his helpless mute girlfriend was sleeping.*

"This is our house, we didn't force our way in here," Nathaniel said. The amusement dropped from his face and he gave me a glare that resembled Rae's, but it only had a fraction of the power.

I shrugged and sat back on the couch.

Whatever you say, I am sure they will buy, I typed. *Why don't you be a good host and serve some tea or something?*

I could feel the anger running off Nathaniel in waves while his twin on the other hand scrambled to run to the door and yell down the hallway for a maid. I gave Nathaniel a shit-eating grin. Teasing him was almost as good as fucking with Rae.

"I see why you run in the same crowd," he muttered and dragged one of the stray loveseats closer to the couch. "Rae has always had a thing for black-mail. Father loves her for it."

I raised my eyebrow. A mischievous feeling was unfurling in my stom-ach. How much could I get out of them? Rae would be pissed and I couldn't wait to see what I could hold over her. She was so against secrets but two could play.

Benjamin also pulled a chair over but angled his away from me and sat much further than his twin. He looked over at me nervously.

But you are the heir, I typed and showed Nathaniel. He rolled his eyes.

A maid came in with a cart of tea and snacks. My mouth watered when I saw the assorted cakes that were placed in an intricate design in the middle. I sent a wicked grin to Benjamin, and he shuddered in response.

The maid poured me tea and placed it on the table in between myself and Nathaniel. She then handed me a plate with a small yellow cake on it. I sent her a grateful smile and dug in. Lemon goodness exploded on my tongue and I had to hold in my moan.

Benjamin dismissed the maid and sipped on his own tea, still looking over at me nervously.

"I am heir only in name. Father would choose Rae if he wasn't so uptight," Nathaniel muttered into his cake. I nodded and decided to dig more after I finished my cake.

What is so important about this meeting anyways? I typed to him and showed him. He let out a huff.

"Father has some guests over. Benjamin and I always ditch those things but Rae's group flock to them. Every party, every meeting, every get-together no matter how small." He took a sip of his tea before continuing. "There are only five people there including the Bennett's and Daxton's parents."

I choked on my tea and had to pound my chest in order to clear my throat. My mind whirled at a hundred miles an hour.

They were here? Right now? I couldn't believe my luck.

"Careful," Benjamin muttered, his gaze averting when I met his eyes.

"Ooohhh have you met them? Let me guess, they hated you?" Nathaniel pried. I shook my head. "They don't? Or you never met?"

I held up two fingers and took a deep breath trying to find my breathing but the pounding in my chest made it harder than necessary.

Nathaniel's eyes sparkled.

"Do you want to meet them?"

God this was too perfect. I had asked to see them and Malik outright refused... Well Malik wasn't here now. I nodded enthusiastically.

"Wait-t," Benjamin stuttered as I stood. "I don't want Rae to be mad, she's here for a reason."

I looked over to his brother; the glint was dampened slightly.

"Maybe from afar?" he suggested. "I mean come on, not introducing your girlfriend even though you are in the same house? Rude." He turned to me. "I wouldn't do that to you sweetheart."

"I don't know Nathaniel..."

"Come on it's from afar." Before there were any other protests I was pulled out of the room by Nathaniel.

Chapter Ten
Daxton

The only perk to this fucking party was that I had Rosie waiting for me upstairs and Eli wouldn't stop whispering ideas every time her arm brushed mine. She wanted to share, badly and couldn't wait to get out of this party so we could put her ideas to use.

Rosie had been different ever since the fight. More open about this relationship, less shy around us. It was perfect in every way. Rae was obviously still pissed that Rosie held a grudge against her but if it meant more pussy for me, I couldn't care less. Rae was the stupid one for saying that shit.

As perfect as those daydreams were, I couldn't get away from the hell that stood in front of me. We were in a small room drinking with the Bennett's, my parents, and Rae's father. Her father watched us carefully under golden eyes. He was in control here and we all knew that. Well... My eyes washed over the annoyingly chatty governor and his trophy wife. Maybe he was still thinking he was in control here.

My parents were on a pair of loveseats to my right. My mother's hand brushed mine as if to remind me of their presence and I shuddered when I felt her slimy magic against mine. I would do anything to get out of here. Turn tail and never look at their ugly mugs again but... Rae was right.

I needed to show here. Let people know I still existed. And most importantly...make sure my parents didn't do anything sneaky. There had been talk about arranged marriages, deals for magic and protection—I didn't need them volunteering my services. It was better this way even if I had to relive my trauma for hours at a time.

Eli's arm brushed mine again.

I can't wait to leave. Her voice flitted through my head. I nodded and took a sip of my drink. It was champagne; of course my parents wouldn't let me have anything stronger. It would taint my magic, they would say.

Everything in their mind tainted magic. Sex, bloodletting, only if it was in the family would it remain pure. And we had to remain pure or else we would fall crazed like those *nasty* witches that liked to attack government buildings. That at least was what they spewed, but I knew it was a control tactic. For people like Governor Bennett...and for me. To keep me under their grubby little fingers.

"It's all the rage now," Mrs. Bennett said to Eli. "Gender changing, pronoun usage, the like. Some witches change their gender with magic constantly."

Mrs. Bennett had a thing for Eli. Whether is was the drugs or the sex I couldn't tell, but her eyes honed onto Eli like a hawk and she would use any chance she got to talk to her.

"We live in a world where magic and demons are normal," she replied with a careful smile. "Changing the way someone presents gender or using pronouns that are more comfortable to them shouldn't be a big deal."

I watched as Rae's father's eyes narrowed in Eli's direction. He pretended like he liked Eli in situations like this but we all knew better. He hated Eli for what she was, a gangster and obvious unashamed pansexual.

"What about you Eli?" she asked leaning closer to Eli and away from her own husband. "Ever feel like you are in the wrong body?"

For the first time Eli's smiling façade faltered. I sipped my champagne and watched her intently. Eli and I may be close but we never discussed anything like this.

"Gender doesn't matter to me," she responded, her smile back full force. "Nor do I feel called to any single one."

"Kids these days," Rae's father muttered with a light tone. I gritted my teeth not liking his tone.

I brushed my hand against Eli.

I didn't know you felt that way, I said. Her eyes twinkled when they met mine.

Change anything for you? she asked in a teasing tone but there was something else there. Something hesitant.

No, I said honestly. *Just need to know what to call you.*

So thoughtful, she mused. *When I make up my mind, I'll let you know.*

"Tell us about your classes, boy," Father interrupted from the other side of my mother. His voice was pleasant, but his eyes were demanding. Apparently, he didn't like our secret conversations.

"They are fine," I said and downed the rest of my champagne only for Eli to push another one into my hand and take the empty one. What a godsend.

"Daxton," Mother chided from my side. My father's magic reached out to me and my own magic reacted by widely fanning out to my sides. I had to grit my teeth to pull it in. Non-magic users couldn't feel or see if but if things started exploding it wouldn't look good.

Father got up and nonchalantly moved to stand in front of me. A scare tactic that still worked. He dropped his voice to a whisper.

"I know you were at the house boy, don't make this harder than necessary and we will forget this happened." He leaned forward as if to give me a hug. "Or do you want to visit the playroom?"

Ice ran through my veins and I felt my stomach twist in a way that made my breakfast reappear in my mouth. My magic flared out even wider and my body shook harder to contain the furious magic that was just itching to blow this entire place up.

"Like you could even get me home again," I hissed low. Rae was watching me closely; her eyes told me to stay quiet. "I will never return. You should be grateful I still show up for these things."

"You will come by yourself," he vowed. "And when you do, I will be ready and I will not go easy on you, boy."

I was ready to pound into him until I felt something play at my senses. A magic. Familiar, tasted like whiskey.

Rosie. My eyes widened and I stepped away from Father. I brushed my hand against Eli's and sent her what I felt. She cursed.

"Goodbye you piece of shit," I hissed at him. I looked towards Rae who shook her head but I didn't care. I wouldn't let my parents get a whiff of Rosie because if they did... My father's eyes were already clouded in a way that made me sick. I didn't want to see what would happen if they felt magic as potent as Rosie's.

"Sorry to cut this short," Eli said with a smile to die for. "Daxton and I have been called back to campus on important business." She lifted her glass to Rae's father who did the same. "An honor as always."

"My pleasure Eliza, glad you could join," he replied in an almost patronizing tone. He seemed to like Eliza better than Eli. It was like he had to remind her she was a girl.

If Eli was bothered, she didn't show it. Instead she just waved to Governor Bennett and pulled me into the hallway. We walked quickly towards where I had last felt Rosie. When we rounded the corner I was surprised to see an annoyed-looking Rosie with Rae's two older twin brothers. I had never liked them, they had everything handed to them while Rae had to fight for her father's attention. Honor student and I have our differences...but I could emphasize with her.

"Look who escaped her room," Eli said with a purr. Rosie sent her a strained smile while tucking a piece of her long black hair behind her ear. The twins were arguing loudly about something, barely paying us any mind. Rosie reached out to touch Eli.

"No not yet," she replied. "Let's wait for Rae up in the room."

I looked over the boys critically. Benjamin turned timid once he realized I was there and Nathaniel just gave me a grin that angered me.

"Why are you talking to her?" I growled at them. Benjamin jumped. He was always scared of witches, ever since I made snakes appear in his room one night while he was sleeping. He deserved it, he was a little shit back then and had said something off-handed to Rae. Nathaniel just shrugged.

"Thought I'd take her to meet the parents," he said with a sly grin. "Sound like she is a dirty little secret."

I didn't respond to his prodding, only grabbed Eli and Rosie and stalked back up to the room. I was too pissed about my parents' audacity; I didn't want to fight with anyone lower than me. It also didn't help that after he mentioned *that place* I couldn't get the feeling of his hands off of me. They were like ghosts touching my hair, my back, my thighs.

"Stop it," Eli growled at me and pushed both of us into the room where we had originally found Rosie. "They will never get you back there."

I took a shuddering breath. I could feel Rosie watching me but I didn't even care anymore. The only thing I cared about was distracting myself. Eli grabbed Rosie and pushed her into my chest. She looked up towards me confused, those big brown eyes wide. I wrapped my arms around her and buried my face in her hair, inhaling deeply.

Eli sucked at comfort, but Rosie knew right away to wrap her arms around my waist and hug me tight. I held onto her trying to get her as close as possible, as if I could swallow her up.

"Just stay like this for a minute," I whispered to her. She nodded against me. Rae's brothers didn't follow us, and I couldn't be happier. If I had to deal with anything else, I felt as though I may actually explode.

"Do you need..." She trailed off but I knew what she was hinting at.

"Maybe later but now, just this," I whispered to her. She nodded again.

"You know I don't think I've ever hugged anyone as much as I've hugged you," she whispered against me. "It's nice you know."

"To hug?" I asked.

"To be needed."

My heart skipped a beat and I felt my chest swell. She was needed. Wanted. I wanted her. After that fight when I watched her tears stream down her face, I realized that I never wanted to see them again and since then...my emotions have been a whirlwind when it came to her.

Eli watched us from her position against the wall. She didn't say anything and allowed us this moment, but her eyes seemed clouded with emotion. I wanted to know what she thought when Rosie said those words, but I couldn't ask.

Rae was knocking at the door.

"We have to leave," she said. "Your parents will follow shortly. I suggest you hurry."

I opened the door behind us and pulled a frozen Rosie along with me. They couldn't find her, I wouldn't allow it. Wouldn't chance it.

Rae gave me a glare but still rushed along with us to get to the limo before my parents could. We made it just in time. As we loaded into the limo and started to drive off my parents appeared from the doorway. They watched our limo leave with distaste.

I swallowed thickly and looked towards Rosie. She had turned herself to watch them from the rear window of the limo, her eyes wide.

"See a resemblance?" I didn't mean for my voice to come out bitterly, but it did. Her eyes didn't move from my parents until they were fully out of view. "My parents." I sighed and gripped her hand in mine. "If you are ever without us and you see them, run."

"Like she would ever come into contact with them," Rae said with a tone. She unbuttoned the first few buttons of her shirt and took her glasses off. "Why the fuck did you run off like that?"

"Your brothers," Eli said with a pointed look, "decided to take her out for an adventure around the house."

Rae glared at Rosie.

"And you let them?" she hissed. Rosie shrugged and positioned herself so she was lying down in my lap once more. There was a small smirk on her lips that she hid from Rae but I could see it perfectly from my position.

It made my cock throb painfully.

* * *

After the incident at Rae's house we went back to our normal routine of classes. It had been two weeks since then and it was easy to settle into, even more so now that I had Rosie to enjoy. Some days I would skip to nap with her in her room. It was nice to be this close to someone and to feel them next to you as you slept. I had never wanted to do this with another witch, but Rosie was just perfect.

"Come on Rosie," Matt whined as we sat down at the lunch table on a Friday afternoon. "Just come visit my family. My younger siblings would love you."

Matt's normal chattering had grown on me and now when he was absent there was a noticeable hole. I didn't like him per se, but I was curious as to how Rosie would fare once he left at the end of the year.

Rosie signed something to him and he gave her a pout. She signed again and he pouted even further.

"That obviously doesn't work, low-level," Eli teased, her eyes shifting to Rosie. She did that often, checked on Rosie. I didn't know if she noticed but I did, and when I caught Rae's scowl I could tell she noticed as well.

I was more open about my feelings. Eli... Eli still had a lot to come to terms with.

"What's the matter?" I asked Rosie. She gave me a scowl but Matt spoke up first.

"She doesn't want to go home for the break next week and she refuses to come to my place," Matt pouted. "They are nice I swear."

Having Rosie alone with the low-level for two weeks didn't sit right with me. It was obvious Matt liked her. Now if Rosie felt the same...

My eyes shifted back to her... Could she?

"Family troubles?" Eli teased only to receive a glare from Rosie.

The conversation we had the first time I stayed over in her room suddenly came to mind. I had a feeling her parents were probably not as bad as mine, but I would hate to see her go back to a place where no one really cared for her.

"I don't go home either," I told her. "If you want you can stay at Eli's apartment with me."

Her eyes widened and I saw a hand shoot out to Eli's under the table. Eli playfully glared at me but I saw a twinkle in her eyes. She would be grateful, and so would I when we were finally alone together.

"You have your own apartment?" Matt asked in awe. I felt myself smile at his antics. That boy was so easy to read and even easier to please.

"Of course," she said. "And yes, Rosie you can come."

Matt muttered and went back to his food.

"Are you sure that's a good idea?" Rae asked from across the table. "That's sensitive information."

"Don't be jealous Rae," Eli said. "You can come if you want."

The tension in the air was palpable and for the first time it looked like Rae really wanted to end Eli.

"I have a home thank you very much," she said with a growl and stood up suddenly. "I have stuff to do."

Without another word, she left.

"What got her panties in a knot?" Matt asked through a mouthful of food.

"None of your business low-level," Eli hissed. Matt jumped with a yelp caused by what I assumed was Eli kicking him under the table.

"Is there a reason you don't want to go home?" Matt asked catching my eyes. "I think I've seen your house win awards or something... It looks nice."

I raised an eyebrow at him. Since when did he do such research?

"I didn't know you held such an interest in me," I murmured and watched as he squirmed.

"Just trying to make conversation," he muttered and sent a glance towards Rosie. "Come get coffee with me tomorrow before you leave. I would like to catch up. I barely see you anymore."

I looked down at Rosie fast enough to catch the blush that spread across her cheeks. There was a reason she didn't meet with him anymore and I felt pride swell in my chest when she looked at me under her lashes. *I* was that reason.

It took all that I had not to force her back into the room and ravage her. My magic had been satiated by all that we had done but it wanted more; I wanted more.

Just a few more days and we would have her all to ourselves. When I met Eli's eyes I could tell she thought the same thing.

"She says okay," Eli spoke for Rosie and made a show of running her hand up her arm to clasp her hand around her slim neck. Rosie's eyes widened at the action. "And I give her permission." Eli turned to glare at Matt. "If I can come with and I can take her right afterwards."

Matt scowled, obviously not liking the idea.

"You are not her keeper, she can do what she wants," Matt said with a growl. His grey eyes flashed with a fire I had yet to see from him.

"You are close to Malik," I noted. His eyes only met mine briefly before flitting away.

"He's in my class," Matt explained. "What does he have to do with this anyways?"

"I don't know if you have some kind of agreement with him—" Eli started but Matt cut her off with a wave of his hand.

"I just want a few moments alone with Rosie," he said his voice sounding almost tired now. "I swear it will be just me and her in the cafe. It's not like Malik and I hang out in our free time."

Eli surprised me by sighing and abruptly standing.

"You will go now," Eli commanded. "For twenty minutes, no longer. And then *you...*" She turned to Rosie and tangled her hair between her fingers. She yanked hard forcing Rosie's head back and leaned close to her face. "...will make good on what you just showed me right after."

My cock stood at attention at the sight of Eli taking control of Rosie. Rosie's teeth were bared as she winced against the pain of Eli's grip but the rest of her was relaxed, ready to be used. *Perfect. So perfect.*

Eli sent me a look and cocked her head signaling me to follow. With a kiss to Rosie's head I did and silently walked into the bustling hallway. People eyed us as we walked but made no move to talk to us. It was better this way, people finally got the memo that we were not interested in stupid college drama.

"We are going to follow her," Eli said and ducked down a side hallway bringing me with her.

"Fuck ya we are," I replied with a small chuckle and peeked over the corner to watch as Rosie and Matt walked out of the lunchroom. Rosie looked around before giving Matt a hesitant smile and led him out of the building.

Chapter Eleven
Rosie

I couldn't relax even as the cafe doors shut behind us and the chatter of the patrons reached my ears. I had been at attention for the last few weeks and there was no distance between me and the trio that could fix that. I had to become a different person in the last few weeks. I tried to hold onto the confident demeanor that I had when I first came back but I lost it quickly, especially when the anxiety of it all came rushing back. I didn't want to ask Daxton for another potion and raise suspicions, but I was starting to feel like I needed to scream and there was no way I would get away with it after being on watch for twenty-four hours a day.

If it was not Eli and Daxton, it would be Amr and even sometimes Rae. Rae almost refused to be alone with me after the incident at her house though, and I could literally feel her glare even if she wasn't in the same room as me.

"I'm not cut out for this work," Matt murmured as we grabbed our coffees off the counter. It was true though, the poor boy had deep purple dark circles under his eyes. I do not know what task they had given him this time but it obviously wore on him harder than the last.

Me too, I signed to him and grabbed my coffee. I looked over my shoulder feeling a sudden burning sensation but when I looked no one's eyes were on me. It made my heart pound even harder.

"Any other update than what I just witnessed?" Matt asked softly as he sat down on a stool near the window. He brushed through his curly hair with his fingers but gave up with a sigh quickly.

I didn't like being so out in the open and ready for anyone to see but it made it easier for me to watch the outside and see if the trio had followed. I still felt the eyes on me with every move I made, but I couldn't place them.

Looking around quickly, I decided to chance talking.

"They have a bad relationship. I don't know much else other than Daxton is very affected by them, and he refuses for me to be around them," I whispered quickly and acted like I was sipping my drink so I could hide my mouth. "I saw them at Rae's house. Met her brothers too."

Matt spat out his coffee attracting the stares of the people around us. He let out an awkward laugh and apologized to them. His sleeves and front of his shirt were sprinkled with coffee stains. He looked around nervously and moved to unbutton his sleeves to roll them. I spurred into action and gripped onto his wrist when I saw the first look at his colorful ink. I sent him a warning glare.

"And your...?" He tried to change the subject looking flustered as he fixed his sleeve.

It's fine, I signed to him. *Daxton helps.*

"Good. Good," he murmured.

I saw him swallow thickly and his eyes searched the area around us. Did he feel the eyes too? With shaky hands he lifted his coffee back up to his lips before finally looking me in the eyes.

"Are you okay?" he asked and let out a weak sigh. "I feel like I am going crazy, I can't imagine you."

I nodded and took another sip of my coffee. Instead of answering right away I took a moment to search the surroundings outside the coffee shop. There were other small shops that lined the area and a few colorful trees that had dying leaves falling off them. This should be a relaxing place. I should feel good to be here, alone with Matt...but I hated it.

Let's go, I signed to him. *I have things to do.*

It was an awkward and stressful walk back. Neither of us dared to speak and only drank our coffee silently. Each step felt like it was being criticized even though I couldn't place where the eyes were. When Winterfell came into view I just about passed out from the relief of it.

That was until something shifted to my right. My head snapped to the sight so fast I felt like I'd get whiplash, but there was nothing waiting for me. I felt it then, a small brush against my magic. I grabbed onto Matt's arm and pulled him to me while looking around for the intruder. It was magic. I didn't know who from... I wasn't that skilled yet but I had felt it.

"Rosie?" Matt asked in a whisper.

I took a deep shaky breath and I felt my throat close up. The panic and fear that had been clawing at me was beginning to get too much for me. This lying and running around knowing that the information was going to hurt Daxton. I didn't care if they had a bad relationship; losing a parent was painful no matter what and even if they were brutish and rude... Maybe I could belong if I tried.

"I think," I whispered but stopped to swallow the scream in my throat as the magic brushed across my back, harder this time. It felt like a warning, or a threat. "I can't do it."

Matt's eyes widened and he looked around before putting his arm around me and walking us towards Winterfell at a faster pace. I knew his gesture was supposed to protect me but it honestly made the entire thing worse because now I had to worry about Eli seeing this.

"Let's talk in your dorm, okay?" he whispered. I nodded and tried to focus my eyes on the ground but the magic I had felt earlier came back full force and I felt it prod at my back, enough to trip me.

I paused and looked around again but there was no one around us. Where were they hiding? Was this Claudine and Maximus? A test? Or was what they had finally warned me about here? Maybe his parents felt my magic and realized who I came from and now they were here to end her bloodline.

I felt tears prick my eyes as the magic enveloped me. I could barely breathe.

"Do you feel it?" I whispered hoarsely against Matt. He pushed us forward with a panicked look.

"I only feel the eyes," he said staring straight ahead. My body started shaking as the magic pressed at all sides.

My breaths came quicker now. My heart was racing like I'd ran a marathon. And I felt a sheen of sweat cover my body. I gripped onto Matt for support.

"What is this?" a familiar voice said from our side. I peered over to see Rae watching us from the grass as we walked by her. She had a scowl on her face and her eyes were narrowed at us. Tears finally fell and I reached out to her leaving Matt's side.

Her face softened when she took catalog of my state and she steadied me against her chest as I reached her arms.

"She said she felt something," Matt said with a thick voice. "We went out for coffee and felt eyes on us; when we got close to Winterfell she said she felt something else."

I buried my face in her chest and exhaled as I felt her power work over me in waves chasing away the panic and fear from my bones. I sniffled into her and gripped onto her not quite ready to show my face to the world.

"Magic?" Rae asked from above me, her voice softer now. Her hand was firm on the back of my head letting me know it was okay to stay like this. I nodded into her.

I felt it again then coming back tenfold. This time it hurt my skin as it squeezed. I let out a strangled whine. My own magic started to move restlessly inside of me. Unlike myself it wanted to fight. It was ready to tear the other magic apart, baring its teeth as it got close like a rabid dog when someone got too close to its cage.

"Make it stop Rae," I begged her pitifully and looked up at her through my tears. Her face was hard as stone, but I saw a flash of something in there. She looked up over my head and her eyes narrowed in on something.

"Stop it," she commanded. "You've had enough fun, look at what you did."

The magic pulled back all of a sudden and I heard Matt curse.

"You fuckers, did you know how scared she was?" he growled. I looked over my shoulder to see Eli and Daxton standing together not ten feet away from us. Eli had a smirk on her face and Daxton's face was unreadable.

They did this? Even my thoughts sounded pained. *Daxton?*

When I met his eyes they did not falter from mine. I couldn't tell what he was thinking.

"We just wanted to mess with her," Eli said and nudged Daxton.

"I wanted to test how sensitive she was to magic," he explained. "Still don't know how you saw through our illusion."

It was them watching us the entire time. I shot a look to Matt and when his eyes met mine I saw an understanding there. We didn't know how much they heard or saw; we were in deep shit if they were inside the cafe with us and heard us talking.

"I didn't," she explained. "I felt your emotions."

Eli rolled her eyes and patted Daxton on the shoulder before walking towards me. I held onto Rae tighter and sent her a glare.

"Don't look so hurt Rosie," she whined. "It was just a game."

I was about to speak but Rae beat me to it and pushed me against her.

"You gave her a panic attack," she said. "I'm worried that if she goes with you she may not come back at all."

"Don't act all high and mighty Rae," Eli hissed at her. "You were the one that said this meant nothing. A deal, no more no less."

I stiffened in her arms at the reminder. I thought I had gotten over it but during the last two weeks I had fallen back into my old habits of trusting them too much. Wanting to be in their crowd. Wanting to be seen.

I pushed against Rae but she held me close still.

"We will go to my vacation home," she said. "I am not leaving you three alone and will not take no for an answer."

Eli let out a groan.

"Is it the one with the indoor pool at least?" she asked. Rae let out a heavy sigh.

"That one can be arranged," she replied.

Eli shifted, looking from me to Daxton. Matt gave me one final look that told me to speak now or forever hold my peace.

I chose to remain silent.

* * *

As Rae had promised she had taken us to the vacation house that topped every other house I had seen. It was just as big as her other one and came with its own wait staff and chef. I couldn't wrap my head around how lucky someone like Rae was to have all these resources at her fingertips. I wouldn't complain though... I went from my old beat-up home to one with five-star meals and a heated pool.

After the incident it had taken me a while to calm myself down. My magic was reaching out almost as widely as it had back in the town and pushed me to release some...but I wasn't ready to go to Daxton just yet. I was hurt by the way he played me.

"This is your room," Rae said as she showed me to a room on the second floor. I didn't even look at the interior as I walked in, still feeling off from the scare earlier. I know it had been a stupid joke but I had never felt my body react in a way like that...at least not since I screamed so loud my ribs broke. It was jarring.

Rae's firm hand squeezed my shoulder causing me to jump. I looked up to her suddenly. Her hazel eyes were searching when I met them. My magic wanted me to latch onto her, pushing me to take a closer step to her...but I knew it was useless. And even though she had shown me some kindness, she still made it clear what she wanted.

She pulled me into her giving me a lingering hug before stepping away. I stopped my hand from reaching out to force her back to me.

"You can stay here as long as you need." She paused looking behind her. "I will keep them at bay if you need it."

I nodded and looked at my feet.

"Just a bit of time would be nice," I said in a meek voice. I wanted to tell her about the magic but Malik's warning rang through my head again. "I just need to calm down a bit."

She nodded and let out a sigh.

"My door is down to the left," she said. "If anything happens just come find me."

"Okay," I muttered and looked up at her between my lashes. The originals pushed me to get close to her but I didn't know what I could do...what I wanted to do.

"We will leave soon," she explained. "You can explore the house on your own then." She pulled out her phone before continuing. "Give us thirty minutes and we should be out of here."

I nodded. Without another word she left me in the room. I let out a sigh and moved to the bed lying on it fully clothed and not bothering to climb under the covers. My phone vibrated in my skirt pocket and with a groan I pulled it out to see who called. I rolled my eyes at the name and answered it.

"Matt told you," I said without a greeting.

"You seem to be having trouble with them," Malik said. There was a bite to his tone.

"If you are worried about me completing my job, don't be," I hissed at him.

I could hear a sigh and then a silence followed by a shifting of fabric.

"I'm worried about you," he said. "I didn't know if I aggravated them *too* much and they decided to take it out on you."

"Of course, they did," I said weakly. "Just..." *Fuck how did I say this?* "They didn't do anything I didn't want. They were just messing around earlier and it scared me. I have it under control."

He let out a sigh and didn't respond for a few seconds, letting my words rest between us uncomfortably.

"Where are you now?" he asked.

"In the vacation house like Matt most likely told you," I replied. "Like *she* asked. In my room. No one is around."

"Good," he said. "Listen, I have to go but if there is trouble call me and we can figure it out from there."

"Sure," I said hastily ready to hang up.

"Wait," he called. "I heard you went to Rae's house."

I let out a groan.

"Yes," I said. "But no one saw me."

"You went against what I said," he said then paused. "Don't do it again."

"Sure," I said and before he could say anything else I hung up and threw the phone across the bed.

I ran my hands over my face feeling the nasty scar. I was just so tired of everything already. I needed to get my hands on more of that calming position because if not, I didn't know how much longer I could last.

Just as the thought echoed through my mind I heard heavy footsteps come down the hallway. I let out another sigh and covered my face with my hands just as the door was pushed open.

"Rosie," Eli growled from the doorway.

What happened to Rae keeping them at bay?

"Leave me alone, Eli," I hissed.

I heard her walk over to the bed and felt her rough hands grab my thighs. She pulled me to the edge of the bed and wrapped my legs around her. I removed my hands from my face to peek up at her only to be met with a glare from her shining blue eyes.

"What's this I hear about you not wanting to see me?" she asked, her voice softer than I expected from her.

She pulled me up by my arms and placed them around her neck, bringing me closer to her. My heart skipped a beat and I felt my stomach heat uncontrollably. This was not helping, with my body and magic already so on edge.

"I just needed some time," I said and averted my eyes. "You guys scared me..."

Eli didn't force me to look at her, instead she trailed kisses from my temple to my jaw. I couldn't help but sigh and arch into her.

"It was my idea," she said against me and continue to kiss downward only stopping to suck lightly on my neck. I tightened my legs around her, bringing her closer. I couldn't stop myself from grinding against her lightly. "I didn't know it would affect you so much."

Her hands ran up my thighs teasingly. I sucked in a sharp breath when her thumbs teased my inner thigh, so close to where I wanted her.

"Well, it did," I hissed still not looking at her. She must have known what I wanted her to do but she didn't move her hands any closer. She was giving me the choice.

"I could apologize, if you let me," she confirmed. "But if you would rather stay mad, I can leave right now. I don't have much time anyways."

I sighed and brought my lips to hers for a lingering kiss. Her hands stayed planted where they were, but she kissed me back eagerly. When I pulled away breathless and worse than when we started, I gave her a hard look.

"This is not a real apology," I said. "Go, Rae will be waiting for you."

Eli gave me something akin to a pout before diving in to bite on my lip painfully. When she pulled away, she gave me a deadly smirk.

"I was jealous and needy," she admitted. "I don't... I have..." She paused before running a hand through her hair, messing up its uniformed look. "I get angry easily when it comes to you. I'm sorry."

Just like back in the dorm my jaw dropped at her sincere apology—or at least it sounded sincere and those words coming out of her mouth were more than I had expected. I didn't say anything, instead just nodded and waved her away.

"We'll be back in a few hours," she said and pulled herself from me only to wink before she left the room. "Don't get too impatient while we are away."

I rolled my eyes and waved her away. With one last smirk she left the room.

I didn't move from my spot for another five minutes and when I did it was only to walk to the window in hopes of seeing the trio leave. I let out a heavy sigh when I saw them board their limo and pull out of the front driveway.

Steeling myself I turned towards my door and marched out of my room before I could lose my courage.

Chapter Twelve
Amr

I let out a sleepy sigh as I stretched on the warm blankets of Daxton's bed.

They had left me here so they could go to Rae's father's house *again*. I tried to leave the room before they left but Rae had told me in a stern voice that Rosie didn't want anyone around her for the time being. If I was in my human form, I would have snorted.

It was *them* that she didn't want to see. *They* were the ones that messed up.

To Rosie I was still a harmless cat that was great only for cuddles and ranting to when no one else was around. I had been excited about the talk of her being a witch. It would mean the end to the secrecy. It would mean I could show myself to someone other than Daxton. I would no longer be invisible.

I had felt her magic and even taken some before the talks of her being a witch even started, but I agreed with Daxton. We needed to wait for the proof before confronting her. It seemed like even she had no idea what she really was, which made this all the harder. If she didn't know anything and I revealed myself to her, I would be jeopardizing the witches' well-kept secret.

Ever since Rosie's magic had slipped up, I had done some serious thinking about what I wanted for my future. The familiars I grew up with were very short-sighted and in their minds the best thing they could hope for was a human who treated them well. Then, after they retired they hoped to find a similar familiar to settle down and have children with.

My own parents had been well over three hundred years before having children. Their witches had both died in a battle between covens and were left stranded; that's how they met. In the midst of blood and chaos. They were lucky. For me though... Daxton was a very powerful witch and the chances that he would die an early death were slim. Not that I would wish that on him... I loved him in my own way. Watched him grow from a teen to a grumpy adult.

But after I met Rosie...

I wanted nothing more than to mate with her and settle down like my own parents had. I longed to feel her the way that the others had, and I burned with jealously when they could touch her so easily. Yet they treated her horribly. I had once thought Rae was an exception, but I was wrong about that.

Now it was only I who stood a chance at giving her the type of love she deserved. And I was stuck as a cat while I did it. That was until we could figure out her true status. If she really was a witch...I planned to change everything.

It had been a lonely existence. If I was honest with myself, I would admit that the idea of being with Rosie was more about my own selfishness to be understood and seen by her. She was special in her own way, and I felt drawn to her. But I was tired of this life. As much as I wanted to be with Rosie and give her all the love I had stored for the years...I wanted to be loved by her as well. As more than a pet. I wanted her to need me, to want me, to trust me as a partner.

I was worried for a moment, when I first met her, that my true self would scare her, but after watching her stand up to the others and accept them...I had hope for me too.

As if the heavens heard my prayers the doorknob to Daxton's door turned and in popped Rosie's blushing face. I sat up and meowed at her to get her attention. I could feel her magic from here and knew that she needed my help.

"Thank god you are here," she whispered and entered the room shutting the door behind her.

I've been waiting, my love, I wanted to say but I settled for meowing again. I climbed into her arms as she came closer, and she sighed as her magic started to fill me.

Unlike other witches, familiars will not go crazy from their magic, nor do we have to get rid of magic or share it to maintain it. It would store itself in my core and come out only when I asked it to. Which I never did with

Daxton around; he was a good witch and almost never picked fights that he couldn't solve himself.

I purred and rubbed my head against her chin, trying to provide her as much comfort as I could. I could feel her stress permeate in the air, almost smell it. She had been a wreck since we came to this house, constantly looking over her shoulder, jumping at every sound.

"They scared me earlier," she whispered to me and left a short kiss on my head. I returned it by licking her cheek. "They followed me when I was with Matt." She took a deep breath before continuing. "I thought someone bad had found us, and when Daxton teased me with his magic..." She buried her face in my fur. "I thought it was all over."

Rage burned inside me. How dare they treat her like that? They knew that she had little to no experience in the magical world. Of course she would be on high alert if she felt someone as strong as Daxton around her. They were selfish creatures that could barely see beyond their own wishes.

My skin itched uncontrollably, a sure sign that I was ready to shift. I tried to steady myself by taking deep calming breaths and inhaling my angel's scent. It had been a while since I had been forced to shift because of my rage; the last time was when she had gone missing with that cotton-ball-haired man, Malik.

But now was not the time. Daxton would surely be mad.

I wanted to comfort her and tell her I would punish them but in this form, I wasn't even a threat. And with the vow still being tied to Daxton...he could punish me any way he deemed fit.

She pulled back and looked into my eyes. She rubbed a spot between them that made my eyes close. A loud purr came from my chest.

"They will be back in a few hours so it's just me and you buddy," she said with a smile. "Hope you don't get too annoyed by me."

How could I ever get annoyed by you? I loved when she would talk to me. Everyone else seemed to just look over me as if I didn't matter. As if I wasn't there to begin with...she was the first one to have conversations with me other than Daxton.

She sighed and looked over the room.

"There isn't anything here," she trailed while walking over to the drawers. "It's just like my own. Nothing here."

She paused and looked down to me.

"Did Daxton bring a backpack or anything?" she asked. I cock my head at her and she giggled lightly. "I am not sure why I expected you to reply."

I would if I could, I wanted to tell her. *If I could speak, the first thing I would tell you is how smitten I am with you.*

She leaned over, squishing me into her chest and searched under the pillow and sheets. With a sigh she climbed back to the bed with me still in her arms. The searched seem to disappoint her.

What was she looking for? I wondered, but I didn't let it bother me. Now was my time with her, everything else could come later.

I stretched out on her chest getting comfortable just like I would have done in the dorm. "I'm just going to take a nap," she said sleepily. "Wake me up when they get here."

She was out in minutes. I waited until her breathing had deepened and her body fully relaxed before moving. I jumped off the bed and onto the floor before shifting into my other from. I had done this before, when she was deep asleep, and from her breathing it sounded like now was one of those times. It was the only time I could fantasize what a life with her in my normal form would be like.

I sighed and stretched when my bones were done painfully pulling in all directions. I grabbed her hand in my own, enjoying the feeling of our bare skin against each other. Her hand was so small in mine, it brought a smile to my face. I knew she could be a hellcat if she wanted to be, I'd seen it in the way she challenged Rae and Eli. But here now she was nothing more than a sweet baby kitten.

I wanted to protect her and shower her with love at the same time. My heart clenched painfully when I realized how far away that dream was. I grabbed her palm and rested it over my cheek trying to take advantage of her skin against mine. I watched her as she dreamed; she was always so peaceful as she dreamt, blind to the real world. I trailed my fingers down the scar on her face lightly, careful not to wake her.

The magic must be taking a toll on her, I could feel it shifting under her skin. It would reach out to me sometimes on it's own, as if to check if I were friend or foe. Magic was funny like that, it had a mind of it's own especially if untrained. Daxton was a perfect example of it, before he took her magic he had gone on rampages devouring every magic he could get and was never satiated. As much as I loathed Eli sometimes... without her oversight Daxton would have gone far beyond what was acceptable.

I noticed that Rosie had been more prone to naps recently even when she got a full night of sleep. It worried me, especially when I couldn't be there to help her through this time. If she made one wrong move, the magical council would be all over her. Daxton was lucky that his parents were such prominent members and he had someone like Rae to help clean up. Without them, he would have been punished for his misdeeds against the other witches no matter how careful they were.

She shifted in the bed and moaned lightly in her sleep. It wasn't sexual but it stirred something in me nonetheless. I frowned at my hardening cock. I had forgotten how easily stimulated a human body was.

I couldn't even remember the last time I had been with another. It had to have been years ago, far before Daxton even needed a familiar. I had been too busy preparing for the moment he would need me. I stayed with my family taking care of my siblings and training until my knuckles bled.

I missed them sometimes, but I knew they were in good hands, or at least I hoped my parents were taking care of them. I would hate to see them become familiars to unworthy witches. Some people thought the rite was the greatest honor, especially if your witch was powerful. They would pay off your family in a lump sum and when you retired and they happened to still be alive by the end of it, you would get double what they paid in the beginning. You would be taken care of, provided for... but all at the cost of your freedom and autonomy.

I sighed and left a long kiss on Rosie's hand.

It had been another hour until I felt the need to wake her. The others said that they would be gone for longer, but I didn't want to chance it especially since she had given me this task. I would prove to her she could trust me, even as a cat.

I shifted back to my cat form and climbed back onto her chest. I meowed a few times before her big brown eyes met mine.

"Is it time?" she asked.

I meowed again for good measure, and she let out a sigh before stretching out on the bed. She sat up with me in her arms and left the room silently, making sure to close the door behind her.

"Well, that was a waste," she grumbled as she walked back to her room.

What was a waste? I wondered. *Was she not there for a nap? To come find me?*

When she reached her room she locked the door and began undressing. I turned to give her some privacy and heard her giggle as I did.

"Such a polite cat," she said and I heard her footsteps disappear into the bathroom. I let out a sigh and spread out on the floor, finally able to relax now that the temptation was gone. There had been many a time when I could have seen her naked, seen her with the others, but I didn't want to breach her privacy like that.

Not five minutes later I could hear the engine of the limo in the driveway. Satisfaction bloomed in my chest when I realized just how good my intuition had been.

Rosie was still in the shower by the time their footsteps sounded in the hallway. I could hear them arguing as they stopped in front of her door.

I padded over to the door to listen.

"I already apologized," Eli growled from behind the door.

"And I would too if you let me anywhere near her," Daxton replied just as unhappily.

"I know what your apologies consist of," Rae grumbled.

"I didn't fuck her!" Eli exclaimed and I heard a smack before I heard the shuffling.

I heard Rosie's shower shut off and looked over to see her walking out with only a towel covering her. She stopped in her tracks when the arguing persisted outside.

"Are they out there?" she asked in a whisper. Amusement tickled at my senses when she expected me to respond. I tried for a nod and her eyes widened as she looked down at her towel.

A small smile crossed her face and she stood straight, the panicked air now turning into one of confidence. My amusement dropped when I realized what she was going to do.

She marched straight to the door and opened it with a scowl.

Rae and Eli were in a heated argument. Eli's hand was wrapped around the collar of Rae's shirt as if she was ready to punch her. Daxton watched them from the sidelines. His gaze was the first to meet Rosie's. I could already feel his magic flare as he took in her attire.

Eli looked next, her eyes trailing down her body with a smirk. She unwound herself from Rae and took a step back as if she wanted to savor the image.

Rae hesitantly looked over her and I could see the knot in her throat as she swallowed. To my surprise a slight blush rose to her cheeks.

"Does this mean you will take me up on my offer?" Eli teased. She stepped forward only to be pulled back by Daxton.

"Only I can help the *curse*," he said with conviction. I meowed loudly causing Daxton to shoot a glare at me.

"Amr has been helping," she said. "Can I ask why you guys came to so rudely interrupt my shower?"

She leaned against the door and the towel opened slightly to show her bare thigh.

That minx, I thought to myself. It was easy to see that Rae was controlling them all with a glare but from the looks of her clenched fists I would say she was having trouble with all the emotions swirling around us.

"We came to get you for dinner." Rae was the first one to speak and stared directly into Rosie's eyes. I watched as Rosie blushed lightly. It made my stomach twist with jealousy. "Get dressed, the kitchen staff already prepared something for us."

She cocked her head and turned back into the room, walking to the dresser and began looking for something to wear.

"These are men's clothes, Rae," she said and held up a large grey shirt that was three times her size.

"I'll find you something later," Rae forced out.

Rosie sent a smile to Rae and in one motion dropped her towel giving us a full view of her stark nakedness. I didn't have time to look away this time like I had the others, and I felt something primal stir inside me. The need to take, the need to protect, the need to bend her over and force her to submit. Her skin was creamy and looked soft to the touch, her hips and backside curved in a deliciously sinful way. I watched with rapt attention as her breasts swung slightly as she searched for clothing. I wanted more than anything to feel her with my human hands.

I have heard that familiars tended to be more feral once they found a mate to claim but I didn't believe it, until now. The little smile she sent the group was full of mischief and only stirred me more. I vowed to myself in that moment that the first chance I got, I would claim her and break my vow with Daxton.

I was left with no other choice. The magic that now swirled violently within me was far older, and more potent than anything Daxton or his family could promise me. I no longer cared what the rules were, I would break them all for her.

She slipped the large shirt on and searched the drawers for something else. She held up a pair of boxer shorts and stepped into them only to pull them up painfully slow.

"Rosie," Daxton growled. "You are asking for it."

She cocked her head and walked over to the group. The way the shirt fell across her body made her nipples all too obvious to the world.

"I didn't say anything," she said innocently. She moved to pick me up but I felt Eli grip at the fur on the back of my neck and pull me up before she could reach me.

Don't think I don't see you cat, she said in my mind.

Don't test me Eli, I hissed back at her.

What are you going to do? Scratch me? she asked. *Don't forget your place.*

I let out a growl at her.

Rosie gave Eli a pout before sending Rae a smile and linking their arms together. There was a growling from the other two beside me.

"You guys are on my shit list," she said and pushed Rae forward. Rae met her with a shocked expression before pulling herself together and pushing up her glasses.

"You won't say that tonight," Daxton growled as Rae and Rosie walked past him.

Rosie sent him a smile.

"Actually, I will be," she said innocently. "Because I will be bunking with Rae tonight right?" Rae froze for only a second before pulling Rosie down the hall.

"That's not fair," Eli whined. "I said sorry Rosie."

Eli pushed me into Daxton's arms and ran to catch up to them. Daxton only sighed angrily and followed them down the hall.

Chapter Thirteen
Rosie

The dinner was silent but far from awkward. If anything, I was amused off my ass. I was frustrated by the way my magic was lashing out, but seeing their twisted and pouting faces elicited a response in me similar to the one I got when Malik got angry.

I was in control here, even if it was just a tiny bit.

Rae was by far the most amusing. She had hidden everything up until now so well...but I saw the blush on her cheeks when I opened the door. She tried to act like it didn't bother her but the killing blow was when I told her I was bunking with her. I thought for sure she would drop dead right there.

I sat in a chair next to Rae happily while I ate the amazing food her family cook had made for us. I knew they were rich but the person they brought in had to be super expensive because every single bite of the food was like heaven.

"Rosie," Eli said while leaning forward. "What are you trying to do?"

I took another bite of my lamb and sneakily rested my hand on Rae's thigh. Her whole body seemed to freeze under me.

"I'm trying to eat, Eli," I said in a light voice, trailing my hand up her thigh.

"Are you trying to tempt us?" she asked in a voice almost low enough to be a growl.

"Not everything is about sex, Eli," I told her.

"Everything a witch does is about sex," Daxton said in a similar tone. It took me a good amount of effort not to freeze. Amr let out a meow from the floor, but I didn't pay him any mind.

"Must be hard for you then," I said with a small pout.

"Don't play," Eli hissed and stabbed her knife into the table. I blinked then turned to Rae.

"Did you guys go to another gathering?" I asked her. "Not sure why you are needed *every day*."

She eyed me while she ate her own steak.

"You don't need that information," she replied.

Typical, yet smart, I wanted to say. And she was right to feel that way. Here I was playing house with them while they were none the wiser to my motives. Just minutes before they came home I was snooping in Daxton's room, but there was nothing inside. Not even a backpack.

This task almost seemed like I was set up for failure. They hadn't specified a timeline, but I needed to get this over with sooner rather than later and then wash my hands of that group and this curse. Maybe then, when I would be finally able to fully explain myself, they would forgive me for lying to them so blatantly.

"I'm tired," I said with a sigh. "Show me to your room?"

Rae didn't respond, instead just nodded and stood up. Her food was barely touched.

"Please don't try to break down my door tonight," she said sternly to the others.

I followed her out of the room with a small burst of satisfaction. Amr padded after us, meowing lightly as we walked.

* * *

We barely spoke as we got ready for bed. Her room had a double sink, so I was able to wash my face and brush my teeth at the same time as her. She had her routine down pat, not like I would expect anything else from her.

She meticulously scrubbed her face with like three different soaps, applied toner, and a million creams. Then brushed her teeth with a fancy toothbrush only to floss for another five minutes then finish off with mouth wash.

And she let me watch all of it.

It felt like I was interrupting something, but I couldn't tear my eyes away from her. I remembered a similar feeling when I spent the night in her dorm not long ago. Everything about Rae was a well-kept secret and every time I somehow came across something, even as mundane as this, I felt like I should look away.

I felt unworthy to be a part of this, I realized.

And you are, a small voice whispered back to me.

"Is there a reason you forced yourself into my bed?" she said as she applied some sort of cream to the ends of her hair. It smelt like coconuts and a flower I couldn't place. My hand twitched and I was overcome with the need to run my finger through her hair.

"Are you unhappy?" I asked and spat my toothpaste in the sink. She eyed me as I did, carefully deciding her words no doubt.

"Nothing will happen if that's what you think," she said. "Last time was—"

I cut her off with a wave of my hand, anger flailing through me.

A mistake. The words hung between us heavily.

I had told them she was not on my shit list but every time she redeemed herself it seemed like she just punted herself back down to the lowest of the list. Not that it was a competition...

"I just want a good night's sleep," I explained. "Like you noted before we came here. They seem hell-bent on destroying me."

I wiped my mouth on a nearby towel enjoying the way Rae grimaced, and then just to annoy her further I reached over to the coconut mixture she put on her hair.

"Be careful with that," she grumbled watching me with a curious gaze as I opened the container and took out a dime-sized amount of cream. "It may be too thick for your hair type."

I was about to rub it on the ends of my hair but her hand shot and grabbed my wrist. I tried to tear it out of her grip but she held firm and scooped the cream out of my hand.

"I can do it myself," I hissed.

"Evidently, you can't Ms. Miller," she murmured. I gritted my teeth at the formal way she called me and sent her a glare. Her eyes twinkled lightly in the bathroom light. She rubbed her palms together smearing the cream across the both of them and reached around to brush it through my hair with her fingers. She started in the middle of my hair and very lightly pulled the thick cream through it.

It felt really good to be touched in this way and I remembered the way she helped me dry my hair in the dorm before. It made my chest warm. This was a caring gesture that gave her no benefit yet she was here helping me anyways.

I looked towards the ground, unable to handle the way the emotions swirled around me. Who knew a gesture as simple as this would be the one to break me? I clenched my fists as she continued to run her hands through my hair. The cream had to be gone by now; she was drawing this out and the longer she did the worse it made me feel.

"Is there something you want to tell me?" she asked lightly. Her voice lost its tone. Its rawness made my throat clench.

"No," I whispered.

Before my feelings got the better of me I turned to head back into the room. Amr waited for me on the bed and I jumped into it with him to smother him with kisses. It was a distraction, a needed one to help me push away whatever had been going through my mind back there. The bed was far bigger than the dorm ones and I had no doubt in my mind that if Rae so chose we could remain separated the entire night.

"You shouldn't coddle him like that," Rae said. Her voice had a twinge of annoyance to it. "He's a *male* cat you know."

I rolled my eyes and sent one last kiss to Amr's forehead.

"Literally everything is about sex with you guys," I grumbled and covered myself with the thick duvet covers. It was toasty inside the house but these covers were so fluffy I couldn't help but wrap them around me.

No doubt something like this would have cost my parents two months' salary. A twinge of guilt and sadness filled me when I thought about the low-levels that raised me. Sure, they were not the greatest but I was still their child. Or I guess... I really wasn't anymore. Living a life with them wasn't easy but if I thought about a world with Xena and my high-level father in it... I couldn't dare understand what type of life that would be.

"What did you just think about?" Rae asked turning off the lights and climbing into bed, making sure to keep a distance between us. Amr curled up to my side purring loudly.

"My parents," I said honestly. That darkness made me feel better, made it easier to digest my feelings. I felt like I could speak here and I was tempted to tell her everything, but Malik's nagging voice in the back of my head warned me not to.

"Do you regret staying here?" she said softly. I heard her shift and felt her eyes on me. It made me panic.

"No," I said quickly. "I was just..." I let out a sigh. "You have a lot of money, my parents never did. So I feel bad that I am here living it up lavishly while they are stuck in their low-level jobs that can barely afford them a decent place to live."

She stayed quiet for a moment and then I felt her power hit me. It was slow as the calming effects rolled over me.

"You are upset," she noted. "In the bathroom, I felt it."

I swallowed thickly. I really didn't want to talk about this. I was one vulnerable moment away from giving away everything...and to someone who thought what we did was a mistake.

"I'm fine," I said.

"Was it because of what I said?" she asked hesitantly.

I shook my head and let out a sigh that seemed to deflate my entire being.

"It was your actions," I said. "I really liked the way you helped me with my hair."

There was a pause.

"Then why are you upset?" she asked.

"Forget it, Rae," I said. The words felt like they took more effort than they should have. "I'm just...really tried."

"You need to relax," she said.

"You say that like it's easy," I said with a humorless chuckle. I turned to face her. Her glowing hazel eyes startled me enough for my breath to catch. "I am a low-level in a huge house full of high-level demons who only want to fuck me until I am an obedient little doll."

I swear I thought I saw the sides of Rae's lips curl but I couldn't be too sure.

"What is it about sharing a bed with me at night that makes you so talkative?" she asked.

I averted my eyes away from her not liking the way her smooth question made me feel.

"I don't know," I said softly curling around Amr.

"Do you need me to help you sleep?" she asked after a pause. I tried not to let her question anger me. It was as if she didn't want me to talk anymore, as if I was annoying her.

"Sure," I said quietly.

There was another pause before her power hit me head-on. Blackness came over me quickly and I didn't open my eyes until morning.

* * *

When I woke up to an empty bed in the morning I decided that this would be the last time I was sleeping in Rae's bed.

At least, until she got over whatever was going on in her head and I got over whatever feeling made me doubt everything last night. I was excited to see that I still had an effect on her last night, but it obviously didn't last long and she was still the same high-level that told me I meant nothing.

There would be no getting close to her, even if the mission asked for it. And I didn't think I could handle it. I was about to pour my heart out to her in the darkness and I knew she would react with nothing more than...

Last time was a mistake.

I ran my hand through my hair; it was softer than ever and the scent of her cream wafted through my nose. It was comforting and sad all at once... At least I knew it was real. That the way she acted wasn't something my mind made up. Deciding not to dwell any longer, I stretched. Amr woke up next to me with a loud yawn and blinked his sleep away. I smiled at the feline and kissed his head.

"It's just me and you today buddy," I whispered to him. He licked my nose in response.

When I ventured out into the house I was surprised to realize that the whole trio was gone. I was a bit hurt that they didn't leave me a note, but it made it better that I had a stack of blueberry pancakes waiting for me on the dining room table.

The rest of my day was boring, but it gave me a much needed rest. I explored the outside of the grounds. The garden was nice and Amr chased a few bugs around causing me to giggle when he failed.

It was honestly perfect, until the trio came home and I was forced to go back into hiding. I know I didn't have to but there was a part of me that didn't want to deal with them. The confidence from yesterday was gone.

It stayed like that for four days. Every morning they would leave and come back during the mid-afternoon. I would spend my days with Amr, and then retire early for the night. It was lonely, but it was good for me. I didn't feel the weight of the task weighing down on me and even as Eli pounded on my door, I felt no need to rush to please her. I was content with myself in a way I hadn't been since being thrown into Winterfell.

Rae had pulled Eli away on multiple occasions and let me know there would be food waiting for me on the table. I never went down at night, only stayed in my room and waited until it was safe enough to create the magic birds. It was better this way.

My magic had gotten worse over the last few days and sometimes at night I woke up in a sweat ready to run out of this room and go find Daxton...but I held off. No matter how much the magic had pushed me. No matter how hot and achy my skin had gotten, I held off. Because I wasn't ready to give up this sanctuary I had built for myself.

Today was another day alone. Rae had stopped by my door an hour ago stating they would leave to visit her father's house again and wouldn't be back until later. The waitstaff were hiding away, busy doing whatever they needed to and didn't bother me. I donned shorts and an oversized shirt as I walked through the house. They kept the air warm in here so I could walk around like this without a problem. I decided to visit the heated pool and sat on the edge with my legs in the water. I let out a sigh and looked up at the glass ceiling. The day was ending, and the setting sun caused the cloud in the sky to appear pinkish.

My magic took that moment to remind me it was there. I groaned aloud when I felt it pulse inside me. It was yelling at me, begging to be let out. It thrashed around violently causing me to hunch over in pain. It almost felt like it was clawing me from the inside out. It caused my breathing to deepen and a sweat to break out over my body.

I looked around the pool house feverishly. There were plants all around the area that lined the walls and partially blocked the windows from seeing into the room. I had made sure to shut the door behind me so there was no chance to be seen. After I checked twice, a third time, I finally allowed myself to conjure the birds.

I didn't stop at one or two—no, I knew that if I wanted to take this edge off, I would need to go big. I focused on blue jays this time and forced them out of my plan one after the other. The small pool room filled with their chirps and wing flaps. They flew together and some even broke out into groups for play fights. A few dove straight down to the pool only to spread their wings right before they hit the water and soar up higher than before.

When one came to pull at my hair, I couldn't help but let out a small chuckle. There had to be at least thirty birds in this room alone. I wondered how many more I could make if I wasn't trying to stay hidden. I thought about making other animals, to test the extent of my magic, but I didn't want to push anything. They were so carefree and had nothing to stop them from exploring new heights.

Their freedom stirred something in me but there was another feeling that filled me when looking at them. Pride. It felt like it would burst through my chest any moment.

It was awe-inspiring, that someone like me could make something so beautiful. It was like a painting had come alive and was now flying over my head. The birds' red was close to that of the setting sun, but that would be gone soon too. I reached out and a bird perched on my hand without even being commanded to. Its beady eyes looked at me quizzically and I leaned forward to place a kiss on its head. I smiled at it as I pulled away.

Its head snapped to something behind me. In an instant my muscles seized, and the birds exploded around me leaving a cloud of glitter in the air. My head snapped behind me, and there was the black long-haired cat I had kicked out of my room the last few nights.

I sighed and relaxed immediately, thankful that it wasn't a waitstaff or the trio coming home early. They obviously already knew but no one dared bring it up and I didn't try to give them any more information that could jeopardize this task.

"Amr, you scared me," I said with a small smile. "Sorry I have been ignor—"

I was cut off short when the figure of the cat twisted gruesomely and began expanding. Pure horror laced my veins and my stomach clenched, ready to force up the measly breakfast I had. The fur shrunk into the fleshy twisting body of the creature and slowly I was met with tan skin and it... *Holy shit, was that a human?*

Finally, the creature started to resemble a human. A very naked, very toned and tanned human that stood before me with hair down to their hips. His eyes were the first thing that drew me towards him; they were the same golden that Amr had.

The second thing I noticed was that he obviously wanted me in a way I didn't expect. I swallowed at the size of this creature's package. What the fuck did I just witness? Was I still dreaming? Did they slip something into my food? Becau—*ohmygod it's coming toward me.* I couldn't move as he advanced on me. It started as a walk and then he full-on ran towards me.

"Wait, wait, wait—" I tried to get up but the man quite literally tackled me into the pool.

I was dunked into the pool for only a second before he pulled me out and pushed me against the pool wall. We were in the shallow end, luckily, or unluckily for my case because now he had me pinned to the edge of the pool with his hips against mine and his erection poking at my belly. He was tall, taller than Eli and his limp black hair stuck to his face. His eyes were so heated that they made me flush.

Holy shit. What do I do? I may have been shocked but my magic wasn't. It was reaching out eagerly to him.

"Witch," he grunted and leaned down to inhale deeply. Just like Daxton did when he first lost control in the garden. "I knew it."

Chapter Fourteen
Rosie

His voice was heavy with an accent I couldn't place but it made this whole thing worse. The cat that I had been cuddling with every night since I met it was now a fully grown man.

This couldn't be happening. This isn't real. Could witches even do this?

"Amr? Is that you?" I squeaked and shakily put my hands on the man's chest to push him away. The man only grabbed onto my hands and placed them over his shoulders pulling us closer together. His bare skin heated against mine uncomfortably and felt even hotter than the heated water surrounding us.

The magic that had a grip on my insides went feral and I could feel my entire body shake against my will. I could feel something, a type of magic that surrounded me so thickly I couldn't breathe.

"If I had confirmed it earlier, I wouldn't have lied to you so," he said as a hand trailed down my back and the other pushed my wet hair out of my face. His movements were sweet, thoughtful, but his gaze told me otherwise. "And I wouldn't have sat by while they treated you so poorly."

"I don't understand," I forced out with a shaky breath. Amr's large hand cupped my hip and then slipped under my shirt. "What are you doing?"

When his hand met my bare skin, I almost lost all thought right there.

"Helping with magic," he explained and tugged at the waistband of my shorts.

"Wait, I need an explanation," I rushed out and removed my arms from around him. His face looked hurt as I did. "You were—are—a cat. Is this something witches can do? I don't understand."

"Rosie, I have waited so long to reveal myself to you." His voice was pleading as he spoke. "Watched them have their way with you, abuse you. I promise to explain. Let me just have this. Let *us* have this. I can feel your magic, have felt it for days. You are close to losing yourself."

"Amr I don't thin—" He cut me off by forcing his mouth to mine. He wasn't rough but his kisses and touches felt like they left a trail of fire as they went. Just like his earlier movements each stroke of his tongue had a purpose; he knew what he was doing. My magic reacted violently and I felt it explode outward. That was when I felt his magic intertwine with mine. I let out a low groan.

I *needed* this, badly. I couldn't stop the sighs that escaped my lips and nothing else seemed to matter as his lips trailed my neck. I pushed my over-sensitive body into his, needing any type of friction I could get.

"I am not afraid of my feelings for you, Rosie," he said against my skin. "I have known since I first saw you that you would be mine. I do not care about the vow. I would break it a hundred times over for you."

When his fingers looped in-between my waistband this time and pulled them down, I didn't stop him. The water between us slowed his movement drastically; he noticed as well and growled loudly in my ear. The action caused another wave of heat to flare through me. He lifted me up onto the edge of the pool and wrapped my legs around him. He was still taller than me in this position and stared down at me with a hungry look.

Never in my life had I been looked at with such desire. Even when Daxton was about to lose control there was something else in there with him, pushing him. But this... It was all Amr.

His fingers slipped between my legs and he wasted no time finding my clit and rubbing fast, hard circles in it. I leaned back and covered my mouth with my fist to stop the loud moan that was coming out of my mouth.

"I promise to take care of your magic," he whispered. His hooded eyes never left mine even as he teased my entrance. "Promise to take care of you. I do not care if these feelings are never returned, only that you are safe and happy."

I opened my mouth to say something, anything, but I couldn't as he chose that moment to push two large fingers into me while his thumb still pushed against my clit. My body tensed as his hand slowly, painfully pumped in and out of me. He took his time watching as I shuddered underneath him. The look in his eyes alone would have thrown me over the edge but then I felt something I never felt before.

His magic entered my body then and I came on his hand while seeing stars. The magic that had been forcing its way out of me snapped back into place but Amr did not stop, instead he continued pumping as I came down from my orgasm.

His magic was different than Daxton's. It was like it had a taste to it that stayed on the back of my tongue and had a spicy yet subtle sweetness to it. Amr leaned forward and removed my hand from my mouth to kiss me once more. His mouth ravished mine like he had been starving and I was his favorite meal.

"Let me show you how important you are," he whispered against my lips. "I'll take you to oblivion with me and when we are done, I will worship the ground where you stand." He lifted my shirt up and over my head. His mouth latched onto my nipple and he sucked hard.

I sent a string of curses his way as he trailed wet hot kisses down my body. I almost screamed when his lips met my wetness.

"I will serve you every day," he groaned against my folds before giving me one long lick that had my back arching. "Treat you like the queen you were meant to be."

I came again when he sucked on my clit so hard that this time I did scream.

"I can't—too much." I tried to form sentences, but I couldn't with the way the magic fought inside me and the way Amr's tongue continued to lap up my wetness.

This is insane. He's insane. I literally felt as though he was about to tear me apart.

"I want to bind myself to you, Rosie," he said against me and stood to bring me to his chest. "Will you accept me? Will you allow me to bind myself to you for the rest of my life?"

I took a deep steadying breath that was sucked right out when I felt the tip of his cock prod at my entrance. When I first saw it I was awestruck and now that it was so close to me, I had no doubt in my mind that it would take some work to fit inside of me. I cursed again but this time it sounded like a moan and even my legs were shaking violently.

"Please," I begged him and threw my arms over his shoulders no longer caring about an explanation for all this weirdness.

"I cannot," he said and kissed my forehead. "I won't until you accept my vow."

I tried to tighten my legs around him and force him closer but his hands on my hips stopped me. I groaned and ground against his tip. It felt good, better than good...but it wasn't enough. I needed more.

"I don't know what that means," I whined. Amr teased me by rubbing his hardened length through my folds.

"It means I'll be yours, forever." His voice was almost a growl. "I will protect you, take care of you, love you for as long as I live. I will belong to you as you belong to me. You will never be alone again."

His words swam around in my chest and heated as they passed by. I had never had someone declare any type of love to me before. No one was willing to be with me through it all. It was the ultimate promise and it scared me as much as it excited me.

"Yes, please," I whined again. "I accept your vow."

Something happened then. I didn't realize until later but when I look back I think that I could feel our magic weave together like two halves coming together with a suture.

He pushed into me with one thrust. I felt fuller than I ever had before, but he was still not entirely sheathed inside me. I let out a strangled whine and tangled my hands in his hair. His hands pushed me into him and I rolled my hips to help and slowly, inch by inch he entered me. When he was finally fully inside I felt myself clamp down so hard on him I thought I would come again on the spot.

He slowly pulled out to snap his hips back into mine. Our moans tangled together, and his eyes never left mine as he brought us to the oblivion he had promised. It was perfect, better than anything I had ever felt before. With the magic intertwined between us it was easy to fall over the edge, again, and again.

I would have kept falling, content letting Amr thoroughly destroy me, if we were not interrupted by the door opening. I barely registered it through my haze but Amr did immediately, his eyes shifting to the intruders and a low growl in his chest.

"Mine," he growled and slammed into me even harder. It was only a few more thrusts until he came, sending me along with him. I felt his seed fill me and for some reason, I really liked the feeling of it. It felt feral and claimed me as his. When the clouds lifted slightly I was able to look back at the group of angry and shocked faces that awaited us at the door.

"Amr shift and get your ass over here *now*." I felt the magic in Daxton's voice as he spoke. It weighed heavily between us. Amr wrapped his arms around me and pulled me closer to him. He didn't pull out yet but I felt him relax inside of me.

"You do not control me any longer, boy," Amr hissed. "I thank you for your care these years but as soon as I learned of Rosie's lineage I made my choice."

"You broke our fucking vow?" Daxton's voice cracked as if he was hurt by this news.

"You refused to let me show myself to her," Amr argued back. "I had no choice or else be forced to hide myself forever while you all *abused her.*"

"No one is abusi—" Eli was cut off by Daxton putting his hand on her arm.

"She's not a witch, you broke our code. You know if the others hear about this they will kill you," he warned in a low tone.

I stiffened against Amr and looked up at him but the smile that spread across his face told me all that I needed to know. *Fuck.*

"Amr wait—" I hissed at him but he covered my mouth with his large hand.

"I saw her," he said. I tried to pry off his hand but he stayed firm. "This has to happen Rosie." His eyes shifted to mine and in that moment I knew everything I had worked on up until now would be thrown to waste. "She can control her magic. She is a witch therefore no code has been broken. How did you think I broke the vow boy?"

I bit Amr's hand hard. He pulled back and stared at me but what I thought was a glare turned into something else as he hardened again inside me. Teasingly he rolled his hips sending a flare of heat through me again.

"She accepted my vow," he said rolling his hips against me again, the water splashing around us. "I bared myself to her and she accepted. I showed her oblivion."

"Fucking her against the pool is not oblivion, cat," Rae hissed at him. "Stop that right now; we have other things to discuss."

"Do you wish for me to stop?" Amr asked me and leaned down to whisper in my ear, "My queen."

After that pet name I wanted him to fuck my brains out right then and there. His finger came down to play with my clit and he trusted into me again. I couldn't think for long enough to even care about the people behind us.

"Please." I was cut off by another hard thrust into me. "Fuck, Amr." This time when he thrust into me I rolled my hips to meet his.

"Please what?" he asked calmly. If his dick was not rock hard inside me now, I would have assumed he was unaffected by what was happening between us. "You're so talkative when we are alone and now you have nothing to say?"

His thrusts picked up and I heard what I assumed to be a sigh behind us. I couldn't get the words out of my mouth, his movements were too intoxicating. My brain was turning into mush and the only thing I could think of was the way his hips snapped into me.

He leaned in close and licked my lips teasingly. I opened my mouth to kiss him but he pulled away and looked at me with a satisfied grin.

"Cat got your tongue?" he asked.

A pair of slack-clad thighs placed themselves on either side of me and I heard Eli's chuckle in my ear. She sat behind me with her chest pushed into my back. A hand easily found its way to my throat and the other pinched my nipple hard enough to make me yelp.

Amr sent Eli a glare but did not slow in his thrusts, instead he went harder and gripped my thighs harshly. He let out a deep growl that radiated from his chest.

I leaned back into Eli feeling like I was about to lose myself already.

"This was supposed to be me, you and Daxton," she said in my ear and bit down on my lobe. "And now I come here to see you fucking the cat after you ignored me so?"

She teased my nipple once more before removing both hands only to hook them under my knees and spread my legs for Amr, allowing him to slip even deeper into me than before.

"Wait Eli, no—" I was cut off by Amr's hand coming back to tease my clit.

"Look at you so eager to suck him into your wet cunt," she cooed in my ear. I couldn't help but look down towards Amr's cock pulling out of me fully only to slowly push back into me, giving me the perfect look at how well he fit inside me. "The only better thing would be if that little curse of yours was working. Imagine your skin ripping open over and over every time you take his dick."

I could imagine it. I had grown to hate my curse, but I really couldn't think of anything better than if this moment had just a bit more pain. Something to intensify the pleasure, bring my clouded mind back to reality.

Eli smiled against me and without warning bit into my shoulder hard enough to draw blood. My cry was choked as I clamped down hard onto Amr. The magic around us snapped back to us violently for the last time, knocking the breath out of me. He let out a string of curses finally losing his cool facade. It only took moments for me to feel his hot release fill me. From my position I could see it forcing its way out of me and dribbling down into the pool.

Amr rested his forehead against mine.

"Maybe I underestimated you, cat," Eli said in an amused tone and dropped my legs and stood.

"Get them some fucking clothes," Rae hissed as Amr pulled himself out of me. He gave me an intense kiss before climbing out of the pool and pulling me into a standing position on shaky legs. I flushed when I looked over at Rae and Daxton.

"Rosie, explain now."

Chapter Fifteen
Daxton

How did my own familiar fuck her before I could? It was hot but I couldn't stop the bit of jealously that coursed through me. Eli had given me a look that told me she knew everything that was going through my mind and then still went to go join Amr and Rosie.

Not to mention that bastard broke our damn vow.

I didn't want my hurt on display to everyone but I only wished he spoke to me about it beforehand. I wouldn't deny it to him; I knew he had some weird obsession with her. Fuck, we all did. If anyone knew how he felt it would be us but *dammit*, I couldn't help but feel a bit betrayed.

Amr had been with me through my shit childhood. He would take care of me when my parents discarded me after they abused me. He would tuck me in while I was convulsing and sobbing and force the calming potion down my throat. He was the only other person that knew what I went through *and* had been there to help me through it. It was like my own personal safety blanket was gone.

I pulled off my shirt with a scowl and threw it to Rosie. She muttered a thank you before slipping it onto her small form. I couldn't bring it in me to resent her. I wanted to. God knew I wanted to be pissed about the whole thing but the worst part of it all was I could understand why Amr was so obsessed with her.

She was just as fucked up as the rest of us.

I didn't pretend to know what her home life was but I knew enough to beg for her to stay with us. And then to find out she was a witch? One that had a violent curse put on her from a young age that forced her into a world of silence. I couldn't imagine how hard it would have been to grow up with unmanaged magic gnawing at your being constantly.

"Show me," I commanded her.

Amr kept a firm hand on Rosie and sent death glares to Eli when she brushed up against her side. Eli just sent him a shit-eating grin.

Rosie lifted a shaky hand and out popped a transparent blue jay made out of shimmering red magic. I could feel the burst of magic on my tongue, and it sent a shock down my spine. The trick she had used was one my own parents taught me when I was young to help get rid of my magic. That could only mean one thing and it raised even more red flags.

"Who taught you that?" I asked watching her response carefully. Eli shifted at my side and Rae stayed perfectly still. I didn't want to doubt Rosie. This whole time I thought that Rae was overreacting, but seeing her use magic so perfectly was suspicious. There is no way she could have *just now* found out she was a witch. This trick, even for children with teachers, took months to learn.

"No one," she said too quickly and looked at the ground.

"When did you find out you could use magic?" Rae asked next. She already had her notebook in her hand.

"After the fight," she answered. This time she looked me in the eyes. They were determined and clear. This was the truth.

"So you are not a low-level?" Eli asked. Her voice held a tone I couldn't decipher. Eli's eyes carefully washed over Rosie, waiting for her answer.

Rosie shook her head.

"I didn't know honestly," she said and grabbed the shirt I had given her. It fell to her mid-thigh and made her look like nothing more than a small child.

"You have a healing trait *and* fire," Eli pushed as if she wanted to convince herself this was impossible. I narrowed in on the scar over her left eye.

"Answer the question, Rosie. Who taught you?" I asked and crossed my arms over my bare chest. It had already taken a great deal of strength to not run over there and take magic from her. This beating around the bush was not helping.

"I read it in a book," she explained. "A while ago when I was researching about witches." She paused then gestured towards Rae. "She saw me there— she can vouch that I was studying witches. I started practicing in my dorm after I realized that it was the magic making me crazy."

I looked towards Rae. She sent me a look before she nodded.

"I saw her there studying with Matt but didn't get a good look at what she was reading," she said.

"I did," Amr's grainy voice interrupted. "I was there with her. Rae retrieved me. She was reading about a witch's history. It went over reproduction as well. I wouldn't be surprised if it was in there."

Amr's eyes met mine. To anyone else they would look dull, unfeeling... but to me I saw the pleading there. He wanted me to help her out, wanted me to protect her when we really should be interrogating her.

"We had an idea," I said. "Like Malik said, we assumed this was the case given how your curse lived in your body for so long. We just needed proof."

"Does this..." She paused looking at each of us carefully before continuing. "Change anything?"

Did it? For me nothing changed except that she now had a hold on my familiar while I was left with nothing. As long as I could keep a hold on Rosie, I wouldn't need Amr any longer. Rosie did far more for my magic than Amr ever had and...she had grown on me to say the least. I had never expected to want her to stay around me but even when I was away from her my thoughts still flitted to her.

I wondered if she had enough to eat.

I wondered if she had her coffee for the day.

And most importantly I would wonder if she had finally gotten enough of me. Had finally seen the monster inside me and decided it was too much for her.

But each time I met her again and her wide brown eyes and easy smile showed...I felt relieved.

"No," Rae answered for me. "Maybe how we approach the curse. We would also need to keep this from the school. It looks better to remove a ten-year curse from a low-level than from a witch."

I didn't know the weight of the others' opinion had been weighing on me so much until she spoke.

"Same here," Eli said and let an easy smile show on her face. "What's another witch?"

Rosie looked to me expectantly.

"No change," I said. "But we should talk about what it means to steal a familiar and reassess how to break the curse."

Her eyes widened and she swayed. Amr held onto her before she fell and she sent him a small smile that made my heart twist. When she looked back at me there was a wrinkle on her forehead and her lips formed a pout.

"You will still help me?" she asked, the surprise obvious in her voice.

"Graduation is still two and a half years away," I responded. "And we have come too far to stop now."

This time she gave me a smile I knew was just for me and secretly I held on to it and placed it in a place no one would be able to find.

* * *

"I'm not saying that you're *going to die,* just that I do have the right to avenge my loss," I teased Rosie as she chugged a cup of water.

After we had gotten them both clothed, we decided it was time for a late dinner. I didn't eat earlier because I had to see my parents *yet again* and around them I couldn't stomach anything, so I was starving. The others always had an appetite so it was easy to come to the conclusion that we needed food. The in-home chef whipped us up Rosie's choice of meal, a super sweet and sticky French toast topped with strawberries and whipped cream.

Eli patted her back lightly and sent me a smirk telling me she liked the reactions I was forcing out of her. Amr was on the other side of her, hand still firmly on her thigh. I was not lucky enough to secure a seat next to her so Rae and I were forced to sit on the other side of the dining room table. Rae looked collected on the outside but that only made me certain she was annoyed on the inside. I didn't care really, I just liked interacting with her and making her freak was a nice touch.

"It is true, my queen." I rolled my eyes at Amr's pet name. Rosie's blush almost exploded on her face at his words. He refused to shift back now that his secret had been outed and it only reminded me how annoying he was.

"I didn't know familiars were that big a deal," she muttered and stabbed at the half-finished pile of sugary bread in front of her.

"We will keep it a secret. As it should be; that is why he cannot shift at school or anywhere public," I explained. She nodded before taking a big bite of her food. Eli and Amr watched her with trained eyes.

How this one tiny witch had us all wrapped around her finger was beyond me.

"So how do we remove the curse?" Rae said while taking a sip of her tea. She had refused a plate of food but sat down with us nonetheless.

"Well, if it is latched onto her magic then we remove it from the source," I said simply.

"How do you do that?" Eli asked. "Is there a way to just suck a curse out?"

"No," I said and chewed on an overly sweetened strawberry. "But there is a way to stop her magic. "

Amr gripped the table hard enough so that a chunk broke off and fell to the floor, silencing all of us.

"Absolutely not," he hissed at me, his eyes narrowing dangerously. "I have watched you grow; I know you are not that stupid."

Rosie looked over to me for an explanation. I let out a heavy sigh and ran my hand through my hair.

"If I take enough of your magic there will be a time where you are almost fully drained," I said. "If we keep you in that state for long enough your curse will have nothing to latch onto and die."

Her eyes widened and a smile stretched across her face.

"Let's do it," she said excitedly. Amr gripped her chin and forced her to look into his eyes.

"This could kill you," he growled. "No to mention your magic is strong and there is a lot of it. Who knows if Daxton can handle all of it."

"But you can," I told him. His glare was almost enough to make me cower.

Familiars may be bound to witches but anyone in their right mind knew not to mess with them. Even when they used to skin them for their magic it would take whole villages to bring a single one down and usually only if they had the element of surprise on their hands.

"You don't want to help me Amr?" Rosie asked in a pleading voice.

I felt a satisfied smirk make its way to my face. Of course she would use my own tactics to get what she wanted. Amr looked about to melt under her gaze.

Smart girl.

"Why don't we just find this witch and make her pay?" he asked in a low voice.

"No," Rosie rushed out. "I do not know where to find her and to be honest I don't ever want to find her. She's dangerous."

I looked away from their intense stand-off to meet Eli's eyes. She was slowly lifting her arm off Rosie and she gave me a confused look. Her leg brushed mine under the table lightly.

I saw something weird, Eli told me in my mind. *A house and inside, this lady.*

An image of a woman sitting in front of a fireplace slithered into my mind. She had long black hair and brown eyes. She was drinking tea and her eyes flitted to what I assumed was Rosie in my mind's eye. She opened her mouth to speak right before the image dissolved.

Who is that? I asked.

I think we both know who it could be, she said.

She pulled her leg back just in time for Rosie to look at me with a triumphant smile.

"Let's do it," she said. Her entire facial expression had changed; she was entirely way too excited about something that could possibly take her life from her.

"We will think about it," I said sternly. "We can talk about it after the break… There is no need to rush."

She pouted but Amr sent me a thankful look. It would seem we both had a similar goal.

Chapter Sixteen
Rae

Eli rarely called an urgent meeting but when she did, I knew that it must be serious and I didn't know if I had the energy for this.

Amr turned out to be a great distraction for Rosie and we were able to slip away unnoticed as Amr followed her to her room. I still didn't expect whatever had happened between them to blossom so fast but honestly, I couldn't say that anything surprised me anymore. Rosie's entire existence was unexpected, and this year had proven that what seemed impossible, wasn't.

I felt a twinge of jealously when I watched the way Amr interacted with Rosie. Rosie had been testing me, fighting me the last few weeks only to let up when she ran to me after Daxton and Eli were messing with her before the break. I was glad that I was there to intervene because those two could feed off each other dangerously. They really had no sense when it came to her.

And then the other night happened in my room...

I spent hours going over my words regretting every single line I had uttered as she slept soundly beside me. I had hurt her *again*. And all just to preserve an image for my father. After that, she didn't look me in the eyes again. Amr was right about one thing—we treated her horribly.

Yet she stayed...but for how long would we be able to keep her?

I brought Eli and Daxton into a spare room and sat down on one of the many couches that littered the room. I was exhausted and all these surprises and meetings really didn't help. Father had called me back home one too many times in the last few months and the pressure of it all was weighing on me.

I didn't want this, I thought staring at the decorated room in front of me. The pressure, the money, the status... I hated it all. I wanted to tell Rosie the other night that I would have traded my *luxurious* life for hers in a heartbeat...but I chickened out.

"I saw something when she mentioned the curse," Eli said as she sat down next to me. Her hand brushed mine and I was hit with an image of an old Victorian house and a witch with long black hair who had an eye for designer fashion and a smile on her lips that made me cringe.

"Who is that?" I asked her. She shrugged and sunk into the couch with a sigh.

Daxton stayed standing with his eyes still on Eli. They had a special relationship but every time Daxton's eyes met mine, I knew that he had a cold calculating side to him that Eli would never understand. But I would, and when he gave me that look right now something didn't sit right in my stomach.

"You know something," I noted. He also gave a shrug.

"Is it so out there to think that was *the* witch?"

"And if it was?" I asked raising a brow at him.

"Then she lied," Eli said. "Again."

"It's to be expected that she wouldn't want to see her," I said all the sudden feeling defensive of Rosie. I didn't appreciate the hidden information but without the right coaxing we would get nowhere.

"It was recent though," Eli said. "I have never seen that memory before even when we talked about her curse."

"Maybe she hid it from you," I murmured staring at the ceiling. I was tired of it all. Tired of acting like the protector. Tired of constantly being on guard. Tired of everything.

"You know it's not easy to hide things from my power."

I took off my glasses and rubbed my aching eyes. Distrust and a small bit of anxiety was rolling off them and coupled with the magic of now three witches in this house I could barely distinguish their emotions from my own.

"Her curse magic tastes like an Original's, or maybe it's hers. I don't know but that means that the woman we saw, if she is the person who cursed Rosie...she may be an Original," Daxton contemplated aloud. It was enough for me to stand abruptly.

"Can't we just leave things as they are?" I asked them placing the glasses back on. "Isn't this enough for you? Why must you look more into this? Into something that may not even be a real issue?"

There was a silence before Eli spoke.

"You are the one that wants to know everything, Rae," she reminded. "Are you really willing to just let this part go?"

I sighed and straightened out my clothing before ignoring Eli completely and turning to Daxton.

"Postpone the removal of the curse. If we are so worried about who put the curse on her then it is best to leave it for now and reconvene when we know more," I said trying to keep the anger out of my voice.

"Are you okay?" Daxton asked. His question surprised me; not once had they ever bothered to ask me something like that. It was Rosie who noticed it first, now Daxton?

"I am fine," I assured him. "We just have a lot to do the next few months before the term ends. Including the end-of-summer gala."

"That's so far away Rae, you want us to wait until then?" Eli whined. I shot her a glare.

"Why do you even care about removing the curse? Don't you like it?" I hissed at her.

"I would if it was working!" she grumbled and crossed her hands over her chest.

"Maybe we can tell her about it before we take it from her," Daxton offered. "A last-minute bit of fun before it's gone forever."

Eli's eyes flashed dangerously. I wanted to fight the idea, shoot it down before it could fester in her mind and become something bigger, more dangerous. If there was a part of me that liked Rosie more I would fight it on her behalf, but the exhaustion continued to wear on me and the effort it would take to fight them was too much for me to handle at this point.

"Whatever," I said with a sigh and moved to leave.

Eli called after me but I refused to look back and headed straight to the garden that lay on the right side of the house behind a maze of hedges. It was a safe haven that I had found the first time I was here with my family, and when pretending to be the perfect daughter got too much I would come here.

It's what I needed. A place to escape the pressures of the outside, away from everyone's needs where I could just focus on my own.

It was a pitiful garden with only a singular stone bench and a few tuffs of bushes that would sometimes sprout colorful flowers. Now they were all dead because of the cold weather. It was a cold that rarely bothered me but as I laid down on the cold stone it felt like it invaded my bones and sent shivers up my spine. I took off my glasses and put them in my pocket. Seeing would just distract me.

The cold was unpleasant, but it let me digest my own emotions after being attacked by everyone else's. Anxiety, stress, discomfort, anger, jealously...and even a bit of sadness. Growing up with tutors that helped me learn how to control my emotions, they made sure to teach me my own emotions first before attempting to understand others. It made me realize just how much I hated how things affected me. I hated the sadness and inadequacy I felt when standing next to my father. I knew everything I felt so well that I couldn't just run and hide from it like everyone else seemed to.

Eli was obviously *still* running from her affections, and not just for Rosie.

Daxton was running from his trauma, replacing it with emotions that were more potent.

Amr was even trying to mask the guilt of breaking the bond.

And Rosie... Her emotions affected me the most because they were a complete mess. A tangled web of guilt, anxiety, hurt, fear, and anger. It was worse when I understood that I was the cause of many of them.

She wanted to belong. She had told me that in the night we tangled together. A night that brought a warmth to my chest that chased away the coldness I had been feeling. And I tore that dream out of her hand and ripped it to shreds. Reminded her she was nothing to us and the fear and insecurity that was buried so deep in her shot up to a height I thought was impossible.

It's so ironic, I thought in my head.

I came here to calm down and gain some space but like always, my mind went back to them. The group we forged for ourselves against all odds. It would be a lie if I continued to believe that Rosie was not a part of it. I knew I was lying to myself; I shouldn't have tried to equate my own lie to the act of trying to protect the group.

I stiffened when I felt a ball of anxiety near the beginning of the maze. Of course Rosie would come to me like a moth to a flame. She seemed to have the talent of being where people didn't want her... Well, that's not *quite* right.

I did want her here. Maybe that's why she was called so strongly.

I held my breath hoping that she would turn back. A twig snapping near the entrance of the garden was all I needed to know that she had seen me. I sighed but did not move from my spot.

"I'm surprised your *fans* let you go unattended to." I didn't know why I wanted the words to hurt but they didn't. She was amused by them.

"I had to sneak out," she confided. I turned to watch her step around the corner. She wore the shirt Daxton had given her in the pool paired with her own sweats. Her hair was still wet and even though I knew she was a stronger supernatural being than I gave her credit for, I worried she may catch a cold. "Said I was going to the bathroom, *alone*."

"And you came to ruin my peace instead," I said and turned back to the stars. This time it hurt her just a bit and then there was the guilt I had become so accustomed to.

"I was just looking for a bit of peace of my own," she explained and I heard her shift. "I can leave."

Now it was my turn to feel a bit of guilt.

"Stay if you'd like," I said.

There was a burst of satisfaction in her chest and before I could think too hard about it she moved to sit on the ground near the bench I was lying on. She laid her head back, resting it on my stomach and also looked up at the sky. She turned towards me and I had no choice but to look straight into her brown blurry eyes.

"Is this okay?" she asked in a whisper.

I nodded and looked up to the sky to try and dislodge the warm feeling she sent through me.

"It's getting too much for you," I noted unable to help myself. "Their attention."

In the dark I couldn't see the blush but I could feel the embarrassment rise in her.

"It's just a lot very fast," she admitted. "I thought handling you, Daxton, and Eli was a lot but Amr takes everything up to another level. I didn't expect *that* to happen."

I let out a snort.

"That's an understatement," I muttered. "You know he fought Eli when you first left us for Malik?"

I should have shut my mouth. Maybe it was the silence that made me more willing to talk or maybe it was the exhaustion, but either way the words seemed to force themselves out.

"Really?" she asked.

"Blamed her and everything. Saying Malik was here for her and that because of her feelings you got in the middle of it."

Guilt. More guilt. And...happiness?

"Eli must have been pissed," she said with a small chuckle.

"Very," I said. "But she also felt bad. Blamed herself."

Rosie paused and a small breeze made its way through the garden. Even though it was cold my body was warming up at an alarming rate with Rosie leaning against me.

"I didn't know she cared that much," she whispered. There was doubt in her heart as well.

Don't say it, Rae, I chanted to myself. *Don't be this stupid. Don't. Don't. Don't. Do—*

"We all do," I said honestly. "In different ways obviously but we all... care." I winced at my words and moved my head to face away from her.

God. The feelings that rose in her were better than any drug I could get my hands on. Addicts chase that artificial feeling of happiness and warmth but Rosie radiated it like a bomb that had gone off. It was almost so strong that I could feel it bubbling up in me as well. Before I could stop it a small breathy chuckle made its way out of my lips.

"Did you just?" she asked and the feelings just kept coming.

"It has been a while since I felt feelings like that so strong and pure." I turned to look at her regaining my confidence. Her eyes were wide and there was the unmistakable ghost of a smile on her face. "Especially from you."

There was a guilt that crept up on her but it didn't outweigh the positive feelings.

"That was nice of you to say," she said and her hand found mine. I intertwined our fingers.

It's okay, I assured myself. *This will be just for us. Just this last time. No one will know.*

"I'm sorry," I said my voice barely above a whisper. "For making you think you didn't belong. For telling you we were only here for the curse... I was wrong."

I groaned when her emotions flared out again. She was going to kill me with this shit.

She leaned forward quickly and pressed a kiss right to my lips. They were just as soft as I remembered. I moved to pull her closer but before I could she was standing up and leaving the garden. I looked over to her dazed.

"Thank you," she said with what I thought was a smile. "I missed talking to you like this."

Without wasting another minute she ran out of the maze and it was almost like she was never there. The only indication was the warmth in my chest but it took me only a second to realize they weren't her emotions. They were my own.

"Me too," I whispered into the darkness.

Chapter Seventeen
Rosie

I had never thought that I would be driven to such lengths but they pushed me to it. In the limo on the way back to Winterfell I was met with an angry face, an amused one, and an indifferent one. Amr was purring on my lap in his shifted form, knowing damn well that he got the best of this deal and that, unsurprisingly, irked the others.

After the pool incident they had been fighting all break to see who would get to sleep in my room. It left many nights where Eli, Daxton, and Amr all suffocated me while they wrestled for room in the guest bedroom. Rae of course just stood by and watched them make fools of themselves, but a girl needed some alone time.

Especially a girl on a mission who had yet to get any good information out of Daxton about his parents. It had been two weeks and I was barely able to get a peep. Matt and Malik would no doubt be hounding me as soon as I stepped onto campus. Cause wasn't that the whole point of this stupid vacation?

"A rotating schedule," I said in a firm voice. "I can't handle you all climbing into my bed at once. Winterfell beds are small and if you won't stop fighting, I will be forced to bunk with Rae and lock everyone here out."

Glares were sent to a shocked Rae. She shouldn't have been surprised though after our conversation in the garden. She was a safe space and she had to have known that after she finally apologized.

"What if we agree to share," Daxton asked. There was a heat to his eyes that made me squirm. I had refused anything sexual with all of them since the pool incident. Amr of course was content with that and chose every time to rub in the faces of the others that he was a man and wouldn't be swayed by such a thing as lack of sex.

"We can arrange it," I said. "But I want to sleep alone three nights of the week."

Eli was going to protest but I raised my hand to stop her.

"And Amr?" Daxton asked with a raised eyebrow.

"Up to him what he wants to do on those three days." I looked down at the cat in my lap and smiled. "Is that okay with you, cutie?"

There were chuckles from Eli and Daxton but Amr stayed unfazed and just nudged my face. I took that as an agreement.

"What the hell?" Rae asked stirring me from my moment. I had rarely heard her curse and when I looked out the window of the limo I couldn't help but curse myself.

The normally bare streets were filled with cars of all different makes and models. Demons and witches littered the area celebrating and cheering as we passed. Some were climbing on cars, others riding the shoulders of another; one witch even sent magic up in the air that burst into light blue fireworks. I had never seen demons and witches so close together and so happy. In the crowd I was even able to make out some low-levels as well.

When we got closer, I was able to make out the crowd of news stations and reporters that were anxiously looking at each car that passed. A thrill went through me. Was something happening? Maybe a famous politician or movie star? I couldn't wait to see for myself. As a low-level I never got a chance to meet anyone famous.

I was waiting on the edge of my seat with excited butterflies in my stomach until the reporters got a look at our car and descended like bats in hell. They knocked on our windows and yelled things I couldn't make out.

"Rae?" I asked in a squeaky voice. "What's happening?"

"For once," she said in an almost worried tone, "I don't know."

I swallowed thickly. Maybe they mistook us for someone? Or maybe Rae's family did something in the government?

When we came to a stop near the front of the school, people were pushed out of the way by people dressed in all black suits and serious expressions.

"Eli, are they a part of *The Fallen*?" Daxton asked.

"Yes," she replied hesitantly.

It wasn't until Malik, Matt, Maximus, and Claudine walked towards the door did I understand what was going on. They were all wearing the same thing: a black button-up that was rolled up to show their tattoos, with matching black slacks. Only Claudine and Maximus showed the clear skin on their forearms but there was no mistaking their part in this.

"No," I whispered in horror. They planned something and I didn't like it one bit.

They lied...again.

I shot a panicked look to Rae but it was too late. Malik forced the door open and held out his hand for me to take it. He had a smile on his face but his eyes told me to move, quickly.

"Let's go, Rosie," he said sweetly. "It's time to introduce you to the world."

He grabbed my hand and yanked me out of the car. The first thing that hit me was the noise. The previous serene environment of the campus was now rowdy and distracting. It made me freeze in place and my heart pounded in my chest. Matt gave me a pitiful look while his siblings just nodded at me. I could hear the trio climb out of the car behind me but my gaze was locked onto the crowd. Amr meowed in my arms but I sent him a look that told him to trust me...even if I didn't trust what was happening.

As we walked the volume seemed to increase significantly. The wall that the men in black had built with their bodies was barely holding back the enthusiast and almost downright frenzied crowd. On reporter with got as far enough to climb on the shoulder of one of them men and yelled at us while throwing her blue microphone. It bounce on the floor in front of us but I couldn't pay attention to it much longer as Malik forced us forward.

Questions were yelled at me from the reporters that were being held back by the black-clad gang members. I couldn't make them out but I could hear a few words like "games," "winner," "low-level," and "hybrid."

"I'm sorry I couldn't prepare you," Malik whispered in my ear. His hand was firm on my forearm. "We are introducing you to the world as a hybrid, a powerful one at that."

"Why would you—" He cut me off with a glare.

"You will still be expected to complete your task but the playing field is different now," he explained. "I will explain it to your harem in a way that looks like you knew nothing. Go along with it."

Did I ever have a choice?

I shot another look down to Amr. *Damn it all.* I turned, hiding my mouth from view.

"This is my new familiar," I told Malik.

His golden eyes held fire in them, and I saw his hand twitch forward like he wanted to throw the cat across the campus.

"Demand his secrecy, *now*," he growled in my ear. It was an order; his magic waved through me in an instant.

"Amr everything you hear between Malik and me must remain a secret," I commanded. The magic swirled around us and he let out a soft meow, but from his eyes it didn't look like he was angry. I only hoped he understood and could forgive me.

"Rosie!" Eli yelled from behind me. I snapped my head to look at the trio. They were behind, guarded by Matt and siblings. Eli's eyes were narrowed and her heaving chest visible even from a distance. She aimed a swift punch at Matt but with a wave of his hand her punch stopped just short of his face. Matt said something to her that made her bare her teeth at him but she withdrew her fist on her own before her flaming blue eyes met mine.

I'm sorry, I mouthed to them.

Eli was obviously pissed, Daxton looked conflicted, and Rae just looked straight up uncomfortable. I had never seen them so out of their element before. When I looked at them they always had their own distinctive air of confidence around them and they always knew what to do. That image of them was shattered as I watched them share a look of confusion.

Malik led us through the campus until we met with a stage that had definitely not been there before. The principal and Mr. Falkner waited there for us with a row of chairs behind them that housed some of the teachers. Below the stage near the ground there was a crowd of both students and spectators that awaited us. My heart stopped when I was met with long dark hair and brown eyes.

"Why?" I hissed at Malik, panic clawing at my throat. Next to her was a familiar set of blue eyes but his hair was black now instead of the blonde that would have been a dead giveaway of his lineage.

"For support," he said. "Don't worry, they will leave right after this. If you haven't already noticed there are hundreds of my men guarding this area. You are safe. They are safe."

I didn't feel safe. I felt seen in a way I didn't want to be. I could barely breathe and he pulled me up the steps of the stage. I felt a calm wash over me that I knew to be Rae's and suddenly I could finally breathe. The action made my eyes cloud, but I tried to shake it off and stand straight.

If I was going to face my doom I might as well look like I was as strong as they portrayed me to be. Amr was plucked from my hands by Matt and given back to the trio.

"Ms. Miller!" Principal Winterfell said as we stood on top of the stage. "There is our champion!"

His purple hair was in intricate braids, and he wore a golden suit that shone in the light. His violet eyes twinkled as we walked towards him. He may have also been a pawn in this game but there was no doubt he would benefit greatly from everything happening today.

Mr. Falkner gave a soft smile to me as Malik led my shaky legs to the center of the stage. I couldn't help but notice that he seemed to be everywhere. In a puff of smoke there were two enormous pictures of me that appeared on either side of the stage. Dirt stained my clothing and face, and I looked utterly exhausted. *It was from the games*, I realized.

On the bottom it introduced me as Winterfell's first hybrid game winner. This was what Malik meant... They were introducing me as a *hybrid*.

"Thank you to everyone who has come out to support such a joyous occasion!" the principal said as he waved to the crowd. His voice was amplified and spread across the square with ease. People began cheering.

"We are here to award our very own champion and introduce her to the world!" he yelled and then looked to Malik with a smile. Malik looked at me and then sent a dazzling smile to the crowd. My breath was cut short when I saw it. Even through his scarring that smile could stop anyone's heart.

"This is Rosie Miller," he said and gestured towards me. "I have been appointed as her spokesperson due to a condition that bars her from speaking but luckily for you, there is a group of highly talented students that have made it their mission to cure her condition. They have made strides in their work and now she is able to speak short sentences at a time. That group is over there."

A magical spotlight shone on the trio. They all had surprised looks on their face, but Rae was the first to snap out of it and wave to the crowd.

I knew Malik, Xena, and Ezekiel had plans that were going to change the world, but was this really what was supposed to happen? I had trouble connecting this with everything they had told me. If anything, this just seemed like a gross show of fanfare, if not rubbing it my existence into the faces of many of the high-level students that filled the crowd. They had already looked at me with such contempt and anger when I won, and now as they are being forced to watch as I come out to the world... well that's just salt on their wounds.

I already felt my list of enemies triple as soon as I walked onto the stage. The eyes in the crowd watched me closely, searched my form for anything array. I knew they were looking for any reason to be unhappy. My anxiety told me to focus on them but as my eyes scanned the crowd I also saw pockets of low-levels and witches that looked overjoyed. Some were jumping with excitement and wide eyes while others just had a smug grin on their face, no doubt ecstatic at the thought of someone liked me beating into those pampered high-level students.

Well now they know why, my mind said wryly.

"Rosie here is the first of her kind," Malik continued looking over the crowd. I met Xena's eyes. She smiled and nodded as if to assure me this was the plan all along. "Under the guise of being a low-level she entered this academy, but I am here to tell you that she is no mere low-level."

Malik walked around me before continuing.

"She is the first ever fully functional witch and demon hybrid." He had finally said the words that I had been dreading. The crowd was silent for a moment before erupting into chaos. There were shouts, cheers, whistles. The reporters on the side were chattering away on their respective news channels and the lights coming from the cameras felt like they were going to blind me. I wanted to curl into a ball and die, or at least cry.

I met Ezekiel's eyes now. His disguise did almost nothing and his expression held a soft emotion that made my throat close.

I didn't want this. I never wanted this.

Rae's power pulled away abruptly and when I met her eyes they were narrowed in my direction.

Calm yourself, child, Ezekiel's voice said in my head. *Trust us. Trust Malik.*

"I will now turn this over to Rosie so you can hear from her yourself!" Malik finished and looked at me expectantly.

Incite them, Rosie, Ezekiel said. *I know you have it in you. I saw the fire. Take these feelings and use them for change.*

I cleared my throat and centered myself. I looked towards the trio, trying to act like it was them that I was talking to and not hundreds of people in the crowd.

Repeat after me, he said in my mind.

"I cannot speak long so this will be short, but the first thing that needs to be said is thank you to the group over there. They have been integral to my success here." I paused to try to stop the shaking in my hands. "This is just the start of my journey. I am here to fight for our rights... *All* our rights and I will not stop until we are equal." I took a deep breath and listened for Ezekiel's words. "All it took was a chance. One chance to prove myself. One chance to show everyone here that I am just like you. For low-levels and humans alike I am here to be that reminder for you. If I can do it, you can too."

When I finished my speech there was a silence once more and then cheering.

"I would like to mention that there will be new security implementation starting from today onwards. Students will have to prove their admission status and there will be a curfew. Reporters and T.V. crews will not be permitted on these grounds. And for the sake of everyone here, please do not try to contact Ms. Miller. We would like her to finish her schooling here so that she can face the world prepared to make a change."

There were a few disgruntled sighs and comments from the crowd but many did not voice their opinions too loud.

"Now," the purple haired manic said with a chilling smile. "For our other announcement!"

The magical posters on the sides of the stage changed to showcase something akin to a stock photo of smiling young adults, but they were all very obviously low-levels. The words on the posters read *The Home of the Melting pot.*

"You'll like this," Malik leaned to whisper in my ear.

If I wasn't so frozen by the stares and camera's on me, I would have smacked him right then and there but the last thing I wanted to be aired was me showing just how *unworthy* I was as a specimen for this role I had been handcrafted for.

"Starting next year, we will be opening enrollment to low-levels and hybrids alike," the principal said, showing his teeth. "Thanks to the trial Ms. Miller went through we are no able to say that it *is* possible for high-levels and low-levels to coexist in one place. We had some bumps in the road but because of her work we are excited to take our next steps into allowing for a more diverse education experience."

I can't tell if this is a good thing or not. Obviously Malik had put this idea in his head, he would never go as far as this... but what's the point of all this?

"Rosie will act as a mentor for these students and help guide them in their paths to full integration in this school." He said giving me a smile. *This sucks.* "A high-level demon and a witch will be named as a spokesperson in the next year so that all three groups will be accurately represented. We are excited for what is to come and cannot wait for next year."

There was a chattering then outrage. There were shouts from the crowd and all the sudden lights started shooting across the crowd. I gasped as Malik pulled me off the stage. My eyes tried to seek out Xena and Ezekiel but they were already gone and in an instant the lights and smoke cleared to show a few demons being escorted out of the crowd by Malik's men.

"You did great Rosie!" Matt said from my side as soon as we descended the stairs.

I could barely register that we were moving into a building. Noises were buzzing in my head and I felt my magic shift under my skin uncomfortably. I needed *out*. The pushed me into a room with couches and chairs, something I had never seen before at Winterfell.

"I didn't know you could actually speak that well," Maximus said with a hint of teasing in his tone.

I wanted to be worried about where I was, if the reporters would follow, if angry demons would follow... but I couldn't catch a single thought.

"Come on, let's sit you down," Malik said from my side.

I didn't even feel like this was happening to me. I couldn't process it. All I knew was that I had just outed a secret to the entire world and now my life would *really* never be the same. When I blinked my eyes a few times Malik's scarred face and golden eyes came into view. He was saying something, but I couldn't focus on it. The only thing I felt was pure blinding rage.

I snapped my fist forward. It connected with his nose with a sickening crunch, but I was not done yet. I tackled him to the ground and straddled his waist.

"You bastard!" I yelled and brought my fist down again. He caught this one. I brought my other fist down; this one connected with his eye.

"Fuck Rosie let me explain," he hissed and struggled to grab both my flailing hands.

"Explain what? That you just outed the one thing you told me not to? Did you even think about how I felt about this?!" I let out a screech and pulled his hands away from his face and reared my head back only to bring it back down onto his.

That was when two strong arms grabbed me from behind. I didn't care who it was; I was ready to kill. My vision was red as I kicked and screamed at Malik. He slowly got up to face me. His eyes were swollen and his nose bloody. I conjured a ball of fire in my hand and threw it towards him. It was doused before it could reach him.

"Calm," Eli whispered in my ear. It was her arms around me. Rae and Daxton stood in front of me blocking my view of Malik.

"I'm going to fucking kill that bastard," I said and grabbed the back of Daxton's shirt trying to force my way through, but no one let up. My magic flared around me wildly. "You lied to me. You told me to trust you!"

"Rosie. Calm," Malik said from the other side of the two in front of me. "I'll explain everything to everyone."

Rae looked back at me, and I was hit with a wave of calm so strong it felt like I had been doused with cold water.

When I stopped squirming Rae and Daxton parted to show me a fully healed Malik.

"First of all, Eli," he started, "I lied...partially. I was here for Rosie *and* you."

"Not surprised," Eli grumbled behind me.

"Second, our gang has been contracted by a client to provide safe harbor for Rosie Miller as she adjusts into her role," he explained. "A role which as you can now see is more important than anything our gang can achieve."

"What is her role in this?" Rae asked with a bite to her tone.

"She will fix the divide in this world," he explained. "She is the first success of her kind. Don't you see? We have been divided for so long we didn't even know it was possible. She is proof our unions are successful."

"You put a target on her back," Rae hissed. "And a target on ours."

"No," Maximus said appearing from the corner of the room I had overlooked. "We did you a favor. Now you are known as the people who have an in with the first ever hybrid. People will flock to you for information. You have the power in this situation."

Rae shifted her stance. Of course, she would love the ability to get a one-up on everyone.

Don't be bitter, we are here to help you, Eli said in my mind. *Your hybrid status was news to us but it seems like you knew as little as us about this show so we are willing to let this slide... But no more secrets.*

"It is an act of good faith," Malik said. Matt showed himself near his side shooting me a pitiful look. "Don't fight us, instead work with us. A truce."

I wanted to scream at him.

"Fuck you," I spat at Malik.

"You have no choice in this Rosie. You haven't had a choice since you were born into this world," he explained with a calm voice but his eyes were narrowed. Reminding me of my place.

I stood straight and relaxed in Eli's grip.

"I'm good," I whispered. "Let me go."

Eli listened and slowly unwrapped her arms from my waist. I searched for Amr and patted my chest when I met his eyes. He jumped into my arms without hesitation. I fed him magic and immediately felt a smidge of anger leave me. I cracked the side of my neck and put my game face on before pushing through Rae and Daxton.

Malik eyed me warily. He and the Originals wanted a martyr to do their bidding, they would have to treat me like a bigger part. I wouldn't forget my role here, but I also wouldn't let them push me around. I am more than just a pawn in their game.

"She scares me," I heard Daxton mutter behind me.

"It turns me on," Eli commented. I heard the smile in her voice.

"You want me to be the face of this *little project*, you talk to me," I hissed at him. His eyes widened before a small smile flitted across his face.

"Just as you said. You will be a face, a light in an otherwise dark world. Your presence will push others to believe anything is possible." The words *even if it's a lie* flitted across the space unsaid. "People in the government will come to you. Try to get you on their side. This is how you will make the real difference."

"I am a nineteen-year-old college student," I said. "I don't know how you expect me to do anything other than be myself."

"That's good enough for us," he said in a sincere tone. "You said so yourself. You just want to see us brought together."

"Who sent you?" I asked. Matt shifted and looked towards the floor obviously not expecting my answer. Not expecting me to still be working for them. Malik knew though and his gaze that was locked on me only fueled me forward.

"A concerned third party," he said. "A friend of your biological parents is all I can say."

The group stayed silent behind me.

"They are letting their own child do their dirty work for them," I hissed.

"I only take the work for the money I don't know what to tell you, Rosie."

He was too good an actor.

"And them?" I asked and gestured at the three behind me. "You expect me to think you gave them this publicity for no reason?"

He cocked his head and shoved his hands in his pants.

"I told you," he said with a sigh. "Don't put me through the wringer. You know me, you can trust me a little. Your *lovers* just tend to get in the way, and I think if we worked together, it would be easier."

Rae put a hand on my shoulder. I gave her a look and she nodded.

"What do you want us to do?" she asked and shifted closer to me.

"Get her closer to influential people of course. Make sure she can use her status to our advantage," Malik said with a smile. "You both have families in the government, no?"

Understanding washed through me. What a bastard.

"Advantage for what?" she asked.

"Just fight for more equal rights," he said with a shrug. "Or at least that's what my employers say anyways. They have no other requirements."

"You're not telling the full truth," Rae noted. "Don't try to fool an empath."

"Fine," he said and held his hands up. "They want her to partner with your father particularly."

His words sent a chill through me. What was this angle?

Rae looked at him hard for a moment before looking towards me.

"We should go," she whispered. I nodded.

"Not so fast," Malik said. "She has to be accompanied by one of us at all times. And we have secured a safe location for her off-campus."

"We are not leaving her," Rae insisted. I felt both Eli and Daxton step closer to me.

"I didn't say you couldn't come." He had a shit-eating grin on his face. "But we will travel separately and in different cars. Rosie will be with me. Eli with Matt, Rae with Maximus, and Daxton with Claudine."

"There is no fighting this," Maximus said to our group. "It is important we keep a low profile."

There was a pause before anyone spoke. Rae looked to me for an answer. I nodded and turned, stepping towards Malik.

"Let's go."

Chapter Eighteen
Rosie

Malik walked me towards a car I didn't recognize after we had separated from the group. He had forced me to give Amr over to Daxton for the time being and I felt like I was walking straight into the lion's den. His grip on my shoulder was hard and only reminded me of the spew of lies we just fed the people who had stood by my side when they thought I was under attack.

"I can't tell you how pleased I am with you," he whispered low in my ear. His tone sent shivers down my spine, but it didn't erase my anger.

"I'll tell you once more, fuck off," I hissed as he opened the door. I sat down in the passenger seat and before I could move, he reached over to buckle my seat belt. His face was close to mine as he paused to look into my eyes.

"We don't need to play pretend anymore, Rosie," he said sweetly. "Though I did like the way you had them wrapped wound that pretty little finger of yours."

I rolled my eyes ignoring the flush in my face.

"I don't need to add to my already full plate of suitors," I hissed. "I'm still pissed at you."

"Yes, they do seem quite a handful," he whispered, his eyes traveling the length of my face. "Maybe wrapped around your finger wasn't the right way to put it." His hand gripped at my thigh. "Seems like you have them wrapped around the sweet cunt of yours."

I clamped my hand over my mouth and tried to lean back into the seat away from him. Coming from him these words were more degrading than embarrassing.

"Don't fuck around," I hissed behind my hand before swatting at his face. He laughed and ducked out of the car to only reappear in the driver's seat a moment later.

"You were the one begging for it in Montnesse not too long ago," he reminded with a smirk. "What happened? Got your fill with the group? Or was the familiar finally the one that satisfied you?"

I sent him a glare.

"What is it?" I asked. "You get turned on after getting thrown around by a woman?"

He shrugged before sending me a smirk.

"Never complained about getting rough in the bed," he replied.

I rolled my eyes. I couldn't tell what I thought about this Malik. He was brash, a little rude even and more similar to Eli than I had ever seen before.

"Did you know he could shift?" I asked. "Amr I mean."

"I guessed," he said.

There was a silence between us as I looked over the crazed people on campus.

"You could have warned me," I hissed. Malik wasted no more time and pulled out of the campus. People were still crowding around but luckily, they couldn't see us through our tinted windows.

"I couldn't have actually," he said suddenly serious. "Rae is right, you really can't fool her power. The only reason you get away with it is because she wants to fuck you."

I stared out the window feeling the tiredness of the last few months weigh on me. If this was my life now, there was no telling how long I would last. I had gotten lucky because the people surrounding me were stronger than me, smarter too. By luck I was born as a hybrid and besides that there was nothing I could offer this world.

"What was the real meaning of this?" I asked in a whisper and wrapped my arms around my hollow-feeling torso.

"You need an in," he replied. "A real one. Not just siphoning information from Daxton."

"I don't know what you expect me to do," I muttered.

He paused and I chose that moment to sneak a peek at the man I once thought was the only person in this world to see me. He was relaxed as ever in the driver's seat, he had even unbuttoned the top few buttons of his shirt. His eyes lazily met mine and he gave me a small smile. A real one. Once that reminded me of the time when we went to the beach. When I was ignorant to the real world.

"What you do best," he said. "Get people to like and trust you. Only then will you get good information. That's when we can strike."

I let out a long exhale and looked back out the window. He drove us through the streets expertly but I could tell we were nearing our destination as he slowed.

"So you are saying the information I gave you wasn't enough."

He let out a soft chuckle.

"You gave us near nothing," he said. "But you did good. You got them on your side. Now when you officially enter their world, they will have no choice but to share information with you or risk you ruining their reputation."

"You don't feel bad about this?" I asked suddenly furious again. "You lie to Eli's faced. My face."

"It's not a total lie," he argued with a small frown. "Just keeping the truth from her until she's ready."

"Like that's any better," I hissed.

"Don't be pissy that you have to do something you don't want to, Rosie." His grip tightened on the steering wheel and his voice turned dangerously low.

"You were the one that forced me into this position by pretending you actually cared for me." My voice cracked when I spoke. "I thought we were friends."

I expected him to soften then but instead he pulled into an underground garage and the car's movements became more violent.

"Don't blame me for this Rosie. Blame the people who are out murdering our own. Fuck, blame Eli even," he growled as he pulled into a parking space and shut off the car. He leaned towards me again, invading my space. The air between us seemed to evaporate and suddenly I couldn't breathe. "If Eli was smarter about her job, listened for once, those bastards would have been dead by now."

"What do you mean?" I asked. The words were small in comparison to his.

"Why do you think Eli even met Rae and Daxton in the first place?" he asked and let out a bitter laugh. "She had the chance to end this while you were still pleasantly unaware of your parentage. If she had, we would have never gone to these lengths."

He moved to open the car door but I gripped the front of his shirt in a panic.

"My parents?" I asked. "The low-levels, I mean."

His face deflated slightly as he digested my question.

"They are in a safe house," he explained. "I paid them a visit with Matt and we moved them into a secure location over an hour away... No one will find them."

I let out a heavy sigh and sat back in the seat.

"You still worry about them?" he asked. "I saw your house...your *father*. I know it wasn't easy on you."

I looked over him hesitantly. His gaze was soft and I was hit with the image of him at the beach, back when things were easier. But then I was reminded that he was a liar... They all were.

They didn't keep the only promise I had asked of them. It was all a lie. A mountain of information hidden under a pleasant, comforting lie that was meant to make me feel better. Feel needed. Feel important.

"That's information you do not need to know," I said.

His face twisted in anger and he left the car with a huff.

Chapter Nineteen
Eli

There was rarely a time where I had chosen to reign in my raging emotions. I never felt the need to, not like I owed it to anyone anyways. If they made me mad, I would make them pay. I would hunt them down and deliver revenge in the most violent way, enjoying the feeling of the person's life slipping from my hands.

It had started to change when Rosie came into my life.

Because she wasn't horrified with who I was, and largely wanted nothing to do with me, I became interested. Obsessed really. All my thoughts turned to her. I wasn't nice about it nor was I gentle but I couldn't get those *fucking* brown eyes out of my mind. On many an occasion I had tried to swallow my anger for her because as much as I loved that fearful pained look on her face... I hated the betrayed one. That one cut deeper than I ever thought it would and when Rae fucked up last time I thought for sure I would never get close to her again.

Now was no different.

I wanted to bash Matt's brains in as I sat mere inches from him as he drove us away from the school. I had fantasied about it in my head millions of times already. I would wait until we stopped and in one movement smash his head against the window so hard the glass broke. He would look at me with his stupid eyes full of shock and I would get so excited—

"You're quiet," he noted as he slowly turned onto a small street. His eyes washed over me suspiciously.

"Just figuring out the best way to kill you," I said with a smile. He raised an eyebrow at me. The *fucker raised an eyebrow* at me.

"Don't like to be the last to know something, is that it?" There was an odd tone to his voice I had never heard before. I sized him up from the passenger seat. He wasn't scrawny but he was always hunched in on himself and his demeanor was as stupid as a fucking puppy. But this was different, he prepared for this and now he was facing me without a care in the world.

"How did you even join Malik's faction?" I hissed at him feeling the anger that I had been holding onto slip. "A pathetic low-level like you would never be seen as an authority figure. They would eat you alive."

He let out a small amused huff as he turned his eyes to the road. That was the thing that set me off. I didn't care that we were driving; I sent my fist flying towards that smug look on his face.

My fist stopped mere centimeters away from his face and his only reaction was a blink and a ghost of a smile that played on his face. Thick plant stems snaked up my arm and forced me back into the seat. I let out a growl.

"Don't disturb the driver," he chided. "It's dangerous."

There was a small light to his eyes when he spoke. He took one more turn into an underground parking garage where I saw Malik getting out of his own car with an angry expression. When his eyes met mine the anger was gone and replaced with the cool facade he always had.

This is weird, I thought as I eyed Matt again. He put the car in park and left the car. Only once his door closed was I free. I kicked the door open slamming it against Malik's. When I stood and glared at both of them they only had a bored expression that infuriated me more.

Rosie got out of Malik's car, our eyes only meeting for a second before she cast them downwards. I was ready to let my anger out on those fuckers but Matt switched faster than I could blink. His bored expression turned into a nervous one and he let a small smile grace his face.

"Rosie," he said in a higher pitch. "You made it in one piece."

That *fucking liar*. He deserved a goddamn award for this performance. How many people did he have fooled? Given Malik's small smile as Rosie walked over to them and the warning look he sent me, I had a feeling he knew about everything.

"Why did the *client*," I hissed the word to Malik, "contact you, and not Damon?"

Malik just gave me a look as if I was asking a childish question. It was the same gesture every time and I had to literally bite my tongue from speaking. His hand was raised, he had a polite smile on his face, and his eyebrows were pushed together. A metallic taste spread across my tongue.

"Because Damon is incompetent, you know that," he said and looked towards the third and fourth car that entered the parking garage. Both Rae and Daxton gave me deadpan looks as they passed.

"Talk to me after the break, you said," I reminded and walked over to Rosie just so I could grab her from his side. "Is that what you were referring to?"

Shock fluttered through Rosie's thoughts and I thought I heard an echoing of Malik's voice but it was gone in seconds as she focused her attention on the way I held her close to me. The way my hand felt as it brushed across her neck.

She was playing with my power and only now did I realize it. Her thoughts turned sexual quickly and it didn't take long for me to understand what her goal was. Looking back at our encounters recently I had been surprised by the confidence she had gained and how much more open sexually she was.

It had all been a way to get one up on my power. I couldn't tell if I was mad or impressed.

"Something like that," Malik said and turned to walk toward the end of the garage.

I pulled Rosie along with me and sent a look to both Rae and Daxton. The two redheads were still on either side of them and when I passed the long-haired man only then did I realized we had seen them before too.

A new feeling started to rise in me. One that I hadn't felt for a long time. Anxiety and a small bit of fear. We played right into their hand. And as the barred glass door came into view with men in all-black suits guarding the inside did I realize how deep we were in.

"Fancy new headquarters," I said in a light voice. Rae met my eyes before repositioning her glasses.

Malik scoffed and walked into the doors that were now being held open by men.

"Each of you have rooms," he said and waited in front of the elevator. One of the goons hurried over and pressed a series of buttons. "Not like you'll use it anyways."

"Her guard dogs are protective," the redheaded woman said in an airy voice. Her eyes shifted over to Amr who was still nestled in Daxton's arms. "Guard cat."

"More like they can't keep their hands to themselves," the man said. He glared at me as he spoke.

Rosie's mind flashed to when he had interrupted us in the hallway. It was out of the way, they had to have been following her to know we were there.

"You didn't enjoy the show?" I asked. "Rosie can be *quite* the performer when she wants to be."

Rosie panicked in that second and I saw it again, the house, the woman... then it was gone.

"You're disgusting you know that? I swear—" The man stopped when Matt turned around and gave him the hardest look I think I ever saw come out of that man. His glare burned with a fire that got my blood pumping and even the temperature around him seemed to drop.

The elevator dinged in that second and gone was the changed Matt and back again was the nervous one. I caught Rae's eyes and I knew she saw it too.

We all piled into the elevator and I pushed Rosie to the back covering her with my form. Her eyes met mine hesitantly and I saw her face flush.

Do you want to give them a show? I asked in her mind. She jumped as the doors closed.

It's not the time Eli, she said her eyes shifting side to side.

That's all you can seem to think about though, I pushed. There was a throat clearing. Malik's, I think.

Not with so many people around. Even in my mind her voice was but a whisper.

A feeling of giddiness swept through me. They thought she was this gift to the world, a treasure that would change the tides...but would they still think that with her riding my hand? I knew by now she would let me do it in front of all these people. She liked to act embarrassed, but she played out the fantasy in her mind. The way my fingertips would tease her thigh and slip under her skirt. Everyone would be forced to watch as she squirmed and moaned my name.

It was perfect. As my fingers started their journey to the place she wanted me most the ding of the elevator interrupted us. Rae's hand on my shoulder was the one to finally pull me away from her after everyone filed out of the cramped space.

Malik gave me a hard look after I left the elevator with Rosie tucked under my arm.

"This whole floor is ours," he explained and opened the door nearest to the elevator. "This is Rosie's."

The interior design screamed Malik and I was disappointed by how much she liked it. The floor was light but the sun shining from the floor to ceiling windows made the material almost shine under our feet. Almost every piece of furniture from the bar stools to the couch was either a dark grey or black. Hell, even the kitchen appliances were black. There were a few rooms blocked off but other than that the open floor plan gave me an unobstructed view of the living area and kitchen.

For the third time Rosie's mind slipped and it was all I needed for me to unwind my arm from her shoulder. She had seen Malik's place. A place I had been to many times before. I knew because when she saw this place she had the same thoughts I had, that the decor reeked of Malik's taste. How else would she know that?

Rosie, unaware of what just happened, stepped forward and flashed a hesitant smile to Malik.

"This is nice," she commented.

"A special request from our employer," Malik replied.

Rosie's smile dropped instantly and her eyes fell to the floor. While the attention was on her I brushed sides with both Daxton and Rae.

We need to talk about her, I sent them. *I saw something.*

Rae gave no indication that she heard me. Daxton's eyes shifted for just a second before landing on Rosie.

"Of course," she said with a nod then turned to us. "I think I will shower and rest, I am a bit tired."

I wanted to point out it wasn't even late afternoon but the words died in my throat. I wasn't hurt by her secrets, I wasn't even mad. But I could feel the divide between us. One that I never felt before. She had been an open book up until now and now everything just seemed to be hidden behind an invisible wall that I could not get behind.

"We will give you time and return later," Rae spoke on our behalf. "Amr can stay with you."

Rosie's eyes lit up when Amr pounced on her from Daxton's arms.

"Your places are the three to the left of this one," Malik said. Rae nodded and left from the door we just came in. The room was tense as we left and Rosie sent me a look that told me she would rather have us stay than be stuck with them... I am not sure I believed that though from her mind and it only aggravated me further.

We ducked into the closest apartment and found it to be almost identical to the one Rosie was in. Daxton shut the door and locked it behind us. He paused a moment, listening before waving his hand in the air. A burst of red magic came out of his hands and shot across the room. It was transparent and more akin to dust than the magic I had seen until now. It seeped through the cracks and Daxton gave a sigh of relief.

"They are not watching these apartments," he concluded.

"I didn't know you could do that," Rae mumbled and pulled out her abused notebook before writing this information down furiously.

Daxton just shrugged as if this wasn't one of the most impressive pieces of magic I had seen him do.

"Had practice...at the house," he explained. I nodded not wanting to hear any more about his abusive childhood. It stirred things inside me I didn't want to remember, things that I tried very hard to forget.

"Speak," Rae commanded, her eyes zeroing in on me.

"She has found a way around my power," I said. Both Daxton and Rae shared a glance. "She focuses on one thing and lets that take control of her thoughts. Something that has *obviously* been distracting me. She slipped though, around the others. I saw the lady and her house again. She has seen Malik's previous house too."

"That lady was at the ceremony," Daxton said.

"Where?" Rae asked without looking at him. Still focused on her notes. Her brows were pushed together and her back hunched.

"You didn't see her? She was like ten feet from us," he said. "Did you?"

I shook my head.

"Most likely the *client*," I mused. "Anything else weird about her?"

Daxton nodded and ran a hand through his short hair, taking a steadying breath.

"She was powerful. She wasn't using magic, at least I couldn't feel it, but I could still taste the magic around her. God, I could even smell it," he said and licked his lips at the thought. "Even just that taste was enough to set my magic ablaze...but I obviously had other things to think of doing that time."

"So the witch Rosie has thought of, met most likely, was there while the news was broken to the world that the first ever hybrid beat a school of demons, is most likely the person behind all this, the same person who now has us all holed up in this apartment building for *safety*," she said in one breath and finally looked up to meet my eyes. "I miss anything?"

"They want Rosie to infiltrate the government," I replied in a deadpan. "Work her hybrid magic and change the world."

"Kinda a big one," Daxton said.

"And they want her to work with my *father*." There was a venom to her voice that made a shiver run through my body.

"I don't get that part," I confessed. Rae sighed and shifted on her feet.

"My father has been integral to the human-demon relationship. He has worked for many years to keep both sides happy...but now we have to add hybrids to that. It only makes sense that they want her in on those discussions," she replied.

"She is an uneducated, untrained nineteen-year-old," Daxton noted.

"We are missing something," Rae muttered.

"She's the face," I said remembering Malik's words. "Just a reminder, nothing more. Someone else will have to do the work."

"She had been in the dark as well," Rae said. "I felt her surprise and anger. She was upset and scared when Malik and his team ambushed her."

"But she knows more than she is telling us," I pointed out.

"Maybe she cannot tell us more," Daxton offered. "Maybe Malik has a stronger hold on her than we thought."

Rae finally slapped her notebook shut and put it in her jacket's inner pocket.

"Looks like we have no other choice then," she said and walked back towards the front door.

"What are you doing?" I asked. She turned to give me a look.

"It pains me to admit that we have no power here," she said. "There is too much unknown and the only way to find out what they *really* want is to play along. So we will wait, observe, and strike when we have enough information."

"And Rosie?" Daxton asked.

"The closer we watch the pawn the easier it will be to see the intent of the player," she said and showed us a small smile before opening the door. "So, keep doing what you are doing. Get her to slip. Force the information out of her in any way you can."

I gave Daxton a smirk before following Rae out of the room.

"Let's have fun with her tonight."

* * *

Malik and his lackeys were long gone when we stepped back into the apartment even though we had been gone for only a few minutes. Rosie was curled up on the dark couch with a grey blanket and was sleeping so soundly I could barely make out the rise and fall of her chest. Amr was curled next to her and gave us a sleepy stare.

Rae looked around the apartment and opened one of the two doors that the apartment had.

"I'll sleep in here," she said in a firm tone. "You guys can sleep with her."

"No need to tell us twice," I said and walked over to Rosie's form on the couch.

Before I could bend to pick her up Amr jumped at me shifting in midair. He towered over me and glared down at me as if I had committed some grave mistake. I had gotten used to his naked form now and seeing it didn't faze me but still my lips twisted in disgust.

It's his personality, I concluded.

"I will carry her," he said and scooped her up in his arms carefully. "Children like you do not know the first thing about being gentle.'

"She doesn't like gentle," I said with a scowl not wanting to be pushed around by a damn cat. Regardless of my feelings I still followed him to the other room.

"It's a bit early to sleep," Daxton commented. He also chose to follow behind Amr.

"No one is sleeping," I replied.

Amr sent me a glare as he tucked Rosie into the bed. She had barely shifted in his arms.

"Let her sleep," he ordered and climbed into the bed, spooning her from behind. I gritted my teeth at the possessive look that crossed his face.

I shared a look with Daxton before jumping into action. I lunged forward fully preparing to take the other open side on Rosie's bed. Daxton's hand snapped out to grab my wrist and force me back. I let out a growl and sent a kick to his chest but he dodged and tackled me sending us both flying to the floor.

"Get off," I hissed at Daxton. I didn't want to actually hurt him but he put his full weight on me and the only way out now would be through fighting.

"You have had your chance," he said in a gruff tone.

"I have not! That stupid cat has been monopolizing her time!" I hissed and hooked my arm around his neck rolling us over.

"You idiots," I heard Amr growl on the bed.

"Are you serious?" Rosie's sleep-filled voice came from the bed. I looked up and was met with both her and Amr's glare.

"Choose now," I ordered. Daxton went slack under me, waiting for her answer.

She let out a sigh and her eyes drifted to Amr.

"Can you just shift to cat form?" she asked.

"Do you not crave my body against yours?" he whispered against her and brushed her hair behind her ear. "It has been too long since I felt your body with human hands."

A blush coated her face.

"It's been a week, Amr," Daxton hissed from under me.

"It is not my fault you children fumbled," he said and placed a kiss on her shoulder. "If you so wish to spend time with them you only need to tell me, my sweet."

I wanted to gag at the pet name but the blush on Rosie's face only got darker.

"Rotating schedule," she said. "You were all in my bed last night, but they are right Amr. You can either stay in cat form so they have room or can sleep on the couch."

Amr gave her a smile and tilted her face towards him and gave her a first small kiss on her lips, then with a sly look towards us he deepened the kiss. Rosie let out a soft moan and relaxed into the kiss. Watching her with him caused my stomach to clench. He was so gentle yet commanding and she all but melted in his arms.

Daxton hardened against me. I sent him a smirk and sent him a mental image of him taking her from behind on the bed. He let out a groan of his own. I could hear Amr's chuckle from the bed.

"We can finish this later," he told Rosie. "Not sure how much longer those kids can hold on. Call me if you need anything."

"She won't," I growled and pulled Daxton to a standing position. Amr left the bed, his erection painfully obvious. Seeing it at his full length I almost asked him to stay. *Almost.* It had been far too long for us to be alone like this, I couldn't give up this chance.

With a wink Amr walked out of the room. I set my gaze on Rosie and she surprised me by lifting her shirt over her head giving me a full view of those soft perky breasts that were just begging for my mouth.

God I was so in trouble with her.

Chapter Twenty

Rosie

Ever since this morning my clit had throbbed painfully every time Eli smirked at me. I remembered all too well what kind of lover she was and she had been restraining herself considerably recently. Daxton on the other hand... His gaze ignited a fire in me that I couldn't control. The way his darkened eyes looked over my form hungrily made me want to cover myself up but instead I gripped hold of the hem of my shirt and bared myself to them.

Amr's kiss had already made me so painfully aroused that the feeling of my shirt against my nipples caused friction that sent jolts through me.

Eli was the first to stalk towards me, her eyes narrowing on my breast and without a moment to waste she swooped down and took a nipple into her mouth. She bit down harshly drawing a yelp from me. I spotted Daxton already stripping the rest of his clothing off, giving me an unobstructed view of the tattoos that lined his torso and chest. Once his pants were fully off he teasingly pumped himself once and ran his fingers over the piercing on his head.

I moaned and arched into Eli's mouth.

"On your side," she commanded. "Face me."

I did as she said and she climbed into the bed with me, her lips leaving a trail from my breast to my neck. One hand came to pinch my nipple while the other dove down my pants. I gasped when she rubbed my clit through my panties. Even though there was a cloth between her and my skin it didn't feel like her motions were teasing. She rubbed my clit with purpose.

Daxton joined the bed behind me, his hands on my hips and his lips leaving a fiery trail up my back and over my shoulder. Eli's mouth met mine and her tongue roamed over every inch of my mouth. Daxton pushed the sleep pants I had been wearing down, leaving me in just underwear.

"This is how I always wanted to take you," Daxton whispered in my ear. "In between me and Eli, at the mercy of us." His hands pushed down my underwear. Eli paused to let them fall only to plunge her fingers straight into me once they were off. My moan was covered by her mouth. Daxton's hand returned to my hips and he guided me against Eli's fingers, pushing me in rhythm with them.

"She likes it like this, don't you Rosie?" Eli asked pulling away from my mouth before she pulled my bottom lip into her mouth to bite down on it. I felt myself clench around her fingers. "You do."

"You don't know how hard it's been to sleep by you," Daxton said. And lifted my leg to hook it around his own giving Eli deeper access to me. My breath caught when her motions picked up, her hand hammering into me harder, faster than ever before. "And not think of how your tight pussy will feel once I finally shove my cock inside you."

I gasped at his words.

"Keep going Dax," Eli purred letting go of my lip. Her gaze watched me as I started to unravel in front of her. "The slut likes it."

"I thought about taking you when you least expected it," he said, his own fingers trailing his hip. Finally, I felt the length of his hard cock against my inner thigh just inches away from where I needed him. "When you were deep asleep, only to be awoken by me pounding into you, just like this..."

Eli removed her fingers, and I felt her guide him into me slowly. I couldn't breathe as I stretched around him. I could feel the cool metal of the piercing as he pushed into me deeper, and deeper, and *holy shit.*

I could imagine it just how he described it. He would do it slowly so I wouldn't wake suddenly, and then when he was fully in he would grind into me just like now. That was when I would wake and boy what I would give to be awoken like this.

"She is imagining it, she likes it." Eli purred. Her fingers found my clit again. "Slowly Daxton."

Slowly Daxton pulled out of me only to fully enter me in one painstakingly slow thrust.

"God you're so warm and wet," Daxton moaned against me. His tongue licked the length of my neck and he thrust into me again, this time harder.

With Eli's ministrations and Daxton filling me like he did, I was going to come fast. I whined when Eli's hand left my clit but I found a new thing to be excited about as she unbuckled her pants. I slipped my hand inside her underwear and was met with her warm wetness.

"Fuck, yes like that," he groaned and picked up his thrusts into me. Eli devoured my mouth as my fingers found her clit. I tried to emulate the furious circles she did on me not too long ago and the most delicious sounds left her lips. It was in-between a moan and a whine, and it sent me tumbling right over the edge.

Daxton's magic entered my body as I lost myself but I was brought back quickly with the sound of Eli's voice.

"You learn quickly," Eli said and gasped when I teased her entrance. Her slickness was intoxicating and I wanted to hear more, see her come undone like she had done to me so many times before. I entered two fingers into her. "Good girl, teach me what you learned."

I heard Daxton groan from behind me.

"Take off her pants," he commanded. "I want to see you fuck her." His thrusts slowed and I pushed her pants down with her help. My mouth watered at the sight of her swollen blonde pussy. I trust my finger in deep and she ground against me hard, her head fell back, and a small breathy moan left her mouth.

"Does that feel good?" I asked softly teasing her without slowing my fingers. Daxton chose that moment to trust into me hard causing me to cry out.

"Yes," she answered, her heated blue eyes meeting mine.

Daxton's hand snaked around, and his fingers squeezed my neck. I shouldn't have liked the way it caused my breathing to slow or my mind to fog but my body had other plans. I loved the way they threw me around, dominated me in ways no one had before.

With newfound energy I pushed my fingers into her faster. Her hips rhythmically met my hand and I could feel her tightening around my hand.

"You're going to come," I said in a teasing voice. Her eyes snapped down to mine and with a growl she pulled out my hand.

Her hand brushed the one Daxton kept on my neck and he chuckled against me.

"You made her mad," he teased and pulled out of me.

Eli grabbed the back of my hair and forced me in-between her open legs, right into her folds.

"You are not in control here," she growled and forced my mouth to her lips. I gave her a long lick only to suck on her clit as hard as she would let me. "Fuck yes, good little slut. So good. Daxton."

At the command he came behind me and lifted my hips entering me in one thrust. These ones were faster, harder, and I knew that if I did not get Eli off right now I would be orgasming the second time before either of them had.

I went to work licking up her entrance and pushing my tongue inside of her but it didn't have as strong of an effect as I wanted. Her hand was still tangled in my hair and I went back to sucking on her clit. When her fingers tightened and her moans became audible I knew she would be coming soon.

I worked hard against my own orgasm, trying to hold on as long as possible. Daxton's nails dug into my hips forcing my back into him. He was feral, demanding, and gave me no mercy. In this position I felt him hit a spot that forced loud whines out of me and made my legs shake. When his fingers came to my swollen nub I couldn't stop myself from tightening around him again.

The magic sharing was different this time. With Amr I could taste it, but with Daxton it was like our two magics combined together before pushing back into us, rocking my body as it reentered. It settled in me providing a clarity I had been missing the last week.

I could hear Eli moan as I attacked her swollen bundle of nerves with my tongue. I wanted her to come...*needed* her to. She did just that as I gave her clit one last suck. Her hands tangled in my hair and she forced me closer to her throbbing pussy. I let her take control of my movements, enjoying the way her hooded eyes looked down at me.

Her eyes wandered to Daxton as he pounded into me still. I was still riding off of our magic sharing when his thrusts became more violent. I couldn't even let out a sound as he took hold of me. Eli smirked down at me and forced two fingers deep into my mouth.

"Don't tell me you are going to come again, are you?" she cooed. I couldn't answer even if I wanted to.

Daxton slowed his thrusts and pulled me back by my hair so that my back was flush with his chest. This time I did yet out a yelp at the pain searing down my scalp. The heat traveled all the way to my stomach.

Eli crawled over to us and pushed my knees apart. I couldn't see him inside me with his hand forcing my head back but Eli's gaze told me everything I needed to know. I was open to her and she had the perfect view. She reached to tease my clit before feeling where Daxton and I connected. Daxton let out a growl as her hand moved lower and I assumed she was fondling his balls.

She straightened out and leaned close to my face, licking my lips but refusing to kiss me. I let out a whimper and began to shake violently as another orgasm was ripped out of me.

"You have a lot to make up for," she whispered against me.

She twisted my nipples harshly as she looked over me. Her gaze was calculating but heated. She was enjoying this, being in control.

"You will not leave this room until we have played out every dirty little fantasy in that head of yours," Daxton said in a low voice near my ear.

Their threat didn't matter to me. If anything, it only pushed me faster over the edge leaving me convulsing between them as Eli watched me with a dark satisfaction.

They really are doing to destroy me, I thought as Eli smiled at me.

* * *

They were not kidding when they said they were going to play out everything. They let me fall asleep in the bed between them but on multiple occasions I was awoken by them to start where we had left off.

The first time was with Daxton between my legs as he ate me out. Eli gave him careful instructions as she watched over us with a glint in her eyes. He followed her every word and only stopped when I was on the brink of passing out.

The second was Eli's fingers as she held me from behind. She was rough, uncaring as she did it but it only made me come faster. Daxton held my legs open as he forced in his fingers alongside Eli's stretching me more than I thought possible.

The third time was just like we had fantasied. Daxton slowly entered me from behind. I could feel it in my sleep state and remained in a dazed sleep-like state, moaning and writhing against him until Eli bit down on my nipple bringing me back to the real world.

The only time when I awoke to something other than their hands was when Daxton lay in the bed breathing erratically and shuddering. He was facing away from me and I could see the tensing of his muscles under the lights. It had to be close to morning as the sky outside the windows seemed to lighten a tiny bit. Thinking it was a nightmare like Rae had, I slowly unwound Eli's arms from my body and wrapped my arms around Daxton's bare torso. He jerked and grabbed my wrist so hard I had to bite my lip to keep the noise from coming out.

"Daxton," I whispered. "It's okay, just a nightmare."

He turned his head so he was facing me. The whites of his eyes were bloodshot and there were tears that still fell from his eyes down his face. Looking carefully, I could see that he had been crying alone in the dark for a while. It broke my heart to see him so vulnerable and hurt; I had never thought someone as put together as him would ever show this side to me. I immediately started to panic. I had no idea how to comfort him, nor did I feel like I had a right to.

"It's not a nightmare," he said with a sniff and pulled me closer to him. "It's a memory."

He continued to shudder and shiver in my arm. I hesitated slightly before rubbing soothing circles in his back. When his breathing was finally under control he loosened his grip.

"It's okay," I said softly. "Just go back to sleep."

"It happens after I am...intimate with someone," he explained, not looking at me. "I know your situation was different, or at least I hope it was. But I feel like you... I don't know, maybe you would understand."

I tried not to freeze at his words. I didn't want him to tell me. I wanted to know because I cared for him in my own sick and twisted sort of way but any information he would give me would be handed over to Malik.

"You can tell me anything, I'll try to understand," I promised.

"My parents use to share magic with me growing up," he said, his breath catching. "My father was more...adamant about sharing and even made a special room for me when I was growing up."

"Daxton..." My voice cracked and my eyes began to sting.

They were monsters, just like Malik had promised. I imagined Daxton as a young witch happy and smiling only for his parents to come in and destroy all of that. *What kind of parents would do that to their own son?*

"They use it to promote their pure magic. People don't know what it really means...but other witches know, and they look at them with disgust. I hate the pity they give me."

"I'm going to kill them," I said surprising myself. I stiffened, waiting for Malik's magic to clamp down on me...but nothing happened.

"I wish it was that easy," he said with a sigh. "I just...wish I wasn't as affected by it anymore."

"You are strong, Daxton," I whispered against him. "They hurt you in ways that parents should never dream of doing. They deserve to pay for what they did."

He let out a soft sigh.

"Thank you," he trailed off. "For listening, and for not pitying me."

This boy was trying to break my heart.

"Anything for you," I whispered.

"Can we stay like this?" he asked burying his head in the crook of my neck. I nodded and ran my finger through his hair. I vowed that I would kill them—if not me, I would be the one to lead them to their painful death.

Suddenly I did not feel bad about what I had to do. Those bastards deserved everything that was coming towards them.

I began to fall asleep like that, with Daxton breathing deeply against me. Eli found us like that not too long later and scooted closer.

The last thing I heard was Eli's voice as I fell asleep.

"You help us more than you realize," she whispered.

* * *

The next day I was the first to wake and I stood dazed near the window looking in the living room, watching the people below start their days. School didn't start for another few hours but there was no way that if I climbed back into that bed we would ever get to school. I had once thought that them together would be too much to handle and I was almost right. They worked together so well laughing and joking as I came undone between them over and over again.

It was hard to forget the way Daxton sounded last night but I knew there was only one way to help him...and I hoped he wouldn't hate me for betraying his trust like this.

Warm arms circled around my waist. I jumped and met Amr's slit eyes. His dark hair fell over his face but I still caught the slight smile that played on his lips. He was dressed now in a loose shirt and sleep pants. I had rarely seen him in clothes and I couldn't help but wish to see him like this again.

"Were they good to you my sweet?" he asked and kissed my forehead. "I hope you are not hurt."

I shook my head and leaned into his warm embrace. He smelled nice but a bit musky, animalistic. I twirled his long dark hair around my finger.

"I am fine," I said. "Just tired."

I looked up at him when he let out a small chuckle.

"I know, I heard you last night," he said. "Come."

I felt my face heat as he pulled away from me and led me to the kitchen. I had been so dazed that I didn't notice Rae standing there until now. She was in her school clothes and leaned against the counter with a mug in her hand. She turned to gather something on the counter as we walked over.

I sat on the stool in front of the bar wincing as the pleasant soreness between my legs intensified. Amr stood behind me, arms circling around my waist and head buried in my hair. Rae turned around to hand me a glass of what looked like iced coffee.

I raised my eyebrow at her.

"I heard you too," she explained. "Looks like we will both need a bit of coffee to get us going this morning."

I took a sip of my drink shyly.

"Don't be embarrassed, love," Amr said from behind me swinging my hair to one side to plant a kiss on my neck. "Your moans are the sweetest I have ever heard. Just your voice alone can send me into oblivion."

I choked on the coffee and was thrown a napkin by Rae. She took a sip and looked over us as if predicting this type of speak.

"It's good coffee," I said wiping up my mouth. "Thank you."

"My pleasure," she said with a lingering look.

The shock that ran through my body was far too big for my dazed and exhausted mind to comprehend. *My pleasure? Didn't she still hate me?* I eyed her suspiciously as I sipped my cup. The night in the garden was something but I fully expected her to forget about it and act like her usual stuck-up self.

"There is a gala coming up that will require all of us to attend," she said casually.

My heart stopped in my chest. Is this *the gala?*

"Can I come?" I asked quickly. A small smile tugged at her lips. It reminded me of the way she looked that night under the stars.

"I was going to ask if you would like to come," she said. "Given your... new status."

"Keep it from Malik and I'll even dress to impress," I said with a teasing tone. Her eyes lit up. Amr's arms tightened around me.

"I'm coming," he said.

"You never came before," Rae said eyeing him.

"Rosie will be in danger. More so now that she is in the public eye," he explained.

"You can act as my date," I said. Rae raised an eyebrow towards me. "I mean no one has seen what you look like right? But they will definitely remember Daxton's cat, no? At least if we have him in human form he can protect me better."

"I'm not supposed to be in this form, Rosie," Amr said from behind me. I didn't like the tone in his voice. I leaned back into him and looked up to meet his eyes.

"Do you prefer your other form?" I asked him seriously. He swallowed thickly before responding.

"It has been all that I've known for many years," he said.

"That's not what I asked," I said and turned to look back at Rae. She was watching us with a careful eye.

"I prefer this one," he said in a whisper.

"Then you can be in this form whenever you please," I told him. "If you would like I can ask Malik to have the principal enter you as a new student so you can attend school with us."

There was a pause. I looked back up to Amr and he captured my lips with his own. It was a sweet kiss but the longer he held it the more meaning it felt like it had.

"Let me think on it," he said. "The school part I mean. I would like to be in this form during the other times."

"Perfect," I said with a small smile and took a sip of my coffee. I looked around for my phone and found it on the counter where I had left it last night. I pointed to it and Rae handed it to me with a questioning look.

I smiled at her and dialed the only number I had on this phone besides my parents'.

"What could you possibly want now?" Malik's grumpy voice came through the line. "Do you know how thin the walls are here?"

"Don't act like you didn't enjoy it," I teased. "I need money."

There was a pause from the other line.

"Why?" he asked.

"Because before this I was a poor low-level with barely anything to my name. Now I have a part to dress for," I said and gave a dramatic pause. "Unless you want me to embarrass your *client*?"

There was a groan and a string of curses from the other line.

"Fine, I'll send it in a few moments," he said with a growl and hung up on me. I placed my phone on the counter with a big smile.

"We will go get you some new clothes after class today," I told him.

"You don't have to Rosie, spend that money on yourself," he said behind me, his voice filled with emotion.

"I only need a bit," I said honestly. "And I want to make sure you are comfortable with me. I guess I'm kind of like your keeper now?"

Amr chuckled behind me and placed a kiss on my head. My phone pinged and I looked to see a notification from my bank pop up. My jaw dropped when I saw the amount that was transferred to my account.

"He must want to impress his client," Amr muttered from behind me.

This was in my control too, I guess. I smiled to myself loving the flush of confidence that flitted through me. I looked towards Rae.

"You have the best style out of all of them, want to help us find some appropriate clothing?" I said.

"How much did he send you?" she asked taking another sip of her coffee.

I turned the phone screen to her and her eyes widened slightly.

"What did you do to get him to send you fifty thousand dollars?" Rae asked eyeing me suspiciously.

"You heard the conversation," I said innocently. "I guess this is his way of saying sorry for outing me to the entire universe."

Rae nodded.

"Ask him for a hundred grand next time," she said and I couldn't help the chuckle that left my lips.

* * *

I was thankful that they had torn down the makeshift stage from yesterday. Reporters still lined the campus but they were much tamer than the day before and instead of yelling and banging on the car's windows they just watched and waited.

We were in the same groups as yesterday and the tension between Malik and I was almost tangible. He barely spoke a word since I got in the car and kept silent as he drove us to school. I noticed he was also in his uniform today.

"Why are you coming today?" I asked.

"The rankings," he muttered in an unamused tone. I looked down anxiously at my skirt. I didn't want to go running around in this thing. I would probably have to stop by my dorm to change. "The winner of the games will remain as one until someone challenges them in the next game and wins."

I let out a sigh.

"That's good news," I said.

"Any more information on Daxton?" he asked.

I weighed my options. I didn't want to breach what he had told me but there was only one way to make sure that they paid. I no longer cared about hurting Daxton by taking away his parents, only hurting him by telling things he would rather keep hidden. By betraying his trust.

"He didn't say it in these exact words..." I trailed off. Malik's eyes drifted towards mine. "But I think his parents abused him."

He snorted.

"Most powerful parents do," he said.

I was enraged by his attitude. He wasn't there to see how affected Daxton was by this.

"No," I growled. "Worse than that. I think..." I swallowed the sourness in my throat. "They shared magic with him. Forced him to share magic with them... Sexually."

The silence only made me feel worse about outing Daxton's trauma in such a way. It wasn't my right to do this. I was lucky to have received that type of information and I should care for it. Care for him...

I'm sorry, Daxton.

"That will work," he said after a moment. "Good job."

Those words were the ones that made me start resenting myself. They made me regret ever sharing anything with this group. I didn't much care for their cause...not if this was what I would have to do to accomplish it.

"You will..." I paused searching for the words.

"Kill them?" he asked. "Yes, slow and painfully. They will pay for what they have done to this world...and Daxton."

I swallowed and tears fell from my eyes.

"Good. *Good.*"

Chapter Twenty-One
Rosie

s usual the students were talking amongst themselves as I entered the classroom but this time all the chatter came to a full stop when I came into view, and then they began whispering amongst themselves as if their voices weren't carrying over to me.

"I thought she was a mute?"

"She lied about being a low-level to seduce Eli."

"It was Daxton she was seducing."

"I heard Rae hates her guts, won't even look at her."

"I bet it's a lie."

"Has to be. Everyone knows witches and demons can't procreate."

A warm hand landed on my shoulder. I jumped and glared at the intruder.

It was Mr. Falkner standing there with the same polite smile he always had.

"You are in on all this aren't you?" I asked quietly.

His only response was a small smile.

"Your *friends* are waiting for you in their usual seats, Rosie," he said in a polite tone. "Wouldn't want to keep them waiting especially after they have helped you so much with your *condition*."

I gritted my teeth and looked over to the seats. As he promised, Eli, Daxton, and Amr were waiting for me. Amr was sitting on Daxton's desk, his tail whipping around him anxiously. I felt a wave of nausea when Daxton sent me a smile that normally would have warmed my heart.

I didn't deserve his attention.

I nodded and walked past the staring students.

"Sit by me today," Eli said. "I'll let you even hold the cat."

I gave Daxton a questioning look. I was willing to take Eli's save but didn't want Daxton to think that what he said changed anything between us. Daxton reached out to brush a kiss across my knuckles then dug in his bag to pull out a bottled coffee. The twist my heart did almost brought me to my knees.

"I'll get you a better treat later," he said. "I didn't have time, the witch was rushing me this morning."

"You're too sweet," I commented. He blushed lightly.

"Alright class, welcome back," Mr. Falkner said and I scurried to my seat next to Eli. "We will conduct the testing of the rankings again today but I wanted to explain some more ground rules and how it pertains to the games."

He gave me a pointed look and I felt the entire room turn to face me.

Eli let out a chuckle and squeezed my thigh under the table.

"The winner of the games will stay at rank one until they get surpassed in the next games. Meaning Rosie, you may sit out of this one. Everyone else must continue and if you have an issue with the current rankings..." There was a light to his eyes when he spoke. "Then just work harder to stand a chance at the games next year."

"A whole year?" some high-level from the middle row exclaimed while shooting daggers at me.

"Weren't you like twentieth?" Daxton asked in a deadpan voice. There were a few chuckles from around us.

"Remember!" Mr. Faulkner said drawing the class's attention. "In our society strength is *everything*. The games are used as a way to determine how well you would survive when faced with a real-world life or death situation. It is our job as a school to prepare you for what awaits you out there."

"We aren't in medieval times," a girl in the front row said with a snort. Mr. Falkner raised an eyebrow at her.

"No we are not," he agreed. "But the fighting between classes has yet to stop. Just because we have grown as a society does not mean we need to stop protecting ourselves. The same could be said for military. Each country needs something to protect themselves from outside threats. You need to train to protect yourself from the same threat." He paused as he looked over the class. His eyes stopped at me meaningfully. "Just because we cannot see the fight, does not mean that it does not exist. But by all means if you think you are ready to face the world, go ahead. This school does not need you or your money."

No one dared to fight back and there was an uncomfortable air that settled around us.

"Alright!" Mr. Falkner said. "Bring your stuff, class will be dismissed after the rankings."

The students got up silently and shuffled out of the classroom one by one.

"I heard we are going shopping after class?" Eli asked and pulled me up with her. Amr meowed loudly and launched himself at me. I scrambled to catch him.

"Yes we are," I cooed at Amr and placed a kiss on his head. "This little boy is going to be getting a full wardrobe."

"You know you are talking to a grown man right?" Eli reminded and ducked close to whisper the rest. "Wait, you know that very well don't you? Weren't you riding his dick not too long ago?

I blushed and refused to speak to her as the memory of Amr taking me against the pool flashed through my mind. My stomach clenched at the thought.

"Why does he need clothes?" Daxton asked pulling me from my train of thought.

"Ah, I will be allowing him to walk around in his other form," I explained. "He may even go to school with us."

"Rosie that's against the rules," Daxton said hurriedly. "The other witches will either get you in trouble or try to steal him for themselves."

"He will always be around us," I said. "We will protect him. And whose rules are you talking about?"

Daxton gave me an exacerbated look.

"The entire witch community?" he said.

Malik's words from the town rang through my head.

If they live outside of this town, they or someone in their bloodline was exiled. As soon as the thoughts showed up in my mind I turned my mind to last night when they woke me up for one of the many other rounds.

Eli chuckled and patted my head before walking us out of the classroom. Daxton jogged behind us and I tried my hardest to stop thinking of his words. Tried to push our sexual encounters to the front but the more that Daxton kept talking the more things slipped.

"I'm serious, Eli, Rosie," he said and brushed my shoulder. I tightened my arms around Amr and tried to shrug off Eli's arm but she kept a hold on my shoulder. "They have a long line of rules that if you don't follow you'll get punished. Tortured, stripped of magic, exiled, anything you can think of. They have archaic rules, ones you shouldn't mess with."

The rules that his family followed may not be the same as inside the town. Thoughts flashed through my mind. Why would they be okay with this type of slavery? I couldn't stop the thoughts of Malik introducing us to the town flow through my mind.

Fuck. Fuck. Fuck. God damnit Eli let go now, I hissed in my mind.

I'm sorry what was that? she pushed back. *Your mind is worse than a sex addict's. I can't make out what you are saying through all that noise.*

A relief so violent crashed through me that I almost tripped.

You couldn't hear me? I asked hesitantly.

"Don't ignore me Rosie," Daxton hissed. "My parents are a big part of keeping witches in line and if they found you not only stole my familiar but are now allowing him to walk around in his other form, they will be angry."

Not for long, I thought but tried to drown it out by anything else. This time it was a loud annoying song.

"Let her do what she wants," Eli said and pulled us out of the building and towards the field. "If your parents have a problem they will have to go through this *client* of ours."

The panic of keeping my thoughts hidden had to have been messing with me because I couldn't help the image of Xena that flashed through my mind. This time Eli paused but did not mention it. Again, I tried to remove her arm from my shoulder, but it was useless. My panic increased, and I could barely keep my thoughts straight.

When Malik and Matt came into view Eli paused.

"Do you know when Matt decided to join *The Fallen?*" she asked. We accidentally bumped into Daxton. I muttered a sorry but kept my eyes on the two I needed the most. They were deep in conversation. Matt's normal happy smile was gone and his eyebrows were pulled together and his lips were pouted.

"I don't know," I replied and tried to walk us forward towards the field but she kept me in place.

You are doing this on purpose, I thought. She didn't respond in my head.

"You must know something," she pushed. "You were with him for a while there."

"No, I was mostly with you all," I hissed remembering the time in the dorm. Amr meowed loudly. His eyes shifted back and forth between Eli and myself. He had to have noticed something going on.

"What about after our fight, you left for hours," she said. And leaned down to whisper in my ear. "Malik's place was blown up during that time."

I made a split-second decision to grab Eli's wrist and burn her hand off of me. Daxton's hand covered mine extinguishing the flame with his magic. I shot him a look but his narrowed eyes told me he was also a part of this interrogation.

The collapsing building entered my mind. *Shit*, I thought.

"So you were there?" she asked.

I dropped Amr on the ground and watched in relief as he bolted towards Malik and Matt.

Thank the heavens, I thought as both Malik and Matt finally looked at us.

"Dirty trick," Daxton muttered.

"Dirtier than you trying to dig through my mind?" I hissed. This time Eli let me shrug off her arm as Malik came closer but kept a firm hand on my waist instead.

"Are you harassing Rosie?" Malik asked with a small grin. "Didn't you have enough of that last night?"

"Just having a little fun," Eli responded. "Rosie's mind can be fun when she is panicked."

"We were warning her the consequences of outing and stealing a familiar," Daxton said as Amr jumped back into my awaiting arms.

"You mean what your parents will do?" Malik asked raising his eyebrows. His gaze shifted to mine, then to Eli's arm around my waist. Understanding crossed his face. "Need help with your mind?"

I nodded feverishly.

"Every time someone you don't want to tries to read your mind they will be met with a loud ringing," he said in a low voice.

His power attacked me like a million tiny cold needles and my mind snapped to a very loud ringing sound. It was weird to hear it in my own head while not actively trying to think of it. It was like an umbrella over all my other thoughts, protecting them.

Eli groaned and removed her arm from my waist.

"What the fuck Malik?" she hissed at him. "No one asked for you to interfere."

"It looks like you were trying to get Rosie to think about stuff she'd rather not," Matt said coming to my defense. He sent me a small smile. "Now she can tell you when she wants you to read her mind."

"Thank you," I muttered to Malik and shot a glare towards Eli. I didn't know how much she was able to pick out from my head but if she heard *everything* we would be fucked.

"Didn't we just make a truce?" Rae said showing up to our right. "Is there already trouble?"

"Not if Eli doesn't start it," Malik said and gave said glowering high-level a glare. "Rosie, you can stay with us today if they are...too much."

"I think I'll actually just take Amr to my dorm," I said hastily. "I want to rest a bit before we get clothes for him later."

"Go to my dorm," Rae offered and dug out a key from her pocket and placed it in my outstretched hand. Her hand curled my fingers over the cold metal with a pointed look. "He can borrow some of my clothes, I have some oversized things that will fit him. We will meet you afterwards."

I nodded and with one look back at the group I carried Amr back to the dorms. When I finally got to Rae's door I shakily opened it and slammed it behind us, locking it as I did so.

I slid down the door to the floor trying to focus on my breathing. My heart felt like it would beat out of my chest. Amr jumped out of my arms and shifted. His shifting process was easier to stomach now that I had seen it multiple times and I was happy to see the face of a person that I knew without a doubt I could trust.

"I'm sorry, I tried," I said feeling my throat constrict. "Eli had to have seen. She was doing it on purpose, I don't know what she saw but whatever it is the town—" I felt a power play at the back of my mind. It felt like Malik's, warning me from saying anything further. "I don't want her to be mad. I don't want them to...get rid of me."

If you betray us you will turn yourself over to me right away. Once the first thought of betrayal enters your mind you will pick up your phone and tell me your location. After that you will not talk until I get you again. Malik really meant any sign of betrayal. I swallowed thickly and gave Amr a pleading look.

"You can't say?" he asked softly. His hand brushed across my cheek. I shook my head.

"I think you can put together most of it," I said with a shaky breath. He nodded and took my hands in his.

"Malik, or this employer of his asked something of you. I have noticed how you speak, you know much more than you let on to the others. Was this what Eli was trying to get at?" he asked.

I nodded.

"I didn't want to do it, any of it," I said honestly. The warning was back again, stabbing at my brain.

"Is anyone in danger?" he asked.

"Not the trio," I choked out. Amr nodded.

"It's okay Rosie," he said and offered a hand to stand me up. "Let's find some clothes and forget about this whole thing. Malik put a stop to Eli's prying and I will be there if they get too out of hand again."

He placed a kiss on my forehead before walking to Rae's closet and rummaging through the lines of perfectly pressed clothes that lie there. I watched as he slipped a light sweater over his head and pulled out a pair of jeans that looked familiar. He also rummaged through the drawers and luckily found some boxer briefs that I hadn't seen before.

"Luckily Rae has good style," he said as he put on the clothes. "Masculine style. Without her the group would look like amateurs. Don't tell her I complimented her, it will go straight to her head."

Even though the panic still played at my mind I couldn't help but smile at his comment. He was trying to calm me down, get my mind to focus on something else. It was a sweet and much-needed gesture.

"Is it true?" I asked. "That the other witches don't want you to shift?"

He sent me a small smile before sweeping his long hair to the side and beginning to braid it.

"Yes," he said. "At least those that are in Daxton's circle. I have heard of other witch colonies from the loose mouths of gossiping women in his parents' circle but I have not seen them myself."

I nodded.

"You know I don't care about that right?" I asked and stepped up to him holding his hands as I spoke. "I want you to do what you want with your life. Not what you are forced to do."

He pulled me into a hug and let out a sigh.

"Daxton was not a bad witch," he said. "And I wouldn't know where to start. The first thing I did for myself in the last few hundred years was take you and demand you make me your familiar. And that was just because I couldn't stand being separated from you any longer."

I stiffened at his words. I didn't know he had lived such a lonely existence.

"We have time to figure it out," I said.

He looked like he was about to speak but there was a knock at the door.

"Done so fast?" I asked and moved to open the door but Amr pulled me back harshly.

"Feel it," he commanded. "It's magic."

I concentrated on the door and he was right. I could feel the magic of whoever was behind the door waft under the crack at the bottom and into the room.

"I don't...recognize it," I said in a whisper.

In a second a blueish light burst from Amr's palm coating the door in a spiderweb-like material just as the door exploded into a million little pieces. The person standing behind the door was unrecognizable to me, but without a doubt, a witch with a plan. And a powerful one at that. You could feel the magic flowing off of him, reaching for us.

He stood tall in the doorway and bared his teeth at us. His brown eyes were crazed and he was dressed in an all-black type of tactical uniform. A red light burst forth from his palms and he readied himself.

"Window!" Amr yelled and pushed us towards the back of the dorm while throwing bursts of magic to the person at the door.

I scrambled towards the closed window and grabbed the chair as I ran and sent it flying. The window shattered into a million pieces as the room was enveloped in a red smoke. I looked back at Amr only to see him fall to his knees. He shakily turned to look at me, blood dribbling down his chin.

"Amr?" I asked and reached my hand out to him.

"Poison," he choked out. "Run. I'll be fine."

I glared at the witch walking through the door. His eyes were narrowed towards me. I wanted to run, my mind was telling me to...but I couldn't leave Amr like this.

I lifted my arm and enveloped the witch in fire. He let out a scream and ran to the open door but didn't make it before I turned up the heat and his body quite literally crumbled before my eyes.

I felt the magic enter my lungs and I began coughing feeling needles in my chest. I covered my face with my arms and helped Amr to a standing position.

"There can't be just one," he choked out. A blue light glowed from his chest much like I had seen Daxton do before.

He was healing himself, I realized.

He stood up straight and pushed us out the doorway over the still smoldering ashes. I tried not to look as we passed; my stomach was already in knots just thinking about what happened.

He pushed me down the dorm hallway to the closest exit. While walking he placed his hand on my chest. The needles were gone and I took a deep gasp of air.

"Who was that?" I asked as we pushed out of the dorm. We both froze as we met face to face with three more of the man we just fought, all waiting for us.

Before they could move I conjured the fire at their feet once more. One was able to jump out of the way and instead of helping the others he lunged at us. Amr stood in front of me and conjured a blue glowing light and slammed it directly into the man's chest.

He disintegrated in midair.

Another one freed himself from the fire and sent a stream of light towards me. I ducked left only for a hand to clamp around my face and something hard to slam into the back of my head. The last thing I saw before darkness was Amr yelling as he tried to reach out to me.

Chapter Twenty-Two
Rae

Finally, after that stupid ranking system was over the whole group walked silently back to the dorm. Malik and Matt insisted on coming with us, and also insisted that they would ride with us to the shopping mall. Acting like a pair of babysitters. Their antics annoyed me but I tried to push down the feeling and just focus on the task in front of me.

As we rounded on the dorms there was a small crowd that gathered in the front, blocking the entrance. There were panicked murmurs from all around and I could feel the fear rolling off them in waves. I got a whiff of an emotional signature that I recognized and pushed towards the crowd in a panic.

"Move," I commanded in a low voice. People parted immediately and I was met with a wounded and hardly breathing Amr huddled on the ground in his human form. Looking around, I couldn't find Rosie and that only heightened my fear.

Daxton dove forward and his hands glowed a light blue while running the length of Amr's body, starting with his head and then moving to his chest. Amr's eyes opened with a gasp and he gripped Daxton by the back of the neck.

"Rosie, they took her," he said. "Witches. Caught us off-guard."

"Do you know who?" Daxton asked and Amr gave him a hard look.

"Your family's guard," he said with a thick coat of venom on his tongue.

Sharp panic rose through the entire group. I jumped as my phone vibrated in my jacket pocket.

"What?" I asked harshly not bothering to look at the ID.

"Don't speak to me like that," my father hissed through the phone. "The Reid's have brought us a gift that I think will interest you."

It couldn't be him? Why would he do this?

My entire life I had watched as he delivered speech after speech about equality and fighting for the rights of both witches and demons. If anything, Rosie's existence should look like a gem to him.

"Why would you resort to this?" I hissed at him. The people around me began to stare and I waved away the crowd. They slowly started to move away obviously wanting to see what the outcome was and trying to linger.

"You should have told me about her before the news went public," he hissed back. "I can't believe my own daughter would keep something like this from me. I gave you twenty-four hours and when you didn't reach out to me I decided to take matters into my own hands."

"What are you planning?" I asked and motioned for Eli to call for a car. Malik shook his head and waved the group to the parking lot. Daxton dragged Amr as he walked behind us.

"Nothing crazy," he said with a small chuckle. "I just wanted to get to know her. I can't promise to wait until you are here though. If you want to redeem yourself, come here and bring the Reid child."

He hung up and I cursed aloud.

"Talk now," Malik hissed as he opened the door to his car.

"Father has her. I am guessing at our place," I said.

"Matt get your siblings, meet us there," Malik commanded. Matt nodded and ran back towards the campus.

I wanted to be shocked at the mention of his siblings but nothing else stuck in my brain. The only thing I thought of was why the hell would Father do something like this?

It didn't match any of his previous actions. I knew he could be a dangerous man but if he had wanted to meet her then he could have simply asked me to bring her. Why must he kidnap her?

There was something way bigger going on here.

I sat in the passenger seat and the others filed into the back seat.

"He was mad that I didn't tell him about her," I hissed and gripped onto the handle of the passenger door as Malik peeled out of the parking lot. "Said it was Daxton's family who helped him get her. I don't know his plan."

"Malik you have to know something," Eli said from the back seat. Her voice was hard but I could feel the worry radiating off of her. Off us all.

"Let me ask you," Malik said with a growl. "Are you two wanting to help her or are you going there to do your families' bidding?"

Daxton was the first to speak.

"I do not stand behind my family's actions," he said. "If anything I hate them. I am going for Rosie only."

Malik's eyes snapped towards me.

"You?"

I swallowed thickly. There should be no doubt in my mind that everything I was going to do would be to help Rosie...but why was I hesitating to answer? Why did I feel odd about going against my father? He had done nothing but berate me up until now and never gave me the time of day.

"I am going for Rosie," I said after a pause. I could almost taste the disbelief rolling off him.

"If you are lying and you betray us in there, I will not hesitate to kill you," he warned.

"Answer me Malik. What's your stake in this?" Eli asked from the back seat. "You seem awfully panicked for just a standard kidnapping. One that you initiated after you threw us under the bus yesterday. You know more than you are telling us."

"Ya, this is your fault to begin with," Daxton hissed.

"She is the future," he hissed. "I believe that firmly and with everything in me." His eyes met mine when he spoke next. "And unlike you I know for sure that I would lay down my life for Rosie. I have lied and hurt her in the past but believe me when I say it has all been for her. Ever since I met her, always been for her."

I was stunned by his words.

"Why does my father want her?" I asked softly. Malik looked back towards the road and his hands gripped the steering wheel so tight his knuckles turned white.

"Is that really something you don't know?" Malik asked. "You are telling me you lived with him your whole life and have no idea what he is capable of? His motives?"

"He does good for the community," I said. I didn't like how sure Malik's words were. If he knew something why wouldn't he spill?

Malik let out a humorless laugh.

"You go home, see what your father has planned and then *you* tell me if he still does good for the community."

* * *

When we finally got to my house we decided to park a ways away behind some trees so the guards would not catch us in Malik's car. Malik sent the coordinates to Matt and in less than five minutes another car pulled up beside us.

"My team will stake the perimeter," Malik said and then gestured towards us. "You go inside talk your parents down. I will sneak in there and free Rosie when there is a chance."

"We are overreacting," I said hurriedly. "He said he just wants to get to know her."

Even as the words fell from my mouth they felt like a lie. Malik eyed me wearily.

"We will do this my way," he commanded. His eyes dared me to fight back... I couldn't bring myself to.

"Let me come," Amr said and pushed past us to stand in front of Malik.

"No Amr," Daxton said pulling him back. "Come with me, you can shift and I can sneak you inside."

"That's the cat?" Matt whispered to his sister.

Amr looked dejected but complied anyway shifting with ease. My clothes fell off him into a heap on the ground. I scooped them up and handed them to Malik.

"Keep this in the car just in case," I said and gestured for Eli and Daxton to follow me. Amr jumped into Daxton's arms and without wasting any time I led them through my property. We traveled through the rose bushes that littered my family estate pausing every time we heard a rustle.

This is stupid, I told myself. *Sneaking onto my own property.*

Malik had to have been overexaggerating. Sure they were disruptive when they took Rosie but could Father really want to hurt her?

"I can feel her in there," Daxton murmured as we finally reached the house. "Her magic is...potent. She was struggling."

"Let's hurry," Eli murmured and I picked up my pace.

When the door was in front of me I slammed it open. There was no one in the hallway at first but Nathaniel's face peeked over the upstairs banister and not a second later Benjamin's nervous face showed itself.

"Why didn't you tell us Daxton's girlfriend was a hybrid?" Nathaniel asked with a pout.

I let out a growl.

"Which room?" I asked.

"The big one," Nathaniel said jerking his head back. "We just came from there."

I hurried up the stairs with Daxton and Eli.

"She's uh..." Benjamin trailed looking nervously at Daxton. "Tied up."

"Are you fucking kidding me?" I asked and pushed past them. They didn't follow after us. *Cowards.*

My heart began racing like it never had before. Well, it had been like this once, when I was younger and still fearful of Father. But now...now the fear of him that seemed so hidden was pushed to the front and I worried for Rosie. Worried about what a monster like him could do... Worried about what he had already done in the short amount of time he held onto her.

Malik was right when he spoke earlier. I did know that my father was some type of monster. I had seen him abuse house staff, cheat on my mother, and there were many times where I had seen him coming home late at night with blood on his clothing. I just never *really* knew what he was doing and when I asked he would state that it was none of my business.

The big room they talked about was one that Father only used to discuss things he wished to keep secret. Being in the business of information he knew there were prying ears everywhere and when he wanted something to *really* be kept away from the public, he would have his meetings in a room that was almost the size of the Winterfell library. The walls were insulated with soundproofing, the room had cameras only he could access, and the lock on the door was impenetrable.

"There is no sneaking out," I hissed at them. "He has it surrounded. If we want to do this right she needs to move rooms. That or Malik will need to tear down the walls."

"This is serious, isn't it?" Eli asked hesitantly.

I looked back at the group before answering. My gut twisted when I thought of what he had been doing to her in that room.

"I'm afraid so," I said.

The double doors came into sight and I picked up my pace reaching out for the doors. Just as my hand brushed the cool metal knob Daxton's hand forced me back.

"Calm," he whispered. "Stay calm, do not let him know this bothers you."

I took a deep breath sending him a grateful look before opening the door. Rosie's muffled screams were the first thing I heard and it quite literally broke my heart into a million pieces.

Opening the door further I saw Rosie flopping around on the ground trying to get out of the restraints. My father was in a chair to the right of her. His eyes met mine as I entered. Daxton's parents were standing over her with magic pouring from their fingertips. Both had magic veins wrapped around her.

His mother, Sirene, had a timid feel to her with her brown hair fixed in a low bun at the nape of her neck. She wore a brown cardigan and a long skirt that covered her ankles, a perfect picture of modesty. Her brown eyes left Rosie to look at us with a hesitant expression.

His father Lars, on the other hand, was dressed in slacks and a blue button-down. His short black hair was cropped close to his head and he had stubble on his face. His brown eyes were set with deep dark circles and he looked over to us with a chilling smile.

Relief crashed through me when Rosie screamed again and I realized it was a scream of frustration and not pain.

"What is the meaning of this?" I asked them as we filed into the room. The door slammed behind us and I heard the metal bolts lock into place, trapping us here.

"I didn't ask for the street rat," my father commented glaring at Eli. His normally calm hazel eyes narrowed, and his mouth twisted into a frown. This was not the image of the perfect, caring politician he showed the public. I could feel the anger burst through Eli at his words. He had tolerated her in public and saved this speak for when we were alone, but it seemed now all facades were dropped.

"She was the one to start this whole deal with her," I fought. "She deserves to be here just as much as I do."

My father let out a hum and looked over Rosie's form. She was staring at us now but I couldn't look in her eyes for fear of what I would see. I felt the betrayal coming off her already; I didn't want to confirm her hatred, her pain.

"You left a man half dead in the middle of school," Daxton hissed at his parents. "You were lucky I was there to clean it up."

Sirene sent him a small smile that was supposed to be warm and motherly but it seemed more crazed than anything.

"I will talk to the guards about being better next time," she said in a light voice. *Next time.* She thought there was going to be a next time?

"Again, what is this Father?" I asked him. "We had her under our supervision we were planning to bring her to the gala to introduce you two."

Father let out a sigh and stood to peer down at Rosie. She sent him a glare that would have made any man's blood run cold but Father just stared at her with little to no emotion, but that was a lie. I could feel the excitement bubbling up inside him.

It sickened me.

"Someone like her needs to be brought in immediately," he said and placed his foot on her back. Rosie let out a muffled groan.

"A hybrid?" I asked my fists clenching.

Father let out a chuckle that enraged me. I hated that tone, that condescending laugh he also did when I was around.

"Daxton knew," Sirene said, beaming at her son. A flutter of pride ran through her as she spoke. "Because he was familiar with the magic. Tell me Daxton, didn't you feel it from her?"

"We didn't know about her hybrid status," Daxton stated. "We really thought she was another low-level."

"Then pray tell, what were you helping her with?" Father asked, his eyes narrowing in on me. Whenever he looked at me like that, I felt compelled to answer. I had a hunch it was whatever power he had locked up inside of him but I never got confirmation. Until now that is.

"A curse," I spoke without a second thought. Even if I wanted to stop the words it was too late now, they were pouring out of me in waves. "She had a curse that stopped her from speaking, we fixed it...for now."

I clenched my fists at my side, digging my nails into my palm, trying to fight against spilling every last detail I knew about her and her curse. The pain helped, a little. It centered me enough to keep from speaking any further. Father let out a noise of interest and looked back down at her.

"Your mother is a smart woman," he said. "She did that didn't she?"

"And how did you fix this curse?" he asked. Before he could look at me Daxton placed a hand on my shoulder, stopping me from speaking.

"I consumed some of it," he said. "Or at least what I thought it was. Turned out it was her magic and taking away some of her magic helped calm it."

"You know that we don't condone sharing magic outside of the family," Lars chided.

Rosie's rage rose sharply, and she aimed a kick at the witches. They simply flexed their fingers and she was bound so tightly the groan she released barely made its way out of her mouth.

"But with someone like her is better than with a dirty witch," Daxton's mother finished for his father.

"Why are you treating her like that?" I asked Father. "We should be welcoming her a place at the table, as a new species. A new discovery. This is history in the making."

Father let out another chuckle and ran his hands through Rosie's hair. I ground my teeth together fighting every instinct I had. I wanted to throw him off her and run out of this room with her. I was seeing red when he yanked at her hair.

"Her kind will never have a seat at the table." He said it as softly as he would talking to a baby. "Especially someone from a heritage as rotten as hers."

"You know something we don't," I said. Panic once again took hold of my muscles, pinning me to the spot.

"A child of an Original witch," he said simply. I felt like my body was hit by lighting. This wasn't possible. "A child of an Original that has been missing for the past hundred years."

Daxton had once said her curse magic was that of an Original but he had dropped it after that, never to mention it again. So, it was never the curse magic that was an Original's... It was hers. I shot a look at Daxton... How would he even know what Original magic felt like?

"How do you know that?" I asked. "Where is your proof?"

He sent me a glare that rooted me to the ground. I wanted to flee. Run out of this room and never look back but my brain wasn't connecting to my body.

"You dare insult me?" He grabbed Rosie's hair roughly pulling her up by it. She let out a deep groan. "She looks just like that *bitch* and that dirty demon of hers. The ones that had turned their backs on our kind and hid like the disgusting cowards they were. And now they gave us the gift of this *beautiful* girl. They thought we wouldn't recognize her but they were stupider than I thought."

"You have to understand, we loved Xena," Sirene said to Rosie. "We would have followed her to the ends of the earth, but then she outcasted us from the clan. Saying we were dirty, saying our ways were twisted and disgraceful."

"We were but third-generation witches, they thought us less powerful," Lars explained. "And when we found a way to grow they outcasted us for it and disappeared. Leaving us to fend for ourselves among the angry humans."

Rosie glared at them and tried speaking but she was still gagged.

"I still don't understand what you want," I pushed. "Who is Xena?"

"Her mother," Daxton's mother replied.

Father turned to me slowly with a smile that chilled me to my core. I had never seen that type of smile cross his face.

"Let's not beat around the bush. We are going to be doing an experiment," he said. "Her magic and powers are bound so she is of no harm to anyone. I hear you have a healing ability is that right?"

Rosie's face paled.

"We did something similar a few years back," Lars explained. "It helped strengthened Daxton's magic tremendously and we are hoping it will do the same this time. I would have hoped to have a full Original but a mutant will do."

Rosie began screaming for real this time. Her brown eyes were wide with terror and tears streamed down her face. I tried to connect the dots but I couldn't see the path that she had. She trashed around violently. What did she know? What was it that I couldn't see?

"Do you know how witches are made?" my father asked as he kneeled towards Rosie. He pulled out a dagger from his suit coat and brushed it against Rosie's cheek.

"From eating demon, dears," Sirene spoke for him. "We tried it on you and your magic flourished. Now that we have a hybrid here it is the perfect time to test what else an Original's flesh can do."

"I never ate a demon," Daxton said in a hollow voice. "I would have known. What kind of drugs are you on?"

"You did," Lars said and nudged Rosie with his foot. "Her father. We couldn't exactly tell you were eating a demon now could we? For weeks we slipped it into your food and your magic since then grew exponentially. Didn't you feel it Daxton? Did you really think it was because you were special?"

"It was because your loving parents took care of you," Sirene said. "Because we knew what would be best for you."

Daxton took a step back. His emotions were stunted for a moment before they went haywire and everything hit him at once. He kneeled over and threw up onto the floor.

"This time we will try it with you as well, Rae. Let's see what an Original demon *and* witch can do for us," Father said and ran the knife around the length of Rosie's cheek. She winced at the pain and Father watched in delight as the wound closed itself.

Where the fuck was Malik?

Chapter Twenty-Three
Rosie

Why the fuck were they just waiting there? Why were they not stopping this? Rae wouldn't even look at me as her father carved into my face. Eli on the other hand couldn't tear her eyes away from me. She was breathing heavily as she stared down at me but did nothing to help me. Where were the people I knew? The dangerous people who would do anything they wanted?

My eyes darted towards Daxton; he was still getting over the sickening revelation that his parents fed a demon to him unknowingly. *My father.* And if what Xena said was to be trusted it was when we were both around ten years old. They were sick, disgusting witches.

Amr was watching me carefully at Daxton's feet. I was glad to see he survived the attack. If anything, at least I could rest easy knowing that. His eyes would dart up to the others as if waiting for a signal and I could have sworn his body was shaking

Rae's father cut off my gag, finally ripping the dirty cloth out of my mouth. I spit right in his face as he did so. He only wiped it off with disgust and gave me a hard glare. His eyes were hazel, just like Rae's. But unlike Rae's I could see the monster behind them, even though their high-level shine they felt dull and sickly. No doubt a reflection of his sins.

"Tell us where Xena is and maybe I will cut off something less painful," he said. "If not, it will be your eye."

His knife came dangerously close to said organ and a small smile tugged at his lips. I had thought that the only ones we had to be careful of were

Daxton's parents but I was wrong. The most dangerous person had to be this man right here. He had acted so calm and collected as I was brought in, yet right now his eyes twinkled in delight. I could tell that he was hoping that I wouldn't make this easy for him.

"Fuck you," I hissed at him. "Stab me all you want; I won't tell you anything."

He leaned back to let out a sigh and shot a look towards Daxton's parents above me.

"At least she is honest," he said. "You know it was Xena and Ezekiel's fault that we are so divided in the first place. After the creation of Xena and the murder of our oldest demons, they went on a rampage. The humans were not so kind after that. They started this and we will end it."

At Eli's father's name I tried to control my expression, but he was too close and too experienced. He saw through it right away.

"Don't tell me you also know Ezekiel?" he asked with a smile.

"Grasping at straws old man. But I think I have this whole thing figured out," I said trying to desperately change the subject. "You must also be third generation because it sounds like you are way too worried about not being accepted by people like Xena. Like really? A grudge after so many hundreds of years? Was it because she didn't even bat an eyelash when you walked by?"

I prayed my panic was not obvious in my tone.

His slap to my face caused me to roll across the floor and land at Daxton's parents' feet. They jumped back in surprise and I felt their magic falter for just a second. With a jolt I realized what I would have to do. Guess I would have to do the hard work myself. I prepared myself before opening my eyes and staring up at Rae's father.

"I was right," I said in a teasing voice and let out a chuckle.

"Rosie," Rae called but I ignored her.

"You liked her didn't you?" I asked. "You liked her and she didn't even look at you? Instead, she settled down with my father and you were so blinded by your own jealously you couldn't see further than what was in front of you and now you still hold onto that grudge waiting for her to notice you." He sent a kick to my stomach pushing me further against Daxton's parents.

"And now you are left to look at the child you could have had," I continued on. "But you know what? She would never even think twice about someone as weak as you."

His face twisted into a snarl and he launched another kick at me. This one was powerful and caused me to accidentally bite down on my tongue.

But at least I could feel the magic weakening with each push into Daxton's parents. They either couldn't stand violence or they didn't do well with the proximity. Either way it would take more of a push to get me free.

I let out a weak laugh and spat out the blood that was filling my mouth.

"Where is she?" he asked. He flipped the knife in his palm, blade now pointing out...towards me.

"Somewhere you will never find her," I hissed. "Kill me, eat my flesh, do whatever you want, just know whatever you do will be your downfall."

He let out a laugh. I used this moment to look back at the group. They shared a collective look of horror. I swallowed thickly and gathered my courage.

"You're a weak man," I hissed. "You think you know it all. That you are all-powerful. But you are nothing more than a coward hiding behind the people who have the real power. You want to control everyone...everything in your life but really it's just to hide that you are nothing. Nothing more than a *weak little bi—*"

This next kick connected with my head and flung me to the other side of Daxton's parents. *Finally.* It was just what I needed. Their magic let up completely and with a throbbing head I jumped to my feet and launched myself at Rae's father.

He let out a gasp in surprise and I dug my thumbs into his eyes while lighting my hands on fire. I couldn't believe that I had once been afraid of my fire...because right now it looked like the most beautiful weapon I could conjure. He pushed me off him violently, throwing me to Rae's feet. While he was recovering from the burn Daxton's hands pulled me to a standing position. He stood in front of me, protecting me from his parent's magic with a blue magical shield of his own.

"You bitch," Rae's father cursed. His eyes were almost fully healed now and they opened to stare at me with a bloodthirsty glare. "Rae hand her over."

I felt Rae's hand on my shoulder. I expected her to step in front of me much like she had when I was fighting with Malik, but this time she did something that broke my heart for the second time. She stepped away from me.

"Rae, don't you dare," Eli hissed from behind us.

I sent a look to Rae but she wasn't looking towards me, she was looking towards her father. Daxton also sent her a look and stayed firmly in front of me, not letting me get pushed any further.

"This is an experiment that could change the course of this world," she said in a hollow voice. "Shouldn't we at least try it?"

"I knew you would see reason," her father praised. "It will. It will change everything we know if we can be successful."

"But," she started and looked over to Daxton's parents, "we do this on our terms. Not yours. She can get the flesh surgically removed and we..." Her voice cracked and her face twisted in disgust. "Will eat it."

Daxton's looked over to meet Rae's gaze. He gave her a small almost unnoticeable nod.

"No need for violence," Daxton added and lowered his shield but stayed firmly in front of me. Amr was at my feet looking at me with careful eyes.

"She needs to tell us where her mother is," her father fought. "That is non-negotiable."

Rae finally looked at me and I felt Eli's hand brush across my back.

Say okay, Rae has a plan, she said.

I inhaled shakily and tried to nod towards Rae's father but my head stuck mid-nod and I felt power course through me. A power so powerful it felt like my skin burned from the inside out. I tried to grab onto Eli, but it was too late. My body was no longer my own as I searched for my phone in my pockets. When I couldn't find it I felt Daxton's pocket and when I finally found the phone I pulled it out to type in a number I didn't know I remembered.

The phone was ripped out of my hand and I was met with Rae's glare. Even though I wanted to back down my hand shot out to grab the phone back. Daxton had to restrain my arms behind me and I flailed against him. Eli came to my side and forced me to look her in the eyes. The loud ringing began playing again and I tried to force it down but I couldn't.

I wanted her to read my mind. I kicked at her but she stayed firm.

Please, I begged my own mind. *Need to call Malik. Malik. Malik. Malik.*

Eli's eyebrows pulled together. The stupid command didn't work. My only chance to save myself.

"What is she doing?" Rae's father asked.

"She's under someone's power, I think," Eli spoke, her eyes watching me carefully. I wanted to say yes but I could only let out a groan.

"Fuck this," Rae's father growled and motioned to Daxton's parents. The ropes that I had just escaped from wrapped around me and pulled me from their arms. The air was smacked out of me as I hit the ground with a thud. "We will do this the messy way."

He pulled out his knife just as the wall towards the back of the room exploded in a flash of light. His head whipped around as Malik, Matt, Claudine, and Maximus came into view. The power holding me disappeared as soon as Malik's eyes met mine and I felt my body relax in the binds, his power finally leaving me.

"Malik?" Rae's father asked. "I thought it was you yesterday, but I couldn't be sure."

"Miss me?" he asked and motioned for those around him to fan out. Rae's father's eyes widened, and he propped me into a standing position while he held the knife to my throat. Malik cocked his head at the act.

"You're a dumbass," I choked out.

"Let's see about that," he whispered in my ear. "I heard rumors you joined their side but no one had proof." He turned his attention back to Malik.

"Because I killed them," Malik responded simply, his gold eyes shifting to mine. "Raphael, come on. Will you let her go or will I have to force you?"

The pounding in my head was getting worse by the minute.

"If you force me I'll have Lars stab her heart," Raphael threatened. "Now tell me where Xena is hiding."

He pushed the knife into my neck hard enough to draw blood.

"I wouldn't do that," Malik said. His posture was relaxed, confident. "We will get out of here even if Rosie doesn't and if you hurt her I will release to the world that the famed Reid family are a bunch of child abusers."

"We did no such thing!" Sirene exclaimed.

I wanted to look at Daxton, tell him I was sorry, but Raphael kept me in his chokehold.

"The many witnesses at your manor beg to differ," Malik said. "Saying that you would constantly magic share with Daxton since he was as young as eight."

"Those are lies," Lars hissed but from my position I could see the panic in his face.

"Nonetheless your career will be over," Malik reasoned. "What we did will be nothing compared to what the public will do to you when they find this out."

"Enough!" Raphael yelled and moved the dagger from my throat to my heart. "Tell me where she is!"

Malik simply rolled his eyes at his actions.

"Let her go," he commanded and Raphael let go immediately. The binds around me loosened only a tiny bit, enough for me to take one step. The knife disappeared from my throat and then I felt a sharp pain from my back. I turned around to see Raphael pushing the sharp metal into my back with a crazed expression.

"I let her go," he said in a satisfied tone. "Lars, now."

A second, sharper pain ripped through me. I could feel the last pump of my heart before it stopped completely. There were shouts around me but they were drowned out. I felt myself fall to the ground but black began clouding my vision. I could feel my magic draining from me, spilling out of my wound. The demon side of me was trying but failing to heal. The magic inside me had begun thrashing about violently, trying to hold on but it was waning.

This is it, I thought to myself. *This was how I would die.*

Was this all I would do in my life? Was this all I was destined for? I had hated the life that was forced upon me but as I felt my body relaxing and my magic recoil, I couldn't help but be grateful for it. Be grateful that I had a chance to finally live a life that was something beyond my wildest dreams.

And to live a life where I belonged somewhere. Because I did belong. I felt it in my bones.

With Rae, Eli, Daxton, and Amr... I belonged. They brought out a part of myself I never knew existed.

And with Malik, Matt, Claudine, and Maximus... I belonged. I had fought it so hard when it was right in front of me. They were my people.

And now...it was gone.

"She can't heal if her heart stops," Raphael said with a chuckle.

I thought I felt a ghost of a hand on the back of my neck, a murmuring near my head, two hands holding mine, and I could feel eyes on me...but they were nothing but an afterthought as I plunged headfirst into the darkness.

A darkness that was so comforting that for the first time in ten years, I felt like I could actually rest. For the first time, I didn't have to fight just to live.

I welcomed the feeling.

THE PRICE OF SILENCE

BOOK 3

ELLE MAE

Chapter 1
Rae

ere I was again, hiding in the shadows like a god damn coward.
I had my chance to do things right, but I couldn't bring myself to. Couldn't watch as the others looked at me with disdain so powerful it singed the edges of my skin.

I could feel it from miles away. The message was loud and clear:

Don't you dare come near.

I wanted to tell them that they had me wrong. That there was no way I would *actually* want to hand Rosie over. I just wanted to be smart about the whole thing and plot our next moves carefully. We were already in deep enough because things were done on a whim, out of panic. If we continued to react out of panic then we would only push ourselves deeper into the hole we had dug. But even as I explained it, I could feel Malik's razor-sharp gaze pierce through my half-lie. He was always too sharp to bullshit.

It was Father who I did not want to upset. It was Father who I obeyed. And as always, it had nothing to do with Rosie or my own personal wishes. It was the way it had to be, the path of least resistance and least damage.

On the other hand, Eli, Daxton, and Amr of course could do no wrong in the eyes of Malik...it was always I who messed things up. This time and last, every time things fell apart among us the only person to blame was myself.

Why couldn't they see what I saw?

The darkness around me was comforting. It felt like a safe space. Like no matter the words I utter they will forever remain between me...and her.

I reached out to Rosie's hand in the darkness. She did not stir, and her hand was cold as ice. The monitor next to her continued to chirp steadily and I could hear her deep breaths. In the darkness, the numbers shone a bright green and there was a pulsing red light above her bed that if touched would signal the closest nurse.

I couldn't see Rosie clearly in the dark, but I knew what she must look like. Her black hair would be sprawled around her like a wave cascading over the pillows, her face would be relaxed as if the events that happened at my house were a mere dream, and the blue hospital gown she was dressed in would bring out the paleness of her skin. The only indication that she had experienced any violence would be the scars they left, the single one on her eye and the massive one now on her chest.

She had lost a lot of blood after my and Daxton's father stabbed her heart. In the moment it took her to fall to the ground I forgot the ties holding me to my father and pushed past him to cradle Rosie's head as she gasped for air. It was in that moment that I realized just how fragile she was, half-witch half-demon or not.

It had been the most horrible moment of my life and one that I would remember for my entire existence, watching her gasp for air while Daxton hastily tried to heal her wound with Amr's help. If they were not as powerful as they were, Rosie would no doubt have succumbed to her wounds.

The second most horrible moment of my life was when my father barked at me to join his side. I *actually* let go of Rosie and moved to him before I could stop myself. *That* was the moment that I knew I wouldn't be welcome among the others any longer. The one place that I had forged for myself would be gone if I did not rectify my mistakes. I had to stand there and watch as they dragged Rosie out of my own house practically dead and stand at my father's side, protecting him as they passed.

I wish they had seen through my weak defense and chosen to end it all.

"Ten minutes," Eli whispered in the darkness. She had let me stew in my own silence for long enough, only to come remind me that we had to leave soon.

Had it really been two hours already?

My eyes shifted to the door where Eli stood. She propped herself up on the metal frame and looked over to me with a guarded look. Her blue eyes glowing faintly in the dark gave just enough light for me to make out her expression.

"I know," I whispered back, unable to take my eyes off of Rosie.

Pity.

Hurt.

Rage.

Sadness.

All of them swirling around Eli in a violent yet slow motion, reminding me of the eye of a storm. Eli stood there strong among it all while her emotions were literally tearing her insides up. The worst thing I felt from her when it all happened, was just plain acceptance.

She saw me leave a bleeding Rosie, walk over to the man that hurt her, and just accepted it as it was. Even worse was that no one would yell at me. They would side-eye me, glare at me, even hiss at me, but no one uttered any words to me about my crimes.

I ran my thumb across the back of Rosie's hand. It was as smooth as I remembered. She had only been here for two days, but my mind was telling me it was much longer. And I knew I needed to see her just one more time before they charted her off to some unknown safe house.

I brought her hand up to my lips and left a small kiss on each of her fingertips, wishing that I could have done this openly before. Wishing I would have taken my chance in the light instead of hiding in the darkness like a coward. My father already knew my feelings for her, it was obvious... So why hide anymore?

I stood slowly and with one last glance I walked to where Eli was resting. She didn't move until I was standing right in front of her, only then did she rest her hand on my shoulder.

They will get over it, she said in my mind.

"They shouldn't," I said and pushed her hand off of me. "I deserve it."

She let out a sigh before walking back down the hallway that we had snuck into hours before. The hospital stood about seven floors tall, and Rosie was nestled into the fifth floor all the way in the corner and was the closest to two of the emergency exits. It was dead during this time of night and all lights save for a few over the nurse stations were off, saving the sleeping patients from the blinding lights. There were not many nurse stations littered down this section of the floor so if Malik had planted any of his spies, they would never know I was here. Matt had been a surprise, and with the addition of his siblings, I had no doubt he had many other spies sneaking in the shadows doing his dirty work. It was almost too easy to find a place where the cameras didn't extend and sneak in through that way. We did it mechanically and without speaking, both lost in our own thoughts.

"Everyone messes up," she said once we were safely out of the building. The cool air was like a slap to the face, one that I took willingly. Eli dug through her pocket, searching for a cigarette. When she found it she paused, looking it over before lighting it up and inhaling deeply. I wrinkled my nose when the burning scent reached me.

"You had stopped for a while," I noted, though this was her third one of the night. Her gaze lazily made its way towards mine and she lifted her head to blow smoke into the night sky, the tense muscles in her neck stretching just slightly.

She had been more affected than she liked to let people notice. Out of all of us I would say that she had been the closest to Rosie once, and to see her like that must have left a scar.

"Yes well," she said. "That was before our little witch-demon hybrid got torn in two."

I couldn't stop the wince.

"Thank you," I murmured, shifting on my feet. "For bringing me."

"Anytime, *honor student*," Eli teased using Daxton's favorite nickname. "I know you felt bad. You should just tell them you regret your actions, and you were not thinking straight."

I let out a heavy sigh.

I may not have been thinking straight, but I knew I would do it again if the situation replayed itself. I had feelings for Rosie...but I couldn't just disobey Father. I could get away with some things, little acts of rebellion here or there but there were other people on the line here...like Mother, Nathaniel, Benjamin.

One mistake with Father would weigh heavily on the entire family. No doubt right now as I was sneaking into a guarded hospital, he was letting his anger out on my mother as we speak.

She was a docile woman that spent most of her time playing house in one of the many rooms. Father treated her as an imbecile even though she had once been the brightest in her class. But that never mattered to him, what mattered was her power...the ability to manipulate emotions.

One which she did not pass on to any of her children.

I had the most similar power to hers while Nathaniel and Benjamin were left with watered-down versions of Father's power...knowing when someone was lying, and a small dash of persuasion for Benjamin. Not that he would ever use it. Mine was empathy and while I could project onto others, it can be easy to differentiate the feelings if you know the signs.

"Where are they taking her?" I asked changing the subject. Eli rolled her eyes and threw her cigarette to the ground in disgust.

"Malik told me I would find out in a few days with *the cat*," Eli said with disdain.

"But Daxton stays?" I asked.

"And you," she said and waved to a car that was approaching. No doubt the same underling that had taken us here, though I was no longer sure if they were Eli's or Malik's. The car stopped in front of us, and Eli opened the door.

"You really have no idea?" I asked and seated myself in the toasty car.

"Nope," Eli said lounging against the seats of the sedan.

The car sped away leaving the hospital, and Rosie, behind in the dust. Eli's emotions held no sourness that would indicate a lie.

There was a silence between us as the lights of the highway passed us by. Amr and Daxton had stayed in her room last night, while Eli stayed on the couch and I cowardly hid inside the adjacent apartment, not even daring to enter her space. Only when I heard of Eli's complaints about them hogging the bed did I come to understand how much it affected both Daxton and Amr. Malik had warned us to stay away, but with one look from Eli she'd told me that we would be breaking in.

It must have been the eyebags from not sleeping all those nights that had caused her to change her mind.

"Will you be back for the gala?" I ask. The surrounding city came into view, lighting up the dark sky and the inside of the car giving me a full view of Eli's face.

"Beats me," she said with a huff. "You see the state she is in. And I don't think Malik will let me leave until she is better."

"You wouldn't want to anyways," I said without thinking.

Eli's expression turned serious.

"No, I don't think I would," she said firmly. Her eyes did not meet mine this time and the words hung heavily between us as well as the unanswered question...

Would you?

I didn't speak to her for the rest of the ride and was not surprised that the car rolled to a stop outside of my family home.

I didn't want to go back. I had been trying to stay away because I was scared of what I would find behind those doors, but I knew for the sake of my mother and siblings I would need to make a reappearance.

"They don't want you back at the hideout," Eli explained with a cold tone. Her shining blue eyes shifted towards me in the dark.

"Only makes sense," I muttered. They had already let me stay far too long. I moved to get out, but she gripped my wrist. I shot her a look.

There is something fishy going on, she said in my mind. *Be careful in there and I'll try to get answers soon.*

I swallowed thickly.

I should be worried about you, I shot back. She gave me a smirk and her eyes glinted in the darkness.

"I'll be fine," she said. *Protect yourself.*

I nodded and shut the door behind me. I stepped back and let the car drive down the empty roads. If I was honest I would admit that I watched Eli go in hopes that she would turn back and come to get me...but she didn't, and the car disappeared down the road.

Looking at my childhood home in the darkness caused an uneasy feeling to stir deep in my stomach. There was an aura that surrounded the house that I had never even noticed before. Maybe it was because I knew the extent of my father's sick obsession now.

And it was an obsession.

I felt the way his feelings swelled when Rosie mentioned the original called Xena. Father was angry beyond belief, hurt and then I felt a small emotion that I sometimes felt come out a Rosie as well. As he spiraled I could feel his emotions expand into something more dangerous and I was sure that if Malik wasn't there...he would be content to keep Rosie instead of Xena.

It scared me beyond belief, and I didn't know what I could do to stop it.

With a sigh and a silent apology to Rosie, I walked up the steps to my house and inside.

I was hit with a flurry of movement and sound as soon as I opened the door. Maids were running with their hands full, male voices were loud from the other room, and there was a huge pile of luggage in the center of the room that stood three heads taller than myself.

This is not good, I thought and jumped out of the way as a maid almost ran into me.

"Rae!" Nathaniel called from the right. I looked over and saw Benjamin strategically positioning himself behind his twin. "We have been looking for you for hours. Father's insisting that we leave tonight."

I froze when I heard Father's voice from the room behind them, even if he seemed relatively happy.

"Where are we going?" I asked and straightened my clothing before walking towards them.

"A different property, this one has been compromised apparently," Nathaniel answered.

"We will be taken out of school for some time," Benjamin said in a soft voice from behind him. "Nathaniel and I."

I focused on him. His emotions were strangely calm. He was usually a flurry of anxiety and fear, very rarely was he ever this calm.

"How long?" I asked and ran my hand over my hair hoping to make it presentable.

"I don't know," he answered.

I nodded and stretched my neck before walking into the room. It was a waiting room we had, usually reserved for guests when we were busy. There was a fireplace surrounded by multiple leather couches and a loveseat that my father usually reserved for himself. This room seemed to be untouched by the madness of the rest of the house. The room was clean and even still had the bar cart out.

It felt like ice was injected straight into my veins when I realized that it was not my father in the loveseat. Instead, he was sitting on the couch with a slimy smile on his face and a drink in hand. Father was put together in a suit and dark red tie, as if he was going to an event even though it was way too late for that. None of these people should be up at this hour.

The person on the seat was someone I had seen only a few times growing up. He was a man with long black hair that was chopped at his shoulders and fell around his face in waves. His face always had some type of scruff on it, but he always kept it neatly trimmed. His golden eyes were the most dangerous I had ever seen, and they constantly haunted my dreams when I was a child. There was something sick and twisted behind them but most of all...they had lost their glow, giving off a dead look.

His full lips curved as he brought the drink to his mouth. He was dressed in more casual clothes than Father but still donned a silk button-up and loosely fitting slacks. If he was here, I had a feeling we were in trouble.

The worst part? His emotions were always locked off to me. He radiated cold, dark energy but I could never get a read on him. There was a time when I was younger that I tried to, and those dead gold eyes burrowed into me so hard I felt him literally squirm around inside me.

Was this why we were moving?

"Rae, finally," Father said in a light tone. "Marques wanted to talk to you."

Shit.

"How may I help you sir?" I asked and tried not to shift on my feet as his eyes looked over my form. I had no idea what his power was, but I was positive I didn't want to know. Just his stare alone was enough to jumpstart my heart.

"Rae," he said. The way he said my name felt unnatural. "I hear you have run into a hybrid."

I swallowed down my fear and walked closer, sitting on the edge of the sofa. Close enough to act like I wanted to be here, but close enough to the door that I could bolt in a second's notice.

"Yes," I said honestly. "Rosie Miller. I was under the impression that she was a low-level until recently."

Why did he want to know about her? Was he a part of the scheme my dad was running?

"Xena thought she was being smart," my father said with a snort. Marques didn't smile at his joke.

"Where is she now Rae?" he asked, not even looking at my father.

I forced my body not to react under his questioning.

"I don't kn—"

My words were cut off as I felt a pain in my side so deep I kneeled over. I felt the pain spread to my entire body slowly. I couldn't breathe and felt tears weld up in my eyes.

Tell him, a voice in my head said. It sounded like my own voice but there was something off about it. *Tell him Rae. Say the words. It'll be so easy.*

My body straightened suddenly, and the pain was gone. I could feel my lips moving, my body relaxing, but it wasn't intentional. Suddenly everything felt like I was in the back seat of my own body. I tried to fight the feeling but there was no point, I couldn't even differentiate up from right and every command I sent my body was ignored.

"Must be Malik's doing," Marques said with a smug grin.

What just happened? I asked myself as the world became clearer.

"I'll send some guys," my father said. "I'll have her delivered to your place."

Marques nodded and made a noise of satisfaction.

"Can't wait to finally meet my niece," he said and let out a chuckle that chilled me to my bones.

I fucked up...bad and now Rosie was going to pay the price. I moved to stand up; I needed to warn Eli.

My body froze on the couch, again putting me in the back seat.

"Not so fast, Rae," Marques said in a low voice. There was a small glint in his usually dead eyes. "We are going to need your help."

I was raging inside my body, trying desperately to get out.

"I hear this *Rosie* has a soft spot for you, is that right?"

Damn it all.

Chapter 2
Rosie

There was nothing and everything all at once.

I could hear things, feel the slightest of touches, but I could never place where I was and couldn't recognize the voices floating around me. I could hear them make words that I should have known but it never reached the part in my brain that understood the sounds they were making. At times I would feel overwhelmed with the things going on around me; the touches were too much, sounds just a bit too loud, my body a bit too cold.

When there was nothing, I was stuck between wanting to float here forever, blissfully in the darkness, and when there was everything, wanting to claw my way to the top.

There was something I was forgetting, something important. And there were times where my chest ached a certain way. When it did the memories played at my senses and I could almost remember it but in a moment's notice it would scatter, and I would be left with nothing.

Things began to clear up when I felt a hand grip mine. I could feel the heat, the pressure, and then in an instant it was gone.

The next time I could make out words. I heard a hushed male tone from somewhere near my side. He was fighting with someone; I could hear it in his tone.

"The longer we stay here the longer she is at risk." This time a female voice spoke.

"It's not safe to move her yet," another voice replied.

I felt a small warm weight rest itself on my stomach and a weight was lifted off my chest.

"Where are you taking her?" the female asked. I thought I could make out some anger.

"Someplace safe," the male replied. I felt something on my cheek, something cold.

"There is no place safe enough," the female voice fought.

I knew these voices. An image of a blonde hair girl made its way to the front of my mind. She was smiling at me. I liked this smile, this smile felt safe...but who was this?

"There is, trust me," the male spoke. "Tomorrow night we move."

I felt something rough against my fingertips.

"Tonight," the female spoke. "I feel her consciousness. We have to act soon or else we may risk her waking up here."

"We are not ready," the male fought back. "If she wakes up here Amr and Daxton can contain her."

Amr? Daxton? I knew them. I felt a warmth when I heard those names... but their faces did not come to me like the blonde woman. It was so close; an image tickled the edge of my brain.

"You have already done enough. Can you please just listen to me this once?" the girl huffed.

...Eli.

Her name shot through me like a jolt.

Eli was here and it made me nervous. Or giddy? Or fearful? I couldn't tell, only that my body clenched.

"You don't know what you are getting into or where we are even going so don't act like you have power here," the male said with a scoff. "Plus, your band of idiots did enough already."

There was a pause and some shuffling, then I heard the clacking of heels against the hard floor.

My heart jumped out of my chest, and I was hit with a million emotions all at once.

Fear.

Hatred.

Anger.

Sadness.

Longing.

Disappointment.

"I know you," Eli snarled.

"Do you now?" Her voice felt like needles embedded under my skin. I *hated* that voice. Hated that she was here right now, but I couldn't place why.

"You cursed her," Eli said. "And if what Rae's father said was right, I am assuming you are not a client?"

There was a chuckle.

"I am Xena."

In an instant my body felt like it heated up. I felt my limbs flail around me, the warmth on my stomach left and I felt hands holding me down. The voices I once heard were gone and I only heard one thing, the voice of my biological mother over and over again in my head.

She was the reason I was here. *She* was the reason for this heartache and pain. *She almost killed me!*

Malik's presence registered to me first. I heard him commanding my body to stop but he was failing.

Eli? I asked in a panic.

There was no response.

Eli can you hear me? Still no response. The fear of not being heard overwhelmed me and this time I tried to push my body forward, tried to command it to move. I needed to warn Eli.

Eli? Eli? Eli? Eli? Eli?

Eli? Eli? Eli? Eli? Eli? Eli! Eli! Eli! Eli! El—

My body flew forward into a sitting position and for the first time I was able to open my eyes. I was met with my mother standing at the edge of my bed with her thin eyebrows pushed together. She wore an awfully extravagant matching suit and skirt to visit her daughter in the hospital.

The second thing I noticed was the blood that stained the cream-colored blanket that was covering the hospital bed. I didn't even care to look down to see where the wounds stemmed from. Instead, I just glared at my mother.

"You fu—" My words became gargled as a frenzy of slashes hit my back at once.

In that moment the ringing I had barely noticed intensified. The room became blurry and the strong hands I felt on my arms became almost like a ghost.

The curse...it was back.

Because of *her*. I narrowed my eyes in her direction and readied myself to use whatever strength I had left to propel myself forward, but Malik's scarred pale face entered my view before I could move.

"Sleep," he commanded. I tried to keep my eyes trained on his golden ones, trying to fight his power but I could not.

I felt my body fall forward before I was thrown back into the darkness.

This time I was more aware of who I was and what happened. I had hoped for a peaceful sleep, but it seemed like that was not in my future. Instead, the time where I almost died played in my mind over and over again.

I was pissed at my so-called mother, but I should be happy that I was alive.

I should be happy.

But I am not. There was a strong disappointment in my bones, in my soul. Because I was alive I would have to go through whatever Xena, and the originals wanted from me. First it was Daxton's parents, then what?

Fear struck my core when I realized that they had Eli here. She would be in danger just like me. But I thought they wanted her to stay far away from this world? Deemed her untrustworthy?

It was because of me, I realized.

It had to be.

I lived through all that just to be punished.

When I was finally able to get up I would have to hurry. Eli's and my time were almost up.

Chapter 3
Eli

With shaky hands and erratic breathing I forced my way outside of the small hospital room. I crashed into a nurse's shoulder as I hurried down the hall but paid no mind to her as she shouted after me. Only when I was safely tucked away in a supply closet did I stop to breathe.

It had been a while since I had seen the curse in action and the only thing I could do to stop myself from taking her right there was to leave the room entirely.

Some part of me had forgotten how beautiful she was covered in her own blood. How sweet the terror felt when combined with her panicked mind.

The best part?

I heard her say my name as she got closer to consciousness...and each time it was carved into her like my own personal brand on her skin. Just the image of my name being carved into her while those big brown doe-like eyes stared at me, begging me to stop while simultaneously getting off on what I did to her caused me to groan aloud and for my belly to heat.

I had been good, docile in the last few months after the fight. I had accepted her curse may never come back and accepted that she was a witch...but only now did I realize how much I had been holding in to keep her around.

Damnit, what was she doing to me? I put aside my own desires to feed hers.

I suddenly regretted how gentle I had been to her. Regretted all of the times I could have made her bleed, but I didn't regret the things I did to her…

Just wished for *more*.

The door tried to open behind me, pushing at my back and pulling me out of my fantasy.

"You never really change," Malik said from the other side of the door. His voice held a hint of humor. "Hiding in a dark place like the little girl you are."

"Don't call me that," I spit at him, my arousal diminished like water to fire. I stepped forward and yanked the door open to glare at him. He had a smirk to his face that only angered me further.

"Little girl?" he asked with a cocked brow. "But that is what you are." His eyes trailed down my form. "Unless I've forgotten something from all those years ago."

"Shut up," I snapped and stepped out of the sanctuary of the closet. "What do you want?"

"Just checking." He paused. "To make sure you're not going off on a rampage."

I rolled my eyes at him and shoved my hands into my jeans.

"I haven't done that since I was little," I said.

He gave me a look that told me he thought that was complete utter bullshit.

"Didn't you just go kick some guy's face in for stealing your money?" Malik asked.

"How did you know about that?" I asked. He just shrugged and turned to walk back down the hallway. I followed after him even though I wanted nothing more than to bash his face in. "Are you going to tell me anything about what you are doing here? Where is Damon?"

He continued to ignore me and led me straight back to Rosie's room. Anger flared inside me. Who the fuck does he think he is?

"You think because I'm below you that I don't deserve answers?" I hissed at him. He stopped in his tracks and turned to look at me with an emotion on his face that I couldn't place.

"You are not below me, Eli," he said in a serious tone. "You never were, and I never thought of you as such."

"Then tell me what's going on," I demanded.

He shifted and gave me a small pitiful smile.

"When we get to a safer place I promise, I will tell you everything," he said.

His voice urged me to believe him, but my brain told me to be cautious. He had betrayed me once before; I would not let him do it again. I was just a naive kid then and now that I have seen the real world I know exactly what type of evil it holds, and the worst types were ones that tried to pass off as being genuine.

Just as I was about to open my mouth to speak, shrill alarms went off, blaring through the hallways of the hospital.

I pushed past Malik and ran the rest of the way to Rosie's room with my invisible hackles raised. It would take an idiot to not understand that this was not a drill, and I would not chance leaving her side empty again. I didn't have time to digest how the thought of her being stabbed again propelled me forward faster than ever, I just knew if I let it happen again I would feel that same pain in my chest as I did when I watched her fall. A pain so deep it felt like my own soul was being torn in two. I couldn't explain it, but I knew that I could not bear it a second time.

When I burst into the room I saw Xena inside a shimmering purple bubble expanded across the room that held both her and the bed that Rosie was currently occupying. She held out one hand where the barrier sprouted from while the other held Amr by the scruff of his neck. Even from my position I could hear his yowls. A cloaked figure pounded his fists against the impenetrable force, but his gaze snapped towards mine when he realized he wasn't alone in the room. I was met with hazel eyes and a snarl. With no warning he lunged towards me, but I was quick enough to snap my fist out and slam it against his jaw.

He dropped to the ground with a thud.

They sent a demon this time.

I kicked the body with a scoff. *How weak.*

I felt a sharp pain to the back of my neck. I turned to glare at the person but was thrown off my feet by an invisible force. I let out a loud growl and tried to lunge at the invisible intruder but felt a sharp elbow come down on my back, forcing me to the ground.

"What the fuck?" I snarled and pushed myself up, but the feeling of a booted foot pushed me back onto the ground.

Malik chose that time to show himself in the doorway.

"Kill yourself," he commanded, his voice reverberating off the walls.

I peered behind me just as the invisible force turned into a person and I was once more met with hazel eyes. This time he fell backwards, his eyes rolling into the back of his head and a white foam began seeping from his open mouth. I searched the room for the other body, but it was not crumpled on the ground like I left it.

"Manipulation trait," Xena said pulling me out of my shock. "Quite strong too."

"We could have pulled information out of him," I growled at Malik. He just rolled his eyes and shut the door behind him as he entered.

"We didn't need to," Malik said. "An enemy is an enemy. We know what they are after."

He dug through his pocket for his phone. Xena was still holding up the barrier and she gave me a look that showed that she wouldn't lower it any time soon.

"Fancy little trick you have there," I noted. She raised an eyebrow at me.

"It's nothing. Child's play," she answered.

"Then why didn't you kill him yourself?" I asked as she looked over her nails. Her attitude pissed me off almost as much as Malik's.

"Not my job," she said sweetly. "That's why we have you my dear but looks like you aren't that good at it yet."

Anger rose in me so fast it made my head spin.

"You think you're all—"

I was interrupted by a flash of light behind me. I jumped closer to the barrier and turned to face the threat, ready to end another life. I was met with the witch with long red hair and a smile on her face. She eyed me, as if assessing me. It was that useless low-level's sister... I remembered her.

Where the fuck did she come from?

"That was fast," Malik commented.

She sent him a smile that didn't reach her eyes. Instead, they looked towards me almost vacantly.

"I have been practicing," she explained. "It's Claudine by the way."

The last portion was targeted towards me. I raised my brow at her.

"I didn't ask," I said and stood up straight, brushing the dirt off my shirt.

She passed me with ease and turned her full attention to Rosie, stepping into Xena's barrier like it was nothing. She took Amr in her arms and sent him a soft smile; he only growled in response.

"You are bad with names," she explained without looking at me. "Come, lift her."

I hesitantly stepped through the barrier, feeling a vibration against my skin as I did so. Xena watched me like a hawk as I leaned down to pick Rosie up, her eyes never so much as wavering. She had always been light but feeling her, now caused a bottomless pit to open up in my stomach. It was like the first time I had seen someone murdered by our gang. I was under Damon at the time and still young enough that I had no *real* idea what went on in our line of business. It was one of our own, who had been accused of being a rat... Damon never took well with those who he saw as traitors. It took a while before that hole closed up, but I had never felt it reopen so violently, until now.

"Sadness. Fear. Anxiety," the red-headed witch said startling me out of my thoughts.

"You see things," I summarized looking at the small witch beside me. She barely came to my shoulder and her bright yellow dress stood out against the white colors of the rest of the room. The whole image of her flowing red hair, smile, and colorful dress made her appear as nothing more than an innocent child. Amr met my eyes and in that moment, even though he was the least likable, I was glad someone was here to experience this with me. To meet someone with such a power would only cause more trouble in the future.

Need to remember this for Rae's little book, I thought.

"You hear things," she said then cocked her head. "Well, I guess you can see things too, in a way."

"You're dangerous," I mused.

She put her hand on my shoulder and without warning I felt a strong pull in my stomach and my vision was blinded by a light. I could feel us twist and turn all sorts of ways until finally my vision cleared. I let out a groan and held on tight to Rosie so I would not take us both to the ground.

"No more so than you are," her light voice said by my side. "Welcome to Montnesse."

I looked up to see an abandoned storefront that still had a sign for a bar in its window. There were more stores on either side, but they had obviously been abandoned for years. The walls were cracked and crumbling, and they looked to be stained with dirt. Some of the windows were even smashed in and you could almost taste the residue the disgusting worn-down place left in the air.

My skin started to feel slimy, and I had a hard time breathing just looking at the area and imagining how much filth was here.

"Hurry," Malik said from my side and placed his hand on my back guiding me to the run-down store.

I made no move to speak, swallowing down my disgust as he pushed me into the shop. While I may not have trusted him fully, I had learned to at least trust him enough to guarantee Rosie's safety. The same stomach pulling sensation swept through me but this time it was quicker than the last and instead of a dusty run-down interior it became a fully functional and clean bar. There was light music playing, some patrons at the bar, and a bartender who looked at us with a pointed gaze.

"I preferred the one that threw up, this one looks like trouble," he commented in a gruff voice.

I wanted to take one of the heavy liquor bottles behind him and smash it straight into his head for that comment, but was pushed forward by Malik so I settled with sending him a glare instead.

"We are not expecting visitors," Malik said hurriedly.

I was just able to see as the bartender grunted and pulled out an automatic rifle from behind the bar, placing it on the counter and pointing it towards the door we just came from. The patrons pulled out their artillery as well, placing them on the bar as we passed.

"Matt is outside with the car," Claire said from my side. Or was it Claudia?

I didn't get my answer because when we went through the back door I was met with a sight that made me stumble. Outside was a bustling city, people everywhere, cars honking, splashes of colors that definitely didn't belong to the town we had just seen. The store front was hiding such a bustling back view, how could I not even tell? Were the shops just a diversion of some sort? Was this like those secret clubs where the entrances were shaped like vending machines?

I looked back to make sure I wasn't hallucinating and saw not just the back door to the bar but the building beside it as well, all looking much more inhabitable than the front view.

"It's magic," a man from the other side of Malik spoke. Behind him was the stupid low-level, Matt, the only person enrolled at Winterfell with Rosie, but this time he was not putting on his stupid puppy dog facade. This time his grey eyes were cold and staring right at me. I shifted Rosie in my arms, holding her closer and shielding her face before critically looking at the man.

He had long blonde hair and bright blue eyes. His skin was on the paler side, and he was currently dressed in a navy suit with a golden brooch on the lapel.

A man with style, I thought wryly and stayed where I was.

"Another seer," I said with distaste.

A smile tugged at his lips.

"No time," Malik said and pushed me again, this time towards the car. "Get to the house."

"Don't fucking push me," I hissed and climbed into the back seat carefully, making sure that Rosie was tucked in.

Matt got in the driver's seat and the blond man into the passenger seat. Malik got into the back while the little witch and bigger annoying witch stayed outside. Amr scrambled to join us, twisting in the witch's arms but her steel grip never wavered.

"We will get supplies with the familiar," little witch called as Malik shut the door. Matt wasted no time speeding out of the parking lot and onto the busy street.

Rosie's bare feet brushed across Malik's lap. I tried to position her so that his *dirty hands* wouldn't be on her, but the space was much too small. His slim hand wrapped around her ankle. The growl that radiated from my chest filled the car.

Matt cast me a glance from the front and the blond man turned to look at me.

"Don't fucking touch her, scum," I hissed.

Malik sent me a smirk and held my eyes as he lifted his shirt, showing his pale stomach, placed her small feet on it, then wrapped her feet in his shirt.

"Just warming her up," he commented.

I pushed Rosie's face further into my chest not liking how Malik had handled her. In truth I wanted him as far away from her as possible until I could prove that he wasn't a threat to her.

"She wouldn't take kindly to you touching her while she's asleep," I hissed at him.

He raised an eyebrow at me and let out a small breathy chuckle.

"I don't think you know a thing about what she wants," he shot back. "Let me ask you, Eli."

He leaned closer, egging me on.

"Malik," the blond man warned.

"Did she ever even ask you to put your hands on her?" he asked. "I mean before you took advantage of her? Did she ever beg you to touch her? Push you until you were forced to?"

I gritted my teeth feeling my body shaking from the violent anger that swirled through me.

"Don't act like you know anything," I said and went to move Rosie's feet from his grasp, but his hand caught me at my wrist.

"Because she asked me," he said. A part of my insides burned and twisted at his confession. I couldn't tell who I wanted to hurt worse, Malik or Rosie.

"Liar," I snarled.

"It's the truth, you know it. That's why you are so mad," he said with a laugh.

"Enough," the blond man said in a hard tone. To my surprise Malik shut his mouth but didn't remove his stare from mine.

"We are here, get out," Matt growled from the front as the car jerked to a sudden stop.

With a huff I brought Rosie out with me and was met with another surprise.

It was the same mansion that Rosie had shown me in her mind. She had come here with all of them before, and never told a single one of us. I looked down at the small body currently curled into me. Her hair framed her face lightly and hung off her, falling towards the ground, swaying with each step. Her face was more relaxed than it had been when she was in her coma, and had a bit of color. All signs pointing to a recovery, but the scar on her chest was a painful reminder that healing would be a long time coming.

What are you hiding?

"Eli hurry the fuck up," Malik hissed by my side and walked towards the house.

"You really think they won't find us here?" I asked making the disbelief obvious in my tone. Malik's jaw twitched. "They found us in Damon's stupid little hospital you think they can't find us here?"

I followed him towards the house and up the stairs that led to a porch that surrounded the property.

"It was mine," he said in a low voice and pushed open a white door.

The inside reminded me eerily of Rae's house and I couldn't help but wonder who had copied whom. I placed my bet on Rae's homophobic father. He seemed impressionable.

"What?" I asked looking around at the people that littered the house; they even had maids here. Was this the older witch's house?

"It was my hospital," he explained with a loud sigh.

"And we share the house," the blond man spoke. His eyes seemed a bit too bright in the moment, like he was excited about something. "Xena and I."

"I don't care," I responded, not liking the way he looked at me.

"Drop the attitude, *Eliza*," Matt said from my side. I shot him a glare. The bastard was enjoying this. He had a smirk on his lips that showed me he thought he was in charge here.

I let a smile rise to my own face and lifted Rosie to my left arm, and in a split second wrapped Matt by the back of the neck forcing his head down. I made sure to grip his neck hard, not as hard as I could but enough to give him a warning.

The little fucker laughed. His grey eyes peeked through his red curls, and I felt something slither under my hand. I jerked my hand back only to see vines thick enough to cover his entire neck protecting where my hand was. He rolled his shoulder and stood up straight, his eyes daring me to move.

"I don't like you," he said. "Never had. And not just because of Rosie."

"I don't like you," I responded. "Someone who has a blood line as weak as yours should have been weeded out a long time ago, *you disgusting little worm.*"

"I didn't know your own name would upset you so much," he teased and put his hands in his pockets. He strolled to a hallway to our right before turning back around. "You should love what your parents gave you."

I had to force myself not to jostle Rosie in my arms. I was ready to explode, and I wanted so badly to take it out on him.

"I'm going to kill you," I hissed at him.

"Children," the blond man interrupted. "We have things to discuss. Stop bickering." His eyes drifted towards Malik. "You too."

I don't know why his tone and sharp gaze caused me to freeze but I didn't argue. When he moved I followed him without so much as a glare towards the other two. He led us to a sitting room on the first floor that looked like a garden threw up all over the interior. There were different patterns of flowers coated on every soft surface while the hard ones got marble, and there was even a god damn skull on top of the fireplace. The maids in there were just finishing placing snacks and tea on the table when we started to file in, and they bowed towards the blond man.

"Master Ezekiel," they echoed. He waved them off and they hurried out the door.

"Place dear Rosie on the couch," the man, *Ezekiel*, ordered. "Just give her some space."

He sighed heavily and poured himself a cup of tea before sitting down on a loveseat closest to the table. I gritted my teeth against his comment and placed Rosie on the couch as gently as I could. I was tempted to sit there with her, hold her head in my lap...but I deemed it too intimate, *too weak*, to do in front of these people.

"Are you going to tell me what's going on here?" I hissed at the group.

Both Malik and Matt looked towards Ezekiel.

So, he was the real person in charge. Not that I couldn't feel how commanding he was. There was an aura around him that told me not to bother him.

"Show her," he said. "Explain our part and Xena will be back soon to explain hers."

Malik nodded and rolled his shoulders and neck before flexing his fists. To say I was surprised to see my long-term mentor, and ex-friend, sprout wings was an understatement. I was floored. I had to freeze in order to keep myself from succumbing to the black spots that covered my vision.

I tried to keep my face as hard as stone, but my mind was racing.

What the actual fuck?

Where did he hide those?

Are they real? Of course, they are real Eli.

Do they work? Stupid, stupid question.

That blonde bitch was right, I thought barely comprehending what I was seeing. The one that showed up to class claiming we were descendants of angels. The one that prodded in my mind. But she couldn't be...could she? No... It was more likely it was just some stupid power they had.

I couldn't stop the breath that rushed out of my mouth when Matt shrugged and did the same thing.

"So, you have wings." I winced at the sound of my own strained voice. "Neat trick."

"It's not a trick, Eliza," Ezekiel said. "Sorry, Rosie told me you prefer Eli now. I'll remember that."

I swallowed thickly and tried to calm my breathing. I wanted to run far, far away; I didn't want to be a part of this. If that teacher was right? Even worse, that was way bigger than I could handle.

God why me?

Why couldn't Rae be the one to deal with this shit? She was better at it than me.

I was saved from having to answer as the pair of witches burst into the room followed by a very mortal-looking Amr, thankfully with clothes on. He paused and his eyes widened as he took in the sight of their wings. Without a moment to waste he stalked over to me.

Thank God, I thought but my relief was cut short when he gripped my arms and forced me to look into his golden slitted eyes.

Trust me, his voice whispered into my mind. *We are in danger, young one. These are dangerous people, and they will hurt us, and Rosie without a second thought.*

He didn't explain any further as he stood in front of me, as if shielding me.

"I apologize on Eli's behalf," he said and bowed deeply to the group in front of us. "She is young and does not know the ways of the world yet."

"Obviously," Xena said. Her heels clacked against the granite floor as she crossed the room to grab herself a tea. She took a sip and her brown eyes met mine.

It had taken me this long to remember Rae's father's words. This woman was Rosie's mother, and this Ezekiel was someone he was searching for, because they were originals. *Originals.* And apparently they not only knew these people but wanted their flesh to make stronger witches...just like he had done to Daxton.

Shit, I thought, *I have been mouthing off to originals.* I looked towards Malik and Matt. So was this what was really behind all of this? We were some lap dogs for the gods of our race?

"She was not raised with her parents, this is expected," Ezekiel said. "Rise, Amr. You do not owe us an apology. We are not as barbaric as we have been rumored to be."

I would believe the cat over him, so his words did not sit well with me.

"We should wake Rosie up for the rest," Malik suggested.

"Cat," the little witch said in a sweet tone. "Do as we told you."

Amr stood straight as a rod then nodded before going around me to kneel at Rosie's side.

"Awaken," Malik commanded.

I turned to get a good look at Rosie but as soon as she woke a bright red light burst from her body. I took a step back and shielded my eyes against the glare. It was a few moments before the light slowly started disappearing into Amr's body. His eyes were closed, and his hands were on Rosie's shoulder, pushing her down into the couch. She stared wide-eyed up to the ceiling.

There was a pause until she looked to Amr, then me. That's when she lunged.

Chapter 4
Rosie

I wish I would have stayed asleep because waking up to all these people in one room, *again*, was a literal nightmare. Not only because they held my fate in their hands but because now I saw two very familiar bodies in here with me.

Without thinking, I lunged towards Eli with my hand out.

I needed to tell her. Warn her who these people were.

"Stop," Malik commanded.

His ice-cold power gripped me hard, stopping me in my tracks. Amr held me up with his strong hands.

"My— *Fuck*," I groaned as I felt a deep cut glide down my back. "Leave them out of my failure."

Each word cut me open, leaving a burning sensation as they healed. I couldn't help the groans, but I needed to say it. Needed to fight for the people I brought into this. There was no telling what *she* would do. She had left this nasty curse on a child once, who was to say she would be any easier on an adult?

"Rosie," Ezekiel said with a sad tone. My gaze darted from him to his daughter... Did she know?

"I know," I tried for a low voice, but the cuts were just as deep. Amr whispered for me to stop but I didn't listen. "I know I blew it, just *please*."

"What made you think you failed?" Xena said as she sipped her tea. "Eli is here because it's her turn. Amr is here by association. No one will harm them."

I gave a panicked look to Eli. Her hooded gaze trailed my blood-stained hospital gown. She had no idea the shit she was about to get into. There was no stopping her from being forced into this hell hole.

A part of me was relieved I could finally share this with someone but the other part...the one that worried for Eli and Amr wanted to bear this alone.

"Curse, now," I hissed at Xena. These cuts were down my arms, and they couldn't heal fast enough to stop the blood from dripping onto the floor.

"Not yet," she said. "Your magic will go haywire. You need to rest first, preferably swap some magic and then we can continue. You almost died Rosie; your magic is extremely unstable. Luckily, Amr can take most of your magic because if not you would have blown the entire house up."

"It needed an outlet after you have been gone for so long," Claudine said with a soft voice.

Where was Maximus?

"One more party should arrive soon," Ezekiel said and watched the door. "We promised we would tell you everything Rosie. Now is the time."

I looked towards Amr; his eyebrows were pushed together but he gave me a small smile anyways. His grip had stayed firm, and I was glad it was him who had held onto me. I hesitantly looked up towards Eli and felt my stomach flip. I knew that look in her eyes. I had seen it many times before and while I wanted to revel in the attention...now was not the time.

"You should have seen Eli, Rosie," Matt said in his normal cheerful tone. I leaned to the right to look past Eli's form to see Matt standing nonchalantly with his wings out. "She was about to faint when we showed her our wings."

This is really happening isn't it?

This was what I had asked for but now that it was here... I was unsure if I really wanted to know *everything*.

"Are you going to explain anything?" Eli asked with a growl. Ezekiel's lips twitched.

"That's a familiar attitude," said a familiar female voice. I moved to peer further over Eli and my heart stopped when I saw a small blonde woman beside Maximus. She was the same woman who spoke in our class all those months ago, who told us about our true heritage.

I had also seen her pictures in the museum of this town. What was her name?

"Sarah," Ezekiel warned but there was a warm smile on his face. Sarah sent one right back to him, her blue eyes gleaming as they met his.

Oh my god, I thought and looked panicked towards Eli. Her brows were furrowed, and her lips pursed. She was also trying to piece it together but hadn't reached the same conclusion I had.

"Well let's start with the elephant in the room," Sarah said and gave a beaming smile towards Eli. Ezekiel stood up, alarmed. Obviously he was ready for a fight but whether that was with us or Sarah, I could not tell and neither option brought me comfort. I dug my fingernails into Amr's arm.

"Rosie?" he whispered.

"You and Rosie are more similar than you think," Ezekiel rushed trying to beat his partner, but Sarah didn't care and cut him off.

"I'm your mother and he's your father," she said bluntly.

Eli's face went stone cold and her whole body froze. The silence was the loudest I had ever heard in my life.

"Sarah we talked about this," Ezekiel said in a hushed tone.

"I know but it's better to just rip the band-aid off," she said in a hushed tone back.

"You can finish the family reunion later," Xena said in a sharp tone.

Unease prickled at my skin. These were the people in charge of this whole thing, originals for god's sake...and they were bickering?

"What you need to know, Eli, is you are descended from an original, like Rosie. And we are currently in the middle of a million-year-long war with people who threaten to erase our existence. They have no remorse and as you have seen, they like to do experiments of their own that are currently going unchecked."

Daxton's face flashed through my mind.

"Rosie, you know most of the rest. The only other thing to note is that Rae's father was also on our hit list; he would have been our next target," Malik explained. "This has been going on for years and the only way to guarantee our safety is to take them out. But they are not the ones at the top. There are more—Eli?"

We all watched as Eli walked straight up to Ezekiel with her hands clenched at her side. They were shaking.

"Eli no," I choked out against the pain of my curse, but I was too late.

She threw her fist straight towards Ezekiel's face only for it to be caught by Malik mere inches away from connecting with his jaw.

"Let her," Ezekiel said. "She deserves to. I deserve it."

"Eli just calm down," Malik said and glared at Eli. "Hear them out."

Eli didn't respond at first, only turned her gaze to Malik. I couldn't see her expression from here but whatever it was made Malik flinch.

"You act like you are more than a street rat," she hissed at him. "What are you doing here with *him*?"

Malik's expression softened.

"I have been a part of this since the very beginning, Eli," he said softly.

"The gang was a front. All for our cause. All to protect the people here. You see my wings Eli, you are smart... Put it together."

There was a pause as Eli lowered her arm.

"You knew this whole time," she whispered in a hollow voice. "That he was here." She then looked back to Ezekiel. "And you know what it was like in that gang. You let me grow up there thinking my father had abandoned me."

"You need real-life experience," Ezekiel said. "This war will not be easy."

"Real-life experience?" she asked with a scoff. She then let out a humorless laugh and stepped away from them. "You never told him what Damon did, did you?" she asked Malik.

"Eli, this is not the place," he warned. His golden eyes were pleading.

"You never told him what you *let happen*," Eli said. "But you knew it, how could you not? And here you are chilling with low-levels and letting Damon ruin my life."

"I didn't know," Malik said hurriedly. "Not until that night, after that I beat him into a pulp. I swear Eli I didn't know—"

"That he was fucking me?" Eli hissed. "That he had been sneaking into my bed since right after I was dropped off? You put a *child* in the hands of people like them and you expect them to be fine?"

There was a gasp from Sarah. She reached out to touch Eli, but Eli smacked her hand away. Eli looked back at me with pain in her blue eyes.

"That's why I wanted you to stay away from him, Rosie. That's why I told you not to trust him...because I wish I hadn't," she said and without another word, left the room.

Malik stood frozen in his place.

"You knew?" My voice was a whisper but the accusatory tone it held to it carried across the whole room. It was as if the room could feel the same two cuts that sliced across my chest. "You let that happen to her?"

He was right before. There were sides I didn't know about, sides I would hate. This one was so disgusting that it made my stomach clench and my magic flare out beside me leaving a red haze around Amr and me.

"I promise you as soon as I found out I put a stop to it," he pleaded. "Rosie, Ezekiel...please."

"I can hear it," he said. "I know."

I stood up. Amr came with me and steadied my sway.

"You were so focused on this war." I had to pause between words to regain myself after the shock of the cuts. It was much worse than last time and I was quickly getting dizzy. "That you didn't give two shits about your children."

"Rosie," Amr whispered. "Let's go with Eli. Don't speak."

I nodded and let him help me out of the room.

"Don't wander too far," Xena called. "You cannot leave the town just yet."

I didn't look back as I left the room.

* * *

I was fuming as we searched the property for Eli. I had been at their whim for so long, my entire life unknowingly was a product of their decisions...but now Eli? How could they just stand there and watch as she was at the mercy of those horrible people? I didn't care about this war anymore, and none of what they said even surprised me anymore. I was just so tired of not being in control of my own life.

Even as my cuts healed I felt weak and if Amr wasn't holding me up I knew that I would have fallen to the ground and never gotten up.

"Rosie they are not people you want to make angry," Amr's accented voice broke through my thoughts.

"I don't care anymore, Amr," I said and gritted my teeth against the pain.

"You should, Rosie," he said in a soft voice. "I just got you back and I plan to keep you. They can stop that from happening, don't you see that?"

My face warmed at his words.

"Seriously cat?" Eli's voice broke through our moment. She came into view as we rounded the east corner of the house. She held a lit cigarette in her hand and looked us over with a lazy stare. There were no tears staining her face, but I could feel the hurt and sadness enveloping her. It was in the way she hunched into herself, and the way her blue eyes seemed to dull. "Throwing pickup lines at a time like this?"

"Eli," Amr said in a sad voice.

"Don't bother," she interrupted. "So little original, what the fuck is going on here?"

I swallowed thickly. I wanted to talk to her more about what happened in there, but I wouldn't push it. Eli deserved as much.

"Do you know what this town is?" I asked trying not to moan at the pain in my side. She rolled her eyes and inhaled again before blowing it towards my face.

"Obviously fucking not," she said.

"Don't be rude," Amr warned. Eli raised her brow at him.

"Rude? You haven't seen anything yet," she promised and for some reason I believed her. Every time I had seen Eli angry she would lash out violently, but this calm and collected version scared me more.

"Time doesn't pass here," I explained. "They told me they are here for protection."

I couldn't carry on like this. My body was growing weaker by the minute.

"From Rae and Daxton's parents," she finished for me. I nodded.

"Malik told me..." I trailed off when Eli snapped the cigarette between her fingers.

"What did that bastard say to you Rosie? More lies? Don't tell me you came here to defend him."

I shook my head.

"No Eli," I rushed out. "He told me it was originally you who was supposed to help them take down their parents, but you got too close to them."

Black spots filled my vision and I leaned on Amr for support. I shook as the cuts on my back healed.

Fuck this curse, I thought.

She shook her head and let out a humorless laugh.

"You want me to believe that my first assignment as a teen, was to bring down this so-called war?" she asked with a laugh. "Was that the failure you spoke about?"

"They had me pry Daxton for information," I admitted.

"Stop speaking Rosie," Amr whispered. I could feel the blood soak the back of my gown.

There was a pause.

"Rae was right," she muttered. "Of course, she was."

I looked towards the ground, but Eli stood over and forced my face up to look her in the eyes. Her grip on my chin was so painful tears leaked out of my eyes.

"Eli, unhand her," Amr demanded.

"Shut up," she growled. "You played us like fools. Sneaking your way in, acting all innocent and shit when really you were planning to stab us in the back."

"No, Eli I had no choic—"

"Shut up," she said squeezing my jaw even harder. She was cracking it; I could hear it echo in my ears. "We were so worried about you. *I was worried about you.*" She threw my head to the side like it was a piece of trash. "I should have left you to rot."

Amr was raging, ready to pounce. I put a hand on his chest and leaned into him unable to stand.

"Let's take you inside," he said softly.

"Don't leave the town," I whispered to Eli.

She shook her head and walked past me.

"I'll be back," she said and when she turned to look at me this time her blue eyes were cold. "But only for the curse. You know the drill. You better be ready for me when I come back."

She left without another word.

And just like that we were back at the start, but this time there was no way we would ever get back the trust I had lost.

* * *

Amr forced me back inside after Eli stormed off. Even though I wanted nothing more than to chase her and force her to listen, I let him do so without a fight.

I didn't really have a choice, by the time I had registered that I was losing consciousness Amr had already picked me up bridal style and walked me into the house. He took me up to my room and I didn't even ask how he knew which one I stayed in last time.

I remained silent as we entered the purple room. He placed me down on the floor of the bed and kneeled in front of me, checking my arms and legs for any unhealed cuts. His hands worked fast but they were careful as they searched for wounds. His golden eyes frantically searched my skin, and his lips were puckered in concentration.

I didn't register that my hand had moved to cup his cheek until he looked up at me, startled.

"Do not be sad, my love." His deep voice was still surprising to me. I couldn't believe that all of this had been hidden from me for so long. I wondered how he survived without a voice, without his own will.

His hand reached out to my own cheek and when he pulled it away I saw dampness on it.

I hadn't even realized I was crying. As soon as I saw the wetness on his hand the tears came down in steady streams. I didn't dare make a noise, but I wanted to sob.

To scream.

It felt like I was being lashed with my own anger and sadness with each silent sob. The anger under my skin, I knew had to be my magic. I had realized that it was much like a beast, or a guard dog. It saw its vessel get upset, get hurt, and it *hated* it.

But I could barely latch onto the anger of what they had forced us into because I was just so overwhelmed by the sadness of Eli leaving. I knew it would happen from the start, when they had asked me to betray Daxton... but I never knew it would end up like this.

"You need magic," Amr said and stood up. Without a second of hesitation, he brought his wrist to his mouth and bit down hard enough to bleed.

"They said no," I choked out. I think those were in my back, but I couldn't tell once he forced his wrist to my mouth.

Take, my magic seemed to demand. *Take. Devour. More. More. More.*

I swallowed a mouthful of blood expecting it to taste horrible but the magic in it sparked on my tongue and warmth spread throughout my body. I moaned into it as I felt it gather in my belly. My whole body seemed to vibrate as our magics combined.

"Take it," he whispered. His golden eyes seemed to have a similar fire in them. "We will not push your body; you will sleep once you take the blood."

I reached forward and fumbled against his pants, needing to touch him. His hand wrapped around my wrist to stop me but instead I pushed forward and grabbed his hardening length through his pants.

He let out a gargled moan.

"Rosie, you are weak," he said but his protests were weak as I squeezed the head of his cock.

A part of me wanted to see him lose control, like he did in the pool. I needed it; my magic wanted it badly. So badly I felt my mouth water.

I removed my mouth from his wound.

"Please Amr," I begged and pulled him closer to me. I was still in the gown, so it was easy to reach under my clothes and take my underwear off. The wounds barely registered, and I guided his hand between my legs.

"You will be the death of me my love," he whispered but his fingers glided up my slit. I hadn't realized how wet I already was until his finger slipped easily into me. I leaned back and moaned as he fit another finger inside me and started slowly pumping into me.

"Amr," I gasped and flinched as a cut ran down my arm. "More."

"Heavens, my name sounds like the sweetest music coming out of your mouth," he said in a husky voice and leaned over to capture my lips. "You're such trouble."

He easily released himself from his pants and without hesitation he pulled his fingers out and pushed his cock inside me. I whimpered against the stretch forgetting just how big he was last time. He kept his mouth on mine even as his hands gripped my thighs and he forced himself fully into me.

He pulled away and his golden eyes burned into me with such fiery passion that I felt myself heat unbearably. My body responded to his and I found myself trying to move my hips in tandem with his.

"You were made for me Rosie," he said as he snapped his hips into mine. "I have waited years for this. For you."

I gasped as his thumb came to rub circles in my clit. I could feel the magic rising around us and I could taste it on my tongue again. It was intoxicating feeling his magic spill into me and after going so long without magic sharing I felt heat rise inside me.

"I don't care what happens, Rosie," he said against me. "It will be me and you until the end. You can count on me to be here, forever."

"Amr," I cried as he hit a spot inside me that caused my body to constrict. The cut down my side only pushed me faster to my oblivion and with a loud growl I felt him spill inside me.

This time when our magic intertwined and came back into my body, my breath was taken out of me and I was thrown into a second orgasm as it pulsed inside of me. I clutched onto Amr to steady myself, but he seemed to be having as much trouble as I was.

When I felt like I could finally breathe he met my eyes with a smile.

"You are one powerful witch, my queen."

Chapter 5
Eli

I had dreamed one day that I would be reunited with my long-lost parents. Dreamed of the days where they would come save me from the hell hole that was living with Damon. Sometimes I dreamed of getting revenge... Other times I just dreamed of them taking me far away. A place where food, love, and warmth were free and abundant. A place where I no longer had to fight just to live.

I had envied the children I saw on the streets. I imagined sneaking home with them and often had daydreams of offing them and taking their place... but obviously those dreams also never came true.

I dreamed until I could dream no more. Until all my hopes, and innocent feelings were forcibly torn from me leaving a jaded, angry teenager in their wake. After what Damon did to me I never imagined that I would ever be leaving The Fallen for as long as I lived, and after a time I was okay with that. Because in the place of a father figure I had someone else who saw me...

Malik.

And then he turned out to be a fucking scumbag just like the rest of them. *That night* he had indeed beaten Damon into a pulp, but by that time I was already well into my teenage years, and I was embarrassed, *ashamed* that he had to see me in such a position.

After Malik had beaten him, I finally took a turn of my own...and then Malik stopped me from the killing blow.

I thought him seeing me like that was enough to send me spiraling but the look in his eyes as he forced me to stop with his power...was one that I would never forget. I vowed now that if I ever had the chance to leave that godforsaken place, I wouldn't stop until I made Damon pay. All this pain, all of this shit I had to go through...and for what? They weren't even a *real gang*. It was all a farce for these stupid originals...

And Rosie just had to run to him. Had to trust him, more than she trusted us.

Trusted him enough to cipher information to him and his group. And now I was stuck here working for him *again*.

Ezekiel's face passed through my mind and made my steps falter.

I didn't realize how far from the house I had gotten until that moment. After Rosie found me I left, running towards the back of the property, down the slope of the hill and into the trees that surrounded the outer edge of the town. I was too lost in my own thoughts. Too lost in the anger that the situation brought. And not to mention...

It was supposed to be you, Rosie's voice whispered in my mind.

I let out a growl and reached to the closest branch and ripped it out of the tree. The tree gave a groan and shook before silencing. I used the branch to lash the side of the tree as hard as I could. With each cut into the tree, I imagined it as someone else.

Malik.

Ezekiel.

That stupid designer witch.

The witch with glasses.

That *fucking teacher*.

I paused when Rosie's face came to mind. My chest felt tight all of a sudden and I threw the branch away from me like it burned.

I wanted to be mad. Wanted to hate her. Wanted to plan her demise just like the rest of them...but I couldn't.

Instead, my first thought was to run back into the house and bury my face in her soft chest. I had never felt the need to do that...*ever*. But now all I could think about was her hands running through my hair and her small sighs as I licked up her throat.

Why? I asked the universe. *Why would she do this...why would they do this?*

I needed to kill something, destroy something. I let out another growl and turned on my heel to continue down the forest but stopped in my tracks as I saw a familiar tuft of white hair. His pale features stood out against the darkening forest.

"Eli," Malik started in a voice that sounded pained. I knew it was a front though. This bastard was nothing if not convincing. He did it to me, to

Rosie, hell I bet that scrawny little shit Matt had no idea who this man really was.

"Don't fucking talk to me," I hissed and lunged toward him.

I expected him to use his power but instead he just let me force him to the ground. The first punch I threw snapped his head to the side and a pained groan left his mouth. There was a cut on his right temple but it healed in a matter of moments. The act only infuriated me more. I wanted him to bleed, wanted him to hurt for longer than a few moments.

I threw another punch to his face, but it was the same response. He laid limp underneath me and just took the punches as they came. I threaded my fists together ready to bring it down onto his head but a whisper from him stopped me and made my blood run cold.

"I'm sorry, Eli," he whispered. "I didn't know."

"You had to," I hissed at him.

His golden eyes shifted to mine for just a second.

"I didn't," he insisted. "But if they would allow it I would gladly let you end me."

I rolled my eyes against the feeling in my stomach. It felt like I had just swallowed lead.

Why didn't I want him dead?

At my pause his own thoughts entered my mind.

Useless.

Piece of shit.

Deserve to die.

How could I fail so badly?

How could I let this happen?

I swallowed thickly and got off him, glaring down as he stayed still in the dirt.

"Even if they let me, I wouldn't," I admitted to him. "Because I want you to suffer the rest of eternity knowing what you caused."

The second part was a lie, but I didn't tell him that. Instead, I continued walking deeper into the forest, not wanting to go back to the house just yet.

"Take a left at the border and follow the fence until you reach the bar," Malik said from behind me. "It's a circle."

Without a look back I continued on.

I didn't know how long it had taken me to reach the bar, but it was completely dark when I saw the first signs of the town. It started off with yellow glowing lights in the distance and as I got closer I realized that I was stepping right into a park, and if I strained my eyes, I could see the line of shops that I had entered from.

A part of me wanted to go back and get Rosie but I couldn't bring myself to go back there. Instead, I headed straight back to the bar. The same group of people were there, and they looked up at me as I entered. There were three men on the stools, two witches and another I assumed to be low-level. The first witch stiffened as he saw me and placed a hand on his guns in front of him. He had scruff on his face and wore jeans and a t-shirt. The second witch lifted his brow at me. He was much cleaner than the other and had a suit on; he looked like one of the businessmen that I had seen line the streets of the city. The last low-level I didn't bother to look at, he didn't deserve my attention.

"You can't leave," the brown-eyed bartender said. He had on a white apron over a fully black attire. "Orders from the top."

"Knew she'd be trouble," the low-level muttered into his glass. "Little girl doesn't know what she got into."

I plastered a smile on my face and walked towards the group. The bartender's eyes narrowed in my direction.

"Look at you," I cooed and shot my hand out to tangle in the low-level's tuft of black hair. I slammed his head down onto the bar and heard a satisfying crunch accompanied by a splatter of blood. "Smart little low-level."

The witch in the suit grabbed my wrist and tried to pry me away from the low-level but I didn't budge and pushed him into the counter harder than before. He let out a gargled groan. He was probably choking on his own blood and the thought made me chuckle aloud.

The witch's palm began sizzling and I felt a jolt of heat go through my wrist. I ground my teeth against it and shot a look at him. I reared my other fist back to punch him in the face, but an invisible force held me back.

"Enough," the bartender commanded. I shot a glare in his direction, but it did nothing to pause him. Instead, I felt the same force peel my hand away from the low-level's head. The witch next to him unhanded my wrist and began working on his face with a blue type of magic.

The rugged-looking witch let out a snort and shot back his brown liquid.

"I think I like this one," he said.

"I'm leaving," I growled and walked towards the door but was pulled back by two invisible arms. I glared at the bartender still standing behind the bar, but he just grabbed a glass, poured a clear liquid in it, and placed it on the bar where the only empty seat was.

"At least have a drink first," he said. "It's customary."

I let out a noise of frustration and pushed forward against the force.

"Son," the witch from behind spoke.

His words froze me in place. I stood straight and turned to face him.

"He's a stupid human that doesn't know when to shut his trap," he explained. "Join us."

I swallowed thickly. There had been only a few times where I had been misgendered and each time it pulled the same reaction out of me. It scared me, caused me to freeze.

It scared me because of how my body responded to it. How a part of me wanted to smile. I had told Daxton that I didn't feel associated to either gender when probed...but *son* just felt so right in the moment.

The one in the suit watched me carefully as I sat down on the barstool. I didn't look any of them in the eyes as I took a sip of the liquid in front of me. It was vodka and it burned pleasantly at my throat. I normally didn't associate with human shit...but this was okay, for now. Just like son was okay...for now.

"I'm Billy," the bartender spoke after a minute. "The one that needs a shave is Javier, the one that has a stick up his ass is Jason, and the human is Earl."

"I am not good with names," I admitted. I don't know why I told them that, but it just slipped out without too much thought. I looked up to Billy, but he only had an amused look on his face.

"I'm not good with them either," Javier said with a throaty chuckle.

"Because you're too shit-faced to remember even your own name at the end of your shift," Earl hissed at him from the end of the bar. He sent me a glare.

"What's a human doing here anyways," I asked with the same amount of disdain.

"I'm the protector of this gate," he said, puffing his chest out as if it was something important.

"Whatever gets your soggy noodle hard, I guess," Javier mumbled and motioned for Billy to refill his drink.

A smile tugged at my lips.

"There we go," Billy said with a smile and poured more vodka into my cup. "Ladies like it when you smile more."

"I'd say the rugged look is what they find more handsome nowadays," Javier said with a laugh. "But I bet a face like that pulls in partners with ease."

Rosie flashed through my mind.

"The girl you carried in before..." Billy trailed.

"She's fine now," I said and threw back the alcohol.

"Trouble in paradise," the one in the suit muttered.

It was more like trouble in fiery hell...but I guess it wasn't all bad when it came to Rosie. I was furious that she lied...but I hated the look on her face as she watched me leave. I had no doubt in my mind that I would punish her, thoroughly... But I don't know how long I could stay mad at her. Even now I felt like it was in the past, and we had much bigger things to handle. The people who I really wanted to hate were Malik and Ezekiel.

"Mind your business," I muttered feeling irritated by his response.

Billy seemed to have deflated a little when I told him Rosie was safe. I raised an eyebrow at him.

"It's just sometimes I never see newcomers again once they leave these doors," he explained with a sigh. "And to see her come in looking half-dead."

"He's more sentimental than he looks," Javier explained with a grin. "Ask him about his picture stash."

Billy visibly flushed but was interrupted by a shrill voice before he could utter a word.

"Eliza Groten I cannot believe you are drinking under the legal age!"

That fucking teacher was back. I groaned and pushed my cup towards Billy. He gave me a sympathetic look and poured more for me.

"We are in a magic town that is outside of our normal time," I said and sent her a glare. "Calm yourself, woman."

She looked the same as last time but at my words she visibly swelled, and her face became bright red. *God I hated her.*

"Woman?!"

I let out a sigh and finished my drink before standing up. I stalked over to the woman in question and glared down at her. She met me with just as much passion.

"You don't get to have a say in my life," I said in a cold voice, devoid of feeling. "Get off your high horse and leave me the fuck alone before I make you regret ever giving birth to me."

"I understand everything now," the human behind me muttered.

She did not break her stare even though I saw the words eating at her. Her left eye even began twitching.

A warm hand clamped on my shoulder. I didn't look at Javier as he addressed *my mother.*

"Leave the boy alone would ya?" he said in a light tone. "He's been through a lot."

"Boy?" the blond woman said with a bit of distaste in her mouth. If not for Javier's hand, warning me...I would have killed her where she stood.

"Unless he tells me differently this is how I will address him," he said and sent me a smile. "My shift is over soon, let me show you around and bring you to some place to let that anger of yours out."

"It's the middle of the night," she hissed at him.

"We're just going to the pit," he said. "Blow some shit up. Ruin some things."

I raised an eyebrow at him, but he just wiggled his brows at me. A bit of excitement ran through me at the thought of destroying stuff, even if it was with a total stranger.

My mother had a look of pure hatred on her face. I loved every moment of it and knew I would call upon this memory whenever she pissed me off again.

"I am taking her home whether she likes it or not," she hissed. Just then two large witches forced themselves through the back door. "I have been sent to retrieve you. Now come back willingly or you will get the same punishment Malik will."

I lifted my brow towards her. Malik was getting punished? For what? I wanted to bash that bastard's brains in, but her words seemed out of place to me. And who was she to threaten punishment?

"Try me," I warned in a low tone. "*Bitch.*"

Her fury-filled eyes and dark smile reminded me too much of my own.

Chapter 6
Malik

The trudge back through the forest was just as painful as Eli's punches.

I owed her more than that, I owed her my life... But they would never allow that. I was too essential to the plan, they needed me just like they needed me a hundred years ago.

Even though this body did not age, I felt the tiredness seep through my bones with each passing year.

I was tired of fighting this war, tired of being the sole person running out into the world and trying to orchestrate this crazy plan while at the mercy of our enemies. I knew it would work, with enough force. While their motives and true intentions didn't sit well with me...I would rather be fighting for my life than turning my back on the people that needed me.

Once this was over though, we would have a much bigger battle that awaited us. Just ridding the government of Lars, Sirene, and Raphael would be the first step. There was someone else, someone bigger that awaited us... and there was no doubt in my mind that Raphael was at that bastard's feet delivering this information by hand. I had fucked up. I had let them live long enough to see me, see my team.

It wasn't supposed to end up that way, but it did and now we were fucked.

It was the other reason I was putting off going back to the house. Ezekiel and Xena were waiting for me in the basement. The scars on my face and back already began aching in anticipation of what was to come. It was easy to tell people that my scars were from rogue witches, and most of them were...but there were some that were a product of my own mistakes and let me tell you, I have made *many*.

This was how they kept their people in line well... Trusted people. Those deemed less important had harsher punishments and as a leader of my own team...I had to set an example of myself to make sure that they would not toe that line, because no way would they even bat an eyelash when it came to punishing them. They were dispensable.

I barely registered the house as I walked the familiar path to the entrance, around the staircase, and down to the basement. It was a stretch to call it a basement. While it was under the house, they had gutted it completely, tearing out the old floorboards, the walls, and windows to make it into its own type of ritual room.

Witches didn't need a special room to do these rituals, but Xena had made this specifically for her and her followers. I never figured out if it was for the dramatics of it all or if they really had a plan at first, but after a while they began to pull the demon blood that soaked into the brickwork and used it to strengthen their magic. They would try and get any demon they could in there as punishment just so they could build up their own power.

The walls were almost pitch black and made out of a magical material that kept all sound, magical signature, and scents inside. It was built for every scenario imaginable, namely for when a hybrid strayed a little too far away from the path. We could easily lock them in here and let them tire themselves out until they passed out or died. But fret not, the walls also absorbed their magic and would store it until another witch called upon it.

Xena...always a step ahead.

The stairs creaked as I descended into the chamber-like room. There were no lights other than the soft glow of a red circle in the middle of the room and a few magically lit torches that littered the walls. Matt, Claudine, and Maximus stood on the left side of the wall while Xena, Ezekiel, and two of their helpers stood on the right.

I was relieved to see that they left Rosie out of this. There would be no way to get her on our side if she had to witness this. Or who knows... She seemed just as angry as Eli...maybe she would enjoy my pain.

Maximus stepped forward as if to say something, but Matt sent him a look that made him fall back in line. This was Matt's first viewing of this, but I was relieved to know he already understood the severity of it. The last time I had been lashed was over a hundred years ago and that time wasn't even as grave as this one.

With a sigh I pulled my shirt off and threw it towards Matt. He caught it with ease.

My eyes drifted towards the inner circle and my stomach flipped. There were new carvings in the ground in the old witch language. It took me a while to understand what it said but I figured it out fairly quickly.

Today was about repentance. Today blood would be spilled and because of my mistake they required something from me. Blood. A lot of it.

I didn't wait for Xena to tell me what to do, instead I simply walked into the circle and kneeled with my back facing them. My own team would get a good look at my face the entire time; it was important they remembered it.

"You messed up, Malik," Xena spoke from behind me, her voice bouncing off the wall.

"I know," I said simply.

"Tell us what happened," Ezekiel said in a solemn voice. He was such a pacifist, he really hated violence. I had an inkling it had to do with the fact that he could read the mind of the person when they were in pain, but I never got the confirmation.

"I underestimated the enemy," I said trying to keep my composure even as I heard their helpers get their whips ready. "Let them take the hybrid. Then when they were still in the same room as us, distracted..." I swallowed as one of the helpers came to stand in front of me, her glowing red whip at her side. "I let them escape."

"Why did you let them escape?" Xena demanded in a cold tone.

"Because I prioritized the life of the hybrid over them," I explained.

The helper witch looked to Xena behind me, and I got no warning before I felt the first lash across my back. I bit down hard and tried to swallow my groan. These whips were magically infused and ate the skin around the wound, leaving burning fire in their wake.

"Why?" she demanded again and this time the one in front of me hit the whip across my face. I couldn't help the whimper that left my mouth. It felt like my face was pushed straight into a burning fire.

I swallowed thickly before answering. I knew Ezekiel knew the truth, how could he not? But to tell it to Xena...that was unacceptable.

"I thought the hybrid would be the key to winning the war," I lied through gritted teeth. This time there was a pause before they both brought down their whips. I fell forward, unable to hold myself up anymore. A pained groan filled the room.

"Try again," she said.

Damn it, I thought. *I wasn't like those children; I shouldn't be acting like this, and I should have been able to separate myself from the situation.*

"I didn't want her to die," I admitted. "She's important."

"The hybrid," Xena corrected. "The hybrid is not important. The hybrid never was, and the hybrid never will be. The hybrid was just a means to an end, as they all have been." She took a deep breath. "What is important?"

It was always the same question and it always caused me to pause because every time it was different. I knew the answer was to win the war, at any cost...but I didn't believe that in my heart anymore. There were things more important...like protecting the people you cared for. Something played at the back of my mind, something important...begging to be let out but I could not pull it forward.

There was more to this.

That's what winning this war will do, Ezekiel's voice said in my head. *Protect the people we care about. She also doesn't want to see another one die.*

Then let's stop this game, I suggested. *Let's all admit we have a soft spot for the newest hybrid and move on.*

It doesn't work like that, he said back. *You know that you know we put this war before anything.*

I know.

"Protecting the people we care about," I said and pushed myself up to look the helper straight in the eyes. She flinched.

"Malik," Xena warned.

The one behind me hit my back again but the one in front stood still, frozen by my stare. I could break out of this, easily if I wanted to. But they would find me and punish me at some point. They had done it once when I was younger and less experienced...when I didn't have a team to look after.

This was the real reason I pushed Rosie. She had acted out, and they knew about it. They would only let me deal with it for so long before they stepped in.

And the last time they stepped in...

I'm tired. My soul is tired.

"The war," I said in a whisper. "Winning the war."

Both helpers sent two more lashes my way before Xena called them off. I leaned forward with my head on the cool floor and focused on my breathing. I could feel the blood pouring out of the wounds and my mind felt dizzy. The ground below me began to soak with my blood, leaving a warm sticky feeling on my face...but we were not done yet.

"Every five minutes we will heal a wound," Xena announced.

"He may die before that," Matt said.

"Matt," I hissed.

"He will heal," Xena said dismissively.

Both Ezekiel and Xena left but their helpers stayed to watch over me. As soon as the door shut the girl in front of me rushed over to me. Her hands were glowing blue before I could even blink.

"Cristy, stop it," the girl behind me hissed.

"Cristy?" I asked peering up at the girl in front of me. The Cristy I knew was a girl that was forever at the age of ten, had been like that for almost a decade. The girl in front of me bore some semblance to her, the same brown eyes, the blonde hair.

"Surprised?" she said with a husky laugh. "I left the town to grow into my body, only took a year for the time to catch up to me. Must be the human blood."

I smacked her hand away harsher than I meant to. She sent me a surprised and hurt look.

"Follow orders," I commanded using whatever power I could muster. She glared at me but was silent. "Tell me about your time out there."

She sighed and leaned back on her feet.

"I was surprised that I aged so quickly," she explained. "I didn't think it was possible to mix human and witch blood and still keep our powers...or at least that's what I assumed happened. I didn't know what else would cause it."

I nodded trying desperately to hold onto the conversation, but the edges of my vision began blacking out. I felt the girl behind me wave cooling magic down my back.

"They are all in the same spot," she muttered.

I didn't need long to put two and two together. It almost made my eyes water, *almost*. I was stronger than that.

"Is this hybrid the one we saw you bring in earlier?" Cristy asked. I nodded without looking at her.

I heard some of my team shuffle, ready to come break me out of the circle.

"He cannot leave," the girl behind me said. "Not at least until he is done healing."

"We can heal him upstairs," Maximus said in an angry tone.

"We collect blood here," Cristy explained. "We need it for our powers."

"I thought it was flesh," Matt said in a voice that gave no indication to how he felt about what just happened.

"This is not a biology lesson," the one behind me spoke and moved to heal my shoulder. I sagged in relief as I felt the wounds close. I was weak still but at least the burning was subsiding.

This was the first time down here that I actually had people around me, trying to help. Every other time I would trudge down here, take my punishment, pass out, then wake up to start the whole cycle over again. I had gotten better after a while; understood the lines I couldn't cross...but this last time I couldn't stop myself from acting out. From the outside it was supposed to look like I was an equal part of this...but that was very wrong.

I hated it.

Hated being a part of this. Hated having others see me in this state.

The door to the far side of the basement creaked open and Xena poked her head in. I tensed waiting for the punishment, but she gave none.

"We require your assistance subduing Groten's offspring," she said.

A sour pit formed in my stomach. I only hoped Ezekiel would be more lenient on his own child, but it wasn't him who needed to be convinced that violence was not the answer. There was still a gash around my face, my lower back, my chest, and part of my left hand but those would have to wait.

I could hear Eli's growl from the room beyond.

"Damn it all," I muttered and pushed myself up and practically ran out the basement with my team following closely behind.

When I rounded the corner to the foyer my heart froze. Eli was on her knees facing towards me, her arms held above her head by an invisible force. Two witches stood by her side. She had her teeth bared at Ezekiel who stood in front of her with a blank expression, Sarah Collins wrapped around his arm with a pout. They both turned to me when I entered.

Xena let out a sigh as she came to my side.

"I hope you have enough power," she muttered. "Seems like the basement will get its fill tonight."

Don't let her, I begged in my mind knowing Ezekiel would hear. *You can't.*

We must, he shot back.

"She won't submit like that," I said aloud for the crowd. Eli sent me a nasty glare, but I ignored her. She jerked against the magical force that held her causing her shirt to spread open more on her chest. The guard to her right looked down at her with a glare that caused my blood to boil. I could only imagine the ways he was thinking of to make her submit.

Disgusting.

"I mean it," I said and stepped forward. Eli's expression faltered as she took in my bloody appearance. "She would hate you even more. Let her throw her tantrum. We know it won't get very far anyways."

"At least make her more agreeable," Sarah said in a snide tone. "Caught her drinking with the guards, had one of them even referring to her as a man." She let out a heavy sigh. "I guess that's what we get for being gone for so long."

"Sarah," Ezekiel chided.

If I wasn't angry before my skin was positively boiling with rage now. I tried to keep a calm facade but with the earlier lashings and just the shit show of emotions...I could barely conceal it. And to make matters worse...a different complication showed up.

Rosie was silent as she and Amr descended the stairs. They must have been called by the commotion. She had her brave face on.

The one she used when I first took her to the beach.

The same one she used when facing Eli's group.

The same one that caused her to challenge me in the tea room so long ago.

This was the face that made it impossible for me to let her go. I knew deep down she was in turmoil with herself. She was always scared and always unsure of what to do. I saw it in the way her eyes shifted when she was asked a hard question. The way her hands wrung the hem of her shirt when she was thinking. But this face...

It was the one she put on even when she felt the most fear.

"Go back upstairs," Xena demanded from my side. "Tell her."

"You get one," I said to her, not meeting her gaze as Rosie stalled on the stairs. "I'm spent."

Eli struggled between the two witches.

"Let me go you fuckers," she hissed. "I'm gonna kill that bitch, I don't care if you birthed me out of your crusty ass cun—"

"Her," Xena commanded jutted her chin out towards Eli.

"Obey me," I commanded towards her. I could almost feel the last of my power drain me.

Ezekiel looked back at me with an expression that told me what I had done did not get past him.

"Fuck off you sad sack of—"

"Silence," I commanded without my power.

Her mouth snapped shut.

"What is this?" Rosie asked from the stairs. She leaned onto her familiar for support as the curse cut her forearms.

"Eli caused some trouble," Ezekiel answered.

"Malik too?" she asked. My heart skipped a beat when she uttered my name.

There was a pause. All the originals looked towards me to answer. Typical that they wouldn't want to tell her how *little* her life really meant.

Should I tell her the truth? I promised I would no longer lie to her...but would she still help after this? We had already pushed her so far.

"I told you," I said with mock confidence and plastered a small smile on my face. "Sometimes witches and I don't get along."

Her eyes narrowed in my direction, but I kept the smile on my face. *Don't ask,* I chanted.

"This doesn't concern you," I said in a more serious tone as she opened her mouth to speak once more. "Leave like your mother asked and rest. You are still not fully healed."

"Dungeon," Ezekiel said in a final tone after an awkward pause. I felt a weight lifted off my shoulder... *Thank god.*

"Ezekiel," Xena hissed from my side. "She attacked Sarah and the witches. Not to forget she tried to escape."

"*They* were out drinking," Ezekiel insisted. I took note of the pronouns and the way Sarah's face twisted. "They deserve some leniency. This is our fault after all."

Was that why she didn't want me to call her a girl? I thought. It almost made too much sense.

"Sarah looks fine to me," I muttered knowing full well that they could all hear me. She sent me a glare.

"Three days," he said in an angry tone. "That is final."

He stormed out of the foyer and into the hallway to our right. Sarah continued to glare at Eli but followed shortly after. Xena was the next to leave and as soon as she did the witches forced Eli up and walked towards me. Past the basement door there was another for the cells that they kept in the house for cases just like this.

I gave Rosie a look before following Eli to the cells.

"Guard her door," I commanded Matt and his siblings. They seemed hesitant, like they wanted to say something but after a moment they just nodded and left.

I stood outside the door as the guards threw Eli into a cell. I heard the one that angered me earlier whisper something to her but couldn't make out the words over the commotion of the other prisoners. When he finally re-emerged and passed me, I gripped his wrist and forced his eyes to meet mine.

"If you ever abuse your position I want you to cut your dick off with a salted butter knife," I growled and fused as much of my power in it as I could.

His eyes widened and he ran away like a dog with his tail tucked between his legs.

At least I could do this much.

Chapter 7
Rosie

We waited until we thought the rest of the house was asleep to venture out to meet with Eli. I had no idea what she would say when I saw her. I knew she was still pissed...and had every right to be.

But for them to force her into a holding cell? And for what? Sneaking off to drink? It didn't sit right with me. I knew there was some weird stuff going on behind the scenes, that much has been obvious since the beginning. But this was just weird.

And Malik...he was a bloody mess when I saw him. We were in a *safe place*, they had told me. So, who would dare harm him?

His nonchalant response should have calmed me down and it would have had I not seen how Maximus and Matt reacted. Claudine had the airy expression she always had but Matt...he wouldn't look at me. And Maximus...

His expression looked downright painful.

Amr stood still at the door, his ear was pressed to the wood and his golden eyes were darting back and forth. He was my rock in all this. He had forced me to share magic even when I was too distracted to even think of it. Without him I knew that when I saw Eli, I would have exploded. My magic was so volatile now that I had trouble keeping a hold on my own thoughts.

In the end it was his steady hand and caress that reminded me to keep my wits about me.

He held out his tanned hand to me without looking over to me. I silently walked across the room, cold rushing through me as my bare feet hit the non-carpeted area. I threaded my fingers through his and brought his hand to my lips. Only then did his eyes meet mine and there was a slight quirk to his lips.

"Let's go, my love," he whispered and opened the door slowly. "The witches are far away from our room and the dungeon."

I wanted to ask about the demons, but I shut my mouth. Now was not the time to test my curse or my magic. It had settled after we shared magic but seemed to go crazy when I began to speak.

Amr snuck us out of the room and down the hall. He was also barefoot, and I only now began to realize how feline he really was. As he pulled us through the halls and around corners, he had a way of moving that was far too graceful for someone of his size. And even as he walked on the marbled floor his feet made little to no sound. He froze as we rounded the corner to the stairs and pushed us against the wall. He covered me with both arms on either side of my head and his long black hair cascaded over us like a curtain.

I heard the voices then but couldn't place them. It wasn't long until the voices began to fade, and we were back on the move again walking down the stairs.

This was the scariest part because we were out in the open. My heart began pounding wildly in my chest and I squeezed Amr's hand tightly. He looked back over his shoulder at me and gave me a small smile. When we finally reached the end of the stairs we hurried down to the hallway we saw them take Eli to. It was hard to see in the darkness, but I trusted Amr to lead the way and tried to stay as close to him as possible.

Amr stopped at a dark open doorway and peered inside. He tilted his head, gesturing me to follow. When we stepped through the threshold I felt a chill go down my spine and tingling all around me...kinda like magic.

And it was like a switch had been turned on. The quiet night was no more, instead the room was filled with curses and yelling from all around us. The long room was decorated with dim lights that lit each one of the cells. I had imagined them to be like old-fashioned cells that you see in pirate movies, but instead these ones were obviously forged by magic. Every few feet there was a hole carved into the wall and a grid of thin red lights covered the entrance like a net. In each cell there was a bed, a toilet, and a sink.

My heart dropped into my stomach when I realized that almost every cell was filled. There seemed to be a mix of demons and witches. Some were older and grey, but I saw some as young as early teens.

Had this been here the whole time?

I had stayed here for weeks, and I had no idea that these people were trapped here like this. It was sickening. Why were they doing this?

Someone in a cage near us whistled and suddenly all eyes were on us. There was a pause before the room was filled with yelling, jeering, and whistles. I felt my face flush and gripped onto Amr for dear life.

I could see the muscles tense in his back as he pulled us forward in search of Eli.

I screamed when a hand clasped my shoulder. Amr turned and reached for the perpetrator but paused when his eyes shifted to the person behind me. I didn't even need to look as the person wrapped an arm around my waist and pulled me back into him.

It was Malik of course. He had a distinct smell and I could see the scars on his pale skin even in this dull light. As mad as I was at Malik I was glad it was him and not any of the other originals.

"A lady should not be down here in the cells," he said, lips close to my ears. "And barefoot? Scandalous."

Let go, I signed to him, hoping he could see from his position behind me.

"I don't think so," he mused in a teasing tone. "You are not supposed to be here, and it is my duty to see to your punishment as fit."

"We just want to check on Eli," Amr said standing up straight.

"Too bad, cat," he said sounding a little too much like Eli.

I took a deep breath and peered up to catch Malik's gaze. His smile faltered just slightly.

Let's see just how like Eli he really is, I thought to myself. My magic came alive under my skin and pushed me forward, igniting sparks in my belly.

I raised my arm up and cupped his cheek. It was the side where his fresh scar remained, just barely healed and still red. He froze at my touch, but I melted back into him.

"Please?" I whispered and jumped when the pain of the cut ran across my belly. "Just a few moments?"

"I told you not to play this," he growled at me. His arm tightened around my waist digging into the fresh cuts. "Do we need a repeat in front of your familiar? In front of all these rowdy criminals?"

He took my chin with his free hand and forced me to look at Amr who had an unreadable expression on his face, then to the prisoners that littered the cells around us. They were watching intently.

I shrunk back not liking their gaze on me. I swallowed thickly.

"It's the least you could do," I said finally after trying to build up my courage. My magic was not as chaotic the last time this happened, so I still felt a tremor of slight fear when I pushed him this time. He was silent above me before he pushed me forward.

"Fine," he spat out, venom filling his voice.

He walked us to almost the end of the room before we stopped at a cell. When I peered inside I saw Eli sitting on the dirty ground. The bed was upside down and looked singed as if it had been thrown at the magic lights that barred her from escaping. Her head was hung until Malik cleared his throat. Eli's head snapped up, and her eyes narrowed as she saw us.

"Caught your girlfriend sneaking around trying to find you," Malik said.

The word girlfriend caused my stomach to flip.

Amr watched us from the corner of his eye, not moving to push Malik away from me like the others would have done. He apparently had more of a reason to fear Malik than the others did, given his reaction to their status.

"If you aren't here to get me out then both of you better fuck off," she hissed as her fists balled.

"Eli I—" I was cut off by her standing abruptly. She stalked to the edge of the cell, just a breath away from the magical grid. She placed her hands on either of the cell's walls covering almost the entire entrance. It felt like she was leaning over me even though there was a barrier between us. I shrunk back into Malik's arms.

"You're lucky they locked me in here tonight," she said in a deep growl. "I was ready to ruin your fucking life, and they only angered me further. If I was in Malik's place I'd make everyone watch as I fucked you against this dirty ground and until that curse knocked you out for good."

Amr tried to step in, but Eli kept going.

"Even then I wouldn't stop, I'd fuck you while you're unconscious only for you to wake up screaming my name." She shuddered. "That would piss them off wouldn't it? Maybe I'd make them watch as I did it, so they knew exactly what type of monster they created."

"Enough," Malik sounded from behind me.

"Don't you dare say anything," Eli hissed at him. "I bet you have a hard-on just by imagining it."

As if to prove her point, Malik shifted behind me.

"I don't get off on sick shit," he growled at her.

Eli let out a chuckle.

"Could have fooled me," she answered. Her eyes snapped down to mine. "I don't need you or want you here. Don't think I have forgotten about your lies. From now on the only thing you are good for is tight ass, and don't forget it."

"Eli, that's too much," Amr spoke finally. "She didn't have a choice, none of us do."

"Shut it," she hissed at Amr. A blonde lock of her hair fell forward and got singed off by the barrier.

"We are leaving," Malik said from behind me. "Even just letting you in here was a mistake."

Panic seized my throat. I turned in Maliks arms.

She'll be alone, I signed to him. *Please let me stay.*

"It doesn't work that way," Malik said in a soft voice. "Let me walk you to your room."

"Get your dirty hands off of her," Eli hissed as Malik pushed us back down the hallway.

I tried to reach out to Eli, but Malik grabbed my arms and forced them to my side.

"Come on Rosie," Malik said. "You need your rest. Tomorrow will be worse for you."

Eli let out a growl as we walked down the hallway and I saw the magic on her cell give off shocks.

"Don't throw shit!" Malik yelled back at her.

The other people in the cells yelled and laughed at us as we passed. As soon as we stepped out of the barrier of the room we were thrust back into the dark and quiet night.

"Is this your town's jail?" Amr asked from behind us. His hand tugged my hair from behind, a sweet gesture to let me know I wasn't alone.

"Something like that," he murmured and gave me a sidelong glance. "How's your magic?"

I twisted myself out of his hold, stopping just before he pulled me up the stairs to the second floor.

"Are we going to act like nothing happened?" I asked him, my eyes stinging as cuts littered my back.

He paused and his golden eyes roamed over me. I gritted my teeth against his actions; he did this before. Usually when he was deciding how much to tell me.

"I truly didn't know what Eli was going through with Damon," he answered after a pause. "When I figured it out I put a stop to it. Eli was, *is* important to me. There is no way I would let anything happen to her like that."

I balled my fists at my side. My magic still lashed out wildly, and my body began shaking at the ferocity of it.

"She's in a cell," Amr said from behind me and placed a hand on my shoulder. I felt my magic flow to him immediately.

"Be grateful she's in one piece," Malik said in a dangerously low tone.

My eyes caught his newest scar.

"Unlike you," I said in a cold tone. He stiffened and looked to the ground before straightening.

"Seems like you don't need my company," he said. "I'll leave you with your familiar for now."

I didn't say anything else as he walked past us. I turned and watched him stalk into the darkness.

"We have to leave soon," I said in a whisper. The cuts were more bearable this time.

"It would be safer to regroup once we can get rid of your curse," Amr said from behind me. He placed a small kiss on my forehead before continuing. "Let's go rest, my love."

I let him lead me up the stairs but all I could think about was the fact that our whole group was now in a whole lot of trouble, and I had no idea when I would be able to see the others again.

Chapter 8
Rosie

I hadn't been able to sleep well knowing that Eli was in the cells *alone*. Even after Amr used his magic in a way that was supposed to be soothing, my mind still wouldn't allow me to sleep.

"I'm sorry," I whispered to Amr after we got out of the shower the next morning.

I had been shy, and probably would have blushed like crazy if it had been anyone else, but with Amr everything was different. I felt comfortable with him and was able to hug him and touch him, something I never would have dreamed of with the others.

"You do not need to be sorry, my love," he said and kissed the top of my head as he wrapped the towel around my body. I watched him in the mirror, trying to avoid looking at the newest and ugliest scar that took up most of my chest. It was like a glaring beacon but with someone like Amr here, it was easily avoidable.

"For thinking about Eli when I'm with you," I said. I watched as red spots bloomed on the white towel. Amr gave me a smile in the mirror and leaned over to plant kisses on my neck. My skin flushed and my magic swirled inside me. His large hands gripped my hips and forced me back against his naked body.

"I'm not in competition with the others," he said in a husky voice, his eyes peering up behind his thick lashes. "At least I don't think it's like that."

"It's not," I promised.

He sent me a smile and nibbled lightly on the sensitive skin of my neck. I couldn't help the breathy moan that escaped my lips.

"I really did worry for you, my love," he said against me. "I was worried I would never see you again. Never hear you. Never feel your warmth against mine."

"Amr—"

He cut me off with a heated look.

"For just that moment my life felt meaningless," he said. "Please work on protecting yourself in the future, if not for you...then for me."

I swallowed thickly and nodded, before pushing myself into him. No one had said such a thing to me before and I had no idea how to react.

"We can finish this after you get some food in your belly," he said with a chuckle and pulled away from me.

I sent him a pout, but he just tugged on my hair playfully and left the bathroom without a thread of clothing on. I leaned over to watch his shapely ass as he walked away. He looked back at me with a raised brow, his hair moving with him as he did to show more of what I wanted.

I could see the color rise to my cheeks in the mirror but instead of shying away I sent him a smile. He shook his head with a laugh.

It wasn't long after we dressed that we were called down to breakfast with a knock at my door. When I opened it I was surprised to see Matt and not Malik. Seeing Matt now, I realized just how little I had interacted with him the last few months. His hair had grown longer, and he had dark purple bags under his eyes. He was wearing a band t-shirt, much like the one I had chosen for myself today, that showed off his colorful ink. He had one hand in his pants pocket and the other quickly went to the back of his neck when I opened the door.

Back to how we started, I signed to him with a hesitant smile.

His eyes lit up and a smile of his own spread across his face.

"Just like the first time, except I have food—not clothes—and you have a half-naked familiar in your room," he replied with a slight blush.

I looked behind me to see that Amr still had not put his shirt on.

"It's too tight," he replied but still grabbed a t-shirt once I gave him a look.

Would you get mad if I said I didn't want to go? I signed to him as Amr and I stepped out of my room.

"I don't really want to either," he admitted.

"How do you know the language that uses hands?" Amr asked him and grabbed my right hand leaving me in between the two men.

Matt gave him an amused type of smile.

"Sign language," he corrected. "I uhh...learned it for her."

My mouth went dry when I realized what he meant. He learned it for his task, not for me. The one where he was charged with getting close to me at Winterfell.

"Winterfell doesn't teach it," he said, still not quite getting it.

Matt looked at me then his eyes shifted to Amr.

"I think you already know most of what's going on here or pieced it together, but it was my task to get close to Rosie at Winterfell," he explained. "Malik and I prepared by learning sign language because of her...curse."

Amr's hand tightened around mine just briefly. I looked towards him, and he sent me a forced smile. I would have to figure out another time to talk to him about this; something behind his eyes told me that he had something to say about all this.

Is Eli okay? I signed to him.

He was about to walk down the stairs, but I stopped him. I needed answers before I could go on.

"Yes," he replied with a frown. "As okay as she could be."

Why was Malik bleeding? I signed.

Matt's eyes widened and shifted away.

"You have to ask him about that," he muttered and without waiting for my sign he walked down the stairs.

I swallowed thickly and pulled Amr along with me. His firm hand was the only thing that kept me planted in this world. I needed more answers.

We followed Matt silently to the dining room. I knew the way by now and had dined here a few times, but each and every time it took my breath away. There were four floor-to-ceiling glass windows that oversaw the garden and the rolling hills near the back of the property. There were two large chandeliers at either end of the room and the white dining table took up almost the entire middle of the room. There were many waitstaff on either end, some had food others had drinks, but they all smiled when we entered.

The click of Matt's shoes was the thing that drew me back from my awe and I stood frozen as he took a seat on the left side of the table, the one with his siblings. Maximus was wearing a blazer, looking clean as always. He met my eyes for only a second before focusing on the food in front of him. Claudine gave me her normal airy smile; she was looking particularly pretty in her pink sundress today.

I looked over to the other side of the table, which held Xena and Malik. I was relieved to see that Malik had the empty chairs next to him and effectively protected me from having to sit next to Xena.

Xena today was wearing Louis Vuitton? I almost rolled my eyes at her actions. She may have said that she was my *biological mother* but nothing about her actions pointed to her wanting to do anything good for me. I may have hated her before, but now that I had an ugly scar in the middle of my chest for the rest of my life because of her...there was no going back.

Malik sent me that soft smile that made my heart twist and patted the seat next to him. He was wearing a loose white shirt and jeans, looking like another young adult you would find walking down the street, save for his arms full of tattoos and his face full of scars. Only now did I notice that his and Matt's tattoos were different from each other. I couldn't make out the pictures but could tell at least they were different.

Gripping Amr's hand tightly I pulled us to Malik's side.

"You look much better," Ezekiel said from the front of the table.

And how could I forget the most glaringly obvious literal *god* that sat at the head of the table? He wore a full-on suit with his signature gold brooch on its lapel. He on the other hand looked like he had not slept well at all. Maybe he was also horrified at the fact that Eli was down in the dungeon alone all night.

I am, he said in my head. *But it is what must be done. Please understand.*

When I sat down on the table with Amr, a waitstaff immediately put down a big pile of blueberry pancakes in front of me and a healthy portion of what looked like a pile of meat in front of Amr. I saw his eyes widen when he took in the sight.

My heart ached for him.

I knew Daxton was constricted by his parents, but I can't believe that they had forced Amr to remain in that form for so long. He never had a chance to interact with his fellow demons, or even enjoy the small pleasantries that came with life. And now he was forced into this mess with me as well. If it was up to me, I would have him spend as much time as he could trying out all different types of foods and go any place he wanted. Amr sent me a questioning look.

I nodded to him with a smile and motioned for him to dig in. He hesitantly picked up a fork turning it once, twice, three times in his hand before stabbing a piece of sausage and biting off a chunk.

The smile that spread across his face almost melted my heart.

Swallowing my feelings, I turned to Malik.

What's the plan? I signed to him with one hand. The other was still holding Amr's and I didn't feel ready to give it up yet.

"It would be easier to explain when Eli is done with her punishment," Malik said.

I rolled my eyes.

"She won't listen to you," I said aloud, wincing as the cuts tore through my body. His eyes shifted down to my uncovered legs and watched as the blood spilled down my thigh. I had chosen shorts for a reason and now it was show time.

"Rosie don't hurt yourself," Amr whispered next to me.

"It seems to be"—I was cut off by a particularly deep cut on my forearm —"the only way."

Malik gave me a hard look.

"Sign it to me," he commanded. I waited for his power to surge through me but instead he was giving me a choice...or at least the illusion of it. That's all it was with these people.

"Lars, Sirene, and Raphael, are probably in hiding," Ezekiel said. My gaze snapped to him; his blue eyes were more tired than I had seen before. "We will need to go to them and complete your mission. You have to kill them."

The blood rushed to my ears and my heart felt as though it would burst out of my chest any moment.

That was not part of the deal, I said to him in my mind. *You said you guys would do it.*

"Plans change," he replied. "What's better is they probably think you are dead or at least out of commission for a long time."

You can't seriously think that I can do this...can you? I asked in my head. *I told you I couldn't do that.*

"You have more duties than that, we can come back to it," he said and paused. "We meant it when we told you we wanted you to be a sort of symbol to people. You will still need to enter yourself into the government. Play your part at Winterfell."

I am not going back to Winterfell, I hissed at him. *Especially not when you just told me I must kill the high-levels who almost killed me!*

"I am glad you are talking but we only hear one side," Xena said. When my eyes snapped to hers, I saw her regret for her words instantly.

"Oh ya?" I asked raising my voice. "I wonder why on earth you only hear one *fucking* side. Maybe it's the—"

I was cut off by Amr slamming his hand over my mouth and pulling me to him.

Malik sent a look to Ezekiel before looking back towards me.

"The curse will be a problem," Amr said from above me. His chest was rumbling as he spoke.

"It will stay until we say so," Xena hissed at Amr, her eyes narrowing in his direction.

My blood boiled and my gaze shot to Ezekiel.

I will scream, I threatened.

"That will hurt you more than it hurts us," Ezekiel said aloud.

I wanted to lash out. Scratch his and Xena's eyeballs out. Scream in their faces. Throw shit. My magic began boiling underneath my skin.

"Rosie," Malik said in a soft tone. "Let's just eat and I can translate for everyone okay?"

I gritted my teeth but nodded anyways. Amr let me up slowly.

"Sorry, my love," he whispered to me. "Just want you unharmed."

I squeezed his hand lightly to let him know I wasn't mad. If I was being honest those words hurt more than the rest and even though I threatened to scream if Amr wasn't holding me, I would have fainted.

Tell that bitch to get her curse off me or I will rip up her favorite clothes, I signed to Malik with both of my hands.

Matt choked on his breakfast, and I even saw Malik's lips twitch.

"She *really* wants the curse off," Malik spoke for me.

I huffed and dug into my breakfast.

"And I told her no," Xena said. "Her magic is unstable."

Shoving a big piece of pancake into my mouth I turned towards Malik.

Then I will not work with you anymore, I signed to him. *This is a give and take, I did my duty and now she must give.*

Malik gave me a look that told me he didn't want to translate it. I leaned over him and gave Xena a small smile.

"I quit," I told her. This time the words barely even hurt as they were carved into my skin.

Xena let out a sigh and leaned back in her chair.

And you know Eli will not listen to you if you don't have me, I signed to Malik.

I gave Ezekiel a look knowing he heard it too.

You are at risk of losing me and Eli. Just lift the damn curse, I pleaded in my mind. It was my last shot; I knew it and he obviously did as well if the way his brow raised had any indication of what he was thinking.

But it wasn't a farce. I would leave. Hell, I was begging for an excuse to.

"After Eli's punishment is over," he said causing Xena to glare at him.

I cannot last two more days, I told him.

"Just eat," he said. "You will do some training, since you insist you are so *unprepared.*"

I raised my eyebrow at him but after that he was content on ignoring me.

With a loud sigh that stung my chest, I focused on finishing the rest of my food though it felt like a cloud hung over us and darkened with each bite.

* * *

A sharp pain in my thigh almost caused the scream that I had been keeping locked in my throat to escape. I ducked behind a tree that was big enough to cover my body without being spotted. My shaking hands covered the now burning flesh of my thigh and with a shaky inhale I focused on surrounding the cut with my magic. I didn't know exactly how to heal a burn, but I tried to imagine building a new layer of skin over the area. The pain subsided almost immediately, and I could finally let out a sigh without screaming. I knew there would be an ugly scar there, but I couldn't keep my mind on that fact as the crunch of rocks beneath shoes hit my ears.

"Come out *little bitch*," came the voice of my attacker. Silent tears rolled down my face.

Each time you win I will answer a question of yours, truthfully, Ezekiel had told me as he brought me deep within the forest behind the property.

They had told me I would be training today but I didn't expect this kind of blood bath; I should have known this is what they had meant. I told them I couldn't kill those high-levels and so this was how they rectified it. I should have said no. I *tried* to say no...but with the secrets of this world dangling over my head I couldn't just let this opportunity pass me by.

When was the next time I would be able to sit down with an angel and get *real* answers?

The man they sent for me was a few paces to my left and only a few feet away from where I was hiding. I could hear the movement of his feet, the rustle of his clothes. Ice-cold fear seized my limbs as I heard the intake of breath.

Let your magic tell you what you need to do, Amr had told me before I left his side to march into the dark forest. But my magic had yet to tell me what to do. I was guessing. Even trying the healing was a shot in the dark.

Let me out, my magic purred. *Let me help you.*

Every time the magic spoke to me, I started realizing that I wasn't alone in my own body. It didn't speak so much in words, though I could guess what it was saying. It communicated more in feelings, wants, desires.

I felt the magic coming towards me before I saw it. It was like a burning pain that forced my legs to shoot out straight and catapult me forward. The tree that I was hiding behind exploded into hundreds of tiny glowing pieces and I saw the horrific sight of the man giving me a bone-chilling smile behind the mess.

He was one I recognized from the dungeon. I couldn't make out his face from the dim light...but the *smell* was something I wouldn't come to forget. He had greasy black hair that fell on either side of his face and resembled noodles more than actual hair. His beard was long, untamed, and his brown eyes were bloodshot. His grey shirt hung loosely off his form and was stained in various spots, making it turn brownish. His black pants had holes in them and light stains on the knees and buttocks.

"There you are," he purred in a voice that made me wince. "They said I could have your magic if you lost. Just needed to take it myself."

My mouth went dry. Before he could stalk any closer I threw a fireball at his face and ran to the right. He diminished it quickly but left heavy black smoke behind. Using this to my advantage I used one of the skinnier trees and turned myself around to his back. His eyes met mine for only a second before I focused on covering his entire form with fire, hotter than I had ever made before.

It was like the games...but instead, this time the tips of my flames were turning blue.

His screams were drowned out by my own heart pounding in my ears. He worked to distinguish the flames but either his magic was too weak, they were too hot...or he was just caught off guard because his screams stopped suddenly.

I diminished the flames before they became too wild and stared at the crisp body on the forest floor.

Was he dead?

My heart stopped and I scrambled over to the body. His hair was all but singed off and he was barely recognizable. With shaking hands, I tried to emulate what I had done to my own leg. I didn't know where to start so I just put my hands on his chest and focused on making the magic as big as I possibly could.

My own tears fell onto my hands and my magic flickered to the tune of my sobs. I couldn't concentrate. I couldn't do it. I had killed the man that was supposed to help train me.

"Enough, Rosie," Ezekiel said from behind me. His hand gripped at my shoulder. "You are hurting yourself."

I didn't notice until that moment that my curse was still working against me. Until he mentioned it the pain had been dulled because I was fighting for my life, and *his*. Now I felt like my entire body was on fire.

"He was meant to die, child," Xena said in a harsh tone from behind me.

This time it was her hand that gripped my upper bicep and dragged me to a standing position.

Her brown eyes met mine. They were hard and her mouth was set in a scowl.

"Meant to die by magic, dear," Ezekiel said. My gaze snapped towards him as his foot came to rest on the man's throat. "Not fire."

The sight of the most powerful man on earth, dressed in a suit, in the middle of the forest, stepping on a fully burnt body will forever be burned in my mind. It was like something out of a horror movie, especially the way his face never changed as he applied pressure and how his soft tone never wavered.

Amr's warm arms pulled me out of my mother's grasp and into his chest. My sobs died down as I stared at the corpse. He didn't even make a sound as he died, just a swoosh of wind came out of his mouth.

"You should have told us that was your plan," Amr hissed. "We wouldn't have agreed."

"Even for all the answers in the world?" Ezekiel asked in the same soft tone and walked toward us. "I will count this one since I wasn't *clear* enough last time. Ask away, then we will start again."

I swallowed all the screams, angry remarks, and tears, trying to focus on the question that was running around in my head this entire time.

How many of there are you? Originals, I mean, I asked towards him in my head.

"She asks how many originals there are," Ezekiel relayed.

"First generation?" she asks with a hum as if she had to think. "Five in this country. Many more throughout, I'd average about twenty or so."

Ezekiel grabbed a handkerchief from his pocket and began wiping off his hands.

"The other countries are more...hospitable to our kind," he explained.

How many were there before? I couldn't stop the question from popping up.

Ezekiel gave me a smile.

"Kill the next one with magic and you will have an answer," he said.

I froze in Amr's arms.

I refuse, I said in my mind. *This is not training, it is slaughter. Please...I will do the task just please don't make me do this anymore.* I was not this person. They knew I wasn't. That's why they put me on information duty at first. What had changed?

My eyes shifted towards the corpse on the floor and questions started to fill my mind.

Who was he?
What was his name?
What did he do to get sent there?
Did he have a family?

"You cannot refuse," Ezekiel said simply. "I will have Malik force you to if needed but we cannot have a situation like *before* happen again."

My breath caught at his tone and my nails dug into Amr's arms. I bit the inside of my cheek to stop the tears from falling even harder.

"You mean her *almost death*?" Amr asked incredulously. His grip on me tightened.

"Yes," Xena spoke and picked at the dust under her nails. Her scowl had deepened. "She was in the perfect position, as were you, to kill the enemies. Yet your own weakness stopped you, so here we are."

I wanted to back away, run from this and never look back. Ezekiel gave me a look that I had once assumed was pity but now I wasn't so sure.

"We didn't mean for it to be like this. Believe us, Rosie," he said and lifted his hands up as if to show me he meant no harm. "But when you go back to Winterfell, go back to your life. You will see them again, and when you do, your task will not be to gather information. You need to know how to use what you have. Remember, *you* were the one who *told us* you were unprepared."

Horror and anxiety gnawed at my gut. I couldn't stop the bile that rose in my throat and I scrambled out of Amr's arms and to the adjacent tree to lose those delicious pancakes from earlier. They were burning as they came up.

"Get Malik," Ezekiel ordered Xena.

I didn't even have it in me to fight them this time.

It only took a few more moments before I heard the two sets of footsteps show up. I slowly raised my head to meet Malik's golden eyes. He was obviously uncomfortable. Amr on the other hand looked like he was seething.

Without a push from the originals, I went to stand in front of Malik, ready for him to hit me with his power. I stiffened as his hand came to the top of my head.

"I'm sorry Rosie," he said softly. "Do your training in earnest, fight those they tell you to fight and for god's sake...use your magic."

This time when the magic overtook me it felt softer than before, at least at first. After a moment it began to feel like my insides were on fire before disappearing like nothing had happened. I almost welcomed the pain and wished for it to go on longer...because then at least I would get what was coming to me.

Malik's gaze didn't leave mine as he removed his hand from my head. I wanted to run into his arms. I wanted to see the Malik I saw at the beach. I needed him and his gaze was teasing me with his ghost.

Ezekiel's hand squeezed my shoulder, breaking my intense stare down with Malik.

"Four thousand six hundred and ten," he said in a solemn voice. "When we reached the eighteenth century we had half, and just this last century we had only six hundred left."

The words weighed heavily in the air.

These were rumored to be the strongest people in the universe. The people who created our race. They should have been undefeatable.

"It would seem that the humans were right," I said in a solemn voice. My cuts hurt but they almost felt numb in comparison to the way my heart was bleeding. I leaned my head back to look straight into Ezekiel's blue eyes. "We really are demons."

Chapter 9
Daxton

"Originals be dammed," I groaned, and I ran to the bathroom for the *fifth* time tonight.

After the sickness ejected itself from my stomach I curled around the toilet in Rosie's bathroom. The cool tile was a relief to my skin. I had shed my clothes hours ago in favor of boxers, just because they were so damn uncomfortable, and the cold seemed to be the only thing anchoring me to this world.

I took steadying breaths as the nausea racked my body again.

It was worse when people were gone. The thoughts came too fast when there was nothing but silence around me.

I remember the day it happened. It came to me in my dream last night.

I sat down with a sigh on my parents' dining table. I had come from hanging out with Eli not too long ago and expected this dinner to be full of arguing.

I couldn't wait to leave this house. Eli had offered multiple times for me to come live with her and her gang...but I didn't want to be involved in that shit. I had seen one too many things when it came to the closed doors with my parents and various other influential parties. Drugs, I could get behind... But the sale of women and children?

It almost made me stop being friends with her completely. Almost. I still needed her and the longer I stayed the harder it was to pull myself away.

"The Bennetts will be here for your seventeenth," my mother said in an

excited tone as she sat down next to me. "And Raphael too, you know Rae's father?"

Of course, I knew Rae's father, I wanted to say but I kept my mouth shut.

I watched as Father took the chair on the other side of me. He did this as a scare tactic. Showing that I would have to go through him if I wanted to leave here. A spike of fear gnawed at my being. Tonight, may be a night where I sneak out to see Eli even though I had been with her not too long ago.

The waitstaff didn't speak as they placed our meal in front of us. It was...a hamburger?

"Since when do you two eat this shit?" I asked and poked the burger with my knife.

I didn't mind hamburgers but seeing them eat something with their hands was unheard of.

"We just thought we should cook something you are more partial to," my mother said with a smile. "Since you haven't been home in a while."

I let out a snort and decided not to think too much about it. I would finish my meal and leave here as soon as possible.

I took a few bites of my burger. It wasn't bad...per se but there was some-thing weird about it. I was about halfway done when I doubled over feeling like someone had punched me in the stomach. I wheezed as I tried to push myself up from my seat, but my knees buckled under me.

Father's hands gripped my arms, trying to steady me but it was no use. The magic that had been bubbling up inside me seemed to be leaking out of my skin and then a flash of light covered the entire room. I could feel myself screaming but I couldn't hear it. All I could see was a white light, and there was a ringing in my ears so loud I was sure they were bleeding.

I scrambled up from the floor and leaned over the toilet again.

After that time, I had woken up a week later, my birthday had already passed and the doctor that came just said that I had a late maturity and that these were my real magic capabilities. I accepted it at the time, but I should have noticed the change in my magic. It was angry, violent, and forced me to take more than I ever wanted. It changed me into the person I am now and only forced me closer to Eli and Rae.

Almost three years ago this happened.

My eyes burned with unshed tears.

I didn't want to believe that I had eaten a demon. A real-life demon with wants and dreams. A family that was missing him. *Rosie's father.*

I couldn't even vomit more if I wanted to. Nothing would come out.

With a shaking form I pushed myself up and tried to clean out my mouth, being careful not to look in the mirror. I had done that last night and it sent my magic awry. I couldn't look at myself anymore, hated what I saw. I wanted to scream and pound in the face of the person staring at me, and my magic sensed that.

It lashed out wildly when I did so and was bent on destroying everything. Amr had been here to help me calm down last night, even if he wasn't my familiar anymore… But I hadn't seen him today. When I woke up from my ten-hour-long slumber, he and everyone else was gone leaving me in Rosie's empty apartment.

The image of Rosie's blood-stained face and gaping chest wound filled my mind. I had to clench my fists against the marble countertop in order to stop myself from crumbling to the ground.

They had told me she was alive…but that was all.

The girl that held me to sleep while I cried in her arms, the one that loved sweets and coffee more than life itself, the one that looked at the world with wide-eyed wonder was currently out of my reach and I had no idea what was happening to her.

On unsteady feet I pushed myself into the room and looked for my phone amongst the sheets. My stomach growled at me and twisted painfully.

"Not now," I hissed.

Hope ran through me as my hand wrapped around the cool feeling of my phone.

I quickly dialed Eli's number but frowned when it went to voicemail. I would call Amr, but we had never given him a phone.

Probably another reason he is better off with Rosie, I thought wryly.

Next I dialed Rae. It was the last thing I wanted to do given her shitty behavior, but I had no choice.

"Are you okay?" she said on the second ring. I let out a heavy sigh.

"Eli didn't answer," I said and sat down on the edge of the bed, unable to hold myself up any longer. "And I need to share magic."

"Well Amr was with her last," she said. I heard some rustling and talking on the other end.

"I know, that's why I am calling you, *honor student,*" I said with an annoyed huff. "Where is she?"

"How would I know?" she said sounding annoyed. Something didn't feel right with her responses.

"Where are you?" I asked.

There was a pause from her. Even the rustling and other voices seemed to go quiet.

"In another property with my family," she ground out. Her words seemed forced.

"Why?" I asked alarmed. Why would she go back to her father's place? He literally killed Rosie—or tried to at least. I could let go of a slip, but this?

"For protection," she said quickly. "Look I got to go. Eli will probably answer soon. Text her or something."

Without another word she hung up on me leaving me to stare at the phone with a foreboding feeling in my chest.

I tried Eli again, but she still didn't answer. With a groan I threw my phone across the room and stomped into the bathroom. There was only one way to get my magic under control.

With gritted teeth I stood in front of the sink and didn't hesitate as I conjured a magical spear in my hand and ran it down my forearm. A scream bubbled in my throat as the weapon singed my skin, but I swallowed it along with my tears.

As blood flowed from the skin, I felt an immediate relief as the magic seemed to pour out of me far faster than my blood was flowing. My shoulders sagged and I felt as though the weight that had been keeping me down on this earth was slowly being lifted. It felt freeing...until I looked in the mirror.

When I looked in the mirror the first thing that I saw was not how messed up I looked standing half naked and malnourished in the mirror, but that my magic seemed to give off this aura that permeated the room.

I could see it gather behind me as if it wanted to create the silhouette of a person. My head swirled and the world around me seemed to tilt and sway. I didn't even register myself falling to the ground until I was looking face up at the shadow of my magic.

The last thing I saw was it smiling down at me menacingly.

Chapter 10
Rosie

I couldn't feel anything as I limped to the chair that sat in the middle of the room. I had been brought to *another* tearoom to heal and calm down from my training. This one didn't seem any different from the others and if I was being honest, I couldn't register anything that was happening. It had lasted the entire day and consisted of five rounds.

Five rounds.

Five witches.

Five deaths.

Every time a body dropped I would be snapped out of Malik's power and just stare at what I had done. It's not like I didn't know. *I knew* what I was doing as I suffocated, cut open, and killed every one of them. But I didn't *feel* until then. I was just working on autopilot and letting my magic tell me what to do.

It would whisper in my ear, show me the way to end things...and it *liked it*. It liked when we spilled blood. Liked when we killed.

Amr crouched down by my side, trying to talk to me but I couldn't hear. My eyes were focused on my now overly scarred legs. I had one on my left thigh, one on my right calf, one on my left knee. And a dozen on my back and upper arms.

I felt the sob being ripped out of me, saw the cut it left, but couldn't feel it.

"Why don't they leave scars?" I asked and wiped the blood from my new cut on my thigh into the blood that the last witch left on me.

It was a shit day to wear shorts.

"Words are the weapon," Xena spoke. "Not the magic. Magic is picky like that. Has rules even I don't understand."

I finally tore my attention from the blood to *her*. Oh god, I hated her so much in this moment.

But I was also really sad. I felt it build up in me like a tidal wave and it weighed heavier than a ship. Why was she like this? To me? I looked towards Ezekiel who stood by her side. Why was he like this?

I killed people.

I killed six people.

And all they gave me were stupid stories?

"You get five questions," Ezekiel said. His blue eyes watched me carefully.

I can't do this, I thought. *I can't be a part of this. Why me? Why was this my fate? Why did I have to be the one that caused these deaths?*

My gaze was taken from them as Matt kneeled in front of me. His red hair was a curly mess around his head and his grey eyes looked at me with a sorrowful expression. He was never good at hiding his emotions and his face told me right now that he would rather be in my place.

Maybe he has been, a voice whispered in my mind.

"Rosie," he said softly. "Stop talking. You used a lot of magic and if you continue to push yourself it will go haywire."

I looked down at my lap to notice the new blood pooling.

Was I saying all that out loud?

I raised my hand and brushed Matt's hair out of his face. How long had it been since we were able to talk like we used to? I wanted to go back to Winterfell with him like before, lie in the grass while we ate our lunch and talked about nothing and everything.

"You need a haircut," I noted playfully.

Anything, I pleaded in my mind. *Please say anything, do anything that will keep my mind away from what I just did.*

"Rosie," Amr said from my side. Finally, when I looked at him I could hear him and recognize the look on his face. *God he must hate me right now.* "Let's go rest. You will feel better in the morning."

I looked towards the originals that stood in the doorway. This time Malik was behind them, and he refused to look at my face. I took a deep breath and looked at Ezekiel head on.

"Are you the bad guys in this war?" I asked seriously. The cuts felt like small stings now.

Xena shifted and stared at Ezekiel as he debated my answer. Malik finally looked up, but he also watched as Ezekiel stayed silent.

"*We*," he corrected, "have played some bad parts." He ran a hand through his long blond hair. "But we have always fought for two things: to keep our race alive and to unite the divide between the races. That is all."

I swallowed the knot in my throat.

"By any means necessary," I whispered. He nodded and moved to the side to let us through.

Just before we left the room, Amr holding my left side and Matt my right, I paused and looked back towards the originals.

"Will you kill any of us if we try to escape?" I asked.

"You have four questions left, is this really what you want to waste it on?" Xena said in a tone that made my blood boil.

Ezekiel didn't look at me as he spoke.

"Escape, betray, fail, slack...all of them will result in death or punishment." When he finally looked at me I could see what the rumors were about. Even though his wings were not out I swear I could feel the aura they admitted. His eyes were sharp as ever and felt like they stabbed my heart. "Blood child or not. We have a war to win, and we can only keep around the best."

I nodded.

"From five thousand to twenty-five," I mused. "I wonder how many of them you killed?"

I didn't wait around for him to answer but I took great pleasure in smudging my blood across the pristine hallway as we walked.

* * *

Sleep didn't come easy that night because the images of the men I killed felt like they were permanently burned into my mind. Every time I would close my eyes and relax for just a second, I would be assaulted by the images of their last breaths.

Amr had fallen asleep with me in his arms and I knew that it didn't take him long based on the deep breaths he took behind me. Since the incident he had stayed by my side and refused to let me go, reminding me that it wasn't my fault and that the feelings would diminish over time.

I was almost jealous about the way that he spoke about the dead. He must have been used to this type of world. But I wasn't. It felt like my heart had been pulled out of my chest, chewed up by the dead's blunt teeth and forced back into my chest.

It felt like I was rotting from the inside.

I slowly unwound Amr's arms from around my torso and stood on surprisingly steady feet. The magic usage had pushed my body to its limit earlier, or so I had thought. Afterwards I felt like death and was ready to pass out, but after I was healed and sat in bed staring at the wall, I felt more awake than ever, and I could feel new replenished magic in my blood.

But this time it wasn't begging to get out. This time it just lay there inside of me, pacified like a tiger relaxing in the sun after a big meal. It scared me when I thought about how much more magic my curse was holding back from me. Would I even be able to handle it?

Maybe *she* had some truth to her words.

Even as I stretched my legs across the cool floor and snuck my way to the door I could feel my muscles and magic stretch with each move. It felt good. It felt satisfying.

That made it even more disgusting.

I opened the door slowly, as to not wake Amr. When his large form didn't twitch I slipped out of the room shutting the door with a light click that seemed to echo in the hallway.

I waited against the door for Amr, but there was no sound. A chilly breeze ran through me, and I snapped my gaze towards the end of the hall, fearing the worst.

I was surprised when a puff of white hair and dull eyes met my stare.

At the end of the hall there was a large window that was currently pushed open, giving an unobstructed view of the starry night. In the daytime it was beautiful to see the sun peek in through this window and if the breeze was hard enough you could see green leaves playing at the corners, but now it was not the scenery that caused me to pause.

It was Malik and Matt.

It wasn't that I was trying to avoid them and that's why I paused, well maybe I was trying to avoid Malik, but it was that they both held lit cigarettes between their fingers. Matt had been in the middle of a drag, his eyes widened, and he tried to hold in his startled cough, leaning out the window to blow out his smoke. Malik was facing towards me, his back to the wall and merely just stared as he took another drag and exhaled without any move to cover his tracks. They hadn't changed out of their earlier clothes, I noticed.

A sudden jolt went through me, and I marched over to them.

Matt regained his composure but stared at me with wide eyes as he watched me descend on them. He held up his hands as if to surrender and grimaced. Malik stayed where he was, and it was perfect for what I had planned.

Without a moment of hesitation, I plucked the cigarette out of his hands and inhaled. My eyes never leaving his as I exhaled, straight into his face.

What are you doing? I signed drawing my attention to Matt. The most likely person to spill. *Scared I'll run?*

"Well, I mean," Matt trailed and gave me a sheepish look. "It was kinda fucked up."

I blinked owlishly at him. *Did he just curse?*

"We can leave after Eli is released," Malik said as he pulled out another cigarette from inside his pants pocket. "We can leave that morning and return to Winterfell."

I am not going back, I signed and took another drag, this time walking towards the window as I did so the cold air could hit my face. It seemed to sink down into my bones and let out a chill in my body that would be hard to get rid of.

"You have to, Rosie," Matt said in a soft tone. And leaned beside me, his sad expression invading my peripheral vision. "You think today was bad? They aren't messing around. They have been far too lenient on you."

"I don't care," I whispered out into the darkness. My belly stung with cuts.

My eyes could barely make out the trees in the distance, instead they just looked like a blob of darkness.

"You'll die," Matt said seriously. He stubbed out his cigarette on the windowsill and leaned back with a sigh. I shrugged at his comment.

Malik's long fingers grasped my shoulder. I refused to look at him.

"You may not care for your life," he growled. "But others do. Eli, Amr, Rae, Daxton. You really want to leave them like this?"

I swallowed thickly.

"They don't care," I said, but even as the words left my mouth I couldn't help but see all their faces.

Amr's vow rang through my head.

I will protect you, take care of you, love you for as long as I live. I will belong to you as you belong to me. You will never be alone again.

Guilt gnawed at my stomach.

"You shouldn't lie to yourself like that," Malik said in a dark tone. "It's unbecoming of your status." I turned to glare at him, but his expression caught me off guard. It was sharp, angrier than I have ever seen it. "You are sulking, whining. Yes what you did was hard, but you need to grow up Rosie. This is the real world and you *do not* have a choice in the matter. You will go to Winterfell, you will complete your mission, and then once it's done you will stay until *we tell you* to leave."

I was shaking. I couldn't tell if it was from the cold or the way his words incited my rage, my magic.

"You—"

"Do you understand?" he asks me, his words cutting mine off.

His grip tightened on my shoulder. A warning. I knew this too well, my father used to do the same. He didn't have to say that the next time we had this conversation he would be forced to use his power.

"You're disgusting," I spat at him and turned on my heel to go back to my room, throwing my still lit cigarette to the ground.

I shouldn't have been surprised when I walked back into the room and saw Amr sitting up in bed. His eyes glowed in the darkness and zeroed in on me. For some reason I felt as though I should apologize but the thoughts of even speaking weighed heavily on me.

"Come to bed," he said in a grainy voice. Instead of walking to my side I went around to his. He stayed still as I pulled the covers back and situated myself between his legs. His warm chest against my back chased away any of the cold that Malik had injected into my veins.

His arms wrapped around me, engulfing me in his scent and pulling me further into him. I could feel something in his chest, a sort of low humming that vibrated my back.

"Are you...purring?" I asked and leaned my head back to catch his eyes. I could see a quirk of his lips just before he left a lingering kiss on my forehead.

"My love needs me," he said. "Even if she does not say it, I feel it." My throat felt tight, and I looked forward in hopes he would not see my eyes fill with tears. "You don't have to be brave. It is just you and me in here. I can put up a barrier if you'd like."

I swallowed the sob that was working its way up my throat. "A barrier?"

His hold tightened on me and I felt his lips against the top of my hair. I could feel his magic playing at my senses, caressing me as if they were hands. They only made the tears well up faster.

"So, you can scream in peace," he said against me.

I sank into his arms like I had deflated and let the tears flow freely. He didn't say anything further, just held me as I realized how fucked this world really was.

* * *

"Rosie?" A voice called me from whatever deep place my mind had wandered into.

It felt like I was submerged under water and then was hit with a blinding light. I brought my hand up instinctively to block it, but it was jerked back with a loud clang.

The first thing that came into sight was a metal bracelet that captured my wrist and the rusted links of chain attached to it. My eyes followed it to where it was bolted into a stone-like floor.

Jerking back with a gasp I looked around me.

I was seated right in the center of a dark enclosed room that was only lit by a few torches and a glowing light from right under me. I looked down at myself and realized that I was in different clothes than when I came in here, and was simply in a long dress that was now pooled around my thighs.

"We can begin whenever you are ready." Ezekiel's voice snapped me out of my trance and made me realize that I wasn't alone in here.

Ezekiel, Xena, and Malik stood in front of me and looked down at me. Ezekiel stood up straight with his arms at his side. He was giving me a look full of mock concern that made me furious. Xena had her arms crossed and looked down at her nails when I met her eyes.

Malik on the other hand, he kept my gaze with a blank face. The scar had seemed to heal nicely and there was no longer an ugly red mark on his face.

"It looks like I'm not the only prisoner," Eli's voice came from my right and I spotted her blond head coming down the stairs, followed by Maximus.

My heart sped when I saw her. She was okay.

Looking further to my right I caught the rest of the group. Matt and Claudine stood near the corner of the room; I could make out just the upper half of their bodies as Amr kneeled right outside of the circle. His face looked pained and when I met his gaze his jaw tightened.

"Three days in that hell hole should have taught you when to speak," Xena snapped at her.

Eli was escorted right up to the side of the barrier and looked down at me with a look I couldn't understand. She also was able to change, and she didn't look as dirty as someone who had been kept prisoner for days would.

Wait...wasn't she supposed to have another day left?

I felt something pry at my brain before I heard it.

Are you missing time, child? Ezekiel asked me.

I swallowed thickly not wanting to look his way. I was pissed and hurt about what they made me do...but there was something else. A kind of hatred that burned in my stomach mixed with a stronger emotion that floored me... Resolve.

What happened yesterday?

I was ready to throw a fit in Amr's arms the other night, couldn't even sleep over what I had done and now...

"Chickened out?" Eli asked, a sly smirk spreading across her face. "Or are you just upset we can't play with your curse ever again?"

That's right, I thought. *This must be what we are doing.*

"Do it," I said in a voice that felt like it belonged to someone much stronger than me. I turned to stare daggers at my *mother*.

I didn't know what I expected the curse removal to look like, or feel like for that matter, but Xena only looked down at me from her spot, lifted her perfectly manicured hand and in one motion flicked her hand upwards.

There was a pause among us that almost made me feel like time was slowed. I looked to Malik, trying to get any indication of what was happening, but I felt it before I could even muster a thought of the words I was going to say.

When the curse magic finally lifted from my body, I felt it first right in the center of my chest. Instead of the tingling feeling magic had left me...this was so much stronger and almost felt like it was vibrating inside me. My body shook with the ferocity of it and then it started to burn. I inhaled sharply and tried to clutch my chest, but my wrists were stopped by the chains.

The fire began spreading, feeling like it was destroying everything in its path as it worked its way up to my brain. I couldn't even scream as it burned hotter and hotter than ever before.

If there wasn't a god, then there sure as hell was a devil and he was making me pay back my sins in the most ironic and painful way he could imagine. I imagined that this was what my father felt when I engulfed the house in flames. Or what the others felt when I beat them in the games.

My body straightened like a rod and my spine bent, forcing me to look up at the dark ceiling. I couldn't stay like that for long though, my body was already nearing its limit. I could see my eyes darken and then one single voice rang through my head.

Whatever you do, stay awake during the ritual. It was Malik's.

When did he say that to me?

I had no choice, even as my body went limp the core in my chest continued to vibrate and burn until my entire body was covered. My mouth was open in a scream, but I couldn't say anything, couldn't scream, couldn't beg for it to stop.

My body jerked with the pulses of the vibration. The only thing that took away from the flame was the tears rolling down my eyes, but even those were boiling from the heat.

I could hear Amr yelling, but I couldn't make out the words. The only thing I heard was a voice that seemed to silence everything in the room, even the fire.

"Not yet," Ezekiel commanded.

In front of me the ceiling seemed to bow until it opened into a dark chasm, and I now no longer knew if I was facing up or falling into the abyss. I reached up to try and feel for it, but my hand was cut off once more.

Then the pain was gone, leaving my body only with aftershocks and noiseless sobs. The vibrating continued but it was no longer stopping my hearing.

The world became clearer, and I could hear the shouts from around me. I felt light, happy, unburdened for the first time in my life. I couldn't help the giggle that made its way up into my lips. Then the full-blown laughter that forced itself out of my sore chest.

The room fell quiet, and my laughs decreased until just a light chuckle.

Against the pain in my limbs, I stood. My knee buckled but that only fueled my laugher and I continued to stand straight. I rolled my head feeling a blast of warm power pushing throughout the muscles in my neck. I did the same with my arms and realized with surprise that the chains now lay broken on the floor.

"Oops," I said with a giggle. As promised, the curse didn't come back. Looking up through my messy tangled hair I made eye contact with my *mother*.

I walked forward but was stopped by a barrier of light flashing in front of me as soon as I toed the line of the glowing circle at my feet. I put my hand against it, barely noticing the burn.

"*Mother*," I cooed with a giggle. "I see why you didn't want to remove my curse."

My movements came as if my magic had a muscle memory that spanned the generations before mine. With ease I drew a complicated version of a cross and sent my mother a smile. With a small blow on the barrier, it shattered into a million light fragments around us.

For the first time I saw that damned woman look at me with fear.

I couldn't really tell if it was my magic or I that liked the fear, but I decided it wasn't important in the moment.

A strong pair of arms wrapped around my waist before I could take a step forward. They were familiar, and a pleasant type of warm.

"Come back to me," Amr whispered in my ear. "Don't let the magic consume you. Reel it in and we leave now."

I wanted to lean back into him, let him whisk me away from here, but watching my mother cower was far sweeter.

"I'd say let her," I said with a smile on my face.

The originals didn't even look at me as I spoke. Probably too afraid to take the chance at letting Rosie get a one up on them. She was not what I expected to come back to, and I think it just about made up for the fact that her curse was no more.

It was different to see her innocent and afraid, but now I had a feeling the mock anger she would put on before had become that much more real.

Amr sent me a glare, but I ignored him. It was Malik who held my attention. He was standing back against the wall of the basement, his hands in his pockets as if the rampaging hybrid wasn't his issue.

"Rosie, let's go," Matt said from behind me. Malik's jaw twitched in response.

Interesting, I mused in my head.

"We can go back to our place," Amr said. "Share magic. Get rest. You don't want to do anything you will regret."

"I won't regret it," Rosie said, but she made no move to attack the witch in front of her. Instead, she leaned further back into Amr.

Malik finally pushed off the wall with a sigh.

"I'll get you pancakes and coffee on the way," he offered and didn't wait to see if she'd follow.

She paused for a moment, her head tilting to the side before taking Amr's arms off her and following behind Malik.

There was a collective shift in the room, but I didn't bother to stay.

Instead, I motioned for the stone-still cat to follow and said goodbye to this goddamn nightmare. I caught up to Rosie just as she reached the top of the stairs and used this as my chance to loop my arm around her shoulder. She sent me a look and the top of her lip lifted in a snarl, much like I had seen Dax do before when he was close to losing it.

I pushed my shaking hand into my pants pocket and looked behind to make sure the cat was still following us. I wasn't surprised to see him right behind us but what I was surprised to see was a thin line of red magic connecting his wrists to Rosie's.

Separation anxiety much? I asked in her head.

She didn't respond right away, instead focusing on navigating the now silent house. Her thoughts were overwhelming and almost unreadable, but I was glad that damn ringing was gone. Malik was tense in front of us even if he didn't show it obviously. His golden eyes looked back at us as he pushed open the front door. When our eyes locked I couldn't help but think about last night.

It was dark in the cells and the people around me seemed to never shut up. I growled and slammed my fist into the rocks at the end of my cell.

"The wall didn't do anything to you," Malik's voice rang out from behind me.

I growled and whipped my head towards the sound of his voice. Just him being there pissed me off. It was like he was waving my freedom in my face. Taunting me with what they took from me.

"If you are not here to get me out then I suggest you get the fuck out of here," I hissed at him.

Instead of replying he forced his hand through the magic barrier, his flesh burning as he did so. He winced and faced his palm up. It was an invitation. I could see his jaw clench at the pain and could hear his bated breath even over the voices of the other inmates.

Curious, I stepped forward and watched to see how long he would let the barrier burn him. He didn't move, didn't groan as I stared into his eyes, daring him to give up.

But Malik was never that person. All shit aside, he was still the person I respected the most. With a huff I took his hand in mine and images flooded through my brain.

Of Rosie, of the people she killed. The way she looked as she realized what she had done.

So, you know, none of this was her choice, Malik said in my mind. Do not hold this against her. Hold it against them.

Coming from their minion, I hissed back at him.

His eyes shifted down the hallway then back to mine.

I will take you back down to our spot and explain everything, he said in my mind.

Without hesitating he pulled his arm back, the disgusting smell of burnt flesh filling my cell. He gave me a hard look before leaving me.

"Did he put you in here too?" a woman from the cell next to me asked in a grainy voice. "He said he was taking us someplace safe...but I should have known it was a lie."

I let out a frustrated sigh and looked to my right. I was met with her long dark hair and dull blue eyes. She was dirty and looked like she hadn't eaten a good meal in her life.

"Don't talk to me, low-level," I hissed.

"I want to go to the one outside of town," Rosie said dragging me out of my daydream.

I didn't realize that we were already outside and walking towards a car. I felt unsteady on my feet and felt grateful that we could take a car instead of trudging down the hill.

"We'll go to the one near Winterfell," Malik said as he opened the driver side door. "Maximus, Claudine, meet us in the pub."

I looked over to the silent and forgotten siblings. Maximus let out a grunt and put a hand on his sister's shoulder and in a flash of light they were gone. I cataloged it in my mind to tell Rae later given that I have never seen Daxton do anything like that before. Rosie didn't even pay attention to them and instead left my hold to pull Amr into the back seat with her.

I rolled my eyes and leaned down with my hands on the hood of the car.

"Move," I commanded. Amr gave me a look but lifted Rosie onto his lap and moved to the far side of the car only to put Rosie back down in the middle. The whole time she didn't react like she used to. I expected her to blush, maybe squeak at being manhandled but instead she just focused on the blank area in front of her and had a death grip on Amr's hand. "It's bad huh?"

Finally, she looked at me as I slid into the back and sat next to her. I took her hand in mine unsurprised that the magic was still raging inside. It was odd to feel her thoughts that were once so quiet to now be raging inside.

"I didn't know it would feel like this," she admitted.

Malik looked back at us in the rearview mirror as she spoke. The annoying redheaded *dog* sat in front and placed that innocent facade back onto his face as he looked over Rosie with concern.

"It can be overwhelming," Matt spoke in a soft tone. "Our bodies are not made to support this level of magic."

"No," she said in a harsh tone as Malik pulled away from the house. "I didn't know that I would like it so much. When I killed"—she took a breath—"those people I couldn't stand it but now..."

She trailed off in her words and pulled her hands out of both my and Amr's grasp to stare at them.

"Now I understand the power. I *like it*," she said in a whisper.

I almost came on the spot.

* * *

I hated low-level joints like this, but it made Rosie almost giddy. I mean...at least it used to.

We sat in our seats silently as we waited for someone to take our order. The booth didn't fit Amr, myself, and Rosie so I had to pull up a chair and sit at the end of the table, much to the waitress' dismay as she finally sauntered over giving us a glare the entire time.

"What do you want?" she asked with a huff.

"Blueberry pancakes," Rosie answered immediately. She cast a look at Amr then turned back to the waitress. "And a pile of every meat you have."

The waitress looked at her with a shocked expression.

"You mean you want steak and everything?" the waitress asked as if Rosie was dumb.

"And bacon and sausage," she said, her eyes narrowing slightly. "You understand what I am asking?"

Satisfaction flared in me at her response.

"I'll take pancakes as well," Matt said breaking the tension. "He'll take eggs sunny side up, and they will take..."

Matt trailed off looking at me expectantly.

They. My lips threatened to pull into a smile.

"Two portions of steak and eggs," I said to the waitress.

She furiously wrote all that down and was about to leave when Malik spoke.

"And some waters," he said with a smile that was probably meant to be charming but with *that* scarred disaster it looked sinister, and she recoiled further into herself and ran away.

"What about the coffee?" Rosie asked with a pout.

Malik gave her a soft smile.

"You don't want what they serve here," he said.

"And it's late," Matt reminded. "Maybe we can get coffee tomorrow?"

535

There was a foreboding feeling that washed over me as I watched Rosie's fists clench against her thighs, her hand no longer in Amr's.

"I've seen that look before," I commented in a playful tone. She sent me a glare. "Let's make good use of Daxton when we get home, ya?"

Her eyes widened for a moment and then her body sagged against the booth. She reached out to thread her fingers through Amr's once more.

When the food finally came I was happy to see mine was one of the first and dug in without waiting for anyone else. I had been holed up in that shit-hole for three days with barely any food.

Rosie remained in a somewhat calm state as she ate her food but no one in the booth had let it fool them; every single one of us had our eyes trained on her every second until she finally finished her pancakes and announced it was time to leave.

It didn't get past me that Malik and Matt had eaten but a few bites of their food before nodding and leaving the place.

* * *

The apartment was the same as when we left it, but I felt as though it had been years since we last visited. It sobered me. The whole situation did.

Rosie had almost *died* then we were forced into this secret town no one knew anything about and that doesn't even cover the revelation that *my parents* were alive and well.

And they were originals.

I knew I was better than everyone else, but I hadn't expected that.

And it weighed on me heavily. The entire time I was in the cell I thought about how I would tear them limb from limb, but when I saw what they did to Rosie...

I just understood in that moment that there were worse things than death and the only way out would be to comply or to find a way out of it.

Rosie paused as soon as she walked further into the apartment, and I felt that same foreboding that chilled my skin.

The air in the room was thick and felt like it was vibrating. The apartment was dark because of the time but it seemed to take on a new type of darkness. It felt *alive*.

I looked to Rosie and Amr, both of their eyes were locked on the door to Rosie's room and Amr's hand was clutching onto Rosie's shoulder so hard, his knuckles began to turn white.

I shot Malik a glance. He was still behind the group and just barely keeping up. He paused as well and looked around the apartment as if also just realizing how dark and sinister the air was.

"Matt, Maximus, guard the door," he commanded. "Claudine, you are with me."

The once frozen Rosie started towards the room, but Amr put his hand across her chest, stopping her. For the first time I saw her anger directed at him.

"I know the signature," she hissed. "You should too."

Amr gave her a look and shook his head.

"Of course, I do," he said softly before looking towards the room. "Just let me go first, I don't like the feeling of this."

I could see the tension sprout in Rosie's jaw before she nodded and let Amr take lead. I was content with wrapping my arm around Rosie, in part because I agreed with Amr, but mostly because I was dying to see what she felt.

As soon as I touched her, thoughts attacked me like a frenzy of flies.

Daxton.

Magic.

Dark.

A lot.

Must take.

Now.

Need—now.

God damn it Amr.

Faster.

Now.

I swallowed down the flurry of feelings that were called forth from me. I loved how needy she sounded and how much the beast that she called magic was pushing her to take. It reminded me much of how Daxton sounded when he was about to lose it.

Amr stalked forward slowly and only looked over when he had his hands on the handle of the door. His amber eyes were hard, and a frown was prominent on his face.

"Daxton?" he asked through the door, his voice louder than I thought necessary.

Just open it, Rosie's thoughts snapped angrily.

I looked down at her with a raised brow, but her eyes were focused on Amr.

"He didn't answer, let's go in," Rosie said and tried to move forward but I pulled her back against me.

With speed that rivaled my own, she sent a punch to my stomach. While it wasn't strong it was enough to startle me. When I realized what happened, I squeezed her shoulder hard enough that I could her bones cracking.

Her silence only fueled me forward.

"Calm yourself before I remind you of your place," I growled. "Original baby or not, you are still just a glorified low-level."

The words came out angry, but I couldn't deny how much her actions thrilled me.

When she whined I let her go and pushed us towards the room.

If you want him so bad, who am I to stop you? I said in her mind.

I pushed Amr out of the way and forced the door open.

With that I lost count of the mistakes I had made that night.

The room was even darker than the rest of the apartment, like a billowing cloud had forced itself into the tight space and because of some invisible force could not get out.

Rosie dashed forward into the smoke, disappearing almost immediately. I called out to her, but Amr was faster and dove into the room not caring about what lay ahead.

A part of me wanted to retreat, because I knew that this was bad news... but a twist in my stomach told me that I needed to check on Daxton. Rosie and Amr had made it clear that he was probably in there and who knows what he was up to.

Malik's cold hand found its way to my shoulder, and I couldn't help but jump at the unexpected feeling. His glowing golden eyes met mine.

Our spot in two hours, he said in my mind. I looked him up and down before shrugging his hand off and walking into the room.

I could see a small glowing light as I pushed through the cloud and as I got closer I realized it must have been the bathroom. I could hear Rosie and Amr talking in panicked hushed tones, but I couldn't make out the words. It was like the cloud was muffling that as well.

When I burst into the bathroom the cloud was lifted. Amr stood up with glowing blue hands, no doubt the one clearing the air, his face was twisted in a pained expression as he looked at the tangle of bodies below him.

Rosie's back was the first thing I saw but as I leaned to the side I then saw her face, which was covered in blood. Her brown eyes were wide and filled with tears. Below her was Daxton. He looked like he had been sucked of life. He was so skinny, and his skin had a sickly pale look to it.

Weren't we gone less than a few hours?

Rosie's wrist was cut open and her blood was spilling all over them. She pushed it into Daxton's face. There was a pause before his eyes snapped open and his mouth latched onto her bleeding wrist. I grimaced at the sight, but it wasn't the act that got to me.

It was the look in his eyes. It was a dead type of stillness.

His moans filled the room, and I could feel a pulsating in the air surrounding us.

"What happened to him?" I asked Amr.

Amr shook his head, his long hair swaying as he did, and met my gaze.

"I have no idea, but it felt like he was drained of magic," he said in a grave tone. He looked behind me, out into the room. "But instead of disappearing, it seemed to have accumulated."

"Like a cloud," I said and looked back into the room. The cloud-like smoke had begun to push against Amr's barrier. "How did you clear the room?"

"I didn't," he answered. There was a moan from Rosie this time. "I just put up the barrier and the smoke in here dispersed."

I looked back down at the two on the floor. Daxton's mouth was still latched onto Rosie's wrist, but he was sitting up now, and his hands were wrapped round Rosie's waist, pushing her into him.

It was hot and made me want to join them...but this whole thing felt wrong.

"You can do that later," I hissed at them. "Dax, what the hell happened?"

Daxton glared up at me like I was the problem.

"Let the magic in," Rosie said in a husky tone. "I think he can absorb it."

"How would you know that?" I said. Her brown eyes stared up at me, giving me no answer, only a glint that angered me.

"It could work," Amr said and without a moment to waste the blue light around his hand disappeared.

The cloud rushed past us like wind and my sight was blinded. Moments later the smoke cleared to show them in the same position, but Dax's hands had already started to wander.

The anger that flashed across me was so hot I could feel my skin heat.

"Fix this," I ordered Amr. "I'll be back in a few hours."

Amr didn't have to be asked twice and he descended on the two.

I let out a noise of disgust as I left the room. Malik and Matt were still waiting in the living room.

"Is everything okay?" Malik asked. Matt stood straight as I approached, his eyes narrowing at me. I ignored his gaze.

"I'm ready now, let's go."

Chapter 12
Amr

I wrestled with Daxton and pulled his mouth away from Rosie's arm. If the stupid boy kept this up she would lose too much blood.

"Fuck off," Daxton growled.

I let out a sigh, picked Rosie up and threw her over my shoulder. She kicked and pounded against my back as I did so. Daxton moved to lunge at me, but I wrapped red strings of magic around him and bound him in place. He bashed angrily against them uncaring of his own safety or the destruction of the room around him.

I could feel both of their magics reaching out and clashing together, fighting to intertwine. They felt like two invisible bodies reaching and lunging, though they were twice as feral-feeling as the two that currently held my attention.

"If I let you two do this," I said in a serious tone, "you have to be supervised. You can't just drain her of blood. Remember yourself Daxton. What on earth happened to you?"

"I need the magic Amr. Now you either give her to me or I *end you*." He sneered at me. I rolled my eyes at his tiny threat. If he really thought that he could take me, he had another thing coming.

Rosie let out a growl of her own and I pinched her ass as punishment. She let out a yelp before relaxing against my hold.

"The only reason I am even *entertaining* that idea is because you were drained of magic—which we will talk about—but if it was not so dire I would make you watch as I make her scream to the heavens." I paused, trying to reign myself in. I needed to be the sane one here. "Now if you two are both good, I will let you share magic, but if not I will leave you here."

It was a lie. Of course, I wouldn't leave him here.

He watched me for a moment before giving me a curt nod.

"You can be here," he said. "Just give her to me damnit."

"Is that what you want, Rosie?" I asked the limp girl on my shoulder.

At least someone was somewhat calm, I thought.

"Yes please," she said in a voice I barely recognized. I could feel her magic humming against mine. It was pleased at what was to come.

"Get on the bed," I commanded while slowly placing her on her feet. "I will bring him to you." I gave her a small kiss on the forehead.

She nodded and bounced out of the bathroom.

I looked towards Daxton. He wasn't being patient but at least he was still.

"Be good," I warned. "I will stop it if it gets too much."

He nodded eagerly. I waited a few more moments before unbinding him. He jumped up and raced out of the bathroom before I could even take another breath. I heard him and Rosie clash before I even walked out of the bathroom.

I knew what was likely to happen, but seeing it compared to imagining it were two different things. When I did finally pull myself out of the bathroom I saw him rid her of her shorts before slipping his erection out of his pants and thrusting into her roughly. They didn't bother shedding the rest of their clothing and it was like they couldn't get enough of each other. Rosie let out a loud moan that went straight to my cock.

I had understood this once before, when I was younger...but I have had control over my magic for most of my life. On top of that, their type of magic was different. When Daxton had told me that the magic tasted like an original's, I didn't fully understand until her magic was completely unlocked and it took over my senses. It was tempting, intoxicating...but I would keep my wits about me, for them.

Daxton wasted no time in fucking her senseless, pounding into her like it was his last day on earth. His hands grabbed her thighs rough enough to leave indentations and I was sure they would bruise if she were human. He let out growls each time his hips snapped into her. The sound of the two of them and wet skin slapping together was filling the room. I clenched my fists, fingernails biting into my palms.

"Oh god, oh god," Rosie's moans filled the room and even though it had only been a few moments I could feel their magics rise sharply before twisting together. But Daxton didn't stop. Even as they came down he lunged forward and buried his teeth into her neck, trying to pull blood from her so he could continue to take her magic.

"Daxton," I growled and raced over to the bed to grab him by the throat and pull him back against me, and away from Rosie. His body lay flush against me, and his head lay on my shoulder. Instead of fighting like I expected him to he froze and pushed himself even further into me. I froze as well when his backside brushed against my hard cock.

No, my brain said immediately. *This is Daxton you are holding.*

I could feel him swallow against my hand and suddenly I felt as though it didn't matter that I watched this boy bloom from a teenager to an adult. Suddenly all I could think of was pulling his shorts down and ramming into him like there was no tomorrow. From my position I could see where he was still buried inside Rosie and it caused heat to course through me and my mouth to water.

Rosie watched us with interest and hunger filling her brown eyes.

"Move please," she groaned. I did not let go of Daxton's throat, but his hips complied and drove into her once more. His hands gripped her legs once more and used them as leverage for his thrusts.

Each time he pulled out—and I knew he was doing in on purpose—-he would slam his ass back into my cock creating a delicious friction between us.

"Amr," Daxton moaned. "Please."

I swallowed thickly. Warning bells were going off in my head.

"No," I said even though the warmth in my belly was almost unbearable now. I moved one hand to his hips to stop him, but I found myself gripping him closer.

"I've wanted you for so long," he moaned against me. This time when he pulled out of Rosie he took a longer time to grind against my cock before pushing back in.

The shock of his words was enough to stir me.

"Ask me again when you are lucid," I said and unwrapped my hand from his throat.

"I am," he said and removed a hand from Rosie's thigh to rub my bulge.

"Fuck," I groaned out. This time I didn't stop myself as I grinded against his ass. "This will not go further than this."

I gripped his hips and began thrusting in tandem with him. I didn't want to admit how much I liked the feeling of his body against mine. How much I liked his little moans when I grinded a bit too hard against him.

And I sure as hell wouldn't admit that I found myself burying my head in the crook of his neck as he came.

I had a sudden need for more.

"Let me finish her," I whispered against him. He nodded and pulled out of Rosie and moved so I would have room.

"Amr?" Rosie asked as I pulled her to the edge of the bed. *God I was going to taste the both of them.* It should have been repulsive, but my mouth watered and I could feel my body start to shake in anticipation.

"I'm going to bring you back to oblivion, love," I said in a sweet voice. "I hope you are ready."

Unable to wait any longer I dove forward into her swollen cunt and dragged my tongue across the length of her. I tasted her and Daxton's mixture immediately and it was enough to bring my overly sensitive and aching body to a fast orgasm.

I had never in my life come without stimulation, but I knew that with the two of them this may be a more normal occurrence if I could not reel them in.

This, the two of them, was pure bliss. Rosie wrapped her thighs around my head, and I didn't taste every inch of her until I had cleaned Daxton's come off her. Even though it hadn't been long since I had tasted her and felt her warmth against me it felt as though I was coming home after a long trip.

And I needed more.

The magic embedded into me was normally calm and didn't affect my mood or actions, but now all I wanted was to feel her around me, screaming as she once had.

She shuddered against me, and I felt the magic pulse around us once, twice, before filling my body deliciously. It roamed around every corner of my existence, and it felt as though it was *her* who fit her way inside me.

Daxton's hand trailed my back and I felt my cock twitch in response. This night was far from over. I stood straight and looked towards Daxton at my side.

It was almost like seeing a new person.

His hair had been short for a while now but all of a sudden I realized just how handsome his face was. His high cheekbones, strong jaw, and the script on his temple that curved so delicately around his eyebrows and brown eyes.

I had never let myself have a moment like this. A moment to take in his beauty. It was looked down upon, even being with Rosie was not how my role should have played out. But I was *obsessed* with her.

And now I could feel the same giddiness I felt when looking at her build up inside me.

The Daxton I once knew was gone and in his place stood a man waiting for me.

Still, I thought. *I must refuse.*

I opened my mouth to speak but Rosie's hand clutching my shirt and pulling me to her stopped me. Her lips crashed to mine with such heat and such need it almost brought me to my knees.

She was another who had changed so drastically in the time since we had met. Gone was the shy angel and now was a vixen whose gaze alone made my legs weak and my head spin.

She pulled me on top of her and I placed a hand on the bed, so my weight wasn't crushing her. Her lips attacked my throat, sucking and biting at the sensitive flesh. By now my dick was fully erect and painfully pushing against my pants. With strength I didn't know she had, she pushed me back onto the bed so that she was straddling me. I expected her to want to ride me, so I moved to unbutton my jeans, but she smirked down at me.

"I want more of your mouth," she explained.

She didn't need to explain anymore, I gripped her bare hips and pulled her sopping wet cunt onto my mouth. She wasted no time in grinding down onto my tongue after I licked the length of her slit. I could still taste Daxton on her.

"Take what you need, love," I growled against her swollen flesh. "Ride my face."

With her head thrown back and her long hair tickling my belly, she did just that. She gasped as she bucked into my mouth, fucking my tongue. I gripped onto her thighs and pulled her tighter onto my face.

I began to lose myself in her. Her moans were the only things I heard; the wetness of her cunt was the only thing I could feel...until I felt the rest of my zipper being pulled down.

I knew those hands. They had stroked my fur in cat form many times before, but I never realized how lithe and perfect they were until they flattened against my stomach, teasing their way down while tugging at my jeans.

I couldn't even think to say no. I wanted his touch so bad. So, when I felt his hand palm my erection through my boxers I let out a groan. Rosie seemed to like that and let out a whimper.

When Daxton finally wrapped his hands around my cock I could feel it throbbing against his hands. He ran his hands up the length of me with a light touch, meant to be teasing, until I felt his thumb brush over my sensitive head. There was a pause and I wondered if he had come to his senses and started to regret what we were doing...then I felt his tongue lick my tip.

"Fuck," I groaned against Rosie. I used my thumb to start rubbing circles in her clit knowing I wouldn't last long.

His hot mouth wrapped around me before taking me fully into him. He only pulled back when I felt the tip hit the back of his throat. His tongue worked at the underside of my shaft as he pulled back before taking me in fully again.

Where the fuck did he learn that?

He set off to work, sucking on my cock and would only pull away to allow his skilled tongue a trip to my tightening sack and then back up. I could hear the obscene wet sounds he made as he greedily took my cock and his small gag when I thrust up into his mouth.

Still, he took it and coupled with the way Rosie was fucking my mouth I found myself bring thrown violently over the edge.

The magic that grew in between the three of us was nothing like I had ever felt in this lifetime and was sure that it was the closest to heaven as I would ever get. I could feel both of their magic swirl inside me, like they were dancing with each other. It felt like we were the only three left in the world and I understood now that this was how it should be. There would be no stopping the three of us any longer and I almost cursed myself for being so stupid for so long.

Rosie lifted herself from my face giving me a full view of Daxton who still had my cock in his mouth. His brown eyes looked up at me and I felt his tongue swirl against me, as if reminding me who had made me come in the first place.

"Don't swallow," Rosie commanded and crossed the bed. Daxton pulled off of me slowly, leaving barely a trail of come in his wake. Rosie then *grabbed him by the fucking throat* and uttered words that made me fall head over heels in love with her for the millionth time. "Show me."

Daxton didn't tear his gaze from hers as he opened his mouth to show my seed. It was obscene, dirty, and without a doubt the most erotic sight I had ever seen.

Rosie leaned forward and pulled him into a deep kiss. I had to grip the sheets in order to restrain myself. Daxton sat at the end of the bed on his knees like an obedient boy while Rosie absolutely devoured him. It was like she was sucking every last bit of magic out of him.

When Rosie finally pulled away a trail of spit connected the two. They both looked towards me. One stare was hot and ready while the other had a glint of mischief that made my spine tingle.

This would be a long night.

Chapter 13
Malik

I didn't know why I was currently trudging through the muddy area near the forgotten side road that led to the bridge that connected Winterfell and the rest of the state. Or why both Matt and Eli were following behind me.

The only indication of what I was doing was the constant chanting in my head.

Go to the spot.

Bring Eli. Go now.

Go to the spot. Be quick.

I had no clue what awaited me in the spot, but I *needed* to go there. It was a need so powerful that it made my skin itch and consumed my entire being. Since I had brought them to the town it had been haunting my every waking moment and even followed me to my dreams.

"Malik," Eli growled from behind me, their voice barely breaking through my thoughts. "Slow down and tell me what the fuck is going on."

Eli's hand grabbed me roughly and forced me to stop in my tracks. Their blue eyes were wide in what could have been fear, but the rest of their face was pinched, showing their true anger.

My gaze shifted to Matt, who was standing behind Eli. His eyes were dark, and his normally red hair seemed dull in the dim light of the moon above us. The shadows on his face contoured him in such a way that looked like he was smiling.

Matt made a low vibrating noise in his chest that carried across the silent area. Eli jumped and glared in Matt's direction, but it was short lived.

Low chants in a language I couldn't recognize reached my ears and slowly I saw a bright light forming in Matt's hand.

"Knock it off, fucker," Eli hissed and lunged for Matt, but it was too late.

The ball of light that was once in his hand catapulted itself across the space and right into my face.

A bright white filled my eyes and all my senses seemed to fall away. Then the memories came.

Memory after memory assaulted my brain. They spanned more than a thousand years and each one felt as though it was being carved into my skull. I saw a man that felt oddly familiar to me. He had long black hair and golden eyes much like my own.

I knew him.

He seemed safe, like someone I trusted. He watched me grow up when my father had died. He had taught me all I needed to know about powers and the world from above. I was happy with him, content to be by his side.

Then the bad memories came.

It was the beginning of the war when the humans had risen against us. I saw the look in his eyes when I volunteered to go directly into the lion's den. I saw how I watched him, and how his friends fought yet failed over and over again. The pain of watching my brethren die felt as fresh as if it happened yesterday.

Each time I came back here, to return to him, and each time I saw the smile fall from his face. It was a reminder that we needed to keep going, a reminder that all the hundreds of years of work could not be wasted and that no matter how many years it took...we had a job to do.

"Stop," I commanded Eli and their fist crashed into Matt's face.

It had taken me longer this time to get used to the memories than last time. Usually, I was blind for seconds but looking at the bloodied state of Matt, I would say it had been minutes and that scared me. I didn't know how many times I could continue to do this and stay lucid.

Eli gave me a surprised look before throwing Matt's limp body to the ground.

"What the fuck is going on?" Eli said, their voice rising.

I looked around trying to find our visitor, but he was not here yet. Or he was waiting.

"Calm yourself," I commanded Eli. They froze trying, waiting for my power, then sagged when they realized I did not use it. "Matt was merely helping me. I brought you here to explain something to you."

"They are too emotional," Matt said from the ground and spit out blood into the mud. "He won't feel safe until they can calm themselves."

"Who is he?" Eli asked, grabbing a handful of Matt's shirt.

I let out a sigh. My head was pounding and the last thing I wanted to do was listen to Eli go off.

"You need to know the truth about your father," I said. This got their attention. They dropped Matt and stood facing towards me with their arms across their chest. "You, Rosie, and the others are not the first experiments."

"Well, no shit," Eli hissed and ran a hand through their hair. "You expect me to believe that someone as old as him only had one kid?"

Truth be told, I was surprised Eli had even thought of this.

"The others—"

"Are dead," Eli finished. "I know. Rosie told me."

"Rosie?" I asked, shock running through me. "How the fuck did she know?" I leaned to the side to look at Matt. "Did you know?"

"Sorry I was too busy trying to not swallow my blood," Matt hissed towards Eli. "I don't know how she found out; she wouldn't tell me. But the last day we were in the town she was hounding me all day pushing me to tell her what I knew. She threatened to go to Ezekiel if I didn't say anything and I panicked and erased the last day from her memory."

"Since when could you erase someone's memory?" Eli hissed.

"It was my mother's gift," Matt said with a cough as he slowly lifted to his knees then onto unsteady feet.

"They don't know," Eli summarized. Matt only nodded his response. "Well, you were too slow, she snuck into my cell in the middle of the night and told me her theories."

"Just that they had other kids?" I asked. A cold sweat broke across me. What else would she have known already? And what did Ezekiel and Xena already figure?

"And that there were probably more out there," they said. "She said it was weird how they progressed with the plan to out her to the world. There was nothing solid, and she sounded crazy...but everything was too weird to be what they said. She said someone she killed had said something...it was right after you came to my cell."

I sighed, the headache intensifying. If they heard her thoughts she would have been offed faster than the others. Before, the shortest running hybrid was six months before they put them down and tried again,

"They use you as bait," I said. "As pawns in the war. Normal high-levels and witches are not enough anymore. It has always been a race to see who could breed the deadliest and most volatile offspring."

"Why didn't Ezekiel breed with a witch?" Eli asked.

I was about to answer but I felt a familiar presence brush across my side. It was small and barely noticeable, but the power it radiated was unmistakable.

"Because they were too bloodthirsty," the long-awaited guest answered as he stepped out of the shadows. He was dressed in a fancy suit and his once long black hair had been chopped to his shoulders. His eyes slid towards mine and I saw the small frown as he looked over my new scars. "Something about his blood at full power that just makes people go insane."

"So, they killed them all," Eli said, their eyes looking up and down the newcomer. "And you are?"

"Marques," he said with a smile that didn't reach his eyes. "And not all, I have one in my possession."

Eli rolled their eyes.

"Marques is an original, like your father," I explained. "He is on the other side of the war that they have been preaching about."

Eli froze at that, and I saw the flick of distrust in their eyes. I readied myself in case they tried to run.

"Am I to assume you are the real reason behind Daxton and Rae's parents' actions?"

Marques let out a scoff. "I merely use them as a means to an end. A way to get what I need to get done. What they do with the information they gather along the way is up to them."

"They almost fed Rosie to us!" Eli growled and flung their arm out as if to gesture the ridiculousness of the idea.

"Yes well," Marques said. "Malik was there to save her."

Eli glared at me.

"Ezekiel and Xena said that they wanted to bring the world together. Humans and low-levels alike. You don't seem like the type of guy who cares about that."

Marques shrugged.

"I don't," he admitted. "Malik does and I know Rosie probably will, but you can work on changing the world later."

"Who's side are you on?" they asked me. "First you are bending your back to save Rosie, then now you are saying everything you have told us is a lie. What's the truth? Who are the bad guys?"

There was a silent pause as their words sunk into us.

"There are no bad guys," Marques answered for me. "We do not have a higher purpose, nor a mission. Only two groups that have two very different views on how the world should look."

"Why are you with this dude?" Eli asked me, their blue eyes widening. "He's just as crazy as the others."

"I just chose the side that was the least cruel," I admitted. "The one that looked the brightest."

"The one that doesn't kill their offspring for fun," Marques said in a smug tone. "I save them, take them under my wing and let them use their anger and power for a better reason."

"Which is what?" Eli asked. "And is this where you ask me to join the dark side?"

Marques let out a wheezing laugh.

"Let me ask you, child. How would you like to slit your father's throat and watch as he begs you to save him?" he asked. A cold swept across the area.

Eli's eyes brightened immediately, and I could make out the smile spreading across their face.

"So, this is your plan? Fight with Ezekiel and Xena? That sounds like a sad little dream," they said.

"I never said I'd stop there," Marques said. "I have been spending the last three thousand years trying to destroy every single original there is."

Chapter 14
Rosie

I awoke with a soreness between my legs that made heat flare through me soon as I came to. My magic felt calmer than yesterday, after many rounds with Daxton and Amr...but I knew it wasn't enough.

Even now I felt it slowly shift inside me as if it had also just awoken from slumber. Instead of pushing me to take magic it settled in my body like a dull ache, reminding me it was there, but not fighting too hard to get attention.

The old me would have been amazed at my change. Would have wondered how on earth I could lie between these two men and make love to them for hours on end...

But this Rosie, while she was surprised, she only craved more. She wasn't embarrassed or ashamed. If anything, once my magic had been unlocked it was like the worries and fear went with it.

Or maybe it was the trauma of killing four grown demons, but I would ponder on that.

Amr was spooning me, his warm breath tickling my neck and his arms circled around me. Daxton's back was pushed into me; his breathing was still heavy.

I knew Amr was having doubts about being with Daxton the way he did last night, but in all truth I had found it to be the hottest thing I had ever seen. Seeing Amr pound into Daxton from behind while gripping at his hair was divine.

I slowly unwrapped Amr's arms and climbed off the bed. Both of their magic, while powerful...was nothing compared to mine. I figured it out last night after they were both spent, and I was still wide awake.

I had once thought that Amr had an endless pit where he could take magic freely...but it turned out mine was just too much.

It was scary and exciting to think about all at once. No longer was I some low-level with a curse. Someone who barely had a say in the world was now a person who could easily take down multiple men at a time.

I shuddered when the images of the decapitated demons entered my mind. I could kill them easily, but a part of me still didn't want to. Though, I assumed it could be turned off if I was angry enough, given how ready I was to pounce on my mother back in the town. Even now the thought of her blood running down my hands made my lips twitch.

This, I realized, *was why she wanted to keep the curse on me.*

I walked into the kitchen to see Eli and Malik sitting at the counter with a bunch of coffees waiting. My mouth watered when I caught the size of the extra-large iced one.

Malik's eyes drifted the length of my body, making me realize that I was in Amr's shirt and nothing else. It fell to my knees so it's not like they could see anything anyways. His eyes darkened before looking away. It made my magic stir inside me; oddly it felt like it was interested in him.

When Eli's smirk showed I couldn't help but smile. This was the life I wanted back, and now as long as we were away from the town, I could enjoy it to its fullest.

Steeling myself, I walked towards Eli and instead of sitting down on the seat next to her, I climbed up on her lap. My mind froze reminding me of the other day.

Them...it's them now.

Eli let out a chuckle and grabbed my hips.

That's a nice sentiment, they said in my mind. *But it would be even better if you told me you weren't wearing underwear under that shirt.*

Instead of answering I reached across the counter to grab the biggest coffee, giving them a view of my bare ass. I looked at Malik daring him to say something. He didn't, instead his eyes shifted back towards Eli. I pouted and sat back down on their lap.

"Thanks for the coffee," I said and took a sip, leaning back into Eli.

"No problem," Malik said.

Eli's hands grazed my thighs pulling up the shirt, giving an unobstructed view of my pussy to both of them. Malik visibly froze.

"Teasing him is not nice," I said in a light voice to Eli, but my gaze remained on Malik.

"He can leave if he doesn't like it. Not like I'd let him touch you anyways," Eli said and licked the shell of my ear. Just as their fingers played with my folds Malik cleared his throat.

"You have school, don't take too long," he said.

My mood was killed instantly, and anger rose up in me faster than I could stop it.

"I'm not going back to Winterfell," I hissed. Eli took removed their hand from me with a sigh and fixed my shirt, realizing that there was no stopping this argument.

"You have to Rosie; you have an obligation—"

"To no one," I said. Malik's eyes narrowed in my direction, and he leaned forward.

"To your mother," he reminded.

"What are you going to do?" I asked in a sweet voice and leaned forward as well. "Force me?"

His jaw tensed.

Fuck that's hot. Keep going, Eli purred in my head. *I love seeing you all worked up.*

"I could but I don't want to," he answered. His eyes locked on my lips before coming back to rest on my own eyes.

I leaned forward even more, almost close enough to kiss him.

"I told you I'm not fucking going. So, you either tag team me with Eli, or get the fuck out," I said sweetly.

Eli took that moment to enter two fingers into me without warning. I was sore so the sudden stretch of her fingers hurt and made a whine come out of my mouth. I pushed myself back onto her fingers.

Malik stood straight and pulled the coffee out of my hands to place it down on the counter, out of my reach.

"You are going to Winterfell whether you like it or not," Malik growled before storming out. Eli wasted no time in pushing me onto the counter and curling their fingers inside me.

"His loss," they said with a chuckle.

* * *

Malik didn't bother me for the rest of the day, and I didn't mind one bit. I was happy to stay in the little bubble of the apartment and lose myself with the people in it. It was better than having to remember all that was against us and all that had happened.

It wasn't until the mid-afternoon as Eli ate me out on the couch that I dared ask.

"Where is Rae?" I asked and let out a moan as she pulled my clit into her mouth.

"At her parents," she said against me before licking the length of my swollen folds. I had lost count of how many times she made me come today. "They don't trust her."

I plucked my nipples and bucked into her face as I felt my orgasm rising up in me. Hands found my chin and lifted my face so that I was staring right into Daxton's eyes. He crashed his lips down onto mine just as I came, sealing us together for magic sharing.

I felt his magic pour into me with ease and it acted like water to a flame, finally calming my magic. The monster inside me finally went back into its hiding place and I could feel my mind clearing, but with that came the remembrance of things I wanted to hide.

"Why didn't you tell us your magic wasn't done?" he asked as he pulled away. His pout looked almost out of place on his usually hard face.

"You two were exhausted," I said.

"Lazy fuckers, it's almost two," Eli said before giving me one last long lick. I shuddered against them.

"It was indeed more that we could handle," Amr said. Daxton pulled away to show me Amr by his side. Amr looked oddly relaxed next to Daxton.

I wonder if they talked it through before coming out?

Amr's eyes told me they did, but if that wasn't enough Daxton shifted so that he was closer to the familiar.

A warmth filled my chest at seeing everyone happy together.

... All except one.

"What happened yesterday?" Eli asked and pulled me to them so that we were sitting normally on the couch.

Daxton flushed.

"I had some trouble with the thought of..." His skin started to turn pale. Amr placed a hand on his lower back they shared a look before Daxton could compose himself enough to respond. "My magic reacted badly to the distress, and I didn't have anyone to calm it with. All I remember is the magic filling the room, trying to get out somehow...then I blacked out."

"Magic is very in tune with emotions," Amr said in a soft voice. "I'm not surprised that it reacted like that when you were under emotional stress."

I frowned at him.

"I'm sorry," I whispered. "If I would have known I would have—"

"Gotten out of your coma and walked over here?" Eli interrupted me.

Be careful, they said in my mind. *They don't know yet.*

We need to tell them, I said angrily.

When we are all together again, Eli promised. *Rae needs to know too. And Malik told me he had used his power against you.*

Shock filled me. *Malik told you?*

They didn't answer, which only heightened my suspicion.

"If anything, I should be saying sorry to you," Daxton said.

An uneasiness filled me when I thought of my parents. I didn't want to think about them, I didn't want to deal with this. There was far too much to digest and on top of the betrayal, my mind was far too calm to handle going through this right now.

"I never knew him, nor did I want to," I said firmly. "Coffee is in the fridge, help yourself."

Daxton paused and shifted on his feet, obviously not taking the dismissal.

"It's kinda a big deal. *You're* kinda like a big deal," Daxton said, his voice expectant. "Child of an original and all."

I shrugged.

"I don't know her nor care to since she cursed me and left me to die," I growled.

"But Eli told us—"

"Let's discuss more when we are all together," Eli interrupted. "With Rae."

"You guys know something," he said, his eyebrows pulling together. *There was that pout again.*

"Amr, Eli, can you give us some time?" I asked. I felt Eli stiffen against me.

What are you up to? they asked in my mind.

He needs some attention, I said. *Let me have a moment with him. The more we keep from him the more he will ask.*

Without another word Eli unwrapped themselves from me and left the couch. I sent a thankful look to Amr when he left without a fight.

I patted the area of the couch next to me and Daxton took a seat without looking at me.

"Are you okay?" I asked and grabbed his hand. I hadn't spoken to him until I found him dying out on the floor and I couldn't help but worry.

"It was hard," he admitted. "To find out that my parents had—"

He shuddered and gripped my hand, unable to continue.

"I understand," I whispered. "It's okay, I just wish I was here to stop what happened. I'll be here next time."

His eyes were shinning when he looked at me next.

"Next time?" he asked with a pitiful laugh. "The only reason you survived was because Amr stopped me. There cannot be a next time. You don't understand this *thing* inside me—"

"I survived because my magic is strong," I insisted and sent him a smile. "It seems like I was the one who wore you out."

After feeling my own magic live restlessly inside me I could understand why he was acting so disgusted by his own magic...but I didn't want him to feel like he was to blame for anything. Dax, like many of us here, got dealt shitty cards and our only choice was to play the game to the best of our abilities.

"Are you sure you are okay?" he asked softly. "I didn't...scare you?"

"I am fine Dax," I said with a small laugh. "You could never scare me."

I felt it then. A rush of warmth rushed towards me. It was his magic; I could feel it tingle at my tongue and worm its way into my heart. It was less aggressive than before and worked through me as if checking on me.

"I thought I lost you," Daxton whispered, his eyes cast downwards. "I thought you had died and then when Eli told me you were in coma...and all I could think about was getting my fix..."

My throat constricted and felt my heart pound against my rib cage.

"Your magic was severely depleted," I whispered back. "Don't beat yourself up over it. Besides I am fine now."

"But..." He trailed off and bit his lower lip. "I should have been able to stop my parents," he said and looked towards me once more. "I just stood there while they ripped you ap—"

The scar on my chest burned at his words.

"You didn't know," I said. "No one did. Now don't blame yourself, okay?"

He swallowed thickly, the muscles in his neck straining.

"And *Rae*... I can't believe she would do such a thing." He said Rae's name with such venom that it left a sharp pain in my chest. "Just leave as you were bleeding out on the floor and protect that bastard."

"I—" I scrambled for words. I knew something had happened and I heard bits and pieces of it while I was in my coma, but hearing it out loud for the first time caused my chest to constrict and the air to be stolen out of my lungs.

She left us. My magic roared inside me. *We could have died, because of her.*

"I hadn't told her yet," Amr said, coming back to the couch with a coffee in hand. He handed it to me to sip on but even as I did I couldn't taste anything.

Daxton visibly flushed and looked down.

"Are you mad?" Eli asked. I looked over at them to find them leaning against the kitchen counter, watching me intently.

Was I? I could feel my magic react in ways that were separate from my own but now I just felt...acceptance.

I had known from the beginning that Rae's father was...problematic at best and if she had to grow up with someone like *that*...well then I wouldn't feel right to hate her for this.

"I don't...think so," I answered softly. "I would like to hear from her before I make any assumptions."

The tension that was so carefully hanging over us seemed to disappear and Amr let out an audible sigh, then gave me a small smile

"Well, you could always meet her at the campus," Amr suggested.

I put the sweetest smile on my face.

"I would rather die than go back there."

After all, living in this apartment in a cloud of denial was far more preferable than having to face the next task.

<h1 style="text-align:center">Chapter 15</h1>
<h1 style="text-align:center">Rae</h1>

She hadn't shown up for a goddamn week.

Eli had texted me to update me about her awakening but since then she hadn't been to school, nor had anyone else. I tried to call Eli this morning, but she refused to answer the phone.

Marques' threat weighed heavily on my mind since he last spoke to me.

Regain her trust, make her come back to you. She is hiding something, and it is your job to figure it out. Once you do, come back to me and I can ensure your family will remain unharmed.

I had known Rosie was hiding something, or at least we were getting close to figuring it out though what unfolded at my house only provided more questions than it did answers.

Even though my mind was plagued by thoughts of what this man could do to my mother and brothers...Rosie had been as prevalent as those thoughts. I wanted, no *needed* to know that she was safe. It wasn't enough to hear it from Eli, I needed to check. Needed to see it with my own two eyes, feel it with my own two hands. I wanted nothing more than to lock her back up in my dorm and hide under the covers with her.

I didn't realize the amount of chances I missed out on with her because I was so worried about my father and what the world would think. I had been so hung up on it while not knowing that her death was just mere months away.

I knew far too well that information had a price...but *Rosie* being that price was almost too much to bear and Marques knew that. That's why he had made it so that I would have to choose the one thing that meant more to me than her.

My family.

At this point I could only pray that his intentions were purer than those of my parents, though I doubted it.

It was on the seventh day when I saw her again.

The morning was comfortable, with only a slight chill to it. A perfect day for an even more perfect surprise. I was about halfway from the dorms to the main campus building when I spotted Rosie being dragged across the quad by Malik. Eli, Daxton, and Amr walked behind them all watching carefully as Rosie kicked and hit Malik.

I could hear the yelling from my place in the quad and their emotions played at my senses. They were all varying degrees of annoyed, but Rosie's anger far surpassed them all and hung over them like a menacing aura. I could also feel the restlessness of her magic, just like I had with Daxton, but now it was Daxton's that was calm and Rosie's that felt like a raging beast.

"Let go of me or I swear to god I will burn this entire campus down!"

Her voice was clear and unafraid, and it was my first clue that something had happened with her curse. My heart skipped a beat because I had never once heard it so loud and clear.

She was thinner than when last I saw her and her skin paler, making her scar stick out more than ever. She wasn't even wearing a school uniform, just sweats and a hoodie. I was thankful that her scar was hidden from view. Even though I had forced myself to look at it while she lay motionless in the hospital, I was worried that it would cause me to feel things that would sway my resolve.

"Don't make me use it," Malik warned.

They walked towards me but had yet to realize I was there, all too focused on Rosie.

"Do it," she growled and went to slap him, but he caught her wrist before it made contact. I could sense it was a mistake as soon as her eyes lit up in delight. Fire exploded from her palm and Malik fell backwards.

Rosie used that chance to run...straight towards me. She was smiling and laughing until she caught sight of me, then she froze. All happiness drained from her face and even as she tried to open her mouth no words came out. The others looked on with shock, finally realizing that I was here all along.

"Rosie—"

"Rae—"

I froze as she spoke. God I had missed seeing her and even now it made my insides shred with guilt.

How could I even navigate this?

"I'm glad to see you are okay," I said in a polite tone. "I was concerned when you didn't show up for school."

There was a red flush that traveled across her face but instead of fighting me she looked down at the ground.

"I don't want to be here," she said softly.

"You could lose your scholarship," I reminded. "And your chance at ambassador next year. Not to mention your curse."

She opened her mouth to speak but Eli wrapped an arm around her shoulders and sent me a smile. Eli still towered over Rosie but with her thinner form it looked like Eli's body was engulfing her.

"Tell me about it we have been trying to tell her that for days," she said. "Yet she has still refused."

The next person to draw my attention was Amr. I had looked over his presence when they first came up, too enamored by seeing Rosie up and walking again to note that he was in human form...and in a uniform.

"Did Amr already get settled with the principal?" I asked looking towards Malik. I didn't easily forget and his hold on the principal was nothing to blink at.

"Going right after we drop off Rosie," he answered, his eyes narrowing slightly in my direction.

He clapped his hand on Amr's shoulder and began to steer the group towards the school.

"What are you thinking of taking?" I asked Amr and glued myself to the side of the group. Daxton chose that time to show himself. He looked sickly, and my mind flashed to the last time I had heard his voice.

"Honor student," he greeted and strode right towards me without even an ounce of hesitancy in his steps.

Anger.

Resentment.

Hurt.

Slight doubt.

In a blink of an eye his fist collided with my face. I was so caught off-guard by the act that I couldn't react, only jerk back as the punch threw me off balance.

I could taste the blood coat my tongue. I spit out the metallic liquid onto the stone ground not caring who looked. I deserved this. I knew I did, for what I had done in the past...and will in the future.

"Ya, I deserved that," I muttered and wiped the spit off my chin with the handkerchief I kept neatly folded in my inner jacket pocket.

"Damn right you did," Daxton hissed. "But all is forgiven." He looked towards Rosie. "At least I think it is?"

Rosie nodded, a hesitant smile forming on her face.

Phase one of the plan, complete, a cynical voice said in my head.

Marques had picked right when he came to me. I almost wanted Rosie to hate me, to yell at me, to never talk to me again. It was only fair.

"Like hell it is," Malik said in a venom-filled voice. "Let's go."

Should I be relieved? Should I be worried? The look on Rosie's face told me that as far as my task went...I should be relieved.

There was a pause around the group, and I could feel their eyes on me, waiting for my reaction.

"So...classes?" I asked Amr once more as I straightened my clothes and continued walking forward. The group began to follow after getting over their shock.

"I don't know," Amr said. "Whatever Rosie is in."

I nodded.

"Only makes sense," I murmured. "With her magic going crazy and all."

There was a pause and a few eyes shot towards me. Rosie's were wide and the air between us filled with panic, self-consciousness, and anger.

"Can everyone feel it?" she asked, her voice soft.

"No," Malik answered quickly. "Just witches and empaths apparently."

I watched her shoulders deflate, then as if she realized she had done so... she tried to fling herself out of Eli's grip.

"We are already here, Rosie," Eli said. "Just fucking get it over with."

Rosie's face scrunched together, and a growl sounded from deep in her chest.

"It's not worth it," she hissed and snapped her elbow back into Elis's stomach. "Nothing will change, nor do I want to act like a pathetic servant."

The attack must have really messed her up, I mused.

"I don't think our parents will pull what they tried to before," I said. "Given the first attempted failed and that they have some form of dignity."

I felt a spike of anger from Malik.

I had spent days after moving from one house to another with my father constantly worrying about the possible attack. Marques was the one that assured us that we would be fine, but I didn't trust him much.

"That's not what I'm worried about," Rosie muttered. "It's—"

She paused and her eyes narrowed in front of her. I turned to look and saw Emma and her group of girls walking towards us. They all had playful mischievous parts sprinkled into their emotions.

"What a group," Emma said in a snide tone looking across us. "Looks like they really have adopted the low-levels—whoops, I mean hybrid now, right?"

"That was quite a shock," a black-haired girl said from behind her. "But we knew something was off about her."

"To the point, ladies," I said in a cool tone. Emma's gaze washed over mine and with a light smile she bounded towards me. I froze when she leaned up and pressed her lips to mine. My gut instinct was to push her off me, but she was gone just as fast as she came, and there was no way I would be caught dead assaulting someone in public.

"Just came to remind you not to forget about our date," she said with a sickly-sweet smile as she turned around once more. "To the gala." This time her eyes slid to Rosie.

I didn't look at Rosie. I couldn't. The emotions she was feeling were overwhelming. Anger, shock, jealousy. A warm flush exploded through my chest then was quickly washed away with a bone-chilling coldness.

I loved those feelings. Craved them. I had never once experienced this before and it had been all that I was waiting for.

But I didn't deserve them.

I wanted to tell her that I promised a date, and not a date with me, but the words died in my throat as I felt Rosie's emotions flare.

I drank them in greedily.

Malik let out a snort and pushed Amr forward.

"Rosie get your ass to class," he called without looking back. "Eli meet me after class."

Eli let out a noise of agreement.

"Why do you get out of school?" Rosie grumbled.

Eli let out a small chuckle.

"*After class*, little original," she said.

The hair on the back of my neck stood up and the world became clearer.

That's right, I thought. *They did say she was an original.*

The image of the black-haired woman passed through my mind.

Was she Xena? The first witch ever created.

"We need to talk about that," I said.

There was a pause.

"After class Rosie can fill you and Daxton in while I am away with Malik," Eli said.

Rosie looked like she was about to protest but dropped it quickly.

"I guess let's get to class," she grumbled.

With another chuckle Eli walked the both of them towards the school. Daxton stayed behind to talk to me.

"They know something we don't," he said in a low tone.

I slowed my pace.

"Obviously."

Daxton gave me a look before fixing his eyes on the couple in front of us.

"Her curse is gone," he said. "Or at least I think it is."

"What makes you say that?" I asked. My finger inched to bring out the notebook that was currently burning a hole through my jacket pocket.

"When she came back her magic had gone haywire," he said. "What you felt is her magic fully satiated. At least as far as Amr and I can take it."

I swallowed the knot in my throat and nodded. This information would be no use to Marques but for me it was obvious... If her magic was hungrier than what Amr and Daxton could handle...then it would be hard for me to get close to her.

Her magic wouldn't need or want me. And then that begs the question...

What if Daxton and Amr could not tame her? Would she go mad?

"What do witches do when their magic is uncontrollable?" I asked.

He let out a sharp breath.

"Well, some people can just fuck until they drop," he said. I didn't like that option. "Others use their magic in more creative ways."

"Like killing?"

"Or cursing."

Daxton didn't elaborate but instead let the words hang between us.

Rosie from here didn't look all that different but the change in her was obvious and it all boiled down to two events.

When my father stabbed her.

And when Daxton's father crushed her heart.

"Maybe she will have some answers for us later," I mumbled.

The hallway to the classrooms was in view now and we would soon be going our separate ways.

"You shouldn't have let Emma kiss you," Daxton said. When I met his gaze, his brown ones were alight. "I know it's not really talked about between us, but Rosie should be it, for all of us, and I know she likes you."

"Are you threatening me?" I asked. A flare of amusement ran through me, not taking his words at all seriously. But truth be told, I had no plans to ever be with another unless that person was Rosie.

But that was harder to verbalize than I wanted to admit.

"I don't need to," he said. "Rosie seems to be more than capable of protecting herself."

I shifted my eyes from him to where Rosie and Eli were waiting. They were both watching us intently. Eli with a smirk on her face and Rosie with a frown.

"I'm sure."

* * *

I entered the office bracing myself for the stale, disgusting air.

"Hello deary!" Tammy said in an excited tone. "How have you been? I hope your vacation treated you well."

"It did," I responded with a smile. "Malik and the new student wouldn't still be taking up Principal Winterfell's time would they?"

Her face scrunched.

"Malik?" She said the name like it was a foreign language. "He should be free, I'm sure you can just go in."

I nodded even though I already could feel the emotions of the two behind the door.

Malik and his damn powers, I cursed in my head.

I quickly walked towards his door and opened it. Inside was just as I expected. Malik and Amr sat in his chairs, both turning to look at me as I came in.

"I don't think there is anything else, right Principal?" Malik asked while still looking at me. The gold in his eyes seemed to come alight as he looked over me.

"Correct," Principal Winterfell responded. "Hello Rae, just in time to show our new student around."

Malik got up and Amr followed throwing me a questioning look.

"Do you need anything?" the principal asked as Malik passed me.

I waited until they both left the room and closed the door just slightly, so they were out of his view.

"Do you know Malik or Amr?" I asked in a low voice.

Principal Winterfell cocked his head, his eyes going dull.

"No, I do not," he said.

I nodded and opened the door to find Malik talking to Tammy with an animated smile, Amr standing patently by his side.

"Who are those people?" I asked.

I saw Principal Winterfell swallow before answering.

"You know your fellow students, Rae. Let's not play games," he answered. "Please show Amr the first-year humanities classrooms when you have a chance."

I grabbed my notebook out of my pocket and jotted down what I learned before leaving his room without another word. He called out a goodbye that I ignored.

Malik gave me a death glare as I approached but continued to bid goodbye to Tammy before leaving the room. I followed after them closely.

"Learn what you need to?" Malik asked pausing just outside the door.

I shifted on my feet.

"Wanted to make sure Amr was settled."

He raised an eyebrow at that.

"Sounds like you don't trust me," he said with a smirk. "And that's okay, I don't trust cowards like you either."

He waved goodbye to Amr and walked down the hall. Just before he got too far away to hear he turned.

"I hope you got what you needed," he said. "Just don't be so obvious next time."

His threat at one point would have worried me, not a lot but it would still hold weight.

Now it was nothing compared to Marques. I was still left with the biggest task of them all: find out what the hell Rosie was hiding.

Chapter 16
Rosie

I had suffered through the entire day in silence, pretending that the curse still had a chokehold on my life. It was annoying and I was far too antsy to sit still at my desk.

I hated the idea of coming here; not only did it mean that I would be closer to having to figure out how to murder both Daxton's and Rae's parents, but it meant I also had to play the sweet little hybrid that was here to change the world as we knew it.

They still had yet to take the posters down that had my pictures on them.

The first ever hybrid! one said.

Winterfell, a champion for change! another said.

It was just sickening and made my stomach twist. How long could I keep up this act when all I wanted to do was blow up this school? How long could I sit here and pretend to be the scholarship student when no one even really wanted me here?

The letter from Winterfell that I held in my hands in my old house, while it had scared me...meant so much more to me than what it truly was. I thought it was a way out, a way to rebuild myself and to create a better future for myself. One that didn't rely on a low-level job that barely made ends meet.

Yet those ideals all turned out to be a lie too.

A part of me wished that I could have been a low-level and stayed oblivious to this entire world...but then I wouldn't have met the people that I had and honestly, I didn't want to think of a world without them.

My thoughts had taken a turn for the worst, and I had thought that at one point I was ready to blow up the entire room. My power even responded and engulfed my hands in flames, but Daxton snuffed them as soon as he caught them.

"There are people in there," he said later as we finally walked from the classroom. "With real lives. Just because you are unhappy with yours, doesn't mean you can ruin others."

I rolled my eyes at him.

"Mr. Faulkner was in on everything," I grumbled. "I just know it."

"Speaking of that," Eli muttered as they wrapped their arm around my shoulders. I was tempted to shrug them off.

I caught Malik's bright tuff of white hair as we rounded the corner. He was leaning against the wall in the band t-shirt I had seen him in his morning. Surprisingly, he was smoking. It threw me back to the night I saw him in the town.

My magic reached out hungrily.

"Remove your power from her," Eli demanded as we walked closer.

Malik's eyes lazily glanced over to me, and the intensity made a heat coil in my stomach.

"Consider it done," he said as he blew out smoke. I felt the power lift from me. I had never noticed the weight it left on me; it felt like I could finally breathe.

There was nothing hindering me from telling the others the truth now. Amr tugged at the end of my hair as if reminding me he was there with me. I looked back and met his eyes. There was something in his gaze and while I couldn't decipher the words he was trying to tell me, I knew they held some comfort.

So sappy, Eli said in my head in a mock annoyed tone. I could feel my face flush.

Don't be jealous, I shot back.

"Thank you," I said to Malik. When he stood to his full height I felt my heart skip a beat. He leaned close, not caring that he was brushing against the others as he did so. The smell of cigarette smoke wafted between us, and my breath caught.

Malik had always been attractive, even with all the scars marring his face, but now that I looked at him so closely, his face held something more mesmerizing...and dangerous. The one light expression that was always on his face was now hard and even though it was still bright out, his face had a darkness to it that made the fresh scar on his cheek stand out.

The one I knew for a fact had to have been caused by my mother.

"I hope you have an idea of what you are doing, Rosie," he said, his eyes running over my face, specifically my scar. His chilly fingers came to lightly run the length of it. "Or at least know what you want." He paused, looking for my reaction. Even though I could feel the others surround us, the world melted away. "Because this isn't a game anymore."

He stood straight and cocked his head, motioning of Eli to come with him. Eli squeezed my shoulder before untangling themselves from me. I felt a chill as they did so, and an emptiness filled me.

I didn't want them to leave. I wanted them to stay here with me. I had the others but without them...I felt incomplete.

Eli paused in their steps before turning around quickly and marching towards me.

"Eli?"

They didn't answer, instead just gripped my chin harshly and forced their lips to mine. I melted into their kiss, but they pulled away as fast as they came. When they pulled back, their blue eyes were lit.

"Don't look so miserable little original," they said playfully. "Or else Dax and Amr will get jealous."

My cheeks flushed.

"Don't fuck around," Malik growled. "And don't call her that in public. Let's go."

Eli sent me a wink before following Malik off to god knows where. I watched them with an uneasy feeling.

Daxton's hand clamped down on my neck, his warm fingers igniting a small fire in me and his magic playing at the area where we were connected. I gave him a small smile and was happy to see he returned it, or at least tried.

Daxton had been having a hard time with what his parents had done, but at least he was trying. His skin was no longer pale, and he looked much healthier than before. Even his tattoos seemed to darken. His uniform was a bit bigger than it once had been and was currently unbuttoned in a way that showed the face of his devil tattoo.

"That was hot," he said playfully.

Amr's hand threaded through mine. I tore my gaze from Daxton to look at Amr. He looked absolutely mouthwatering in his school uniform.

He had borrowed one of Eli's but even then, it was far too tight. He was slightly taller than them, so the white button-up looked like it would rip if he got too wild with his movements. And don't get me started on the pants that sinfully hugged his figure, though they did stop just above his ankles.

"Rae will be waiting for answers," he said in a deep, calming tone. "After that we can share magic again."

I lit up at the thought.

* * *

Talking about the last few months of my life, including being introduced to the town and having to kill demons with my own two hands...was harder than I thought, but not in the way I thought.

Amr was next to me on Rae's bed and held my hands as I spoke. It was a comfort I didn't know I needed and was probably the only thing keeping me sane during this time. He would squeeze my hand when my voice got shaky or rub patterns on the back of my hand with his thumb when I came across a particularly hard part to talk about.

I was sure as soon as I got to the part about my parents disappearing there onto being forced to spy on Daxton, that I would be in tears and begging for forgiveness. I had more than once wanted to throw myself at his feet and confess everything, but now that it was actually here I could only wait for his outburst.

Instead of sadness that filled me after I was done speaking, it was an uncontrollable rage. I felt it eating up my whole being, destroying anything else in its path. I could feel myself heat in response and I knew that if I did not share magic soon I would turn into something that scared me.

Daxton and Rae stood in front of us. Rae had her arms crossed over her chest and didn't even look like she was breathing. Her stone-cold gaze stared down at me in a way that felt like she was ripping me open.

I knew it, I imagined her saying. *I told the others we couldn't trust you.*

Daxton on the other hand was looking up at the ceiling and refused to make contact with me. He was strangely relaxed and even had his hands in his pockets and leaned back into a causal posture. When his brown eyes finally looked towards mine, I only saw an acceptance in them.

"Thank you for telling us," he said in a voice devoid of emotion. Shock rushed through me. *Thank you?* "It must have been hard for you to keep those secrets for so long. I know because I have my fair share."

I nodded and opened my mouth to speak but Daxton held up a hand to stop me.

"That being said, I am disappointed that you played me like you did," he continued. "I understand the circumstances, but I told you things that no one outside of this room knows...and you sold that to our enemies."

I bit my tongue. *They may not be good guys but they sure as hell aren't enemies.*

"And you said Eli is now dragged into this? Did they do the same thing to her? What's her task?" Rae asked.

I swallowed thickly.

"*They* originally failed their task," I said. Rae lifted a brow at my words, but I saw it click pretty fast. "The goal was always to get to your parents, both of them."

"And so, they picked you," Rae said in a bitter tone. "A hybrid that can't even use their powers. Oh sorry, I mean couldn't. Let's not forget the time where they took you to a secret magic town and forced you to kill demons in preparation for your next task."

I flinched at her tone even though I knew I deserved it.

"You act like we lied to you," Amr said for me when my words failed to come.

"If it is true the whole motive seems stupid," Rae said. "Why have you thrust out into the public like that? Why not just send you to kill our parents when they are least suspecting it? They made you a target and nothing else. It's like they *want you to die.*"

Something, a memory tugged at my mind, but it was hidden behind a cloud of smoke. I felt as though I had something to say about it, but I couldn't form a coherent thought around it.

"Maybe they did," Daxton mused. "They almost got their way until Malik came to rescue her."

"But Malik is on their side," Rae said back. "So, if that was their plan why would he come to save her?"

"They were caught off guard," Amr said from beside me. His hand squeezed mine. "They didn't plan for them to act that fast."

Rae let out a sigh and ran her hands through her curly locks. Her hazel eyes narrowed in on me.

"And what are the next steps?" Rae asked.

"Find a way back to your parents," I said in a weak voice. "And kill them."

Daxton stiffened at my words. Rae gave him a look.

"That's impossible," Rae said, "...at least when they are together."

A prick of hope lit my chest.

"You're willing to help?" I asked. This time it was me who was squeezing Amr's hand.

Rae shrugged.

"It's either my dad or Eli," she said. A knife twisted deep in my stomach. I nodded.

"Right. *Right...*" I whispered. My hurt and anger mixed together, trying to push my magic to the front.

Take. Take. Take, it demanded. *Show them your power.*

I swallowed the raging emotions inside me.

"I have one condition," Daxton said pulling me out of my own pity party.

"Anything," I whispered.

"I have to be the one to kill them," he said, his tone absolute. His eyes were lighter than I had seen in months and for the first time a *real* smile tugged at his lips.

This was it. *The way out.* If he agreed to kill his own parents then there would be no blood on my hands, and I wouldn't have to relive that awful experience I had in the town.

But there was still...

I looked towards Rae.

Would she just stand by as I murder her father?

"My father will be my responsibility," she said, surprise running through me.

I squeezed Amr's hand, unable to breathe.

"Deal," I said in one breath.

Rae nodded while Daxton visibly swallowed.

"How do we even start?" Amr asked from beside me.

Rae shifted before pulling out her notebook.

"I would like to avoid making a scene at the gala later this year," she murmured and flipped through the pages of her book.

I looked to Amr for an explanation. I had heard about this gala multiple times yet had no clue what it really was about.

"End of summer gala," he said softly. "Rich people from all over gather and flaunt their year's achievements, get drunk, and spend money. Sometimes they have charities lined up but it is mostly a face thing."

"And it's at *my father's* house," Rae said. "Not a great place to be on equal footing."

Daxton cleared his throat.

"My parents share magic once a week," he said. "They have a sort of *ritual* that they like to do. If we can catch them *before* that ritual...they would be open to an attack."

My heart picked up speed in my chest.

"Wednesday nights?" Rae asked. Daxton nodded and his eyes shifted from mine to Amr's.

"That's soon, Daxton," Amr said, his deep voice filling the room.

Daxton shifted on his feet and his right hand came to scratch at his arm.

"Are you... ready for that?" I asked.

I should feel guilty for having them take care of my task for me, but instead I only felt an intense amount of relief and it only solidified my feelings towards the two in front of me.

They would do this, *for me*. Tears pricked at my eyes and my throat constricted.

"I have never been more ready for something in my life," he said, his voice steady and sure.

I nodded.

"My father will be more difficult," Rae said. "I will need some time to figure out how to deal with him but as long as they will not be together, then we will not run into a problem...like last time."

This was it, I thought. The beginning and the end of this thing. I had put it off long enough and now it was finally here. There would be no turning back, or else I would need to face Xena and Ezekiel and let them know of my failure.

"Let's prepare," I said. "Amr and I will accompany Daxton and then we will wait for your signal, Rae."

There was a tense silence among the group, the weight of what we planned finally bearing down on us...though it was no longer mine alone to bear, I still felt as though the weight of it all was doomed to crush us.

Chapter 17
Eli

Tonight, was the night.

The night that I would end it all.

I had been careful, after all I could only kill Damon once. Every night, when Malik and that fucker Marques didn't *require my attention* I would sneak away and watch as Damon ran the streets.

He hadn't changed in the months that I had been absent. Instead, he looked to be flourishing. He now had two pieces of arm candy instead of one, his guard duty tripled, and I spotted a new Rolex on his wrist every other day.

He had changed his schedule since I last saw him though. He was known to be secretive and constantly in hiding, but it would seem that he had forgotten there was a bounty on his head by literally every demon organization alive. He now didn't shy away from going out in broad daylight and even had the balls to stop off at a strip club three nights a week.

I stood outside of that very same strip club, hidden by the shadows as I watched his men guard the building. There was one on every corner and two circling the block. I had gotten past one layer of protection very easily but now it came to the second layer.

The anger had festered deep inside me since I learned that everything I had been fighting for had been a complete and utter lie, and that the originals just sent me off to the wolves for a bit of *character building*. I didn't take myself as anyone special, nor did I think that just because I was the child of an original that I deserved to be born with a silver spoon in my mouth...but I would be dammed if I let them treat me like nothing more than a dirty rat.

I shifted the gun in my hand, flexing my numb fingers to get the blood flow going again. I was severely disadvantaged when it came to my power and with this many men, I had to take precautions. The gun held magic-infused bullets that would make wherever you shot a deadly wound, because demons would not be able to heal it as the magic spread across their bodies and destroyed their insides. A sick sense of satisfaction fluttered in my chest when the men started to move. This was the time to strike, the shift change, and I had two options:

Walk in like an old friend.

Or shoot them.

The black-suited men laughed as they passed each other and exchanged a few dirty jokes. It was done in minutes and Damon's defense was almost ready except for...*there.*

The one man who was supposed to be guarding the rear exit was late... Well his body was actually being disintegrated in a toxic soup inside a hotel bathtub, but Damon's men didn't know that.

And just like I had predicted, they all moved closer when they realized there was someone who didn't show up.

I let out a laugh and raised my gun. *Idiots.*

I jumped when a hand was placed on my shoulder. I spun around and aimed the gun at the intruder's face only to be met with familiar grey eyes and an annoying smirk.

"Get out of here you low-level bitch," I snarled at him. He only cocked his head to the side and peered over me to look at the strip club.

"That'll cause a lot of attention," Matt said and started walking towards the club.

I let out a growl and pulled him back. His smirk dropped for only a moment.

"This is *my thing*," I hissed. "My moment. Don't come barging in here and acting like you own the place just because you sucked some original dick."

He raised his eyebrow before letting out a light laugh. A rapid heat flared around my skin, and I didn't even have time to think before I aimed the gun and shot it at Matt, point-blank.

The gun jammed.

Turning the gun, I saw a series of thin vines growing rapidly from inside the chamber and quickly spreading towards my fingers. A yell tore itself from my mouth and I threw the gun on the floor where it shattered to pieces. The vines continued to grow and wriggle on the ground like a dying animal.

I glared at Matt with more hatred than I had ever experienced in my entire life.

"Marques has given you a gift," he said then jerked his head towards the strip club. "Why don't you just go and check it out. You can walk in, no one's stopping you."

I paused, looking over to the door. The men were back in their places and acted as though they hadn't heard the commotion or just didn't care.

"I didn't need his help," I growled. "Who are you with anyways? Malik? Marques? Ezekiel? You seem to play every part very well."

He blinked rapidly and dropped the smirk, putting on his oblivious expression that he had fooled the others with so easily.

"I am in it for myself, Eli," he answered simply. "As are you, as is Malik, as is Marques." He looked towards the club and let out a breath. "I just don't fancy planning, I'm more of a doer."

"So, if Marques told you to get on your knees you would," I said with a snort.

He shot me a smile.

"I sure would," he said. "But he wouldn't need to tell me that."

I gritted my teeth against his response. *Stupid, stupid, low-level.*

Without responding to him I stalked toward the entrance. The men didn't even look at me as I approached and even when I stood right in their line of vision their eyes rolled over me as if I were invisible. With another growl I kicked open the door feeling thoroughly irritated and disappointed that the work that I had done up until now had been for naught.

The club had music blaring, and lights flashing, but there was not a soul in sight. The inside even looked more spotless than it had in the previous years that I had frequented this place with Damon. I slowed my steps as I walked down the hallway to the main area, a slight chill running over me. The area smelt fresh as if recently cleaned and I could see spots on the wall that were still drying as if they had been scrubbed vigorously.

Peering around the corner I saw that only the main stage, placed in the center of the room, was lit up. My breath caught and the sound of my blood rushing throughout my body was almost deafening.

Damon was kneeling there, naked as the day he was born, with his arms held up by two ropes fastened to opposite sides on the stage. His white hair was wet and clung to his skin, bringing out the stains of red that littered his body. When his eyes met mine I saw that he was also gagged. His body had already been shaking but when he saw me he began trembling even harder.

A buzzing filled my body and I felt lighter than ever as I crossed the space between us. I no longer cared that Marques had intervened because here Damon was...waiting for me like a beautifully wrapped present. And now I just needed to open it.

My excitement intensified as I saw that next to Damon lay tools for my usage. An electric razor, a blow torch, a taser, and a baseball bat. I am sure there were more tools lying around here but this was already better than any dream I had imagined.

I let out a loud laugh, that only intensified when Damon jumped and began struggling in his restraints. I gripped his hair and forced his head back so that he had no choice but to look into my eyes and watch as the same person he ruined now paid him back in full.

He tried to speak around the gag, but it only came out as muffled sounds.

"You really thought I would just let it go?" I asked him. He tried to jerk his head out of my grasp. I let his hair go only to deliver a punch to his jaw that caused him to go slack against the binds. "That won't do."

Picking up the taser I tested it once before lowering it straight to those disgusting balls of his and watched as his body went straight as a rod, eyes flashed open, and a scream forced itself out of his throat.

A flush of warmth shot through me so hard I thought I would be the next one out on the floor.

"A present indeed," I said with a laugh. "I may have to rethink my relationship with originals if *this* is my reward."

I stood up and looked over the tools all while being serenaded by Damon's cries.

Maybe Matt was on to something. I was in this for myself, always, and if Marques could ensure that I would have Damon and that disgusting shit of a father at my whim...then I just might be on my knees for him too.

"Let's have some fun."

Over three hours later I was still laughing as I hauled the bloody bag up the steps of the empty building that held the Demon Regulation Society's main office. They had an extremely classy office in the middle of downtown that was a bitch to find parking for, but at this time of night it was easy to break in and make my way to their front office.

When I reached the fifth floor I kicked open the door and was welcomed with two glass doors with their logo plastered on it. With the baseball bat in my other hand, I smashed the doors in on my third try.

The alarms didn't even sound, I thought smugly.

Without a moment to waste I tossed the bloody bag into the office. It rolled across the floor leaving a satisfying red streak. But I was far from done.

With my laughter echoing the empty space I stepped into the office and used Damon's blood to write on the pristine white wall behind the receptionist's desk.

A present, I wrote and stepped back to admire my work. It was a beautiful mix of gore and revenge all tied into one and last I checked his head was worth around a million dollars.

But I didn't want the money.

With the bat still firmly on my shoulder I set around the office smashing anything that I could find. Computers, paintings, glass walls.

I was a sweaty panting mess by the time I was done but the feeling that it left in my chest was second to...

Well, maybe not none, I thought as Rosie's flushed face entered my mind. Her image sobered me for a moment as I looked over the destruction I caused. There were papers and blood everywhere and I knew that I had done more than what I needed to.

I froze when I heard the crackle of glass under a foot. Snapping to look at the intruder I was met with a group of three.

Matt, Malik... And Marques.

"Come to bring me back from the edge?" I asked and threw my bat down the hall. "Don't worry, I was just about done anyways."

Malik's golden eyes slid to mine but it was Marques' dead stare that sucked me in.

"It was a show of good faith," Marques said. "Before the real work starts."

I raised a brow at him.

"Do I get more shows of good faith?" I asked.

A smile played at his lips.

"If you help with some of the work," he said. "I'll do what is in my power if you do what is in yours."

I nodded, the giddy feeling of killing Damon still running through my veins.

"You got yourself a deal," I said and walked towards him, holding out my bloody hand for him.

I expected him to eye it in disgust like the other originals would, but instead he placed his hand in mine and we shook on it.

Chapter 18
Rosie

I couldn't bear the thought of Daxton going in there alone, no matter how much he had begged me. There was no way that I would send him to be at their mercy *knowing* the type of people they were.

"I refuse," I whispered angrily as we rounded Daxton's property.

It was much bigger than I imagined and the magic that was weaved through the grounds was so potent I could taste it. Now that my magic had been freed for quite some days, I found myself more in tune with the surrounding area. There were no longer vibrations as the magic passed me, but I could feel it intertwining with my own, feeling if I was friend or foe.

And it came just at the right time because tonight, we would be sneaking into the Reids' house and murdering his parents as they were at their most vulnerable.

"I'm just saying that if things *get bad*," Daxton whispered back while he ducked behind some hedges. I followed suit tucking Amr in my arms. We had decided that it would be easier for Amr to be in his cat form and only shift if necessary. After all, two people were easier to hide than three. "Amr has to get you out before they turn on you."

I let out a huff.

"Just focus on the mission," I said through gritted teeth. "I can feel their magic moving in there."

It was like two blobs of slime moving through to the floors. The aura they were emitting was disgusting and made my stomach clench painfully. I could feel them moving downward and only assumed that they were going into the basement.

Daxton let out a sigh before pushing us forward, through the garden and alongside the south side of the house.

"Last time, they found out we were here in about ten minutes," he said. "If we can be quicker than that then we can get out without getting harmed."

I swallowed thickly. My palms were already a sweaty mess, and I could feel the overlooking cloud of despair coming on quick. We had only mere minutes until our lives were in danger.

He brought us to a metal door on the side of the house that creaked lightly as he pulled it open. Just beyond there were stairs that led further into the ground and just beyond I could see a light glow... I could feel their magic radiating off of it and had to clamp my hand to my mouth to keep from vomiting.

Daxton took a deep steadying breath and glanced at me just once before tiptoeing down the stairs. I followed suit trying to keep my magic as close as possible, though when we got closer I could understand why they were so vulnerable.

I could feel them in the act of sharing magic as we walked down the dim hallway and one peek into the room at the end told me that I was right.

In the middle of the room, they had a circle much like what Xena had in her basement and it was glowing a bright blue. They were placed in the middle, naked and covered in blood. There were slashes on each of their palms, and they wrote on their bodies and spoke in a language I did not understand.

All my life I had been told that witches were crazed, frenzied, and would do anything to wreak havoc...and I never truly believed it...until I saw this. The act was utterly barbaric, and I could feel the waves of disgusting magic seep out of them.

A rage so powerful swept through me when I remembered the look on their faces as they bound me. How they laughed with Rachel as I struggled. And finally the look of utter satisfaction as he pushed his magic through my chest.

I pushed closer without thinking; all I could feel was the rage burning my insides and my magic wanting to get revenge on the people who had hurt me. I imagined storming in there and letting it all out on them, forcing them to feel what they made me. I felt my foot twist and my world tilted.

I was falling forward, and right into their sight.

Daxton's hand grabbed at my collar but even as he stopped my fall it was too late, their gazes snapped over to us. Sirene tried to cover her naked body while Lars jumped into action, lunging at us. His face was twisted into a terrifying snarl and the noises that came out of his mouth were animalistic.

Ice-cold fear shot through my veins, and I found myself frozen, unable to move even as he descended on me. Daxton was the one that pulled me back and shifted us so that he would take the onslaught of his father's attack.

We tumbled to the ground and they collided, and Amr fell out of my hands. I had to blink a few times for my vision to clear, but when it did I saw Lars with a bone-chilling smile on his face as he began to strangle his own son.

"I thought you would have learned from last time," his father spat at him.

Daxton struggled under his father, fear filling his face as he jerked under him.

What was he doing? I thought panicked. Daxton was stronger than this. I knew he was. But he continued to struggle under Lars.

I stood frozen on the ground, unsure what to do. The images of those dead demons filled my brain, and my breath was stolen out of me, my previous rage blew up in smoke.

Could I do this again? My limbs felt like jelly as I pushed myself off the ground. My pants came in pained breaths as I called forth my all too eager magic. *I can do this,* I thought as Daxton's face turned purple. *I can fight him. Kill him.*

A blur pushed past me, and I only caught a glimpse of Amr tackling Lars to the ground and pummeling him with his fists. Bright bursts of magic exploded from his hands with each punch, and I scrambled towards Daxton, pushing him up.

Looking into the room I saw Sirene leaving out the door of the basement and into the house. My stomach dropped.

"We have to go!" I yelled towards Amr. His wild face looked back at me; there was blood splattered across his face. "She is getting help!"

"Two more minutes," he growled. "I can kill him."

"No," I said, my voice stern. "Daxton wanted to."

The man in question froze suddenly.

"Shit," Daxton muttered as we felt two balls of magic on the property above us. "Amr, the hounds."

Amr froze and glanced at Lars before pushing himself off him and running back to us.

"Through the house," Amr commanded. "Take one of the cars."

We ran into the room, and toward the way that Sirene had escaped. There was a short climb up the stairs before we burst into the main room.

There were waitstaff already waiting for us up there, their fists glowing with magic and ready to fight us.

We all froze when we came face to face with the sight.

The only way away from them was through fighting or back through the basement, but there were things waiting for us out there.

Feeling no choice, I also called forth my magic with trembling hands. I didn't want to hurt these people but if I had to...

Then the man in front stood straight and cleared his magic. The others followed immediately. He watched us before stepping aside showing us the front door.

"There is a car outside, Young Master," he said and bowed. "I suggest you hurry before they catch wind."

"Kevin..." Daxton whispered. It looked like he wanted to say more but Amr pushed us forward forcing us to leave them behind. They watched us as we left.

Like they had said, a car was waiting for us and it appeared to already be turned on.

"The hounds are out there," Daxton whispered. "On the count of three..."

"One."

"Two."

"Three!"

We piled out the front door and sprinted to the car. I could feel the magic running towards us, yet I did not dare look back. Amr was the first to the driver's seat and Daxton and I dove into the back seat.

When I looked back I caught sight of a giant menacing-looking dog that was sprinting straight towards us.

"Go!"

Amr hit the gas and steered us towards the path that had led up to the property, the hound still following us. The car jerked and the ceiling started to cave inward. Amr cursed and tried to straighten the car.

Big yellow eyes peered through the rear window, looking straight into my soul. Withholding a yelp I did the only thing that I could think of and pushed a beam of pure magic right into its face.

The hound let out a blood-curdling yowl and fell off the car, causing the other hound that had been following us to tumble over him. Amr only sped up and did not slow down until we were on the main road.

That was when I could finally breathe a sigh of relief.

Looking over at Daxton I could see that relief started and ended with me. His brows were pushed together, and I could see a faint shimmer in his eyes.

"I—"

"It's okay," I said in a light tone. "Next time."

Though even as the words left my mouth...I didn't know if there would be a next time.

Chapter 19
Amr

By the time we had gotten to the apartment there had been a tense silence that surrounded us. Daxton and Rosie had refused to communicate the entire way and even without magic you could feel the waves of shame rolling off of Daxton.

Even as we dumped the car a few blocks away from the apartment and walked in the darkness, each of us peering over our shoulder scared of being followed...no one dared to whisper about what happened. It was like they were both in their own thoughts, both beating themselves up about not completing the task.

His reaction to it all made my chest hurt for him. He shouldn't have taken this on to begin with, neither of these children should have...because at the end of it all, that's what they were.

Both Rosie and Daxton were inexperienced in the ways of the world and especially in the face of witches of their caliber. Even the escape tonight was a miracle in and of itself. To think that the originals had wanted her to do this *alone* didn't sit right with me and for the first time I began to curse them instead of fear them.

I didn't want the people I loved to have to go through this. Didn't want the weight of the world on their shoulders. They deserved a happy and healthy life unburdened by death and corrupt witches.

...and I should have been the one to shield them from this pain. I shouldn't have stopped when Rosie yelled at me to because we were going to be stuck with an even bigger problem, now that they knew we were after them. I couldn't help but blame myself for this mistake. I was much more experienced than them yet I still let them get themselves into such a tangle.

We got ready for sleep in silence. There had been an unspoken rule that the three of us would stick together while the others had been off doing god knows what. And it was easier to keep track of them this way, after all without the others I was the only defense that these two had. I may have only been bound to Rosie but my loyalty for both her and Daxton went beyond the magical bond that tied us together.

"We must pull back," I said as neither Rosie nor Daxton showed signs of sleep. "I should have put a stop to it from the beginning. I have failed you."

I could hear the heavy breathing of Daxton on the far side of the bed.

"You did fine Amr," Rosie said quietly next to me, her small hand reaching out to intertwine our fingers. Even just such a simple act caused my heart to soar. "I should have thought this through more. Next tim—"

"There cannot be a next time," I said in a firm voice. I could feel her eyes on me, but I fixed my gaze onto the ceiling memorizing the bumps and textures.

"Amr, they will kill—"

"We will find another way but neither of you can continue this," I said. "We are not at their level and even escaping was a miracle. I cannot risk you dying *again*."

"It is *my* task," Rosie growled. She sat up on her elbows to glare at me. I could feel the heat from her stare burning holes in the side of my face. I looked away. "And I am tired of people telling me what I can and cannot do."

"Do you want to kill them?" I asked finally looking at her. "Do you want to go through this task?"

Her face faltered but I continued.

"You need to think about the others we got involved, love," I said trying to soften the blow of my words. "Think of yourself. Have a little bit of self-preservation."

Rosie's lips pursed and she looked towards Daxton who had been oddly silent.

"What do you suggest?" she asked.

"We need help from Rae," I said after a moment. "Maybe even Eli and Malik. We tried our way, now we should get her involved. She could be better at planning than us. She could find a way to do this in a saf—"

"I want to try again," Daxton said, his voice rough with emotion.

Neither Rosie nor I spoke.

"It was my fault it didn't work," he said. "So, I want to try and redeem myself."

"I was the one that outed us," Rosie said in a soft voice.

"I could have killed him," he said. "His magic was weak...we all felt it. It would have been simple."

"I also could have killed him," I muttered remembering the satisfying way his bones cracked under my fists.

Rosie averted her gaze.

"I was the one that asked you guys to leave him to me," Daxton said. "And I want to do it."

"At school, let's tell Rae," I propositioned. "Then we can rethink a plan that is safer than sneaking into their house."

"It wasn't that bad of an idea," Daxton grumbled in a low tone "You agreed to it too."

I almost wanted to laugh at his childishness.

"Let's figure it out tomorrow," I said in a light tone and turned to reach my arm around both Daxton and Rosie and pull them tightly to me. Rosie let out a light laugh.

* * *

It was morning again when we came across another problem. I had thought that failing the task was the worst that could happen but a knock at the door proved me wrong.

We had been gathered around the kitchen island eating breakfast and chatting sullenly. The mood from last night followed us into the next day and still hung over us like a dark cloud.

I was the first to get up from my seat while I motioned for the others to stay behind the kitchen counter. I couldn't feel any magic from the other side, so that was *somewhat* of a relief but I wouldn't put it past Lars to send a demon to do his dirty work. I steeled myself with each step, prepared to pull open this door and defend the people behind me.

I looked through the peephole and relief crashed down on me.

It was Rae.

Opening the door, I caught sight of her. Her uniform was meticulously well kept and her overall demure told me that she was still on that high horse of hers. If I was being honest, I preferred the company of Rae over Malik or Eli. She was calm and smart and even though she often thought way too much of herself, her confidence was never misplaced.

"You guys messed up," she said in a grave tone and shifted on her feet, as if unsure what to do.

I opened the door wider and gestured for her to come in. She did not. I raised a brow at her.

"I will stay out here," she said.

I could hear the shuffling of feet as Rosie and Daxton left their spots to come join us. I didn't miss the way Rae's eyes followed Rosie and the way the muscles in her throat constricted.

I looked at Rosie, she was still in my shirt and her hair was tousled with sleep. I loved seeing her like this, overpowered by me, my clothing; it made her seem small and the urge to protect her only intensified.

I was so obsessed. I thought the words, but I couldn't bring myself to care.

"Sorry," Rosie said with a grimace. "We thought we could handle it and it just got...out of hand."

Rae watched her for a moment.

"My father is now on high alert so the plans for tonight may be more difficult than I thought," she said.

"Is that why you came here?" Daxton asked. "Or is it just to throw it in our face that we fucked up?"

Poor Daxton, I thought. *He probably still thinks we blame him for this. But there is no one to blame. No one except those originals. They sent us on a death mission, I am sure of it. They never once intended for us to come back.*

"I don't think you need me to do that," Rae answered.

There was a standoff between the two, both probably figuring if it was worth it to keep up this fight.

"So why are you here?" I asked, trying to keep my tone light. Her hazel eyes shifted to mine; a small glint shined in them.

"To tell you there is a possibility *I* may fail as well," she answered. Rosie stiffened next to me, and her hand found the hem of my shirt. "Given that my father knows you are back and realized that I have probably had contact with you, the chances of failure are too high to ignore."

Smart. Rational. Safe. I liked her more and more each day.

"So, what do we do?" Rosie whispered.

I swear I saw a bit of panic flash across Rae's face, but it was gone before I could make it out.

"If I fail tonight the only other time that we can get all of us in a room with them, *safely*," she said then paused. "Is the gala."

"You said before—"

"I know what I said before," Rae said cutting Daxton off. "But I am not the one who froze while I had a chance to kill their father."

Daxton let out an angry puff ready to charge at Rae, but Rosie put a hand on his chest, stopping him in his tracks.

"How did you know that?" she asked.

Rae raised an eyebrow.

"What do you mean? You guys failed and the only reason had to be because Daxton couldn't finish his task."

"But you said froze," she insisted. "How did you know he froze?"

Rae didn't move, didn't even look like she was breathing. I desperately wanted to know what her brain looked like inside right now because I could just see it whirling. Then, she let out a sigh and looked down at the ground.

"They came to the house last night," she said. "That's how I figured you failed in the first place."

"That's not a hard thing to say," Rosie said softly. "We wouldn't be mad. At least you came to tell us right?"

The tips of Rae's ears flushed.

"Did they say anything we should be worried about?" I asked.

She gave me a grateful look, thanking me for saving her from her own embarrassment...but it wasn't for her.

"Just that Rosie was way more healed than they thought possible and that they were planning to retaliate," she said then wavered for a moment. "It was my father who told them to let it be."

"*Your father* told them to not attack us?" Daxton asked, the surprise running through us all evident in his voice.

"My father may be rash and sometimes a bit insane," she said. "But he is not stupid. They almost lost last time."

"Almost," I said. "If not for you." A muscle in her jaw flexed. "And they still trust you even though they know you are talking to her?"

"I told them that they would have a better chance if they could get Rosie alone. They seemed to accept that."

A raging hot fire burned inside the pit of my stomach and all the positive feelings I had for her seemed to go up in flames.

"I would never let that happen," I growled.

"I know," Rae said calmly. "I *know*. So just keep doing what you are doing and under no circumstance can Rosie ever be alone."

"She never will be," Malik's voice came from down the hallway. "I thought you were told to stay away?"

Rae took a step back and looked towards Malik. I had to lean over the threshold to see his form and when he came into view I had never seen him more disheveled than now. His clothing was ripped and looked like it had been worn for years, his hair standing up all which ways and his dark circles made his skin look almost translucent.

"I was just leaving," she said and sent us a nod before turning back the way she came.

Malik watched her go before coming towards our door.

"Where is Eli?" Rosie asked.

Malik almost seemed to deflate at her question though his normal reassuring smile came to his face with ease.

"They are resting in my place, we thought it was too early for them to come to yours," he answered. "Would you like to check on them?"

He stepped back and motioned for her to step out, but she shook her head.

"Just tell them no matter how late, to please come back to our place, so I know they are safe," Rosie said.

Malik nodded.

"What are you guys doing anyways?" Daxton asked.

Malik shrugged.

"Gang stuff I guess," he said. "It's been a while since Eli has been...unoccupied. So, I require their help."

There was more we wanted to ask; I could feel the questions raging between us, but no one dared to speak.

"We need to get to school soon," I said and looked down at Rosie. "Let's get some breakfast in you."

I shut the door in Malik's face with a smug sense of satisfaction.

Chapter 20
Rae

The house was quiet as I walked through the upper floors, winding through the abandoned hallways. No one came up here except for a few house staff, and my brothers and me on the rare occasion that we found ourselves wanting to meet with our mother.

Dust clung to every surface, and it was a far cry from the tidiness and absolute perfection the lower levels needed to be. I made a mental note to myself to find one of the staff and order them to do some cleaning up here. Just because my mother was shunned by Father didn't mean that she needed to be treated in such a way.

After they had a few kids and father realized that none of them would take her powers in the way he wanted he stopped caring for her completely and moved on to a different obsession. Only now did I realize that it was probably about consuming the flesh of an original.

I found myself standing in front of her door in less than a few minutes, but I still had to take a few moments to collect myself. This part was always hard, and I was never a hundred percent prepared no matter how many years had passed. Taking a deep breath, I pushed open the door.

My mother had always been a fanatic of florals and that was one thing that my father indulged her in still to this day. From the old rug to her comforter, to even the tablecloths, were always in patterns of beautiful and colorful flowers. I had once tried to ask her about her favorite flower, but my ask fell on deaf ears.

She was perched on her rocking chair that faced the window outside.

She had a perfect view of the sunset and even though she couldn't tell me her likes or dislikes, I knew that when she looked out at the sunset, she had a tinge of warmth that radiated from her chest.

I knew she heard me because the muscle in her jaw twitched but she made no move to turn and look at me. I walked up beside her chair, like I always did, and lowered myself to her side so that I could see her but still not block her view.

"Hello mother," I said in a soft voice. Her eyes had long ago lost their glow and they didn't even move to look at me, instead just stared out of the window.

I had wondered what would make a demon lose the light in their eyes. Was it when they were close to death? Was it something to do with the loss of powers? I had once thought it was something that only happened to my mother after years of trauma, but seeing Marques made me question it even more.

"I will ask the house staff to come clean this floor up," I said. "It's dirty. Have you been okay?"

It was always a one-sided conversation but sometimes I could feel a flicker of emotion still inside her, though it was always very small, almost nonexistent.

I would sit there and tell her about my school, tell her about what was happening in the world. I never shared the secrets I collected but she was the one exception to that rule. If my mother could talk, if she could think, she would single-handedly be the most powerful person in this world. The stuff she had seen during her time with my father coupled with the information I fed her was enough to topple even the most influential demons.

But today was not about that.

"I will get you out of here soon," I vowed. "Me, you, Nathanial and Benjamin will be rid of Father once and for all."

I waited for anything. A flicker of surprise, even happiness...but there was nothing.

I grabbed her hand but reeled back when I felt how cold it was.

"Bastards," I muttered and stood up to go get her smaller blanket from the bed and drape it over her. "I'm going to have a talk with your nurse about this."

I carefully placed her hands underneath the blanket making sure that she was covered. Her body was frail and would get cold easily so it was imperative for her health that she stayed warm. A creak of the floorboards made me freeze in my tracks.

"How the mighty have fallen," Marques said as he let himself in the room. He looked around the room with mock interest. Those dead eyes seemed to see every fleck of dust, every crack...and it made me angry. "Your mother could have been very powerful if she stayed away from Raphael."

I stood up and watched Marques carefully. When his eyes finally landed on me, I could feel a chill run through me. Though he hadn't used his power on me since that night...I still felt uneasy around him.

"I am not going to hurt you or your mother, Rae," he said then moved to sit on the end of her bed. It was an utterly human thing to do but looked so performative when he did it. "Calm down a little."

"How can I help you, sir?" I asked choosing my tone carefully.

Marques let out a breathy laugh, a smirk pulling at his lips.

"No need to be formal, Rae," he said then blinked slowly as if waiting for me to correct myself.

I tried not to shift on my feet.

"Did you need an update?" I asked after his silence became too much.

"About Rosie?" he said. "No, seems like you have been getting a bit closer to her, though you still have a long way to go."

I swallowed thickly; my eyes glanced towards my mother.

"Why do you want her?" I asked.

His smirk became a full-blown smile.

"Her mother and I have history," he said. "And I think her powers could be put to...good use."

"So, you don't want to..."

"Feast on her flesh?" he asked in a light tone. "Of course not."

"But my father—"

"Can get a bit eccentric," he said. "So, what's your plan?"

"Well, we are already on speaking terms, so I just need to continue—"

"I mean for killing your father," he interrupted.

I froze and my eyes darted to the door. A million excuses filtered through my mind but none of them seemed to matter. I could run through the door but then I would be leaving my mother here. The window behind me was old and could be broken easily with enough force. The fall would hurt but I would survive and whatever damage I sustained would heal in minutes.

Marques let out a barking laugh that stirred me from my thoughts.

"What an imagination you have," he said, his voice still filled with laughter.

"You can read thoughts as well?" I asked and shifted so that I was closer to the window. "What is your power really?"

"That's a secret worth at least ten originals," he said. "Originals, right? That's what you call us?"

"Yes," I muttered.

"It's all you have been thinking about for the last week, though I was disappointed when I realized you weren't going to go through with it."

"Whose side are you on?" I asked. "You and my father have different goals and you don't seem to be with Xena and Ezekiel."

"I am in it for myself," he answered simply. "And I think they have lived a long enough life. Not to mention they are trying to murder the poor hybrids."

I raised my brow at him.

"Are you trying to tell me you care about Rosie?"

He let out another laugh and stood up.

"God no, I just need her for the future and your father is trying to ruin that," he said. "Listen, tomorrow tell Rosie you failed to kill him."

"Why would I—"

"Hush child," his tone was cool, but his words sent a bolt of fear down my spine. "Tell her you have a plan for the gala—good excuse by the way— but in order for it to work she cannot know—"

"I can't keep lying to her," I said, my voice pleading.

"You can, and you *will*," he said. "Now where was I?" He paused and looked up at the ceiling before a smile spread across his face. "Yes, you failed so you will do it at this gala. She cannot know the plan, if she asks just to tell her you cannot chance it going wrong because it is your last chance—or something like that. You have a good imagination; you can figure it out."

I took a deep breath.

"They will kill us at the gala, last time she almost died," I said.

"Last time you didn't have me," he said and stalked towards me. When he put his hand on my shoulder, I couldn't help but shiver underneath his touch. "I will help little Rosie with her task, so all you have to do is *show up*."

Help Rosie with. Her task? It is too good to be true. What does he gain out of this?

"I gain nothing," he said then shrugged. "At least not yet. And Rosie will never be able to kill them without help, though their attempt was impressive."

"You speak so easily about killing someone you are close to," I said, though I didn't fully understand why.

"You're the one who wants to kill her own father," he said then turned his back to walk away. He paused as he opened the door. "Not that I'm judging."

"How can I trust you?" I called.

He sent me a smile.

"You can't, just know that if I wanted to kill you or your friends I would have done it by now," he said. "The shabby apartment they got would be far too easy to break into and I would be in and out before you even knew they were dead."

He left me with those words hanging in the air. My father didn't pry me for the address to the apartment, I had carefully hidden it from him with an excuse that Rosie was still at Winterfell dorms...but Marques already knew where it was, and kept it to himself. My mouth went dry when I thought of him walking the halls, sneaking into the apartment... Would they even notice him? I could barely feel his emotions so how on earth would Rosie, Daxton, and Amr protect themselves from him.

When I was sure he had left the vicinity I fell to my knees and buried my head in my mother's lap. The emotions, the fear, the lies...it was too much. But there was one resounding emotion that brought me to my knees and made tears spring to my eyes.

Relief.

It burst through my body and in that moment, I had never felt more relieved in my life. This wasn't on me to figure out anymore. As soon as I heard of this plan from Rosie I knew that we would never be able to pull it off, that we would die in the process. But now the answer was here, right in front of us and while I may not be able to trust him, he was by far the most honest of any of the people we were involved in now.

The only cost was simply just *one more lie.*

* * *

"It failed," I lied through my teeth as Rosie looked at me expectantly.

I had found her the next day as soon as she came onto campus. She was jittery and I could tell that the task had been weighing on her. She was barely eating and the dark circles under her eyes resembled that of Malik's. Daxton and Amr were at their usual spots beside her, and they stiffened at the news.

"Their defense was too much, and I risked getting caught if I acted rash," I explained though it sounded more like an excuse. Daxton eyed me wearily.

Rosie looked up at me under her lashes and I felt my heart clench.

"Are you sure the last chance is the gala?" she asked.

"Yes, but give me time to plan," I said. "Once it's ready I'll get an invitation for everyone here."

"Why would they let us anywhere near them?" Amr asked.

"To save face," I explained. "The biggest news of the century just hit, they would not risk having Rosie *not* make an appearance. Think about it, my father is in charge of interspecies relationships, you really think he would take that hit?"

"The gala is far away," Daxton said. "Is there a timeline that you need to have this done by?"

The last question was aimed towards Rosie. She shook her head.

"So, it works out," I said. "But let me plan it out, I don't want to chance it again."

Amr looked from Rosie to me then back to Rosie before stepping forward. I raised a brow at him, but his answer was not to grip the front of my shirt and pull me close to him. He let out a growl that started deep in his chest. The distrust was rolling off him in waves and was almost suffocating.

"If I find out you are lying to us and we cannot trust you then I swear to you I will end your life," he threatened. "I have always liked you Rae but consider this your last warning. This doesn't smell right, and you still have a long way to go for us to trust you again."

He let his threat simmer in the air before pulling away and going back to Rosie's side.

"Can you please not fight?" she asked, a small pout forming. "I have forgiven Rae and I know she just has what's best in mind."

Amr gave me a warning look before murmuring something to Rosie that caused her to blush. I was shocked when I saw that Daxton was still watching me.

Even if there was still this one lie, I knew that at the end of the day, Rosie would thank me for this because this lie was the only thing saving our lives right now.

Chapter 21
Rosie

It had been two months since our first failed attempt.

Two months I was left to wither at Winterfell.

Two months I was left to sit through classes and act like I gave any shits about school even though I knew at the end nothing would come out of it.

The anxiety of the upcoming task was becoming unbearable and coupled with the festering anger at the originals that put me in this position, I could feel myself falling deeper and deeper into despair.

I wanted to trust Rae; I *did* trust her. But having this task that my life depended on and being completely unavoidable made me regret my decision to get every else involved.

I mean, Daxton *almost died* for god's sake.

It didn't help that Malik and Eli had been secretive about their tasks. I knew that they had to have been given something, because these two months Eli has been glued to Malik's side and wouldn't come home until late. I had tried to ask multiple times, but I was always given dismissive answers and Malik had even threatened me when I didn't want to give up.

It tied my hands and made me feel lonely.

Though I wasn't *totally* alone in this...I had Daxton and Amr but more often than not we were the only ones together. Even after we had agreed with Rae on the plan, she did a total one-eighty and began avoiding me like the plague.

Not to mention that even Matt, Claudine, and Maximus have totally disappeared as well. It was like the very carefully crafted farce that Xena and Ezekiel had built was up in smoke. I had thought at times that I had seen his familiar curly hair in passing during my time in Winterfell but every time I lingered to catch a glimpse, it was gone.

It was like another part of me was gone and never to be seen again.

I didn't mind spending time with Daxton and Amr, if anything I was happy that our relationship could get so close. It was like I could finally slow down and understand the people I was spending my time with. Every moment I was learning more and more about them and no matter what I learned I was just so amazed by them. Their reliance, their magic, their likes, dislikes, it was perfect.

Every day after class we would head back to the apartment and do whatever we wanted to for the day. It was freeing to not have to be on any deadlines or be hustled by originals or violent high-levels. It could be watching movies, playing board games, and even practicing magic.

When I was with them it felt like the perfect time to really grow into the witch that I was supposed to be. It would start with small tricks like levitating objects, making things out of nothing, and making things disappear. It was exciting especially when I saw their eyes light up when I did something correctly.

It also made me realize just how wrong we were about witches. Yes there were some people that used their magic for bad, but the majority didn't.

Though there was always a pause when I asked about curses. They would say that we weren't there yet, and it required complicated magic, but I vowed to myself that I would keep pushing because after all, I had plans for after this task was done.

But no matter how busy we were, how fun the time was...the gaps were too big to ignore. Rae, Malik, and Eli were always missing, and it was obvious when they were. Sometimes when I didn't know how to answer something I would look for Rae, only to find that the spot where she would be was empty. Other times I expected to hear a snarky remark or feel an arm sneak across my shoulders when I wasn't looking, though Eli still wasn't there. Sometimes I would wake up to find them coming home in the early hours of the morning and they would crash on the couch. It was what I had asked of Malik, and Eli came home without a fight...but the exhaustion on their face was hard to get over.

"It feels like you are ignoring me," I said one night as Eli snuck in through the front door. "Or cheating."

I had chosen to slip out after both Amr and Daxton had their fill of magic. Even if I practiced all day, when it was time to share magic, they would still get worn out pretty quickly and I was left wanting. It was not to say anything about their lovemaking capabilities and had everything to do with my insatiable magic. It would wake me even from the deepest sleep with its restlessness. I could feel it even now, moving inside me asking for me to reach out to Eli, but I pushed it down...now was not the time.

Eli paused as they shut the door softly. I could see their blue eyes glowing softly and the light that shone from them highlighted the stains on their cheek. No doubt blood, there had rarely been a time where they came home with clean, bloodstain-free clothes. As much as my rational side hated the look of them bloody, my magic was quite the opposite.

"It's just work," they said with a sigh and trudged over to the couch only to sprawl across it and rest their head in my lap. "And don't act like you own me, little original."

My throat tightened. I had been waiting to have this time with them for so long, but I didn't want to scare them away. Instead, I settled for running my hands through their hair. It was hard to verbalize the fact that I missed them, it was nothing I had been able to say before. But then again, there were many other things I didn't know how to say.

I miss you.

I worry about you.

I wish we had more time together.

I'm scared.

I lo—

Eli's deep breath shook me out of my thoughts. Their eyes were already screwed shut and their chest moved with the deep breaths they took.

They must have been exhausted.

I used this time just to stare at them. I remembered when we first met, how cocky and sure they were. They used to never let me this close, nor touch their hair...but less than a year later here we were and regardless of all the pain and death we went through, I wouldn't change anything if it meant that I could be here with them right now. I leaned down and left a kiss on their forehead.

I heard a shuffling behind me, breaking my little moment. I turned to see Daxton with messy hair and sleep clothes coming out of our shared room. He walked over to the couch, his feet shuffling lightly as he walked. I smiled softly at him and motioned for him to be quiet. I caught a whiff of his musky scent as he leaned over the couch to look at Eli.

"Watch and learn," he whispered to me and waved his hand in the air. I turned to Eli and watched as a sheer watery type of magic washed across their face, taking all the blood and grime with it. With another wave the clothes were changed to a pair of boxers and large shirt.

Eli didn't even twitch at the feeling of the magic.

"You have done this a lot," I noted.

Daxton let out a noise before placing a kiss on the top of my head.

"I forgive you," he whispered. "I just wish you could have told me from the beginning. I would gladly have told you anything you needed."

I am not sure how long I had waited to hear those words, or if I really understood how much I needed them. I knew at times that what I did, regardless of the circumstances, was shitty and he didn't deserve any of it. The tears that had been pooling since Eli's return finally poured over. I looked up towards him, and he gave me a soft smile.

"Will the magic always make me feel like this?" I asked.

It had many implications that I was sure he would understand.

Would it always make me so angry?

Make me feel so out of control?

Be unpredictable?

Be so bloodthirsty?

"Mine was," he said. "Until I met you."

I nodded and looked back down at Eli. A lone tear fell onto her cheek, and I wiped it off quickly.

"So, there is no hope," I said bitterly with a humorless laugh.

"I wouldn't say that," he mused. "Though I am not partial to adding Matt to whatever it is we are doing."

A smile formed on my face.

"It likes Eli," I said. "The magic. Rae too but she has been..."

"I see," he trailed. "I have an idea that honor student would totally hate."

I looked back to him only to see a smile light up his face.

"Wouldn't I want to get on her good side?" I asked.

He chuckled.

"The only way to make Rae pay *more* attention to you is do something she thinks is utterly reckless," he said. "And it helps if those fucking originals would hate it too."

I liked where this was going.

* * *

I rubbed the still sore inked area on my inner wrist and frowned. I really did want to get Rae talking to me again...but maybe letting Daxton talk me into getting a tattoo wasn't a good idea.

"Stop touching it," he hissed and pulled my arm away. "Just because it was done with magic doesn't mean it is healed already."

He paused to look down at the raven on my wrist. After looking at his I had somewhat of an idea on what to expect, but it turned out much different than I thought it would be like. It was darker—and bigger—than I had originally planned to get but after seeing it fully done I couldn't help but fall in love with it.

I had trouble picking something that I wanted. At first, I wanted to find something that was filled with meaning, but the more that I looked back on my life...the less I wanted to permanently brand a reminder of how shitty my life had been on my body. So, I picked something that I knew would look cool and suit me well at the same time.

It was actually Amr that had first given me the idea. It was a night where we were practicing my magic before bed and while they had taught me many magic tricks over the last few months...the birds remained my favorite. He had watched the raven in fascination and said that it would be a pretty painting...so I decided to get it tattooed on me.

"And this will help with my magic?" I asked ignoring his glare. "Are you sure?"

He rolled his eyes.

"Yes it's just like another way to keep your magic under control," he answered. "It's done with someone's magic and so until the magic wears off it'll be like a constant dose of magic."

I raised my brow, still not quite getting it.

"How long does the magic stay?" I asked.

"Well," Daxton said with a sigh. "If the witch is strong it can stay for a few months, maybe a year. The magic is working along with your own but it's not like someone's magic can stay in your body that long...especially if you use a lot of magic."

"Is that why you have so many?" I asked.

The area around us went quiet and his face told me he would rather not answer that question. It was okay, we all had things that we didn't want to share so I would let him keep this, though I wish he would feel comfortable enough to tell me.

A breeze passed by, and I shivered lightly. The area was desolate, and it only seemed to make the wind even colder. We were outside the confines of Winterfell in a run-down place that wasn't even near any of the towns in the area. The sun had set long ago so it really felt like it was just the three of us out here. Another bit of anxiety hung over me like a cloud. This was a safe area...*should be safe.*

As long as you are not alone, as Rae had said.

Though part of me, the untamed part wished for them to come. Wished that they would even try because I was ready to take my revenge. I had to look at my scar every single day and remember the way those faces sneered down at me. The more time passed the more I regretted leaving this in the hands of Rae...and she *still* had yet to give us any insight to what she had been planning all this time.

I tried to not let that, coupled with her absence, affect me.

Shaking the dark thoughts out of my head I looked over to where Amr waited for us by the car. It was one of Malik's that we had found the keys to in the table by the door. We took it without a second thought.

"It looks good," he said as we walked up.

"You should have got one," Daxton said. "A neck tattoo would suit you."

Amr shook his head with a slight smile.

"Not my thing," he answered. "I'll leave that to you."

"We will see," I said teasingly. "Maybe we can convince you what, fifty years down the road?"

His eyes twinkled in the dim light.

"We will see if we can live that long," he said. "I have a feeling that this is just the start of a *very reckless* future."

He got into the car without waiting for a response while shaking his head. My stomach flipped anxiously when I realized that we would once again be riding home with Amr. He was a smart, dangerously handsome, and an all-around perfect partner...but anything dealing with modern technology, especially vehicles...was not his strong suit. I didn't notice it when we were literally running for our lives, but it was obvious when we were not in a rush that you were not supposed to drive over a curb, or run multiple red lights, or swerve out of the way of oncoming vehicles because *we* were going the wrong way on the highway.

"I'm scared," I whispered to Daxton in terror.

He visibly gulped.

"Sucks that you're in the front this time," he said quickly and dove for that back seat door.

My mouth dropped and I tried to reach for the back of his shirt to pull him back, but he easily slipped out of my grip and into the back seat before flipping me off.

I slowly looked towards Amr's smiling face through the driver's seat.

Fuck.

I shakily crossed over to the passenger side and entered, but not before taking a deep breath and praying to whatever god there was that I would live through this experience for a second time.

"Don't be so dramatic, love," Amr said with a smile, obviously enjoying this all too much.

He turned on the car and sped out of the parking lot before I could even put on my seatbelt.

Chapter 22
Rosie

"Maybe this is too far," I whispered as I poured magic into the stones at the bottom of the Winterfell tower. I focused on filling every crack and hole just like Daxton had taught me. I focused on making the magic as light as possible, visualizing it as a type of slime that could fit through any space. The visualization helped, I realized, just like Ezekiel had said...though I didn't want to admit that him or Xena were right about anything.

Daxton scoffed from somewhere far behind me, I could hear his shuffling echo in the space. The Winterfell tower was hollow inside, filled with only empty space and a single rusty staircase. I had seen pieces of trash and discarded books, but besides that it was a wasteland.

"Don't pussy out, Rosie," he said in an annoyed tone. "Did Rae notice the tattoo yet?"

"No," I grumbled and clenched my fists, nails biting into my palms.

It had been a whole week since I had gotten the tattoo and Rae didn't even look at me anymore. It didn't matter if I was standing right in front of her, if we were eating breakfast, she simply would avert her gaze and move along. Even this morning I had tried to get her attention, waving my bare arm around, putting it out on the table casually, and still nothing! At first it hurt me that she was ignoring me, after all I had thought we had put this behind us...but now it was starting to anger me, which is why I agreed to this stupid plan.

Though I couldn't deny the buzz of excitement that ran through my body.

It was past eleven at night and far beyond the curfew the principal had enforced for Winterfell after my hybrid nature came to light. Though the news vans and reporters lingered around during the day, they were almost never seen at night. It was a relief because we would no doubt be stuck in the confines of the campus until daybreak when we could sneak out without being noticed. But for now, the campus was swarming with security and every rustle or other small noise would send a jolt of adrenaline through me.

"Are you sure this is safe?" I asked after I finished my section. I was checking it and poking at it with my magic to make sure I got everything. We had one shot at this, *one*. And we couldn't afford to mess this up.

"It's *fine*, Rosie," Daxton said with a huff. "The tower will fall to the east where there is nothing, but the open space of the quad and the magic will slowly eat at the brick."

"What if there are people walking around?" I asked.

"It's past curfew Rosie," he reminded. "No one should be here."

I nodded and continued to add magic into the brickwork. Amr was adamant about not partaking in our *rebellious games*—as he liked to call them—and stayed outside to guard the area. This time though, he remained in his cat form in case he was spotted.

"I'm done," I whispered after packing as much magic into the brickwork as I could. The bricks that lined the inside of the tower were already falling apart and it looked like even a strong wind could send this tower falling.

I heard Daxton shuffle behind me before bringing me to my feet.

"Let's get a good spot," he said. "Maybe closer to the dorms in case people come to find us, then we can just say we were getting fresh air."

I nodded and walked out of the tower with him, my eyes darting around the dark to catch any sign of life. Amr meowed once he saw us and jumped into my arms without hesitation. I let out a small laugh, then nuzzled his face for just a few seconds until he was ripped out of my hands.

"You have a healing tattoo," Daxton growled playfully and kissed Amr's head. "And he's a dirty animal."

Amr playfully swiped at Daxton's face, causing me to giggle even more. Their relationship seemed to be the easiest to repair, though I was sure they had a long way to go even now. I would catch them whispering sometimes, sharing their own jokes, there were also a few sly touches here and there... but it never bothered me. If anything, it only made my heart grow for them.

We walked quietly across campus to the dorms with only a whisper of a joke here and there and would pause around every corner.

"Hold on," Daxton said in a hushed tone and grabbed me by the back of my sweatshirt, pulling me into his chest. Moments later I heard the shuffling of feet mere feet from us, right around the corner I was going to turn.

Daxton's breathing hitched when I pushed myself back into him and spread my magic out to his. I teased him as we waited for the guards' footsteps to leave. I heard him pause for a moment and my breathing stopped completely.

Amr let out a soft growl as the footsteps sounded again, though this time they were walking in the opposite direction. I sent a look back towards Daxton, who had a slight frown on his face. I sent him a wink.

"Let's see if we can get back into my dorm after this," I whispered and turned the corner quickly.

I heard him curse and chase after me.

Even though I had expended a good deal of magic I felt my skin itch with anticipation at the thought of sharing with them once more. I have gotten used to living as though there was another being inside of me because I had realized that our wants were really not that far off from each other's.

When *it* wanted to share magic, I knew I wanted it too. When *it* became angry, I knew deep down that I was too even if I didn't know it at the time. And when *it* wanted to hurt someone...

I stopped dead in my tracks when we rounded on the dorms. Outside was a set of familiar piercing hazel eyes that shone in the darkness. Rae was leaning against the wall with her notebook in hand, her pen pausing on the paper like we had just interrupted her writing. It was odd to see her like this shrouded in the darkness with only the dim lamp outside the dorm entrance to light the area. It looked painfully lonely and only now did I realize how lonely she had to have been this whole time.

Eli was missing constantly so I doubted they would have reached out to Rae. Not to mention Matt and his siblings were off who knows where...and she was just here attending class all alone. I wondered how often she went back home to see her family and if this was her routine now that we had left her.

"Aren't you supposed to be in the apartment?" she asked.

"Aren't *you* supposed to be in the dorm?" Daxton shot back. "Or maybe back in that hell hole you call home?"

The words I had wanted to say died on my tongue.

"Let's not be *rude*," I hissed towards Daxton. He gave me a look as if to say, *I am not the one she's ignoring, you should be the rude one.*

"What are you doing here?" she asked. "It's not safe."

"We're fine," I choked out, unable to look at her. Suddenly her eyes were too much to handle, and my magic shifted inside me, pushing me towards her. "I can handle myself."

She raised a brow and the chilly air around us dropped at least five degrees. I shivered in Daxton's oversized hoodie. It was all black and baggy, great for causing trouble in the dark, but it wasn't that thick, and I hadn't bothered with a shirt underneath it.

God I was stupid and underprepared.

This was for her, to get her attention, and to get back at the originals that wanted to control my life...but now that I had gotten what I wanted I found myself floundering.

"Sure, you can," she said and snapped her notebook closed, walking towards us. "And look how well that turned out for you last time."

Daxton nudged me in the side painfully. I cursed at him but then forgot it immediately as I hear a loud grinding sound. Turning, I caught the tilting of Winterfell tower just in time. The normally proud structure that had been a staple of the academy was now preparing to fall to its doom. Even though the tower was not the end all be all for this academy, the falling of the tower felt oddly therapeutic.

My stomach dropped to my feet at the same time that a pure unfiltered giddiness bubbled inside me.

"Oh, this is good," Daxton said with a chuckle.

"You didn't," Rae growled.

"We did," Daxton and I spoke in unison.

Rae's hand grabbed at the back of my hoodie yanking me back with such force that I lost my balance.

"Inside now," she hissed.

I flailed and tried to smack her hand off but was unsuccessful. The tower was just about to break, and I didn't want to do this all for nothing. All the magic and time I had wasted on this only to leave right when things got good would be unthinkable.

"Let me go!" I growled back.

I felt her pause before circling her arm around my waist and shoving me over her shoulder. I let out a yelp which was followed by Daxton's chuckles.

"Hey! What are you doing over there?" a security guard yelled from across the quad. "It's past cur—"

He was cut off by the final crashing of the tower which cut through the air with a sharp whistling sound before the shattered bricks flew all across the quad, the chunks landing in the grass with a thud.

With a flurry of curses Rae began running, but I didn't see Daxton follow us. I was bouncing atop her shoulders with each stride as she turned to go back into the dorm. I could only catch glimpses of the now disinte-grated tower as we ran, but it was enough to pull a bubble of manic laugher out of me.

"They will find us there!" I yelled through my giggles, but she continued forward.

I could barely tell where we were going but we ran past her dorm and down a hallway I have never been before.

I was ready to yell again when I heard the security guards enter the dorms, but Rae ducked into a dark room and forced me up against the wall, sealing us in the dark. It was cramped, based on how close she was to me and that the legs that wrapped around her waist were touching the other end of the room. I could feel my elbow brush against something, but I couldn't pay any mind to it, her angry gaze shining in the darkness was all my muddled brain could comprehend.

The giddiness and laughter from earlier left me entirely and I was left to feel the tensions rising between us in the small space.

"Where are we?" I whispered.

"Are you really that fucking stupid, Rosie?" she asked ignoring my ques-tion. "You know how much trouble we can get in? And how much it will take to get you out of it?"

Her angry voice caused my stomach to clench and warmth to gather between my legs. *God I loved it when she was angry.* The way her hard gaze looked at me and the way her hands tightened around me were enough to send me spiraling, even in this situation. This was the closest I had been to her in months, and I couldn't help but lean into her touch. One hand was on my waist while the other held the left side of my head. The protective gesture didn't slip past me easily. We had to have been kneeling on one knee because when she reached up to lock the door I felt her knee push into my core.

I sucked in a sharp breath and her eyes narrowed at me.

Take. Now, my magic whispered. It wanted nothing more than for me to close the gap between us, it even knew Rae could not help with the magic... but it didn't seem to care. It was just as hungry as it was with Daxton or Amr, and I had to admit, I had been dreaming of when I could be with Rae again. Even after everything, I found myself missing her touches, missing the calm and collected way she held us together. I trusted her more than anyone else and even now I could feel that the trust between us was stronger than ever.

I grinded on her knee unable to help myself. The jolt that shot through me pulled a whine from my throat. My hands trailed up the front of her shirt but just as they got close to her breasts the hand on my waist moved to grab them.

"Don't," she warned.

"Rae, I—"

She clamped a hand over my mouth and not seconds later I heard feet run by our little hiding space.

Oh god.

This was too much, and I had been waiting for it for too long. She looked down at my wrists and froze. Just barely, because of slight light shining underneath the door, you could see a black blob where my tattoo was supposed to be.

I swallowed thickly when her eyes slowly met mine. I could feel the electricity between us, and it was becoming harder to stay still. Those eyes had the ability to pin me in place without even uttering one syllable and I have never in my life been more thankful for Daxton than in this moment. I drank in her attention greedily, loving the way her eyes were devoted to my form. The muscle in her jaw stood out and I could hear her teeth grind together.

"Please tell me you didn't," she whispered, but still did not remove her hand. Her eyes trailed down my form and I tightened my legs around her. The groan that escaped me filled the room. "I'm not doing this with you."

She finally let go of my mouth but we both froze as more footsteps sounded. We waited and listened as they passed us twice before disappearing. Her hand moved to my hip.

"You have been avoiding me," I said in a whisper. Her eyes cast downward. I followed them looking at where we were touching. She had to have noticed it too right? The electricity passing through us. This tension couldn't have been one-sided. "You can't ignore me here."

"Watch me," she muttered.

"We will be here for another few hours until it dies down," I noted. "We might as well talk through the issue."

She let out a huff.

"The issue?" she asked then looked towards me. "You lied and did exactly what I said you would. This isn't something we can just get over."

I swallowed the hurt down.

"I thought we were over this," I said. "You even agreed to help with my task which you still didn't—"

She let out a light growl in warning.

"Fine, then let's not talk," I said.

"You liter—"

I cut her off by diving forward and forcing my mouth to hers. When her lips parted slightly in surprise a moan escaped my mouth. I felt my body literally melt into her, feeling a warmth consume me. I had almost forgotten how it felt to be with her. How soft she was no matter how cold she liked for people to believe. How it felt to feel her projection when she was happy, shocked, and in this case aroused. Her whole being was overwhelming, like a delicious secret that I just couldn't stop myself from becoming addicted to. Her lips were soft against mine and they responded for a few seconds before pausing. She pushed me back against the closet and placed her hand over my mouth once more.

"Rosie we are in a fucking supply closet," she hissed.

I shrugged and pulled my arms into my sweatshirt to undo my bra.

"What are you—stop," she said, panicked. I pulled my bra out and threw it somewhere in the closet beside us.

I tried to pull it off, but her hand stayed glued on my mouth leaving the material trapped around my shoulders. Her eyes zeroed on my exposed breasts, and I felt my nipples tighten in response.

"I told you that's not what this is," she said her voice getting weaker.

I smirked against her hands and made a show of caressing my stomach and dragging my hands up and over my breasts. She groaned when I began plucking my nipples. I let out a sigh and arched towards her.

"You have changed, Rosie," she whispered and leaned forward. "But so have I."

She engulfed my nipple and fingers with her mouth, then bit down. I whimpered behind her hand and removed my hands from my nipples only to thread them through her curly locks and pull her closer. Her tongue traced the areola before flicking at my erect nipple. Her free hand went to grip my ass and pull me closer.

I couldn't keep my moans in as she began sucking on them. I closed my eyes and leaned back against the wall. She left a trail of kisses from one nipple to the other before biting that one lightly as well.

I froze as I heard more footsteps coming and stifled my moans, but Rae didn't stop. A jolt of fear ran through me.

What if they caught us in here?

Not only would it out Rae but they would easily identify my clothing.

"Keep quiet," she whispered against my nipple with another teasing bite.

The jolt of pleasure that shot through me was unbearable. Her fingers dipped into the waistband of my leggings. I have never scrambled faster to get my clothing off, but in the tight spacing I was only able to lower both my underwear and leggings to mid-thigh. But it was enough for Rae's hands to dip in-between my legs and feel the wetness accumulating between my folds. With one swipe from my entrance to my clit she then pulled her hand away from my mouth and shoved her finger in my mouth.

Shocked by her actions it took me a minute to catch up. The footsteps walked right by our door once more. This time I didn't freeze. Instead, I bit down on Rae's finger. Her eyes widened and she pulled her finger out of my mouth before leaning closer. Her warm breath fanned across my face as she spoke.

"I'll keep my hand off for now, but Ms. Miller," she whispered. "When I say you need to be quiet I mean it, or this stops faster than you can bat those pretty little lashes."

I nodded feverishly and was rewarded with two of her fingers massaging my clit. A shaky breath left my mouth. I tried not to buck against her or let any noise out, but it was getting harder with the mounting pressure she added to my clit.

She quickly unbuttoned her shirt and exposed her shoulder to me.

"Bite it," she commanded.

Fuck yes. The way my mouth watered when she said that was unreal. I leaned forward and bit into her just as she entered two fingers inside my aching pussy.

My noise was muffled by the bite, and she pushed in her fingers as far as they would go before hooking them and playing with a spot that made me jerk against her. Tears pricked at my eyes, but I only gripped her closer.

When she was sure I wouldn't make any noise she pulled them out only to force them back into me. The feeling of her thumb hitting my clit with each thrust was so much of a shock throughout my entire body that I grabbed onto the wall behind her.

Loud wet noises filled the small space as Rae pumped her fingers into me without mercy. Gone was the girl who had been gentle and caring with me the first time we are together. This was a girl who knew what she was trying to do. Each thrust harder than the last and there was only a pause when she heard someone coming, but she never stopped. Her movements turned shallow, and she would leave kisses on my shoulder as we waited for them to leave. As soon as they did she would resume her pace.

"Fuck, Rae," I moaned and leaned back against the wall to catch my breath. I was going to come, hard, and I was sure I would make a noise. The hand that was twisting my nipple came up to my mouth and she pounded into me at an animalistic pace.

I couldn't help the sob that came out of me as she violently pulled an orgasm out of me.

I heard more footsteps and I expected them to pass our door but instead, they paused.

"Did we check this?" a male guard asked.

"It's just a janitor's closet," another called.

I could see the shuffle of shoes beneath the door and froze.

If they opened that right now I would be fully exposed. My sweatshirt was pulled up over my shoulders and with my back arched against the wall they were fully in view. My bare ass was hanging out and Rae's hand was still buried inside me.

As if reminding me, my own pussy clenched around her fingers. In response she circled my clit again. I shot her a look but didn't say anything.

They tried the door but thankfully, it was locked.

"Do you have a key?" he asked.

Shit.

Unbothered, Rae began slowly pumping in and out of me again. I wanted to hate it, wanted to be fearful of the people on the other end...but I couldn't bring myself to think of anything other than Rae's fingers inside me. And then I felt a wave of arousal so strong from her I could feel myself pulse around her. My pussy had to be dripping all over her by now because I was so painfully turned on.

I rocked my hips against her hand with the next thrust, and my eyes rolled into the back of my head.

"Nah," the other guy responded. "Just leave it, it's usually locked so they probably aren't in there. Not like it could fit three people anyways."

There were a few more back and forths but Rae had already resumed her pace, the slaps of her hand against my wet pussy now even louder than my heartbeat.

"You liked that," she whispered then chuckled. "Who turned you into such a bad girl, Ms. Miller?"

I shuddered and felt a tingling heat spread through my core and across my body. My magic responded to my orgasm, and instead of feeling like it was trapped in a cage I felt it flare out around us. The small room filled with red specks of dust lighting up the dark space. Now I could see the sweat dripping down Rae's face.

"That doesn't usually happen," I mumbled against her hand.

She let out an uncharacteristic snort and began to pull my pants back up.

"I don't have anything to clean you," she whispered.

"It's okay," I said and begun to pull down my sweatshirt, but she stopped me and sucked on an already overly sensitive nipple.

"These are so perfect," she murmured and gave enough attention to both leaving me writhing against her. When she was done and I finally pulled my sweatshirt on, we moved to a more comfortable position.

Me straddling her.

I looked at her, unable to read her expression.

"I won't tell anyone," I said quickly. "We can keep it between us just... please don't avoid me anymore." I swallowed thickly. *Here it is.* "I missed you."

Her eyes widened and she forced my lips to hers. She kissed me with more passion than I had ever felt from her before.

"Again," she commanded.

"I missed you, Rae."

She sighed against me.

"I thought about you a lot," I admitted. "I felt incomplete without you with us. I would always look for you when we were together, but you were never there."

"I know."

"Your room is still there," I whispered against her lips. She pulled away.

"They don't want me there," she said.

"I do," I said. "I'll make sure Malik doesn't bother us about it anymore."

She thought over it for a moment then nodded. I moved to kiss her again.

"Don't," she said. I pulled away immediately but her firm hand on my back held me in place. "Don't keep it a secret I mean."

"Are you sure?" I asked, shocked.

"I'm tired of hiding," she said. "I don't care if you're a hybrid, low-level, or girl. I just don't care anymore."

I dove forward sealing our lips together.

We were interrupted by a knock. My magic fanned out in a panic, but I relaxed when I could feel Amr's magic pulsing on the other side.

I stood and unlocked the door for him. His golden eyes were the first thing I saw, then his soft smile. I could tell that he knew what happened, or at least felt the magic.

"Let's go home you two, they are too busy to catch us now."

"What did you do?" Rae asked standing up behind me. I could feel her buttoning up her shirt and the motion didn't go unnoticed by Amr.

"Set the cafeteria on fire," he admitted as easily as if he were discussing the weather.

I shook my head and followed him out. When Rae didn't follow I turned and shot her a look. Her curly hair was disheveled, and her glasses crooked.

I smiled and reached my hand out towards her.

"Let's go home."

Chapter 23
Malik

It had been over thirty hours since I had last taken something akin to a nap. I had replaced my blood with magic, thanks to Matt's plans, and it has kept me somewhat human…at least until I heard what Rosie did at Winterfell.

They thought they were slick and snuck in during the light hours of the morning, but I was already there, waiting for them. Not only was Claudine able to follow them and keep tabs on everything that they did…but she also had to report it back to Xena and Ezekiel.

Cue an angry phone call from Xena not moments after the tower fell.

Now I was here staring at the dirty, disheveled group of people that will single-handedly ruin everything that I have been working for the past few hundred years. If Ezekiel came snooping around it would severely delay our timeline and Marques didn't have any more time to wait, especially with another hybrid in his clutches.

I eyed Rae as she stood straight next to Rosie. Her chin was high and her chest was puffed out like she wasn't staring into the eyes of the one person that could end her right now. I knew what she was doing.

Hell, I helped Marques come up with it, I thought bitterly.

Well…I didn't say the words directly but more mentioned that it would be safer if neither I nor Matt took her away from the group since I had long known that they began to suspect me. It was when the whipping started; they were known to only use pain on their captives and those who they found a threat…now look at me, *look at my fucking face.* The evidence of their trust had littered my body and every time Matt had to unlock my memories, I was set alight with a fresh dose of rage.

Rae would prove to be a problem if she continued to act like that. She had already been walking on thin ice and I would need to be careful in case she even got a whiff of what my role was.

I wanted to live, after all.

"What the hell were you thinking?" I growled towards Rosie. She looked like an utter mess standing in between Rae and Amr. Her hair was sticking out every which way, her sweatshirt had dust on it, and there was a hickey on her neck. I couldn't tell if the hickey was fresh or not but paired with all of the mess of her clothing it didn't matter, it still painted a horrible picture that would just end Xena.

Daxton was off towards the end of the group, next to Amr. He opened his mouth to speak.

"Silence," I commanded. It almost hurt to use my power. I had used it far too much in the time that I had been awake and now I felt an ache spreading across my body.

Rosie frowned silently causing me to cock my brow at her. I expected her to fight, to yell, but she seemed oddly docile now. I almost wanted to see that raging spitfire that I had seen in the town...but maybe reality had finally caught up to her.

That's kinda sad...and disappointing. I like a woman with a bit of fight. The thought came out of nowhere and shocked me. I liked Rosie, more than I probably should have but that thought was out of pocket. I blamed it on my tiredness.

"I didn't think it would be a big deal," she answered. Her eyes met mine before dropping to her feet.

"You didn't think destroying the symbol of the most prestigious demon academy would be a big deal," I said with a humorless laugh. My hands clenched around the granite countertops, and I was thankful that there was something in-between me and that group because if not, I was sure that I would tear into them.

"It's not like you guys care," she said in a voice that was slightly raised. Her cheeks flushed and it looked like it had finally dawned on her how much trouble she could get into. "You just want me to go to Winterfell, complete the—"

The countertop crumbled with a loud crack between my fists. They all stared at me wide-eyed. I had half a mind to chuck it at them and embed this countertop into that wall behind their heads.

Warm fingers wrapped around my wrist. I slowly turned to Matt beside me. I had forgotten he was here.

Damn I really needed to sleep.

"Amr, Rosie," Matt said. "You will report for your punishment tomorrow evening. Before then, get some rest."

"Punishment?" Rae asked. "You don't own them."

I rolled my eyes at her and dropped the pieces in my hands to the floor with a thump.

"They are under my care, they do work for me, I pay for their living expenses," I said, narrowing my gaze to her. "I own every part of them until they are no longer under my service. *Like hell* I don't own them. Try that tone again Rae, see what happens."

I saw Rosie shiver next to Rae. I was too tired to think of how that made me feel.

"There is nothing else to say about this," Matt said, cutting Rae off. "We will leave now. Don't leave the apartment."

Matt let go of my wrist, allowing me to make my own exit.

* * *

I slept like the dead until Matt rose me the next night.

"Malik, it's time to talk to the others."

I groaned and blinked away the sleep from my eyes. I eyed Matt. His curly hair had grown much longer than I had seen it in years and it brushed the tops of his ears. It would have given him a boyish look if he didn't have scruff on his face and deep-set eye bags.

This whole game between the originals was too much for the poor boy... and it was far from over. Even though the biggest fight yet was in sight, there would be much to do after it to not only finish this but keep everyone alive while we did so.

"When was the last time you slept?" I asked.

Matt stood straight and gave me a forced smile. It reminded me of the way he interacted with Rosie. Even though it was an exaggeration of his character, it made me have a bit of hope that he could return to a normal life after this.

"I caught a few hours yesterday when you passed out, but was worried I wouldn't be able to wake you in time," he said, his voice grainy.

"I have an alarm clock," I muttered.

"Which you slept through," he noted.

Scrambling for my phone on my nightstand I saw that he was indeed correct. All my alarms were off, and I had many missed calls from Maximus, Xena, and one from Rosie.

I let out a deep sigh.

"I'm sorry," I said and stood. "You rest tonight, I'll cover for you."

Matt's eyes widened.

"You cannot. Marques will—"

"He only cares that the work is done," I said. "And anyways we got the most troublesome across the threshold last week. Tonight, should be a piece of cake."

It was a lie, and Matt knew that.

"I'm coming."

"Don't make me use it," I warned. His eyes narrowed but then quickly he sighed and ran his hand through his hair.

"Maybe take one of the others?" he suggested.

I shook my head.

"Your brother and sister need to be on lookout and baby-sitting duty," I said.

"I meant Daxton or Rae," he corrected. "Doesn't Rae live with the guy anyways?"

I walked past him and slapped my hand on his shoulder.

"The less they know the better," I said. "Let's keep them out of it until the very end."

Matt nodded.

"Good luck."

It wasn't long until I found myself walking into Rosie's apartment and I was more than relieved when I saw them all waiting for me *and* wearing clothes. There had been times where I had accidentally walked in on them in less than appropriate attire and while it stirred something in me, I needed to ignore it.

I was an old demon that had much more to think about than getting my fix, though it had been far too long if I was being honest.

Rosie was leaning against the island eating pancakes while Rae leaned against the opposite counter. She had an apron on and a cup of what I assumed was coffee in her hands. Daxton was sitting on the bar stool, his hand running through Rosie's hair and only paused to shoot me a glare. Amr was in his cat form on Daxton's lap and Eli was the furthest from the group and they were definitely drinking coffee.

More like guzzling it down, I thought as I saw them throw the whole cup back then motion for Rae to pour some more. She rolled her eyes but grabbed the pot anyways.

"You wanna tell us why you and Eli are dead on your feet?" Rae asked. Her hazel eyes were sharp behind her glasses, and I worried that she would catch on too soon.

"None of your business traitor," I said in a bitter tone. "Everyone except Amr and Rosie leave."

I didn't use my powers, but it would seem they knew by now that I wasn't fucking around because Daxton and Rae walked towards the door. I knew that they knew what was going on...but I was willing to play the fool for appearance's sake.

"We will wait for you in the car," Rae called to Rosie while stopping right next to me. We stood shoulder to shoulder, and I knew she was doing it to anger me.

"Where are you going at this time of night?" I asked.

Rae watched my face intently before turning to look at the door.

"None of your business...*traitor.*"

The last part was whispered so that the others couldn't hear. My body wanted to freeze but I pushed back against the reaction and instead lazily shifted my gaze to hers.

"You really think you did something there, huh?" I asked. "You should try harder to get a reaction out of me."

She rolled her eyes and then promptly left with Daxton out the door. Eli stayed, watching the interaction carefully.

"They are going to teach me etiquette," Rosie said standing up straight only to scoop Amr in her arms and place a kiss on top of his head. "We are going to sneak into Rae's old property and use the space there."

"Why would you need to learn that?" I asked, my words coming out more venomous than I meant.

"The gala," she answered simply. "You know, *mother dearest* would just love the opportunity for me to show the other influential high-levels that I mean business." She paused. "And murder people of course."

I swallowed thickly then nodded.

I knew the plan like the back of my hand and was thankful that this time we had Marques on our side. I was hesitant to send her in there without my protection, but I had trusted Marques so far, and I had faith in him for at least a little longer. My gaze shifted towards Eli. They were obviously very unhappy with the prospect of putting her out there like that.

Me too, buddy.

"Good luck with that," I said. "Hopefully you won't die this time."

She let out a huff and a pout graced her perfect lips.

"Unbelievable," she grumbled. "And here I thought you cared for me."

"Only sometimes," I answered simply.

She held my gaze, not backing down. It was that stupid brave face again and I was starting to hate it.

"Sit on the stool," I commanded.

She looked at the car hesitantly before sitting. Eli took action and crossed the space to grab Amr by the scruff of his neck, the feline hissing at their actions. Rosie gasped.

I walked over to her and grasped her hands. Her large brown eyes looked at me with so much emotion that it was intoxicating. I could see the anger etched on her face, the magic shifting beneath her eyes, the confusion, and most importantly the fear.

"Rosie," I whispered. "Please believe me when I tell you that everything that I am doing is to help you and that the originals do not give two shits about you or me." She opened her mouth to speak but no words came out. I squeezed her hands harder. "You want to wreak havoc? You want to fight them? Go ahead but remember that them forcing you to kill those prisoners, it wasn't training, it was their last and final warning to you. They only care about one thing: themselves."

"But then why did they go through so much trouble?" she asked.

"It is not trouble for them," I explained. "These are beings that have lived millions of lives and yours is but a blip in their memory at the end of the day. Money? Power? It is but a carefully structured plan that was put in place a decade ago."

Her eyebrows furrowed and I wondered if she was trying to reach the memory Matt took from her.

"You have a job," I said before she could get any ideas. "Just complete it and you can ensure safety for yourself and the people you care about."

Her eyes shifted to Eli immediately and it made something ugly twist inside me.

"Why are you telling me this?" she asked looking back at me.

I sighed and placed her hands back in her lap. I was tempted to brush her hair behind her ear, but I stopped myself.

"Because you have grown on me and I would like to see you live a long healthy life," I said truthfully. "But I cannot do that if you continue to cause problems for us."

A delicious blush coated her cheeks and finally she nodded.

"I'm sorry, Malik."

Damn.

"It's okay," I said. "Just please don't do anything stupid tonight and focus on the task at hand."

I stepped back and motioned for Eli to follow me. They nodded and threw Amr back to Rosie, kissed her full on the lips then followed me out the door.

"A kiss goodbye, huh?" I asked, teasingly.

"Where's Matt?" they asked, ignoring my question.

I frowned.

"I made him stay home to rest."

Eli surprised me by nodding and saying, "That's probably for the best. Weak and tired people will only slow us down."

"Too true."

I paused as a shrill tone filled the hallway. Pulling my phone out of my pocket I felt my palms start to sweat when I saw it was a private number.

"Malik," I answered after clearing my throat.

"The boy is coming tonight," Marques said from the other end of the phone. "Prepare the other one, would you?"

"Of course," I replied and not a moment later he hung up on me.

Eli looked at me expectantly.

"You're meeting him tonight," I said.

Eli's eyes widened and a smile spread across their face.

I didn't much like that smile.

* * *

We met the boy near the town. Far enough to escape if needed but close enough to start our night's work.

Eli stood next to me, putting on a nonchalant air but their eyes were trained on the figure that approached. He was wearing all black clothing and looked to be a male version of Eli with buzzed hair.

"God Malik," he said in an exacerbated tone. "Get someone to fix your damn face."

I didn't let him get under my skin. The Grotens were known to try and push their boundaries and I was much too tired to indulge any of them.

"This is Eli. *They* currently go to Winterfell and are under my care," I said. Eli didn't make any move to introduce themselves.

"Charles," he said, beating Eli to it. "Let me guess, Father never told you he had another kid?" He didn't give Eli time to answer. "Of course, he didn't. The less you know the less you can fight back."

"I didn't ask," Eli said, their eyes shifting towards mine. "Are we doing to do this or what?"

"Let's get started," I said trying to hide my smile.

Eli was ultimately the better choice between the two.

Just like every night, we snuck into a weak part in the barrier on the east side of the town. The thinner part of the barrier was carefully placed by Matt and me a few years back in an area of the woods that no one visited. There were many places that were off limits to the townsfolk, but we needed a place even the originals wouldn't think of.

"God, he had told me you picked a sewer, but I thought it was a figure of speech," Charles whined as he caught sight of where we would enter through.

I gave him a look, but he just brushed it off.

"From here on we have to be quiet," I said. "This whole thing is blown if they catch onto us."

"Sure, sure," Charles said and waved his hand in the air.

I looked back to Eli, thankful that they were able to keep it cool even during this time.

I motioned them forward and ducked under the tunnel. I had long since learned to not breathe while we made the trek, but the rank scent still permeated the air and clung to every part of my being.

It would take days, if not weeks for me to feel clean afterwards and even now I could feel the dirt crawl up my body and settle in a film across my skin. This would be one of the last times we would have to do this, and the thought gave me somewhat of a comfort...though I couldn't say the same for Charles.

The trek was no more than a few minutes, but Charles complained as if it had been three miles.

"This will be our last run," I said just as the shimmering border came into view. "We have a handful of protectors we are going for."

"How do we tell which ones to take?" Charles asked.

I paused.

Maybe bringing him was a bad idea.

"They are marked, with a blue handkerchief somewhere on their body."

Charles let out a snort.

"So, what do I do?"

Eli let out a sigh.

"Go up to them and tell them they left something at your house the last time you saw them," Eli said. "If they start to panic you may discreetly knock them out and carry them across the border. Many know it is coming and will come along willingly but some...panic."

"How many times does it end in a fight?" Charles asked, a smile in his tone. I gritted my teeth.

"It should never end in a fight if we can avoid it," I growled. "Remember we must be discreet."

"I saw we just pick them up and run, if they want to fight, that's on them," Charles said.

I turned back to look at him in the darkness.

"If that is the way you think, go back to Marques and tell him I refused to let you help," I said. I watched as his eyes shifted between Eli and myself as if Eli could save him.

"Fine," he grumbled. "I won't start anything."

Pushing through the barrier I felt a chill go through me. The magic that kept the town stuck in time was always like this in its pure form. It felt disgusting, evil, and there was no wonder why the place was as horrendous as it is. Just like the magic, the town within was shiny at first glance, perfect even, but the insides were much darker and more sinister than they would have you believe.

I stilled and pushed back against the opening, stopping the others from leaving. The air felt different tonight, like there was a buzz of energy waiting for us.

I prayed that tonight would be easy...for our last night doing this, the least the universe could do was make this easy on us.

I let a few more heartbeats pass before moving to allow the other two through. Eli exited the tunnel in silence while Charles continued to grumble under his breath. I led them along the south side of the town where the protectors were known to hang out after their shifts. The last of the passage germs would be there today and it was crucial that we got these people out.

They would hang near the pit and let off steam after work; it was something akin to a black hole where all their trash, and bodies, would go. The protectors like to throw shit in there and get drunk off their asses. It wasn't an original-approved method of letting off steam, but they let them get away with it.

When the rusted chain link fences came into view I paused, hearing the rowdy voices of some of the protectors. There were seven voices, two more than we were scheduled to bring back...and one of them was a troublemaker.

"Why is he always here?" Eli growled. "I swear that human just likes to get his ass beat."

"Be careful," I reminded. "Matt's not here to *correct* any mistakes this time. If he sees us and causes problems he will go to the originals."

Eli shifted then stood up straight.

"A dead man can't talk," they said and pushed past me. My arm shot out to catch theirs.

"Eli, be careful, please."

They gave me a lingering look before tearing their arm out of my grasp.

"Don't touch me," they hissed.

I watched helplessly as Eli swiftly climbed over the chain link fence, the sound filling the dead air.

"So, you let her have fun but not me?" Charles asked from behind me.

I bit the inside of my cheek to keep from saying something I shouldn't. I watched as Eli appeared in the darkness. The voices caught sight of them immediately and there was a pause before I could hear the groans of the one human that just seemed to really hate Eli.

I let out a long sigh. I had no idea what Eli had done to this human but every time they saw each other there was no hesitation and they charged at each other like wild animals.

When I heard Eli let out a pained groan in the darkness I moved forward to help, but Charles' hand on my shoulder stopped me.

"Let me help sister dearest," he said with a smirk before running full speed to the fence and climbing up it with ease.

I heard more shouts before there was a quiet that settled in the area. I looked around and listened for any rustling or leaves of snaps of twigs, but there was nothing.

The universe must have heard my prayer, I thought... Then I heard the arguing.

I walked forward towards the fence and peered in the darkness to see Eli carried not one, not two, *not three, but four fucking bodies.* Charles was next to them and was dragging someone by their arm. The body was limp.

"Pick him up *fucker,*" Eli hissed. The closer they got the more I was able to make out the damage. The only one that seemed to be hurt was the human Charles was dragging. Though Eli did have blood stains on them, I knew it wasn't theirs.

"Why?" he asked and let out a small huffing laugh. "Aren't you going to kill him after this?"

I could see Eli's snarl in the dim light. Without a second thought I began trying to pry the chain link fence apart with force. I was strong, but not as strong as Eli so pulling apart the metal still caused my skin to burn like crazy.

"Malik," Eli said as they stopped on the other side of the fence. "I'm going to throw them."

"Don't you even think about it," I warned. There was a smirk on their face and I barely had a moment to prepare myself before Eli literally grabbed the limp, injured man from Charles and *fucking threw him over the fence.*

The man's arm almost got caught on the top of the fence, but I was there waiting with my arms open as he tumbled towards the ground.

I let out a groan as his full weight filled my open arms before carefully lowering him to the ground just in time to catch another one.

When Eli was down to one, they climbed over the fence with the protector slung over their shoulders instead of throwing them with the rest. I gave them a look, but they only shrugged it off.

"Charles take one," I said. "We are taking the human with us."

"They are not marked," Eli said as their eyes lingered on the battered body.

"I will make an exception," I said and motioned for Charles to pick one of them up.

"You mean Marques will make one?" he said with a smile before picking up a body haphazardly.

I let out a growl before lifting two over my shoulder; Eli did the same with the remaining. It was an even longer and more painful trek back through the sewer with Charles complaining. He had even dropped the human *twice* and by the time we had brought the protectors to the drop-off location, he was looking worse for wear.

The collector was always someone different, but I was surprised to see Cristy waiting for us in all black. She had a black sedan parked ten feet away and a smile spread across her face when she saw me. I didn't remember it when I saw her in the basement, but I was there for her year in the outside world. I watched her becoming trapped in a child's body, watched until it drove her mad. She was even considering ending her life at one point because she had just had enough...and then I had to forget it because it was the very reason that brought us here today.

"Nice work boys," she said with a smile and motioned for us to load them in the back. My feet were aching as I did so but when the last person was finally loaded I let out a sigh of relief, feeling a mountain of weight go with it.

This was it, I thought. *This was the final stage and now we just had one more task until this phase of the plan was complete.*

Cristy handed us each our clothes and waved a goodbye before getting in the car. Shedding any type of insecurities, I shed my clothing. My torso and back looked even worse than my face and I heard Charles let out a low laugh.

"Damn, they really did a number on you," he said. Ignoring him I changed my pants as well. "I bet the ladies love it." He paused. "Or maybe that hideous face of yours scares them away."

I looked towards the van that had yet to leave and caught Cristy's eyes in the side mirror. She had an unreadable expression on her face before I caught the pull of her lips. She rolled down the window.

"Check your pockets!" she yelled before speeding out of the area.

I checked mine but there was nothing. Eli did the same and then looked towards Charles who was still putting on his pants. He looked up with a smirk then moved to place a hand on Eli's shoulder.

"Not bad little sis," he said. "Seems like you will be more beneficial to the cause than the others."

"Charles," I warned, glaring at him.

He rolled his eyes.

"It's not like it's a secret, she had to have figured it out by now."

"Leave them alone, we are tired and need to get back," I hissed.

"Don't boss me around," Charles spat back then looked at Eli. "Why are you still hanging with him anyways? Just come with me and we can do this all by ourselves. Maybe we can even eradicate those pesky low-levels while we have a chance. "

Eli looked down at Charles with a blank expression. They reached into Charles' pants pocket, ignoring his shouts, and pulled out a white paper. When Eli unfolded the paper, a heart-stopping smile spread across their face.

"I now see why Ezekiel never mentioned you," Eli said.

In a blink their fingers were wrapped around Charles' neck as he flopped around, trying desperately to break their hold. I could only guess what the paper said but I knew what was about to happen and leaned back to enjoy the show.

Charles had been with us for many years but after the first few times I had met him, I refused to work with him and Marques found some other use for him. Just like Eli he was brash, uncaring, and *annoying as hell*. But unlike Eli...he had nothing to fight for which made him far more unstable and dangerous.

"Let me go you *bitch!*"

Eli let out a deep chuckle and inhaled deeply.

"God, I have been wanting to do this all night," they said in a crazed voice.

"Eli, maybe think this through," I said, but even as the words came out, I had no intention to stop her, maybe just move her to a more discrete place. We were still near the border of the town, and I was worried that someone would catch us.

"R-right," Charles choked. "Marques will be upset."

Eli let out a loud sigh.

"No, he won't."

A loud snap echoed in the darkness and Charles' body went limp against Eli. I expected them to drop the corpse to the ground but instead they proceeded to lay the body on the ground and rip the head off violently only to throw it as far as they could towards the way we came from...towards the magical border of the town.

"Ezekiel will love that," I said with a snort.

Eli looked down at their clothing with a frown.

"I'm hoping that teacher bitch will see it before him," they murmured.

I couldn't help the laugh that left my lips.

Chapter 24
Rosie

When Rae had slapped an invitation to a gala on the counter, I would have never suspected that just mere hours later I would be forced to slow dance with her while both Amr and Daxton tried, unsuccessfully, to keep their laughter in.

My face burned and my anger was rising fast.

Rae held me in the position normally reserved for the leading partner and had a blank expression on her face as I stepped on her foot for the fourth time in the last five minutes.

"If you are so amused, why don't you come here and dance with me yourself!" I hissed to Daxton as the chuckle he was holding back slipped through his lips. He held up his hands in a position of surrender and continued to chuckle. Amr, now in his human form, shot him an amused look.

"Pay attention, Ms. Miller," Rae said clicking her tongue.

As she stared down at me with a cold expression, I had the distinct impression that she would be one hell of a teacher.

I pushed myself closer to her and trailed my hand from her shoulder to tease at the buttons of her shirt. The hand on my waist tightened and I smiled at her.

"Please Rae, let's be done with this," I said with a pout.

Her eyes trailed the length of my face and for a moment, I really thought that she would give in. I even saw the sides of her mouth twitch just slightly.

"If you want to embarrass yourself in front of every person at that gala, then be my guest; but do not get your feelings hurt if I refuse to rescue you when you make a fool of yourself," she said in a cool tone.

Her words stung, but they had some merit. I sighed and stepped back into the position that she had taught me with my back straight and my chin raised. She continued to lead me through the steps with no music to accompany us, only the sounds of our shoes squeaking against the floor, and the dying chuckles of Amr and Daxton.

The house looked much more daunting without the furniture. Sure, I knew that it had to have been huge but without anything in here it looked like a wasteland, and I felt as though a ghost would pop out of a doorway any minute.

It didn't help that I had felt an odd tingle on the back of my neck since coming here.

We had taken the old living room on the first floor as our place to practice. The once rugged area that I had seen only a glimpse of as I was pushed around the house was now granite that stretched across the whole area. Besides the light wallpaper there was nothing on the walls that drew the eyes. The only really remarkable thing besides the sheer mass of the space was the floor-to-ceiling windows that covered the back of the room and overlooked something that looked like a garden, but I couldn't be too sure with the darkness outside.

"I've always liked spaces like this," I murmured to Rae as she spun us around, giving me a perfect view of the moon shining behind the glass.

"I'm sure you can ask Malik to buy one for you," she said.

I don't know why the sentence bothered me, but it was enough to fix my eyes to the buttons of her shirt.

The room became silent and even the chuckles from the other two stopped. I peered over to where they were previously to see that they had left. My heart skipped a beat and a sharp panic rose in me.

"They left two sets ago," Rae said, noticing my panic. "They are in the other room; I can feel their emotions. I'm sure you could also check if you tried."

I pushed my magic out, past the walls of the living room and sure enough, I could feel them near the entrance.

"You don't like other people to see you like this," I said remembering her words. "Vulnerable."

You will be the only one to see me like this, I remembered her saying.

"There is nothing vulnerable about teaching a person with two left feet how to dance," she said. Her voice betrayed no emotion. I smiled up at her before leaning into her and resting my face on her chest. She was warm and her fresh scent filled my senses reminding me so much of the nights I had spent with her.

I had missed this.

"Thanks for teaching me," I said. "But if the gala is not far away I am not sure how much I can improve by then."

"You'll be fine," she whispered. Her hand placed mine on her shoulder so that it could push my head further into her. The action made my eyes sting. "I didn't mean what I said earlier."

"I know."

"I also am not taking Emma, if that's what you were worried about."

I smiled into her.

Stupid empath abilities, I thought.

"She seems to think so," I murmured.

We had stopped with the routine and merely swayed back and forth. It was the closest I had been touching someone that wasn't sleep or sex...and it was refreshing.

"I told her I would get her a date," she said. "Not that it would be me."

I nodded.

"I visited you," she said. "In the hospital."

I swallowed the knot in my throat.

"You did?"

"I did."

"Malik must have been pissed," I said with a light laugh.

"Eli snuck me in," she confessed. "I don't think Malik knows."

I scoffed.

"Malik knows everything."

She let out a hum.

"Will you hate me?" I asked unable to keep the words inside me any longer. "After the task?"

She paused.

"I am not a fan of colors in the house," she said.

I paused and tried to look up to her, but she pushed my head back into her chest.

"What?"

"Or flowery patterns."

"Rae," I warned.

"Minimalistic is clean, predictable, more my style," she said.

I sighed giving up on the question. If this was her way of politely telling me that our relationship may be as good as over afterwards, I might as well enjoy this time while I had it...though it did make me sad.

"I like darker colors," I said. She made a noise of agreement.

"We can work that into a minimalistic design," she said. She stopped our movements and twirled me, so I was facing the windows. She pointed towards the empty space next to them. "A bookshelf for the books that no one will ever read."

"And the biggest comfiest couch you have ever seen facing the window," I said, playing along.

"It would look a bit awkward but I'm sure whatever designer that is chosen could work with the space," Rae said. Her voice was nonchalant, but I could swear I heard a smile hidden in it.

"The wallpaper would have to go," I said with a sigh. Her arms wrapped around me, and she placed her chin on top of my head.

"It is quite ugly," she murmured.

"Is there budget to change to wood flooring?" I asked.

"Of course," she said.

"Of course, there is," I scoffed.

A smile had made its way to my face without even knowing it.

"If you get a projector you can have movie nights here," I said.

"Or we could build an in-home movie theater," she replied.

I let out a small laugh.

"I am surprised you don't have one already," I confessed.

I paused enjoying the feeling of her against me.

"If I call my agency tomorrow we can probably get this whole place done before summer vacation," she said.

"Rae..."

"It will be mine anyways," she said. I stiffened against her. "Well maybe my brothers' since Father loved them so much, but a will is easily forged."

I swallowed thickly. The playfulness that had once filled us was now replaced with tension so thick I tasted it on the back of my tongue.

"This probably isn't—"

"I won't hate you, Rosie," she said so softly I almost didn't hear it. "And don't you dare ask Malik for anything. We will move here as soon as it's ready...if you don't mind that is."

I turned around to face her. Her expression was still blank not betraying any emotions. No words came to mind.

"I don't know if you are happy, angry, or sad," she said.

"It's possible to be all three," I said. "Are you okay to stay here... afterwards?"

She cocked her head to the side.

"I have been here for years. I only ask you because you almost died here

Rosie, that is not something you would easily forget if you were forced to live here."

"But you would really do that?" I asked grabbing her hand and bringing it to my chest. "Let me stay here?"

"All of us," she corrected. My eyes widened. "You didn't think I would leave them out would you?" I opened my mouth, but she held up her hand. "Don't answer that." I snapped my mouth shut. "I have grown to understand that the group is inseparable, and it would just be more beneficial for us all to stay together, but we do need a bigger home and this one will be mine soon... so why not?"

My mind was whirling. Out of all people I never would have expected this out of Rae. She was cold, uncaring...or at least that was what she liked to give off. Yet I had seen now multiple times where that outer shell wasn't the entirety of her being.

"Rosie?"

Without another moment I launched myself into her so hard that we started falling to the ground. She groaned as I fell on top of her, but I stopped her by planting my lips on hers. Her hand tangled in my hair and pushed me closer, deepening our kiss.

She sat up so that I was straddling her waist but didn't break the kiss.

"I take it this makes you happy?" she asks against my lips.

"So happy," I groaned as she kissed my neck. "Will Amr and Daxton be mad if we make them wait a bit longer?"

"Why do you ask?"

I know she knew, but I could play along and give her what she wanted. I grabbed her hands and forced them up my sweatshirt so that she could feel that I wasn't even wearing a bra.

"I want to fuck you so hard the neighbors think this place is haunted," I groaned.

Her eyes widened and then slowly a smile formed on her face before I heard the first breathy chuckle that came out of her mouth. I was mesmerized by it and turned on at the same time.

"We don't have neighbors within hearing distance," she said. "And as much as I'm ready to ravish you..." She twisted my nipple, pulling out a yelp from me. "I would like to finally do it in a bed once more."

I pouted but she just leaned forward and planted a kiss on my lips.

"I'm sure Amr and Daxton would be happy to help you on the way though," she offered.

I sent her a devilish smile.

* * *

"Fuck, I can't—Rae please," I begged as Amr pushed into me in one thrust. By now his size didn't even give me pause but I already felt my body start to shake violently.

Rae, true to her word let them take care of me in the car, but then it moved to the counter, then now the couch. Amr and Daxton took turns fucking me in all different positions all while Rae watched and jotted down notes in her stupid fucking books.

I had never taken Rae as someone into group sex until now. I had always just thought that she never meant to walk in, but with the gleam in her eye now...I am starting to think I don't really know her at all.

I was laying on the couch with my ass up, forced to stay in the position while Amr and Daxton rested. To prolong the experience Rae hadn't let them fuck me together. That's right, *let them.* They were actually listening to her.

"I can't hear you," she mumbled and read over her notebook, as if ignoring what was happening in front of her. She had taken the loveseat across from us so that she had a full view of what was going on.

Amr gripped my hips harshly and began thrusting into me at an animal-istic pace. I couldn't help my cries.

Amr pulled me back further and I angled my ass back only for him to hit a spot that made me start sobbing.

"Damn," Daxton murmured from the loveseat adjacent to Rae. He was already palming his hard cock in his hand. My mouth watered at the sight of it.

I knew the old me would be beyond embarrassed by now, but I couldn't even bring myself to flush. Being at the whim of them was just too intoxicat-ing, too addictive.

Amr's name and strings of curses began coming out of my mouth like chants.

"Flip her over," Rae commanded, finally looking at me.

I imagined what she was seeing. I had to have been a mess by now, I could feel the tears running down my face and cum had been drying in my hair and on my chest. Even though I had come so many times already, wetness was dripping down my legs. I wondered if Daxton's bites on my thighs left marks that she could see.

Amr flipped me over, more gently than the pace of his trusts, before picking up speed again. His cock moved inside me with such ferocity that I was sure I would break. That was until he placed his outstretched hand on my lower stomach and pushed.

"You feel that my love?" he asked. His hair fell over us like a curtain and I could feel the beads of sweat dropping off him and onto my already heated skin.

He thrust again and my eyes rolled into the back of my head. With his hand pushing against my stomach, I could feel his cock pushing against my upper walls sending jolts through my entire body.

"Yes. *Yes*," I moaned.

"Head slightly off the armrest. Daxton," Rae commanded.

Amr moved us so that I was in the position she outlined, and Daxton stalked over to us palming his cock. He had an indecent smile on his face.

"Tilt your head sweetheart," he purred. "Let me try that mouth again."

Oh god. I didn't know I could get any wetter, but I could feel myself reacting to this.

Amr groaned and slowed his thrusts.

"Now."

I did as they asked and tilted my head so Daxton could slide his throbbing cock into my mouth. He titled my chin even further as he slid in for deeper access. I could feel the cool metal piercing play at the back of my throat.

"Yes, just like that," he cooed once I took him as deep as possible. Amr picked up his thrusts. I whimpered around Daxton's cock. "Damnit, stay just like that."

He was gentle as he gripped my throat and then gave two experimental thrusts. When I held in my want to gag his trusts picked up in line with Amr's.

Drool escaped my mouth as he forced his cock into me and began fucking my face in earnest, but I didn't care how messy this was. All I cared about was the feel of his piercing against my tongue.

Amr's thumb circled my clit and the tears fell freely. Heat rose up in me and I felt my orgasm start to build.

"Don't let her come," Rae commanded.

I let out a muffled protest as his hand moved but it was quickly forgotten as I felt Daxton swell inside me.

He pulled out just in time for his hot seed to shoot onto my face and chest. I licked my lips as I looked up, tasting him.

I then shot up to grab Amr by the neck and force his lips down to mine. He moaned and with two more thrusts I felt him spill inside me.

I fell back into the couch, exhausted. Amr laughed at my reaction and slowly pulled out only to place his hand back on my stomach, this time with a glowing light.

"I am assuming that's a magical form of birth control?" Rae asked from the loveseat, unfazed.

"It is indeed," Amr replied.

"So that's what that is," I replied sleepily.

"I'm surprised you didn't ask earlier," Daxton said and left a wet kiss on my mouth.

"I'm not," Rae said, standing. "Alright boys, good work, now let me help her clean up."

"Yes, sir," Daxton chimed sarcastically.

I reached my arms out to Rae as she approached. She didn't hesitate to pick up my dirty naked body and walk us to the empty room.

"She will be with me tonight," she called back. "Get some rest, we have school tomorrow."

I barely registered as she brought me into the dark room then straight to the bathroom. I was blinded when she turned on the light.

"You have your own tub in here?" I asked. "I'm jealous."

"It's your apartment," she reminded. "Come in here anytime you'd like."

She leaned over to turn on the tub but did not let go of me.

"I didn't know you were into that stuff," I said with a sniffle. "Usually, Eli is the one giving orders."

"They would listen to me too, in that situation," she said. "Though we will need to think of the logistics behind more than three."

I smiled.

"I have many holes and two hands," I joked. Her gaze darkened.

"We can think about it," she said. "Though I think I will prefer you alone, at least if I am not just watching."

"Whatever you need," I said and kissed her cheek.

"Though I am sure Malik will probably be the same," she mused. "Or maybe he and Eli will get over their feud for you."

I froze at her insinuation. She lowered me into the bathtub's hot water before stepping back to take off her own clothes. I watched in rapt focus as she did. I had seen her naked in darkness before but seeing her in the bathroom light was breathtaking. She had muscles, of course, but her clothes hid the slight swell of her breast and mark of her hips. As well as the delicious tuft of curls in between her legs.

"Malik isn't on the table," I said.

"That's not true," she said putting aside her glasses then stepping into the bath with me. Her legs brushed across mine and I realized this tub was probably too small for the both of us. Her nipples peeked out above the water and even though I was exhausted I wanted nothing more than to taste them.

"I guess it's not," I said. "When I was first adjusting to the news of my status, I was in the town, and something almost happened."

She raised her brow.

"Describe almost."

"Well, it was making me antsy, and I just tried to push him." I had the audacity to flush. "To try and take it out on me, punish me."

"Sounds like he didn't take the bait," she murmured.

"No, he scolded me instead," I said. "Though he has dropped hints but..."

"But what?" she asked.

"But I don't feel right thinking of that when not everyone is here," I said.

"Eli you mean."

I nodded.

"Do you know what they are up to?" I asked hesitantly.

Rae shook her head and leaned back with a sigh, her neck muscles stretching.

"If I did I would have told you," she said. My silence caused her to look up at me quizzically. The eyes that were normally guarded by her glasses were now bared to the world giving me a rare look at her full face.

We didn't speak as she moved to grab a washcloth from the other side of the bath. She wetted it in the water and began cleaning my face. I leaned into her touch, not breaking eye contact the entire time.

These moments were just for us, and I reveled in them. I could feel the words that she was trying to say through these actions, feel the emotions she was trying to pack in with it. It was more tenderness than I had been awarded in my entire existence and I tried not to let the tears fall over.

"Eli is back," she murmured and tilted my head to clean my neck. "They're...impatient."

My heart jumped when I heard their name and no sooner did the devil burst into the bathroom. Rae's gaze shifted to mine then she continued to drag the washcloth gently against my skin.

"Get out," they demanded.

"This is my time Eli," Rae said in a calm tone. My gaze flitted to a bold and wild-looking Eli.

Their blond hair fell into their eyes and was stained dark red in places as was their face and clothing. I could tell with a glance they were unhurt, but the blood caused something to shift deep inside me.

"I'm not waiting," they growled and stalked towards us, but Rae stopped them in their tracks with a glare that caused me to shiver.

"Go wash in the other room then *maybe* I will consider letting you in tonight," she growled.

I could feel the tension filling the room, suffocating me and the others. Eli glared at Rae and took not one but three deep breaths before turning on their heels and walking straight back out the door.

"Are you sure?" I asked.

"I did that for you," she said. "If you want to spend the night with them then I will not stop you, but they seem volatile... They may hurt you."

A part of me wanted a feral Eli. Wanted to be ravished by them as they lost control of themselves. I had been denied an orgasm and was waiting to continue it with Rae but...

"I can handle it," I said. "But you..."

"I will leave you two to it," she said and leaned back with a sigh. "I had hoped I could spend more time with you but that can wait."

I gave her a small smile before leaning forward to place a light kiss on her lips.

"You are a selfless person," I said. "Thank you."

She stiffened slightly before pulling away.

"They are already waiting outside the door," she said. "Go to them."

With a fluttering in my stomach and a tight chest I did what she asked.

Eli was waiting for me, dressed in a clean t-shirt and boxer shorts. Daxton and Amr were watching with interest from the couch, though they were both slouched over as if they were exhausted. Amr gave me a look and I knew he was telling me to let him know if he needed to intervene.

Eli gave me a heated stare as I walked closer in nothing but a towel. Their hand shot out to mine and gripped me with such force that I had to swallow my yelp in pain.

"Be careful," Rae said from the doorway behind us. I looked back to give her a smile, letting her know that I would be fine, but Eli pushed me into the opposite room without warning and slammed the door behind us.

"Fucking *finally*," they growled and yanked me to them. Their hand buried itself in my damp hair and pulled harshly so that I was forced to meet their piercing blue eyes. They forced their lips against mine and continued to give me a bruising kiss that sucked the breath out of me.

I lost the grip on my towel and let it fall to the floor and wrapped my arms around their shoulders. It was easy to get lost in their touches, but I still couldn't get over how much I had missed them. How much their touch seemed to seep into my bones and finally fill the hole that has been growing since their absence. I pulled their body closer to mine unable to bear the thought of any more space between us.

I missed you. I missed this, I told them in my mind. I knew they heard me, but their only response was a deep growl and to hoist me up. I wrapped my legs around their waist and scraped their bottom lip with my teeth.

They turned to drop us on the bed and only then did they pull away, panting heavily to look at me. There was a frown on their face when they met my eyes.

"There is a..." they trailed then looked away before continuing. "My chest it—*damn it.*"

I cocked my eyebrow at them.

"Are you okay?" I asked. The tension from before still hung in the air and their hand in my hair tightened...but there was something else.

They gave me a glare.

"It's because of you," they growled and leaned forward to bury their teeth in my neck. Their free hand clamped on my mouth to stop the whine. They pulled away and licked the area before meeting my eyes once more. Their hand ripped away from my hair and went straight to my sore pussy. Without warning they forced two fingers into me. I let out a noise that was muffled by their hand.

They pumped their fingers into me slowly, building up to a slow aching pleasure that curled in my belly and made me like putty in their hands. They watched me intently, still with a frown on their face.

I wanted to ask more but I couldn't. Not with their hand stopping me from speaking and the way their fingers were expertly teasing me. They brushed across my clit, just barely causing me to whine.

"You make me feel things," they said picking up their pace. I arched into them and positioned my hips so the heel of their hand brushed against my clit with each thrust. "Things *I hate.*" They spit each word out like a curse. "I don't want to feel this way. I don't want to think of you when I am gone. I want it *to stop.*"

They were ruthless with her movements and leaned down again to bite me in various places, but each time it was more and more controlled, as if they were holding back. I felt my stolen orgasm coming up fast, but I didn't want to be so far from them.

Eli, I said in my mind. Their eyes peered up at me, their mouth hovering just over my nipple. *Kiss me, please.*

They paused as if considering not doing it, but with one movement they removed their hand and brought down their mouth to mine to give me a passionate kiss that sent me straight over the edge.

Just like with Rae, I felt my magic bubble up and explode all around me, but this time I didn't stop kissing Eli to look. Instead, I brought them closer not knowing when the next time I would be able to do this with them would be.

When they finally pulled away and removed their hand from between my legs, they lay their head down on my chest and rested their entire weight on me. I was caught off guard by the action and froze before I hesitantly brought my arms around their form and held them in an embrace.

Do that thing to my hair, they commanded in my mind. With slow movements I did as they asked and started to run my fingers through their slightly damp hair like I would do when they were asleep.

I swallowed thickly, unsure how to continue.

"I feel the same way you know," I said softly. "When you are not around...I miss you, *a lot*. And I worry so much that it drives the others mad."

They let out a snort.

"I doubt you have much time to think when you are moving between Daxton, Amr, *and* Rae," they said.

It hurt that they didn't know how much they meant to me. How much I had waited for them to come home and pass out on the couch just so I could see them for just those two seconds. Those few minutes that I could watch them sleep and know that they were safe with me were more meaningful than I could put into words.

They let out a groan.

"I get it," they said. "Just stop saying those things, it makes my chest feel weird."

I let a small smile spread to my face.

"Maybe Rae can give you a class about emotions," I told them.

"Never," they said with a huff.

I don't know how long we had stayed like that, but soon my vision began to blur, and I found myself falling asleep to the small patterns that Eli was drawing in my skin.

Chapter 25
Rosie

emons and witches alike were bustling with excitement all throughout Winterfell for the last few weeks of the school year. There were more smiles and laughs filling the hallways than I had seen all year. And on top of that no one even seemed bothered about the Winterfell tower, though there were a few who were amazed by such a feat and even weeks after it had made a small flutter of pride fill my chest.

Though along with the excitement of the year ending, came a shift in the people around me and their attitude towards me. The same demons who had looked at me with such spite and hate were now chatting with me, sharing smiles, and just treating me as more than the low-level that I was first introduced as.

I wanted to chalk it up to the fact that everyone was just excited to be leaving for summer. That they had gotten over their differences and finally understood that no matter the species, race, or sexual orientation, we were still people stuck on this god forsaken planet and the only safe harbor was the walls of Winterfell.

But I knew it was because they now knew my real heritage and that as soon as the other low-levels came to this school, they would be treated the same as I once was.

I also have come to learn very quickly that the wall that kept us inside this school may be the most valuable thing on this earth. After all, not many knew of what the world had waiting for us outside. I was just one of the lucky ones that got forced into it.

So, while I could enjoy being treated like one of the demons who belonged here...I knew that it was only a matter of time before the shadow from the outside seeped into the carefully crafted gates of Winterfell.

I was brought back to reality with one painful reminder.

"So, you are going to help other low-levels get settled in, right?" a brown-haired, green-eyed demon asked me. He leaned across his lab table as if wanting to catch every single syllable that I uttered.

I leaned back on my own table and shot a glance to Daxton and Amr. They were currently on the table behind me going over the class notes. Amr's brows were furrowed as he tried to understand what Daxton was spewing.

To my surprise Daxton actually paid more attention to the class than I ever had and even had his own set of notes... Ones that I had never seen him write before. Every day I watch him I come to the realization that I don't even know him all that well. I had a general idea of what he liked and disliked, his trauma, and his sleeping habits...but it was barely scratching the surface.

Amr on the other hand...he was an open book. Loved everything to do with life and freedom. Was obsessed with me—and Daxton—and would do literally anything he could to make sure we were happy.

Eli of course was absent and while I had once felt that we had made strides...all of that seemed to disappear with them. I was right to savor that one night together because the next day, everything was back to normal, and I would go days without seeing them.

"Rosie?" the demon asked, calling me out of my daydream. I jumped and felt Amr's magic reach out to me, as if checking that I was okay.

"Yes." I cleared my throat. "I will be helping the low-levels next year as their..." *Shit what was it called?* "Sort of like their ambassador."

"Do you know who the demon ambassador will be?" he asked, his eyes lit with excitement. "Maybe they will do a drawing and then I will be lucky enough to get to work with you."

I rolled my eyes.

"I would choose a safer target for your affections," I said.

"Ya dipshit," Daxton called from the table. "Back off. Didn't you hate her before?"

The demon spluttered and sat up straight, putting as much space between us as possible before turning the other direction and ignoring me completely.

I would have hated the way the trio dictated my life but now I found myself just leaning into the idea of them being the only important people in my life.

And it wasn't because I didn't want any friends...but instead I just didn't want to see anyone else hurt. I had no idea what waited for me out there and after this task, nor did I want to bring some unprepared innocent into this.

Sometimes I still dreamed of the men I killed, but I found quickly that there were other ways to occupy my mind when those thoughts start to take over. And when I did, I think I really started to understand Eli and Daxton more.

I looked over to Mr. Faulkner as he sat at his desk, looking over papers and typing on his computer. It was a free day for study, even though most people took it as something else, and he had let us know that he would be creating our final exam.

He was another person that I could not figure out.

Was he with Malik?

Or was he controlled by him?

Had he been to the town?

Or was he just in the dark as the rest of the people here?

The more I thought about his involvement the more I thought about the sheer amount of people behind this, yet I had only come face to face with a few. This may have been an operation for thousands of years, but I felt as though I barely scratched the surface.

And it was dangerous for all of us.

Even telling Daxton and Rae would get us in trouble...yet Malik just removed his powers just like that. It was odd and completely unlike him.

Another brush of magic at my side told me that I had been staring at Mr. Faulkner for far too long. I looked behind me to see both Daxton and Amr waiting for me.

"I still don't understand why we must test," Amr grumbled. "Are the hours accumulated in this classroom not enough? Is there nothing else to be graded on?"

"You have the rankings tomorrow, and then the actual exam the day after that," Daxton said. "If you can win the rankings you can probably pass even if you fail the exam."

"I'm forfeiting the rankings next year," I said.

Daxton nodded then shot me a smile.

"Ya I plan to grow my hair out again and I would like to not get the Rosie special next time," he joked and ran his hand through his hair. It was a bit longer than before but didn't cover any of his boyish features or the scripted tattoo on his temple that I saw my gaze being drawn to more than once.

I returned his smile.

"I like it short," I said and twirled a short lock around my finger.

"Me too," Amr said with a smirk. "Not every demon is as capable as I am when it comes to hair growth." He made a show of combing through his long dark hair.

I rolled my eyes at the horrible joke.

"I'll think about getting a *real* haircut over the summer," he said. "Are you ready for next year?"

For the low-levels? was unspoken but I heard it loud and clear.

"We have a few months to handle that," I said. "We will get to it when we get to it."

In truth, I had no idea what I was supposed to do, nor any idea of how to help anyone if they came to me. Sure, I looked good on paper. Scholarship, games winner, hybrid...but I didn't know what they wanted from me.

Anger shifted deep inside my belly when I realized just how powerless I was. I don't know how we were going to change the tides, but we needed to start, and fast before the new year started.

* * *

The rankings came and went.

Amr won and had actually enjoyed beating the absolute shit out of all the weak demons that surrounded us. He would throw them around like they weighed nothing and egg them on as they cowered in fear.

It was nice to see him letting go a bit and allowing himself free reign.

But alas, those times never last and I found myself staring blankly at the exam that Mr. Faulkner had prepared for us. It only had one question that he had promoted at the start of the class, and I didn't even know how to answer.

Where do demons come from and how were they created?

I knew a bit about where Ezekiel and the other originals hailed but would that be too much to put in this exam? Would that count as betraying them?

Students started answering quickly and leaving just as quick. I felt both Daxton and Amr leave their seats to hand in their papers. Eli, who had shown up for just this class was sitting next to me and I could feel their stare.

"What a double-edged question, huh?" Eli whispered.

"I think it's fairly obvious actually," I whispered back in a bitter tone.

Eli shifted their paper over to me and I came face to face with a fairly artistic drawing of horned demons pulling themselves out of the fiery pits of hell. The drawing was extremely detailed, and each ugly line of the demons' faces was etched into the page.

It was good, *really good.* I looked up at them in shock.

"I didn't know you were an artist," I commented, and they gave me that beautiful smirk I had been missing so dearly.

"There is a lot you don't know about me," they answered and got up to hand in their paper.

I sighed and stared down at the paper once more before scribbling my answer and racing after them.

Mr. Faulkner accepted my paper with a smile that quickly turned into a frown when he saw my answer.

"Rosie," he said with a disappointed sigh.

"Don't act like I won't pass," I said. "I think I already know the game too well by now to even think that's an option."

He just waved me off with another sigh and I walked out of the class with my head held high.

* * *

The perfect way to start of a birthday was to murder someone— *of course.*

I had played around with the idea of telling the others but instead I let it go, knowing that right now was not the time to celebrate such a thing. Nor did I want to celebrate it if I was truthful.

After all, what good had come from my birth?

It had snuck up on me and I didn't even notice it until it was staring me in the face this morning. A time that was once coveted by people my age now became this gnarled and twisted nightmare.

"Why is it called the End of Summer Gala when summer has just begun?" I asked Rae as she walked over with the choice of dresses I had.

I hadn't slept well for days knowing that the Gala was coming soon. Every time I closed my eyes I could still feel the way it felt to be torn in two by their magic.

"It's used to be at the end of summer," Rae explained. "But the old wealthy participants stated that it was too far in between events so they would like to push it forward."

I rolled my eyes.

"Of course."

I looked over the flowy and no doubt expensive material in her hands. Even now the thought of wearing those left a pit the size of Mount Everest in my stomach.

"Which one?" she asked and held up a long, emerald green gown that would no doubt drag on the floor behind me as I walked. The one in the other hand was a deep blue, so dark it almost seemed black if not for the shimmers that caught the light, showing its true color.

"The blue one," I murmured and looked at myself in the mirror.

Rae had brought in makeup and hair people to help me with everything and looking at myself now, I couldn't even recognize the low-level I once was. The only thing I recognized were my large brown eyes but even those were shrouded in heavy makeup. My hair was no longer cascading limply down my back and instead I was left with an updo that was starting to cause a dull ache in my head.

She stood behind me, the scent of her cologne invading my senses and the heat from her body seeping through my thin robe. She swept the dress in front of me, her arms just barely brushing across mine as she held it up for me to look. Her sharp eyes watched me in the mirror, and I knew she was cataloging every minute expression and reaction.

She nodded then let out a hum.

"It suits you well," she said.

She was right, I thought.

The dark blue brought out the paleness of my skin and matched the makeup perfectly. I looked sultry. Powerful. Like I belonged at the table with those corrupted high levels. The deep neckline and straps would give the perfect view of the scar on my chest.

It hit me then, that I would have to act like I was friendly with the people who had once killed me.

"Are you scared?" Rae asked.

"Can't you feel it?" I asked running my hand across the dress.

"Yes," she whispered, her breath fanning across my neck. "But I feel something else too."

I swallowed thickly.

"Yes there is something else."

"Excitement?" she asks.

I nodded.

"To see them? That can't be right."

"To destroy them," I said and watched as a smile played at my lips in the mirror.

Her smile dropped for just a moment before she leaned forward and planted a kiss on the top of my head.

"Hold on to that," she paused before looking at me in the mirror. "Happy Birthday."

"Of course *you* would remember," I teased around the thickness in my throat.

"It is in my best interest to know things," she said with a small smile. "Soon, we can celebrate in peace."

* * *

Daxton had a death grip on my arm as we walked up to the house that seemed to rival the White House. It was built in an old European fashion with windows that decorated the entire exterior of the house. The house on the outside showed an exposed brick that looked as if it had been polished just for this event and shined even in the dark night.

Spotlights were spaced evenly on the pathway leading up to the house as if guests would not be able to find the entrance to a monstrosity such as this. Guests walked the pathway with light conversation and by the glow of their eyes I could tell that they were all demons. I had yet to see another witch here.

On top of that no one even noticed that we were here and continued to walk around us as if I was not the only hybrid in the world. I mean...I knew it wasn't true...*but they didn't.*

"This doesn't really look like hiding," Daxton muttered.

I nodded in agreement. For people who *really* didn't want to be found, this was quite an obvious choice of living. It was almost as if they were goading us to come in.

I shivered at the thought.

I looked past Daxton to Rae and Amr. Like Daxton, they were both dressed in suits. Amr's hair was gathered in a low ponytail giving everyone a full view of his chiseled face. His eyes met mine and he sent me a reassuring wink. Rae on the other hand had her curls slicked back and she had put on a special pair of glasses that I had never seen before. Her eyes were trained on the open doors and the butlers that were seeing the guests in.

I couldn't help but focus on the empty spot. Eli was *still* not around, and I found myself really put off by it. Out of all nights *this* was the one that they chose to miss even after the talk that we had that night.

I tried not to let it bother me.

After all, I couldn't afford to let my makeup run when I still had a job to do. They would smell weakness from a mile away and for what I had to do, I had to be strong.

This night would mark the end of all this terror, and the completion of my task and hopefully the freedom from the originals.

"Remember the plan," Rae said without looking at us.

Separate them. Kill them. Clean up. Then leave like nothing ever happened.

Rae and Daxton both wanted a stake in this, but it had only taken one look at Rae to know that she could probably not go through with it. It was nothing against her or her character, but I could tell her bond with her father was different than anyone's here and that this would not come easy to her.

But that was okay.

Because I planned to intervene when it came down to it.

I steeled myself and pulled from the magic around us. Daxton's and Amr's magic swirling around mine only solidified my resolve. Without another word I pulled Daxton forward towards the open door.

"Mr. Reid, Ms. Miller," the butler on the right with short brown hair and bright blue eyes greeted as we came up. I didn't let the shock of them knowing my name show on my face, but I felt a sense of uneasiness creep up on me.

This is normal, I told myself. *To be seen. To be known by these people.*

I gave them a once over then looked further into the party. Demons of all kinds were walking around with drinks in hand and chatting away. The most shocking though was the mix of humans among the group, yet there were still no witches. I knew the greater public had thoughts about witches and I had seen some coverage about the uprisings...but they couldn't be *this hated* could they?

"Mr. Reid and Mr. Ashwell are waiting for you in the main room," the one on the left continued.

I swallowed thickly. Word must have gotten around to them that I was still alive, I really shouldn't be surprised. What is surprising is that they were inviting me so publicly to see them.

"Perfect," I said in a sweet voice and smile. "Show the way please."

Just go with whatever happens, Rae had told us on the ride over. *I have it planned; you just have to trust me.*

I did trust her. *Of course, I trusted her...*but it didn't stop the uneasy feeling I got in my stomach when I realized that in just a few moments I would have to face them, and I knew literally nothing of the plan.

Daxton's grip only got tighter as we were led through the bustling area and people started to look at us. I hated attention and could feel myself crumbling under all the stares but it would seem that Daxton was worse off than me. I could feel the tension rolling off of him and his magic was lashing out. I could feel it grabbing onto mine and trying to spread out and feel the people around us.

I tried to understand his response. After all, these were the people who were supposed to love him and take care of him, yet they continued to betray him and use him over and over again.

My own rage sank low in my chest, rising as we took each step. The plan started now, and we had but hours to complete it.

I paused in my steps when I spotted a familiar female demon on the arms of a person I did not recognize. Their full lips were formed into a pout, and they sent a glare to Rae as we passed. It was Emma and she looked extremely unhappy to be tangled to an elderly low-level. His low-level status was apparent by the way his hair greyed and skin sagged. I almost wanted to laugh and felt a flare of satisfaction when I saw it, but it didn't override the anxiety that was gnawing at my gut.

With each step my heart rate got faster, and I found it harder to breathe. My stomach was threatening to empty its contents and my hands started to visibly shake. It was different than last time. They knew we were coming. We were in more danger here than ever, regardless of the people in the party.

But my magic loved it. It thrived off of the dangers and I could feel it shifting within me, getting ready for the fight that was about to happen.

Kill. Kill. Kill. Take. Take.

Over and over, I felt it trying to push me forward, but I used Daxton as an anchor.

The main room as they called it was closed off to the rest of the house and as the butler stopped in front of the doors, every moment of the last school year flashed through my mind. On the other side of these doors were the people that started the "war" the originals were so adamant about winning. They were the ones who had forced Xena's hand and gave me the curse that wrecked more than half my life. It was their fault as much as the originals' and this would be the first step into reclaiming back my life...and finally getting back at them.

My magic rose sharply, and I could feel the air crackle around us. Rae's hand nudged my back, but I ignored it, zeroing in on the space behind the door as it opened.

I first saw the disgusting face of Lars, then Sirene. They were both smiling and laughing as if they did not single-handedly ruin the man next to me. Their eyes snapped over to us and their smiles died.

The next was Rae's Father. He was looking off towards the corner of the room, but his expression hardened after he caught sight of us. My rage was rising sharply when I finally caught sight of them and the scar on my chest burned as though it was fresh.

When the doors were fully open I caught sight of who they were talking to. A man, with shoulder-length black hair and golden eyes that rivaled Malik's...though his were dull and had a haunting shadow in them. These eyes alone looked like they had seen both the creation and destruction of the world. These eyes were haunted with demons unseen, and they left a chill in the air. He was dressed in a fancy suede suit and a smirk graced his full lips. When our gaze met I felt something tie us together and blood rushed to my ears. It was as though I could feel the connection and to touch it would be as easy as reaching out to grab it. When I was unable to take the attention any longer I looked at the space occupied next to him. My heart stopped and with it the noises of the crowd fell away until there was a ringing so loud I thought my head was going to explode.

Familiar curly red hair was the first thing I saw. Then paired with grey eyes and a surprisingly sullen expression. He was dressed in a suit just like the others around here, but I couldn't pull my eyes from him. Matt, my first friend in Winterfell, was standing in a room with the people who tried to murder me. He was the one who got me into this, took me to the town under a guise that hid his true identity.

Who the fuck was Matt really?

Chapter 26
Daxton

I knew I didn't like that little shit.

Well... I was willing to give him a chance, it was Eli who hated him, but I should have known to trust Eli after all these years. They were always right.

I glared at him before turning to my parents.

Tonight, would be the last time that I felt their slimy magic on me, the last time I would be forced to breathe the same air as them, and the last time I would have to listen to their bullshit.

"Rae," the black-haired man spoke. "Look at how well you did. I knew you could follow orders."

There was a pause from Rosie. She stilled completely, and her magic stilled with her. She turned her head to look past me and towards Rae. I followed her gaze. Rae was looking at the ground, Amr's hand around the back of her neck and his teeth were bared at her.

Seeing Amr's reaction made my magic flip and I felt Rosie's magic explode between us. Usually even the most powerful witch's magic is clear unless they are actively using it and can only be felt by other witches, but this magic was the darkest red I have ever seen and billowed out of her like smoke.

She was mad, she had to be. I was pissed, upset, *scared*. Rae brought us here with a plan, one that we took in blindly, not asking any questions. I should have known that we couldn't have trusted her since last time.

I stiffened and looked over the room. This would be worse to escape than the last time, especially knowing that the closed doors behind us held wait-staff, but I knew they had to double as guards. We were fucked, there was no way that we would be getting out here alive.

I watched as Rosie's magic spread across the room, slowly covering it. Maybe if we could pull the magic out of her, we could stand a fighting chance but... I looked towards my father and mother. He had healed nicely since last time and my stomach dropped to the floor when I realized once again I would have to try and fight him.

I can't do this, my thoughts echoed.

"I don't think we have been introduced," Rosie said, the smile dropping completely from her face.

"No, we have not," the man said with a smile and handed his drink to Matt. "You may call me Marques."

"So, you are the one pulling the strings?" she asked.

Marques raised his brow.

"Excuse me, child?"

"You don't expect me to believe that these weak ass people are the ones behind the big conspiracy?" she asked waving off my and Rae's parents like they were a fleck of dust. Between my nausea and panic I felt a bit of pride rise up within me. She had to have been as scared as I was yet...here she was playing the part she was always meant to without hesitation.

"There is no conspiracy," he said and took a step towards us. In an instant fire roared to life mere inches from his feet stopping him in his tracks and singeing off part of his hair. He sighed. "I am not here to fight you."

"I am," Rosie hissed. "I came here for one reason and one reason only."

With a wave from my mother the fire was extinguished. I could hear Rosie grinding her teeth together.

"Oh, I know the reason," he said with a chuckle. "And to clarify, I have no plan to stop you." He paused and looked towards my father. With one look my father's eyes blurred over, he then stood and walked towards the space between us before kneeling with his head bowed. "A peace offering if you will."

My mouth went dry. I looked toward Mother, and she seemed to be fighting against an invisible power while Rae's father seemed content to sip his wine. I could feel a power so strong rise in the room that it played at my senses. Never once had I come into contact with a demon power that I could feel so tangibly like this before.

He's bad news.

"Matt, explain," Rosie commanded not moving from her spot. I could feel her shaking under my grip.

I looked towards Rae.

"Please," I whispered. "What is this?"

"Just go with the plan," she spat back.

I met Amr's eyes before looking back towards Matt. The normal goofy look on his face was gone and we were left with the shell of the person we used to know.

"He won't answer to you," Marques said and then walked forward and placed his foot on my father's back before putting all his weight onto the kneeling man. I could hear the bones on my father's back crack, but no noise came out of his mouth. "Go on now. Isn't this what you wanted?"

"We don't even know you and you expect us to kill someone in front of you?" Amr asked.

"You can trust me more than that *bitch* Xena that's for sure," he said. "An eye for an eye. This is to show you that you can trust me; it is not meant to be held over you."

Rosie looked towards me, and I saw the beast of her magic barely being restrained behind those brown eyes.

I could hear the question without it being asked.

What do you want to do?

She was offering herself in my place. Of course, she would be willing to step in for me even though I had sworn I would be the one to do it. I didn't deserve someone like her, but I also wasn't sure that I could go through with this anymore. I swallowed and took one step towards my father, leaving the comfort of Rosie's side.

Then another.

Then another.

And another until I was right in front of my kneeling father. Marques lifted his shiny polished shoe off my father's back, and I was met with wide eyes and an expression that showed only hurt.

I couldn't breathe.

I couldn't move.

It was the same thing I had felt even as he was on top of me, squeezing the life out of me. I had been waiting for this moment for years. It had been in my dreams when I was still in that hell hole. Everything about this situation was too perfect...yet there was something in my chest tugging me back. Begging me to go running to the hills. It reminded me of all those dark nights in my room alone when I had felt like there was no reason left to live in this world.

I knew the look in his eyes. I had seen it many times in my own. Even when I wanted to end it all I was always left with *that look.*

The one that wanted so desperately to live. Even without speaking I knew that he was begging for his own son to save his life. No matter how much he had tortured me as a child, he still had the audacity to beg me to live...*and it was working.*

I couldn't do this, I thought even as I walked around my father.

I shouldn't do this, I thought as I tangled my fingers through his greasy hair and pulled his head back sharply, exposing his throat.

Just because he did it doesn't mean... I looked back at the group. Amr watched me with a tense expression, Rosie stood straight with one foot out, ready to jump in...and Rae had a dead look in her eyes.

She too was thinking about what she would have to do in the next few minutes.

I knew that he was bad. I experienced it. I knew that this was the only way to stop it once and for all. This was for years of abuse and torture at their hands.

I readied a magical blade in my hand and placed it at his throat. Tears began to leak from his eyes. I closed my own eyes, unable to look. My hand was shaking violently, and I felt my breathing turn shaky.

I can't do it, I thought. *After everything I was still just as weak as they thought I was.*

A warm hand grabbed my own, pulling the blade away from my father's throat. I opened my eyes to see Rosie staring down at me, a soft smile spread across her face and her hand brushed across my cheek.

"This is my job to do," she said. "I'm sorry I put you through this."

I paused and opened my mouth to refuse but no words came out of my mouth. I knew now, in that moment that no one understood me more than her. That even though I had opened my mouth to protest she knew in her heart that this was something I could not walk back from.

Again, she had acted as my savior, while I just stood there.

Her hand covered my eyes, and I heard a sick squelching and a burst of hot liquid sprayed on my chest. I swallowed thickly, not wanting to think about the body that awaited me. But even as she used the magic to wipe away the blood and burn the body, she never removed her hand from my face, saving me from having to see the one thing that would haunt my nightmares.

I could feel the tears running down my face, but I couldn't feel the sadness that followed. Instead, my entire chest felt numb. When her hand finally removed itself from my eyes the only thing left between us was the stain of my father's blood on the carpet.

There was a light clapping from behind us.

"Quick, clean, effective, perfect execution for someone who knows little to nothing about her magic," Marques said from behind me.

I knew I should be mad, but I couldn't be. I could only feel the intense guilt that filled me knowing that I failed the one thing I asked Rosie to let me do.

"I failed you," I whispered to her. She leaned forward and left a kiss on my forehead.

"It was I who have failed you," she said. "Go back with the others. Let me finish this."

"Listen to her, child," Marques said. I could feel myself get up and move without telling my body to and when I blinked next, I was standing next to Rae looking on as Rosie stood in front of the dark-haired man.

"So, you don't care for them," Rosie said. "Then why are you here?"

"I like to collect things," he said with a hum and walked around her. "Like hybrids. Though you seem to be one of the better mixes."

"I'm not a toy," she hissed and glared at him, though she made no move to fight him.

"Collect is the wrong word, I guess," he muttered. "I take in those thrown away by Xena and Malik."

"I was not thrown away," she said, standing straight.

"Not yet," he said in a light tone. "Tell me, what is your next task, hm? Did they tell you what happens after this?"

"I—"

"Or did they just send you here with no other directions and you just listened like the weakling you are?" he asked narrowing his eyes at her. "Or did they show you how little you meant to them, and you finally got it in your head that you're better off just listening to them until your untimely end comes?"

"What do you—"

"Don't answer," he said. "I already know." He let out a sigh and looked towards us. "You got yourself quite a group. Did you ever ask yourself why you and they were born so close in age? Did you ever ask if you were the only child they birthed?"

"She did," Matt said, speaking for the first time of the night. "She asked and figured it out. Understood they were the enemy...but I took care of it."

Marques sucked on his teeth.

I shared a look with Amr.

"Well good luck with that," he said and began walking towards us. "Let me know if you get tired of working with them and want to do something worthwhile for once. I can't promise you will change the world for the better but at least I will be honest." He paused when he got to my shoulder before looking back to Rosie. "And I won't force you or try to kill you. It's up to you." He looked towards me once more. "And the invitation is only for you."

He left with Matt trailing after him and back into the party. Once the door was closed the power that had a chokehold on my mother was lifted and she burst into tears before crumbling to the ground screaming bloody murder. I shot a worried look towards the door, but it remained closed even as her screams echoed off the walls. I could hear the music from just beyond the door and wondered how long we had until someone came to find them.

"Stick to the plan," Rae said in a hard voice.

With one look Rosie forced a shard through my mother's chest much like my father had done to her before. Feeling my stomach flip I covered my mouth and turned around, unable to watch any longer.

Rae left my side and Amr's warm arms surrounded me.

"It's okay, it'll be over soon," he said before cupping my ears, muffling my mother's screams.

When he removed them next I turned to see Rae breathing heavily while standing above her father with a bloodied magical knife in her hand. Rosie paused looking over the dead body, then with a snap his body burst into flames leaving only a pile of dust where the person ruling our lives used to stand.

Rosie walked over to Rae and pulled the knife from her hand before vanishing it in a cloud of smoke. They shared a long look, both breathing heavily and stained with blood. It was obvious that they would share something after this that I would never understand.

"Time to clean."

Chapter 27
Rosie

"Rosie, ple—"

"Silence," I hissed at Rae as we walked—more like marched—up to Malik's apartment.

"Let me explain," she insisted. Her hand reached out and turned me around to face her. I pulled my arm out of her grasp with a growl.

"I have listened far too many times for you," I spat at her. "You kept this from me."

She scoffed and crossed her arms over her chest. Daxton and Amr walked behind her, Daxton still looking sickly pale with tear streaks down his face. I didn't realize he would take it as hard as he did, and I felt bad for putting him in that situation.

Rae on the other hand, she had surprised me and actually went through with it but had been lying to all of us until this whole point. I didn't know what it is with this group, but we seemed to never be able to get out of this web of tangled lies that we have built for ourselves. I wanted us to get past this, wanted us to fully be able to trust another, but how could we do that when every single one of us had been lying?

"Don't act like I was the only one keeping any secrets," she said through clenched teeth. "I did what I had to do to keep everyone safe while you *literally* plotted murder!"

My jaw dropped at her accusation and an angry breath left my lips.

"I was doing it because I had to! Did you not listen to anything I told you? As *soon* as I had a chance I spil—"

"Hey!" Malik yelled from down the hall. "Stop yelling and get over here now!"

With my anger rising I turned and bolted straight towards Malik and for the second time in my life tackled him to the group before ramming my fists into his face.

"*You! Lied! To! Me!*" I growled the words with each punch. He laid there limply taking each punch until I faltered. I lifted him up by his shirt and forced him to look at me. His normally pale skin was stained with crimson blood. "I killed those people for *you*. For *them*. And it was all a lie?"

"Rosie, loo—"

"Where is Eli?" I demanded. "You get Matt involved, did you get them involved too? Did you know we were set up?"

"They are fine Rosie," he said with a sigh. "If you just list—"

"That man said they wanted to kill me," I said my voice wavering. It was easy to remember the way Xena's eyes narrowed and the unfazed way they disposed of the bodies I killed. And all those people in the prison? My mind was whirling. "I finished the task...is that it for me? What about Eli? Why did they lie? Why did they act like I...mattered?"

Malik's heavy breathing filled the air, and I could hear the shuffling of feet behind us.

"Rosie," Amr's deep voice came from behind me, but it was Rae's firm hands that pulled me off of Malik and into her arms.

"You knew this whole time," Rae said.

"I like to pride myself on knowing *everything*," Malik said and groaned as he got up. "Hybrids are...a commodity to them. This"—he stood a shuddering breath—"*war* is not really just an old family feud filled with originals who are just too afraid to die."

"We do the dirty work," I muttered against Rae's chest. My throat began to close, and my eyes stung but I refused to let it out. "I knew that to a point but..."

"But you didn't realize how little they regarded their children's lives," Malik finished.

"Giving people a sense of purpose is a form of control," Rae said from above me, her arms tightening around me as if I would run. "Control the narrative, you control them."

"What was the point?" I asked. "Of all of it?"

"To kill Marques' people before he killed them," Malik said.

"So, they weren't really...?" My stomach tied in knots. *Did we kill the wrong people?*

"No, they were bad," Daxton spoke up. "Don't twist it."

I sniffled against Rae before turning to face Malik.

"What do we do now?" I asked, my heart aching with each word.

He opened his mouth to speak but there was a flash of light between us. Claudine appeared instantly with blood all over her.

"The operation," she choked and fell to her knees. Malik dove to catch her as she fell. "Need to go now. Eli, Matt holding them off—"

"Let me come," I insisted. "I can help."

"No," Malik growled. "Stay here until I give you the signal. If they know about your contact with Marques *you will die.*"

He nodded towards Claudine, and she closed her eyes. Just as her body started glowing, a stupid *stupid* plan formed in my head. I dove forward and gripped her free arm. There were shouts all around me, but they died as my body was pulled all different ways.

When my vision cleared next I saw Eli sitting on the ground with their eyes wide and their clothes dirty, staring at what was once Montnesse.

Now the same rundown town was on fire and just beyond it we could see the disintegration of the barrier that kept all the people of Montnesse safe, up in flames. I knew that type of roaring fire all too well. The sight, so bright it blinded you. The smell so potent it would reside in your lungs for days. The heat so powerful it could fry the skin and melt the muscles off your body.

Then the screams came and that was when I realized that the fires had started from the inside and the barrier had acted as a container until finally it couldn't handle anymore.

Even if what Malik said was true…those people… *Oh my god the people.*

I pushed myself forward, running towards the bar that lined the parking lot remembering the man that greeted me the first time in the town, remembering the tour guide that laughed and joked with us, remembering the children that played in the parks… They couldn't deserve this horrible of a death.

It was Eli's rough hands that pulled me back. I snapped back to look at their smoke-stained face. Their mouth was moving but I couldn't hear any of the words over the sounds of the fires and screams.

Their hands gripped my face.

"You stupid girl!"

I blinked rapidly as the noises around us distracted me.

"The people," I choked out. "We have to save them—we have to go—"

"This was the plan, Rosie!" they yelled, their eyes reflecting the light of the flames.

Malik grabbed us harshly and pushed us away from the entrance to the town. I tried to fight against him but with Eli by my side forcing me along I was but an angry kitten in their hands.

I caught sight of Matt, still in his suit from earlier, running up to Malik. His eyes were wide, and soot covered his face. Malik was talking to him, but I couldn't hear their words over the screams.

Matt's grey eyes met mine and I froze. Gone was the laughing boy I knew. The one full of life and love, and in his place was a cold, unfeeling person.

They walked towards me, and I kicked and screamed in Eli's arms, but they held onto me with an iron grip. My scream was pulled out of my throat only to be muffled by Matt covering my mouth with his hand.

"I'm sorry Rosie," he said as he leaned closer to me. "You can't know this yet. Please forgive me."

There was a low muttering that came from his mouth and his free hand covered my forehead. I felt an uncontrollable heat coming from his hand that felt like it was working its way into my entire being and lighting up my entire body.

My screams died then and the last thing I saw before the fire took over me was Matt's frown.

THE PRICE OF SILENCE

BOOK 4

ELLE MAE

Chapter 1
Malik

Exhaustion weighed on me.

I no longer felt like the unbeatable demon I once had been. I was once blinded by my power, thought that I was above everyone and anything in this world. After a millennium, I finally realized that I was just as much a pawn in this game as everyone else.

I should have been upset or angry that my time in the limelight was taken from me...but instead I was relieved. It was *tiring* to try and prove to the world that you were the one in charge and woefully unfulfilling, even with a power like mine.

I didn't want people to run and hide, or cower when they looked towards me. I wanted them to run to me. I wanted to be trusted and to trust others... and I didn't realize how much I was missing out on until I saw Rosie interact with the others.

She had a power that was undeniable, and it had nothing to do with her heritage.

She had an intenseness to her that seemed to attract people like moths to a flame. *I* wanted that. *I* wanted to not just be around her and soak up the light, but emit it as well.

It was Xena and Ezekiel who had taught me that personalities like Rosie's were a weakness. They taught me that you needed to grab the world by the throat and make it submit and you were permitted to do whatever you wanted to make people bend, just because you had the power to do so.

But they were so wrong.

They instead tried to say that *they* were at the top of the food chain. The Originals, the first demons and witches of this world who had single-handedly changed the course of our world for good.

But they too were blinded by their power. They were too cocky in their ways and had full faith that their plan to rule over the world would succeed. The years they had lived unharmed and surrounded by their demon-shaped armor had lulled them into a false sense of security.

But if this worked, they wouldn't live to see the end of this year, and I would make damn sure that they would never hurt my people *ever* again.

If I could attain that...this exhaustion was well worth it.

The coolness of the dark, empty room settled around us. There was a slight bite to it, warning us of colder months that lay ahead, but that wasn't all it warned of.

The air around us was charged with magic so powerful even as a demon I could feel the tingle of it run across my skin.

It was a warning that someone powerful lay ahead.

I shifted my gaze, noting the glowing eyes beside me. This time, it was no longer just Matt and his siblings. Now we had backup and that same jolt of magic could be felt through us all, binding us to our fate here.

The others, they had given up a lot to come here with me. There was no guarantee that this would work and in all honesty, the chance of us showing up dead to our next meeting with Xena and Ezekiel felt far more likely.

But I knew Marques, trusted him enough to know that if the demons next to me wanted to risk their lives, it wouldn't be him delivering the killing blow.

The others shifted and waited for a sign that we were welcome.

A pair of glowing hazel eyes met mine and even through the silence I felt the threat of their unspoken words.

We had come further than I had imagined, all of the pieces were coming together and we were just waiting on one more final piece to settle before we could move...and end this thing once and for all.

That was the hope I was holding onto.

The once dark room lit up without warning, jolting my senses. I scanned the room, looking for a threat but all I saw was an empty foyer in front of us. A sense of relief washed through me when I saw that the group I had come with, still had all of their limbs.

Eli, Matt, Maximus...and Rae all stood next to me in various levels of discomfort.

Rae was scanning the place as well before her gaze met mine again. She was patiently waiting for directions, a move that was astonishing coming from anyone that allied themselves with Eli.

It was risky to bring Rae, but I had a feeling that she would only continue to hinder us if she was not brought into this as well. She had caught on too quickly to our actions before and we couldn't chance someone as cunning as her falling to the wrong side.

Eli was standing next to Rae, but their gaze was glued on Matt. They were...displeased to have to continue work with the redheaded hybrid and insisted that erasing Rosie's memory of the burning town had been a mistake.

*Maybe it had been...*I thought.

But that thought came out of my weakness for her. I knew, logically, that we were too close to the end to leave any possible stone unturned. Any liability would need to be dealt with and that came to our meeting today...

We had used Claudine's power to get us across the border into Canada where Marques's main base was kept. Deep within the woods stood an impossibly old manor that was surrounded by a blue shimmering barrier that would cut the intruders in half if they tried to force entry.

It was a strong piece of magic and one only capable by a very talented witch. The same witch that stood next to Matt with his arms crossed and a scowl on his face.

Maximus was a hidden gem that had taken years to cultivate. Without him, there would have been no way for us to accomplish such a feat as this. I would rely on him heavily for what was to come.

His brother, Matt, looked my way and sent me a triumphant smile. The one that I was starting to understand as the most dangerous expression he had.

The man we had been waiting for entered the room with long strides, from an open door to our left. His black hair hung limply at his shoulders and he was dressed in a suit and tie. With each step his aura radiated out of him and I fought to keep from flinching as his dead eyes met mine.

While I knew this man, grew up with him, I had seen him commit the types of sins that I could not stomach. He was not one to be messed with, no matter what our relationship had been.

He stopped a mere twenty feet away from us, his head turning back to watch as Claudine entered the room the same way he had come from.

Her red hair was bouncing with each step and her bright pink dress clashed against the dark interior of the manor. She smiled at Marques as if they were best friends.

Marques did not return the gesture.

"Let's cut to the chase, shall we?" Marques asked, his voice cutting through the silence and slashing us harder than the cold air had.

"I don't know what you expect from Eli and me," Rae said in a tone that aired her displeasure with ease.

I had relaxed too soon, I grumbled in my head.

Leave it up to Eli's group to mouth off to the most powerful being in this world.

"I don't *expect* you to do anything," he answered, his eyes looking over Rae carefully. I felt her shift next to me. "You are here because I require assistance and in return you get something from me. It is a mutual exchange."

"I already killed my parents," Rae said without a hint of remorse. "There is nothing else you can give me."

There was a pause between the group and my mind went into overdrive.

I may not care about the girl next to me as much as I did Eli...but Rosie would be heartbroken if Rae was taken from her so soon and even just the thought of Rosie in pain caused my chest to twist.

"We need your help," I said before Marques could speak.

Rae shot me a look as if she didn't believe my words.

"Xena and Ezekiel are at their weakest and this will be the only time that we can finally be free," I continued. "We need as many people on this as possible and I hate to say it...but you are talented when it comes to scheming."

The flash in her eyes betrayed her emotionless face.

"You have had years to plan this," Eli interrupted. "Centuries even...and you expect me to believe you have no plan? We free the people from the town, force the Originals out of their hiding spots, and then what?"

"They are going to kill them," Rae said. "No... You want us to kill them. To do your dirty work just like they asked of Rosie."

"A mutual exchange," he reminded. "Eli is willing to kill their father, or has that changed since the last time we spoke?"

Eli shoved their hands in their pants pockets and shrugged.

"That was the plan," they replied with an air of disinterest.

"What makes you think Rosie will want to kill her mom?" Rae asked. "Matt erased her memory, we have been keeping secrets from her, how are we any different from them?"

I looked down at my feet. It was a long shot to believe that Rosie would bend over for people she hardly knew.

People who wanted to turn her into a murderer.

It wasn't ideal, nor was it what I wanted personally for her. I wanted her to stay out of this as long as possible, leave the hard stuff to me and the others while she lives the life she never could.

But right now, we need to end this.

"She has a choice," I said. "Like you all do. The memory...it was necessary."

But the more I thought about it, the less I agreed. It was a split-second decision and it was made out of pure panic.

But then again Matt didn't know what we knew. I caught Claudine's gaze and she sent me a nod, confirming what I knew all along.

Leave it to the twins to save the day, I thought.

The tiredness in my bones lifted enough for me to catch my breath.

"They watch her," Matt added. "Because of her blood. She is useful because they think they can use her as a shield."

"And Eli?" Rae asked. "Daxton? He ate her father."

"Daxton's magic will be the death of him," Marques said. "They are sure, as am I, that his magic will corrode him from the inside out. His body was not made to handle this power so he is not a threat. And Eli..."

"They have lost faith in me," they answered for the Marques. "That much I know. To them I am useless, too reckless."

Rae was silent at their admission.

"She has to know," Rae insisted. "I refuse to let her go through this blind."

"It's not you—" Matt started with venom slipping through his words but I stopped him with the clearing of my throat.

"We can arrange something," I said. Any further arguing and I was not sure that we would get out of here before the others noticed. "I agree that it is wrong to have her so in the dark especially when her role is so vital." Rae's shoulders relaxed at my compromise. "But not now... They are too close to her at the moment. We need to wait until we can safely separate her from them and then we can explain the plan to her. She can decide then if she wants to continue down this path."

Rae nodded.

"And then what?" Eli asked. "When do I get to kill him?"

Marques smiled at them.

"I think it would be more satisfying to get your mother first, don't you?" he asked.

Eli tried to hide their smile but I saw the twitch of their lips. It was a troubling sign.

"What if she doesn't want to kill them?" Rae asked.

"Stop worrying about her," Matt said with a huff. "Just go with it, make your demands, and have Rosie figure it out on her own."

The ice-cold glare that Rae sent Matt was enough to start my own heart.

"In a room full of snakes, at least *one* person needs to look out for the key to this plan," Rae hissed then turned back to Marques. "Because that's what she is, right? No one is worried about Ezekiel."

Marques eyed her for a moment before speaking.

"No," he confirmed. "Not a soul is worried about Ezekiel, at the moment."

The weight of his words was felt around the room.

"So what do we do?" Rae pushed again.

"I will get Eli's mother," Marques said. "When I have secured her I will send you a message, that is when the plan starts."

"And the others?" Eli asked.

"First," Marques said. "Hide your mother's body where it cannot be found. The longer they do not know, the better. Then since they are still at Winterfell, just as school starts, we need to corner them."

"Why when school starts?" Matt asked. "Why not sooner? They are just sitting ducks."

"They will have less chance to move if the campus is overflowing with students," I murmured.

I felt Marques's power grab ahold of me and the plan unfolded in my mind, but it would only work with Rosie.

And a particularly volatile Rosie. Then when they were busy with her... we would attack alongside Marques.

It was simple, just needed to be kept from them long enough so that we could slowly tear off each of their strongest warriors, and it started with Eli's mother, and then I would take care of her handmaidens.

"Easy," I said and crossed my arms. "We target the mother first, I will put the rest of the plan in place and then we pull Rosie away from them and get her on board." I turned to Rae. "That will be your job."

"Is that enough to establish trust?" Marques asked and held out his arm to Claudine.

She conjured a bright pink dagger and held it to his skin.

"If I take the oath," Rae said. "How much access will you have to my mind?"

"More than what you are comfortable with, child," he said. "But understand I only do this for your benefit and safekeeping. With this your powers will increase and if anything were to happen, I can intervene."

Rae swallowed and did not dare to step forward.

"I am not getting on my knees," Eli said stepping forward. They sent a look to Rae. "I told them to fuck off last time they offered, but now it seems we don't have a choice."

"You do," I interjected. "You have a choice, but we are so close to ending this that we cannot do this half-assed. *Everything* is on the line here. Rosie's life, your future, they know everything and have eyes everywhere. There is no escaping."

"Will I have access to you as well?" Rae asked.

Marques smiled at her.

"To an extent," he said. "If you need me I am but a thought away."

Eli closed the space between them and Marques and nodded towards Claudine.

Marques didn't even flinch as she brought down the dagger and drew a solid line through his forearm, dark blood pulsating out of the wound.

"You should get that checked out," Eli murmured and leaned down to lick the blood from the wound.

They reeled back and began coughing immediately before falling to the ground in a heap. Their body convulsed as they clawed at their neck. Their mouth was open but no screams sounded.

"Eli!" Rae yelled and dashed forward.

"Wait," I commanded. Her eyes met mine just long enough that my power was able to hit her and she stopped in her tracks.

Eli's body stopped convulsing and the same aura that came out of Marques in waves started to flow from them. Slowly they crawled to their knees, a manic laughter filling the space. With shaky limbs they stood and reared their head back, their blue eyes wide as they looked up to the ceiling.

"It's there," they said between their giggles. "I feel it."

Rae took a step back, her eyes wide as she stared at Eli. Her hand clenched into a fist.

"What do you feel?" Marques asked.

"The power," they replied. "You and...the thoughts."

They turned to look at me and walked towards me slowly. Their hand came out, stopping mere inches from my head.

"Like I can just..." they made a plucking motion with their fingers and their eyes lit up before meeting mine. A chilling grin showed on their face. *"Take it."*

I knew the effects would simmer down after a while but there was no way in hell I wanted to deal with this monster.

Chapter 2
Rosie

I do not remember the last time I had a full night's sleep.

Before the gala I was hopeful that this summer would be the best one of my life.

Rae had offered up her family's house for us to live at and I truly believed for just a moment that we had a chance at all being happy together. No one would feel the weight of a task on their shoulders, we could just retire there and finish out our schooling in peace...but I should have known that that dream would never see the light of day.

I ran down the empty Winterfell corridor with my arms full of magical potions created by an exhausted Daxton and Amr. We had taken advantage of the empty school and ransacked the multiple science wings to use their magic gathering equipment so that we would have supplies to heal the injured.

It was hard work that left us all exhausted, and since the main ingredients in these potions were magic...we all had to donate more than our bodies could handle.

My magic was easily replenished, and I found myself less strained than the others, but Daxton and Amr were a different story. They would work themselves until they had not a drop left they could spare and then if I was able, I would share magic with them.

Though it wasn't ideal.

I burst through the double doors that led to the cafeteria and was immediately assaulted by the sheer noise of the room.

The cafeteria which was once filled with rows upon rows of tables was now emptied out to fit hundreds of cots and blankets where the injured people of Montnesse stayed. Young, old, magical, demons, we had every type of person under this roof...and all of them were in different states of dying.

Late on the night of the gala, we were hit with the news that the town had been attacked, burned from the inside out, trapping most of the people inside its barriers and cooking them alive.

When they began to pull out some of the survivors, it was worse than I imagined. I couldn't hold back the gags when I saw the state of some of the demons and witches that were wheeled into Winterfell. Because of the fires, their skin had literally begun to melt off of them and many had burns all across their bodies.

Apparently a magical barrier and fire was a hell of a combination.

Principal Winterfell, under the obvious control of Malik, had accepted the survivors with open arms...and the Originals that came with them.

I had never had any magical medical training in my life, but I was quickly put in charge of tending to the various injured people by my one and only mother, Xena.

She had insisted that I work with my *friends*, as she liked to call them, and help to heal the injured.

I refused at first but when I saw just how awful it was...I couldn't stand by and watch as they died.

Xena had a gang of witches that also volunteered to help out, but there were only a total of twenty helpers...and three hundred people.

Out of the entire town that spanned miles and housed people for centuries, only three hundred people made it out alive.

While we were short-staffed, with our magical capabilities I was hopeful that we could heal them. I had seen Daxton heal himself, I had even done it a few times on myself so I knew it was possible, but just like everything else in this world, it wasn't as easy as it seemed.

Because of the sheer amount of people with injuries, we were forced to treat only life-threatening injuries at first, but as the months went on we saw people dying of injuries that we hadn't been able to see at first. It was like one moment they were healthy and fine, and then the next day they looked as though they needed to be rolled into their grave.

I weeded through the crowd of people and to the corner where my current patient was waiting for me.

Amber, a young woman looking not much older than myself, who had been one of the people to drag the others out of the burning town. Just last week she had started sleeping more and today I found her with grey skin, and her once beautiful long brown hair had turned into a silver-grey.

She was currently in her cot and huddled under a pile of blankets that the others had donated.

I dropped to her level and carefully put the potions to the side. I unwrapped the blanket from her and was met with her pained expression. Her eyes fluttered open and her bight green eyes looked dull in the morning light.

"Rosie," she croaked.

"Hey Amber," I said in a light tone. "Can you sit up for me?"

I watched as she tried—and failed—to sit up on weak arms. I smiled at her and helped her into a sitting position. She had lost a lot of weight while I wasn't looking. It pained me to see someone so young, so like myself...dying so horribly.

"I feel like shit," she groaned.

I let out a forced laugh and grabbed the shiny blue potion that Amr had made that morning.

"This will calm you and help with some pain relief," I said and pulled the cap off with my teeth, making sure to keep one hand steady on her back.

I pushed it to her lips and watched as she downed the entire thing.

I wasn't sure what percentage Amber was, but the potions seemed to not be doing any good for her. Each day she got worse and worse and I was afraid that I would lose *another* patient.

"I think I need to sleep," Amber said in a weak voice. Her eyelids were already drooping again.

"Sure thing," I said and carefully laid her back down. "I'm sorry this is happening to you, Amber."

She let out a weak laugh and pulled the fur blanket close to her.

"It's okay, love," she said. "Anything is better than that hell hole of a town they kept us in. At least now I can feel *something* even if it is death."

"Don't say that," I hissed around the knot in my throat.

There were so many things I wanted to ask. So many things I still needed to know about the Originals and the magical town they kept. This wasn't the first time someone had uttered something about the town, but I could never get the information before they died.

If Amber didn't live through this, she would be my thirteenth patient to die under my care.

"Maybe in the next life I can have a group of lovers that dote on me like yours does," she joked, her voice trailing.

"You can get one when you get better," I promised.

She just smiled and drifted back to sleep. I let out a deep aching sigh and set to work. The other potions I brought could be applied on the skin. The issue was we couldn't tell where her injuries were coming from, so I had Amr and Daxton think of anything they could.

In the middle of work a warm hand cupped my shoulder.

I wasn't surprised to see Amr sitting next to me and Daxton next to him. They were always here to bring me out of my spiral and I couldn't thank them enough for their support the last few months.

"Let her rest," Amr said, his deep accented voice barely above a whisper. "Xena wants to see you."

I swallowed thickly and worked on sealing the potions back up. Before we left I handed them to the witch on duty and ask that she look after Amber for the time being.

With a last look at the blanket-covered body, I left the room with both Amr and Daxton by my side.

"Are you okay?" Daxton asked as we walked.

I smiled at him and threw my hand through his. He, Amr, and I had our fair share of time together the last few months while the others were still off doing god only knows what. I got to see a side of them that I had never seen before and it only made me realize how lucky I was to have them even when I had acted so horribly the last year.

I had expected Daxton to carry a grudge for what I had to do to his parents...but if anything he seemed much happier than before. It had been helping with my guilt, though I wasn't sure it would ever go away for as long as we were together.

After I had some time to think about what I had done, and the high of it all had worn off... I came to realize just how much of a monster I was. I felt guilt because I hurt Daxton, not because I murdered someone in cold blood.

The people who had made me into such a monster were currently residing in the highest part of Winterfell, at least the one that was still standing. They had yet to remake the tower after we had destroyed it last year though I doubt someone like Xena would be caught dead in the towers. Instead, they chose something much more fitting and ironic.

A remnant of a human worship center.

It was the second-highest part of the campus and gave them the perfect view of the campus. If anyone came in or left the campus, their guards would see and be able to alert them if necessary. They stated it was the safest for them, but I knew deep down that they didn't care much about safety.

While I was in low-level school I had met with children who used to go with their human sides of the family to these worship centers and pray every week. The half breeds, as they called them, were not very welcome. But sometimes I heard stories about the humans seeing it as a sign of repent for what our kind had done to the earth.

I wondered briefly if Xena and Ezekiel were using it as a way to repent for themselves...but I doubted that was the case. They did not have a single shred of humanity in them that would make them understand the gravity of what they had done and the people they had harmed.

When we finally made it to their dwelling I had to take a moment to calm my erratic heart.

No matter how much I hated these beings, no matter how much I resented them for what they had done to my life...they still had that very life between their fingers and could at any moment snap it.

I had finished my task after all... I wouldn't put it past them to see me as a useless burden and hope to get rid of me as soon as possible.

We were treated by a few of the handmaidens that Xena kept by her side. From their brown eyes I could tell that they were witches, but the most shocking was that they looked to be no older than the age of thirteen. They were identical twins that I had seen a few times during my visits and they had a tendency to mirror each other's movements.

It sent shivers down my spine. Something about it just seemed unnatural.

They smiled at us and bowed before letting us into the renovated space.

Before the Originals had taken this spot as their home, it had been a rundown wasteland of space filled with spiders and cobwebs. I would know, because they had me scout it with her handmaidens before they even stepped foot on campus. Now, the large space had been lit up with magic lights that floated high above our heads and illuminated the entire space, and showcased the mural that was painted on the ceiling above it.

Splashes of green and blue made up the intricate ceiling and what I thought was once a depiction of some Great War between the gods and the people of this earth turned out to be the story of fallen angels. There were five that I could count, all of them bloodied and injured, and many with a portion if not all of their wings cut off. It was painted in colors that looked light and magical, but the image itself held a darker tone that hung over us with every step we took.

The once fully open space had been designed into a parlor, where they entertained guests. A few rooms on either side of the place were separated by walls that were built by magic.

It was just as extravagant as their previous house and I was annoyed that they just didn't pick a place outside of the campus. I didn't realize how much worse it was to be so close to the people that held my life in their hands. It's like it wasn't enough for them to force me to this school or commit crimes on their behalf, but now they had to be here and watch my every single step as well.

Amr's hand found my wrist and I sent him a grateful smile.

I wasn't looking forward to meeting the Originals. There had only been a handful of times that I had been summoned, though it was becoming more often as the semester neared, but each time I felt like it was another test. Like they were just checking how obedient I was, making sure I hadn't strayed.

They had refused to leave this place, even as their own people were out here dying leaving just me and a few others to help out with the dying patients. They were too busy licking their wounds and hiding from the embarrassment of finally being caught.

The walk through the makeshift home was short but felt like forever. Each time I was summoned to meet them I felt as though I was walking to my death. There was no telling with these Originals.

One minute they were welcoming me with open arms, giving me an apartment, giving me more money than I'd have in a lifetime, and the next they were forcing me to kill their prisoners as punishment.

They had set up their sitting room similar to the one in the town with floral imprints on every surface, a very large fireplace, and a table that was just big enough for the two Originals and their tea.

My mother had her long hair braided in an intricate fashion on the back of her head and even though her entire wardrobe had been burned to a crisp, she was still able to salvage some of her priciest clothing decked with gold thread that made her shine in the dim fluorescents.

Ezekiel on the other hand looked to at least have somewhat of a care about what was happening in the outside world. His normally shiny blonde hair had lost its luster and I could have sworn that there were bags under his eyes. He wore a blazer and slacks, looking as though he was off to some business venture.

He shot me a small smile as we walked in and I felt the intrusion in my mind before I heard it.

It has been a tough time for us all, child, his voice weighed heavily in my mind.

"Rosie," he said aloud. "Nice of you to join us. I know that it is out of your way."

"Yes," I said with venom laced in my tone. Amr's hand grabbed mine harshly, reminding me that there were consequences for speaking to an Original like that.

"Oh please," Xena said with a huff. When she looked over towards me her brown eyes narrowed, much like my low-level mother used to do after I had been cursed. "It's in the same campus."

The wall in my mind that I had forgotten even existed seemed to erect itself within moments, warning me not to get close. Warning me that those eyes were eyes that brought pain, not joy.

It warned me that getting too close, too vulnerable would cost more than I was willing to pay.

"How can I help you?" I asked in a tone full of mock politeness.

"We just want a status update about the patients," Ezekiel said, cutting in before my mother could.

I was in no way in charge of what went down there and couldn't help but think of this as an excuse to check on me and keep me in line.

"We have lost—"

I cut Amr off.

"They are dying," I growled. "Healthy ones, they all of a sudden get sick and die out of nowhere while you just *sit* here doing *nothing*."

"We cannot *do* anything," Xena hissed. "It is what happens when the weak stay frozen in time forever. They are *bound* to die."

It was like my body was hit with ice-cold water. They *knew?* They knew that this was going to happen and they still forced me to sit there and watch them, try to save them even when they knew it was a lost cause.

Amber's silver hair and smile flashed through my mind.

"All of them?" Daxton asked, his voice steady.

I used my grip on his arm to steady myself as my magic boiled inside of me. I couldn't be seen as weak in front of them, wouldn't dare to have what happened before happen now.

If I let them know how much this affected me, what would they do?

Kill them all at once? Make *me* kill them?

My stomach twisted and turned uncomfortably with the thought.

There were children there. People who had full lives ahead of them and deserved to have a chance of a life outside of the town and away from the Originals that controlled them.

Ezekiel's piercing blue eyes met mine.

"Most," Xena said nonchalantly. "Not all, but most. There are many in there without pure blood, and for those who find themselves unlucky, they will perish."

"You don't care about them?" I asked, unable to help myself.

Those narrowed eyes met mine once more and I knew she was trying to figure out a way to punish me for that comment. My magic welcomed the fight, growled and gnashed its teeth at Xena. I wanted her blood on my hands. I wanted to destroy her and watch as she begged for mercy.

I saw red.

I know she felt it, she had to. Because I could feel hers. It was cold and snake-like, just waiting to wrap itself around me and strangle the life out of me.

"We cannot save them, child," Ezekiel said. "They knew this when they entered the town with us. It was either that, or be hunted down by those who hated us."

I simply nodded at this, unable to find the words to fight anymore. Regardless of my unstable magic, I knew that attacking her here and now would only be the end of me.

"They are dying," I whispered. "But there are a few who have gotten better, and the rest still remain stable."

Xena nodded at this and took a sip of her tea.

"Will we keep them in the cafeteria for long?" Amr asked. "Winterfell starts its session soon."

Ezekiel's gaze shot towards Xena, his eyes wide. I wonder what thought could make the creator of demons look that scared?

"We will get them dorms," Ezekiel said, still staring at Xena, as if that gaze alone held her back from uttering anything. "For the families, we will find other accommodations."

The weight that was weighing on my shoulders dissipated and I wanted to thank Ezekiel for his mercy, but his sharp gaze told me I was better off not saying anything.

You have more questions you can ask us, he sent to my mind. *A deal is a deal.*

Images of the mangled dead witches flashed across my mind. I even remembered how their flesh smelt after I had burned them, how their screams sometimes still haunted me in my memories. For what I did, I was given a set amount of questions that they had to answer truthfully.

A life for a single question from an Original with a track record for lying.

I am okay, I shot back.

"If that is all," Daxton said, gripping my arm. "We have a funeral to get to."

The sly smile that spread across Xena's face was one of nightmares.

"Have fun."

Chapter 3
Eli

I fucking hated suits.

I tugged at the too-tight fabric that itched at my skin silently pleading that someone in the heavens would stop this event from even happening. It was a waste of time.

It was all for the image and no one was really there to mourn the fallen. And to top it off the white-haired bastard told me I had to behave.

I didn't mind most of the gatherings because neither Daxton nor Rae really cared what I chose to do while I was there.

Drugs? Totally fine.

Fucking the governor's wife in the bathroom? Have at it.

But none of that today according to Malik. Rosie would be there and I had to be on my best behavior even though it had been far too long since I last saw her.

I felt my fingers just remembering the way her skin felt against mine. All I wanted to do was be alone with her for five minutes, was that too much to ask?

Growling, I tugged at the stiff fabric trapping me. Not only did it have a death grip on my limbs, but the discarded tie that lay before me on the floor was its own death trap. I had tried, one too many times to get that stupid rope tied, but each time it looked worse than the last.

I caught my gaze in the mirror and frowned.

The high from Marques's blood had left me, but the power that now rested inside me was just as intoxicating. It swirled inside me at all times and taunted me with what was possible, but continued to stay just out of reach.

The thoughts it pulled from other people would hover at the edge of my mind like a small butterfly landing on a flower. They were innocent, delicate, and totally unaware of what I longed to do to them. I wanted so badly to grab those butterflies by their wings and tear them open, forcing them to tell me all the delicious secrets they kept.

They taunted me. Told me that if I wanted to beat Ezekiel that I could, but they remained just far enough away that I was enticed to chase them.

Catching Malik's golden gaze in the mirror, I picked up the once discarded tie at my feet and worked to try and tie it again. My eyes kept wandering to him as I felt the fuzziness of his thoughts reach me.

They were *right there*. So close that I could taste the tingle of them on my tongue.

He wanted something, but I couldn't tell what.

The normally white hair that stood on all ends was slicked back, giving me a rare look at his entire scarred face. I remember when I was young how cool I thought they looked. He fit the mold of a gangster perfectly and was everything I wished I could be.

But now I knew how his face came to look like that, and their meaning.

Thinking of what my own father did to Malik, made a sharp pain twist in my chest. I felt the same prick in my chest when I saw Rosie almost die. Albeit, it was much smaller now, but the pain was still there.

"Let me help," he said. There was no sigh, or laugh in his tone, just a simple statement.

It made it hard to get angry at him and I gritted my teeth in anger as the thoughts kept flying at me. The closer he got the easier they were to feel, but *why* were they not coming to me yet?

I sighed and turned to face him. He didn't hesitate, grabbing the limp tie from around my neck before tugging my collar upright and trying again.

"Now I know why you always wear your shirt unbuttoned," he murmured. "I thought it was a fashion statement but here you just didn't know how to tie a tie."

"Say one more word and I cut your head off," I grumbled.

"I have no doubt," he said in a light tone, his eyes shifting to mine.

I stayed quiet for the rest of the time it took him to tie the stupid tie, and just watched him.

When did I stop fighting him? When did his scarred face being to make me feel warm again and not furious? Why did I suddenly want to understand the thoughts that lurked under the surface?

It couldn't have just been Marques's blood in me that started this change.

If anything his blood made me more restless, not the same calmness I felt when interacting with Malik.

"I don't think I hate you anymore," I said, my tone as indecisive as I was feeling.

He looked up at me, then back down to the tie, then stepped away before looking at my face again.

"I am glad," he said then cocked his head. "I have always cared for you, regardless of what has happened. I hope you know that."

Heat flashed across my face and before I even registered my actions I had backed up to the door behind me and swung it open. Leaving him alone in the room.

* * *

It was unnecessarily cloudy when we arrived at the cemetery where Daxton and Rae's parents were to be buried.

Apparently this cemetery was for the best and most prominent figures in the world, and both Daxton and Rae had slots next to their parents for when they passed as well.

To the world the story was:

Both Rae and Daxton's parents left the party, never to be seen again. Rae and Daxton, with some help from prominent political figures that helped fund some money, hired a search team. The search team and police had been investigating the disappearance but after three months with zero evidence... they had to assume they had died.

Of course it wouldn't have been possible if we didn't have Malik's help to *persuade* the police force and search teams to give up...but it ended up working out well enough that the entire world now believed they somehow went missing and wound up dead.

No one even questioned the validity after Malik was done.

I mean, why would they?

If the head of the demon regulation came out and stated that there was nothing fishy going on, the world would just turn its back and focus on the next biggest thing going on in this world.

There was a crowd that surrounded the area and as expected, instead of quietly mourning there was a low chatter amongst the group. I recognized many of the faces here as those who had done dealings with *The Fallen* throughout the years and it made it all the more obvious when they blanched at Malik and me as we walked by.

Their thoughts too played at my senses, teasing me with the secrets they were keeping now that their superiors were laying cold in their caskets.

It was so tempting, but also infuriating.

"I don't even get why *I* have to be here," I grumbled to Malik and searched the crowd for my favorite hybrid.

It had been many weeks since I had alone time with Rosie and that ache was back in my chest.

I didn't much care about the secret-keeping, but I had to admit...Rae was right. She always was, but more so now than ever. The lies had to stop at some point because if not, I had no doubt our little Original would be more pissed than the time we were hiding the curse knowledge from her.

I personally wanted to see her angry. Wanted to see the murderous spitfire I had seen in Rae's memories as she slaughtered Daxton's parents. The restlessness inside me demanded a fight, demanded bloodshed, and it would be all too sweet if it was hers.

Even just thinking about it caused a warmth to flush through my body.

But...that same spitfire was carving her own path out from the prison she had been placed in.

She was no longer the shy, mute low-level that had no idea of this world. She was ready to fight, and that fight was what put me on edge.

What if this was the final straw? What if after this she finally saw what it meant to be with someone like me? People like us?

My thoughts were stirred by the brush of Malik's arm against mine. His golden eyes peered into me as if reading each thought that crossed my mind.

"They are here," he said and jutted his chin toward where the crowd was parting.

I saw Amr's long black hair that had been tied into a bun before Daxton and Rae's heads came into view. When the crowd finally parted I saw the small hybrid nestled right in between Rae and Daxton while Amr stood behind her.

Rae looked oddly calm for someone who had taken a mouthful of Original blood. Her eyes scanned the crowd, keeping close to our prized possession as if her life was at risk.

I knew the point was to protect her, and from an outsider's perspective it looked as though they were crowding her...but it was so much more than that.

What they didn't see is with each movement Rosie took, the others would follow. If she so much as shifted her gaze, both Rae and Daxton would search to find what could possibly call her attention. And in this moment, it was me.

She met my eyes with a small smile and I soon felt the others' eyes as well, but I did not spare them any glances. Instead, I took in the woman in front of me.

Her black hair was pulled up in an intricate twist on the top of her head, showing off a shimmering pair of earrings. Her face was bare with only a hint of shine on her plump lips. She wore a long black dress that covered her from her neck to her wrists and ankles.

It was a modest dress, and that made it all the more intoxicating for me.

Here she was, acting as if she was the picture-perfect hybrid, innocent to the core, someone the people could trust...but they never got to see the look on her face as she stood over the burning bodies of her lover's parents, nor did they see the way she begged to be used by us.

The stark contrast made my mouth water because for once in my life...I had something all for myself.

She walked towards us, stopping right in front of Malik and me.

She held onto her smile but I saw the glint of anger boiling just under the surface of her perfectly crafted expression. Unable to help myself I brushed my hand across her cheek, my body on edge and begging me to take a look inside that mind of hers.

I don't like this, she said to me, her wide brown eyes meeting mine.

Her thoughts were a flurry of emotions, anger, sadness. She was tired and still thought of the townspeople that littered Winterfell. She cared for them, hurt for them.

On one hand I couldn't wait to tell her it was I who had burned down the town, but on the other...I was *afraid.* That damn emotion had a choke-hold on my being and threatened to force me to my knees so that I could beg for her forgiveness. I was afraid she would shun me, ignore me.

But I would never let that happen, I growled internally. *I will never let her try to leave even if she pleads.*

You and me both, I said in her mind and pulled her between Malik and me so that I could drop my arm around her. *So many fake bastards.*

They don't even care, she agreed in my mind. *They never did, they are all here for show.*

Rae, Daxton, and Amr stopped in front of us, each murmuring their hellos. The funeral that they had arranged was not scheduled to start for another few moments, so we were forced to wait for her under the scrutiny of the demons and witches around us.

I could feel their eyes on us, watching us intently and waiting for their moment to take Daxton and Rae away. After all, if they wanted to get in with the future leaders they would have to take advantage of when they were naive and vulnerable.

The first came up mere moments later, a balding man that I remembered as the governor of this state. They exchanged pleasantries and then dragged both Daxton and Rae away, much to Rosie's dismay, if her internal complaining held any indication of her mood.

I leaned closer to her, brushing my lips against the shell of her ear. She shivered in response.

"How does it feel to have all these people mourn those you killed?" I whispered loud enough for Malik to hear.

His hand clamped down on the arm that held Rosie and he began to squeeze.

Do not make me use my power, he threatened in my mind.

I didn't care about his anger, I only cared about the way Rosie flushed and the thoughts floating in her mind.

She thought of all of them, wondering what happened, where they disappeared to, all while the killer lay among them. She thought about the power the secret held, the weight. But she was not upset, nor was she sad.

She was satisfied, and felt pleasure from the sickness of the secret she kept from them.

I almost couldn't hold in my groan as heat flashed through me.

If we weren't out in the open with everyone watching us, I would pull that dress up and bend her over the nearest headstone and make her recount the sick feeling her crimes left in her while I forced her to cum over and over again on my tongue.

I sent her the image and watched as her breath hitched and face flushed. She let out a small whimper and pushed back into me.

Amr watched with rapt attention as her deep breathing made her chest rise and fall rapidly.

I was tempted to show him the same dirty daydream I was showing Rosie, but I let myself enjoy it. I wanted to bathe in her moans, lock her up so that only I could hear and feel her.

I was selfish like that and I didn't care who knew.

Malik's hand gripped mine harshly. I shot him a look. He obviously wanted to fuck our little hybrid, I don't know why he suddenly got cold feet.

"Don't feel so left out," I murmured with a smirk and pushed the same image to him. His eyes clouded over and he stiffened.

I had done this once before, with Daxton and a shared witch but never with Malik.

I knew he wanted her and she him, so I wasn't surprised when his grip lightened after seeing what I was projecting into Rosie's head.

We would have to do something about this sooner or later, I mused.

"Eli," Amr growled.

I shot him a look.

"Mind your business, cat," I growled back.

"The witches can feel the spike in her magic," he explained in a hushed tone.

Looking around I saw a few select people watching us with disgust written all over their faces.

It angered me, made me want to give them an even better show...but for once I listened to the cat and pulled the scene from both Malik's and Rosie's minds.

Rosie whined and looked up at me with shining eyes. Her cheeks were flushed and her mind was telling me how wet she was underneath that dress.

"How disgusting," I murmured in her ear. "You getting off on your crimes. You almost came in front of everyone, didn't you?"

I expected her to turn away, unable to handle this talk in public, but instead she only pouted.

"Almost," she admitted. "But you stopped too soon."

This time it was I who had to grip on to Malik, to center myself.

Control yourself, Malik chided in my mind.

"Rosie," Malik growled. Rosie turned to him. "Behave yourself."

I saw the thought pop into her mind just before she took action.

I watched as her hand slipped into his pocket and she batted her eyelashes at him.

This was the Rosie I wanted to see. *This* was the one that ignited that uncontrollable fire in me.

"Only if you help me out a little," she whispered. "Tell me, Malik. Have you ever made a girl come with your power?"

The thoughts that ran through Malik's head before he distanced himself from us were sinful. Oh he *had*, and he wanted to do the same thing to Rosie. Punish her for that beautiful mouth of hers. He bent down to look her in the eyes, much like you would expect of a parent when they were scolding a child.

"I am one more word away from taking you back to Winterfell and making you regret the day you were born," he growled. "Do not test me, Rosie."

She held his gaze for a few more moments before she huffed and leaned back into my side.

"Don't worry," I said with a smirk. "I'll make it up to you later."

A small body pushed against my back and slipped under my arm. I growled aloud and was ready to break the neck of the person who separated me from Rosie, but then long red hair and brown eyes filled my vision.

The seer, I thought in a venomous tone.

"The mind reader," she said in the wistful tone that she normally spoke with.

Even though she acted as if there was a cloud over her consciousness, I knew better than to assume she wasn't paying attention. She had to see more than the average witch or demon and in all honesty, that power angered me so much because it was all-seeing and there was nothing I could hide from her.

But not for long, I thought in a smug tone as I felt the buzz of thoughts around her head.

They were frenzied, ready to burst out of her skull. I was so ready to hear them, finally.

Finally, there would be nothing she or anyone else could hide from me.

She looped her arm around Rosie's waist and held her close. Rosie shot her a shocked look before laying her hand atop the one that fell near her hip.

Since when did these two hug?

"I am sorry," Claudia whispered to Rosie. "I know it's hard."

Rosie's face dropped and I shared a look with Amr.

"Come on, ladies," Malik said and stepped forward to lay his hand upon Rosie's head. "The funeral is starting."

With that he ushered the group forward, but I caught something that would have made any heart skip a beat. Rosie looked over her shoulder at me and I could have sworn I saw a fiery glint pass her eyes, but it was gone in a second.

Interesting as always, my lovely hybrid.

Chapter 4
Rosie

I have never been a religious person, even after the truth about our heritage came out. If anything it pushed me further away from this idea of having one omnipotent force.

But even so, I had been praying this day wouldn't come. I would sit in my bed at night, staying up after my partners were asleep and just hope that the world would show some type of mercy...but I should have known by now that wasn't how the world worked.

Even when I expected the worst, that didn't stop the pain.

It was eleven o'clock at night and I had finally convinced Daxton, Amr, and Rae to leave me with Amber for her possibly last night on this earth.

Eli and Malik were, of course, off doing god knows what so that left me all to myself for the time being. And while I could feel the loneliness that permeated my soul...I also felt a sort of relief.

I was truly alone now. The only time where I could fully indulge my thoughts, even the darkest ones that tried to hide in the recesses of my mind during the day.

There were no medic witches about, and everyone was sound asleep except the sliver-haired girl that lay in front of me, shivering under the mountain of blankets she was wearing.

I do not know why *this* patient was the one that was threatening to break me, but it felt like claws were gripping at my throat and squeezing the life out of me as I watched over her. I couldn't move, couldn't breathe, all I could do was just sit by her side and watch as the parts of her soul wasted away.

"Amber," I croaked out and reached under the blanket to cover her cold hands.

I knew that even if I tried to ease up her pain, there would be no change. It was far too close to the end for her.

"Hey, love," she whispered, her eyes blinking open. "I am glad you are here with me."

I swallowed thickly and squeezed her limp hand, willing it to squeeze mine back.

"Of course," I said. "Anything for you."

She let out a sound that was akin to a laugh but sounded more like a rough cough as it wracked her small frame. It was painful to watch.

"It's the end, love," she said.

"I know."

"They knew this would happen," she continued. "That we would die, yet they still didn't let us leave."

"Why?" I asked finally, the questions that had been circling my head were screaming at me to get them answered.

"I thought they were trying to save us," she said. "But now I just see that they wanted to control us. They were scared we would revolt if we learned of the outside world. Learned that there was nothing to fear. *Not even them.*"

I gritted my teeth, begging the tears that were gathering not to fall. I needed to be strong for her.

"I don't get why they would do it," I said honestly.

"Because they are not royalty here," she said and let out another laugh. "But *in there,* they were gods. They were the almighty people who had saved us from the power-hungry humans that threatened our existence. Though they didn't want us to realize that it wasn't them that held the power anymore, but ordinary people like us. They didn't want them to know we *didn't need them.*"

"Save your strength," I said as another coughing fit ran through her. I was so afraid she would break right then and there and I still had the foolish hope that she could live through this. That small hope hung between us like a glowing thread, but it was thin and torn... It was at the end of its life.

"There is nothing to save," she said and then with strength I didn't know she possessed she jerked me forward, our faces inches apart. "Gather the healthiest of us, love. I have a feeling something bad will happen and you need to get them out."

I shook my head.

"They are being relocated already, don't worry about this," I whispered. "I will watch over them."

The sigh that escaped her lips seemed to carry the weight of the universe with it.

"And take care of yourself too, Rosie," she whispered. "I cannot tell you how much it means for you to stay by my side all this time."

I watched in horror as her eyes closed and the light grip she had on my hand loosened.

I don't know how long I waited in that cramped space, pleading for her to take another breath, but when my form started shaking under the pressure of the awkward position I was forced to sit back up and look once more at her shell of a body.

The tears silently fell down my cheeks.

"Please," I whispered. "Please come back."

There was no answer. Her body remained still and my magic spread out, trying to feel for something, any type of vibration to indicate a life...but there was none.

My magic was threatening to tear down the entire building, it was begging for me to let it out, gnashing and snarling against the shell it was caged in. The only thing holding me together was that people, just like Amber, littered the places beside me and I couldn't bear to see them hurt.

Swallowing my sobs I put a magical barrier around her cot and with a single thought, I burned the body until there was nothing but soot in its place.

I had done this so many other times that I didn't even have to think about cleaning up the leftover debris with magic and slowly standing up to leave my spot amongst the sleeping people.

As I walked I saw a few glowing eyes peering out at me, but I couldn't hold their stare.

They saw what happened, they knew everything.

When I finally was able to force myself down the empty hallways of Winterfell, I found myself unable to catch my breath. It felt like the air had been knocked out of my chest and the sobs that I had been hiding from the sleeping bodies forced their way out of my mouth.

I was devastated about Amber, about all the others...but all I could think of was...*why?*

Why did this have to happen?

Why did they have to die in a world where anything was possible?

Why didn't I feel this way about the others I killed? The witches in the town? Daxton's parents?

Why didn't it hurt then? Why is this so different?

I leaned against the wall and let myself slowly fall to the ground; the cold tiles acted as a perfect way to calm my racing brain.

I felt his presence before I heard him. The sounds of his shoes padding across the stoned floors echoed through the hallways and his warm hands found my shoulder first. He pulled me to him and whispered in my ear.

I looked at him through my tear-filled eyes, seeing a familiar grey set of eyes and red curly hair.

Matt, what perfect fucking timing.

I threw my arms around his neck.

"I know it's hard," he whispered against me. "But you did all that you could."

"Where were you hiding?" I asked through my sobs. My hand found the side of his neck and I leaned back to look him in the eyes once more.

He sent me that famous sheepish smile of his before answering.

"Just down this hallway," he admitted. "I'm on Rosie duty tonight."

I smiled at him through my sobs. I wasn't planning to do this tonight, but this moment was too perfect. No one was in sight.

"I know."

He lifted a brow and tilted his head to the side.

He played such a good puppy, I thought.

"You know?" he asked.

I nodded and called my magic into my palm. He stiffened when he finally felt the swirling magic against his skin, the same magic that was threatening to burn a hole in the side of his neck.

He swallowed, his throat coming dangerously close to the magic in my palm. His eyes widened and then another second passed before his eyes narrowed at me. No longer did I get to see my best and only friend at Winterfell, instead I got an eyeful of the *real* person Matt was.

"What gave me away?" he asked.

His whole demeanor changed in that moment, and into a person that I didn't recognize, but one that I knew intimately. I had seen the change happen, even if I wasn't fully aware it was happening. It was in the little things, the way he fought with Eli, the way his eye would narrow when he thought no one was looking.

I knew the type of person this was because I had done the same. It was a front to keep people from knowing what was really going on.

For me it was the Originals' task... And for him...

I cannot afford to be kept in the dark any longer.

"You think that when I already was missing a day in my memory I wouldn't take precautions?" I asked.

It was a half lie. I didn't take any precautions and relied only on luck and my intuition and a single person on my side.

As the bright light blinded me I fell to the ground, acting as if I was affected by the magic that Matt threw at me. My heart was pounding and I could still hear the roaring of the flames in the background.

"I will take her back," Eli said from afar.

"I will be faster," Claudine's sweet voice said from right near me. I could already feel her hands across my back, rubbing in soothing motions. "We will meet you at the apartment."

Without another moment to waste I felt the same stomach pulling sensations and then the cool ground beneath me.

"You did good," she whispered.

I finally sat up to notice that we were not far from the ruins of Winterfell tower. The cool night breeze seeped into my body and I couldn't help the shudders.

"How did—I don't under—"

She grabbed my hand and showed me the glowing symbol she had left on me. It was smudged and barely visible to the naked eye.

"I had to act fast," she said. "I knew as soon as you grabbed onto me that most likely he would try and use his powers on you."

"You helped me," I said in a hollow voice. "Was he trying to take my memories?"

Panic rose in my chest when she nodded.

"How many times?" I asked. She gave me a pitying look.

"I know of four, but I suspect more," she answered.

"Four?" I whispered and cupped my hand over my mouth. "I thought it was only once." I felt like I was going to be sick.

Who was this person? How did I miss this?

"Listen, Rosie," she said hurriedly. "We don't have time. I need to teach you how to protect yourself."

She slipped my hand over and I watched as she drew an intricate symbol into my palm with purple glowing magic.

"Remember this symbol. I did it for you before, but remember it for next time," she said. "If you think he will use it, draw this symbol somewhere on your body with magic and you will be fine. Better yet if you can get it tattooed. Do it."

"How did you figure out..?"

She gave me a sad smile and I couldn't help but feel pity for the little girl that had to grow up around a memory manipulator.

"Will it uncover what he has done before?" I asked.

She gave me a sad smile.

"Only he can do that," she answered.

"Thank you, Claudine," I whispered.

"It's my pleasure, though to be honest Marques was the one that suggested it," she said with a smile of her own. "Now let's take care of those pesky mind readers."

I did exactly as she had recommended and went to the same tattoo artist with Daxton and Amr and made us all get matching tattoos. They had asked many questions, but dropped it when I told them to just trust me. I had yet to bring it up to Rae and Eli as they had both been absent and would probably have a run-in or two with people that could do harm with this information.

It was sad to think about how little trust was between us now, but I had to do this to not only keep myself alive...but all the people around me as well.

Matt's jaw clenched and I watched as he thought through all of his options, his eyes scanning every inch of me.

"What do you want?" he asked after a pause.

"Take me to him," I demanded.

A smirk spread across his face.

"To who?"

I pushed the orb of magic into his neck and watched as his face flushed and pain spread across his expression. He let out a groan, but did not give in.

I pushed the orb in harder.

"Fine," he grunted. "But I have to call my sister."

"Do it," I hissed. "Now."

He patted his pockets for his phone and typed out a message to her.

I didn't know what it said, but I didn't need to. She warned me about this earlier today, it was the whole reason I was here so late anyways.

She appeared in a flash of light and looked down at us with an unamused expression.

"What a precarious—"

"Shut up and do as you are told," Matt hissed at her.

For good measure I pushed the ball further into his neck. Claudine's lips twitched and she placed a hand on us both.

This time I was prepared for the feeling of my stomach being turned inside out. When the light subsided I was hit with a chill before I saw the massive space we were in. We were in what looked to be a ballroom, but the interior seemed darker, more mysterious than those ones I had seen on TV growing up.

Claudine gave no rest; she disappeared in a flash of light.

Matt used that chance, and my moment of distraction, to push me to the ground as he straddled either side of my hips. I felt a thick rope-like object wrap around my wrists and force my arms over my head. I looked towards them to catch sight of thick vines that made their way down my arms as if they had minds of their own.

I glared at Matt and he met me with a smirk.

"Not so tough now, are you?" he asked. I felt the vines slip into my clothing and wrap around my body much like I imagined a giant snake would.

"You don't scare me," I said in a defiant tone.

"No?" he asked. "I can be very scary if given free rein."

I kept his stare down. There was no way I would be scared of him, I wouldn't allow myself to even as the vines wrapped around me and began squeezing my body.

I saw the flash of light over Matt's head and smiled before lighting the vines on fire in one burst. The ones that had snaked through my clothing fell limp and Matt frowned when he realized what happened.

He sat up and looked over at the very people we were waiting for. Right next to Claudine's form stood the man that single-handedly saved me from dying at the hands of the Originals because of my failed task.

He stood tall and dressed in a sweater that hugged his body and loose slacks. His dark hair fell in his eyes and he had scruff on his face. His dead eyes looked over the two of us without any indication of his emotions.

"I heard you took a little hostage," he said, a smirk finally spreading across his face.

"Little indeed," I scoffed and sat up only to push Matt off me. I could tell he allowed it for the second because as soon as I stood, he had my wrist in a death grip.

"Don't get too comfortable," Matt hissed behind me.

"I should say that to *you*," I hissed at him.

"Malik will hear about this," he threatened.

"What will he do, huh?" I asked and stepped closer to Matt. "Make me kneel? Bind me with his power? *Fuck off*, Matt, and don't hide behind someone else's power."

My magic was rising with each word and I had trouble controlling the shakes that traveled through my body. It dared me to treat him just like I had with the other witches in the town. I knew I could do it, it knew I could do it. The only thing holding me back was the front that Matt had shown me when I first got to Winterfell. The one that stood by me through the hard times as a friend and slowly introduced me into this world.

Turning away from him and snatching my wrist out of his hands, I walked towards Marques with my hand still throbbing.

"I wanted to first say thank you," I said. Shock ran through his face for just a moment before he composed himself. "Second I wanted to ask whose bright idea it was to kill hundreds of people by setting the fucking town on fire."

"That was Malik and Eli—"

I turned back to Matt and sent a fireball barreling towards him. He scrambled out of the way before regaining his composure and sending me a glare.

"I know it was yours," I said to Marques. "I have been trying to save them for days and they—"

"Just die," he interrupted. "I know."

I was stunned by his honesty and found myself unable to find the words to continue.

"Come, Rosie," he said and held a hand out to me. "I will explain over some tea maybe?"

I squared my shoulders and placed my hand in his.

"Some alcohol would be better," I replied.

He laughed at this and led me into the next room.

Chapter 5
Rae

Tonight was the last time that we could meet with Marques before the start of the term and I hated to admit it, but I was nervous.

Nervous that the Originals would catch on. Worried that Rosie would get hurt. Worried that the world would crumble...because after killing my father, it felt like it had.

There was nothing in my control anymore. From the state of the house to the mountains of letters arriving at my door from all of my father's close colleagues, I had no idea what to do with the mountain of attention we were getting and no way to separate it from the looming threat of the Originals.

Tonight would be the night where we would plan the demise of the people who turned my world upside down. My father...was not a nice demon, but I knew that if somehow he had been able to separate himself from the clutches of the Originals, he wouldn't have been in this position and neither would Mother.

Speaking of my mother...

I stood from my place in my father's study at his desk. It had taken me far too long to comb through the condolence letters and I had to hurry if I wanted to meet Mother before I set out.

Taking a look at my phone I sighed and left the room with only ten minutes to spare.

I had moved Mother to a more comfortable space on the second floor. The room was much more vibrant than the other and I made sure it was always warm enough for her. It was the least she deserved after all the years of torture she went through.

On many nights I stayed up thinking about how awful it must have been to be confined to such a space with no one to talk to. Even the maids had forgotten about her at one point as if she was no more than a ghost.

Opening the door, my heart skipped a beat as I saw the newly hired nurse lifting my mother onto the four-poster bed. Hiring a nurse was a straightforward decision, the right one...but it was far from easy. Our finances were not in a good place and hiring her was another burden on the family.

You would think that his life insurance and the payout from the government would be enough to hold us over for years to come, but one thing I was starting to understand was Father was reckless with our money.

"Let me help you," I said in a light tone.

The nurse jumped at my sudden intrusion, her green eyes widening, but her face quickly relaxed and she sent me a soft smile. She was not much older than me but experience wasn't an issue when she had a power like hers.

"That would be wonderful," Callie replied.

I walked around the bed and helped my mother into the bed. Callie moved around me to help cover her with blankets.

I watched my mother's face for any flash of recognition...but there was still nothing.

I turned to Callie, noting her bright yellow scrubs. They had printed flowers on them that matched the ones decorating the walls of this room. There was a stark contrast against her dark brown hair and scrubs, washing out her skin tone.

"She likes them," Callie explained, probably noticing my stare. She sent me another soft smile. "Her mind has had more activity as of late and when I wear yellow...well let's just say her mind lights up."

I swallowed thickly and nodded. A sort of bitter relief washed through me.

Callie's specialty was that she could see the activity in the mind of others. She explained to me that it was like the mind was painting a picture, filled with vibrant colors and each of the colors had a meaning.

"Good," I said and straightened my clothes. "I will be leaving, see your-self out whenever. I just wanted to check on Mother before I left."

"I can leave you two for a moment," she said and without waiting for my reply turned to leave the room.

As soon as the door closed a heavy sigh escaped my chest and my shoulders caved in. Looking over to my mother I let the powerful emotions that I had been so carefully locking up fill my body.

Sadness.

Anger.

Disappointment.

Fear.

All of it swirled around my being. It had been so hard to keep up this facade around the others, especially when they were already dealing with such volatile emotions themselves. It helped that most of the summer we stayed apart. It let old wounds heal, anger die down, and everything was almost as it once was...

I don't regret killing my father.

If I had the chance to I would do it over and over again... I just wish I hadn't been so naive.

And even now, I knew what I had to do, but each step towards a normal and balanced life for me and my family seemed harder and harder.

I was torn out of my thoughts by a prick of emotion that was not mine.

It was a familiar feeling and full of pity and sadness.

My eyes trained on my mother's vacant stare.

"Was that you?" I whispered.

She gave no indication that she heard my words.

Marques's blood had indeed strengthened my powers, but not as much as I believed it would. Instead emotions just carried further, felt stronger, but I had yet to have the chance to see if I could manipulate emotions just yet.

Maybe if I could figure it out...

I rolled my shoulders and with one last lingering look, I left my mother's side and went down to the front of the house.

I smiled at Callie as I passed, not slowing my pace.

I let my emotions crowd my senses too long, and now I was late for my meeting.

"Where are you going?" Nathaniel asked as I walked through the foyer.

I stopped in my tracks and looked over at my brother. He looked pale, and worse than I had seen him before. While the demon blood in his veins healed most of his bags and dull skin, it couldn't magically make him healthy again.

He had been neglecting himself in Father's absence.

None of us liked Father, that much was apparent, but I never realized just how sheltered they had been until I asked them to take on some of the family tasks. I couldn't do it all, but I was starting to think that I may have to given their inexperience.

"I'll be back soon," I promised.

He shifted on his feet and ran his hand through his hair. He was frustrated, worried, anxious, and I could feel it packing the room enough to choke me.

"Mary was asking about repairing some of the cracked drywall in the cellar," he said. "But mentioned that it would be out of the budget they had been allowed for this quarter."

After my father's death, all of the managing of the household came down to me and my brothers, which none of us fully understood how to take care of. The maids, housekeepers, and accountants all turned to us now for any little thing that used to set my father off.

"I'm going to hire a manager to run this property at some point," I told him and straightened my jacket. "I don't know how Father managed to approve and look over all these expenses without one for so long."

He looked down at his feet.

"Are you sure we have money for that?" he asked slowly.

I could feel the anxiety rolling off his chest in waves and it surrounded the empty room, making it hard to breathe. I sent him some calming waves and his shoulders relaxed almost immediately.

"I am sure," I said confidently, even though I had had the same worry just a few days ago when I realized the cost of running all my father's properties.

I planned to sell off the properties if we had to, but until then I would pull from where we needed to and start undoing the unnecessary costs our father had put on this extravagant lifestyle.

"Don't worry about the money," I said in a softer tone. "I have already thought it through and have a plan for us."

There was a relief that washed through Nathaniel. He flashed me a grateful smile.

"Alright," he said with a sigh. "I guess don't get home too late, young lady."

I shook my head and let out a light chuckle before pushing out into the summer night.

* * *

I met the others at the designated area only a few miles away from the apartment Malik had provided Rosie. Eli and Malik had insisted on living there as a way to escape the Originals, but Rosie didn't have a choice as she was now bound to them in a way that made it hard for her to escape them.

We gathered in a small alleyway between two large warehouses that smelled distinctly of rotting fish. My nose curled as I walked towards the group that was already waiting for me and noticed with a start that we were missing Claudine.

"Where is she?" I asked waving to the empty space between Maximus and Eli.

Maximus crossed his arms around his chest and shrugged.

"We will leave in a minute if she doesn't show," Malik said, his eyes shining in the darkness.

I looked to Eli. The way they kept flexing their fingers and the restlessness inside them was affecting me already. They had been in this group longer than I had and even if they didn't admit it, I noticed how much leaving Rosie's side affected them.

When they were finally reunited at the funeral their anxiety dropped to almost nonexistent levels. The emotions of the group at times had been almost too hard to handle, and when you pair that with the dying refugees in the campus... Let's just say there was a reason why I was avoiding that part of Winterfell.

I tried not to blame Eli and Malik for the burning of the town. I knew with or without them Marques would have found a way to do it...but it really took a toll on us all.

"Let's go check on the others first," Malik suggested. "Then if she still isn't here, we flag it."

There were a few nods and we set off down the alley and to an adjacent warehouse that unbeknownst to the public was heavily warded by Maximus.

When Maximus came no more than ten feet away from the warehouse, he began muttering something under his breath and the bright red barrier became clear for only a moment. We took our cue and rushed towards the door in silence.

Eli was too slow and I heard a hiss of pain signaling the place where the barrier singed them. Looking back I saw them send a glare to Maximus while they rubbed their arm.

"In, now," Malik hissed as he pulled the heavy door open, screeching metal filling the silent air.

We filed through the empty warehouse until we stood right in the center of it. From an outsider's perspective, it looked like a normal everyday abandoned warehouse... The secrets it held were unbelievable.

Malik knelt to the ground and rolled up his sleeve so that his forearm was bare to the world.

"You'll have to recharge later," he murmured to Maximus. "Sorry to put so much stress on you."

Maximus shrugged and opened his palm where he conjured a magical spear that lit up the dark space.

"I can handle this," he said and without hesitation dug the spear into Malik's forearm.

I could feel his pain, but he never uttered a sound. We watched silently as the blood poured from his wound and onto the hard ground. As soon as the first droplets hit the ground, a bright red light surrounded us and slowly, the real secrets of the warehouse began to show themselves.

The once dark, empty space turned light and filled with warmth. The sound always came first and tonight, that sound was laughter. Slowly the world hidden behind the veil of magic appeared.

We stood right in the middle of the makeshift dining area. Unsteady tables surrounded us and at them were the smiling faces that I came to know as refugees from the town the Originals had been hiding in.

"Eli my boy!" came a voice from behind us and just like every other time, a rugged-looking man was the first to greet us.

I felt the small spark within Eli when they heard their name being called, but made a point not to stare at them too hard. It was rare to feel that type of feeling from them, I wanted them to enjoy it as long as they could.

Eli scowled as they looked the man up and down.

"We give you a shower, a bed, free food *and* clothes, and you still can't clean up?" Eli grumbled.

The man let out a laugh and waved over to the corner where the others were watching him with apt attention.

"Come!" he yelled. "Let's have a drink!"

Eli gave him a look but followed him towards the corner anyways.

"Let's make our rounds," Malik said to Maximus and me.

I nodded and began the routine we had made for ourselves this summer.

We would go through the dining hall while Malik talked joyfully to the people there. His whole persona changed and instead of the conniving serious demon, he turned into a warm sort of caretaker for the refugees.

He would ask them how they have been, if their supplies became low or if they wanted anything special.

Many of the times they would brush him off and say that the witches here were plentiful and supplied everything they needed, but Malik would still push and Maximus would end up conjuring a handful of items the others were too weak to do on their own.

The second stop, was the infirmary.

This one always took a toll on me.

I was proficient at separating myself and blocking out the stray emotions...but the infirmary was filled to the brim with fear, anger, sadness, and all the other potent emotions that came with dying.

And now that Marques's blood was coursing through me, I had to keep my own emotions locked away or else I would be susceptive to outbursts. Though the aftereffects of keeping them in for too long wasn't ideal either, many times as I lay awake I would be shaking with the potent emotions still playing at my mind, and couldn't sleep until the last of them left my body.

From Malik's words, they had *stolen* one of the lone doctors the town had on staff and was now using them here. He was an older graying witch that had been alive for as long as Malik had, though we are still unsure how he managed that feat.

He was at the end of the infirmary, hovering over a patient.

As I passed the beds I noted the bright pink chart at the end of each.

Miller

71.33% Demon.

Power: Unknown

Status: Rapid Decay

A memory played at my mind, but I was too crowded with the emotion in here that trying to pull it to the front made my head hurt. I pulled my gaze from the glaring chart and to the rest of the bodies that littered the area. Almost every bed was filled.

Each of the sixteen beds was full with those who had a little too much human blood in them. There was no way to stop the decay; it was a sure fact that if you had human blood in you, you would age right after you left the barrier and stopping it was an impossible work of magic.

"I can sense you," the doctor said from afar, stopping Malik from getting too close to one of the patient beds where a sleeping low-level lay encased in a magic-type film that glittered in the light.

"Nice to see you Richard," Malik called back with a light tone. "What's the update? Need anything?"

The doctors stood and looked back at us with a small smile.

"I have some good news," he said and waved us over.

In front of him was another low-level encased in the same film but this time...his eyes were open and looking towards us.

"Get Eli," I said and looked toward Maximus. He nodded and left the room only to come back with an annoyed Eli a few moments later.

"Exactly what I was thinking," the doctor said smiling at me. "He has been awake but unable to talk. I need to know what he is feeling."

"Pain," I answered for him. "Though Eli can probably tell you why."

Eli gave me a look and pushed past me, towards the low-level.

"Welcome back from the dead," Eli said with a smirk and wrapped their hand around the low-level's arm.

There was a pause.

"Well?" Malik asked.

"He's mad at me," Eli explained. "And currently cursing my existence. For that I should let you stew in your injuries, would you like that?"

The low-level's eyes widened.

"Eli," Malik warned.

They rolled their eyes and removed themselves from the low-level.

"His injuries were not healed," she explained. "His leg is still hurt and he says something in his back and head hurt."

"I thought we...?" Malik trailed.

The doctor gave him a sad smile.

"I can only heal with magic what I know to be the issue and because we do not have equipment..."

There was a heavy aura settling around the room. I turned to look at the beds around us. Did this mean all of them were subjected to this pain the entire time they remained asleep? I could feel pricks of it here and there, but nothing like the man in front of me.

"Try to replicate what you did with him," Malik said. "And we will bring the mind reader and the seer next time."

"Give me a few weeks," the doctor said. "And I'll try to have an update for you."

Malik and he bid their goodbyes and we moved onto the next round.

As we were walking down the makeshift rooms, Maximus froze in his tracks.

"Claudine passed the barrier," he announced. "Something is...off."

Malik shared a look with him and without another word he dropped to the ground, preparing to take Maximus's spear.

Maximus wasted no time and stabbed the spear into his arm.

The world in front of us vanished faster than it came and we were plunged into the darkness of the warehouse.

I could feel the joy coming off of Claudine before I turned to face her.

"Marques requests you all," she said in a light voice and practically skipped her way towards us.

Eli looked at me and their emotions told me that they were suspicious of this and I couldn't help but agree.

"Why were you late?" Malik asked, his tone commanding.

"You'll see," she said in a sing-song tone. "Hands on me."

She pushed herself in the middle us of and I slowly placed my hand on her shoulder praying that nothing was burning, destroyed, or dead.

"You'll be pleasantly surprised, Rae," she said and in a flash of light, the warehouse was gone.

Again the first thing I heard was laughter. A high-pitched female laugh that rang through the warm space of Marques's mansion. The second thing I felt, even through the laughter, was a deep pain swirled with sadness.

But it was familiar, it was...

"Rosie," Malik and I growled in unison when our eyes both traveled to the couch where Rosie, dressed in her sweats and a loose t-shirt, sat laughing with a drink in hand.

Her laughter stopped and a small smile spread across her face.

"Welcome back," she said and took a sip of her drink. I spotted Matt right behind her, his eyes narrowed at her and his mouth twisted into a grotesque scowl.

His anger was almost as strong as her pain; it spread across the small sitting room and tried to seep into my bones.

"Look at you," Eli cooed and walked over to the couch, ignoring the dead-eyed Original as they sat next to Rosie and wrapped an arm around their shoulder. "How naughty."

They leaned forward to whisper something in her ear that shot a pang of arousal through her.

I looked at Marques, trying to figure out anything but he looked us over with a blank face and not a prick of emotion through him.

"How did you even get here?" Malik growled and stormed towards her, pushing Eli away and grabbing Rosie's chin.

I found myself wanting to do the same thing. I was angry, shocked, and nervous that she had been here with *him* alone.

She had risked so much to come here. Did she know this man could kill her in seconds? Did she know that without the proper precautions every-thing we worked for up until now would be for nothing?

I was almost as worried as I was angry.

"She cornered me," Matt spit out. "Bitch fucking fried my neck and burned my veins."

Eli was ready to pounce and Malik's head snapped over to Matt. I had never felt the two so angry before in my life and after the stint in the medical bay... I felt my head swoon.

"You're just mad you got caught," Rosie said with another laugh and pushed Malik's hand away from her so that she could down the rest of her glass.

She was tipsy, enough to affect her mood and I was worried what would come out of it. I had never seen her like this before. Not to mention her guard was down next to the most dangerous man in this world.

"So, shall we start?" Marques asked. "Rosie has quite a few topics to address it seems."

"Hell yeah I do," Rosie said and stood up. "First, you."

She pulled Malik forward by his shirt and hit the side of his face so hard the slap reverberated around the space.

"Don't ever try to erase my mind ever again. I don't care if it was Matt's power, you were the one in charge and to hear that my memory was taken from me *four* times—"

"Six," Malik interrupted. "Six times we took your memory from you."

Rosie slammed her jaw shut and I thought that she was going to slap him again but instead she smiled.

"There was the Malik I missed," she said. "Never again, got it?"

"Understood," he murmured, his eyes trailing the length of her face.

I cleared my throat and Rosie sent me a small smile.

"Right," she said. "Now I hear, you have a little refugee hideout, is that correct?"

Her devious smile told me all that I needed to know, and man did it stir something in all of us.

Chapter 6
Rosie

The honesty from the group was...refreshing.

It had taken a lot to get here and I literally had to force my way into this space, but I was grateful they finally caved. If not I would be forced to take more drastic measures and I didn't want that after we had come so far.

"The doctor there is working on a way to save them," Rae said, the first one willing to divulge more than I asked. I sent her a smile.

"We will have the results soon," Malik said and shifted on his feet. "I hope."

Only Eli, myself, and Marques dared to sit and drink on the couch. The others spread out around the room in various stages of discomfort.

It didn't get past me that Claudine, Maximus, and Malik were the closest to Marques. It spoke volumes for their true ties. Matt was standing behind us, still leaning against the wall and grumbled his opinion every now and then.

"And why are they the only ones involved?" I asked Marques. "Me, Daxton, Amr, we all want the same thing, to end this just like everyone else."

Jealous? Eli teased in my head.

Pissed, I corrected.

"Xena and Ezekiel care about them the least," Marques said and took a sip of his drink. "They were the easiest to pull away."

"We were going to tell you," Malik spoke up. "Rae wouldn't have agreed to it if we didn't have a plan to tell you."

My eyes traveled to Rae. She was standing there with her arms crossed and her head high. A warmth spread through my chest when I thought about her standing up for my right to be involved.

I had forgiven her long ago, but to know that even after we had been separated for so long, she still fought on my behalf? It almost made me tear up.

"Then what's the plan?" I asked. "Go after the Originals? They are at Winterfell now with loads of guards by their side. Not to mention they are worth at least ten of us each."

Marques's lips twitched.

"I can help with the power aspect," he said in a tone that made my skin crawl.

"We drank his blood," Eli said with a grimace. "It hurts like a mother-fucker but it works. I have been able to hear some thoughts without touching people."

What? I asked in my mind. *You can hear everyone now?*

Just sometimes, they explained. *It takes practice.*

"Me too," Rae said. "Emotions are stronger, clearer than before, though I have yet to try to control them."

"Something we can rectify in training," Marques said with a smirk. I noted the way Rae's jaw clenched.

Their power got stronger through...drinking blood?

How was this possible? Was this his power?

No... It couldn't be, could it?

My mind swam with the information and possible ideas of why this was possible.

Demons' bodies reacted to other demons' blood? Or was it just Original blood?

I looked at Marques, ready to word vomit all the questions that were running through my head...but his hard gaze stopped me.

In that moment it felt like the world had fallen away and it was just us in this room. I couldn't see his mouth move but it felt like I could hear him.

And he was warning me to not ask the questions that plagued my mind.

"I want it too," I said in a serious tone.

"Rosie," Rae chided.

Marques gave me a grin.

"I knew the daughter of Xena would outshine her one day," he said. "Come here, child."

I left Eli's comforting embrace to walk over to Marques. All eyes were on me and my steps echoed through the room. I didn't know if this was the right choice or if it would push me further into this world that I hated so much... but all I could hold onto was the hope that this would be the thing to turn the tides.

That this would finally make me the demon I was yearning to be.

Finally help me be strong enough so that never again would I be subjected to this fight.

"You think too highly of me child," Marques said with a smile as I stopped in front of his seated form. "I am merely a conduit."

"We will see, won't we?" I asked.

Claudine came over with a magical knife, grabbed his arm and without hesitation slashed his skin. His blood was like nothing I had ever seen. It was dark, and sticky. My stomach twisted but even as my mind yelled at me to run back I slowly picked up his arm and licked the blood off his wound.

Pulling away I watched his expression only to see his eyes already locked on me.

"I don't—"

Just as I was about to speak a sharp pain went through me and I was thrown to the ground. All the cells in my body felt as though they were vibrating and I couldn't stop my body from convulsing against the cold floor.

Warm arms wrapped around me and I was pulled into Rae's embrace. I held on to her and tried to breathe through my mouth as I felt the blood attacking my system.

My magic which had normally been lashing out and begging for some action quietly sat back and seemed to let the blood run through my body. Like even it was terrified of what I had just done.

"Why is it taking so long?" Rae asked from above me. "She should have been fine by now."

I let out a groan as a flash of white-hot pain radiated through my body.

"Soon," Malik spoke from somewhere near. "Claudine and Maximus had the same reaction."

Slowly as I listened to their words, my body began to relax and the pain started fading.

"I thin—*shit*," I groaned as another wave of pain shot through me. "I think it's ending."

Even as I lay there with a weakened body, Rae never let go of me and for that I was grateful. It was embarrassing and shameful to be seen like this in front of everyone but with her strong hold, I felt like I could do this.

When the last of the pain washed away I stood up with the help of both Rae and Malik.

"We are not done here," I said in a pained voice as I tried to walk back to the couch.

"You need to go back—"

I cut Malik off with a look.

"Tell me—*in detail*—the plan, and then we can go," I demanded.

I practically snuck into the couch. My body was still feeling the aftereffects of the blood.

"I'm going to kill the teacher bitch," Eli spoke up in an excited tone. They sent me a smirk as I gave them a disbelieving look.

"Your mother?" I asked then threw my head back into the couch. "God we have issues."

* * *

I do not know how many hours we spent talking, but we were interrupted by the sun peeking through the dark space.

For the first time I could say that everything was out in the open and I finally knew what the fuck we were going to do next. I don't know if it made me relax or angered me because of how simple it had been.

I looked towards Marques, for some reason thinking that the sun would just destroy his frail frame but he just smiled at me. He had not moved from his chair the entire time, letting Malik do a majority of the talking while he sipped on his alcohol.

The demon with the magic blood and powers I didn't really understand looked oddly homey.

"Time to get back," he said. "Xena and Ezekiel will be worried if you are gone too long."

"Worried," Eli said with a huff next to me. I pulled myself from their embrace and stood with the rest of the group.

We were all various levels of tired, but my eyes fell on Malik, watching as he swayed. His eyes shifted to mine and he straightened as if brushing off what I had just seen.

I searched for the familiar redhead that should have been cursing my entire being in the corner but to my disappointment, he was gone. It hurt to think of how he had played me, and somehow hurt even more now that his actions lined up with the real him. I expected the Matt I knew to stick around, maybe talk about our misunderstanding...but I didn't think it was a misunderstanding to begin with. This was planned and I needed to accept that.

"Was the goal of this fight always equality?" I asked Marques as he walked us to the door. I half expected him to just shoo us away but instead, like a real host, he saw us out.

He gave me a small pitiful smile before answering.

"No, it never was," he said, his honesty stunning me for a moment. "I knew we were an abomination by the time our feet touched the ground of this plane. Others thought themselves as righteous, as saviors, as higher beings...but that is far from the truth."

I stood still, unable to pull myself from his intense stare.

"And do you remember heaven?" I asked.

He smiled at me, an all-knowing one and I couldn't help the flush of awe that rose in me. This man was the one with all the answers to everything, the Originals, our way of being, and even beyond...and here he was indulging me.

"I do, cursed one," he said. My lips twitched at his nickname.

"Is it..." I struggled to find the words to describe what I was asking.

"A word of advice," he said and paused before walking towards me. The others stepped back as if afraid of his actions. His cold hands found my shoulders and I found myself frozen in place by his eyes. "Stay alive as long as you can. You have seen the types of monsters they throw out of there... Do you really want to see what still resides there?"

"You have a point," I whispered, a smile tugging at my lips even after everything. "And hell?"

A grin slipped to his face.

"You are living it, darling."

A small bubble of laughter came out of my mouth. Though the alcohol had long been burned off by my demon blood, I still felt light and airy. Though that could just be the feeling of finally belonging somewhere.

"You are not wrong," I said. "I'll see you in practice."

A smirk played at his lips.

"I think you would prefer me to stay out of that, but I will see you soon," he said and leaned forward to place a kiss on my forehead. When he did, something like a memory zapped through my body forcing my hair to stand at all ends.

It was him alone in a chair, looking towards the forest outside. I could feel the weakness that hung over him and the tiredness that clouded his brain. Even breathing seemed like a tremendous task and with each inhale I felt the weight on his back double.

"I see," I said in a solemn tone.

I looked into his eyes, now seeing not an all-powerful man, but someone vulnerable and in pain.

He was *dying.*

How did I not see it sooner? Even his eyes had lost their shine.

"See you soon, cursed one."

* * *

Eli's hand dug into my shoulder as we arrived at Winterfell. Claudine had used her powers to transport us here and even though she played it off well, by the sweat accumulating in her forehead, I knew she must have been straining.

Don't even think to run off to god knows where, she said in my mind. *I have plans for you.*

They sent me an image of me tied to the dorm bed, nude and writhing.

My mouth watered. It had been so long since I had had proper alone time with Eli. Let alone in an area where they had full control.

I was exhausted after the assault of information earlier this night, but it made the idea of being under Eli's control all that more enticing. I needed a break from it all, needed to get my mind away from the pain and death. For once not think about the steps I needed to take to make sure that I wouldn't die the next day.

And I couldn't think of anyone better to do the job.

I would much rather spend the time with you, I said in my mind.

Their eyes shifted to mine briefly.

"Alright," Malik said. "Disperse and don't let me see you again until next time."

The group gave a round of agreements and Eli began steering me away, but not before I caught sight of a familiar redhead walking up to our group.

Where had he gone?

I sent a glare to Matt, which he wholeheartedly returned. Malik noticed and smacked the side of his arm and Matt's glare dropped.

Unease twisted in my stomach as I watched the two.

How had Matt changed so quickly? It couldn't all be fake, could it?

Our time at Winterfell, while fake...had felt like a real friendship. Our laughs were real, the warmth I felt from him was real, the comfort...

It was never real, Rosie, Eli said in my head. *He has always been a snake, you just never knew until now.*

My last look was to Rae, who had stood silently on the side of the group. I wonder what she was thinking, feeling, during this time. Her eyes gave no indication though I could feel something simmering beneath her skin whenever I came close.

I was tempted to ask her to join us, but that was quickly shot down when I realized how little time I had spent with Eli. Rae nodded as if understanding my thoughts and turned to leave, her glowing hazel gaze lingering on us.

"Rae," Malik said in a light tone. "Can we talk?"

Rae raised a brow towards Malik but nodded anyways and followed him in the opposite direction. I wondered what the two of them could possibly talk about, but I gave them the benefit of the doubt, even though inside I wanted to turn around and demand what other secrets they were keeping. Steeling my raging magic and unsteady emotions, I tried to focus on the person that held me tight against their side.

At last, we turned away as well and set forth with Eli across the dead campus.

There was much to discuss still, but none of it safe for the prying walls of Winterfell. I have learned now that getting answers quickly was impossible, and if they came fast...well then they were probably lies.

And after the change in Matt, I had realized that there was not a person besides those I have kept around that were worth trusting, and even they sometimes had proven to break that trust.

The silence that spread across the place was eerie and held a weight to it as though we were walking in a graveyard and the dead lay right below our feet The only thing that calmed me somewhat was the undeniable thrum of magic underneath us as we walked and the traces of magical signatures left by the refugees.

"Stop being so dramatic," Eli teased, their hand moving to twist a strand of my hair. I leaned into their warmth and inhaled their familiar scent.

I had missed this much more than I thought. Eli, while brash and sometimes unhinged, had been a constant never-changing person that I could rely on to keep me grounded.

Even through everything that happened, I found them staying true to their nature in an ever-changing world.

Their strong hands continued to guide me and even as they sent explicit images of what was to come, I found myself comforted by them. I was safe in their arms and I couldn't imagine a place where I would rather be in that moment.

"I did it," they said. *The town.*

"I know," I replied.

"How did you hide it from me?" they asked.

I wondered how long the question had been gnawing at them.

"The memories?" I asked looking up at them.

They nodded.

"I just tried not to think about it when you touched me," I said truthfully.

"And how did you stop him?" they asked.

"I had help," I said and looked out at the still campus. "I will show you more later."

They nodded and dropped the conversation after that.

The rest of the way was quiet, except for the scenes in my head. Each one sent a flood of arousal through me and my magic, which had been laying low, sprung to life.

Living with my magic now, was almost like second nature.

Daxton and Amr had done wonders when it came to exploring this side of me...but it was pushy about what it was missing.

Never before had the others heard of a witch's magic being expelled with a demon's help, but mine craved a demon's touch.

Specifically, Rae's and Eli's.

Eli quickly opened the door to their dorm and the first thing that hit me was how clean the inside was. There was mostly darkness until they flipped the switch for the lights, and something I had never seen before came to life.

Winterfell dorms were all the same, to my knowledge, so I was familiar with the exposed brick and muted tones of the room, but what was out of the norm were the shelves decorating the walls and the paintings that hung on all four sides.

My mouth dropped open when I got a look at the shelves.

There were *pictures* of Eli and the others, all frowning while they seemed to be at a party not unlike the gala we had gone to together.

My mind whirled with this information.

Eli kept stuff like this?

"There is a reason I didn't want you here," they grumbled.

"I just—"

They cut me off with a tug on the back of my hair, forcing me to look up at them. Their blue eyes shimmered in the dim lights that lit the area.

"You can gawk at my dorm later," they growled and nipped at my bottom lip.

Their free hand trailed up my arm to grip onto my neck, forcing my body closer to theirs. The roughness of their skin only added fuel to the fire that was slowly burning up my insides.

I melted into their touch, submitting fully to whatever they planned for me. I trusted them enough for this, at least.

"I don't have my curse," I murmured against their soft lips.

Their lips quirked.

"I have a plan for that," they replied. "Now strip. I want you kneeling before the bed naked and ready for me."

A shiver ran through me. I thought about fighting, just for the thrill of it. Talking back, hitting, pushing away, just to see how far I could push them as I remembered the first night we ever had together and how the roughness of their touches stayed with me for weeks. But I decided against it.

Instead I stepped out of their grasp and slowly peeled my clothes off, giving them a view of my fully naked body before turning and walking towards the bed.

"Facing me, this time."

I did as they told and knelt down with the bed behind me. Even though the air was warm in the room, I couldn't stop the shivers that wracked my body. I couldn't stop the way my nipples hardened under their gaze or the way my pussy began to throb.

All it took was one pointed look from them and I was already becoming a puddle at their feet.

They walked closer towards me, the height difference causing me to shift my gaze upward. I could feel the ends of my hair brushing my bare ass. Their gaze ran up the length of my body and I found my breathing becoming quicker.

My magic was reaching out wildly trying to wrap around Eli and force them to our side, but I stayed put.

Their hand came to rest on the side of my face and I leaned into it. Their mouth quirked at my actions.

"This will be rough," they said.

I swallowed down the nervousness rising up in me.

"I know," I whispered. Their thumb traced my lower lip. "I want it rough."

Their gaze became hooded and they pushed their thumb past my lips to push down on my tongue. I closed my lips around it and sucked lightly.

"It's not like before," they said. "Back then... I didn't feel the way I do for you now."

My heart pounded so hard in my chest that the sound of it began to drown out everything else.

"I feel like I am being torn in two when I am away from you," they said. "I loathe the people that hurt you." They took a deep breath as if trying to calm themselves. Their gaze was wild now, with a smile spreading across their lips.

"I want you, no—I *need* you now," they continued. "More than ever."

"Eli," I tried to say around their thumb.

"And that means I just want to *hurt* you more."

There was a bit of fear mixed into all of this, but that only spiced up the arousal that was coursing through me. Sitting like this in front of them, so vulnerable, and waiting for them to ravish me... I was positively dripping.

And on top of it, it was *my choice*.

My choice to be here in front of them.

My choice to hand over control.

They kneeled down so they were at eye level with me.

"Hurt you because of the things you make me feel," they explained. "Because how *dare* a hybrid who grew up parading around as a dirty low-level bring me to my knees like this. How dare that same person turn and viciously murder her lover's parents, and not give a damn."

"Eli—"

"I am not done," they growled and removed their hand only to fasten it around my neck.

"I do not know if hating you," they said, "...or whatever this is, is worse. But there is no going back and I swear to you if you ever think about leaving my side I *will not* show you any mercy."

My mind exploded.

Is this...is this how they tell me they love me?

Before I could think of any other thoughts their lips crashed against mine and their rough hands forced my legs apart. Their fingers immediately found my wetness but instead of starting rough like I expected, they slowly trailed the length of my slit, only stopping to rub circles in my clit before continuing their teasing touch.

I continued to kiss them, our tongues intertwining with each other, but in my mind, I was screaming.

I love you, I sent them. *I don't care, hurt me, bind me, torture me...my heart still beats for you.*

"Good," they purred against my lips. "Because me feeling for you, does not mean I will give you a break. I am not a good person, Rosie."

"And I don't ask you to be," I said in return.

They sent me a devious smile.

"Face down on the bed, ass up."

* * *

I didn't know how much longer I could handle in this position. I was face down in the bed, with my ass up in the air, fully naked. I could not stop the shaking in my legs as I sobbed through the intense pleasure that was shooting through me.

Eli had brought back the toys in full force.

Not only did they get real cuffs that tied me to the opposite ends of the bed, but that damned egg was back as well. They had turned it on the highest setting, sat back on the opposite side of the room and watched to see how long it would take for me to break.

I was close to my breaking point now, three orgasms in and it was hard to find my grip on reality because as much as my magic begged to be let out, it wouldn't settle for this stupid toy. It wanted a real demon between my legs as I came.

My wetness had gathered and I could feel it leaking down my legs.

My back was aching and I tried to shift in order to get to a more comfortable position, but Eli's stern voice gave a firm warning.

"Is that all?" they teased.

I shifted, the cuffs clanking against the metal of the bed frame. I peered over to them, my hair was damp with sweat and made it hard to make out the demon's form in the dim light.

I silenced my whines when I caught sight of the toy in their hands.

I had been so caught up in my own pleasure that I didn't notice that they were fully naked, their sleek skin simmering with sweat under the light and a toy was placed between their legs.

The toy was quiet, barely noticeable over the beating of my own heart.

They looked at me with hooded eyes and pressed a button on the side of their toy. I watched in fascination as their chest puffed and their head was thrown back, a deep moan escaping their mouth.

The sight alone caused my body to heat up and I found myself falling faster over the edge than I had the entire night. My entire body was stiff and I couldn't help but thrash around in the sheets calling Eli's name.

"Please," I begged them. "Please, no more."

They took a few deep breaths before they threw the toy across the room and stood from the seat. They silently walked over to the shelf, taking their time as if I was not just pleading for them to end me.

They rummaged through the boxes on the lower levels of the shelves before pulling out a dark purple dildo. My jaw dropped at the pure size of the toy. It was even bigger than Amr and had to be almost the size of my forearm.

"Eli, no," I said and pulled against the cuffs that were holding me against the bed.

"In that case," they murmured and reached back into the box to pull out a much smaller one. Almost *too* small...and then I watched as they fastened it above the other one with expert precision.

"Eli, I've never..."

"I know," they answered with a smirk. They fastened the harness around their waist before bending down to get a bottle of lube. I relaxed a bit and finally let my hips drop to the bed. "I didn't say you could relax yet, little Original."

I let out a whine and lifted my hips for them.

They walked over to me chuckling lightly and I felt the bed dip when they positioned themselves behind me.

"This will hurt," they warned. I flinched as they spread my cheeks and poured cold lube onto me. "But remember you asked for this."

I let out a sob and pushed myself back into them, feeling the large head of the dildo rest at my wet entrance. Their fingers pushed inside me to retrieve the toy, relieving me from the harsh vibrations for mere moments before I felt the first tip push against my entrance.

The stretch was fine at first, and it glided in easily, then I felt the prick of pain followed by a stinging sensation as I began to fill more than I ever had before.

I took a deep breath and arched into the pain, trying not to freeze when I felt the smaller dildo line up at the puckered ring of flesh that hadn't been abused by any of the others yet.

"That's right," they breathed. I let out a high-pitched whine as the second dildo pushed past the barrier. "I know. *I know.*"

Without warning their hands gripped my hips, nails digging into my flesh and forced me back to them, sheathing both toys side of me. A hot flash of pain shot through me from head to toe as I got used to the feeling of an object inside of me.

They didn't let me rest there though. I should have known this was an act. This whole time, they were prepping me for the harshness of what they were going to do to me.

They pulled out fully before they snapped our hips together once more.

"Fuck Eli," I groaned as they began to pound into me at a pace that forced the breath out of my lungs.

I had never been so full as I had in that moment and with each thrust into me I found the pain changing into something far more pleasurable, but instead of letting me get used to it, they began fucking me harder. Their hand pushed my back down into the comforter allowing them deeper access.

I could feel each thrust hit the back of my cervix and for a second, I really thought that Eli may ruin me.

I held onto the cuffs and buried my face in the pillow to conceal my sobs. No doubt if anyone heard us they would think I was being murdered with the amount of screams that had been coming out of my mouth.

Eli's hand left my hip to rub circles in my almost forgotten clit. The bundle of nerves was so sensitive that just a single touch caused the heat that had been gathering in my belly to start to explode outwards, pushing it along my entire body.

"I can't wait until the others realize that *I* was the first to fuck this tight hole of yours," they said from behind me and moved their hand from my back to push at the abused rim of flesh with their thumb, stretching me even further. "I'll take pleasure in knowing that you will not be able to sit without being reminded of who was here first."

They pushed into me and rocked their hips in a gentle swaying motion. Their hand left my clit to pull on my hair and force my head back at an awkward angle.

"You love it, don't you?" they asked. "Being filled to the brim. Tell me."

"Fuck, Eli. I love it, so much," I groaned and pushed my hips back against their thrusts. "Harder, Eli."

They let out a laugh and pounded into me at an animalistic pace.

"I forgot how much of a slut you were," Eli laughed and pulled on my hair. "I saw in Rae's head what you looked like as Amr and Daxton tag teamed you. *So needy.* Taking their cocks like you were starving."

Their hand left my hair and came down my ass with a loud smack. Pain and pleasure vibrated through my body and left me shaking.

"Again," I gasped as I felt the sting radiate through my body.

They brought their hand back down on my ass again.

"God I missed this," they grunted from behind me. "I am not going to let you get an ounce of sleep today you hear me? You fall asleep and you will be waking up with my cunt in your mouth."

"Fuck, I can't anymore Eli," I whined as they brought their hand back down on my ass.

They pulled out without warning and flipped me over only to reenter in one swift movement. The second dildo shining with lube and juices rubbed against my clit as they fucked me.

"Your magic," they groaned and splayed their hand across my stomach. "Here."

I grabbed onto their arm, barely keeping up.

"What?" I asked.

"Here." They pointed against my lower stomach. "I want my name carved in your body, forever, but knives will heal."

I sucked in a deep breath but conjured a magical spear all the same, but instead of doing it myself I handed it to Eli.

"If you brand me, then I brand you," I said.

Their thrusts paused and without hesitation they grabbed the spear. I heard the burning of skin as they held it over my stomach. Their hungry blue eyes flitted to mine before they brought the spear down onto my stomach.

I threw my head back and fisted the sheets at my side, a groan filling the room. My chest heaved as the burning pain of the knife slicing my skin filled my being. After Eli finished carving the first letter I bit back my scream as they spread the blood from the wound across my stomach.

As the blood leaked from my body so did my magic. I felt it releasing into the air and saw through my blurry eyes that it created shimmers.

"Beautiful," they murmured. "You were always so beautiful in red."

Their bloodied hand found my clit and they rewarded me with a few shallow thrusts. The intoxicating mix of pain and pleasure made my mind swim.

"Next," I gasped.

Eli chuckled and then went to work on the next letter. It was deeper than the last and I felt blood pool on my stomach.

"*So. Fucking. Beautiful,*" they bit out with three hard thrusts. Their bloodied hand gripped my thigh, their nails digging into the soft flesh, no doubt drawing blood of their own.

"Next," I commanded again.

The dot on the eye was excruciating and I almost felt my consciousness falling away if not for Eli's careful circles on my clit, bringing me back. I felt the lost orgasm start to blossom.

"Quickly," I moaned.

They finished off the letters without removing the spear from my skin. I came as soon as the last letter was finished and Eli threw the spear across the room. The magic that came with this orgasm, while less intense, sent a warmth through my body as it burst out of my skin.

Never before had I been so whole fully satisfied with my magic resting and going silent inside of me. The beast that was residing in my skin had finally had enough and my body was able to relax into the bed.

"Amr may be onto something," they murmured with shallow thrusts as they continued to spread the blood up my stomach and around my erect nipples. Each movement was ripe with pain but slowly, it mixed together providing a hum of euphoria that ran through me. "Cause right now, I wouldn't mind kneeling before you and calling you queen."

Chapter 7
Daxton

I hated mornings.

They reminded me of the shitty life I now had to live.

Every morning I would wake up and stay as still as possible as to not disturb any of my sleeping partners. This was the time when I would replay the last four years of my life and go through every single mistake I had made.

It was the only time that I had absolutely alone, with no one to snap me out of my depression spiral.

Ever since the night my parents—

I couldn't even think about it on the bad days.

On the good days I would think about what my life could be. What this freedom with the others finally meant. I could dream about the days where I could just lounge on the couch with Amr and Rosie and sleep the day away.

During those dreams, nothing was ever bothering me and it was like my parents didn't exist. It was like it was a single bad nightmare that never bothered me again.

But on the bad days... I *missed* them.

Missed the family that I wished I would have had.

Today was a day where I loathed them. I hated what they did to me and the way they made me feel all those years growing up and was relieved that I no longer had to look at their disgusting faces anymore.

In this moment, I was grateful for their deaths... But my magic only held onto the anger.

It amplified the small bit of anger that was residing in my stomach and fanned it outward and suddenly, I was angrier than I had ever been. It *loved* the darkness inside me, wanted to see how far it could take it, mold it into something more dangerous.

The magic pushed me to destroy, pushed me to destroy the peace of Winterfell and all the students that just happened to arrive early this year.

It wanted blood.

It wanted death.

It wanted to—

A familiar warmth engulfed my being, and strong hands gripped my hips. I leaned into Amr as he left lazy kisses down my throat.

"We have to get up and find Rosie," Amr murmured into my neck, but against his words his hands trailed down my stomach and teased the hem of my boxers.

This is what I needed. I needed to calm my magic and be in the company of someone I trusted.

"If she hasn't found us by now then it means she needs more time," I said and leaned back into his warmth, soaking up the feelings that flittered inside of me.

"You're right," he said and licked the length of my neck causing me to shudder. Heat had already begun to pool in my belly because of his sleepy touches.

He reached down and ran the length of his hands up my already throbbing erection. I whimpered and reached my arms around and turned my head so I could bring his mouth to mine.

"We will go in a bit," I whispered.

"In a bit," he agreed and ran his thumb over the head of my cock. "Just a taste."

I let out a groan.

I tried not to think about what my growing magic meant, though deep down, I knew it was chipping at my existence. I had been around enough witches to know that this was not normal and nothing that awaited me could be good.

I remembered the way Father and Mother used to talk about crazed witches, but I never saw them. Not until I looked in the mirror.

"Are you here with me?" Amr asked pulling his hand away.

I quickly grabbed his wrist to stop him from moving.

"Yes," I whispered. "I am here."

The words felt like a lie.

* * *

Luckily school was not in because if it was, Amr and I would have been hours late.

I kept waiting for Rosie's messy hair to pop through the door, but she never came. When Amr and I both decided that she had had enough time to herself, we ventured out into Winterfell.

A handful of students had begun to arrive early and they shared looks when they caught Amr and me walking side by side. They would whisper and point but when I glared at them they just ran in the opposite direction.

"Must be the news of the funeral," Amr said. His strong hand came to massage the knots out of my shoulders.

"Or the hybrid," I murmured and watched another pair of high-level demons stare at us from a building mere twenty feet away from where we stood.

Did they think we couldn't see them?

When one of them gasped I felt my magic surge. The feeling of it rising up in me made my head swim and my body tense.

My magic roared and pushed me to go fight. With every fiber of its being it thrashed around inside of me as if it had been starving for a decade. Its bloodlust was overpowering and for once, I felt as though I had something completely separate from my magic.

As if there *really was* a beast inside of me after all.

"I feel her," Amr said, pulling me out of my red haze. I looked over at him, taking in his beautifully tanned skin and long dark hair that was pulled back into a ponytail.

He sent me an understanding smile.

I took a deep breath, closed my eyes, and sent my magic out looking for her.

"She is back with the refugees?" I whispered.

"Maybe she never left," Amr murdered. "Something feels off her magic..."

As if his words had the ability to predict the future, there was a flash of magic that spread across the campus.

It was so strong I stumbled back as it clashed against mine.

We shared a look before bolting in the direction of the cafeteria.

With each site the magic Rosie was emitting became more and more potent and instead of running to save her, my magic was pushing me forward to consume.

It was racing with me, trying to see who could have more control over this sack of flesh before the other. It was roaring, telling me to tear apart the magic user and eat the magic core raw.

Amr beat me to the doors of the cafeteria and flung them open. He stepped in front of me as we were blasted with a fresh dose of magic.

The room that was once filled with the bundled refugees was now empty, save for four people in the middle of the room.

Eli stood to the side. They were the first to look at us as we entered.

Rae was across from them and her eyes never left Rosie.

Malik was slowly approaching Rosie with his hands up.

Rosie was in the middle of the group but it was hard to make out her form through the oozing black cloud that radiated out of her body. It was thick and fell to the ground in waves before spreading out across the floor and right towards us.

The biggest attention grabber, besides the magic pouring out of Rosie... was the bright red letters that lined every surface of the place.

"Traitor," was written all along the walls and from the small pulsing from the fresh blood, I could tell it was witches they had used for the blood.

The refugees missing with the fresh blood lining the walls was enough to break the bit of sanity that was holding me to the ground below me.

The same people we had been working the entire summer to save. Pouring our magic into potion after potion... It was *their* blood that painted the walls.

"Don't," Amr growled, but I wasn't sure if it was for Malik or myself because all I could think about as I bolted forward was how sweet the magic smelt.

I could even taste it on my tongue.

That sweet old magic that was as aged and delicious as the first day I had ever tasted it. I clawed at Amr's arm as he stopped me from running forward.

"Rosie," Malik said in a voice almost too low to hear. "Look at me."

"Did you know this would happen?" she snapped at him, her voice much louder, more powerful than his.

The tone sent me into a frenzy.

"Daxton, calm," Amr's voice commanded.

I sent a kick to his leg but he easily dodged and circled his arms around me.

"Did you know?" Rosie asked when there was no reply. *"Fucking answer me, Malik!"*

There was a pause before anyone spoke. The only sound filling the room was my growls.

"We were aware of the possibility," Rae said in a dark tone. "Though we thought with the effort—"

"I don't want to hear any more *lies!*" she yelled, her magic flaring out.

The monster inside me liked the way the others shrunk at her voice. Liked the fear rolling off of them.

Half of Malik's body disappeared as he kneeled in front of Rosie.

"Open your eyes!" he growled.

"No!" she yelled. "You are just going to manipulate me and hide things from me *again*. And I can't take another minute of it!"

She swung her arm and the black magic shot out and threw Malik across the cafeteria.

Go. Run. Feast.

This was our chance.

I struggled against Amr's hold.

"You're making this worse for everyone," Eli said. "Cat, do something."

"I have my hands full!" Amr yelled from behind me.

I dove for the floor as the black magic finally reached our position, but Amr yanked me back and held me in a headlock.

The world started to dim as Amr's hold on me tightened.

"Let me go," I choked out.

"I am sorry," Amr whispered from behind me, his voice barely audible over my own growls.

The last thing I saw as I sunk into darkness was the dissipation of the black magic and Rosie's body going limp only to be caught by Malik's awaiting arms.

Chapter 8
Rosie

"They ran for it," Malik's deep voice flitted through my fuzzy brain. My limbs were heavy with sleep and I couldn't make sense of up or down. My head swam and the world began tipping around me. Below me was soft fluffy material which I assumed was a bed, though there was an itchy material that was laid on me.

"I didn't expect anything else," Eli said with a huff.

I peeled my eyes open and was hit with a blinding light. The smell of chemicals filled my senses and burned my nose.

As my vision cleared I sat up in a flurry and pushed back until my back hit a cold wall.

The man that had been leaning over me jumped up and straightened his spine, my sudden movement taking him off guard though his surprise quickly wore off and a small smile rose to his face.

My gaze darted towards the group on the bed next to me.

Eli was sitting on the bed with their legs hanging off the side. Their arms were crossed and they were scowling at me.

Malik was standing behind them with a small smile of his own on his lips, and Rae was behind the two. She wouldn't look at me.

"Amr, Daxton?" I asked, my throat burning as the words were forced out of my mouth.

Eli jutted their chin forward. I followed the motion and looked to the left, and just beside me was Daxton asleep on the bed next to me and Amr was sitting next to him. He sent me a smile.

"How are you feeling, love?" he asked and reached out to grab my hand. His warmth seeped into my skin and a breath escaped my tight chest.

"I just—"

My words caught in my throat.

How could they? They had said they would find a place for them...

Was this what Ezekiel was scared of? Did he know Xena would do this?

When I woke up, I ran to the cafeteria, ready to take all of the refugees out of that hell hole and to a place where I knew they would be safe. Malik had told me that there was a place for them, and as long as we could sneak them out, Xena and Ezekiel would never be the wiser.

It was a chance to save the dying group of people that never knew any better than the trapped lives they were given.

A chance to change something.

A chance to do something *good* for once.

And then I saw the blood splattered across the walls, and that message...

"How did they know?" I asked and looked towards Malik.

He was the traitor in their mind too now.

No longer could he play the manipulator for their side, now they knew the truth.

"I do not know," he answered, the smile dropping from his face.

"But you knew they would do this," I said, a small bit of venom filling my voice.

Amr squeezed my hand.

"Not in relation to defecting," Rae said, calling my attention back to her.

At the edges of my being I could feel the familiar push of her emotions. The same ones she used when we had slept in her dorm.

They were warm and caused tears to well up in my eyes...but it wasn't enough to quench the fire that was burning through my veins. The hatred for those monsters had been festering silently below my skin, waiting for its final blow...and this was it.

This was the moment it had been waiting for.

It was ready to wreak havoc. It wanted to tear them apart and make them pay for what they did to those poor people.

"In relation to what then?" I said in a softer tone, letting her powers ease over me.

The bunched muscles in my back relaxed.

"They were always going to do it," Eli said with an annoyed tone. "Don't you get it? They didn't care for them, and now that they are fleeing they don't need the extra mess."

"And they knew it would mess with you," Malik added on.

I swallowed thickly.

"A weak enemy is one they do not have to worry about," Rae continued. "They preyed on your unhinged magic. And probably Daxton's in turn, knowing yours would call to his."

I turned from them to the doctor that was watching me with interest. Or at least I assumed he was the doctor. His hair was almost fully grey except for a few strands of black. He had a pair of circular glasses that inched down his nose, giving me a good look at his brown eyes.

"I'm sorry," I said in a low voice. "I was…"

"Startled," he finished for me with a smile. "Don't worry. Does anything hurt?"

"No," I said quickly and looked over to a sleeping Daxton. "What about him?"

The doctor's face fell slightly.

"His case is…a bit different," he said and then there was a pause.

"Which is?" I asked.

"We shouldn't talk about it until he is awake," the doctor said with a forced smile.

Anger sparked deep in my belly. I deserved to know, I wanted to help him.

"His magic is killing him," Eli spoke out.

I froze, every nerve in my body on edge.

"You're lying," I spit at them.

They met me with a disbelieving stare and a raised brow.

"I am the only one telling you the truth, mutant," they growled back.

The nickname pulled a growl out of me and I felt my magic spike wildly around me.

"It's not killing him," Malik hissed and hit the back of Eli's head.

They glared at him and stood to fight but Rae cleared her throat. They both sent her a look before frowning and turning away from each other.

"The Original magic is having adverse effects on his natural magic," the doctor said with a sigh. "His life could be in danger, if he is not careful. If his magic is calmed by that of an Original then he can last longer, though I have never seen a case like this before if I am being honest."

I nodded and sent a helpless look at Amr. We couldn't lose him, not after all of this. I couldn't even think what a life without him would look like. He didn't deserve all this. He was the victim in this situation and I felt even worse that it was me who brought him into this.

If I would have just completed my task without him, maybe we would have been better off.

"We will figure it out," he whispered.

I let out a sigh, though I was anything but relieved. This whole thing was a mess and the rage that was so carefully hidden within me came tumbling to the surface.

"Am I good to go?" I asked the doctor. "Maybe take him with me?"

"There is not anything else I can do, so feel free to leave but you are more than welcome to stay."

I gave him a small smile.

"I am not much for hospitals," I said with a grimace, remembering the last time I awoke in a hospital.

He sent me a look before looking towards Malik.

"We are not in a hospital, Rosie," Malik said.

As his words sunk in my heart picked up speed.

"The safe house," I breathed.

"The safe house," he confirmed a light twinkling in his eyes.

A spark pushed its way through my body, lighting up a once desolate darkness.

I looked around and noticed more than a few beds filled. Squinting I saw that patients laying in bed had this sort of magical film on them that shimmered in the light.

"What is wrong with them?" I asked.

"They are aging fast," the doctor responded and looked over at his patients. "The magical barrier protects them from aging while I figure out how to save them."

"There are less here now," Rae noted, her eyes snapping over the empty beds with a furrowed brow.

"Yes," the doctor said and cleared his throat. "Those who have been rapidly decaying even with the barrier have been moved to rooms where they can be more comfortable."

I swallowed thickly.

"So those ones are lost causes?" I asked, a lump forming in my throat.

Was there really no way to save them?

"I wouldn't like to call them lost causes, Ms. Miller," he said with a frown. "Though some have families and would like them to be comfortable in case they pass."

I nodded, no one else spoke and just let me stew in my own thoughts.

"Show me the rest of the safe house."

* * *

After confirmation from both Amr, Rae, and the doctor that they would watch over Daxton while I was gone, I set out to explore the hideaway that Malik had built for the others.

I was almost tempted to stay with them and explain all that had happened in Marques's manor...but that would have to wait. That would be a long conversation and I couldn't wait another second to see the people who were saved.

I needed it after what I just witnessed.

The rooms were mostly empty save for a sleeping child or breastfeeding mother. The real crowd was in the "main room" as Malik liked to call it.

When we entered it my mouth dropped.

"An old warehouse served as the perfect hideout," Malik said from my side.

The space was huge and the ceiling spanned on forever. Tables littered the area and I caught a scent of delicious smelling food that made my mouth water.

People of all ages were surrounding the tables laughing, and joyfully talking as if they had not just been imprisoned for years on end. Though I could understand it.

They finally escaped the grimy fingers of the Originals and had a life where they were safe and free to live however they wanted.

The laughter and smiling faces warmed my heart, but the bitterness in my mouth didn't leave.

They were the lucky ones that still had a life to live while the others were murdered without remorse. I tried not to let my anger sour the mood; the people here deserved to be happy.

"How long do they have to stay like this?" I asked.

While I was beyond ecstatic to see them happy, this was not a life.

"Until those fuckers are dead," Eli growled next to me.

Their voice was loud enough to turn a few heads and I felt a jolt when I recognized the smiling bartender that was once in charge of the portal to the town.

"Eli!" he yelled. "Bring your lady over!"

My heart skipped a beat as Eli threw an arm over my shoulder and dragged me towards them.

"Wa—it, Eli *no*," I stuttered trying to look cool as a whole crowd of people turned to look at me. Some faces were recognizable but mostly it was just the bartender that I remembered.

"Son, what a catch," a man with a beard and long hair said. He chuckled as he lifted the drink to his lips.

"It's good to see you again," I said mostly to the bartender.

He sent me a smile and motioned for the others to pour me a drink.

I took the glass from a random witch with shaking hands and a wavering smile.

Don't be so dramatic, mutant, Eli sneered in my mind.

So this is what you meant when you said you would be worse? I egged on. *A nickname?*

They sent me an image of me tied over a school desk with that Winterfell skirt pulled up over my waist. I watched as they slapped my bare ass.

I would leave you there, they said. *For all students to see. Let them do whatever they wanted to you as I watched.*

I shuddered.

Don't test me, they warned.

"So what took you so long?" the bartender asked.

The image of "traitor" written in blood all over the cafeteria filled my mind.

"I—"

"Had a breakdown," Eli finished for me.

I sent them a glare.

"You are horrible," the bearded man muttered with a slight laugh.

"You get an extra," the witch that handed me my drink said while lifting a bottle of whiskey to my cup.

"Rosie," Malik's voice interrupted.

A wave of relief washed over me as I realized I was being saved from this hell.

As I turned I sent him a grateful smile, but it quickly turned into a look of horror as I saw the woman standing next to him.

"Oh, *it's you,*" Eli said as they turned to look at the newcomer next to Malik.

"How do you...?"

The words wouldn't come out. They dried up in my throat as did all of the assuredness and confidence I worked on in the last year. Every raging emotion in me plus my magic seemed to silence when her blue eyes met mine.

"She was next to my cell," Eli said. "Don't you remember? It was when you came to my cell—"

"This is what you took," I said, the air rushing from my lungs.

My low-level mother looked exactly the same as I left her. Her black hair still fell silkily over her shoulders and her small frame was crouched over as if she wanted to bury her existence.

The same mother that made my life hell as the curse ran rampant through my body.

The same mother that cared more about image than her daughter.

"Yes," Malik spoke. "I asked Matt to remove both yours and Amr's memory."

"Rosie," she said in a soft voice.

It was softer than I ever heard.

"You said a safe house," I accused.

He gave me a look that told me I should know better by now.

You should kill this one too, Eli said in my head. *Count it as practice.*

Oh god, I felt as though I was going to be sick. Her eyes flitted to the drink in my hand and with the only strength left I brought it to my lips and tilted my head back, drinking the entirety in one gulp.

"If this is you trying to redeem yourself, I don't want it," I growled at Malik.

"Rosie," my mother chided. I froze on spot.

I can't deal with this, I sent to Eli as I felt my skin heat to extreme levels. The once silent magic was boiling under my skin.

Why was she here? I left her—them—oh god, is my father here?

I thought Winterfell would be my ticket out, but here she was looking as healthy as I left her. Her long black hair was pulled into a low ponytail and she wore a beaded shirt and pants that looked far too expensive to be here in this safe house.

The walls felt like they were closing in on me and the noise from the people around us became louder. A layer of sweat appeared on my skin and I had to push myself into Eli in order to steady my swaying legs.

First the death of my patients and then this?

How could I even begin to explain how this happened? She had to know at least some of it right? Did she remember Xena?

I need out, please.

When they didn't answer I began to panic.

Please, Eli I beg you.

"Let's come back," Malik said with a smile to my mother. She frowned but nodded.

"Find me before you leave Rosie," she said. "We need to talk, as a *family*."

We are not family, I thought bitterly. We never were and never would be. The moment I stepped out of their life and into Winterfell was the best moment of my life and while fraught with challenges and pain...I preferred it to their company.

She eyed Eli with a scowl before turning and walking back to the hallway that kept the rooms.

"Rosie, I didn't realize—"

"Let's not talk about it?" I said quickly cutting Malik off. "Please."

He nodded before sighing and looking around.

"The clam chowder guy is around here somewhere," he muttered. "Let's get you some food."

I nodded and looked up towards Eli.

"You didn't help," I snapped.

Their eyes slowly shifted to mine and I was faced with an expression more serious than I had ever gotten from Eli before.

"I'll kill her," they said. "Will that make you satisfied since you cannot find yourself to do it?"

A cold shock ran through my body. I searched their face looking for any sign that this was a joke.

A smirk.

A twinkle in their eyes...but there was nothing.

"No-o," I said, caught off guard by their offer. "I don't want to do that."

They looked back towards where my mother had walked away to.

"I think you do want that," they murmured. "She was a horrible mother anyway and will only hold you back. The last thing we need is another loose end."

My mouth went dry and my heart went into overdrive.

"Please don't," I begged, not liking the eerie stillness in their expression. It was intense and I knew that they were weighing the decision heavily in their mind.

"I am," they said. "I just don't understand, I thought you were stronger than that." They looked back towards me. "Maybe I need to teach you."

"Let's go eat," I said quickly, trying to move away from this subject.

Whether or not I decided to forgive my mother was one thing, but there was no way that I would let Eli near her.

Chapter 9
Malik

Xena and Ezekiel fleeing was both the worst thing that has happened in my existence...and also the best.

The weight of their presence disappeared in the night with them and as I stared at the joyfully laughing demons around me, I couldn't help but think that even through all the bad...we did something good.

After all the years of death and pain, there was *finally* something I could proudly say that we did right. It took a while for us to get here, and the path here was gnarled and filled with broken glass, the people were less than honorable...but *we did it*.

And now, we had everyone right where they needed to be. The Originals were missing but we couldn't let that put a damper on our plans. If anything, it was the break we needed.

It would give us time to train those who had ingested Marques's blood, and once they were ready...it would be a piece of cake.

My chest ached and a shiver of excitement ran through me. We were so close.

I shifted uncomfortably against the wall of the makeshift dining room and searched for Rosie.

My heart melted when I saw her sitting with Eli and eating clam chowder out of a chipped bowl. The demons around her were chatting away and she was obviously failing at trying to keep up with their tempo.

She would take a bite then smile with her mouth full and nod as if the man who was talking to her was saying the most interesting thing in the world. Then, when there was a pause she would dip back down and eat again.

I had lost count of how many times they had asked her if she was enjoying her food.

I realized in that moment, that this was the life she was supposed to live. Going forward she could be a normal college student and live her life without interference from crazed Originals.

I couldn't take this away from her, I thought. *I couldn't steal away her last hope as a real college student. The others be dammed, they had had their fair share of life, but her...*

I promised I wouldn't lie to her, and I wouldn't anymore. But I would be dammed if I let her be dragged into this plan. As much as she wanted revenge for the refugees and to get back at her birth mother...I would try and shield the weight for as long as I could.

And it started with finding where those fuckers were hiding.

The faster I found them, the faster Rosie and the other would be able to live in peace.

I caught Eli's sidelong glance and raised a brow at them.

Their lips quirked before turning back to Rosie. By the look on her face and quickly reddening cheeks I could tell that Eli was no doubt filling that mind of hers with dirty thoughts.

My curiosity for her never wavered. How could someone so young be so resilient? Someone who had magic that was far too powerful for their body sitting amongst all these people and eating clam chowder as though it was a family reunion, when not an hour ago she was bursting at the seams?

I pulled myself out from my thoughts and with a prayer that Rosie wouldn't hate me, turned back to the medical bay. With the rowdy crowd, it wasn't hard to silently slip out and in between bodies until I found myself closing in on the room.

Here goes nothing.

As I peeked in I saw that Daxton was now sitting up and talking to Amr while Rae was sitting in the bed Rosie was once occupying. They were in deep conversation and Daxton's eyebrows were pulled together. Amr had a blank expression and his arms were crossed.

Looking at Daxton, I couldn't help but feel for him.

His parents had to be the worst of them all, and even though Marques had no intention of having them fuck up Daxton's life as badly as they did... there should have been something we could do.

We weren't saints. We had killed people, lied, stolen, anything illegal you can bet that we already did it.

But we never harmed kids and Marques would never have allowed it if he could stop it.

It had been a shock when Rosie told me what they did...but somehow there was something in me that wasn't surprised at the cruelty of those people.

I was too caught up in the double life and preparing for Rosie's introduction into the world that I never thought to think about the others who were just as affected by the Originals' cruelty.

Even Eli...

Rae looked up at me through her glasses as I walked past and stopped her talk mid-conversation only to go back to her little black notebook and begin writing furiously. I tried to lean over and catch a glimpse of what she had written, but she snatched it back with a glare.

"If you are here to ask us to help you, we refuse," she hissed.

I sent her a smile.

"How did you know?" I teased. "Maybe I should have come to you all along since you are so *all knowing.*"

She let out a huff and slipped the book back into her jacket pocket. The little comment seemed to upset her and she turned her head away from me.

Such children.

"Can't you just stop this?" she asked.

"Stop what?" I asked with a raised brow. "You mean trying to figure out a way to get rid of those homicidal Originals? The ones that forced you to kill your parents? Those ones?"

Her tone pissed me off more than Eli's ever had. With Eli it was like dealing with a kid, but Rae was more on Rosie's level of annoyance.

They both had that one look like they knew what they would say would get under your skin, but Rosie found entertainment out of it and Rae... She just stated it matter-of-factly.

That was much more infuriating. She acted like I hadn't been around for a millennia before her. Like I hadn't *literally* built this would with my bare hands.

"Stop creating a *bigger mess,*" she said with conviction, her eyes finally meeting mine.

"A mess?" I growled. "The *only* reason you are still alive is because *I* allowed it!"

The doctor who was currently hovering over a patient cleared his throat and sent me a knowing look. I swallowed my anger and gave Rae an expectant look.

"If we are not *all* involved, we cannot help," she said in a calm voice.

"You think it's not possible that Rosie will find out again? Do you realize how mad she was I kept something? *Again?* And you just want to do it again? What if next time she gets hurt because of her lack of knowledge? You said anyways we would try to get her onboarded to the plan, what changed?"

There was a sigh and I turned to see Daxton glaring at me.

"Don't act like we are not here," he growled. "You forget that we have been just as ignored as Rosie. It was *my* parents that were on the hit list. We deserve to know what's happening too."

I shrugged and sat down on the bed next to Rae. She made a noise and shifted away from me.

"The more people that know—"

"Don't pull that," Daxton interrupted. "We don't trust you for shit and we need to know going forward that we *will not* be kept in the dark any longer."

That little— Trust? He literally doesn't understand all the lashings and beatings I had to go through to keep these fuckers safe.

Rage began boiling under my skin and my hand clenched into fists, nails digging into my palms.

I was trying to keep it together not only because of the witnesses, but because I knew that brave little hybrid had a soft spot for these children and would never forgive me if I hurt them...but I was on the edge of showing them what my power could *really* do.

"I cannot trust an uncontrollable witch and a familiar—"

"Do not speak as though we are below you," Amr said with a sneer.

I hadn't been around him enough to know much about his personality but I knew enough to understand that the familiar must really hate me.

He probably only feels comfortable enough to talk back because the Originals are gone. I will never forget the way he stood in front of Rosie and bowed on her behalf as if that pitiful show would ever protect them.

"Well," I said with a slight smile. "I *am* much older than you."

Rae let out an annoyed sigh.

"It doesn't matter anymore," Rae said. "They will be involved from now on."

"You can't just make that—"

"I didn't," she said, her hazel eyes burning holes into my face. I could feel the tension between us rise sharply. We were mere inches away from each other and it would be so easy to cross this distance and force her to obey. "I asked Marques, and he approved it."

"You went behind my back," I said, grinding my teeth together in order to keep myself from yelling out.

A part of me thought that she was lying, but I knew with a simple check with Marques he would say the same. After all, he wanted the results. It was me who he left most of the groundwork to. If he thought this would guarantee a win, he would support it.

"I did," she confirmed. "Told them the whole story and then some while you were flaunting Rosie around to the others. Trying to win her over."

"I wasn't flaunting," I scoffed and looked at her.

Her sharp eyes met mine and suddenly I felt small.

It was as though her gaze alone made the world around me double in size and a spike of fear shot up my spine. The same annoyance and anger turned into something far more potent.

I began to sweat and my heart picked up pace as if I had just finished fighting hand to hand with a witch.

"*Remove* your power before I show you the strength of mine," I threatened.

Her jaw twitched and the fear that had wormed its way into my body dissipated.

"I removed it because I am tired of fighting, not because you told me to," she clarified, her eyes never leaving mine.

She knew how my power worked and so for her to meet my eyes it not only told me that she wasn't afraid of me, but that she had the audacity to think that even if I did use my power that no harm would come to her.

I swallowed my retort.

"Are you not tired, Malik?" Amr asked.

I shifted my gaze to his. His chocolate eyes bore into mine and only then could I see the years of struggle behind them. Being stuck in that cat's body must have been hell for him.

"I am," I admitted, my voice coming out more hoarse than I'd like.

"Then let's do this right," he urged. "You need our help and we refuse to do it without her."

I don't need your help, I hissed internally.

But I did.

Matt was no longer reliable. I understood that now after seeing his reaction to Rosie. I knew to an extent the act was a facade, but the coldness in his eyes...

I could not chance putting my trust in the wrong people this late in the game. And if Rosie could trust these people, then I would have to too.

"I want her to have a normal college experience," I said truthfully. Saying it out loud made me cringe. "I don't want her to fight, or fear any longer. This wasn't how it was supposed to be... I just wanted to keep her alive."

The truth. This was it. Words and sentiments I had never spoken aloud to anyone else before. An admission that I was thinking of her in a way that was not just for the better of our world.

I was no longer thinking of her as *just the hybrid*—the mindset forced upon me by Xena and Ezekiel as I got too close to each and every hybrid they created.

It had been hordes of them and while I could remember every one of their faces, I couldn't get attached. Wouldn't allow myself to because in the end it always hurt.

But with her...

From the start there was something different with her.

Amr's gaze finally slid from mine to the floor. Daxton's locked on his hands and I watched as they clutched the blanket so hard his knuckles turned white.

"While I know the others concur with your sentiment," Rae said drawing my attention back to her stoic face. "No one here has the luxury of normalcy anymore. And I for one do not want to see what happens when she finds out we kept this from her."

I too was worried about what would happen if she put this together on her own. Would the magic in her finally explode? Would she go on a rampage?

This was also a risk we needed to consider and I couldn't be blinded by my affections when it came to this.

"Fine," I said with a sigh. "We will rest, and when it is safe we will discuss the plan."

I swear I could feel Rae's satisfaction rolling off her in waves.

"Why rest?" Daxton asked, an edge to his voice.

I looked him up and down with a raised brow.

"You both ended up in the hospital," I said. "And if you want to get through the first week of school, I suggest you *both* stock up on magic."

He let out a growl.

"But the longer we wait the better they will be at hiding," he spat.

A silence filled the space between us as I tried to swallow my annoyance.

"He's right," said a voice from behind us.

God damn it, I cursed internally.

Looking over my shoulder I wasn't surprised to see Eli and Rosie standing mere feet away from us.

How much did she hear?

If she heard that I wanted to keep this from her...would she be angry?

I searched her face for a reaction but there was none. That brave face was back for all to see and I hated that face so much in that moment.

I wanted her to be angry, be scared... Just anything other than ready to face the trial that lay ahead.

Too many people have died with that same exact face and I can't let that happen to her.

"If we do not try to catch up to them, we may never find them again," she said.

Anger boiled up in me as I heard a grunt of agreement from Daxton.

"Who said the plan was to go after them, hm?" I snapped.

Her eyes widened just a fraction before her jaw twitched. Her brown eyes never wavered from mine as if just like Rae, she was challenging me to do my worst.

"They killed the refugees," she argued. "Made our lives hell and forced us to kill needlessly. We just let those demons run wild? Marques himself said that they are an abomination so why the *fuck*—"

"They are probably long gone by now," Rae spoke up, cutting Rosie off. I watched as her mouth slammed shut and she sent a glare towards Rae.

"The blood was fresh," Daxton countered. "They can't be far."

"Exactly!" Rosie chimed in.

"You really think they would do their own dirty work?" Rae asked raising an eyebrow at Rosie. "After what you went through you *really* think they would want to get their hands dirty like that? Think about it. They were long gone before you even stepped foot in the cafeteria."

The tension was rising fast and I could feel it prickling against my skin. A dull throb started near my temple.

"Finding them isn't an issue," I said finally. "We have the strongest of their team with us. We can reach them whenever we want... But the fact remains, we are not ready to fight the Originals."

Eli let out a huff of a laugh.

"When will we ever be?" they asked.

"That's why we work with Marques," Rae interjected. Suddenly I was glad to have at least someone with a rational thought by my side. "He can help us prepare. If we rush this, we die."

I noted the blood part of this deal was conventionally left out of her words.

"Let them get comfortable," I said with a small smile. "We will hit them when they are least expecting it."

Rosie's gaze fell to her feet.

"Okay," she said in a small voice.

"Okay," I said with a sigh.

I watched as she shifted uncomfortably on her feet. No doubt wanting to retreat back into that persona I had the pleasure of knowing when we first met.

"Who is the strongest?" Amr asked stirring me from my thoughts.

A smile spread to my face.

"My favorite pair of magical siblings," I said. "When we are ready, they can help us find them."

Chapter 10
Rosie

I was less than thrilled to find myself in Winterfell—*again*. A part of me wished that I could just run away from this cursed place forever, but Winterfell had claws and each time I came back they dug deeper into my being and tied me to this place in unimaginable ways.

A place that was once so full of light and hope, had become stained with the sins of the Originals and was no more the reputable demon academy that everyone sought after.

As I walked the halls I felt a sort of acceptance wash over me. The darkness that was intertwined with the bricks of Winterfell no longer felt frightening. It felt like I was coming home. As much as I tried to reject this part of Winterfell, as much as I tried to turn a blind eye and run in the other direction...it felt like I was meant to be here no matter how much my brain told me otherwise.

My body relaxed as I felt the familiar old magic that built Winterfell brush across my senses.

The footsteps of Malik, Eli, Rae, Daxton, and Amr echoed behind me, none of them stopping me from where I felt compelled to visit.

I had planned to stay away from the cafeteria for as long as I could, but my body had a mind of its own and my feet began to guide me to the burial ground.

When I pushed open the doors to the cafeteria a rush of magic hit me and I had to grit my teeth in order to steady myself as my own magic tried to lash out. The aura of the place was dark, even though the walls were now free of blood, and settled uncomfortably in my belly.

Claudine and Maximus were in the middle of the newly cleaned cafeteria and turned to us as we entered. Claudine's bright smile sent a warmth through me and I couldn't help but return it.

She had been a surprising ally and friend that I didn't know I was lucky enough to have.

"I am sorry, Rosie," she said in a wistful tone as she walked towards me. "I know you cared for them."

I swallowed the lump in my throat. Maximus looked us over with an unreadable expression and I saw his gaze flicker when Eli's arm wrapped around my shoulders.

I don't know if Eli knew how much the simple gesture comforted me, but even something as little as this grounded me to this world.

"Thank you," I replied and leaned into Eli. A warm hand found mine and I immediately knew it was Amr's. His magic brushed against mine in a comforting manner and I felt my throat tighten.

"At least we are ready for school," Amr said from beside me. "You have a lot to handle this year."

I nodded and looked over the new cafeteria. Not much had changed from the semester before but every surface had been polished and shone lightly as the morning sun cascaded through the window. The tables and benches now covered what used to be hundreds of beds for the refugees and at the very end there was a buffet and checkout.

Last night we came back to Winterfell late and even as I slept between Daxton and Amr, I could feel this place call to me in my sleep, begging for me to come take a look.

A part of me hoped that I was being called to this place because there was something waiting for me. Maybe a lost refugee that escaped, or a scrap of something that proved that hundreds of people lived and suffered here this summer...but there was nothing except the small barely visible traces of magic that they left.

The absence hurt more, I realized.

Because now, the lives that I tried so hard to save, just faded away into the dark history of this place, never to be seen again and leaving only a handful of people with their memory.

I wished I had asked them about their families, wished I could have found a connection to the outside for them...but I was too late. Now no one would know how they suffered.

And it was all her fucking fault.

Xena's smirk filled my mind and anger exploded inside me. She used me. Made me believe that she actually had a plan to help out the refugees.

I was so stupid.

Eli let out a snort.

Hold on to that anger, they said. *It's very sexy.*

My lips twitched at their words, but it was the reminder I needed.

I needed to hold onto this anger and mold it into something useful. Now that they had fled, we had a lot of work to do in order to bring them down, and make them pay for what they have done to not only our lives, but the countless other lives they had erased due to their own cowardice.

"Can we just take back the program?" I asked and turned to catch the white-haired demon behind us.

Since last night he had been silently following behind us. My guess was he either had nothing to do now that the Originals were gone...or was just worried that we would fuck something up while he was gone.

My bet was on the latter.

Even though the Originals were gone, that didn't mean we could stop pushing forward, and who knows what they had planned? I didn't really buy that they were just hiding away.

Xena and Ezekiel were cowards that much was for sure, but they weren't weak.

Malik gave me a sad smile. The same one he had shown me so many times before. It was a small glimpse of the demon I had become so comfortable around.

My chest tightened.

"It was already announced to the public. Going back on it would not do well for Winterfell's image," he said. "Just entertain them for a while as they get used to the school."

"It's not just entertaining," I grumbled and shifted my gaze.

In between saving the refugees and meetings with the Originals, Principal Winterfell sought me out and explained exactly what my duties entailed. Needless to say, I was horrified.

I was a mentor to all of them. I was supposed to explain the rules, show them their dorms, and help them navigate this new world full of angry high-level demons. I would have to be there at all hours and at their beck and call.

I didn't have the time, nor desire to mentor a bunch of new students after I spent so long trying to fight for my life. I didn't want to pretend anymore that this place was the magical academy it pretended to be. I knew the truth now and I would hate having to lie to innocent low-levels who had no idea what they were getting into.

They were going to come here excited, hopeful that *they* could change the world... Just like I had been. And I had to watch as their dreams were crushed right before their eyes.

I was stuck between two conflicting desires.

Retreat into a hole and never come out.

And scream at the top of my lungs at the incoming low-levels. Tell them to run. Tell them that none of this was worth it and that it was all a fraud.

"How many are there?" Amr asked, his hand squeezing my shoulder.

"Two hundred thirty-seven," Malik and I said at the same time. I turned back to look at him. The sad smile was still on his face.

"The first semester will be the worst," Rae said from beside Malik. "After that they should get the hang of it."

God I fucking hope so, I groaned internally.

If I had to hold their hands for the entire year I might as well be considered useless when it came to our plans.

"When are they coming?" Amr asked drawing my attention back to him. His voice was soft as he asked, obviously one of the only people realizing just how nervous I was.

On cue the doors behind us opened and a flustered Rhonda walked in.

I hadn't seen our lunch lady friend for a long time and my chest tugged painfully when I looked at her sweet face. She had been the first warm person that I had the pleasure to meet and I wished that I would have made more of an effort to get to know her.

Close behind her followed her staff, about fifteen low-levels all wearing aprons and looking equally as flustered as her. Rhonda didn't even look at me as she passed our group.

"Food won't be for a while!" she yelled back at us. "Go lounge somewhere else."

I tried not to feel hurt at her dismissal.

"They will be here soon," I murmured to Amr as I watched Rhonda bark orders to her staff. "Some are coming tonight actually."

Claudine turned to me with a smile.

"Have you thought of what to say to them when they come?" she asked.

I shook my head.

"The first meeting is in three days, then most if not all the students will have—"

"The cafeteria is closed!" she yelled back at us. Not a single flash of recognition spread across her face as we locked eyes and I understood now that Matt's power had to be the most sinister of them all.

"Let's go," I whispered.

As we walked out of the cafeteria Claudine, Maximus, and Malik were about to give their goodbyes but I stopped them.

"Malik, Rae," I called. Both turned to me with a questioning gaze. "Can you stay to talk?"

Eli's nails dug into my arm.

Why are you pushing me away? they asked in my mind.

I just want to question them about when we are going to Marques again, I said. *They work better in a smaller group.*

There was a pause as they weighed my words.

"Fine," they spat and pulled their arm from my side. Amr leaned down to leave a kiss on my head which was followed by Daxton's lips at my ear.

"Don't take too long," he whispered. "You heard what they said about sharing magic."

A shiver ran up my spine and I sent him a look as he left. My magic lashed around me, trying to follow him down the hall but I stayed in my spot, ignoring the two demons in front of me until everyone else had left.

"I need a date," I said to them, finally looking over to where they stood.

Malik had his arms crossed over his chest while Rae stood to the side, an arm resting on her hip.

"For?" Malik asked.

"You know what for," I growled. "Curse training and planning."

He straightened and looked back down the hallway.

"Before the first set of rankings," he said in an annoyed tone.

"A date," I hissed.

A scowl marred his scarred face and I could have sworn I heard the grinding of his teeth from across the hall.

"Three Wednesdays from now," he spit out and closed the space between us.

I stood my ground and stared at him, even as his golden eyes glared at me. His breathing was heavy and his chest almost touched my own.

His warm scent filled my senses and I had the urge to fall into him, but I kept my face blank and my feet planted. If I caved now, none of these demons would take me seriously regardless of my bloodline. I needed to show them that I was not one to bend easily, and that went for all of them.

Matt had been a sole example of that, taking advantage of my weakness and playing me like an instrument. On top of that, Malik already tried once more to keep me out of the planning, I was lucky to have someone like Rae and Daxton to push for my inclusion. Now that we had come so far, I couldn't chance any more time in the dark. It was time to take control and fight for my freedom.

"Seems perfect," I purred and let a smile tug at my lips. "Unless there is something bothering you?"

He swallowed, his eyes trailing my face before he spoke.

"We need to clarify some things," he said finally.

"We seem pretty clear," I said with an even bigger smile. "Now if you'd excuse me, I have some things to talk to Rae about."

His eyes flashed and his hand came up to grip my chin. It wasn't enough to actually hurt but he put enough pressure to remind me that he held my life literally between his hands.

"*I* am in charge here, Rosie," he spat. "Don't get cocky because you snuck into his hideout. That was Matt's fault for not being diligent. And don't think your little trick with Claudine passed right by me."

My eyes widened at the mention of Claudine's name.

"That's right," he said. "Who do you think she came to for help, hm?"

With my face still in his hands he ripped open the remaining button of his shirt. There, right under his heart, was the same symbol I had tattooed on me.

"How long have you...?" I trailed. My mind was having trouble forming coherent sentences.

My mouth went dry at the image of him half shirtless in front of me. The tattoos didn't stop at his arms and instead littered his torso as well, but there was more than that symbol that interested me; right next to it was one that I didn't recognize.

"Not long," he admitted. "I couldn't, not with *them* watching me. My mind was too open, and I couldn't risk them learning of Marques's plans. Wiping my mind was the safest way."

I swallowed thickly and nodded. I couldn't imagine what it was like to entrust Matt with erasing my memory...and *so much* of it.

"Do I need to get that one too?" I asked, my eyes still fixated on his bare torso.

I wanted to reach out so badly and run my hands up the planes of his stomach. There were scars that slashed his body spelling out his pain with the Originals and I couldn't help but think how similar he and I were.

If my mother was just a bit more careless I may have ended up looking like him.

"No," he said in a soft voice. "I think what Claudine taught you was better. Or am I wrong?"

The mind-reading, I realized. He really knew it all.

"Just a way to clean up the mind," I said with a small smile. "No magic involved at all but it does the trick."

A bit of meditation, surprisingly enough. Claudine taught me how to compartmentalize my thoughts so that it would be harder for people like Ezekiel, who read surface thoughts, to get anything out of me.

It was a work in progress, and something I was far from proficient at, but it helped enough to keep me safe.

His scowl finally broke and he let go of me.

"Don't do anything stupid while I am gone," he said and paused before continuing. "And give your all to the low-levels, Rosie. You know all too well what it was like coming into a school where everyone hated you."

I remembered it all too clearly, actually. And I remembered him helping me out, even under the guise of something completely different... He was there when I needed him.

But that wasn't the Malik I craved now, I wanted the one that threw me against the wall, the one that got angry if I talked back. That was Malik in his truest form and I loved every minute of it.

"I'll try," I said in a weak voice. He nodded to me then to Rae before leaving us.

I watched as he walked away, wishing that he could stay because unlike the others, I had no idea when he would be back. And I had no idea if he would be safe.

His and Eli's life still remained a mystery to me. I didn't know what to expect when they came home after whatever it was they did. Would they come home bloody and beaten? Would they keel over from lack of sleep?

The worries never stopped.

I heard Rae stand next to me and looked up to her with a smile.

She didn't smile back fully but I saw the corner of her lips twitch. I grabbed one of her hands and squeezed it. It had been far too long since she and I had time together and I was grateful that she even allowed this much.

We hadn't been able to talk much, but I could see she was struggling. She would leave us often and only come by every once in a while, and even when she did...she seemed distant with her mind focused on other things.

I didn't ever bring up what happened last summer. Why would I?

I understood better now. None of the others had a choice and all thought they were doing what was best for us. And I had seen her advocate for me with my own two eyes.

"Are you okay?" I asked her. "Your siblings?"

Her eyes widened and I watched her swallow twice before she moved to answer. I waited patiently letting her gather her words.

"We are fine," she said in a voice hoarser than normal. "We did not expect the amount that Father had taken care of when he was alive."

"Work?" I asked. She shook her head and ran her thumb across my knuckles.

I recognized it as a soothing gesture but it wasn't me who needed soothing.

"The house, the finances," she admitted though her words came out slow and forced. "He was in charge of seeing to it before and now it is only my brothers and me."

"I can imagine that they would be a bit hard to work with," I whispered remembering the way Nathaniel and Benjamin had been as they accompanied me for the short time I was in Rae's house. They were mischievous and adventurous enough that I doubt menial work like housekeeping and crunching numbers would keep them entertained for long.

"Yes, well." She let out a heavy sigh, her eyes falling to our intertwined fingers. "They are doing better. Though I am very busy. I came here this morning to make sure you and the others were alright, but I will have to leave soon."

I swallowed my disappointment and sent her a smile. Standing on my tip-toes I leaned forward and planted a light kiss on her mouth. As I pulled away her hand slid into my hair and pulled my lips back to her.

She gave me a hungry kiss that stole the breath right out of me. She had packed the months of our little interaction into this kiss and kissed me like her life depended on it. It wasn't the sweet comforting kisses I had once experienced from her, these were starved and wanting.

I ate up the attention greedily and pulled at her shirt forcing us closer than we needed to be in the middle of the school hallway. I didn't care who saw us or what they thought. Rae was more important than any one person's thoughts and I wanted to show her as much.

She pulled away leaving me breathless and panting. There was a glint in her eyes.

"I'll bring you home before the end of the year," she promised. "Just let me get everything cleaned up and we can do this again."

I nodded and stepped back from her.

"Walk me to my dorm?" I asked.

She let out a small chuckle.

"I'll do you one better and walk you to Daxton's."

Chapter 11
Amr

I had seen my fair share of witches growing up in a family of would-be familiars. We had to get accustomed to working with them anyways, so my parents would drag me and my siblings along wherever they could. It was normal and each time I would shake a witch's hand I would be simultaneously sizing them up and trying to see exactly what type of employer they would be. Those meetings were where I figured out all the different types of witches that littered this earth, and I got pretty good at seeing the secrets they tried to hide.

Some were openly evil. They fell deep into the darkness their unmanaged magic grew inside them and they were the easiest to pick out. Their magic was sticky and felt uncomfortable as it stretched across your skin. *Dirty*. That happened when a witch got far too consumed in the darkness their magic carried. It was easy if they were not careful, they could be changed by their magic. Those were the witches shunned by our society and it was all too obvious as soon as you came across them. They were forced underground and they had little to no chance to live a normal life, and while some hid it better than others, their path was almost certain from the moment they first lost themselves.

The more I watched Daxton, the more worried that I became that he was on that same exact path. I had tried to watch over him, take as much of his magic as possible...but it never seemed to suffice. He seemed to come back with magic even stronger and angrier every single time.

But I would be damned if I let anyone take him away from us.

I am sure Rosie felt the same, but there was no denying that Daxton was changing and it was only a matter of time before people started to notice. Daxton was shielded somewhat by his parents because they were corrupted and wanted people to look anywhere but inwards, and now that they were gone...he was the person in the limelight. He was the last known witch of his immediate bloodline and there were already people lining up to talk to him about his future.

It was terrifying.

I watched this boy grow into a man. I watched his parents abuse him and use him however they deemed fit. Even through all that he had still remained resilient. He held onto Eli and Rae, pushing forward in hopes of a better future for himself, one away from his parents.

But now that his parents were gone...he was spiraling. There was nothing to keep him in check, no matter how much I or the others tried.

It was the little things that stood out to me the most.

The lack of sleep, the short fuse, and the insatiable magic.

He thought that I didn't know that he woke up hours before I did and just stared into space. But I did because I was awake too, just waiting there to see what he would do.

During those times I felt him reaching out his magic, draping us in it. It would stay there around us for hours sometimes and I didn't understand the point. Was he checking on us? Was he trying to get rid of excess magic? Protecting us?

I do not know why he felt the need to hide his magic as such. We knew that he had far too much to keep inside of him. I expected it...but he always pulled it back as soon as he felt us stir.

And now as I watched him with Rosie...I couldn't help the tingling sensation running up my spine and making my hair stand on end.

I was already on edge around him since Rosie had her outburst in the cafeteria and when Rae stood outside our dorm with her, I had a gut reaction to push them away and deal with Daxton's magic myself.

Daxton's normally cozy dorm room was now filled with an electric tension running through the three of us. Magic had already started accumulating in the room due to Rosie and Daxton's playing.

I couldn't bring myself to join just yet even as my cock strained against my pants.

I sat silently in the chair adjacent to the bed they were on, watching them intently.

Rosie was kneeling on the floor between Daxton's legs as he sat on the bed completely naked, as was she. His eyes shone with a glint that I had recognized a few times in the years that I had been with him. He had been rougher than was necessary with her, his hand already pulling at Rosie's hair.

From my position, I could not see her face, only her tense back and ass as she teased him. Even without a perfect view of her, I knew the moment that she took Daxton's cock into her mouth by the way he threw his head back and moaned aloud.

I watched as his chest heaved up and down as he panted. His skin was slick with sweat already and his muscles rippled as Rosie's hands began to explore his chest and stomach.

They were magnificent together.

The way their bodies and magic easily intertwined. It was like they were connected in a much deeper way than the others. They didn't even need to speak, just were somehow so in tune with each other that they knew exactly what the other needed.

Even outside of the bedroom, I noticed the way Daxton and Rosie would orbit each other, even when Eli would lead Rosie across the room...Daxton was never far.

I should have noticed it since the first day we encountered her, but I was too wrapped up in the goddess of the woman in front of me that I completely wrote off Daxton's reaction to her.

I shifted uncomfortably in my seat as Daxton's low moans filled the room. I gritted my teeth when he pushed her down so hard on his cock that she gagged. A smirk tugged at his lips and he thrusted up into her mouth.

His eyes were hooded but I watched as they narrowed even further as Rosie took him as deep as she could. He was enjoying watching her struggle.

He used to be embarrassed when he handled her roughly, but now he was leaning into his wilder side. Even fucking her mouth wasn't enough for him and he pushed her head down even further so she couldn't move.

When I heard her choke I let out a growl. Daxton looked over towards me with hooded eyes, his smirk widening, before he thrust up into Rosie's mouth.

He was egging me on. He knew I didn't like when we were rough with her. I was furious when I saw what Eli did to her perfect skin. I was ready to blow, but I reigned myself in and waited for a time when I could show Eli what I *really* thought of their actions.

"Do that again and I'll make you sit there—*alone*—while I fuck her," I threatened.

He gripped Rosie's hair back and forced her off his cock. A line of spit followed her as he did. She gasped for air and stared up at him with wide doe-like eyes.

"He thinks I'm being too rough on you," he said with a small frown. "Do you?"

She shook her head wildly. He smirked and let go of her hair to lean back on the bed. Rosie watched as his hand ran the length of his hardened cock.

I would be lying if that gesture alone did not make my cock pulse with need, but he took it one step further.

"Come here," he said and patted his lap. She crawled up onto the bed and without instructions sunk slowly down onto Daxton's cock. She let out a whimper that filled the room. Daxton's hand came up to her throat and he pulled her to his lips.

They both fell flat to the bed and Rosie began to ride him, her ass slapping against his thighs as she fucked him. I bit back my retort and rubbed myself through my jeans, unable to help myself.

I couldn't deny how much I loved seeing them together and how much it turned me on. A dangerous and enticing dance that they did and I could watch them forever if they let me.

"Amr," Daxton called from the bed.

I watched as his hand traveled to Rosie's ass before spreading her cheeks and giving me a show of the rarely used puckered hole. He wasted no time pushing his fingers into her, pulling a moan from Rosie.

"Damn it all," I growled and stood to strip off my clothes.

I walked to the bedside drawer that held a bottle of lube that Daxton and I had used on occasion. I hesitated going to them until Rosie sat up and looked at me. Daxton's hands moved to grip her hips as he rammed into her from below.

She reached out to me, begging me to come closer even as the words came out garbled due to Daxton's ferocity.

I walked over and positioned myself with one leg between Daxton's and the other bent on the bed. Her arms lifted behind her to wrap around my neck. Her skin was sweaty against mine and her back slapped into me with each of Daxton's trusts.

I put the lube bottle on the bed next to us and wrapped my arms around her so that I could use one hand to roll her nipple between my fingers and the other to rub her clit. She gasped and threw her head back against me. Loud mewls came from out of her mouth and I could feel the magic in her spike rapidly.

"Are you sure you want this, love?" I asked and nipped at her ear.

I trailed my hand lower so I could feel where they were connected, squeezing Daxton in warning as I did. They both shuddered at my movement.

"I want *you*, Amr," she gasped against me.

I chuckled and kissed the side of her sweaty face. My cock was begging for action and each time they met Rosie would brush against me, shooting sparks through me.

"Right after you come," I promised and trailed my hand back up to her clit, putting more pressure on the forgotten nub than before.

She cried out and Daxton groaned.

"She's going to come," he forced out. "Keep going."

His eyes met mine for an instant and I got a look of the Daxton underneath it all. There with his hair sticking to his face, and his skin shiny with sweat, I saw the man I had fallen for.

"*Ah*— Faster, Amr!"

I complied and she let out a strangled sob as she came around Daxton's cock. Her magic flared around us and I felt the sweet potent magic that she had hidden inside her spill into me.

Each time I was taken aback by how addicting the feeling of her magic inside me was.

My own magic rejoiced and I could feel them swirling together until they settled inside of me. But instead of being satisfied, I wanted more.

I took the lube and spread a generous helping on both my cock and her backside. I shuddered as I rubbed my cock down the length of her. I was already so swollen and my balls were so tight with unspent release that I knew it wouldn't be long until I spilled inside of her.

"Prepare yourself love," I whispered and unwound her arms from my neck, to angle her more towards Daxton. "This may hurt a little."

"It's not my first time," she said with a mischievous glint back at me.

I looked down at Daxton with a glare.

"It wasn't me," he said defensively, pausing in his thrusts so I could line myself up at Rosie's entrance.

"Eli," she said. A small bit of anger unfurled inside of me when I realized I wasn't the first but I brushed it away.

This wasn't about me.

I pushed into her slowly at first and then with her encouragement I placed my hands over Daxton's and pulled her down on my cock as far as she would go. I groaned as I felt her squeeze around me. She engulfed me in warmth and fit me so perfectly that I couldn't fathom how I stayed away from this for so long.

She sucked in a sharp breath and I rubbed the length of her spine in a comforting manner, grinding my hips against her lightly. I was easily starting to lose myself. My magic, hers, and Daxton's played at my senses begging me to fuck her senseless.

"How does it feel?" I asked her, my voice dropping deeper. "To be filled by both of us?"

She let out a small whine as I pulled out a little just to push back into her.

"Now I know why Eli calls you a little slut," Daxton purred from underneath her. He thrust up into her once. "I always thought that was just her attitude. But you really are one aren't you? You're gripping onto me so tight that if I didn't know any better I would say you were about to come again."

Rosie sat up, pressing her back against me and pulling me further inside of her.

"Fuck me," she commanded.

With a light chuckle Daxton and I resumed our pace, albeit much slower than before. Rosie's head fell back onto my shoulder as I thrust into her.

"You take us so well," I cooed and reached over to play with her swollen clit. She let out a sob.

"It's too much," she whined as I pinched her clit.

"I know," I whispered in her ear and left kisses on the side of her face. I thrust a bit harder that time and was rewarded with a moan. "But you are doing so good. You don't want us to stop do you?"

She shook her head and tried to stifle her noises but the harder we became with her the less she was able to hide it.

Daxton and I easily found a rhythm that allowed us to pound into her with ease and as I said, she was good at taking us both. Even as her second orgasm came close she didn't shift or move in a way that would disrupt us.

"*Fuck*," she cursed. "I'm coming."

"Me too, *shit*," Daxton hissed.

I continued to play with Rosie's clit until she came with Daxton not far behind her. Just before he fell over the edge Daxton's hand found mine and I was hit with a dose of both of their magic.

It was so strong that my vision went white for a moment before I could regain myself.

"Be a good girl and go kiss him," I whispered to her.

She did as I asked and as soon as their lips met I pulled her hips back to mine, fucking that tight hole harder than I probably should have while I chased my own orgasm.

Her cries were muffled by Daxton's mouth and I felt a warm tingling sensation start low in my belly.

Before I knew it, my magic exploded inside of me and I came inside of her.

I pulled out of her slowly before falling back onto the bed where they both watched me with a smile.

I couldn't help but groan aloud.

These two are insatiable.

* * *

The days passed in a blur and suddenly on the day Rosie was supposed to welcome the low-levels...I found myself getting up in the middle of the night and watching them as they slept.

I couldn't stop thinking about how much they had suffered at the hands of this cruel world. They had changed because of it, barely holding a smidge of the people they once were. Of course, I would support them and care for them no matter what, but I was afraid.

Afraid they would lose themselves.

Afraid they would hate themselves for what they have become.

Afraid that they were in danger.

And afraid I wouldn't be able to protect them from the people who sought to destroy us.

If allowing the low-levels into Winterfell wasn't a ploy thought up by the Originals themselves, I would feel much better than I did now.

But instead, I thought of all the ways this could be a trap for us.

I mean, why else would they do this?

They spouted nonsense about her entering the government, but they knew that after the murders of both Daxton's parents and Rae's father, there would be spots for them to fill. I hadn't heard much about their positions as I stayed with mostly Daxton and Rosie, but they couldn't keep those positions long, right?

They also couldn't just wait around for them to be done with their school. They still had almost two years left.

Which made their entire plot ridiculous, unless...

The goal was to kill Marques's people, Malik had once said.

The same person that Rae had told us was on the other side of this war.

The more I thought about it the weirder it got. This was a suicide mission from the start, but if hybrids were so valuable to them, why would they chance it?

I was stirred out of my thoughts by a shuffling outside our door. I waited a moment, listening closer.

Then I heard it again.

My senses went on high alert and the hair on the back of my neck stood up. I ran towards the door and threw it open, ready to end the person that was trying to hurt us.

The dim hallway was empty and I let out a growl as I scanned the area. Just in case, I sent my magic out to feel if there was a witch nearby, but there was nothing.

As I slowly backed into the dorm I saw a flash of blue in front of me and I bust out into the hallway with my magic ready.

Two breaths went by and there was still just me in the empty hallway with only a small glimmer of magic, proving to me that I wasn't crazy.

But it was so small I couldn't determine a signature from it.

"Amr?" Rosie called.

"Coming," I muttered and looked twice over my shoulder before returning back into the dorm.

Chapter 12
Rae

I had said that I would help Nathaniel figure out some stuff today, and told him I didn't have much time...but he seemed to be in a bigger mess than I originally thought. What I believed would have taken me just a few minutes had now dragged on for hours.

Nathaniel had been struggling and as much as I wanted to groan and complain about him not being able to do it himself, I couldn't bring myself to do it. He was struggling too in his own way and had been left virtually uneducated on the ways of this world due to Father's pampering.

His was messy, unorganized, but he wasn't unfeeling. Even through the mess of the papers and contracts in front of me, I could see by his notes in the margins that he put time and effort into trying to understand what was going on here.

Nathaniel had always been like this as a kid. He tried to act aloof and like he didn't care, but I could feel it and see it in his actions. He did care, he was trying... He just didn't know how to show it and even coming to me for this must have taken a lot from him.

Father had brought us up in a way that made it almost impossible to ask for help and because my younger siblings were men, they didn't have much to prove and whenever they struggled Father would just hand whatever they needed to them and that was the end of it. They never had to learn to actually ask or try to figure out their own issues.

It was me who had to fix it for everyone.

I sighed and took a sip of my father's prized aged bourbon.

I was in his office looking over the contracts with the various agencies we hired, including the maid service that Nathaniel was supposed to take care of, and found that he still had a bottle stashed in his bottom drawer. I was not a drinker usually, but today I would make an exception.

The weight of our problems weighed on me, threatening to pull me into the ground and swallow me whole. I was supposed to fix and take care of everything for my family *and* I had to think about the looming threat of Xena and Ezekiel coming back to end us all.

We knew too much. They should want us dead in order to preserve their legacy.

I thought back to the way Rosie *literally* infiltrated Marques's hideout. And how Daxton had almost lost his damn mind when it came to his magic.

And don't get me started on Eli's habit of disappearing and committing heinous murders.

Damon's murder had been all over the news and who else would have made such a mess of his death? And right on the stairs of the Demon Regulation Society nonetheless.

On top of it all we had to act like our parents *suddenly* disappeared and they were never seen again. Without Malik's power I do not know where we would be now. I hated to admit that I also hadn't thought of what we were going to tell the public. I foolishly thought that Marques would fix it all for us.

Daxton and Eli especially were all fueled by their dark need to destroy and bring havoc wherever they went. I always knew when they were planning something; it would start with a burst of curiosity that played at the edges of their emotions and would soon morph into an unquenchable hunger that would only be solved by burning or toppling something.

The Winterfell tower *just* started being repaired again in time for the new semester. A glaring reminder of just what happens when these crazed people were let loose.

My head was pounding even thinking about it.

I had a special place for them in my heart, hell I knew I cared for Rosie, maybe even *loved* her...but a demon could only take so much.

I looked up from the papers, took off my glasses, and rubbed my sore eyes. Leaning back into the old leather chair I looked towards the clock that seemed to mockingly stare down at me. The hands told me it was nearing two o'clock and almost time to leave.

I wasn't anywhere near done so I would have to come back later and figure it out.

Rosie had the orientation today for the low-levels and it was something that I couldn't miss. I wanted to be there not only to see her through it...but to watch as new people infiltrated Winterfell... It made me feel uneasy.

The low-levels themselves weren't the issue, but continuing on Xena and Ezekiel's plan even after they called us traitors and continued to threaten our lives was a risky move. Any of them could be there on the Originals' orders and we wouldn't know until they had a knife to our throat.

Pulling out my phone, I opened it to call our driver and my heart stopped when I realized it was past three o'clock. Rosie would have already been meeting the low-levels and I would be the *only* one not there.

I jumped up and stared back at the clock only to notice the minute hand stuck on something, unable to move forward.

Grumbling under my breath I sent a text to Eli letting them know I would be coming soon. They texted back immediately with a suggestive-looking emoji and my anger fumed.

I wouldn't have been stuck here if Nathaniel just did his *fucking job*. Why did I always have to be the one to pick up all the pieces?

"Father couldn't even get his fucking clock fixed?" I growled and stood to take a closer look at the clock.

There was something poking out of the number "2" stopping the hand. I reached up to brush off what I suspected was some type of fuzz or part of the paint chipping, but it didn't move. I tried to grip it and to my astonishment, a small folded piece of paper came with it.

My phone buzzed again but I ignored it as I carefully unfolded the tiny paper. On it was a list of ten names that I had never heard before.

I looked back at the now unstuck clock.

Why did my father put that in there?

It was hidden and no one but me would dare come in here before this... So was this note for me?

I didn't have the choice to sit and think of all the reasons why my father would do this. Though I already had a million reasons in my head, I had to get to Winterfell. Instead of dwelling on it I carefully folded it and put it in the middle of my notebook, before leaving the room and the mess of contracts behind with it.

* * *

I was lucky that Rosie had planned the big speech near dinner instead of when they first arrived. It gave me enough time to not only drive the few miles from my house but also cross the school to get to the cafeteria. By the time the doors came into view, a light sweat covered my forehead and I was over two hours later than I should have been.

Pushing open the doors I couldn't help but pause as I was met with tables and tables of low-levels. Hearing the number was different than actually seeing the bodies in seats. Many were already in deep conversation but some spared curious glances at me.

Emotions attacked me from all ends and I almost regretted taking Marques's blood in that moment. All the excitement and anxiety sunk deep into my bones and I could already feel my body vibrating with anticipation that was not my own.

I searched the room and right at the front and center of the entire cafeteria, was the small woman that had nestled her way into my being, and she was *smiling*.

Like *really smiling*.

Normally, crowds like this can mess with my ability. Emotions would run together and jumble up inside me until it was too much forcing me to retreat to a quiet place...but I felt hers loud and clear. And it was comforting. As soon as I felt it the anxiety rising inside me disappeared and my body relaxed.

Nathaniel's contract and my father's note was all gone, and all that was left was the way Rosie smiled at her low-levels.

Her happiness was no longer shrouded in despair like it had been since the murder of the refuges. No longer buried so deep I was sure I would never feel it again... It was *here*, right now for everyone to see and feel.

A part of me wanted to sweep her away and lock her in a spare classroom so I could greedily eat up all this happiness. It had been so long since I had been able to feel something so pure and warm. I wanted it all to myself and felt robbed that it was here on display.

But *god*... She was radiant.

Today, she picked a light lilac dress that matched her skin tone perfectly, probably a gift from Claudine. It didn't match her usual style at all, but it fit her figure perfectly and I yearned for her to wear more clothes like this. Her hair was up in a ponytail and her skin was clear and free of dark circles.

She looked like she didn't belong in the old, chipped hallways of Winterfell and instead in some farmhouse where she could run and lounge in the grass. This Rosie was free of the worry of the Originals, and free of bloodshed and pain. *This* was the Rosie that was finally happy.

To see her so radiant again took my breath away and planted me firmly to the floor.

I was only pulled out of it when her wide brown eyes lifted to mine and she smiled then waved me over. I clenched my hands into fists, digging my fingernails into my palms, hoping the prick of pain would pull me out of my stupor.

Only then did I notice that the rest of our group, Eli, Daxton, Amr, and even Malik were sitting at the table to the far left. They were also watching her. They looked comfortable even in the room full of low-levels and it looked like they didn't even bother getting up to socialize with her.

So not only was she happily chatting with low-levels, but she was even doing it alone?

My gut twisted painfully. I wanted to help her as much as I could. She had been so nervous and scared about this moment, the least we could do was be there for her...and I was late.

I walked towards her suddenly feeling the eyes of the room on me. It wasn't bad before but after Rosie waved me over many of them looked over to see what she was waving at. I squared my shoulders and put on a small smile, not letting the sudden spike of curiosity throw me off balance.

She beamed at me as I came up and turned back to the rest of the low-levels she was talking to. It was an unremarkable group with not any one person standing out but I smiled at them anyways.

I held onto Rosie's feelings and forced myself to remain calm as a wave of nervousness fluttered through her.

Was it me that caused her to get nervous so suddenly?

My chest bloomed at the thought.

"This is Rae," Rosie said. "You'll see her a lot with me. She takes government-focused classes and is a great resource for all things Winterfell. She *literally* knows everything you could think of asking."

I tried not to grimace at the thought of low-levels coming up and talking to me as if we were friends. Even high-levels stayed away from me. I wasn't very social...but I would change for Rosie. I had changed so much already, so what's the harm in one more thing?

"*Oooh,* so we have another one Rosie-bear?" one of the guys in the front asked.

I noted his playful tone and smirk. I immediately made a mental note to jot him down in my book later. I didn't like the way his eyes lingered on Rosie and while I couldn't feel anything suggestive...his focus on her made my gut burn with jealousy.

His messy black hair curled around his head and hung into his eyes, giving him a moody look that rubbed me as more unkempt than stylish. His purple eyes were dull, not surprising given his low-level status. And his skin was slightly tanned, just covering up the freckles that lay beneath.

"What's your name?" I asked.

"Ren," he said and held out his hand, which I noted was scarred. On even closer notice I saw that he had darker freckles splattered across his hand and they almost seemed to run in some sort of a pattern, though I couldn't recognize it.

"Is that a tattoo?" I asked ignoring his outstretched hand.

He smiled shyly at me and withdrew his hand hiding it in his jacket pocket.

"Ya-a," he stuttered and tried to play it off with a sheepish laugh. "If school didn't work out I was going to become a tattoo artist for the humans, this was just a test with my machine."

I had no reason not to believe him, but for some reason I didn't. I kept quiet and nodded before I looked down at Rosie.

"Should we sit with the others?" I asked hoping she would take my offer. I still wanted to eat up all these emotions and hated the thought of being so separated from her.

"Soon," she said. There was another spike of nervousness and panic rising in her. "I have the announcement."

I nodded and sent her calming waves. *So that's what she was worried about.*

It makes sense, Rosie until now never had to really speak in front of a crowd, besides the one Xena and Ezekiel forced upon her. And this time she would be all on her own. It must have been nerve-racking.

"I will be watching from the side."

She nodded and I left to sit by the rest of the group. They watched me as I came up but didn't speak right away. I used this time to look at the low-levels surrounding us.

"I don't like the boy either," Eli grumbled from behind me after a moment.

The low-levels were spaced far from us, as if scared to get any closer. It was better this way. I had more patience than the rest of the group and Rosie would be pissed if Eli started beating up her newest arrivals before the semester even started.

"Ren?" I asked and looked back to him and Rosie talking.

She was happy again and so was Ren. He talked with her excitedly and used his hands a lot. His laughter echoed through the room and Rosie flushed, embarrassment rising in her.

"The goofy one," she corrected. "You know I'm shit with names."

"He tried to hug her and Eli got jealous," Malik said with a light chuckle.

There were a few spikes of anger from the people around us but most surprising was my own.

"Is hugging as a greeting a low-level thing?" Daxton asked.

"No," Malik and I answered at the same time.

I was too tired to glare at him. He nodded and smiled at me.

"He wants to fuck her," Eli growled.

"I don't think so," I said after deciphering the feelings around us. "I think he is just excited, happy, grateful...though he is a bit nervous."

Eli snorted.

"Sure he is," they responded.

We were interrupted by a flash of magic that flew out of Rosie's hands.

"Uhh, attention," she called.

Embarrassment was flowing out of her in waves. I sent some calm emotions to her but I couldn't help but be enamored by the whole thing.

This girl had faced high-level demons when she was still cursed and her words tore into her skin. She looked us in the eyes back then and told us to *fuck off*.

She may have been riddled with fear and pain but she still stood there in front of all of Winterfell and held her head up high even as we threatened to destroy her.

And here she was, scared, embarrassed, worried all over some low-level students.

The irony of it all was too sweet.

And then I realized that even though she never wanted any part of this... here she was doing the best she could. To help the low-levels, to help our group, all at the cost of herself.

...and now it was my turn to do the same.

I didn't realize how much of a coward I had been until I watched her in this moment talking to the low-levels as if they were her friends.

She may have been disgruntled about this, but here she was still standing tall with that pretty smile of hers and that lilac dress.

All this time I had been so focused on protecting Eli, Daxton, and myself from anything even remotely bad for our reputations, that I didn't realize the power that exuded from her was all a product of the growth she had to do in order to stay alive.

"So," she said pulling me from my thoughts. "You will all be given your schedule on orientation day. The class that you are assigned to will be your class for the next *three years* so I recommend you start off on the right foot with your classmates."

Eli let out a small snort.

"Look how that ended up for her," they snickered.

I think it ended up pretty well, I wanted to say, but I held my tongue.

A hand shot up from the back. Rosie looked taken aback but motioned for them to speak.

"Is it true that you are a witch demon hybrid?" a girl from the back yelled.

There was a silence that descended on the cafeteria as we waited for her response. A small smile spread across her face.

"Yes," she answered with conviction. "Now moving on..."

There was light laughter from some of the low-levels but nonetheless they listened with close attention as Rosie walked them through the workings of the school, the money they receive, and the dos and don'ts of this new world they were in.

"To put it bluntly, high-level demons can be jerks—*most of them.*" She sent a pointed look to our table and I heard Daxton and Malik laugh lightly. "And with a school like ours, where our rankings can be determined by the Winterfell Games... You can bet that if you even rub someone the wrong way, they will come after you during the games."

"Will they kill us?" another person asked.

"No," Rosie answered with a smile. "But it will hurt, *a lot.*"

"Is bullying a problem here?" another boy asked.

Rosie grimaced before answering.

"It won't be easy," she admitted. "But I am hoping with more and more low-levels here, the stigma behind the classes will change. Back then, it was only myself...and one other student. I am sure it will be different now."

Chatter broke out amongst the low-levels. Some panicked others disgruntled.

"Any more questions?" she asked.

"What is your power?" one called.

"Fire," Rosie answered with ease.

"How did you find out you were a hybrid?" another asked.

"I blew up the top floor of a building," she answered again with a slight smile. "Giving me this guy."

She pointed to the scar that marred her face. There were some collective gasps.

I heard a strangled laugh from Malik and sent him a glare. Eli was also glaring at him.

"I thought you said she wasn't responsible for blowing up the hideout?" they hissed under their breath.

"I lied," Malik replied with a smile.

It wasn't a very convincing lie anyways, we all suspected it.

But I wouldn't put it past Eli to want to believe their former mentor.

"How did you get the high-levels to respect you?" another called.

Rosie straightened her shoulder and a real smile spread across her face with pride rising in her.

"I beat them all in the games," she answered.

There were some claps and cheers from the low-levels and some groans from our party, but her happiness was starting to wear off on me.

"Are you happy here?" Ren asked suddenly, drawing Rosie's attention back to him.

They had an intense stare down and I felt the conflict rise in Rosie. The bit of sadness and anger was rising again in her. I wanted to make that annoying boy pay for interrupting her happiness.

"I have found happiness at Winterfell," she said in a light voice, though her eyes did not show the same light they once did. "And you all will too."

A bell chimed from behind her and the low-level lunch lady nodded to Rosie.

"Let's eat! Principal Winterfell will stop by later so get your fill now, you will need it."

I watched her as the low-levels came up to her one by one before getting their food. The others behind me had started talking amongst themselves but I couldn't pull my eyes away from Rosie as she smiled and laughed with strangers.

Was this how she would have been if the curse did not ruin her life? I wondered.

Was this what it would be like if we didn't step in?

The bench I was sitting on moved as Malik sat next to me. Even though I did not look up at him I felt his emotions swirl next to me. They were calmer, more collected than the majority of demons I had been around. Like he had compartmentalized them and only let a few slip out when he needed them.

It was impressive...though I would never admit that to him.

"This was the Rosie I saw too," he whispered next to me.

A prick of anger and jealousy played at my chest.

"When?" I asked in a low voice.

I caught Rosie's awkward laugh as she motioned for people to get in line for the food.

"I took her to the beach once," he answered. "She was different there, somewhat like this, though this version is much happier."

I nodded.

"But this isn't completely real," I said as Rosie's eyes met mine. She was struggling to keep her smile up now and the sadness and anger that Ren ignited was getting stronger by the second.

"It's real enough," Malik said. "Though the spitfire has to be my favorite version of her."

I finally tore my eyes from Rosie to look at Malik. He had a small smile on his face as he watched her. There were warm emotions unfurling inside him that caused my throat to tighten.

"I stayed away too," I told him.

He looked at me with a raised eyebrow.

"I am an empath, there is little you can hide from me," I said.

He sighed and shifted in his seat.

"Since when do you have this type of conversations with the others?" he asked.

"I don't," I admitted and looked back at Rosie. She finally got the last low-level in line and let out a heavy sigh. "I am just so tired of lying."

I let him stew in the silence for a bit longer until I dared to breach it.

"Who is Mary Langworth?" I asked in a whisper.

The folded-up paper burned in my pocket.

I felt the panic inside him but it did not show on his face, instead he kept the same facial expression with his eyes locked on Rosie.

"Where did you hear that name?" he asked, his tone low and deadly.

A sliver of fear ran up my spine.

"My father," I lied. "Was babbling about her and a few others before..."

Malik's head slowly turned and I was met with a cold stare. *This* was the face of someone ready to attack and it made me regret inviting him into my house at all. I was sure that tonight I would be woken up by that same exact face though this time, he would have a knife in his hand.

"Never speak that name again," he threatened. "You are smarter than that and smarter to think you could lie to me."

"I am not—"

His eyes narrowed.

"End of discussion," he growled and turned back to Rosie.

Maybe I wasn't the only liar after all.

Chapter 13
Rosie

Talking was proving to be exhausting.

Since I was ten I never had the chance to talk as much as I did now and every word felt like I needed to pull it out with all my strength.

My throat was sore.

My feet were killing me.

And I was starving.

Principal Winterfell showed up and spewed his bullshit to the low-levels at the welcoming feast, but didn't do much else. Like everything he did, it was all for show. Many of the low-levels ate it up, just like I had when I first joined, though now I was the one that was continuing the lie on his behalf.

I tried to catch him before he left and ask about the demon I would work with, but the low-levels ran to me as soon as we concluded the session and I had to watch as he weaved out of the crowd expertly avoiding me. I knew he was doing it on purpose too because just as he gripped the door, he turned back and smiled at me.

I bottled up my annoyance and tried to focus on the eager low-levels for the rest of the orientation.

I was happy to have been a part of this, I realized after I talked to the low-levels.

I was happy to finally talk with people who came from a similar background as me and who understood the hardships of growing up in a low-level household...but that's where it stopped.

As I stood in front of all of them telling them what Winterfell was all about, I realized that they were no longer my people.

The wide-eyed excited young people that were just coming into this academy had no idea the extent of shit I had gone through this past year... and it caused the hole in my chest to spread open.

Suddenly it felt like *I* was the imposter in this room.

Here I was a demon-witch hybrid, helping the students become like me... But they couldn't become like me, could they?

I was lying straight to their faces about the wonders here and in reality I should have been telling them that they made a huge mistake in coming here.

But how could I have done that?

How could I have told the girl who gushed to me about how excited she was to finally be able to make a living for her single mom and three siblings, that a girl that I was in charge of taking care of died right where she was sitting not days before.

How could I crush all of their hopes and dreams and feel okay about it afterwards?

Unlike me, these low-levels still had a chance in life to be the change that I was supposed to be.

"Do you ever stop thinking, and just live?" Eli asked, dropping their voice to a low whisper.

Between helping the low-levels around campus and getting them settled in their dorms, the days flew by and all of a sudden, it was time for orientation.

The high-level demons showed up the day before orientation and since then I was constantly on edge.

Many had nodded to me in the hallway even as I showed the other low-levels around, showing me that they still remembered who I was and that they would be fighting me in the games this year.

It was a relieving thought, but I knew it wouldn't last forever.

Now there were many more targets at their disposal, and none of them had a gang of demons and witches for their protection.

"I know, I know," I whispered back.

We were all seated once again in the auditorium. This time it was magically expanded to fit all of the new arrivals and the noise was deafening. Demons and witches alike were chattering and shooting glances at the new arrivals all while waiting for Principal Winterfell to make his grand entrance.

The stage remained empty as people filed in and found their seats. The low-levels navigated through Winterfell and to the orientation by them-selves, but as soon as they saw me many ran to crowd the space around me, only moving when asked by a disgruntled demon or witch.

Eli was to my left and Daxton took my right while Amr Rae and Malik were forced to sit behind me.

Matt, Claudine, and Maximus had yet to show and now that the Origi-nals were gone, I guessed that they no longer needed to pretend to be students. Though Matt did say that he was a third-year last year, so he wouldn't need to be here anyways.

I had wished for the time back when there was a buzz of excitement and nervousness around us, when we thought that it would be only us against all these high-levels for the rest of the time we were here.

It was sweet and innocent, or at least I was led to believe it was...and that only hurt more.

I wanted to have the happy-go-lucky best friend that laughed with me in the courtyard of Winterfell and gave me purple flowers when I was sad. I wanted someone there with me who knew the struggles of my upbringing and still tried to make every day the best it could be.

I tried to push those thoughts out of my mind and focus on the way he changed. The anger and hatred I saw when his eyes narrowed at me, and the way it felt to be held down by him in Marques's manor.

"Can we tell them to leave us alone?" Daxton whispered in my ear. His hand clamped down my thigh and I felt his magic sink into my skin.

I shivered at his tone.

"They aren't even bothering us," I hissed back.

And just as I said that I caught dull purple eyes and a teasing smile from a row ahead of me.

"Rosie!" Ren whispered loudly and waved at me.

I forced a smile to my face and leaned forward.

"Yes, Ren?" I asked in a polite tone even though I had no energy to keep up this facade.

"Can you please show me my class after this?" he asked.

Swallowing my annoyance I nodded.

He beamed at me and leaned back in his seat. The girl next to him turned to look up at me as well.

"Mine too?" she asked.

Daxton let out a chuckle from behind me while Eli growled.

"Of course," I replied.

She sat back down in her seat with a wide smile.

More heads turned to me and suddenly I was in charge of showing more than twenty people their classrooms.

"They aren't even bothering us," Daxton teased as I leaned back in my chair.

"Shut up or I will make you take a group as well."

His mouth snapped shut and I heard Eli snicker.

"You too, Eli."

"You couldn't make me even if you tried, mutant," they responded.

A gasp sounded through the chatter around us and I looked around only to catch a low-level staring at Eli with wide eyes.

"It's okay," I assured them, heat crawling up the back of my neck as low-levels turned to stare.

I didn't need to explain my relationship with Eli or the others, but it wouldn't look good if they saw them walking all over me when I was supposed to be an advocate for our safety and equality.

"You have a problem, low-level?" Eli growled.

"Stop," I hissed at them. They smirked and leaned closer to me, a fresh wave of their scent filling my senses and putting me on edge.

I hated to admit how much this part of Eli affected me.

"Make me," they tested.

Slowly a smile made its way to my face and with a brush of confidence I didn't know I had I turned to the group behind us. Amr, Rae, and Malik were watching the scene play out before them, each with their own reaction. Amr was scowling at Eli while Rae looked indifferent and Malik... Well, he looked slightly amused. I batted my eyes at Malik and watched as a triumphant smile flashed across his face.

"Behave, Eli," Malik said in a low tone.

Eli frowned and squeezed my arm.

"You can't throw his power around like that," they hissed at me.

"But she can," Malik said and leaned forward. "Now, *behave* and listen to what Rosie says, hm?"

I could hear Eli's teeth grind together and they were forced back into their seat. They sent nasty words into my mind through our connection but I couldn't help but laugh at them and leaned into Daxton's side.

He shifted so that his arm was on the back of my chair and I could lean comfortably onto his warm chest. I could feel his lips hover on the top of my head and the whole moment filled me with warmth.

"Good pet," I teased, just to get an extra rise out of them.

Before they could fight back the lights dimmed and out walked Principal Winterfell. His bright purple hair and eyes were the first thing that drew my attention. The second was the disgustingly extravagant suit he wore that had millions of green flashing squiggles on them.

Even from afar they hurt my head.

"Here we go," I groaned and sunk into my chair.

* * *

Right after the orientation, myself and the others, plus a good majority of the low-levels, gathered in the halls of Winterfell. The other demons and witches gave us dirty looks as they pushed past us and I heard more than a few muttering about taking up space.

I was lucky enough to have dealt with this kind of sentiment with Eli and the others to keep a cool expression on my face even though I was seething inside.

Me winning the games and acclimating into this academy should have shown them by now that there was no need for those comments, and that their own ideas about bloodline and purity were conflated.

But I knew better than to expect them to change in such a short time.

It made me rethink the plan to join the government and fight for low-level and hybrid rights...but I already had too much on my plate.

"Okay so we have," I said looking at the group in front of me, "Demon History and Culture to the left." Only a handful of people moved. "Government to the right." A majority of the people moved. "And Mathematics and Science in the middle."

Many of the low-levels seemed to lean towards the government portion and while I was surprised, it made sense.

These people were here to change the course of this world, where better to start?

"I can take Government," Rae said from my side.

I jumped, not even noticing her presence until that moment. Her hazel eyes stared down at me and I felt a chill run through me. Even though we were not touching I felt a pull to her.

It had been so long since we had any alone time together and that kiss in the hallway was currently playing in my mind on repeat. I swallowed thickly and tried to find a somewhat coherent sentence.

"You want to help?" I asked in a weak voice.

The side of her lips twisted, a devious-looking smile if I had ever seen one.

"Of course," she said and looked at the group in front of us. "Each major is on a separate area of the campus, unless you refuse?"

"No, that's fine—great even," I said tripping over my words.

Why was I getting so nervous and flushed?

I cursed internally and wiped my sweaty hands on the sides of my skirt. I had known her for over a year now, seen her intimately…why would she still pull a reaction out of me.

She nodded though her eyes were alit, almost like she could see right through me.

I felt oddly naked in front of her.

"I'll take science and math people," Malik interrupted, coming to stand at my other side.

A warm feeling shot up inside me and for some reason, it made me want to burst into tears. *Finally,* I wasn't alone with these low-levels.

"Alright," I said.

"It won't get you brownie points," Eli grumbled in a low voice from behind us.

Malik gave me a smirk that told me he knew it did.

"Demon History and Culture, with me then," I said and waved people off.

Ren broke out of his government section and ran towards me.

"Can we talk after?" he asked. "I have some more questions about the games."

"Sure," I said. "I'll find you afterwards."

He gave me a smile and ran off with the group that was now being led by Rae. She had already jumped into a lecture on the hall they were going to and the history of the school. Her enthusiasm, even if obviously forced, made me smile.

"Well," Malik said and shifted next to me. "I don't know—*or care*—about the history of Winterfell but if you stick around I can tell you where each of your powers originated from."

There were a few gasps before the low-levels started rambling off about their powers.

"Um," I stalled as the low-levels eyes looked towards me. "I guess I am the boring one. Let's go to our classes."

There were a few chuckles, but they followed me nonetheless. As I walked them to the hallway I pointed out my own class and showed them to their classes as well.

Eli, Amr, and Daxton followed me silently and didn't interrupt even as the low-levels bombarded me with questions that had nothing to do with their classes.

I understood that to them, I was some sort of commodity, and of course they would take advantage of my time. I would too if I was in their position, but it made it all the harder to hold onto my energy.

Talking and interacting was something I haven't been able to do at scale for more than ten years of my life and I could already feel the soreness gathering in my throat.

To my relief none of them were in my class, though I knew soon enough many would pop in to find me at some point now that they knew where I was most of the time.

As soon as they were settled and began dispersing, Eli grabbed me by the arm and forced me to walk in the direction of the dorms. Their grip on me was powerful, and I had to swallow my whines as they dragged me.

I had almost forgot about the earlier anger because they were so quiet during the tour.

"First you use Malik's power on me, then you fucking entertain those low-levels for two hours?" Eli hissed in my ear.

"Eli," came Amr's voice. "Calm yourself."

"I *will not* listen to a dirty cat who thinks that just because Rosie takes your di—"

"Eli," I said in a serious tone, cutting off their angry rant.

My magic flared inside of me and there was a crackle between us. Eli's eyes widened and they jumped away from me, ripping their hand from my arm.

Their eyes filled with anger and hurt as if I had just done the worst thing imaginable to them.

"Did you just...?"

"Yes," I said and squared my shoulders. "I have a duty to those low-levels and why do you think it's okay to talk to Amr like that?"

Their blue eyes narrowed in my direction and they began taking deep breaths.

"Let's go get a celebration coffee," Malik's voice said and his arm wrapped around my shoulder, pulling me further from Eli.

I was caught off guard by his sudden appearance but I didn't mind, not in this moment where Eli was on the edge.

I could take the bullying, I could take the cuts and pain...but I would be dammed if *anyone* talked to Amr like he was not worthy of his place on this earth.

Amr had been trapped in his familiar body for *years* because Daxton's parents thought of him as *lower* than the other witches. He deserved far more than verbal abuse. No matter what Eli's normal temperament was, this could not be excused.

Eli glared up at Malik and their body tensed like they were ready to pounce.

"It's a nice day, Eli," he said. "Let's keep it that way."

My heart was beating in my chest like crazy because not only did I know that Eli was going to punish me later for this, but the way Malik's arm was holding me to his side was surreal.

I used to have to pull his reaction out of him through pure anger...but here he was giving in to it without me even having to ask, though I wish it was under a better circumstance.

"Let's get the frozen one," Daxton said, appearing from behind Eli. "I bet you haven't had one of those, have you?"

I shook my head and he smiled at me while putting a hand on Eli's shoulder.

I looked towards Amr and grabbed his hand. He sent me a warm smile but by the creases near his eye, I could tell that he was unhappy with the way Eli spoke to him.

"Let's go," Malik said. "Someone text Rae."

He began to pull me towards the opposite side of campus.

"Oh wait—" I said and dug my heels into the ground. "I have to meet Ren."

"He can wait," Malik said dropping his voice low.

It caused shivers to run up my spine and his thumb began drawing patterns in my arm. I swallowed thickly and tried to reign in my magic as it fanned out, begging for me to take things further.

It wanted the white-haired demon far more than it should have.

Ever since that moment in the town where he forced me to kneel in front of him, my magic had been on the hunt. It pushed me closer to him every time, begging for me to sample him.

His hand gripped my shoulder and it was far too easy to imagine them in my hair, imagine his scarred body over mine, sweating.

Amr tensed in my grasp and I tried to reign in my magic.

"Okay-y," I stammered and let him guide me towards the parking lot.

Chapter 14
Eli

I stormed down the hallways of Winterfell with anger coursing through my veins. My skin felt like with any drastic movement, it would rip in two.

Every face that passed was one I wanted to slam into the concrete until they were unrecognizable. Every laugh or whisper made me want to scream and every stray thought that brushed up across my mind made me want to rip my hair out.

Not only had all activity with *The Fallen* been canceled, but Rosie had been ignoring me for weeks forcing me to suffer this pain alone. I thought for sure with her help I could be happily distracted from the mundane life that I was forced to live now, but even that was too much to ask of her.

I tried every day through every class to get just a smidge of her attention but each day she was swept away by a series of low-level demons that demanded her time. Low-levels that she thought were apparently more important than me.

I didn't take myself as a jealous person, but how dare she treat those monstrosities as more deserving of her time?

Malik, Rae, Daxton, even the *fucking* cat would have been better than those damn low-levels.

You would think that once those useless sacks of skin finally started that their insistent yammering would stop, but no.

It just got worse.

Now Rosie was still fielding complaints and even as we reached our second full week of school it had only gotten worse.

Apparently Principal Winterfell had *forgotten* to name a demon representative and so there was no one to hold the demons back from their attacks on the low-levels. Forgotten may not be the right word—it's more like Malik didn't use his powers on him and no one here wanted to step up and name themselves as the one in charge of these rampant demons.

The attacks were well deserved in my opinion, but that didn't stop them from complaining to Rosie.

Rae and Amr had stepped in to help talk to the demons who had been bothering the low-levels but Rae was tired and Amr.... Well, Amr was not well received in the demon community as a witch.

As I rounded the corner to our classroom I found one of my current annoyance leaning against the wall, whistling as he watched others enter the classroom.

That purple-eyed kid.

Everything from his black messy hair to his wrinkled shirt, to his fucking horrible posture made me irate. It's like he was born to irritate the shit out of me. He had been by far the low-level most attached to Rosie, meaning that I saw him all the *fucking* time.

His face dropped as he caught my gaze and his whistling fell short.

"Eli, hey," he said in a nervous tone.

"Don't bother her today," I growled at him.

His thoughts were in a flurry and shot out every which way as if even they were trying to escape the shitty situation he was in. Even they could understand that they were in danger.

My breath caught as one of the thoughts became clearer. It was useless, but it was more clear than I had ever heard it before without touching another person.

Oh shit, his thoughts whispered.

I wanted to hear more, I needed it. Because finally that bastard's blood was working. Finally, I was just a smidge closer to that useless sperm donor.

"I just have a few questions," he said with his hands raised in surrender. "I haven't been able to talk to her for weeks."

Join the club, I thought wryly. I wracked my brain trying to think of anything to say or do that would make his thoughts pop out again like that.

But just as I was about to give him a verbal beating, a hand shot out and grabbed the hair on the top of his head, forcing his head back into the concrete wall. I heard the crack of his skull and while that should have excited me I was more annoyed that the hand got to it before I did.

Because I heard another thought.

A small, *What the?*

I looked at the high-level demon with a scowl. I didn't recognize him though he seemed to recognize me, and he nodded and laughed as if I was enjoying this.

How dare they pull out a thought that I barely managed to do myself. My blood boiled and I began to see red.

How many times today did the universe need to tell me I was useless?

How many more times would I feel as though I was trapped in my own skin?

My haze fell away and I forced my jaw to unclench.

I smirked at the unsuspecting high-level and gripped their wrist.

"I was having a talk with this one," I said in a polite tone. Though I put a significant amount of strength behind my grip and they let go immediately.

His face dropped and their pained thoughts reached my mind. I scratched my neck and looked down at them through hooded eyes.

This was what I needed, I realized as the throbbing in my head began to subside.

A small calm washed through me and in an instant my mind was clearer than it had been in weeks. I understood now what this power, *his blood,* required from me.

It makes sense that Marques's blood would react better to this. React better to violence, fear, and pain because after all...that's what he was forged out of. I wouldn't pretend to know what it took to survive among his kind and then forcibly be cast out like him, but I would grasp at whatever shining string was left for me.

Yes, I thought. *I understand this now, maybe Rosie wasn't the only way to cure my boredom.*

I squeezed harder as they let out a groan, tears welled up in their eyes and I couldn't help the bubble of excitement that floated through me.

"Please, Eli I'm sorry, I thought you hated them as much as we did," he sputtered. "Please, I'm sorry."

I squeezed harder and watched as he fell to his knees. A sick pleasure shot through me.

"I was *busy* with him, or did you not see? And the more you mess with the fucking low-levels the more they interrupt me, does your puny brain understand that?" I asked. "Do you realize every single one of them runs to Rosie about this, hm? Next time tell the other dumbasses to *fuck off* or I swear I will visit you in your sleep and slit your god damn throat."

He tried to hold in his groan but as I snapped his wrist in my hands he couldn't help but cry out like the weakling he was. I reveled in the way he jerked against my hold, trying so hard to get away but still remaining just as trapped as a rat.

These types of high-level demons made me sick. They made low-levels look like god damn saints and it was disgusting that they disgraced us so horribly. *We* were the ones that were supposed to be superior. *We* were the ones that were untainted and remained as much a part of heaven as our Original ancestors.

Except you are also tainted by that blond bitch...

The thought hit me and caused me to pause.

"Get out of here," I growled and threw his limp hand back at him wishing internally that it would heal wrong. He deserved much more than the leniency I gave him, but that would be for another day, and another time.

I turned to the annoying boy still clutching his head. He looked up at me with a pitiful expression, his blue eyes wide and scared.

His thoughts were burrowed back into his head forever gone from my power.

"Don't fucking bother Rosie ever again," I warned and walked into the classroom without another word.

I wasn't surprised to see Daxton and Amr in their seats already but I scowled when Rosie's seat remained empty. She must have been busy with the low-levels again and I couldn't stop the growl that left my chest.

Tonight, I would change that. Or at least blow off some steam with her, I thought. It was the only thing that pulled me further into the classroom.

Mr. Falkner, or should I say *Original scum,* was seated at his desk, looking over some papers as students filed in. He hadn't left with the others and it made me all the more suspicious. I would have to remember to ask Malik if his inclusion with them was purely because of his mind control or if there was something deeper.

After all, he could be reading back information to the Originals.

Felling extra aggravated this morning I walked over to his desk and slammed my hand down on his shoulder.

He looked up at me, blinking a few times before he spoke.

"Yes, Eli?" he asked.

I leaned forward with a smile.

"Don't think I forgot where your ties lie," I whispered in a low voice to him.

His mind remained blank and I was tempted to cause a scene just to pull something useful out of his head...but I didn't want to chance Rosie getting mad at me.

"I don't know what you mean Eli," he said in a smooth voice and brushed my hand off his shoulder. "Now don't ever try to intimidate me ever again."

I smiled and stood back up to peer down at him.

"We will see about that," I said with a smirk and turned to walk to my seat.

Daxton's arm shot out and gripped my wrist as I walked by.

Did you get anything useful? he asked in my mind.

Nope, I replied back and looked over my shoulder at Mr. Falkner who, as was no surprise, was watching me back. *Still nothing from him.*

We should ask Malik tonight, he said.

I sighed and pulled my wrist away to sit in my seat. I didn't need to be told what to do, by Daxton no less. I had been in this far longer than him, ran back and forth from the magical town, met and killed my brother for god's sake. I knew what I needed to do.

Tonight, was the night we visited Marques's place to discuss the plan.

It was about time. I was tempted to destroy something if I didn't get any action soon. No outings with Malik, no Rosie, no talk of a way to get back at those Originals.

I gripped the side of the table when I thought of Ezekiel. He'd tried to play it as though he was the nice guy in this situation. Tried to stand back and make it seem like Xena was the crazy bloodthirsty one...but I saw inside that mind of his.

I saw the way that he thought about me and the other children.

He didn't care one bit for us.

He only saw us as players in his game and didn't mind if he lost a few pieces while he was at it.

Seeing my blood brother only confirmed it.

This family was fucking insane and had no idea the hell I was going to reign in on them when I finally got my hands around his throat.

I had a plan for him. If Rosie and Malik took too long to prepare, I was ready to seek them out and end this myself.

I saw Rosie's flustered face enter into the classroom. I could never get enough of her school uniform and I couldn't wait to rip it off of her as soon as I got her alone. Watching her stride across the room, her skirt rising with each step was almost enough to make me jump out of my seat and take her right there in front of everyone.

"Sorry," she murmured as she brushed past me.

As soon as she sat down I grabbed her stool and dragged her closer to me, not caring that it caused a loud noise to fill the room.

I could feel the stares but I knew they would be gone soon. I clamped my hand down on Rosie's bare thigh and sent her the collection of fantasies I had been feeling about her lately. It was the only thing I could do to stop my hands from wandering.

Bent over a desk, taking my strap while Daxton fucked her face.

Tying her to the bed and denying her an orgasm for hours.

Forcing her to wear a vibrator in her underwear while she attended her classes.

Her face flamed a bright red as I hit her with fantasy after fantasy.

"What has gotten into you?" she whispered under her breath.

The bell rang and I used this as a chance to duck lower and speak into her ear.

"After the meeting tonight you and I are gonna have a talk about how you have been ignoring me these last few weeks," I whispered.

Mr. Falkner called the class's attention and jumped straight into his lecture as he always did. I paid no mind to him and focused on sending Rosie mental images of all the dirty ways I wanted to violate her tonight.

"Eli, we are in class," she whispered and tried to focus on the teacher.

Feeling her unhappiness I pulled away and vowed to myself that tonight, would be a night she would never forget.

* * *

The plan was to meet at Rae's house before we set out and I arrived with Rosie early in hopes to see my plan come to fruition before we had any real work to do.

My mouth was watering at the thought and I knew Rosie would go crazy for what I had in store for her.

"We should have waited for Daxton and Amr," she grumbled as we climbed out of the car.

"I have a surprise," I said with a smirk.

She raised a brow at me and that quickly silenced her complaints. A small light of curiosity lit her eyes and I knew she was hooked.

"What kind of surprise?" she asked as we ascended the stairs to Rae's house.

I didn't knock and just opened the door without warning. No one was in the front room and this made it all the better. No one would stop us on our way to my surprise.

I hadn't fully believed it would work, but I wouldn't complain that it did.

"You'll like it," I said. "Trust me."

She would like it for sure. And it would fulfill at least one of the fantasies I had with her and hopefully tide me over until I could carve into that beautiful skin again.

I led her to the hallway to the left of the entrance and down a short corridor to the last room on the right. I was taken aback by the absence of maids, but Rae had told me a bit about their troubles with the contracts. There was no shortage of struggles now, but I wouldn't let it distract me.

She also told me another interesting little secret. A change that happened after the Originals had cast us out of their light.

I listened outside the door and when I heard nothing I pushed it open.

A flutter of warmth spread through my belly as I realized the main room was empty. Looking closer I saw that there was a light shining from the bathroom door and I could hear the water running from inside.

So perfect. Even better than I expected.

Her mind was in a frenzy as I pulled her into the room and shut the door softly behind us.

"Closet," I whispered.

She looked at me wide-eyed.

Is there someone in here? she asked in my mind.

"Closet or I leave you here to find out," I whispered.

That spurred her into action, and I followed her silently to the shuttered closet. Closing the door behind us, I peered out into the room. The slitted shutters gave us the perfect view of the bedroom without being in the open.

"Perfect," I whispered and turned to Rosie and without warning attacked her lips with my own.

She didn't hesitate to wrap her arms around my shoulders and push her breasts into me. It would seem that even the Rosie, who had all of us at her will, had been longing for some type of release. Her nails dug into me and she clung to me as if I was the only thing keeping her in this world.

Her eagerness made me absolutely feral and only exacerbated the itch I had been feeling the last few days. I *needed* this. Needed her. She was the only constant release that I could count on, and the only one that made this boring life worth it.

I gripped at her shirt and pulled it open. The buttons snapped and flew everywhere.

The closet was cramped and clothes were brushing across us, but I didn't care. All I cared about was getting these annoying clothes off of her.

She gasped against my mouth and worked to undo her bra. When she finally threw it to the side I leaned down and brought her erect nipple into my mouth, sucking on it before biting it.

I never got tired of the taste of her. Every time it pushed me forward, pulling a ravenous state out of me that I could barely control.

She let out a soft moan and threaded her hand through my hair.

"Fuck, *Eli*," she cried as I pulled her underwear down with one hand.

I stood back up and gave her a scorching kiss before I finally decided to put my plan into action. I grabbed her and forced her in front of me, turning her so that she could look out and into the bedroom.

The closet was small, but had just enough room for me to fuck her against this door without the hindrance of the closet. I couldn't wait anymore.

I unzipped my pants and pulled out the strap. It was the same one I used on her before. It was large to use without lube, but I was sure she would be drooling all over herself in mere minutes when her gift arrived.

Plus, I knew she liked the pain that came along with it.

Kicking her legs apart I slipped two fingers into her already soaked pussy. She arched back into me and I watched in amusement as her hand came down to rub her clit.

"Where is that sweet, innocent Rosie, hm?" I teased and removed my fingers to rub the head of the strap against her lips. "The one that acts like such a good girl in front of everyone? Who knew you were so wet for me already."

"Hurry," she whispered. "We have to meet them soon."

Just then the water stopped and she froze.

"Eli?" she whispered.

I hushed her and grabbed her chin so she was looking out into the bedroom.

I couldn't see much but I could hear the familiar sound of wet feet against the wood floor and then the carpet as my surprise left the backroom.

Is that...?

An image of Malik fully nude and using a towel to dry his hair flashed through my mind.

I had noticed Malik coming and going with Rae on multiple occasions and it only took a little persuasion for both to give me all the details. Poor Malik wanted to keep an eye on Rosie, ergo coming and going with our favorite blackmailer every day to school and conveniently living in her house.

After all, we were both out of a job.

Hard times indeed, but perfect for this.

"Surprise," I whispered.

"Are you sure this is what you want?" Malik's voice from earlier flitted into my mind.

"Yes," I said with an annoyed tone. *"Not like I haven't seen your dick before."*

I swore Malik flushed and looked down at his feet.

"And Rosie?" he asked in a small voice.

"She will fucking love it," I said with a wicked smile. *"And don't forget that you owe me."*

His eyes flashed and he let out a sigh.

"As long as she will like it."

And she did. Rosie was frozen in front of me but in her mind I could see how her eyes roamed Malik's body. How they stopped at his hips before taking in his erect cock.

Rosie was not innocent. Rosie was a dirty, horny little Original and she was all *ours.*

Chapter 15
Rosie

li's hand covered my mouth and they thrust slowly into me.
I gripped onto the sides of the closet, trying to keep my noises to a bare minimum.

The stretch was painful but god damn was this everything I wanted and more.

I had so many questions, starting off with:

Why the fuck was Malik here?

And secondly:

How did Eli even come up with this?

But I was too distracted by the god in front of me to even care about how this worked.

Taking in every single detail of Malik's body as he dried his hair. My eyes ran down the side of his torso as I followed the trail of his tattoos and scars to his firm ass. It wasn't long until my eyes narrowed in directly on his mouthwatering cock which was already standing erect.

It looked swollen and painful like he had been denied for far too long and I couldn't help but imagine kneeling in front of him again, this time taking it all into my mouth.

I heard Eli's taunts in my head and they began slowly pumping in and out of me. Each time their hips met mine they paused to rock our hips together, starting small sparks deep in my belly. They knew the thought of being here, watching him while Eli fucked me silently was turning me on immensely.

My pussy was so wet that even with the size of the strap, Eli moved inside of me seamlessly. They picked up their pace as I stayed quiet, rewarding me for good behavior.

That's right, Rosie, they purred in my mind. *Stay quiet so Malik doesn't catch us. We don't want this to end early do we?*

God no, I said back and moved my hand back to my clit.

Malik paused for a moment and my heart jumped into my throat. Eli was careful to not thrust into me hard enough that the slap of skin could be heard, but I was so wet that it was almost impossible to disguise the sound of them fucking me.

I bit back my whimper as Eli delivered a harder thrust, almost knocking me into the door.

Suddenly, Malik turned to sit on the edge of the bed, discarding the towel as he did so. He leaned back and looked at the ceiling and finally—*finally*—his hand came to stroke his erect cock.

Eli leaned over me to peer out of the closet and slowed their thrusts. Each time Malik's hand would travel base to tip, Eli would follow suit matching his pace.

The veins in Malik's neck stood out as he threw his head back and let out a loud groan that filled the room. I couldn't stop the whimper that escaped my mouth as both Malik and Eli sped up.

Malik started out slow and calculated in his movements but in an instant they turned harder. So hard I could hear the sound of his hand hitting the base of his cock with each pump.

His eyes were closed and his mouth remained open, small pants coming through his plump lips. I wanted—*no needed*—so badly to be on his cock. Be the one that was riding him as he made those noises. *I* wanted to be the person to draw this reaction out of him.

Jealousy suits you, Eli said in my mind with a chuckle. They slammed their hips into me harder, the sound of them fucking me becoming louder. Far too loud for Malik not to hear.

But he stayed, with his eyes remaining closed, furiously pumping his cock in his hand.

A warmth started to expand deep in my belly and I found myself falling faster towards my climax than I had before. Eli pulled me back to them, both hands over my mouth as I came around their strap.

The orgasm was so violent and sudden that I jerked against them. Quickly with one hand on Eli's wrist I brought the other down to my clit to ride out the orgasm, watching as Malik grunted and came all over his stomach and chest.

His golden eyes flashed towards us in the closet and I thought for sure he heard me and was going to come end us. But instead he simply took the towel he discarded, cleaned up and went back into the bathroom.

Eli grabbed some of the fallen clothing and something from the hangers around us before ushering me out of the room in only a skirt.

* * *

The walk of shame through Rae's house wearing my skirt with soaked panties and a random sweater found in Malik's closet had to be the hands-down most embarrassing moment of my life.

"You should have told me!" I hissed to Eli as they steered me through the house. I was far too embarrassed to even comprehend the layout of this place, let alone think about anything else than Malik's soft pants and groan as he jacked off.

"Don't act like you didn't like it," they teased.

"Should have told him then!" I hissed. "That's a total invasion of privacy and consent."

They paused, stopping outside of a double door, and looked down at me with a playful expression.

"Don't worry about him," they replied and pushed open the doors.

Everyone was already there except me, Eli, and Malik.

Heat flamed my face as all attention was turned towards us.

"Finally," Rae muttered.

"Once Malik shows his face, I will transport us into the wards," Claudine said with a smile.

I hide my gaze from the group suddenly feeling like what we had done was all too obvious. Eli walked us over and positioned me between them and Rae.

I sent Rae a small smile and she looked me up and down with a curious look. Her brows were pulled together like she was trying to locate a missing piece of a puzzle.

"Is that...?"

The doors were pushed open by a freshly showered Malik, his hair still wet. He wore a t-shirt and jeans, similar to what I saw him in when we went to the beach.

I swallowed thickly and looked back at Rae.

She looked from me to Malik, and then Eli before looking down and pushing her glasses up. A flash of understanding crashed her eyes.

That was the missing piece, I guess.

"Of course, that's what you do with the information I gave you," she muttered and if I didn't know her any better I would have assumed she was holding in a bout of laughter.

"It was fun," Eli said with a laugh.

If my face got any hotter it would have caught flames.

"Hold on to me!" Claudine yelled impatiently.

We each stepped forward and placed an arm on her. Her warm smile filled my vision and I felt a sense of relief fill me. When the last person gripped a hold of her, which happened to be Malik, we were engulfed in a bright light.

I had to steady myself against Eli and Rae as I felt the pull of magic at my core. You would think that after all of the times of using this to travel, I would have gotten used to it, but it was still the same twist in my stomach and flash of nausea that caused me to groan aloud and lose my balance.

Unfortunately, right after I blinked the blurriness from my eyes, the first eyes I met were Malik's. There was an unreadable expression in them, and I had to look away in embarrassment, my face heating uncontrollably.

I suddenly felt far too toasty in the sweater and wanted to run for the hills at the first chance that I got.

Fucking Eli, I cursed in my mind and heard their light laughter.

Malik would be pissed when he found out and I worried if this crossed too far of a line with him. I would have liked to cross the line with him myself, but bringing Eli along made it feel all the more serious.

Looking around I noted that we were in the front hall of the manor again. A cold spread through the room and I shivered, pulling Malik's sweater closer to me. The manor, just as before, held an aged and almost creepy vibe to it that made my skin crawl.

I spotted familiar curly red hair waiting for us near the adjacent room.

Anger burned inside of me and all the unshed magic seemed to boil under my skin.

Of course, he was here... Why would I expect any different.

Though if truth be told, inside I was happy to see him again even if my magic was more angry than not.

He sent me a smirk.

"Welcome back," he said in a cocky tone. "Let's get this over with shall we?"

Eli's arm wrapped around my shoulders as I glared at Matt.

My magic was raging inside of me. Throwing itself against the confines of my skin like a wild animal in a cave.

Besides Xena, I have never wanted to hurt a single person so badly before. I imagined a thousand deaths for him, each of them more gruesome than the last.

A fresh wave of hurt slashed through me.

As I watched the low-levels interact these last few weeks, I couldn't help remembering what we used to have. The way he helped me through the first few months at Winterfell.

He stood up for me.

Pretended to be the friend when I didn't have one.

He was the single person that introduced me to this world and now he just stood there laughing down at me.

Don't mind him, Eli said in my mind. *We have bigger things to take care of.*

And just as the words were uttered the black-haired dead-eyed demon showed himself. His head peeked out from the threshold and he smiled at us. It was almost a playful act that humanized one of the strongest beings on this earth.

"I hear we have some planning to do," he said in a light voice.

"Unfortunately," I said and freed myself from Eli's arms to walk towards Marques.

"I am sorry to hear about your beloved patients," he said in all seriousness.

"Thank you," I murmured. "I can rest easy once we have a plan on how to deal with this going forward."

"That's easy, dear," he said and waved for the others to come over. "We wait."

I grimaced at him.

"I assume the familiar and rampant magic users are aware of what we do here?" Matt asked, smugness filling his tone.

Instead of giving in to my urge to smash his face into the wall, I let the others answer for me.

"As aware as anyone else here," Rae spoke on their behalf.

"Welcome," Marques said with a smile. "Get comfortable, this will be a long talk."

* * *

"We will never match up to the strength of an Original," Daxton said to Marques. "Even if they have your weird-ass blood or not, we will *die.*"

We had gone in circles for hours now and finally I realized why it was better for a select group to make the plans because at this rate, we wouldn't be leaving this place until the morning.

We had found a side room complete with a fireplace that helped ward off the chilly atmosphere and had enough chairs for us all to sit, though Claudine, Maximus, Malik, and Matt unsurprisingly wanted to stand.

They acted as though they needed to be battle-ready in minutes and while it put me on edge, it also calmed me to know that they were there for us.

Eli was sitting next to me on the couch, an arm around me at all times, while Amr sat on the other side of me and Daxton by him.

Rae sat off to the side in a single love seat and I saw her shift a few times and reach to grab her notebook, but with a firm look from Malik, she would scowl and drop her hand to her lap.

Marques of course, had his own love seat as well and had been patiently answering all of our questions...though I knew he was tired by now.

Daxton was...reasonably upset at the information shared and had no problem airing those concerns.

"And you are still against giving us some of your blood?" Daxton asked, his hand clenching into fists that rested on his thighs.

"I do not know how it will affect magic users yet," Marques replied with a cool tone. "And given your already, *fragile* situation... I do not want to chance an overload on your system."

There was a silence.

"Because it's tearing me apart," Daxton muttered bitterly.

My heart squeezed painfully as I watched in real time, him coming to terms with how bad his magic was. I didn't want to think of what it meant for his magic to run rampant, I couldn't bear it.

"Rosie's will help keep it together," Marques assured. For the first time his voice softened, as if he was talking to a child.

Daxton didn't reply, just simply nodded, and relaxed back into his seat.

I wanted to reach out to him and grab ahold of his hand, but didn't want to upset him further, so I stayed seated.

"Why is it you cannot fight them?" Amr asked, his voice cautious.

"I have been trying for years," he said. "And sustained many injuries since, I am not the young demon I once was."

He sent me a knowing look. *He was dying* and no one here would know. No one could know...because if they did, he would be the first one they would go after and we would lose the only bit of protection that we had.

"How do we know when we are ready?" I asked him.

He sent me a grateful smile.

"You will never be *fully* ready for what faces you out there, but defeating me would be a good start," he said.

Rae stiffened beside me.

"Don't worry young one," he said. "I won't hurt her."

I looked between them. *Was he speaking to her?*

"What is your power?" I asked.

He just leaned back and cocked his head to the side.

"In the real world, demons will not come up to you and explain their power before they tear you to shreds," he said.

I grimaced at the imaging of Xena ripping me apart in my mind.

"We know Ezekiel's power," Daxton said. "And since Xena is a witch, it is pretty straightforward."

A slow smile spread across Marques's face.

"Is it?" he asked. "Are you sure that is the only power he holds?"

Eli let out a scoff.

"Trying to scare us?" they asked. "My power was passed down from them, I should know if they had anything else."

Marques leaned over to grab his cup of wine and brought it to his lips. His silence settled louder than any words could.

"Can demons that are not hybrids have multiple powers?" I asked Marques. Again he didn't answer. I turned to Malik with a questioning stare. "You must know."

Malik shifted uncomfortably, his actions only confirming what I was scared of. If the Originals, or any other demons for that matter, had two powers...then how could we possibly defeat them?

And how the hell did they get the second power in the first place?

For hybrids, I could understand the power in combination with the magic and how it expanded their arsenal...but regular demons too?

"That is something you'll have to figure out yourself," he said in a forced tone.

I sat back slowly and looked at the group. A sick feeling settled in my stomach and I felt a sourness rise in the back of my throat.

We weren't safe here.

The thought scared me to my core.

Even here in the place of one of the last demons still wasn't safe enough to speak such things out loud.

And if here wasn't safe, then where was?

"So we train," I said breaking the heavy silence. "And find them when we are ready."

And from Malik's previous words, in a place where we were safe, Claudine and Maximus were powerful enough to help us with that.

I looked towards Matt wondering if he had ever been to the safe house. If he had, and was not a suspect...

They are listening.

"Finally, you get it," Malik said in a teasing tone. "We train at night and on the weekends so everyone can keep up with school."

"I will take the demons," Marques said. "Maximus will take the witches."

"And I will take the hybrid," Malik said with a grin.

My face flushed when I realized how close we would have to be in order to train.

God what if he made me tell him what happened?

"So you already had this planned?" Rae asked. "What was the point of even discussing this."

"You insisted," Malik replied with narrowed eyes.

Chapter 16
Daxton

It's not that I didn't trust the others. I did. I trusted them with my life and there was no one else I would rather have by my side during this time...but that didn't mean they knew everything.

Both Malik and Rae liked to act as if they knew everything, but neither of them was a witch and I would be damned if I went to Matt with this issue.

And after the way Marques had looked at me with those haunting eyes... I couldn't chance going to him either.

I still can't believe that they all just rolled over and changed their bodies so drastically because of him. They were now connected with him for as long as they lived, and literally could not keep anything from him.

From my perspective, that didn't make him any better than Xena or Ezekiel and we were right back where we started. It was all a game of chance and we didn't truly know who had our best interest in mind, though I doubt Originals could see past their own desire to rule this earth.

Even just thinking about the Originals and how fucked up this entire thing was caused my magic to boil under my skin. I was used to the way it would lash out, but that didn't mean I just overlooked it.

It was different now...and it had been bothering me.

I could feel it at night when I was sleeping. It would wake me up with a start in the dead of night as if someone was attacking me. My heart would be beating so hard I swear my bedmates could hear it, and when I blinked the sleep from my eyes, around me would be a cloud of black billowing smoke.

It never woke up Amr or Rosie, but it would hover over them as if taunting me. Never touching, but just getting close enough to feel the vibration of magic against their skin, take wisps of it as they slept, leaving them none the wiser.

It would be so easy to take them now, it would whisper. *So easy to just rip them open and find their magical cores to eat them whole.*

It scared me. I would lay there terrified that it would act on its own and hurt them. I would stay up for as long as I could, watching its next moves as it expanded and filled the room to the brim. Sometimes it would brush across their skin and draw a reaction from them, but then slowly it would pull back inside of me and I would be left staring at the ceiling for hours until exhaustion pulled me back to sleep.

Neither of them could know. If they did, they would ask to go to Marques and the last person on earth I wanted to trust with this was a demon. They wouldn't understand the complexities of magic, or understand how it felt to be at the whim of something so bloodthirsty.

They didn't know that it was like being in the backseat of your own body and unable to say or do anything to stop it.

And while Marques had said that Rosie's magic would help me keep mine in control...that was only true to a certain extent. Right after we shared, I was fine... But the intervals between when I needed to share became increasingly shorter each time.

So that left me only one choice...

I had traveled in the dead of night to a place miles from Winterfell. A place where the buildings were crumbling and the air smelt like a sewer. It was a district that poor and disadvantaged witches often found themselves, especially if they pissed off any high-levels as of late.

The ground was wet though it had not rained recently and I made sure to keep my eyes downcast as I navigated my way through the narrow streets and alleyways.

I had heard of this place in high school from some of the witches who got caught distributing a sort of magical elixir that made demons see colors and run around as if crazed. That was when I first started to understand that there was more out there for witches than stuffy prep schools and government titles.

That was when I first started to understand that I had only called forth a smidge of my power, and this place had offered me the dream of more.

I shifted on my feet as I came to a stop at the rundown bar in front of me.

There was no signage to indicate the business that they did here, but thanks to those witches from so long ago, I knew that inside was a place where any answer you were looking for could be surfaced if you knew the right people.

It was a bar and fight club all in one, and while no one was coming in or out of the place, I could feel the magic seeping out of the ground below my feet, enticing me to come in. If I was in a different situation, I may come here to let off some steam and lose myself in the army of magical potions they offered here...but I needed to be ready to face the person that awaited me down there.

They were not patient, and I didn't want to keep them waiting and risk losing my chance for some answers.

Showing myself to the side door I flared my magic and waited. Only those who didn't belong here tried to use the obviously fake front door. That was lesson one with dealing with witches such as these: the front door was almost always fake and had some kind of a magical trap on it.

Slowly a person materialized from the brickwork and shook off their camouflage just enough so I could make out their face and eyes. They were tall and radiated powerful magic, but not as powerful as mine. They seemed to realize that as they looked me up and down with dark brown eyes before waving their hand.

The wall where they were camouflaged sunk into itself and a set of dark stairs appeared. Loud music filtered out into the silent alleyway we were in, swirling around the dead space bringing small bits of magic with it.

I nodded towards the man and headed towards the stairs. As soon as the wall shut behind me I was assaulted by sweet-smelling magic that permeated the air. It was similar to that of a sickly sweet hard candy that used to make my teeth hurt as a child, but now that I was older and had been around these types of places, I came to realize that it was a special aroma made by the various owners of these establishments to loosen up their patrons. Excite them.

My own magic shifted inside of me as if awaking from a long sleep. I inhaled deeply, enjoying the way the bursts of magic filled my being. It was addicting, that was the whole thing that kept people coming back here to spend their money.

Pushing myself forwards, I navigated down to the underground where witches of all kinds were drinking and talking loudly without a care in the world. Many had tattoos much like myself, others had scars that seemed to span their entire body.

This was a place where those with less than legal lives chose to have fun and right in the middle of the dark, wet space was a caged-off area where two magic users were already going at it. The interior was not much different than the outside. It was grimy, wet, and only smelled slightly better because of the magic in the area.

I navigated my way to the back of the place where I knew the person I was looking for would be waiting. A few people stopped to stare at me as I passed, no doubt feeling the magic that resided inside me. Their brows would furrow and they would look as though they were trying to place where exactly they had felt my magic before, but it would be lost to them.

If this was before the incident, I would feel worried that they may try to fight me, but their stunned expressions told me they were more wary of me than anything else. My magic, of course wished that they would try to fight me. Maybe drag me into the ring and give me an excuse to unleash this angry demon inside me...but no one dared.

The back of the establishment was the only place with full booths. They were made out of dark cracking red leather and the table was always sticky with some type of residue and shined in places where people spilled their precious magical elixirs after having one too many.

Normally, I had not seen too many people use these booths. When I saw them filled, I usually chalked it up to business and sex dealings.

But tonight it was me who decided to take a booth.

I stopped at the booth at the very end, the one that was shrouded in the most darkness as the lights above had long since burned out. From afar you couldn't tell that there was anyone occupying the booth, but as you got closer the unmistakable thrum of magic was there.

As I approached the figure hiding in the shadows did not even so much as look at me, but I could feel their magic stir and reach out to mine.

This was an assessment, I realized. I stayed still as their magic prodded against mine, and when it finally pulled back I slid into the booth on the opposite side of them.

"I need a contact," I said in a low voice.

They moved then, giving me a glimpse of the inside of their hood. She couldn't have been older than twelve, with bright pink hair and brown eyes that seemed to pierce my soul.

I would have assumed she was just some kid, if I hadn't seen her look exactly the same years before. She was the person who had met with me on my first visit here; for some reason she had wandered up to me as I watched the witches pummel into each other.

We talked for a short while, then she disappeared but not before leaving me with one lingering message.

Come find me if you require assistance.

I could tell by the look in her eyes that she was remembering the same moment I was.

"Daxton," she said in a polite tone. "You have got into some trouble have you?"

I swallowed thickly. Trouble was an understatement.

"Trouble found me," I said. "My magic, I mean."

She nodded with a hum.

"I can see that," she said, her eyes trailing my form.

She could visualize magic, I knew that much from our short conversation...but everything else remained a mystery and a lot of the rumors about her were chalked up to an urban legend. They called her Cumae in the rumors, as a reference to some sort of oracle, stating that her powers were nothing like anyone in the world had seen.

I was lucky she took pity on me all those years ago, or I would have never been able to find her now. It was simple, if she didn't want you to find her, you never would.

I never told anyone that I had met her in fear that she would never appear in front of me again.

"I just want my magic to go back to what it once was," I said in a whisper.

She was my last hope; I needed this to work.

She cocked her head and hummed. It was a low but musical tone that floated in the space around us and sent a shiver down my spine.

"I don't know if that's possible," she said. "The demon inside you is rather...clingy."

I shuddered at the idea of Rosie's father living inside me.

"It's not him it's his—"

"I know, boy," she said in a curt tone. "I can find you a contact that can help remove it, but I cannot guarantee what their price will be. That will be up for you to negotiate."

I shifted in my seat and looked at the witch in front of me.

I was no stranger to these deals, but now that I had Rosie in my life, I was hesitant to jump straight into this in fear of fucking up everything we had been working on up until now.

What if they asked me to deliver on something I couldn't? What if they tore me from her?

The family I had worked so hard to surround myself with was something I couldn't lose.

The alternative is being eaten alive by your magic, you feel it don't you? a small voice in the back of my mind said.

"And your price?" I asked.

"If this works out I expect to be introduced to the Original that is feeding you magic," she said in a dark tone.

I bit my tongue to stop myself from correcting her. She didn't need to know Rosie's true heritage.

"If it works," I said.

She nodded and then turned so her face was once more hidden by the light.

"You will be contacted with the next steps if they agree to meet you," she said.

I knew a dismissal when I heard one and slowly got out of the booth and hightailed it out of there before anyone else could stop me.

Chapter 17
Malik

Rosie let out a loud groan after unsuccessfully trying to mold her magic into a curse form.

To keep safe, we went to the refugee hideout and sectioned off a small part for ourselves. It was by far the best place for us to be while we prepared, even though the noise of the people seeped through the walls. This was our long-awaited training time, both of us sitting on the cold concrete ground as Rosie tried her best to curse me.

I knew little about wielding magic, but I have been around long enough to understand what was happening in her body right now.

Untamed magic ran wild and only cooperated when she was in some type of grave danger, hence the games she was subjected to in the town. Fortunately, I was not like those monsters and would never make her do something like that again...but I would need to push her.

I acted as though we had all the time in the world, but on the inside I was antsy. I was worried they would get suspicious, or even bored and come looking for their *beloved* hybrid.

Was it wrong for me to hope that there was some poor sod already pregnant with their next batch? Maybe this time they would succeed in separating them from their family.

"I wanted to talk to you about something," I said, breaking Rosie's concentration.

She looked up at me with a raised brow.

"Am I in trouble?" she asked innocently.

I bit back my suggestive retort for something more along the lines of what I wanted to say.

"You know if your mother had returned you…" I trailed, letting her soak up my words.

She dropped her hands and her shoulders slumped forward as if a weight was just put on her back and was far too heavy for her to bear.

"I know," she said softly. "I probably would have ended up dead like the others, am I right?"

I nodded solemnly.

"You are the strongest I have seen so far," I said. "But that doesn't mean that it would have ended differently. Same with Eli."

She peered up at me between her lashes.

"Why did he abandon Eli?" she asked.

I leaned back and looked up at the metal beams above us. This was a hard conversation to navigate, but one I should have had a long time ago… with both of them.

"I don't know what the main reason was," I said. "Maybe a combination of things. They were always so methodical in the things they did. There was a reason for everything. When you were born, who you were born to, your task after you were taken and even—"

"Our death if necessary," she finished for me. I gave her a sad smile.

"I have to think it was that you did not show up. The children are raised together so it would have been a hassle to do another batch so soon," I said. "It takes *some* effort from them too. Not to mention Sarah refused to let Ezekiel have other partners."

"She birthed all of them?" Rosie asked, her jaw hanging open. I let out a light laugh.

"Unfortunately, though she was never really a caretaker," I said with a smile. "She liked to hand them off to the handmaidens."

Rosie nodded thoughtfully.

"Maybe they realized their methods didn't work," she offered.

"I may have also been part of the issue," I admitted and let out a big sigh. "I was, tired of watching them die… At least at *The Fallen* I could have seen them grow away from this world but…"

I let the silence hang between us. There wasn't anything else I could say, nothing I could do to get the guilt of what I have done to Eli, to Rosie, to all the others out from my system.

"I understand," Rosie said with a small smile and looked back up to me. "How many were there?"

I shrugged.

"I lost count," I said. "Truly."

She nodded and went back to her magic.

I was grateful she didn't try to push me on it because in all honesty, while I did forget how many...if I stayed here long enough and tried to remember each of their faces I am sure I could come up with a number.

But I was already so exhausted and worn out, that I didn't think I could handle any more of the death.

I watched as her magic gathered around her, red sparkles becoming visible in the air, floating around on silent winds.

This was my favorite part, and always so mesmerizing. The way her brows pulled in concentration, the way she would pull her plump bottom lip into her mouth and bite it.

I was jealous of those teeth. *I* wanted to be the one to do that.

"How is your body reacting?" I asked unable to help myself.

She sent me a smile and the magic around her disappeared. She held up her hand and in the very middle sprouted a flame, but it was no longer red. Instead it was a pure black that sucked the light from the surrounding areas into its body.

I had seen this once before, with her father.

"The flames of hell," she said with a slight laugh to her tone. "At least that's what Marques told me to call it."

I swallowed thickly.

"Your father called it that too," I said. "Sorry for the interruption but glad your body is adjusting okay."

"Me too," she said. "I was worried about my magic, but it seems normal."

"That's good," I said with a smile.

I liked this portion of our relationship. It was easy, simple. Though I wouldn't deny the pull I felt, especially when she gave me *that look*.

I would eat up every moment of my time here, even if it was on these conversations about nothing. As long as I could get this time, I would be happy and not try to push for anything more, even though my body had been pushing me to.

I had messed up quite a few times with her and now that we were so close to the end, a part of me was worried... But after remembering Rae's words, I also couldn't get the idea of her out of my head. So much so that I let Eli talk me into something completely insane, something that would make the way I viewed Rosie change forever.

Even with her so close to me, it was easy to get lost in my daydream of what I wished to do to her. I couldn't get those wide brown eyes out of my mind, couldn't get the way she was pressed up against that closet out of my mind, her pert nipples peeking out through the slits.

"I can't do it," Rosie said with a pout after trying once again to call on her magic.

I swallowed thickly, the air suddenly feeling much heavier than it had been.

"It takes time," I said in a light tone, not trying to discourage her.

"Malik." She turned to me with a serious face. The sweat that had once been a light sheen was now pouring down her face and her hair clung to her skin. "It has been weeks."

"It takes time," I repeated and tried not to watch as a stray drop of sweat fell down her face, following the curve of her neck and into her cleavage.

She moved to sit down on the ground next to me, her arm brushing mine.

I tried not to react as it sent a course of electricity through me.

God, she was so tempting.

"Tell me about school," I said, cringing as I realized how weird the words sounded.

She sent me a shit-eating grin as if she had the same thought.

"Yes, *Dad*," she teased. The word caused my body to heat and I had to shift my gaze away from her.

"Behave," I growled.

She let out a heavy sigh.

"The low-levels are getting better," she said. "They just went through their first ranking."

I looked towards her with a raised brow.

"How did that go?" I asked.

Her smile dropped a bit.

"Many scored really low," she said.

"But that's normal, given their status, right?" I asked.

"Ya..." she trailed. "Except this one boy..."

She surprised me by leaning her head against my shoulder. I swallowed thickly and allowed myself a short inhale of her flowery scent before turning away.

Keep it in your pants for god's sake Malik, I cursed to myself.

"The boy?" I asked.

"Forget it," she said with a sigh. "Can we go to the beach again?"

My heart ached. I would love nothing more than to go and watch the waves lap the water at her feet until the sun set, but...

"It's not safe," I said.

"Nowhere but here is safe," she grumbled.

Elle Mae

She wasn't wrong. There really wasn't a place where we were safe so long as Xena and Ezekiel stayed alive. Though they were probably just as scared as we were.

They were cowards who left their hybrid experiment running around without a leash. She was bound to tap into her full powers sooner or later and go hunt them down.

It was the cycle, yet no one but Rosie had the drive to do it just yet.

"Let's start again," I said.

She grumbled but moved so that she was sitting in front of me. Her forehead creased as she concentrated and I waited a few moments for her to gather her magic.

"Why is Claudine not teaching me this?" she asked.

I sent her a smile.

"Stop procrastinating," I said. She sent me a look and my heart warmed.

I watched as she let out a deep breath and straightened her spine. Her face took on a calm expression and her breathing evened out.

I had seen Claudine do this on more than one occasion, though I didn't know the point. It was stupid in my opinion even as Claudine insisted it did wonders, I never fully believed her. I thought it was just new-age bullshit...

And then I felt it.

My finger twitched on my right hand.

Then my arm lifted.

Her eyes shot open and a brilliant smile spread across her face as she realized it worked finally.

We started easy.

A curse that allowed someone to control another's movements. I had seen it used in many battles, cause many deaths, but it also was the easiest to control by Claudine's expertise.

She leaned forward, crawling towards me, and looked at my raised arm.

Today she was wearing her school uniform and the top buttons were unbuttoned enough that I had a perfect view of her lacy white bra which was now dampened with sweat.

I shuddered no longer able to keep the image of Eli fucking her out of my mind. She tried so hard to make sure she wasn't caught, but I heard it, *all of it*. And loved every dirty minute of it.

I loved knowing that she was getting railed behind that door to the image of me jerking off. Knowing that she wanted me so bad in that moment that she was willing to be fucked in a closet.

It was a stupid, stupid idea, I hissed in my mind as I felt myself harden.

Rae was right about one thing, the barrier between us would not last.

I had dreamed of this moment, where I would finally get this spitfire under me. I watched in jealousy as the others wasted their time with her.

All I wanted was to take that beautiful face in my hands and force her lips to mine...but I couldn't do it. Couldn't move.

I watched as her throat constricted as she swallowed.

"Try again," I whispered in a husky voice. Her hooded eyes trailed to my lips and then lower and lower. "Try again."

This time I repeated it with a bit of my power mixed in.

"Damn you," she hissed.

"*This* is why I am here," I said. "Your magic knows what to do, you just have a mental block."

She smiled at me and I felt my body lean forward, towards her.

My pulse began to quicken, and my mouth watered when I realized what she was doing.

She stayed utterly still as I leaned forward, closer to her. I could feel her breath fan across my face and smell the sweet candy she must have had before this.

I wanted so badly to *taste* it.

"Practice is over," I said when I was just a hair's breadth away.

She let out a loud growl and stood, giving me a scowl as she did so. As she turned to walk away, I was flashed with white panties that matched her bra.

She fucking came prepared, I realized and groaned internally.

* * *

I ran to catch up to Rosie as she stormed through Winterfell campus.

It was dark and she didn't want to wait for the others to finish their training. Instead she demanded that I take her back that instant.

She was running away, putting herself at risk all because I rejected her back at the hideout.

Anger coursed through me at her idiocy.

The Originals were still out there and she had the audacity to make me chase her down. Did she not realize that they could be hiding anywhere, Winterfell included?

"Rosie," I called and followed her through the small intricate paths she took me on.

I thought I knew Winterfell pretty well but as she led me through turn after turn, I had to admit that I was completely lost.

She stopped dead in her tracks when we finally reached a small clearing where the purple rose bushes had far outgrown their normal height.

She turned to face me; her face was stone cold and her shoulders were squared.

I didn't like that look one bit, but I was too angry to think anything of it.

"You reckless demon," I growled and infused every word with my power. "Listen to me and go back to your fucking dorm, *now*."

With jerky movements she walked towards me and then took a sharp left.

"I fucked Eli in your closet," she yelled.

"Stop," I commanded. Her body obeyed.

All of the anger and frustration was beginning to be too much. I couldn't sit there and think about disciplining her while she brought *that* up knowing how bad I wanted to brush it from my mind, but couldn't.

That image of her would be the death of me and I felt it tearing at the seams of my control.

If I was any less of a demon I would make her submit right there where she stood and fuck her senselessly against the wall until she was screaming for mercy.

Teach her some respect.

Damnit all, I groaned internally. *Why couldn't she keep this to herself?*

It would have been much easier if she just listened, and silently went to her dorm. The consequences of her being angry at me was something I could deal with...but this went way farther than I was capable of handling.

"After you showered," she said. "I saw you—"

"I know," I admitted.

Her head whipped to the side to give me a shocked look.

"You know?" she asked.

"Rosie," I growled and walked towards her. She was still frozen in her spot and I used her stillness to trail my hand lightly on her shoulder. "I *fucking* saw you through the slits in the closet door."

Her face turned a bright red before looking at her feet. I ate up the facade in front of me knowing there was a spitfire just waiting to break free.

"Where did that fight go, hm?" I asked in a low voice and tugged on the end of her hair. "Embarrassed that you're caught in a lie? Or embarrassed I caught you being railed by Eli?"

"Why didn't you say anything?" she asked.

I walked around her so that I could stand in front of her, our chests mere inches apart. I trailed a single finger underneath her chin and forced it up so that she had to look me in the eyes.

Watching her stew in her own shame shouldn't have been as enjoyable as it was, but sure enough I felt myself harden and this time I was so close it brushed against her stomach.

I let out a content sigh and leaned closer to her, our lips once again centimeters apart. I couldn't control myself anymore. Each moment it was like I was fighting against my own restraints but instead of chains, they felt more like flimsy strings, just willing me to give in. Begging me to take her.

"Because I wanted to see how you would react when I was around," I whispered.

Her mouth opened slightly. The tension between us was so thick it was overwhelming.

The year's worth of electricity between us was putting me on edge and I was beginning to shake just from the intensity of it.

I was so close I could taste the sweetness of her on my tongue and wondered how her pussy would taste. Wondered how she would feel as I fucked her late into the night, not letting her go until all these months of waiting had finally been accounted for.

"I wanted to see how many times you looked at me." I tilted my head and lightly licked her bottom lip which she immediately brought back into her mouth, sucking my taste off her. "And imagined being fucked by me. Even with everyone around. Acting like the innocent girl you pretend to be, but inside you are like a dog in heat panting for a good fuck."

Her eyes flashed in anger and a scandalized gasp left her mouth.

"There she is," I cooed and gripped her chin. "Do you ever get tired of pretending? You really thought that if you stormed out of there, that it would be the thing I needed to give you this?"

I pushed my swollen cock against her letting out a groan.

"You're fucking—"

"What?" I asked dangerously and pulled her lip into my mouth before tugging on it. When I let go her eyes were once again alight with the anger I loved so much. "Use your words like a big girl."

"Nothing," she said with a smirk. "I was just curious, but it seems I will be left with another disappointment."

Her eyes trailed down my body and when she reached the obvious erection pushing against my jeans she let out an exaggerated sigh.

It was all I needed to push me forward.

"You are so cocky now," I said and gripped her chin harshly. "We have to fix that don't we?"

She rolled her eyes.

"I don't want your puny dick," she hissed.

I chuckled. She wanted to act like she wasn't as affected as I was? Like she wasn't begging me to take her?

She had another thing coming and there was one thing I knew for certain... I was much more cruel than Eli.

"I'll give you one chance to take that back," I said in a low voice. "And *trust me,* you won't like what I have in store for you."

Her jaw clenched and her hands balled into fists at her side.

"*Fuck you,*" she growled. "You don't get to berate me and treat me like I am lower than you. You can do whatever and I won't care. Make me kneel again, *just see* how that ends up for you."

"Oh no, I have much worse for you," I said and leaned back to look in her eyes. "You can't come until I say so."

Her mouth dropped open as she felt my power wash through her.

"You didn't," she gasped.

"Maybe when you have learned how to control your attitude," I said and took a step back. "Maybe I will forgive you."

"Malik my magic—"

"Will be fine," I growled. "Now march that bratty ass of yours back to your dorm room."

She let out a loud groan as my power worked through her.

"Come to me when you have less of an attitude," I called after her and chuckled when she flipped me off.

I would be lying if I said I didn't find this game of ours the best I ever played.

Chapter 18
Eli

The familiar itch was back again.

It started from the base of my spine and trailed up to my head.

It made me want to rip my fucking skin off. Made me want to destroy everything and anything in my path. I didn't care who or what it was, but I needed *something* to get rid of this fucking feeling or I was bound to go crazy.

It made my blood boil, my teeth ache, and my legs restless.

It was pure boredom and it grated my nerves until they are overstimulated and sent jolts through my body.

"Is that all you can manage?" Matt asked me, his voice cutting through my concentration.

It was my task from Marques to try and make the images he was seeing in his head as real feeling as possible and right now we were cycling through a few of my favorite scenes, one of which involved him being torn in pieces by many horses.

This was the stupid training I had to deal with. It did nothing and was probably just an excuse to watch us and make sure we weren't off doing anything that would call unwanted attention to us.

I had foolishly thought that working with Marques would give me more freedom, but I found myself just as confined as with the other Originals.

In times like these where I was trapped like a wild animal and had no other place to turn to get rid of my boredom...it called for drastic measures.

"Shut up," I growled and squeezed his shoulder harshly in warning.

We had tried before to do this from afar, without touching, but Marques's blood had yet to affect my power all that much yet.

Another fucking failure.

"Let's take a break," Marques said from behind me.

Marques's manor had become a hot spot for us, and we were dragged here every time they decided we needed to test the limits of our power. And instead of a nicely cleaned and comfy space for us to practice, they had put us in the ballroom, and had us sit on the dirty floor like peasants. I looked to Rae to see how she was holding up under these inhumane conditions and noted her stoic expression.

Of course she wouldn't outwardly show her disgust, not when someone like Marques was around her. She had a thing for keeping up appearances and even that was another thing that got on my nerves.

Matt stood up and pushed my hand off his shoulder with a smirk, before walking to the other side of the room. I gritted my teeth as I watched him stretch his arms and back like he had been doing all the hard work when in reality, he just sat here and made snide comments.

He knew what he was doing.

When his eyes met mine and that knowing smirk made its way to his face, I knew that he specifically was sent to torture me. I should have known it when I first met him; no one was that happy and bubbly and now that his facade was gone, he was filling with a disgusting amount of cockiness for someone of his genetic heritage.

He had made this whole training even worse than it already was with his comments and stares. For some reason, Marques wouldn't let Matt out of his sight so we were forced to interact with him.

I was ready to break out of this training. It was useless. I didn't *need* any training to strangle that bastard of a demon. All I needed was alone time and enough of a window to tear his head off.

Much like how I wanted to do to Matt.

I let him sit for a few minutes while I listened to Marques's teachings.

"Your mother had this ability," he said to Rae. "And I have seen it in you too."

"No one in my family inherited her power," Rae said with conviction.

"Don't be so sure," he said.

There was a pause before Rae went back to her training.

"Don't see them as your own emotions, child," he said in a softer tone than I had heard him use before. "You feel mine, use those instead. Bend them to your will. You are not trying to push your own emotions onto me but change the ones I already have."

Not being able to stand the dullness anymore I walked over to the space Matt was currently occupying.

His brow lifted.

"I may have something interesting for you to see if you meet me at Winterfell tomorrow," I said in a low voice and leaned against the wall, my gaze shifting to his.

He looked to Marques with a blank expression.

"What are you playing?" he asked.

"Nothing," I lied. "I have just...come to some terms with some things."

He looked me up and down, taking his time to answer.

"Why would I trust you?" he asked.

"You don't trust *me*," I said and smirked. "Trust that I am bored."

His eyes lit up and I knew I had already caught my prey.

"5 a.m. inside the new tower," he said.

"Deal," I said and pushed off the wall.

Marques gave me a look as I passed him and I felt the intrusion of him in my mind before I heard it.

You are playing a dangerous game, he warned. *Actions like these have consequences, ones that can hurt you and your loved ones.*

I scoffed aloud before continuing across the room and sitting back down next to Rae for the remainder of my training.

* * *

I didn't even sleep that night in preparation for this meeting.

I was too excited about what awaited me to even attempt to, and of course I needed to be wide awake for this.

When I finally snuck into the tower I leaned against the cool brick and lit up a cigarette.

This tower had finally been erected with barely any time to spare before the semester started, and now it was as if Rosie and Daxton never went on their rampage to begin with.

Learning about their own boredom never failed to amuse me. They were more like me than they wanted to admit, but I saw through them. I read their minds and knew that just like me, they wanted something more from this world. They couldn't stand the boring Winterfell Academy life. They didn't want to sit in class with a fake teacher and learn about things that would never benefit them after they graduated.

They wanted to explore. Test the boundaries. And fight against the world that damned them.

Which is exactly what I planned to do.

The morning air was cool and the sun hadn't even begun to rise. There was a silence that fell across Winterfell as everyone slept soundly in their beds, dead to the world and unknowingly sleeping through what was about to be the greatest experiment I have ever run.

A shiver of excitement ran up my spine and I couldn't wait to find Rosie after this. She would see the real monster after this. I had nothing to hold back anymore, she accepted this part of me and tonight... I planned to show her in detail what it was really like to pair with a monster like me.

I felt the flurry of his mind before he showed up. I could just barely hear his thoughts and smiled when I found out he was just as excited as he was suspicious of my motives.

He too was bored and hoping for something to move along his plans. Though I was not privy to what those plans entailed, I reveled in his thoughts nonetheless.

"I feel you," I said aloud.

His curly head popped into the opening of Winterfell tower, mostly shrouded in darkness except for the red light of the torch that was placed above the door.

"You came prepared," he said noting the light.

"Of course," I replied.

He stepped in fully and looked around the place with his hands in the pockets of his hoodie. When his eyes finally landed on me I couldn't help but smirk.

"So, what is it you wanted to show me?" he asked.

His thoughts became clearer then, cutting through the night.

He was hoping I had some secret... A secret he could use against Marques and Malik.

"Malik has been on my nerves recently," I said with a sigh. His face lit up as I played into his little fantasy. "Marques too, I just don't want to follow old senile men anymore."

I wondered if said old senile man was listening to my thoughts now. Wondering if he was panicking while listening to what I was going to do.

Matt let out a small chuckle.

"Is this the boredom you were talking about?" he asked.

"Something like that," I muttered and inhaled my cigarette.

I held out my free hand to him; he did not move from his spot.

"You think I'm stupid?" he asked. "Don't think for a second I trust you."

"And you shouldn't think for a second that I trust you," I growled. "I just want to be aware of eavesdroppers."

He shifted on his feet, taking far too long to decide whether or not he was going to go through with it.

"And what about Marques?" he asked. "He can hear you can't he?"

But not you, I thought in a smug tone. *Because he refused you, didn't he?*

"What can he do?" I asked with a small chuckle. "Come kill me?"

I heard his indecisiveness. Heard how worried he was that this was a trap and that he should turn and leave right this second before things got out of hand.

But it was the curiosity that pulled him back to me. After all, what could Eli possibly want to tell Matt? The one person I seemed to hate the most.

I ate all the thoughts up hungrily.

"What the hell," he muttered and walked towards me.

At least if worst comes to worst, I can erase her memory, he thought.

I smiled at his idiocy.

Just a few nights before, Rosie had a wonderful surprise for us that involved a tattoo parlor and a bit of magic. There would be no memory loss even if he tried.

His slimy hand clasped mine and I immediately used all my strength to crush the bones in his hands before that pesky power of his could start to work.

He fell to the ground with a yell, his face twisting into an ugly snarl.

I took the cigarette and forced it into his open mouth and let go of his hand to send a punch to his jaw.

I had to be quick or else those *stupid* plants would come after me in a moment.

When he hit the ground I was surprised he didn't get back up.

I hesitated for a moment, listening for thoughts...but there were none.

I let out a laugh and stalked to the dark corner of the tower where all my supplies were stocked.

I made quick work of gathering them before turning back to the unconscious hybrid.

"Too easy," I said with a laugh.

I regretted those words as soon as a body slammed me to the ground and a fist connected with my cheek.

I flailed to catch the fists flying at me.

"I knew you were full of shit," Matt hissed at me.

I felt the vines of his power trail around my torso and up my chest. I panicked and shot my hand out to grab hold of his neck and flip us.

The sun was just starting to slip through the cracks of the tower and I caught a full look at his anger-filled face.

Fucking bitch, I am going to bring her to Xena and Ezekiel and watch as they skin her alive, his thoughts rang out loud and clear in my mind.

I tightened my hold on his neck, his mouth gasped open as he was trying to pull air into his lungs, but it was useless. His vines fought to reach my neck but they slowed as his consciousness was ripped from him.

When at last, his lids fluttered closed, I rolled off his body and dove for my ropes.

I made quick work of hog-tying him.

When I successfully tied him together I rummaged around in my bag and a crazed laugh left my mouth as I brought out my favorite new human gadget.

I didn't even wait until he had a chance to wake up. I shifted the plastic box in my hand and aimed it right at his back. Two strings shot out and embedded into his back. I watched in fascination as they lit up as if infused with magic and his body jerked to life.

His scream echoed through the tower and after a few seconds I turned it off and listened carefully.

His curses were hard to drown out but once I did I smiled as his thoughts began to push to the surface. They were clearer than I had ever heard before.

They were trying to escape, as if they wanted me to hear them... They just needed a little help.

A little push.

I turned it on again, the flashing magical lights hitting him in the back. His body went stiff, his screams silenced by the intensity.

When I turned it off next, his entire body fell limp.

With a scowl I discarded that toy and moved on to my favorite.

With a knife in hand I bent down near Matt and ran the dull side up his arm, making sure not to touch him with my hands. He was unresponsive.

"Come on, Matt," I provoked. "Where is that fight of yours?"

When he didn't answer I dug the tip into his arm.

His eyes shot open and I felt the vines of his magic weakly prod at my sides.

If I don't get out of here soo—

"You will die, yes," I cooed. "That's the point."

"I thought you said his blood—"

"Didn't work, right well," I interrupted and dragged the knife down his arm. "I found pain." I twisted the knife, enjoying the way his screams filled the empty air. "And fear, helps a bit."

His thoughts were so vivid in the moment a sick satisfaction filled my body.

I needed to signal them quickly, he thought. I saw the image of him sending out a shot of magic to signal his precious Originals and without hesitation I dug the knife into his skin deeper than before.

"Well, I guess I got my answer," I said with a sigh of disappointment. I wanted to play with him longer. Make him scream just like I had with Damon...but I guess I just had to wait for Rosie.

I removed the knife and threw my leg over his back. One had threaded through his hair pulling his head back so his neck was bare and ready for me. The other held the knife.

"Any last words?" I asked and prepped the knife at his throat.

"We are going to make you pay," he spat. "There are people on our side just waiting for a chance to scoop Rosie up and I swear to you we will skin her and send her bones back to you in a box but not before we test that tight—"

The rest became garbled as I ran the knife across his throat, his skin splitting open as easy as cutting butter.

I let go of his hair and he fell face-first into the ground.

It wasn't long before he drowned in his own blood. I sat next to him enjoying the images that were pouring out of his mind. They were mostly memories and now I understood when people talked about their last moments flashing before their eyes as their life slipped from their body.

I did see pictures of him and his siblings but I was surprised to see Rosie as well, during the time when they first came to Winterfell.

He had been happy then as well, oddly enough.

He liked the carefree version of himself. Free from burden and able to enjoy a life that he never had before. He felt like a real college student with her and wished that he could have stayed her friend just a bit longer before the whole thing blew up in his face.

Pulling out my phone I called Malik.

"It's too early to be hearing from you," Malik groaned from the other line. His voice was heavy with sleep.

"The spy was Matt," I told him and threw the bloodied knife into my bag of tools.

"How did you—*tell me you fucking didn't Eli.*" Malik's voice rose in pitch and I couldn't help but laugh.

"Someone had to," I said playfully. "Now come be useful and clean up for me, will ya? Winterfell Tower."

I heard a few curses from the other end.

"I will go wake Rae," he said with a groan. "Stay there, I will need your clothes."

"No," I growled. "I am going to visit Rosie."

"You most certainly *will not!*" Malik yelled. "Stay there or I swear to you I will lock you in Winterfell's jail myself."

"I didn't know Winterfell had a jail," I mused.

"Shut the fuck up Eli," he growled. "You fucked up, real bad and you better hope Claudine doesn't come after your ass."

"The seer?" I asked. "She can't do shit to me."

"God damnit Eli," Malik groaned. I heard a door slam. "Stay there, I will be there in ten."

* * *

I didn't stay, obviously.

Right after I hung up the phone I waltzed out of the tower.

It was still too early for the students to be out so I was able to freely walk around campus, even with the hybrid's blood staining my clothes.

I walked back to my dorm, showered, and changed clothes, discarding the other ones in the trash can before leaving to find Rosie.

An unbearable heat had settled deep in my belly. I wasn't anywhere near satisfied with killing Matt.

He had been but a small annoyance in the grand scheme of things... The person I really wanted?

Sarah.

That fucking disgrace of a demon was next on my list and I couldn't wait until my present was delivered to me, and if Marques took any longer, then I would be forced to take it into my own hands.

On my way to Rosie's dorm I was stopped in my tracks as Daxton left his dorm. He gave me a shocked look.

"You're up early," he noted.

I simply nodded and ran my eyes down his form.

He was dressed in a hoodie and jeans, obviously not ready to go to school.

"Are you sneaking out?" I asked.

He gave me a sheepish look and ran a hand through his hair.

"I wanted to see Rosie," he admitted. I let a smile form on my face.

"Me too, though I was thinking..." I trailed and his eyes lit up. "Maybe we can spice it up a little?"

His excited thoughts buzzed around me.

"Fuck ya we can spice it up," he said.

With a laugh I led him down the empty hallway.

My blood was already pumping but instead of the crazed feeling taking over me, I felt a sort of calm wash over me.

My head was clear, my rage had subsided, and I felt invincible.

When we reached Rosie's dorm I didn't hesitate to break the lock for the second time.

"Maybe she will just finally stay with us after this," Daxton joked. "I don't even know why she even tried to have her own place. She spends most of the time in our dorm anyways."

I let out a noise of agreement and stepped into the dark room.

As my eyes adjusted I noted a lone figure sitting up on the bed.

The anger that was a mere shadow of itself came back with a roar when golden eyes met mine.

"You are far too predictable, Eli," Malik chided.

He stood to his full height and looked both of us over with obvious distaste.

"Where is Rosie?" Daxton asked, anger and a bit of panic seeping into his voice.

Malik cocked his head.

"Ask Eli," he said. "They were the ones that fucked this up."

I felt Daxton's eyes on me.

"What do you mean?" he asked. "Just tell me where Rosie is, you fuck. I don't trust you and I am not above calling for the others."

Malik let out a laugh and shook his head, his white curls bouncing with each shake.

Daxton's thoughts were worried. He thought Malik had taken her, done something horrible to her. His mind went in a spiral...

All while Malik's thoughts stayed on me.

His were far clearer than they ever have been, giving me a rare look at the inside of his mind.

He saw me as a coward. As unhinged. He was angry...but also disappointed.

"*I* did good work," I growled. "He was a rat and was obviously going to hurt Rosie. And I *know* he was the one who caused the refugees' death. You should be thankful that I did the job you couldn't bring yourself to do."

There was a pause as Malik looked me over.

"I knew," he said.

"You knew what?" Daxton asked. "Eli? What happened?"

I ignored him even as his hand cupped my shoulder.

"You knew and you let him put us in danger?" I asked.

Why a hypocrite, I thought angrily. *These people act like I am the bad one here when they were putting our lives in danger the entire time!*

"It's not that simple, Eli," he said in a soft tone that only made me angrier. "There is more to this than you think. You can't just go murdering people. Especially those who have ties to Xena and Ezekiel, we told you we were going to give you Sarah, why couldn't you jus—"

"Why can't you just tell us the truth?" I growled. "If you knew he was a traitor why didn't you say anything?"

"Eli—" Daxton started but was interrupted by a voice coming from the hallways behind us.

"What is going on here?" Amr's deep sleep-ridden voice came. "Students will wake soon and I can hear you from down the hall."

"God damn it," Malik growled and ran and hand through his hair. "Rosie will be staying with me and Rae from now on, and Eli..."

"Don't you act like you're in charge here," I hissed and stepped towards him.

"Stop and stay there until I am out of range," he said, his voice threaded with power. My feet froze to the ground, stopping me in my tracks. "You will not be allowed near the house until you can control yourself. Rosie will be escorted by me when she is in school and if you kill another person—"

"I am going to fucking kill you," I growled and tried to grab him but he was just far enough out of reach that my fingers brushed the fabric of his shirt.

"If you kill another person I will see to it to have you punished," he said. "And not by me."

By me, Marques's voice warned in my head. *I told you this action would have consequences, child.*

Malik took a long look at me before passing me, his shoulder bumping into mine on purpose.

I turned to catch Daxton's hand grabbing the front of Malik's shirt. Malik's hand slammed into the side of Daxton's head and pushed him away.

Amr let out a growl and stood up to him next.

"Regardless of what Eli has done you cannot—"

"I can," Malik interrupted in a low, dangerous tone. A chill fell over the room, one that I hadn't felt in a long, long time. Malik was angry, but not in the explosive type way that we had seen since working with him, but in a cold calculated way.

This was that Malik that scared me when I was younger, this was the Malik that earned my respect. Grown demons would cower in fear when

Malik's stone-cold face was shown, and this time I knew he was not joking around.

"You better hope this issue ends here, Eli," Malik threatened. "Because if it doesn't... I am not sure we have a chance of winning this war."

There was no other push to stop him from leaving. Both Daxton and Amr were silent and finally after what seemed like forever my muscles relaxed and I could move.

"Eli..." Amr said in a low voice. "Who did you kill?"

I turned to face his accusing stare.

"The fucking rat," I hissed. "Matt."

Amr's eyes widened and his gaze shot to Daxton whose gaze was currently fixed on me.

"He was for sure on their side?" Daxton asked.

Anger and betrayal flooded my senses.

"How long have you known me?" I growled. "Why are you acting like I fucked up? *I* eliminated a threat, he was thinking of signaling them to come to Winterfell—"

"Did he ever say that he was on their side?" Amr asked. "Did he ever tell you why?"

Swallowing my urge to fight I pushed past both of them and left the dorms without a look back.

Chapter 19
Rosie

Being woken up by shaking hands was not the best way to welcome the day...

Nor was being magically transported to Rae's house at an ungodly hour, with everyone panicking around me.

It was Malik who had awoken me from my slumber and it was a shock to see him in my bedroom. The last time I had spoken to him was almost a week before, when we had an explosive argument that led to him rejecting me—*again.*

So to see those golden eyes over me in the middle of the night, I was sure it was a wet dream.

But he quickly shot that down when he forced me to get up, explaining that I needed to leave Winterfell right this instant and Claudine would be taking me to Rae's house.

I had mere minutes to come to my senses before Claudine appeared and in a flash of light I was pulled in all different directions only to land right in the middle of Rae's foyer.

She had sweats and a hoodie on, her hair was a mess around her head, and she was missing her glasses. I was shocked to see the missing glasses but was quickly pulled out of my awe by their conversation.

"Malik will be back soon," Claudine said. "Maximus and I will clean up and..." Her voice became thick. "Hold a funeral." Her eyes lingered on my face before she disappeared in a flash of light.

"Rae, what is—"

"We are not going to school today," she said in a grave tone. Her hazel eyes searched my frame and with a small frown her arm wrapped around my shoulders and she steered me to the stairs.

Panic and fear clawed my throat. A funeral? Clean up? Who died?

"Rae, please," I said and gripped her hoodie forcing us to a stop. "Please tell me it wasn't one of the others. Amr, Daxton, Eli? Are they okay?"

She paused, and my mind went to the worst.

"It's not them, just…" She let out a heavy sigh. "Please, let's get you warm and back into bed. I will explain in a bit."

"I don't want to go to bed!" I yelled. "No more secrets remember?"

She swallowed and her tongue shot out to wet her lips.

She was stalling.

Rae didn't stall. Rae always knew what to do and what to say. She was the one who had everything together and helped us through this shit show of life… What could make her change so drastically?

"I don't want to chance your magic going crazy," she said and started pulling me up the stairs. "You can rest easy knowing that Amr, Daxton, and Eli are not hurt and are fine at Winterfell."

A part of me did calm at the thought of them being safe, or it could have been Rae's power worming its way into me. But that still didn't answer the question and knowing that, my magic may go crazy.

Anger boiled under the surface. They were secret-keeping again, though this time it was important enough to drag me from Winterfell in the middle of the night and hide me miles away.

"I need to know, Rae," I growled, though I didn't stop her from leading me to her room.

I knew it was hers by the decoration. Everything was in dark greens and satins. It smelled fresh, like the shampoos she had back at the dorm.

"I know," she said in a slightly annoyed tone. "I don't know much either if I am being honest. I just know the bare minimum, I am still awaiting details. Let me get you some clothes."

I had to bite my lip to keep from fighting with her. She left my side and disappeared into her closet to come out with a large sweatshirt and some sweats that would have to be tied at the waist.

"The bathroom is over there," she said and motioned to the other side of the room but I had already started undressing, taking my tank top off in one motion.

"Nothing you haven't seen before," I said with a smirk and grabbed the sweatshirt from her hands first. The cold air had hit my upper body and I could feel my nipples harden. By the look on Rae's face she had noted it too.

"What are you trying to do?" she asked.

"Change," I said and pulled the sweatshirt over my head. Next I dropped my shorts and hurried to put pants on my freezing legs.

"Rosie, I thin—"

The door to her room burst open and I saw Malik standing there in all his glory, a cold expression on his face.

That expression caused the blood to pump harder in my veins and I felt the already chilly room drop a few degrees.

"Did you know?" Malik asked and crossed the room towards us.

I turned and stepped back only to run into Rae's front. Her hands grasped my shoulders and pulled me closer to her.

"You're scaring her, stop," Rae growled as Malik came to a stop in front of us. He looked down at me with more anger than I had ever seen. "Of course she didn't know."

"What happened?" I asked. "Why did you guys—"

He cut off my words by grabbing my face with one hand.

"Rosie, you better not be lying to me because if you knew this was going to happen, I cannot go lenient on you," he warned.

Fear settled in my belly, but also something else. Something darker. My neglected magic thrashed inside me, unable to get out.

It was angry, it was tired, it was panicked, and most of all...it was *famished*.

"Stop, this isn't the time Malik," Rae said. "Her magic cannot handle this and I am afraid..."

"That she'll blow up the god damn house again?" Malik asked, his eyes traveling above my head, presumably to meet Rae's gaze.

"You know the situation," she said. "We don't have the liberty to afford these repairs right now."

Repairs on Rae's house? What, they were having issues with money?

My thoughts were shaken as Malik's molten gaze met mine and his hand squeezed my face harder.

"When was the last time you shared magic?" he asked.

I used all my strength to smack his hand off my face, enjoying the way his eyes lit up with anger.

"Not since before you fucking took away my ability to come," I growled. "I tried to blood let but it only made me weak and my magic angry. I tried with Amr's help but I *can't do it* and it's your *fucking fault*."

"Are you kidding me?" Rae growled.

Malik's face twitched and I saw a glimpse of what looked like regret.

"Are you sure bloodletting didn't work?" he asked.

"This is my magic, you really think I am that fucking stupid?" I hissed.

I wanted so badly to pounce on him but my magic was stopping me; it was waiting politely to see what Malik would do. It was excited at the prospect of being so close to these two and wanted so badly to take things further.

It had lost all the panic and fear and was now raging and clouded by lust.

"You let her go a week without sharing magic?" Rae asked. "I thought you were smart but you are just as reckless as the others."

Malik's gaze shifted to hers and there was a pause between the two.

"I think I am going to do something she won't like," Malik said.

"I highly advise you don't," Rae said, her hands wrapping around my front and pulling me closer into her. "Give me some time, I can help her with her magic."

Yes, my magic purred.

"No time," he said. "We need to do this fast and now before it becomes bigger."

His hand gripped my face once more and I saw his eyes light up with something dark.

"Malik," Rae warned.

"Rosie," he said his voice dropping low and I could feel the power radiating from his chest. "Come."

I couldn't even look away if I tried. My entire body froze and in an instant an intense heat filled my body, gathering deep in my belly. I couldn't stop the whine as I felt my pussy throb with a sudden orgasm. It was intense, and I had to grip onto Malik's arm to steady myself.

Even without being touched it had felt just the same as any other orgasm and I found myself beginning to shake as my neglected magic began swirling inside me.

But...it didn't escape.

Even as I shook against Rae's hold, my orgasm drawing out moans from my mouth, it stayed put...but boy was it hungry.

Shame and embarrassment filled me as Malik watched me come down off of the orgasm. I wanted him, badly, but never thought it would be like this. I imagined us hate fucking against a wall after I pushed him one too many times, or on my knees as he fucked my face...but not this.

"It didn't work," Rae muttered from above me.

"Fuck you," I hissed.

Malik growled at me, his eyes flashing.

"*Again*," he commanded.

"I swear to god Mal—" My protests were cut off by a sharp spike of pleasure running through me. My hips began bucking wildly as the heat rose in me and just like before I found myself falling over the edge without a single touch from the two.

I could feel the wetness that was accumulating between my thighs and I rubbed them together as the aftershocks of the orgasm rocked my body.

"Useless," Rae muttered and removed Malik's hand from my face so she could force me to look up at her. Shame filled me violently and I felt awfully exposed.

I didn't want Rae to think I wasn't trying, and I wouldn't want to cause her any more trouble. I didn't know much about her situation, but from the simple sentence I could glean that it wasn't ideal.

"I'm sorry I—"

"Not you," she whispered in a soothing tone. "I feel you, understand you. You just need a little help. Will you let me help you?"

If I wasn't wet before her words definitely had an effect on my body.

"Yes," I whispered. "Please help me."

"I am not much for group things," she whispered and leaned down to nip at my bottom lip. "But I will make an exception for you."

"Rae, I—"

"Let's teach Malik how you liked to be touched, hm?" she asked.

"I don't need to be taught how to touch a woman," Malik growled. His hands grabbed my hips and pulled them to his.

I let out a strangled moan when I felt his erection grind into me. My magic was going positively feral no matter how mad I was at him.

"You can't rush things," Rae said and then planted another kiss on my lips before removing her hands and lifting my sweater, exposing my bare chest to Malik.

I flushed and closed my eyes, not liking the attention on me.

Rae's two fingers pushed past my lips and I began to suck on them, heat filling my body as I felt Malik's hands trail from my hips to my stomach.

I was shivering between the two now, and it had nothing to do with the cold.

Rae may have been onto something about taking it slow, but I have never yearned more for their hands on me than right in this moment.

"Take her pants off," Rae commanded.

"You're lucky I have been waiting a lifetime for this, because if I hadn't I would have kicked you out by now," he growled, but his hands slipped into the waistband of my pants and began pulling them down. Only then did I peek and look at him through my lashes.

My stomach clenched when his golden eyes met mine. He started to kneel down with the pants and didn't stop until he was eye level with my swollen pussy.

The air hit my wetness and I shivered when he gave me a predatory look before ripping my pants off and throwing them across the room. Rae's wet fingers traveled from my mouth to my nipple where she pinched one lightly between her fingers.

A light moan came from my mouth but I couldn't take my eyes away from Malik, especially not as he took one of my legs and picked it over his shoulder and stared at my throbbing pussy. His stare darkened and I felt myself get wetter under it. Rae's hand traveled down my stomach and to my lips where she pulled them apart, giving Malik a perfect view of my sopping wet hole.

I threw my head back as those same fingers came to circle my clit.

"Now," Rae commanded, her free hand forcing me to look at Malik.

His golden eyes met mine while he leaned closer to my folds.

"Come," he whispered, his hot breath fanning across my wetness.

I couldn't keep his stare as the violent orgasm ripped through me. I threw my head back against Rae's chest and shook as a tingling heat spread through me.

My magic exploded around me, filling the room with red sparkles. It was a weight off my chest and I felt like *finally* I was no longer being held hostage by my magic...but I was far from done.

"God," Malik moaned, his tongue licking up my inner thigh. "Please let me taste."

I shuddered at the hunger in his voice. Rae's hand moved from my pussy and she grabbed my hand only to thread it through Malik's messy white hair.

"Do you want him to taste you, Rosie?" she asked. "It would be cruel to deny him at this point."

I gripped Malik's hair and pulled him closer to where I was aching for him.

"Please," I whispered.

He wasted no time, his tongue licking up the length of my folds slowly before pulling my clit into his mouth and sucking.

"That's it," Rae coaxed, her voice in a low whisper. She left kisses down the side of my face. "Do you like this, Rosie?"

"I do, I do," I gasped as he sucked once more on my clit. He let out a groan that vibrated against my lips.

"Tell him," she whispered. "Tell him how much you have wanted him to do this to you."

"Fuck I—" Malik cut me off by inserting two fingers into me while still sucking on my clit. I bucked against his hand and Rae's hands fastened around my hips to stop my movements. "I wanted you so bad, Malik."

I was rewarded with a groan and he began to thrust his fingers into me.

"Say you wanted to come on his mouth," Rae commanded. Her tone was strong yet soft at the same time. I had no choice but to comply.

"I wanted to—*ah god.*" Malik sucked on my clit in hard intervals pulling sobs out of my shaking mouth. "Come on your mouth."

"Seems like you are almost there," Rae said and ground my hips against Malik's face causing sharp bolts of pleasure to run through me.

"I am, *I am,*" I moaned as once more magic rose up inside me. "Harder, Malik, *please.*"

His fingers pounded into me harder and with each suck on my clit I found myself hurdling faster towards my orgasm. A bright red light flashed through the room and I shuddered against Rae as I came.

Malik dropped my leg and stood, his lips crashing to mine. As his tongue sunk into my mouth I could taste my own release.

His free hand began to undo the button of his pants, then he paused and pulled away. There was an unreadable expression on his face.

"*Shit,* I am sorry Rosie," he said his tone heavy. "I took this too far. It's not..."

"Appropriate," Rae finished for him.

My stomach dropped. Did this mean he didn't want me? That he didn't want to touch me that way?

"We need to talk about—"

"I will tell her while we clean up," Rae said. "Just...go get a hold of yourself, and be ready because we will both have questions."

I watched as Malik's throat bobbed. Wordlessly he leaned down and stole another kiss from me, leaving Rae and me alone in the room.

"Let's go take a bath shall we?" she asked in a light voice.

I swallowed thickly and looked up at her.

"It's bad, isn't it?" I asked.

She gave me a pitiful look.

"I really hope you don't blow up this house," she said. "But yes, it is bad."

"Are you...having problems with money?" I ask.

She sent me a strained smile.

"A topic for another time," she said and ushered me into the bathroom. "Your magic feels better, though I do wish we had a witch to take more of it."

Her bathroom was even bigger than in the other house and had a big jacuzzi tub.

"Are Amr and Daxton not able to come?" I asked.

She left my side to turn on the tub. I watched as she meticulously poured in shimmering powders and swirled it around.

"It's magical," she explained, avoiding my question. "It has healing properties and the person who I got it from told me it helps curb magic, though I don't know how true that is."

My chest felt tight.

"You got this for me?" I asked.

Another unanswered question. She motioned for me to get in and slowly started undressing, joining me in the tub as well.

"You know if my magic goes crazy, this is a horrible place to be," I said.

"That's why I will tell you after we get out," she replied and stepped into the tub only to pull me against her.

Her hand came to massage my scalp and I relaxed into her.

"Listen Rosie," she said her voice trailing. "You're going to have to stay here for a while."

I nodded into her chest and let out a sigh.

"I don't mind," I said. "The others will come soon right? It would be nice if they could all have their own rooms. They deserve better than Winterfell dorms."

As I sunk further into the bath I could feel the light vibrations of the magical powder start to sink into my skin. My already somewhat satiated magic began to calm further and I felt my body get heavy.

"Daxton and Amr may be able to come soon once we gather the facts," she said. "But Eli..."

I shot up and turned to her. Her face was expressionless and my stomach filled with lead.

Hold a funeral... Claudine's voice rang through my head.

"Eli is fine though you said," I said, my heart beating faster. "Why would Claudine mention... *Oh god.*"

Murder was not something new to this group but...who exactly did Eli murder?

"For your safety we removed you because Eli wasn't in the right—"

"Eli wouldn't hurt me," I interrupted.

How could they think they would ever hurt me? Eli wasn't a good person, nor did I try to kid myself into thinking they were, but I knew they wouldn't hurt me *like that.*

Rae's lips turned down.

"You don't know that," Rae said. "They compromised us all by their actions and even though they were warned not to do it, they still went and did it anyways."

"Just tell me," I begged. "Please Rae."

She studied me carefully.

"They killed Matt," she said in a voice barely above a whisper.

Chapter 20
Rae

I expected rage. Blinding fury that threatened to destroy not only the structure we were in but the whole world if allowed.

It was what had been hiding deep inside her, coming up to the surface in bouts while the rest had stayed carefully concealed until the right moment.

I thought this would be the moment, but the more I watched Rosie as she digested the news, the more I came to understand that I don't know her well enough at all.

Matt had been a liar, someone we couldn't trust...but I knew Rosie had forgiven him just as she did everyone else. He was no exception to her kindness even if he didn't deserve it, so I assumed when she was told that the person who had been with her all through her beginning at Winterfell, had been murdered by someone she loved... I expected chaos.

But instead she simply leaned back and stared at me, the water coming up just below her breasts as she digested my words. Her lips were pressed together firmly and her breathing was erratic. It was building up; I could feel it gathering under the surface.

There was a sharp anger and then in an instant...it was gone and instead I was left with a hollow feeling. It was as if Rosie's emotions were swallowed by a black hole and there was nothing left for her to feel.

"Eli killed Matt," she repeated. The words came out slow and felt odd as she spoke them, as if speaking an unknown language.

I nodded slowly, cataloging her reaction. Then I felt the prick of sadness and guilt, but nothing else. It was too fast for even her facial expression to change.

"We were worried the shock—"

"I understand now," she said. "I—"

She took a deep breath, sinking further into the bathtub, her legs brushing against mine. I didn't let my own emotions, the lust, cloud my judgment.

Like I said to Malik in the room mere moments ago, it was inappropriate.

Rosie deserved time to feel like a normal being with emotion and pain, instead of just this toy that was passed around between us. We all cared, that much was obvious, but that didn't make the actions and lack of grace any better.

If we cared for her as we said we did, we should learn how to be with her.

"It was the right choice," she said in a voice that was far too calm. "I just don't—"

"Malik will explain later," I said in a soft voice and reached for her. I grabbed her hand in mine. "It's a lot, I know. And we still don't understand Eli's motive so it's okay to feel angry, even hurt."

"No, I mean." She paused, looking for her words. "I don't understand why my memories haven't come back."

Her response stunned me to my core and for the first time I found myself without a response. I sat back and stared at her as her neck tilted and her head leaned against the back of the bathtub. She acted as though this was just a way to unwind after a long day, instead of like someone who had just heard that her best friend was murdered.

"Also, the games are soon," she continued and lifted her leg, watching as the water droplets fell off and back into the water. "I have to be back for those."

I nodded again. She was not wrong, though that wouldn't be my first thought.

Mine was more along the lines of...*what will Xena and Ezekiel do now?*

"How about we finish up here and go talk to Malik about what happened, hm?" I asked her.

She nodded and without another word stood from the bath.

* * *

A silence spread over us as we listened to Malik explain every detail of the crime. Both of us kept looking to Rosie to make sure she was handling it well...but her face never changed. She just sat and stared at Malik as he spoke, eyes never wavering as if she was worried she would miss an important detail.

After the bath I had taken my time to help her dry her long hair and apply the creams she liked so much, just in case the emotions would explode out of her. But even as I watched her intently in the mirror, her expression never changed and her emotions stayed level. She would just stare at us in the mirror and sometimes I even saw the tilt of her lips when she met my eyes.

It must be shock.

Now we talked in a sitting room not too far from my room. I was hesitant to go into this spare room because of how close it was to my mother and Callie, but I trusted Rosie enough now to know that when she looked me in the eyes and told me she was okay, that she was okay.

"So we knew—or suspected that he was the rat?" Rosie asked. "I am not surprised given his sudden change when I outed him."

Maliks gaze met mine and worry was practically spilling out of his pores.

"Ya, well." Malik shifted and cleared his throat. "We don't know how Claudine and Maximus feel, not to mention if there will be any revenge—"

"Matt was horrible to them," Rosie said in a firm tone that told us we could not refute her. "They may hurt for a moment but from what Claudine mentioned, I would have trouble believing this would push them over to the other side."

Neither Malik nor I dared to speak.

I knew Rosie and Claudine had to be closer than meets the eye when I saw how she talked about her to Malik, and the random hugs they gave one another. Not to mention how she all dragged us to get tattoos that Claudine designed to protect us from Matt.

It was my first tattoo, and I was against getting something that marred my skin so permanently...but I knew the consequences of not getting it outweighed the inconvenience of getting it. I didn't fully understand just to what extent his power worked and how on earth Claudine figured out that *this* was the answer, but I was thankful it was over now...

Even if it hurt Rosie.

I didn't approve of Eli's ways and was angry that they didn't come to me first. If they did, I would have thought of a better plan than this. One with more tact, something that wouldn't involve us separating them from Rosie... but Eli was unstable. They always had been, though since Marques shared his blood it felt worse. Their anger and restlessness just continued to build and I guess this was the result of it exploding.

...though I would be the first to admit that they did good.

"As far as revenge from the Originals..." she trailed. "If he was important to their plan, maybe, but I have a hard time believing that they would give up their comfy hiding space for a single hybrid."

"You are..." I didn't know what I wanted to say. "Are you okay?"

Her brown eyes met mine and I couldn't help but flinch at the sharpness of them.

"I am hurt," she said. "I thought maybe he could redeem himself but..." She let out a heavy sigh. "I don't think Eli is wrong to do this, though I do want to understand their motives. I have a hard time thinking that Matt accidentally outed himself to Eli but none of us."

Malik shifted in his chair and grimaced.

"From what Marques told me, Eli had been planning it because they were bored," Malik said slowly. "In training he heard their thoughts and—"

"So, he knew but he didn't stop it?" Rosie said, her tone sharpening. She was glaring at Malik but even I felt her words cut me.

"He warned them," Malik said his eyes shifting to mine as if I could help him out of this mess.

"He's being awfully quiet now," Rosie noted and cocked her head. "Why are we so worried about this when he obviously couldn't care less?"

Malik's rage spiked sharply and I shot him a look.

"She's not wrong," I said, even though I didn't want to fight the Original either.

I would choose my battles and one with someone like Marques was not at the top of my to-do list.

Malik narrowed his eyes at me before turning to Rosie.

"Marques has his reasons—"

"Or does he just want us to do the dirty work?" Rosie asked. "From my perspective he doesn't seem much different than the other Originals. Sitting comfy in his home while we do the hard work."

"Rosie," Malik warned, his voice low and his anger rising steadily with each word out of his mouth. His hands balled into fists on his thighs and his jaw was clenched.

Such a short fuse, I thought wryly.

"Sounds like this was his plan actually," Rosie said and leaned forward, a smile pulling at her lips.

I could feel the satisfaction flowing off of her. She *liked* this type of reaction from him.

Malik stood so abruptly the chair behind him rocked. He crossed the space between them and placed his hands on the armrests trapping Rosie.

"You forget who you are talking about," Malik growled. "Do you have no sense of self-preservation?"

Their emotions were far too powerful for this room and made my head ache. The anger and lust swirling around them began to choke me.

Just as I felt myself sway the door was pushed open and I was met with a panting and panicked Callie. Her brown hair was in a messy bun on top of her hair that threatened to topple over and today her scrubs were bright pink with yellow ducks.

"Rae, I am so sorry—"

"It's okay," I said quickly and stood. "What's the problem?"

I was just glad to have something break up the emotions in this room.

Malik and Rosie were both watching, curiosity filling them.

"Your mother, her eyes moved," she panted out.

I froze, unable to think of what to do next.

There wasn't supposed to be a chance for Mother's recovery, she had been all but a lost cause…and I didn't want to fool myself with hope only to have it crushed.

"Let's go see her," I said and turned to the others. "Work out your problems yourself. It doesn't seem like the issue here is Eli's actions."

Malik stood up and cleared his throat, pulling his gaze from Rosie.

Rosie looked like she wanted to say something but I left them to their own devices.

* * *

Callie had stayed with me an extra hour, but Mother's eyes did not move again.

Even as she left with a soft goodbye I stayed planted to my mother's side and tried to pay attention to the black hole of emotions surrounding her. Hoping that I could feel something different for once.

Sighing I looked up to the ceiling and tried to enjoy the lack of emotions in the space.

Marques's blood had only continued to develop my power and the emotions were starting to get to be too overwhelming. I found myself visiting my mother's room more often than I used to, just to get away and decompress.

His training had helped a bit with emotional control as well, but not enough for me to do anything real with it.

A prick of nervousness, sadness, and guilt played at my mind as Rosie walked down the hallway. Malik was nowhere near her and I was glad that I only had to deal with one of them at a time.

...but I still wasn't sure if I wanted Rosie to see this part of me.

None of the others had seen my mother and even when they asked about her, I always deflected. It was not something you talked about.

Having a mother that was so abused by your father that she turned comatose and now was bedridden for the rest of her life.

Though it was only speculation, I knew Father had something to do with her state now.

Rosie knocked on the door and I quickly decided that it was time to stop hiding this part of my life.

"Come in," I called and turned my head to watch Rosie's head peek through the doorway.

Her eyes met mine before falling onto my mother's form and her brows furrowed.

"Is it okay if I am in here with you?" she asked, her voice barely above a whisper.

I nodded and held out my arm for her. She closed the door behind her and came closer. Her movements were slow and hesitant. She was also unsure what it meant for her to share this with me.

I pulled her into my lap and buried my face in her hair, inhaling her scent deeply. Warmness enveloped me and I realized that I enjoyed her company here over the thought of sitting alone in this room with no one by me.

Even though she had received the news of Matt and had been holding in her anger the entire day, I still found the familiarity of her comforting.

"She has been like this for a long time," I said against her hair. "Without the proper care I never understood exactly what was wrong with her, still don't."

Rosie leaned into me and her fingers threaded through mine.

"The girl that came in, she was her caretaker?" Rosie asked. "She said something about eye movement?"

I nodded and left a kiss on her head, not really having the words to respond at the moment.

"She looked like a demon though," Rosie continued and twisted to look at me.

"She is," I confirmed. "Her power to see brain activity is to help my mom. I have never used witches for her care before."

Rosie's brows pulled together and she looked back at Mother.

"She has magic on her," Rosie said.

My insides froze over and I felt a chill run up my spine.

"What do you mean?" I asked, panicked.

Rosie stood and walked closer to Mother's bed, leaning over her.

"I can feel just a tiny bit," she murmured. "But it's a very small amount, too small to recognize a signature."

I stood and moved to her side.

"That's not possible," I said, my breath getting caught in my throat. "We don't have any witches in the house."

Rosie stood straight and gave me a look that told me she was almost pained to say so.

"I think I need to call Claudine," she said.

I shifted and tore my gaze from her to my mother.

Even allowing Rosie in here was a big step, now inviting others in?

But she said there was magic on her...

"She is probably busy," I said quickly. "With Matt's funeral preparations... Let's wait a few days and see if maybe the magic wears off by then."

Rosie's warm hand found my face and forced me to look at her. She met me with a small smile.

"It must have been hard for you, all these years," she said in a soft voice. Her eyes searched my face before she leaned in and planted a chaste kiss on my lips. "Let me know when you are ready and we can see about having her come over."

I nodded and swallowed thickly, trying to push down the sudden tsunami of emotions that filled me.

Even without a power like mine, Rosie had read me better than anyone had my entire life.

Chapter 21
Daxton

I do not know how I got here. But I know why.

After the talk with Marques and the trainings with Claudine and Maximus I just...

With a sigh I grabbed the glass cup in front of me and threw the burning magical liquid back. It singed as it went down, but it barely fazed me anymore. I had had my fair share of drunken nights as I tried to deal with my parents' abuse, so even though I had been here for hours I knew that I could continue.

Not like I wanted to go back anyways. Rosie was still gone and I had to suffer through school with a pissy Eli and overly depressed Amr.

My body relaxed in my chair as a warmth spread throughout my body.

This club, while not in the main magical area that I liked to frequent, had proven to be a welcome surprise. They had plenty of witches in here and even a few low-levels, all looking to waste their night on something better than their reality.

The music was loud and wisps of magic swirled around me, dancing along with the music. Every time it brushed over my skin a jolt of magic passed through me. Bodies were packed in the place sweating and grinding against each other as they moved to the music, leaving little to no room for anything else.

Only I and a few other depressed losers sat on the stools, probably wallowing in their self-pity as well. I didn't pay attention to them much, just continued to throw back drink after drink, trying to get away from my own demons.

Cumae had yet to get back to me and it wore on my patience because now that Rosie was not with us, I could feel my magic getting restless. So here I was, stuck relying on someone other than myself to make sure that I could live to see the next day.

Useless, useless boy, my mind hissed. *Couldn't kill your bastard parents, now you can't even help the others with—*

"Another," I commanded and tapped my glass against the bar. Purple swirling liquid filled the empty cup and I wasted no time bringing it to my lips.

Magical bars will always far surpass demon ones. They know that if you are there to drink your life away, you don't want to have to talk to a fucking bartender each time. They would have probably cut me off by now, anyways.

Images of my father's eyes begging me not to move forward with ending his life flashed through my mind on repeat. The dreams have gotten worse, even though they are long gone. Some of them were completely real scenarios like before he died, others were images of him coming back from his grave to ruin me.

Often I remembered when they would share magic with me, but I would be on the outside looking down at the whole thing.

That made it worse.

Because I could see the fear in my eyes...it was the same fear I saw on his face when he finally realized he was going to die.

I wondered if he saw that too before the died? Did he realize it finally?

He always had a smile when he did it. The lines on his face would deepen and his brown eyes became so dark I thought they would turn black.

He deserved it.

But Mother...

She would sit there on the sidelines watching while he committed the heinous act. I would see her grimace sometimes but, she never stopped anything and after a while it just became the norm.

If the other witch organizations knew that their biggest spokespeople were doing the unthinkable...there would be a revolt.

That's why they kept everything hidden and used mounds of cash to pay off all the employees. Only after I saw the transactions on the bank account after they died, did I understand how much they tried to cover it up.

"Who are you going to vote for?" a witch with slurred words asked to my right, his loud voice breaking through my thoughts.

"I don't know..." the other trailed. "I am thinking to move out west, actually. I heard that witches have an easier time there getting into science and tech-based industries."

"The least you can do is vote for Perkins before you leave," he grunted. "At least then the people left here have a smidge of their dignity."

Christa Perkins, the next witch to take over my father's work, and the one that was supposed to work alongside Rae's father... Though they have yet to vote someone into office for that position either.

Perkins was by far the youngest and most qualified candidate I had seen take the stage. She believed in uniting demons and witches, getting rid of the stereotypes of crazed witches which my parents had worked so hard to push...

And she wanted to bring awareness to sexual abuse that was abundant in the magical community.

I was not the only one who had dealt with this, that much I knew. But from her statistics she stated that one in every *ten* had experienced some type of magical abuse and over half of that was sexual in nature.

Still...I could not shake the hold my father's eye had on me. Could not get away from the constant screaming of uselessness in my head.

And it made it all the worse that Rosie wasn't here as a distraction.

I drank the rest of the liquid in one gulp and slammed the glass down on the table. I must have hit it too hard because the glass cracked into my hand.

The two drunkards who had been gossiping silenced their conversation and I felt their gaze on me. I was tempted to fight them, but the sane part of me held me back. I would be too powerful for them anyways and I didn't want to go on a rampage.

Before they made themselves known, I felt Eli's presence.

Ever since Marques had given them their blood I had begun to notice when they tried to invade my brain. It felt like a small push and then pressure. After that, my brain felt more crowded than usual.

It only enraged me more on top of everything else.

They stood to my right and slid a wad of cash on the table. In a flash of shimmering light the money was taken and stored in the bar's underground bank.

"I don't need your money," I growled.

"It's not mine," they answered. "It's Original scum."

It didn't make it any better who it came from, just that it was another dig at my uselessness.

"What are you doing here?" I asked not trying to hide my distaste.

"The cat is worried," they explained. "Thinks you're on a rampage."

I snorted at Amr's mother-hen-like attitude. Ever since we fucked he hadn't removed himself from my side. Always fussing, always making sure I was taken care of...

It made me feel even more *useless*.

"I for one thought you were out of money and being held somewhere to work off your debt," they continued. Their voice had a teasing edge to it. "I hoped it was a strip club but thought I would try this place first. It wasn't hard to find you, just asked a few people if they saw a huge tattooed witch that looked like their cat just drowned."

Their joking fueled my rage and I had to clench my fist, nails biting into my palms in order to calm myself.

They spoke as if they didn't *murder* someone. Someone that was important to the people who wanted us dead. Who was important to the only people who had the ability to save us.

Who knows what Matt's death will bring us? The Originals were unpredictable and I didn't want to chance their wrath anymore.

...but they were right about the money.

I was lucky my parents had paid for this education up front because if not, I couldn't afford this year or next.

Ever since they had died, I didn't have the balls to withdraw any of their money. It felt gross. They had a fund for me, I knew about it. And they had been hoarding their wealth for years giving us no shortage of money but I just couldn't...

"Do you still have the house?" Eli asked.

I let out a sigh.

"What will it take for you to leave me alone?" I complained. I was too tired and fed up for this. I came here to lose myself, not to be reminded of the shit world that waited outside for me.

"Let's go do some stress release, hm?" they offered. "The cat can wait a bit longer."

I stared at the broken glass in front of me. Parts of it shone under the dim light and I saw my dull eyes being reflected on the surface, right next to Eli's bright blue ones.

"What do you have in mind?" I wondered, my curiosity getting the better of me.

"Well..." They trailed and put a hand on my shoulder. "If you still have the house..."

An image of the house ablaze lit up my mind.

You can get rid of it once and for all, they said in my mind. *And then move on with your life.*

"Why are you doing this?" I asked and turned to meet their eyes.

For once, Eli looked tired. Their hair was a mess on top of their head, blonde hair once combed back neatly fell limply around their head. Dark circles seemed to be permanently etched under their eyes and their cheeks seemed a bit more hollow than normal.

I know I didn't look much better, but I was a witch. Demons could heal on their own so for Eli to look like this...

"I want you to stop acting like a limp dick," they growled, their eyes coming to light. "And I'm *fucking bored* okay?"

Were they bored? Or were they going crazy that the one thing that they cared for was taken away from them?

From the beginning Eli had a tie to Rosie that went beyond their normal actions. Eli was a person who refused to form ties with anyone, and did not trust a single soul. It took years for them to even trust me fully and here they were, killing themselves over a girl they had known for just a year.

"Fine," I said and got up from my chair, stopping to stare Eli in the eyes. "But don't think I forgive you for taking her from us."

Eli's jaw clenched and I could feel the tension vibrate between us.

"She will be back soon," they spit out behind clenched teeth.

"Not soon enough," I said. "I am *dying* Eli. You think I don't understand how this works? I have lived with this magic for *years* and here it is eating away at me, leaving no crumbs in its trail. Without her I am dying and I know you know it too. Rae was kind enough to spill all the gossip while none of you were looking, while none of you *care—*"

I took a deep breath to stop the shaking in my voice.

"While none of you cared to tell me," I finished. "You just looked right past it and forgot about it, but I can't okay?"

Eli's stone-cold expression dropped and on their face was a rarely seen frown.

I hated that face. I knew it was pity. What else could make Eli make a face like that?

"Let's see what we can do to make those feelings go away, hm?" they asked in the softest voice I ever heard from them and wrapped their arm around my shoulder, then guided me out of the magical bar.

In that moment, no matter how mad I had been at Eli...I was grateful to have them by my side because *finally* someone could see my struggles.

* * *

I sat in front of the cold structure that had been empty for months now.

All of the magic that my parents had fused into the ground, the plants, the structure...had gone cold.

The places used to be intertwined with my magic and I remember the feeling of running through it when I was a child. The feeling of it tickling my senses.

I was in awe of magic and what it could do. Back then the feeling of being surrounded by magic was comforting. It was like a warm blanket was placed over the area. It felt like it was protecting me.

I only learned much later that it was there to trap me, not protect me like I had once thought.

Now all that magic was gone, and the ground was cold.

It was as if it never existed. As if *we* never existed.

My parents were gone.

Their hold on me was gone.

This empty house that spanned far too large and desolate ground were proof that they were no longer here...

Now it was just me here left to deal with the ruins.

"I hope you don't need anything in there," Eli muttered by my side.

"The accounts are under my name now, Amr had it dealt with for me..." I said. "I just haven't touched them.

Guilt weighed heavy in my gut when I thoughts about how caring Amr had been the last few months...all while I left him back at Winterfell to worry his poor head off.

"Any prized family heirlooms we should sell?" they asked. "Anything black market worthy?"

I shook my head.

"I don't think I want anything to come out of there," I said in a weak voice.

"Do you want to go in?"

I shook my head.

I allowed myself two more deep inhales before I held out my hand and created a perimeter around the house.

It wasn't hard to set the house alight, but it did take a lot of magic.

I watched as in one flash the house was engulfed by flames.

It was an old house with dried bushes and splintering wood. It didn't take long for it to start to crumble.

The fire licked at the bright blue perimeter but never went beyond it.

The magic inside me turned hungry. It liked the act of destroying and it wanted *more*. It didn't want to stop until every last thing in its path was destroyed.

It took me more than a few moments to reel myself out of the magic haze and pull my gaze to Eli.

They were watching me intently.

"The cat will be worried," they said.

I nodded.

"Just a few more minutes," I said and turned to watch the structure collapse, and along with it every painful memory my parents scarred me with.

Chapter 22
Rosie

I had gone to sleep the night before with a head full of worries and an empty, unfeeling chest. I only wished it would stay that way; maybe if the universe looked more highly upon me they would have allowed me to stay in that state.

But given my parents, I knew that the universe wouldn't give me a break. Who else would pay for their sins?

I was awoken by my magic in the early morning. A restlessness filled my being and practically flung me from the comfort of Rae's bed.

Even as my magic woke up inside of me and started to ignite a path of fire, the only thing I could think of was how dangerous it would be if I was stuck inside with Rae and her mom.

The others would live, but I worried for those who were too close and could not defend themselves.

I blindly ran down the hallway and bolted down the stairs, pushing my clumsy legs faster as my magic clawed at me.

I found myself barging through the side door and out into some sort of garden area. Everything passed by me in a blur as I tried to get as far away from the house as possible before I fell to my knees into the damp ground.

A cold passed over my overheated skin and without a second to rest I conjured a magic knife and ran it down my forearm. Thick blood started to leak from the wound but it was slow-moving and inside my magic was building up faster than the blood fell.

Rae's shirt stuck to me as I panted and sweat poured down my back.

Holding in the blast of the magic was painful; it was stretching against my skin and threatening to take down everything near us.

I lifted the shirt away from my thighs, never more grateful to have not worn pants to bed, and began leaving deep cuts as I hurried to get the magic out. Each cut burned less than the last, the pain from the magic overtaking it all.

Tears clouded my eyes as I slashed at any naked skin I could get to.

Please, please, please come out, I begged my magic.

"Please," I cried and lifted the knife above my head with both hands and brought it down to my stomach.

A pale hand shot out from the darkness and caught it just as the tip bit into my skin.

I let out a cry and flung my head against the attacker only for them to grab my head and bring it close to their chest.

"Get away," I moaned against them. My body was shaking now. "*Leave!*"

I felt the first wave of magic roll off of me and out of my cuts, but it didn't do much to stop the crazed magic inside me.

I pounced on the person, throwing us both into the dirt. I raised my hands ready to bring them down on my target but froze when Malik's golden eyes shone in the darkness.

He sat up suddenly, his hand coming to grab my wrists and force them to my side.

"What the fuck do you think you are doing?" he growled at me.

I struggled against him and threw myself backwards, trying to get away. He was in the line of destruction now and even though he had survived last time, I doubted that he would be able to survive this time.

"Get off me!"

Malik pushed us back so that he was now straddling me and forcing me into the dirt below us. He overpowered me and left not an inch for me to fight him off.

I bucked, kicked, tried to fling my arms about but there was no escaping him.

"Rosie if you do not stop this right now I will have to use my power on you," Malik warned. "And this time you will not like it."

I knew by his tone that he was serious, that I would not like anything he was about to do to me...but my magic wanted more.

"My magic," I choked out through my sobs. "It's too much. It woke me— hurts—I don't know—"

"Then do some magic or something!" he yelled. "Conjure those birds or some shit. We need to get you inside, where it is safe."

I shook my head violently, my vision swimming to keep up.

"Too slow!"

I felt the thick blood trickle down my body and into the ground beneath us, the magic swimming around us. The ground below me heated to a point where it felt like it was burning.

And then finally like a sigh of relief, the next wave of magic washed out of me and I could feel the open cuts ache as blood started to pour from them.

Malik's eyes trailed my form and he sat up slowly, noting every single new cut on my body.

"The bloodletting," he murmured as if the thought just occurred to him.

Exhaustion fell over me and I felt myself sink further into the ground.

"It didn't want to come out," I whispered, my voice hoarse as if I had been screaming.

Had I been? Was that how Malik found me?

"It's coming out normally now," he said and lifted my wrist, inspecting the deep wound that now marred my beautiful raven. It would be disgusting and gnarled after this, even if I did heal it with magic...but I wasn't done yet.

Just because I made it in time to not blow up Rae's house, didn't mean that it wouldn't happen again.

And now that I knew how bad the effects of magic could be, I refused to put the others in danger.

"It was dark, thick," I said. His gaze stayed planted on my arm and blood started to flow towards my face, dripping and staining Rae's shirt even more. "Like *his.*"

Malik slowly dropped my arm back to the ground and looked down at me. His mouth was turned downwards and there was an air around him that displeased my magic.

He's unhappy, I noted.

My skin heated as I thought about his obvious disappointment. He didn't have a right to judge me on what I needed to do to keep the others safe. I did what I needed to do and there should be no shame in how I dealt with my magic.

"Heal it," he said in a low tone.

"No," I hissed. "I need to let more magic out before I go back."

Malik's eyes narrowed and his hand gripped my chin, forcing me to look into his eyes.

"Do it," he commanded with his power. "You can go expend magic another way, wake Rae for god's sake."

Blinding fury was all I felt as my arms raised by themselves and began magically healing my wounds. It was slow and painful as my mind was torn between remembering the way to stitch my own flesh together and how to get back at Malik for this.

He moved off me so that I could sit and heal the slashes on my legs. I grimaced as I saw the amount of damage I had done. My legs, which were already littered with scars from the bloodbath in the town, now had fresh scars running up them, ruining my once smooth skin.

Dirt was caked onto every surface and I felt it dry and crack as I healed myself. Once the last cut was healed and I felt Malik's power leave me, I turned as fast as I could and launched myself at him.

I was far from proficient in my curses but I trained enough with him to be able to focus my power on his hands and force them over his head.

I straddled him and gripped his chin much like he had done to me moments ago. His eyes widened and his expression was a mix of shock and anger as he realized that his hands were now stuck.

"Fine," I said in a sickly sweet voice. I ran my hand down his throat and grabbed it tightly, enjoying the way his Adam's apple nodded as he swallowed. "Let's burn some magic, shall we?"

I moved down so that I was directly straddling his half-erect cock and began grinding against him. With even such a little move magic burst through me and I found my hands flailing to come tear off the fabric that separated us.

My concentration must have slipped because Malik sat us up and threaded his hands in my hair, pulling it back hard enough to pull a yelp from my mouth.

His hot breath fanned over my face and our chests were brushing together with each pant.

I smirked down at him, noting the dark look on his face. He tried to play it off in the room, acting as if he regretted his actions, but I saw the look he gave me.

He was just as hungry as I was.

"Do you still taste me?" I asked and let out a gasp as he stood, throwing me to the ground.

"Get your ass inside or I will have you sit out here making magic birds for the rest of the morning," he threatened.

I looked up at him with a glare only to see that his back was to me.

"You wouldn't," I dared.

He turned, his golden eyes flashing under the moonlight. An excited tremor ran through me.

"I would," he said. "And if Xena and Ezekiel come to finish their job? I would let them."

I was left with my own shock as Malik walked towards the house.

"Don't tell Rae!" I yelled after him.

* * *

Malik was becoming an even bigger dick than usual since the incident the other night, though I was glad that he didn't tell Rae about my almost tantrum.

Today was a prime example.

I was sitting with Nathaniel and Benjamin as they asked me question after question about my hybrid status and life at Winterfell. It wasn't what I wanted to be doing with my free time. I would much rather be with the others at Winterfell...but I was stuck here until it was *deemed safe.*

My anger had not simmered down quite as easily as I would have liked. Instead I found myself dreaming of how to get back at Malik, about finally bringing down Xena...and of course about Eli.

"I'm not saying I don't *believe* you..." Nathaniel trailed, a smirk spreading across his face.

Benjamin visibly paled as he sensed the tension between us rise.

The brothers were interesting and I still couldn't get over how similar to Rae they were. In looks anyways—their personalities were totally different.

"I am just saying it is not very likely," Nathaniel continued. "All studies showed that the fetus miscarried. So how is it that you flew under the radar for so long?"

I sighed and leaned back in my chair, my eyes floating to Malik. I had come here for him, and when I heard he was in the family's library I thought it would be the perfect time to talk to him.

I had planned to ask him to bring Daxton and Amr here so I could get rid of some of my magic, but to my surprise both Nathaniel and Benjamin were already here with him.

Malik was settled across a bench right underneath a floor-to-ceiling window that overlooked the property. His eyes were skimming a very old book in front of him, seemingly stuck inside a world of his own.

His aloof attitude annoyed me and made me only want to push him further, demand that he pay attention to me. His disregard...hurt after all.

I had been attracted to him for a while but beyond that, he had been the first one to show me some care and treat me like I mattered for the first time in my life. And then all of a sudden, after taunting me with his words and advances, he puts a hold on it and acts like I am nothing once more.

"Because I didn't know," I said with my gaze still planted on Malik. "But Malik did, didn't you?"

His hand froze as it was about to turn a page and his head cocked to the side.

"I found out when you did," he lied.

I huffed and rolled my eyes. When I turned back to Nathaniel I saw a devious look spread across his face.

"Malik," Nathaniel said in a mock astonished tone. "I never took you for a liar."

I raised an eyebrow at Nathaniel.

"I am not lying," Malik said from behind me. "Anyways, it's not your business."

Nathaniel leaned back in his chair and threw me a grin.

"You should know better to lie to someone whose whole power revolves around it," Nathaniel said.

What I would do to have his power, I mused. *It sure would have helped with Xena in the early days.*

"Whatever," Malik grumbled.

"Anything you want to ask him Rosie?" Nathaniel asked. "Maybe his bank PIN, or maybe why he has suddenly found the library very interesting even though he has never been here before three days ago?"

"I can add a dash of persuasion," Benjamin chimed in shyly.

I opened my mouth to decline but Malik's voice cut through the silence.

"Out," he commanded.

I sat in my seat refusing to leave as both Nathaniel and Benjamin left with heavy sighs. When the door closed I turned back to Malik. I jumped when I was met with his torso.

He had come much closer as I was watching Nathaniel and Benjamin leave and his sudden closeness caused me to jump in my seat.

"I need Daxton and Amr," I said quickly before I chickened out.

Leaning back to look at his face my breath caught in my throat as finally after days of ignoring me, he looked me straight in the eyes.

"You need to use what you have," he growled.

"But you said—"

"Eli is *not* in the right headspace to be around you," Malik cut me off. "And I don't think for a second that Daxton will listen to me, so he has to stay away too."

Heat engulfed my body and I wanted so badly to tackle him, just like I did the other night.

"Eli *would never* hurt me," I growled.

Malik leaned down and put a hand on my shoulder, stretching me out against the couch. With his free hand he ripped up my shirt to showcase my bare belly and jagged scars that spelled out Eli's name.

"They already have," Malik said. "They were on a rampage and ready to do more damage. Just because you get off on their abuse doesn't mean that we can chance you getting killed by them."

My mouth flopped open like a fish and I was left without words.

"I don't—"

"Rosie," Malik said in a tone so soft it made my chest feel tight. "Stop being so *selfish* and go ask Rae for some help."

Embarrassment flooded through me.

"I have been," I growled. "But it's not enough if you would just listen to me—"

"No," Malik growled. "*You* listen to *me.*" His grip tightened on my shoulder. "You need to understand that just because the Originals are not here with us, does not mean life is back to normal. I am in charge for a reason and you do not get to disobey me just because you feel like being a brat."

My eyes trailed down to his lips, remembering how he kissed me in Rae's room. It was feral, needy...and I wanted to feel it again. I wanted to turn the man in front of me into nothing more than a beast that couldn't control himself.

"Then you help me," I said, a warmth pooling in my belly. "You haven't touched me since that night, but I know you want to. Why can't you just get over yourself already?"

I knew I fucked up by the way his face hardened. He stood abruptly and stared down at me for a moment, as if deciding if I was worth a response.

It hurt and angered me at the same time.

I guess he found me unworthy because he just turned and stormed out the door of the library.

* * *

Days had passed since the library incident and I found myself angrier than ever.

I had explored the place from basement to ceiling. Spent time with Rae's brothers, and mother. I even tried to read in the library to pass the time but it did nothing for me and just started to bore me.

That boredom turned very quickly into something much hotter and soon I was seething.

It wasn't all because I was cooped up in the house, though a lot of it had to do with my magic.

I was still mad at Eli. Mad that they decided to take Matt's life and consequently tear me from them, Daxton, and Amr.

I was mad at Matt for being a traitor and lying to me about who he really was when all I wanted was a *real* friend.

And most of all I was pissed at Malik.

Ever since the incident in the garden, followed by the library, he became even more distant and now it was like trying to find a ghost. The only reason I knew he was still in the house was because I saw him in passing, though it wasn't the same as before.

We would have breakfast with everyone in the house and he would be there, eating breakfast and chatting with Rae. Sometimes I saw him talking outside with Claudine and Maximus, but they never came in and would disappear soon after I caught them.

Never again did I see the way he looked at me as he kneeled between my legs. All that passion and need was gone and I was left with only a shell of the person I once knew.

And that *fucking* infuriated me even more.

You keep me here, away from the others but don't have the audacity to finish what you started?

That was the thought that spurred me in my decision tonight. I needed to get this magic out and since he was the one that put me in this position, he would be the one that finished it.

It was well past midnight when I slowly unwrapped myself from Rae's arms. She had fallen asleep over an hour and a half ago but I wanted to make sure that she didn't awake when I left so I waited until she was deep asleep.

As I slid out I listened for any sign that she would wake, but she still remained peacefully asleep and unaware of what was about to transpire. I tiptoed across the room, the uncarpeted parts of the floor sending shivers through me as my bare feet made contact with them.

The house was silent, so silent I could hear each hinge strain as I slowly pushed open the door and slipped out of the room.

The outside hallway was even colder than the room and I had to hug myself to create some warmth, as being in nothing but Rae's shirt, did shit for warmth.

Walking down the hallway as silently as I could, I peeked around the corner and tried to peer down into the foyer and make sure that Malik wasn't having one of his late-night meetings with the witches.

I let out a sigh when I saw that it was still empty and made quick work of descending the steps. As my feet touched the cold marble of the front room a chill fell over me and the back of my neck itched. I searched around the dark space, but found nothing alarming.

Ignoring the lingering feeling I hurried towards the other side of the house and to where I knew Malik's room was. Thankfully, the excursion with Eli prepared me to find his room and an excited rush rose in me as his door came into view.

Just as I was about to take another step further, my body was slammed into the wall by a hard force. I let out a pained groan as a hand came to crush my face against the wall.

"*Shit,*" Malik cursed from behind me, his hands loosening just a bit. "Rosie I thought you were an intruder."

"Would an intruder really be walking around in just a shirt in the middle of the fucking night, Malik?" I hissed at him and tried to push him off but his grip tightened after my quip.

Warmth radiated from his body, fighting off the shivers that spread across my cold skin.

"Watch the attitude Rosie," he threatened, his breath fanning across my face. "Now why don't you tell me why you are sneaking out in the middle of the night?"

"I am not sneaking out," I growled back and struggled against his hold.

I suddenly regretted my decision tonight. I could have chosen any way to get back at him but instead I let my body choose for me.

"Right, so if I search the perimeter right now I will not find Eli waiting for a fuck?" he hissed.

I gritted my teeth and gathered magic in my hand. Suddenly Malik's golden eyes entered my field of vision.

"No magic use for you," he said. "Not until you tell me the truth."

His power was warm as it washed over me and even as it bound my powers, I let out a sigh in relief.

I could feel the hard planes of his stomach against my back and I arched my back, gasping as my ass brushed across his front.

His erection told me he was just as affected as I was.

Fucking liar.

The truth was that I wanted him to fuck the living shit out of me since he had been such a bastard as of late. Leading me on with no intention to actually go any further with me than he had while Rae was with us.

"I was not meeting anyone," I insisted.

He raised a brow and spun me around so that we faced each other. He grabbed both my wrists and pinned them above my head using his free hand to grip my chin and force me to look in his eyes.

The movement caused a fire to spread throughout and I found myself spreading my legs, but he did not come any closer.

"What were you doing then?" he asked. "Midnight snack with no under-wear on?"

My face flamed and humiliation burned inside of me.

"Do you really want the truth?" I asked and glared at him.

"That's why I ask," he replied, his words laced with venom.

I shifted against the uncomfortable wall and glared daggers at him, all of my confidence burning away into anger. This was *not* how it was supposed to go.

I wanted to sneak into his room and surprise him while he was half asleep; I didn't expect him to attack me in the fucking hallway.

"Your silence tells me I am right," he said with a dangerous tone. "I thought you were better than this Rosie. I thought you would listen to orders for once in your life and just sit back while Eli calms down. You know we planned to bring you ba—"

"I was coming to fuck *you*," I said with a confidence I didn't know I had. His eyes narrowed in my direction before trailing the rest of my body. Fueled by the desire in his eyes, I continued. "I was going to wake you with your cock in my mouth and suck you off until you found the balls enough to *fuck me*—"

He launched himself at me. The once omnipotent and controlled demon was gone and in his place was a wild and famished beast. His mouth claimed mine brutally, his teeth biting into my lower lip, forcing my mouth open for his tongue to explore.

The hand on my chin moved in between us and I felt him pull his cock out before grabbing both my thighs and hiking them up around his waist.

Whatever thread he had been holding onto had snapped and *finally* I was met with the Malik that I wanted to meet. The one that took what he wanted with no remorse.

With my now free hands I swung them around his shoulders and pulled our bodies closer together. I positively melted under his attention and found the raging magic in me exploding as his hands gripped my thighs so hard I knew they left bruises.

His rough touches anchored me and allowed me to fully melt into his kiss. In my anger I pulled at his hair as if I was trying to rip it from his head, but he only pushed harder into me. Even as I nipped at his lips and scratched at his arms, he continued to devour me. When he let out a pained groan as I scratched at the bare skin of his neck, I tried to buck my hips against him, looking for some sort of friction to release the pent-up energy inside of me.

He was not a sweet or attentive kisser. Malik liked to claim with his mouth, liked to bruise. Through his kisses and touches I could tell that he wanted me to remember this moment, remember how he controlled my body, remember who it was I was about to fuck.

He ran the tip of his cock from my entrance to my clit and then back down, sliding through my wet folds with ease. From the time he forced me against this wall, I had been ready for him, my body begging for him to touch me, and *finally* it was happening.

He pushed me hard against the wall and lined himself up at my aching core before entering into me with one thrust. It was a brutal, powerful thrust that I wasn't prepared for, but nonetheless I took it and enjoyed finally feeling Malik inside me.

The sudden stretch was only slightly uncomfortable but as soon as he reared back and began snapping his hips into mine, I forgot all the pain.

I threw my head back, not caring about the pain of my head hitting the wall and let out a silent scream as he fucked me relentlessly.

"You look at me as I fuck you," Malik growled as his hips met mine. I peeled my eyes open to catch his snarling face.

The position was uncomfortable, but I couldn't find myself to care as the feeling of being filled by him was far more addicting than I ever imagined. I was used to the brutal ways of Eli and even some of Daxton's rougher times...but this was different.

Malik acted wild and positively feral.

"You're going to come on my cock right now and then I am going to take you into my room and fuck you until you can't walk straight do you understand?" he asked, his power bursting through me like a raging fire.

His hand clamped over my mouth as I screamed through my orgasm. His thrusts never paused as my orgasm rolled through me, each thrust feeling deeper than the last and pulling scream after scream out of me and I clenched down on his cock.

Without warning his arms wrapped around me and he walked us down to his room, while I still rode him, each step jolting me against him causing bursts of pleasure to go through me.

He opened his door with ease, shut it behind us and laid me on the bed.

"Safe word is red," he groaned and he pushed me into the bed with one hand, using it as leverage to pound into me. "Tell me you understand."

I tried to respond but I couldn't as the ferocity of his movements stole my words from me. I nodded and gripped at his arm, nails digging into his skin. I wanted to hurt him, wanted to make him groan in pain as I squeezed the life out of his cock.

His hand gripped my face, forcing me to look into his golden eyes. There was nothing but the small bit of moonlight seeping in through the windows to light his face. It caused his scars to shimmer in the light.

He gave me no moment of rest.

"I have wanted to be inside this cunt of yours for so long," he groaned and leaned down to capture my lips. His free hand came to rub circles in my clit. "I dreamed about it. Fucked my hand and imagined it was this tight pussy."

He left a trail of kisses from my lips to my chest and caught a nipple through my shirt, sucking on it before biting. I let out a moan and tangled my hands in his soft hair.

"You. Were. Just. Too. *Fucking. Tempting.*"

With each word he thrust into me harder and harder pushing us up until we were in the middle of the bed.

No words escaped my mouth no matter how badly I wanted to tell him I had waited for this moment as well. I yearned to feel his mouth on mine, to feel his touch.

"I knew you were doing it on purpose," he said pausing his thrusts to grab a pillow and place it under my ass.

He did an experimental thrust that caused my eyes to roll back into my head. The head of his cock rubbed exactly right against the place that made my body shudder with pleasure. His large hand came to push down on my lower belly right above my pelvic bone.

My hands flew to my mouth to stop the loud sobs being pulled from my mouth. The pressure from the outside combined with his slowly calculated thrusts right against my walls was going to tear me apart.

"Testing me," he said his eyes trained on me. "Pushing me." He pushed my legs apart and his eyes narrowed in on where we were connected. I leaned up to watch as well and felt myself clench as I watched his cock, coated with my release, disappear inside of me in one slow thrust only to be pulled back out again.

"Did this this cunt get what she wanted? Hm?" he asked. My body froze as the words sent a shiver through me.

Malik chuckled and picked up the pace of his thrusts, the wet slopping sounds obscenely filling the air.

"Tell me Rosie," he demanded, pinching my clit.

"Yes!" I cried out.

Malik smirked.

"Now you are going to sit there," he trailed. "And every time I make you come you are going to have to apologize for being a brat. You got that?"

I glared up at him.

"Like hell I wi—"

"Come," he commanded, stopping my protests in their tracks.

My body jerked as the orgasm ripped through me with the help of his thrusts and firm thumb on my clit. Magic burst out of me in waves as I clenched around him.

"Say it Rosie," he commanded pinching my clit. "Apologize to me."

I glared up at him.

"I don't have anything to—"

"Come."

I flailed, my hand coming to grip onto the comforter looking for something, anything to ground me as my world was blinded by red lights right before my eyes.

"It's not that hard Rosie," he said teasingly. "I mean, isn't this want you wanted? You have been pushing me for days to give this needy pussy what it wants. Just say sorry and I'll let you catch your breath."

"You're worse than Eli," I sobbed.

Malik clicked his tongue and shook his head slowly.

"You're not listening to me Rosie," he said in a low tone. "Maybe I have been too easy on you. After all, I bet the others have raised your tolerance. I could always stop you from orgasming instead..."

"Please don't," I said panicked.

He slammed his hips against mine.

"Then are you going to say sorry Rosie?" he asked in a mock sad tone, a smirk spreading across his face.

"I don't have—"

"Taking orgasms away is too cruel, I agree," he mused ignoring me completely. His thumb was rubbing lazy circles in my clit. "What's your record with the others, in one session?"

I sent him a look.

"I don't count," I answered.

"Hmm, pity," he said. "Let's start with five, shall we?"

He leaned down to plant a small kiss on my lips.

"Now you are going to come five times with five second intervals in between, each orgasm stronger than the last," he whispered. "Starting... now."

A cry was torn out of me as the first orgasm was torn out of my body.

"Count the time between the intervals," he said resuming his thrusts. The thumb on my clit in time with his thrusts sent a frenzy through me that was almost too much to handle. Tears leaked from my eyes.

As soon as the waves of the orgasm subsided I did as he commanded.

"One, t-two, three four—*Ah!*"

My back bowed as the next one ran through me, my magic exploding around me. My sobs were silenced as my body shook violently from the orgasms.

"Ohhh," Malik chuckled. "That was a nice one wasn't it?"

"Please Malik," I begged. "That's enough make it—"

"Count," he commanded his tone serious. "You know the safe word."

I did know the safe word...but even as I cried out and begged him to give me a break, I didn't want this to end. I wanted him to give me his worst. Wanted him to destroy me if he dared.

"O-one, Two—"

I was too late. The next one came sooner than I could finish counting. A scream pulled itself from my lips.

"*That's right,*" he moaned looking down at me through hooded eyes. "Let everyone hear how well I am fucking you."

I grabbed his hand to stop his attack on my clit.

"I'm sorry Malik, I'm so sorry for not listening to you I swear—"

His hand came down on my mouth as the next orgasm ripped through me. Tears were falling down my face and I swore my vision went white for a second before his golden eyes found mine again.

"Last one, baby," he cooed. "I'm coming with you this time and I want to hear you scream my name at the top of your lungs as you come, you got it?"

I couldn't answer him as he slammed his hips into mine and the last orgasm seized my body. I tried my best to scream his name from behind his hand but it came out muffled and more like a beg than a cry from an orgasm.

Malik let out a deep growl and froze inside me as he released his seed. He was breathing heavily and he leaned over me, his arms resting on either side of my head, the sweat from his forehead dripping down onto my shirt and my face. His once curly crazed locks were sticking to his face, damp from sweat.

"We are not done here," he warned me, his eyes locking me in place. "I promised you I am going to be fucking you well into the night and I keep my damn promises."

* * *

When I awoke next my head was pushed into a naked chest and strong arms were wrapped on either side of me. Not wanting to get rid of the warm body, I snuggled further into Malik and let out a content sigh.

All the fighting, the pushback, if it was worth this I would do it ten times over.

Malik had been...a dream.

A calm experienced hand that watched me fall over the edge time and time again giving me little to no rest in between. He wouldn't give in to my pleas no matter how many times I begged him.

Malik let out a low groan and his hand rubbed down my spine, eliciting shivers from me.

"Don't think this changes anything. We both have jobs to do and the safety of this group comes first," he growled and planted a kiss on my head.

"I know," I whispered.

I understood, I really did. It was the same with the others, regardless of what was going on between us, we had to remain safe with our heads clear.

It made me understand a bit more why Malik took the actions he did, when it came to Eli.

I didn't want to be separated from the group, and even though I knew Eli wouldn't hurt me, it would be best to have them cool down before we meet.

Though I knew that wasn't the complete reasoning as to why they tore us apart. Now that my head was clear and my magic had subsided, I could see the situation more clearly.

This is a punishment. Eli's punishment.

His hand trailed down and cupped my ass lifting my leg over his. I felt his erection slide against my folds.

"*Fuck*, why did I stay away from this for so long?"

"I tried to tell you," I teased and lifted my head to kiss him.

He lazily thrusted against me, his length rubbing against my clit and pulling small whimpers from my mouth.

"That didn't take long," he mumbled against my lips as wetness pooled between my legs. With help from his hand he guided his cock to my entrance and entered me slowly, pulling the breath out of my lungs. "Heads up, we are going back today."

"We are?" I asked staring up at him. He gave me a small smile.

"We are," he confirmed.

"Then we have to go, we wi—" He cut me off with a thrust. I was still sore from the frenzied fucking last night, but as he slowly moved against me the pain started to dissipate.

"Rae will wait for us," he said. "Probably glad someone can take this needy cunt off her hands for a night."

My gasp was quickly muffled by his mouth.

Needless to say, we were not going to get out of this bed anytime soon.

Chapter 23
Eli

My whole body was on edge after Rae texted me and told me to skip class with Daxton and Amr today. Not like I had planned to go anyways; I had taken to skipping most of them because it was too hard to concentrate.

And it's not like I needed them anyways. After I finally killed that bastard I would spend my time doing whatever I wanted.

I hadn't taken much time to think about what I would do after school—if I even finished it, that is.

I thought maybe reviving *The Fallen* would be a fun endeavor. I knew the workers didn't just disappear off the face of the planet once Malik told them to disperse. They were also likely to be hurting for cash, so as long as I could provide *that*...

I kicked at the gravel on the ground, unable to keep my body still. A buzz of anticipation ran through me as we waited in the old worship center the Originals once occupied.

All the decorations and walls were destroyed, leaving this place in shambles. One look at it told you that a raging Original had been the one to tear down the interior, but surprisingly they kept the structure intact.

Amr and Daxton stood by my side, seemingly better off than I was but I knew inside they were just as anxious to be reunited with our hybrid.

I wanted to laugh, but the sound didn't come out of my tight chest.

We were so obsessed with her.

Elle Mae

It was funny how a little hybrid, who was once no better than the dirt under our shoes, had come in and changed our lives so suddenly.

Demons of this school cowered when we walked by and refused to associate with us if they knew there was even a smidge of their being that we would deem unworthy.

They didn't want to chance it. They saw how easy it was for us—*for me*—to snap.

Not to mention the rumors of what Daxton did to that witch previously were still embedded into the minds of every witch in this school.

Yet Rosie, a *weak* annoying low-level turned Original offspring didn't fear us, nor care about the rumors.

I doubt she even heard them. She was too busy with us that she didn't even glance at the other students.

Maybe that's why we were so drawn to her.

"They are taking for-fucking-ever," I growled and turned to pace beside Daxton and Amr.

I knew they were bringing Rosie back. I mean how obvious could you be? Rae wouldn't tell us to skip class for nothing. She had a high standard and moral compass of a saint, like hell she would actually *ask* us to leave class.

She did murder her own father though.

A hypocrite, like they all were.

Rae and Malik thought they were being smart, thought this would finally get me to obey them. They saw my weakness for her and preyed on it like vultures.

They knew it would fuck me up yet they used the action as a guise for her *protection*.

Them taking her from me only left me with built-up tension and I would fucking *destroy* Rosie as soon as I got my hands on her just to prove a point. I had thought of all the ways I could have her while she was gone and I was forced into a dark empty dorm room with nothing but my own thoughts to occupy me.

They thought it would make me realize my actions were wrong, but it was *them* who were wrong.

And I planned to pay Malik and Rae back in full when the time was right. It would have to be *big*, make them realize that they couldn't leash me like a dog. I had a few ideas, but would have to tread carefully as my mind was unsafe.

Amr and Daxton were also still mad, though they blamed everything on me, instead of the people who actually took her. Luckily, they had come around slightly when they realized I wasn't going on a murder spree, though I still caught the cat glaring at me on occasion.

But the best thing?

Matt did help with one thing…

Pain, panic, and fear make it easier for me to read thoughts, and I planned to test the extent of that theory in time. And you bet I would make it Malik's and Rae's problem.

"Watch yourself," Amr muttered as I shifted yet again.

I sent him a glare. There he goes again on his self-righteous act he puts on. Does he really not get how annoying his entitlement is. Does he really think that just because he doesn't have his hands stained like the rest of us that he is *somehow* better?

"I only let you live because of Rosie." I paused and then jerked my head towards Daxton. "And this guy. Don't get comfortable."

Amr let out a low growl.

"Don't think you were the only one suffering because of this," he growled.

I was about to respond but finally the doors were pushed open and Malik and Rae showed up. Right in the middle, was a very angry Rosie.

A jolt of excitement ran through me as she fumed. She tried to be scary, tried to intimidate us, but it was obvious she was no more than an angry kitten with her guard dogs beside her that did all the work.

As soon as Rosie's eyes met mine a frown marred her perfect face and she stomped over to me. Her brown uniform skirt bounced with each step, pulling my eyes from her face.

When did she get those scars?

I had seen the others before, but there were obvious new ones that littered her skin. They looked deep and painful.

Both Rae and Malik called out to her but they did not dare follow as a wave of red magic exploded in front of them, keeping them frozen in place.

"Eli!"

I stayed in my spot as she came to a stop in front of me and connected the palm of her hand with the side of my face.

The force was enough to turn my head and spread a small bit of pain through me, but not much else.

I couldn't help the smirk that formed on my face at the action and the heat that coursed through me from the feistiness of her. It would be so satisfying to watch her break down later.

Her chest was rising and falling with each inhale, her face starting to flush, and there were tears behind her eyes.

I paused when I saw them.

Why was she crying? She hit me so she must be mad at me... But the death of Matt, a man who hurt her...would make her sad?

I didn't pretend to understand the emotions of the people around me. Sometimes I got lucky, but others, like now, seemed to be lost to me.

A part of me felt like I should comfort her...but the other part felt angry.

I wanted to make her cry, make her beg...scream even, but not *like this*.

This was a face I had seen only a few times from her but this one was the most painful.

And I wanted to stop it...but I was the one who caused it.

"You shouldn't have done that," she whispered. "We should have probed him for information at least before the killing, but I hear we didn't get anything useful? Did you even question where Xena and Ezekiel are?"

I cocked my head to the side, stunned at her words.

Was she mad I killed him? Or mad I didn't do a good enough job at killing him?

"You're not sad about—"

"I am *mad*," she interrupted. "Furious, that you would endanger us like that without even thinking through the consequences. Thinking about how it would affect our plan."

Her voice cracked towards the end and I felt the same pain rip through my chest. I didn't like this, not one bit.

"I apologize for making you mad," I said.

She straightened and let out a sigh, a small smile forming on her face as she wiped away a few of her tears.

"Promise you'll let us know before you try to kill anyone again," she demanded.

"I will," I lied.

Sorry, Rosie...after this one. After my payback for them taking you from me, I will tell you everything.

Rosie looked from me to Daxton and Amr with a sad smile.

"I missed you all," she said. "It wasn't that long but, it was still—"

There was a ringing that filled the still air, and everyone turned to look at each other.

Rosie waved away the wall of magic separating Rae and Malik from us then stepped back looking for the noise.

I caught Rae's glance; we didn't need to check where it was coming from. I heard it last year and I wouldn't forget it again.

"Is that...?"

"The games," Rae and I finished at the same time.

"They are early," Rosie said, a hint of worry in her tone.

Her thoughts reached out to me without any prompt. They were frantic and swirled around me as if needing my comfort

It has to be Xena and Ezekiel's work.

"Tread with caution," Malik warned and began to back away towards the entrance. "I will call the others and search the perimeter."

"We will go," Rae said and reached out to grab Rosie's arm, who in turn gave her a worried look. "You're last year's winner, and have to show your face. We will watch you from the crowd."

"Take me," Amr insisted and without warning shifted into his cat form running full speed towards Rosie's open arms. She caught him with ease and pulled him to her chest, planting a kiss on his nose.

"But the games, he is in the top twenty," Daxton said from beside me.

"This will be fine, if he doesn't show up, they will just forfeit him," she said to Daxton then her eyes shifted upwards, taking everyone in. "For those on the sidelines... We need to be on the look out for anything they have planned *and* we are dealing with the low-levels' first game. I suspect that we are going to see the worst of the high-level cruelty."

The sudden change in her confidence took me even more by surprise than her acceptance of me killing her once best friend. Now her shoulders were back, her chin high, and eyes narrowed at us. No longer was she the enraged kitten but a grown woman who had a plan and was trying to lead us into the unknown.

"Sure," I said with a shrug and tried to walk forward and pull her into my arms but Rae walked over and pushed me away with a glare.

"Don't think I don't know you, Eli," she growled. "I can feel what is building on the surface and until that goes away, you have to keep your distance."

I looked down towards Rosie and she just shrugged.

"We don't have time to discuss this," she said and turned towards the open door. "Let's go."

* * *

All the students began filing into the bleachers, with varying levels of excitement and interest. There were far more students than those that made it into the top one hundred so it was like a free tournament for them, instead of a brawl.

The idea of the games excited me, but the execution was subpar.

You couldn't kill anyone.

People relied too heavily on their powers.

And of course I had to watch Rosie get pummeled into.

She only made it by sheer luck and I doubt it would happen a second time.

There were no seats available in the front, but that didn't stop me from walking over to the laughing high-levels that occupied the seat I wanted and glaring down at them.

"Move," I demanded.

The stunned demon looked up at me with wide yellow eyes.

"I'm sorry?" he asked, his voice cracking.

I felt Rae stand beside me and his friends turned to look at us, their eyes widening as well. Their faces got noticeably paler and they scrambled to leave.

I tilted my head to catch Rae's glance.

"Laid it on a little heavy, didn't you?" I asked and plopped down into the now empty chair. The uncomfortable plastic dug into my skin through the thin Winterfell slacks.

Rae and Daxton sat on either side of me, all of us focused on the mess of a PR sent in front of us.

There was a stage set in the back center of the field, leaving just enough room for the students to fight without worrying about stray powers or magic. On the stage sat the principal, Mr. Falkner, and Rosie along with at least five or six cameras stationed behind her. I couldn't see Rosie's expression that clearly from how far away we were, but I noticed her jerky moments and the way she shifted under the gaze of all the students and countless people.

There were more cameras to either side of us and a hoard of news people who were trying to grab students to interview before the games started.

"For such an abrupt start, they sure were prepared," Daxton muttered next to me, eying the cameraman that was currently making a beeline towards us.

"Mr. Reid, Ms. Ashwell!" he called. "Care to talk about your first games with your parents gone? Any plans to take over your parents' roles after you graduate?"

Rae glared daggers at the cameraman and I watched as his face twisted and he took a shaky step back.

"We don't feel like speaking now," she said in a low voice. "Thank you though."

Even before the words left her mouth the man was turning and running back in the direction he came from.

I let out a small laugh and looked towards Rae.

"What's with your power? Seems like your blood is working better than mine," I said.

Her eyes shifted towards mine and I caught something there that made me pause.

"It hasn't changed much," she muttered.

I hope you are hearing this, but find me after this. I need help.

Curiosity burned at my senses and I found myself unable to wait for this shit show to be over.

Chapter 24
Rosie

Last year's games did not even hold a candle to these ones. In comparison, last year's was a low budget version of a pathetic underground fighting ring while these were some sort of shiny televised event broadcasted to the entire world.

Everything about this caught me off guard.

Mere hours earlier I was cocooned in Malik's embrace, excited to finally see the others after being separated again and the games were not even on my mind.

The games weren't supposed to be scheduled for another week and none of the low-levels were thoroughly prepared for what they would have to face.

I wasn't prepared either, truth be told.

Not to have to fight someone again.

Not to have to watch the low-levels get beat by people way stronger than them.

And I definitely wasn't prepared to be showcased to the entire school like a medal, nicely polished and put behind glass to be viewed at their pleasure.

Only in this case it wasn't glass, but a magical barrier and instead of casual viewing, the cameras all around me zeroed in on me like hungry dogs, just waiting for the moment I messed up.

I was lucky Rae insisted I wore a proper uniform and get ready as if I was actually going to school, or else I was tempted to show up in Malik's shirt and Rae's oversized sweats.

I shifted uncomfortably as Mr. Falkner moved to sit next to me with a smile. I still didn't know what his deal was or why he was even still in this school to begin with. His employers left, so he should have too.

Unless he was here for something else.

"Are you ready for the games Rosie?" he asked.

I looked at him critically, as he faced me. He had been here standing next to me for each game and event that Winterfell had held, like he was some sort of chaperone though he made no effort to talk to me when the others were around. All of it just added to my list of growing suspicions.

Amr gave a clear warning growl pulling Mr. Falkner's gaze from mine.

"Hello, Amr," he said pleasantly. "I see you have changed into something more comfortable."

I froze at his words. His eyes slowly met mine and I saw a glint of something sharp pass through them.

I sat back in my chair with a smile. I knew his act was bullshit.

Probe him about Sarah, child, Marques's voice said, filling my mind.

I almost jumped at the intrusion but forced my face to stay neutral.

"You know, Mr. Falkner..." I trailed. "I haven't seen that Sarah teacher around. You know, blonde hair blue eyes? I was really interested to hear about her theories last year, is she coming back?"

Mr. Falkner's smile dropped and his eyes searched my face carefully.

"No unfortunately," he replied and turned to look back at the field. "She has been quite busy recently and doesn't have time to teach."

Fourteen-fifty.

Telekinesis.

Margret.

Repeat them to him, Marques ordered me.

I did as he said and watched as Mr. Falkner became rigid. His eyes stayed in front but I watched as they darted back and forth, searching for something I suspected would never come. A small bead of sweat trickled down the side of his face.

Then he relaxed in his chair, and crossed his legs at the ankle.

"This semester we will be focusing on the path the Originals took and the settlements they created along the way," he said in a strained voice. "The ones of particular interest are the ones all along the east coast of this continent as based on our previous assumptions about wings, we are to assume they flew there and landed somewhere in Nova Scotia. So there is no need to look at hypothetical fossils anymore." His eyes shifted towards mine. "Because we already know they are there."

Noted, Marques said in my mind.

I didn't relay anything else to Mr. Falkner and was just happy to watch him wallow in his own panic.

I already knew what Marques's plans were with Sarah, and was excited that I could finally lend some help, no matter how small it may be.

Malik does not sense the Originals there, child, Marques said in my mind. *But be careful, I doubt this was caused for nothing.*

Understood, I relayed back.

Also, Marques trailed, sounding uncertain. *Watch your lovers, they are scheming.*

My eyes shot towards the group closest to the field. While I couldn't see their faces, I knew those three figures from anywhere. I caught Eli and Rae looking at each other while Daxton's eyes were focused on Amr and me.

Scheming indeed, I thought to myself.

"Welcome everyone!" Principal Winterfell called causing me to jump in my seat. I sent an apologetic look to Amr as he was jostled but he just cuddled up to me purring loudly against my chest. "This is the second annual Winterfell games!"

There were cheers that erupted from the crowd.

"To note this is also our first year that we are going to televise the games, all to welcome our newest addition to Winterfell academy," he continued, his voice echoing across the field. "The low-level demons have been proven to be one of our most successful integrations yet. With zeros dropouts and with many of the new low-levels scoring in the top six percent of all grades, we cannot believe our success rate."

There were more cheers, but not as much as before, showing that a majority of the demons in the crowd did not feel the same way as the principal.

"Now, how this will work is two stages will go at once until the final battle with our beloved Rosie Miller." The crazed purple-haired maniac smiled and motioned towards me. I sat up straight and looked into the crowd, not smiling or waving.

In my peripheral I could see my face being broadcasted on magic screens that floated in the air.

"Now there is a representative that will watch over each field and declare a winner, and please remember *no killing,* that is something Winterfell will not be held liable for!" His cheerful voice was starting to annoy me. "Now let's begin!"

Two floating numbers appeared on either side of the field and I had to squint to see the names on either side.

I sat up straight when I saw a shy low-level descend from the bleachers and stand across from what I assumed was a high-level. I remembered the girl from orientation; she had come up to me and shyly asked questions, because raising her hand in front of everyone else scared her.

I hadn't heard from her since and I had to watch her now fight someone.

Please forfeit, please forfeit, I chanted in my head over and over again. Praying that someone was out there listening.

As the numbers counted down on the one side, my eyes were pulled to the other side where another low-level I recognized made it to the field.

My heart started racing as I tried to keep the two in sight.

The girl, to my dismay, did not forfeit and instead lifted her fists as if she really wanted to fight the man. The laugh from the high-level could be heard even from where I was sitting and I watched in horror as he readied himself and lunged forward just as the numbers disappeared.

The girl had no chance, his ability was speed and he tackled her to the ground. Without hesitation he threaded his fists and brought them down onto the girl's face.

I stood abruptly and moved forward. I didn't know what I was going to do, but I couldn't watch as this girl was being so brutally pounded into. My head snapped to the other direction as the other boy screamed.

I gasped as the high-level was trying to pull off the low-level's arm.

Mr. Falkner's hand wrapped around my wrists and tugged me back down to my seat.

"They can forfeit if it's too much," he said. "But you cannot stop this."

I looked up at him in shock. Amr growled aloud letting me know his own displeasure.

"This is not a game anymore," I argued. "They are using this as an excuse to torture the students."

"This is the way it is Rose," he said. "Now sit back and wait your turn."

With a heavy heart and a sadness I watched as both the low-levels in front of me forfeited, leaving the two demons to now fight amongst themselves.

As I watched another low-level descend I felt my stomach twist.

This was going to be painful.

* * *

I watched every single match with barely so much as a blink in between.

The results were the same. Each time the high-level would use whatever means necessary to get them to forfeit, but not until they were done having their fun.

I felt like I had failed them and on many occasions I watched as their hands reached out to me, as if pleading for me to save them from this brutality.

I wanted to so badly, wanted to go down there and put a stop to this but Mr. Falkner's stare stopped me from moving.

I wanted to tell them that I knew all about what they were feeling, that I had been there as well before but as more and more low-levels were tortured in front of me I realized...our experiences were not the same at all.

I was protected by the monsters that found me. I somehow successfully turned the most vile and bloodthirsty of the high-levels into people who now protected me and watched my every move...the others didn't have this opportunity.

They were stuck fighting on their own as the people who hated them laughed at their tears.

"Here," Mr. Falkner said. In his hand was a water bottle. "You look like you're going to throw up."

I was in no state of mind to reject him. Instead, I just opened it and gulped it down as fast as I could.

In the middle of the water bottle I paused and tore it from my lips. The effect was almost unnoticeable at first but the familiar vibration of magic as it passed through me was unmistakable.

My magic went stone-cold inside of me before lashing out wildly. Luckily it was still not visible to the eye, but I could feel it fanning out, searching for other magic users, intent on consuming everything in its path.

"What was in that?" I growled and pulled Amr closer to me, hoping he could take the magic.

I felt him start to pull magic into him...but my magic was growing far faster than he could handle.

"A stimulant," he answered in a low tone.

His eyes glanced over to mine and a small smirk played at his lips.

"Good luck, Rosie," he said. "Your turn is soon."

I looked towards the field and watched in horror as Ren and Eli faced each other. From Eli's stance I could tell that they were ready to fight the low-level. I wanted to scream to them, tell them they had caused enough damage, but the words wouldn't come out of my mouth. All my energy went into making sure that the magic would stay tucked inside me.

With great relief I watched as Eli called out a forfeit as soon as the numbers disappeared.

Rae and Daxton followed their lead and quickly left the field one by one. Rae glanced at me and held my stare for a moment too long before turning back and walking to her seat.

It was supposed to be Malik's turn now...but after a few minutes passed Principal Winterfell stepped up to the mic.

"Now we have our champion, Rosie going against our newest low-level recruit, Ren!"

There were cheers and with stiff limbs I walked down the stage steps and across the field.

"Go to them," I whispered through clenched teeth to Amr. "Tell Eli."

Amr meowed in protest but did as I said when I came to stand across the floating number.

I could see only half of Ren's face but what I did see caused me to pause.

No longer did I see the smiling face of the low-level that had greeted me on the first day. Instead his purple eyes were narrowed and his mouth set into a deep frown.

When the numbers gave way I lifted my hand to forfeit only to have to dodge a black ball of...fire?

Did he just shoot fire at me?

I stared at him with wide eyes.

As if to prove I wasn't just seeing things he did it again, causing me to dive to the ground. The fire just brushed past me and I could feel the heat of it singing the back of my uniform.

My magic angrily thrashed inside me, pushing to get out of my skin, begging to rip the boy in front of me in half. It acted as though in front of me was not the harmless low-level, but a witch with a core that I needed to consume.

It saw him as an enemy, one that threatened the existence of myself and the people I loved.

I jumped to my feet and lifted my arm again but this time I found myself knocked over by a bright purple light of magic that singed my cheek.

Magic?

The air was knocked out of my chest and the world came to a screeching halt as I looked up at Ren. I could feel it now, why couldn't I feel it before?

The thrum of magic was vibrating next to mine as he walked towards me. With each step I felt a flare of magic spread out and rock my being. *I was scared.*

Scared of this magic.

Scared that this was the person who was going to end it all for me.

The crowd's screams and chants were muffled as he came to stand over me, his shadow blocking out the blinding sun. A crazed grin spread across his face, much like the one I had seen spread across Daxton's when he was lost to his magic.

"Hybrid," I breathed.

He let out a small chuckle.

"Say hi to Father, would you?" he asked and with a snap of his fingers blackness engulfed me.

I was too stunned to get my barrier up in time and felt the fire burn into my skin. Using my magic I built a barrier around myself and watched as the flames fought to pry open the magic.

The ground below me started to melt against the heat the fire was emitting and a slick sweat covered my skin. With shaky arms I pushed myself into a sitting position and tried to think of a way out of this.

My skin healed itself but I didn't even pay it any attention as my mind whirled.

Black hair, purple eyes, freckles... He was my brother? But I was told there were no others from Xena and my father.

A memory from when I was training with Malik hit me like a train.

"How many were there?"

Malik shrugged, a dark look overcoming his face.

"I lost count," he said. "Truly."

Was it possible one survived? Even after they tried to erase their sins, one still persevered?

If he escaped, then why is he trying to hurt me?

The flames disappeared and I used the surprise to my advantage and quickly tried to pull my magic together, concentrating on covering his form and then snapping my magic as close to his skin as I could.

I watched as his eyes widened and he struggled against my magic.

I made quick work of my magic and forced his body to the ground. He howled as he bucked wildly against my hold like an animal caught in a trap. Fear and panic were slapped across his face and my heart began to ache.

He was working with them...he was afraid I would end him, or they would on my behalf.

I had been there, I knew the pressure that came with working with them. At least Marques had never tried to hold that power over us.

Luckily for Ren, my magic wasn't as matured as it should have been and the more he struggled, the weaker my hold got.

He broke out of my hold and I felt wisps of magic wrap around my ankle, pulling me closer to him. I flailed my arms out to the side and dug my nails into the ground, trying to hold onto anything that would keep me as far away from him as possible.

"Why are you working with them?" I yelled.

"Why are you *not?*" he asked and readied another fireball.

I quickly turned and shot one of my own at him before pushing myself up to my feet and tackling him head-first.

I did not wait for a second and created a bubble of magic around his head and sucked the air out of it. A trick that I learned from the cruelty of Xena and Ezekiel's test on the town.

I couldn't watch as he struggled and instead just focused on holding him down as his hands grasped at me and tried to pull me down with him. By mistake my eyes wandered and I caught sight of his purple face. His eyes were wide with tears tracking down them and his mouth was open in a silent scream.

When his body stopped moving I removed the bubble and looked directly towards Mr. Falkner. Displeasure was evident on his face even from so far away.

My magic was still roaring inside me, ready to kill the hybrid below me. It didn't care that this was Xena and Ezekiel's doing, all it saw was that we were in danger and the danger was still very much alive and breathing underneath me.

But my mind was the one to tell me that Mr. Falkner needed to be taken care of. If I had not let out some magic beforehand, I wouldn't have been able to stop myself. They thought that I would turn into a rampaging beast, hell-bent on destroying my own blood.

But what I couldn't figure out was...was this supposed to be my disposal or his?

Cheers echoed the field as I was announced the winner, but I didn't pay them any mind. Instead I motioned for Eli to come help me pick up Ren and waved the nurses away as they gathered around us.

"They wanted us to kill each other," I whispered as Rae came up to my side. "If you didn't notice he has the same power as me."

"I noticed," she answered. "I made the connection."

"Come with me," Daxton said, his hands full with Amr. "Malik will wait for us in a classroom."

"Here take this guy," Eli said passing off the unconscious hybrid to Daxton. Amr yowled and launched himself at me. I gladly opened my arms for him. "Rae and I will be busy."

"Where are you going?" I asked.

"We will tell you when we get back," Rae said.

Elle Mae

I eyed her suspiciously but chose to trust them.

"I need to share soon," I told Amr and Daxton.

Daxton nodded and without another second to waste we walked off the field trying to dodge both news anchors and students alike. I heard my name being called by the principal but I paid no mind. I had bigger things to do now.

Chapter 25
Rae

I knew that I was really pushing the boundaries of Rosie's trust when I refused to tell her what Eli and I were up to, but I didn't want to give anyone false hope.

There were still many unknowns and I had to put my effort into the biggest one. The names hidden in my father's clock meant something. I had suspected that he knew he was going to die, he wasn't stupid after all, and used his last chance as a way to blackmail yet another person.

If I ask you about Mary Langworth, would you tell me the truth? I asked in my head hoping it would somehow make its way to Marques.

No, he answered back right away. *Though feel free to snoop, not like I could stop you.*

I sent Eli a look, and they merely raised a brow at me, indicating they heard nothing of this conversation.

Why was Malik worried? I asked.

There was a pause before he spoke. The only thing breaking the silence was our steps against the concrete halls of Winterfell as we rushed to the office. Cheers and music were still playing at the field but given our abrupt exit, I doubted the crowd would stay there much longer.

After all, their star was gone.

Malik wants to protect me, he answered. *This information could be dangerous if it falls into the wrong hands.*

Protect Marques. Malik wants to *protect* the oldest known being on this planet. The same one who could end all of us in an instant.

But you won't stop me, I shot back.

We turned down the hallway and the Winterfell Office was in sight. I paused with my hand on the cool metal door, waiting for his answer.

You can say that you have earned my trust, he replied, his voice holding a slight bit of amusement. As if he knew that I was the last person on the earth he could entrust this secret to, but he would anyways because this option was better than anyone else finding out.

I paused to look at Eli. Their face was blank and their posture and jerky movements told me I was wearing on their patience. It would have been better for me to bring someone else given how pissed they still were at me. The anger fanned out around them and hung over us like a dark cloud. I don't even understand how they kept it all in.

...but there was no one else that I trusted more. They would have my back regardless of what happened in there.

Without a word to them, I threw open the Winterfell door and stepped into the dimly lit space. The dry air hit my skin and the first thing I saw was Tammy's flushed face. A smile spread to her face.

"Not enjoying the games, ladies?" she asked.

I felt Eli's spike of anger next to me.

"No," I said in a polite tone. "Just waiting for Principal Winterfell to get back so we can talk to him about some stuff."

Tammy visibly cringed when she met Eli's glare.

"Well, his calendar is booked so unfortunately—"

"Listen here, lady," Eli growled and took a step forward.

I made the snap decision to send as much exhaustion to Tammy as possible and jumped when that panicked face of hers thumped right into the desk, knocking her out cold.

Eli paused and there was a silence that fell over us. The clock on the wall behind Tammy clicked a few times before either of us stirred. Carefully they eyed Tammy, stepping forward just a bit but not too much, like they were scared of getting too close. Their eyes met mine and they stood straight, casting one last glance at Tammy.

"You saw that wasn't me, right?" they asked.

"That was me actually," I said feeling my face flush, and cleared my throat. "Let's wait in his office."

Eli looked at me with a shocked face before a smirk pulled at their lips. Amusement exploded inside them. With a huff I turned around and walked towards Principal Winterfell's office, which was to our luck, unlocked.

There was nothing special about his office, just a desk, a file cabinet, and a few bookshelves, but I knew that the principal of the most prestigious demon academy had to have something valuable in here.

Eli wasted no time making themselves at home on the office chair and propped their feet on the desk, scattering some of the loose papers.

I pushed their chair to the side earning a glare from them, then bent to look through the drawers. By the third one, I had found nothing but an obscene amount of chapstick and hair ties.

With a heavy sigh I moved to the file cabinet adjacent to the desk.

I came across the student files and quickly sought out the section labeled "low-levels." There were not many low-levels as of yet so this made the search much quicker.

I was actually surprised to find Ren's folder, thinking that Xena and Ezekiel were being careless. After all neither Matt nor his siblings had one, but I am sure that they had to do what they could when they lost Malik's power for good.

"To what do I owe the pleasure?" Principal Winterfell called from the door. I didn't even look at him as I flipped through Ren's file. As promised, everything from past school records to address and more were listed, but I would need Malik to check if they were legit.

"Sit," I said and moved to stand behind Eli, only then glancing up at the principal.

He watched me with careful eyes, and I could feel anger and fear rolling off of him and clouding the small room. Principal Winterfell was a disappointment of a demon and really only used his place here to get his dick sucked by underage students.

While the trick with Emma was a good piece of blackmail, she no longer came close to our group after the gala last summer, so that leverage was as good as gone.

When he didn't move I sent more fear towards him and watched as his face lost all color. He looked back towards the door, his hands wringing his jacket before he stiffly sat down opposite us.

Now he was in the student chair and I couldn't help the low thrum of satisfaction that ran through me when I peered down at him. He looked so minimal and powerless from this perspective and I found I rather quite liked being on the other side of this desk.

"You seem comfy behind there," he said in a light tone, though his chuckle afterwards was forced. "Don't tell me you are vying for my job?"

"Maybe I am," I said in a noncommittal tone.

Eli stayed silent next to me and I handed the file to them without a word.

"Are you going to tell me why you are here?" he asked.

I looked down at him, noticing the way he squirmed in his seat.

"I am going to give you some names and you are going to tell me what you know about them," I said and threw a little more fear his way to ensure I got what I wanted.

His Adam's apple bobbed and he nodded his head, the thoughts of denying us seemingly having vanished in thin air.

"Mary Langworth," I said.

He paused; his knee started to shake. His sudden spike of panic and recognition told me what I needed to know.

"Jon Abbot," I said.

Same reaction.

I continued to list off each of the names that I found on the list my father was hiding. By the time I was finished, sweat dripped down his face and his color had turned sickly.

"They were, not people I knew personally," he said quickly.

A sour taste filled my mouth. *A lie.*

"Eli," I called.

Without needing to say anything Eli lunged over the table and grabbed Principal Winterfell's hand, crushing it without hesitation.

Principal Winterfell's screams echoed the room and I quickly moved to shut the door, hoping Tammy would stay asleep.

"Try again, James," I said and walked up behind him. I didn't dare touch his slimy skin but I let my hand brush over the chair he was sitting on.

"S-ssorry," he sputtered. "I knew them. But they were much older than I was when we met. I hadn't even started the school yet—"

"You met all of them?" I asked.

He shuddered as he felt my hands grip the chair he was sitting on. Eli sent him a devious smile.

"Yes," he answered.

"What was their relationship with my father?" I asked.

"Your father?" he echoed. "None, I don't think."

Then why did my father have their name on a piece of paper hidden in his study?

I hummed and sent a look to Eli. They reached over and Principal Winterfell let out a shout.

"I don't know anything about your father and them I swear!" he cried.

"Then how are they all related?" I asked.

"They um…" He let out a shudder. "They were *very* old. Much older than me. They migrated here from up north but I don't know much else."

"Their powers?" I asked.

Principal Winterfell paused and Eli lifted a brow.

"I'm thinking, okay? I am old now it takes me a—"

Eli grabbed his hand.

"Okay!" he cried. "I think one could search your memories or something like that, and uhh, one could put you under hypnosis, he used it to get people to tell him the truth, I think... But I don't remember the others I swear!"

My whole body froze and suddenly, I was back in the study between Marques and my father, unable to move. A sweet voice trailed in my head, persuading me to give up my secrets.

These were powers that Marques had, or at least what I think he had. But how did that work? How could a demon have powers another demon had?

"Where are they now?" I asked.

"They disappeared a long time ago," he said with a quiver in his voice. "That's all I know, and I have never seen them again. I swear."

It still doesn't make any sense...

"That's a secret that will cost you at least ten Originals."

I stood straight and stepped back from the chair.

Is it true? I asked Marques, but there was no response. I didn't need one. The world became clearer and now I understood why Marques's blood had so much effect on us.

But if the world found out demons could eat other demons and take their powers?

We'd be fucked.

"Let's go," I commanded Eli.

They threw Principal Winterfell's hand away like a piece of garbage and stood, knocking the desk as they passed.

We walked out of the office without another word.

"I heard what happened," Eli said as we walked down the hallway. "About the Original."

"Good," I grunted and pulled out my phone. There was a text from Daxton that told me the room number they were in.

I let out a sigh of relief when I realized it wasn't too far away.

When I opened the door the last thing I expected to see was Rosie standing in front of Ren with a knife in her hand.

He was bound to a desk with glowing ropes that burned into his skin, the sound and smell of his smoking flesh filling the room. His pain was immense, though no sound left his mouth.

I shot a look to Malik and he just held my gaze, giving me no indication if he had allowed these events to transpire. Daxton and Amr watched from the corner. The magic was building up inside Daxton and for a moment I thought we may have another situation like the cafeteria on our hands.

"Fuck you," Ren spit at Rosie, anger flaming his eyes, though I could feel the panic and fear settling underneath his skin.

He was also sad. A sadness so heavy I could barely stand in the room.

It was the same sadness Rosie was trying so hard to keep in right this moment.

Chapter 26
Rosie

I turned to Rae and Eli as they walked into the classroom.

They both looked me over, Rae with a tense expression while Eli's was of obvious enjoyment. In their hand was a thick manila envelope that looked to be of particular interest.

Even though we had been waiting for them for a while, Ren had just barely woken up, and was already proving to be difficult. He refused to answer even the simplest of questions and seemed hell-bent on dying in this very classroom.

And if my magic had its way, he would.

"Welcome," I said in a calm tone. "Malik, let's finish this."

Malik, who was standing against the wall on the opposite side of the door, walked slowly towards Ren. Said hybrid jerked against the chair, trying to get as far away from the man as possible.

He obviously knew the power the man held and knew that his fighting now, was useless.

I wanted to give Ren a chance to answer for himself before we went down this route. I didn't plan to actually hurt him, nor did I want to cause him any discomfort, I just wanted him to come clean because he *wanted* to, instead of being forced to do it.

I for one, knew how it felt to have all of your will taken from you and used against you horribly. Being in the backseat of your own body in this situation was horrifying and if he could just gather himself and tell us the truth without us having to force him, *maybe* there was a way to build trust between us.

We were apparently blood-related, after all. Shouldn't I want to trust him?

But there was another reason that had nothing to do with Ren. It was Malik.

Even as he walked the short distance to the small desk that held Ren, I could tell that he was exhausted.

He used his powers a lot last night, and I don't fully understand the extent he had gone to search Winterfell before the games.

He was important, to me and this mission so I needed him in his best state if we were to continue.

Malik grabbed Ren's chin and forced him to look in his eyes.

"Where are Xena and Ezekiel?" he asked.

Even from afar I could feel his power swirl around us and while it was woefully inappropriate...it kinda turned me on. Seeing the way he commanded his attention, the way his power brushed against me as if reminding me of its presence.

I shivered along with the magic inside me.

"I don't know," he said, trying his hardest to fight Malik's power.

"Where did you meet them last?" Malik asked.

"Montnesse."

"How do you contact them?" I asked.

He sent me a glare.

"Answer her question," Malik growled.

"I wait for their signal," he spat out. "A witch comes to find me."

"When is your next meeting?" Malik asked.

Ren's face turned bright red as he struggled against the power.

"Six weeks from now."

"Where?"

"My dorm room," he said. "If I wasn't taken by the demon regulation society before then."

His tone held some bitterness in it and all I could think of was how alone he had been in all this. They expected him to either die, or get taken to jail because he killed a student.

He was just another pawn in their game, and they really didn't care how much they lost.

I was lucky to have those around me by my side through it all, but he was all alone and had no protection against Xena and Ezekiel... If I were in the same position as him, I might have ended up the same.

"Did you grow up with low-levels?" I asked.

His eyes widened and he forcefully ripped his chin from Malik's grip to lock eyes with me.

"Why don't you just end me already, hm?" he growled. "Isn't that what your people do anyways? I know about what you did to the people of Montnesse after you didn't get your way."

"What are you talking about?" I asked through gritted teeth.

My already raging magic spiked sharply and I felt lightheaded from the sheer intensity. I reached back to steady myself on the teacher's desk.

"You killed them," he hissed. "You slit all their throats, and painted the walls with their blood."

His words swirled around me, invading my mind and repeating themselves over and over again.

You killed them.

And...maybe I did.

It was my fault anyways, I was the one who decided to corner Matt and force my way into Marques's hideout.

A warm hand gripped my shoulder.

Looking up I caught Amr's gentle smile.

"Is that what Xena and Ezekiel told you?" I asked, taking the strength Amr was giving me.

"No, I saw you leave the cafeteria in a rush and when I entered everyone in there was already dead," he said.

My body froze.

"When did you arrive at Winterfell?" Malik asked.

"A month before the orientation," he said with a struggle.

"Were you watching me?" I asked shocked.

"Yes and when I saw you run out I knew it was bad news so I flagged to Xena and what would you know, they were all dead when I—"

His words faded into the background and I couldn't hear them over the rush of my own blood running through my ears.

It was never Matt, a pitiful voice spoke in my head.

I couldn't even bring myself to look over at Eli even though the only thing I wanted to do was tell them how hurt I was they lied.

They told me he was the rat, but now that seemed less likely.

"Why did they move the games up?" I forced out.

There was a pause before he answered.

"They said your magic would be vulnerable," Ren answered.

"How would they—"

I was cut off by my own realization.

Because Eli killed Matt.

I looked up to meet Malik's eyes, realization dawning on him as well and he cast his eyes downward.

They knew him better than we thought.

"Keep him somewhere he cannot be found by the Originals," I said in a hollow voice. Malik's eyes drifted back to me. His face was set in a deep frown. "Do not tell any one of us where he is kept."

Malik nodded. There was no need to speak about why we couldn't know. We both understood that there were too many unstable people here and one slip up would end in his death.

Whether that be by our hands, or the Originals.

"We should think abou—"

I raised my hand to stop Rae from speaking.

"We are changing things, a little," I said. To my surprise no one fought me.

"In six weeks' time we will bring Ren back to here and meet the witch," I said. "Before then we will all take shelter in Rae's house. Malik, get Claudine and Maximus to build us a barrier. I do not think we should be here until we—I— recuperate. Ren is one in a million and since we have just welcomed hundreds of low-levels into this school, all with complete access to my time—"

"We cannot chance it," Rae added on.

I nodded and looked around the room.

"Any objections?"

There were none.

Good job child, Marques said in my mind. *You take after your father.*

I couldn't help the way my eyes snapped to Daxton. His eyes burrowed into me and his magic brushed up against me.

"Alright," Malik said and pulled out his phone. "Let me call for reinforcements."

Amr pulled me against his chest as Ren glared at us with so much hatred it made my heart feel like it was shriveling up. I wanted to help him, I wanted him to be on our side and get free of those psychos...but it would take time.

"You're growing into your crown, my queen," Amr whispered in my ear.

"Thank you," I whispered, tearing my eyes away from Ren to look at Amr.

He had a small, encouraging smile on his face that lifted a weight off my chest. He was here still, after everything, just like he had promised.

"Do not burden yourself with this worry, let's get you taken care of," he said.

In a flash Claudine was in front of us, and she met me with a pitiful look. I longed to reach out to her, to confide in her like I once had...but now wasn't the time.

Now was the time to stand strong. We were the closest we had ever been and if I had not been as prepared as I was today...the cycle would start over again but this time it would be Ren, and he would be alone.

"Thank you for your help," I said to her.

She sent me a wide smile, her eyes sparkling in the light.

"Anything for you," she said with a wink then turned to face Ren. "It's a pity things didn't turn out differently for you."

Malik walked over to her and placed a hand on her shoulder, his dark gaze meeting mine.

"I will be back," he declared.

"We will be busy," Daxton said and pushed off the wall to come to my side. "Take your time and don't interrupt us."

Malik's eyes shifted to Daxton and he smiled.

"Be gentle with her," Malik said in a dark tone. "I was rather hard on her last night."

Claudine let out a giggle before taking both Ren and Malik away in a flash of light.

Daxton's hand gripped my shoulder and he moved to cover my line of sight. I had to tilt my head up to meet his gaze.

"You let him put his hands on you?" Daxton growled.

"Daxton," Amr warned, his grip on me tightening. "Rosie is free to care for who she wants. You said so yourself."

Daxton's eyes flashed towards him before gripping my chin, a warning gesture. My magic reached out to him, trying to pull him closer.

Take, now, my magic seemed to say.

I had already waited long enough, and with the elixir I was handed my magic was barely keeping itself together. I had wished that maybe we could have done this under better circumstances, when my heart wasn't as beat up as it was now, but I couldn't chance an incident again.

"I can share," he said in a dark tone, his head dipping to mine. "In fact I love watching you with the others...but that *bastard*—"

"Come on Dax," Eli said from the door away and moved to stand next to Daxton, throwing an arm over his shoulder. "We knew this was bound to happen, you're just angry she was taken from us."

Eli's tongue came out to lick their lips and I shivered under their stare.

"And who's fault is that?" Rae said stepping closer.

My heart started pounding in my chest and my magic stirred inside me.

Never had they been as close as this. Never had they all been here when I needed to share magic. My mouth began to water and I rubbed my thighs together, heat flashing through me.

"I know," Eli said with a huff. "But doesn't mean we didn't miss her. Isn't that right Dax?"

As Eli spoke their rough fingers traced my collarbone and began to unbutton my top.

Amr's hands began to wander down my back, to my hips and then dipped under my skirt. I gasped when his warm hands played with the straps of my underwear.

"We did," Daxton said and moved his hand from my chin to my throat.

"Is this okay, Rosie?" Amr asked, his hot breath fanning my face.

Heat pooled low in my belly and my knees felt weak. If I was not leaning against him I would have fallen to the ground.

It was more than okay, this was everything I dreamed about. The way their hands tugged at my clothes and brushed across my skin left bolts of electricity running through me.

I shot a look towards Rae. Her eyes were hooded and there was a slight quirk to their lips. They sent me a sharp nod.

"We can take turns," she suggested. "I am sure with your...*condition*, it will take more than normal to settle you. Am I wrong?"

Eli finally unbuttoned my shirt and spread it open, their hands coming to cup my breasts. Even through my bra, by the smirk on their face I knew they felt my hardening nipples.

"As long as I can go first," Daxton muttered, removing his hand from my neck to pull my skirt up, giving them a view of my soaked pink panties.

"Is this what you want, my love?" Amr asked and slowly pulled down my panties, exposing my swollen pussy to Eli and Daxton.

I let out a whimper.

"You'll let them take care of you like a good girl, hm?" he asked.

Eli let out a dark chuckle and in one motion ripped my bra painfully off.

"I prefer it much more when she's bad," they said.

"Good girls don't let people like us have their way with them," Daxton said and without warning kicked my legs apart and forced two fingers inside my wet folds.

I leaned back into Amr with a loud moan which came out strangled as Eli twisted my nipples.

"Good girls also don't like to get punished," Eli chuckled.

Daxton began pumping his fingers inside of me, all while his eyes never left my face. Both him and Eli were watching me intently as if they enjoyed watching their destruction.

"Cat, switch with me," Eli commanded.

To my surprise Amr just let go of me with a small kiss to my temple and moved to stand by Rae.

I felt embarrassment flood through me as I realized they were all watching me. It felt oddly vulnerable and safe all at once, knowing that with all of them here they were safe.

We were safe.

Eli clicked their tongue and took Amr's place but didn't stop there.

"We are getting on the desk," they commanded.

Daxton gave them a smirk and pulled his fingers out of me, the sudden loss of them pulling a whimper from my lips. I felt Eli hoist me up with ease and place us on the desk, with me between their legs. They scooted to the far back of the desk and Daxton wasted no time perching himself between my legs.

"This should be a good enough view," Daxton said and pulled me closer to the edge of the desk by my thighs.

"Unzip his pants Rosie," Eli whispered in my ear.

I did as they said and quickly undid his pants before reaching in and grabbing his stiff cock. I fingered the metal of the piercing, tugging on it slightly.

He groaned and helped me push his pants down.

"Are you sore?" Daxton asked as the head of his pierced cock ran through my folds.

I winched at the stretch as he pushed into me. There was a slight burning but nothing I couldn't handle.

"A little," I admitted

At my words Daxton used my hips as leverage to slam into me. Eli covered my mouth with their hand and pulled me back to them. I wrapped my hands around Eli's arms as anchors.

"Good," they said in my ear with a throaty chuckle. "Do your worst Dax."

Daxton grunted and began slamming our hips together, each time eliciting a new pained moan from my mouth as the soreness increased.

"That's it," Eli cooed and grabbed my left thigh only to place it over theirs, giving Daxton deeper access and giving our audience a better view.

"Oh god," I groaned as Daxton fucked me harder than before.

He was ravenous, angry. I could feel his magic clinging to me in almost a cruel fashion, as if they were sinking their claws into my entire being and getting deeper with each thrust.

Eli's hand came to rub small circles in my clit.

"You can't leave like that ever again," Daxton hissed. *"You. Hear. Me?"*

With each word Daxton snapped his hips to mine so hard the desk we were on began screeching as it was forced across the floor.

"I feel left out of this party," Eli said. "Flip her."

Daxton pulled out of me abruptly and pulled me off the desk and turned me around.

"Hands," he commanded. I was out of breath and disorientated but did as he said anyways and put my hands behind my back. With a single hand he grabbed both wrists and with the other bent me forward so he could enter me from behind.

He used my hands to force me back into him, my whole body jolting as he did so.

Eli chuckled and climbed off the desk to remove their pants.

"Look at these tits," Eli said and slapped one before climbing back on the desk.

They wasted no time grabbing a fistful of my hair and pushing me down into their wet pussy. Daxton's animalistic thrusts made it hard to stay still but I tried as hard as I could to lick the length of their slit while meeting their blue eyes.

They tasted just as sweet as I remembered and suddenly I couldn't get enough of them.

"You're not coming until I do," they growled. "So you better put some work into it."

"She already feels like she going to come," Daxton chuckled from behind. "Looks like Malik left her wanting."

"Or she's just that much of a slut," Eli chuckled and pushed my head further into her wet lips.

I latched on to her clit and began sucking. Their hand pulled roughly on my hair, telling me that they liked what I was doing.

Daxton's zipper bit into my ass as he slammed into me. I could tell he was going to come soon by his frantic patterns.

Please let me come, I begged to Eli in my mind and sucked on their clit. Their eyes narrowed at me and I felt a thrill go through me as I pulled a moan out of their mouth.

"Not yet," they groaned and their hips bucked against me. My hands were behind my back so I couldn't indulge them as much as I wished but from the looks of it...Eli liked it better when I was restrained and they were in full control of what I was doing.

"I'm gonna come," Daxton groaned from behind me.

"Then we switch you out," Eli said with a grin, which fell off as I gave their clit a hard suck.

Daxton let my hands go and instead grabbed my hips as he pumped his release into me. The magic that snapped between us made me groan. It overtook us and I was momentarily blinded as it rushed into me and mine rushed into him.

The magic felt familiar, felt soothing, like I had been missing him this entire time and didn't even really know it until now.

I used my free hands to spread Eli's lips as I attacked her wetness.

"Amr," Rae commanded.

I felt Daxton pull out of me and felt familiar warm hands knead my ass cheeks then slowly trail down and pinch my clit.

"Are you ready, my love?" Amr asked from behind me.

I tried to nod but Eli's hand stopped me.

"She says yes," Eli grunted back.

Instead of going straight to fucking I was surprised to feel Amr's tongue swipe my wet folds, not doubt licking up Daxton's release.

Heat rushed through me as he paid extra attention to my clit. My legs began to shake and I didn't know how much longer I could hold on.

"A little more," Eli said, their head falling back.

I worked on their clit like a hungry woman, giving them no break. I felt their thighs clench around my head and was surprised by their sudden release on my tongue.

Eli cursed and pulled my head back, Amr held onto my thighs not allowing me to move from his mouth as I began shaking violently in his grip.

"Good slut," they whispered. "You can come now."

I did exactly as they asked and kept their gaze as Amr pushed me over the edge.

The magic sharing was different with Amr. It was calming, more comforting and less abrupt than with Daxton. The magic slowly rolled me into another orgasm as I held onto Eli, engulfing me in a pool of warmth.

"Rae," they called. "Do you want in on this?"

Amr stood back up and pulled me to him. I turned and caught his lips in mine.

"Yes," she said. "Go entertain yourself with Daxton."

I felt Eli's presence leave and heard some shuffling and the scrape of a chair.

Amr let me go as Rae came close. She leaned against the desk and looked at me critically, her hand coming to feel my jaw. I winced as she touched a sore spot.

"Barbarians," she said with a soft voice.

"But we aren't like that," Amr said and left kisses down my neck finally pulling off the rest of my shirt while Rae tugged off my skirt.

"No," Rae whispered, her eyes trailing to my lips. "We aren't."

When her lips met mine I melted into her body, enjoying the shift from rough to sweet. Amr ran his hands down my body and began massaging my abused pussy lips.

"Are you sure you want to continue?" he asked against me, though I do not know if it was to me or Rae.

I pulled away and looked up at Rae, giving her the choice.

"You spoil me," she said and reached down to massage my clit. "Always giving me that look. Having me decide on everything. It would be a lie if I said I didn't love it. The power you give me."

Her words caused butterflies to fly free in my stomach.

"I am ready when you are," I gasped as Amr's fingers entered me.

"No need to rush," Amr murmured.

Rae leaned down and captured my lips once more. As our tongues intertwined I couldn't stop thinking about how lucky I was to have her, *everyone*, here with me.

My magic, while still swirling around restlessly in my body, would have been so much worse if I wasn't surrounded by people like this.

I was the spoiled one.

With Rae's and Amr's ministrations it wasn't long until I felt myself on the cusp of another orgasm.

"It's okay," Rae whispered against my lips. "Let go."

I shuddered and pushed back into Amr, wanting more than the gentle orgasm I was receiving right now. I loved the way they touched me but I felt far too empty and my magic was begging for more.

Amr lined his cock up at my entrance and left scorching kisses up my back as he entered me. Rae left kisses down my chest and bent to pull a nipple into her mouth.

I moved to undo her pants but her hands stopped me.

"This is about you," she said and lightly bit my nipple.

Amr gave his first experimental thrust then gently pushed my back forward.

Rae stood straight and pulled me closer so my hands could rest on the edge of the desk on either side of her.

"You're so perfect love," Amr growled and thrust into me again.

A strangled moan left me and Rae's eyes lit up. She reached down and started to circle my clit once more.

"I think you can go faster now," Rae said.

Amr didn't have to be told twice and began fucking me in earnest, each thrust hard yet not too fast as to overwhelm me.

I wanted to pull my gaze away from Rae as Amr fucked me. It was intimate, almost too much and reminded me of the first time Rae and I were ever together.

We were different now though, and I tried to embrace the feeling I got as her hooded eyes stared down at me.

"You handle your magic so well," she cooed and brought her free hand to trace my open lips. "Asking for help when needed, letting us take care of you."

I let out a whine and gripped onto the desk.

"Keep going," Amr said from behind me, his thrusts picking up speed. "She likes it."

Rae's eyes lit up.

"Were the others too mean to you?" she asked.

I heard a protest from Daxton and Eli but she waved them off.

"Did they not tell you how in love they are with this pussy?" she asked and pinched my clit. Tears welled in my eyes. "Or how good you feel? *Taste?*"

Rae paused her ministrations on my clit to drag her fingers across my bottom lip. Without hesitation I pulled it into my mouth and moaned at the taste of me on my own lips.

"You're so beautiful like this," she cooed. "When you let us use you. The way you silently plead for more. This face is one I cannot forget."

"*Fuck,*" I cried as she moved her hand back to my clit.

"Yes, my love," Amr moaned. "You feel so good, come on my cock."

Rae's lips crashed to mine as the orgasm ripped through me.

Amr gave a few more thrusts before I felt his hot release inside of me and we both shuddered as our magic fluttered between us.

"Damn I missed a party," Malik said from the door.

Shocked, I looked up to see him slipping in and closing the door quickly behind him. Rae leaned forward and her arms circled around me, shielding me as I came down from my high.

"You had enough time with her," Daxton growled.

I turned to see both him and Eli close together, glaring at Malik.

"I am here to take you back to Rae's house," he said. "We have work to do."

Chapter 27
Malik

I t was a horrible day to die.

Even as we were hurdling closer and closer towards the warmer months, there was a chill in the air and clouds had covered the sky all day. I had thought it would rain, but it didn't. The clouds just loomed overhead as if taunting us with what was to come. Like it knew that nothing good could come from this day and moved in just to set the atmosphere.

I stood in front of the man I had entrusted with my life over and over again, with unsteady legs. It hadn't been the first time that I had to face him with my nerves eating me alive, but I was saddened to think that it would be the last.

The last time his dulling golden eyes stared into my soul.

The last time he and I would share a consciousness.

A frown pulled at my lips, even as he smiled up at me. He was relaxed in his chair, hands on the armrests and his chest moved with each shallow breath. While he had come to terms with this, I for one, had not.

I knew this day was coming soon, but somehow through our years together I had lost track of time. He told me long ago, and never seemed to *fucking* let me forget, but now that it was actually here...

I felt like the young untamed demon I once was, though at least this time I could keep my tears inside me. They fought hard to spill over, but I didn't want his last image of me to be sobbing at his feet, begging him to find another way.

Elle Mae

I couldn't help but remember our times before, when he had first hinted at the idea and how different our roles were now.

I didn't know how long I had been sitting out here, looking over at the clueless town below me. The people in there going along with their day, happy as could be, thinking they were safe from the impending doom that the humans brought onto us.

I had sat on this hill many times before, when the world seemed too much. I would contemplate if the life in this bubble was worth it, or if I would just be better off defending myself against the humans.

They had calmed down in recent years and every time I went out, I was attacked less often, but that didn't stop the fear of another fight breaking out... though at this point, I wasn't really sure who started it in the first place.

They took my father and mother, fed them to other humans...but why? Why would they come up with a measure so cruel?

I doubted they thought of it on their own after witnessing the cruelty of the ones that came before me.

I leaned back on the damp grass, knowing my pants would be stained but didn't care. This was the time when I needed to be alone with my thoughts or else they would threaten to tear my insides up.

I couldn't do it anymore.

I couldn't lie. Couldn't repeat the cycle. And for god's sake I couldn't keep sending those children to their deaths over and over again.

Guilt clawed at my throat and made it hard for me to breathe.

Ann—

I couldn't even let myself think of her name. A child barely over the age of eight, and already deemed a failure.

She was number eight, and I had sentenced her to her death because she could not use her magic as well as Xena had requested. Too much diluted blood in her, we needed something purer.

I wanted to take her and run away from this cursed place. I had no idea what it meant to raise a child, but I wanted to do it for her.

It was my own cowardice and self-preservation that stopped me from following my heart on this one and I knew that it would stay with me for as long as I roamed this earth. This wasn't why I stuck with them. This wasn't what I wanted to do with my time on this earth.

I would much rather spend the rest of my time in exile, fighting off everyone outside of this hell hole. While my chances were slim, at least I wouldn't have to murder children.

I felt Marques's power before he sat down next to me on the dirty ground. I hadn't expected him to follow me. He was always the stoic voice of reason, never getting too involved but making sure to speak up when he saw an issue.

...but this time he just stood there.

For some reason, him being here made the invisible claw on my hand tighter and my eyes began to water. I was far beyond the age of crying but with him by me I was reminded of everything he had done for me since my parents were taken.

Xena and Ezekiel couldn't care less about me, but he saw through my mask. Saw the immature, hurt demon within and made sure I was taken care of.

If he was a man that hugged, I would dive right into his arms this instant.

"I am going to do something that will change the way we do things around here," he said, his voice cutting through the cloud of emotion surrounding me.

"What?" I asked with a scoff. "Xena getting too much for you, or is it the experimentation and murdering of children?"

When he didn't answer I shifted my gaze to him, taking in his tired expression. Marques was always quiet and reserved, but never had I seen his face look so tired before. His whole body bowed as if carrying some type of invisible weight.

His glowing golden eyes met mine. Little did I know that after this, those eyes would slowly begin to lose their luster.

"You are old enough to know that the threat to the survival of this world is not the humans," he said. "We have been hidden in this bubble for over a thousand years; if humans were a threat, we would have been extinct by now."

I swallowed thickly and looked out into the city.

This spot was my favorite, because it was one of the only places that you could see the entirety of the town we were stuck in. At times, when I missed the outside the most, I would squint and pretend that the magical barrier that lay right over the horizon was the ocean.

I used to love visiting the ocean. Having the sand run through my toes, jumping into the freezing water...

And most of all I loved to spread my wings and fly over the waves, swooping down to get close and pulling away just before they crashed into me. It was a thrill and comfort all at once.

Thrilling because the waves threatened to take me under, deep below the surface where no one had ventured.

A comfort because I knew what to expect from the ocean. It was deep, angry and misunderstood. I found solace in something so powerful yet delicate because it proved that it was real and had a life as much as anyone else did here.

But now the barrier seemed too prominent, and I began to feel claustrophobic.

He was right, of course he was right...but that didn't mean we could change it as easily as he imagined.

"Why are you telling me this?" I asked.

Marques had been the one to raise me in the absence of my father and mother. He had a firm hand, and rarely talked about emotions...but I knew deep down if he didn't care that I would have ended up at the whim of Xena's short fuse.

"I want you to be prepared," he said seriously, a wistful smile forming on his face. "For when you come to hate me. For when I do things that are unforgivable. For when you come to believe that I am the worst evil this world has ever known."

I paused, unable to find my words.

"What are you going to do?" I asked. My stomach felt heavy and sourness spread across my tongue.

"I am going to save the world, by watching our people burn," he said in a joking tone, though I did not think he was joking one bit.

I shifted on my feet as Marques's hacking cough filled the room. It sounded painful and I kicked myself internally for not noticing his rapid decline.

Since the last I had seen him, he was a mere shell of himself. His skin was ghastly pale and sunken in like he hadn't eaten in weeks. He couldn't move without help from Claudine, who patiently stood by his side with a solemn expression.

"Is this when we finally save the world?" I asked.

The sides of his lips curled at the old joke.

"That was a silly dream," he said and let out a huff, something I came to realize was actually laughter. "But I will do my part."

I didn't want to think about what was next, didn't want to believe that we had finally reached this stage.

...but I also couldn't let myself think of the world that awaited us if we *did not* take these steps.

Rosie, Eli...they wouldn't be safe, none of us would. We needed a push to help us defeat the Originals that awaited us.

"We will keep the barrier up around the house," Claudine said. "But it will not fool them for long, Malik. We have to work fast. Once they figure it out..."

"I know," I said in a soft tone and sent her a smile.

The poor girl, not only did she have to suffer the loss of her brother but now...

"Ensure that Rosie doesn't fight this, hm?" Marques asked. "That girl is too much like her father."

"With a healthy dose of Xena," I said in a dry tone. Even though we were joking, it did nothing to lift the weight on my heart.

"Will Rosie experience the issues you do?" Claudine asked, her brow furrowed.

"I am not sure, child," Marques spoke. "Though I would like to think that I took the punishment of all ten of my sins and she, well..."

"Will take just the one," I finished for him.

Marques nodded.

"I should be mad that you are shortening her life," I said.

Marques smiled.

"If she is lucky, she can live as long as that blond bastard," he said. "And with her track record, I would say she's pretty damn lucky."

"Or unlucky," I muttered and shifted on my feet.

"Well," Marques trailed. "Shall we get on with it?"

I froze, every single point in my body on edge, but nodded anyways.

"Do you...want me to tell her anything?" I asked. "She's your last of kin."

Marques merely shook his head and smiled.

"Rosie has heard enough from me to last a lifetime," he answered. "Though I only wish I could have learned more about her. Give her the family she deserved."

I nodded, my throat constricting. I would fight to give her the same thing, even if it killed me.

I took stiff steps towards him until I stood directly in front of his chair.

I didn't even have to tell him to look into my eyes, he met me straight on and didn't waver. He had been waiting for this moment for lifetimes.

"Thank you," I whispered. "For giving this reckless demon a chance."

Light caught his dead eyes and I saw tears begin to well in them.

"Thank you," he said. "For trusting me, and please don't hold onto this. Go home, hug your loved ones and know that *you* are making it possible for them to continue to live happy, healthy lives."

I let out a shaky breath.

"Anything else?" I asked.

"Just can't wait to see you on the other side," he said. "Though don't hurry, enjoy yourself. You deserve it after everything."

I wanted to look away. Wanted to run and hide and never look back, but

I stood my ground. He had built me up for this and now I had a job to complete.

"Sleep, have the best dream you could possibly imagine," I said, sadness ebbing into my words. "And then stop your heart."

His eyes fluttered closed and a smile spread across his face.

His body was so weak that it just sunk into the chair. I didn't dare move to touch him, I couldn't pull my eyes away.

A hand clasped my shoulder.

"Claudine and I will—"

I cut Maximus off with a wave of my hand.

"This is my burden too," I said. "Let me."

Chapter 28
Eli

The cold air seeped into my clothing, pulling a light shiver from me.

I leaned back against the side of Rae's house and shoved my free hand into the pocket of my hoodie. The other hand held my half-smoked lit cigarette, and I brought it back to my lips to take another drag.

I had tried to stop, but since we had been laying low...I was getting bored again and needed *something* to tide me over.

The night was quiet, and there was no sign of any life just outside of the magical barrier Maximus had put up around us. Sometimes a stray bird or squirrel would try and get close to the barrier but it had been a few hours since I had seen any other life form.

I was starting to think that we had overestimated Xena and Ezekiel's capabilities. They were supposed to be the strongest beings of this world, the ones that started everything. Couldn't they just take what they wanted? Were they *that* scared of a bunch of college students getting the upper hand?

Maybe we were the cowards.

But on the other hand, Rosie had made the right call. I may be itching for action, but I would stay put if it meant ensuring her safety. I was reckless, not stupid.

I exhaled the smoke into the cool air, watching as it dissipated, wishing many problems could just float away with it.

Rosie was still mad at me... Well, I wouldn't say mad.

She would give me this look sometimes. There would be a frown on her face and her eyebrows would be raised, usually followed by a sigh.

She was *that*. Whatever *that* was, was beyond me...but I didn't like it. I had thought to punish her when she first gave me that look, so that I would never have to see it again...but the constant presence of the others warned me not to.

They had continued to keep their distance, with only Daxton daring to seek me out. But even he was occupied with the cat and Rosie.

I didn't like how it made my chest feel cold; after all, I know I did the right thing. Matt was trouble, and he would have pulled some shit, even if he wasn't the one to snitch on Rosie.

The first thought in my mind after we found out that purple-eyed low-level was actually spying on us and planning to kill Rosie, was to tear him to pieces and give his corpse to Rosie as a gift.

But then when he was hidden, that ruined my plans.

So fucking boring.

"I didn't know you took guard duty so seriously," Malik said, his voice cutting through the silence.

I turned to see him materialize, stepping out of the darkness of the back entrance as if my bitter thoughts about him called his presence to me. Even in the dim light of the moon I could tell that his skin had dulled considerably. When I tried to reach out to his mind, none of his thoughts were clear enough for me to understand, but I could hear them swirling around.

He was thinking something heavy, something he didn't like to think about. It was dark and I couldn't help but wonder what would pull that type of emotion out of him.

"I don't," I answered simply and took another drag of my cigarette.

"I don't believe you," Malik said with a teasing tone. It was one he used to get on my nerves, but this time it didn't hold the weight it once did.

I looked at him critically.

Malik, who used to act all-powerful and all-knowing, seemed much more solid now and less of a god-like figure that always seemed out of my reach. I knew him almost as well as I knew myself by now and if I had to put my money on it, he was probably bored out of his mind too.

"Believe what you want," I said and shrugged. "Are you taking over?"

A twig snapped and my head snapped to the intruder.

Maximus appeared just outside the light blue barrier that separated us from the rest of the world. He was wearing surprisingly casual clothes and his long hair was pulled into a bun on top of his head.

"I will be," he said and slipped past the barrier with ease. The same barrier that I had seen shock a bird to its death mere hours earlier.

"And you are coming with me," Malik said drawing my attention back to him. "Your present has arrived."

An excited thrill ran through me causing all of my hair to stand up on end. I threw my cigarette down and stomped on it with my foot before practically running to Malik's side.

Finally, some action.

"So that dusty bastard finally kept his promise?" I asked with a laugh.

A sort of buzz overtook my senses and I couldn't wait until I actually got to indulge myself.

Malik's eyes shifted from mine to Maximus's then back to me.

"Yes," he said in a thick tone. "He kept his promise."

Without waiting for my reply he turned and walked out past the barrier and into the night.

Without looking at Maximus I followed after Malik with a growing excitement tingling my limbs.

* * *

Kept his promise indeed, I thought with a smug tone.

Malik had brought me to a secluded warehouse not far from where we kept the refugees, and presented me with the person I had been waiting to tear apart.

I couldn't help but think it was all kind of fitting, somehow.

The blonde-haired blue-eyed teacher was chained and sat in the middle of the cold dirty warehouse. The space was empty except for her and a few scraps of metal. Underneath her was a large plastic tarp. A long black fabric was wrapped around her eyes, but her head turned as soon as our steps sounded in the warehouse.

I could hear her fear. It was so clear, I could almost *taste* it.

Malik stood aside silently and let me walk to her.

She struggled against the chains.

I have to get out of here, her mind screamed. *I can't die like this.*

"How does it feel?" I asked and brought my booted foot to her chest. "To be trapped against your will?"

I kicked the center of her chest and laughed as she hit the ground with a thud.

"Eliza!" she yelled.

I bent down and removed the blindfold from her face and was met with wide blue eyes. I had seen that look in the mirror more times than I would like to admit, though that was with Damon... Now this was something I controlled.

How could my own daughter do this?

I growled and grabbed her face roughly.

"Don't call me that you *cunt,*" I hissed.

Her body began shaking in my hold. Gone were the dark stares and sinister smiles, now all that was left of the woman that ruined my life was a whimpering sack of useless skin.

"Eliza, please, you don't have to do this," she begged me.

"What do you think I am going to do?" I asked and threw her head to the side.

I stared straight and looked down at her with disgust. The tears and snot were running down her face, making a mess of a once perfectly respectable demon.

Why wasn't she angry? Why wasn't she fighting.

I didn't want to hear her beg for mercy, I wanted her to yell at me. I wanted to see that cunt of a woman that I saw when Ezekiel was still backing her.

That was the woman I wanted to end.

This was supposed to be the moment I was waiting for. I was supposed to love the idea of toying with her. Love ripping her apart as she cursed for mercy...but I found myself disgusted by her and wished that Marques would have done the dirty work himself.

There was something different about this one, as opposed to Matt or Damon. With them, I found myself getting high off of watching the life bleed from their eyes. I wanted to hear them beg and then just when they thought I was going to give them mercy, take it away right before their eyes.

I didn't even want to touch her.

"Please, Eliza," she sobbed.

"Did you like my present?" I asked. "You breed annoying children did you know that? I didn't even have to strain to tear that head of his right off."

Her sobs increased and I felt an uncomfortable pressure in my chest.

I didn't like how they bounced off the walls. They grated on my nerves and I found myself flinching as her volume raised, practically screaming for mercy.

Malik's hand clasped my shoulder and I jumped at the suddenness. I didn't even hear him come up. Normally I would shrug him off right away, but his hand felt like it was cemented to my shoulder, forcing him closer than I would allow.

A part of me wanted to move closer to him.

"Is there an issue?" he asked.

I gritted my teeth not wanting to explain the mixed emotions tearing apart my psyche.

I wanted to kill her, *god* I fucking hated this bitch and had been waiting for this moment for a lifetime.

But...

"Malik, please," she pleaded, eyes wide.

I couldn't stop my face from twisting.

"Not so tough after all, hm?" Malik asked, though while his words were meant to be joking, there was no humor in his tone.

His eyes were curious and his tone not as condescending as I needed it to be in order to see this task through.

"It's not the same," I said in a thick voice.

"Let's hope you don't think the same when we face your father," he muttered and sunk down to her height. "Stop breathing."

I watched with disgust at the woman on the floor as she struggled to gasp for breath. Her face turned a bright red and then she stopped moving entirely.

It was quick and easy, but it left an uncomfortable weight in my chest.

"Disgusting," I muttered.

Malik stood and faced me with a frown.

"I'm glad," he said in a low voice. He spared another glance at the woman on the floor before meeting my eyes again.

"You don't seem like it," I noted.

"Just surprised—confused," he said, his eyes burrowing into mine. "Though I am glad you haven't lost yourself completely, yet."

Yet.

The word hung between us uncomfortably.

Chapter 29
Amr

Even though I had spent many years in my cat form, I still found it to be comforting, especially in Rosie's hold.

I was comfortable enough with myself to admit when I needed some love and attention. I thrived on physical contact and couldn't get enough of the way Rosie's nails scratched under my chin *just right*.

Today we were in Rae's office as Rosie helped her brothers pour over their finances. It was a move that even I didn't expect.

Rosie had made it clear that she was not an expert, but then went to Rae and insisted that she become of some use to their situation... Rae reluctantly handed her over to Nathaniel and Benjamin with the instructions, *just help them figure out why we are spending so much*.

That had been an hour ago and I spent the whole time on Rosie's lap.

"You're wasting money because you were hiring witches and high-levels," Rosie grumbled as she looked over the stack of papers on the desk she was sitting on.

Rae had scowled when she saw her disregarding the chairs in the room to sit on the desk, but left soon after that with a small smile on her face. Benjamin and Nathaniel sat next to each other in a pair of office chairs, each with stacks of papers that they were combing through.

Though Nathaniel didn't seem to be much interested in doing any work. I caught him multiple times stifling a yawn and leaning back to watch as Rosie sifted through her own stack.

"Are you saying we hire *low-levels*?" Nathaniel asked, the disgust evident in his voice.

I didn't have to look at Rosie to feel the death glare she gave him. His and Benjamin's reaction was enough. They both cringed and looked to each other for an answer.

"They can do the same job, if not better," she said. "And they would absolutely foam at the mouth when they realize they could work for such a prestigious family."

Benjamin shifted uncomfortably.

"Well, it would be better than the witches," he mumbled.

Nathaniel reached back and slapped the back of Benjamin's head.

My gaze shifted as Rae's form slowly came into view as she leaned against the door frame watching Rosie interact with her brothers. A small smile played at her lips.

"Hire them," Rosie said. "And you should start auctioning off the furniture in the empty rooms."

"Wait I think that's a bit—"

"It's fine," Rae spoke from the doorway. Rosie jumped, obviously not noticing Rae's intrusion. "We don't need it anyways."

"Next you are going to say we need to get rid of the summer property," Nathaniel said with a forced laugh.

When no one responded his eyes widened.

"Really?" Benjamin asked. "I mean I knew it was a possibility...but really? Now?"

"Already sold," Rae confirmed. "Three properties have been sold and the money is deposited into the savings while the other is being prepared as a rental property."

Rae's eyes glanced towards us when Benjamin and Nathaniel failed to form coherent responses.

"Are you done here?"

"Yep," Rosie said and scooped me up before jumping off the table.

I cuddled into her and began purring as she walked towards Rae. I was addicted to this woman and I couldn't find it in myself to be bothered by it.

When I told her I would stay with her regardless of the circumstance, I meant it. I would follow her to the ends of the earth and was prepared to take any bullet for her. I would be her shield if she needed it, but after seeing her slow and ever-evolving sense of confidence, I had a feeling she may not need me as a shield.

Which was fine by me.

Guard cat. Assistant. Familiar.

I would be anything for her.

Her magic spiked as Rae's hand came to rest on her shoulder and I ate it up greedily. It had been a few days since I was able to share magic with Rosie and it felt like I was missing her far too much.

But I had to admit, everyone together under one roof for the last few weeks had been a godsend for Rosie's magic. No longer were Daxton and I the sole people to take all of her magic and it gave us a much-needed break.

"Are you prepared?" Rae asked, her words weighing heavily on us both.

"I don't know," Rosie muttered in a soft voice. "Many of the students will be there and I am just worried..."

Tonight was a gala hosted by the governor to welcome the low-levels into Winterfell. Another complication we did not expect. We would have to tread carefully as just tomorrow night, we would have to stake out in Ren's dorm and hope that Xena and Ezekiel would send the witch as planned.

"We will be on the lookout," Rae said. "Malik, Claudine, and Maximus will be there for backup."

It had been quiet since the games. Six full weeks had gone by and there was not a peep or stir from the Originals, Marques included. The older demon had not reached out to us once since we arrived and even when Malik went to go check on the refugees, there was no news of him.

"Does Marques know about this?" she asked.

Rae frowned lightly.

"I tried to reach out to him but he has not responded," Rae said. "Malik and Claudine told me he knows, but is just taking the time to adjust his plans accordingly. They assure me he is fine."

There was a pause.

"They are hiding something again," Rosie said with conviction.

"Let's confront them tonight," Rae offered. "But we have to get ready first."

* * *

Suits were uncomfortable and itched terribly. They were a complete waste of fabric and I didn't understand why we had to dress up so formally for a simple trip to the museum. It's not like it was the clothes that impressed people, but rather that magic and power embedded inside you.

I stared down at Rosie as she fixed the stiff collar near my neck with delicate hands.

"My love," I whispered.

A small smile spread across her face and she peered up at me through her dark lashes. Gold glitter was brushed across her eyelids and made the lighter tone of her brown eyes come forward. Her hair was pulled up into an intricate updo with a few strands falling into her face and curling around her neck. I preferred her natural face, but she had done a beautiful job at decorating herself today.

I looked down at the deep red dress she was wearing, my magic stirring inside me as I took in her figure. It hugged her body well and left a lot of her skin open. My eyes lingered on the scars on her arms, particularly the one that slashed through the raven tattoo. I hadn't asked about the scar, I wanted to give her some sort of privacy, but I noticed it along with the ones on her legs.

The slit in the dress showed a bit of her leg, showing me the deep scars that tugged at my heart. Just a year ago her skin was smooth, but because of the selfishness of the people around her, her body began to pay the price.

I bottled up my hurt and locked it inside me because I knew that to Rosie, it was a sign of her strength, her journey in this world. She should get to show it off to the people that doubted her.

Some may not understand, like the low-levels she oversaw... They would whisper when she wasn't looking and stare at her body with fear. Afraid that they would end up like her, but they didn't know what she had to go through to live up until now.

"Yes?" she asked, her sweet voice spreading warmth across my chest.

I trailed my fingers up her arm and cupped her cheek, careful not to smudge the paint she worked so hard to apply. When she leaned into my palm my heart jumped in my chest.

"Promise me, if you see anything wrong, you will let me take care of it," I said in a serious tone. Her eyes widened.

She may have wanted to lead, take charge of what was going on here... but I was not sure she was ready and tonight, I wanted to make sure that I protected her in any way that I could.

"What do you mean?" she asked.

"I have a bad feeling about this," I admitted.

The bad feeling had started ever since the start of this semester and looking back I believed it was foreshadowing the murder of the refugees and fled...but it started again ever since we moved into Rae's house.

It started at night, when I would wake up in a cold sweat thinking that someone was in the room watching us. When I searched for the culprit, I found nothing but empty hallways. Still the feeling never left me. It became like a dark cloud that hung over us at all times...ever since then I have never let Rosie without one of us by her side.

"Me too," she said softly. "But we won't know until we find out hm?"

"Just stay with me okay?" I said and leaned down to capture her lips in mine. "I can't lose you."

She smiled against me then pulled away.

"I love you Amr," she said.

"I love you too," I said and leaned in again but was interrupted by a throat clearing.

Malik and Eli were watching us from the doorway, both with different levels of amusement on their face. Eli was wearing a suit similar to mine though they forwent the jacket and of course had a majority of their chest showing, no doubt trying to piss off the stuffy demons we were about to meet.

Malik on the other hand at least tried to look prepared. He even had his hair slicked back, showing us a rare look at his entire scarred face.

I couldn't help but think how perfectly he matched Rosie and while she may have been okay with her scars, it would do well if she wasn't the only person whose body showed her struggle.

"I knew the cat would be taking all her time," Eli said with a smirk.

My eyes lingered on Malik, thinking back to the conversation Rosie and Rae had earlier.

What would he have to hide any longer? We have been through hell and back only to end up right here with one another... Why keep secrets?

Rosie followed my gaze and I felt her stiffen.

"Is it time already?" she asked and turned to them.

"It is time," Malik spoke.

Like Rosie and Rae had noted, there was something off. Malik's usual cockiness was gone and he sort of deflated into himself.

It could be the exhaustion of it all, but my gut told me it was something different.

My gut told me to beware.

Chapter 30
Rosie

Ideally, I wanted to ask Malik what was going on before the gala because he deserved the benefit of the doubt after everything we had been through...but I never got the chance. We were always surrounded by people and the last thing I wanted to do was question him in front of the others.

It was enough for me to have this feeling of doubt, but I didn't want to corner him and throw the group into chaos.

I wanted to trust him and deep down I did, I trusted him more than anything. But his behavior had led me to believe something was wrong and I was scared of falling into another trap.

Quiet chatter filled the limo as I stared out the windows. While it was getting warmer, the leather seats sent a chill across my skin and I shifted uncomfortably in my seat.

The dress I was wearing was jaw-dropping, but it wasn't very practical.

I had planned to go a bit more casual but when Rae walked into my room with this beautiful dress in her arms...I couldn't deny her.

The limo slowed as we rounded the corner and drove into the city. We had to pass parts of downtown in order to get to the venue where the gala was being held, and it gave us a perfect view of the protests.

Normally, I would have been excited to explore parts of the city and come face to face with parts of this state that I hadn't been able to in the past; after all I had been stuck in either Winterfell or Rae's house for a majority of the school year.

But looking at the people that crowded the streets with signs and angry faces, yelling at cars to pay attention to them, made me want to turn right back and hide.

I wasn't following the election as well as I should have been, but the low-levels and witches were very unhappy with the prospects. The last time I had seen them so riled up was when my status was announced.

They blocked the sidewalks and the cars in front of us started honking at them. I heard a few shouts but couldn't tell if it was from the drivers or the protesters as all the noise outside the car started to jumble together. I wondered if I had never been introduced into this life, or been cursed to begin with, if I would have somehow found myself in line with them, fighting for the future of our dreams.

Would I be brave enough to yell in the face of the demons who shunned me? I grew up timid and scared because of my power and curse. I never wanted to hurt anyone and always found myself hanging on the sidelines, so how could I stand up like them?

Though maybe in a different life I could be like them.

I envied them, I realized. Envied their drive and passion and ability to scream at the top of their lungs for their rights. Even if I was reserved, I couldn't help but feel enraged on their behalf.

I wanted to be there with them, change the world in a way that mattered.

Instead I became the worst version of myself...one that thrives on pain—my own and others'—and murdered multiple people for no reason at all.

A rough hand squeezed mine and my gaze was drawn to Eli. They had stolen the seat next to me while Malik sat next to them and Daxton, Amr, and Rae sat further down in the limo.

They were wearing a button-up and dress pants that matched the others, leaving only me in a dress. I didn't mind though. They were all positively mouthwatering.

Every time I looked toward Eli, I had to take a breath in order to continue because no matter how many times I saw them, I still found them breathtaking.

It wasn't just their looks that caused my heart to pound in my chest though. It was the way their eyes never left me and how a hand always rested somewhere on my body. It was comforting and maddening at the same time.

"Don't tell me you regret coming to Winterfell," they teased.

Malik leaned forward to watch my response, his expression curious if not a little hurt. The chatter was silenced.

"No," I said truthfully. "Though I will be happy when this is all over."

"This?" Malik asked with a raised brow.

"Originals," Rae answered for me.

I sent her a small smile. For the first time in a while, her glasses were off and I was given an unobstructed view of her chiseled face. Her features seemed sharper under the limo's light and her eyes darker.

"That's not a tonight problem," Malik said in a light tone and smiled, though it didn't reach his eyes.

"Are you sure about that?" I shot back without thinking.

His face fell before he quickly plastered the smile back on his face. I watched as Eli's eyes shifted towards Malik then back to me.

"As far as I am aware of," he said.

The car slowed, halting the conversation. Peering back outside I realized that we had arrived at our destination. New reporters and other media personnel noticed our car and began waving for their partners to catch up to us.

I swallowed my nervousness and squeezed Eli's hand for reassurance.

I still wasn't a fan of the attention, no matter how common it had become. I wished for them to just get bored and move on. I didn't have much to offer and their constant pestering only made me feel even more alienated than I already was.

Relax, Rosie, Eli said in my mind, their voice oddly soft.

I took a few seconds to pull myself together and then without prompting, the limo door was opened for us.

Amr was the first to exit, his eyes lingering on mine as if he was reminding me of his words. He was acting as the protector tonight...and for now I would let him, but I knew soon I would have to stop hiding behind everyone and take charge for myself.

I followed after him but froze as I was met with a scene I didn't expect.

Tonight's gala was in a museum that the governor had recently opened, stating that this had been ongoing for years. The guise was that this would be the first-ever museum to hold all of the demon and witch historical arti- facts known to our kind and the first thing he wanted to do when it opened?

...bring the school's newest low-levels in as a way to "promote a healthy and prosperous future together."

It was huge with white columns holding up the main portions, causing it to look like something that came out of Rome instead of the United States. On the stairs was a fancy black carpet that high-level demons were walking up and on the sidewalk, were the press...and protesters.

The press I expected, they were always around...but why were the protesters here?

As the rest of the group filed out of the car, I reached my hand out for Malik's. With a stunned expression he came to my side and wrapped his arm in mine. I leaned into his warmth and inhaled his spicy cologne.

I gave Eli a look and they rolled their eyes.

Trying to be sneaky? I heard their voice in my mind, though it sounded distant.

What did you hear? I asked.

Pulling Malik to the stairs I tried to keep a smile as people yelled at us left and right.

I couldn't make it out, but he was worried about something, Eli said. *If you are worried about him starting something, come here. We will keep you safe.*

I didn't reply right away, focusing on the stairs underneath me.

It wasn't that I was worried he would hurt me, I trusted him more than that. But I was worried there was something I should know.

"Rosie! I heard you won the Winterfell Games again!"

"Rae, how have you been handling your Father's death?"

"Rosie, is that your spokesperson?"

I tuned them out and sent one last sentence out to Eli.

If there is something he knows about, I said. *I am the one that needs to be by his side. I cannot hide behind you all forever...plus Malik couldn't scare me if he tried.*

"You are far too silent to be up to anything good," Malik whispered in my ear as we reached the top of the stairs. His deep voice sent shivers down my spine.

He unwrapped his arm from mine to rest his hand on my lower back, his light touch sending waves of heat through me.

With my head held high I sent him a smile.

"I have a soft spot for you Malik," I said and leaned in close to him. "But I said I was done with lies and I meant it, so if you have anything to tell me, you should do it now."

His jaw twitched and I swore I could feel the anger rise up in him, then the tension between us becoming thick.

"Not here," he said simply. "But we will have a talk before tomorrow's meeting."

"Malik," I trailed in a disappointed tone.

"It's not bad it's just..." He sighed and shook his head. "You will understand when I explain."

I looked at him then nodded.

Turning to the others I switched to Daxton's arm and led him through the museum.

"I am honored," he whispered with a smile.

His smile warmed my heart as it had been a while since I had seen it. He seemed much better in the last few weeks. His skin was clear and soft and his eyes were almost glowing. My eyes trailed his face noting the growing length of his hair that now covered the tattoo on his temple.

"Let's get wasted," I whispered, a thrill running through me.

He gave me a mischievous smile.

The museum was packed with both students and non-students, each dressed in their fanciest clothing. You could tell the difference between the low-levels and the high-levels by the quality of their clothes...and how they stopped what they were doing to wave at me.

I weaved us through the crowds trying to avoid heavy conversation until I got at least one drink in my hand.

I stopped at the bar and let Daxton order for us. I knew nothing about alcohol so would defer to him for what to choose. My mouth dropped when the bartender grabbed two empty glasses and placed them on the counter, purple swirling liquid rising from the bottom of the cups.

When I lifted it I tried to look for a spout or anything that would show me where the alcohol came from, but there was nothing except the smooth countertop and the now full drink in my hand.

"I don't think they will look kindly on underage drinking," Rae muttered as we turned back to the group.

Eli watched us with a smirk while Malik and Amr seemed to have the same sentiment as Rae.

"It's not like I am trying to impress them anyways," I said with a smirk and took a sip of the glowing liquid.

As soon as the liquid hit my tongue a fruity flavor burst into my mouth and sent tingles down my body. It danced with my magic and left dull electric tingles throughout my body.

Rae's head snapped to the side and she cursed under her breath before grabbing the drink from my hand and turning around, while keeping the drink behind her back.

Peering to the side I saw a soft-faced, gray-haired man walk over to us with a blonde woman on his arm. The woman was staring at Eli as they approached.

Jealousy burned in my stomach and I caught Eli's smug gaze.

"Rae, Daxton, glad you could make it!" His booming voice caused others near us to turn and I caught a few of them whispering behind their hands.

"We couldn't miss it," Rae replied with a smile.

"Oh my, is that...?" The woman on his arm leaned over and met my gaze. "The hybrid!"

I felt a dull ache in my head form and was two seconds away from taking the drink from Rae's hand and finishing it in one gulp.

"Hello," I said in a polite voice. "I am not sure we have had a formal introduction yet."

"I am Clara," she said in an excited tone. "And this is my husband, Governor Bennett."

I gave the man a once over, confusion filling me. He was a low-level from the looks of it, how did someone like him get his position?

I guess for the image of collaboration.

"Rosie Miller," I said though I doubted I needed to. "Nice to meet you both."

"I am sure we have more time to chat later," she said with a smile and sent a pleading look to her husband. "Let's make rounds and before we know it, it will be time to eat."

They said their goodbyes and as soon as they were out of sight I grabbed the drink from Rae who sent me a glare.

Ignoring her, I turned to Daxton. I smiled at him and pulled him along with me into the museum.

"Let's have some fun," Daxton whispered as we came to look at a painting.

He nudged me to look at a couple not too far away from us. I watched as he sent a little wave and the guy was pushed into the girl next to him who gave him an annoyed look in return.

I let out a small laugh and focused my magic on the boy.

"Watch this," I whispered and tried to grab hold of the man's motor functions.

Sure enough, his hand slowly started to creep towards the woman's ass, who saw his hand and slapped it away.

"Enough," Malik's voice came from beside me. His hand gripped onto my shoulder leaving a flash of heat where his skin touched mine.

I turned to look at him and shrunk under his dark gaze.

"How annoying," Daxton mumbled from beside me.

"We aren't causing any harm," I said and tried to push his hand off, but he stayed strong.

I felt the magic buzz near us before I felt the shake of the museum. It was old, potent enough...and unmistakably Original. It crept along the floor of the museum and lapped at my feet.

Looking around I noticed the other demons in this hall looking for the culprit. We were all thrown back as another wave rocked the museum. This time the magic blew into the hallway. It was so thick it began choking me.

I held onto Daxton as we were thrown again into Malik who wrapped his arms around us to stop our tumble.

"An earthquake?" Rae asked.

"Magic," I, Amr, and Daxton replied in unison.

I met Malik's panicked eyes.

"Original," I said.

It was all Malik needed to jump into action.

"We need to get you all in a room," he said in a hushed tone. "And call Claudine."

People around us were panicking and trying to push towards the front of the museum. They were yelling and screaming. I heard some talk about this being from the protesters but now I was sure that it was all one death trap.

Xena and Ezekiel had to be close.

And then another wave hit us.

"This way," Rae said and pushed past us.

We all followed her without complaint. Everyone was running past us, going the opposite way that we were, but I knew in my heart to trust Rae and whatever was making the museum quake, was probably out there waiting for us.

We dipped into an unfinished exhibit and Amr and Daxton worked to secure the door.

Malik was on the phone and before he even finished Claudine appeared right next to me in a flash of light.

"Grab on," she commanded.

Without thinking I reached towards her, then paused just before our skin touched.

"What about the low-levels?" I asked.

Eli's growl sounded from behind me and they forced my hand to touch Claudine.

"They don't deserve your worry," they grumbled.

Just as the others were gathering around us a violent crash sounded just beyond the room and was so powerful it caused us to jerk forward, falling on top of Claudine in a mess.

"It's okay, it's okay," she gasped. "Just make sure everyone is touching me!"

She lifted her arm and Malik, Rae, Amr, and Daxton touched her skin. I felt the magic shimmer around us and the pull at my stomach.

Then, a claw-like grip tangled in my hair and pulled me away from Claudine. Pain burst across my skull and my hands went up to try and pry the claws from me.

When I realized that they were pulling me away from the group I flung my arms out, trying to reach for whichever body was the closest to me. Eli's shirt was the first thing that my fingers made contact with but I was dragged across the floor, causing my fingers to slip.

I let out a scream and started kicking and clawing against the person. Their grip loosened just enough for me to launch forward and grab the hem of Malik's jacket.

Slim hands wrapped around my ankle and pulled both Malik and me away from the group. I had no choice but to gape at the group, horror filling my body as light engulfed them and when it was gone, no one remained in place.

Malik and I were stuck.

Original magic slowly crept across my skin like a thick slime. It slowed my movements and blurred my vision. Malik's eyes narrowed above me and he bent down swiftly to hold onto my arms.

"You have been hard to get close to, my dear," Xena's voice rang out from behind me. It was her hand that had the death grip on my ankle.

When I turned to meet her brown eyes, all the rage and hate that I had pushed down so deep came bubbling up to the surface. I wanted to attack her right then and there. I wanted to make her feel the pain that she caused others.

I knew that if I let my powers go that I could blow up the entire place, Xena along with it.

But if the low-levels didn't get out...then there was a chance that they would be caught in the blast too.

...and so would Malik.

But what other time would I get so close to ending it all?

Another pair of hands shot out and gripped my arm and Malik's leg and in a flash of light the museum around us was gone and replaced with a dark sky.

I recognized the surrounding area... We were back at Winterfell, specifically the grass of the quad where the tower had once fallen. The environment was a shocking silence; the loud noises and screams from the museums were still ringing in my head.

The world tipped around me as I was pulled into a standing position.

"We have to go," I croaked out and turned to look at Claudine, whose hand was still fastened around me.

Sweat fell from her forehead and she was breathing heavily. The trip must have cost her a lot of magic.

"They will be here soon," Malik spoke in a hurried voice. Then looked towards Claudine. "We have to skip the next phase, do you still have enough magic to get Maximus here?"

"She already thought ahead," Maximus's voice sounded.

My head whipped towards him and I saw him kneeling down on the ground with Rae and Eli sitting next to him. Amr and Daxton were off to the side giving him a suspicious look.

That's when I felt it. A thrum of Original magic...but this was different than what I felt from the museum. It was fading.

All eyes were on me.

"What's going on?" I asked Malik, panicked.

Claudine's cool hands found the side of my face and forced me to look into her eyes. She was scared and panicked, just as I was, but she was taking deep breaths and asking me to do the same with her eyes.

"Marques had once entrusted you with his secret, do you remember?" she asked slowly.

I nodded and felt my blood run cold.

"He's dying," I croaked out. Claudine nodded.

"And his last wish was to ensure you could kill Xena and Ezekiel," she said speaking each word slowly.

"Last w-wish?" I asked, unable to find my words. "He's not—he didn't—"

"He's dead, Rosie," Claudine spoke in a harsh tone. "Xena and Ezekiel figured it out, that is why they are coming now."

"I *can't*."

"Hurry up," Malik growled from beside me. "We don't have time, she is probably already on her way here."

"If he is dead how can we win?" I cried.

Claudine gave me a pitiful smile, her eyes softening as if she understood me. But how could she?

How could she understand me if *I* was the one that had to kill the Originals. I didn't even think it was possible. I didn't have the amount of control over my magic to go up against my mother let alone Ezekiel. And their powers far surpassed mine, they had millennia of experience and I didn't even have two full years.

Maximus's hand holding a small bag invaded my vision. The bag was an originally black one, but I could feel the Original magic radiating from inside of it.

"Eat this," Maximus said.

I grabbed the baggy and felt bile rise in my throat. I already knew what was in here.

"Are you stupid?" Eli asked. "We are demons, this should go to the witches."

"No!" Malik growled.

I jolted at the noise and looked up to Malik. His eyes were narrowed at Eli.

"It doesn't work on witches," Maximus explained. "Like Daxton their magic will just go haywire."

"But demons can absorb his power," Rae spoke, her tone low and barely reaching my ears.

I stood on shaky legs with Claudine's help and stared at Rae. Her expression told me she was dead serious.

"I shouldn't be surprised," Malik muttered.

"Ten powers," Rae muttered. "Anything else I should be aware of?"

There was a pause before Maximus cleared his throat.

"The blood sharing should have prepared you for some," he said. "But the worst is yet to come."

I watched in mute horror as Rae opened her bag and without hesitation lifted it to her mouth and threw her head back.

Eli took one look at her, and then did the same thing.

Was I the only one who thought this was crazy? Consuming the flesh of a demon was no small feat, and who was to say we would even absorb these powers.

Rae was the first to start convulsing on the grass, her body becoming rigid after some time. I could feel the aura surrounding her. It was much like Marques, one that overpowered everything and hung over us like a threat.

I tried to run to her but Claudine held me back, and soon Eli was doing the same.

"Your turn," Malik said and grabbed my bag for me.

"Wait," I said panicked. "What about you?" I then gestured to Claudine and Maximus. "Them? How do we know this will even work?"

"We don't want to chance it," Claudine said. "We have too much magic in us."

"I already took mine," Malik grunted and opened the bag with a wince. "I wanted to try it out on myself before you guys."

"That's why you have been distant," I gasped.

"Yes," he answered. "Hold her."

I tried to fight as Claudine held my arms but once Malik's hand gripped my face and pried my jaw open, I quickly lost the battle.

I tried not to think about the flesh that fell into my mouth or how it felt to chew. Malik's strong hand gripped my mouth and then pinched my nose, forcing me to swallow.

He watched over me and lifted his hands. I pulled in a deep breath, sickly sweet air rushing through my lungs before my body began to convulse. Inside it felt as though every cell in my body was vibrating intensely.

My knees were the first to buckle and I fell right into Malik's open arms.

I whimpered as my magic rose sharply and my head was assaulted with memories, thoughts, and feelings that were not my own. My head felt like it would explode from the sheer size of the memories.

Images flashed through my mind, almost too fast to catch. I saw the world when it was still young, when demons, humans and witches all existed together... And then I saw the downfall.

I saw the war, the killings, and I saw the demons and witches who once looked over the humans become twisted and start attacking them.

Were these Marques's memories?

I could feel his exhaustion weigh on me. I couldn't comprehend how many years he lived and suffered through. I saw his grief, saw his pain. I saw when he murdered, saw when he loved...but at the end all that was left was exhaustion.

...and then I saw Malik crying over me as Marques died.

Take care of them, he had whispered in his mind, but it never reached Malik's ears.

With a loud gasp I pushed Malik off of me and fell to the damp grass.

The magic and power was shooting through me like shots of electricity. They couldn't meld together and instead focused on attacking each other, fighting over the little amount of space I had left for them in my body. The pain became worse than anything I could imagine, but even as I tried to scream nothing came out of my mouth.

I clawed at the damp grass, trying to put out the sudden heat that spread across my skin. My back arched and my limbs twisted painfully.

Tears were already pouring down my face, so much that I felt like I would drown in them. I couldn't breathe, I couldn't think...

I wanted it to end.

Then it was over.

"They are here," Malik said as he lifted me from the grass and rushed me over to the group.

Eli and Rae had already composed themselves and reached out to me. Their power and the magic that surrounded us was a shock to my abused system and pain radiated through me as Daxton and Amr's magic tangled around me.

"I don't know what to do with this power," I said through chattering teeth, phantom pain still jolting through my body.

The power, it was living and breathing inside me, much like my magic. It wasn't a part of my being like my fire that belonged to me fully. It was almost like these powers knew that they did not belong inside me and just settled to swirl around inside me, carefully avoiding my magic.

"Just let it guide you," Malik said looking back at where we just came from.

I peered over my shoulder and saw a small army of witches heading towards us, all with their magic already lighting up their hands.

They were far too young to be fighting for the Originals. Many seemed to be my age or younger and had fear written all over their faces. My heart ached for them because I knew that there was no way they would come out of this alive.

"I only know something about memories, and hypnosis," Rae said. "But that is not enough to tap into the power."

"Use your own for now," Malik said through bared teeth. "On the signal pump them with as much fear as you can, and for once please *do not* look me in the eyes."

I signaled for Amr and Daxton to come to my side. Without hesitation they dove for us.

Claudine and Maximus stood in front of us. The noises from the witches got louder as they prepared their magic.

"Don't look at him," I said to Daxton and Amr.

Malik took one step forward and I could feel his power whip around us, a strong wind pushing us around.

Rae's hands covered my ears from behind and pulled me to her chest.

"Combust!" I heard Malik's voice yell, and I could feel the magic whoosh past us. It was unlike any power I had felt before.

The loud explosions sounded immediately. I couldn't count how many because of the abrupt suddenness of it all.

When I pushed away from Rae and peered around Malik I saw at least a third of the army was wiped out, leaving a clear path to the two people that stood in the middle.

Xena and Ezekiel.

There they stood, as if above the rest. Xena was wearing her fancy brand-name clothing and looked at us with a sneer while Ezekiel had his face cast downward to the grass. I could make out some type of blazer and slacks.

"Rest," Claudine commanded.

I put my hand on Malik's arm and peered up at him. His face was paler than I'd ever seen and there was sweat pouring down his face.

"We need to attack," he said.

Blood trailed from his nose.

"Witches next," I said and didn't wait for his confirmation before turning to the rest of the group. "Magic users, take out as many as you can and Rae, Eli and I will push forward. I will try to take out as many as I can with fire."

"They need to stay in front," Rae spoke. "Long-range attacks will create a hole for us, but we will not be able to get them unless we are closer."

"You need to save your magic until we get close," Malik said.

"Two people cannot defeat—"

"Someone has to kill them!" Malik yelled. "And if I do not have the power to do it you must, so you have to save your magic. Get back."

"No Malik—"

"Back!"

That was the only warning I got before he sent out another wave of power. I shut my eyes as tight as I could and only opened when the explosions stopped, but this time they already caught on to the trick and not nearly as many were taken out.

At least half still remained.

"It will work," Claudine said in an airy voice. "Maxi."

Maximus let out a noise and I watched in fascination as he set up a magical parameter around us just as a few beams of magic came pummeling towards us. They burst in the air as they came into contact with the barrier.

"Move as a group," Claudine said.

I felt Eli's hand find my shoulder and push us forward.

As we got closer the army began attacking us with magic.

Claudine was throwing magic at them left and right but there were far too many. Calling my magic to me I peered around Malik and set my sights on the biggest group of witches and without hesitancy called forth black flames that engulfed them.

They didn't even have time to scream.

"I told you—"

"It's okay," I said to hush Malik. "It wasn't a lot."

"Rae," Claudine spoke. "Immobilize them. Daxton, Amr, some help would be nice."

**

I could feel Daxton and Amr's magic fly past me and see when they hit their targets, clearing a space for us, but my eyes were locked on the figures that awaited us.

It was bold of them to come alone.

"Take the hybrids alive!" Xena yelled.

Blinding fury lit up my entire body and I focused on Xena's snarling face. She was still yards away from where I was comfortable using magic, but my rage pushed me forward and my magic begged for a chance at her.

So I let it free.

Magic burst from me so strong that I was thrown against Eli. It had been waiting for this moment, begging me to let it out, and now that I finally did, it easily narrowed in on its target. Xena's face dropped as she felt the burst of magic rush towards her, but her reaction was too delayed.

Black flames engulfed her body.

The fool in me thought this was it, I had done enough, but for once I didn't listen to that voice and continued to pump magic towards her. I could feel us moving forward, but I didn't register it, all I could see was her flailing inside of my flames.

All I could think about was what she had done to us up until now. How she had brutally murdered the refugees after they escaped her clutches. How she had forced me to take the lives of so many without even blinking.

It was all a game to her. *I* was a game to her.

She pretended to want to be my mother. Lied to get close to me and turned her back on me when I started to question her motives.

She deserved this. She deserved to burn for her sins and deserved the most painful death possible. If this was what she had accomplished in two years, what had she done her entire life?

I thought of Ren...what about the others? Where was their justice.

This was for them.

It was for every single person that was affected by their cruelty and hatred. I kept the flame lit for them and them only because they deserved this as much as I did.

Warm hands covered my eyes.

"That's enough, Rosie," Amr said.

With the connection lost I felt my magic shut off abruptly. He waited for me to catch my breath but with each inhale I felt more and more power escape me. I was burning my magic and newly acquired power too quickly and my body was starting to feel the effects. When he removed his hands, I saw the utter destruction we had left on Winterfell.

The grass below us was charred, the trees that lined the outer edge of the quads were still on fire, and there were charred dead bodies all over the place.

My fire did not stop at Xena.

No, I was lucky Amr stopped me when he did because *we* would have been the next targets.

I looked to the spot where my mother should have been, but saw nothing but charred ash, and next to it a petrified and shaking Ezekiel.

We were close enough now that I could see the pain that etched his face as he slowly knelt to the ground.

Eli pushed past us, leaving the safety of the barrier. I was too exhausted to call for them. All thoughts and words escaped me as I sagged against Amr.

The fire from my father, the gift I had hated for my entire existence, was the one thing that I could do to end this battle. It enraged me and satisfied me all at once. All the pain and fear that went into this power, my curse... was suddenly gone.

Xena was gone.

My biological mother who had forced me into this life of pain and suffering...was gone.

Eli stopped walking when they reached Ezekiel and as much as I tried to hold on, my eyes began to flutter shut. I couldn't hear what they were saying, or if they were talking at all, but I could just barely make out Eli grabbing their father's head and violently ripping it off with all their might.

They then turned and lifted the head, their hungry blue eyes meeting mine. Then they threw the head up into the air and my last and final effort for this fight, was engulfing Ezekiel's twisted face in black fire.

I let my eyes close to the image of Eli's bone-chilling smile, and then tearing off the arm of Ezekiel's headless body and tearing the flesh off with their teeth.

Their laugh followed me into the darkness.

Chapter 31
Rosie

Screaming echoed in my mind. Bloodcurdling painful screams that made your bones ache and your ears ring. Images of black burning fire filled my mind along with the melted faces of the hundreds of witches I killed.

Xena's eyes as she was consumed by my flames flashed through my mind. They were horrible, painful. Those eyes followed me through my dreams and my day-to-day life...but I wasn't upset.

No...I *liked* seeing her in pain. I liked seeing her realize that her last moments on this earth would be the worst she had ever experienced.

And I found joy when it was I who brought her to her demise. I liked how she silently begged for me to let her go. The power and control I had was nothing like I experienced before. It settled deep within me, and for once my magic was quiet because finally it was satisfied with my kill.

A hand coming down on my head pulled me out of my thoughts.

I peered up to Billy's warm smile.

"You seemed lost there for a moment," he said in a light tone, but I could hear the worry underneath it. "Would you like to take a break? I am sure we can manage."

I shook my head and sent him a strained smile.

"I am good," I said quickly and pushed his hand off me. "*Fine.* And we barely got through the pile."

I looked out at the warehouse in front of me. People, papers, and random items were everywhere. It was moving day for the refugees and there was a buzz of excitement and laughter that filled the once empty space.

Demons and witches alike loaded up their belongings and were ready to start their new life.

We had them in groups, people who they were the closest with or friends they had made here, all got a place to live together. We supplied them with fake IDs courtesy of Malik and his new—*and improved if he was to be believed*—section of The Fallen.

We had used the last of Rae's properties as a place for the doctor and his remaining patients while the others all got stipends from Malik.

Apparently after years of running an illegal gang, he had quite a lot of it stashed.

The refugees were still gathering all their stuff with the help of Eli, Rae, and Malik while Daxton and Amr helped stabilize the patients. I wished I could stay to listen in on what they found out about the rapid decay of the patients, but they assured me that they still needed a few more months of testing and that I was more needed in other places.

Which left me, Claudine, and Maximus in charge of the paperwork. The folding table in front of me held everyone's passports, IDs and log-ins to bank accounts and other documents that they would need to live a normal life. Looking down at the mess of bags and folders in front of me I felt anxiety itch at my skin.

There is no way we will finish by the time the sun sets.

"We won't," Claudine said from beside me.

I looked over to her and watched as she smiled and sifted through the piles of paperwork, a mother and child waiting for her with a blinding smile. The small child peeked out from under the mom's dark hair, their large hazel eyes meeting mine.

"She will get a new lease on life thanks to you all," Billy said from beside me.

I watched Claudine intently; Maximus was beside her and I could feel his gaze boring into me, though I didn't pay him any mind. Claudine was wearing a light blue dress that fell to her knees. It covered her shoulders and had virtually no shape, but still, she made it look so pretty, so clean...so unburdened.

But how could she be like this after everything?

I didn't understand after what we saw, and did, how she would be able to move on like nothing happened while I got attacked daily by Marques's memories.

Sometimes I got lucky, and saw a happy one...but other times I got flashes of death and violence. Some so bad it made my stomach twist.

What will you do now? I wanted to ask her. *How will you live after this?*

...but the words didn't escape my mouth.

I felt someone come up to my table and I looked towards them. When blue eyes met mine, my heart skipped a beat, but unlike before I didn't feel glued to my spot.

My low-level mother was wearing a flowy shirt with a lace collar in front. Her long hair was pulled back and she was looking towards me with a sad smile.

She was pushing a wheelchair, and seated in it looking worse than ever... was my father.

His scarred face was the only thing that stayed the same, but somehow in the years I was gone he had aged considerably. His once firm hands were now shaking as he gripped onto the side of the wheelchair and his hair had turned fully grey.

I knew where their file was, I had seen it when I first shifted through them.

I could feel the stare on me as I found theirs and held it out to my mother. She took it in hand and gave me an expectant look.

"Inside is everything you need and directions to your new place," I said. "Since you'll probably need help with transportation you can wait over there until someone is free to take you."

I gestured to the area where most of the others waited. Malik had rounded a few of his ex-gang members to act as chauffeurs for the day and drop people off at their new locations.

My mother's was too close to Winterfell, in the same building I had occupied not long ago coincidentally. Though now that the Originals were dead, we didn't have to fear going back to that place and in turn all of the refugees could now use the space.

It was far better than what I had grown up with and I knew that they would be comfortable there.

"Your new surnames are Moore," I said. "With this money and housing you will be able to live for a long time without having to work."

"Will you come with us?" my mother asked, her voice hesitant.

Father's eyes watched me carefully.

"No," I answered without hesitation.

My mother's face dropped and she gripped the pile of folders in her hands so hard the plastic folder creased.

"Rosie here has to finish school, don't you?" Billy asked, his tone light. I had almost forgotten he was here.

"Rosie if you could just—"

My father cut my mother off with a growl.

"Why do you refuse to help your parents?" he asked, his voice gruff and far too loud.

I heard the conversation around us lull and I could feel the eyes weighing on me. Normally, I would have been embarrassed. My cheeks would have flamed and I would have bucked my head to hide my shame. I would have tried anything to make sure my father wasn't mad. Tried to make sure that I wouldn't get punished.

But that was then, and now...I was different.

Marque's years of knowledge and power lived inside me, strengthening my previously weak resolve. My experience with the Originals had shown me that dealing with my parents, was nothing more than a minor inconvenience and *for me,* one of the last Original hybrids still alive on this earth, to feel *shame* and *embarrassment* because of the people in front of me...well that would just be laughable.

"What other assistance do you require?" I asked and cocked my head to the side. My eyes trailed up to my mother. "There is nothing in that pile that needs my help."

"You said yourself, the money will not last," my father huffed. My mother looked away, blush coating her cheeks. "And I am not as healthy as I used to be—"

"The demon regulation society can help with disability," I said, cutting him off. "With these files you are new demons, with full lives ahead of you. They wouldn—"

"Rosie!" my father exclaimed. His face reddened and soon he was taken over by a coughing fit. Mother rushed to pat his back, but I just stood there, staring down at them. "We have done *so much* for you. Provided for you. Sent you to school. And not to mention dealing with that curse after you burned down our—"

"Are you done?" I asked in a calm tone.

I felt Billy shift beside me and Claudine placed a hand on my shoulder. Only when her hand made contact and her magic brushed up against mine did I realize how much my magic had spread out around me.

The witches in the room would be able to feel it, but if you looked closely you could see the way the air rippled around me.

My father puffed up and was ready to retort but I lifted my hand to stop him.

"I am no longer under your care," I explained. "I do not *owe* you anything for taking care of me. As someone who wants to help people affected by the Originals' cruelty I am here helping you get back on your feet, but that is where my relationship with you stops."

I caught my mother's sad gaze.

If she returned you to Xena, you would have ended up like the others.

There was something to be grateful for, but I wouldn't force a relationship with them if they continued to treat me like property and something to make money off of.

"There should be room in the next car," Billy said with an awkward laugh. "Why don't you guys go wait in line?"

My father sent him a glare.

"I wouldn't be dying if it wasn't for you," my father spat at me, his words filled with hatred. "So much for *helping us.*"

My eyes flitted to behind them where Eli towered over my mother. Their glare was burning into me and a dangerous smile passed their face.

"If I had my choice," Eli spoke, causing my parents to jump and stare back at them. "I wouldn't have dragged you from that cell."

"But you don't," I reminded, not liking the way Eli's eyes roamed my parents. They met my gaze with a smile, calling me out on my bullshit. It's not like I would be able to stop them anyways.

"It's mine," I continued, looking down at them. "It's *my* choice to decide what happens from here on out and *I* chose to help you out. Now please leave so I can get the others their papers."

Eli leaned down near my mom's ear and said, "You know she killed her blood mom, burned her to a crisp. Not even bone fragments were found. *That* was her choice too."

My mother paled and her eyes widened.

After the threat they ran to the side and refused to make eye contact with me.

"Don't go scaring people," I said to Eli as they walked up to the table, their hands brushing over the piles of sensitive documents. I could feel the thoughts of destruction behind them.

Can you? they asked in my head. The side of their mouth turned upward into a smirk. *Do I have another mind reader on my hands?*

I rolled my eyes and looked up to Billy with a small smile.

"Can you please take over from here?"

He nodded though his smile was gone. I turned to Claudine to apologize but her sweet smile stopped me.

"Go rest, Rosie," she said. "You deserve it."

Chapter 32
Rosie

Where are you going?

I jumped as Eli's voice entered my mind suddenly. I turned around, my hand still resting on the cold metal doorknob as I peered up at the stairs. Claudine shifted beside me, but did not make any noise, no doubt also sensing that we had been caught.

It was early in the morning, at a time when everyone else in Rae's house was deep asleep. The morning was silent and the barest hints of the sun rising spilled through the many windows that littered this place. The cool morning air brushed across my skin as I locked eyes with Eli who stood just on top of the stairs leading down to the foyer.

They were dressed in a hoodie and sweats, indicating that they may have just crawled out of bed, but their slicked-back hair told me differently. Their blue eyes shone in the dim light and they crossed their arms while they stared down at me. A tension rose between us and I could feel the argument that was about to break out.

"You already know, don't you?" I asked, though did not raise my voice, worried that the others in the house might hear and wake up to see what was going on.

Eli cocked their head and let out a huff. They stayed silent as if contemplating their next move. The brash Eli that I once knew was no more after they had eaten both Marques and Ezekiel's flesh; they wouldn't get as angry as they once had. It was like a switch had flipped and now they were calmer and more calculated than ever.

I knew what Marques had passed on, and while I had yet to really try out the new powers, the memories and knowledge that came with it were enough to change a person. And on top of that, I had no idea what they had taken from Ezekiel.

What did Ezekiel know about this world and its demons? What were his plans before he died? What did he tell Eli right before he was torn to pieces?

"I do," they said. "And I want you to take me."

"I refuse," I said without a moment of hesitation.

Their eyes flashed and they took one step down and paused.

"It won't be like Matt," they said. "I just have some questions for him."

I paused and stared at them. I had planned to do this with only Claudine by my side, not wanting to risk any more deaths, but having Eli there to read their mind was...enticing.

"Get Malik," I whispered to Claudine. "If Eli comes we need reinforcements."

Eli's face twisted and they walked down the rest of the stairs. Claudine disappeared in a flash of light leaving just the two of us in the space. Slowly, Eli crossed the space, their sneakers against the floor the only thing that broke the silence.

I stood tall, with my shoulders back as they came to a stop in front of me, the heat of their skin brushing across mine.

"You know he cannot stop me from doing what I want," they said in a low voice.

"I know," I said back, my eyes trailing the length of their face.

"And if I kill him?" they asked, their voice dropping to a whisper.

I didn't know if they meant Ren or Malik, but I didn't want either to die.

"I cannot forgive you forever, Eli," I said in a firm tone and took a step back to put some space between us.

They merely smirked and we waited in silence for Claudine to come back.

Another five minutes passed in silence before Claudine came back in a flash of light, an angry Malik by her side.

"Rosie just because they are dead now doesn't mean—"

I sent Malik a look that stopped his complaining in its tracks. I wasn't in the mood to fight. Any other time I would love to push his patience until he exploded, but now was the time where I needed to be listened to.

Malik's golden gaze searched my face and when he finally relaxed I grabbed onto Claudine's arm and nodded towards her.

"You know the drill," Claudine said in a tone far too light for the amount of tension in this room.

Eli smirked and complied but made sure to step close to me, their front brushing across mine as they reached out to grab a hold of Claudine's arm. I locked eyes with them and refused to back down.

I like this version of you, they cooed in my mind. I could feel the satisfaction rolling off of them.

Without warning Claudine transported us in a flash of light and the world around us tipped. Even as the power exploded around us and twisted my stomach, I held Eli's gaze.

Watch yourself, Eli, I growled in my mind.

Feisty, they teased back. *But I will let you have this...for now.*

I was the first to look away as the world came back together around us.

I was surprised to note that we were in a *very* familiar apartment. The sound of a door opening came from behind me and I turned to catch Ren looking at us with wide eyes in nothing but his boxers and a t-shirt.

"So this is where he was," Eli murmured.

"He was here the whole time," Claudine said. "We moved in right underneath him and we were none the wiser. I just merely gave him his apartment back."

"With a fucking magical tracker that tries to kill me every time I leave," Ren grumbled and ran a hand through his messy black hair. "What the fuck are y'all doing here?"

I swallowed my nerves and turned to him.

"Come back to Winterfell with me," I said.

Shock flashed across his face which he immediately tried to hide with annoyance. He ran his thumb across the small tattoos on his hand and paused, taking in my offer.

"Why invite him?" Eli asked. "He has no intention of complying with what we ask of him, I can hear it."

Ren shot Eli a glare, but his face softened when his eyes met mine.

"I am not asking him anything," I said. "I just want to give you a chance at a normal life. Malik can help get you situated and you wouldn't have to worry about—"

"Where is our mother?" he asked, cutting me off. His voice was hesitant and had a weight to it that sat uncomfortably in my chest.

"Dead," I answered. "I killed her. Now that she is gone you can live your life however you want."

Ren deflated and his mouth dropped into a frown.

"And if I choose to go back to my father's house?" he asked. I assumed he meant his low-level father and nodded.

"You can do whatever you wish," I said. "Though I wished that the offer to attend Winterfell was real, for me at least. And I wanted to give you the chance to make it real for you too."

Malik shifted, causing Ren's eyes to dart to him. I stepped forward and reached my hand out to him.

"No ties," I said. "I wish to know you and to understand what you went through, that is all. From experience I know it must have been difficult. I want to be there for you. But if you want to run as far away from me as you can, I will accept that."

Ren remained silent and his eyes fell to the floor.

"He's quiet because they treated him well," Eli spoke from behind me. "They didn't force him to kill prisoners, or ask him to take down government officials. All they asked of him was to watch you and then end it during the games. That is all."

I swallowed and a sour pit appeared in my stomach. Bitterness filled me and I wanted nothing more than to destroy this entire floor...but a part of me inside realized that I couldn't hold my own jealousy against the boy in front of me.

"One kill is still something," I said, though my voice sounded forced. "Regardless I just came to tell you this. I planned to come with less people but..."

I let my sentence trail and sent Ren a small smile. He shifted on his feet and stepped forward to take my hand in his. I felt our magic connect. It was warm, comforting, and familiar. His eyes looked up at me hesitantly.

"I would like to know more about what happened," he said. "If you would like to stay for breakfast that is."

A warm bubble filled my chest and I couldn't stop the real smile from spreading across my face.

"I would love that."

Chapter 33
Daxton

I had suspected for it to be hard to sneak away from the group after the battle between us and the Originals, but everyone seemed too distracted about the consequences of eating some of Marques's flesh to even pay attention to anything beyond themselves.

A more sane and put-together version of myself would have been bitter that I was being ignored, or maybe I would have wanted to help...but I couldn't help it as my own panic began to take hold of me.

My magic was getting worse by the day.

Instead of hanging over me like a dark could in the middle of the night, I felt it take form. I felt it leave my side and wander about the house.

It never got far, but the idea of my magic working autonomously sacred the living hell out of me.

It was violent and angry. It wanted death and destruction and nothing else.

And it was free to roam around,

Cumae had finally reached out to me through a magical carrier pigeon with nothing more than an address and instructions on what to do when I got there.

I didn't know if I could trust her fully, but now that the Originals were gone, I knew there wasn't much else out there to be afraid of.

If anything, the witches of this world should be afraid of me next. Who knows what my magic would do once it got enough strength to interact with the world on its own.

I was hopeful though, that finally I would get some answers.

I found it hard to believe that no one had run into my situation before this. The demon and witch history spanned on for years and years; there had to be a mess up somewhere. The people of this world were greedy and craved power like a drug, of course they would try and experiment much like my parents did.

Cumae had given me the address of another bar, though this one I had never been to before.

It was just a few miles away from the one where I had met her and this one spanned multiple stories. The place was cleaner as well and had a well-lit front entrance that showed the patrons inside, but I ignored it and rounded the bar for the hidden one.

The street beside it was wider, but smelled just as sour as the place before it. When I felt a flash of magic by my side I paused and called my own.

A door opened for me, this time no bouncer appeared out from the wall and I walked straight into the place.

It was much like any other magical bar I had seen, though this one was full of people who gave me death glares, even as they felt the powerful magic inside me.

I scoffed at the immature reactions and walked to the back of the bar like the note had told me. The stairs creaked under my weight and I was sure I would fall straight through the wood, but even so, I made it up the stairs in one piece.

There was a long, dimly lit hallway that smelt of cigarettes and sickly sweet magic.

The same type of magic that made my own coil in disgust.

The people here were not using their magic in good ways...meaning they were just like my parents.

I would recognize this type of magic anywhere. It haunted me in my dreams and caused sour bile to rise up in my throat.

Shaking the feeling off I walked down the hallway slowly, feeling the signatures of the people that I passed, worried that there may be someone beyond these rooms that I knew.

When I reached the room at the end of the hallway I eyed the stained and torn doorway critically. The numbers on there read "333" and stood out to me like a bright warning sign.

In the witch community those numbers were supposed to signal that I was on the right path, that the decision ahead of me was one that would change my life, in a good way...

But I am not sure I believed it.

It was almost too good to be true.

I felt a small spike and then there was a pause before the door slowly creaked open. There was little light in the room and I could only just barely make out the shadows of a table, chair, and bed.

I took two steps in and that's when I realized there was a person sitting in the shadows. I suspected a witch, based on the way my magic reacted violently inside of me, but the signature was off...something was wrong with it.

"Glad you could make it," said a woman sitting near the corner of the room. Her face was shrouded by shadows and I watched in interest as she leaned forward, the dim light shining on her face giving me a perfect view of her twisted burned face, the entire left side of her face burned beyond recognition.

Her dark hair peeked out of her hood but that too was fried and stuck out in every which way.

The door closed behind me and I shifted on my feet.

When she turned I finally got a good look at the other side of her face and my heart stopped dead in my chest. Ice-cold fear was injected into my veins and my legs planted themselves to the cheap stained floor, barring me from any fast movements.

Xena did not die in the battle.

I swallowed thickly and looked around the room for anything to help my escape...but there wasn't even a window in this room.

Xena had somehow survived the entire ordeal and sat right in front of me. While she may not have been in perfect condition...she was *alive*.

Was Cumae trying to kill me?

"This is a mistake," I said in a grave tone. I willed my body to leave, but not even a muscle twitched.

"No mistake," she said, her voice raspy like she had been smoking for years. "Your friend reached out and I said I would help."

"I don't trust that you would want to help," I said. "You tried to *kill* us."

"No," she said and stood, her cloak falling to the ground behind her giving me a look at her entire burned left half.

I had to swallow my bile.

"I just wanted my daughter back," she said. "But I truly am not here to punish you for that. Though I will require a payment from you once my work is complete."

I took a step back with tremendous effort and a sweat broke out on my skin.

"I won't give anyone up to you," I growled.

Xena let out a harsh chuckle.

"I never said that's what I wanted," she replied.

"Then what do you want?"

I shouldn't even be considering this. I should be turning around and running back to the others, getting as far away from this psycho as possible.

But a part of me wanted to hear her out. I *needed* the help.

"I will tell you if this goes well," she said. "After all I don't even know if this is possible."

I gritted my teeth and tried to take calming breaths through my nose.

"If you won't tell me I am leaving," I insisted.

The tight cord that was holding me to my spot snapped and I turned towards the door, but paused as soon as my hand hit the sticky doorknob.

"Do you want to die?" she asked. "Because with the way your magic feels, it seems like you don't have much longer."

Damn it all.

"How long?" I asked.

She let out a humming noise that ground on my nerves.

"Once the magic takes over I have seen people last anywhere from three months to two years, though if you have rapid signs of growth you can expect a few weeks. Those are usually the hardest for the host."

"What are the signs of a more extreme condition?"

Another pause.

"Your magic controls your every move, develops a mind of its own, its own wants and needs," she said. "Once it becomes corporeal you have little to no time left. It will come for your core."

Damn it, damn it, damn it.

"I won't allow you to hurt any of them," I vowed and turned back to her.

Even in the dim light her brown eyes shone.

"I don't have a plan to," she said.

Rosie was going to hate me.

We made such good progress and here I was confiding with the enemy that had literally tried to kill us.

And if Malik or Rae ever found out...I would be as good as dead.

But if not, and I went home *right now*, I wouldn't have long with them anyways. I would die a lonely and meaningless death, unable to live out my dreams of a happy life with them.

"Fine," I spat.

"Good, *good*," she purred. "Now let's get started shall we? Since you seem to be in a hurry. Can't *wait* to let that little monster out."

She raised her hand, a large magic knife took shape and in my mind all I could think of was the lonely meaningless death and how that seemed to be a much better option now.

Before I could move, darkness shrouded the room and that was when I felt her lips against the shell of my ear.

"This is going to hurt," she said with a chuckle.

The last thing I felt was the knife sinking into my chest.

THE PRICE OF SILENCE

BOOK 5

ELLE MAE

Chapter 1
Rae

I didn't detest school.

If anything, I really enjoyed learning. I loved being able to expand what I had previously thought to be impossible and learn more about this chaotic and ever-changing world we were in...because knowledge is power.

With knowledge, you could make every one of your dreams come true.

Want to be a scientist? Go to school, get a degree, learn about your field.

Politician? Same thing. Go to school, get a degree...then blackmail people until you get a seat at the table.

Even teachers had to hurl around a dirty secret or two to get their way.

If a kid was misbehaving?

A good, honest teacher may have gone straight to the parent, or principal... But a *smart* teacher would have used it against the student.

Threaten to get them in trouble and the student would have done a complete one-eighty.

That was the type of power I was after.

And it all started with getting a good degree and getting as much dirt on my fellow students as possible, so someday, when I needed it, I could rise to the top because of my own ingenuity.

I wouldn't admit it if anyone asked, but I was excited about Winterfell. And not just for the power I would hold by the time I graduated.

I was excited about *finally* completing my education and proving to Father that *I* was the rightful heir to his kingdom. Regardless of how useless my brothers had made themselves, I had been living in their shadows. At times, I thought they were being useless on purpose. I had seen them grow up and knew that they both had something behind their eyes, but they had never *truly* shown me their cards.

Attending Winterfell was going to be the thing that changed my life forever...and it did. But not in the way anyone could have thought.

Hybrid demons, Originals, and having to murder my own father were not on my list.

So slowly, the hate for all things Winterfell started to creep up on me.

To this day I cannot pinpoint when I started to hate this school. Maybe it was when I found out how much of a sham the principal was. I had come here excited to flex my knowledge and force that annoying demon's hand. I could control him; I knew I could.

I had prepared for this moment over and over again. I had worked for years to understand his reign at Winterfell and what made him tick, but it would seem someone had already gotten to him before I could.

Malik.

Maybe it was *he* who had ruined Winterfell for me.

I remember the day he walked into this campus, poised and ready to whisk Rosie away.

That day felt like so long ago, and the fear that came with it was now muted, but when I learned that Malik had gotten his hands on Rosie...I felt like I had failed. I couldn't admit back then just how much our little hybrid had wormed her way into my entire being, but I could admit it now.

Rosie was the start and end of all things beautiful and deadly in this world.

Her laugh and smile would fill me up with a warmth that I hadn't felt in years, while her anger and uncontrolled magic had left me weary of her.

Weary of *them.*

But now that I too held some of Marques inside of me...I found my fear, anger, and drive to be on top of the world slipping from my fingers.

I no longer wished to control the world around me, or make the demons respect me. I didn't want anything to do with the government and hated to think about what came after graduation. I still loved learning and holding onto all the secrets I could get my hands on...but it wasn't the same. Back then it was all fun and games, but now it was for survival.

Marques's own exhaustion and lack of will to live had transferred over to me and made the rest of the world...so dull. Demons, no matter how far advanced the world had become, never changed.

Humans would forever try to fight everything unknown and would jump at any chance for them to rid the earth of us.

Witches—there had been some times when they surprised Marques over the years, but they hadn't changed much either. Those who were in control of their magic used it normally, but didn't make huge contributions with it because the uncontrolled magic users had ruined their reputation.

Everything was the same, even after thousands of years, and I knew that no matter what I did here, there would be nothing I could do that could change the world. The world would continue to be dull and boring and hold zero interest to me...

Except for Rosie, of course.

She was the *only* thing keeping me going. The only thing in this world that I still couldn't understand, and it wasn't because of her hybrid status. It was because of *her*. The ever-changing and evolving woman that had taken over every thought and action I had taken since I met her.

She was the only thing in this world that pushed me to want to learn more and made my life worth living. It was pathetic and almost embarrassing to admit that I had become so enamored by her...but I couldn't stop.

No matter where I went or what happened to this world...I would forever be at her side.

The feelings were so strong for her that even thinking of my own family paled in comparison. They used to be the only people that I thought about. They used to be the ones that plagued my mind at night. My mother, my brothers, they were everything, until they were not.

After all, how could they understand what had become of me?

The answer was: they couldn't. And they never would.

As soon as they realized that I had killed our father, and he hadn't *disappeared randomly* as the reports mentioned, they would see me as a complete monster.

And I was. I accepted that part of myself.

I needed this monster inside me to survive. I needed it to make sure the people I loved and cared about were alive and well. But there was a bigger monster out there, one that made me want to take Rosie and run for the hills.

One that even Marques, in all his years on this earth, couldn't have expected.

It was the first weekend back at Winterfell, and the start of my third and final year at this academy. I was somewhat relieved to be walking on campus again, but only because I would be done with everything soon and never have to look back.

It was the beginning of the end.

Elle Mae

Students were smiling and laughing as they walked the corridors, excited for the start of school. Even with all the changes in the past few years, the school's reputation hadn't decreased, and high-level demons and witches were foaming at the mouth at the thought of getting invited into this place.

The low-levels had found solace in one another and the ones that came in the year prior helped the newest ones out. They would walk around with the low-levels, protecting them from the high-levels. They were filling the classes and had proven to give the witches and high-levels a good amount of competition. Principal Winterfell had added an additional three hundred and forty low-levels this year, making their presence undeniable.

After the first few days that were filled with complaints and groans, the high-levels seemed to understand that this was the new norm. Many avoided them when possible, and there weren't as many that were out for blood. Maybe it was because of Rosie's influence, or maybe it was because of Eli constantly beating up the high-levels that attacked the low-levels. They *hated* when their time with Rosie was interrupted.

Some high-levels and witches even began to seek out the low-levels. I had watched them approach, shyly at first. The low-levels would cower, or get ready for a fight, but after a few days I would notice the same group laughing as if they were best friends. It was the type of change Rosie would have wanted.

A change that Marques would have been surprised to see.

But of course, that couldn't last.

I normally wouldn't have come to school on a weekend. The others had moved in with me, causing the once empty mansion to be filled with noise and warmth. It would be a lie if I said I was annoyed by their presence.

Maybe sometimes I wished that Eli wouldn't steal my time with Rosie, but besides that, everyone was living together happily. We had enough bedrooms and enough food to go around so it was the perfect setup, so I found no need to venture out except for school and the occasional trip.

But that day...that day I was called here.

Call it a hunch, or maybe it could have been Marques's power in my veins. Sometimes I still felt connected to Eli and Rosie in ways even I couldn't understand. It was like there was an invisible thread tying us all together and I could feel their energies sitting comfortably in the back of my mind. Sometimes, a strong tug or a sinking feeling would cloud my mind and I knew it was from them. It was as if Marques was the one who tied us all together.

That's the reason I came.

In search of Eli.

Whatever bond we had was going haywire and begging me to find them. It started in the morning, and I brushed it off, thinking it was some sort of tension headache.

But then it went on, and *on, and on,* until I couldn't deny it anymore. Then when I focused on the pain, I could distinctly feel Eli and I dropped everything to come find them.

When I stepped onto Winterfell campus, everything seemed normal, and it made me really doubt whether or not the bond that I was feeling was real. And then, as I walked through the campus watching the students laugh, something changed.

It was like a powerful gust of wind had violently ripped through the campus, but instead of tearing up the foundation and toppling buildings, ice-cold fear traveled through each of the students. So overwhelming that I had trouble separating their feelings from my own.

It wasn't long until I followed the overpowering feelings and stopped right in front of Winterfell Tower. There was a large group of students standing at the bottom of it, whispering and pointing up at the clock tower. There were some shocked and tear-stained faces, but *that* chaos didn't hold my attention for long.

Instead, my gaze was immediately pulled up to the top of the tower.

It was impossible to miss the two dangling bodies that jerked with each movement of the hands of the clock. They had been tied well enough that their bodies wouldn't fall, but not tight enough to stop their arms and clothes from flying around.

It was a gruesome sight. The pure white face of the clock had been stained with dark red blood, and with each passing second more and more blood fell to the students below as the bodies were dragged against the stone.

They were beat up and bloodied, but you could still make out the face. I am not sure how many people could recognize them, but right away I knew who they were.

Mr. Falkner and...Emma.

I froze in that moment. All thought and emotion fled from me as if even they were afraid to stand there and watch the downfall of everything.

I once prided myself on knowing everything and I had really thought that there was *nothing* in this world that Marques hadn't seen or had an explanation for...but this was something neither of us could have guessed.

Why? I wondered. *Why Emma?*

Panic rose through me as I thought of who could be responsible, but I knew in my heart that the reason our bond had called me *here* today was because Eli had done something. But this?

This wasn't something they did. They didn't murder indiscriminately *and* make a scene.

Mr. Falkner I understood. He was with the enemy and had proven so by how he tried to *literally* get Rosie killed in the last Winterfell games...but Emma?

She hadn't hurt anyone.

"She kissed you," Eli said, appearing by my side.

I tried not to flinch at the coldness in their voice. I hadn't even felt them come up. I was too busy trying to wrap my head around the sight in front of me.

People were screaming now, openly. More people started rushing to see the bodies. People were taking pictures.

The emotions began to get too much, and I felt my stomach twist and bile rise in my throat. The only thing keeping me rooted in my spot was Eli. As they stood next to me they began to pull in all the emotion, much like a dark hole. They had a shockingly large hole where the emotions *should* have been, but there was nothing. Just complete and utter emptiness.

Slowly I turned to them to see their eyes fixed on the bodies above. Even as they looked at the screaming students below there was not a bit of pity or guilt in their being.

"Eli..." I trailed, my mouth dry.

They turned to me, their blue eyes strangely dull.

"That hurt Rosie," they said, then turned back to look at the bodies. "Her kissing you."

I swallowed thickly and looked back up at the dead student.

She didn't deserve this. No one did.

"Anyone who hurts Rosie will die," Eli vowed next to me. "Like it or not, *Honor Student*, she has changed me, so if you are looking for someone to blame, blame *her*."

Eli left me standing there in my own shock and in the chaos of the students around me. I was vaguely aware of a purple speck in the corner of my eyes as it advanced onto the tower, but that wasn't what controlled my mind.

All I could think was *I needed to call Malik.*

Chapter 2
Rosie

Sometimes the magic roaring inside me combined with the voices of Marques's past threatened to consume me. They were like two very different opposing forces that were confined in such a small prison that they barely had enough space to move. Sometimes it would wake me up in the night, drenching me in a cold sweat. Other times it would stop me in the middle of what I was doing and force me to take a deep breath as my body was stretched with the power.

It was painful at times, overwhelming.

But here, I found my mind and body at peace.

"Ready?" Malik whispered in my ears, his voice almost drowned out by the sounds of the waves crashing on the sand and the wind swirling around us. It was chilly up in the air, but I made my mind more present.

A giggle forced itself out of my lips. I tightened my hold on his neck and buried my head in his chest, inhaling his scent.

It was comforting to be this close to him. Even though I knew that Malik was just as scared and torn up about the world as I was, it helped to be around someone who could understand everything I had gone through.

Well...he understood most of it, at least.

"Ready," I said, my voice muffled by his clothes.

He gave me no other notice before he dropped us from fifty feet in the air and wiped all the heavy thoughts from my mind.

A scream was lodged in my throat as gravity plummeted us towards the sea. Wind whipped past us, causing my hair to fly around us and hit my arms and neck. Malik's hands gripped me tightly and there was a moment where I thought this might be our last time doing this.

My stomach twisted and just like every other time, I was ready to fall into the cold sea in Malik's warm embrace, but as soon as we got close enough to the waves to feel the light spray of saltwater, he pulled up.

My stomach dropped down past us and back into the ocean, and I was pulled forcefully up. I clung to Malik for dear life as he brought us back into the sky. Then, just as we paused in midair, he turned his body, and we were plummeting again.

"Malik!" I squealed.

His laugh echoed in my ear, and he jerked us upright once more, his brilliant white wings flapping behind him. It took me a few moments of gasping for air to catch my breath before I could pull back and glare at him.

His normally pinched face was relaxed and the biggest bright smile I had ever seen on him spread across his face. His face, for the first time in centuries, was unburdened and he looked like he was actually *happy*.

Before I could stop, the words spilled out of my mouth.

"It is nice to see you truly smile again," I said with a smile.

I was hit with a memory of a young Malik flying over the sea and laughing.

I think he was about eleven or twelve. His wings were three times the size of his body and weren't quite synchronized but still, he was managing to do the same thing he did now. He would fly up high, *so* high, and pull his wings in, allowing himself to be pulled down towards the blue depths of the water just to open his wings back up and glide across the water, and back up into the air.

Marques, unbeknownst to Malik, had watched him do this for hours. He would sneak out every single time Malik did and sit in the shadows, enjoying the laughter that spilled out of the young boy's mouth. He found it cathartic in a way, watching him live a life he never had. While Marques was sure he was a boy like that once, he didn't remember much of his childhood.

The fall and the time before it, he remembered vividly, but if you asked him to recall his own father's face...he couldn't.

So, he found solace in watching him live the life he wished he could.

He hadn't seen him do that in more than a decade.

Malik leaned forward, his soft lips brushing mine. I leaned into the kiss, only slightly worried about the vast space below us.

When he smiled against my lips I froze. He let out another chuckle and without warning pulled his wings in once more, allowing us to plummet.

This time, my laugh escaped and fell with us.

* * *

I let out a content sigh as I laid down on the warm sand.

It was a bit warmer in the sand than it was in the air, and I was soaking up every bit of the sun I could. Malik was at my side lying down next to me, his hand threaded into mine.

We were at the same beach he took me to the first time he ever pulled me away from Winterfell. When we had visited this place last, I didn't know what was waiting for me, and sometimes I wondered if I had just listened to the others and stayed away from him, if I wouldn't be here now... but my experience with Xena told me no matter what, he would have found me.

I tried not to think too hard while I was here, with him. I wanted to enjoy this moment instead of wondering about all the questions that plagued my mind.

The beach was empty for the most part. Whatever stray demons or witches that came, Malik would easily use his powers on them and make them turn back so we could enjoy this moment. It helped because even after everything, I knew he was doing it so people wouldn't see his wings, but I still felt a bit of nervousness creep up my back when strangers came near so I was grateful we were alone.

Malik rolled over so that he was almost on top of me, his scarred face blocking the sun out. I couldn't help the smile that formed on my face.

It had taken Malik and me a long time to get to where we are now and sometimes I don't even fully believe it's real. Before this I had hoped that I was more than a nuisance to him. I hoped that he wanted me the same way I wanted him. But after spending time with him...I realized there was something much deeper here.

His rough hand cupped my cheek and his eyes trailed down my face.

"You're very gentle today," I noted with a slight playfulness in my voice.

His demeanor changed in an instant. His hand left my face to grip my chin and force my face up. His eyes narrowed and his lips parted ever so slightly.

I was suddenly all too aware of how sticky and uncomfortable my clothes were.

"That sounds like a complaint, Rosie," he said, his voice low.

I smiled at him and ran my hand through his tousled white curls.

"Just an observation," I said and tried to bring him closer, but he stayed still even as I pulled at his hair.

"Did you enjoy yourself today?" he asked.

There was something in his tone. Something akin to worry. Though I did not fully understand what Malik had to be worried about.

"I did," I breathed and ran my hand down his neck and to his back, feeling the muscles jump under my touch.

As if reading my mind, slowly his wings appeared behind him. They were a brilliant white but if you looked closer, they were scarred, much like the rest of his body. If I looked closely, I could probably bring forth a memory of each of these scars, but instead I just drowned out the noise in my head and reached out to touch the soft feathers.

Malik's breath caught as I ran my hand across his wings.

"You like that," I murmured and applied a bit more pressure to the appendage.

He let out a low groan and dropped his head, burying it in the crook of my neck.

"They get sore if I don't use them," he explained and left a burning kiss on my neck.

"You need to stretch them more," I murmured and focused on massaging his wings. He shuddered against me and let out another groan.

"Wings aren't supposed to be out freely," he said and left another kiss on my throat. "It's dangerous."

The image of humans ganging up on a screaming demon and brutally cutting off her pure white wings, staining them with her own blood, flashed across my mind. I knew it was an image from Marques's past right away, but I never could stay in the moment for very long. I wanted to stay in that memory, understand what was happening at the time. I wanted to know who he was with and maybe see what they looked like, *before* war and death had changed them for good.

But I never did.

"They almost got you a few times, hm?" I asked and ran my finger across a particularly deep scar in his wings where the feathers refused to grow. I reached for the memory, tried to coax it out of the millions of other ones swirling deep inside me...but nothing came.

"Should I be nervous about what you see?" he asked, pulling away from me so our eyes met.

"Only if you are hiding something from me," I murmured, my eyes lingering on his lips.

His lips quirked and his eyes shone as if the secret he was hiding was no more than a small joke in the grand scheme of things.

"I was an embarrassing young demon," he said. "And Marques was privy to all of it."

"So, you're not lying to me about something?" I couldn't help but ask.

After all, up until the very last possible moment, he had hidden his biggest plan from me. The one that literally cost a man his life.

"I told you I only did that because I had to," he said his voice dropping to a low whisper. His eye searched my face, probably for a hint of what I was thinking, but I made sure to keep my face as still as possible. "I wanted to keep you safe. I *needed* to make sure that you lived through this. Rosie, I couldn't risk losing you."

If this was another time, in another situation...I may have yelled at him. I may have forced him to relive the moment he lied to me. I may have stormed away from him in hopes that he would chase after me and show me just *how much* he needed to apologize.

...but I wasn't that girl anymore.

Sure, I was angry at what had transpired, but I also understood him. Maybe even better now that the memories of the only person he had ever trusted in this life were burned into my brain.

I saw more of him through the eyes of Marques than he had ever shown me himself.

I watched him fly over the sea with tears streaking down his face after his parents had been murdered.

I watched as he anguished over each of the children's deaths until he became numb.

And I watched how the little bit of life that he had seemed to triple in size after he was sent to retrieve me from Winterfell.

"Marques was my uncle," I said in a soft tone. Malik's eyes widened, and they darted to the side, unable to hold my gaze.

"He was," Malik said in a grave tone.

I had seen it after I had gotten his memories, but hadn't had the courage to bring it up until now. In Marques's memories, my father's face was never fully clear, but their relationship was. Even in his blurry memories of his childhood, he knew there was someone by him.

"My father..." I trailed, not sure what I was trying to ask. "Can you tell me about him?"

Malik raised a brow at me.

"Can you not see it through Marques's memories?" he asked.

I shook my head.

"It's not very clear," I said.

Malik paused and looked up at the sky before bringing his gaze back to me.

"He was fun at times," he said. "More carefree than Marques ever was.

The kids, myself included, would flock to him whenever we could, hoping to get his attention."

"At times?" I asked and tried to pull a memory from Marques, but nothing came.

"He was..." Malik trailed his eyes, searching my face. "Let's just say him and Xena were a match made in heaven."

I swallowed thickly and nodded.

"So, most likely a murderer," I said in a cool tone.

"More than that," Malik said with a sigh. "He was awful to the humans, sometimes even the witches. I don't know what happened to them before the fall...but it changed them. He would lose his temper quickly and when the humans attacked—"

He couldn't finish and I didn't force him to.

"Promise you won't lie to me again?" I asked.

He swallowed thickly and nodded.

"I promise, Rosie," he whispered.

There was a tense silence that filled the space between us and his face dropped. His hands dug into the sand, and I saw something flash in his eyes.

This was the look of a man who had been sorry for what he had done. A part of me wanted to push him harder, make him beg for forgiveness...but instead I let it go.

I let it go because it was what I needed to do to heal from this. What *we* needed. There wasn't room for this type of fighting anymore. There couldn't be. We had been there before with Xena and Ezekiel, but now wasn't the time to continue this.

"Have you...seen anything?" I asked hesitantly.

His eyes shifted and his face hardened.

"I see some things," he admitted. "But nothing I haven't seen before."

"And the powers?"

He paused for a long moment.

"I don't feel them," he said. "Maybe at times, but never enough to grasp onto them."

Digesting his words, I nodded.

"I believe you," I said and lifted my hand to brush his cheek.

The magic underneath my skin fanned out and curled around him, as if it too wanted to assure him of my words.

He leaned down to brush his lips against mine and a shrill vibrating sound filled the air.

He groaned and fished the phone out of his pocket before cursing under his breath and holding it up to his ear.

"If you are calling me I assume I will not like the next words out of your mouth," Malik said in a serious tone.

The playful softness in his expression had hardened and in front of me now was the Malik that had slain thousands and ruled the world—and the Originals—with an iron fist.

"Two bodies were found hanging from the clock tower," Rae's said, her voice coming from the other side of the phone. There was a pause on the other line, some type of screaming.

"And?" Malik asked, his voice tense.

"And it's Mr. Falkner and Emma," she said. "You need to get back here. Bring Rosie and the witches."

"Emma?"

"Emma?"

Malik and I echoed at the same time.

"Who would—"

Malik was cut off by Rae's low voice, but I couldn't hear the words she spoke. Malik's eyes widened, and they shifted to mine.

A chill ran down my spine and I knew that whatever he was about to say would single-handedly ruin my day.

"It was Eli," he breathed, disbelief written on his face.

Fuck.

Chapter 3
Amr

I was the type of witch who would die for the ones that they love.

I didn't care how much they messed up, how cruel they were, or if they hated me as much as Daxton seemed to hate me right now. As long as I loved them, I would go to the ends of the earth and back for them. I would fight their battles. Care for them.

No matter what it was, I would do it because losing *them* was worse than death.

But I would be stupid to overlook the issues that could endanger their lives. I work my hardest to make sure that I can keep them in my life, but if they are the ones causing their own downfall...then I have to step in.

Daxton was glaring at me from across the cafeteria table, a lit cigarette in his hand. His brown eyes were surrounded by the dark circles under them.

There were times that he would disappear. The first time this happened he had disappeared for days and came back with an excuse that he had been visiting his parents' land...but I didn't believe it. He had been too tired, too sickly looking for me to believe that the change in him was from visiting a burnt-down house. He looked like he had been on his deathbed.

He begged me not to go to the others, to keep this between me and him... and because I loved him, I did. But I was starting to realize how stupid it was. What was even more stupid was how he thought no one else would notice his disappearance.

After the first disappearance, things started to escalate. He wasn't even mentally here. He would avoid me and Rosie for hours on end and looked like he was struggling to hold on. He was pushing away everyone that had come to care for him and had been building a wall between us that was becoming impossible to break down.

To be frank—he looked like shit. Like he hadn't slept in weeks. Though I knew that couldn't be true because I was cuddled up to him every single night. I made sure to stay awake long after he fell asleep just in case he woke up with hungry magic.

I had seen it happen a few times, felt it. The magic would hang over us like an ominous cloud...almost like it was watching us. Every time I shifted, the magic would come with me. Every time I tried to open my eyes, it felt like it was staring back at me.

But it had stopped not too long after we had banished the Originals from this plane of existence and sent them back to their homeland...or at least I *think* that's where they would go.

No one really had any answers anymore.

Malik and Rae's bank of information on the Originals had run dry. We knew that there were more out there, but they didn't try to find them. I assumed it was because we all wanted a chance to live a normal, happy life.

The others wanted a chance at school.

A chance to live together.

A chance to *love*.

But Daxton...he didn't seem like he wanted to love. It seemed like he wanted to disappear.

Every day I woke up next to him and saw the bags under his eyes get darker, his skin lose its luster, and the light in his eyes dim.

His hair had grown out to almost his shoulders now and I was afraid that if I took my eyes off him for too long, that he would disappear altogether.

"If you don't want to eat at home," I said with a huff and pushed the full, untouched plate of food towards him. "Then you *must* eat here."

He made a noise of disgust and inhaled his cigarette deeply.

It took all my strength to not smack it out of his hand. Witches and demons may have been the closest thing we have to immortals in this world, but we couldn't chance it and him smoking while looking like *that*...well, he was just begging for the gods to take him.

"It's not *home*, Amr," he spat at me and put the cigarette out right on the dark wood table. With my magic, I sent a quick droplet of water to where the cigarette met the wood, hoping that he wouldn't be stupid enough to burn the cafeteria down *again*.

"Home is gone," he continued, his hands balled into fists. There was a sharp rise in his magic...though it wasn't as strong as before. *That* magic would have consumed the entire cafeteria and called forth all the witches in the area. "Destroyed. There is no *home* left for us here, Amr."

My heart ached for the man in front of me.

Didn't he understand that Rosie and the others were our home? That *I* was his home?

"Home is not just a place," I said and leaned forward to grasp his hand, but he pulled away from me with a noise that could only be described as disgust. It tore me in two to hear that. "Wherever you are, Rosie, the others... *that's* our home. We could live in a shack, in a dorm...it would all be a home for us because we are together."

His eyes shifted to mine. There was something unreadable in his expression, but it was gone in an instant.

"Don't get sappy on me," he growled and averted his gaze to one of the only other groups that were in the cafeteria.

It was mostly empty, which made it much easier to get him comfortable here, but apparently it wasn't enough to get him to open up about what was going on.

"What's the matter, Dax?" I asked in a low voice. His jaw clenched and I could feel the shadows of his magic wrap around me, but instead of comforting, it felt violent. "Talk to me."

"Nothing's wrong, Amr," he said and quickly stabbed his fork into the potatoes on his plate. He shoved it in his mouth and the fork back onto the table. The metal bounced off the wood and clanged on the floor, pulling the attention of the others around us.

He motioned to the plate with an eyebrow raised as if to say, *See?! I ate just like you asked! Nothing is wrong!*

"Daxton," I said, dropping my voice into a whisper. "I can see something is wrong. You aren't eating. You seem to be sleeping, but your circles are darker than my fur. *Tell me.*"

His glare hurt me more than his words ever could. He looked at me like I ruined his life. Like *I* was the problem here.

I tried to pinpoint a moment when his heated gaze turned into one that rivaled hatred, but I couldn't. It had been a slow, subtle change that left me reeling.

"Don't fucking sit there and act like my father or some *shit*," he growled and leaned forward. "I think we both know that I have had enough of his shit, and I am not ready to replace it with yours."

I swallowed thickly as I digested his words. I knew the right course of action was to give him space, maybe to get Rosie involved as well. Let her know what I have been seeing, what he has been saying...but I didn't want to betray his trust.

I knew that as soon as I went to Rosie about this, he would feel like I broke his trust, and I couldn't chance that. If I broke that, then there was no telling what would happen to him. What if he just disappeared altogether?

I didn't understand why he couldn't just *tell me*. Logically, I knew it probably had something to do with the delayed reaction to his parents' passing. After all, he had taken it as though it was nothing, even though inside I knew he was suffering...how could he not?

It didn't matter how cruel they had been to him. I watched him over and over again look at his parents with hope in his eyes. Hope that they would change. Hope that they would become the parents that they were when he was just a boy.

I may not have known Daxton during his entire childhood, but I knew the pleading look he had given to them all too well. After all, I had seen it in the mirror many times.

When my parents left my siblings and me at home for months on end, sometimes to fulfill their contracts, I would be left there pleading with them not to go. I was a child too back then. How could a child take care of two other children?

It's why I didn't get mad at him now. Why I tried not to take offense at his words.

"We don't have to talk about it now," I said with a deep sigh. "But trust me when I say I want to help. If it's about your family—"

Daxton let out a loud growl and brought his fist down onto the table. The people in the room silenced their talks and I could feel the pressure of their attention weigh on me.

"What do *you* know about my family, Amr? What do you know about what I have been through? How I feel about this?" he asked me. "You act like you weren't just a goddamn pet for the last four years of your life. Don't try to act like you're better than me."

A small smile spread across my face even as my chest tightened.

"Is that all I am to you, Daxton?" I asked. "A pet?"

His eyes widened as if he just now started to understand the implications of his words.

I stood, ready to pull Daxton out of this cafeteria, but then I felt a spike of magic brush across my skin.

It was slow at first, just a trickle of magic, probably from far away. But then it came in waves, stronger and more potent than before. It wasn't all from one person. It was a combination of many magics all coming together to form a ball of sharp, potent magic.

My eyes shot over to Daxton, finally understanding where the magic was from.

"Fear," he breathed, as if reading my mind.

His own magic spiked, and he stood abruptly, only to freeze as his eyes trailed behind me.

I turned to see Rae and Eli standing in the open doorway of the cafeteria.

Rae's dark curly hair was neatly combed, her glasses shined in the light, and her uniform was as pristine as ever. To the outside world she would be seen as their put-together honor student...but when my eyes shot down to the black notebook that was in her hand, I knew something was horribly wrong.

Her hand gripped onto the notebook so tight that her knuckles had turned white, and the leather cover was bent and starting to bow in her grasp. Her stance was powerful, but I saw the tremor in her hand as she waved us over.

This was not the Rae that led us through battle after battle with the Originals.

She was *scared*.

When my eyes shifted to Eli, I knew all too clearly why she was scared, because Eli's eyes had never seemed more dangerous than when they shone in that moment. They knew *exactly* what they had done.

I had no doubt in my mind that *they* were the ones causing the fear of the witches in Winterfell. And they relished in that power.

The corner of Eli's lips twitched, and they held their head up high as if they were looking down on me.

Because I am, their voice said in my mind. *You think you wouldn't enjoy it when people shook in your wake? You think you wouldn't crave the way people's eyes and minds filled with fear because of you?*

I am not like you, I hissed back and motioned for Daxton to follow me.

I made sure to maneuver myself in front of him so that Eli wouldn't be tempted to charge at him.

Like I would be so crude, they said in my mind. *And Rosie would be mad. Anyone that shares a bed with her should be safe...for now.*

Their words swirled around my mind, and I wanted nothing more than to launch myself at them.

"Mr. Falkner and Emma have been found tied to the clock tower," Rae told us in a low whisper as we approached. Her eyes darted around to the people still in the cafeteria.

"Emma?" Daxton asked from behind me.

Dread filled me so quickly it was like a punch to the gut. I didn't have to ask who it was. I knew it was the blue-eyed smirking demon next to us, but they entered my mind anyway.

Scared?

No, I shot back, but it was a lie and we both knew it.

Chapter 4
Eli

Death tended to scare people.

I think it was probably because it was a reminder of their own fragility. Demons and witches liked to think that they were these higher beings who had to bow to no one...but they were wrong. Demons were just as fragile as our human counterparts, and I have come to realize that I took great pleasure in reminding them of that.

When they came face to face with a dead body, they all did the same thing. They would still, their eyes wandering the corpse's body, searching for any indication of life. No matter how mangled or bloodied the corpse was, they would still try to hang onto that useless sense of hope that seemed to live in us all.

When they found out that the bloodied, mangled body in front of them had lost its soul, *that* was when the fun would start. I could hear their thoughts spiraling. The horror of the realization that the dead body in front of them used to be a living, breathing person.

Then, all of the sudden, they would be reminded that death was still very possible for our kind. It would shock them to their core. Many would grip their chests as if they could feel the pain of their own life being ripped from them. They would think of everything they had to lose and everyone they would leave behind.

And then they would feel a sharp relief that it wasn't them who was hanging on the top of Winterfell tower, their blood spilling over all the spectators like a shower of thick, wet rain.

That was the thought that would jar them enough to start screaming.

But Rosie...she was different.

She stormed into the small classroom that we had managed to work our way into with her eyes flashing and her nose flaring. The small space seemed to become even more cramped as her thoughts and presence filled every nook and cranny.

She was *angry*.

Even if her expression wasn't obvious enough, I could hear it in her thoughts. She had been good at learning a way around my power, but right now, it came at full force. I drank them in greedily, feeling them invade my mind and cause a shiver to run through my body.

"Why did you think *murdering* people and stringing them up for all of Winterfell to see would be a good idea?" she asked as she walked towards me.

Malik was hot on her heels, glaring at me as he came in. His thoughts were filled with anger...but also disappointment, and I didn't like how it made my chest feel, so I focused back onto Rosie. Malik tried to reach for her and pull her back to him, but she came here with a mission and there would be no one to stop her.

Daxton and Amr were sitting in the seats in front of me. Both of them had been waiting in silence for her to arrive. Their thoughts had come and gone, but there was something there that they both wanted to keep hidden. If I had been even a bit more bored, I may have tried to pry, but I didn't really care about them at this moment.

Rae was to my left; she had refused to leave my side. In her mind, she was doing her duty and making sure that I wasn't going to run, but we both knew that wasn't in my plans. I *wanted* to see what would happen. I wanted for the others to know what I had done.

I leaned into the desk and crossed my arms over my chest as Rosie stood in front of me. Her angered thoughts swirled around us, drowning out all the others. It only excited me more and I was positively vibrating as she came to stand before me.

"They hurt you," I said simply. Her angry mask crumbled then, and her angered thoughts went silent.

"Emma?" she asked, her eyes flitting to Rae.

Did she realize that whenever there was something she couldn't understand or handle, that she would always seek out Rae? Heat flared inside me and before I could think twice, I gripped Rosie's chin and forced her attention back to me.

She looked back towards Amr and Daxton, her eyes lingering on Daxton a bit *too* long for my liking. She was worrying about him, even when I was *right* here in front of her with blood still under my fingernails.

"She hurt your feelings," I explained, calling her attention back to me. "Took what was *yours*. I just thought it was time to get payback."

Her eyebrows pushed together, and her mind was a crazed mess. She tried to balance every interaction she had with Emma in her mind while also trying to keep her focus on me, instead of worrying about how horrible Daxton looked and how long it had been since she had last seen him.

My anger rose sharply, and I was two seconds away from exploding on her. I looked over Rosie's head to take in Daxton.

He was looking worse than I had ever seen him. Even during our high school days, he had never looked *this* beat up. It was like someone had stripped him of everything. Magic, food, light, even his own thoughts seemed dull in comparison to what they used to be.

I *almost* hated him for it.

Almost, because there was once a time where I was closer to him than anyone else, Rae included. I couldn't hate him after he accepted me, after Damon and his gang treated me like they did.

"She kissed me," Rae said from my side, most likely feeling my emotions bubbling under my skin.

Ever the fucking savior, I shot towards her.

My attention was pulled as two forms crowded the open doorway. Both Maximus and Claudine looked on towards Malik, nodding when he met their gaze before pulling it back to me. I meet the seer's eyes and cringed.

I fucking hated her.

Her delighted thoughts told me she and I were on the same wavelength.

Turning back two Rosie, I was met with her wide eyes and scowl. Flashes of Emma coming up to kiss Rae were zipping across her mind. Rosie had just about forgotten what had happened, too busy trying to make sure we lived through the Originals' wrath to even remember that another woman had done that to a person she was openly with.

But *I* didn't forget...and I never would. Because no one acted like that around us.

They may have forgotten. Think that we have grown soft, but I was here to remind them they were wrong.

Marques's memories were good for one thing and one thing only. He reminded me just how out of hand things could have gotten if people underestimate you.

But I guess it would have been a total lie if I used that as my excuse.

"She has a family," she whispered. Her hands balled into her fists at her side.

My fault, her mind whispered. *I didn't put a stop to this. I should have known.*

"So does Mr. Falkner," I said, interrupting her pressing thoughts. "And Matt."

His name rolled off my tongue and tasted like something dark and forbidden. He wasn't my first kill, but he was one of the most satisfying. I hated that *fucker* since the day I laid eyes on him, and I still fully believe that his murder was worth it.

I had known since then that Emma and Mr. Falkner would be my next targets to experiment on. I had promised Rosie that I wouldn't act on my desires, but it was a lie. I knew that then, and I held onto it until I saw my chance. And I made sure *every fucking second* of it counted.

Now that I had my father's power raging through me, there was no barrier between me and their last dying thoughts. This time I made them bleed out slowly while I sat in between their bodies and listened to every last rampant thought that flew through their mind. They were pleading up until the very end, just *begging* for me to forgive them. To show them some type of mercy.

But it wasn't me who they needed to ask because frankly I didn't give a fuck. I wanted to feel that sweet rush of adrenaline and power that I got with listening to them as they bled out by my side. I wanted the high of them realizing that everything that stood between them and death was *me* and *me* alone.

In that moment, I was their God *and* their devil, all wrapped in one. They didn't know whether to please or curse me. Mr. Falkner obviously fought me more than Emma had, but he too had broken down after a while and would have kissed the ground I walked on if it meant that he would have been set free.

It was surprising to hear what they cared about when they were moments away from death. Some of it was mundane stuff but almost always they thought of who they were leaving and what their life *could* have been if they just made a single choice differently that day. Maybe if they didn't show up to school, or if they had escaped last year when they had a chance.

But it was fate that we ran into each other, I just knew it.

"But you don't care about them, hm?" I asked and wrapped my arms around her. She melted into my arms without so much as a fight. As if she didn't smell the blood and sweat on my skin and I was still the Eli that had come to her all those years ago. "I did this for *you* Rosie. You should be thanking me. And just know that I would kill any other demon, witch, or human that dares to hurt you ever again."

The people in the room shifted. All of them had the same single thought running through their mind.

I was no exception.

They didn't know that I wouldn't hurt them if it would hurt Rosie...but if they so much as harmed her without her consent, I would make sure that they paid. After all, there were other punishments that didn't result in death.

"You can't just kill people, Eli," Rosie said pushing me away. "And in front of the entire school. The students saw what you did."

I shrugged and crossed my arms over my chest, angry that she was pushing me away *again*.

Memories were just as fragile as human lives. If Ezekiel's memories had taught me anything, it was that the memories of the creatures in this world never really outlived their host. Thoughts, feelings, memories, they would all leave us at some point in our life so whatever I did right now, in this moment, would be nothing come twenty years from now.

"I cannot erase the minds of so many people," Malik growled. He walked over to stand by Rosie, his hand brushing across hers.

I wanted to call him out on the intimate gesture, knowing how much it would anger him, but instead I just leaned back with a smirk. I would have time to annoy him later. All I wanted right now was to get myself and Rosie out of here.

"They will forget about it in a matter of weeks," I said with a shrug. "You worry too much."

Malik's jaw clenched and the jumbled angry mess of thoughts swirled around his head like a storm. His body was shaking from the pressure of trying to keep things bottled up.

He was going to burst.

He didn't want to do it here, not in front of everyone and especially not in front of Rosie.

A twinge of excitement ran through me at the thought of fighting Malik. It had been years since I had really had him as an opponent and the blood-lust that filled me from the last few kills was far from gone.

Which was why I needed to get Rosie out of here so I could fuck her until she forgot her own name. I needed to feel her blood run through my fingers. Hear the wall vibrate as she screamed my name and begged me to stop.

I fucking needed her to pay attention to me.

She had been avoiding me after the incident with the refugees. I knew the power we shared scared her, but it shouldn't have been a surprise. After all, she had part of Marques too. Ezekiel had brought me a wealth of knowledge. His memories of the evolution of our kind and the destruction of the humans had calmed me, but it did not remove the bloodlust that Marques's memories brought.

His powers would sometimes shift inside me, as if begging to come out. I had tried—*and failed*—to test them on both Mr. Falkner and Emma but I knew as soon as I could tap into his powers…I would be unstoppable.

She knew that too. That's why she was looking at me as if I had just committed the gravest sin. Though she wasn't crying, or screaming, or even that angry anymore. She just stood there, staring at me with those dangerous brown eyes all while her mind tried to work out why I would have done such a thing.

"What pushed you to do this?" she asked. "I understand *why* them, but *why* now?"

I opened my mouth to speak but Amr stopped me. He stood, pushing himself out of his chair.

So, the cat wants to play? I sent him. It only angered him more.

"Why when the school was just recovering from the damage we inflicted on it?" he asked. "Why after we had finally gotten rid of the Originals? Was what we went through not enough for you?" His hands balled into fists at his side and in his mind he was already lunging at me and gouging my eyes out with his claws.

"We *finally* got some time to just *live*," he continued. "Rosie and Daxton have been through enough. We can't have you continuously put us in harm's way. Don't you even care about anyone other than yourself?"

I shifted and stretched the side of my neck, feeling a slight pain as my stiff muscles stretched. Mr. Falkner had proven to be more difficult than I imagined, and I would be feeling the ache for at least another few hours while my body healed itself.

"Watch your words mongrel, or I may have to take back my vow to leave you unharmed."

Don't, Rae warned, her thoughts far louder than the others'.

She tried to send a wave of calm towards me but what she didn't seem to understand was that I *was* calm. Even the bloodlust that was building up inside me, was no longer enough to make me lose my cool. They thought that they were dealing with the old Eli. The one that would burst if prodded hard enough. The one that had their anger as their biggest weakness.

But that wasn't me anymore.

If I chose to kill the cat, it was because *I* chose it, *not* my anger.

The anger that had been boiling underneath Malik's skin had burst and in a flurry of motion he lunged towards me, pushing Rae and Rosie out of his way.

Rosie yelled after him, Rae tried to grab him, but they were too late. His hands wrapped around my throat and squeezed. He got close to my face, his hot breath filling the space between us. His eyes were lit with the molten fire that I had yearned to see.

"Come on then," I choked out, keeping my hands at my side. "Make the first move."

He paused, his eyes taking in my face. He hated the smirk that was currently plastered on my face and wondered where he had gone wrong with raising me.

His thoughts sent a surprising wave of hurt through me and I couldn't help the growl that ripped out of my throat.

Malik growled and squeezed harder before Rosie came to his side and placed a hand on his arm.

"Don't, Rosie," he growled. My own growl rumbled in my chest at his harshness towards her.

"Let go of Eli or I will *make* you," Rosie commanded, her voice was powerful enough to stop both of our growls and plunge the room into the silence. "I *am not* my mother, so please *both* of you, don't make me act like her."

I almost moaned aloud when her fury-filled eyes met mine. She looked so *fucking* delicious like this. Even if she didn't want to admit it, she was more like her mother than she realized. She had waited for the perfect moment to jump in and use that tone that made everyone in the room bend to her will.

She was calculating, angry, and everything the witch who came before her was.

She pulled Malik's hands away from my throat and pushed him away from me. Her glare dug into him, and fury erupted inside of me as she continued to dismiss me.

"That's it?" I egged. "Rosie sure did tame you, huh?"

He looked like he was going to burst again and in the corner of my eye, I saw the witches move further into the room.

"Eli," Rae said as she moved back to my side, her lithe fingers wrapping around my forearm.

I didn't back down. I *wanted* this.

"Eli," Rosie growled. "You are in deep shit. I wouldn't act like this if I were you."

I almost laughed aloud when I heard her.

"Or what?" I asked with a smirk.

Now *that* really set Rosie off, but instead of lunging at me like Malik, she combed through every possible way to make me pay, and settled on the one thing I *hated*. She wanted to force my hand. Something that would make me regret my *"childish tantrums"* as she dubbed them.

She let out a sigh, then looked back to Malik.

"Use your power on them," she commanded. "Make sure that they cannot kill anyone anymore."

Malik shifted, his eyes shooting towards me.

My hand balled into fists, and I tried to take a step forward but Rae's grip on my arm stopped me.

"Eli," Malik started, his tone low.

"No," I growled and tried to turn around, but wisps of red magic flew at me and held my face forward.

I let out a pained groan as the magic burned my face and glared daggers at Rosie. Malik stepped in front of her, his eyes on me.

"You will not murder anyone from now on," Malik said, his voice filling the room and his power swirling around me. I felt it lock into place and I let out a deep growl that filled the silence in the room.

How fucking dare they.

Rosie's magic left me, and I rubbed my free hand across the burning flesh. Pain shot through me, and I couldn't help but feel like I had been betrayed.

"You fucking *cunt*," I growled at him. "Fucking fight me."

Malik just shook his head and looked towards Rosie. His face was hard, and his mouth was set in a straight line. His thoughts told me that even though he didn't want to do this, he would listen to Rosie.

Rae squeezed my arm, drawing my gaze back to her.

You can't just go killing people. This will put us in danger if we cannot keep up with everything. We no longer have an easy entrance into the govern-ment and police force. If you really wanted to do this for Rosie...you would be safe about it.

I shook off her hand and let out a noise of disgust.

"Leave us," I commanded, my eyes shifting to Rosie's.

There was an outrage across the various minds in the room, but Rosie's stayed calm and focused. She had expected this as well.

"I'll be okay," she said, her voice barely above a whisper. For anyone else it might be seen as a sign of fear, or weakness, but her voice rang across the space, pulling everyone's attention and just like a switch had been flipped, they started to shuffle out of the room.

Daxton was the first. He didn't even meet my eyes as he passed. His gaze locked on Rosie's for seconds before he turned back towards the door and left. The other witches had already disappeared before I could even catch them.

Amr was close behind him, sending me a glare as he walked past.

Malik looked at Rosie, but when she smiled and nodded at him, he left with a small, lingering look between us. He was pissed and made sure I knew it as he stalked out of the room.

Rae was the last to step forward. She stopped in front of me, covering Rosie's frame from my sight.

"If Rosie hadn't okayed it," she said, her voice dropping to a low tone. "I would have brought up a different punishment as a discussion point. Don't let this happen again."

I felt something probing at my brain. It was soft at first, but enough to make me realize that whatever power Marques had acquired through his years, may have more easily transferred to her than Rosie and me.

"Run along," I said in a tone that mirrored hers. "Rosie and I have some things to discuss."

Her nostrils flared and her jaw clenched, but even as her mind was screaming at her to attack, she just shook her head and left, just as the others had.

There was a silence that fell across Rosie and me as we sized each other up. I didn't like the disappointment on her face. I thought she would at least be relieved to see those two gone...but she seemed almost upset.

The bloodlust and anger simmered down, and I could think a bit more clearly without all those noises fucking thoughts in my mind.

"That was a little overboard," I said and rubbed my jaw. These would for sure scar.

"You needed to be taught a lesson," she said with a shrug, her eyes falling to her feet. "You and I have both seen what happens when societies let their strongest run wild."

She was referring to Marques's memories, though I was sure she wouldn't have thought the same if she had seen my father's memories.

"You should be happy," I growled. "I killed them for you."

She shook her head and took a step forward.

"You killed them for *you*, Eli," she said, her tone soft. "I know who you are as a demon. And I wouldn't try to change that...but you *cannot* be this reckless."

I reached out to grab her arm with the intent to pull her closer, but she maneuvered just out of my grasp.

"I want you," I growled, feeling a spike of anger inside me. It was hot and brought a wave of recklessness that felt almost nostalgic.

"No," she said in a firm voice.

"*Need*," I corrected. "I *need* you. Right now."

I didn't wait for her to reply and lunged forward to tangle a hand through her hair with the other gripping her throat.

She let out a noise of protest as I crashed our lips together, but I ignored it and attacked her mouth with my own. As soon as my tongue swiped across her bottom lip she opened up for me with a breathless moan.

It was all I needed to haul her back around and force her on top of the desk. Her hand came up to my chest pushing me away from her even as her tongue fought against mine.

She was still trying to deny this even though she so obviously wanted me. It was laughable.

Then the burning started.

Pain lit up the entirety of my chest and I was forced to pull away from her.

My hands flew to my chest, and I began wildly patting it down as my skin burned, but when I looked down there was no sign of fire.

I glared at Rosie just fast enough to catch her purple glowing hand. Her face was hard set, and her brows were pushed together. Yet again, she was disappointed in me.

"Reckless *children* get punished," she said and hopped off the desk.

I tried to grab her as she passed me but a glowing wall of magic burst in front of me causing me to jerk back, the magic just barely missing my face.

I let out a loud growl, but Rosie just looked back and this time, she had her own chilling smirk that spread across her face.

God, I thought as heat flashed through my body. *I can't wait to pull that little spitfire out of her again.*

Chapter 5
Rosie

"You feel different."

Ren's voice caused me to jump and the magic that I had been so carefully building in my palms dissipated into thin air.

I let out a sigh and ran the back of my hand across my forehead, wiping away the sweat that had begun to drip down my face. My skin felt like it was on fire and my lungs were aching with each deep inhale.

With shaky limbs I pushed myself into a standing position and turned to look at Ren. His purple eyes shone in the dim light of the warehouse. Moonlight flitted through the high windows, giving me just enough visibility to notice that he was in his school uniform.

The tightness in my chest seemed to ease just a bit when I realized he had taken my words seriously and decided to come back to school and finish his education. I never knew what being a *big sister* would mean, or how I would even go about acting as one...but I knew now that it was my duty to make sure he could have the life that I couldn't.

I wanted more than anything to form a bond with him. Something that I never felt with my low-level parents and definitely not with Xena. Both of them had left me looking for something more...maybe *that* was how I fell into such a helpless hole all by myself. I had been so enamored by all the attention I was getting from them and wanted nothing more than to be able to accept them as my own.

That was probably why I had been almost killed multiple times.

I wanted a family that I could do everything and anything with. A person that I could protect. Someone who would be there with me no matter what happened and would have my back when push came to shove.

I wanted to show them the love I wasn't able to get growing up and teach them that even if the world was gnarled and ugly, that they didn't have to become that way too.

Malik, Rae, Dax, Eli, and Amr...they were becoming a sort of makeshift family but there was something about the thought of having a blood brother to love and protect that made my heart skip a beat.

For the first time, I was nervous again. Nervous of what he would think of me. Nervous that he wouldn't want to be around me. And nervous that I couldn't protect him from the horrors that had been forced upon to me.

I had been searching for him since school had started, but hadn't seen him. It didn't help that we had to take a small *mental health break* from our courses because that had only prolonged the time that I would be away from him.

Classes had resumed after two weeks since the incident, but it was hard to pull myself away from the others. I was worried about Eli and Daxton also, which made it hard to actually go to classes.

I had seen the teacher a few times, but I had been so focused on running around the campus looking for Ren on the times that I did go to school that I barely had time to study.

I was pretty sure he had been avoiding me. I tried to chalk it up to him visiting his low-level father...but I didn't know how true that was, especially when he looked at me like he did now.

It wasn't hatred or anything like that, but there was *something* behind those eyes that made me feel like he resented me.

"My magic?" I asked and wiped my sweaty palms on my jeans.

I had chosen casual clothes for today, not feeling like showing up at school. It got harder to show up the longer he avoided me and the longer I stayed in my perfect little bubble. I had tried to pull myself out of Rae's arms this morning, but each time I thought of stepping out of our safe space that was her room, I got scared.

And it wasn't Eli that I was scared of...

It was me.

My thoughts had run rampant during the last few weeks and didn't let me rest. It would always remind me of the powers swirling around inside me and how easily I had commanded the group to listen to me. I was scared I was turning into someone I wouldn't recognize.

Ren cocked his head and took a step closer, right into the moonlight. His eyes held a light that I had seen everyone around me lose and it comforted me knowing that there was still life in him after everything after all.

"A little," he admitted and then paused, as if no words could describe the change in me. "It feels...heavier, *dangerous.*"

I nodded and held my hand out, commanding magic to pool in my hand.

Black sparkling magic began to swirl in my hand, pulling more and more from the shadows until it was an orb the size of a basketball in my hand. Even though it was my own magic, I could feel the aura around it.

It wasn't clean.

"I started to practice," I said and commanded the magic to move. Ren took a startled step back as the magic swirled around him. "And after a while...it turned to this." I called the magic back to myself, and Ren let out a gasp when it turned red. "Though I can't keep it up for long."

Ren swallowed thickly, the sound of it filling the warehouse.

"Is that...why you called me here?" he asked.

I sent him a small smile.

"No," I said, and motioned for him to come over. "Let me see your hand."

His movements were hesitant as he crossed the room. His footsteps echoed in the empty space and his magic was spiking with each step he took closer.

He's nervous, maybe even scared, I realized after taking in his slightly shaking hand as he lifted it to me.

I didn't need to ask for the tattooed one. He already understood what I wanted.

I brought his hand closer, taking in the small specks. When I ran my fingers over them I felt the magic inside them buzz to life and tingle under my skin.

"Did you really do this yourself?" I murmured and looked up into his eyes.

His gaze faltered and he let out a shaky breath.

"Yes," he whispered.

"You're not in trouble Ren," I said in my softest voice possible. "I need your help, but I also need you to be honest."

Ren nodded. A small sheen of sweat already covered his face.

"I have seen something like this in Marques's memories," I said. "And I need to know if you can replicate it."

The memory had come forth on a random morning, when I had been trailing my fingers down Malik's back, tracing the tattoos there. It was so small, and I would have missed it if I wasn't paying attention.

It was just one question really, paired with the image of a tattoo machine.

If you don't stay put I will put a permanent tracker on you.

There was nothing else to indicate that *this* tattoo had been what was in Marques's memories, but I could make my own conclusions after locking myself in a room for hours on end with nothing to entertain me.

"I just need a sample of their blood or for them to feed magic into the ink," he said, pulling his hand away from mine. "It's not hard."

I nodded and took a step back, allowing Ren some space.

"Who taught you that?" I asked. "And who are you tracking?"

I had a feeling I knew the answer, but I wanted to hear him say it.

"I had watched a friend when I was younger do something similar," he said and forced his hands into the pockets of his school slacks.

There was a silence that fell upon us, and his gaze fell to his feet. He mumbled something under his breath.

"Again," I commanded, feeling my blood run cold.

Slowly his eyes met mine again. This time there was a small glint in his eyes that I sometimes saw in myself.

"Mother," he spoke louder. His voice was strong, clear, and deadly.

It wasn't Eli who I was afraid of... It was myself, and now Ren.

* * *

I stood in the corner of the room watching as Daxton funneled magic into the black ink Ren had laid out in little caps on his table. Everything was wrapped in plastic wrap. Ren made sure to wrap and clean his machine and wear gloves.

We decided the best place to do this would be his dining room table in the apartment my mother had first confined him in. It was far away from Winterfell, and no one would interrupt us once we started.

Rae, Eli, and Malik would probably come by to see what was happening if we had stayed at Rae's house. I couldn't chance Eli reading my or Ren's mind, so we were forced to find a more secluded place.

The apartment was quiet as Daxton did his job. Neither he nor Amr asked any questions when I had told them that I wanted to intertwine their magic with mine. My excuse was that I wanted them close at all times, and I thought this would be a nice sentiment.

They didn't even bat an eye at it and had no problem telling me that they didn't know what was about to happen once their magic was tattooed into my skin. I was surprised someone like Amr hadn't heard of this before, but I counted my blessings.

Ren had already charmed the ink so as soon as Daxton added his magic they would work together to create a thread between me and him. It would be quick, easy, and semi-painless. I watched Ren as he adjusted his gloves and watched Daxton mix in his magic.

If I didn't know better, I would assume he was a pro at this.

Ren's eyes met mine as Daxton moved onto the next cap, allowing this magic to fall from his palm and intertwine with the ink. Ren's hair was tied back showing his purple eyes and light freckles splattered across his nose and cheeks.

He was a better actor than I could have hoped for.

"No offense," Daxton said as he pulled away from the ink. "But are you sure you want *your brother* to do this? I have a professional, you know."

Amr shifted next to me, the arm that was on my waist tightening.

"He'll be fine," I said with a smile. "It's just a small tattoo. I wanted to match the one on his hand. Something to tie us together as well."

The lies flowed out of my mouth smoothly.

"Amr," Daxton called and jerked his head towards the table. "Your turn."

Amr left my side with a kiss to the cheek and Daxton walked to my side, though he didn't try to touch me. I leaned into Daxton, inhaling his scent, and sinking into his side. He stiffened before relaxing against me with a sigh.

"Are you tired?" I asked him.

It had been obvious that Daxton was not sleeping well. It was part of the reason for what spurred this. He had become but a fraction of himself in the last few weeks and I was worried, especially when he kept brushing me off as if there was nothing wrong when there so *obviously* was.

"I'm okay," he said in a voice low enough not to let the others hear.

Amr was concentrating on the ink in front of him and Ren was lightly coaching him, telling him when to stop and move onto the next.

"Are you sure?" I asked and snuck a peek at his hard-set jaw. His dark eyes were staring at Amr and his lips were pushed into a straight line. His skin had paled and there was a light shadow on his cheeks and jaw. He had lost a significant amount of weight, making his face almost look sunken in.

Just like I suspected he would, Daxton began to withdraw even more than he already had. His face relaxed and his eyes zoned out like he was stuck in a daydream.

"I already told you I am fine," he grumbled and straightened, forcing me off him.

I looked back over the table to see both Ren and Amr staring at us.

I shook off the hurt that spread throughout me and walked over to the table with a smile.

"Let's do this," I said to Ren.

He nodded and motioned me to sit in the chair across the table.

I did so, but made sure to angle my chair towards Amr and Daxton who were leaning against the back of the couch. Daxton's expression had darkened and there was something guarded behind his eyes that twisted my gut.

I will save you from yourself, I vowed while holding Daxton's gaze. The first prick of the needle wasn't horrible, but the magic working with the charm had quickly sunken into my skin and sent a burning pain shooting up my arm.

Ren warned me it would hurt, and I assured him I was fine...but this pain was far more than what I had expected. But I would take it and with each prick of the needle through my skin I hardened my resolve.

I will save you from yourself.

Mark my words.

You may hate me for this, but it would all be worth it in the end.

I wouldn't let *anyone* ruin our happiness...not even the people I loved.

Chapter 6
Malik

I pushed back the cafeteria doors so hard the hinges creaked. The sound of the door hitting the wall echoed the room and while a few demons met my eyes, others seemed to sense that they should mind their fucking business.

Rage was burning hot underneath my skin and I knew that if I didn't find Eli soon, I would burst.

I hadn't been able to get ahold of Eli ever since Rosie had asked us to leave her alone with them. Eli had contently disappeared, and it only made the whole situation worse.

For days after the event the agents from the Demon Regulation Society were circling the area, cataloging the crime, and interviewing students. Rosie and Rae had told me to let Eli do their thing, but as week two came and went and classes resumed, I was worried that Eli had gotten into some trouble.

After hours of searching the house and questioning Daxton, I decided to search Winterfell. I didn't bother trying to disguise myself as a student anymore, so I didn't have a chance to check on them during class. Daxton had insisted they showed occasionally, and he was all I had to leverage because Rosie had been ditching as much as possible.

Another fucking pain in my ass. Neither of them seemed to want what I tried so hard to create for them.

I let out a growl as I walked into the cafeteria and scanned the area. If Eli had even gone to school, their classes should have been out by now, but the cafeteria was oddly empty and there was no sign of Eli's familiar blond hair.

I spied a familiar purple-eyed hybrid sitting in the corner with a few other low-levels and made a beeline toward him.

When he looked up to see me walking towards him, he dropped the bottled coffee in his hands, causing it to spill all over the table. The people at his table yelled and quickly got up so they could get some napkins to wipe it up.

Ren stayed in his seat, not caring to run after them, which left us alone for the most part.

Perfect.

"Where is Eli?" I asked, but out of respect for Rosie I didn't use my power on him. I knew that would have pissed her off.

She had confided in me one night as she lay in my arms that she had wished to grow closer to him, and I would try my best to make Rosie's life better than when I had entered it.

He raised a brow at me and shook his head.

"Why would *I* know where they are?" he asked, venom lacing in his voice.

It was my turn to raise my brow at him.

"Where the *fuck* did that attitude come from?" I asked.

His eyes widened for just a split second before he stood abruptly. His friends passed when they saw me talking to him. Bunches of napkins were in their hands and their faces had gone pale.

"I said I didn't see them," they said again in that goddamn tone that rubbed my nerves raw.

I stared him down, not willing to move from my spot. I wouldn't be disrespected. Not by him, not by anyone.

I had a life of following orders, and it was time that I finally left that in the past. I had a life now that I actually wanted to live but I knew that I would fall into the same pattern over and over again if I continued to be soft.

History had taught me that much.

"Bullshit," I growled and slammed my fist against the table. The wood splintered and the table groaned. *"Tell me."*

There was a silence that passed between us, and his eyes were glaring into me, begging me to push him.

At times like this, I wished that I had harnessed Marques's powers so I could dive deep into his mind and force the memory out of him...but I knew I was better off without the power.

Having the power would be more of an indication that I was going to die a slow and painful death like Marques, and I needed all the years I could get with my loved ones.

"I know where they are," his friend squeaked. I turned to look at the low-level. Their green eyes were dull, and they had a splash of freckles on their face similar to Rosie's.

"Speak," I commanded and crossed my arms over my chest.

They jumped at my voice and shot a look towards Ren.

"I saw them near the tower," they said in a weak voice.

Heat flared through me, and a growl ripped from my throat.

"Thank you," I huffed and turned on my heel to go find them.

As I walked to the tower I took out my phone and quickly dialed one of my old employees. There was no time to sit on this any longer. I needed to make sure that Eli hadn't done anything reckless and as much as I tried to stay out of it for Rosie's sake, I just couldn't anymore.

Not when the health of our unit was at stake.

"Boss?" he answered on the second ring.

I hated to admit that I may have missed my time with them in *The Fallen* and I was glad to have it back.

We weren't up to how we used to be and were still relatively small as compared to when I was working with Xena and Ezekiel...but it was good for now. It covered our expenses and I had made it clear that I only wanted them to go after corrupt and horrible people.

Damon may have run his sector like a madhouse, taking advantage of the youth and pumping drugs into children barely old enough to drive, but I didn't work that way.

I wanted everything we did to have meaning and an impact on the world...and it started with getting rid of those corrupt fuckers who give our gang a bad name.

"Hey," I said in a low voice. "Please tell me you are assigned to the Winterfell murders."

There was a pause from the other end and a shuffling before he spoke.

"Of course I am," he whispered. "As soon as I heard about them I jumped on it."

"I need you to do me a favor," I said. "Do your usual. I can have payment ready if you are willing to drive to Winterfell for it."

His *usual* in this case has always been clean up. He would help make sure none of my people went down for anything. The Demon Regulation Society were a bunch of old fucks in stuffy suits and while they may be horrible and slow at their job, they have been more than annoying when it came to catching some of my best guys.

"You got it," he said then cleared his throat. "I'll be there in twenty."

I said my goodbyes just as I came across the tower. Eli was standing right beneath it looking up at the stains of blood that the bodies had left. Their face was relaxed, but instead of a smile like I would have expected from a murderer visiting their crime scene, there was a small frown on their face.

It made my stomach turn.

I had been ecstatic when they didn't kill their mother, hoping that some of their humanity remained...but they had proven me wrong as soon as I took my eyes off of them.

But not anymore.

They turned towards me as I walked closer to them.

"Malik," they greeted, and flashed me a smirk.

"Dorm" I growled. "*Now.*"

"And if I say no?" they said, a teasing edge to their voice.

I ran my hand through my hair and let out a loud sigh.

"Don't make me use it," I pleaded. "Just come with me."

They shifted on their feet, their blue eyes staring into my soul. They were reading my mind, I knew it, but I wasn't scared of what they would find anymore. I was an open book.

They let out a snort.

"What a joke," they drawled then jerked their head to the side. "Come with me, I have to get my stuff anyways."

When they turned towards the dorms I felt my shoulder drop as the tension left me. *This* was half the battle and I hoped that the rest would be just as easy.

* * *

"Thank you," I muttered as I took the thick envelope from Claudine's hands.

She sent me a soft pitiful smile before turning to glare at Eli.

"If you keep on this path," she said in a low tone. "You will end up like one of your victims soon."

Eli raised a brow at her and shifted on their bed. I had let them start packing their stuff first before jumping right into business. It gave me time to get Claudine here and hand me some of the money we had stored away for things just like this.

Their dorm was now barren. The small pictures and...*toys* they had stashed were all neatly piled into their duffle bag along with any additional clothes they had left here.

I suppose it was a good sign that Eli was seeing our living arrangement as something permanent. Maybe meant that they would get used to being in this type of environment and hopefully cause less problems...but that was only an old man's hope.

I couldn't tell what the future had in store for us.

"You mean like your brother?" they asked.

"Eli," I warned.

Claudine shook her head, her small laugh filling the room.

"You will never change, Eli," she said and turned back towards me. "Watch your back before they take everything from you."

With that grave warning she exited with a flash of her magic.

I took a deep breath and was about to give Eli my speech, but they cut me off by clearing their throat.

"I'm sorry. I won't do it again, please forgive me," Eli said in a flat tone.

Their eyes were dull, and their facial expression gave me no indication that they actually meant their words.

The anger that had become almost non-existent rose to the surface.

Did they think this was a joke?

Did they not understand what was at stake for us if this got out?

"You can just clean it up," they said in a bored tone. "I don't know why you are acting like it's such a big deal."

It was a big deal.

I couldn't command the students to forget about what they had seen, nor could I just use random people from *The Fallen* to clean up this mess. I was being serious when I told Rosie that this was the improved version of the gang, and I couldn't risk it. I was a single demon and even my power had a limit.

There were three short raps on the door, and I gritted my teeth to stop the scream of frustration that was bubbling in my throat. I turned to the door and opened it quickly. Clean-up was here and luckily I didn't have to tell him to not wear his Demon Regulation Society uniform here.

"I will have it cleaned by Monday, boss," he said in a low voice. His eyes shifted to behind me and lingered on Eli, no doubt remembering how much of a hothead they were when they worked with us.

"Thank you," I mumbled and handed him the envelope that Claudine had brought me.

There was one thing the Originals did right, and that was hoard a treasure trove full of money and jewels that would fill our bank accounts for years to come. And with Eli acting like they did...I may have to use a chunk of it for things like this.

"Anytime, boss," he said, and his eyes flashed back to Eli. I didn't catch if Eli had glared at him, or said something in his mind, but the demon visibly flinched and turned back to me with a forced smile. "I will let you know if there are any updates in the case."

I nodded and waved my hand, dismissing him. I had never seen a demon run back down the hall faster than he did that day.

"I cannot keep cleaning up your mess, Eli," I growled and turned back towards them.

They exhaled loudly and leaned back onto the bed, while looking up to the ceiling. There was a small smile on their face. This was the posture of a child who knew they had just gotten caught and enjoyed the thrill of it, not someone who just got in trouble for murdering two people.

"Because I am not in trouble," they said, their eyes lazily meeting mine. "You will make sure of that."

I gritted my teeth and forced my hands to my side, worried that if I let my control slip for just a moment, that I would lunge forward and pummel Eli into the mattress.

"Do not use my love for Rosie as a weapon," I growled.

Eli arched their brow and straightened their back, their eyes running down my form. The act made me feel small.

"You can't *love* Malik," Eli said in a cool tone. "You just don't want her to throw you out in the cold when she realizes that you are not the all-powerful god you pretend to be."

White-hot rage flashed through me and before I knew it, I found myself lunging forward and gripping Eli's shirt. My knee was on the bed, and I leaned over them, panting as I glared at them. I forced their face close to mine and bared my teeth.

"You don't know *anything* Eli," I spat. "I have worked to save you—*us*—from harm for years and you doubt me? What I feel for Rosie? What I feel for you?"

Their eyes widened and then narrowed before their hand wrapped around mine and began to squeeze.

I would have liked to think that I was stronger than Eli. I had been alive for far longer than they had, and I made sure to exercise my body and power when I could...but as soon as they began to squeeze my hand I knew that they had surpassed me.

With ease they squeezed my hand until we heard the cracking of my bones filling the empty classroom. I gritted my teeth, refusing to show them that they had hurt me, but the smile on their face told me that they already heard every single thought that had entered my mind.

"I know you can't love because I have *seen* it," they growled and pushed us back as they climbed off the desk. "You think Ezekiel gave me nothing but his power?" They pushed me back until my back hit the wall. They were shorter than me but the power they exuded in that moment made it feel as though they were towering over me.

I gripped their wrist with my free hand, ready to pry them off of me, but they quickly grabbed that hand and forced it back onto the wall.

"I *saw* you, Malik," they whispered. "I saw you grow. I saw you fall in and out of love with every single hybrid that crossed paths with you. This is not love. You *could never* love Rosie."

Not like I do.

I don't think Eli intended to project the words into my mind, but I heard them. They were only a whisper, but they held pain and so much anger that I could feel it take over my mind.

"You're jealous," I breathed.

Eli's mouth turned to a frown, and they pushed me away before taking two steps back. They took a shaky breath before meeting my eyes.

"I'm not jealous," they growled. "That's fucking stupid."

It was my turn to smile at them. I couldn't help it.

Eli was acting out because they were *jealous*. No wonder they had been looking at the tower as if it had offended them.

"You were mad that she didn't like your show of affection," I said with a gasp. I couldn't help but chuckle at the thought of Eli being so strung up over Rosie scolding them for killing people that *this* is how they would act.

Without hesitation I looped my arm around their neck and pulled them to me. I laughed as they struggled against me. I inhaled their scent and leaned into them.

When did we ever hug like this?

We don't, Eli growled in my head, but they didn't push me away. I let them go after a few more seconds and sent them a soft smile.

Their ears turned bright red, and they averted their gaze to the ground.

"I am just tired of being outcasted," they grumbled. "Rosie hasn't come to school for days. She has been avoiding me."

She *was* avoiding him, this much I already knew, but...

"Maybe she just needs extra time—"

"We were allowed *two weeks* off," they growled and ran a hand through their hair. "And when she is here she won't go anywhere near me."

"Eli—"

They let out a loud growl.

"I don't want your *pity*," they said. "I just want you to see that I am doing this to protect her. Those people *hurt* her. Why can't I just wipe them off the face of this earth? And besides her I have...*nothing*."

I swallowed thickly while trying to collect my thoughts.

Eli had held it together for a long time after consuming both Marques's and Ezekiel's flesh...but maybe it was time for them to finally let out the simmering emotions that were buried deep down inside them.

But they couldn't do that if they were parading around as an academy student. They needed to work off their boredom and anger. Do something they thought was meaningful...

"You can't just murder people, Eli," I said and took a step forward. "In *The Fallen,* we had jobs. We were discreet. But this is not that." I paused and watched as they pouted. "I can see about calling more men back and giving you a sector...but we can't have you doing whatever you want. If we do this, we need a structure. We need a plan."

To this day, I don't know what I saw in Eli in that dorm that made me offer to put Eli in charge of the gang I had worked so hard to resurrect. Maybe it was the way they looked at me when they admitted that they were just trying to help, or maybe it was the realization that they had nothing besides Rosie to look forward to anymore.

After all, I had brought Eli up with the intention of taking over a part of the gang, or at least that was what they always thought and now that our world had been turned upside down by the Originals, they had nothing to turn to.

I understood them because I felt the same.

My life revolved around a single hybrid that had wormed her way into my life.

Their eyes lit up and their lips twitched.

"I could be in charge?" they asked, their question hesitant, as if they were scared to even speak the words.

I nodded.

"You can be in charge. I just need you to build the structure and plan *with* me," I said. "No rampaging."

They looked up towards the ceiling, digesting my words then nodded.

"No rampaging," they promised.

I let out a sigh and ran my hands through my hair.

"*You* will have to be the one to tell Rosie though," I said quickly. "And if she says no then it's a no."

Eli frowned but nodded anyways.

"I didn't know she was our keeper now," they grumbled but there was no heat in their words.

"She's more than our keeper," I said with a smile. "She's our everything."

Chapter 7
Daxton

My body felt like it was on fire.

Every movement. Every inhale. Even every fucking thought seemed to hurt in some shape or form. Even though my chest had sewn itself back together and my body had recovered, it still felt like the pain of being ripped in two never went away.

That damn witch had said nothing to warn me about this. Not like it would have deterred me anyways, but a warning would have been nice. At least I would have had time to prepare what I was going to tell the others instead of snapping at them every other second.

At least now I had a chance at life.

I didn't know how much longer I would have to deal with this pain, but at least I knew that I could spend the rest of my days with the people I cared about. It was better than being a ravenous monster and not knowing if which day would be my last day on earth. That is...if they ever chose to forgive me after this.

I had been horrible to Amr and cold at best to Rosie. They didn't deserve it, but I was worried that with each passing moment my resolve to keep this secret inside of me weakened.

Rosie and Amr had mentioned on more than one occasion that they were looking forward to this *new version* of our life and I didn't dare try to ruin it by telling them that not only was Xena alive, but I knew where she was and had to visit her on a weekly basis in order to make sure her father's magic had been fully purged from my system.

How would I even begin to explain this kind of betrayal? And after everything Rosie had done to me?

She *murdered* my parents for God's sake and what did I do to repay her? Fraternize with the enemy right behind her back?

I pulled the fluffy black comforter closer to my body feeling a chill settle over me. It was just around three in the morning, and I had missed Amr's body heat. With everything that happened to my body, I found myself relying more and more on his body heat as mine dwindled.

I froze when I heard the door open but relaxed when I felt Rosie's magical signature.

It had been difficult to feel for signatures now that my magic was half of what it was. Just *another* thing to add to the growing pile of things to be self-conscious about, including how my body was rapidly deteriorating.

Without talking I turned over and caught sight of Rosie sneaking into the room. It was pitch black except for the light of the moon giving me just enough visibility to see that she was in a long t-shirt and nothing else.

I lifted the comforter for her, and she wasted no time climbing into my bed and pushing her frozen feet against my legs.

I let out a hiss and wrapped the blanket around us. Her hands found my waist and she buried her head in my chest. Her nose was so cold I could feel it through the shirt fabric.

"Take a midnight walk?" I asked, keeping my voice low.

I would bet money that half of the house was still up at this hour. Everyone had been restless since Eli had taken to murdering our teacher and classmate and whenever I went out to get myself a glass of water, at least one of the residents was there as well.

Rae liked to sit on the edge of the kitchen island, black book in hand, with a freshly brewed coffee at her side. She was never much of a talker and just nodded to me as I passed before turning back to her book and writing down whatever scheme was in her mind at the moment.

Eli tended to wander the outside garden, close enough to the wards that still protected the house that at times I was worried they would hurt themselves.

Malik...well if Malik was ever awake, it was usually because he was with Rosie and damn...did he give me yet another reason to be self-conscious. That demon could literally make Rosie orgasm with his power alone.

I had never had a problem with libido, or any type of sexual encounters... but I was aware of the drastic change in my appearance as much as everyone else. I didn't want to be seen as weak. I didn't want to be frail or sickly...even if it was at the cost of my life.

It was the only thing I regretted about my decision.

"I was searching for you," she said and snuggled further into me. "You were not with Amr."

I swallowed thickly.

"No," I admitted. "I may have crossed the line earlier."

I should shut my mouth. I should shut this whole thing down before it gets too far.

But there was something about being in an almost completely dark room with the woman I loved in my arms. Her warmth radiated around me while her magic tangled with mine. It was *safe,* comforting...everything I had ever wanted.

It made my lips loose.

"I know," she whispered. "He told me."

I leaned down and placed a kiss on top of her head. A warmth spread through me as I inhaled her scent.

It had been so long since I had her like this. All alone and cuddled up to me.

I missed it. *I missed her.*

"It's been a while since we slept together," I noted, then quickly added, "alone."

She shifted so that her eyes could meet mine and there was a small smile on her face.

"Getting tired of sharing?" she asked.

I made a show of rolling my eyes.

"*Never*," I whispered, and leaned forward to brush my lips across hers.

It was a soft kiss. That was all I intended it to be. Until she sighed into me and deepened the kiss. Her soft tongue darted out to tangle in mine, and I couldn't help but moan into her.

It really hadn't been *that* long since I had shared this with her...but damn, did I forget how crazy she made me.

Even with most of my magic being taken from me, the rest of it still roared to life under her touch.

More, it begged as it felt the ancient magic rise around us.

I gripped her hips and pulled her to me. Warmth spread in my belly as her leg hooked over mine and she began to grind on me.

"You came for a hookup," I teased and bit her lip playfully.

I pulled up her shirt and my hands traveled to her ass. Imagine my surprise when I also realized she wasn't wearing underwear.

All thoughts of self-consciousness left me as I grabbed her thigh and turned us over, so I was on top of her. She wrapped her legs around my waist and used her free hand to tug at my sleep pants.

"I just wanted to spend some extra time with you," she said breathlessly.

I worked quickly to take off her shirt and only broke our kiss so I could pull her nipple into my mouth. Her soft moans filled the air, and her hand came to grip at my hair.

I accidentally bit her nipple a bit too hard, and the pain from her pulling my hair coursed through me.

Lucky for me, she like it rough and arched into me, begging for me to bite her again. I moved to the other nipple, trailing my tongue around the bud before taking it fully into my mouth.

My hand came to cup her pussy and I took in a sharp breath when I felt how wet she already was.

"Rosie," I growled and peered up at her.

She looked at me with hooded eyes and flushed cheeks. Her mouth was open and soft pants came between her swollen lips. She was absolutely perfect, and I became painfully hard at the sight of her under me.

Without hesitation, I plunged two fingers into her folds. Her head rolled back, and a shaky moan filled the space between us. I leaned forward and licked her lips, thrusting my fingers into her one more time.

My self-control was waning. Even with the magic gone, I began shaking as I tried to hold back from plunging into her.

"Dax," she moaned as I circled her clit with my thumb.

Her hand slipped between us, and she pulled my hardened cock out of my boxers before stroking it. I let out a loud groan as her thumb rubbed my sensitive head.

"This is my favorite," she said against my lips and fingered the piercing on my cock. I shuddered when her movements became more erratic.

I quickly shed the rest of my pants and positioned myself in between her legs, but before I could thrust into her she pushed me to the bed and straddled me. My back hit the soft mattress and I couldn't have been more grateful for her. Not only was my control almost nonexistent...but I could feel my limbs start to shake as they begged for a break.

I wasn't as recovered as I should have been before doing this...but I needed to be inside her *now*.

She met my eyes with a mischievous grin and held my cock in one hand as she slowly lowered herself onto me.

I bit back a groan as her pussy clamped down on me. She was so warm and wet already, I probably wouldn't last long.

She gave an experimental swivel of her hips, causing her to sink down even further.

"Let me do this for you," she said with a light moan. "Just lie back and let me make you feel good."

I tried to reach for her, but she ended up grabbing both of my wrists and forcing them above my head.

I couldn't help the chuckle that slipped from my lips.

"Is *this* what you like?" she teased, though her voice was husky and her eyes roamed over me like she was famished.

God.

I felt my mind go fuzzy as she moved on top of me. The light sound of her wet thighs hitting my hips filled the room. I couldn't even find the right words for what I was feeling. The control she exhibited on top of me as she rode my cock and kept my hands above my head was absolutely delicious.

"Fuck," I managed to whimper.

Her lips came to trail hot kisses against my chilled skin as she ground against me, pulling bursts of pleasure from me. Her lips trailed all the way to my nipple before she looked up at me with hooded eyes and gave an experimental lick.

I let out a shaky moan and arched into her.

Never had a lover ever played with my nipples like she had and with stark clarity, I realized just how much I had been missing out.

"Ooh," she teased with a smile before covering my nipple with her mouth and giving a slow suck. The groan I let out was pitiful, but with the way she was causing my body to light on fire with each movement, I couldn't find myself to care.

The pain was quickly chased away with the heat that was rising in me with each thrust of her hips. I felt myself swell inside her and my body began to tremble. She straightened and began to ride me in earnest, her head tilting back and moans spilling out of her mouth.

I joined her, not caring if we woke the entire goddamn house.

"Fuck, Rosie," I groaned and gripped her hips to meet each of her thrusts. "I'm going to come."

"Come inside me, Daxton," she commanded. "Fill me to the brim so when I wake up tomorrow, your come will be running down my thighs."

I couldn't even groan out a curse as I came inside her. My entire body went rigid as she rode me until every bit of my seed had been emptied into her.

Whatever magic I had swirled around with hers and when hers entered my body, I felt like a new life was breathed into me. The magic filled me to the brim, almost painfully. Before, I couldn't get enough of this but now...her magic was almost too much for me.

She looked down at me with a smug expression, then climbed off me and curled into my limp arms.

She had just pulled all my remaining energy out of me, and my eyes fluttered closed before I could stop them.

"I'll make it up to you," I mumbled and pulled her closer.

"This was for you," she reminded and as she peppered kisses on my chest.

* * *

When I awoke next I stayed still as Rosie curled into me. Her breathing was even, and she let out a low moan as she dreamed. It was the first time in a long time that I had a moment with her. A moment so quiet and still that I could hear the groans of the house as the wood settled.

The air around us had a chill and we were plunged into utter darkness. Rosie was warm as she curled up to me. A comforting warm that should have filled me with joy and lulled me back into sleep, but instead it hurt my skin.

The way her hair brushed against my chest shot low vibrations of pain through me.

The way her fingers curled into my skin caused electric-like shocks to wrack my body.

And even her breath, once a tickle on my skin, caused it to itch.

But none of that mattered because finally, she was here. Finally, I had her all to myself. And finally, the dreams had been chased away.

I pulled the blankets closer to us and planted a soft kiss on her head. I wrapped my arms around her and held her as close as I possibly could. I didn't want to miss a single moment of this.

I didn't care if I was slowly decaying or if my skin felt like it was on fire.

I needed this...*her*.

"I'm sorry," I whispered into her hair.

Alone, in the darkness, I felt like I didn't have to hide anymore, at least not in this moment. I didn't have to conceal my thoughts, or make sure the pain wasn't evident on my face.

Here I could just be.

It was all I ever wanted. Ever since my parents—*stop*.

I didn't want to think about that right now. This wasn't what this was about.

"My magic..." I trailed in a whisper, my throat aching. "It's never going to be the same and I don't know what to do about it."

I paused, waiting for any indication that she was going to wake, but she stayed still in my arms. It gave me the courage to speak.

"I didn't want to disappoint you," I said. "That's why I didn't tell you. I had no idea—"

My words were cut off by a lump forming in my throat. I swallowed thickly and blinked rapidly as tears stung my eyes.

Fuck.

I didn't want to be like this anymore. I wanted to be better than...*this*. Be the person Rosie and Amr could rely on. Be the person that would contribute to this family we were building...but I couldn't.

Xena had asked me to do something, now that she was sure that what she was doing had worked...I tried not to think of it around the others...but when I was alone, it was all that I could think of at times.

I was no longer just fraternizing with the enemy.

She looked down at me with a smirk.

"This is good," she purred and took one long lick of her blood-covered hand.

I couldn't even stand and was forced to lie on the bed as I bled out.

"Your terms," I choked out with a groan.

Her smile widened and showed her blood-stained teeth.

"Just keep disappearing," she said. "Keep up our meetings...and sooner or later, my curious little daughter will come to find you."

I tried to sit up, but the pain was too unbearable, and I found my consciousness slipping.

"You promised," I groaned.

"I won't hurt her," she said with a chuckle. "I just need to...talk to her. Need her help, actually."

And since then, I had done what she had asked of me. Rosie hadn't yet tried to follow me, but I knew it would happen soon and, as if the universe wanted to prove my point, Rosie woke up.

She turned with a groan and peeked up at me with her large brown eyes.

"How long have you been awake?" she asked in a voice that was still thick with sleep.

"Not long," I muttered and leaned forward to kiss her lips. She let out a soft sigh and melted into me before returning the kiss.

When she froze, I pulled away and squinted into the dark, trying to catch a small glimpse of her face. I think she was frowning.

"If I ask you a question..." she trailed. "Would you tell me the truth?"

My heart pounded in my chest, and I tried to keep my panic locked inside me.

"Trust issues?" I asked with a small smile, keeping my tone light.

She had every reason to worry, and I wouldn't put it past her to have already put together that I was hiding something. She was smart, smarter than anyone gave her credit for, but I knew in there, just like Amr...she had her doubts.

She forced a smile, and something flashed across her face before she spoke again.

"Does your disappearance for that period of time have anything to do with why it looks like your body is falling apart?"

Ice cold panic filled my veins, and I had the powerful instinct to push her out of the bed and run for my life. There was something in her voice that the old Rosie didn't have before...something far more dangerous than I had expected.

She knows. She has to know. Why else would she ask this? Why else would she ask this right now?

Did Marques's powers have anything to do with this?

I cleared my throat.

"I didn't think you noticed I was gone," I said truthfully. "Given the new powers and the refugees and everything."

Her frown deepened.

"Of course, I noticed," she said. Her tone was high pitched and there was an edge to her tone that told me she was offended by my assumption.

"I was visiting my famil—*my* land," I said. It was a half-truth. I spent time recuperating in the bar's upstairs room and one night, when the guilt of what I had done almost consumed me, I limped my way back to the land my parents had bought and sat in the burned ruins of my own home.

It was painful as I walked the same paths that I had when I was a child. I could still remember everything so clearly, from the way the fresh linens smelled to the noises of the familiars wrestling in the yard. It had once been a beautiful, carefree place...but selfishness and greed had ripped it away from me.

The memories didn't hurt...at least not much anymore. And not because of my parents' murder, they hurt because I had destroyed any chance of being able to experience them again...but this time with the people that actually cared about me.

Rosie's eyes widened and her hand came to cup my cheek.

"I'm sorry Daxton," she breathed. "I didn't know you still went there."

I shook my head and held her close.

"Rosie..." I trailed. "Can I tell you something?"

She nodded and tried to look back up at me, but I didn't let her. If she looked at me I would lose all the courage I had built up in the darkness and never be able to face her again.

And this may be one of my last chances to do this.

"I love you," I whispered. The words were barely audible even in the silence of the room.

Her breath hitched, and I felt her magic swirl around us.

"I love you too Daxton," she said, her tone light. I could feel her smile into my chest, and I let out a sigh of relief, though it didn't ease my guilt.

I just *needed* her to know that I loved her because there was a chance that I may not make it out of this alive, and I wanted to make sure that I didn't die with any regrets.

Including telling Rosie that I loved her.

"Again," she commanded.

I smiled and kissed her head.

"I love you, Rosie Miller."

Chapter 8
ROSIE

"Again," the doctor said in a gentle voice, his soft brown eyes looking over my palm as the black magic spilled into my hand.

He gasped as the black magic grew so fast he had to jerk back in order to not get burned.

"Pretty scary isn't it, doc?" Ren asked in a teasing tone and leaned into my side.

My heart skipped a beat when I realized that this was the first time he had ever done such a thing.

I couldn't help but look back at Malik and Rae. They were both sitting on the hospital bed behind us, their eyes lingering on me. Rae had a slight smile on her face while Malik's expression was blank.

It was my idea to take them here today. After showing Ren my magic the other night, I couldn't get his reaction out of my head. My magic *did* feel different, and I didn't want to chance letting it consume me like Daxton's had.

The doctor and his remaining patients had taken one of Rae's properties and had begun to use it as a rehabilitation center for those who were still recovering from their stint behind the barrier. The dining and living room had been combined to fit all the medical beds and gave a great view out into the garden.

It would have been perfect if there weren't so many decaying low-levels in here. Well...they weren't decaying anymore.

The magic had taken a toll on their bodies, and they were no longer able to live the lives they used to. As I turned back to face the doctor, I saw some of the low-levels still lying in their beds. There was one sitting upright behind the doctor, his eyes were glaring into us. His hair was scruffy and fell to his shoulder, he had a matching white beard, and his skin had a greyish tint to it.

"Where's the blonde?" they grumbled, their voice coming out hoarse.

"Eli didn't come today," Malik called from behind us. "Will you ever let go of that grudge? We saved your life."

"You almost killed me!" they shot back. They lurched forward as a cough wracked their frail body.

The doctor's gaze dropped to him, and he rushed over to his side, only to be pushed aside by him.

"Don't fucking touch me you—"

The low-level's yells were interrupted by another round of coughs that went through him.

"Doctor Svensson," Malik called. "Glad to see your patent is alive. Good work."

Doctor Svensson sent him a small, forced smile before taking a step away from the low-level.

"Andrew," he said and lit his hands up with magic before motioning for my hand once more. "Call me Andrew."

I placed my hand in his, palm up, and tried to focus on bringing forth the black magic once more.

"Why does he look like that?" Ren asked.

His question startled me and caused my magic to flicker. I sent him a look.

"Don't ask that," I whispered.

Ren sat back up straight and leaned to look over at the man.

"I couldn't stop the effects from aging entirely," Doctor Svensson said in a solemn tone. "I tried my best to and while his insides may be in better shape than they were before, his outer appearance has changed drastically. They all have."

The image of Amber dying in the cot flashed through my mind. I tried not to let the guilt overtake me as I realized that if we had gotten her to this man sooner, she may have lived. There were many deaths during that time, but *hers* had stuck with me the most.

Ren nudged my arm, and I was torn out of my thoughts.

"Sorry," I muttered.

Doctor Svensson gave me a small smile and held my hand in his.

"I think that's enough," he said. "You're fine for now, though I would hope in the future you will stop...partaking in cannibalism."

I flinched and tore my hand from his like it was on fire.

I didn't have to look at Malik to know that his eyes were burrowing holes into the back of my head.

"Is that all it's from?" Rae asked, her voice closer behind me than I remembered. Her hand lightly squeezed my shoulder and I leaned back into her.

Doctor Svensson paused.

"I am hoping so," he said. "Though this is all very unprecedented... and I can never be a *hundred* percent sure."

"We will have to watch it," Rae said and then shifted. "Is the kitchen still as it once was?"

Doctor Svensson gave her a smile.

"Exactly as it once was," he said.

"Let's have an afternoon coffee, shall we?" Rae asked.

I tilted my head to look up at her and my heart skipped a beat when I realized she was already looking at me. She must have felt how affected I was by his words.

I appreciated the gesture, and it was a distraction I needed at the moment.

"That sounds great," I whispered.

She sent me a smile that made my heart pound in my chest.

"I was a barista once," Ren said and jumped off the bed, calling my attention towards him. His eyes were lit with mischief, and he had a sly smile on his face. "Though I did get fired for spitting in a high-level's coffee."

My jaw dropped and I couldn't help the laugh that spilled out. I pushed myself up and wound my arm through his.

"Well," I said with a smile. "Let's hope I haven't done anything to upset you as of late."

He rolled his eyes at me.

"I think we are past that now, Rosie," he said and pulled me along with him to the kitchen.

* * *

I took a sip of Ren's overly bitter coffee and grimaced when it hit my tongue.

True to his word, he had made me coffee. But he had insisted that I take it without any sweetness because it "ruined the flavor."

To appease him I accepted it without complaint but by the look on Rae's face, I knew she understood all too well how I felt about it. For the first time, I had to watch as Rae tried to hold back laughter.

She had no problem drinking her own coffee and looked perfectly content, but I was dying.

"Is it true you own a gang?" Ren said suddenly.

I shifted in the hard chair and looked towards Malik to watch his reaction. We had moved to the garden outside. The sun shone down on us, warming my skin. The air around us smelt fresh and there was a distinct scent of roses from the neighboring bushes.

Malik and Rae sat next to me and Ren across. There was a small table that separated us, and I was surprised that there was no awkwardness between us. It was the tamest I had seen this group to date. It was refreshing, calming even being able to sit here among them and just *be*.

"Where did you hear that?" Rae asked before Malik could answer.

Ren gave her a look and turned back to Malik.

Maybe I spoke too soon.

"I guess you could say that," Malik said with a sigh and lifted his mug to his lips. "Who's asking?"

The insinuation was clear in his tone. Ren placed his cup down on the table with more force than was needed.

"You think I'm a rat?" he spat.

I swallowed thickly. The mask that Ren was holding on to was now gone and in front of me stood the same boy who had tried to murder me during the games. It was scary how fast he could switch...but so could I.

"Why are you angry?" I asked and cocked my head to the side. "Is it so wrong for him to think that you are a rat when you were before?"

Ren slumped in his chair and held his hands up in the air.

"Sorry," Ren said and gave me a sheepish smile. "I guess you can say I don't favor scarred gang members. Nor do I respect them."

Anger burst inside me, and a growl ripped from my chest.

"Ren," I warned.

He let out a sigh, his whole body seeming to deflate.

"Okay," he said, exasperated. "Sorry. I will behave."

I nodded and sent him a look. Seconds ticked past us in silence, and I waited for him to start something again. When he didn't I sighed. I was tired of the fighting. Tired of the secrets. I didn't want this resentment and anger to follow us for the rest of our lives.

"I saw someone leave Eli's dorm," Ren confessed. "And he didn't look very...friendly."

Malik stiffened in his chair and his jaw ticked. I had seen the same look on his face more than once, though this may have been the first time I had seen it hold such a weight in a long time.

The air around us was tense as Malik took a few deep breaths. My eyes shot to Rae but hers were locked on Malik.

"You were spying?" he growled.

Dread filled my stomach.

"Old habits die hard," he said with a shrug. "I was just curious as to why you were so angry."

I looked back towards Malik.

"Why were you in Eli's dorm?" I asked.

Eli and Malik were on better terms now, but I wouldn't have expected them to be so close that they had allowed him in. Especially when I had just been allowed in myself after all these years together.

Unless... Eli didn't act out again, did they?

He pressed his lips into a tight line.

"I was talking to Eli," he said, and his eyes narrowed towards Ren. "About what they did."

I cleared my throat and looked towards Rae. Her jaw was clenched, and her fingers were clasped tight around the mug.

"They didn't...do anything, did they?" Rae asked.

Malik shook his head. Relief burst through me.

"Nope," he said. "Thank God, but you should stop ignoring them Rosie." His eyes burrowed into mine and there was a heavy emotion there. "They miss you."

I averted my gaze towards my cup with a frown.

"I know," I whispered. "I miss them too."

Chapter 9
Rae

I looked at the glowing red numbers next to my mother's bedside tables and sighed when I realized that it was almost five in the morning. The night had fallen into morning quicker than I had accounted for. I enjoyed being in the silence, and found myself getting lost in it, and my own thoughts. The house had fallen asleep and there was no one here to bother me.

I had been here for the latter half of the night when I realized my personal sleeping aide wouldn't be with me tonight. As it turned out, I couldn't sleep very well without Rosie by my side.

Even though her magic had at times gone haywire and her emotions had been volatile...it seemed like that was in the past and now her normal thrum of contentness had been what lulled me to sleep.

I knew it was selfish of me, but sometimes I wished that I could keep her every night. She had been visiting me more often now that she had been ignoring Eli...but even then I found myself wanting more.

I was becoming obsessed.

But I knew that my sleepless nights had more to do with Eli than it did Rosie.

It had been four weeks since that incident and thankfully Malik had been there to help us clean it up...but that didn't mean I didn't worry about what was to come. I knew that it was a matter of time before his power couldn't cover the extent of Elis's recklessness, especially if they continued in this direction.

He may have used his power to make her stop killing, but they could do many other things without breaking that rule.

I let out another sigh and leaned back in the chair, feeling my bones ache. I had sat in this position for far too long. I stretched my neck and arms, hearing each of my joints as I did. I took off my glasses and rubbed the bridge of my nose. The stress had given me a nonstop headache the last few days and with everyone's volatile emotions I felt the control of my own emotions waver.

It was why I chose my mother's room in the first place. It was the furthest from the others as I had specifically requested that they stay away from her. I didn't need Eli stirring up trouble, especially when it came to my mother. There were many things I could tolerate from them…but anything to do with my mom was off the table and was not something I could forgive.

No matter how small it may be.

Tonight, was a night where Marques's memories and powers threatened to tear me from the inside out. I had been careful to keep it under control and made sure to distance myself whenever I was on the verge of losing myself.

Sometimes, I felt like I was on the verge of a breakthrough. Maybe a memory would flash through my mind, or maybe I felt like I could understand the rampant powers that lay deep inside me, just waiting for me to finally understand how to awaken them.

It happened once, when I was in the classroom with Rosie and Eli.

Without me even commanding it I felt myself pushing into Eli's mind, and by the way their eyes widened, I knew they felt it as well.

I knew Marques had some type of mind power. He had used them on me once, which led to the situation at hand and the downfall of all the Originals we had known.

But I didn't know enough to control it and when I continued to push, I found myself facing a wall. During the night while I tossed and turned, I tried to think of what I would even do if I was able to reach into their mind… but nothing came to mind.

The room was silent as I stewed in my own mess.

Please, Marques, I begged, though I didn't know if it was to the dead Marques who had made his home in hell, or if it was the one that was still alive in my memories.

Show me something useful. Please.

I wanted to know how to use these powers. How to distance myself from the painful memories that lay behind an iron curtain. I was *scared* of what lay waiting for me. I didn't know if I would be able to handle what Marques had seen. I had seen how it changed both Eli and Rosie...and I couldn't risk being changed in the way they had been.

I needed to keep my head straight for this fucked up little family we built together.

If I were so overtaken by the memories, or the powers, I would let something slip...and it would be too late.

I had just worked out with Nathaniel and Benjamin how we could profit on our multiple properties enough to pay for *all* of our lives without having to dip into the dirty Original money. They would keep a few, and so would I, but everything would be shared equally...and we would support each other.

That was my rule.

No matter what they decided to do or where they decided to go, we needed to continue to support each other. It was the least we could do after what our father had put us through.

Malik had offered, multiple times, and while I had used the money for urgent things like house repair and a property management company...I didn't want to use it forever. I *would not* let the fucked-up situation we had been forced through make me complacent.

As much as I hated my father, I would upkeep our family values. Even if *he* couldn't.

Nathaniel and Benjamin were finally starting college and surprisingly enough, they both decided that Winterfell wasn't for them. It had been Father's wish for us all to attend, but now that he was gone I guess they were free to choose whatever. And at least I didn't have to worry about them ever being separated again—they were as close as twins could get.

They came home often to check in on me and Mother, but they both seemed more than happy to put some space in between them and the horrors of this house. I could feel their emotions dampen as soon as they walked in through the door.

This place wasn't for them anymore.

I didn't blame them. They had a god-awful childhood, and they hadn't taken well to Father's death and the responsibility it put on them. I hoped in time, they would accept it and learn how to live a happy and safe adult life. I didn't mind being the person they ran to for everything, but I needed to know, for my own peace of mind, that they could survive in the world.

I rubbed my eyes hard enough that white stars exploded in them. When I put my glasses back on I looked over Mother's frozen frame with a frown.

"Benjamin is doing well in school. Good grades as always," I said to her, even though I knew she wouldn't hear it. "Nathaniel is...not doing as well but he is trying." I let out a heavy sigh. "I mean I hope he is. Their tuition was expensive."

I paused and let my eyes wander to the dark garden that surrounded our property. The sun would rise soon, and it would be a great place to watch it rise over the hills.

"They left this place as soon as they could," I continued. "It's best that they did. I have enough on my hands with Eli and Rosie." I paused, a sourness filling my stomach. "Daxton has some issues of his own...but I don't know how to help him with it. And to be frank...I don't want to. I think it's witch stuff and I—"

I was cut off when I was hit with a wave of emotion and a rustling of sheets. The air stilled around me, and my chest squeezed so tight that I couldn't breathe. I snapped my gaze over to Mother and ice-cold fear filled my veins when I realized she had shifted so she was now lying on her side. Her eyes were wide open and looking *directly at me.*

I jumped out of my chair causing it to fall to the ground with a loud thump.

Then my mother blinked. She *fucking* blinked.

Against the fear rushing through my veins, I dove forward, kneeling by her bedside.

"Mother?" I asked in a soft voice.

I watched for any reaction at all, but when she stayed there motionless my mind started racing for any possible explanation for what I just saw.

Maybe the pillow was lopsided, and she fell off it?

Maybe she had been that way the whole time?

I am sleep-deprived.

Yes...I have been up too long, and I am seeing things.

I shook my head and tilted my glasses so I could rub my eyes again, but when I blinked away the stars, her eyes moved again and this time her mouth moved as well.

"Cur—" Her words were choked and barely audible.

She didn't sound like the mother in my memories. Her soft voice was now hoarse and sounded like she had smoked for years.

"What?" I asked again and leaned closer.

"*Cursed.*"

* * *

"If you don't behave in here I will see to it that your entire bloodline is wiped off this planet," I threatened as my hand gripped the metal knob to my mother's room.

Eli rolled their eyes at me.

"I'm not heartless," they said and pushed my shoulder.

I growled in warning and pushed the door open.

Callie, my mother's nurse, was already near the windows, scribbling down wildly on her notebooks. She jumped when we entered and gave us a strained smile.

The room seemed much more lively in broad daylight as opposed to last night. Last night it had been something of a nightmare and I was almost relieved to see Callie's colorful flowery scrubs. They still stood out horribly in comparison to the neutral tones in the room, but I wouldn't complain. Not if we were getting results.

Rosie sat on the side of the bed with my mother's hand clasped in hers. She was wearing a bright yellow dress that I had never seen her wear before, and her long black hair was pulled up into a high ponytail on top of her head.

She looked out of place in that dress. It was too innocent for her, made her look too much like the young adult that she should have been.

It was a painful reminder of how much we had been through.

"Trust me, you have *never* seen someone try harder to hide something than a low-level child afraid to get caught by the high-level demons they just stole an expensive pair of headphones from," she said then let out a laugh. "I think I was around seven during that time and my friend, Marissa? I think that was her name. Marissa was trying to hide me behind a trashcan outside the cafe. I wasn't a kid that took a lot of chances, but she was *so* popular, and I wanted her to like me...so I guess...I just went with it."

I looked towards Callie with a raised brow, and she put a finger to her lips, motioning for us to be quiet before turning back to Rosie.

I pulled Eli in and closed the door softly behind us.

"You can bet I never tried that again," Rosie continued, her tone light. "They chased us for almost *three miles.* Can you believe that?"

I felt a flicker of something warm in my chest and my gaze shot towards my mother. She was lying motionless in the bed, her eyes vacantly staring at nothing as if the moment we had last night was all in my head. But I knew I felt something from her in that moment. It was weak...but it was there. Proving that last night *wasn't* all in my head.

I had tried to pry more words out of my mother but when it turned out to be futile, I quickly called Rosie in here and impatiently waited for Callie to start her shift. As soon as Rosie walked through those doors my mother turned back into her comatose state.

I felt crazy as I explained what I saw to Rosie...but she believed me with no hesitation. I couldn't feel any whisper of disbelief in her system.

She was more than I could have ever asked for, and I was glad that she was here to help me with this. If not for her...I would have surely gone mad by now.

It was her idea to bring in Eli, to see if they could figure out anything. I didn't like it, but Rosie had a point, and I was too close to figuring something out that I couldn't chance it.

When there was a lull in Rosie's story, Callie looked over to us and motioned for us to step forward but Eli's hand on my shoulder stopped me.

"Tell her a sad story," Eli commanded. Rosie's head whipped around to us, her eyes wide and her face becoming flushed. "I thought I heard something when you were telling her about hiding. I think it was worry but I couldn't tell."

"I felt something warm," I admitted in a soft voice. "She liked your laugh."

Blush coated Rosie's face and she looked back to where her hands were intertwined with my mother's.

"Let's try sadness first," Callie said. "Whenever Rosie talks I see light flashing, but there isn't much of a correlation to what she was saying. I suspect sadness is easier to pull out than happiness."

Swallowing thickly, I nodded and motioned for Rosie to continue.

"I don't know where to start about a sad story," she admitted. "My life has been pretty sad, but I think the first time I ever truly realized that my life was messed up was when I overheard my mother sobbing because of what a *freak* her daughter had become." She let out a pitiful laugh. "She didn't care about the curse that was ripping me apart, nor did she care that my father's face was burnt to a crisp...just how people would think about it."

Eli's hand dropped from my shoulder, and they went to stand over Rosie's shoulder.

"More," they commanded, their blue eyes locked onto my mother's.

I felt a rush of emotions burst through me, including guilt for how I thought about Eli recently. I knew they could hear everything I had felt and suddenly seeing them help me just proved how shitty I had been to hold what they did against them for so long.

"I don't know what else to say," Rosie said, though we all knew it was a lie. There were plenty of things in her life she could share...but she was ashamed. Her shame was potent and heated my skin as if it was my own.

"It's okay," I said then shot a look to Callie. "I can ask her to leave if you don't feel comfortable."

Rosie shook her head, her hair bouncing back and forth. Eli and I both looked towards it and just as their hand moved to pull a strand. I cleared my throat.

Don't ruin this, I growled inside my mind.

A frown marred their face but for once, they listened to me.

"It's okay," Rosie said and took a deep breath before speaking. "I have never had a real family. My biological mom cursed me and tried to murder me. I *literally* stumbled into this new...*family,* I guess, but that doesn't change the one thing I want the most." She paused again, this time taking longer to gather her thoughts.

I could feel the emotions tearing at her insides. She was hesitant to share what she was thinking and worried, probably, about hurting our feelings.

"I really value my blood brother," she whispered, her hand squeezing my mother's. "I want to protect him with everything I have...even after he tried to kill me. Can you believe that our mom pitted him against me? He was supposed to assassinate me."

"We don't have to—"

Eli cut me off with a wave.

"Say it," Eli growled.

"No one's mother is left," she whispered. "All parents have been either murdered by the people in this room, or an Original that only used them to further their plans in destruction. And it's all I wanted. A blood mother. I grew up without someone I could put my faith into."

She let out a shaky breath.

"There was no one to run to," she said then paused. "You know when I told you about those demons? Well, they caught us and made me pay. I came home with cuts and bruises and even then before the curse, they didn't care."

Rosie shifted on the side of the bed.

"We need a mother," she whispered. "All of us. So, if there is something inside you that is stopping you from coming back to us, *please* try your hardest to fight it. We need you. Rae needs you. Nathanial, Benjamin. Please fight it."

I stepped forward. I didn't like the way her words made my chest feel. Eli raised their hand high in the air causing everyone to freeze.

"You still feel magic?" Eli asked Rosie.

Rosie nodded.

"It's small but it was always there," she said.

Eli turned to me, their face stone cold.

"I don't know if I should congratulate you or apologize," they said and lowered their hand to run it through their head. "I caught some of her memories. Just barely with a bit of thought. She *is* cursed, said so herself."

I cocked my brow at them. My mother had told me she was last night, but I don't know if I believed it. With everything we knew about curses it would be impossible for her to *still* be cursed after all these years.

"We went over this with Rosie," I said. "Curses can only work for this long if the witch is near."

"Unless it latches onto other magic," Eli said and cocked their head to the side.

There was a pause in the air, and I cracked my head to the side.

"It's her magic," Rosie breathed, her head whipping to look at me. "She has magic. Rae…"

"Congrats, I guess," Eli muttered, a small smile showing on their lips. "We have another hybrid on our hands."

Chapter 10
Rosie

My mother never changed, even after she was burnt to a crisp.

She dressed in the most expensive clothes, her neck and fingers were decorated with intricate gold jewelry, and she was wearing heels that were far too high. Her nails had been perfectly manicured and there was not a hair on her head that was out of place.

Maybe when they dragged you back down to hell they healed you before they tortured.

I found myself in the room that had started it all, in the town that never aged.

The fireplace was roaring, far hotter than it had been when I visited before. The room around me tilted as the flames from the fire began to spread so uncontrollably that the walls began to melt from the heat.

The picture frames that hung on the walls began to catch fire and the oils in the paintings kickstarted the flames. They burned so hot their golden frames melted down the wall and into a puddle on the floor.

"You think you got rid of me that easily?" she asked and stood. Her heels clacked against the burning floor beneath her feet. She seemed unaffected by the flames...maybe it was because she had created them.

Her smile told me that she had.

I tried to step back but when my back hit the wall, white-hot pain clouded my senses as the melted wall fused to my back. Her claw-like hand came to grip at my throat and she lifted me with a strength I didn't know she had, efficiently cutting off the air to my lungs.

I gasped for breath and tried to claw at her wrist, but she only let out a wretched, evil laugh.

"I spent *decades* preparing you to help us finally become the gods we were supposed to be and I *will not* have that erased because you decided to have a fit," she growled, and I felt the tips of her nails pierce the side of my neck.

I tried to call for my magic, or even my fire...but nothing came. I was left to my own devices with no power or anything to help me escape from her. In her grip, I was nothing more than a human with the hands of a literal devil around my throat.

"I'll see you in hell," she said with a twisted grin.

My world went black, then I surged forward out of the bed, panting.

I woke up with my heart racing and my back burning. I struggled to find my breath and reached for Rae, but the bed beside me was empty and cold. I looked around the dark bedroom, trying to calm my racing brain and remind myself that I was *not* back in the town with Xena.

Damn dreams.

My magic swirled around me wildly, leaving red glowing light in the area. I cursed and tried to pull it back to me, but it was being stubborn.

It had been a while since I had lost control of my magic in this way, and it only made the whole situation that much more unsettling. It wasn't the first time that I had dreamed of my mother since her death, but this was by far the most real feeling. And definitely the most painful.

Usually, it was a flashback. Sometimes it was my memories, sometimes it was Marques's.

Marques's memories though...were surprisingly more painful than my own. Because in his, Xena seemed like a real person.

She laughed, smiled, and loved. She was not the same witch that I had experienced when she was still alive. She was...unburdened. She was capable of caring for people and was not the cold-blooded murderer I had seen in my nightmares.

It made my stomach twist when I thought about it because I didn't like to think of Xena as anything other than a monster. It made me wonder what the tipping point had been because through all of the times I had seen her in Marques's memories...I never saw the moment that everything had changed.

I wish I had, because instead of feeling some type of *pity* for her, I could hate her.

And I did hate her. I hated her enough to *kill* her...but I didn't want to understand her. It was easier to see her as a monster and I wanted to keep it that way.

Maybe that was why Ren had begun to hate us so much. Eli's words rang through my head, jarring me.

He's quiet because they treated him well.

Did Ren still think of her as a savior instead of the devil I saw? If he did though...there would be no reason for him to have a tattoo that tracked her. *That* was something I still hadn't come to understand.

And how he even got close enough for her to give him her magic or blood?

It scared me.

I shook the thoughts out of my head and jumped out of the bed, not caring to put on additional clothing as I exited the room. Everyone here had already seen me in various intimate positions so just wearing a t-shirt that fell to my knees was almost considered well dressed. I rushed down the halls and the stairs, trying to get to the kitchen. It was the only place I felt safe and the only place that I knew Rae frequently visited when she couldn't sleep.

The marble floor was cold against my feet and the sound of my bare skin hitting the ground rang out through the silent house. My heart was still pounding in my chest and my magic was steadily building up inside my chest. It wasn't enough to need to share just yet...but I knew soon if I didn't calm down there would be some consequences and I hoped to whatever god was out there that I wouldn't blow up the fucking house.

I rushed so fast to the kitchen that I barely recognized Daxton's magical signature, just beyond the walls that separated me from the kitchen. I burst into the kitchen to see Daxton leaning against the counter with Rae across from him, sitting on the other side of the island furiously writing in her notebook. They both looked over when I entered, each holding their own level of surprise.

Daxton looked a bit better than the last I saw him. His skin had regained its natural hue, his eyes were well-lit, and he had a cup of what I assumed was coffee in his hands. He wore a loose t-shirt and sweats that hugged him tightly.

It was impossible *not* to notice how much weight he had lost, but at least now he wasn't trying to hide it. It gave me some hope that things were getting better.

I hadn't talked to him since the other night when he told me he loved me, and by the shifting of his eyes I could tell that maybe it wasn't the right time to talk about it.

I averted my gaze to Rae, who was still staring at me intently. She was wearing the same sweatshirt and sweatpants she had on when she had fallen asleep, and her hair was tousled as if she didn't even pause when she rolled out of bed and just came straight down here. Her glasses were slightly foggy and there was a cup of coffee in front of her.

"Nightmare," I explained and walked towards Daxton before stopping in front of him and turning to face Rae.

Without hesitation I pulled the back of my shirt over my head, exposing my bare back to Daxton.

"Nice to see you too—"

"Check," I commanded. "For magic, burns, anything."

I heard his intake of breath before his chilled hand brushed across my upper back. I winced as a dull ache spread throughout my body. I wasn't crazy. That dream *felt real* and the pain that radiated up my back was too real to ignore.

"I don't feel anything other than your own magic," he said from behind me.

I let out a groan and pulled my shirt back over my head.

"Come," Rae commanded. Her eyebrows were pushed together and there was a small frown on her face.

I walked around the kitchen counter and allowed her to pull me between her legs. She sent light, calming waves to me as her hand ran through my hair.

"Thank you," I whispered into her chest and leaned my head against her.

"I'm sorry I wasn't there to help with your nightmare," she said and planted a small kiss on my head.

I shook my head and inhaled her clean scent. Rae always knew what to say or do when I was feeling distressed. Whether it was a shower, or brushing my hair, or helping me clean up...she always knew *exactly* what I needed and in this moment, I needed her comforting touch.

As much as I hated to admit it, I was a big baby when it came to nightmares. I leaned into her further, enjoying her fingers running through my hair and scratching my scalp.

I remembered when she was so closed off when we first met that she wouldn't have been caught dead hugging me like this in a place like this, in front of anyone. But here she was doing the most because I had a nightmare. It warmed my insides and sent a burst of happiness through me.

This was how it was supposed to be.

"What was it about?" Daxton asked, pulling me from my thoughts.

I pulled away from Rae to peer over her arm and to Daxton. He took a sip of his coffee, waiting for my reply. I swallowed thickly as his magic brushed across my skin.

It was weak but felt comforting. He too, in his own way, was trying to help me through this.

"My mother," I admitted. "She came back."

Daxton stiffened and quickly brought his cup to his lips, taking another sip. I waited for him to say something, but he didn't speak and just continued to drink his coffee.

"She's dead," Rae murmured from above me. "You don't need to be scared anymore. The Originals will never hurt you again."

I let out a shaky breath and nodded but I couldn't take my eyes off of Daxton. He had paled considerably and there was a slight tremor to his hand.

I was about to ask him what was wrong, but he stood straight and sent me a smile. His magic pulled away from me abruptly; my own magic tried to reach out to him, but he was too fast.

"I think Rae has got you from here," he said, walking towards the door. "Amr will get worried if I am gone from his bed for the fourth time this week."

I nodded and stayed still in Rae's arms as we watched him go.

"What was he feeling?" I asked when I felt his signature disappear.

"Panic," Rae answered. "Pure panic."

* * *

I shuddered as Rae's lips found the spot where my neck and shoulder met. Her hands gripped my hips and pulled me back into her with a light groan. Her hot breath fanned across my bare skin and caused my skin to tingle.

"We are supposed to sleep," I said in a light tone, not at all caring about my sleep schedule.

"I just drank a cup of coffee," she said, her words muffled, and she continued to kiss the length of my shoulder. I wrapped my arm back around her neck pulling her closer to me and arched into her, and her hand trailed from my hip to my stomach, spreading bursts of heat through me. She pushed up my shirt as she went, exposing me under the covers.

"Then you should have thought of that before coming back to bed with me," I said and turned so I could capture her lips with my own. She melted into me, and I felt a fan of warmth blooming from my stomach and moving fast towards my core.

"You sound like you don't want me to thank you," she said against my lips before pulling my lip into her mouth and sucking on it lightly before letting it go.

The action caused my body to heat. Her hooded eyes roamed my face, the glow from her glowing irises lighting up her face.

Whenever I caught her unguarded like this, without her glasses, my breath was always taken away. She was so beautiful like this. No one else was privy to this version of her and I ate it up hungrily because in this moment she was all *mine*.

Her eyes trailed my face, pausing on my lips before licking her own. She looked like she was ready to pounce on me and my mouth watered at the thought. An uncontrollable Rae was a treat.

"Thank me for what?" I asked and let out a gasp when her fingers pinched my nipples.

"For being you," she said. "For helping...with my mother earlier."

She paused in her ministrations to meet my gaze. The air between us was tense as she waited in silence for my answer.

"Of course," I said quickly. "Anything I can do to help I will. You don't need to thank me for that, Rae."

She bit her lip and her eyes shifted. This was one of the few times that I had really seen Rae hesitant to say what she was thinking.

"I didn't know that I—"

"Was a hybrid?" I asked with a raised brow.

She nodded, though no other words left her mouth.

"Maybe it's too low of a percentage for you to feel any of the magic," I said. "I barely felt it from her so I wouldn't be surprised if the demon in you overpowered the witch."

She let out a sigh and frowned.

"But I thought...she and father were third generation," she said. "Meaning that she would at least be a quarter. How could a quarter of a witch not have any magic?"

"I didn't say she didn't have magic," I said. "I just feel very little of it. Plus, we don't know what she knows or if she has practiced magic."

Rae let out a sigh and leaned forward.

"Let's not think about this," she said and bit down on my lip. "I would very much like to fuck you now."

I let out a laugh and rolled over to push Rae on her back before disappearing into the sheets. She let out a noise of protest as I began to pull off her shorts, but I shushed her.

"I'll make you think about something else," I said and trailed kisses down her inner thigh.

I couldn't see her pussy in the darkness, but my mouth was already watering at the thought of tasting her again.

"Rosie," she groaned as I licked the length of her folds.

She tangled her hand in my hair and pushed me closer to where she wanted me. I laughed and began devouring her. It had been so long since the last time I had tasted her that I forgot how addicting it was.

I easily found her clit and gave it a hard suck. Her back bowed and she let out a string of curses.

"Ah yes," she hissed as I continued to suck on her clit. I teased her entrance with my finger, not surprised to find her already dripping wet. Slowly I pushed a single finger in and pumped it in and out in time with my sucks.

When she let out a whine I inserted another finger. Her hips began to buck wildly against me, and I had to push my hand down on her lower stomach to hold her hips in place.

"Just like that," she gasped as I picked up the pace of my thrusts. "Fuck that feels good."

I gave up on her clit for just a moment to peek above the covers and take her in. Her arms were spread out across the bed and her head was thrown back. Her chest was rising and falling rapidly as she panted and moaned. Her back bowed as my thumb found her clit and I felt her squeeze around my fingers.

"Come for me, Rae," I whispered and trailed kisses back down to her clit before latching onto it and sucking on it hard.

She let out a muffled cry as she came around my fingers. Before I could even compose myself she was pulling me back up the bed and forcing me onto my back.

Her hazel eyes were wild as she looked me over.

"You are getting far too good at that," she murmured and leaned down to taste herself on my lips and tongue.

Her hand gripped my throat, not enough to restrict the flow, but hard enough to keep me in place as she attacked my mouth. She didn't stop until she had licked her own come off every surface.

She pulled up my shirt but didn't try to remove it as she kissed down my chest. She latched onto my nipple and gave it a hard suck and light bite before moving on to the next one.

I gasped when her fingers found my clit and she began rubbing hard circles in it. The orgasm, instead of relaxing Rae, had only made her that much more ravenous and she began playing with my clit so hard and quick that my toes began to curl.

"Fuck, fuck, *fuck*," I groaned as a surprise orgasm overtook me.

I hadn't even felt it and suddenly my body went limp, and heat flared through me, lighting up my body as it ran through me. The burst of red magic filled the dark room illuminating Rae's face.

She didn't pause to let me catch my breath and instead chose that time to enter two fingers inside me.

"You're driving me crazy Rosie," Rae growled. Her movements became so rough I couldn't even buck my hips to meet her thrusts for fear that I would lose the delicious heat that was coursing through me.

"You are a gift, one that I do not deserve but I refuse to let anyone take you from me," she said and tightened her grip on my throat. "I should be angry that you barged in here, throwing my life into its own special sort of hell, but I can't."

I opened my mouth in a silent scream as another orgasm started building in my stomach. I felt like my skin was on fire. Rae was feral as she fucked me and more ruthless than she had ever been, but this time it felt like I was seeing the part of her that she never showed anyone else before.

The crazed, uncontrolled side that only showed when the cool and collected mask fell off.

"Rae," I managed to choke out.

"You are the best thing that has ever happened to my life Rosie," she said, her words sincere but they came out like a curse. "Even through all this shit, I have never been more proud to call you mine."

I let out a choked sob as a powerful orgasm overtook me.

"*I love you,*" I yelled out through my orgasm. I tried to watch Rae's face, but I couldn't as my eyes shut, and my head was thrown back.

A burst of heat exploded in my chest, but it wasn't the same as the fiery orgasm I had...this was soft. It was a soothing type of heat that caused my entire body to relax.

When I finally pried my eyes open, I was met with Rae's wide ones.

"Again," she whispered, as if she was afraid that her words would break the warm spell that had fallen over us. "*Please.*"

"I love you, Rae," I whispered. "And I will spend the rest of my life trying to find a way to thank you for all that you have done for me."

The heat in my chest grew and a smile, a *real* smile pushed itself onto Rae's face.

"Is that you?" I whispered and placed my hand over her chest.

She nodded and then slowly lowered her lips to mine.

"I love you too Rosie," she whispered. "But it is me who will be spending an eternity at your feet, thanking you for how you have changed me—*us.*"

I lunged forward and connected our lips together. I didn't give a damn about school or about the others. I deserved this time with Rae, and I would do away with anyone who tried to take it from us.

"Again," I commanded as I straddled her.

"I love you," she said, this time louder and without hesitation.

"That's right," I said with a smile. "And I love you too."

Chapter 11
Rosie

School was exhausting.

Every time I stepped back onto Winterfell campus I expected to get used to the anxiety and fear that filled me, but it would return with a vengeance each time.

The last few years had been ingrained into my soul and I would never forget the horrors that happened here...but I also couldn't ignore how it had changed my life, for the better.

As I walked the halls, greeting the low-levels and demons alike, I found myself getting more exhausted by the minute.

I wasn't scared of the students or the faculty...this place just felt off, still. I thought that after I had killed off the Originals, that my life would go back to normal, or at least a type of normal. But I still felt like there was a divide between me and the others in this school, and I didn't think I wanted to change that.

The divide was the thing that had kept my loved ones and me safe, and every time I got close to someone or opened up...there would be consequences. *That* was the fear that I was still living in.

I stood outside of the main office, hesitating to go in.

I had only a few more minutes before classes with the new teacher started and I didn't want to have to walk into the classroom late and be scolded by him.

He was an aging demon and while he looked no older than thirty, he sure as hell acted like a grumpy old man who severely hated his job. He would berate the students that came in late, embarrass them, then move on to teaching like nothing happened.

Maybe the other students could brush it off, but I couldn't. I hadn't been in the spotlight for long so even something as simple as that still caused my anxiety to flare.

Even with the Original inside of me.

With a deep breath I pushed through the office and was hit with a blast of cool air. Tammy, the main receptionist, was sitting behind her desk with glasses perched on her nose and a book in front of her.

Her dull eyes peered over the page at me and when she put her book down she was smiling.

"He's free if you need him, dear," she said and waived to Principal Winterfell's closed door.

"Thank you, Tammy," I said and walked toward his door.

"Oh!" she said suddenly. "I forgot to ask, how is everything with the newest batch of low-levels?"

Guilt washed through me, and I turned stiffly to give her a forced smile.

"They don't come to me that often anymore," I admitted. "But I was planning on holding something small for them to help with networking. It's what I wanted to talk to Principal Winterfell about."

Her face lit up and she nodded.

"That sounds delightful dear, go on!"

I swallowed thickly and sent her another smile.

It was a half-assed attempt at trying to help the low-levels. It had been true that the low-levels hadn't been coming to me as often anymore...but that was partly because I was avoiding school and when I was here...I would avoid them as well.

They would come up to me, say hi, talk about their classes...but after the first year's trial run they had begun to fit in here pretty easily. I still had to show them around on the first-day orientation, but even during that time, the other more senior low-levels had shared the burden, leaving me with nothing to do other than to watch them go.

I didn't know if my stomach felt sour, and disappointment filled me because I *wanted* to be the one to help them or if I had finally realized how useless I was.

I was once seen as a status symbol. As something new and great...but even the cameras had stopped coming around as often as they once did. I was beginning to go back to the invisible low-level I once was...and a part of me was terrified because of it.

I knocked three times on the principal's office before I heard his voice.

"Come in," he said in a low voice.

I pushed the door open and stepped into the familiar office. Principal Winterfell sat behind his desk, his purple hair in braids and for the first time in a while, he met me with a genuine smile. The room around him was in a sort of organized chaos and there were boxes lining the back wall near the windows.

I closed the door behind me and hesitantly took my seat in front of him.

"So, you want to hold...something for the low-levels?" he asked and leaned back in his chair. The leather squeaked softly, the only noise filling the silence that spread between us.

"I heard you from outside," he added quickly, sensing my hesitation.

I took a breath and leaned back in my own chair.

"Yes," I breathed. "Just something going forward once a year where they can all meet and connect. I think the opening was good for new students in the beginning of the year but maybe something later? After the games?"

Principal Winterfell watched me as I squirmed in front of him. He had a soft look in his eyes and a small smile on his face.

"Let's do something for graduation, shall we?" he suggested. "After all we have quite a few who are graduating this year, yourself included."

I nodded and gave him a forced smile.

"That I am," I said, my voice trailing off towards the end.

He didn't say anything for a few moments before he stood and walked over to one of the boxes at the very back of the room. I leaned over to see what he was looking for, but he stood abruptly and walked back over to me before I could get a good look.

He walked around the desk and sat on the edge, his legs almost brushing the side of my chair.

"Here," he said and handed me a thick leather-bound book. As soon as I touched it I could feel the old magic thrum to life in its pages and gasped aloud. It was strong magic, maybe even stronger than Xena's. "I don't think I will need this anymore, but you may."

I gave him a look before opening it.

Welcome to Winterfell Academy.

1634

I was careful to turn the page and was hit with an intricate drawing of Principal Winterfell, and next to him were two men. One of them had black hair and had a stare that made a shiver run down my spine.

"This is the first year our school was opened," he said in a soft tone. "Next to me you see the two strongest demons I have ever met. They were the ones that helped build this school."

His finger stopped on the man on his left.

"This witch helped us build everything from the ground up and continued until his death in 1856," he said, then his finger trailed towards the other. "This one helped source students from affluent and powerful parents. From Originals. He believed strongly in education and wished for a future where we could live peacefully amongst each other. But he knew education came first if they ever hoped to achieve what we dreamed."

"Why are you giving this to me?" I asked and looked up towards him.

His smile had dropped, and his expression turned solemn.

"Because I believe it's time you start thinking about what comes next, Rosie Miller," he said and folded his hands in his lap. "You are no longer a cursed low-level whose life expectancy was cut short. You are here for the long run, and you care about the students more than you can admit to yourself. I have seen it. Use what they gave you for good."

I froze and the air around us stilled.

"How long have you known?" I asked.

Principal Winterfell smiled and stood to sit back in his chair.

"I don't know what you are talking about," he said and sat down.

I leaned forward.

"Yes you—"

"My time here is coming to an end," he said, interrupting me. "I am old, I have made some mistakes, and I think it is time for me to turn in my seat."

The air rushed out of me.

"You can't—"

"I *can*," he said. "And I will. My only hope is that the person I want to take over for me accepts, and I know that they will need a strong fire user by their side who only wants to see this place succeed. It worked for me."

I looked down at the page, feeling a headache bloom behind my eyes. There were memories begging to be let out, but they were being blocked by something.

Damn it.

* * *

Daxton didn't show up today, so I sat by Amr and tried to avoid Eli.

I couldn't even focus on the lecture; I was too busy thinking about the book that was now weighing down my bookbag.

Correction: I was thinking about the man next to Principal Winterfell.

At this point, I didn't care what Principal Winterfell knew or didn't. I was shocked that he was leaving his office, but that was where my thoughts about that man ended.

I knew the man next to him in that drawing had to have been my father... or at least someone related to him. He looked more like Marques than I had originally realized, and the pieces had started to fall together too perfectly to ignore.

Look alive, Eli said in my mind. *Or else risk being called on by the asshat.*

I shifted in my seat and focused my eyes back onto the professor, whose eyes had just passed over me for a second before turning them back to the class.

Thanks, I shot back.

Eli sent me an image of an easy way I could thank them, and heat coiled in my belly.

Stop it, I growled in my mind.

Their warm chuckle reached my ears and I had to stop myself from giving in and letting them continue to assault my mind with delicious images of us together. Not only would my magic be on edge for the rest of the day, but Eli still hadn't officially apologized or even cared about what they had done to Mr. Falkner and Emma.

Rosie, they chided in my mind, but I ignored them and focused back on the lecture.

"So, tell me..." The professor trailed, his eyes combing the class for an unexpecting student. "*Henry,* why do you think the divide between humans and demons really started?"

Amr and I both bristled when he conveniently left out witches. It was one thing to have a teacher educate the students about the history of how we came to be, but it was an entirely different issue when they knew a bit *too much* about the stories that were supposed to be kept private.

To the world, we were demons that crawled up from hell and took over the world slowly while dominating the humans. Witches were more mysterious in how they came to be...but no one was thinking about how they cannibalized Original demons in order to gain their powers.

Nor did they understand that we were *not* the demons that they thought we were but instead, we came from a much higher, yet seemingly just as corrupt place.

Now *that* information could cause a riot.

"The humans were scared demons held more power than them," he answered quickly, his cheeks flaming. This was one of the newer low-levels that had joined my class this year. He sat next to a high-level demon that gave him an encouraging smile.

"Right," the teacher said then paced the front of the room. "The *humans* were scared. The demons had a power that they knew could end their existence, but what about the demons?" When the class was silent he continued. "I mean what do we think the demons wanted out of the humans?"

"To control them," another high-level muttered to my left.

"But why?" the teacher asked. "These are demons that had *everything* going for them. They didn't *need* the humans to survive...so why try to control them? Why didn't they just live on their own? Create their own colonies and live separately? Why did they *have* to try and integrate into human society?"

There were a few murmurs but none of the answers seemed to please the teacher.

"*Because* they wanted families like the humans had built. They wanted the freedom to grow and live their lives the ways the humans had...and do you know what else the humans had that the Originals didn't when they first came here?"

Another silence fell over the room.

"Come on guys!" he said and leaned against his desk. "It's not hard! Think about it."

"Gods," Eli spoke from behind me.

The professor's eyes narrowed in on them and a small smile spread across their face.

"Gods," they confirmed with a nod. "Kings, queens, clergy, priests, royalty...they did have a class system. No demon was any better than their counterpart. *That's* what they wanted from the humans."

"And witches?" the low-level, Henry, asked.

The teacher's eyes lit up.

"They come in when the humans decided they didn't like how the demons were trying to control them," he said and crossed his arms over his chest, letting his words settle over the crowd.

He knows too much, Eli said in my mind.

Marques's memory of a very human-looking Xena getting fed a dead demon ran through my mind and I had to clamp my hand against my mouth to hold back my own bile.

"Rosie," Amr's voice trailed, his arm running down my back. His magic mixed with mine and I took a deep breath.

"I'm okay," I whispered.

Let him be, Eli. I shot back. *Let this one be.*

I was met with silence.

Chapter 12
Rosie

The cool air whipped across my skin and chased away the fire that traveled up my arm.

The dots that had been carved into my skin with ink and magic were glowing in the darkness and grew hotter as I ran through the cramped alleyways.

The patter of Amr's paws behind me was barely audible through my own pounding heart and blood rushing through my ears. Just as we reached the mouth of the alleyway I leaned down and scooped Amr into my arms. His bright golden eyes watched me as I took a moment to regain myself.

Whatever Ren had done to my hand paled in comparison to the pain that my curse brought out. At times it felt like the magic coursing through my veins was actually burning me from the inside out, but nothing showed on the surface of my skin.

Amr's paw came to pat my face gently. I gave him a forced smile then brushed my lips against his forehead.

I hadn't planned to drop everything and try to find Daxton tonight, but he hadn't shown up to school and Amr said he hadn't heard from him for hours. Amr pulled me aside after class and stressed to me how worried he was about Daxton.

In a rush he had told me that Daxton had been acting weird lately and he just couldn't keep it inside anymore. After that, I had no choice but to come clean about the tattoos Ren had given me and beg him to join me.

Amr had been too understanding for my own good. Maybe it was his own guilt eating him alive that forced his hand...but he brushed it off as if it wasn't even a minor inconvenience. As if tracking your lovers with magic was something I would normally do.

"There are witches," I whispered feeling the brush of magic coming from all around me. It played at my senses and awoke a dark part of my magic that I once thought had been completely gone forever. "We should be careful."

Amr let out a loud meow and I stagnated as I felt a magical signature come towards us.

I pushed us out of the alleyway only to almost run straight into a male witch. He gave me and Amr a grimy smile before trying to grab at my hoodie. I slapped his hand away and pushed past him into the street.

He let out an annoyed huff and disappeared down the alleyway we had just come from.

The buildings that surrounded the street were in various states of decay and there were people littering the streets who looked at us with a slimy type of interest that made my stomach churn.

The rest of the street was empty, sticky, and smelled sickly sweet.

I hadn't been to a place like this in my lifetime, but Marques had. His memories flashed through my mind as I took in the rundown area. During his lifetime, places like this had been used for underground deals and illegal magic, including the testing of new curses.

But there was nothing else that came to mind as I walked down the street with Amr in my hands. Maybe it was because the burning had grown even hotter and started to cloud my mind with pain.

"He's here," I said through gritted teeth as I came to a stop in front of a bar that spanned a few stories. Unlike the buildings around it, the entrance was well-lit, and I could spy a few witches drinking inside.

I looked around, noting that the witches spread around outside were watching me. None of them made any movement to get any closer, just kept their eyes focused on me. I felt a few of their magics circle around me and brush up on my sides, but I couldn't tell who it had come from.

Shaking off their gazes I walked towards the entrance, only to stop when I felt a strange chill rush down my spine. My heart skipped a beat and I felt a heavy dread fill me.

This isn't right.

Amr let out a whine as I took a step back. I turned to look back at the witches who had been watching but my heart dropped when I was met with an empty street. Even more of a sign that what was happening here wasn't right.

I walked towards the side of the building with the intention of ducking into the alleyway and trying to center myself, but I was caught off guard when I felt a small amount of magic on the wall of the building.

My magic lashed out wildly around me, responding to the possible threat of attack. I held Amr close to me and took a step back, my eyes darting around to find where the magic came from. Without a warning, the wall opened up and showed me a glimpse of the bar inside.

A wave of magic hit me, and I felt bile rise in my throat as its sticky film coasted my skin.

What the hell kind of place was this?

I stepped into the bar and there was a silence that cut through the patrons as soon as my booted foot hit the wooden floors. I looked around the dim underground bar, noting the booths to the side of the room. Many other standing tables were littered throughout and there was a staircase to the back of the room.

The bar was to my right, where a male witch looked me over warily. Even as my hand started to burn uncontrollably there was no sign of Daxton, meaning...

He wasn't upstairs was he?

I walked towards the stairs, ignoring the eyes and swirling magic of the patrons. They had started to resume some of their conversation, but it was obvious that I wasn't supposed to be here. Even after the doctor had told me eating Marques would come at a price to my magic...it was still too pure to be in this place. In comparison to some of the people here, my magic was like a shining beacon giving me away to anyone within a few feet of me.

A small hand grabbed the back of my hoodie and I turned around to come face to face with a pink-haired child. She had a cloak that covered most of her face, but I could still make out her brown eyes and vibrant hair.

I opened my mouth to speak but stopped when I realized the child in front of me, wasn't a child at all. There was an unmistakable old magic flowing out of her that couldn't have belonged to someone of her age.

"I have been waiting to meet you," she said in a low voice and motioned to a nearby booth. "Let's chat, shall we?"

"I have to meet—"

"After you speak with me," she said in a curt tone. "He is too busy for you now."

Hot, unbridled anger flashed through me.

"Who are you to—"

"You can call me Cumae," she said. "And I am owed a conversation with you. In return, I can answer any question you may have. "

I raised my brow at her.

"I don't need anything from you." I sat and tried to shake her off, but her grip stayed firm on my hoodie.

"I can tell you what your little reckless witch is doing up in those rooms," she said. "Or I can take you. But I need you to talk with me first."

I shifted Amr in my arms.

"And if I don't?" I asked.

A small smile spread across her childlike face.

"You don't really have any choice," she said. "I was being polite but if you would rather I not be, then I can let you know that the *boy* bargained *you* to get into the room upstairs."

I gritted my teeth and tried to breathe through my nose as uncontrollable magic began to flood my system.

What did she mean he bargained me? And what the fuck was he doing up there? In a room?

There were a million scenarios that ran through my mind, none of them good.

But there was nothing I could do, not when someone as powerful as her stood in front of me. I either listened to her, or needed a plan to fight for my, Amr's and Daxton's life...which I didn't have.

I nodded and let her lead me to the booth. I slid in and begin to pet Amr as he gave the girl across from me a low growl. Her eyes flashed to him, and an amused smile spread across her face.

"There aren't many of them anymore," she said. "Familiars, I mean. You should take good care of him or someone just might *scoop him up.*"

I knew the history of familiars a bit from what Amr had told me, but it didn't sit right with me how easily she threatened to hurt him like that. No one should be bound to servitude. Witch, familiar, low-level...no one.

"Get to the point," I growled.

Her smile faltered, obviously not used to being talked to the way I talked to her.

"You share magic with that boy," she said and waved her hand in the air. I watched as the bartender across the room scrambled to bring her a drink. "Original magic."

The bartender ran over to us at breakneck speed to put a glass of pink swirling liquid in front of her. She waved him away, her eyes still narrowed on me.

"I don't think that's any of your business," I said and gripped my hand as a flash of burning pain went through it.

My mind just about exploded as the pain increased. The multiple magic signatures swirling around didn't help either. I could feel my once calmed magic starting to thrash inside me, begging for a release.

It wanted to fight.

It was hurt that Daxton could do something like this and furious that I was stuck here instead of finding him again. It wanted answers...from Eli, from Daxton, from Marques, even from this little pink hair girl but *no one* was willing to spill.

"I am looking for someone," she said and took a slow sip of her liquid. "I think you may know them."

Like I would know anyone that she knew, I growled internally. *What was she even up to?*

"Someone with your magic wouldn't have trouble finding anyone," I said and took in her small frame.

Her magic alone was one that rivaled my mother's. It was potent, electrifying and every time it brushed across me I felt bursts of power run through me. It was addicting.

"I would if they were somehow protected by a magical barrier," she said and pursed her lips. "One that so happens to be stuck in time."

I sucked in a sharp breath of air. I wished for nothing more than to be able to harness Marques's powers and delve into that mind of hers. Everyone who had known of that town should have been dead or relocated and as far as I knew, there were no other Originals in this area.

On top of that, I couldn't pull forth any of Marques's memories that would indicate the child—*Cumae*—would have lived in that town. So how the *fuck* did she know about this?

"How old are you?" I asked, licking my suddenly dry lips. I ran my hand through Amr's fur, trying to calm myself, but it wasn't working. It was all too much; I was losing the battle.

With a bitter sigh I pulled my magic back from my hand. A violent relief crashed through me as the burning in my arm finally ceased.

"Second generation," she said quickly and took another sip. "I am looking for a girl that goes by the name of Amber."

I don't know what was more surprising, the fact that the child in front of me was as old as Malik or that she knew of the one person from the town that still haunted my nightmares.

"She is dead," I said, swallowing back the prick of sadness that filled me.

If Cumae was upset, she didn't show it.

"And the barrier?" she asked.

"Gone."

She nodded and ran her finger around the rim of the cup. The bar around us had gone back to its rowdiness, but I could still feel the eyes on us, and Amr let out a low growl.

"How did you know her?" I couldn't stop the words from tumbling out of my mouth.

She sent me a small smile.

"I lived in the town with her for a time," she admitted. "Though I was exiled when I spoke out against the Originals. My only regret is I didn't bring her with me."

I nodded, unable to find any words. If Cumae had escaped the town, there had to be more people as well. The town was supposed to be the Originals' best kept secret, but it would seem that nothing stayed a secret for long.

I wanted to ask more about Amber, about her life there. She insisted she had no family but how could that be true? There were so many things that were left unanswered, but I knew I would have to be careful with my asks.

The world had taught me enough for me to understand that secrets came at a price, sometimes ones that were too high to pay.

"I have two questions," I said. She waved for me to continue. "What is Daxton doing in that room?"

She paused a moment before speaking, her brown eyes shifting to the stairs.

"He is getting rid of the demon inside him," she said. "Well, most of it is gone now."

"Getting rid of..." I trailed, unable to wrap my head around her words. Until...

Father.

Cumae nodded and drank the last of her swirling liquid.

"I found a specialist that could help him," she said. "An Original."

I froze in my seat and looked down to Amr.

"There shouldn't be any other Originals in the area," I said. Cumae just shrugged but did not elaborate.

"I want you to show me to his room after you answer my next question," I demanded. She waved for me to continue. "How do I remove a curse if I cannot feel for a signature to identify the witch?"

She raised a brow at me.

"You can't," she said simply. "Identify the witch. They remove it or you kill them. As simple as that."

I shifted in my seat.

"Could you?" I asked. "Identify it I mean."

She paused.

"For a price," she answered.

"Which is?" I asked and leaned forward.

"Share your magic with me," she said, a wicked smile spreading across her face.

Disgust coiled in my stomach, and I stood abruptly.

"Take me to him," I commanded.

"It's too late," she said, her brown eyes boring into mine. "He already left."

I growled and commanded my magic to the tattoo on my hand. A slow dull burning made its way up my arm, nothing like the fire that had been there moments ago.

"You did that on purpose," I growled, and she shrugged.

"Not my fault you took too long with your answers," she said.

I slammed my fist down on the table and leaned over her. Amr let out a loud growl.

"Take me to your contact," I said.

"No," she said quickly. "But you are free to go exploring up in the rooms yourself."

Without wasting another moment I left the booth and ran up the stairs, with Amr held tight in my arms.

"I'm sorry," I whispered to Amr.

As soon as I reached the top floor I could feel Daxton's weak signature. It was coming from the end room. The rest of the rooms had their own potent magic, but I ignored it.

I marched towards the room and without hesitation threw it open.

There was no one in the room but I could feel two distinct signatures. One was of the man that I loved, and another was from someone that I thought I would never see again.

...Xena?

A burst of magic came from behind me, and I was thrown to the ground. Pain flashed across my entire body, and it was so powerful that white spots covered my eyes. The last thing I heard before darkness overtook me was the sound of heels and Amr's growls.

Chapter 13
Malik

The world has put Xena's spawn in this world to punish me.

At first I thought it was just Rosie's temptation that was going to be my downfall...but once I had her I knew there was no way I would be letting her go.

It took me a long time...but I accepted that.

I knew that no matter how long I may live that it would only be to be by Rosie's side. I would be happy with her. If I could hear her content sighs, watch as a real smile spread across her face even after all the shit she had been through, I would be happy.

She gave me a reason to live again. Because of her, my breaths came easier. The weight on my shoulders was lifted. And for the first time I was happy in my life. And I didn't even mind the others. If anything, I found myself enjoying their company as well.

I could see a clear future with us where we were all happy and living the lives that we wanted...

And her *fucking* brother took that all away from me.

If Rosie was supposed to end it all for me, her brother must have seen that as a challenge.

"I wanted it to be just us," Ren said as he looked between Rae, Eli, and myself. His purple eyes shifted quickly, and he began to fidget.

"Don't try to hide your thoughts from me," Eli growled from next to me.

I leaned against the cool kitchen counter in the apartment the Originals had bought for us and looked around the place. I hadn't wanted to come back here. Too many painful memories. I wanted to focus on the now instead of what had happened. But when an unknown number texts you asking—no—*begging* for me to meet him at his place, I had to come.

Especially when I found out it was Rosie's brother.

I didn't have to hear her admit it for me to understand that her brother was important to her. I saw it in the way she looked at him. In the way her face had lit up when he agreed to have breakfast with her. She spilled everything and then some in that breakfast with him, no doubt in hopes to mend whatever part of their relationship they could salvage.

And by the look on his face, it may have just worked.

"I am assuming this has something to do with Rosie," I cut in, trying to save Eli from making yet another disastrous mistake.

They were a ticking time bomb, and I didn't want Rosie's brother to be the thing that set them off.

Ren nodded and rubbed his hand before lifting it up, palm facing him to show the tattoos that marred his skin. Slowly, they turned a bright blue.

"I asked you about this before," Rae said. She left her spot next to me, stepping closer to Ren but he pulled his hand back quickly and gave her a look. "You said you did them yourself."

Her voice was softer the second time and he nodded slowly before taking a deep breath.

"It's used to track others," he said. "If infused with blood or magic, I can track a person wherever they are in—"

"Shut up," Eli growled. I quickly shot my arm out and grabbed onto their arm to stop them from charging at Ren. "You're a little fucking *liar*."

"I'm not," Ren cried and raised his hands to cover his face. "I wouldn't have asked you to come if I wasn't sure! I only asked you because I can't get in touch with Rosie."

I shared a look with Rae. I hadn't seen Rosie for a few days. Usually when this happened I assumed she was with another lover, and since I was still trying to rebuild *The Fallen* I was busy with them for the last few days. I never...

"When was the last time anyone has seen Rosie?" I asked, panic rising in me.

"The day before yesterday," Rae answered quickly. "Last night was supposed to be Amr's night. I assumed she was still with him and Daxton."

Eli stiffened.

"Daxton left yesterday," they said, their wide blue eyes shooting towards me.

It hadn't been often that I had seen Eli scared, and when I did it caused my own chest to stir. I tried to remain calm and keep myself grounded for the group, but all I could think about was Rosie.

"Where did he go, Eli?" I growled.

"I don't know," they answered. "I just assumed he went out to drink. He didn't go to school the next day. He does that when...he is having a hard time. So, I thought he was just going to get wasted."

A growl ripped through my chest.

"Call Daxton *now*," I commanded.

"Already on it," Rae said as she put the phone to her ear.

I turned back to Eli.

"Has she still been avoiding you?" I asked.

The way their eyes shifted told me she had.

Fucking damn it.

I turned back to Ren.

"You said that tattoo can track others?" I asked. "Can it lead you to Rosie?"

Ren was silent, his eyes shifting towards Eli.

"Spit it out," they growled.

Ren jumped and ran a shaky hand through his hair. His skin was slick with sweat, and he was practically vibrating with how nervous he was. This wasn't the same low-level that tried to fight me in the cafeteria and gardens. This one was deathly afraid for his sister.

"Mine isn't used to track Rosie," he said.

Rae let out a huff and slammed her phone on the counter.

"Daxton didn't answer," she said.

I launched myself forward and grabbed Ren by his shirt. I couldn't help the growl that burst out of my chest, or get the ideas of how I could hurt this little hybrid out of my head. This wasn't a joking matter and if one more person interrupted him I was going to lose it.

"Who does it track, Ren?" I asked with as much venom in my voice as I could muster.

"Xena," he choked out.

And with that single sentence, another one of Xena's offspring had brought me to my knees.

I would have liked to say that I was a strong demon. That I could serve as leader of this makeshift family we had created...but I was wrong. I was weak for her.

As soon as my knees hit the hard floor I knew that there was only one reason why Rosie wouldn't answer our calls. If we assumed that she hadn't been seen since early day yesterday…it had already been twenty-four hours since she had been gone.

So many things could have happened in twenty-four hours. She had to have been taken, that was the only possible reason as to why she wouldn't be with us right now. And I couldn't believe that someone as strong as Rosie was, now with Marques's blood flowing through her veins, would be taken by a random person off the streets.

Rae's hands grabbed my upper arms and forced me back to my feet.

I heard her and the others trying to speak to me, but I couldn't decipher any of it.

It had felt like my head was dunked in ice-cold water. My body was frozen. My mind was hazy. And I couldn't hear a damn thing over the sound of my own heart beating.

Then pain exploded on the whole left side of my face.

My blurred vision cleared, and I saw Rae's firm expression in front of me.

"Get a hold of yourself," she growled. "Call Maximus and Claudine. We are going back home to reconvene. We do not know anything yet. Do you hear me?"

"There is only—"

"We know nothing yet," she repeated, her eyes ablaze. "Get them on the phone *now*."

Her harsh voice stirred me into action, and I found myself numbly pulling out my phone and texting both Maximus and Claudine to get to the house in ten minutes.

"Why didn't you tell us she was alive sooner?" Eli growled.

I blinked twice before turning my head to see that Eli now had their hands on Ren's neck. The boy clawed at their hands and kicked, trying to get free, but they were no match for Eli's strength.

"I didn't know," he gasped. "It only tracks her when I tell it to."

"Let him go," I commanded Eli.

I didn't have it in me to use my power, but Eli dropped him like I had.

"Both of you get a hold of yourselves," Rae growled and stepped between us. Eli was glaring at me from the other side of her and looked like they were ready to pounce. "We don't know *anything* yet. For all we know she could be at school. Or with Amr somewhere."

"She doesn't just go to school for fun," Eli growled, their eyes still piercing into me. "That's the *last* place she wants to be, and you know it."

How could you let her slip through our fingers? they hissed inside my mind.

You are the one that is supposed to protect her. You are the one that is supposed to know what to do. It was your job to make sure that the Originals have been killed.

"How did you *not know* that Xena was still fucking alive?" they bellowed, continuing their verbal assault out loud.

"She was burned alive," I forced out. "I saw her. We *all* saw her."

"Stop!" Rae growled. Her own anger flaring out around us was so hot my skin began to warm. "We can hash this out at home *with* the others."

A tense silence spread across us as Eli continued to glare at me.

You are a pathetic excuse for a demon, they said in my mind. *If Rosie was hurt in any way, shape or form because of this fuck up, I am coming after you.*

Good, I said back. *I would deserve it.*

* * *

We didn't make it further than the foyer when we arrived back home. Claudine and Maximus had been waiting outside and now all we were waiting on was Daxton. We were all worried sick and none of us had our favorite moderator here to make sure we didn't rip each other's heads off.

It didn't take long before the tense silence turned into something more volatile.

"Eli," Rae said with a sigh. "This fighting is not helping. We have a bigger issue at hand here."

"Because of him," Eli growled and tried to cross the room, but Maximus was there, his hand spread out wide towards Eli.

"Don't make me intervene," Maximus warned.

Maximus wasn't a person who lost his cool easily but this whole mess seemed to be getting to him and Claudine as well. None of us knew what to think. We may have all worked on some gut-wrenching horrible things through the years...but we never expected a woman to literally rise from the dead.

Not when we all saw her burn in front of us.

"Like you could fucking do anything," Eli hissed at him. "You and your freak of a sister are just as responsible for this. You three had direct access to Xena for *years.*"

"It isn't their fault, Eli," Rae hissed. She was standing in front of me, as if she could stop Eli's descent. "If Xena got away it was because Xena was powerful—"

"You act like you don't care that she is nowhere to be seen!" they hissed and tried to take another step forward, but it was Claudine who took a step in front of them.

"It hurts, doesn't it?" she said in a low voice. "It's because you care for her. That's why you are so angry."

Eli flinched as if they had been punched and took a shaky step back. The hurt was clear on their face and their chest puffed as they took deep angry breaths.

"You are just looking for someone to blame," Claudine continued. "But right now, there isn't anyone to blame because we are not sure what happened. Hold onto that anger until the time has come to use it."

Eli's jaw clenched and they shifted their gaze back to me.

"Don't get inside my mind, seer bitch," they growled.

Maximus shifted at the insult, but Claudine smiled. She turned around, her eyes looking past me and to the door. At first her face was twisted in confusion and then slowly it changed to horror.

The rest of us all turned when the front doors opened, revealing a pale and sweaty Daxton. His hair and clothes were sticking to his face and he was wheezing as if he had just run a marathon. He froze when he saw how many people were in the room. His brown eyes widened, and you could hear the sound of him swallowing from across the room.

"What happened—"

"Have you seen Rosie?" I asked, not waiting for him to finish. This was far too important and even just waiting this extra twenty minutes had weighed heavily on me.

"She was with Amr the last time I saw them," he answered and closed the door behind him. His hand was shaking, and his shoulders were hunched over as if he had been carrying a heavy weight on them.

"Which was?"

"Where?"

Rae and I spoke at the same time and Daxton's eyes flitted between the two of us.

"I don't know," he said. "Sometime yesterday? What's going on?"

Ren opened his mouth to speak, but Eli beat him to it.

"Where were you?" they asked. "I thought you had gone to a bar, but you look like shit so it couldn't have been that."

He rolled his shoulders and stretched his neck.

"I was in a bar—"

"Xena's back," I said quickly as I felt my last bit of patience slip. "Well, I guess you can say she never died and with Rosie now missing, you can see why this is a cause for concern."

"Xena?" he asked, his gaze dropping to his feet.

Eli pushed through the group.

"What was that?" they growled.

Daxton jumped as Eli stood in front of him. Their hands were in fists at their side, and I had never seen Eli look at someone besides Ezekiel with so much hatred. It was strong. So strong it felt like an aura had surrounded them and begun to spread across the room.

"Nothing," Daxton said quickly and took a step back.

Eli's hand shot out to tangle in his hair, and they forced his head back.

"You were out fucking another woman while Rosie was missing?"

A deathly silence fell over the crowd as Daxton tried to find his words. My own fists clenched, and I felt a white-hot rage flash through my entire being, burning up every single cell with it.

How dare he?

"It's not like that, I wasn't there to—"

"Why were you on the bed?" they asked. "And why were her hands—*oh.*"

Eli froze and even without a power like Rae's I could feel their anger explode around us. All it took was a second of realization for them to decipher whatever they had seen in his head and snap. In an instant Claudine and Maximus were at their side pulling them away from Daxton. They jerked as their hands came to pull on their arms.

"Don't you fucking touch me!" they growled and tried to lunge towards Daxton, but a magical wall was quickly erected between them.

"Eli!" Rae yelled and took a step forward but then Eli's next words rang out.

"He was meeting with Xena the whole time!" they growled. "The person that he was with was *that bitch!*"

Muffled silence. That's all it was when their words sunk in.

Daxton met Xena. Daxton had been meeting Xena.

He knew Xena was alive.

For how long? How many times?

Did she know where Rosie was?

Had she used him?

Did he give her up? Was that why he was so weak?

No, Daxton wouldn't. He couldn't.

Daxton loved Rosie, just like we all did. I knew that much. She had helped save him from his parents' iron grip. She had been there with him through it all. She shared her magic with him, even when he was uncontrollable.

No, *no*.

"No," I breathed and took a shaking step towards Daxton.

Eli was screaming at him, and I vaguely heard Ren and Rae trying to talk to him as well but I couldn't decipher their words.

I pushed myself towards Daxton and when I reached his form I couldn't help but fall to my knees. He tried to run away but I held onto his hands.

"Please," I begged. "*Please* tell me it's a lie."

He looked down towards me and tears filled his eyes instantly.

"I'm sorry," he whispered.

And with that, for the first time in all my years...I had no clue what to do.

Chapter 14
Rosie

I came to with an unbearable pounding in my head. My body was weak and there was a distinct metallic taste in my mouth. The air around me was charged with something electric though I could feel the dust that had been accumulating around the room with each inhale.

My magic felt...off, and not in the way it had since I had changed because of Marques. It felt like I was constrained and at the same time empty. I had all of my magic bubbling up inside me like a tornado...but it was also just out of my grasp.

The floor was cold beneath me, and it had begun to seep into my bones. My teeth were chattering and the tips of my fingers had become numb. The only thing that stirred me awake enough to pull my thoughts together was Amr's magical signature. I could feel him. He was *so* close. I shakily sat up, my head swirled, and bile rose in my throat.

I didn't have much time to process the room as I pushed myself forward and lost the contents of my stomach. My throat burned and tears rolled down my eyes as pain shot through my entire body. I didn't know what had happened after I was hit with the wave of magic, but it felt like my body had been flung off Winterfell Tower.

I wiped my blurry eyes and looked around the room to realize that I wasn't in a room at all.

I was in a type of dungeon.

The walls and floor were made of concrete and there were dark iron bars where the fourth wall should have been. When I squinted into the darkness

I could just make out Amr's form. He had shifted, fully naked and back into his mortal form. He still lay in a heap on the ground, his chest barely moving. To his right, there was a blanket and when I looked around my empty room, I realized there was one for me as well.

I tried to reach my magic out to feel if there was anyone around us, but as soon as I did I got violently nauseous and was forced to stop or otherwise risk throwing up my stomach acid.

"Xena!" I yelled at the top of my lungs.

Fury ran through me hard enough to cause whiplash. That *fucking* bitch had decided to mess with my life *one* too many times. I thrashed around and screamed loud enough to cause my ears to ring. My voice bounced off the walls and echoed down the hallway.

Silence filled the room but that didn't stop me from slapping my hands against the cold concrete and screaming until my voice grew hoarse.

I had heard her just as I was blacking out back in the bar. The clack of her heels. The same ones that used to haunt my nightmares as I grew up. The same ones that now echoed in my brain and pulled snarls from my chest.

She had to be hiding somewhere; I just had to draw her out. She was probably waiting until my fit was over. She hated putting any effort into anything and God forbid she have to face her rabid daughter.

I kicked myself for not realizing sooner that she was still alive...but there was no sign. Even as we cleaned up the campus and prepared for school, there was not a single thread of evidence that Xena could have survived that blow.

I was the one that tried to burn her to a crisp, but apparently I couldn't even do *that* job right.

With a growl, I stalked over to the bars and gripped them in my hands, hoping to try and pry them loose, but as soon as my hands wrapped around the cool metal my body flew back as magic exploded in front of me.

My head hit the concrete floor with a sickening crack, and I let out a pained groan. My hands were on fire as the magic began burning my skin. I tried to heal myself but again when I called forth my magic, my stomach lurched.

"Amr!" I yelled. "Amr!"

He stirred and in seconds he lunged forward to empty his stomach, much like I just had.

"Rosie?!" he yelled, his eyes flashing. My heart dropped when I got a look at his face. It was almost sunken in, and he was paler than I had ever seen him.

As soon as his eyes met mine he tried to run for me.

"Stop! The bars have magic on them!"

He skidded to a halt mere inches from the bars. With a growl he bent over and paused. He stood there for a few breaths, the sound of his breaths filling the air between us. Finally, after minutes of silence, he let out a groan and looked back up towards me with a pained expression.

"I can't shift, Rosie," he said, his voice hollow.

I opened my mouth to respond but the clicking of high heels against the concrete floor stopped me. They echoed down the hallway and each clack of her heels only worsened the heat inside me.

I saw red, my magic was rising and becoming uncomfortable. Even though I wasn't calling it, it was trying to force its way out of me and because of that there was a looming threat of pain and nausea over me.

In seconds Xena stepped in front of the bars. To see that she was dressed in designer clothing with freshly painted nails didn't surprise me. What surprised me were the burn scars that covered the left side of her face. Her black hair fell around her in waves and covered a majority of the damage.

So, I did burn her...but how did she escape?

I stiffened when I felt her magic wash over me...but there was something else intertwined with it, something almost familiar. I knew what it was, and the answer was teasing me. It lingered in the back of my brain but no matter how hard I tried, I couldn't place what it was.

"I almost can't believe you, someone as stupid as you, came from my eggs," she said with a smug tone, her eyes dropping to my burnt hands.

"You should be dead," I growled and stood up. I walked over to the bars, commanding my legs to be as strong as possible. I couldn't let her see how much she had affected me; it was the only thing I had left.

She sucked her teeth and sent me a look of disappointment.

"Like you could actually kill me," she said with a huff. Her tone caused something to stir in me, but I tried hard to clamp down on my anger as a wave of pain washed over me.

"What do you want with us?' Amr asked with a growl.

Xena's eyes shifted to him, but only for a moment. I don't know if it was his nakedness that bothered her, or just him, but she looked at him as though he was a mere speck of dirt on those shiny heels of hers.

"I wanted Rosie," she said simply. "For her magic, though I guess you coming with her doesn't hurt. I need extra."

I could feel Amr's gaze on me, but I kept my eyes locked on Xena.

"Why mine?" I asked.

When her eyes rolled over my body I felt a shiver of disgust run through me.

"Because you are the closest thing to an Original witch I have here," she said and reached through the bars, gripping my wrist. "If you are still, the bars will not hurt you."

She pulled my hand and wrist through the bars and conjured a magical knife. She didn't hesitate to bring it down onto my skin, right on my raven tattoo. She dragged the knife across my skin, ruining the tattoo entirely.

I bit back a scream as pain flashed through me. Tears pricked my eyes and I had to cover my mouth with my free hand to keep in the sobs.

Magical pain was far worse than anything a regular knife could do, and she had gone extra deep, punishing me. She did this on purpose, trying to pay me back for the burn on her face.

As my bright red blood fell to the floor, the floor lit up. Much like the floor in her basement, there were intricate carvings in the floor that could only be seen when called forth by magic. The room lit up a bright red as drop after drop was sucked into the floor.

She left my hand in midair to walk over to Amr's cage. When she held her hand out for Amr's arm, he just growled at her.

She sent him a chilling half-smile and snapped her fingers. I watched in mute horror as Amr's body contorted and he was forced into his cat form. She then snapped her fingers again, a burst of her magic filled the air and then suddenly Amr was growing back into his mortal body, his bones snapping together loudly.

She let out a laugh before snapping her fingers again, forcing him back into his cat form before he was even finished shifting. Amr let out a pained howl and she snapped her fingers again.

"Stop!" I yelled. "It's hurting him!"

The act of his bones growing and snapping together just to be shrunk again, over and over again, must have been excruciating and I couldn't bear to see Amr in pain.

"Then he should listen," Xena said and extended her hand once more. Amr shakily stood to his full height and slipped his hand through without any retort.

"How did you do that?" he asked then winced as Xena tore through his skin with a magical dagger.

"You're cursed," she said simply.

My blood froze.

"You didn't," I growled, though I couldn't do anything but stand behind the bars and watch as she turned to smile at me.

"I didn't curse him directly," she said and waved me off. "It's in the bloodline, didn't you know? Gosh you're such a disappointing project. I wonder what I ever saw in you."

Her words hurt, but the information about Amr's heritage was more important than my bruised ego.

"I don't understand," I said, pushing for more information. "His bloodline?"

She rolled her eyes.

"Everything started somewhere, right?" she asked, though I know she didn't expect an answer. "A group of witches long ago betrayed me and so as a punishment, I turned them into animals and bound them to other witches to do what they pleased with."

My stomach turned sour.

"You're disgusting," I spat at her.

She shrugged and turned back to me.

"Maybe I will do the same to you after I have bled you dry," she said and waved her hand over my wound. Her magic swirled around my arm and began stitching the wound closed. To my surprise, she healed my hand as well. "I have been craving a good chicken dinner. Hard to get good service around here when you look like a freak."

She pulled away and turned to leave but my growls filled the space between us.

"Him too," I commanded and jutted my chin out towards Amr. His wound was still bleeding and if I felt faint even from just that bit of blood, I knew he wouldn't make it much longer.

She lifted her unmarred brow at me.

"He can bleed out for all I care," she said and turned back down the hall.

"Wait!" I yelled. "You can't leave us here!"

There was no reply back and moments later I heard a door slam shut.

"Rosie," Amr breathed. I turned to look at him. He pulled his arm back into the cell and was trying to use magic to heal his arm, but his face had gone sickly pale. Moments later he was forced to bend over and vomit on the floor.

His eyes met mine and my heart froze.

"I can't use my magic," he said. "I can't—I can't—"

His words were cut off by painful coughs.

Shit.

Chapter 15
DAXTON

Three days. It had been three days since Rosie and Amr disappeared. If I wasn't sure before about their fate, then I was now.

"Damn it!" I yelled and threw everything off the desk.

The notebooks and papers scattered across the floor. Normally, this bit of destruction would be enough for me, but now I needed more. I needed to destroy everything I could get my hands on. Turn this pristine place into one that matched my insides.

I kicked at the desk. Tore out the drawers and threw them to the ground. Anything breakable I could find would be thrown at the walls. I didn't care when glass and shards of wood flew at me, nor did I even feel the sting when some of them scraped my skin. All I saw was that the world looked too perfect for something as ugly and monstrous as me to live in it.

Guilt and anger raged inside me. It gave me no rest, even when I was sleeping. My dreams were filled with Amr and Rosie looking at me with horrified and betrayed expressions and I would wake up to their curses in my ears. When I was awake and I found my mind wandering after days of not sleeping, I swore at times I saw them in front of me.

They would berate me, yell at me...but other times they would just look at me in disappointment. The worst hallucinations I had were when I thought I could feel their touch or their magic across my skin. It felt so *real*... but soon enough my mind would clear, and I would be left to realize what I had done.

As soon as I tried to pick up the desk, exhaustion weighed over me and a wracking cough spilled from my lips, burning my chest. I took heaving breaths and kneeled on the floor. The pain from Xena's last purge was still fresh and my body ached with each breath I took.

Another reminder of how much I had fucked up.

I sat back on my heels and looked over my now destroyed room. It was a mess. There were shards of glass scattered across the floor, paper was everywhere, and ink stained the wall from the various pens I had thrown at it.

Rae would be pissed if I didn't clean this up soon. One more thing that I couldn't allow to happen. I had fallen so low in the group that I couldn't chance another fuck up or I knew I would be testing their patience.

They hadn't done anything to me yet other than a few altercations and some choice words...probably out of respect for Rosie, but that didn't mean I wanted to chance it.

Rosie could only protect me for so long.

I raised my hand and called my magic to me, but even such a simple task caused a shooting pain to burn through my chest. Xena had done horrors to my magical core. She had assured me it would heal over time...but I was starting to understand just how much of a liar she really was.

Even with my out-of-control magic, I didn't feel *like this*. I knew it was a lot to handle and I sometimes lost myself...but at least it didn't feel like I was decaying every day.

The door opened, lighting the room with the light from the hallway. I slowly looked over to see Malik looking at me from the doorway. His hair was pulled into a messy bun on the back of his head, he had dark circles branded onto his face, and he looked paler than usual. He was dressed in the same clothes I saw him in for three days again: a ratty band t-shirt and black sweats.

His and Rae's reaction had been the worst.

At least Eli took their anger out on me. I could punish myself while their fists connected with my face...but Malik and Rae, they just stared.

Malik looked like I had ripped his soul in two when he learned of what I had done. He hadn't been the same since, his eyes had hazed over, and he had a faraway expression that told me he was probably with Rosie in his daydreams.

It hurt because I wanted to be there too.

I didn't want this life. I didn't ask for my parents to do this for me and I just wanted to *help*. That's all I wanted yet it turned into something horrible.

Something I could never come back from.

"We are trying something," he said in a hollow voice. "We need your magic."

I opened my mouth to tell him that my magic was as good as gone but stopped myself when I realized it would just disappoint him even more.

I nodded and stood slowly. He watched me struggle to get up and walk over to him with a blank face.

"Listen, Malik—"

"Let's go," he said interrupting me and turned down the hall.

I stared at the now-empty space in front of me, guilt overtaking me. With a soft sigh I exited the room and followed him down the hall.

Just like on *that* day, everyone including Maximus, Claudine, and Ren had been in the foyer. They all looked towards me when I approached the top of the stairs.

Eli outright glared while the others just seemed...dejected.

"Come," Claudine said and held out her hand towards me.

I descended the stairs quickly, the slap of my bare feet against the hard floor echoing through the room. They waited for me in silence, and I could feel their eyes glaring holes into my face, probably figuring out how best to kill me. Malik was waiting for me at the end but did not say anything as I pushed past him.

"I am going to pull your magic from you," she continued. "I am hoping that if Xena or Rosie's magical signature is still inside you, then I can try and track their location."

"I didn't know that was possible," I said and put my hand in hers. Her magic brushed across my sides, and I knew it was supposed to be comforting, but it stung as it washed over my oversensitive skin.

"It may very well not be," she said.

I called forth my magic to my palm; the same shooting pain exploded in my chest. I winced but tried to keep the magic flowing as long as possible.

Claudine made a low humming sound before closing her eyes. Her own magic swirled around her plunging the room into a tenseness. She pushed her eyebrows together and made a strangled groan. After a few moments in silence her body started to shake.

I didn't know how much longer I could keep this up. The pain in my chest was excruciating and there was sweat dripping down my face. White spots flashed across my vision and my knees shook.

She let out a sigh and her eyes popped open. Her magic was called back to her, and a small frown marred her face. Before she could even utter the words that would have for sure disappointed the group, a hard force slammed into me.

I was forced to the cold ground, my head slamming against the hard surface causing pain to explode through me. I couldn't even make a pained noise as the air was pushed violently out of my chest.

I looked up at my attacker through blurry eyes, expecting Eli but instead I got Malik. He looked down at me with narrow angry eyes. The once dejected mask was gone and finally we saw the raw pain he was feeling underneath.

I gripped my head and tried to stand but Malik's bare foot came down on my chest, pushing me back into the ground. My skin was still sensitive and the small act set my skin on fire. I gasped trying to regain control of myself, but I couldn't help the pained groan that forced its way out of my throat.

"Why?" he asked, his eyes trained on me. "Why wouldn't you tell us Xena was back?"

I swallowed thickly, trying to push through the pain that wracked my body.

"I didn't know it was her until after our first session," I confessed. "And after that it was too late."

"How was it too late?" he spat. "You could have stopped this any time."

Anger, disgust, and hurt clouded my mind. I could have stopped at any time. I could have turned back and forgotten about everything.

...but then it would have cost me my life.

It would have cost Rosie and Amr their lover...and Eli their brother.

But it would have been a lie if I stated that those were the things that had motivated me. Yes, they played a part and haunted me every waking moment, but the truth was that I was scared.

I didn't want to die.

"That *demon* was killing me!" I choked out. "I would have died if I continued to live with it."

Malik's hard gaze faltered before he pushed his foot harder into my chest. I couldn't contain the pained sob that tore from me. My entire body was on fire and black spots burst across my vision.

"Many are in the same position," Malik countered. "Others have put their lives at risk to make this world—"

"I was a *monster!*" I yelled. My words caused the world to fall silent.

I heard the others around us shift and by the sound of the footsteps I could tell that one person was getting closer, but Malik shot them a look.

After a pause, Malik slowly took his foot off my chest, and I gasped for air. Only then did I realize how long I had been holding my breath because the pain was too severe to even breathe.

My body relaxed as Rae sent calming waves into my body and I felt her hands grip my upper arms to pull me into a standing position.

I hated how I melted into her hold, but I couldn't pull myself away.

"All of you just *forgot* about everything," I spat as I clutched at Rae's clothes. "Once you thought the Originals were dead you just forgot that I had one *inside* of me this whole time!"

Malik's eyes shifted and his jaw clenched. His hands were balled into fists so tight that his knuckles turned white.

"He was eating away at me," I whispered. "Every single cell in my body was being disintegrated by him and the only thing that helped was Rosie's magic...but for how long? How long would I have with her? With Amr? I was a ticking time bomb!"

Rae's hands tightened on my arms.

"Daxton," she whispered. "Let's save your strength. You're in a lot of pain."

Eli was the one to let out a harsh laugh. I couldn't even bring myself to look at them. We were once so close...how did it come to this?

"This pain is your own fault," they snapped. "I should have known there was something wrong when you began to avoid me. Rosie I understood, but you? If you would have just told—

"No, I couldn't have," I said with a bitter laugh and finally met their narrowed blue eyes. "Don't you see it? What would you have done? Would you even take it seriously?"

I could feel the hatred from both Malik and Eli filling the room with tension. No one else dared to say anything to combat it, not even Rae.

Because she too was still blaming me.

"She was playing you," Claudine spoke, her whimsical voice cutting through the air. I turned to her. She was looking up towards the ceiling, her eyes far away. "You cannot separate a demon from your body. It's in your core. She was just stealing your magic."

Pain.

Pain so bad that it caused my knees to buckle and my chest to convulse shot through me.

"No," I breathed, tears filling my eyes.

This *couldn't* have been for nothing. I couldn't have gone through this pain to have it mean nothing. I couldn't have been going behind my friends' backs for *nothing.*

Please have it be a lie. Please. Please. Please.

"In theory," she continued. "I guess if they were powerful enough and the magic had a mind of its own it *could* exist outside the host...but it is unlikely and there would never be a way to get all of it out."

My magic rose in me sharply, tearing at my insides and heating my skin.

No, this couldn't have been—

Malik's rough hand gripped my chin and forced me to look into his golden eyes.

"Sleep," he commanded.

I welcomed the darkness.

Chapter 16
Amr

"Please don't," I begged as Rosie approached the bars for the fourth time.

Her eyebrows were pulled together, and her mouth was set into a frown. She was determined, yet she knew that as soon as her skin came into contact with the bar, the magic that had been infused in it would send her flying back into the wall.

But nonetheless, she had persisted.

Each time she would peel herself off the wall and even though her body was weak from no food and her magic was nonexistent, she stood on steady legs.

It was terrifying.

I hated watching the girl I had fallen in love with be in so much pain. I knew I shouldn't have resigned myself to sitting here and waiting. I knew I should be the one trying to force a way out of here...but I just couldn't bring myself to.

My mind was heavy.

With Daxton, with Xena's news about my bloodline, all having some sick sort of curse that had enslaved us to years of cruel witches that wanted nothing more to do with us than to abuse and use us how they pleased.

I had grown up with horror stories and seeing proof of just how cruel witches could be to our kind. I had thought that Daxton was my lucky break.

A good family.

He was nice, even if I was ignored.

I *thought* I was free...but I was so wrong.

"I think I got it," she said and slowly lifted her hand towards the bar. Her entire arm was shaking, and the palm of her hand had been burnt so badly it was barely recognizable. My own palm and forearm had been healed by Xena but only just barely. Each time I felt the pain burn through me and was sure it was the most pain I had felt in my life until she came for the next round.

Yet Rosie didn't even flinch as she extended her hand, the burnt flesh stretching and cracking as she did so.

I wanted to look away, but I couldn't tear my eyes from her. I never could, I realized. Even from the very first moment I had seen her sitting in that cafeteria. Back then, she had curled into herself. She was hiding from the world, hiding from her curse. She was a scared and weak low-level and I couldn't help but be drawn to the power that lay inside her.

Now I was drawn to the strong warrior in front of me. The one that fought for the people she loved and persisted even though she knew that the world, and *literal gods* were out to get her. I loved this woman so much... which was why it was so hard for me to watch her hurt herself.

Slowly, she wrapped her hand around the bars and for a second, it looked like she had actually succeeded. There was a stillness in the air, even my own heartbeat paused as Rosie and I made eye contact.

Then bright red magic filled the room, filling my eyesight and blocking the love of my life from my view. I heard her hit the brick wall with a thud.

I flinched and waited for the magic to disperse.

This was always the scariest part. I would wait, unable to breathe, and see if this time was the time that she had finally knocked herself out. Even as a demon, a body could only take so much.

When she let out a pained moan my body sagged with relief.

"Stop it," I growled and took a step forward, pain shooting up my legs. "Stop hurting yourself."

I had spent a long time crouching near the ground, thinking of all the ways our life had gone so horribly, so standing and walking so suddenly brought me pain that I couldn't heal from. At least not while my magic was still bound to me. My skin ached and I was freezing because of my lack of clothes.

She ran her hand through her messed up hair and winced. Her once perfect hoodie had been charred to bits at the selves, showcasing her now scarred forearm. Even though Xena had healed her with magic a few times, she made sure to leave even more scars on Rosie's perfect skin.

"I will heal soon," she said and stood up once more. This time she was slower to stand, and her chest heaved as she struggled to get up. Her eyes were narrowed and set on the bars in front of her once more.

I loved and hated her determination. Any other time it would have made me fall to my knees, but not here. Not now.

My heart twisted and pain shot through my chest as she took another step forward.

I can't watch this.

"Make me shift," I blurted out.

Her eyes snapped to mine, and a frown marred her face.

"I have never—"

"We have a bond," I reminded, my voice desperate. "If you wanted to you could command me to shift, and I could slip between the bars..."

It was the only way we could get out of here. If I could shift, at least one of us would be able to get out of these cells and Rosie wouldn't have to continue to hurt herself like this.

"It requires magic," she said in a low voice and stared at her hands.

I swallowed thickly. We hadn't been able to use magic for four days. Every time we had tried we would get violently ill, and pain would spread throughout our bodies. The pain was so unbearable it made it impossible to even think while we were trying to conjure magic...but if Rosie could command the magic on my behalf, I was sure it would work.

I had never experienced something as strong as what Xena had done to us, but I wasn't surprised anymore. I knew that the Originals were dangerous, but I had underestimated their cruelty.

"Only a little," I partially lied.

It would require little for her, but a lot more for me. But I could take it. If it meant getting us out of here, I would take any pain. It was our only chance at this point.

Her only chance.

If we didn't get out of here now we would either starve to death or Xena would use every last drop of our magic. Every day Xena would throw us some random food through the bars. Today's was a banana and a child's packaged lunch. Yesterday's was a pack of instant noodles, with *no* water.

Then when we were just about exhausted from the day, she would come in and force us to bleed on her enchanted floors. It was never-ending and as much as we tried to fight it, Xena would always get her way.

We were already starving. And if we stayed here any longer, I don't know if we'd make it out alive. We were hanging on by threads, which was probably why Rosie was so adamant about leaving today.

Exhaustion threatened to take us both and if that happened we would have no way to fight Xena.

Sometimes at night when the cells were dark and Rosie was asleep, I would curse Daxton. The man that I had loved had turned on us so horribly and I had no idea why.

Daxton loved Rosie and me as much as we loved him, I knew that even if he couldn't say it. All this time, I knew something was wrong...but I never thought *this*. It didn't take long for me to connect what the mysterious child-like witch had said and what had happened in the room with Xena, but it felt *wrong*.

Daxton wouldn't do this. If he had seen Xena he would have told us. If he was struggling with the demon he would have confided in us. After all, weren't we the people he trusted the most?

It *hurt* to realize how we had been betrayed by him.

He had to have known that going to Xena would have been a death sentence for Rosie. Going to Xena, regardless of the reasoning, would lead her straight back to us, but it didn't seem like he had thought about these consequences at all. He walked straight into that death trap even after seeing firsthand how bloodthirsty the Originals were.

Sometimes those thoughts would control my mind and they were all I could think about even as Rosie lay sleeping in the cell next to me. I would toss and turn all night remembering what it felt like to sleep next to them, snuggled tightly in the blankets instead of lying on the cold ground, but then my mind would freeze, and I would remember that *he* was the reason we were here.

She had been taking this far better than I was, or at least I assumed she was. She would fight with Xena, curse at her, but she would still meet each day with optimism, like she *really* thought we were getting out of here.

I on the other hand, was spiraling.

We were trapped.

And I would be stupid to underestimate Xena any more than I already had. She had no plans of ever letting us go. An Original like her couldn't take a loss and this would be her *biggest* loss yet.

Her daughter, that she had so carefully groomed into being her next pawn, developed a mind of her own and an army of followers that would do anything for her.

Even kill.

Rosie's fists clenched at her sides and her mouth was pushed into a thin line. She knew I was lying but she didn't yell or berate me for doing so. She knew what we had to do.

"We need to escape," I whispered, my eyes shooting down the hall. Xena would be here soon and if we were caught speaking of this, I had no idea what pain she would inflict on us today.

"I know," she said with a small sigh, her shoulders hunching. "It's just… it'll hurt."

Her brown eyes shifted to mine and trailed the length of my body.

Yes, it would.

But at least I would be doing *something* to help get us out of here.

I had stood by doing nothing and she would still wake up every morning and assure me that today was the day that we were going to escape. But then just like every single day, Xena would come, and she would show us that we were never going to escape.

And so, for *her*. For Rosie. I would take this pain.

Shifting made it feel like my skin was being torn apart and my bones were being snapped all at once. But to push through that *and* supply the shift with magic? It would hurt.

Whatever curse Xena had used on us made our magic useless, or at least it made our bodies so wracked with pain that we couldn't even think of using magic.

"I'm a big cat," I said with a small smile.

My heart soared when a small smile pulled at her lips.

"Let me know when to stop," Rosie said. Her gaze was much darker than her words.

"I will," I lied.

Her eye narrowed at me as if she could feel the lie.

"Just do it," I said quickly. We had wasted too much time already. "Just use a bit of magic and command me to shift. It'll work. *Trust me.*"

Rosie let out a loud sigh, her eyes lingering on me for just a second longer before she turned, her back facing me. Her shoulders were tense and her hands balled into fists at her side.

"Please," I breathed.

She took a stiff step towards the middle of the room, then another, then another until she sat down on the ground, right in the center of the room. She braced herself on the ground, her palms resting against the concrete. Her entire body stiffened and with a sharp intake of breath, I could feel her magic spiking around her.

It was weaker than it had been before, but there was no mistaking the potency of it. It was dark and exploded on my taste buds. I shivered as it passed through the cold space, feeling it leave a burst of heat through me as it brushed across my skin.

I took a shaky step back and braced myself on the ground, just as she had.

Rosie took a deep breath, her face contorting in pain. Then I felt it in the air, stronger this time. Her magic was coming towards me slowly, creeping across the bars of her cell and into mine, heating up the cold dungeon.

"Shift, *Amr*," she commanded and immediately, her magic wrapped around me. Any other time I may have enjoyed the heat of her magic...but right now it made me feel sick.

The magic started in my toes, then slowly made its way up my body. It spread through me, tingling at first, then it quickly turned to pain as each one of my bones cracked and my body was forced to shift.

It was pulling magic from me, and I had to focus on feeding it more or else I would be left here with broken bones and a half-shifted body.

I tried to breathe in through my mouth. Focus on the sounds around me.

The sound of Rosie.

The sound of my heartbeat as the pain shot through my body.

The sound of my pained gasps for air.

After a while I couldn't hear what Rosie was saying. I could hear her voice, but I didn't know if she was screaming. I didn't know if Xena had found us. I was blind to everything but the pain.

Except the muffled sound of her voice.

It was like I was underwater. The pain was so intense that even the ground beneath me had disappeared and left me floating in a dark cocoon of pain.

I let out a groan as my back contorted and I felt my skin tear. I was shrinking. I could feel it in the way my body was forced in on itself.

And then suddenly, as my eyes were screwed shut, and I was panting...I felt it.

I shifted.

Blinking the stars away from my eyes, I found myself closer to the ground than before and just beyond the bars of my cell, I saw Rosie staring at me with tears in her eyes.

The world around me had turned more vibrant. The coldness of the dungeon no longer bothered me, and I found myself cuddled in soft warm fur. I could smell Rosie's sweat and the slight burst of old Original magic floating in the air around us.

Thank the Gods.

"Thank *God*," she breathed, echoing my thoughts. Her eyebrows pushed together, and she looked to be a moment away from falling apart. "Why the fuck would you ask me to do that if you knew it would hurt you so bad?"

Of course I couldn't answer her, but I wouldn't have anyway. We both knew why I did what I did and there would be no changing it now. So instead of wasting more time, I walk towards the bars. My body ached with each stretch of my muscles in this new body, but I didn't let it deter me. The bars were buzzing with magic that began to reach out to me as I neared, coiling around my body.

I didn't want to think of what would happen if I was hit with the exploding magic while I was in *this* form. All I knew was that there was only one chance to do this and if I made a single error...it may just be my last.

As long as I don't touch it, I'll be fine, I said in my mind, though to be honest, I wasn't too sure anymore that this had been the right approach.

I braced myself and put one paw out from the bars and took a deep breath. Slowly, I pushed my head through. Once my head was through I felt a violent wave of relief fill me. That would be the hardest part, but thankfully I had lost some weight because of Xena and could slide through the bars with just enough space.

I could feel Rosie's gaze on me, but I couldn't look at her or else risk my concentration. I could feel the magic around the bars buzzing around me and even in this form I started to sweat.

Then slowly, I tried to pull my hind legs and tail through the bars.

Just in time for the tip of my tail to escape the cell, I felt Xena's magic right above me.

When my gaze snapped to Rosie, I knew she had felt it too.

"*Hide*," she whispered. "Hide *now*."

Ice cold panic froze my veins and even as I felt our captor come closer, I couldn't move.

Leave Rosie?

I wanted to tell her no, scream at her, but I couldn't.

"Now," she growled, her eyes shooting back to the ceiling.

Xena was getting closer and our time together was ending.

I knew I should listen to Rosie. Even as my mind screamed at me and my heart pounded in my chest...I knew she was right. One of us had to get out of here and if Xena found me before I could get to the others...

I turned down the hallway and ran towards the opposite direction.

It didn't feel good to run.

I felt like a coward. I wasn't the familiar Rosie needed. I should be back there fighting Xena.

But I continued running until I reached the end of the hallway and luckily, there was a small barred window that I could jump through.

I pounced and as my paws hit the windowsill I heard a roar behind me.

Xena had found out.

I rushed out of the window, dropping straight into a muddy bank below. There was a large hill in front of me that seemed twice its size now that I was in my cat form. It towered over me. Without pause I tried as fast as I could to run up the hill of mud and grass, my paws slipping in my haste. I clawed myself up as the feeling of Xena's magic getting closer to me played at my senses.

My mind had gone blank. Everything else had been forgotten and I only focused on a single thing:

Getting over the peak of this hill and running like my life depended on it.

Her magic was getting closer. Stronger. She was angry.

I could feel it in her magic, in the way the world around me shook and in the way that my own magic recoiled in response. It pushed me to get to the top of the hill faster, not even caring how the mud began to seep into my wounds.

When I finally reached the top of the hill, I felt her magic pull back so violently my entire being was left hollow. I froze at the top, looking over the scene in front of me. The grassy hills that surrounded us paled in contrast to the towering brick buildings that stood up straight and tall in the distance.

I was at Winterfell.

And as if to prove my point, the clock tower, which was facing away from me, let out a series of chimes indicating the turn of the hour. They were muffled from here, and the tower wasn't anything but a distant silhouette in the setting sky...but it was there.

I took off running towards it.

Hang in there Rosie.

<h1 style="text-align:center">Chapter 17
Rosie</h1>

For some reason, I wasn't shocked when Xena kept looking at me even as Amr escaped down the hallway. Her brows were furrowed, and her eyes were narrowed at me. She may have flexed her powers like she cared that Amr had run away from her, but the slight tilt of her lips told me that it wasn't just anger she was feeling.

Her magic grip took hold of me and for the first time, I realized I felt something different about it. It was darker, but noticeably weaker. It was not as intimidating as it used to be...

She was dying.

Just like Marques had been.

I felt the familiar dark magic waft around me and I shifted on my feet, walking closer to her. There was something tugging at the edge of my mind, enticing me to get closer. It was darker than her magic and far more intoxicating.

A thrum of electricity ran through me and in my mind a fuzzy picture started to show itself before quickly disappearing as Xena's eyes shifted back down the hallway.

"Why are you still doing this?" I asked her, needing her to focus back on me. "Haven't you had enough already?"

I called upon my own magic. I didn't care that the magic was burning my chest and tearing up my skin, instead I used it as an anchor to call forth the deep deadening magic that resided in my core. It spread through my body, and I watched with a sick satisfaction as Xena's eyes widened before quickly concealing her reaction.

The magic inside me coiled deep in my belly, and all I wanted to do was launch myself across these bars and strangle her until I watched the last of her life bleed out into her eyes. I did not know how she escaped the fire but *God* I wish more than anything that she had perished in there.

My hatred of her before paled in comparison to my hatred now.

The only solace I got was that Amr was escaping. If Xena was with me here, then that meant Amr would live and while that comforted me, it didn't make me any less angry because I was still stuck in here with *her*.

I didn't know what she wanted anymore.

Was it my magic?

Even in her deathly state, she still had more magic than any witch on this planet. She was *the* Original witch and yet...she still tried to take what wasn't hers.

"I'm doing this because it is my right," she growled still not looking at me.

"Your *right*?" I asked. "*You* have no right to *me*, or my *magic* or anyone else's *magic*."

She threw her head back and let out a bitter laugh. Her sharp voice echoed down the hallway and grated on my nerves.

The scarred side of her face was on show in the dim light and paired with that disgustingly twisted smile, it made this all the more bone-chilling.

"I *made* you, child," she said after she caught her breath. "Without me, you wouldn't be here nor would any of the other witches on this planet. I have a *right* to take whatever I want."

"Give it up," I growled at her and stepped closer to the bars. I could feel the magic vibrating against my skin reminding me that if I stepped any closer, I would be thrown back into the wall behind me.

"I will give up when I die," she said, her voice full of venom. "I may be the last of the Originals in this area, but I am not the last in this world. I will do what I need to survive. You out of all people should know the struggle that comes with just trying to survive."

There was a silence that fell between us. I didn't know what to say.

On one hand, I understood because deep within Marcus's memories I had seen the struggle. I felt the fear—it was more than just a fear of humans. They feared for the competition of the other Originals. Ezekiel had once told me that there were hundreds of thousands out there, but would they be as cruel as the ones that I knew?

Would they try to tear her down?

I fucking hoped so.

"Don't you try to manipulate me," I growled at her.

She took a step back and cocked her head.

"I don't need to manipulate you to control you," she said. "If I wanted to *manipulate* you, I may have told you that if your friends ever set foot near this place, I would kill them...but I even let one of them go, didn't I?"

Panic soared through my veins. My throat constricted and I felt the pain stab my chest.

She didn't even try to disguise her threat.

I tried to clamp down on my reaction, knowing that as soon as she saw my panic she would make it worse.

I needed to think of a way out of here. With Xena knowing that Amr had escaped and that there would be others coming for me, I wouldn't put it past her to move me...but if that happened I would lose any chance I had at escaping.

Then just as her eyes met mine the same dark feeling that played at my mind hit me with full force. I focused on it and tried to imagine pulling it towards me and a flash of white covered my eyes. I was thrown back in time as memory after memory of Xena's journey after she had been defeated raced through my mind.

Fire.

Black fire so hot that it had begun melting my skin consumed me. I looked back to see Ezekiel's terror-stricken face. His mouth was open, and he was trying to say something to me, but I couldn't hear him, not over the roar of the flames that surrounded us.

In a split second I made my decision to leave, though I didn't realize how close the fire was to me until I was miles away, back at the foot of the burnt town that hid my existence for more than a thousand years. Even though the cold air had seeped into my bones, the burns from the fires set my skin alight.

I opened my mouth to scream but no sound came out as I tried to call for help.

"Anyone," I choked out as my nails drug into the soft dirt. "Help."

There would be no one to come for me though. There never would be. I would be stuck all on my own just like every other moment in my life.

Blackness enveloped me like an old friend, and I passed out to the sound of my own burning flesh.

When I awoke again I was still alone, but the sun had come out. I managed to pull myself together enough to try and start healing my wound... but I wasn't powerful enough. At least not in my current state.

And so, just like every other time, I pushed myself to my feet and began to walk.

I watched through Xena's eyes how she survived those first few days cowering in fear every time she heard a twig snap or felt the brush of magic against her skin...but it wasn't just me she was afraid of...

It was other Originals as well.

In her memories, she was sure the other Originals had heard about her defeat and were ready to come after her. She thought back to the countless times she had been hurt by them throughout the years and feared for her life.

That was when she started to visit the underground witch areas. She needed safety so she could lick her wounds and devise her next plan... Then Daxton fell right into her lap.

She shifted, the sounds of her heels against the stone calling me back from the recesses of her mind. Before me was no longer the unbeatable god. The Original witch was no more than an urban legend.

Now she was just a person who was so scared of other people paying her back in kind for what she had done, that she was resorting to the only thing she knew how to do.

But I didn't feel pity for her...no, I was angry.

Angry that she thought she could get away with everything. Angry that she saw Daxton as a way to rebuild herself, a way to take advantage of a poor suffering boy.

But I was also giddy with excitement because she had given me the single most powerful leverage I have ever had over her without even knowing it. She had given me everything I needed to know about her by simply just looking me in the eyes.

I let out a hum and crossed my arms over my chest. Pain from my wound shot up my arm but I used it to steady myself and the raging magic inside of me.

Just like me, it was ready to bring down this abuser once and for all.

Xena raised a brow at me, keeping her calm facade...but I saw behind it all.

I saw the terrified woman underneath. The one that knew what she had done to her own daughter and now was worried that she would have to pay the price.

Her most powerful person had left her for me. Her partner had perished in the fire she selfishly escaped from. She had *no one* and she was completely vulnerable.

"You have lived quite the life, haven't you?" I said, my eyes trailing her perfectly made-up clothing.

"You don't want to anger me," she growled, baring her teeth at me.

Her magic flared out around her, brushing against my sides, and burning my skin as it swirled around us.

She wasn't angry though. I had seen enough in her memories to know as much. She was *scared*.

I flared my own magic around me, pushing down the need to throw up the sorry excuse for a lunch that she had given us earlier. I focused on calling forth the darkest magic I could, pulling at the strings of the powers that Marques had left me, and pushing it towards Xena.

I had no intention of actually hurting her; I couldn't do anything with her magic still ripping up my insides...but I could scare her.

"What is your goal?" I asked her again, ignoring her glare. "Why are you doing this? What do you need? Do you need magic? Do you need safety? If so...let's make a *deal*."

She scoffed and rolled her eyes, but I didn't miss the small change in her expression. She needed safety more than she liked to admit. She was a person that from the beginning was at the bottom of the barrel. She *needed* a helping hand now more than ever and while she wouldn't admit it, the act of someone offering to *help* her was something that she had been silently begging for her entire life.

What she didn't know was that I knew her better than she even knew herself. I knew that in this moment she was thinking of all the ways that trusting me would kill her...but also help aid her.

That was why she alone was standing in front of me. Her kingdom had fallen and now she was forced to the front line, just like all of the hybrids she had taken.

"What could you possibly give me that I cannot get right now?" she asked, her eyes narrowing in my direction.

"Don't speak like you aren't on the run, Xena..." I trailed and took a step back, acting as if I wasn't panicking about being stuck in this cage forever. "You and I both know that people will come for me, and you are the lone witch here to guard this place. Don't think I haven't noticed the lack of magical signature."

She opened her mouth to speak but I raised my hand, motioning for her to pause. To my surprise, she actually listened.

"It could be my friends...or maybe even other Originals," I continued with a shrug. "If they found out that *the* Original witch was here, wasting away...why wouldn't they take advantage?" I stepped forward as I felt her magic waver around me. "Think about it Xena. You were lucky you even got me in here in the first place."

She let out a huff of a laugh and rolled her eyes.

"It's true," I fought and took another step forward. "It was my own oversight. But that doesn't mean that you are off the hook. You know as well as I do that keeping me here is only going to reflect badly on you. *But...*" I looked her up and down with a smirk. "Unlike you I have a soft spot for my family."

"Don't act like you are doing me a favor," she growled.

"Oh, but I am," I cooed and ran my hand over the bars close enough to feel the magic radiating off it. "Malik has revived *The Fallen,* did you know?"

She shook her head and let out a lighter laugh, but the tension was still in her shoulders.

"I am not afraid of a *stupid gang,*" she said and waved her hand. "Seriously Rosie? That's all you got."

"You don't have to be afraid of them, Xena," I said with a soft smile. Satisfaction rolled through me as I realized I had her *right* where I wanted her. "They can help you... Don't you want a little help after all those years of struggles?"

Her eyes flashed before they narrowed again at me.

Gotcha.

"Get to the point before I force you to," she hissed. I sent her a smile.

"So," I said and ran a hand through my tangled locks. "*If* you make a deal with me. *If* you let me leave...I can make sure that doesn't happen. I can set you up in a comfortable place safe. I can give you magic every so often. Even if it's not me I can find people to share magic with you...but you *have* to let me go. If you don't let me go then I can't help you and they *will* come after you. It's just a matter of time."

She scoffed again, acting like it was the most ridiculous thing that she'd ever heard but I saw the look that passed her face. She was seriously considering it. And I knew she would because the most potent thing that you could use to manipulate someone was hope.

And I learned it *directly* from her.

Chapter 18
Rosie

My muscles ached as I shifted Amr in my arms. My legs were screaming at me to stop, but I wouldn't allow myself to rest, not until I knew was safe. Xena may be leaving me alone in the meantime, but that didn't mean she would play by the rules.

She was narcissistic and psychotic. There was no rule book when it came to her and even if I had successfully used her own manipulation tactics against her, that didn't mean anything when she still needed me.

I had not only been her worst project yet, but I had humiliated her, berated her, and given her no reason to trust me. But that would have to change because for the first time, she had given me the key to her own demise.

The walk to Rae's house from the Winterfell campus was much longer than I remembered, or maybe I was just so exhausted and worn down from everything with Xena that the short walk felt like miles.

My heart was beating erratically, there was a sweat coating my body, and I was already out of breath. Amr had whined and whined for me to put him down, and probably had been pushing for me to rest, but I didn't listen to him.

I needed to get to the others and let them know what had happened before *she* did.

When I found myself on the edge of Rae's garden, I let out a deep sigh feeling all of the tension and panic leave me.

In front of me, trees were sprawled across the perimeter of the house;

beyond them were rose bushes and other well-kept flowers that made the area smell wonderful. A welcome change from the dusty dungeon she had kept us in. It had no doubt been left over from when the school was first built and forgotten about for long enough that Xena took refuge there.

Though she would leave now that her hiding place was known, that much was obvious. After all, even with our deal intact she was still a woman on the run.

The magical barrier that surrounded the property was vibrating in the air and sat against my skin comfortably. It was warm, comforting magic that I had come to recognize over the years and was now associated with my feelings of home and security. It was the only thing separating me from the others, but my own erratic thoughts kept me from crossing it.

Once again, Marques had shaken me to my core.

For the first time, I was able to access his power and the bloodlust that it emitted had scared me enough that on the walk home I started to doubt if it was even safe to come back here.

I knew that I would *never* hurt those that I loved...but it scared me when I realized how little control I had over his powers or memories. Suddenly, I had been filled with memories and feelings of a person who was not me.

It was like the first time the curse had been lifted and I was able to access my full powers. I felt unstoppable. I was ready to tear Xena down and I didn't care how many people I hurt in the process, including myself.

At least this time I could remember my goal. I knew I had to get back here. I knew Amr was running for his life and Daxton was just beyond these walls wilting away because Xena had been feeding off of him. I saw as much in her memories.

She was trying to remove my father from his core...but she was also trying to strengthen herself. She was using him as much as he was using her, except he was going to die if she had not stopped.

Amr and I were his only defense. The only reason he was able to escape Xena.

I hated myself for letting it get this far.

Amr meowed again, calling my attention to him. I pulled him closer and placed a kiss on his soft forehead.

"Just a few more minutes," I said softly. "And then you can shift."

It hadn't been long until I caught up to him after Xena had let me go. Luckily all I had to do was flash my magic and let him know I was alive, and he had come running back. I felt bad when I saw just how beat up his paws looked, but it had made it all worth it when he jumped into my arms and allowed me to heal him.

Getting rid of her was just the first step, but now I had to figure out how to get us out of it. I need to figure out how to turn the tides in our favor or else be stuck with her forever.

With a sigh I shifted, feeling the magic stick to my skin.

The curse that affected our magic would wear off soon, that much Xena had promised me. It was going to be our first test.

If the curse didn't wear off…she couldn't be trusted, and I would be good on my threat to have her destroyed. But in return I had given her something too…

I paused just as I was about to walk through the barrier. Apprehension filled me. I didn't know what lay behind those walls, waiting for me.

Were they angry?

Were they upset?

What about *Daxton?*

My chest twisted when I thought about him. I gave a lot of thought to what I was going to do when I saw him but I could never settle on one thing. I was mad. Of course, I was mad. How could he go behind our backs like this?

After everything that we've been through…after everything that we've worked on, and he went straight to *her*.

I wished those angry thoughts could stay for longer. Ignite my fury and make my blood boil like they once had…but I couldn't stop thinking about how much pain he had to be in to do this.

When the witch in the bar first told me that he was up in a room with another witch, I thought he was *cheating* on me.

What a stupid thought.

But who would have thought he would have gone to my mother and asked to pull my father's demon out of him?

It would have been better if he had just been cheating.

I still didn't know what I was going to do when I saw him. I didn't know what I was going to do when I saw *any* of them.

I knew I had to tell them. I knew it couldn't wait. But…would it be so wrong if I just asked for us to forget about it in that moment and just *be?* To just lie in their arms and sit in the warmth of the love they provided me? For a moment…I just wanted to forget.

I think today marked the fifth day that I had been gone. The fifth day I had been held captive. The fifth day I had been separated from my loved ones. And the fifth day I had not been able to use my magic.

I wouldn't know it would go crazy when Xena's curse lifted. I could already feel it shifting beneath my skin, waking from its deep slumber. It was angrier than I could muster in my exhausted state and quite frankly, it scared me.

In my peripheral vision I spotted Maximus's figure coming towards me. He walked out from behind a tree, his eyes zeroing in on me. His long auburn hair was pulled into a low ponytail and his glasses shone in the sun. His mouth was set in a deep scowl and his arms were crossed over his chest.

We stared at each other for a moment before he took a step forward.

"Rosie," he said in a low tone. No other words came out of his mouth, but his eyes watched me like a hawk, as if he was afraid I was nothing more than a ghost that would disappear the moment he moved too fast.

"It's nice to see you again, Maximus," I greeted with a tired smile. "If I asked you not to let anyone know that I was home yet...would you listen?"

He averted his gaze and looked towards the house that towered over us in the distance. The sun had set by now and the lights in the house and in the garden lit up the night around us. From the outside it looked like the perfect home, complete with white trim and shiny windows...but inside I knew it must be a mess of emotions that would threaten to overtake me as soon as I stepped through those doors.

He shook his head, his eyes still focused on the house.

"Fair enough," I said with a sigh and walked straight through the barrier.

I didn't stop until I was at the back door and even then there was no hesitate in my steps as I passed over the threshold and into the house..

As soon as I opened the door I was hit with a comforting sense of familiarity. The air smelled clean with a hint of something warm and sweet that made my mouth water and my stomach twist with hunger pains. The surface was polished and shone in the warm light of the house.

As I walked through the halls I could feel how dirty I was compared to the pristine place and for the first time in a long time, I felt a bit self-conscious of how I may look.

I had been gone for only five days but in those five days I had come to miss this place and the people that I surrounded myself with more than I ever could have imagined. Coming *home* was the best feeling that I've ever experienced even as the thoughts of Xena and Daxton weighed on my mind.

I belonged here.

Suddenly Amr jumped out of my arms and began shifting. I let out a heavy sigh of relief when he shifted with ease, meaning that Xena's curse had left us. It had been painful to watch in the dungeon as he slowly tried to force himself into the body of a cat. The snapping of his bones and then his groans still echoed in my mind.

He stood straight in his human form and turned towards me. His inky black hair hung in his face, covering his golden eyes. His hair was so long it almost came to his hips now, but it did nothing to cover how his body had changed.

Only now in the bright lights of our home did I understand how much he had gone through in the past few days. Our lack of food showed in how his face had slimmed; our lack of sleep was shown through the deep dark circles under his golden eyes.

It pained me to see him like this.

Without speaking he grabbed my hand and pulled me down the hallway. He only paused to try and open every door we came across. Many were locked but finally when one opened he pushed us into it. It was a small study with a bookshelf and a desk near the windows. It smelled like old books and was warm enough to chase away the coldness of the walk. It was shadowed in darkness, the only light coming from the moonlight that entered through the windows that overlooked the garden.

"Amr," I protested. My voice was filled with exhaustion and even that little protest took far more energy than I could muster in that moment.

Only now as I felt myself being wrapped in a cocoon of warmth and protectiveness did I realize how tired I was and how much it took out of me to walk from Winterfell to here. My entire being felt like it was being pulled to the ground and my bones ached with each step.

As soon as he shut the door locking us in this room alone with our thoughts and exhaustion, my knees buckled. His warm arms wrapped around me and held me tight against him.

He held me like he was afraid that I would leave him again.

He held me like he had lost me.

"Rosie," he breathed, his warm breath spreading across my scalp. "I love you." His arms wrapped around me tightened. "I'm *sorry*. I love you. Just stay here a moment with me *please*."

Beside myself, I feel the familiar prick of tears in my eyes.

"I almost lost you," I whispered with a bitter laugh.

We were silent for another moment. Just taking in each other's warmth. I pushed my face into his bare chest, the sound of his heartbeat calming my fried nerves. The bloodlust from earlier was far gone; the only thing I felt now was utter relief that we had made it out.

"We need to talk about it," he said from above me.

"I know," I whispered but he didn't push me to talk about it and for that I was grateful.

He let another few moments pass between us. The house was silent, though I knew it wouldn't stay that way for long.

"I made a deal," I whispered against his skin. "When we are ready we can talk about it with the others."

He nodded and took a step back. I felt his magic wash over my skin in a cooling wave. I looked up to him with a raised eyebrow.

"I do not know when the next time we can get clean will be," he said. I nodded and stayed silent as his magic washed over my body, face, and hair. The film of grime that I felt on my skin was gone in seconds and I exhaled heavily.

"Thank you," I whispered and sent him a small smile.

His eyes darkened and he leaned forward to place a kiss on my lips.

"I think I need to go see Daxton," he said then paused. "Are you ready to come with me?"

I shook my head. I still needed to gather my thoughts, to just be here for a moment before I had to face the world. He gave me a small, understanding smile then grabbed my hand.

Just as he was about to pull me back towards the door, it burst open showing a wild-eyed Malik. His golden eyes searched the room before landing on me and without a moment to waste he stalked across the room.

The tension in the room skyrocketed and I found my heart racing as Malik eyed me. His presence had taken over the entire room, making him unavoidable. My hands itched to reach for him, and I wanted nothing more than to bury my head into his chest.

Amr let go of my hand and stepped out of Malik's way, though I was sure if he hadn't, Malik would have run him over.

Malik's arms wrapped around me, pulling me to him. His hand tangled itself into my hair and the other had a tight grip on my waist. He inhaled sharply and buried his head into the crook of my neck.

"I'll give you a moment," Amr said and silently left the room.

I tangled my hand through Malik's hair and held him close to me. He pulled away from me and began searching my face. Then my neck and chest. Then he started pulling at my clothes, his hands running over my scarred skin.

"I am not hurt, I have been healed," I told him in a soft tone. "Just drained of magic."

His eyes flashed and he cursed under his breath.

"I am going to kill that fucker," he growled.

A stab of guilt filled me. This was my fault, not his.

"Don't give him too much of a hard time," I said. "He didn't know this would happen."

His eyes flashed and a strong hand gripped my chin, forcing me to keep eye contact with him. I was reminded all too well of the Malik long ago that was in charge of my safekeeping. The one who had fun buttons to press. The one who would do anything to protect me.

He must have been so scared. After finally getting rid of the people who held his life captive for years, his lover had been taken from him so brutally, it had to have scarred him.

"He sacrificed you, Rosie," he said, his voice full of hatred. "He went behind all of our backs and put you in danger. He didn't even tell us that Xe—"

I quickly covered his mouth with my hand.

"*Don't* speak her name," I hissed. "I am cursed. She will hear."

His eyes widened and he slowly nodded. I tried to pull my hand away but his was already there, holding my wrist. He brought my hand to his mouth and left a gentle kiss on my knuckle.

The action caused butterflies to soar in my stomach. He paused, his eyes searching my face.

"Can I be selfish?" he asked.

I couldn't stop the smile from spreading across my face.

"You can be," I said and just as the words left my mouth he dove forward, crushing his lips to mine.

I let out a shocked gasp which he used to explore my mouth. I wrapped my arms around his shoulders and let him pick me up and push me against the cool windows. He gripped my thighs and forced my legs around his waist.

"I'll be gentle," he murmured between kisses that he trailed down my neck.

I tugged his hair.

"I don't want you to be," I said.

He growled against my neck and quickly began removing my clothes.

"I was going to wait," he said as he threw my hoodie across the room. I hissed as the cool glass hit my back, but I didn't let it stop me. I helped him undo my bra and let out a strangled moan as his lips clasped around my nipple. His tongue circled my nipple before he sucked then bit it lightly. When he pulled back, his lips were wet with his own spit. "But as soon as I saw you standing here I couldn't think of anything other than being inside you."

His words made heat unfurl in my belly.

He leaned back down to trail more kisses on the other side of my neck until he reached my other nipple. This time he bit down harder, eliciting a pained moan from my mouth. The pain quickly mixed with pleasure as he began sucking on it.

I arched into him, wanting more of his mouth on me.

His hands trailed down my sides until they reached my hips and ground me into him. He was already hard, and his erection rubbed across my aching pussy deliciously. It had been far too long since I had felt him against me and far too long since I had had my magic satiated. I needed him more than I realized.

"Then just do it already," I said with a moan as he pushed my hips into his.

He unlatched himself from my nipple and looked down at me with dark, glowing eyes. A small smile tugged at his lips.

"You have been gone for *five* days going through God knows what," he said. "And you *still* have an attitude with me?"

The edge in this voice set my body alight.

"*You* were the one that asked to be selfish," I reminded, a smile also spreading across my lips. "Seems like you're all talk though."

He growled and brought his hand in between us to cup my pussy. I bit my lip to stop the moan from escaping. He raised his brow and began massaging me through my pants. When the heel of his palm dug into my clit I let out a breathy moan.

"Don't push me, Rosie. I would like to remain in control, and I can't do that if you act *like that*," he warned. "I'm trying to not be an animal."

"Maybe I want you to be," I shot back.

All I wanted right now was to have him make good on his promise. I needed him. Needed the distraction. Needed the assurance that he had missed me. I didn't want to think of the problems that awaited me, nor did I think I had the strength.

It was my own form of cowardice, I knew it...but I couldn't bring myself to care. If this was how I would begin to heal, then so be it.

He leaned back, a mischievous grin spreading across his face.

"You're lucky I like giving pleasure rather than taking it away," he growled in a low voice. "Come for me, Rosie."

His power washed over me, running down my back like hot molten lava and sending sparks throughout my body. I let it take me, relaxing as I felt my body tighten and warmth spread throughout my belly. I let out a low moan as my pussy contracted around nothing and I was thrust violently into an orgasm.

This time, my magic had been too used up to even stir at my orgasm, but I could feel it slowly rising with each second that passed.

He used my distracted state to slip his hands into my pants and rubbed circles on my clit. I jerked against him and pulled at his shirt. He let me take it off of him as he continued to play with me. I marveled at the body he hid so well underneath his clothes. The scarred skin, the tattoos, all of them coming together to make something so undeniably *Malik.*

He's beautiful.

He watched my reaction as he pushed two fingers into me. I threw my head back against the glass, making sure to hold eye contact with him. It was a dare, and he knew it.

"Look at you," he cooed. "Are you not afraid of my power anymore?"

"Not in this lifetime," I said and let out a groan as his heel dug into my clit with each thrust of his hand.

He let out a chuckle.

"You feel so good," he moaned and leaned forward to brush his tongue across my lips. I tried to lean forward to capture his lips in mine, but his hand gripped my chin and forced me to stay still.

He circled his finger inside me and I had to break eye contact as I felt a sharp rise of pleasure run through me.

He clicked his tongue.

"Look at me," he commanded.

I forced my eyes open to meet his.

"Come," he commanded. "And don't stop until I am coming with you."

I couldn't even protest as his power filled me because I was thrown off by such a fast and powerful orgasm that it made my toes curl. I let out a choked moan as he pulled out his fingers from inside me and used them to circle my clit as the orgasm wracked my body.

He took his time tugging off my pants and underwear from one leg. When I was bared to him he inhaled sharply and used his fingers to spread my folds.

I had no rest between each orgasm. I was thrown directly into another one and was forced to grip onto Malik like my life depended on it.

"So beautiful," he whispered, his eyes still locked on my pussy. "You're coming so hard you've left a puddle on the floor."

Those words shouldn't excite me like they did but they only added to the flame that was building up inside me.

"Please, Malik," I begged.

His eyes flashed back up to mine and he held eye contact as he pulled his cock out of his sweats. He pushed his head up to my entrance but instead of sinking into me like I desperately wanted, he dragged his head along my folds and up to my clit.

"So, you do know how to be polite," he teased. "But I am not sure I believe you."

I let out a choked sob as another orgasm shot through me. He positioned his cock at my entrance and pushed in just enough so I could feel the slight stretch, but he didn't move, nor did he sink fully into me.

"Please," I begged again. "I need you. It's too much."

"You can take it," he cooed. "The safe word is there when you need it."

By the look in his eyes, he knew *damn* well I wasn't going to use it.

"*Please,*" I cried out and he rewarded me by entering me in one thrust. My eyes rolled in the back of my head and his hand covered my mouth to muffle my screams.

He let out a sigh as I clenched around him.

"Fuck," he groaned. "I could stay in this tight pussy forever."

I writhed against him as he slowly thrust in and out of me. He was taking his time, letting orgasm after orgasm run through me. It was pure torture, but in the best kind of way.

All thoughts about the outside vanished and I was here with him alone in our pleasure.

"If you squeeze me like that our game will be over," he warned with a chuckle as another orgasm burst from me. Sobs poured out of me, and I shook in his hold.

I was about to answer him, but the door pushed open to show Rae's concerned face. When she took in our position her face quickly contorted into fury and she crossed the room.

Malik didn't even pay her any mind.

"None of you can keep your dicks in your pants," she growled.

I expected her to stop and watch us, or try to interrupt, but she continued her descent until she was right behind Malik, her chest pushing into his back.

Her hand came to rest against my head on the window and she pried Malik's hand off me so she could capture my lips.

"Hypocrite," Malik said but even as Rae ravished my mouth with her tongue, he didn't pick up his pace. Neither of them seemed to mind what was happening.

I came again, sobbing into Rae's mouth.

"Damn it, Rae," he groaned and pounded into me in short hard thrusts. "She's squeezing me so hard. I wanted to take my time."

Rae pulled away, her hazel eyes searching mine.

"We don't have time," she said and took a step back.

Malik's lips replaced hers and with only two more thrusts he was coming along with me. He leaned his head against mine and let out a deep sigh. I let out my own exhausted sigh and sunk into him, enjoying the feeling of him still inside me even as I felt his seed leak out of me.

Malik let out a soft chuckle before letting me down. His golden eyes watched me as I tried to stand on unsteady legs.

"I'm not sorry," he whispered and fixed himself before bending down and helping me back into my pants.

"Me neither," I said and gripped his hand as he stood. He left a soft kiss on my forehead before pulling away. It was Rae who handed me my bra and sweatshirt. She watched me expectantly but didn't push me any more than she had and stayed silent as I continued to dress.

It would have been uncomfortable if I was not already so at ease with the two of them.

"Thank you," I whispered with a smile.

Her eyes shifted to Malik.

"Daxton, Amr and the others are waiting in the foyer for us," she said. Her eyes shifted back to me. She held out her hand for me and a warmth burst through my chest. I slipped my fingers through hers with ease. "Don't be nervous."

I swallowed thickly.

"Let's do this."

Chapter 19
Daxton

I thought I may have just died and gone to heaven when Amr walked into my room fully naked, looking like he hadn't slept in days. It had been jarring at first and I was sure that I was just having a nightmare, but when his magic brushed over my skin my heart caught in my throat.

He's real.

I tried to move, tried to force my mouth to make a sound...but I was just too taken aback by his sudden appearance. His eyes searched the room until he found my hunched-over form in the corner. I hadn't found the strength to pull myself to my bed after the questioning from the others a few days ago and had just resigned myself to the corner.

I hadn't eaten, slept like shit, and had hallucinated about Amr and Rosie coming home so seeing him in the doorway really felt like I had been dreaming. Though in my dreams he looked just as angry. His chest puffed and his eyebrows furrowed as he took me in.

A part of me was disappointed that *this* was his reaction...but another part of me understood it. He and Rosie had every right to be mad. I had fucked up big time and even him being here right now was much more than I deserved.

He was marching over to me in an instant and dropped to his knees when he got close enough. His warm hands clasped mine and the anger turned into a look of concern. His skin against mine was so hot it hurt and the pain from Xena's last session flared through me.

I held on and kept his gaze, marveling over my lost lover.

He had definitely been through hell.

His normally tanned skin was paler, his face almost sunken in, and he had lost weight. Instead of being gone for a week it looked like he had been gone for months. Even his magical signature felt different against mine.

"Daxton," he whispered, his voice low and grainy. "What have they done?"

I couldn't stop the bitter laugh that spilled from my lips. This man had probably been tortured and almost killed by Xena, but his first thought was to ask about how *I* was.

My inner child rejoiced. I was ecstatic to see that *someone* finally could see my pain and wanted to know about it...but it was all wrong and I didn't deserve it.

"It was all me," I said and let out a groan as I sat up straight. My strength was slowly coming back to me, but my body still ached like hell. "How did you—"

"We will discuss that later," he interrupted with a frown. "I came to make sure you were okay."

I rolled my eyes at him and tried to stand but couldn't due to the pain radiating up my legs. Without a word he steadied me and helped me to my feet. I could feel his questioning gaze and my face heated as I realized how pitiful I must look to him, but I was grateful he kept his questions to himself.

"Rosie?" I asked hesitantly.

When he paused my stomach flipped and guilt hit me like a tsunami. It was mere seconds that he had stayed silent, but it was enough to turn my fried and exhausted mind into a mess of anxious thoughts and images of Rosie dying over and over again. If Amr hadn't been holding onto me with such a fierce grip I would have fallen to the floor.

"She is fine," he answered then cleared his throat. "Malik is with her. Tending to her."

A part of me was relieved that Rosie was safe, but the other part was furious. I wanted Rosie to come for me as quickly as Amr had. I wanted her to be worried. I wanted to see her and make sure she was okay...but maybe she had just been avoiding me.

Maybe it was too hard for her to see me, and she was somewhere else in this house, planning on unleashing her anger on me. Maybe that's why she didn't come with Amr. Maybe she was protecting me from her angered magic.

But I didn't want that. I just *wanted* her...no matter how she felt about me in this moment.

I scoffed and rolled my eyes, trying to ignore the pain that went through me.

"Of course, *that bastard* had swooped in and taken her before anyone else could," I grumbled, though it was halfhearted. I wanted to hate him for how he treated me, but I couldn't because inside I knew they were all going easy on me.

Amr gave me a sad smile.

"She needs some time," he explained. "I don't even know all that happened. All I know is after she helped me escape, she worked something out with Xena too. Or at least I think that is what happened. We will only know for sure if we gather with the others."

I let out a sigh and leaned into his warmth. We could count on Rosie to get us out of this mess. She wasn't the same person she was a few years ago, not after that curse was lifted and not after she had tried to kill Xena.

"Let's get you some clothes first," I said, though I much rather would have preferred to lie in bed and drink up his warmth.

He let out a grunt and helped me to the bed before searching my closet for clothes. As I watched him dress I couldn't help but dread the upcoming conversation.

It had been horrible when the others were all against me...but what about Rosie?

She must have been upset and given how she had reacted before to us hiding things...I would assume that I would not be let off easy this time. I had messed up too bad and it didn't matter if they were able to escape unscathed, they shouldn't have even been taken in the first place.

But you deserve it, don't you? Their anger? Their hatred?

The little voice that had been telling me what a piece of shit I was came back with a vengeance.

I deserved her anger. All of their feelings of betrayal and hurt were warranted...but I didn't *want* her to hate me. I wanted to go back to normal, that was why I did this whole thing in the first place.

I wanted to have a chance to live out a life with the people I loved without being afraid that they were going to get hurt because of me. I saw what was happening to me and finally I took the chance to stop it, but it all backfired.

"Do you hate me?" I asked as a fully dressed Amr came to help me up from my seat.

He paused, his golden eyes meeting mine.

"I could never hate you Daxton," he said. The heaviness in his voice caused my chest to ache. "I think you made some poor decisions, but Rosie and I are alive. And I think I can understand why you did it."

I averted my gaze to the floor.

"But that doesn't make it right," I said and gripped onto his arm.

He gave me a small smile.

"No, it doesn't," he agreed. "But I am not a person who determines right or wrong."

I let out a light laugh that sent bursts of pain through me.

"Then who is?' I asked.

His eyebrows pushed together, and his lips formed a pout.

"Long ago I would have said the Originals..." he trailed. "But I don't think that's true anymore."

"Then who should I look to?" I asked, my heart pounding in my chest.

"Yourself," he answered. "Look to yourself for the answer."

* * *

I began to hate this foyer.

Even if we got past everything, I may not be able to look at this place again.

In front of me stood Rosie. Her hair was a mess and she had deep-set bags under her eyes. She had looked just as bad as Amr, and I didn't miss her ripped clothes or new scars on her arms. By her side were Malik and Rae, both of their arms brushing across hers. They were overpowering, both of them staring into me, though I couldn't decipher either of their expressions.

Eli was to the side of Malik, their eyes trained on Rosie. Even without a power I could hear the thoughts running through their mind and prayed that Rosie could get at least some time to heal before Eli released their pent-up anger on her.

Maximus and Claudine were to my right, their magic swirling around them and ready for any other fights, though I hoped it wouldn't come to that. Amr was to my left, his magic engulfing me like a blanket. His hand was threaded through mine, and it was what gave me the strength to look Rosie in the eyes.

I didn't like what was happening here. I didn't want us to fight like this.

There was a clear division amongst the group, and it weighed on me heavily that *I* was the one to cause this. We weren't perfect before, but at least it wasn't like there was a *war* dividing us.

"I made a deal with her," Rosie said, her voice bouncing off the walls of the foyer. "From now on we do not speak her name. She has cursed me, so if I spoke her name she would be able to listen in and if she wanted to, find us."

The group shifted, their eyes darting to each other. My heart lodged into my throat and my mouth went dry. We were not safe here; we were not safe anywhere.

"I had promised that we protect her from other Originals," Rosie continued, her eyes trailing to Malik. "We use *The Fallen* to provide for her, and I share some of my blood with her and find willing witches to share with her."

Malik looked obviously uncomfortable at the thought of using his gang for Xena, but he nodded slowly anyways.

"I can contact some of my guys," he muttered. His eyes darted to Eli then back to Rosie. "Get her shelter and food, but I can't promise witches."

Rosie nodded.

"We will have to figure something out when the time comes," she said. Her hand came to rub the tattoo on her forearm, and I only now noticed how gnarled and ugly it had become. The once beautiful raven was barely recognizable due to all the deep scars on her skin that ran right through its center.

"What do we get?" Eli growled. "This is a lot of trouble to go through for a fucking *Original*."

I didn't say it out loud but I agreed with Eli. Xena was more than capable of taking care of herself. She had proven as much by literally kidnapping Rosie and Amr. Just one look at the state of them was enough to know that Xena was still a *very real* threat.

"To remain free," Rosie grumbled, her eyes narrowing at Eli.

"Where is she now?" Rae asked with a sigh. Her eyes flashed to Eli and gave them a warning look before looking back down at Rosie. Her face softened when Rosie's eyes met hers and another stab of guilt hit me.

Rosie faltered, her eyes passing to Amr's. There was a silence that fell upon us and Amr shifted closer to me. Rosie looked back towards the ground before she spoke.

"She had us in Winterfell, though I do not think she will remain there," she said and there was a powerful tidal wave that seemed to go through the group, raising all of our invisible hackles.

She was at that fucking school this whole time?

If I wasn't held up in my room maybe I would have been able to feel her and save her from everything she had gone through, instead of her having to make this God-awful deal with Xena.

"You were in Winterfell this whole time?" Eli growled.

Malik lifted their hand, as if that gesture was enough to calm them but it only made Eli's face contort even more.

"In the dungeons," she said. "There is a forgotten section of the school behind Winterfell. She kept us there, rigged it with her magic. I didn't know until she had let us out."

I had to avert my gaze to my feet as all eyes swung to me.

"I'm sorry, Rosie," I said in a low whisper.

"Sorry?" Eli scoffed. I heard their feet across the floor as they walked towards me. "You should have thought of that before you went to that son—"

"Silence," Malik spoke. I could feel the edges of his power tickle my skin and leaned into Amr for strength. "Get back."

Eli's footsteps receded but I couldn't look up as all eyes were still on me.

A dungeon. A fucking dungeon.

I heard Rosie cross the room. Her magic was weak, but it still tried to curl around me, to comfort me.

Her delicate hand, the one that was so soft yet so deadly, gripped my chin and forced me to look in her eyes. She trailed it to my cheek and I closed my eyes waiting for the slap but instead she just cupped it.

"You must be hurting," she whispered. "I am sorry that I wasn't there to listen to your troubles."

My eyes shot open and I was met with her sad smile. My chest exploded and it became hard to breathe.

"*No,*" I breathed. "Don't say that."

Please, please don't say this to me.

I wondered how I had not been drowned by my own guilt. It consumed me, tore at my insides, and brought me deep into the abyss with it. She watched me fall apart in front of her. Tears filled my eyes and for the life of me I couldn't figure out how to make my lungs work.

"It was hard, wasn't it?" she asked, her eyes trailing down my form. "And you were all alone through it all."

Please don't comfort me. Please don't understand me.

"If I had known how much you were hurting. How *scared* you were of losing yourself and your life to your magic," she said. "Then I would have worked harder to stop this from happening. That's why you did it, isn't it Daxton?"

I swallowed thickly and opened my mouth to speak but no words came out.

"It's okay," Amr said by my side.

I nodded while gritting my teeth. Sobs threatened to pull out of my chest as they comforted me.

"I thought so," she said in a low tone. Her face dropped, sadness seeming like it was carved into it. "I'll be better. I am sorry I overlooked this. You have been so kind to me, so loving, yet I couldn't even see your struggles... I am sorry Daxton."

Her words were like a punch to the gut and were the final thing that forced the tears out of my eyes. I didn't care that the others saw me like this. All I cared about was that Rosie was here, in front of me, and while it may have been easier for her to be mad at me, she had decided to forgive me and understand my struggles instead.

My entire life I had felt like my struggles were invisible. My parents hid what they did and only until I met Eli and Rae was I able to finally be with people who *saw* me...but this was different. Amr and Rosie saw me like no other. To them I wasn't this strong witch with uncontrollable magic that would burn everything in its path.

I was just *Daxton*.

Scared, upset, hurt Daxton, but Daxton nonetheless.

You don't deserve her, Eli said in my mind. My eyes shot to them to see that they were glaring daggers at me.

I don't, I said back because it was true. I never deserved her.

Watch out because even if she forgives you, I sure as hell do not, they growled in my mind.

Rosie stiffened and looked back towards Eli.

"I don't know what you are saying to Daxton," she said, her voice dropping low. "But whatever you just said to me was unacceptable. Don't forget that not too long ago you had killed two demons in cold blood. Daxton didn't sit there and berate you and I will not allow you to do it to him."

Eli looked like they wanted to murder the both of us, but their mouth stayed shut due to Malik's power.

Rosie turned back to me with a smile.

"Now," she said and took a step back, turning around to look at the group. "I think we have some planning to do."

Chapter 20
Eli

I f Rosie didn't make my chest hurt as much as it did, I would have fucking killed her by now.

How could she just forgive Daxton like that? *And* have the audacity to look at me as if *I* was the bad person.

She was willing to forgive Daxton for *literally* handing her over to Xena, but wouldn't forgive me for taking out the people that had hurt her?

It wasn't fair and she had gone back to ignoring me.

But I would change that soon enough.

It was night and it had been a week since Rosie had come back from Xena's torture chamber. For the last few days, I had watched her leave every bed that she crawled into and make her way into the library.

I waited day after day in the shadows to see what she had been up to, but after a while I had come to the conclusion that she had just been reading. Tonight, I had waited for an hour and a half in the corner of the dark library and watched as Rosie grabbed the same book she had been reading two days ago. It wasn't a large book by any means, and I could tell by her thoughts that she had read the same thing over and over again, but I didn't understand why.

I stalked through the bookshelves careful not to alert her of my presence. I paused when I was twenty feet away and listened for any sign of her hearing me, and quickly sidestepped in between the bookshelves closest to me, making sure my entire body was concealed by books.

A picture of the empty library filled her mind. She focused on the shadows of the library further down and the possible monstrous things that they hid...but she wasn't scared.

She was intrigued and she already knew that I had been waiting.

I let her stew in her own thoughts, enjoying the way she imagined me lurking in the darkness.

Even though she knew I was there, I didn't want to give in just yet. I wanted to catch her off guard. For once, I wanted to wipe that smugness right out of her and make her pay for ignoring me.

She went back to reading her book and I waited a few more minutes before slowly peeking out from around the corner. Her back was to me, and she was curled onto one of the love sofas. Her hair was up in a messy bun and she was wearing an oversized shirt. I hoped she had nothing else underneath.

I stalked closer to her, my heart beating rapidly in my chest. A buzz of excitement ran through me as I realized that she was just where I wanted her.

God I couldn't wait to have her all to myself.

All of the anger and panic that had taken control over my mind while she was gone began to rise directly up to the surface. I had to clench my hands and dig my nails into my palms to stop myself from lunging forward and taking her right here and now.

I took a deep, silent breath and closed the gap between me and her. I clamped my hand down on her mouth and used my other head to squeeze her throat. Her mind was panicked as she tried to understand what was going on.

She knew something was in the darkness waiting for her.

She knew it was a monster.

She knew it was *me.*

She relaxed against my hold and tried to peer up at me but I used my hands to keep her head in place.

"You really think that you could leave me like that? Ignore me after everything?" I asked. She tried to talk against my hand but it came out muffled.

What are you doing? she asked in her mind.

"I am here to remind you of my existence," I said. "I am here to get payback."

Payback for what? she asked in her mind.

"Payback for you *ignoring* me," I growled. "Just because I murdered some people you think it's okay to give me the cold shoulder. Yet, when

Daxton literally sells you out to the person who *ruined* your life, you treat him like a *kicked puppy.* Tell me how that makes sense."

She didn't answer. Even her mind was silent. She was only thinking of how tightly I was gripping her throat. How my hot breath felt against her skin...and how utterly *drenched* she was.

"Tell me," I demanded again.

You and Daxton are different, she said in her mind.

Her heart was pounding. I could feel it against my hand that was clamped tightly on her throat. But that didn't dampen how excited she was. If anything, the fear *fueled* her desire.

She knew I was stalking her in the distance, and she was waiting for me to take advantage. She had been waiting for days and finally I'd come to give her what she needed.

"How are we different?" I asked dropping my voice to a whisper. I rubbed my thumb against the expanse of her throat, reveling in the softness of her skin.

You know how, she replied in my mind. I removed my hand from her mouth and squeezed her throat tighter. She took a sharp intake of breath and arched her back off the chair.

"I'm gonna take my time with you tonight," I threatened.

A powerful shot of heat ran through my body when she thought of exactly how I was going to punish her tonight. She thought of all the times that we were in my room together, all the times I made her come over and over and over again while she begged me to stop.

She liked it. She *liked* to be treated like this. But only because it was *me.*

"In here?" she asked.

Instead of answering her I pulled her up by her throat and swung her over the chair. She tried to fight me, but it was no use. I took her and slammed her up against the nearest shelf. Her pained thoughts filled the room as her head hit the hard wood, but they were quickly wiped from her mind when it became obvious where I was going with this. My hand slipped underneath her shirt and I wasn't surprised to see that she only had a pair of skimpy panties underneath. Without prior warning, she threw her head back as my thumb brushed across her clit.

She tried to pull me closer.

"Right now," I growled. "Is only going to be a little *taste* of what you can get. Think of it as me showing you how much I've *missed* you. And the punishment...will come later."

She swallowed thickly, her brown eyes washing over my face.

"Tell me," I continued and rubbed the length of her wet folds slowly. "How long were you sitting there in your own wetness?"

She shuddered and gripped onto the wrist that still held her throat. When she didn't answer I lifted her up higher, making sure her feet were off the ground.

I made sure not to choke her hard enough that she would lose consciousness, but I wanted her to know how close the line she had been walking was. I wanted her to know how many times I had wished she was anyone else so I could have ended it all by now.

She let out a whine as I pushed two fingers into her tight hole. She tried to put her leg up on one of the shelves but quickly lost balance. I pumped my fingers into her lazily and held her gaze as her big brown eyes widened and swam with tears.

God she was so perfect like this.

Her pink lips were parted and her breaths came out in small pants as I fucked her slowly. I had always been so fast and hard with her, but I realized something slow and painful like this would be just what she needed for later.

I brushed my thumb across her clit and she jerked in my hold.

"How long?" I whispered. "Don't tell me you came to this place just to tempt me?"

She let out a pained whine and spread her legs as I thrust into her, pulling me in deeper than before.

"The whole week," she said in a strangled moan. "I knew you would come. I wanted you to come."

I let out a laugh and rewarded her with a brush of my thumb over her clit.

"You can pull my hair," I whispered and placed a kiss on her lips before putting her back on the ground and falling to my knees in front of her.

Her face was filled with confusion until I began pulling her panties down.

She quickly stepped out of them and I was eye level with her perfectly swollen cunt. I licked my lips and ran my hand up the length of her right leg. She shuddered as I trailed kisses on her inner thigh.

"In my hair," I growled and nipped her thigh.

Her hands flew to my hair and pulled at the strands like her life depended on it. I met her gaze as I dove forward and trailed my tongue from her entrance to her clit. I couldn't help but moan into her as her taste hit my tongue.

It hadn't been long, realistically I knew that...but in that moment it felt like I hadn't been able to touch her for years.

Hunger, desire, and heat flared inside of me and I found myself unable to hold back. I attacked her core, sucking on her clit, fucking her tight entrance with my tongue, and gripped her bare ass while pulling her impossibly closer to myself.

"Eli!" she whined and arched into me.

I couldn't remember the last time I had hungered for her so fiercely. Of course, Rosie was everything to me, but right now in this moment, I felt like a raging beast.

I sank two fingers back inside her so I could fuck her while sucking on her clit. She began shaking against me and I picked up the pace.

I wasn't gentle. I devoured her. I didn't care if I was too rough as I entered a third finger. I didn't care if anyone heard her and came to investigate as I curled my fingers inside her. And I sure as fuck didn't give a damn when she began to scream my name at the top of her lungs when I bit down on her swollen clit.

She came violently, her juices dripping all over my face and she clenched around my fingers, but I couldn't bring myself to stop. I *needed* more. I needed her to beg me to stop. To lose her mind with me. I needed her to think of nothing else but the way I felt inside her.

"Elie, *Eli*," she moaned. "Please. *Enough.*"

She was writhing under me as I continued to fuck her with my drenched hand and mouth over her clit. The grip on my hair became stronger and she curled over my head, her pants filling the silent library.

"Ah *fuck*," she groaned and began to sob as I gave her clit another long suck. "Shit, if you don't stop I'm going to come again."

I let out a growl and continued to suck on her clit.

That's the point, little Original, I said in her mind. *Come for me and I will let you rest.*

"I can't," she moaned aloud and her cunt began to flutter around my fingers. "My magic—it's not—"

She cut off mid-sentence and threw her head back, causing a loud bang to ring out into the library.

This time when she did come there was bright red sparkles that filled the air, but if you looked closer you could see every few sparkles there was a pitch-black one that barely showed in the dim light of the library.

Instead of mentioning it I stood up, pulling my fingers from Rosie and made her watch as I sucked off her juices from my fingers then leaned down to give her a taste of it.

"It's going to be a long night for you," I whispered against her lips.

* * *

I have found that I rather like tying Rosie up and watching her struggle while I make her come.

Maybe it was the helplessness in her eyes. Or the fact that for once, in this room she was all mine and couldn't do anything but take what I had given her.

After we had finished in the library I carried her to my room as I continued to finger her swollen pussy. After all, I needed her ready for this moment.

I had her tied to the bed, with her ass in the air. Her knees were shaking as I forced them to spread even further so I could get a look at her dripping pussy. The sight of a bejeweled plug between her cheeks caused heat to swirl in my belly.

"Are you ready for it?" I asked her as I spread her folds open with my fingers.

Her face had been pushed into the blanket and all I heard from her was a muffled groan.

She wasn't ready, not for what I had in store for her.

I brought the wand vibrator to her clit and turned it on the highest setting. She writhed and tried to move away from it. Her clit was painfully swollen and even just this light touch sent her mind into a frenzy.

I held her hips in place with one hand and forced her to stay still as I pushed the vibrator hard into her sensitive nub.

"*Fuck!*" she screamed into the blanket and just as I felt her body clench, getting ready for an orgasm, I pulled it away.

She let out a string of curses and let out a pained sob. We had been doing this for the last twenty minutes and I made sure that she didn't come, not even once. I dipped my fingers into her and let her rock her hips back into my hand.

"You think you can come like this?" I asked her as she began fucking my hand.

She widened her knees trying to take me deeper but as soon as she tried I pulled my finger out of her. She cursed at me again.

"Eli, please," she begged and tilted her head to the side to look at me behind her. Her face was tear-stricken and there was a tremble in her voice.

"It doesn't feel good to be strung along, does it?" I asked and cupped her pussy before pulling away and hitting her clit with a light slap.

"Fuck," she groaned. "Do that again."

I let out a chuckle and leaned down so I could lick her dripping wetness off her leg. She arched back, giving me a perfect view to her aching pussy. To be nice I gave her clit a small kiss.

I stood and started to undress before climbing back into the bed, but this time I lay next to Rosie and sent her a smirk. I reached towards the vibrator that was discarded on the bed and turned it on full blast. I let her watch as I brought it towards my own clit.

I let out a low moan as pleasure burst through me.

"You're gonna watch as I take what you can't have," I said and let out a breathy moan. I arched against the bed feeling the powerful vibrations wrack my body.

This whole time while I had been punishing her, I had been positively aching and needed release if I wanted to continue.

She tried to tug at her restraints but frowned when she realized how tightly I had tied them.

"Let's share," she said quickly.

I shook my head feeling my orgasm quickly sneak up on me after so many weeks of being denied.

"Please, Eli," she begged. "I want to come with you. Let me be on top."

I let out a harsh laugh that came out choked as my body froze. Heat spread throughout my limbs before settling deep in my belly.

"Turn over," I ordered.

She quickly twisted her restraints and turned so that she was on her back. I placed one leg between her legs and the other on the outside of her hip. With one hand on her hip I angled us so that our lips were almost touching, then pushed the still vibrating toy between us.

She let out a choked scream as it assaulted her clit. I let a low moan and forced our hips closer together. Even as she orgasmed I continued to keep the vibrator between us, intent on both of us getting a second orgasm.

I leaned over her, unable to keep myself up as heat swirled in my belly.

"Fuck, fuck, *fuck*," I groaned. "Rosie, I'm coming."

"Keeping going," she moaned. "Come with me, Eli."

And I did. I came so hard I saw stars behind my eyelids and fell onto her sweaty chest afterwards. I threw the vibrator across the room, not caring that it was still on.

"I love you," she breathed.

Warmth exploded in my chest.

"Do you?" I asked panting. I didn't want to look in her eyes. "Even after everything?"

"Even after everything," she said.

I fisted the comforter next to us, feeling a sudden anxiousness fill me.

"Even if I am not the...*girl* you first met?" I asked, unable to add on anything else.

I had never spoken these words, not like this and I didn't know how she would react. Hell, I didn't even know *how* I would react. The words just spilled out of me without thinking and there was no way to take them back.

"I love Eli for Eli," she answered. I felt tears prick my eyes. "Eli doesn't even have to love me back if it's too hard. *That* I would understand but nothing, and I mean *nothing*, will stop me from loving you."

Tears fell freely onto her overheated skin. Never in my life had I felt so vulnerable and protected at the same time than I did right now.

"And if...*Eli* did l-love you?" I asked.

The answer lit up their mind so bright that it hurt.

"I would be overjoyed," she answered. "But Eli can love me when Eli is ready to."

I nodded and buried my face into her soft skin.

"I'm sorry," I breathed. "I thought it would make you happy."

I *know,* she said in her mind.

In that moment I saw how clearly she saw me. More so than anyone I had ever met in my life. She saw right through the surface level Eli and knew exactly want I needed and why I acted the way I did.

It was frighteningand I wanted to run, but against every wish I stayed curled up in her arms.

"I forgive you," she said. "But it's not just up to me. Just like Daxton, you endangered the others as well."

"Please don't ask me to beg them for forgiveness," I groaned.

She let out a laugh.

"I won't," she said. "Though I would push you to be more agreeable to them."

"Fine," I grumbled. "But only for you."

"That will do," she said and ran her hands through my hair.

"I really do love you Eli," she said in a whisper.

"I know," I answered, and for now...that was enough.

Chapter 21
Rosie

This time when I went to the bar in the middle of the magical district, I went alone.

Not because I wasn't worried about my mother, I was, but I didn't want to bring anyone else into this. Bringing Amr in last time was a mistake and I couldn't forgive myself for fucking this up again.

It was about three in the morning and the street was still littered with seedy-looking witches that stared at me as I passed. I could feel their magic brush up against my sides, trying to get as much of a feel of me as possible.

Even though it felt invasive and their magic stuck to me in a way that made my skin crawl, I didn't give them a second glance as I rounded the side of the bar. I quickly flashed my magic and the hidden door opened to my right. Just like before, a small steady stream of magic poured out of its doors, inviting me in. This time I didn't hesitate to step in.

As soon as my foot passed over the threshold, there was an audible still in the air and the many witches there all turned to stare. I should have been used to the attention by now, but my gut reaction was to still duck my face and hide from them. Instead, I squared my shoulders and searched the place.

My eyes stopped at the same booth I had been in last time and just like before there was a hooded figure, presumably waiting for me. Her magic was the most notable and even though my magic had yet to return to its full capacity, I could feel the powerful aura she exuded.

If I was any wiser, I would walk straight out of here and get as far away from this person as possible...but tonight I was going to act recklessly because there was no more time to waste. Xena had taken me *and* the people I loved. She had torn apart my life and many others' just for her selfish desire to be worshipped. Hundreds of people still tried to move on with their life after the town had collapsed, but they were in a new world and had no idea how the environment around them worked.

The effects of her cruelty would last on for millions of years to come and I was not about to let it go on for any longer than I already had.

With a deep breath, I signaled the bartender. He was standing behind the black bar polishing some glasses. He had not taken his eyes off me since I had walked in and jumped when I made eye contact with him. Unlike the people that were in here, he didn't seem like he belonged. If anything, he looked like he would fit right into Winterfell.

A pity.

"Two of her regular," I ordered, jerking my head to the occupied booth before turning and walking towards it.

She didn't even stir as I walked around the booth and sat across from her. There was a small smile that spread across her lips as her eyes met mine. I had worn a hoodie today and pulled the hood up so I was hiding my face. The action seemed to amuse her. After all, both of our magic was so powerful that a hood—or a cloak in her case—wouldn't do us much good. As soon as we got close, people could feel our magic. Perhaps even from miles away if they were proficient.

I had tried to search Marques's memories to get a glimpse of this girl, but that had ended up failing me. The small glimpse of his power had been but a taste of what I was really capable of and I prayed that I would be able to access his power once more before I faced Xena again.

The fire trick would only work so many times.

We didn't speak until the bartender came over with our drinks. The familiar swirling pink liquid greeted us and without hesitation I brought it to my lips and took a hearty gulp.

Instead of the expected burn of alcohol, the liquid spread a delightful warmth in my mouth down my throat and to my belly. It was a sweet liquid, but didn't taste like any fruit I had eaten before. Something like a mix between a lychee, a mango, and a...strawberry?

"You knew I would come," I noted and her hand popped out of her cloak to grip the drink. There was no drink in front of her and my seat was cold, meaning that she had been here for quite a while doing nothing.

"That *is* my specialty," she said with a twinkle in her eye. She took a slow sip, watching me with interest. Her tone was playful and it took me a moment to realize that she was playing me.

I took a deep breath and gripped my cup harder than I should have. The witches around us were watching and it only added to my anxiety.

"I've come to see if—"

"The answer is no," she said cutting me off, and took another sip. Her expression was cool now, all of the playfulness lost and I was met with the same girl I had met when I first came here.

My mouth dropped open and I gave her an incredulous look. Panic and disbelief ran rampant through my body.

"It's an *Original*," I hissed, leaning closer and dropping my voice to a whisper.

A smile spread across her lips and she leaned in closer as well.

"I am not *interested* in sharing magic with her," she said, matching my tone.

Anger pricked at my senses and my magic sprang to life inside me. It was hot and burned my insides. It wanted me to rush forward and destroy this girl, even though we both knew I would lose.

"She has stronger magic than I," I countered, hoping to sway her.

This was supposed to be our last chance. Our one-way ticket out of here.

"It's *tainted*," she said her voice full of disgust. She leaned back and sent me a look. "And yours will be too if you don't stop partaking in *cannibalism*."

I shuddered at the thought of eating more demon flesh. She watched me as I took in her words. She knew I was desperate, but how could you sway someone like her? I had no leverage or anything I could offer her...

"Bloodletting then," I said. "But I need two things from you."

A sinister smile spread across her face.

"*That's* more like it," she purred and leaned forward. The hood slipped just enough for me to get a glimpse of her impossibly young face. "I will agree to identify the curse but I *will not* be getting anywhere close to your mother."

I grumbled and took another drink of my liquid.

It was impossible to keep anything from her now.

I had come here with the intention of having her help me set up my mother, but apparently that was a no-go. I could understand her hesitancy, but at this point I was feeling like I was running out of options.

"You're on the right track," she said suddenly, her fingers trailing the rim of her glass. "But trapping her only works if she trusts you enough to stray from her path."

I tapped my fingers across the sticky table, cringing.

Getting Xena to trust me would be impossible, especially after I had proven how much I hated her. I tried to kill her for God's sake and the way she let me go was with a promise to tend to her forever and a fucking curse on me.

"But she won't," I grumbled and leaned back against the bar seat.

The bar around us had returned to its normal hum of conversation, leaving us completely forgotten in our dark corner. I wished at times to be as oblivious as the witches around me. To enjoy sharing magic and all the perks that being a witch brought, but I didn't dream for too long because as much as I wanted to forget and move on, Xena would end up following us forever if I didn't do something.

"Not if you give her something she wants," she said, her tone low. "Maybe a certain freckled hybrid?"

My body froze and I sat up straight. My magic flared out around me and I had to dig my fingernails into my thigh in order to keep myself seated.

"*No,*" I growled.

The witch shrugged and took another sip of her drink.

"Then good luck trying to convince her otherwise," she said. "Unless you have another Original handy, it would be in your best interest to use something she *actually* wants."

"We can track her," I said. "The issue is just—"

"Catching her before she runs," she interrupted. "I know."

I ran a hand through my hair and sighed.

"Look," the witch said and leaned forward, her voice dropping into a low whisper. "I have seen *every* possible outcome for this fight and let me tell you, *this* is the only way that you will be able to get out of this with *all* of your loved ones alive."

I paused and looked her over. It was a surprise that Xena and Ezekiel had not gone after her. With a power this powerful I started to wonder if there was anything she *didn't* know.

I leaned closer to her as well. Her magic wrapped around me and while it felt warm, I wouldn't mistake her actions as friendly. In front of me was someone even more dangerous than Xena.

"Why are you even helping me?" I asked. "This goes way above blood-letting."

She gave me a sad smile.

"It's for Amber," she answered.

Amber's sickly face flashed through my mind and I tried to avoid thoughts of her burning body. It still hurt to think of her, even after so long. I wished to have done more.

"What was she to you?" I asked. "She told me she didn't have any—"

"An unrequited love," she answered quickly then sat back. "That's all."

I cleared my throat feeling my cheeks flush. So even beings like her could love.

"Rosie," she said in a serious tone. "Take my advice, please. Use him and get your loved ones out alive. She may be weak now but even in my mind's eye I can see her hiding something."

I swallowed thickly and nodded.

"I will think about it," I said and moved to stand. Just as I was about to leave the booth her hand shot out to catch my wrist.

"Don't take too long," she warned. "Whatever it is she was using your blood for is now almost complete."

* * *

I stared at Rae's mom, with the conversation from earlier running through my mind.

I refused to use Ren as a pawn. I couldn't chance him going through the same thing that I had. He was my *brother* for God's sake.

We had just begun to build a relationship I so desperately wanted and now this fucking seer witch was asking me to throw it all away?

As if she had heard me talking about her, I felt a burst of familiar magic at my side.

"You're going to get us in trouble," I warned and shot a glance at the intruder.

She wore her hood even during the day, but this time I got a good look at her deep red dress she was wearing underneath. Her eyes narrowed on the body in front of me.

"Too late," she said and in an instant there was another flash of magic at my side.

I shot out of my seat quickly and placed myself between the small witch and the newest witch.

Claudine gave me a look when she saw me trying to protect the intruder.

The door burst open and a panting Maximus stumbled into the room, followed by a concerned-looking Rae. Her eyes drifted towards her mother and she let out an audible sigh.

"She is here to help," I said quickly. "I have a deal with her."

Amr and a pale-looking Daxton pushed into the room not a moment later.

I rolled my eyes and let out a sigh as I felt a pounding headache bloom behind my eyes.

"She is here to *help*," I hissed as low growls filled the room.

The witch leaned to the side and by the look on Daxton's face I bet she was smirking at him.

"Cumae?" he asked, then his eyes shot towards me. "Please tell me you didn't—"

So that was her name.

"I wouldn't if I were you," Cumae sang from behind me.

I sent her a look.

"Can you please do what you came here to do?" I asked, feeling the rising tension in the room grate on my nerves.

She lowered her hood and for the first time I caught a full look at her bright pink hair and young face.

"What is a child doing here?" Eli's voice rang from the doorway.

I let out a deep sigh and rubbed my finger over my temples.

"She's not a child," Rae and Maximus growled in unison.

"Can everyone just trust me for a minute?" I huffed and shot a glare towards the group.

Even Malik had come up and stood towards the back, behind everyone else. He was the first to speak.

"Do what you need to," he said and sent me a forced smile.

I nodded towards him and turned back to Cumae. She was sitting on the edge of Rae's mother's bed and was leaning over her, meeting her vacant expression.

"What did you do to deserve this?" she muttered and then leaned forward, inhaling her scent. Her eyes widened and a low chuckle rose from her.

"I won't like this will I?" I asked.

Cumae leaned back and met my gaze with a smile.

"Say, what kind of trouble do you have to be in to be cursed by an Original?" she asked, then her eyes drifted towards Rae. "I would say your mother knew something she shouldn't, though only the Original could tell you that."

Rae stepped forward to speak but I motioned for her to wait.

"There is only one Original witch left in the area," I pointed out.

Her smile widened to show her gnarled and grey teeth.

"Seems the problems with your mother don't just stop at you and your brother, hm?" she asked and jumped off the bed to stand in front of me. She reached out a childlike hand for me.

Without hesitation I gave her my arm. She pulled a palm-sized jar out of her cloak and popped off the lid with her thumb.

I conjured a weapon with my magic and winced as I dug it into my own arm. I vanished the weapon and waited. Blood slowly flowed from the wound and she used the small jar to collect it.

"This is much better than I thought you intended," I said.

Her eyes met mine for a brief moment and she focused her gaze back onto the falling droplets.

"No one wants to do *that* with someone stuck in a child's body," she said, bitterness laced in her voice.

"Is that what happened with Amber?" I muttered, not caring about our crowd.

She sent me a look.

"Not exactly…" she trailed and ran her hand over my wound, healing it for me. The jar was only filled up halfway but I didn't mention it. "I stayed this way hoping one day when we ran into each other she would recognize me, but alas your mother has continued to ruin every single life that she has touched and now I will be forced to wander this earth in this form, looking for a lover whose body has long grown cold in hopes to find her soul one day."

My heart twisted when her sad eyes met mine. I swallowed thickly, not ready for the onslaught of emotions that hit me like a train. I didn't know Amber had someone to care for her, and in some sick way it made me feel better that she didn't leave this world without someone loving her.

"I hope you find her one day," I whispered and brought my arm to my chest, rubbing where the cut had just been.

"Me too, cursed one," she said.

Marques's old nickname jarred me and a memory of a flash of pink hair ran through my mind. Marques may have not known her but he had seen her once, long ago when the world was still young.

"I won't see you again," I said, coming to the realization that her job here was just about done.

She shook her head and gave me a small smile.

"Not that I can see," she said and got a dreamy look in her eyes. "Though even I cannot see every path this future has for us. So until next time."

I nodded and took a step back, watching as she disappeared from sight.

"Remember what I said," she whispered, her voice wrapping around me like a warm burst of magic. I could still feel her in the room but her magic had slowly begun to disappear until we were left alone in this room.

"So what now?" Eli asked, breaking the spell her words had put me under.

I sent them a shaky smile.

"Now we end this," I answered with a weak voice. "But we have to prepare, gain her trust, then when she is least expecting it, strike."

"When is the first drop?" Rae asked.

"Tomorrow," I answered and wiped my sweaty palms on my pants. "And you and Malik are the ones coming with me."

"Why not us?" Amr asked, his voice filled with outrage.

I swallowed thickly.

"We are getting her to trust us," Malik answered for me. "And what better way to show up than with her ex-lackey and the person who is in charge of all our assets?"

A still fell over the room.

"That's asking for her to strike," Eli grumbled.

I didn't have answers, because yes, that was the whole point. If she chose to take us out there the rest of the group would be fucked. We would have no home, no money, no protectors. The only thing that would be here would be Maximus and Claudine, but they could just as easily wash their hands of everything and be done with it.

"It's the right choice," Daxton said, his voice husky as if he hadn't drank water in days. "Risky, but it would show her that we are willing to work with her."

I nodded and took a deep, calming breath.

"If there is no more discussion I would like to rest," I said and looked towards Rae.

Without a word she held her hand out for me.

"Let's talk."

Chapter 22
Rae

I looked down at Rosie as her anxiety flared out of her in waves. A part of her was ready for what we were going to face tomorrow, but another part, the old her...was scared to face the mother that had cursed her again. I could feel both of them clashing inside her and along with her magic, it was a volatile combination.

I couldn't blame her though. I had my own reservations about the whole thing and at this point...I didn't even fully believe in what Xena had said. After *years* of trying to take control of a hybrid and bring them back to the powerful beings they once were, she just...let Rosie go?

That was not the Xena we knew.

Especially not after we had tried to literally burn her to death. It was suspicious at best and I wouldn't be surprised if there was another surprise waiting for us tomorrow when we met.

Malik was next to me. Our poses were the same, arms crossed and a scowl on our face; he was just as unhappy with this situation as I was, though he wouldn't show Rosie that. He needed to keep a cool and collected persona. He had exploded one too many times and each time it had cost us. He knew this now and so did I.

Right now was the make-it-or-break-it moment.

Rosie sat on the bed staring up at us with wide eyes. Whatever she was going to say was on the tip of her tongue, but she had refused to utter anything for the last ten minutes. She was being controlled by her thoughts; I could feel it in the way her emotions shifted every few seconds.

God, I wished Eli was here.

"Out with it," Malik demanded, though there was an obvious lack of his power in the air.

She let out a sigh and looked at her hands in her lap.

"That witch," she said. "She said she saw only a few ways that we would win this war with Xena and I wanted to tell you two before we mention anything to the rest."

My curiosity spiked along with Malik's. Rosie had made it clear that she didn't want any more secret-keeping.

"Why can't you tell the others?" I asked, raising a brow at her.

She shifted on the bed, her eyes darting to the floor. There was a spike of anger and worry inside her.

"Because she says I need to use my brother," she spat. "Give her something she wants in order for her to trust me."

Gods, I groaned internally. I gritted my teeth and balled my hands into fists. This wasn't good. I didn't know who this witch was, but this couldn't be the way.

"How do we even know we can even trust her?" I asked Rosie. "What if she is just going to hand you over to Xena? Or keep you to herself?"

She peeked up at me, her lips pulled into a pout.

"I told you," she said with a sigh. "I don't think she is in it to betray me or just for the blood."

There was something coming over her, a deep type of sadness that made my heart clench.

"What is she after, then?" I asked with a raised brow.

"I will give her blood..." she trailed. "But she said she also knew Amber."

I couldn't help the sigh that came out of my mouth. I wanted to trust Rosie. I really did, but I didn't like this witch.

"And why can't you say this to the rest of the group?" Malik asked.

There was a silence that fell around us, and no one wanted to speak.

It was because of Eli, I realized. They were the reason she couldn't let this get out because no doubt they would take her brother without even thinking about it. If they trusted Rosie and this witch, they would no doubt be the one to offer him up first.

They did it because they loved her in their own way...but they were impulsive and didn't know the difference between right and wrong. To them the world revolved around ending their boredom and Rosie...there was nothing in between.

"They will act on their own," Rosie said in a low voice. "I don't want to chance it or put anything in their head. But you two...I know you two will think through this rationally with me. I trust you."

Damn it.

She knew just what to say to make me bend for her.

"You should do it," Malik said in a hard tone.

I took my glasses off and rubbed my hand down my face. Frustration played at my mind and the exhaustion that had weighed on me from losing Rosie to now this seemed to double. I was ready to fall straight into bed with Rosie, only to wake up when this whole ordeal was over.

"Malik," I warned.

He was too much like Eli for his own good.

"What?" he asked sending me a look. "I believe Rosie when she says this person can be trusted. It's not every day you get a seer like her, couldn't you feel her power?"

"What about Claudine?" I asked and pinched the bridge of my nose.

"She's not as powerful as that one," he said. "She can't see into the future, she just *knows* things. It's different. If she could see into the future we wouldn't have gotten into any of this mess."

"Then can't she *know* a better way out of this?" I snapped.

"What's your issue?" Malik growled and turned towards me. He took a step forward, a growl erupting from his chest.

"My *issue* is that when Rosie mentions giving up her brother it feels like her chest is being torn in *two*," I growled but quickly pulled it back and looked towards Rosie. "Sorry I didn't mean to—"

"It's okay," she said cutting me off with a wave. "It's true, I don't want to hurt him and I would think that after your experience Malik, you would see my way."

Now *that* hurt Malik.

"I do," he said quickly. "I just care about you more."

Guilt rose in him quickly when he realized what he just said.

"I understand," she said and let out a heavy sigh, her shoulder slumping forward with the weight of her task. "I just *need* some time to think of something different."

"We have time," I said quickly cutting Malik off. I held my hand up and sent him a warning look. "We still have to gain her trust, right? Let's start to do that first *then* we can talk a bit more about how to end this."

Malik looked like he wanted to argue but instead sat down on the bed next to Rosie and laid down with a loud sigh.

"I'm staying with you all tonight," he said. "And don't you try to convince me otherwise, Rae."

I rolled my eyes and placed my glasses back on my face.

"I won't," I grumbled then held out my hand for Rosie. "Let's take our shower, shall we?"

Rosie perked up right away and stood up quickly.

"What's with you and showers?" Malik grumbled but stood up as well. "Don't think you pulled a quick one."

He sent me a glare and I simply smiled in return.

"I wouldn't think of it."

* * *

"Does that feel good Rosie?" I asked as her head fell into my chest.

She nodded and shuddered when I angled the showerhead slightly to the left, right onto her clit.

Her hands were digging into my arms as she let out a light moan. Malik let out a small laugh as he pulled her hips back into him, burying himself to the hilt inside her.

His hands were gripping her hips, right over some scars I had yet to have seen. They were both soaked, though I couldn't tell if it was from sweat or water at this point. Malik's colorful tattoos stood out against his skin and the all-white bathroom, and his white curly hair stuck to his face.

Rosie's long hair was sticking to her body and she looked up at me with a dazed expression. Her mouth was open and soft moans spilled out of her as she let us have our way with her. She fit snugly between the two of us and as much as I may have detested Malik mere minutes ago, I had no problem bringing him in here if he could make Rosie look like *that*.

"Now I know why you enjoy these showers so much," he said and pulled out of Rosie before burying himself inside her with a slow thrust.

I grabbed Rosie's chin and forced her to look in my eyes. Their arousal was so thick it threatened to choke me.

"Use your words, love," I whispered and placed a light kiss on the side of her mouth. She let out a moan as Malik thrust in again. "Slowly, Malik."

"Yes, ma'am," he growled and lifted her right leg to sink into her even deeper, both of their groans filling the bathroom.

"It feels so good, Rae," she moaned and as a reward I let her chin go and pulled on the handle to the showerhead, upping the water pressure. "Ah, yesss."

I brought my hand into her hair and ran my nails against her scalp, allowing her to put her head back on my chest. She let out a loud whine when Malik thrust into her again.

"Shh, you're doing so good," I cooed and kissed the top of her head. "Let us take care of you, hm?"

Malik listened to me, making sure each of his thrusts was painfully slow. I could see and feel that he was struggling against his instinct to fuck her like an animal, but I wanted this to be better for her. She had been through a lot and I wanted her to be able to enjoy this in a way she hadn't been able to.

I wanted her to feel the warmness that radiated from my chest as she shuddered into me. I wanted to show her that we could take care of her no matter what.

I wanted to reward her for trusting us so much.

"Yes," she panted. "Please take care of me."

Malik let out another chuckle and laid his head on Rosie's, both of them leaning into me.

"You really have her trained, don't you Rae?" he asked. "She's nothing like this when she's alone with me."

I felt Rosie's anger rise and I quickly pushed her head down into my chest and pushed the showerhead harder into her clit. She didn't hesitate to bring my nipple into her mouth and give a single long suck.

Pleasure shot straight to my core and I let out a light moan as her tongue circled my nipple.

"She just needs a bit of love, don't you Rosie?" I cooed and ran my fingernails across her scalp.

She let out a low groan and switched to the other nipple just as Malik gave her a sharp thrust, causing her to bite down.

I let out a hiss and Rosie tried to pull away, but I forced her head back down.

Malik met my gaze and I nodded. His white wet hair was stuck to his face, almost covering the devilish smile that crossed his face. He pulled Rosie's leg out even further and anchored her hips with his other hand before he began pounding into her.

Her mouth unlatched from my nipple but I still pulled her head to my chest and ran my fingers through her hair as he continued to thrust into her from behind.

"Fuck," she cried and I winced as her nails dug into my skin.

"That's it," I cooed. "You take him so well. Show us how good you'll be for him and come on his cock."

It wasn't long between the showerhead and Malik's thrusts that she came.

"Damn it," Malik groaned and thrust into her twice more before he came in her with a shudder.

I forced Rosie to look at me and planted a kiss on her lips before turning her head so Malik could claim one as well.

When it got a bit too heated I brought the shower up and let the water cascade down their heads. They broke away, both with differing looks of shock.

"We need to get cleaned and get ready for tomorrow," I said and turned to place the shower head back where it was supposed to be mounted. "The last thing we need is to be exhausted."

I handed them the shampoo bottles and focused on wetting my own hair. It wasn't a wash day but it had already gotten too wet while we played to let it go.

When I turned back, a warmness spread through my chest as I watched Malik lather Rosie's hair with shampoo with a small smile on his face. Rosie reached out and grabbed my hand, forcing me to step out of the spray.

Without having to ask, I bent down so she could reach my head. She gave me a beaming smile and poured a generous amount of shampoo into her hands before lathering it all over my hair. The warmth that radiated off the both of them was enough to make my head spin.

"You're happy," I noted. Her smile faltered and I used that chance to wash the shampoo out of my hair.

Malik pushed Rosie closer to me and I pulled her under the spray with me, helping her rinse out her shampoo.

"She deserves to be," Malik said as he lathered his own hair.

"You too," I said and grabbed the conditioner I kept for Rosie in my shower.

She accepted it with a smile and moved to give some to Malik, but I stopped her.

"He needs my type of conditioner," I said and reached behind me for it. It was made from coconut oil and shea butter; it worked better on our curlier hair than her straighter hair.

Malik sent me a look before pushing us both out of the way to wash his own hair.

"I never used this type before," he muttered, grabbing the conditioner from me.

"Obviously," I grumbled and took it from him to run it through my hair with my hands.

"You should give him that cream," Rosie said as she ran her own conditioner in her hair.

"I will," I said and sent Malik a look. "How long have you been on this earth and you still don't know how to take care of your hair?"

Malik rolled his eyes and dove forward to grab the conditioner from my hand, but I pulled it away from his grip.

"Let me do it," I said quickly. He raised a brow towards me but surprised me by leaning forward so I would better be able to run it through his hair. His golden eyes flashed with something akin to mischief.

"Is this my aftercare, Rae?" he asked, a smirk gracing his face.

It was my turn to roll my eyes.

"I just feel like I have a duty to teach you how to do your hair now that I know you had no idea," I said and poured a generous amount of conditioner on my hands before running it through his white strands.

He let out a deep groan as my nails scraped against his scalp. His eyes fluttered closed and he leaned into my hands.

"God," he moaned. "I'm showering with you from now on."

"Don't get any ideas," I growled.

He let out a chuckle.

"Let me guess, you find me repulsive?" he asked, his eyes opening to peer up at me.

I scoffed.

"I just don't like *dick,*" I growled.

Rosie let out a light laugh and wrapped her hands around my waist, her cheek against my back.

Malik let out a chuckle and stood. I quickly grabbed his wrist and pulled him out of the line of the water.

"You have to leave it for a few minutes," Rosie sang from behind me.

Malik frowned but folded his arms across his chest and leaned against the shower wall.

I did the same but pulled Rosie to me and helped her apply the conditioner to the ends of her hair.

We stewed in our own comfortable silence, listening to the water fall around us. Rosie let out a sigh and leaned into me. I felt a small spike of sadness from her and I quickly pushed her head into my chest.

"It's okay," I whispered and ran my hands down her arms and back. Malik shot me a look as Rosie wrapped her arms around my waist. "We are almost there."

"I thought it was over," she whispered, her voice barely audible over the falling water.

"It's okay," I said again as her sadness spiked even higher. I looked forward through the glass that separated the shower from the rest of the bathroom. I could see all of us in the shower, Rosie curled into me, hiding her face as she started to cry, and Malik staring at us unsure what to do. I could feel his anxiety rising by the second.

He *hated* when Rosie was upset.

"She's planning something," she said. "The witch can feel it."

I suspected as much. She let Rosie go too easily. In the past she would have kept Rosie and fought for her until her last dying breath, but if what Rosie said was true...it would point to a weakness that Xena wouldn't dare allow to be shown.

It was too convenient. The timing too perfect. And she hadn't even bothered us since the day Rosie walked out of her dungeon.

"We will live through it," I vowed, though it had no conviction because even I couldn't be certain.

"Are you sure?" Malik asked from my side. His eyes met mine in the mirror.

"No," I admitted. "But if we are smart, if we prepare...I am sure we can make it."

Rosie's sadness felt like a punch to the gut and when she stepped back to look at me with tears running down her face, I felt like my own heart was ripped out.

"I'm scared," she said.

"She's weak," Malik said and looked down towards Rosie. "We can take her if she ever tries—"

"Not that," I muttered once I felt Rosie's guilt rise.

Rosie sent Malik a strained smile.

"Sometimes Marques's memories make me..." She paused trying to find the words.

"Feel like a different person," I finished for her. "Make you feel invincible."

She nodded and sent a sheepish look towards Malik. Guilt filled his body so heavily it hung in the air around us.

"I caught myself, and Eli," she said. "Sometimes we act like different people and I don't want it to be our downfall."

I could feel the question before Malik asked it.

"Have you noticed that too, Rae?" he asked.

I shifted.

"Do you?" I asked back just as quickly.

I was met with silence.

"Wash out your hair," I said then looked back towards Rosie, wiping the tears from her face. "I can feel it, though I don't think I am as affected as you, Rosie and Eli seem to be. Even the memories don't bother me at times."

The lie was sour in my mouth, but I didn't want them to worry any more than they had to.

"And the powers," Malik asked as he washed out his hair. "What about those?"

I sighed and pushed Rosie towards Malik who accepted her with open arms.

"I think I can feel them at times, but I also don't know what I am looking for most of the time," I admitted.

"I—" Malik took a deep breath. "I think it has to do with how diluted it was. Marques was dying, his powers weren't as strong and he *ate* more of them than we did."

Bile threatened to force its way up my throat.

So we had some type of extra powers that seemed to help us in only the moment of consumption, a portion of his spotty memories...and that was it?

There had to be more, didn't there?

We had committed the greatest grievances our kind had done and this was what we were left with?

Marques's frail and breakable body flashed through my mind.

He had waited a long time to give himself to us and maybe it could have been in order to protect us, or save us from the hell that awaited those who feasted on Originals.

"Wait," I trailed. "But my...*magic* wasn't affected."

Rosie's eyes shifted to mine. There was a tension in the room. None of us had really discussed it *since then* but here it was now and out in the open. We couldn't hide from it now.

"It's also probably too weak," Rosie said.

Malik nodded along and crossed his arms over his wet chest, his skin glistening in the light of the bathroom.

"We got lucky," he said in a low tone. "We don't *want* what comes along with consuming an Original. You *saw* Marques. It was a death wish."

For the first time, I had no words for them and I had no answers. I was just as dumbfounded as them and I couldn't do anything but sit in silence, the sounds of the shower in the background.

"I saw some," Rosie admitted after a moment, saving me from the awkwardness. "Of Xena's but I can't control it. I haven't felt much else. What else is there?"

"The ability to access someone's memories, hypnosis, deflection, and a few others but those were the ones that came in the most handy," Malik said.

"There were ten names," I reminded him.

His eyes snapped to mine.

"It was more about taking out Originals rather than collecting their powers," he said.

"What's deflection?" Rosie asked.

"It's what made Marques so hard to find," he said.

A crashing feeling of dread filled me so violently I almost lost my balance. If this knowledge got into the wrong hands…

I refused to think of it. Instead I just washed off with Malik and Rosie and continued to enjoy my night with them as much as I could, trying desperately not to think of what was going to happen when we met Xena.

Chapter 23
Malik

"Did Eli ask you about *The Fallen?*" I asked Rosie as we walked towards Winterfell.

Even though the sun had been shining on us, there was a chill to the air. Every demon, witch, and human we had passed had been going on with their lives like nothing was wrong. It almost felt surreal to see them just living their lives.

Xena was a problem that had possible consequences for the entire world...but no one here knew any the wiser. No one here knew that the people they were amongst, were some of the most dangerous and oldest on this continent and could wipe them off the planet in mere moments.

To anyone else it may have made them feel powerful, and maybe it had once made me feel that way as well, but now...now I just felt tired and if not for the demons at my side, alone as well.

I took a deep breath of the cool air, feeling it freeze my insides as we walked. We had decided it would be best to walk the short way to the school, instead of taking a car. Maybe it was a way to get rid of the nerves that had been building up since last night...or maybe it was just to protect from any further damage to life.

We didn't know what to expect from Xena anymore and even just getting close to her was a risk to our own lives; we had no idea what type of destruction she had caused since she had been on the run.

Maybe this time she would decide to blow up the entire school just to get back at us. I wouldn't put it past her.

"No," Rosie answered with a small frown. "What were they going to ask about?"

Rae shot me a look, disapproval already radiating off her in waves. I cursed Eli internally. I didn't know what they were waiting for, but I would have assumed that they would have begged for Rosie to let them join as soon as I gave them the okay.

Maybe they were affected more by Rosie's disappearance than I originally thought.

"They were...getting bored," I said and looked at the silhouette of Winterfell as we arrived. It stood in stark contrast to the darkening sky around it and had a foreboding aura surrounding it, though the students and faculty seemed ignorant to it as they walked the campus. "They wanted to resurrect the gang."

Students and faculty alike were walking around campus chatting and some even stopped to wave as they saw Rosie. It had been a while since we had all come back to school together—no one had the motivation to pretend anymore. The others had at least tried enough to reach the minimum number of days in class to get their degree, but they all knew I would use my power against that purple-haired weirdo if they couldn't graduate.

Ever since Eli had killed those two, there was tenseness that had built in that group and no one really dared to go back to the life that they had had here in Winterfell.

After all, why did we even need to pretend anymore?

Even if the people around us didn't get it, it still felt like we had constructed this exhausting lie and at some point it had just gotten too hard to keep up. I desperately wanted Rosie to live a normal life, go to school, and maybe even get a good job...but Xena's return had shattered that dream.

"Well," she said with a sigh. "Eli isn't much of a school person, I don't know why we would force them to go through it if they weren't happy here."

I was shocked to say the least at her reaction and by the look on Rae's face, she was too. Rosie's gaze was locked on the school in front of us. The only thing separating us from the school was the dark metal gate, but even that seemed tiny compared to what lay waiting for us.

The reporters had long since gotten spared of Rosie's constant avoidance and since there was no Xena and Ezekiel to fan the flames, there was no need to keep her in the limelight. The reporters and Demon Regulation Society instead put their attention into finding more hybrids, though based on my sources inside the society, they had yet to find anything.

"You don't think it's dangerous?" Rae asked, her voice dropping into a low whisper as we passed the school gates. Her hazel eyes trailed the grounds around us but when they found nothing of interest, they darted back to Rosie.

"I think Eli being bored is dangerous," Rosie said, her eyes shifting to both of us. "And besides at least this way they can help provide for the family so it's not just you and Malik."

I swallowed thickly. *The family.* It has been the first time I ever heard her talk about us like this. It hurt and caused my heart to soar at the same time.

I often thought of what would have happened if I had the balls to bring Xena and Ezekiel down years ago when I had the chance. Marques had insisted that there never had been a chance from the beginning, but I knew that there were many times we could have implemented these plans instead of using the newest generation of hybrids and Original children to bring them.

By waiting, we had single-handedly destroyed the lives of the last generation of Original children. All of them had been thrust into a war that they didn't need to be a part of and had done and seen things that would live with them for the rest of their lives.

Guilt ate at me daily and I knew nothing I could do would ever be able to let me redeem myself. Rosie aside, what I had done to Eli was unspeakable. I was supposed to protect them, love them, nurture them, but I threw them away just like everyone else in their life.

And yet Rosie, who had known Eli for only a few years, knew their wants and needs far better than I ever had.

"Have you thought of what you wanted to do...after this?" I asked hesitantly.

Rosie's eyes widened and her steps faltered.

"I don't know. Principal Winterfell asked me the same thing as well," she said slowly, as if also digesting the words.

Rae raised a brow at her.

"When did you talk to him?" she asked.

"A while ago," she said and paused in her steps. "He is retiring this year and is looking for a replacement."

"You?" I asked with a surprised tone.

Why would he want her to take over for him? Him leaving his position was even more surprising.

Rae was silent next to me; her steps had also paused.

"Not me," she said quickly. "But he showed me the welcoming book of him and a couple other people. I think my father was there as well. Says I can help the next principal, be there for the low-levels I presume." Her eyes shifted to mine. "You wouldn't know anything about that, would you?"

I shook my head and pushed my hands into my pockets.

"I stayed out of his business," I said. "I knew they had ties though I wasn't close to your father."

Nor did I want to be...but I didn't tack that on. He had seen me as a worker and nothing else, until the very end.

"You would like to stay here?" Rae asked, breaking through my thoughts.

"Don't you?" Rosie shot back. Rae held her gaze a moment before looking off into the distance, towards Winterfell tower.

"I haven't given it much thought," she said, but there was a clear frown on her face.

"Liar," I said and wrapped an arm around Rosie. "Though we have time to think about it. Let's just get this done."

* * *

Xena was waiting for us behind the tower as she had promised.

The once bare, dirty area had been redone and was now filled with colorful plants of every single color, some towering over Rosie. It reminded me so much of Matt that my chest began to ache. When he was younger he would practice his powers by creating rose garden after rose garden, trying to make every color imaginable. It was Claudine's favorite time with him. I remembered their laughter filing through the windows and whenever I would peek out to see them, I would see Matt handing her a different colored rose.

Even though he had turned on us...I so desperately wished it hadn't had to end the way it did. He hadn't had an easy life as he tried to care for his siblings while trying to navigate the tasks handed to him by the Originals. He didn't get to have a real childhood and had been at the whim of Xena and Ezekiel's anger for his entire life. I don't know when he started to turn...but I wish I had paid more attention to him. Maybe I could have stopped him and maybe he would have still been alive if I had just taken my role as caretaker more seriously.

Xena shifted, her eyes trailing between the three of us. When her brown eyes and half-scarred face turned towards me, I had to hide my flinch. Her glare was so powerful it made my insides curl. To her, I was probably her biggest regret besides Rosie. I had played her for years and now it was all out in the open.

No more pretending.

She stood in the middle of the small garden wearing a bright red blazer with a matching skirt and heels. Her long hair was pulled up into a sleek ponytail, showing off the burn that marred the side of her face, but for all intents and purposes...she looked like she had recovered nicely. Her skin had a glow and she stood strong on her own two legs. I could feel the power radiating from her and even if it was weaker than before, there was no mistaking it.

Which didn't fare well for what we needed to do.

We needed her weak and crippled so that we could end this once and for all.

But that wasn't what worried me the most. What worried me the most was that she wasn't alone. It was ironic. For someone who needed the protection of my gang, it was odd to see her so close to a being that had the ability to end her existence.

Next to her was a woman that wore a loose-fitting all-black dress that fell to her ankles. Her stark grey hair fell around her in waves and her bright blue eyes drilled into mine as we strolled up. Her eyes were as bright as Ezekiel's and even from across such space my hackles raised and my fight or flight instinct was telling me to flee.

There was very little in this world that could cause such a reaction in me, and two of their bodies were already cold and in the ground. But this woman...

I knew her...or at least had seen her.

Long ago, so long that my memory from that time had run fuzzy. I couldn't make out when or where I had seen this woman...but I had once, there was no mistaking it. I knew her.

I shot a look towards Rosie and Rae to see if they could also pull something from their memory banks...but they met the two with a hard expression, not even giving me a hint that they noticed anything wrong.

Did they see something in Marques's memories that I hadn't?

"Blood," Xena commanded and held her hand out for Rosie.

Rosie walked forward and both Rae and I followed closely behind her. The woman with long silver hair stepped forward, peering around Xena as Rosie got closer. My breath caught when she tried to reach out to touch her and I let out a low growl.

She flinched and pulled her hand back like I had bitten it. She looked towards Xena for an explanation but Xena's eyes stayed locked on me.

"Malik," Xena cooed in the condescending tone she always used. Anger exploded inside me and I gripped onto Rosie's shoulder to steady myself and remind myself why we were here to begin with. "I didn't know you had lowered yourself to a bodyguard."

"Shut up," I growled.

Xena scowled at me.

Rosie conjured a knife and quickly ran it along her forearm. Xena's eyes snapped towards the wound and she conjured a magic jar, similar to the one that forever-young witch had, and began collecting her blood.

"I need a witch to share magic with," she said as we all watched Rosie's thick blood fill the jar.

"There is a whole bunch of them just a few miles to the west," I said before Rosie could say anything. "Why don't you look there for them?"

Xena openly sneered at me this time.

"Stay out of this," she growled. "Or should I show you your place?"

Anger flashed hot across my skin and I took a step forward, losing myself in it, only to be jolted back to myself by Rosie's words.

"Hurt any of the people I love and I will personally see to it that this deal is over and every Original in a three *thousand* mile radius knows that a weak Original is here for the taking." Xena let out a warning growl but it didn't stop Rosie. "Or *maybe* I will leak the information that witches can gain powers from eating your flesh to the Demon Regulation Society."

"They will die as soon as my flesh hits their stomach," Xena muttered, her eyes flashing dangerously to Rosie.

Rosie shrugged.

"They won't know it is a lie until your body has been torn to shreds," she said meeting her mother head-on. "I wouldn't test me, or the hundreds of impressionable, desperate students in this university."

Xena let out another low growl and Rosie stepped away from her, healing her arm with her magic as she did.

"Since you want to act like this," Rosie said with a cool tone. "Then we are done today. Let me know when you have had a change of attitude and we can come back."

Xena's expression turned to one of outrage, but Rosie ignored it and simply turned her back on her. Rae and I shared a glance before following after her and leaving a fuming Xena alone with her silver-haired friend.

"Don't forget the rest of the deal!" she screeched as we left.

When we got far enough away from them, Rae was the first to speak.

"That was too risky," she said. "Don't do it again."

Rosie let out a huff and rolled her eyes.

"I won't if she can act like a respectable witch," she said, her eyes flashing to me. "I am sorry you had to be reminded of that."

I shrugged.

"Did Marques show you?" I asked my voice low. A small creeping self-consciousness crept up on me.

"A little," she admitted. "But not a lot. Just enough for me to understand what had happened."

I nodded and let the silence fill the space between the three of us.

"Who was that silver-haired lady, anyway?" I asked. "Did Marques meet her before? I swore I saw her once before...but I can't remember her clearly."

There was a pause between us and Rosie stopped walking.

"What silver-haired lady?" she asked.

My veins turned to ice and my head spun. I had to dig my nails into my palm hard enough for pain to flash through me in order to contain myself.

"Please tell me you saw her too," I asked Rae, but she quickly shook her head.

I cursed and ran my hand through my hair in frustration. If that was the case, we were more fucked than I thought. Whoever I had seen must have been Xena retrying to be sneaky...but she didn't even look at her; it couldn't be a third party could it?

It was too much of a coincidence to be. Xena had to be trying to pull something.

"There was someone else there?" Rosie asked. "Who?"

"I have no idea, I just know that I had seen her once before," I said and tried to pull the memory forward but it still remained fuzzy.

"What power makes her invisible to only some of us?" Rae asked.

I hung my head in defeat and let out a bitter laugh.

"I have no *fucking* clue."

Chapter 24
Eli

I had waited patiently for Rosie, Rae, and Malik to return.

I knew the rest of the house was probably all waiting for any sound that indicated our favorite obsession was home, but not a soul in here dared to even breathe as we waited.

I had passed by Daxton and Amr's room earlier and listened to their thoughts as they spoke in hushed voices.

Daxton was still beating himself up for what he had done to cause this. His thoughts were painful to listen to but they still angered me. The person who I had once been close enough to share all of my life secrets with had betrayed us—*me*—in such an unforgivable way that I didn't see how we would ever get through this.

Amr had similar sentiments to mine, though he was delusional enough to at least pretend like the thought of Daxton single-handedly almost killing Rosie was something he could get over.

That cat was almost as much of an idiot as Daxton.

Only an hour and a half after they had left, I heard the front door open, and the soft chatter of Malik and Rosie rose up the staircase. I had hidden myself down the hall on the second floor and was in the perfect spot to catch any of their conversation that they may have wanted to keep from the rest of us.

I knew that they would probably debrief us, but I wasn't stupid enough to think that they would tell us everything. I had heard Rosie and Malik's hesitancy when they looked at me. They tried to hide it but failed miserably.

They thought I would act on my own. They thought I would go against their wishes...and they were probably right, but keeping it from me only made me want to try harder to find out what they were keeping from me.

I had yet to breach the conversation with Rosie about *The Fallen,* so that left a whole lot of nothing for me to do and the thought of Rosie keeping something from me only fueled me to find out exactly what it was. That and fucking her until she couldn't think straight were my only two ways to get rid of the boredom at the moment and the others would be pissed if I took too much of her time...so here we were.

Footsteps echoed in the empty room as they entered and I cursed when I realized that they were heading to the kitchen and not upstairs like I had planned. I had originally planned to hide out in one of the hallways or rooms as they passed, trying to get into their minds as they passed, but I would have to improvise.

I tried to make my way down the stairs as silently as possible and tried to stay as far enough out of rage to make sure that Rae didn't feel any of my emotions. Our ranges were pretty similar, but I had the advantage. As soon as she was able to pick out my emotions I would have enough time to back far away enough so I would be out of range, but it wasn't foolproof. I still needed to remain as calm as possible.

I tried to clear my mind, to make sure that there was nothing angering me or bothering me. It was easy to get excited as the thrill of sneaking up on them filled me, but I pushed those feelings down and tried to focus on clearing everything from my mind.

Anger and sadness seemed to be the things that Rae picked up the most and everything would be ruined if they knew I was eavesdropping. I could still hear Malik and Rosie talking, but it was Rae who spoke up and told me something that I wouldn't have known if I had stayed in my room like a good little demon.

"It's dangerous, Rosie," Rae said with a sigh. "Xena doesn't seem like she's going to be giving up anytime soon. I think we can keep this up for a little bit, see if we can make her more...agreeable. But her attitude combined with this unknown silver-haired woman, I don't know how much more I want to risk our safety."

"Rae," Rosie breathed.

I could hear their thoughts running back and forth. They were like whispers on the edge of my mind. They sunk into my mind with ease, like they were just begging to get out into the world, to make their presence known. It was my favorite part about Ezekiel's power, the ease of getting everything you needed in mere seconds.

Malik was thinking at a hundred miles per minute. He was trying to remember something about the silver-haired lady they had mentioned and why she had looked so familiar. A jolt of familiarity ran through my mind as well when I saw her face, probably from Marques's memories, but I couldn't pinpoint where exactly he had seen her...

Maybe it wasn't him who had seen her after all. Maybe it was another demon he had eaten...maybe that's why it was so hard to remember her.

Rosie's thoughts were dangerous. They were angry but not an explosive anger. It was like a slow rumbling that began deep inside her brain and started to come up for air.

She was hurt.

Hurt that Rae would suggest this. She had thought that Rae would understand because Rae had told her that she had understood just the night before...but now she was taking it back. *Just. Like. That.*

Rae on the other hand, was the most logical one here. She understood that handing over something important to Rosie to Xena as a bargain, would make her hate Rae for the rest of her existence.

But she was willing to chance it because she was *terrified*. She was terrified of facing the unknown and she knew that we were at a disadvantage. The deal Rosie had made would only harm us in the long run and Rae was the sort of person that would try to fight for her own survival and the ones she loved above all else.

She didn't want to risk the fight...and neither did Malik. It was only Rosie who had a hesitation.

A sort of excitement bubbled in my chest and giddiness rose in me when I realized that they had thought of handing over that annoying, hybrid brother of Rosie's, to *Xena* of all people.

They were thinking of using him as some sort of sacrifice as something to keep Xena entertained while they thought of a better way to take her down. Well, at least that was Rae's thought.

Malik had a similar idea, but his was more cruel, more in line with what I was thinking.

He wanted to leave Ren. He didn't care about the brother, any least not in the way that he cared for Rosie. Malik knew that he would be torn apart for his magic, but he didn't care. He didn't care that this would hurt Rosie. He wanted to give him right to Xena and be *done* with it. And he fully accepted that Rosie would hate him.

But there was still something in the back of his mind that told him he couldn't cross that line because he couldn't chance having Rosie leave him over this...

But *I* could.

Because I had done the same thing so many times over and over again and she had proved to me over and over again that she doesn't hate this *Eli*. No matter what I did she had promised that she would love me no matter what.

And that thought alone was all I needed. I didn't stick around to hear them talk about it. I let them stew in their own emotion, in their own thoughts, and left swiftly out the back door and didn't look back.

* * *

I had taken the seer with me.

Well, I didn't *take* her. She tagged along. She had already been waiting for me outside the barrier because for some reason, she knew that this would happen.

She had a sad look on her face, and when I gave her a look, she simply stated that she had been expecting this.

I didn't ask when. Because frankly, I didn't care. All I had the capacity to care about in this moment was what I was going to do tonight, would make sure that we would be safe for all eternity.

Because I knew that Xena would not stop.

Rae knew, Malik knew, and even Claudine knew...it was just Rosie who refused to take this one extra step. But it was okay, because where she lacked, I would come in and fill all of the gaps. I would do that for her, because even if she hadn't realized, she had done that for me too.

I was going to walk at first. Trying to make it as inconspicuous as possible but Claudine already had all the transportation I needed. And so without a word, she held on to my arm and transported us right into his apartment.

His TV was on and blaring through the dark apartment. He was watching some type of boring drama on the TV where the girl's shrill voice exploded out of the speakers and they threw drinks at each other.

He only knew that we had broken in when it was too late.

As soon as I saw the back of his head on the couch I lunged forward and wrapped my hands around his neck.

He struggled and started kicking against my hold. He was bucking like a wild animal and began screaming at the top of his lungs. In his mind, Xena and the Originals had come back. They were here to take him and bestow upon him the same pain that they had his sister.

Boy will he be in for a surprise.

"It's me," I said in his ear with a chuckle.

Flashes of when I had murdered Matt, Mr. Falkner, and Emma flashed through my mind. I wanted so *badly* to end everything right here. I wanted to slit his throat and be done with it but with Malik's stupid fucking power I knew my hands were tied...but they never said anything about harming him...I just couldn't *kill* him.

The excitement of all of it was barely containable inside me and threatened to spill out, taking this hybrid with me. But I knew that that would ruin the plan, so instead of giving in to my desires to paint this apartment with his blood, I quickly covered his mouth and nose and held it until he stopped struggling.

Malik's power was in my veins, struggling against me as it felt my intention shift from killing the hybrid to simply just knocking him out. It knew I was moments away from taking his life.

"That is enough," Claudine said from behind me when the fight left him.

I sent her a look, but let go of him nonetheless. His body flopped onto the sofa and fell to the ground in a heap.

"Rose is going to be mad at you," I sang to Claudine, still feeling the high of almost suffocating that bastard hybrid. She shot me a look. In her mind she was furious at me for making light of this situation.

She didn't want Rosie to hate her. She had found a friend in her and wanted to keep her around as long as possible, but she knew that even after everything, this might be the thing that would tear them apart for good.

Because unlike Matt, Ren had done *nothing* wrong.

"What changed?" I asked. Suddenly, I was curious as to why this witch was helping me. After all, I had killed her brother.

"The witch that came in to look at Rae's mother," she said. Her voice was weak and shaky. "She was far more powerful than anyone I have ever felt. Even Xena didn't compare. It was her idea. I saw it clearly when we were in the same room together but I couldn't say anything. I didn't want it to come to this."

"But she's second generation," I said. She paused and looked at the body behind me.

"There's something about this witch," she said. "As a fellow seer...I can understand her a little bit and maybe to other witches she may not feel like she's more powerful than Xena...but to be able to see the future *and* the outcomes of choices that we *haven't even fully made yet* is something that I do not want to play with." She took a deep breath, her eyes drilling into mine. "So even if Rosie hates me for what I am about to do, I will trust her."

The heaviness of her words silenced the room and weighed upon my shoulders. I walked around the couch and reached down to pick up the hybrid's lifeless body and throw it over my shoulder.

"So," I said. "Do you know where Xena is right now?"

Her only response was a raised hand. Excitement bubbled through me and without hesitation I grabbed it. In a flash she had brought us right back into Winterfell. As I turned I noticed that we are right behind Winterfell tower and not moments later, I saw Xena approach us. She had come in the same flash of light that we had and she glared at me through the darkness.

She was shocked when her eyes trailed to Ren's body. The woman I had seen in Malik's thoughts was here as well, standing directly behind Xena. Her blue eyes watched me intently and when I smiled at her she flinched.

Weak.

"What a surprise," Xena said, her voice dripping with condescension.

"Somehow I think you knew I was coming," I said and I threw Ren's lifeless body down into the dirt. He didn't even twitch as he landed with a thud.

"In exchange," I said. "I don't want you ever going after Rosie or the others ever again."

She cocked her brow and tilted her head.

"What makes you think that you can give me these orders?" she asked, venom lacing her words. She looked down at her perfectly manicured nails and flicked invisible dirt off them.

I let out a bitter laugh.

"Because if you have him," I said and jerked my head towards the hybrid's body. "You don't *need* Rosie, just like you don't *need The Fallen.* And if you dare, we are just one step away from ruining your entire existence. So, take your prize and leave us the *fuck* alone. And if I see you back here again, I will tear off your head exactly like how I tore off my father's."

"What did you see in that head of his?" she asked, her eyes trailing my form.

I was giddy with excitement, it was so powerful it made my head spin. I had been away from this type of action for too long and now that I had it, my body was beginning to vibrate with need.

"I saw how *weak* you were," I hissed. "I saw how *greedy* you were. And I saw how *all of it* led to *your* downfall. While my father just sat there like a *coward* and watched you *ruin* everything you worked for." I took a deep breath trying to control myself, and stop myself from launching across this space and bashing her head in. "*Now,* I *will not* repeat myself. Don't you *ever* fucking come back here *again.* You or that creepy weirdo behind you."

Xena shifted abruptly, turning towards the silver-haired lady.

"You can see me?" the lady behind her asked. Her voice was small in comparison to Xena's and barely reached my ears even though we stood a mere thirty feet away from each other.

"I can," I said with a smirk. "And we'll remember if you ever come around here again. Now take him. I will watch you leave, and don't you ever *fucking* come back here again, seer."

"You sound like a broken record," Xena muttered and her magic lit up the space between us before coming down on the hybrid and lifting him into the air. "Tell Rosie that she knows where to find me if she needs me."

After that, she disappeared in a flash leaving no trace that she or the other lady had been here in the first place.

"Like hell I will," I muttered and kicked the dirt.

"You need to go home," Claudine said in a panicked whisper. "They will be looking for you soon. *Please* don't say anything."

I shrugged and reached out to hold her wrist.

"Whatever, seer."

Chapter 25
Amr

"Just stay still," Doctor Svensson mumbled as he leaned towards Daxton's chest.

The doctor's face was towards us, but his eyes were closed and his cheek was so close to Daxton's chest with just a small movement it would look like he was lying his head down on him.

Daxton sent me a look from his hospital bed, distaste obviously written all over his face. His skin had regained some of its color and his hair fell in waves around his face instead of hanging limply like it once had.

It had been weeks since he had last had to give Xena magic and his body was slowly helping itself...but it wasn't enough. His magic hasn't bounced back to normal and it was beginning to worry us.

Even before eating an Original, his magic had been more than the standard witch's due to his family's blood purity. They were revered for being some of the last remaining whites with a traceable bloodline back to the Originals...but to lose it was a blow.

A witch's magic was a part of them as much as the blood in their veins. To any witch, this would have been a big blow and it only made us wonder...

What if Daxton never got his magic back?

That's why we had dragged him back to this makeshift hospital. At this point we needed answers and there was no one else to go to.

The hospital beds had been almost all cleared with only a few of the most serious patients still lying in their beds. I was sitting on the bed across from Daxton, holding Rosie's hand as we watched the doctor check him over.

Rosie's grip on me had become so hard that pain shot through my arm, but I didn't mention anything. I understood her and would act as her rock.

Daxton's eyebrows pulled together and his head tilted back against the pillow. The cords on his neck became taut and there was a groan that escaped his lips. His hands grasped the white bedspread under him and his knuckles turned white.

When his body began shaking both Rosie and I stood up.

"Don't," the doctor warned, his eyes still closed. His eyebrows had also bunched together and there was a low whispering from his lips but I couldn't make out any of the words.

His magic had plunged the whole room into an ice bath as he forcefully pulled Daxton's magic out of him.

The thick black cloud of smoke-like magic began oozing from Daxton and hanging around us in a cloud until it was almost impossible to see.

"Daxton..." Rosie whispered next to me, her own magic lashing out wildly.

It had been a while since I had felt both of their magics so powerfully around us. It excited my own magic but also scared me.

We were still surrounded by vulnerable people who had escaped the towns with their lives barely intact. If they *both* blew up there would be not a scrap of this place left unharmed.

Daxton let out another groan, but his magic had covered both him and Doctor Svensson from our view. Then just as quickly as it started, the black smoky magic snapped back into his body.

When everything cleared Daxton had remained lying on the bed, but he was now drenched with sweat. The doctor was no longer leaning close to him but instead had his hands on either side of Daxton, his eyes staring directly at Daxton's chest. He was panting wildly and it took a few moments for him to call his magic back to himself.

He cleared his throat and stood straight.

Daxton glared at him and let out a groan as he tried to sit up.

"You greatly underrepresented the pain, *Doc*," he growled.

Rosie and I ran to his side, both of us scrambling to help him up. I expected him to brush us off but instead we were met with silence as we helped him up.

The doctor hadn't spoken for a few moments, his eyes still trained on Daxton's chest.

"Doctor Svensson," Rosie called. "What have you found?"

His eyes snapped towards hers and he took his glasses off to rub his face.

"Out with it, Doc," Daxton growled. "Why don't you tell them how fucked up my core is."

My eyes snapped to Daxton. His face was hard as he glared at the doctor. His jaw was clenched and his hands were still gripping the white sheets like his life depended on it.

"I can't," the doctor said with a sigh and placed his glasses back on his face. "Because then that would mean you still have a core."

His words were like a punch to my gut and the room plunged into silence. There was a tearing that filled the room before Daxton lunged towards the doctor. Rosie acted quicker than I did. She lunged towards Daxton, wrapping her arms around his waist, anchoring him to his spot. Her magic exploded between us and in an instant, black vine-like wisps of magic wrapped around herself and Daxton.

Daxton let out a pained howl as his fingers were just out of reach of the doctor's face.

"You lie!" Daxton growled. "You fucking piece of shit. I'm going to kill you for—"

I walked over and helped Rosie push Daxton against the bed as he cursed the doctor. Rosie's magic was helping keep him in place, but Daxton seemed to have tunnel vision, only seeing the doctor. No one else was in this room with him and his pained howls filled the void.

They hurt *so* much. I wanted to claw out Daxton's pain and take it on his behalf.

I was trying to get rid of my own shock at his words.

How could a witch not have a core?

The core was where we held all our magic. It was the start and end of all our lives. It was the beginning of our existence here on this planet and the only thing that allowed us to use and share magic.

Without that....

Without that it was like a bird with its wings cut off. The magic was an extension of yourself, your entire being, and to have that be taken from you so cruelly and without remorse was worse than any curse that could have been put on him. After this...I failed to see how he could even live anymore.

"Doctor," Rosie groaned as Daxton fought against her. "Please explain. You can't just leave us with that."

I was too busy holding Daxton down as he kicked and flailed to look at the doctor's face, but even through Daxton's yells and growls I heard what he said very well.

"His core has been obliterated," he said. "The magic that he still has is only a mere remnant of what it once was. If I were to guess, he has only ten percent of his original core left. That's why it is so painful for him to conjure magic. His body may heal, but it is no longer suited for magic."

"You fucking liar," Daxton growled. "I can feel *it*. I can feel everyone's magic, it's still there."

Even Daxton's growls became silent as we digested the information.

"But for how long is the question we are facing now," Doctor Svensson said. "I don't know and I have never seen someone's core so destroyed like this. I have seen some cases of damaged cores but this..."

Daxton stopped struggling and sank into the bed. I hesitantly pulled away to see him staring blankly at the doctor. There was not a flicker of emotion on his face. Rosie recalled her magic and shot me a look before cupping Daxton's face, trying to get him to look at her.

He didn't move.

"Is it possible for it to heal?" Rosie asked, her eyes still trained on Daxton.

I looked towards the doctor now. He hadn't moved from his spot and his mouth was pushed together in a firm line.

"I have seen some instances of core healing, but these were in people who only had a slightly damaged core," he said. "To go from the core you had less than a year ago to now...the person who did this to you is very cruel indeed."

I was numb. I didn't know how to comfort Daxton or what to say. This... *this* was the worst possible outcome.

Daxton gave the doctor a nod and jerkily swung his legs over the bed and stood on surprisingly steady feet.

"Thanks doc, sorry for the outburst," he said, his dead eyes flashing to us. "We don't want to miss the games. Let's go."

"Wait," I said quickly and rounded the bed to stand in front of him. "You need to rest. We don't need to go to the games. We will automatically forfeit, it's okay. Just lie—"

"This is our last games, Amr," Daxton said in a hard tone. "And I, for one, want to participate before I never get a chance to again."

"Daxton, you can't," Rosie said from behind us. "Your magic cannot sustain something like the games."

Daxton's eyes darted behind me. I saw a flash of hurt go through his handsome features.

"I will," he said. "You don't have to come if it's too painful for you."

With that he left us both standing there slack-jawed and staring at him as he exited the room.

Chapter 26
Malik

*T*he Fallen would be different this time.

I planned to keep my word to Rosie.

I didn't want to go back to that scum-infested gang that I once had. Even thinking of it made my skin crawl.

Back then, I did what I had to.

I lived for myself and myself alone.

Even when I did things to help the people stuck in the town, or the work I did with Marques...it was all built out of the need for my own survival.

Back then I didn't have anything—*or anyone*—to live for.

I walked on this earth like I couldn't wait for my expiration date. Sometimes I would wander the night, picking fights for no good reason, just to feel something.

Maybe that's what caused the gang to become the way it did.

After all, people learned by example. They saw me behaving recklessly and therefore they thought they could too.

And that's when that *bastard* Damon was born.

I regretted everything I did back then, now that I had come to my senses. After Rosie and the death of Ezekiel, I had many things put forcefully into perspective for me.

That's why I was here right now. And that's why I was letting Eli do *that*.

A loud groan filled the empty living room that we had taken refuge in for the day. I let out a sigh and looked over to Eli.

They were in the middle of the plastic-covered room, a man on his knees in front of them, and they were currently...pulling his teeth out.

Our men stood around them, watching as they tortured the man for information, though I think we had long since passed that. I think now they were just having fun.

Some of the men flinched as Eli pulled out a molar. Blood splattered the plastic-covered floor and the tooth went flying, only to land near the foot of one of our men.

A couple of them looked to me for help but I just shrugged.

Now, when I told Rosie we would be better, it didn't mean that I would change our ways so completely that we wouldn't be *The Fallen* anymore... but we would change the *why*.

"I have a horrible memory," Eli said with a crazed smile. Blood was splattered all over their face, but they didn't care. They thrived in the mess and loved the way the man screamed. "Write them down."

Eli held out their hand to the men surrounding them and many of them tried to fish for a pen and paper from their pockets. The one that finally got it rushed to give it to them and promptly kneeled at their feet.

Eli's eyes shifted to them for the first time this night and while I couldn't see their face from this angle, I saw the face of the man at their feet pale.

"Thank you," they cooed and even patted the man on the head before tearing the paper and pen from his hands and throwing it at the bleeding man at their feet.

The man scrambled to catch it and began writing furiously on the paper.

"Not just ones that bought the children," I called out from my spot on the wall. Eli may have been okay to get blood on them, but I wasn't. I had a reputation to uphold and I wouldn't walk on the streets looking like I just murdered someone, even if I had. "Adults too. Hell if they so much as even stepped foot inside here I want their name on *that* paper."

His eyes shot to me and his face paled.

"That w-will take a lo—"

He was cut off by Eli's boot smashing into the back of his head so hard that his face planted into the hard floor and his nose exploded.

He let out a pained scream and Eli only let up after I gave them a look.

"Get to writing," they growled.

The man flinched.

"I never wanted this you know?" he sputtered out. "I didn't want to be involved in this. Damon he—"

"Damon's dead," Eli growled and bent down so that they were almost at face level with the man. "Speak his name one more time and I do exactly what I did to him, to you."

Eli's words were so cold they sent a shiver up my spine.

The man we were with today had a track record with Damon. They worked closely and in exchange for *product*, Damon would protect this fucker. But little did he know that there was a change of management and we didn't sully our names with dirty shit like that.

See Rosie? I said in my mind, a small smile pulling at my lips. *We are different this time.*

"Hurry up," I called and turned towards the door, a few men following me. "I have something to show you after this."

Eli gave me a look but I shook my head and tried to keep my mind as blank as possible.

It's a surprise.

* * *

"I wish you would have just talked to her about this instead of making me the middleman," I grumbled as I showed Eli the newest headquarters. I was tired after today's outing and wanted nothing more than to go home and cuddle with Rosie, but I knew it was time to show Eli.

I had been working on this for a long time, even before Eli had shown interest in joining once more and I was happy to show them what lay in wait.

I bought a large building in the city, much like my last one but instead of a living space at the top, it was our office and every other floor under it would be used for our various dealings. This time we would be as legit as we could get.

That's right, *our* office.

Something I thought may never be. Yes I knew Eli's capabilities, but I never thought we would be this close again after so many years.

"I was going to mention it to her," Eli grumbled as we entered the main office space, though we both knew it was a lie.

Eli was probably worried that Rosie would reject them. I mean, even I was surprised when Rosie easily gave in. I thought that she may be wary of Eli losing themselves again, but I was glad to see that we could give them something they wanted.

She was right.

If Eli didn't want to go to school or enter the workforce, then we shouldn't force them to.

Forcing Eli away from the darkness inside them was like separating the magic from a witch, or getting rid of Winterfell. They would be here to stay and denying them would only make it worse for all parties involved.

When I picked this office, I had made sure that this time all of the main walls had been made of glass. I wanted to be able to see the city below us and imagine what it would be like to fly over the area. I wouldn't be able to of course, not without risking my image to the public, but a man could dream.

Some days I would lie in bed and remember what it was like before we had reached this point. I remembered what it felt like to soar over towns and villages, waving to the people I passed. That was before the humans retaliated and before the Originals divided.

A simpler and freer time.

No one cared about showing anyone up. The Originals were still new to this earth and they were having an exciting time learning the ways of this world. Sure the humans were scared, but there were many that accepted us with open arms.

So this would be for me, as a little reminder of what was.

The main office had two rooms, both with their own desks, chairs, and couches. They both had separate spaces with a door but were close enough that if we needed anything we would just be a door away from each other.

I wanted to make sure that they wouldn't feel too annoyed with our shared space or feel like I was keeping tabs on them. I wanted them to know that this space would be theirs and theirs alone.

The rest of the space was open and had a full kitchen and living space. Mostly meant for if Rosie or the others wanted to come over. I wanted to make sure that no matter where our job took us, that we would have space for them to be here.

"That one is yours," I said pointing to the one towards the right. It had the best view of the sunset. I imagined Eli sitting there with a drink, looking over the area they ruled, though that was all a dream.

I knew that Eli would most likely like to be on the ground, doing the dirty work instead of sitting up here in a cozy office. Seeing how they acted today was just a reminder of that.

They belonged in the field, exercising their powers.

"Mine?" they asked with a raised eyebrow before taking in the space. Their body was stiff and their face gave no indication of what they were thinking.

I nodded.

"Don't act like you didn't hear it in my thoughts," I said. They shrugged and took a step towards their office. I wished so badly to be able to read their mind.

Did they like it?
Did they hate it?
Was it all too much for them?

"Are you sure?" they asked and turned to look at me. "Are you sure you want me in this position? You should know not to expect me to act like your lackey."

I stepped forward and put my arm around them, ignoring the way they stiffened next to me.

"You will be my partner," I said. "You will help me build this place back up to what it should have been. We will do it right this time and I want your help."

They were silent for a moment before speaking.

"Are you doing this because you feel guilty?" they asked.

"Partly," I admitted and removed my arm so I could face them. Their blue eyes were digging into me and suddenly my soul felt uncomfortably bare to them. "Maybe about letting you join again. But the decision to make you in charge was a long time coming. You have worked hard to get here and I wanted to give you a position you deserved."

Eli held my gaze before letting out a huff.

"You just don't want me to kill people," they said, their gaze looking back to their shiny new office.

"You can't," I said with a smile. They growled at me in return. "Though I will give that back to you in time."

They had to earn this back. They had been better up until now, but that didn't mean we were in the clear. I had trusted them to behave accordingly once and then they hung two dead bodies on the Winterfell tower.

I wasn't stupid.

"Now," they said abruptly. "Remove the power now."

I took a step back, searching them.

"Who are you planning to kill?" I asked.

They opened their mouth to speak but was cut off by my phone ringing, a sharp vibration that filled the silent air around us.

They glared at me, as if the phone vibration was my issue. I knew that as soon as I was done with this call, they would give me a verbal lashing.

I dug it out of my pocket and my heart dropped when I saw that it was Rosie. She never called me. I sent Eli a look before answering. Their anger was gone in a flash and they stood up straight as a rod.

"Rosie?" I asked. "What's wrong—"

"It's Amr," the deep voice on the other line came. *Shit.* "Get Eli and come to Winterfell. The games have started and Daxton is not doing well."

For once, Eli looked just as worried as I felt.

"What do you mean not doing well?" I asked.

"He's put two high-levels in the hospital," he said. "Ren is facing him next and I don't think this looks good."

"He wouldn't hurt Rosie," Eli said grabbing the phone from my hands.

"Eli—"

"He wouldn't hurt her," Eli repeated into the phone. Their eyes widened when they took in what Amr said next.

"Get the seer," Eli ordered me. "We need to get there *now*."

* * *

Black smoke filled the arena. It was so thick that it blocked out the blue sky and made it impossible to see more than twenty feet in front of you.

The faculty were panicking and yelling at the students to evacuate. I stood there for a moment, taking on all the chaos.

Students were running.

People were screaming.

There was a distinct smell of burning flesh and I could feel a tremor of dark power brush across my skin.

Magical sirens filled the area and it was so loud it caused my ears to ring. There was a booming voice that echoed through the area, asking students to evacuate immediately, though it didn't say why.

Where the fuck is Rosie?

It was a mess from the start trying to find anyone from the moment we appeared on this campus, but not being able to find Rosie was my literal worst nightmare come true. I had flashbacks of hearing about her kidnapping and an ice-cold hand gripped my throat and caused my blood to freeze.

My first instinct was to believe that Xena had finally come back to take what we refused to give her...but then what did Amr mean by Daxton?

Claudine and Eli were both by my side and I motioned for them to follow me. Eli's eyes were set on the growing cloud of black fog in front of us. Their eyebrows were pushed together and their fist clenched at the chest of their shirt.

"Eli," I called. They shuddered and took a step forward.

"Just ahead," Claudine said, her eyes snapping towards me. "It's potent magic. Mostly Original in origin...I think it's Daxton."

I swallowed thickly as I looked over the scene in front of us.

The smoke had entirely cut off light from entering the area and we were plunged into darkness, with only a bit of the light that shone behind us to light our way.

Without another word, I guided us further into the fog and against the crowd that ran past us. Screams still filled the air as the thousands and thousands of students that had been in the arena before we arrived tried desperately to get past us.

Many succeeded but I saw a few that tripped and fell. My hands ached to help them up but I knew that if I delayed any longer...Rosie may pay for my actions.

As we pushed through the crowd and got closer to the field I realized quickly why people were running.

This was not ordinary black smoke.

Just like Claudine had said, this smoke had magic in it and as we got closer it began burning my skin. It was small tingles at first and then it began to actually create burns.

"Shit," Eli cursed and staggered back.

When my eyes darted towards them I was met with their quickly reddening skin.

"Get back," I growled and pushed them in the opposite direction. "It's magic, you will never be able to heal those.

"Does it look like I care about that?" Eli growled at me, their blue eyes flashing.

"I do," I growled and took a step closer to them. When I pushed them back their hand clamped onto my wrist tightly.

"Don't you dare," they warned.

"I don't want you to get hurt," I confessed.

Normally I may not have been able to admit this, or say it with such ease, but the situation called for it.

Please, Eli, I begged in my mind. *I need you safe.*

But Rosie—

We were cut off from our mental conversation by Claudine closing the space between us.

"We don't have time for this," she said, her voice harder than I have ever heard it.

She grabbed my arm and with a burst of light, a bright blue magic began traveling up her arm and to mine. I flinched as it came close to my skin but it didn't hurt, instead it was cooling and stopped the burning from the black smoke that surrounded us.

I let out a sigh of relief as the pain that had been crowding my brain finally left.

"It's a protective magic," she said and threw a look towards Eli. "That should be no more than a sunburn for a few days."

Eli nodded.

I turned to look into the smoke but I couldn't see anything from beyond.

"Rosie's in there, isn't she?" I asked Claudine, unable to shake my gut feeling.

It was like Rosie to run straight to danger.

At times I wished for the shy little low-level back at my side. The one that clung to me and Rae, afraid of the world beyond and whole fully unaware of what lay ahead of her. *That* Rosie would have never run headfirst into danger...but this Rosie?

She didn't just run straight to danger, she fucking exuded it.

Ever since she had wormed her way into the Originals' nest far before she needed to, she was nothing but trouble.

And this time I was afraid it would follow her if I was not diligent enough to keep an eye on her. I wanted to trust the others, and I did to a point...but how could I leave her around them when *this* was what happened if I were gone for a mere day.

God damn it Rosie.

"Yes. I can feel her—"

Claudine was cut off by a screech that was more akin to an injured animal than anything that should have been in this arena.

The students had mostly cleared and their screams had been silenced, so this one cry had pierced through me and the silence that had descended on us.

"Where is he?!" came Daxton's voice from the abyss.

Without hesitation, I pushed through the smoke and towards his voice. I didn't bother to check if the other two were following me.

Something was terribly wrong.

"Evacuate the field immediately," the voice called from all around us. I only now realized that it was the principal's voice. "The games are over. I repeat, the games are over. Leave the area immediately."

In the corner of my eye I saw a similar blue glowing orb of magic. Inside I could make out Amr and Rae, standing together, both looking deeper into the smoke.

They were both wearing their Winterfell uniforms and had been covered from head to toe in soot. They were speaking to each other but it was too far away to make out.

I strained my eyes to see what they were looking at and my heart dropped when I made out Rosie's form. She had a film of magic around her as well, but she was pushing closer to the darkest part of the smoke, instead of running away from it like she should have.

Her hair was spread out around her and her uniform clothes and skirt were torn. She looked like she had been thrown around, but that couldn't be right.

"Rosie!" I called and tried to push forward, but Eli's hand grasped my wrist, forcing me back.

She didn't even pause to look at me, just kept pushing forward.

"Daxton!" she yelled and lunged forward, her magic-covered hand grabbing something in the darkness.

Her magic slowly started to expand across the form, revealing Daxton, but the film that connected them quickly became polluted with smoke, hiding them from sight. The fog around them began to disperse showing a ruined field.

All the grass and dirt had been dug up and large pieces of the foundation underneath had been thrown around all around us.

It looked like a bomb had fallen on Winterfell...

"No!" I growled and broke free of Eli's grip.

Claudine tried to stop me from leaving the safety of the magic barrier but I didn't listen to her. I couldn't. Not when Rosie was going to be devoured by the same smoke that had begun burning my skin.

It was more painful the closer I got. It started in my outreached hand, burning my fingertips, then traveled up my arm.

Just as I was about to reach the barrier that held Daxton and Rosie, the black smoke around us snapped back into the barrier. I stumbled forward, my hand brushing across the blue barrier that separated Rosie and Daxton from me. Inside was still filled with smoke but the space all around us had been spared.

I heard my name echoing around me. The others came to my side trying to pull me away from them, but I fought against them.

Then the barrier broke and along with it the smoke disappeared, showing us an unharmed Daxton and Rosie.

Daxton was on his knees, his head on the ground and his hands covering his head. Rosie was on top of him, covering his entire body with hers as if shielding him.

"It's okay," she whispered against his back. "We will figure it out. It's okay."

It took me a few moments to realize that Daxton was sobbing under her. His entire body shook with his cries and his wails got louder with each passing second.

I could hear the crowd coming back now. Their chatter was reaching my ears and they were nothing that Daxton nor Rosie should hear in this moment.

"Take us home," Rae said as she kneeled down by my side. Her hand came to rest on Rosie's head.

Rosie peered up at us, her eyes filled with tears. She sniffled and reached her hand out to Claudine, who stepped forward without hesitation and took Rosie's hand in hers.

"Grab on," she said.

It was the only warning we got before she began to transport us.

Chapter 27
Rosie

Magic danced around us, lighting up the darkness of the room. The air was warm but there was a sharpness to it indicating that as soon as the magic settled, the chill would probably seep in again.

We had taken one of the bigger rooms in Rae's house. Amr, Daxton, and I could stay in one room all together, but for now it was just me and him. It was better this way and allowed him the grace to be alone without feeling alone.

Sometimes too many people just got too much for him.

I didn't blame him, though. After all, his whole life had been taken from him and in its place was the knowledge that he may never again be able to use his magic.

Going on a rampage and causing the whole school to get evacuated while overboard, was also understandable. Though I could empathize with him, I could never truly understand how he felt.

He had grown up with his magic. He had learned that his whole being and existence was only important because of the magic his parents passed on. So how could he possibly learn to live now that it was all so cruelly taken away?

Sometimes I wished that I didn't have my magic and now I cursed myself for even having such stupid and reckless thoughts, especially when I saw how much it had affected Daxton.

Daxton lay by my side in his magically induced sleep. It was the only time he would fully relax after what happened. It had become a routine and took up all my time for the last two weeks.

We would feed him, help him bathe, tend to his magic and then he would go to sleep. At first Amr and I felt uncomfortable sharing magic with him in his state, but it was the only thing that seemed to bring a bit of himself back. And it's not like he was *here*...he was just struggling to get the thoughts of his magic slowly dying out of his head.

It had been affecting Amr as well, so I asked him to take the night off, letting me take care of Daxton for the time being. I was curled in the bed with him, running my hand through his still damp hair. His arms were around me and his face was pushed into my chest. His breathing was deep and he grew slack against me as he fell into *hopefully* dreamless sleep.

But I knew that it was unlikely.

I tried to keep my anger inside me. Tried not to think of how my shitty mother had done this to him. She had lied to him, told him that she would help him get rid of the magic that was eating him alive...but instead she took his whole goddamn core with her and destroyed whatever was left.

She had single-handedly taken a witch's sole reason to live.

He meant it when he said he didn't want to miss out on the last games. He ran through participant after participant. He didn't care how much he strained his magic or how much he hurt the others, all he was trying to do was exert as much magic as possible.

I guess in his mind he was trying to use it before it was gone once and for all.

It hurt to see him like that. The pain was obvious on his face. He was grieving the loss of his magic, probably always would.

When he was deep asleep, I gave him a soft kiss on the forehead.

"I love you. Wait for me, I'll fix this," I whispered against him and slowly began to detangle our limbs and slipped out of bed.

I walked the hallways feeling for magical signatures and made sure to avoid the kitchen where I knew Rae and Malik probably were. They had taken to late-night chatting there, waiting for me after Daxton had fallen asleep, though I would only visit them for a few minutes before heading back up to take care of Daxton.

Instead of going down to the kitchen I snuck out back where I knew another demon was probably up waiting.

As I stepped out of the back door the cold air brushed across my skin and I shivered. I was only in a t-shirt and socks, making it a less-than-ideal outfit for this weather.

I looked towards my left and spotted Eli leaning against the brick, with a lit cigarette in their hand. Their blue eyes glowed in the dark and watched me as I approached.

"Miss me?" they asked as I leaned against the wall beside them.

I sent them a forced smile and took the cigarette from their hand. I inhaled it deeply, the smoke burning as it went down. I couldn't hold in my cough.

They let out a chuckle and snatched the cigarette from my hand.

"Don't try to be something you're not," they said and took a drag of the cigarette before moving so that they were in front of me. They placed the hand with the lit cigarette on the wall behind me and used their other hand to grip my chin, forcing my face up.

I opened my mouth for them and they leaned forward to ghost the smoke into my mouth, their lips just barely brushing across mine. I inhaled the smoke, and even though it still burned, I tried hard not to cough as it went down.

Their hooded eyes watched me and they licked their lips before taking my bottom one into their mouth and sucking lightly.

"I missed you," they said in a low voice.

I swallow thickly.

"Daxton needs me," I said.

They nodded.

"Which is why I haven't barged in there to take you," they said. "But this time *you* came to me. You can't fault me for just a taste can you?"

They placed the cigarette in my mouth before kneeling down in front of me.

"I wanted to talk to you," I said and steadied the cigarette in my mouth with one hand.

Their hands began roaming up my legs before they caught the hem of my shirt and lifted it. The cold air hit my bare pussy and we both inhaled sharply.

"Look at you," they cooed and used their hands to spread my legs. "Still so swollen."

I used my free hand to grip their hair as they leaned forward and kissed my mound, causing a burst of heat to explode through me.

My magic began coiling in my belly, wanting more of their mouth.

"I was serious," I said and stifled my moan as they leaned forward and licked the length of my slit.

"After this," they said and kissed my clit before taking one leg and putting it over their shoulder. Their hands came to grip my ass and without warning, they descended on my pussy.

"Fuck," I groaned and tried to arch away from Eli as they sucked on my clit, but their hands kept me anchored.

I took a drag of the cigarette and exhaled, though it was cut off by my own cry as their teeth grazed me. I looked down to meet Eli's gaze as they looked up at me. I removed the hand from their hair and shakily lifted my shirt so I could see their mouth on me.

God.

The sight of them with my pussy in their mouth as they smiled up at me made my knees weak. Too bad it had to be cut short.

Their eyes widened in surprise as I called my magic and trapped us in our positions. Black dangerous magic was circling around us and if either one of us chose to move we would be zapped with the magic so hard it would leave a scar.

They growled against me.

"I didn't do anything," they said and bit the side of my thigh.

I let out a shaky breath and took another drag of the cigarette, this time to calm my nerves.

"Eli..." I trailed. "I love you."

They lifted a brow towards me and tried to pull back but the edge of their hair was burnt off as it touched the magic.

"That's not what you want to say," they said and left a kiss right where they just bit me, as if to apologize for their rash actions now that they knew I had them cornered.

"I do love you," I said, stronger this time.

Their eyes narrowed at me.

"But..."

I took a deep breath and looked up to the night sky.

"Xena hasn't contacted me," I whispered.

The stars were pretty tonight. They shone brighter than I ever remembered seeing them...but then again when was the last time I had a moment to look up at the stars and just admire them?

"That's a good thing," they said and licked the length of my slit.

I shuddered and tried to stay focused on what I wanted to say, but when two fingers entered me my mind went blank.

"Enjoy it while it lasts," Eli said and curled their fingers inside of me. I let out a loud whine as their thumb came to rub circles in my clit as they began to finger fuck me.

I cursed when the pleasure of their ministrations caused me to lose focus enough for my magical barrier around us to disappear. It was only a few seconds but it was enough for Eli to stand up and force me against the cold brick wall, this time with my back to them and my face biting into the brick.

They pushed themselves into me, their lips at my ear. The surprise change in the position caused me to lose grip on the cigarette but they stomped it out as it fell to our side.

"Don't want Rae to get pissy, hm?" they teased in my ear, their voice causing shivers to run down my spine.

They kicked my legs apart and forced their arm between me and the brick to rub fast, hard circles into my clit.

I let out a cry and pushed myself against them, but they were too strong.

"Where is that fight, hm?" they asked. "Is there anything you wish to tell me, little Original?"

I did. I had so much I wanted to talk to them about but I couldn't formulate the words as Eli's skilled fingers brought me closer and closer to the edge with each passing second.

They buried their face in the crook of my neck, their lips brushing my skin before inhaling me deeply.

"Or maybe I should say accuse?" they asked, their voice low.

Heat began to build up inside me so quick I knew that if I didn't stop Eli, I would be coming in mere seconds.

Then abruptly, they pulled back from me. I tried to follow them but they pushed me against the wall with one hand.

My entire pussy was throbbing as the stimulation was brutally paused. I was so close to coming that my entire body had already gone taunt, only for Eli to pull away at the last second.

"Say it," they growled. "Say what you came here to."

I swallowed thickly, unable to think of a coherent sentence.

"Ren," I choked out after a few moments. "He didn't show up to the games."

Eli let out a bitter laugh.

"A good thing too or else he may have been killed by your favorite," they spat. "I bet you wouldn't come to any of the others with these types of accusations. Why is it only me, Rosie?"

Guilt flooded my system, but I didn't let that stop me. I sent out a large flare of magic, something akin to a beacon, hoping it would reach the intended audience.

"I just wanted to make sure," I cried out. "If you know where he is then tell me. I already asked Malik to look at his apartment but it looked like he hadn't been there for *weeks*. Eli...please. There was a struggle. We saw the state of his apartment."

They pushed me harder into the wall.

"So Xena kidnapped him or something," they growled. "How the fuck should I know?"

Eli's hand disappeared, and I fell to the ground.

Rae's warm arms surrounded me and forced me back onto my feet. She sent calming waves towards me and I gripped her shirt tight. I peered over my shoulder to see Eli struggling against both Malik and Amr.

Taking a deep breath I unwound myself from Rae's arms and conjured a magical cage over them. Malik and Amr let go just in time not to get hurt by the bars of magic that had been brought down around Eli.

Eli let out a growl but knew better than to launch themselves at the bars.

"What are you doing Rosie?" Malik asked, his eyes locked on Eli.

"I wanted to ask—"

"Accuse!" Eli growled. "Accuse me of doing something with that stupid brother of yours."

All eyes were on me now.

"Xena has been quiet and Ren missed the games," I said. "He wouldn't miss the games. Malik, I asked you to check—"

"But you shouldn't accuse Eli of doing something if you have no proof of it," Malik cut in, his voice so hard it caused my chest to ache. "Yes, I checked his apartment and he was gone but that doesn't mean—"

"You know what that witch said!" I cried and gripped onto Rae for support. "No one would take him. No one except—"

"Me," Eli finished for me.

They let out a humorless laugh before turning and glaring at me.

"Eli," Rae warned. "Whatever you are thinking don't—"

"If you want me to be the villain for saving our asses, then so be it Rosie," Eli said cutting off Rae. They looked up to the sky with a crazed smile.

"I took him," they admitted.

Those three words caused me to freeze to the ground. My heart stopped beating and there was a violent sickness that ran through me.

"I took him and I wanted to kill him *so* badly," Eli said. "He was so fucking annoying. You know it's your fault right?"

They looked back towards me and stepped closer to the magical bars that kept them in place.

"What are you saying, Eli?" Malik asked.

"I heard you, all of you," they growled. "After you came back from your meeting. Rae and Malik wanted to hand him over too, did you know that Rosie? You act like they are literal gods walking on this earth but they are just as *fucked* up as me. They only didn't because they knew you wouldn't love them anymore. But not me. You will always love me, isn't that right?"

My stomach lurched and I had to hold onto Rae for support.

"Stop it," I whispered.

I knew they had all thought it would be easier to just hand Ren over and run for it...but I never thought they would take action. I tried to keep it a secret just because of this and now...

Images of a beat-up and bloodied Ren entered my mind.

Would Xena throw him in a cell like me?

Would she make him bleed?

Would she heal his wounds?

I had Amr and the others surrounding me every time I had faced Xena but Ren...he had *no one*.

Oh my God how long had he been with her?

"Some sister you are," Eli jabbed. "He has been missing for a *month*."

"Eli," I moaned, tears filling my eyes. "Please tell me you didn't. Please, Eli."

They sent me a wicked smile.

"I did and later you will thank me for it," they said confirming my worst thoughts.

The magic that had been bubbling up inside me began to heat my skin. I tried to focus on controlling it, but the thoughts of Eli betraying me had taken over my mind and I lost control.

The barrier around them dropped, and I pushed Rae away from me. I lunged forward, falling to the ground.

I needed to get out of here.

I tried to get up and run but Amr's warm hands were on me. I could feel him taking some of my magic, but it wasn't enough.

Everything since Xena had captured me until now had been carefully building up under my skin. It was threatening to take down everything around me. If I didn't escape now, it would destroy everything.

"Claudine," I choked out. "Get her here *now*."

Amr's grip on me tightened.

"Give me more," he said quickly.

"Rosie," Malik's voice came from above. "Let me help you."

Felling Rae's calming emotions, passing over me was my final straw.

"Everyone back the fuck up now!"

Amr's hands left me so quickly it was like I shocked him. I could hear the others scattering away and I stood slowly, taking in everyone.

Malik was in front of me, his hands up in front of him. Eli was to my right, staring at me with a smirk. I could feel Amr behind me and I assumed Rae was next to him.

"I won't ask again," I said through gritted teeth. "Get me Claudine."

Malik nodded and made a show of getting his phone. The magic stretched under my skin painfully and I let out a groan.

"Get her to get me some clothes as well," I ordered.

"Rosie, let's think this through —"

I cut Rae off with a growl.

"There is no more thinking through," I growled and shot a glare at Eli. "They ruined that when they decided to hand over my brother."

"If you just would have told me—"

They were cut off by Claudine's light of magic flashing between us.

She was wearing sweats and a hoodie, something I hadn't seen her in before. In her hands was a pile of clothing and there was a sad smile on her face.

"You are about to burst," she noted and handed me the clothing.

I quickly put on the hoodie and leggings she gave me, deciding that not was too much of an emergency to put on shoes.

"Rosie—"

This time it was Amr who tried to call me but I raised my hand to stop him.

"One more person tries to stop me from going, and it will cause me to explode and none of us want that to happen," I said. "Now whoever wants to come, grab onto Claudine. If not, you stay here with Daxton."

I wasn't surprised when all but Amr stepped forward.

"Take care of him for me," I told him.

He nodded.

"We will text Claudine when we plan to come over," he said. "I will attempt to wake him, then meet you there."

I shook my head.

"Watch over the place," I said. "I don't know what Xena is up to. Make sure Rae's mother and Daxton stay safe."

Rae's eyes widened before they sent a panicked look towards Amr.

"Rosie—"

"Please, Amr," I said. "Please."

His eyes widened and his form slumped forward.

"I love you, Rosie," he said. "If you don't come back to me you know I have no choice but to follow you into the next life."

I sent him a sad smile. I wanted to console him. Let him know that I would be back as soon as I could…but honestly I didn't know what Xena had planned, so I couldn't for sure say that I would be back.

"Keep the bed warm while I'm gone," I said and gave Claudine a nod.

There was no more time to wait. My magic was becoming so painful to hold back that white spots started to appear in my eyes.

"Where to?" she asked.

"Where it all started," I said. "Take me to Winterfell."

Chapter 28
Eli

Chaos.

As soon as we landed in Winterfell, it became chaos.

The entire campus had been covered by a disgusting type of film that quivered under our feet as we walked.

I knew it had to be some type of magic but it was more akin to a slime monster than anything else. It was warm, sticky, and covered every single surface.

Disgusting.

The thoughts of the people varied around me, but all of them had been just as taken aback by the scenery change as I had been. I had expected Rosie's anger...but I hadn't expected Malik's disappointment.

I heard in his mind very clearly that he had also wanted to give up Ren, so why was it suddenly a problem when I fixed everything for them?

He acted like I had just committed the gravest sin even though his mind was singing my praises just days ago when I was with *The Fallen.* The whiplash had me reeling and angered me beyond belief.

I knew they didn't like it when I acted on my own like this, but could they really not see what I had done for them? How I had gone out of my way so whatever it was that we had here could be safe?

Did they not realize that *I* was the person who had saved us all from Xena's reign?

Without me they would have been at her beck and call. They only complained now because they found out how they had all failed, but they hadn't said anything the month he was gone while we lived in peace. Because they enjoyed it too much and they *never* thought of the cost of a peaceful life.

The only reason that I was coming now, even though I really just wanted us all to leave it, was because I knew that Rosie was about to do something crazed. Against our better judgment all of us listened to her when she ordered us not to go against her and followed her into this battle.

It was a suicide mission...but for her we would do it.

Claudine looked back at me, her thoughts racing. She was trying to take in all the information around us and all the new things her power was picking up. But there was one thing that stayed in her mind.

Why didn't you tell her I helped you? she asked in her mind.

Because I can live if she hates me, I said. *Though I don't know about you.*

She hesitated before looking at Rosie and I saw a flash of a memory I hadn't seen before. Rosie in a dress far too bright for her and sitting in a garden. She was conjuring those magical birds she used to and there was a warm smile on her face.

I don't know why, but in that moment everything had changed for Claudine. She hadn't given much thought to Rosie's friendship before that point, but in that moment whatever she felt or saw changed things drastically.

Including Claudine going against her own brother to save Rosie.

So no, Claudine couldn't handle it.

"That doesn't look like it's coming from our meeting place," Malik said from my side.

I followed his gaze to see a bright light that was shining up into the night sky. It was so powerful it looked like the light was punching a hole through the darkness of the sky and the thought of it settled deep in my bones, causing the hair to stand up on the back of my neck. Even from so far away I could feel the power that was radiating off it. It was near the tower, but slightly further away and closer to the dorms.

"The garden," Rosie breathed. "She's at the garden."

"What's going on here?" I asked. No one answered so Claudine turned back towards me.

"I can't tell," she admitted. "But it's strong. Whatever she did to the campus feels...old."

Rosie hummed and looked at the ground. The slimy black tar-like substance had stuck to her socks and when she lifted her foot, the tar kept her sock with it.

"It feels...familiar," she said and looked out to the distance. "If you can, ask Maximus to strengthen the barrier around the house."

"On it," Claudine said and pulled out her phone.

"The students?" Rosie asked, her eyes shooting towards the direction of the dorms.

"I think that's the last thing we should worry about," I growled.

She sent me a heated look.

Don't be cruel, she warned in her mind.

"Eli's right," Malik spoke up, surprising me. "We don't have time to worry about them."

Rosie's face hardened.

"Rae?" she asked.

Rae's face stayed rock solid and then she quickly shook her head, but did not elaborate.

Rosie let out a sigh and looked back up to the light.

"Let's go," she said and pushed forward without any more fight.

It was hard to walk in the slime but each of us made do. By the time we had gotten closer the slime filled my shoes and traveled up my pant leg. It was disgusting and unclean. It caused my skin to crawl and it took everything in me to hold onto my lunch.

The slime...it moved like it was alive. It latched onto your skin and felt like it was trying to burrow inside of me. I swallowed thickly and tried to focus on Rosie's back as she led the group.

Her hair flowed around her and jerked with each step. Her hands were balled into fists, and there was an unmistakable aura around her.

One I had only felt once before and led to the destruction of my father.

It had taken five minutes longer than normal to get to the garden, but when we did I had to hold in a shocked gasp.

In the middle, the fountain was still there but it was now the source of the black tar that surrounded us. As we walked closer it came up to our ankles and had a putrid smell. The light was also shining from the fountain and there was a black elongated blob that floated above the fountain.

Squinting, I could make out that it was moving, much like the substance that was at our feet.

Rosie let out a gasp and tried to run to the far side of the garden, though the tar clung to her, making it hard to cross the space.

Around the corner, and covered in tar, was Ren, though you could barely make out the hybrid under all the gunk.

"Rosie, stop," Malik said and ran after her but he was too late.

The light that had been shining over the fountain exploded and threw all of us back against the adjacent wall.

Claudine's body flew into mine and Malik crushed my arm against the brick building.

Rae landed somewhere near, if her groan of pain was any indication.

I blinked rapidly. I tried to locate Rosie, but the bright light had taken over the entire area, blinding me.

With a growl, I pushed the two bodies off me and crawled through the slimy tar in search of Rosie. If I strained, I could hear her soft voice just over the groans and yells of the others. I used it as my guide, pushing through the gross material. It came up to my elbows now.

My mind was whirling and my chest had begun to burn. I couldn't breathe. I couldn't think. Everything in my entire body and soul pushed me forward to do the only thing it knew how to.

Find Rosie.

"Rosie!" I yelled and started to claw at the tar as it began to rise.

Then as quickly as it came, the light disappeared. My eyes took a few moments to adjust but when they did my yells lodged in my throat.

Rosie was on the ground, in front of her brother while Xena stood in front of them.

The silver-haired lady kneeled at her feet with her hands clutching the tar around her.

"This is enough Xena," Rosie growled. "Stop this and let him go."

She let out a laugh and turned to kick the woman at her side. She tumbled towards the ground and I watched in horror as the slime tried to consume her limp body.

Rosie's nostrils flared and she moved to lunge at Xena, but she was stopped with a powerful glare from the Original.

"Finish the ritual," she commanded. "Now that we have *two* of his offspring this should be faster."

"Xena," the woman moaned and shakily tried to sit back up. "It's too much. The magic, it's consuming me. I can't hold on—"

"You will stay here until the job is finished," Xena threatened, her manicured hand coming to yank at the woman's hair. "Or should I bring your daughter to come finish the job?"

The woman visibly paled and shot a glance towards Rosie and Ren.

Panicked thoughts ran through her mind and I saw a glimpse of white hair. She was scared, so scared that she was about to do something that would surely take her life.

But she didn't care about her life. Only her children's.

She was never a demon. She was a fucking hybrid witch.

"Xena!" Malik yelled from somewhere behind me.

In her mind, Xena knew not to look at him so she kept her eyes planted on her daughter.

Her thoughts disgusted me. She thought of her children as nothing more than a means to an end and thought that they were a disgrace. She had put time and power into them only for them to disobey her and scar her face.

She never had any urge to make peace with us. It had all been a farce so she could get enough blood from her offspring without killing them. That was the real reason she let Rosie go. She didn't do it because of what Rosie had offered; it was only because she knew that she had lost and that there was no way to keep her long enough so that they would be able to finish this.

That's why she had been so quiet.

She was bleeding Ren dry. Only keeping him alive so that she could use his blood. But now the hard part was done and she needed just one last sacrifice to make this work.

When her eyes flashed to the tar below her and she recognized the magical signature...everything kicked into place.

"She's a necromancer!" I yelled to the others. "She's bringing back an Original!"

Xena's fury-filled eyes flashed to me and before I had a chance to dodge, her magic shot out at me. It wrapped around me like vines and forced me into the ground. It took all my strength to keep my head from going under the slime, but the burning from the magic was almost too much for me to bear.

Tears welled in my eyes and my breath constricted.

Rosie's eyes flashed to mine and her cry for me was the last thing that I heard as the magic finally pushed me under. I tried to hold my breath but the slime had a mind of its own and forced its way into every crevice and into my mouth and nose, making it impossible for me to breathe.

The magic had disappeared, but it was useless to try and push myself up. The slime had wormed its way inside me, making it hard for me to focus. I lost control of my limbs and even the thoughts of the people around me began to disappear.

I had once enjoyed the thoughts of others when they died. I had found it fascinating what they chose to think about when they knew their life was slipping away from them, but I found myself no different than them.

I fought like hell to regain control of my body. I cursed Xena and her *fucking* nerve to do this to us. I cursed the gods. I cursed this school. I cursed Rosie for making it so hard for me to leave her.

And most of all I cursed myself because if I had just left everything as it was, I wouldn't be dying.

Most people when they died worried about what would become of their loved ones, but I was different.

I was selfish.

I only worried about what would happen after I died.

Malik, Rae, and Rosie would all die with me, that was a no-brainer...but would I ever see her again. Was that argument the last time we would ever speak to each other again? I didn't want this to be the end.

It couldn't be.

I was scared that I would never see her again. Never hold her.

It was selfish but all I wanted was her.

I wanted to feel her skin against mine. Feel the way her nails scratched my scalp when she thought I was asleep. Hear her whispering in my ear as we lay in bed.

I wanted to hear her say she loved me, *and I wanted to say it back.*

This couldn't be it, right? I couldn't have my life taken from me so easily, could I? We had just started this fight. I had just started realizing who I really was and this? This was it?

Damn it all.

Just as I felt my consciousness slipping, a strong hand grabbed my arms and forced me up. I could feel the cool air from the outside hit my skin. The slime from around me fell off my skin, but it was still *inside* me.

Then something strong and akin to a punch rocked my gut.

Once.

Twice.

Three times and the slime ejected itself from my body.

I forced my arms to wipe the tar off my face and with shaky, barely responsive hands I finally was able to wipe it clear, but Rosie was no longer in front of me. My eyes darted to the fountain, though my vision was blurry and it made it hard to see. In anger I wiped my eyes hard and the next time I blinked them clear I finally saw her.

Her eyes were wide as they looked towards me and her mouth formed a snarl as her limbs flapped around wildly. Xena was over her, her manicured hands gripping at her head and body, pushing her closer to the fountain until she was just next to it.

And then Rosie tilted.

The hands forced me up again and I looked up to see Malik. His gaze was set on Rosie and words were coming out of his mouth but I couldn't hear him. The slime had wormed its way deep into my ear canal making the words muffled.

I forced my limbs to move and pushed forward, towards the fountain, desperate to get Rosie out of her grasp. My legs were clumsy, but with enough force I made it to the fountain and gripped the witch's hair in my hands.

Her eyes widened when they met mine and she let out a shriek which was short-lived when I forced her to the magic fountain. Rosie fell from her grasp and into the tar below but Rae was there, catching her before she sank.

Xena fought against me, but I kept a strong hold on her. I tried my hardest to push her into the fountain, hopefully killing her but there was a powerful burst through me and I found myself immobilized. No matter how close she was or how much I wanted to end her pitiful life...I couldn't.

Malik's power.

Xena quickly fought back against my frozen body and I couldn't do anything other than stand my ground. I tried to search for Malik over my shoulder, but I couldn't do that and keep an eye on Xena.

"Malik!" I yelled. "Your power!"

Xena's magic burst against my side and a white-hot burning covered my entire right side. I let out a choked groan and glared at the *cunt*.

She may have been fighting for her life, but I saw what she was really feeling in her eyes. She thought she was winning. She had assumed that we would never beat her and now her assumptions proved correct. She thought she had us cornered. Thought that we would bend. When I pushed against her, her mind took an abrupt shift.

Her thoughts were panicked. Jumping back from me, to Rosie, to Malik, back to Rosie, then to the body that was growing above us. She was piecing together a plan, even as she struggled against me.

"Fuck you," I growled.

Her eyes flashed and a sinister smile spread across her face.

"You're just as weak as your father," she screeched.

Her magic kicked up and just as I saw dark spots flash over my vision, Malik's hands came to grab ahold of her alongside me.

"Eli," they growled, barely audible. "I release you from my power."

And just like that I felt the powerful force that had been holding me to the ground snap and we pushed her closer to the fountain. As soon as the light brushed across her skin she let out a screech. I couldn't make out much given how powerful the light was but if the burning smell of flesh told me anything, this would do the trick.

Xena couldn't even finish her scream as we pushed her into the fountain. Her magic disappeared, and I let out a relieved sigh. I didn't dare look down to see the damage on my body but I knew by the feel of it, I would be in a hospital bed for quite some time.

Beyond the light, I caught a glimpse of her bubbling power and a flash of the brown of her eyes, but nothing else. Everything else had been disintegrated and that was all that was left of her. Malik's power rose around us so powerfully, the air was stifling. I couldn't hear the words he spoke, but they were clear enough in his mind.

Die and stay dead, he had commanded her.

The light of the fountain exploded once more and we were all thrown back. This time I had enough of a warning to brace myself and instead of staying on the ground I crawled over to Rosie.

She and Rae were on the ground a few feet away from us. They had recovered quickly and were speaking to each other, but their voices didn't reach my ears.

I grabbed Rosie's face and forced her to look at me.

"I can't hear," I tried to choke out but her thoughts told me that it came out jumbled and husky; the tar had done worse damage on my throat than I realized.

I tried again but both of their gazes were pulled back to the fountain.

I felt the insane thrum of power before I saw it and my gaze snapped back towards the fountain where the black tar blob on top had become a full-fledged body. Then, in an instant, the light cut out and all the tar around us began returning to the body.

The tar that was deep in my ears was pulled out so hard that there was an intense ringing and pain shot through my head.

I cried out and fell into Rae's and Rosie's hold.

I could hear the world around us better now, but it was still muffled and felt as though I was hearing everything from underwater.

When new thoughts filled my mind I looked back towards the fountain to see the body standing fully erect at the top, looking up at the stars.

It was a man. His long black hair fell to his waist and his purple eyes shone in the darkness; he was marveling at the sky just like Rosie had a few hours ago. His thoughts were structured better than anyone I had ever met and there was a clear path to it. He was old, as old as my father...but he was dangerous.

Marques's memories inside me lit up and I knew for a fact that the man standing in front of us was Rosie's father, and it wasn't a good thing that he was here instead of Xena.

My gaze caught Claudine on the far side of the fountain. She was kneeling over the necromancer, who was but a lump on the ground. Claudine's thoughts told me that she was dead. Behind Claudine was Ren's unconscious form. He had been saved from injury but even from so far away I could tell that he had been starved to the brink of dying.

"What a pity," I could hear the man on top of the fountain say. He rolled his shoulders and white wings burst out of his back. His purple eyes shifted to look down at us, then looked over to Malik.

I follow his gaze to see Malik still recovering from the blast. At first I thought he had just been knocked to the ground like me, but his injury became obvious when he sat up fully to meet the man's gaze.

There was a large piece of the fountain sticking out of his abdomen, and normally with demon healing that wouldn't be cause for concern...but it was much bigger and took up a majority of his torso.

With a grimace Malik took the stone with both hands and pulled it out of his stomach.

"No!" Rosie and I screamed.

He threw the concrete slab to the ground and shakily moved to his knees and into a submissive position I had seen only in Marques's memories. He placed his head onto the dirty ground and breathed in deeply. From my position I could see his sides healing, but blood was still pouring out of his front.

"Malik," the man said in a tone that was smiler to a parent expressing disappointment in their child.

The man jumped from the fountain and came to stand in front of Malik.

"Zuriel, forgive me," Malik said, pain evident in his voice.

"How could such a lowly little bastard be the one to end me?" he asked and stepped on Malik, forcing him to the ground.

Malik said something but his voice was too low for me to hear, but Zuriel heard it just fine.

"A life for a life then," he said and removed his foot before stretching his hand out, black fire gathering in his palm.

"No!"

Before I knew it I was rushing towards Malik and covering him with my body. Zuriel paused, his eyes on me. He didn't extinguish the fire in his hand, but I heard his thoughts loud and clear.

"Don't," I pleaded. "Malik is the last one left of your circle, the last one on your side. Without him, you would be alone in this world, vulnerable to other Originals. You *need* him, need *us*."

"Don't play with me low-level," Zuriel growled and the black flame grew in his hand. "Your life ends here."

I felt the heat of the flame just as I was thrown to the ground. I closed my eyes ready to get taken by the flame, but when it didn't come I pried my eyes open to see Malik's pained expression on top of me.

His wings were out and spread around me, protecting me from the flames. But I couldn't say the same for him. His wings and back were on fire. His feathers were falling off in clips and the skin of his wings began to melt.

His sweat dripped onto my face pulling my eyes back to him.

"I'm sorry Eli," he said.

"Malik..." I choked out.

For the first time for someone besides Rosie, my chest began to ache. It was so powerful it caused tears to weld in my eyes and a panic like I had never felt exploded inside me. His thoughts changed. He was no longer thinking about the pain, but had only wished to do what was best for me.

He failed me. His biggest regret was that he left me with Damon to rot and in his mind...this was penance.

The fire stopped suddenly and I heard Rosie from over Malik, but I couldn't hold onto her. All I could do was hold Malik's gaze as he went over every single moment of his life that he regretted.

He left me with one single thought.

Thank you for allowing me to love you this last time, Eli.

Chapter 29
Rosie

"Father, Father!" I begged at the man's feet.

His eyes darted towards me and a scowl marred his face. He looked just like the drawing in Principal Winterfell's book and hadn't aged a day since.

His power spread out around us and now I realized why that disgusting tar had such a familiar magical signature. It's because it was him.

The same magic I felt from Daxton.

The same magic I felt from Xena...

It was all *him*.

I had an image of what my father should have been and even if I never admitted it, I had hoped inside that he would be different from Xena. That he would be the person I dreamed of. The parent that would show me that everyone else in my life had been wrong.

Malik and Principal Winterfell had given me a hope that he would be different. A hope that he was better than the rest and that he wasn't the monster Xena portrayed him to be.

I wished he could show me what a parent's love could really be, but when he looked at me with those narrowed eyes I had a sinking feeling that he would be just like the rest.

"Please, you know me, right?" I asked and gripped at his free hand. "It's Rosie. I'm your daughter. Ren, your son, he's over there. Please let's just talk—"

His hand connected with the side of my face. A sharp burning pain flashed across me and I had to bite my tongue to stop the groan of pain from my lips. Rae's hands pulled me back to her and I was left clutching my face and staring at him in shock.

His chest puffed and his wings flapped around him. Now I understood why Malik had immediately lowered himself in front of him. This demon made all the others that came before him seem like children.

Everything about him screamed otherworldly. His aura, the way he looked down on you, hell even his features seemed far too perfect to be human.

But it was a nice package for a devil. No one would suspect him otherwise.

You have seen the types of monsters they throw out of there... Do you really want to see what still resides there? Marques's words swam through my mind.

No, I really didn't want to know but it seemed like I was going to get a taste whether I liked it or not.

"You act as if I was not present through everything you and your disgusting friends had been doing," he spat, his eyes full of anger. "I watched as you single-handedly destroyed everything that we have worked for. Do you know how many years we had to work to get this done? And you think just because you are Xena's daughter that you have the right to throw away everything?"

"Father I—"

I was cut off by another slap. My eyes filled with tears and I couldn't stop the pained moan from escaping from my mouth.

"You are a pitiful excuse for a daughter," he growled and his eyes shifted to Eli and Malik. "And he is a disgusting excuse for an Original's offspring. He doesn't deserve your or anyone's mercy and I cannot wait until his head is on my stake."

I gripped at his hand once more.

"Please," I begged. "This is not how we want to end things. Please don't hurt anyone else. All we want is to live in peace."

His eyes snapped towards Rae.

"Try that again and I will cut your head off," he threatened.

This was not the demon Principal Winterfell had told me about. This person was a monster. All the originals were. No matter what lies they had passed on to the generations before them, none of them were true. Each and every one chose their own destructive path and didn't give a damn about who they had to hurt to get what they wanted.

All they have ever cared about was themselves... there truly were no good guys here.

"Father—"

"Don't," he growled. "I am sick of your whining, and you are no child of mine."

He paused to look over Eli and Malik and there was an awkward pause before he let out a heavy sigh.

"I thought you were worth something, Malik," he growled and looked back up at the sky. "You were so perfect. So obedient. So powerful. You were all of our dreams and *this* was what you turned into? Marques corrupted you and turned you into a disgusting excuse for a demon."

His eyes traveled back to me.

"You may think that consuming Marques would give you power, but that is not true," he said. "All it does is corrupt you. Weak, *pitiful* bodies like yours were not made to house such power which is why even in this moment you are *nothing*. You will never be an Original, no matter how you pretend. It was disgusting watching you pretend."

"I never tried to be anything other than what I am," I growled, unable to stop myself. "I never wanted this. I never *asked* for this."

Rae's hand gripped my sides.

"Don't," she growled in my ear.

Father let out a huff of a laugh.

"You think we asked to be sent here?" he asked, his voice turning hard. "You think I asked for the humans to despise us? You think I asked for them to take all of our children and force us to watch as they dismembered and *ate* them?"

I shuddered at the intensity in his voice.

"You can't be a monster," I forced out. "I heard about you, what you did for this school, for the children—"

"You know nothing!" he growled, his wings flapping and causing the air around us to shift. "I am not the man in their memories. I haven't been since the ones I protected and fought for betrayed me."

He paused, looking back towards Malik, his breathing uneven.

"It's not too late," I said and tried to reach for his hand again but he slapped it away. His eyes bore into me.

"For a short while, I thought you would live up to our expectations," he muttered. His hand slowly cupped my cheek and I couldn't help but flinch as his cold skin touched mine. "You were much like her. Shy at first, but when you got a taste of that power..." He let out a dark laugh before it was cut off abruptly. "You could have done so well. And now she is dead."

"Father, I'm sor—"

His hand gripped my chin harshly and stopped me from speaking. My jaw began to ache but I didn't dare fight him, not when he held my pitiful life literally in the palm of his hand.

He was angry. I had angered my father and one of the most powerful Originals to walk on this earth. I had but a few precious seconds to prove that I wasn't a stupid disappointment like he had assumed and I had just about thrown them all away.

It was also the thing that would determine whether or not the loves of my life could live on. The only thing stopping the horror that awaited us. And I couldn't seem to get a word out, not with his grip so hard on my chin that I could feel the bruises bloom under my skin.

"Don't lie to me child," he growled then threw my head to the side. His eyes shifted back to the fountain. "But if it consoles you, I am not the least bit hurt. Xena was once beautiful and powerful...but she has lost herself and there is only you to blame."

It didn't console me. If anything it made me feel worse.

"Father—"

"Consider yourself lucky that I leave you be," he growled, his eyes shifting back towards me. "You have disgraced me and your entire heritage. The only reason I am going to leave you alive is so that someday I can take back the power I have *wasted* on you."

He crouched and without another word launched himself into the sky, his wings flapping in powerful gusts bringing him up higher and higher into the sky until he was nothing more than a speck.

I didn't have time to think of the way his disappearance both caused a weight to lift off my shoulder while also causing the dark pit of despair inside me to deepen. I launched myself towards Eli and Malik. Eli had shifted Malik so that he lay in their arms, his eyes already closing. Rae followed me, keeping a steady hand on my back.

"Fuck, Malik," I whispered and ran my hands over his body. His wings were burnt to a crisp and his entire back had large burns across it that melted his skin. The wound on his stomach had mostly closed but there was a noticeable drop in his healing speed.

His eyes fluttered open and he looked towards Eli before his eyes traveled towards mine.

They were no longer the vibrant gold they had once been and instead were now so dull they were almost gray.

It scared me. I wasn't ready to go through this and couldn't help but regret ever pushing us to come here. It was my fault that Malik ended up this way and it would be my fault if anything happened to him.

"I'm sorry, Rosie," he choked out.

"Stop," I said tears filling my eyes. "Don't be sorry. Claudine!"

I called the witch over, hoping we could salvage him. Most of my magic had been taken out by Xena but I would give him every last drop if I knew it would save him.

"Rosie," Rae said from behind me. "This doesn't look good."

Claudine was by us in an instant, looking over his wounds.

"We need to take him home," she said. "To Maximus. I don't—I can't... He's dying."

"Take him," I said quickly. "Take him and if you can Eli. They both need medical attention."

"Rosie," Eli said, their voice far louder than it needed to be.

I knew their ears were messed up and I prayed that Maximus could fix them too.

"I'll try," Claudine said. "Meet me at home with Ren."

Then, just like that, they were gone.

Chapter 30
Rosie

Three months later

The ticking from the clock on the wall had begun to annoy me as we sat in these chairs. My back had begun to ache and my overexerted magic had begun to shift under my skin, begging to be released.

It had been a long few months, between caring for Malik, Rae's mom, and Daxton. Every day I would heal one of them or share magic with Daxton and even though we still had four other magic users under our roof—plus Ren if he was feeling generous—it was still getting out of hand. I didn't have an ounce of magic left for myself and more often than not I found myself unable to even leave my bed after the day's end.

Malik had remained in a coma for the last few months as his body healed from the burns. The only thing that gave me hope was that Eli could hear his dreams and Rae could feel his emotions. There was nothing that those dreams or emotions told us other than that sometimes he still felt pain and had a nightmare now and then.

Doctor Svensson had been more than willing to help the man that saved his life and was constantly over, helping me pour magic into his skin. Every day we would sit around him and focus on healing his extensive injuries. At first we didn't know if our magic would react badly to his skin and just make it any worse than it already was, but after a while he had shown a great deal of improvement.

But still it wasn't enough. He remained stuck in that bed and away from all of us.

Eli had taken over for him with *The Fallen*, and combined with that and the investing Rae had done, we were well off and would be cared for even if he remained that way for years to come.

But that didn't mean that we didn't need him and it didn't mean that it hurt any less to miss him.

I thought about that night over and over for the last few months, reliving every small detail.

I remembered the way the slime felt against my skin. The way it felt to see Ren's frail body after a month of being stuck in Xena's claws. I remember how it felt to see Eli getting taken by the slime and how it felt to see my father burn Malik's wings clean off.

That would be hard to explain to him as well, though I knew that when all the memories of that night came back to him he would remember that my father had literally melted his wings off as repayment for the betrayal of him and Marques.

If there was anything I could change about that night it would have been that I had broken out of my bubble sooner.

I shoulder have paid attention to what was going on around me. I should have seen the signs. And if I had, maybe Eli wouldn't have done what they had and Malik wouldn't have been in a coma for the last few months.

It wasn't fully Eli's fault though. I had come to realize this after they came to me and apologized.

It had taken months for us to start talking again and even now I found myself still doubting whether I could trust them...but I believed in second, maybe third or fourth chances in Eli's case.

I rolled my sore shoulders feeling a shooting pain running up my arms from my everyday stiff posture of pouring magic into the patients. Doctor Svensson and Claudine gave me a break for the last few days so I could recuperate in time for the end-of-year banquet, but if I was honest I was still ready to collapse and I was in no way prepared for the event tonight.

Rae shifted behind the desk and let out a loud sigh.

"I know," I mumbled and reached over the desk for her hand, giving it a little squeeze before letting it go. "It's almost over."

She let out a huff of a laugh.

"Or it's just the beginning," she said in a tone that matched my exhaustion.

She had had a hard time as well, always running around and making sure everyone was taken care of. She didn't show it but I know even after everything, she was ecstatic to have her mother back. At this point, her mother could barely stay awake for more than a few hours but the hope was that as she was able to regulate her body again, she would be able to get up and move around.

She was the mom everyone needed, just like I had thought.

She was surprised to see how many people Rae surrounded herself with but was happy that someone was "taking care of her babies" as she put it. Yes *babies,* though I was ashamed to say I had almost forgotten about Rae's brothers since they had been off to college.

I left them alone most of the time but there would be times where I would catch Rae, late in her room at night, whispering to her with a smile that I had rarely seen myself. We hadn't told her brothers yet for fear that everything would fall apart as soon as we uttered the sentence, but in time they would find out.

He's coming, Eli's voice said in my mind,

I straightened in my seat and gave the office a once over.

Principal Winterfell's stuff was still piled against the walls and gave no indication that he was going to move it anytime soon, no matter what he had previously said about leaving this role behind. This day had taken some planning and pulling from various resources, but surprisingly between Rae, Eli, and myself, we were able to pull some strings without the use of Malik's power.

The door opened to show the purple-haired Principal and his smile dropped as soon as I turned towards him.

I sent him a smile and both Rae and I stood.

"Have a seat, James," I said and waved to the seat next to me.

He raised a brow and shook his head.

"I think this is the second time I caught you in my seat, Rae," he said and stepped towards the desk. "Aren't you supposed to be at the banquet, Rosie. You look oddly casual for it?"

I stuffed my hands in the pocket of my hoodie and shrugged.

"That doesn't start for another few hours," I said. "Plus, this is far more important."

Rae shuffled through the desk drawer and pulled out a stack of papers. The silence of the room gripped us by the throats and I could feel the tension roll off Principal Winterfell in waves. I was sure if I strained I could probably also hear Eli chuckling and as if to prove my thoughts, their laughter filled my mind. A smile threatened to tug across my lips.

I saw Rae's eyes light and her lips twitch as well.

"Hey!" Principal Winterfell protested and crossed the room to grip Rae's hand.

She glared at him and I felt the room drop in temperature. His hand slowly unclasped from her wrist and he shakily stood up.

She turned back to the stack of papers and started shuffling through them.

"Sign here," she said and handed him a pen.

He took the pen with a shaky hand but as soon as his eyes landed on the paper, he snorted.

"You're kidding," he said, his eyes shooting towards me.

"Nope," I said and crossed my arms over my chest. "Sign it."

He rolled his eyes and sent a look towards Rae.

"Was this your plan all along?" he asked. "Let me guess, you have something else up your sleeve and if I don't sign this you will hold it against me? If you haven't heard yet, I am going to be leaving soon. I don—"

"Ah yes," Rae said in an exaggerated tone. *As if* she actually forgot this part of the plan. She dug into the desk and pulled out another thicker stack of papers and flipped through them before pointing to where he needed to sign. "Here as well."

Principal Winterfell threw the pen across the room. It cracked and exploded against the wall leaving a large black stain on the wall.

"We will have to clean that," I said with a frown.

"Tammy can do it," Rae said quickly and produced another pen for him. "You fucked a student who was murdered here, James. Do the wise thing."

His eyes widened and he gave me a look, as if I could stop this whole thing.

"You can't be serious," he said with a panicked tone. "I thought we were done with this?"

Send him in, I said in my mind.

Got it, Eli replied and only moments later did a member of *The Fallen* open the office door in his Demon Regulation Society uniform. He looked right at the shaken purple-haired man and smiled, showing all of his pearly white teeth.

"Gods," Principal Winterfell moaned. "Please tell me you are joking."

"I am not," Rae said. "Now sign here or we will let the nice man take you back to his office to ask you some questions."

Principal Winterfell looked over to the uniformed demon and with a sigh grabbed the pen from Rae's hand before signing the paperwork.

Rae let out a hum of approval before flipping the pages for him and pointing out where he needed to sign.

The uniformed guard sent me a smile and a wink, and I let my own smile form on my face.

Let him do that again and I will cut his hands off and make you walk with a limp for a week, Eli growled in my mind.

I shivered and turned back to Rae whose eyes were also on me. There was a heat in her gaze that made my knees weak.

She wants to fuck you on that desk, Eli explained. *I asked her if I could watch.*

It took all I had in me to stifle down my giggle.

Enough, I shot back.

Principal Winterfell set down the pen with a loud sigh.

"I had a plan for this," he grumbled.

"Yes," Rae said with distaste. "A high-level demon with a more dirty laundry list than you and your many side pieces."

Principal Winterfell flushed but cleared his throat and extended his hand out to Rae.

"Congrats," he said as she shook his hand. "In a few months' time this seat will be yours."

Rae gave him a smile.

"You don't read your contracts do you?" she asked and signaled for the officer to take him.

Principal—well I guess it's just *James* now—spluttered and tried to fight him as he stepped closer.

"But I thought you said—"

"Cooperate or I will add resisting arrest into your sheet, James," the officer said.

James let the officer cuff him all while staring at us with his jaw open.

"Goodbye James," Rae said with a smile. "It was a pleasure doing business with you."

"Take him out through the quad," I told the officer. "Let the students see."

"Yes ma'am," they said with a smile and left with a shell-shocked James.

I walked over to Rae and planted a kiss on her lips.

"Congrats, Principal Ashwell," I said with a purr.

She smiled and pulled me closer.

"Eli will be here soon," they whispered against my lips. "Lie over the desk would you?"

I couldn't stop the giggle from my lips.

* * *

"Dance with me," Eli said in my ear as they pulled me to the dance floor.

Elle Mae

We had emptied one of the unused ballrooms and used it for the end-of-the-year banquet I had promised the other low-levels. We filled it with the best catering we could find, and allowed the students to have just a bit of alcohol. It was a hit.

I had originally wanted to keep it to low-levels but after some choice complaints from the high-level demons, I had chosen to extend it to all students and I was glad I did.

Demons and witches alike all chatted and danced with each other in a way that wouldn't have been possible just two years ago. For the first time, there was no fighting between the groups and a few of the high-level demons had even come up to thank me for inviting them.

I may not have accomplished much at Winterfell, but this was one thing I think I could safely say was my biggest achievement.

"I didn't know you danced," I teased, but made sure to say it louder than usual. They still had trouble hearing after the events in the garden, though hopefully in time it would get better and if not...Eli seemed pretty comfortable using their mind-reading powers to make up for it. I let them pull me to the dance floor, but just as we were going to step on, a hand shot out and gripped Eli's wrist.

We both looked over to see Ren standing there with a forced smile.

"I think I can call in my favor and say you owe me this," he said and sent a glare to Eli.

After he had awoken, he had been understandably unhappy with Eli and still was. I didn't have to force Eli to apologize to both him and me, but it was still hard to get over.

Ren had made it obvious that he had no plans to be friends with Eli, but he at least forgave them enough to be civil...and to be honest I think he liked throwing something in their face after all the shit he went through.

"I guess you're right," Eli said and leaned forward to place a lingering kiss on my forehead. "Find me when you are done, I have a *surprise.*"

I raised a brow at them but they only smirked and left before I could ask.

I gave my hand to Ren and we easily slid into the flow of the crowd. Light classical music filled the air and people on the dance floor swayed and pulled along their dates, careful to not bump into anyone beside them.

While I may not have come from a family background like most of the people here who probably had some type of training on this dance, I joined my brother with ease. For once I didn't care if we messed up, or if the people in this room looked at us weird. Hell, I didn't even care if we downright embarrassed ourselves because I was happy to be here with him.

With a content sigh I leaned my head on his shoulder, enjoying his warmth. It had been a rough few months of his recovery but he was finally back to looking like the healthy demon he once was.

He stiffened before leaning into me as well.

"I wanted to tell you I am leaving Winterfell," he said from above me.

My eyes shot open, but I didn't try to move from his hold as he brought us around the dance floor in tandem with the music.

"Is it too much?" I asked, images of his almost death and resurrection of our father running through my mind.

I could feel his hair brush across me as he shook his head.

"No," he said softly. "I have actually just decided to do some traveling."

I pulled back to look at him; there was a light blush covering his face.

"Traveling?" I asked. "With someone?"

His blush deepened and he looked off in the distance.

I let out a scandalized gasp.

"Ren you are dating someone and I didn't know about it?" I asked. "I am offended you didn't tell me! Who are they? I need to meet them before you go off to God knows where with them."

He cleared his throat before looking down at me.

"I think you know them very well," he said and paused in his steps to turn me around.

I gave him a look and looked into the crowd, but I couldn't see anyone that stood out.

"Who?" I asked.

He let out a deep sigh and pointed to the very corner of the room where both Claudine and Maximus stood in the corner talking to each other.

I had invited them but I didn't realize they would come. They were both dressed up beautifully and—

"Both of them?" I asked with a gasp, my own face heating.

"Claudine!" Ren hissed and pulled me out of the dance floor. "I just wanted to tell you. We will be leaving after this and won't be back for a few weeks but as long as Maximus is here the ward—"

I cut him off with a hug, which he slowly returned.

"I'm glad," I admitted, feeling a weight lift off my chest. "I'm surprised it's her, but I am glad you found someone to be happy with."

"It's nothing serious yet," he said, pulling away from me. His face was flushed so bright it clashed with his eyes.

"*Yet*," I reminded and patted him on the arm. "Now go. *Apparently*, Eli has a surprise for me. Make sure to check in often, okay?"

He nodded and turned to look at Claudine, who waved at him.

"I'll see you around, Rosie," he said with a small smile.

"Until next time," I said and sent him off with a small wave.

It was bittersweet watching him go but if this was what would make him happy, I wouldn't make him stay.

With a sigh I looked for Eli but couldn't find them right away.

I weaved through the crowd greeting those I knew and congratulating the seniors on their upcoming graduation. I almost lost myself in all the chatter until I saw a flash of blond hair near the back end of the room. I just made out Eli's face before they disappeared down the hallway.

Feeling a giddy excitement fill me I rushed after them and into the hallway that led out to the adjacent courtyard.

We had decorated it with lights and tables for those who wanted to get away from the party and I was glad to see that there were a few people out here, but Eli was conveniently missing.

To your left, they said in my mind.

I looked over to see them at the edge of the courtyard and near another small corridor, though I knew this led to a smaller ballroom, one that we had chosen not to use based on the amount of people on the invite list.

A familiar heat started to build in my stomach when I realized where this was going and hurried over to them.

Catch me if you can, little Original, they said and disappeared down the corridor.

I followed them with a small chuckle. When I rounded the corner I didn't catch sight of them, but I did feel a familiar magical signature.

"Daxton..." I breathed and hurried down the corridor, where I saw a single door open to the second ballroom.

Without wasting time I barged into the room and in front of me was Rae, Daxton, Amr and Eli.

Rae and Eli had dressed up in suits for the event but Daxton and Amr kept it casual. Daxton had a healthy glow to his skin and for the first time in months he was up and out of the house... There was even a small smile on his face.

They blew my breath away.

I heard a shifting behind me before cold hands covered my eyes and a familiar scent filled my senses.

"You look ravishing," Malik whispered in my ear.

My heart lodged into my throat and I whipped around to get a good look at him.

I must be dreaming, I thought but when I turned Malik's golden eyes looked down at me and there was a smile on his face. He was much skinnier than he had been before his coma but he was *here* and he was standing by himself.

Tears stung my eyes and began streaming down my face before I could even register them.

"Malik," I whispered and reached up to touch his face. My hand shook as I traced the familiar scars on his face.

"Have you missed me?" he asked with a devilish grin.

I launched myself at him and captured his lips in mine.

His hands gripped my waist and pulled me impossibly close to him. I threaded my fingers into his hair and deepened the kiss. He groaned against me and entered his tongue into my mouth. His kiss caused an explosion of heat to go off inside me and my exhausted magic sprang to life.

I missed him so much. So much more than I thought possible. Even though he had been laying in that bed protected by all of us, it hurt every single second that he was in that coma.

"I'm sorry," I whispered against his lips before continuing to kiss him.

Rough hands grabbed my shoulder and neck and I was pulled off of him. Malik's flushed face and heated gaze was on me even as Eli pulled me off him. He had worn a hoodie and sweats and even though I was ecstatic to see him and wanted to make up for lost time, my heart hurt when I saw how frail he looked compared to his form before.

"Easy, little Original," they cooed in my ear and bit down on the soft flesh of my lobe. "The man just got out of his hospital bed."

I reached back out to Malik and pulled at his hoodie. I wasn't ready to let him go.

"There is no need to be sorry Rosie," he said, his hand coming out to grip my own. My heart started pounding in my chest and Eli gripped my throat harder, making it more evident just how fast my heart was racing as it pounded against their hand.

"We are not here to hash out what happened," Eli said in my ear.

"Then what are we here for?" I asked and tried to look back up at them but they gripped my chin and forced it back to Malik.

"I need some help," Malik said with a shrug and took a step closer, sandwiching me between them. I pushed back into Eli and their hand trailed down my arm and to my stomach, pushing me closer into them. "I couldn't wait to see you but they had me in that fucking bed until I was strong enough to see you again."

Anger flashed through me but as soon as it rose it was gone and replaced with something *much* warmer.

A soft, lithe hand gripped my cheek and softly pushed me to look to my left. Eli's hand moved from my chin to my throat, allowing Rae to make me face her.

"You were busy and he was weak—still is," Rae explained in a soft voice. When her eyes trailed down my form I couldn't help but shiver. "So we decided to bring him *here* and *lend a hand.*"

Eli stepped away from me and I tried to look towards them but Rae stopped me by forcing her lips to mine.

I let out a whine as she devoured me. Malik's hands pulled my dress up enough so that his palms could roam up my thighs. I almost forgot about Eli until there was something soft that hit the back of my legs.

In an instant I was pulled away from the both of them and forced down onto some sort of cloth-covered bench. It was taller than the seats we had filled the other room with and laying on it made me come to almost waist height. Eli's hands kept me down on the bench, their blue eyes glittering as the others came to stand around me. Rae stood at the end of the bench, her knees brushing against mine. Malik was towards my right, his eyes looking hungrily down at me and his hand already on the tie on his pants. Daxton and Amr stood next to Eli towards my left. Amr's hands had already begun roaming Daxton's body and heat coiled in my belly when Daxton's breath hitched.

"Me first," Malik growled.

Eli's hands grabbed me and positioned me so that my legs were towards them. They kneeled in between them, their rough hands roaming up my thighs and to my lacy underwear.

"Head back Rosie," Rae commanded, her hand coming to push my chin up.

Shakily I did what she asked and I was met with an upside-down version of Malik staring at me. He kneeled down just as Eli began moving my panties. He planted a kiss on my lips before leaning back to look at me. His fingers traced my lips and he let out a shaky sigh.

"I love you Rosie," he whispered and then forced two fingers into my mouth just as Eli's face was buried between my legs, their tongue running across my length. Malik's fingers muffled my moan. "But I'm going to fuck this mouth of yours like I *loathe* you."

God.

His words startled me as much as they turned me on.

Eli sucked on my clit and Malik removed his fingers, causing my moan to ring out through the empty room. He trailed his spit-covered fingers down my chest and pushed my dress down just far enough so that my breasts were exposed.

He pinched my nipple, pulling a pained moan out of my mouth which Eli only turned into heat as they entered two fingers into me.

"These are for Rae," Malik whispered, his voice husky. Then he stood slowly, his eyes trailing my body. I couldn't stop the moans from spilling out of my mouth as Eli fucked me in earnest, their thrusts so hard it caused the bench below me to screech against the floor. I gripped onto the bench but I felt Rae's hand pull at my wrist and force my hand into Eli's hair. Eli hummed appreciatively, their mouth vibrating against my clit at the action.

Malik wasted no more time and pulled his erection out of his sweatpants and settled closer to me. My mouth watered as I got a good look at him. I had seen it clearly only one other time, and even then I yearned to taste it and *finally* here it was.

I opened my mouth for him and his hand caressed my face before he thrust into me. His size made me gag, but it didn't seem to bother him. On the contrary as soon as he heard me his soft hand left me and he pulled back only to slowly enter me again with a growl.

"Fuck Rosie," he growled and pulled back again to thrust in, harder this time. I let out a choked moan as Eli sucked hard on my clit.

Combined with them finger fucking me and Malik's ministrations, heat was pooling in my stomach so fast that if we didn't slow down I would be coming soon.

The next moan that was out of my mouth seemed to stir something in Malik and he began thrusting into my mouth without rest. I arched feeling my orgasm ride through me, but Rae's hand pushed me down and helped Malik go even deeper down my throat.

Malik cursed and I felt teeth bite down on my nipple, throwing me violently into my first orgasm. I sobbed around Malik's cock feeling the tremors of my orgasm run through me. My magic exploded and bright red spots filled the air around us.

Eli left my legs and before I knew it I felt the push of another cock at my entrance.

"God you're so wet," Daxton groaned from above me.

I could feel him lean over us and with one hard thrust he entered me.

If I had thought Eli and Malik were ruthless, that pair was nothing compared to the way Daxton and Malik fucked me together.

Malik was unhinged, his thrusts short and powerful, making it impossible to breathe. I had spit and tears running down my face all while he fucked me exactly like he said he would. My jaw hurt but I loved the way he overpowered me, the way he owned me.

And Daxton...he fucked me like this was our last day on earth. His thrusts were timed with Malik's and he pushed both of my legs as far apart as he could so he could go impossibly deep inside me.

When Malik's thrusts became short and frenzied Daxton slowed but only to rub my clit at an unbearable pace. I tried to close my legs and stop the violent move that was causing me to lose control of my body but two other pairs of hands pulled them open for him.

"Swallow," Rae commanded. And that was the only warning I got before Malik came in my mouth in short spurts. It was hard to swallow as he fucked me, riding out his orgasm. I knew some had escaped but even if it did, when Malik pulled away he didn't seem to mind.

"Messy," Eli complained and dropped one of my legs.

Eli leaned over me even as Daxton continued to pound into me and gripped my neck, forcing me to meet their lips.

I screamed into their mouth as Daxton pulled another orgasm out of me. I writhed against them as I clenched around Daxton. Daxton let out a groan.

"Daxton on the seat, Rosie will ride you," Rae spoke from somewhere to my right.

Eli pulled away from me after they devoured Malik's seed from my mouth. Their eyes glistened and their tongue licked their lips, akin to a feline who just had the most delicious meal in their life. I shivered at the hunger in their eyes.

Eli moved away as Daxton lifted me in his arms only to sit back down and force me down onto his cock.

I threw my head back and let out a loud whine as his hands guided my hips.

"Amr," Rae called.

I heard a shuffling before I felt Amr behind me. The pleasure was too intense, I couldn't keep my eyes open to check on the others.

But maybe it was better this way.

Every one of my senses was heightened and my body was at its breaking point. Everything they did to me just forced me further and further into a place that was so full of pleasure and comfort that nothing else in this world existed besides us.

"Are you ready for me, love?" Amr whispered in my ear, his body pressing into mine.

My dress was already pulled up to my hips, so his hands were able to easily brush across my bare ass. I felt his cock dig into my back and I swiveled on Daxton's cock so I could grind against Amr.

"Ah fuck," Daxton cried from below me. "Hurry, Amr."

Amr let out a deep chuckle that caused my entire body to vibrate.

I felt a cold splash of liquid on my ass and Amr's fingers pushed into me softly.

"You came prepared," I said with a chuckle, though it was short-lived as Amr began stretching me with the head of his cock.

"Always," he replied and sank into me. "Though I may be with Malik on this one, my queen. I am awfully hungry tonight."

"Please," I whined, and it was all the encouragement he needed.

He growled and pushed me into Daxton, who wrapped his arms around me while Amr fucked me from behind. Daxton timed his thrusts with Amr, driving up into me with a force I didn't know he still had.

My whines rang out into the air, embarrassingly loud. My eyes were screwed shut, but when I felt a hand in my hair I opened them to meet Malik's golden eyes.

"Come for us, Rosie," he commanded.

My body seized and with a cry, I came around Daxton's cock.

"Bastard," Daxton growled. "I'm going to come."

And not moments later did his thrusts turn to a frenzied pace as he came inside me.

I whined as I felt him shift underneath me, his come leaking from my pussy.

"I'll take over," Rae said.

Amr paused in his thrusts so Daxton could pull out. But before he left Daxton gave me a deep kiss, sighing into my mouth.

"I love you Rosie," he whispered, but before I could return it I was forced back onto my knees as Amr rammed into me. Rae came to my front, gripping my face and forcing her lips to mine.

She surprised me by trailing her hand to my aching pussy and gathering Daxton's seed as it dripped out of me, only to push it back in.

I shuddered at the act.

"You're ours now Rosie," she said against my lips and pulled back to watch me struggle as she played with my clit.

I was so oversensitive that tears streamed down my face and every movement felt like it was violently throwing me into my next orgasm.

I didn't know how much more I could take.

"Look at Malik, baby," Rae cooed.

I turned my head to meet Malik's golden gaze.

"Go easy on me," I begged and arched so Amr plunged deeper inside me. He cursed at my action and Malik's eyes gleamed with mischief.

"You were awfully reckless Rosie," Malik reminded. "I don't think you deserve leniency."

"She doesn't," Rae said from my side.

"Come until Amr does," he commanded. His power seized hold of me and I had to turn back to Rae and bury my head in her chest to muffle my screams.

Rae plunged her fingers back inside me and curled them in time with my orgasm, sending heat coursing through my veins.

Even if I wanted to keep quiet, I couldn't. These orgasms were violent and almost painful as they ripped through my body. Even my magic didn't have time to keep up.

"There you go, love," Amr groaned from behind. "You're doing so good."

I whined aloud and Rae clutched my head to her chest.

"Almost there," she murmured.

Then when Amr shuddered against me I felt a blinding last orgasm rip through me. I collapsed into Rae as Amr pulled out and took a deep breath as the aftershocks of the orgasm shook me.

"Fuck," I moaned and tried to push down my dress...

There was laughter around me.

"Aw that's cute," Eli cooed.

I moved to glare at them but Rae kept me stationary.

"It's cute that you think we are done," Malik said and leaned over my sweaty back, leaving kisses down my spine. "We are just getting started *brat*."

Epilogue
Six years later.

I groaned as another plate was put in front of me.

"*Mom*," I groaned. "I am bursting."

I looked up to see Rene—Rae's mom—looking down at me with a beaming smile. Her curly hair spread out around her, only contained by the yellow bandanna she fastened to her head. She was so beautiful, even in her flour-covered apron and sweaty face. She had a way about her, she pulled you in, made you feel warm and tingly inside even if she was just standing next to you.

It made me realize why Rae had been chasing after that warmth for so long. Just in the short time that I had known Rene she had become the single most important maternal figure in my life. I absolutely loved her to death, and she did the same for me. For all of us.

"You say that every time," she said with a light tone. "But if that was true then you would have gained weight, but from what I can see my daughter is overworking you."

I let out a laugh.

"If anything it's me overworking her," I said and stood to place a kiss on her temple.

Rae's mom had made strides in her condition after Xena's curse was removed from her.

She was understandably dazed at first and it had taken time for her to get used to how the world had changed, but she got the hang of it and before you knew it she was the mother we all wished we had growing up. She would fuss over us, make us breaks, lunch, and dinner because she was adamant that we hadn't been eating enough.

She sat with us for hours listening to all the *clean* details of how we met and how we narrowly escaped the clutches of the Originals that threatened to end our existence. And Rae... Rae was almost a completely different person after her mother came back.

I mean, she didn't change *that* much, but she allowed herself to live in the warmth and care that Rene provided. She allowed herself to take a step back from the world and just *live*. She was still a control freak and had used her blackmail to get us ahead in more ways than one during her reign at Winterfell, but she was happier.

"If Amr doesn't eat that I will have some words for you," she warned as she noticed me picking up the plate. I let out a light laugh.

"He's been with the newest batch all day so I know he's starving," I said and sent her a small smile. "Sadie, the littlest one, doesn't like green beans. She was very adamant I tell you."

Rene rolled her eyes and shooed me away as she turned back to the connected kitchen.

I sent her a wave and left the large dining room that was at the top floor of the home.

It had been empty for the last few hours as the others awaited their dinner, which gave me some time to snag a bite before anyone else took it. The kids were ravenous—for good reasons—but it was always easier to get distracted by caring for them and making sure they didn't hit anyone with their magic or turn the food into some type of monster that had a hunger for children.

I walked down the hallways, smiling as I passed the drawings after drawings that had been hung on the wall.

The once pristine and sparkling newly built house had now been well-loved and used by its residents. There were burns from magic on the wall, the boards were warped in places where a water demon had lost control of their power, and there were holes that we had to patch in the ceiling due to the children throwing up spears of magic and seeing if they would stick.

They didn't stick though.

They pushed right through the soft material of the ceiling and struck Eli in the back one night.

Daxton had decided that after years of his family's land being used for nothing, he wanted to work towards building a home for witches and demons alike. We accepted all kids, no matter what their story was, though many came from homes like Eli's and Daxton's and were just looking for a place to stay safe.

We worked with the Demon Regulation Society and registered as a home for those they deemed particularly at risk, and Amr and Daxton would work their magic on them. We made sure they had a safe place to grow up. Enough food to fill their bellies. Good schooling. And when they were ready...they would leave, but not a moment before.

We hired many people from *The Fallen* to help us and surprisingly enough, we found a good batch who cared for the children just as we had. They would help with childcare, bringing them to school and back, and everything else you could think of.

I walked down the stairs and rounded the corner to the playroom where I knew Amr and Daxton were probably waiting for me. I caught sight of three of our newest children all surrounding Amr. They were around the ages of four to six and all came from magical families.

One was on his back and the other two tried to tackle him as he pounced around on all fours. When he playfully tackled the other two on the ground they let out squeals of delight.

I caught Daxton's eyes and laughed. He was standing in the corner and one of the children had decided to draw extra tattoos on his face.

"Amr!" I called and held up the plate. "Food is ready!"

The kids paused to look at me and Amr helped them down. They screamed and all ran for the door.

"Careful!" Daxton yelled and conjured a blue bird in his hand that followed the children out. "Follow the bird to the dining room!"

They yelled something back but I couldn't make out what they said.

"Impressive bird," I said and smiled towards Daxton. He flushed lightly and ran his hand through his hair, giving me a rare look at the script tattoo that lined his forehead.

He had done a lot in the last few years to build up his magic again, and I was ecstatic to see that he was able to make some progress. It had been hard to get him motivated, but after Xena had been pushed into that fountain, something changed in him.

He was no longer stuck in bed, afraid of his future. After that he worked hard to graduate on time, without Malik's help, and was able to stand on stage with all of us.

Before the home he played some roles at the Demon Regulation Society and worked with many of the magical activist groups to make sure they unearthed people like his parents and made them pay for what they had done. It was what led to the idea of building a home.

"Oh, heavens I love Rene," Amr said and grabbed the plate from me but not before placing a soft kiss on my lips. "But not as much as I love you of course."

I rolled my eyes. Amr hadn't changed much but he did try to help both Daxton and me as much as possible and split his time between the low-levels at Winterfell and the children here at the home. I pushed him to go out more, maybe travel and make up for lost time, but he was perfectly content with just spending his time with us.

Another perk of Xena's death was that Amr was no longer forced to shift at the command of the person he bonded to. It had taken a lot of trial and error to see if he still had the power to shift but after many *many* mishaps, we had discovered that it was possible, but not just for familiars.

Magic was really just as unlimited as they rumored. You just had to be a particularly strong witch to harness that type of magic.

I held out my hand for Daxton and sent him a smile.

"It's time," I said.

A light lit up his face and he took a step forward.

"Let's see what Rae has in store for us," he said with an amused smile.

"I'm sure it will look beautiful," Amr said by my side and plated a soft kiss on my head. "But Daxton should wash his face before we go, or he may just steal the spotlight from you."

* * *

The air at Winterfell had a buzz of excitement in it. The students were walking around the campus, chatting and joking as they usually would, but there was something that hung in the air all around us and sank deep into my bones.

Even though it had been eight years since I had first stepped foot in Winterfell Academy, each day felt exactly like the first.

Nerves and excitement flowed freely and the old thrum of magic made shivers of excitement run up my spine.

A majority of the others were waiting for us at the base of the tower as Amr, Daxton, and I walked up. Rae was dressed in her suit, her glasses shining in the sun that hung over us. She smiled nervously as we approached.

Malik, on the other hand, seemed amused. His wide smile and scarred face were absolutely glowing and the black of his cut-off t-shirt and jeans only made his white hair stand out even more. His tattooed arms were out for all to see and if I cocked my head just right I could see the pitch-black feathers that trailed up and around his neck which led to two wings that were tattooed right in the middle of his back.

He never did get his wings back.

He stepped forward and pulled me into his arms before deeply kissing me. I sighed into him and wrapped my arms around his waist, not caring if the students or other faculty saw us.

"I missed you," he murmured against my lips before pulling away. His dull golden eyes looked over me and a small smile spread to his lips, the action causing my heart to beat rapidly in my chest.

"It's only been a day," I said with an eye roll. "But I missed you too."

Rae cleared her throat.

"Are you ready?" she asked.

I gave her a forced smile and looked back to Amr and Daxton, who were holding hands and smiling at me. Amr nodded and sent a look to Daxton, who gave me a thumbs up.

"I think it's a bit overboard," I admitted, looking back towards Rae. "But I guess I'll never be more ready than I am now."

Rae shook her head and turned towards the large structure that stood at the base of the Winterfell tower. It was currently covered with a sheet, but I knew what was behind there and it made my stomach fill with butterflies.

I had been the type of girl who had hidden my entire life. I didn't want to be seen. I didn't want to make friends. I wanted to be left alone and that was it. But my time at Winterfell and with the people that surrounded me now had forced me out of my shell and into the spotlight.

Some of it hurt.

Some of it had me feeling like I was flying.

But it was what made me who I was today. And for the first time in my life...I *loved* me.

I loved me for who I became. For whom I loved. For those we lost and found.

I wouldn't allow myself to hide anymore. Regardless of what we faced, or how ridiculous the declarations of love may be.

"Where's Eli?" Daxton asked from behind me, stirring me from my thoughts.

"On a job," Malik said. "We can start, and he should be here shortly; he said don't wait up."

I nodded but didn't let the disappointment show on my face.

With a deep breath I nodded towards Rae and she walked towards the structure and took the sheet in hand.

"Ready love?" Amr asked, his voice close to my ear. He left a burning kiss on the side of my neck.

"Do it," I said and with a smile Rae pulled the sheet off to show a large, bronzed statue of...me.

It was when I won the first games, though I looked much more ethereal there than I did in person.

My hair was spread all around me and I was looking up at the sky. Instead of the school uniform, Rae had insisted that I be in a flowy dress that hugged my body, and I couldn't help but be grateful for the change.

I looked like a goddess.

Below it was a sign that said.

Celebrating our first Champion and hybrid.

Rosie Miller.

"Oh my God," I said and hid my face in my hands. Laughter rang out around us, and I felt my face heat.

"You become principal, and *this* is what you do?" Eli's voice rang from behind me. There was a sprinkle of amusement in his voice.

I jumped as his arms wrapped around me and they left a kiss to my temple, their facial hair scratching at my skin.

I was proud of Eli.

After everything they continued to run *The Fallen* and as Malik and he had promised, they turned it into a respectable organization that focused on doing good...though that didn't mean that their ways have changed.

More often than not the both of them would come home covered in blood and laughing like they had just had the time of their lives.

Eli had never fully regained their hearing and continued to have issues when in groups, but they made do with their power and of course used it in the bedroom, claiming they couldn't hear me even though I knew very well they could. *That* had been an embarrassing conversation the next morning.

I was proud of his change—of all of theirs.

They had been through hell and back but after some time we were able to create our own safe haven with each other.

It may not have been as luxurious as traveling the world or fighting Originals...but it was ours and we were happy.

Rae pouted and gave him a look.

"It looked good!" she insisted throwing her hand back to the statue behind her.

"I like it," Malik said with a shrug. "And I think it's the least she deserves."

I flushed further and leaned back into Eli, feeling a mix of embarrassment and glowing pride in my chest.

"It was a hard time," I whispered, and all eyes snapped to me. "Ugly and painful…but I couldn't have asked for a better, and more beautiful reminder of everything we have accomplished since then. Thank you Rae, truly."

I held a hand out to her and she stepped forward with a frown marring her beautiful face.

"I love it," I said and pulled her down for a kiss.

"Just like you love us," Eli said in my ear.

I broke our kiss to look up at him. His blue eyes were shining in the light and there was a light five o'clock shadow that covered his jaw. There were a few faint scars that littered his face, but if anything it added to his handsomeness.

"I think I love you all a bit more than that thing," I said and Eli threw his head back to let out a laugh.

"Wait," Rae said turning serious. "Please don't tell me you recruited my brothers into your gang."

I turned in Eli's arms to see Nathaniel and Benjamin walking this way both decked in *The Fallen's* all-black uniform. They hadn't changed much through the years, though they did have a few more tattoos of their own now.

They held themselves with a confidence that they hadn't before. Even Benjamin, the once scared demon, was now bursting with power I didn't expect from him.

It had been over a year since they had come to see us last and while I knew that Rae had probably kept in touch with them…I didn't realize the change in the way they held themselves until they walked towards us.

The air shimmered around them, and my eyes were pulled to the space between them. Something flashed before my eyes and I thought, for just a moment, I saw a small silver-haired girl between them but the next time I blinked there was no one there.

"They work really well," Eli said and waved them over.

"Rae's gonna be mad," I sang and slipped out of Eli's arm. "You can deal with that on your own."

Daxton wrapped his arms around me and pulled me between him and Amr.

"So, what now Rosie?" he asked and nuzzled the side of my head pulling a giggle from me. "How should we celebrate. A drink? Visit your favorite cafe? You name it."

I looked around at the others, feeling the warmth in my chest explode.

"Let's go home."

Smiles broke out around us, and I couldn't help the own smile that formed on my face.

At the age of twenty-four, I had finally found a place that I could call home and people that would love me unconditionally. The world may have been cruel to us on our journey, may have punished us for the sins of our parents, but it was a world that I was grateful for and a world that allowed me to *finally* be the person I had always dreamt of becoming.

THE END

Want exclusive NSFW art?

For NSFW POS art (and other series as seen above) join my Patreon!
There is also a few shorts and deleted scenes of the couple that you can take advantage of!
Check it out here or go to https://www.patreon.com/ellemaebooks

About the Author

Elle is a native Californian who has lived in Los Angeles for most of her life. From the very start, she has been in love with all things fantasy and reading. As soon as Elle found out that writing books could be a career, she picked up a pen and paper. While the first ones were about scorned love and missed opportunities of lunchtime love, she has grown to love the fantasy genre and looks forward to making a difference in the world with her stories.

Loved this book? Please leave a review!

For more behind the scene content, sign up for my newsletter at https://view.flodesk.com/pages/61722d0874d564fa09f4021b

 x.com/mae_books

 instagram.com/ellemaebooks

 goodreads.com/ellemae